A number-one be [...] around the world, a [...] million copies in the UK a [...] recent novels, including *A Lesser Ev[il]* [...] *Remember Me*, are published by Penguin. Lesley Pearse lives near Bristol, has three daughters and one grandson.

Find out what your favourite author's been up to by signing up to her newsletter. Go to www.penguin.co.uk. Type your e-mail address in the 'Join our newsletter' panel and tick the box marked 'Lesley Pearse'.

LESLEY PEARSE

Perfect Partners

TRUST ME

REMEMBER ME

PENGUIN BOOKS

PENGUIN BOOKS

Published by the Penguin Group
Penguin Books Ltd, 80 Strand, London WC2R 0RL, England
Penguin Group (USA) Inc., 375 Hudson Street, New York, New York 10014, USA
Penguin Group (Canada), 90 Eglinton Avenue East, Suite 700, Toronto, Ontario, Canada M4P 2Y3
(a division of Pearson Penguin Canada Inc.)
Penguin Ireland, 25 St Stephen's Green, Dublin 2, Ireland (a division of Penguin Books Ltd)
Penguin Group (Australia), 250 Camberwell Road,
Camberwell, Victoria 3124, Australia (a division of Pearson Australia Group Pty Ltd)
Penguin Books India Pvt Ltd, 11 Community Centre,
Panchsheel Park, New Delhi – 110 017, India
Penguin Group (NZ), cnr Airborne and Rosedale Roads, Albany,
Auckland 1310, New Zealand (a division of Pearson New Zealand Ltd)
Penguin Books (South Africa) (Pty) Ltd, 24 Sturdee Avenue,
Rosebank, Johannesburg 2196, South Africa

Penguin Books Ltd, Registered Offices: 80 Strand, London WC2R 0RL, England

www.penguin.com

Trust Me first published by Penguin Books 2001
Remember Me first published by Michael Joseph 2003
Published in Penguin Books 2004
This combined edition published 2005

1

Copyright © Lesley Pearse, 2001, 2003
All rights reserved

The moral right of the author has been asserted

Printed in England by Clays Ltd, St Ives plc

ISBN-13: 978–0–141–02737–1
ISBN-10: 0–141–02737–1

TRUST ME

To all those children everywhere who suffered the indignity and brutality of orphanages. My heart goes out to you, and I hope that in some small way this story will acknowledge the sadness of your past and help you to put it aside.

Acknowledgements

To Bruce Blyth in Perth, Australia, for your help, knowledge, advice and enthusiasm. Without your passion and commitment I could never have written this book. But then you've been helping the survivors of Bindoon for years, an unsung hero, a man of integrity and compassion. After you all men will fall short. My hero and friend.

To Ted and Betty in WA, for allowing me to pick your brains and trawl through your memories and your knowledge of farming. Come to England soon!

To Faye and Geoff in WA, for putting up with a greenhorn jill-a-roo and her many naive questions. I will remember my time on your farm with great affection. If I've made mistakes in the farming details, forgive me. I'm just a townie.

Thanks to the Child Migrants Trust in Nottingham, England, for sending me invaluable news clippings and advising me on books for my research. The Child Migrants Trust is devoted to searching out relatives of the children sent to Australia and helps to fund travel expenses for them to meet up. Thanks to Margaret Humphreys, its director, a great many people have been reunited with family back in England. I thoroughly recommend her book *Empty Cradles* to anyone who wishes to know more about the Child Migration Scheme.

Finally, extra special thanks to Peggie Rush, Mary Eather, John Carvill and Paddy Dorrain. I can hardly find the words to express my admiration for each of you, sharing your blighted childhoods with me so that I could write this book. Things you told me stayed on in my memory long after I'd returned to England. I needed no notes to remember. I have wept for each of you, and for all those other children who lived through those evil times. I hope my tears, and those of the readers, will soothe some of the pain and injustice done to you all.

Part One

1947–1955

Chapter One

Edna Groomes and Iris Brown paused in their gossiping as Anne Taylor came tripping along Leahurst Road. Her high heels tapped out a staccato message, *Look at me, look at me,* and so they stared, hating her for her beauty, blonde hair, trim figure and youth.

Edna and Iris were both only in their early thirties, no more than six years older than Anne, but their crossover pinnies, headscarves knotted like turbans and sagging, overweight bodies made them look much older.

'She'll be off to the 'airdresser's again,' Edna said accusingly, shaking her tin of Brasso and bending over to finish polishing the letter-box she'd started before Iris came out of her flat next door. 'She's always in there. All she thinks of is 'ow she looks.'

Iris put her hands on her hips and smirked as Anne came closer. ''Ow's the little 'uns?' she asked with some malice. 'Stuck indoors as usual?'

'The children are fine, thank you,' Anne replied without even breaking her step, her nose firmly in the air. 'And yes, they are indoors. I don't allow them to play in the street disturbing the neighbours.'

It was the crisp, cultured voice and the snipe at Edna and Iris's children who were playing a noisy game of cricket further down the street which momentarily stunned the two older women. By the time Iris had managed to open her mouth again, Anne had already disappeared around the corner into Manor Lane.

'Stuck-up bitch,' Iris spat out.

3

Edna laughed. 'You asked for that one, Iris. If she weren't so bloody posh she might 'ave whacked you.'

'She might be posh but she's no better than she should be,' Iris retorted, sitting down on the low wall which gave a mere three feet of front garden to the two-storey flats. 'She's bin carrying on with Tosh down at the pub for months now. I've two minds to slip Reg the wink.'

'I wouldn't if I were you,' Edna said, abandoning her polishing to sit on the wall beside her friend and drawing a packet of Turf out of her pinny pocket. 'I reckon 'e'd knock you out.'

The two women lit up their cigarettes, enjoying the warm spring sunshine on their faces. It was the first warm day of the year. Nineteen forty-seven had been the worst winter on record, snow lying on the ground from January right through to early April, and it was only now, the first week in May, that they'd been able to come outside without a coat.

But apart from the sunshine, there was no real evidence of spring in Leahurst Road, for there were no trees, and the tiny front gardens were used to house dustbins and bicycles, not flowers. Even further down the street nearer to Hither Green station where the long terrace of Victorian houses was broken by a bomb-site, the weeds and grass hadn't yet begun to grow. Across the street was Lee Manor School, but as it was Saturday the gates in the eight-foot fence were closed, shutting out the sight of pots of daffodils on the window-sills.

Edna drew hard on her cigarette before speaking again. 'You sure she's carrying on with Tosh at the pub? I can't see someone like 'er messing with a creep like 'im. I wouldn't touch 'im with a flaming barge-pole!'

'Well, 'e's loaded, ain't 'e,' Iris said with a sniff. 'She thinks she's too grand to live around 'ere, 'spect she thinks he'll set her up somewhere more to 'er liking. He won't, though, he's as tight as a monkey's balls.'

Edna laughed. Tosh, the landlord of the Station Hotel, was famous for his meanness. They joked that moths flew

4

out when he opened his wallet. He was also nearly fifty, balding and paunchy, an ex-boxer with a broken nose. It was surprising enough that Anne Taylor, with her stunning looks and hoity-toity manner, should even work for him as a barmaid, but although Edna would like to believe what her friend was saying she thought it extremely unlikely that Anne would stoop to having an affair with him too. 'Why would she want a man to take her away from 'ere anyway? Reg ain't a boozer, and he's always in work,' she said.

Iris rolled her eyes with impatience. 'Are you blind and deaf?' she exclaimed. 'Everyone knows they fight all the time. Mrs Gardener downstairs to them says they are at it hammer and tongs most every night.'

'Me and Sid fight all the time an' all,' Edna retorted. 'Specially when he stays in the pub and his dinner's ruined. That don't mean I go looking for someone else.'

Iris moved closer to her friend. 'She neglects those kids,' she said conspiratorially. 'Back in the winter when the snow was on the ground sometimes they was waiting on the doorstep with their teeth chattering for hours for their mum to get back. If it weren't for Reg I don't reckon they'd ever get a decent meal or clean clothes. She spends all the money on clothes and hair-dos, and why would she do that if it weren't to catch a new man?'

Edna knew it was true about the two little girls waiting on the doorstep in the cold after school, she'd taken them in a few times herself, but she thought Iris was being a bit malicious about the rest so she made no comment. She liked Reg Taylor. He looked like a thug with his big shoulders and hair cut as close as a convict's, but he'd been the first to come round to offer help when her pipes burst in the winter and Sid was working away. Just the way Reg talked about his little girls showed how much he loved them, and she didn't believe he would stand for his wife neglecting them.

'Oh, I know Reg is a good sort,' Iris said as if she'd read Edna's thoughts. 'But she's a bad 'un. Fancy 'er leaving those little kiddies cooped up in that flat all day while she gets 'er 'air done. It ain't never right.'

The Taylor girls didn't think it was right either. As their mother was walking up the street they were watching her from the window. They saw her pass Mrs Groomes and Mrs Brown, and once she'd gone round the corner, they grabbed the spare key from the mantelpiece and skipped out, knowing she wouldn't be back for at least two hours. They were making for Manor House Gardens, the pretty park with a lake only ten minutes away. Within an hour they had joined some other children down in the mud on the banks of the River Quaggy, which ran through it, until the park-keeper spotted them.

All six children involved in building a dam across the river jerked up their heads in alarm at the sound of his outraged shout from the bridge some twenty yards away. Dulcie Taylor didn't stop to see what her companions would do, just grabbed her younger sister May's hand, hauled her up the river bank and squeezed first May, then herself, through the same bent railing they had entered through.

'Quick, hide under there,' Dulcie gasped, shoving May beneath a dense shrub on the other side of the pathway, then, with only the briefest glance around, crawling in too.

Seconds later, the park-keeper in his brown uniform came riding past on his bicycle. Dulcie put her hand over May's mouth and whispered that she wasn't to move until he was out of sight. As they could hear him yelling at the others, no more than thirty or forty feet away from their hiding-place, they stayed crouched under the bush, both panting with fright.

Dulcie was eight and a half, May had had her fifth birthday only two days ago, and they were very alike, with blonde hair which they wore in plaits, pale skin and wide blue eyes. Yet May was always referred to by neighbours as 'the pretty little one'. It wasn't that Dulcie was plain, though she was rather thin and gawky, with new front teeth which looked a little large for her small face, merely that May endeared herself to people by smiling readily and chatting, and she didn't look permanently anxious as her older sister did.

Dulcie *was* an anxious child and it was quite out of character for her to suggest slipping out to the park while their mother was out, or to do anything as reckless as playing in the river. Normally she was a timid and obedient girl, and took responsibility for the safety of her younger sister seriously. But today's warm sunshine after months of bitter weather had caused latent feelings of resentment towards her mother to boil over. She couldn't see why she and May should be expected to stay indoors on such a nice day while *she*, who couldn't even be bothered to make them something for dinner, went off to the hairdresser's.

Dulcie wasn't prone to thinking she was hard done by. She knew that everyone in England had had to endure severe hardships all through the long, bleak winter. Animals had frozen to death in the fields, old people had died of cold sitting in front of an empty grate. Food rations had been cut again, lower even than during the war years, and the heavy snow prevented much of the food from being distributed.

Young as she was, she appreciated that her family were lucky to have a decent place to live, for many people were still struggling to repair bomb-damaged houses or living in temporary accommodation. Dulcie had grown used to having to wear a coat and hat in class during the winter – her teacher had explained that coal for the boilers was difficult to get hold of – she didn't even mind that she and May often had to get into bed as soon as they got home for the same reason. She had put up with chapped thighs, feet and hands and conditioned herself to ignore the rumblings of hunger in her stomach, but what she couldn't accept or understand was her mother's apparent total lack of regard for her family.

Anne kept on buying new clothes for herself instead of

food. She sat around all day painting her nails and reading magazines instead of cleaning up. It was perfectly under-standable to Dulcie that Dad got mad when he came in from work and found there was no dinner, or when he had to wash and iron their school clothes because Mum hadn't done them. Like him, Dulcie had come to the conclusion that Mum didn't care about him or her children, and night after night when she had to bury her head under the pillow so she wouldn't hear the bitter rows, she almost wished Mum would make good her constant threats to leave – at least then they'd get some peace.

Just that morning in Lewisham, Anne had bought another new dress for herself. Dulcie had pointed out that both her own and May's shoes were pinching their feet, but she'd snapped at them and said they must put up with them for another few weeks. On the way home Dulcie had asked if she'd take them to the park in the afternoon because someone at school had said there were baby ducks on the lake. But Mum had just clouted her round the ear, said she was always asking for something, and anyway she was going to the hairdresser's.

Dulcie knew it was pointless asking if they could go alone. Dad didn't allow it, and he wouldn't let them play in the street either. She understood why. Dad had been a street urchin himself and he always said he wanted something better for his girls. Besides, he was fair, he was never too tired to take them to the park or up to Blackheath when he was home. Even if he'd planned to do something else, if it was a nice day he'd drop it for them.

That was why Dulcie decided to defy her mother. It was a protest against her selfishness, coupled with a desire for adventure and freedom.

She wished she hadn't now. Her shoes were wet through and covered in mud, and May was in an even worse mess with mud all over her skirt and cardigan. If the park-keeper caught them, goodness only knew what he'd do to them, and Mum would go mad when they got home.

At last Dulcie saw the park-keeper moving away. He

was pushing his bike with one hand and holding one of the boys by the ear with the other. Once she was satisfied that he was too far away to see them, the girls crawled out of the bush and Dulcie said they must go home.

'But I don't want to go,' May said petulantly. 'We haven't even seen the ducks yet. Mum won't be back for ages.'

Dulcie sighed deeply, hoping May wasn't going to have one of her tantrums as she often did when she didn't get her way. She was reluctant to go herself, she'd wanted to see the ducks too, but she had no idea what the time was, and it was imperative they got their clothes and shoes cleaned up before Mum came in.

'We can't stay now, Parky will get us,' Dulcie said, taking her sister by the hand and almost dragging her towards the gates.

'What would he do to us?' May asked. She looked intrigued rather than frightened.

Dulcie had no real idea. As she'd never been to the park before without an adult watching over them, all she knew about Parky was hearsay from other children. They said he clouted children, whipped them with a stick for picking flowers; one girl at school claimed he'd taken her into his shed and forced her to hold his willy. Dulcie didn't really believe *that* story, but the way he'd shouted at them earlier and the way he'd dragged Stephen off suggested he could be very nasty.

'He'd lock us up in his shed, then he'd get Dad,' she guessed.

Just the mention of her dad made them both really frightened. He wasn't a cruel man, he never, ever belted them like some kids' dads did, but he would be very angry that they'd slipped out without permission.

Dulcie was an observant and thoughtful child, and when they visited Granny in Deptford, she could see why her dad wanted something better for her and May than he'd had. Deptford was a slum area, with nasty old tenements and dirty streets, and many of the dilapidated little terraced houses like Granny's housed several families. Dad

9

had once told her that most of the boys he'd played with as a child had become thieves and rogues, and the reason he'd always worked so hard when he was young was so he could get away from there. Dulcie supposed that he'd married Mum for much the same reason, because she was beautiful and she had a posh voice.

Yet that didn't always make sense. Mum was always saying cruel things about how rough and uneducated Dad's family were. Dad usually struck back by saying hers were mean-minded snobs and they hadn't equipped her for real life. Dulcie often wondered what on earth had made them get married in the first place if they disliked each other's families so much.

As they turned into Leahurst Road, to Dulcie's horror she saw that their dad's bicycle was in the front garden. Either it was much later than she thought, or Dad had knocked off work early. He was a builder, at present working on a site in the Eltham Road, and normally he didn't get home before six on a Saturday. But now they would be in serious trouble. Mum would probably only have given them a clout, she wouldn't have told Dad what they'd done because he would have been mad with her for leaving them on their own. What on earth were they going to do?

'Dad's home,' Dulcie said fearfully to her sister who hadn't yet noticed his bike. 'We're in for it now.'

May pulled a couldn't-care-less face. 'It's not my fault. It was your idea to go.'

Dulcie felt like slapping her. It was quite true it had been her idea, but then May always wriggled out of any blame. 'Well, at least don't go and say we went in the river,' Dulcie said. 'We'll say we fell over on the muddy grass.'

May stopped in her tracks. 'But that's a lie!' she exclaimed, opening her blue eyes very wide. 'You'd have to confess it!'

Dulcie had taken her First Communion and perhaps unwisely had told May all the sins she was supposed to tell the priest in the confessional.

'It's only a very tiny lie,' Dulcie said. 'And it's a kindly meant one because Dad will be very upset if he thought we were playing somewhere dangerous. I will confess it in church, but don't you dare tell on me.'

May gave her a sly look. 'I won't if you give me half your sweets.'

Dulcie sighed at this blackmail. If she didn't agree, May would go out of her way to get her into worse trouble. Dad always brought them home sweets on a Saturday, but they wouldn't get them tonight anyway, they'd probably get sent to bed without any tea, so half of nothing wasn't much to give up. 'Okay,' she said. 'But don't you ever ask *me* to help you when you're in trouble!'

They walked on then, Dulcie's heart thumping loudly with fear. Dad had never given her a good hiding before for anything, but maybe he would for something as serious as this.

Dulcie didn't use the key to the door, Dad would think it even more sneaky if he knew they'd taken that. She rang the bell and a few seconds later heard his footsteps coming down the stairs.

'Not today, thank you,' he said as he opened the door and saw them standing on the step. He closed the door again.

This was one of his little jokes, pretending he didn't know them, it showed he was in a very good mood, and he probably thought they'd run ahead of their mother. Usually when he did this, Dulcie would say, 'Let me in, little pig' through the letter-box, and he'd reply, 'Oh no, Mr Wolf, not by the hair of my chinny, chin chin, I won't let you in.' But Dulcie couldn't bring herself to play out this game today.

She took a deep breath and lifted the flap of the letter-box. 'Let us in, Daddy, we've been naughty, we went to the park when Mummy told us to stay home.'

The door opened immediately and there he was, looking down at them with a frighteningly stern expression on his face.

11

Reg Taylor was a big man, six foot two with shoulders like a barn door. He had the kind of tough appearance that made other men nervous of getting on the wrong side of him, fair hair cut very short on top, cold, pale blue eyes, pitted skin and a strong jaw-line. As his neighbour Edna had observed, he did look like a thug, that was until he smiled and showed the warmth of his real character. But anyone, even his children, was inclined to back away when he looked as he did now.

'I'm sorry,' Dulcie whispered. 'But it was so nice outside and we just wanted to see the baby ducks.'

Reg looked the pair of them up and down, noting the mud on their clothes and shoes. He realized immediately that they had been in the river. 'Come on in,' he said. 'Take your shoes off and leave them there, I'll sort them out later.'

He walked on back up the passage towards the stairs while they took their shoes off, but stopped suddenly to look back. 'Where's your mother?' he asked.

Dulcie gulped. Whenever her dad used the word mother instead of mummy it was a sure sign he was cross with her. 'At the hairdresser's,' she said.

He gave a sort of grunt and disappeared up the stairs. The girls took off their shoes, placed them neatly on the mat and holding hands, nervously crept up too.

The flat consisted of three rooms, a bathroom and kitchen. When they'd moved here eighteen months earlier from just two rooms in New Cross, they'd all thought they were in heaven. Back in New Cross the stove and sink were on the landing, they had to share the outside lavatory with several other families and go to the public baths. It was so exciting watching as Dad painted and papered, turning a gloomy, dirty place into a real home, to go with him to choose furniture, to see Mum sewing curtains and cushion covers. It didn't matter that the furniture was second-hand, or that there was no stair carpet. Dad kept saying that they were on the way up.

Everything had seemed so perfect then. Dad had joined

up in the army at the start of the war and had been away in the fighting for almost all of Dulcie's early years, but now he was home for good, taking up building work again and coming home every night. Lee Manor School was right across the street from their flat, there were nice shops down the road by Hither Green station, the park and the library to go to. But best of all was that Mum had been so very happy, dancing around, singing, laughing and cuddling Dad. Dulcie had thought it was going to be that way for ever.

But it didn't stay like that for long. Soon Mum gave up laughing and singing and lay around in her dressing-gown, chain-smoking the way Dulcie remembered she had so often done during the war. She stopped cleaning the flat, the washing and ironing mounted up, she didn't seem to care about anything other than how she looked when she went out.

'Come on in here,' Dad called out once they'd reached the landing outside the living-room.

They slunk in to find their father sitting on the couch. It was a large room with a bay window overlooking the street. At night when the curtains were drawn, a table-lamp lit and the fire roaring away, the cream wallpaper with gold scrolls looked so very posh. It looked nice too in the mornings when the sun came in, but the sun was gone from the windows now, and in the gloomy light the room looked as sad as her father's expression.

Dulcie realized almost immediately that he had been home for some time. He had changed out of his work overalls into his grey trousers and a clean shirt, and he'd cleared the grate of last night's ashes and laid it with kindling ready to relight later when it got cold.

'I'm not going to ask why you disobeyed your mother,' he said, looking at them with cold eyes. 'I know why. But I want you to think what would have happened if you had been run over by a car, or fallen in the river.'

Both girls just stood there, hanging their heads.

'That's why I make rules about you not going out alone,' Reg went on. 'You see, if either of those things happened I wouldn't know where you were. Can you imagine what it would be like for me and your mother if you just didn't turn up? How would I know where to look for you? Little girls sometimes get taken by bad men, that's why it's important we always know where you are.'

He held out his arms to them, and the girls, realizing he wasn't going to smack them after all, ran to them willingly. He pulled them on to his knees and cuddled them tightly.

'You must never, ever do that again,' he said with a strange kind of croak in his voice, his cheeks rough against their smooth ones. 'You two are the most precious things in the world to me, and I'm only strict with you because I want to keep you from harm.'

'Are you going to spank us and send us to bed without any tea?' May asked, her voice trembling.

'Not this time,' he said, and Dulcie heard the faintest hint of amusement in his voice. 'But if you do it again I will, make no mistake about that. As it happens I've been home for over an hour. If you'd been here I would have taken you to the park myself, and we might have had an ice-cream too. But there'll be no ice-cream or sweets this weekend now.'

He sent them to their bedroom then to change their clothes and put on dry socks. As they left the room Dulcie saw him going over to the table and picking up all the bottles of nail varnish and other cosmetics their mother had left on it this morning.

A long narrow passage ran from the living-room past the stairwell, Anne and Reg's bedroom, the kitchen and then the bathroom before reaching the girls' bedroom right at the back of the house. They loved their room, even though the double bed they shared took up most of the space. There was pretty paper with pink roses on the walls and a pink eiderdown on the bed. They could look out on the gardens that belonged to the ground-floor flats, and their bedroom's distance from the living-room meant they could play noisy games without their parents complaining. Afternoon sun shone through the window and it was invariably warmer than the living-room as old Mrs Gardener who lived downstairs kept a fire going in the room below them.

After changing their skirts, cardigans and socks, they stayed in their room to play, climbing up on the bed with their dolls. May seemed completely untroubled, chatting to her doll Belinda as she pretended to feed her with a toy bottle. But Dulcie still felt very anxious for she knew that once Mum came home a row between her parents was inevitable and she was ashamed that this time it would be all her fault.

She didn't have long to wait. Just after the clock chimed four-thirty along in the living-room, Mum came up the stairs, her high heels clicking on the painted boards.

'I'm back, girls,' she called out.

May went to jump off the bed and go to her, but Dulcie stopped her. 'Wait until Daddy's spoken to her,' she whispered.

They heard Dad say something sarcastic about her hair, then they must have gone into the living-room together and closed the door because the girls couldn't hear their voices any more.

Dulcie gradually relaxed when the expected shouting didn't begin. She picked up the Enid Blyton book she'd borrowed from the library, lay back on the bed beside May and began to read.

'Why didn't you arrange to have your hair done when the kids were at school?' Reg asked Anne as he handed her a cup of tea and sat down opposite her in an armchair. He didn't want to start yet another row with her, but when he'd told her what the girls had done she had merely laughed as if it didn't matter. 'It was hardly fair to expect them to be shut in here on a nice sunny day.'

'It's you who insists they can't play outside,' she said

haughtily, lighting up yet another cigarette. 'Besides, I needed my hair done today, I'm working tonight.'

Reg bristled at this piece of news. Just the way she sat, so poised and elegant, her legs crossed, one shoe swinging loosely from her foot, irritated him intensely. Yet irritated as he was, as always he was struck by her classic oval face, features as perfect as a china doll's, the big speedwell blue eyes and soft, sensual mouth.

She had been merely pretty when he first met her at a dance at the Empire, Leicester Square in December of 1937. Just seventeen, all eyes and soft blonde hair. She had made him think of a baby deer, and he'd felt so big and ugly next to her. Even now that he knew how heartless, selfish and cruel she could be, he was still awed by her beauty.

So many young mothers had lost their good looks during the war – the hardships, danger, anxiety and lack of nutritious food had turned them into drab, worn, prematurely middle-aged women. But not Anne. She was more curvy now, her soft floaty hair had been styled into Hollywood glamour, the pretty but bland features had matured into striking beauty, and there was a bold, challenging look in her eyes. Even though he bitterly resented her constantly buying new clothes, cosmetics and getting her hair done, he did feel proud that she kept herself looking so good.

'Working tonight!' he exclaimed. 'I told you I was going to take you all to the pictures.'

She merely shrugged and puffed on her cigarette. 'We can do that another night. You didn't tell the girls we were going.'

'Would it have made any difference if I had?' Reg said, his voice rising. 'Since when did you care tuppence about letting them down? I agreed you could work at the pub lunchtimes. Not bloody Saturday nights.'

'Tosh needs me there, and besides, I need the money,' she said, her tone more defensive now.

'Oh, Tosh needs you there, does he?' Reg said sarcastically. 'It doesn't matter that your husband and children have to spend the evening alone. And it makes a lot of bloody sense to spend what you'd earn for one night on having your hair done. Dare I ask what we are having for tea tonight? Or are we to go hungry because you are swanning off to work behind a bar?'

Reg knew by the way she looked shiftily away from him that this was in fact true, and the last of his good humour left him. 'You'd better have bought some food, Anne!'

'Oh, calm down, Reg,' she said, getting up from the couch. 'I just didn't have time to get anything for tea. I'll send Dulcie down for fish and chips.'

It was the way she was making for her handbag which made Reg suspect she had something more to hide. He leaped up and reached it before she could, snatched out her purse and spilled the contents out on to the table. All there was were two half-crowns, a two-shilling piece, a sixpence and a couple of coppers.

'I gave you eight quid last night,' he said, his voice trembling. 'What have you spent it on?'

When he got in from work he'd gone into the kitchen to make himself a sandwich, and all the kitchen cabinet contained was half a stale loaf, one egg, a tiny piece of cheese, milk and margarine.

'I bought some beef for tomorrow,' she said defiantly.

Reg caught hold of her arm and dragged her out to the kitchen to prove this. There was a tiny piece of beef in the meat safe, but Reg knew by its grey appearance it came from the market and would be as tough as old boots. 'So what are we supposed to have with it?' he said sarcastically.

'I'll get vegetables tomorrow,' she said, trying to get free of his hand. 'The kids were playing up and I forgot about getting them.'

'Show me what you bought for yourself,' he commanded, hauling her by the arm along to the bedroom.

'Oh Reg, don't be like this,' she pleaded, starting to cry. 'I just had to have a dress. I'll pay back the housekeeping out of my wages and I won't buy anything again, I promise.'

'Show me!' he said, pushing her towards the wardrobe.

She brought out a blue dress and even though Reg knew little about fashion he knew it was an expensive one by the embroidery which ran down the bodice and across the front of the skirt.

It was too much for Reg. He knew the girls both needed new shoes, their underwear was threadbare too, and for the first time ever he slapped Anne hard across the face.

'You vain, selfish bitch,' he hissed. 'You'd let your children wear shoes too small for them and go hungry just so you can show off in that pub.'

She just looked up at him, big blue eyes full of shock that he'd struck her, and it made him feel like a maggot.

'I didn't mean to hit you,' he said hurriedly. 'But my God, you deserve it, Anne! Stay in here. Get yourself tarted up for bloody Tosh, he's just about your level. I'll feed the children and take them to the pictures on my own.'

He turned on his heel and walked out, slamming the bedroom door behind him.

Anne *was* severely shaken by the slap Reg had given her, so much so that she lay on the bed with the eiderdown wrapped around her, shaking like a leaf as she listened to him getting the girls' coats and shoes on to go out. Part of her wanted to get up and go and apologize, say she wouldn't go to work tonight and promise faithfully she'd never spend the housekeeping money on herself again. But the other part wouldn't let her.

It was always like this for her. Part of her was happy enough just to be a wife and mother, grateful she had a sober, hard-working husband, a nice home and the security of being loved. Yet the greater part resented the mundane chores, living on a tight budget, trapped in a life that never changed. This wasn't what she'd expected when she fell in love with Reg, she thought he'd take her to a world completely different to the one she'd grown up in, and instead all he was doing was trying to make a replica of it.

Anne's parents were over forty when she was born. Their only other child had died of meningitis when he was two, and they had all but given up hope of ever having another. Throughout her childhood Anne had been all too aware that she was everything in the world to them, and she felt stifled by their over-protective ways. She never got to play with other children, instead her parents played with her, board-games every night, jigsaw puzzles and reading books. They took her to the circus and the seaside, on walks and for boat rides, but all she really wanted was to be allowed to run around with other children, to join the games of rounders in the street, to walk along the high street and look in the shops on her own.

Their house was a semi-detached one in Eltham, in a quiet, tree-lined avenue, and all their neighbours were as genteel and restrained as her parents. Anne's father left for his office in the City at exactly eight every morning, wearing his bowler hat and dark suit and carrying his furled umbrella. She and her mother kissed him goodbye at the door and greeted him again when he came in at six in the evening. He would ask over tea how their day had been, and as young as seven or eight Anne could remember wondering why he always asked because each day was almost identical. Taken to school and collected later, half an hour's piano practice, laying the tea table, and that was all.

On summer nights she would lie awake in bed hearing children's voices in the distance. She knew they came from the nearby council estate, and from what her mother said they were all under-fed and neglected, but it seemed to her that they had much more exciting lives than she did.

At sixteen she was sent to a private secretarial college in Catford, and all at once she was travelling alone on the train each day and not having to wear a school uniform. That was almost enough in itself, but to her delight it led to making new friends that for once her parents approved of. Most of the other girls had parents who were wealthier and further up the social scale than her own, and she was invited home to tea and even to stay overnight at these girls' homes. Ironically, her parents' trust in professional people was misplaced, for they couldn't really care less what their daughters got up to as long as they kept out of their hair. So while Mr and Mrs Hobbs smugly imagined Anne was mixing with the elite and being carefully chaperoned, she was in fact learning to put on make-up, making eyes at boys, trying alcohol, and out exploring the West End.

It didn't amount to anything very wicked, just wandering around giggling when boys tried to pick them up – the farthest they went was a few kisses before catching the last train home. But by the time Anne was seventeen it was autumn and too cold to spend evenings outside. She had soothed her parents into complete trust so that they no longer constantly checked up on her when she said she was staying with someone overnight. So when one of the girls suggested going dancing at the Empire in Leicester Square Anne was only too eager.

It was just the third time she'd been to the Empire when she met Reg, and she fell for him right away. He was as opposite to the kind of man she knew her parents would approve of as it was possible to be – he was a builder not an office worker, his accent was strong South London, he wore a sharp, hand-tailored suit, the kind spivs wore, and his face looked as if it had been moulded by fists. When he took her in his arms to dance, for the first time in her life she suddenly knew what desire was. There was something animal and raw about him which made her feel all weak inside, and even though one of her friends drew her aside later and warned her he was too old for her and probably dangerous, she didn't listen.

He walked her and her friend Marianne to Charing Cross station later to catch the last train to Petts Wood. Just before the train came in, he caught her up in his arms and kissed her with such passion that she knew she'd keep the date they'd made for the following Monday, even if she had to lie to her parents to do it.

Anne got up after Reg had left with the children. She ran a bath and held a cold flannel to her inflamed cheek while she waited for the bath to fill.

'I'm only twenty-seven,' she said aloud to her reflection in the mirror. 'Surely I'm entitled to more than this?'

Later, as she lay back in the bath, her hair protected by a scarf, she looked down thoughtfully at her naked body. Not a stretch-mark, her breasts as firm as they'd been at seventeen.

'If only I hadn't got pregnant,' she murmured.

It wasn't persuasion from Reg that pushed her into making love, it was she who instigated it. He wanted to wait until they could be married, but kissing and petting wasn't enough for Anne, just as meeting him in secret wasn't either. Perhaps it was as her mother claimed, that she knew the only way her parents would tolerate him was through disgracing herself.

Anne winced as her mind went back to that ugly scene on a summer's evening in 1938 when Reg had come to the house to share the responsibility of telling them the news.

Her father had remained standing for the whole time, his back to the fireplace, his mouth set in a straight line of disgust.

'She's having your baby!' he exclaimed. 'You must have raped her, my daughter wouldn't allow an animal like you to touch her willingly.'

Her mother was even worse. She sat on the couch weeping as if she'd just been told her child had been savaged by a mad dog.

Yet Reg was wonderful, he kept so calm and insisted they heard him out.

'I know you disapprove of me because I'm ten years older than Anne, a mere builder from Deptford, and you wanted a lawyer or a doctor at least for your daughter.

But I love her, she loves me, and we want to get married right away.'

Her father ranted and raved, her mother wept and insulted Reg by saying he was a common upstart. Yet still Reg stayed calm. 'Give me a chance to prove myself,' he said. 'I will take care of Anne and our baby. She will never want for anything, but meanwhile just give Anne permission to marry me if you don't want the disgrace of having a little bastard in the family.'

Of course her parents did give their permission. As Reg had put it so succinctly, they didn't want the shame of an illegitimate child. But they never even tried to like Reg, they turned up their noses at the tiny flat in Lee Green he found for himself and Anne, and refused to visit them there. By the time Dulcie was born in December of that year there was talk of war, men being called up, and Anne always had the impression that her parents were pinning all their hopes on Reg being killed, for that way they could get their daughter back home where they believed she belonged.

But Reg survived the war. It was her mother who was killed in an air raid during the Blitz, caught while scurrying to a shelter while shopping in Lewisham.

'Oh Mummy, you were so narrow in your outlook you wouldn't even try to see the good in Reg,' Anne sighed, standing up to soap herself all over. 'If you'd just forgiven me maybe everything would have turned out different.'

As Anne sat down in the bath again she thought back to when her mother was killed. Anne had been evacuated to Sussex when Dulcie was seven months old, billeted in a big country house near Hastings with three other young mothers. With them for company, and older women in the village to give advice and help, she felt secure and happy, and for the first time in her life she was making decisions for herself, learning to become independent. When Reg came to see her before being sent overseas with the army, they talked about finding a permanent home in

Sussex once the war was over. Yet the happiness she found there shattered when her mother was killed in September 1940.

Her father couldn't bear to be alone, he made Anne come back and keep house for him, even though it was so dangerous to be in London. He kept crying all the time and expected her to wait on him the way her mother had, complaining about everything Dulcie did, insulting Reg. All the while bombs were dropping, turning every night into a living hell.

It was impossible to stay with him. She wanted to go back to Sussex, but her sense of duty compelled her to find somewhere near to her father, so she took the poky flat in New Cross. Yet when he died three years later, he proved how little he'd thought of her sacrifice or her future, because he left everything, the house and his savings, to his younger brother and nothing to her and his grand-daughters.

Anne got out of the bath, her eyes swimming with tears. Reg had said dozens of times that she ought to let the past go, and she wished she could, but it just wouldn't let her. It was slowly poisoning her, making her into someone she didn't want to be.

Before Anne began dressing she took out the bottle of gin she kept hidden in the back of the wardrobe and drank directly from it. It burned her throat and made her eyes water but the warming effect was instantaneous, pushing back the bleakness inside her.

Two hours later, at eight o'clock, she was behind the bar at the Station Hotel smiling and pulling pints as if she was the happiest woman in the world. The saloon bar was packed as usual on a Saturday night, as was the public bar next door, and a private party was in full swing in the function room at the back.

Tosh, the landlord, stood at the corner of the bar with a large whisky in one hand and a cigar in the other, watching Anne. He liked to see her breasts moving up and down as

23

she pulled pints, and the curve of her pert little arse under that tight dress, and to know that he'd have her again before the night was over.

No one, least of all Tosh, knew how he'd got that name – his real one was Albert Bright. He was born in Stepney in 1900, and he had taken his childhood nickname with him when he turned to professional boxing. Although he'd never reached any dizzy heights in boxing circles, he had made enough money to buy a little pub in Mile End, and by branching out into black marketeering during the war, he got enough to buy this place.

Situated on the corner of Leahurst Road, directly opposite Hither Green station, the large Edwardian premises were a little goldmine. The immediate area was short on pubs, travelling salesmen found his rooms upstairs a convenient base from which to travel to the City and the West End, and he had two function rooms he let out for parties and weddings.

Tosh had been married, but his wife had run off with a sailor twelve years ago. He hadn't missed her, only his pride was hurt, but it had made him wary of women ever since. He knew he wasn't much to look at, short, stocky and balding. His nose had taken a few too many punches, his teeth were bad and he had a big gut. Yet women were always making a play for him. They claimed it was because he had style and made them laugh, but he knew only too well they were mostly only interested in his money.

Anne Taylor was no different. She was just looking for a way out of a marriage which bored her. She was barking up the wrong tree with him, though. She might be the most thrilling screw he'd ever had, as beautiful as a May morning and ladylike to boot, but he wasn't about to get himself saddled with two kids and a man like Reg after his blood.

He was prepared to play the game for a little longer though. Just the thought of pushing his cock into that sexy mouth made him quiver and when he saw there was a slight lull behind the bar, he beckoned her over to him.

'Want a break for a while?' he asked. 'Janet will come in from the public bar to take over. We could go upstairs for a drink.'

Anne groaned inwardly for she knew exactly what Tosh really wanted, and not for the first time she regretted embarking on an affair with him. She had begun working lunch-hours at the pub last December, and Tosh made her feel good because he was always saying how beautiful she was. Before long she was staying on after the pub closed for the afternoon, and over a couple of drinks he would tell her about his boxing days, the elegant night-clubs he went to, and all the glamorous people he used to mix with. She sensed that he still hankered for that kind of life, and it seemed to her that if he had the right woman on his arm, he'd go back to it. She found herself thinking about him constantly, imagining herself as that woman, stepping out for a night on the town in a fabulous evening dress and a mink coat.

It turned bitterly cold at Christmas, and then the snow came. The flat was freezing, the windows iced up even on the inside, it was an ordeal just to get undressed and have a bath, let alone try to wash clothes, dry them and find something in the shops to make into an evening meal. Reg didn't seem to notice the cold, and it irritated him that she just couldn't stand it. If she hadn't had her job to go to at the pub, she thought perhaps she might have gone mad, for it was warm there, and a few drinks, a bit of flattery, took the edge off her despair.

Tosh was so attentive, so caring. He often gave her a few chops or some mince to take home when she'd used up her meat ration, and he would shove a pound note into her hand and tell her to pop over to the hairdresser's and get her hair done, but most of all it was his appreciation of her, rather than desire, that lured her into having a little kissing and cuddling with him.

It was mid-February when she finally let him make love to her. Even that came about because the water pipes were frozen up at home, and he suggested she had a bath upstairs in his flat. It was heaven in his bathroom, a big radiator kept it warm, the water was piping hot, and the couple of large gins she had before getting into the bath transported her into a blissful state where she didn't care about anything but the moment. She had been wallowing in there for almost an hour when Tosh walked in with a hot, fluffy towel for her in one hand, and another large drink in the other. He wrapped her up in the towel and carried her into his bedroom, and even if he wasn't a great lover, the wickedness of it, the sensuality of the warmth and comfort, and the gin, made it quite delicious.

Anne was very glad she wasn't a Catholic like Reg, or she'd have been compelled to confess her adultery. But she got her punishment in other ways, because each afternoon after going to bed with Tosh, which was never so good after the first time, she had to go home again and face the girls and Reg. She knew she was failing them all by not having meals ready and letting the flat get so dirty and untidy, but instead of guilt making her try harder, it seemed to have the reverse effect. The more Reg complained, the less she did, and each night when she went to bed her dreams were all of a glamorous life, with her dressed in silk and satin, diamonds around her neck, and being with a man who wanted to show her off.

She knew it was wicked, but sometimes she even had fantasies about Reg dying. It wasn't that she actually wanted him dead, all she wanted was freedom, just as she had as a child. Maybe that was why she riled him so often by buying new clothes – she had never consciously thought about it, she just wanted to look stunning, but perhaps it was a way of making him get so exasperated with her that he'd leave her.

'Come on then!' Tosh said impatiently, repeating his suggestion they went upstairs for a drink.

Anne forced a smile. 'A break would be nice,' she said, even though she had no heart for even speaking to him, let alone sex tonight. She knew it was a mistake to get involved with Tosh, but she needed to keep him sweet just in case Reg did take it into his head to slam the door on her.

Tosh poured her a large gin and tonic upstairs in his sitting-room. There had been a time when Anne admired his flat with its ostentatious flock wallpaper, the cocktail bar, radiogram and sumptuous couches, but tonight it looked as vulgar as he was. He had barely poured her the drink before he unbuttoned his fly, pulled out his flaccid cock and suggested *she woke John Thomas up*.

'I'm not really in the mood tonight,' she said, looking away. 'Reg and I had a fight today, things are going from bad to worse at home, he actually hit me.'

She thought that Tosh would put his cock away, come and sit beside her and reassure her he would take care of her if necessary, but he didn't. Instead he moved right in front of her, caught hold of her head and pushed her mouth down on to him.

'Fill your mouth with this,' he said, and held her head so she couldn't move away. 'I've been watching your tits jiggling all evening and I'm as horny as hell.'

It was vile – no tenderness, no loving words, no thought for her, just bestiality. He smelled musty, he kept muttering filthy things, and he was pushing himself so far into her mouth it made her retch. He didn't even have the grace to withdraw when he came.

Anne turned away and spat into her handkerchief, then quickly took a large gulp of gin. Tears of humiliation welled up in her eyes, and when Tosh slumped down on the couch beside her and tried to put his arm around her, she shrugged him off.

'Don't you dare ever treat me that way again,' she hissed at him. 'I'm not some old tart.'

'Sorry, doll,' he said, not even looking vaguely ashamed. 'I got carried away. I'll make it better for you later.'

'I can't stay later,' she said, wishing she could go home right now. 'I told you already, things are bad at home. I think Reg might even throw me out.'

'Well, you can always share my bed for the night,' he said as if it was just a joke.

Anne riled up. 'Don't you care about me at all?' she asked indignantly. 'I've already told you Reg hit me once today, I'm hurt and scared and all you've done is make me feel worse. I wish I'd never come here to work, I've had nothing but trouble since I did.'

'Come on, babe,' he said, pulling her into his arms and kissing her. 'You know I think a lot of you, I'm just not much good at the sloppy stuff. But you've got to make the peace with yer old man, you've got the little ones to think of. Now sit there, drink yer drink and have a fag till you've calmed down. I'll have to get back to the bar.'

Anne did as she was told, but Tosh's words and his actions had done nothing to reassure her, just stirred up even more resentment and bad memories.

Reg held his two girls' hands as they walked through the dimly lit subway under Hither Green station. They had eaten egg and chips in a café and then gone to the Park cinema. This rather elderly picture-house rarely showed new releases, but instead packed people in by putting on a double programme of old, well-loved major films. Tonight's were first *Dumbo* and then *Daddy Long Legs* starring Shirley Temple, but although both girls were riveted to their seats during *Dumbo*, May had begun to fidget in the second film and Reg had no real choice but to leave. All the way down the hill Dulcie had been complaining that May had spoilt the evening.

'That's enough now, Dulcie,' he said finally. 'May's only five and she can't concentrate for long. We'll get to see *Daddy Long Legs* again one day.'

Dulcie shut up then, it had after all been a lovely surprise going out with Dad. When she heard him raise his voice to Mum about her dress she'd thought they were all in for another miserable evening.

'Can we go in and see Mummy?' May asked as they came out of the station. They weren't often out when it was dark and the Station Hotel, all brightly lit, looked and sounded very inviting with music wafting out through the doors.

'Of course not,' Reg said. 'Children aren't allowed in pubs.'

'But I didn't see her in her new dress!'

Dulcie looked sharply at her younger sister – sometimes she could swear May was half-witted. Surely she knew the new dress was what had made Mum and Dad argue again today? She'd soon be telling Dad how the park-keeper chased them.

'I expect she'll put it on again tomorrow,' Reg said, and to Dulcie's surprise he didn't sound angry, so maybe he'd forgiven her. She thought her parents were very odd sometimes, Granny had said more than once that they were *chalk and cheese*. When they weren't fighting they were all lovey-dovey, kissing and hugging each other. That embarrassed her almost as much as their fighting disturbed her. She wished they could be like Mary Abbott's parents a few doors away. They were just nice to each other all the time, neither sloppy nor nasty. But then Mr Abbott was a very little man, and his wife was big, fat and plain. Perhaps that was why?

'Into bed quickly,' Reg said once they got indoors. 'While you're getting undressed I'll make you some hot milk.'

As he waited in the kitchen for the milk to warm, Reg looked around him and winced at the state of it. The walls were greasy, the lino hadn't been washed for weeks, and the tablecloth and curtains were filthy. He'd painted it all glossy white when they moved in eighteen months earlier, the kitchen cabinet and the window-frames bright yellow. Anne had been so pleased with it that she'd made the yellow gingham tablecloth and curtains and bought a couple of plants for the window-sill. Why had she let it get this way? Didn't she see the dirt, or was it just that she didn't care any more?

He didn't understand her, but he still loved her every

bit as much now as he had when they got married, the dreams he had then were all still intact. He intended to start his own building business in a few years and buy them a pretty little house out in the suburbs. Maybe when Anne was back where she belonged she'd start being glad about things again.

Reg was one of eight children. His childhood and adolescence had been overshadowed by hunger, poverty and a drunken, violent father. Yet even as young as seven or eight, Reg sensed there had to be a way into a better world, and he spent his time looking for it. While his siblings were content to kick a tin can round the dirty streets or make mud pies on the banks of the creek, he used to take long walks up through Greenwich Park to look at the grand houses in Blackheath and admire their beautiful gardens.

His mother seemed to understand how he felt, and when he was fourteen she persuaded a master builder to take him on as an apprentice, even though this would mean further hardship for her. While Reg's old playmates were already moving into crime, he stuck tenaciously to his work. Even after a twelve-hour day humping bricks and mixing concrete, he still attended night school too. He wasn't satisfied with learning mere brick-laying, but mastered plastering, carpentry and plumbing, and because of this he managed to keep in work right through the grim years of the Depression and support his by then widowed mother and the younger children.

He was twenty-seven when he met Anne, and though there had been other women before her, he had never taken any of them seriously. Anne, with her sweet-smelling hair, dainty manners and posh voice, gave him the same feeling when as a child he'd looked at those beautiful houses up in Blackheath. He found himself blushing like a sixteen-year-old, his pulse raced, and he hung on every word she said. Yet it was the same for her too, she would jump on a train or bus to meet him anywhere, she sent him love letters when he worked away from London, she enveloped him in the kind of sweet romance that until then he'd thought only existed in fiction. He asked her to marry him after knowing her only a few weeks, before they even made love for the first time, for he believed they were made for each other.

They'd had it tough, there was no getting away from that. The hostility from her parents, the separation during the war. Then Anne losing her mother, and all the unpleasant stuff with her father when she was trying to cope with two small children. But then all women had it hard during the war, she wasn't unique, and it was over now, they had a decent place to live. The girls were bright and healthy. So what was it that made her stop caring?

The milk was warm enough now, Reg poured it into two mugs, stirred a spoon of sugar in to each and carried it in to the girls. They were sitting up in bed waiting for him and he had to smile, they looked like a pair of angels with their just-brushed blonde hair all silky on the shoulders of their white nightdresses.

'Prayers first,' he said, then sat on the end of the bed watching as they said the Rosary. It made him smile again to see May peeping through half-closed eyes at her sister and trying to copy her. She could never remember the words, just moved her lips and muttered 'Hail Mary' now and again, but Dulcie was word perfect. It took him back to when he was her age – his ambition then had been to be an altar boy, for the church was his favourite place. He loved the serenity, the smell of incense, polish and flowers, he could remember praying hard for a miracle, that his father would stop drinking and beating his mother, and that they could move away from Deptford to somewhere beautiful. His prayers were ignored. He was seventeen before his father was found dead in a back alley where he'd had a heart attack while staggering back from the pub. There was no money to move away, the only solace for the children was in knowing they would never have to see their mother with black eyes again.

As he watched Dulcie he wondered if she had a secret

31

prayer too. She was a thinker, an observer, happy to stand on the side-lines and watch others take the centre court. Yet she had so many abilities, she was the best reader in her class, she could draw and paint, sew almost as well as her grandmother, and she had only to be told something once and she grasped it.

May was very different. She wasn't half so advanced as Dulcie was at the same age, but perhaps that was because her older sister did so much for her. May liked the limelight and she stole it effortlessly with her ability to chat and laugh. He felt that even if she never matched her sister's intelligence, she would be the kind to grasp opportunities, for even now at only five she could be very determined.

He loved them so much, and he was all too aware that the rot which had crept into his marriage had to be stopped before it damaged them.

'God bless Granny,' Dulcie said when she'd finished the Rosary. 'And please make Mummy happy again.'

A lump came up in Reg's throat and his eyes prickled. He bent over the girls, kissed them and said goodnight, then quickly left the room. It took a child to hit the nail right on the head. Anne wasn't happy, and perhaps he ought to try to find out the root cause of it.

Reg had dozed off, but he woke when he heard Anne's high heels tapping up the street. He got out of his seat and pulled back the curtains a crack to watch her. Even when she was tired after a long evening, she walked so elegantly, head held high, shoulders back. Her hair glimmered under the street lights, her figure was so curvy and desirable in the new dress. He didn't really care now about the money she'd spent on it, all he wanted was for her to come in and hug him and tell him she loved him, the way she used to.

He slipped out into the kitchen and put the kettle on. Maybe if he talked to her now they could sort things out and then go to bed and make love.

The kettle was just coming to the boil as she came up the stairs. She looked more than just tired, completely drained and care-worn as she slung her handbag over the newel post on the landing, and his heart went out to her. 'I'm just making some tea,' he said before going back into the kitchen. 'Go and put your feet up, I'll bring it in.'

She was slumped on the couch when he came in and she looked nervous as if expecting more harsh words.

'I'm very sorry I hit you,' he said, handing her the tea.

'I provoked you,' she said. 'It doesn't matter.'

'What's gone wrong with us?' Reg asked, sitting down on the chair opposite her. 'We've got to work out what it is because we can't go on like this.'

'It's not you, Reg, it's all me,' she said wearily. 'I'm no good for you. I can't be what you want me to be.'

'What do you think I want you to be?' he asked gently.

She didn't reply for a moment, just frowned as if trying to get it sorted out in her mind. 'You want a perfect wife and mother,' she said eventually. 'One who scrubs and cleans like your mother does, has the dinner on the table when you come in, and never sees beyond the four walls.'

Reg laughed. 'If I wanted that I could live with my mother,' he said. 'That's not it at all. I can live with a bit of mess, and having to wait for my dinner. But I want to come home to a wife who's pleased to see me, to a mother who talks and plays with her children, and I want a wife who shares my dreams for the future and doesn't spend the money I'm trying to save for that.'

'But that's just it, Reg,' she suddenly burst out. 'It's all in the future with you. Save money, be sensible, wait and wait. I can't stand it, I want to live now.'

'With me?'

That question shot out, he wasn't even aware of it forming in his mind. But once it was out he realized it was the crucial question. Did she or did she not want to live with him?

She hesitated, and that in itself cut him to the quick. 'You don't want to live with me,' he said. 'Do you?'

She put her hands over her face. 'Why did you ask that?' she said through her hands. 'It's impossible to answer.'

'It's not. Just a yes or no will do.'

'But it isn't black or white,' she said.

'Why not?' He was surprised he could sound so calm.

'Because sometimes I'm happy to be with you.'

'And sometimes you aren't?'

She nodded.

'Well, let's talk about the times when you aren't then,' he said. 'How does it feel?'

'Like I'm trapped, like a mouse in a cage with only the wheel to go round and round on,' she burst out.

'Well, I could say the same myself.' He shrugged. 'I have to go to work every day, that's like a treadmill. I'd rather be sitting at the seaside, or driving a motorbike down an empty country lane, or even getting drunk down in the pub, but I have to go to work or we'd all starve.'

'I knew you wouldn't understand,' she said sullenly. 'You always bring everything back to how hard you work for us.'

'I don't, I go to work willingly for the good of us all, and I dream of the time I might be able to buy that motorbike or lie in the sun in our own garden. My dreams are for all of us. What do you dream about?'

'Being free!'

Anne's voice rose as she said that and Reg knew it came from the heart.

'Free of me?'

'Yes. No. Oh, I don't know,' she said, and promptly burst into tears.

Reg allowed that to sink in for a moment. Instinct told him the first reply was the one she really meant, but she hadn't the courage to go through with it.

'Are you trying to tell me you want a divorce?' he said in little more than a whisper. 'To end it all after nine years of marriage? Why, Anne? What about the children?'

'Why did you have to start in on me again the moment I got in?' she suddenly snarled at him. 'I'm exhausted, I can't think straight.'

This, or something similar, was how she wriggled out

of all confrontations. Reg usually let it be then, but tonight he had no intention of doing that.

'But you *can* think straight,' he insisted. '*You* know why you are unhappy, all you have to do is explain it to me, or how can I help you? Try looking back and thinking about when it all started.'

She gave him a cold stare. 'When Mummy was killed, I expect,' she said. 'Everything was fine until I was forced to come back to London and live with Daddy. From then on it was just one crisis after another, and you were never there.'

'I couldn't help that,' he said evenly. 'It was the same for everyone. I know it must have been tough with a baby, the rationing, the bombs and everything. I came home as often as I could.'

'But it wasn't enough,' she blurted out. 'I was scared and lonely, Dulcie was a little misery, Dad was always moaning, I never got a decent night's sleep. I used to panic each night we went into the air-raid shelter that I'd be killed and there would be no one to look after Dulcie.'

Anne brought up this period of the war every time they had words and Reg felt there was nothing new to be dragged out of it.

'But things improved once you'd moved out to New Cross,' he said. 'You seemed much happier with those two girls downstairs for company.'

'Those bitches,' she said sharply.

'You said you liked them!' Reg exclaimed in surprise.

'That was before I knew what they were really like,' she said. 'They were just tarts, they were laughing at me behind my back.'

This was a new slant, Anne hadn't said anything about the girls before.

'Why?' he asked.

'Because I was always trying to make that place nice, and waiting for you. They jeered at the way I spoke and dressed, they kept saying all soldiers were unfaithful to their sweethearts and wives. They made me feel so childish.'

Reg recalled that on that leave he had been a little worried that Anne had made friends with these two factory girls. They were in their mid-twenties and were fast types, who made crude jokes when he passed them on the stairs. He got the impression they had rather too many men in and out of their flat. Yet they did seem to have cheered Anne up. But now he came to think about it, by his next leave they'd moved out, and Anne had given up on trying to make the flat homely. Did something unpleasant occur in the interim period that she'd never spoken of?

'Did something nasty happen then?' he asked. 'Maybe if you tell me it won't bother you any more.'

'It will bother you though,' she replied darkly.

'I don't think I can work up much steam about an incident six or seven years ago,' he said with a smirk.

'Well, if you must know, they persuaded me to go out with them one evening,' she blurted out. 'When we got back there was a policewoman in the flat. A neighbour had reported I'd gone out and left Dulcie alone.'

When she saw Reg's shocked expression she began gabbling that she'd only been gone an hour, that she'd never done it before or again, that it was just the pressure from the two girls that made her do it.

Reg guessed that it couldn't have been the first and only time. It was very unlikely anyone would notice a mother going out and leaving a child, not unless they repeatedly heard the child crying. Yet while it was reprehensible that a mother should leave her child alone at a time when air raids were an almost nightly occurrence, there was no real point in ranting about it now, so many years later. What puzzled him was why she'd confess to it now.

Reg was reminded of times he'd made a confession and spilled out one sin to the priest, while leaving out a far more grievous one. It was a way of exonerating himself of at least part of the guilt. Was this what she was doing?

He watched as she took out a cigarette. Her hands were trembling so much she could barely strike the match, and clearly he had stirred up some painful old memories. He leaned over, took the matches from her and struck one for her. 'Suppose you tell me the truth about what happened at that time?'

'I just have,' she said defiantly.

'You've told me part of it,' he said. 'My guess is that there is a whole lot more, and you're just afraid to tell me.'

'Why do you always have to be so bloody righteous?' she snapped at him. 'You're smug about not ending up like your brothers, for being a craftsman, for every bloody thing. It makes me sick.'

'Well, I'm sorry,' he said with heavy sarcasm. 'Maybe you'd like it better if I got drunk every night and beat you up? Or if I was a dustman or a road-sweeper and you had to live in the East End?'

She gave him the oddest look, her eyes were half closed, her mouth twisted in a sneer, and he knew immediately she was going to tell him something he wouldn't like.

'If you must know, I had an affair with an American airman. Now, how does that make you feel? Are you glad you got it out of me?'

He felt as if he'd just been kicked in the stomach. Yet it wasn't purely the content of what she'd said, it was the way she'd delivered it, coldly and deliberately with the intention of wounding him.

Reg could only gawp at her. Her eyes were like blue ice, no fear or remorse in them.

'Okay, so you had an affair,' he said after a moment or two's silence, his voice croaking with emotion. 'But I'd like to know why you chose to tell me this now. Is it because you want me to hate you so you can be justified in leaving me?'

'You asked what was wrong, I told you,' she said with a toss of her head. 'If you can't take the truth you shouldn't have asked.'

A picture formed in his mind of Anne swanning down

the stairs of that seedy house in New Cross on an airman's arm, with Dulcie lying upstairs alone in her cot. The picture then moved to Anne making love to this man while Dulcie sat watching, thumb in mouth. It was too much to bear.

'You cold-hearted bitch,' he hissed at her, getting up from his seat and walking across the room towards the window. He turned back to her, tears rolling down his cheeks. 'I could stand knowing you'd been unfaithful if I thought you'd confessed to it because you were tormented by guilt and you knew the only way to save our marriage was by bringing it out into the open. But you don't want it helped, do you? You want to destroy it and me!'

'Oh, poor, poor Reg,' she taunted him. 'You pounced on me the minute I came in the door intent on digging out something. Now I'm supposed to feel bad because I let you! I was twenty, for God's sake, my mother had just been killed, my father had turned against me, I was struggling to cope with a two-year-old and my husband was away. I just turned to someone else for comfort, that's all. It's hardly a hanging offence.'

Reg sank down on to a chair, resting his elbows on the table, his face in his hands. Part of his mind said she was right. He couldn't even count the number of friends he had who'd found brief comfort in the arms of another woman during the war, there were so many. He'd been sorely tempted himself on many occasions.

He looked at her through his fingers, hoping to see tears, some sign she was sorry. But she was yawning, twiddling a strand of hair. She clearly couldn't care less.

The truth came to him in a blinding flash.

'You're having it off with someone now! Aren't you?' he said, springing off the chair towards her. 'You want to go to him?'

'Of course not,' she said, looking startled.

He leaned over her, his hands on the back of the couch either side of her head, his face right up to hers. 'I know I'm right. I may be slow but I always get there in the end. The new clothes, the hair-dos, the boredom with me and the children. That's why you admitted to that affair in the war, not because it was really troubling your conscience, but because you hoped it would make me mad enough to throw you out. Admit it! You bitch!'

She didn't have to admit it, he could see it in her face. She had never been a successful liar, she always coloured up, her eyes took on a hunted look. 'No, Reg, you're wrong,' she bleated.

Reg moved back from her, and she leaped off the couch, backing away from him towards the fireplace.

'Swear on the children's lives, then maybe I'll believe you,' he demanded.

They faced each other, both panting and wild-eyed.

'Swear,' Reg commanded. 'I don't think even you are low enough to swear on your own child's life if you aren't telling the truth.'

He could see her indecision, mouth opening and closing, wanting to swear, yet afraid to. 'You can't do it, can you?' he taunted her. 'You'd leave a small child alone while you go out with a Yank, you'd take money from my pockets when I'm asleep, you'd buy clothes for yourself when your kids need shoes, but you aren't quite evil enough to swear on their lives.'

Her mouth began to quiver and her eyes to fill with tears. That was all the confirmation he needed.

'Don't turn on the waterworks,' he snarled at her. 'Just get out of this flat now and never come back.'

'You can't throw me out at this time of night,' she whimpered. 'Oh, please calm down, Reg. I'll go in the morning, but don't make me go now.'

'Why don't you want to go now? Won't your lover be pleased to see you?'

She seemed to wilt before his eyes.

'Who is he, Anne? Where do you go with him?'

'Does that matter?' she said, tears running down her cheeks.

'It matters all right,' he said. 'You see, if he's another poor sap like me who fell for your posh voice and your pretty face, he needs warning what a calculating, lying bitch you really are. On the other hand, if he's been laughing up his sleeve as he knocks you off, then he needs his head kicked in. If you want to ever see the kids again, you'd better tell me who he is.'

Anne knew in that instant that she'd seriously mis-judged Reg. The gentle way he had started probing about the past when she got home from work had made her think he was looking for a amicable solution to their problems. Divorce was what she had in mind, and in her stupidity she'd imagined this would be arranged the way she'd seen other couples part, with her staying in this flat with the children, and Reg finding another place of his own.

But she should have known better, a tough man like Reg wasn't going just to give up without a fight, it wasn't his way. He'd fought for everything he wanted through-out his life. What a fool she'd been to try to wound him with her infidelity, all it had done was strip him of all his illusions about her, and now he was wounded he'd move heaven and earth till he got at the whole truth.

But she couldn't let Reg rush around like an enraged bull questioning every Tom, Dick and Harry. There were too many people out there already whispering that there was something going on between her and Tosh.

'It was a man I met at the pub,' she blurted out. 'You don't know him, he's a travelling salesman, he doesn't come from round here.'

Reg's face grew dark with anger, his eyes mere slits as he came towards her.

'You bitch,' he screamed at her. 'You were off in the afternoons having it off with him while I'm working my socks off to keep you in new clothes and hair-dos. How could you?'

'I couldn't help it,' she sobbed. 'I was feeling so mis-erable.'

'What sort of an excuse is that?' Reg raged at her. 'You've made me miserable too, but I never looked at another woman. Get out of here now. Go on, go, before I hit you again.'

'No, Reg, please don't throw me out,' she whimpered. 'I'm sorry, it's all over with him now.'

'I don't care whether it's over or not. You are going this minute and I'll never let you in the door again,' he roared at her. 'You won't take your bag, your coat, the key or anything. You can go to him just as you are.'

'But the children,' she tried to plead with him, knowing that was his one weak spot. 'You can't do this to them.'

'Better for them to live without a mother than to know she's a whore,' he retorted, pushing at her shoulder, edging her towards the door. 'Out now!'

He pulled the door open and pushed her through it on to the landing, and by putting one hand on either door jamb, barred her way from getting back in.

'If you do this to me I'll fight you in the courts for them,' she screamed at him. 'I'll get them back from you, you'll see, and I'll take them somewhere you'll never find them.'

She was about to go down the stairs when she realized she had no shoes on. Turning to plead with him, she saw he had moved back from the door, and she made a move to rush back into the living-room to retrieve them.

He caught her by both shoulders and shook her.

'What reason could you possibly give the courts so they'd let you have them?' he shouted angrily.

'May isn't your child, for one,' she screamed in his face. 'She's the child of the airman.'

Even as the words came out of her mouth Anne knew she'd gone much too far. It was true, the real reason she felt so much guilt and unhappiness, but it was a secret she'd always vowed to take to her grave.

Reg gave a bellowing roar and made a grab for her. Stunned by what she'd revealed, terrified of what he was going to do to her, Anne ducked under his flailing arms and sped for the stairs. He caught her at the top, his hands gripping her round the throat, and as his fingers tightened on her windpipe, she tried to kick his shins with her stockinged feet.

Reg looked down at her bulging eyes, saw the terror in them as her feet kicked out at him, and instantly released her. 'Get out before I kill you,' he yelled and turned away.

There was a gasp, a thump, and Reg spun round. To his shock she was hurtling head over heels like a ball down the stairs. All he could see was a glimpse of stockings, suspenders and white knickers, then her blonde hair flying out like a mass of gold Christmas tinsel.

'Anne!' he yelled, running down after her. But with a loud crash she hit the hall wall at the bottom of the stairs and landed on the floor. She looked like a broken doll, one leg stuck out at a strange angle.

'I didn't mean it,' he said, crouching down beside her. 'Stay there, don't move, I'll get an ambulance.'

But a trickle of blood was running out of her open mouth. Her eyes were glassy. Reg slumped on to the floor and roared out his anguish.

Chapter Two

Dulcie woke at the sound of her mother's raised voice. She heard her saying something about fighting in courts, and taking someone to somewhere where Dad would never find them. This didn't make any more sense to her than most of their other quarrels, and she was just about to pull the pillow from under her head to cover her ears when Dad's voice roared out.

'What reason could you possibly give the courts so they'd let you have them?' she heard him say, as clearly as if he were standing at the end of her bed.

Suddenly Dulcie was wide awake, for it sounded as if he was talking about her and May. The bedroom door was open just a crack and the landing light was glimmering through it. As she moved to sit up, May woke up too, but only snuggled closer to her sister.

'May isn't your child for one!' Mum yelled out, loud enough to wake the whole street. 'She's the child of the airman.'

There was a wild roar of rage from her dad, and a scuffling sound as if they were struggling together. 'Get out before I kill you,' she heard Dad shriek, and then a second or two later she heard a peculiar loud thumping noise. It sounded as if something heavy had been dropped and it was bouncing down the stairs.

When Dad yelled out 'Anne!' Dulcie knew her mum must be falling. At the same time as she heard Dad pounding down the stairs, May clutched at her in terror. Dulcie pushed her away and ran out on to the landing to look down over the banisters.

From where she was standing she could see nothing but

Dad's feet and a bit of his bottom sticking out, as if he was kneeling down in the hall where the stairs ended. But as he began to bellow, a terrible, wild sound, she ran along the landing and started down the stairs after him.

'Daddy!' she screamed involuntarily as she saw him bending over Mum.

He turned his head towards her, and even though there was little light there, she could see his face was all twisted up like a monster's. In terror she ran back up the stairs, grabbed May who was just coming along the landing sleepily rubbing her eyes, and fled back to their bedroom, shutting the door behind them.

'What's the matter?' May asked, her voice squeaky with fright in the darkness. 'What did Mummy say about me?'

Dulcie switched on the light and reached out for her sister to hug her. She had no idea what to do, she felt she couldn't even breathe she was so scared. She had heard with her own ears Dad say he would kill Mum if she didn't get out. Had he killed her?

Yet that didn't seem possible, and even in the midst of her own fright she knew she must look after May. This had always been her role since she was born. It had been she who rocked the pram to get her off to sleep, she who told Mum when her nappy was wet, and as May got bigger she'd played with her, fed her and prevented her from hurting herself.

'Get back into bed,' she said. 'I'll look after you.'

She got back into bed beside May and cuddled her tightly, straining her ears to hear what was happening downstairs. Dad was still making that horrible roaring noise, but all at once she heard the click of the front door opening, then silence, as if he'd gone out.

This was even more frightening. Had he run away and left them? Was Mum still lying down there all hurt?

There was complete silence now, and after few minutes' thought she decided she'd better try to be brave and go and look. She whispered that May was to stay in bed and that she wouldn't be long, and made her way back along the landing and down the stairs.

Mum was still lying there at the bottom, her back against the hall wall. A cold wind was whistling up the stairs, fluttering Dulcie's nightdress as if the front door was open.

She crept down nervously. 'Mummy!' she called out softly. 'Can you hear me?'

By the time Dulcie had reached the fourth stair from the bottom she could see her mother clearly. Her eyes were wide open, her mouth was too, and something dark was coming out of it, trickling down on to the bodice of her new dress and staining it.

She so much wanted to go right down and touch her, but she was too frightened. When children fell in the playground at school they always cried. Why wasn't Mum making any sound?

Not knowing what else to do, she sat down on the stairs, put her hands together and closed her eyes. 'Holy Mary, Mother of God,' she began, but then found she couldn't remember what came next because all she could think of was that Mum was showing all her stocking tops and the lace on her knickers. She wanted to go down and cover her legs up, if the door was open someone passing might see her, but her own legs wouldn't seem to move.

Dulcie was still sitting there when her father came rushing back in. He stopped stock-still when he saw her.

He was still wild-eyed, as though he'd been crying, but he didn't look scary any longer. 'What are you doing?' he asked.

'I don't know, Daddy,' she said, for a moment thinking this was just a horrible dream and he was going to carry her back to bed. Yet she looked past him and Mum was still lying there. 'Can you cover Mummy's legs up?'

She watched as he returned to Mum, observed the tender way he stroked her cheek and pulled her dress down over her knees, and suddenly Dulcie realized.

'Is she, d-d-dead?' she stuttered, hardly able to get the word out.

He nodded and came back to her, squatting down before her on the stairs. 'It was an accident, sweetheart, she fell down the stairs. I just went for help.'

Dulcie began to shiver and Dad took her hands in his. 'I want you to go back to bed, sweetheart. Any minute now someone will come to help. Will you look after May for me?'

Dulcie nodded.

'The police may take me away with them,' he said and his voice sounded shaky. 'If they do and I don't get a chance to speak to you again, you must get them to take you to Granny's.'

'But why would they take you away?' she asked. 'Did you do something bad?'

He leaned forward and rested his forehead on her knees which were tucked up under her nightdress. 'I didn't push her, Dulcie, you must believe that even if some people tell you otherwise. We did have a fight, but she fell down there.'

'I heard you fighting,' she whispered. She didn't know whether to say she'd heard him say he'd kill Mum if she didn't get out.

He lifted his head and looked right into her eyes. 'I loved her, Dulcie, she made me very angry, but I wouldn't have hurt her.'

Dulcie didn't have to say anything more for she heard the sirens coming along the road.

He kissed her on the forehead and lifted her to her feet. 'Go back to bed now, don't be scared. Trust me, it will be all right.'

Dulcie tried very hard not to be scared when she heard all the men's voices drifting up the stairs. May had fallen asleep again by the time she got back into bed, but she knew she wouldn't be able to sleep. She felt cold right through to her bones, and her head ached with all the questions she wanted answering.

Someone opened her bedroom door and looked in, but she shut her eyes tight and pretended to be asleep. Then she heard men going into all the rooms, their voices low rumblings in the distance.

'Of course I didn't throw her!' she heard Dad shout out at one point.

There were sounds of doors opening and closing, then she heard a vehicle drive off, but still she could hear Dad's voice and other men's, and it seemed to her they were up in the living-room now.

It was then she began to cry, for suddenly it struck home what Mum's death meant. Who would look after her and May? Surely they couldn't stay with Granny for long? How would they get to school? And what had Mum meant by *May isn't your child*?

Dulcie was still crying when the bedroom door opened and two policemen came in. She sat up in bed in alarm, putting one arm across May who was still sleeping.

'It's all right, don't be frightened,' one of the men said, coming closer to the bed. 'Your mummy has had an accident, and your daddy has asked us to take you to your granny's.'

'I want my daddy,' Dulcie sobbed. 'Where is he?'

The policeman sat down on the bed. 'Daddy's gone down to the police station now to answer a few questions. We can't leave you here all on your own, can we?'

Dulcie just looked at him in horror.

'You must be Dulcie, and your sister is called May, Daddy told us,' he went on, putting one hand on May's shoulder. 'Will you help me wake her up and get her dressed? Then we'll put a few of your things in a bag and go.'

Some ten minutes later they all went downstairs, the policeman carrying the bag they'd packed, their two dolls sticking out of the top. May was unusually quiet, she didn't even ask any questions, but as Dulcie got to the place where her mother had been lying, and she saw someone had drawn a chalk mark round it, she began crying again.

'Did you see what happened tonight, Dulcie?' the policeman asked as they went towards the door.

'I saw Mummy lying there after I heard the noise,' she sobbed.

'Then maybe you can tell me about that once we get to your granny's house,' he said, taking her hand.

'Gawd almighty, what's happened?' Granny exclaimed as she opened the door to her house in Akerman Street and saw the two policemen with her grand-daughters.

'We're sorry to wake you in the middle of the night, Mrs Taylor,' one of them said. 'But it was an emergency.'

The children broke free of the hands holding them and flung themselves at their grandmother. 'Mummy's dead,' Dulcie blurted out. 'She fell down the stairs. Daddy said we had to come here.'

Maud Taylor was seventy-five, a small but rotund woman with a face so lined she often joked she looked like a dried prune. Laughter was her way of coping with the hard life she'd been dished out with, and her eight children had rarely seen her fazed by trouble or disaster, yet she looked amazed by what Dulcie had just said and clutched the two children to her tighter, looking to the older of the two men for confirmation.

He just nodded, for he hadn't realized until now that Dulcie was aware of the outcome of her mother's fall. 'I'll explain inside,' he said, noting the old lady was wearing nothing but a flannel nightgown. He nodded to his younger companion to wait in the car.

PC Hewitt was forty-two, a warm-hearted, stout man with a shock of prematurely white hair. As a father of four himself, and a veteran of hundreds of cases where the news of a sudden and often violent death had to be broken, he was an ideal choice, but added to this he had a reputation for getting at the truth in awkward family situations.

The senior officer who had attended at the scene of Anne Taylor's death was of the opinion Reg Taylor had hurled his wife to her death following attempted strangulation. His fingermarks showed clearly on her neck, and even though Reg had freely admitted he'd caught her by the throat in anger seconds before he claimed she fell backwards down the stairs, and appeared utterly devastated by her death, he refused to say what had started the fight. Indeed, his only real concern was that his children should be taken to his mother's as soon as possible.

Hewitt's brief was to discover if the children had overheard the fight, and to find out whether the Taylors' marriage had always been a violent one. As Maud Taylor led them into her home, he noted the smell of mildew and mice. He had been stationed briefly at New Cross during the thirties and had been appalled then at the squalid conditions in Deptford. He could remember calling at tiny houses like this one and finding a whole family in each of the three rooms.

Yet once Maud had lit the gas light in the kitchen, he was surprised by its cleanliness – a clean cloth on the table, a dresser crammed with well-dusted china and ornaments, a well-scrubbed draining board and gleaming white sink.

Maud staggered to a chair, sat down and drew both the little girls on to her knee. 'Where's my Reg?' she asked, looking up at Hewitt with tear-filled eyes.

A lump came up in his throat. He'd met her breed of woman so many times, hard as nails because of what life had thrown at them, but fiercely protective of their children, even if they were now grown men. She looked so vulnerable in her nightgown, she hadn't even realized yet she hadn't got her teeth in. Judging by the pride she took in her home, she'd be horrified when she did remember.

'He's being questioned down at the station,' Hewitt replied. 'You can see him tomorrow morning, I expect, but for now we just had to get the children settled.'

Maud looked from one to the other of them, perhaps noting May's puzzlement and Dulcie's tense frown. 'You two go upstairs and get into Granny's bed,' she said. 'As soon as I've talked to the policeman I'll be right up to you.'

May got up off her knee immediately, but Dulcie clung to

the old woman. 'I want to tell you about it,' she whispered.

'You can in just a little while. I'll bring you up some cocoa. Just go on up now, I won't be long.' She lit a candle for Dulcie to take with her and nudged her towards the door.

Hewitt noticed the agonized look on the child's face and guessed she could tell him a great deal. But the fatherly side of him couldn't bring himself to insist on questioning an eight-year-old at three in the morning. It could wait a few hours.

'Thank you,' he said, once Maud had watched the girls go up the stairs. 'I didn't want to tell you about it in front of them, it's been enough of a shock for them already tonight.'

He went on to tell Maud what the police found when they answered the emergency call. 'I'm afraid your daughter-in-law was dead on our arrival, we won't of course know the exact cause of death until the post mortem. Your son admitted they'd had a bitter quarrel, but he claimed her fall was an accident.'

'Well it would be, my Reg ain't a wife beater,' Maud said stoutly. 'Though 'eaven knows that little floozy was enough to drive any man to it.'

'Would you know what they might have been quarrelling about?' he asked gently.

'She were a slut and a spendthrift,' Maud spat out. 'But Reg never slagged 'er off to me, 'e adored 'er. I tried to put 'er straight many's the time, but she'd stick 'er nose in the air and tell me to mind my own business. She thought she was too good for the likes of me, she were from a snotty 'ome up in Eltham.'

'Would you have her parents' address?' Hewitt asked. 'We'll have to inform them of her death.'

'She ain't got none now,' Maud said. ''Er ma was killed in the Blitz and 'er dad a few years later. There was an uncle, but she didn't 'ave no truck wif 'im 'cos her dad left everything to 'im instead of 'er.'

Hewitt was very relieved he hadn't got to call on any

more relatives, and he was instantly curious as to why Anne's father should disinherit her. After sitting down and making the customary sympathetic remarks about Maud's shock, and attempting to reassure her that anything she chose to tell him about her daughter-in-law would be off the record at this stage, he probed deeper.

'Did she quarrel with her father too?'

'I dunno. Anne said 'e cut 'er off 'cos she didn't stay wif 'im after her ma was killed. I always reckoned there were more to it than that though. Still, we ain't gonna find out now, are we?'

Hewitt agreed they weren't and suggested he made them both a cup of tea.

'I'll do it,' Maud said and got up from her chair. As she filled the kettle she explained that Reg was one of eight, the fifth child, and how he'd always been different from the others. 'I'll tell you now, because I know you'll soon find out, all my boys 'cept Reg 'ave got themselves in trouble before now. They're like their dad, boozers, without a brain between them. But Reg was always different. He used to look after me when the old man beat me, supported me and the younger ones once 'e was dead. See it's all decorated nice in 'ere? Reg done that an' all. 'E's always trying to get me to move somewhere nicer, but me old chums and me memories are 'ere. Reg's one in a million, 'ard-working, sober, kind and generous. You can ask who you bleedin' likes and you'll 'ear the same. Right good dad to the girls an' all. So don't you go thinking 'e's a murderer.'

'What did he do in the war, Mrs Taylor?' Hewitt asked.

'Joined the army, didn't 'e? Didn't even wait for 'is call-up, 'e reckoned it was every man's duty to fight for their country. 'E saw all the action over in France, 'e was at Dunkirk and at Normandy, a bloody good soldier too, got made a corporal in no time, and then a sergeant.'

'Anne must have found it difficult in the war, Dulcie would've only been a baby when it started and then May born in 1942,' Hewitt probed. 'Anne was very young too.'

51

'Yeah, she found it 'ard,' Maud agreed. 'It were tough on 'er when her ma died. But I was around, I 'ad Dulcie 'ere any time she needed a break. But she got matey wif a couple of girls soon after she moved into a place in New Cross, and she told me to piss off once when I went round to see 'ow she was. We never got on after that, I reckon she was ashamed of me.'

Hewitt thought it sounded as if Anne might have been up to something, but he didn't say so. 'How were things when Reg came home after the war?' he asked. 'Lots of men I know said their kids were scared of them, and it was difficult for a while.'

Maud chuckled. 'There was a lot of that round 'ere too. Specially those who had a new kid which couldn't 'ave been the old man's. But it were all 'earts and flowers with Reg and Anne. 'E got that place for them up at 'Ither Green, did it all up, Dulcie went to the school across the road, they was as 'appy as sandboys for the first year.'

'But then it changed?' Hewitt prompted.

Maud didn't answer for the moment and turned her back to get some cups and saucers from the dresser. Hewitt thought she was struggling not to cry, but at the same time selecting the best cups.

'I don't know what got into Anne,' she said eventually. 'She 'ad bleedin' everything a woman could want. Reg earned good money, 'e didn't drink, 'e made that place like a palace for 'er. But she just let it go, never washed up, cleaned or anything. Reg used to do it when 'e got 'ome. Always spending money on 'erself, dresses, shoes, having 'er 'air done. Never knew where she got the coupons for the clothes, I got a job to scrape together enough for a new skirt.'

Hewitt weighed this up. 'Do you think there was another man, Mrs Taylor?'

'That ain't fer me to say,' she snapped at him. 'That's their private business. But I do know that once she got the job at the pub she got less inclined to do anything for Reg and the kids.'

Hewitt made a mental note to make inquiries at the pub.

'Could you tell me what Anne was like? I mean her personality, her interests.'

Maud snorted and banged the cups down on the table. 'Dancing and clothes was her only interests,' she said tersely, but suddenly her face softened a little. 'She was a beauty though. I remember the first time Reg brought 'er 'ere, I thought 'e'd got the fairy off the top of the Christmas tree. Big blue eyes, lovely blonde 'air, the sort that don't come out of a bottle. And she talked real nice an' all. She were nice then, used to bring me a few flowers or chocolate, she'd get me to 'elp her with 'er knitting for the baby, ask me stuff about 'ow it was going to be when 'er time came. I was 'urt that her folks 'ad no time for Reg, but I s'pose they was mad 'cos he got 'er up the duff. But anyway I was that pleased for Reg, even if it were a shotgun weddin'. Anne 'ad class, you know what I mean?'

Hewitt nodded. Even dead, with a tear-stained face, Anne Taylor looked beautiful. Perhaps she was just too young and beautiful for Reg, maybe she'd got a better offer from a rich man and was about to take off. If the old woman was to be believed she probably led him a dog's life, maybe she even deserved what she got. But sadly Reg would pay the price for her death – even if murder couldn't be proved, he was bound to be charged with manslaughter. By the time he got out, his daughters would be grown women, he'd be too old to find himself another woman as lovely as Anne.

They drank the tea Maud made, while Hewitt asked if the children could stay with her for the time being.

'They ain't going anywhere else,' she said sharply. 'I might be getting on, but I can look after them all right. Don't you go getting any funny ideas about taking them off me.'

'Of course not,' Hewitt said with a reassuring smile. He didn't think the Welfare people would approve of such an old woman taking care of the girls, but she clearly loved them. 'Anyway, I'll be back later on today to talk to Dulcie.

She might be able to throw a little more light on what happened.'

Maud took the stairs very slowly after the police were gone. She was shocked to the core that Anne was dead, frightened for her son and for her grand-daughters. All her sons with the exception of Reg were violent men, just as their father had been, and she knew Reg with his brutish looks would be tarred with the same brush. She was certain Anne had another man, and that Reg had found out, and if that came out in court he wouldn't stand a chance.

She stood on the tiny landing between the two bedrooms, the candle in her hand, tears rolling down her cheeks. This house had once been crammed with children, boys in one room, the girls and her and her husband Albert in the other. At night it quivered with snoring, snuffling and rustling. She could remember nights too when the kids cried with hunger and she sobbed as well in desperation. Eight was a great many children, yet she'd borne eleven, three dying before they were even one.

Reg had been the only one who always gave her joy. It was always he who came home with wood for the fire or a few vegetables left at the end of the market. As young as seven or eight he'd earn a few pennies selling papers or cleaning out stables and bring the money back to her. There were so many times when he bathed her black eyes and split lips, or washed her hair for her when she couldn't lift her arms for the bruises. He always told her that when he was grown up he'd take her away from here.

She never mourned Albert's death. How could she? He'd been such a cruel and wicked man. She just wished she'd found a way of leaving him years before he'd made the older boys just like him. But Reg, with his gentle ways, big dreams and the ability to work hard, had cheered her. Thanks to him, Maria and Rose, her two youngest children, had shoes on their feet, food in their bellies and weren't haunted by the misery their father had inflicted on the others. They were both in Canada now – Maria had gone first at eighteen, and then Rose joined her. They became nurses, got married and had a child each. Maybe they had more than one now, for neither of them wrote home any longer. Alan and Raymond, the two oldest, didn't keep in touch either – for all she knew she could be a great-grandmother. So many, many children, seventeen grand-children that she knew of, yet it was only Dulcie and May she had close contact with, Reg had seen to that.

How was she going to comfort them now? Anne might not have been a good mother, but they loved her. And to be deprived of their father as well, that was too great a loss for them.

As she went into the bedroom and saw them huddled together, fast asleep, arms around each other, her tears fell faster, for reason told her she was unlikely to live to see them leaving school.

She sat on the edge of the bed, reached for her rosary and prayed. For Anne to rest in peace, for Reg to be cleared of any crime, and for God to give her the strength and endurance to make a good replacement mother for as long as she was needed.

Blowing out the candle, she slipped into bed. It was warm from the girls' small bodies, and it gave her a little comfort. Through the gap in the curtains she could see the first rays of daylight creeping into the sky above the roof of the house opposite.

'Sleep tight, my little loves, Granny's here,' she mur-mured. 'Don't you worry either, Reggie, I'll take care of them for you.'

Maud woke at her usual time of seven, and force of habit made her get up. The girls were still sleeping, May buried in the crook of her sister's arm. Maud pulled on her dressing-gown and pushed her feet into her slippers. It felt very cold.

Downstairs, she put her teeth in, lit the fire in the parlour, and turned the gas cooker on to make the house warmer. She was sitting sipping a cup of tea when Dulcie came into the kitchen. She was dressed, but with the buttons on her cardigan all askew, and she was ghostly pale.

Maud didn't speak, just got another cup and poured some tea for the child too. For all her personal experience of death, she didn't know what to say to her.

'Did the policeman say what will happen to Daddy?' Dulcie asked after a little while. Her voice was as pale as her face, flat and toneless.

''E couldn't, sweetheart, not yet. But 'e's coming to talk to you later today, maybe 'e'll know something then.'

'Why does he want to talk to me?'

'Well, because you were there,' Maud said with a shrug. ''E'll want to know what you 'eard and saw.'

'I only heard them shouting for a little bit, then the noise of her going down the stairs,' Dulcie said, her voice dropping to a whisper.

'What were they shouting about?' Maud asked. 'Can you tell me?'

Dulcie dropped her head. 'If I say it, it might make things worse for Daddy.'

Maud felt her stomach turn over. What had the child heard?

'Suppose you tell me what you think you 'eard,' she said, patting Dulcie on the hand. 'Telling me don't count for anything. Maybe you was 'alf asleep and got it all wrong.'

Dulcie's head came up slowly. 'I don't think so, Granny, it keeps on going round in my head.'

She told what she'd heard all in one gulp, starting from the bit about the court, her mum saying May wasn't his child, and then on to how Dad roared at her and the sort of scuffling she heard when he screamed *Get out or I'll kill you*, then finishing with the noise her mum made as she fell down the stairs.

Maud was severely shaken. She knew if Dulcie was to say all that to the policeman, Reg was as good as hanged. But how could she ask a child to lie? That wasn't right either.

'Granny!' Dulcie exclaimed when the old lady didn't reply immediately. 'Are you worried that it makes Daddy sound bad?'

Maud nodded. 'But I know 'e ain't,' she said. 'I threatened to kill your grandfather many a time, but I wouldn't 'ave done it.'

'Shall I tell the policeman I woke because they were shouting but I didn't know what they said?'

Maud just looked at her. 'I can't tell you what to do,' she said wearily. 'But maybe it would be better if you forgot what you think you 'eard. That ain't the same as lying, love. Yer dad's an 'onest man, 'e'll tell the truth about what went on.'

'He told me it was an accident and that she just fell. He said whatever people said I was to believe that.'

'Then you must believe it, because it will be true,' Maud said.

'What did Mum mean about May not being his child?' Dulcie asked, looking perplexed.

Maud forced a laugh. 'Well, that was plain silliness, she just wanted to get 'is goat. 'Course May's 'is, look at the pair of you, like two peas in a pod. Now, why don't yer go in the parlour by the fire, there's some comics in there. I'll get us some breakfast.'

Maud sat for a while thinking after Dulcie had gone into the other room. It was the bit about May not being Reg's child which was eating into her, for she had always suspected that might be the case. Reg had only got leave twice in 1941, first in February, just after Anne moved out of her father's house to New Cross, and then again in October. May was born in early May, named for the month too. Anne claimed she was early, but Maud was too long in the tooth to believe an eight-month pregnancy could result in a seven-and-a-half-pound baby.

But she'd never said a word, not even to Anne. Reg loved that baby from the first time he held her, and she couldn't bring herself to cause her son any pain. As it happened, May was so like Dulcie that it would never cross anyone's mind to doubt they were full sisters. Silently she cursed Anne for her revelation, for that would certainly have been enough to push Reg over the edge. He had always idolized May, often making more of her than he did of Dulcie because she was such a little show-off with her giggling and chatting. The trouble was, this was going to be like a sodding time-bomb. Dulcie didn't understand about how babies were made yet, she probably still imagined the doctor brought them along in his bag. But one day when she did know what was what, she was going to remember what she'd heard, and suddenly all the events of last night would take on a whole new meaning.

Maud caught a bus to Lewisham police station during the afternoon, leaving the girls with her neighbour. On her arrival the duty officer informed her that Reg still hadn't been charged with anything, because as yet a solicitor hadn't arrived, so he said she could speak to her son in an interview room alone.

Reg's eyes looked sunken, his cheeks hollow, as if overnight he'd lost a stone in weight. 'I didn't push her, Mum,' he said immediately he was brought into the room. 'She fell, I swear it on the girls' lives.'

'I know you didn't,' she reassured him. 'But tell me 'ow it all came about. Get it off yer chest.'

Maud's heart felt as if it was being squeezed as he explained the events of the previous day. He broke down as he got to the point when he realized Anne was having an affair with another man, and sobbed uncontrollably. 'I trusted her, Mum, I thought she was all mine. But the way she was last night I saw she'd never really been that, only a part of her, the rest was always waiting for someone better to come along.'

'There ain't no one better than you, son,' she said, wondering why he hadn't spoken of the business of May's birth. But she couldn't tell him she knew, not without saying that Dulcie had heard it. 'She were a fool, 'er bleedin' 'ead stuck up in the clouds.'

'I'm scared shitless,' he admitted. 'I don't want to go to prison for even one day. What will the girls do without me? They'll be too much for you. How will they go to school? What if I get hanged for murder? What will that do to them?'

Maud braced herself. 'Get a grip on yerself, son. When that solicitor gets 'ere, you tell 'im everything what 'appened. Tell 'im you was really angry with 'er, don't leave nothing out. 'E'll see the truth in it, just as I can, and I bet there'll be dozens of people down Leahurst Road what will tell him what you was, and what she was.'

PC Hewitt came back to Maud's house at six o'clock. He was tired, he'd got his head down for around three hours, then he was back up to Leahurst Road interviewing the neighbours. After a cup of tea with Maud and both the girls in the kitchen he took Dulcie into the parlour to speak to her.

'Did you hear Mummy and Daddy quarrelling last night?' he asked.

'Sort of, when I woke up,' she said, frowning intently.

'Could you hear what they were saying?'

She shook her head. 'It was just noise. Then the sound of Mummy falling and Daddy calling out her name and running down the stairs after her. That's when I got up.'

'Were you scared?'

She nodded again and then went on to tell him how she saw her mother lying in the hall and she was so frightened that she ran back to bed with May.

It struck Hewitt that she was a very controlled little girl. She hadn't run out of the flat screaming when her father left. She had stayed in bed all the time the police were in the house. He didn't think his own children would have done that, unless of course he'd ordered them to.

Had Reg told her to say nothing and stay there? Could she in fact have witnessed everything?

He sincerely hoped she hadn't, for that would weigh very heavily on a child's mind.

Hewitt went on to ask her about her mother, and Dulcie readily told him about the many rows, and what caused them. 'Did Daddy ever smack Mummy?' he asked. 'You know, when he was really cross with her?'

She looked surprised by such a question. 'No, of course not. He never even smacked me and May, not even when we were really naughty.' She illustrated this by telling him about how she and May had gone to the park the day before and how he'd said he just got scared they would be hurt.

Hewitt didn't think a child of her age would be able to make up something like that. He didn't think either that a man who took his kids out to the pictures when his wife was working sounded like a bully. All the neighbours had verified this too. Apart from the landlord at the pub where Anne worked, who said Reg had hit her the previous afternoon, no one had a bad word to say for him.

Reg wasn't a drinker, a gambler, a womanizer, he'd come from an entire family of blackguards from the slums in Deptford, yet he'd no previous convictions at all, not even petty crime as a young lad. He was a hard worker, a skilled craftsman and a good father. But as Hewitt knew only too well from the many domestics he'd been called out to in his time, appearances could be deceptive. Reg could be an intensely jealous man, maybe he tried to keep his pretty wife in a cage, resented her buying nice clothes or going out because he couldn't bear other men to look at her?

Sarge back at the station had said Reg still wouldn't admit what the row was all about. Why not? Because he didn't want the content of it to become public knowledge? Or because he knew that it would only make him look more justified in killing her?

Several of the neighbours had said there was gossip about Anne carrying on with Tosh, the landlord of the pub. Maybe that was true, after all he was the only person who claimed Reg was a brute. He needed interviewing again.

Hewitt was just about to wind up his talk with Dulcie when May came into the room.

'Hello,' she said with a wide smile. 'Don't you want to talk to me too?'

Hewitt hadn't noticed much about May the previous night, she was sleepy and silent, and as she appeared to have slept through all the action he'd had no real reason to make any kind of assessment about her.

'I always want to talk to pretty little girls,' he said with a smile.

'Have we got to stay here with Granny?' she asked.

Hewitt glanced at Dulcie while he considered how to answer that question. To his surprise she was giving her sister a filthy look.

'This is the best place for you both at the moment,' he said carefully. He wondered if Dulcie's hostility towards her sister was just at that remark, or whether it was long-standing sibling rivalry.

'I don't like being here,' May said with a pout and without any hesitation clambered on to his knee. 'The toilet is outside and it's really scary. Granny hasn't even got a bath or real lights either.'

'May!' Dulcie exclaimed, looking very embarrassed. 'Granny will hear you and be upset.'

'I don't care,' May said, turning towards Hewitt and snuggling up to his chest. 'Mummy never liked Granny, she didn't like us coming here, so why can't we go somewhere else?'

In a flash of intuition Hewitt realized that he was catching a glimpse of Anne Taylor through her younger daughter. Both girls had inherited her looks, but in the older girl there was nothing of the flirty 'I'm-gorgeous-so-I-can-do-and-say-what-I-like' that he'd picked up about the mother from her neighbours. May might be only five, but just the confident way she'd plonked herself down on him and spoken her piece suggested she was used to getting all the attention and intended to keep things that way.

Dulcie was very different. Hewitt sensed that she had worked out exactly what she was going to say to him before he arrived. He felt she had heard at least the last part of the quarrel between her parents, but she'd decided that by repeating it she wouldn't help her father's cause. Her loyalty to him was touching, and that in itself proved Reg was no brute.

'Mummy's dead, and you'll stay where Daddy said you'd got to go,' Dulcie snapped at her sister. 'And if you say anything else nasty about Granny, I won't play with you any more.'

May looked stunned for just a moment, but then she turned her face up to Hewitt. 'She's just being mean to me because of what Mummy said last night.'

'What was that?' Hewitt chuckled. It was impossible not be enchanted by this outspoken little madam.

'She said, *May's not your child*. I heard her shout it at Daddy! Dulcie knows that meant she liked me best.'

'That's rubbish,' Dulcie shouted, leaping off her chair and rushing towards her sister to strike her. 'You didn't hear anything, you were asleep.'

It was the first time Dulcie had lost her control and in doing so she'd inadvertently slipped up.

Hewitt caught hold of Dulcie's arm before she hit her sister. He sent May out of the room, then drew Dulcie close to his knee. 'Don't be upset by what she said, of course it didn't mean your mummy liked her best.'

'Mummy did like her best,' Dulcie said, looking right into his eyes. 'I didn't mind, everyone likes May because she's cute. I was only cross with her because she didn't really hear anything, she just made that up to get your attention.'

Hewitt felt like pulling her into his arms for a cuddle, the way he would his own children, but he sensed this prickly little girl would reject him. May had undoubtedly heard her mother make that statement, and in her innocence of what it really meant, she had let in a shaft of light on the whole sorry business. He very much doubted that

Dulcie understood the remark any better than May, but he knew by her swift reaction she'd heard it said too, probably along with a great deal more which hadn't registered with May.

'One of my daughters is a bit like May,' he said, hoping to gain her trust. 'She's nearly eighteen now, but when she was little she used to hog the limelight all the time, my other children called her "Twinkle" because of it. I think they all thought she was her mother's and my favourite, but she wasn't, parents don't have favourites, they like each of their children equally, but for different things. I expect your parents valued you for being clever, loyal and very caring to your little sister.'

Dulcie shrugged and stepped back from him. 'Can I go now? May's bound to be making something else up to Granny.'

Hewitt smiled at her. His respect was growing for this child, she was bright, intuitive and brave. Through talking to her he felt he'd got an insight into her father's character. His gut reaction was that the man hadn't killed his wife, it was just an accident.

Chapter Three

It was Tuesday morning before PC Hewitt could get to Leahurst Road to interview the headmistress of Lee Manor, the primary school Dulcie had attended, and to re-interview Albert Bright, known locally as Tosh.

Reg had made a brief appearance at Lewisham Crown Court the previous morning. He pleaded not guilty to murder, and despite an appeal from his solicitor to grant him bail so he could take care of his children, he was remanded in custody and sent to Brixton prison.

Hewitt already knew Miss Willoughby, Lee Manor's headmistress, as he'd called at the school before after a break-in. He had formed the opinion then that she was a typical middle-class spinster, stern, humourless and very narrow-minded. But as such characteristics usually come along with complete honesty, he was hoping for a fair appraisal of the Taylors as parents.

The first thing that struck him once he'd been seated upstairs in Miss Willoughby's office was what a worm's-eye view she had of the Taylors' flat. There were three schools under the name of Lee Manor – Infants, Primary in the middle, and Senior girls at the end of Leahurst Road. They were basically single-storey buildings, each surrounded by a playground, but each had just a couple of small rooms used as offices set up in the roof. Miss Willoughby's was right opposite number 294, and had the curtains been open she would have been able to see right in.

The second thing which struck him was her excitement at being so close to a crime scene, she was quivering with it. 'I had such a shock when I heard about the tragedy yesterday morning,' she said breathlessly, her eyes gleaming behind her thick glasses. 'I can hardly bear to think of that lovely woman being hurled down the stairs.'

She was in her fifties, with iron-grey hair cut off abruptly about her ears, a plain, moon-like face, and a stout, bolster-like body beneath her tweed suit. Not the type of woman Hewitt would normally expect hysterical behaviour from.

'There is no evidence as yet that she was hurled,' Hewitt said quickly.

'Oh, but I've heard about the fearful battle they had,' she insisted. 'They say she was pleading with him not to hurt her, over and over again.'

'Who is *they*?' he asked.

'Everyone,' she said, throwing her arms wide as if to encompass the whole street.

'Miss Willoughby, the facts are that the whole thing happened without anyone hearing anything,' Hewitt retorted. 'The lady downstairs did report she was wakened by a thumping noise as if something heavy was falling down the stairs, but that was all. It was Mr Taylor who telephoned the emergency services, and until the ambulance and police came to the street, everyone was sound asleep.'

She seemed momentarily deflated by this. 'Well, it's been common knowledge for months now that all wasn't well with the family. Terrible rows two or three times a week, many's the time Dulcie has come to school with dark circles under her eyes.'

'Did you ever ask her about them?'

'In a roundabout way, yes. But of course she'd been drilled by her father not to speak out.'

Hewitt sighed. He could see that he wasn't going to get an unbiased view from this woman after all.

'How is Dulcie doing at school?' he asked.

'Oh fine, one of the brightest in her class. Excellent reading, way beyond the norm, quick at arithmetic too and exceptionally well-behaved.'

'Aren't troubled children usually slow at school?'

'Sometimes, but that's not always the case.'

65

'I know Dulcie has only been at this school for eighteen months, but have you met both parents?'

'Of course,' she said. 'I interviewed them together when they wanted Dulcie to start here.'

'That's rather unusual for the dad to come too, isn't it?' Hewitt said. He didn't think he'd ever been with his wife to any of his children's schools.

'Well, he's a bossy man, isn't he?' she said with a sniff. 'I doubt he trusted his wife to come alone. I knew right away they were a disaster in the making. He was so common and rough, a frightful accent too. She was a real lady, beautifully groomed, well-spoken and well-educated.'

Hewitt groaned inwardly at this snobbishness.

'Did you see either of them after that interview?'

'Yes, on parents' evenings, they both came at first, but recently it was only him. I never spoke to him of course, that's the teachers' job.'

'So you only spoke to either of them the once?'

'Oh no, I spoke to Mrs Taylor at the first carol service after Dulcie started here, she was an angel in the Nativity play. I spoke to *him* several times. He was the most extraordinary man.'

'In what way?'

'He would come here to fuss,' she said, folding her arms on her chest. 'The first time was about a year ago. Dulcie fell over in the playground and he wanted to know why her knees hadn't been cleaned and dressed. I said I imagined it was because she hadn't asked for them to be. He had the cheek to tell me that I had a duty to all the children in my care and they should be attended to after an accident whether or not they asked for it. He said even grown men in the army got looked after when they were hurt, and so should a little seven-year-old.'

Hewitt agreed with Reg entirely on that matter, but he just raised an eyebrow as if he was taking Miss Willoughby's side.

'And then,' she said with a gasp, 'in February he came

marching in here one morning and asked why I hadn't done anything when I knew both his girls were standing on the doorstep in the snow for over an hour the day before. I ask you! As if it's my place to check every child gets into its home after school!'

Hewitt glanced out of the window and saw the front door of number 294 and wondered how anyone, particularly a teacher, could see two children standing there shivering and not go over to ask where their mother was.

'What did you say to that?' he asked.

'That the children were only my concern until four o'clock. He was so rude to me, accused me of being heartless and it was no thanks to me they hadn't died of the cold. It was around that time I heard about all the rows going on over there. I felt so sorry for that poor woman, living with a brute like that.'

PC Hewitt had heard enough for one day. He sincerely hoped that whoever was sent by the Welfare to investigate the suitability of Maud Taylor as the children's guardian wouldn't take any advice from this appalling snob.

He thanked her for her help and asked if he could speak briefly to Dulcie's teacher. She rather curtly reminded him teachers couldn't be interrupted in their work and asked that he come back in the lunch-hour.

Within ten minutes of talking to Albert Bright the second time around, Hewitt knew he'd definitely been Anne's lover. Bright had been shocked by the news of her death the first time he called, he was hung over from the night before, and he looked rough. Even though Hewitt had been told of the gossip about him and Anne before that first interview, he couldn't take it seriously because it seemed impossible that such a lovely young woman would entangle herself with someone so repulsive.

But this time Bright was shaved, cocky and full of himself. He took Hewitt up to his sitting-room on the first floor, offered a glass of whisky which was refused, then poured himself a very large one.

'Call me Tosh,' he insisted. 'I can't be doing with all that Mr Bright.' He sat down on his plump velvet couch like an Eastern potentate. 'Anne and I were mates. She used to tell me all 'er troubles. Reg didn't like 'er working fer me. 'E's the sort that likes 'is woman barefoot and pregnant in the kitchen, know what I mean? I used to tell 'er about me boxing days, the clubs and all that, we'd 'ave a drink or two and she'd cheer up.'

He kept saying what a looker she was, how she brightened up the bar, and how Reg ought to have appreciated her more. Then Hewitt asked him point-blank if they'd become lovers.

'What!' Tosh exclaimed. 'Do you really reckon someone as gorgeous as 'er would go with an old geezer like me?'

'It doesn't seem likely,' Hewitt said, intending to rile the man. 'But then Reg Taylor is no oil painting either, and ten years older than Anne.'

'Reg's a wanker,' Tosh muttered.

'You knew him then?' Hewitt said.

'He came in for the odd pint now and then,' Tosh replied. 'When 'e first moved 'ere we used to talk sometimes, but 'e weren't my sort of bloke. Typical bloody army type. You know what I mean.'

Hewitt guessed that meant Reg took a dim view of ablebodied men who hadn't joined up during the war. Several neighbours in the street had mentioned that Tosh evaded subscription and bought this place with black market money. 'Did he come in here with Anne?'

'Hardly ever, only if they'd got a babysitter and were out fer the evening. If he'd taken 'er out more maybe it wouldn't 'ave come to this. She were the kind fer the bright lights.'

'So how did she come to work for you then?'

'She come in one day last November. She'd only popped in for a packet of fags, but it was quiet and I asked if she wanted a drink. She stayed, we got chatting and she said she'd always fancied working behind a bar. As it 'appened

I knew one of my girls was leaving, so I offered 'er a job. She started first week in December, three lunchtimes to begin with, then as it got busier she did more and an occasional evening.'

'You said you were mates – did she used to stay on after the bar was closed?'

Tosh smirked. 'Yeah, we'd 'ave a few drinks and a chat. I felt sorry for 'er. She could 'ave 'ad it all if she 'adn't married Reg. Ought to 'ave found 'erself an office worker or sommat, not a bleedin' builder.'

'But she married him for love.'

'That soon flies out the winder when you've got no money,' Tosh retorted. 'I see it every day in 'ere. Anne used to say to me, "Tosh, I'm tired of waiting for the good times. It just gets drearier and drearier every day." She used to tell me that sort of stuff 'cos she knew I weren't one for the routine, the ordinary.'

'I expect she found the sex was boring with Reg too,' Hewitt said.

'Too right. She used to say he was a Friday nighter. Always the same, predictable as Big Ben.'

'No wonder she fell for you!'

Tosh jerked his head up, sensing sarcasm.

'Come on, Tosh, I knew right away the first time I called you were lovers. It was written all over your face. You have a right to grieve for her too, and you can't do that unless you admit what she was to you.'

Tosh looked wary.

'She's dead now, Tosh,' Hewitt said in the same gentle, reassuring tone he always used with the bereaved. 'My job is to get at the truth about the circumstances. Don't you owe her something? At least the truth.'

Tosh swilled back his drink and grimaced. 'Okay, we was 'aving it off, and I feel bad if you must know because I should have listened to 'er when she said Reg 'it 'er. But I didn't take it serious, I thought it were just a little slap. But 'e's a big bloke, and deep too – Catholic, yer know, never misses 'is Mass every Sunday, they're always the worst ones. They bottle things up, and when it comes out it's with a big bloody bang.'

'Had you made any plans with Anne for the future?' Hewitt asked.

Tosh suddenly sat bolt upright, an expression of horror on his face. 'Plans for the future! Of course not, she were a married woman with two nippers. Gawd almighty, mate, whatcha take me for? We just 'ad a bit of fun together. She were a great screw. But I wouldn't want to be saddled wif 'er.'

'Why not?'

'She were a schemer. Oh, I fell for the big blue eyes and the sexy ways of 'er in the beginning. But there was sommat wrong wif 'er, like she didn't really care about anyone, not even that much about 'er kids. 'Er life weren't a bad one, she 'ad more than most round 'ere. But I reckon even if you gave 'er the sodding moon she'd be cryin' out for the stars too. I was just a stand-in till someone better came along.'

Tosh paused to get up and pour himself another drink. He stood by his big mirror-lined drinks cabinet and swigged it down in one.

'But I still wish I'd taken her a bit more serious on Saturday. Maybe if I'd bin a bit nicer to 'er she wouldn't have gone 'ome and picked a fight.'

Hewitt knew the time had come to leave. He'd got what he'd come for – Tosh was the lover, and a dirty little affair it was too.

Back at the school at twelve o'clock, Hewitt was ushered into a classroom by another stern-faced middle-aged teacher and asked to wait for Miss Sims.

All the classrooms, and there appeared to be just three, were partitioned off from the assembly hall with wooden panelling up to five feet and then glass up to the ceiling. A handful of children were having lunch on tables out in the hall, he assumed the rest of the children had gone home for theirs. The school had the same smell he remembered from his youth, a mixture of chalk, floor polish and small bodies that perhaps weren't washed well enough. But there the resemblance ended – his school had been a grim, gloomy place, the only decoration on the walls a map of the world and a set of canes.

Children's bright paintings covered the walls here. There were displays of handicrafts, a nature table with a vase of sticky buds and a bird's nest, and up on the blackboard the teacher had written a series of words connected with spring. Hewitt thought perhaps the children had been asked to write an essay using them.

He saw a painting which had Dulcie's name on it, and he moved closer to get a better look. Again the theme was spring, as for all the pictures, and hers was by far the best, with trees covered in blossom and lambs skipping around beneath them.

'Dulcie is very good at painting and drawing.' A gentle, refined voice spoke behind him, making him reel round in surprise as he hadn't heard the door open. The owner was young, no more than twenty-five, small, with light brown hair caught back in a bun at the back of her neck.

'I'm Susan Sims, Dulcie's teacher,' she said, transferring a cup of tea into her left hand and holding out the right. 'How are she and her sister? What a terrible business this is. I've been so worried about them.'

There was real compassion in her soft brown eyes, and a sweetness in her face that made Hewitt think of heroines in old-fashioned books.

He shook her hand, introduced himself and asked her to sit down. She didn't ask him any questions about Mrs Taylor's death, but instead said she was relieved to hear the children were with their grandmother rather than in a children's home.

The absence of any snooty remarks was cheering, especially as Miss Sims was clearly out of the top drawer herself. Her brown and cream print dress, though very plain and demure, looked expensive, as did the cream leather belt around her small waist.

She said Dulcie was one of her brightest children and very willing to learn. If she had a problem it was only that she never pushed herself forward. She allowed other children to shine when she could probably outdo them.

'And what can you tell me about her parents?' Hewitt asked, perching on one of the small desks.

It was the first time she faltered. 'Say whatever you think,' he prompted her. 'I'm trying to build up a true picture of the family.'

'Mrs Taylor rarely came here,' she said. 'I believe she did when Dulcie first joined the school, but then she's only been in my class since last September. Since then the mother only came once, and only then when I sent a note home asking her to.'

'Problems?' Hewitt asked.

'No, the reverse. Dulcie is such a good reader, I wanted the parents to let her join the library. Mrs Taylor came in with rather a bad grace I'm afraid. She seemed to think I was exceeding my role of teacher. She said she didn't have time to keep going up to the library with Dulcie, and surely there were plenty of books at school she could borrow.'

Hewitt raised his eyebrows.

'But Dulcie did join, her father used to take her after he got home from work. Almost every week she'd show me what she was reading. She said her father often read them too.'

'How did he seem to you?'

'Not the way people are portraying him now,' she said firmly. 'I thought he was a good man, a loving father, and he tried hard to give his girls all the things he'd been denied as a child. Did Miss Willoughby tell you about him calling here to complain about them standing on the doorstep in the snow?'

'Yes, she did.' Hewitt replied.

She blushed and looked down at her hands. 'Well, please don't repeat what I'm going to tell you, but I thought Mr Taylor was right to complain. I was away from school that day, and I'd certainly have brought the children over here if I'd seen them waiting in such cold weather. Maybe it was a bit high-handed of me, but I dropped in to see the Taylors a couple of nights later.'

'I don't think that was high-handed, just kindly,' Hewitt said.

'I'm glad I went,' she said. 'You see, rumours were flying around about Mr Taylor being a brute even then, and I wanted to reassure myself they weren't true. Mrs Taylor was working that night too, and he'd just got the girls ready for bed when I got there. We chatted by the fire, he was sitting in one armchair, with both girls on his lap, I was in the other, and I could see for myself that this was how he was all the time. A man who loved his family and home. I do not believe for one moment that he killed his wife.'

'What did you talk about?' Hewitt asked.

'All sorts, books, the bad winter, how the government was letting everyone down by not rebuilding houses fast enough, even the new Health Service. But mostly about school. May had only started at the Infants in January, and he asked me how he could help her along with reading at home. May made us both laugh because she said she wanted to be a film star when she was grown up, and you didn't need to be able to read for that.'

'How long did you stay?'

'Over an hour. I was shocked it was that long when I looked at my watch, I'd only intended to stay a few minutes.'

'It sounds as if you really liked him.'

'I did,' she said softly.

As Hewitt drove back to the police station he was very disturbed. He felt he knew Anne Taylor now, and he didn't like her one bit, a self-centred, neglectful mother, an unfaithful wife and a heartless bitch. Yet the saddest, most disastrous part of all this was that every new fact that emerged about her gave more credence to Reg deliberately killing her. He could just hear the prosecution banging home to the jury how impossible she was, they'd get to hate her, and sadly at the end they would judge Reg by what they knew they would do faced with the same circumstances.

The black Wolseley glided to a halt in Deptford High Street in front of a greengrocer's. Mr Sims turned to his daughter. 'Are you quite sure this is wise, dear?' he asked.

It was Saturday morning, four days after Susan Sims had been interviewed by PC Hewitt. She had thought of little else but Dulcie and May since then, and she'd woken early this morning determined to visit them at their grandmother's house.

'I don't know that it's wise, Daddy,' she smiled. 'But I must do it. Pick me up again here in an hour.'

'Why won't you let me drive you to the house at least?' he said in a pleading tone.

Susan tickled him playfully under his chin. To her he was just Daddy, but she knew his clothes, bearing and voice displayed that he had an important position in the City. 'Because you and this car will just create more attention,' she said. 'Now, stop worrying, I'm going to see an old lady and her grand-daughters, not an ogre.'

She got out quickly and walked away. She had telephoned Hewitt and got the address – fortunately he'd seen no good reason why a teacher shouldn't go and see her old pupil and had given her directions. But he had warned her that she would find the area very unpleasant.

Susan could see exactly what he meant once she was off the High Street and into the labyrinth of narrow streets which led to Akerman Street. There were no front gardens here, front doors opening right on to the pavement, and as it was a warm sunny day, most of them were wide open giving a glimpse of a world she had no previous knowledge of. Dank, unpleasant smells wafted out, mingling with worse ones that appeared to come from drains. Yet it was the level of noise which affected her most –

babies crying, women shouting both inside the houses and out on the street, bringing home to her that almost all these houses held more than one family.

As she turned into Akerman Street she saw May jumping a skipping-rope turned by two big girls. It was quite obvious she didn't belong here, for there was a glow about her – rosy cheeks, shiny, neatly plaited hair, and plump legs. She was chanting breathlessly as she jumped, her short dress leaping up to give glimpses of white knickers.

Dulcie was sitting on the doorstep, watching her sister. Her shoulders were hunched, arms clasped about her knees. She looked so very sad.

But as Susan came nearer, Dulcie glanced round, saw her and leaped to her feet. A wide, wide smile spread across her face and she came tearing down the street to greet her.

'What are you doing here, miss, have you come to see me?' she asked, her blue eyes wide with delight.

'Now, what else would bring me down this road if not to see you?' Susan said with a smile. 'How are you?'

'Okay,' Dulcie replied, her eyes sliding away from her teacher's face. 'Did you get told Mummy died?'

Susan nodded. 'Yes I did, Dulcie, and I'm so sorry.'

'Daddy didn't kill her,' she snapped out, as if needing to get that straight immediately.

Susan put her arms around Dulcie and held her tightly for a few seconds, overwhelmed with sympathy for the child. 'I know, dear, I liked your daddy very much and that's why I came today. I hoped it might make you feel a bit better,' she whispered into the child's hair.

May came running up then. 'Did you see me skipping?' she asked in a shrill voice. 'Beryl and Janice have been teaching me.'

Susan gulped, sensing in that moment how different the two girls were. May was too young to grasp the gravity of what had happened, Dulcie was bowed down by it.

'Shall we go in to see your granny?' Susan asked.

May disappeared almost as soon as she'd checked that nothing in Miss Sims's bag was for her. Susan had brought two pots of blackcurrant jam made by her mother, a quarter of tea, sugar and some home-cooked ham.

'My mother and I thought you might be finding it a bit difficult if you haven't got the children's ration books yet,' she said to Maud by way of an explanation. 'I hope you aren't offended.'

'Offended! 'Course I'm not, it's good of you, miss,' Maud said, looking delighted. 'I 'ave got the ration books now, 'cos that policeman took me up to 'Ither Green on Thursday to get some more stuff for the kids. It's right kindly of you to come and visit us too. It means a lot to Dulcie, don't it, girl,' she said, nodding at her grand-daughter.

Susan drew Dulcie on to her knee. 'Well, we're old friends, aren't we, Dulcie, and in times of trouble we all need friends.'

'Will I be able to come back to school soon?' Dulcie asked.

'The funeral's on Monday,' Maud said pointedly, making a gesture to Susan as if she wanted to have a word with her in private. 'I keep telling Dulcie that I can't see 'ow she can go back to your school after that. It's too far away.'

'Granny's right,' Susan said. 'It is, and I'm sure the school here is just as nice.'

Dulcie's lower lip trembled. 'But I liked Lee Manor, and you.'

Susan found she had a lump in her throat. She had known this visit wasn't going to be easy, but she hadn't really prepared herself for what this tragedy meant per-sonally to Dulcie. 'Well, I still care just as much about you,' she said. 'I'll come to see you if you want me to. Maybe I can go and speak to your new teacher too, so she knows how clever you are, how about that?'

Dulcie nodded, and her eyes looked a little less bleak.

Susan got out her purse and pulled out a shilling. 'Now,

suppose you and May go and buy an ice-cream,' she suggested. 'I need to have a little chat with Granny, and I can't stay very long this time because my father is meeting me in an hour. While you're gone you can think about anything special you want to tell me.'

Maud gave Susan an appraising look as Dulcie left. 'You're a real nice woman,' she said. 'I bet that snooty headmistress of your'n don't know you've come down 'ere.'

Susan smiled at the old woman's intuition. 'No, she doesn't. But Dulcie was always a bit special to me, Mrs Taylor, and like I said to Dulcie, I liked your son too. I wanted you all to know you had my support, and if there's anything I can do to help, just ask.'

Maud jiggled her teeth up and down thoughtfully. 'Can you help wif the Welfare?'

'How do you mean, getting extra money for the children?'

'No, I can sort that out meself. I'm scared they'll take the kids away from me. Could you put in a good word?'

'I'll do my best,' Susan said. She could see for herself that this house with its gas lighting and lack of bathroom wouldn't be considered ideal. But it was Mrs Taylor's age which was the real problem, and the fact that Reg wouldn't be tried for some weeks yet. 'I'm sure I can convince them it's better for the children to stay with you at least till the trial. But I can't make any promises further than that.'

She meant if he got life, or worse still was hanged. But she couldn't say that.

'PC Hewitt said that the coroner said Anne's injuries were consistent wif a bad fall and 'itting 'er 'ead on the wall at the bottom of the stairs,' Maud said, her eyes filling up with tears. 'But even if they didn't find no other injuries, like she'd been given a pasting by Reg, there was still the fingermarks on 'er neck, and the coroner couldn't say if she were pushed, thrown or just tripped and fell.'

Susan reached out and patted her arm. 'I know he didn't push her or throw her,' she said firmly. 'He thought too much of his children to do that, however angry he was with Anne. We have to trust the lawyers to make the jury see that.'

'But everything's stacked against 'im,' Maud said sorrowfully. 'Anne were a cow, she were carryin' on wif someone, she taunted 'im she were going to take the kids away from 'im. 'E even looks like a thug. 'Ow the 'ell can we get round that?'

'I have every faith in British justice,' Susan said more firmly than she felt. 'I shall speak up for him if I'm given the chance.'

Maud smiled. 'Gawd, I feel better for you comin' round.'

Dulcie accompanied Susan down to the High Street later on. May had returned to her skipping game. Over tea and fruit cake, it had been decided that they were Susan and Maud now. Maud had spoken of her apprehension about the funeral on Monday – she had no wish to go herself and she didn't feel the girls should be put through it either. But Anne's uncle who lived out at Crayford was arranging and paying for it, and as he was sending a car over for them she supposed there was no way out of it. Maud had explained briefly how this same uncle had inherited Anne's father's money, and Susan felt that he might be trying to make amends, and also that it could be beneficial to the girls in the long run to meet their great-uncle.

'Daddy never let us play in the street,' Dulcie said suddenly. 'Do you think I should tell Granny that so she stops us?'

Susan felt as if her heart was being squeezed. It was too bad that this little girl felt she'd got to try and hold on to all her father's old standards, on top of everything else she had to cope with.

'I think you and May will be happier if you can play outside,' she said carefully. 'Granny's house is very small after all, and she's a bit old for little girls running around making a lot of noise. But maybe you should speak to Granny about it and make rules, like not going beyond your street. That's what grown-ups call a compromise.'

'Daddy hated living in Deptford,' Dulcie said, looking up at Susan. 'He must be really worried because we're here now.'

'No, he won't be. He knows you are safe and well looked after with Granny. So don't worry about that, Dulcie. What he'd want you to do is to try and like your new school, keep up your reading and carry on taking care of May the way you always used to. Do you think you can do that?'

'Yes, miss,' Dulcie said. 'But what's going to happen to Daddy?'

'Why don't you call me Susan now?' the teacher said as she thought how to answer the question. 'I can't tell you what the outcome of your daddy's trial will be, no one could. Do you understand what a trial is?'

Dulcie shook her head.

'Well, it's a special way of finding out exactly what happened the night Mummy died. Everyone who was involved in any way, like the police, neighbours, even me maybe because I know your family, get questioned by people called lawyers. Then the jury, that's a group of twelve people who are specially picked because they don't know anyone personally, listen to all sides of it all, and they decide whether your daddy did push Mummy, or didn't. If they decide he didn't, then Daddy will be free to come home again.'

'But what if they decide he did push her?' Dulcie asked, looking very frightened.

Susan sighed. It wasn't known yet whether Reg would be charged with murder or manslaughter. She couldn't possibly tell such a small child what the ultimate punishment for murder was, but she knew she must prepare Dulcie in part at least. 'Then he will have to be punished, probably that will mean going to prison.'

Dulcie didn't make any comment on this, but it was obvious she was mulling it over in her mind because her small brow was furrowed with frown-lines.

They had reached the High Street now, and Susan's father was waiting in the car.

'I have to go now,' Susan said, bending down to kiss Dulcie. 'But I'll be back next week to see you.'

Dulcie clung to her briefly, then turned and ran home.

'How did it go?' Susan's father asked once she was in the car. He looked anxious, as if she'd been on his mind for the whole hour until he picked her up.

'I was right to go,' Susan said. 'They need help.'

Mr Sims gave a deep sigh, glancing round at her, dark eyes full of concern. 'I suppose that means you've committed yourself to be the one that gives the help?'

'I have to, Daddy, there's no one else.'

Chapter Four

On a sultry day in August Susan Sims broke off from a family holiday in Broadstairs to come back to London to visit Reg in Brixton prison. She arrived just after two and stood apart from the large group of women gathering outside the prison doors, all too aware of the cold, hard eyes scrutinizing her and that the low whispers and occasional sniggers were about her appearance. She had thought her light grey suit and matching small-brimmed hat would make her inconspicuous, but they were all wearing gaudy cotton-print summer dresses, with bare heads, and to her dismay she realized her sober appearance had only defined what she really was, a middle-class, out of her depth, frightened Good Samaritan.

Glancing up at the high grey walls, she shuddered. Even in bright sunshine the prison looked bleak and forbidding. For a man like Reg who had worked outside for most of his life it had to be terrible to be locked in a cell day after day.

Susan had never imagined when she first called on the children at Maud's home that her involvement with the Taylor family would take over her life. First she had gone with the children and Maud to St Thomas's Catholic School in Deptford to enrol the children there, and then visited Miss Denning, the Welfare worker for the area, to make sure they had no intention of removing the girls from Maud's care. Maud could barely read or write, so rather than take the chance that she might be manipulated or led astray by family, friends or neighbours, Susan became her adviser, secretary and confidante.

Writing to Reg to keep him informed of how his children

were was all part of this, and it was a natural progression that Mr O'Keefe, Reg's lawyer, should ask Susan to be a witness for the defence. The police had dropped the murder charge in favour of manslaughter, but O'Keefe seemed optimistic that a verdict of accidental death would be returned.

The first letter Susan received from Reg touched her deeply for it was so courteous and brave. Not one word about his own predicament, no snivelling or attempts to convince her of his innocence, just deep concern for his girls and his mother, and gratitude that Susan was helping them. Before long she found herself writing back to him far more than was really necessary, and as the weeks passed and she learned so much more about his past from both him and his mother, her admiration for him grew.

Maud had told her how it was when her husband died. Her four older boys all callously cleared off, unwilling to give any of their wages to keep their mother and younger brothers and sisters. Reg was only an apprentice builder at that time, yet he got odd jobs in the evenings and on Sundays and managed to save the family from starvation. It was he who later paid the fares for his two sisters to go to Canada. Even after he'd married Anne, he still helped Maud out, he always made sure she had enough coal for her fire, decorated her house, and during the war when he was overseas, he sent money back for her.

A sudden surge towards the prison door startled Susan. She had expected that the large doors would be thrown wide open, but instead only a small one within it opened, forcing the jostling crowd to form an orderly line. One by one they filed in, and Susan reluctantly joined them.

A door to the left of the lobby was clearly the way in to see the prisoners. A burly warder stood behind a counter, and as the other visitors were holding up their visiting orders as they approached him, Susan copied them. The man barely looked at the orders, just nodded the women through the door as if he knew their faces. Yet when it was Susan's turn, he stopped her.

'First visit?' he asked curtly.

'Yes,' she whispered.

He took the order from her and studied it. 'Are you his wife or girlfriend?'

'No, his daughter's teacher,' she said.

'What have you got in that bag?' he asked, looking down at the small shopping bag on her arm.

'Some books, fruit and cigarettes,' she said. 'Is that all right?'

He practically snatched the bag from her and rummaged through it, then placed it under the counter.

'Can't he have it?' she asked.

'We'll decide that later, when we've checked it,' he said curtly. 'Go on through there.'

The corridors and gates seemed to go on for ever and she followed the women in front of her, feeling more intimidated by the minute, for it smelled awful, of disinfectant, stale sweat and damp. Finally she came to the last door, and yet another officer asked who it was she was visiting.

'Mr Reginald Taylor,' she said.

'His number!' he snapped at her, as if this was obvious. Susan didn't know it and had to take the letter from Reg out of her pocket to look it up.

'Five four seven nine,' she said.

'Five, four, seven, nine, Taylor,' he yelled out, and a few seconds later the same cry was repeated by someone unseen further down in the room. 'Number twenty-five,' he said.

That meant nothing to Susan, but someone behind her nudged her forward and pointed out numbers on each of the long line of booths ahead of her. As she walked along the narrow passage, booths either side of her, she got caught brief glimpses of men in prison grey beyond a metal grille. Each one of them had his hands up to it, desperate to touch his visitor even though the holes in the grille were less than a quarter of an inch square.

Twenty-five was empty, no one behind the grille. She sat down on the bench and waited for what seemed for ever. The seat was shiny with age and endless bottoms polishing it, names and messages had been scrawled on the walls either side of her, and she could hear a woman crying nearby, and a male voice trying to comfort her. Then suddenly Reg appeared behind the grille.

'I didn't think you'd come,' he said breathlessly. 'I couldn't believe it when they called out my name.'

He looked much thinner and paler than when she had last seen him back in Leahurst Road. His pale blue eyes had lost the sparkle she remembered and his hair was cropped even shorter. Yet it seemed to her he looked less brutish now, but whether that was because she knew him better, or whether it was that circumstances had really altered his appearance she couldn't say.

'But I promised I would visit today,' she said, trying to smile.

'People's promises don't mean much to me any more,' he said with a shrug. 'But I should have had more faith in you.' He smiled then, and suddenly his whole face changed, making him almost handsome.

'We don't get long to talk,' he said, moving close to the grille. 'So tell me about the girls.'

'They were very happy last week when I saw them,' she said, going on to describe how his mother had got one of her neighbours to make them each a new dress. 'Miss Denning, you know, the Welfare lady, was going to take them to Greenwich Park the next day for a picnic, so they were really excited.'

'Is Mum coping with them all right? It's not getting too much for her is it, what with the holidays and everything?'

The truth was that Susan had noticed a decline in Maud's health in the last weeks. She wasn't sleeping well at night with anxiety for her son, and by day she felt she couldn't sit down and rest in case the girls got into mischief. Her biggest fear was that the girls would be taken into care, and this had robbed her of her appetite. Her legs swelled up alarmingly in hot weather, and though she tried to hide that she found even a short walk exhausting, she didn't fool Susan.

'She's fine,' Susan lied. It wasn't fair to add to Reg's worries right now. His trial was set for the middle of September and she felt he had to be kept buoyant until then.

'I can't begin to tell you how grateful I am for all you've done for my family,' he said, his voice cracking with emotion. 'I don't know what we would have done without you.'

'That's what friends are for,' she said. 'And speaking of friends, O'Keefe telephoned me last night to say your commanding officer is prepared to act as a character witness for you.'

'Captain Duncan!' Reg's bright smile came back. 'Bless him!'

'Mr O'Keefe's written to tell you all about it, but he wanted me to give you the good news today. Now, tell me how things really are with you. You never say in your letters.'

'What is there to say?' His smile vanished, even his voice went flat. 'I'm doomed, Susan. I didn't push Anne, but no one's going to believe me.'

'I believe you, and your mother does,' she said stoutly. 'O'Keefe and Captain Duncan do too, I think PC Hewitt does as well.'

'But they won't be on the jury. You can bet the prosecution will find dozens of people that will say I've got a nasty temper. Even if Captain Duncan does speak up for me, if they cross-examine him he'll be forced to admit I got in a few fights in the army, and let's face it, Susan, I don't look like a choir boy.'

He didn't, but Susan knew from Maud he had been one, and an altar boy, and that made her want to cry. 'Oh Reg,' she sighed. 'I wish I could do something more to help.'

'You've already stuck your neck out far enough for me,' he said with a half-smile. 'I bet that headmistress of yours isn't best pleased. O'Keefe reckons the prosecution will call her as a witness. If he challenges her, and he'll have to, where's that going to leave you?'

Susan suddenly saw the explanation as to why Miss Willoughby had become so unpleasant to her before the end of term. Clearly she'd been told of her teacher's support for Reg. 'I'll get another teaching job,' she said defiantly. 'Lee Manor isn't the only school in London.'

'You're amazing,' he said with open admiration. 'I bet until all this happened the nearest brush you'd had with the criminal world was when someone swiped the milk off your doorstep. What on earth do your family make of you visiting a man in prison?'

'They brought me up to believe in fighting for the right,' she said simply. 'Of course they were anxious about me coming here today, but they wouldn't have tried to stop me.'

Before Reg had a chance to say anything more, a warder suddenly appeared behind him, announced the visit was terminated, and yanked Reg away, not even giving him time to say goodbye.

All at once Susan felt the real horror of his predicament, treated as a criminal even before he was tried, and slammed back into a cell without a chance to end the visit with dignity. As she hurried away from the prison, tears rolled down her cheeks for him. She guessed he had wanted to know a great deal more detail about the girls and his mother. He hadn't even had time to give her any messages for them.

Maud had told Susan once how as a child Reg used to go up to Blackheath to look at the rich people's homes, and Susan felt a twinge of conscience that her family home was probably one of the very ones he'd admired. It was a pretty Georgian villa overlooking the Heath, the front garden a profusion of flowering shrubs. Her childhood had been idyllic. There had always been nursemaids for each of the four children as babies, a woman came in daily to clean and wash, so her mother had plenty of time to spend with her children. It was a secure, happy home, the days marked by Father leaving for the office at eight-thirty and returning at six. School was a small private one nearby, they had a large playroom, a sand-pit and swing in the garden, all of them learned to play the piano, and Susan and her younger sister Elizabeth had dancing lessons too.

Every single August the entire household went down to the same large house in Broadstairs where they would be joined by various aunts, uncles and their children too. Hunger, debt and lack of warm clothing were unknown to her family. While there was no wild extravagance, her mother was a careful housekeeper, there were always good hearty meals, fires in each room in winter, toys and books. Yet her parents were modern in their thinking, the children were allowed to play ball games on the Heath, to ride bicycles, to bring schoolfriends home, and on many a night the house would resound with the sound of laughter as the children put on plays or concerts.

In 1938, when Susan was just seventeen, her elder brother Stephen, who was up at Cambridge, brought a friend home for Christmas. Susan took one look at Douglas Broadhurst, and although she'd always been shy of young men before, fell for him instantly. Everything about him, his height, slender body, dark floppy hair and clear blue eyes was perfection to her.

By the time Christmas had passed, it was clear to both her parents that there was a blossoming romance, for they'd noticed the way Susan sparkled and fizzed with Douglas, and that he looked equally entranced. They gave Susan a serious talking to, reminding her that she was very young, that she had yet to start her teacher training, and that Douglas had to concentrate on his studies. But right through the spring and summer of 1939 she and Douglas wrote to each other, and he often came as a guest for weekends.

But in September the war came, and both Douglas and Stephen joined the airforce, determined to become fighter pilots as they had both previously had a few flying lessons. It was then, at Christmas of 1939, that Susan's parents gave their permission for her to become engaged to Douglas, on the understanding they would wait until the war was over before they got married.

Douglas was shot down over the English Channel in March of '41, his Spitfire plunging into the sea before he could bail out. When Susan heard the news she wanted to die too, and in the months that followed she fully believed she would never laugh, dance or be happy again. It was her parents who pushed her back into finishing her teacher training, encouraging, cajoling, telling her that Douglas wouldn't have wanted her to grieve for ever.

So teaching became the new love in her life. It filled the empty feeling inside her, pushed the loneliness and hopelessness away. She didn't want or need a new man in her life, children were enough. Her brothers teased her sometimes, saying she would end up an old maid. But she didn't mind, maybe she was in a rut, but it was a warm, comfortable one.

Then along came the Taylors, and suddenly she was jolted out of that rut, bombarded with new experiences that were often far from comfortable. She might have known love and grief, taught working-class children for some years, but she had no real knowledge of what it meant to be poor. To avoid embarrassing Maud she had to watch and learn how she ran her life. This meant groping her way through an almost alien language to understand the real meaning of what Maud said, because down in Deptford what often sounded like an insult could be an endearment and vice versa. She had to say goodbye to her own standards of hygiene, soon discovered that Maud would go hungry to feed the children and her fierce pride could not accept charity. Susan couldn't buy a meat pie from the shop to give to Maud, that was insulting. But to bring something cooked from home and to say that it would go to waste if it was kept another day was okay. Likewise an old jumper would be accepted with pleasure to be unpicked and knitted up for the children – new wool was suspect. Yet as Susan found her way through this often baffling maze she began to see that Maud's way was a good one, she kept face, she had standards that were never broken. Maud would never dream of stepping out into the street without her battered felt hat and her proper shoes. She went to Mass every single Sunday, and for that she had to put on her corsets, best dress and gloves too. Pride was everything when you knew you were very close to the gutter. It made you whiten your doorstep every day, clean the windows once a week, and always keep a few dried goods at the back of the pantry so that if there was an emergency in the street, a sudden death or sickness, you'd have a little something to offer your neighbour.

After Douglas died Susan really believed she'd sealed her heart up, but she soon found this wasn't so. What began as mere affection for a couple of motherless little girls was fast growing into love, and with that came the question of how she would fill the emptiness if they were removed from her life. Then there was Reg. She knew she thought about him more than was natural, that she shouldn't be building her life around his trial and his family. Yet they had all found a way into her heart, and try as she might, she couldn't distance herself from them.

It was teeming with rain as Susan and Maud came out of the court, one of those typical September days when the summer ends abruptly and without warning. Susan felt the weight of the old lady leaning on her arm, heard her laboured breathing and silently cursed all twelve jury members for their blind stupidity.

Reg had been found guilty of manslaughter and sentenced to twelve years' imprisonment. At a stroke they had robbed two children of a loving father and destroyed his mother.

Maud had fought with the only weapon she had, her

sharp tongue. *'You bastards,'* she'd yelled at the jury after they gave their verdict. *'I 'opes you never get another night's sleep knowing what you've done. You call this justice!'*

Susan had tried to restrain and quieten her, and the judge ordered that she would be removed from the court if she said another word. But Maud continued to hiss and swear, and so they both had to leave and wait outside. They didn't hear the judge's comments as he passed sentence. They had to learn from O'Keefe that the judge felt some sympathy that Reg had been so wantonly provoked by his wife, and that was the reason he was giving a lighter sentence than was usual.

Maud didn't agree it was a lighter sentence. As she pointed out to O'Keefe, even with good behaviour it would be eight years at least before Reg would be free, Dulcie would be sixteen then, May thirteen, and she'd be pushing up the daisies long before.

Three months ago Susan wouldn't have agreed with that last remark. Maud looked indestructible then, but now as she felt her leaning on her and saw the distress in her eyes, she sensed Maud was right. She had lost so much weight in the past few weeks that the skin on her cheeks and neck hung in folds, her legs were badly swollen, her blood pressure was sky high. But worst of all she'd lost the will to live because she knew she really couldn't look after the girls satisfactorily any longer.

'I pinned all me 'opes on them deciding it were an accident,' she said in little more than a whisper. 'I really thought my Reg would be 'ome tonight and all we'd 'ave to do was find 'im and the girls somewhere new to live. Why did that bastard 'ave to say my Reg was a scrapper? All blokes is, ain't they?'

In his summing up Kirkpatrick, the prosecution lawyer, had laboured the point of how beautiful Anne was, that she was better educated, ten years younger than her husband. He pointed out that maybe Reg could have continued to live with her lack of housewifely talents, even the occasional neglect of him and the children, but when he'd discovered she had a lover that was too much for him to bear, so he used his thirteen stone against her eight, attempted to strangle her and then tossed her down the stairs in a fit of understandable rage and jealousy.

O'Keefe had nothing so strong to fight with, all he really had on his side was Reg's unquestionable love for his children. He put it to the jury that no father who cared so much would harm their mother. While he agreed that there were fingermarks on Anne's neck, and that Reg freely admitted he had caught her momentarily by the throat a little earlier under extreme provocation when she said she was going to take the children from him, the facts were that she was killed as the result of a fall. He pointed out the speed at which Reg ran for assistance immediately after it, stressing this wasn't the act of a guilty man. He finished up by reminding the jury that no one had actually seen what took place, and therefore if there was any doubt at all in their minds that Reg pushed or hurled his wife, they must pass the verdict of Not Guilty.

But by then it was clear the jury were convinced that hurling or pushing was exactly what Reg had done.

Susan hailed a taxi and helped Maud over to it. She felt broken up herself inside, she knew she had no way of comforting Maud or the children. It was shameful that none of Reg's brothers or sisters had come to the trial to offer support for their mother, brother or young nieces; even the priest from the church Reg had worshipped at in Hither Green had declined to speak up for him. Yet the one thing that stood out most in Susan's mind was the stunned expression on Reg's face when he heard the jury's verdict. That, she felt, was going to stay with her for all time.

In January of 1948, hailstones rattled against the windows of the first-floor conference room at the Welfare offices in Lewisham. The air was fuggy with smoke from one of the men's pipes and a single naked electric light bulb cast a murky yellowish light down on to the central table and the six people seated around it. Each of the three men and three women had an open file in front of them. The topic for their discussion was the Taylor children.

One of the men was Father O'Brien, the priest from St Michael's, the Roman Catholic church in Deptford which Maud had attended all her life, and latterly the children too. The remaining men and two of the women held positions as Children's Officers. The last woman and the youngest by at least fifteen years was Susan Sims, and she was there only under sufferance because Maud and Reg had requested that she was to put forward their views about the girls' future care.

Almost as soon as Reg had been convicted, the local Welfare bureau had stepped up their interest in the family, making several impromptu visits to the house in Akerman Street. In a report they had found it to be damp, infested with mice, and the lack of electricity, bathroom and outside lavatory concerned them. But their primary concern was Maud's age and failing health.

'Both Mr Taylor and his mother believe a foster-home is the best solution,' Susan said firmly. She had stated this right at the start of the meeting almost an hour earlier. Since then the discussion had gone round and round in circles and she was very afraid that nothing would be resolved today. 'They have no behavioural problems, they are doing well at school, and they will be much happier in a family environment.'

'But fostering is an expensive way of caring for children, and really only suitable in the very short term, Miss Sims.' The most elderly of the women looked disdainfully over her glasses at Susan. 'Also the Taylors are Catholics, and most of our foster-parents are Church of England.'

Susan couldn't really see why the religious denomination of foster-parents mattered. But Father O'Brien had already gone on at length that they should be kept in 'the Faith', as he put it.

'It's my belief that the father should be compelled to

offer them for adoption,' one of the men insisted, not for the first time during the discussion.

Susan's blood ran cold each time this man spoke. His name was Arkwright, a big bully of a man of around sixty, with eyes as dead as those of a fish on a fishmonger's slab. How he managed to become a Children's Officer she couldn't imagine. He appeared to have little liking for children, even less knowledge of their needs, and no understanding of parental love.

'In all likelihood the girls will be adults before Mr Taylor is released from prison. Why should the taxpayers be compelled to keep his children during that time when we have dozens of prospective adoptive parents only too willing to take one of these girls?'

'But that would mean they'd be split up,' Miss Denning spoke up. She had had considerable contact with the girls during the summer months, taking them out for trips and picnics, and she was the only person in the group who was backing up Susan. 'I believe May could manage quite well without her sister, but Dulcie would certainly suffer enormously.'

Susan shot her a look of gratitude. The woman looked formidable, thin as a stick, with a long pointed nose and a very unflattering short grey bobbed hairstyle which only accentuated the length of her face and nose. But she was intelligent, a staunch believer in keeping families together at all costs, and the only one here today who hadn't spoken of Reg as if he was a degenerate.

'It seems to me the ideal solution all round is for the children to go to the Sacred Heart Convent,' the second of the two men from the Children's Department volunteered.

'Hear, hear,' Father O'Brien applauded, his already bulbous eyes almost popping out of his head. 'Untold damage has already been done to the children by their immoral mother and their bully of a father. Their great-uncle isn't the least bit interested in them either. At the Sacred Heart the Sisters will see that they are both spiritually and physically cared for. They will be able to put aside the regrettable memories. It is a small convent with beautiful grounds, and the children will attend a school outside. I know too that Mr Taylor and his mother will find this an acceptable solution.'

It was true Reg and Maud had tentatively agreed to accept this convent if a good foster-home couldn't be found, mainly because Father O'Brien had been so voluble in its praise, but Susan had visited the place, which was situated in South London between Lee and Downham, and found it cheerless, the nuns dour, cold and unimaginative.

'Well, we really cannot spend any more time discussing this matter,' Miss Denning said, glancing at her watch. 'We must make a decision today. We have agreed that we are likely to run into problems with fostering, and adoption is out of the question, which leaves only children's homes.'

She paused to look around the table. 'I have spent some time with Dulcie and May, and weighing up everything I know about them, their individual characters and the family's strong religious views, I believe the most suitable home *is* the Sacred Heart. I suggest we have a show of hands if you are in agreement.'

Susan was unhappy that a decision should be made so hurriedly and she was reluctant to agree with something she didn't support wholeheartedly. Yet she was here only to present Reg's and Maud's views, not her own. They believed the convent was a good one, they had faith in Father O'Brien's judgement. As everyone but Arkwright raised their hands in agreement, she added hers to them.

Father O'Brien looked triumphant. The motion was carried.

'Would you like to accompany me when I tell the girls?' Miss Denning asked Susan as the meeting closed and the others began to pack their files away. 'I'm sure your presence would reassure them.'

Susan glanced around the room. The rest of the group were chatting amongst themselves as if nothing more important had been discussed today than what they should eat for dinner tonight. She wondered if any of them was really aware what this 'solution' would mean to Dulcie and May. They had lost their mother in the most shocking way, their father had been imprisoned and their family home was gone for ever. They had barely come to terms with the idea that their father wasn't going to come home again for many years, and now they were to be snatched from their loving grandmother and the school they'd only just settled in. Perhaps it might be for the best in the long term, but she was terribly afraid that for two such young, vulnerable children it was going to look very much like abandonment.

'Yes, I'd like to come,' she said, tears prickling at her eyes. 'It wouldn't do for them to think I'd stopped caring too.'

Miss Denning put a comforting hand on Susan's shoulder as she saw the young teacher's eyes swimming. 'Don't reproach yourself about anything, my dear. You have been a good friend to the family and you did your best for them today. I can't count the times when I've felt, as I'm sure you do now, that I've only reached a compromise rather than perfection. It saddens me, but then this isn't a perfect world.'

Susan looked up at Miss Denning and saw real understanding in her eyes. All at once she knew this woman wasn't entirely happy with the decision either.

'When are you going to tell the children?' she asked.

'As soon as possible.' The older woman sighed. 'It's better to get it over quickly. They have room for them now at the convent, and they'll adjust to the new school better if they don't miss too much of this term. Could you come with me tomorrow afternoon? I could pick you up in my car after school.'

When Susan arrived home and found her mother sitting by the fire in the sitting-room putting the finishing touches to the two little tartan pinafore dresses she'd made for

Dulcie and May, she began to cry. She sank down on the settee beside her mother, allowed herself to be drawn into her arms and sobbed out her disappointment.

The fire crackled, table-lamps cast pools of soft light on to the Persian rug and the heavy dark green velvet curtains. It was a beautiful room, the furniture well-loved family heirlooms, the many fine paintings on the walls all of exquisite pastoral scenes. But it was very much a family room, childhood photographs of the four children crowding the mantelpiece, Daphne Sims's sewing-machine on the table, more needlework equipment strewn on the floor, Christmas decorations spilled out of a box waiting to be put away for another year.

Daphne bit back her own tears. The girls had been to tea here several times in the past months, they'd had a special tea party on Dulcie's ninth birthday in December, and she'd been charmed by them. But in her heart of hearts she was relieved that a long-term arrangement for their care had been found for she was worried by her daughter's ever-increasing involvement with this family and the depth of her feelings for Reg Taylor.

'I think it's for the best,' she said reassuringly. 'You'll still be able to visit them, they'll be going out each day to school. You know May finds friends everywhere, and I really think Dulcie will be a great deal happier with an ordered, sheltered life.'

'You always seem to know everything,' Susan said with a deep sigh. 'Even what I'm thinking.'

Daphne laughed gently. 'No, your thoughts are quite safe from me, but any mother watches out for danger, and in the past few months I've seen how much all this has changed you.'

'I thought I'd changed for the better!' Susan said indignantly.

Daphne took her hand and squeezed it. 'So you have, darling, you've finally learned that this house and our family isn't the axis the world turns on, and that out there are many new challenges and experiences for you. Find a new job, Susan, soon, get to know new people. You can still see the children, maybe see Maud too. But let Reg go.'

When Dulcie heard a car coming up Akerman Street on Friday evening, she ran straight into the parlour to look out of the window. Very few people in Deptford owned a car, there were none at all in her grandmother's street, and in the seven and a half months Dulcie had lived here, she'd come to see that cars invariably meant trouble for someone. A doctor calling on someone who was very sick, the police trying to find someone, or the Welfare, sticking their noses into other people's business.

It was pitch dark although it was only five o'clock, yet Dulcie recognized the green Morris as Miss Denning's car straight off, and her heart sank. It wasn't because she didn't like the lady, she had after all taken her and May out several times, and she seemed very nice. The only reason for her trepidation was that Gran wouldn't like her coming again, she claimed Miss Denning was a busybody who peered into corners and asked too many impertinent questions.

But when Dulcie saw Susan was in the car too, she instinctively knew it meant something bad had happened. She adored Susan, if she'd been walking up the street alone Dulcie would have run to greet her – even Granny, who was suspicious of anyone posh, liked and trusted her. But in the time Dulcie had been living here, one of the things she'd had drummed into her was that when a Welfare person called with support from someone else, that was something serious.

Dulcie ran into the back room to warn Granny. She was dozing in her chair by the stove, May was sitting at the table doing a jigsaw, squinting at it because the gas wasn't turned up properly.

'Granny, it's Susan and Miss Denning,' she said, shaking her shoulder. 'Wake up!'

Maud's eyes shot open. Dulcie repeated herself as she pulled the old lady forward in her chair and snatched off her dirty pinafore. Then, going over to the window-sill, she got her teeth which were soaking in a cup. By the time the knock came at the front door, Dulcie had turned up the gaslight, but that only made her notice some mice droppings on the floor.

'Maybe I should take them in the parlour?' she suggested.

'You can't, it's too cold – besides, they'll see how bad my legs are,' Maud said. 'I'll move over to the table and they won't see anything.'

'Won't see what?' May asked, carrying on with the jigsaw as if nothing unusual was happening.

Dulcie wasn't going to explain. May was oblivious to such things as swollen legs, mice droppings and black mould creeping up the walls, but if she was asked not to speak of them, she would go out of her way to mention them.

'Hello, Dulcie,' the two women chorused as she opened the door to them.

Dulcie made herself look really surprised and pleased. But she noticed immediately that Susan wasn't herself. She usually enveloped her in a tight hug and bounced into the house, so jolly that none of them ever considered she might be looking around her and thinking what an awful place it was. She had the bag in her hand which usually contained all sorts of little treats for them. But her wide smile was missing, she was stiff and holding back.

'Miss Denning offered me a lift so I could come and see you with her,' she said. 'I hope Granny won't mind us turning up when it's nearly tea-time?'

'She hasn't started it yet,' Dulcie said. 'We were all doing a jigsaw together in the kitchen. Come in there because we haven't lit the fire in the parlour yet.'

By the time they got into the kitchen, Granny was sitting at the table, her legs tucked away. She greeted both women as if there was nothing unusual about them coming together, then asked if they'd like some tea.

'I was hoping for a private chat with you, Mrs Taylor,' Miss Denning said, looking pointedly at the two children. 'Maybe Dulcie and May could find something to do upstairs for a little while?'

All hope that this was purely a friendly visit vanished then for Dulcie. Grown-ups only got children out of the way when they had something serious to discuss.

'Go on then, buzz off, you two,' Maud said in a jocular manner, giving Dulcie a nudge. 'You can come down in a minute when I call you and make us all some tea.'

'I don't want to go upstairs,' May pouted. 'It's cold there, and there's nothing to do.'

'We'll play tents,' Dulcie said immediately – she didn't want May to start showing off on top of everything else.

'You've come to take them away, ain't you?' Maud said once she could hear the girls in the room above the kitchen.

Susan couldn't reply, she let Miss Denning tell her. But as she saw Maud's wrinkled old face crumple and the bleakness in her faded eyes, she knew this old lady had nothing more to live for.

In her many visits to the house Susan had come to see Maud was like a crab, a hard shell on the outside, inside as soft as marshmallow. She wouldn't cry today, not in front of Miss Denning, she'd bottle that up until after the children were taken, then she'd let it go. She guessed too that Maud was sitting at the table instead of in her usual chair just to hide her legs. Last time Susan had come they were swollen to twice their normal size and she could barely walk, but she'd made light of that just as she made light of the struggle it was to keep the girls' clothes and the house clean, and to do the cooking and shopping.

Susan knew now that when Reg was arrested, Maud's pride took a severe tumble. He was the one she could boast about – his craftsmanship, his honesty, sobriety and the fact that he had always looked after her. While she had lost none of her love for Reg, and strongly upheld his innocence to her neighbours, she was dented, and the only way she could keep her head up was by transferring all that fierce pride to his daughters, and caring for them. Without them she would be like a three-legged chair, unable to hold her head up in her community. The girls' removal would be like signing her death warrant.

'How soon have they got to go?' she asked when Miss Denning had finished. She seemed calm and collected – to an outsider it might have been taken as complete acceptance. But Susan knew it was her pride holding her together – everything she felt, the pain, anxiety and the humiliation, would be suppressed for the children's sake.

'I thought it would be best to collect them in the morning,' Miss Denning said. 'As it's Saturday they'll have the whole weekend to settle down before starting at their new school on Monday. But you can visit them there, Mrs Taylor. It's quite close to Downham station.'

'I wish they were going to a family,' was all the old lady said.

Susan took Maud's hand and held it tightly. 'I do too, and Miss Denning. But it is only a small convent, and the grounds are lovely.'

Maud seemed to rally herself a little and she straightened up in her chair and tried to smile. 'You'd better call the girls, Susan, it's enough to freeze the balls off a brass monkey up there.'

Susan felt like Judas as the girls came down the stairs. Whatever was said now by Miss Denning, Dulcie at least was going to believe it was she who had failed them.

It was Susan who put the kettle on after seeing Dulcie back up to her grandmother and slip her arm around her shoulders. She might not know what was coming, but she'd sensed her granny was upset.

May knelt up on a chair and began her jigsaw again, but even she kept taking surreptitious glances at Miss Denning.

'Well, girls,' Miss Denning began, her voice rather too loud for such a small room.

'I'll tell 'em,' Maud said, giving Miss Denning a scathing look.

The Children's Officer nodded.

Susan found it so very touching how Maud reached out for May and drew her off her chair so she had both girls right in front of her. She put one hand on each of their cheeks and gently stroked them.

'You gotta go to a new home,' she said, her voice cracking with emotion. 'It ain't 'cos I don't want you 'ere, only that I'm gettin' too old to mind you. It'll be better for you anyway, lots of other kids to play with who ain't ragamuffins. You'll have proper baths again, and go to a nice school.'

Neither child said anything, just stared at Maud with wide, unwavering eyes.

'I'll let Miss Denning tell you the rest,' Maud said, turning them around so they could face the woman, but she still kept a hand firmly on each of the girls' shoulders.

'It's the Sacred Heart Convent,' Miss Denning said. 'You might even have seen it before because it's close to Chinbrook Meadows, not that far from where you used to live. You'll be very happy there, it's got a lovely garden and an orchard. You'll go out each day to school and you can have visitors on Sundays.'

'Will Granny come to see us?' May asked.

''Course I will,' Maud said quickly. 'It's only a little train ride.'

'Does Daddy want us to go there?' Dulcie suddenly burst out, looking suspiciously at Miss Denning.

'Yes, he does,' Miss Denning replied. 'He knows you will be safe and well looked after there. So you must be good girls, work hard at school and make him very proud of you.'

'I don't mind going there,' May suddenly said in a cheerful voice. 'I don't like it here, the children are so rough and dirty and I hate the outside toilet. It stinks.'

Susan and Miss Denning exchanged glances. While it was good to see that May didn't appear upset by the news, her remark must have been so hurtful to her grandmother. Neither of them knew what to say.

'Fair do's, May,' Maud said, surprising them both. 'The kids round 'ere *are* rough and dirty. That's why I want you to go somewhere better. But what about you, Dulcie? Will you be pleased to 'ave a garden, and go to school with nice kids who don't pull yer 'air? No more finding me teeth for me, or going out to the lav in the rain?'

Dulcie wound her arms round the old lady's neck and buried her face in her shoulder. 'I want to stay with you,' she mumbled. 'You need someone to look after you.'

Maud looked up at Susan, her lips quivering. 'You'd best go now,' she said. 'I'll 'ave 'em ready for the morning.'

Susan didn't think she'd ever seen such courage. What Dulcie had said was true. Maud did need someone to look after her, and the child had been doing just that ever since she came here. Maud knew it too. She might be relieved of responsibility and hard work, but she was going to be lost without them.

'My mother made you both a pinafore dress,' Susan said, opening her bag and getting them out. 'Why don't you wear them tomorrow to look really pretty?'

Later that night she was struck by the different way the two girls reacted to those dresses. May was thrilled, she jumped up and down holding it against herself. Dulcie on the other hand politely asked her to thank her mother for them, folded it up neatly, and gave her a look which said she felt she'd been betrayed.

Chapter Five

Dulcie's first thought as Miss Denning led her and May up the gravel drive to the Sacred Heart was that maybe it wouldn't be *quite* as bad as she feared. The big red brick house looked kind of grand with its large windows, pointed eaves and wide steps up to the big porch. She knew that to see anywhere on a cold winter's day was to see it at its worst, but the huge trees all around the front garden suggested that it would be pretty in summer, and the other big houses in the tree-lined avenue all looked as if they were the homes of rich people. It certainly didn't look the kind of place where anything bad could happen.

She hadn't been able to sleep last night because she felt so afraid, so she left May in bed and crept downstairs. Granny was sitting by the stove drinking cocoa laced with brandy, and she made Dulcie a cup of it too, then took her on her lap to cuddle her.

'You're a right little Jonah,' she said teasingly. 'Always expecting the worst. People wot do that get it an' all. Try and be like our May, sweetheart, she always looks on the bright side. She went off to bed 'appy and excited about the convent, and you can bet yer boots she'll get in there tomorra with a cheerful grin on 'er face, and she'll bowl 'em all over. But if you goes in there with that long face, lookin' like you've got a stink under yer nose, you ain't gonna make any friends. Then you will be lonesome.'

'But I'm so scared,' Dulcie whispered, snuggling closer to the old lady.

Granny tipped Dulcie's face up to look at her. 'Whatcha got to be scared of?' she asked. 'There ain't gonna be no bombs dropping up there, no floods, fires or plagues of the Pharaohs! Just some little old nuns, a bunch of other kids wot ain't got no one, and you and May will be the prettiest, smartest ones there. I reckon that'll give you an 'ead start!'

'But what if the nuns are nasty to us?' Dulcie whispered, looking right into her grandmother's faded blue eyes.

Granny snorted. 'They'll have me to reckon with if they are,' she said fiercely. 'I'll be up to visit you, and Susan will an' all. We ain't casting you off, love, you's only goin' there 'cos they don't think it's nice enough 'ere. We'll both still be watchin' over you.'

Dulcie felt reassured at that and reached out for her cocoa. The brandy made it taste like medicine, so she supposed it would make her feel better.

'Good girl,' Granny said approvingly. 'Now, tomorra you got to put on an 'appy face, not for me, nor May, or anyone else, just for yerself. 'Cos that's a magic trick I learned a long time ago, if you look like you're 'appy, you soon get to be.'

Remembering Granny's words, Dulcie thought it was time she put her advice into practice. She looked up at Miss Denning and smiled. 'It looks nice,' she said.

The social worker was caught unawares for a moment by her small charge's apparent change of heart. Dulcie hadn't said a word on the drive here from Deptford, but her expression of profound misery had revealed everything she was thinking. In fact Miss Denning shared some of the child's anxiety for she knew the convent had a rather harsh regime. Yet it was a beautiful place in spring and summer, and Deptford with its squalor and poverty was no place for two gently brought up girls like these two.

The house had been built back in 1880 by a wealthy businessman as a family home, and the extensive grounds which included an orchard, tennis court and a formal rose garden were renowned for their beauty and cared for by a team of gardeners. In the twenties it had been a select preparatory school, and the grounds equally well kept, but when the Church had bought it during the early thirties to turn it into an orphanage, they dispensed with all but one gardener, and as he was unable to keep up the previous standards on his own, he concentrated all his efforts on the front garden to maintain appearances and barely touched the gardens at the back.

Inside the house all signs of its former glory were gone too. While the oak-panelled hall and wide staircase must have been so gracious in the days when the polished wood floors were softened with carpets and lit by a chandelier, now the floors were bare, and the lighting miserly. Rows of iron beds filled the once sumptuously appointed reception rooms, worn cheap cotton curtains had taken the place of the heavy velvets and brocades which once adorned the vast windows. Distemper had replaced hand-printed papers, the only pictures now were of a religious nature, and as the boiler which heated the house was erratic, it was often very cold.

Most of the girls placed here at the age of five had never known a real home, many had been in orphanages since birth, and those who had come later had usually been taken from their mother because of neglect or problems in the family, so few of them had any idea what they had missed out on. Miss Denning knew it wasn't possible in an all-female environment to simulate an average family home, but she knew the Sisters and wished they would make more of an effort to be kindly, affectionate and sympathetic to their charges.

Yet it was Mr Taylor's wish his girls should go here, he believed that the cloistered world the Sisters offered, the spiritual guidance and the high standard of education in the school his daughters would attend daily would give them a better chance in life than he'd had. So, hoping he was right, she swallowed her reservations and smiled down at Dulcie.

'That's the spirit, Dulcie,' she said. 'You will miss your granny of course, but you'll soon make lots of new friends

and I know you are going to like your new school just as
well as Lee Manor.'

She ushered them up the three steps to the front door
and rang the bell. A few seconds later the door was opened
by a fresh-faced nun who appeared quite young.

'Good morning, Sister Grace,' Miss Denning said,
pleased they should be greeted by the most pleasant and
kindly nun in the convent. 'This is Dulcie and May Taylor,
Mother Superior is expecting us.'

The sister gave them a beaming smile, urged them to
come in, and said Mother Superior would see them in
her sitting-room. After asking Miss Denning to leave the
suitcase by the door for the time being, she led the way
across the wide wood-panelled hall and knocked at a
closed door.

Dulcie's eyes swivelled around, trying to take everything in all at once. She thought the hall was a bit bare and
gloomy, but the life-size statue of the Virgin Mary on the
turn of the huge staircase was quite comforting, as was
the large picture of Jesus surrounded by children on the
wall. The utter silence was daunting, however – she wondered where all the children were.

Mother Superior's small sitting-room was very warm,
though as bare as the hall, furnished only with a battered
desk under the window, four fireside chairs and a bookcase. She was disconcertingly old, and the small face
encased by the tight white wimple was as wrinkled as a
prune. She stayed by the fire, only turning her head to
look at them as they came in. Apart from greeting the girls,
and telling them to say their names and ages, she then
spoke only to Miss Denning, asking what childhood diseases they'd already had, not even asking the girls if they'd
like to sit down.

Dulcie glanced nervously at her younger sister as they
stood there. May had chattered and giggled all the way
from Deptford, she'd even callously said she was glad to
be leaving there because Granny's house smelled funny.
But she never could stand being ignored, and Dulcie could

see by the way she was sticking out her chin and looking daggers at the two women talking that she was working up for one of her tantrums.

To try to avert this, Dulcie sidled nearer her and took her hand, but instead of the gesture appeasing her, it had the opposite effect. May's mouth began to quiver. 'I want to go home,' she wailed pitifully.

Both women turned their heads in surprise to look at her – it was as if they'd completely forgotten the children were in the room.

'That's quite enough of that,' Mother Superior said sharply. 'This is your home now and you must behave as all my other girls do. I'll call Sister Teresa and get her to take you out to meet them.'

'But I don't like it here,' May retorted, squeezing out a few tears.

'Now, that's silly,' Miss Denning said, picking her up in her arms and cuddling her. 'You haven't even seen anything yet.'

It surprised Dulcie that May stopped crying, normally she persisted for some time when she had an audience, but perhaps getting Miss Denning's attention and seeing Mother Superior rise from her chair to ring a bell by the fireplace was enough for her.

Almost instantly the door opened and in came another nun. Mother Superior informed her that they were the children they'd been expecting.

'I'm Sister Teresa,' the nun said. 'Now, say goodbye to Miss Denning and then come with me to meet the other girls.'

She held out her hands to the girls, a welcoming and friendly gesture, yet Dulcie shrank back. She didn't know why, the nun wasn't particularly ugly or very old, she was just a big middle-aged woman with a slightly yellowish complexion and very dark eyes like two pieces of coal.

Sister Teresa smiled at her and took a step closer. 'Everyone's a bit frightened on their first day,' she said, and her voice was soft with a faint Irish lilt. 'But it soon passes.'

She came closer, leaning down to their level, smiled and asked them to tell her their names, and even assured them they would see Miss Denning again soon. May smiled back at her and readily took her hand, so Dulcie had no choice but to follow suit.

'That's better,' the woman said. 'Now, let's go and meet all the other girls, shall we?'

Miss Denning gave them both a kiss on the cheek and said they weren't to worry about their granny, and she'd be back to see them soon. Her hand lingered on Dulcie's head, and she murmured something about looking out for May and helping her to write letters to her granny.

May became excited again and she started talking to Sister the moment they were out of the room. She told her she had a new pinafore dress under her coat, seven new pairs of hair ribbons in her suitcase, and that Granny had told her she wasn't to forget to brush her teeth or they'd all go black.

Dulcie thought it was strange that Sister Teresa didn't laugh, she'd never met anyone before who didn't laugh at May, but in fact she didn't even appear to be listening, just hurried them down a long narrow passage. As they got to a half-glazed door at the end and May asked when they'd be having dinner, she stopped short and looked down at her.

'You are very full of yourself,' she said sharply. 'I don't like that in children.'

Dulcie often thought May was too full of herself too, but she didn't like anyone else pointing it out. She opened her mouth to retort that May was only five and a half, and a chatterbox by nature, but she closed it again as she saw the woman's expression.

It was as if she was sucking a lemon. It chilled Dulcie right to the bone, and it seemed to make sense of why she'd shrunk away from this woman earlier. All at once the hand holding hers felt more like a claw and she was reminded of the old lady in the gingerbread house who invited Hansel and Gretel in, then turned into a witch.

'She's just a bit scared,' Dulcie said in her sister's defence.

'No I'm not,' May said indignantly. 'I'm not scared of anything.'

Sister Teresa gave her a look that would turn milk sour, let go of their hands, unlocked the door, and nudged them both out into a small yard surrounded by single-storey outhouses. Beyond this they could see children in a fenced-in playground.

'Off you go.' Sister Teresa gave them both a further nudge in the back. 'You stay in the playground until the bell rings for dinner.' With that she blew a whistle, and the playground grew still and silent. 'Carol!' she yelled. 'New girls. Look after them!'

That was their introduction to the Sacred Heart. They had to walk across the yard alone, go into the playground and be surrounded by around fourteen other girls ranging from five to eleven, all dressed identically in navy-blue gabardine raincoats, grey wool ankle socks and brown lace-up shoes.

Dulcie was heartened by the warmth of their smiles and how they all clamoured at once to find out the sisters' names, ages and where they had come from. Carol, the one Sister Teresa had ordered to look after them, appeared to be the eldest; she took their hands and told them all the other girls' names.

Carol was very thin and plain, her brown hair cut off abruptly on a level with her ear lobes, and her front teeth stuck out like a rabbit's. She admired both Dulcie and May's blonde hair, and their wool coats, but spoiled the moment for Dulcie by saying she hoped that Sister Teresa wouldn't cut their hair tonight at bathtime, and that tomorrow they'd be wearing the same uniform as everyone else.

'I'd better tell you the rules,' she went on. 'We have to

stay in here.' She waved one hand at the wire netting surrounding the playground. 'Go outside into the garden and you'll get the stick.'

May's eyes nearly popped out of her head at this and she immediately ran over to the fence and looked longingly at the vast, somewhat overgrown garden beyond it.

'I mean it,' Carol said, looking anxiously at Dulcie then across to May. 'You'd better make sure she understands because the Sisters watch us from upstairs. Helen went out there a week ago to collect some conkers. Show us your hands, Helen!'

A girl of about eight with carroty hair and freckles held out her hands to Dulcie. Her palms still held faint brown weals from a cane. 'It hurt so bad, and they still ache,' she said. 'You wouldn't catch me going out there again.'

Carol then went on to explain more. 'We get sent out here every Saturday and every day in the school holidays after breakfast, unless it's raining. You have to go to the toilet before we come out because we aren't allowed back in except at milk-time. One of the Sisters rings a bell at dinner-time, then we all get in a line. You mustn't talk then at all. We hang up our coats, go to the toilet and wash our hands, then wait for another bell before we can go down to the dining-room. That's in the basement. If you speak even once, you have to stand in the corner till everyone else has finished their dinner, then you get yours afterwards. But it will be cold and even more horrible than it was hot.'

She paused to laugh after she'd imparted that. 'Saturday's dinner is the worst. It's always macaroni cheese,' she went on. 'But make sure you eat it, otherwise you'll get it cold again tomorrow.'

Dulcie assumed the girl was pulling her leg.

'I won't eat the dinner if it's horrible,' May said. She'd just returned from the fence to hear the last part of the conversation.

'Then you'll just get it again and again until you do.' Carol looked down at the small indignant face looking up at her. 'I once had to eat a meat pie with mould on it. I was sick afterwards.'

There was a chorus of similar horror stories from the other girls and all at once Dulcie realized they weren't pulling her leg. 'And we can't speak either?' she gasped.

Carol shook her head. 'Not a word, apart from grace, or answering a Sister if she speaks to you, not until we get out here again in the afternoon.'

'That will be hard for May, she talks all the time,' Dulcie said, making a brave attempt at humour.

Carol looked down at May and smiled, the way everyone who ever met May did. 'Save it up till you get out here again,' she said. 'If you upset Sister Teresa she'll pick on you all the time, even if you are only little.'

May blanched, for once stuck for words.

'I thought there would be more girls than this,' Dulcie said, looking around at the group, not wanting Carol to tell May any more awful things.

'Oh, we're just the Juniors,' Carol replied. 'The Seniors are all inside.' She thumbed towards the house. 'They do work instead, the laundry, cleaning and stuff. I can't wait for my eleventh birthday next month so I can join them.'

Dulcie couldn't understand then why Carol should want to be inside, but half an hour later she began to see why. The sun was shining, but it was biting cold, and there was absolutely nothing to do in the playground. There wasn't a ball to play with, a skipping-rope or even squares for hop-scotch.

By six that evening Dulcie was very relieved when Carol said it would soon be time for bed. She was weary of forcing a smile, of answering endless questions from the other girls and trying to stop May from speaking when she wasn't supposed to. She wanted to cry, to find someone, anyone who would put their arms around her and assure her that this was all a bad dream which would soon be over.

She had seen little of the convent, just the dining-room, cloakroom and now the playroom, which was on the first floor. One of the other girls had said that the Sisters slept up here, and that the bathrooms and chapel were on this floor too. Apparently the four girls' dormitories were all downstairs. Maybe if she'd just been shown around so she got her bearings she wouldn't feel quite so scared.

She'd somehow managed to eat the disgusting macaroni cheese for dinner, she'd coped with being cold out in the playground all afternoon, she'd got over the disappointment of only bread and margarine for tea. After all that she wasn't even surprised when the 'playroom' they were herded into after tea turned out to be a bare room, furnished with nothing more than two old couches and a single box of useless broken toys. At least it was warm. The Senior girls had only just joined them for they'd had to stay downstairs to wash up the tea things and lay the tables for breakfast. They were cheerful, giggling as they fought for places on the couches, but Dulcie had observed several pairs of sore-looking hands, and she guessed the work they had to do was very hard.

Dulcie wished she could be more like May, she didn't seem troubled by anything, in fact at dinner-time she'd given the Sisters such beaming smiles that she'd had her head patted. Being with so many admiring older girls was her idea of heaven, and Dulcie had no doubt that before the week was out she'd be almost everyone's pet.

She watched as May went over to the group of Senior girls. They wore similar grey wool skirts and maroon jumpers to the younger girls, but they looked more individual as some had adult bosoms and their hair was better cared for than the younger ones'. Dulcie had learned this afternoon that all the girls who had their hair cut brutally like Carol's had not kept it tidy enough for the Sisters' liking. They would allow long hair only if it was well brushed and plaited. Carol recommended that Dulcie hold on tight to her rubber bands, as Sister Grace, the nun who had let them in today, was the only one who would ever find replacements. Dulcie had no intention of allowing her hair or May's to be shorn, she just hoped she would have enough time in the mornings to plait both her own and May's. Carol had said there was always an inspection before the morning service up in the chapel, and quite often Sister Teresa got out her scissors then and there if a child's hair wasn't to her liking. It seemed Dulcie had been right to be nervous of that nun, all the girls were really scared of her.

From her position leaning back on the hot pipes Dulcie couldn't hear what May was saying to the Senior girls but within just a few seconds she was sitting in the lap of a big girl with curly auburn hair. Dulcie felt a pang of jealousy, she couldn't remember ever being babied the way May was, except of course by Granny. She supposed now she was nine she never would be again. But it made her feel sad.

It was less than half an hour later that May threw the biggest tantrum of her life, and any jealousy Dulcie might have harboured vanished in the need to protect her.

When the bell rang for bath-time the Junior girls lined up in size, the smallest ones at the front. May was third, Dulcie eleventh, and Sister Grace who came in to collect them led the crocodile along the upstairs passage towards Sister Teresa who was standing in front of an open cupboard. As Dulcie looked over the heads of the smaller girls she saw the first being handed a pile of clothes, then she trotted off towards the bathroom for her bath.

Like earlier in the day there could be no talking, so when it was May's turn to collect her clothes, and she spoke, everyone's head jerked up in shock.

'Those aren't my clothes,' May said in a loud clear voice. 'My nightie is white with little pink flowers, Granny made it.'

'You wear what I give you,' Sister Teresa replied.

'But I want my things, they are in my suitcase,' May retorted belligerently. 'My dolly's in there too and I want her before I go to bed.'

Dulcie shuddered at her sister's impudence. It would be rude to make a demand like that to anyone, but to say it to Sister Teresa, who'd they'd both been told was dangerous to cross, was downright foolhardy.

'Any toys in your suitcase will be shared by all the children tomorrow,' Sister Teresa barked back at her. 'And another word from you tonight and you'll be punished.'

Dulcie didn't think she minded too much sharing her books and games with the other girls, but she knew May would never accept anyone touching Belinda, her baby doll. It wasn't just a toy to her, it was her whole world. She'd been given it when she was three, and she loved it passionately – it had a complete wardrobe, including nappies made by Granny. She took it to bed every night and Dulcie doubted she'd ever go to sleep without it.

Sensing that the worst thing May could do was make a scene about it now, she willed her to stay silent, but her sister had never been one to let anything go without a fight.

'I want my dolly now. I'm not sharing her with anyone,' she screamed out at the top of her lungs. She began to stamp her feet in rage, hurled the pile of clothes she'd been given at Sister Teresa and continued to scream that she wanted to have her doll.

A buzz went along the line of girls, everyone craning their necks to see what was going on. Even the playroom door opened and half a dozen Senior girls popped their heads out.

Sister Grace came running out of the bathroom, fluttering her hands as if she didn't know what to do, and still May continued her tantrum. Her face was bright red with the exertion. 'I won't stay here unless you get me my dolly and my own nightie,' she yelled at the top of her lungs, then to Dulcie's horror she began to dart backwards and forwards, pummelling Sister Teresa in the stomach with her little fists.

'May! Stop that at once!' Sister Grace called out, trying to catch hold of the child. 'Such behaviour just will not do.'

It was Sister Teresa who caught May, grabbing her

shoulders, and she shook her violently. 'Stop it, you wretch,' she yelled, her coal-black eyes glinting dangerously and her yellow skin becoming flushed.

Dulcie darted forward, her only intention to stop May before she did anything worse. But by the time she got to her, the Sister was shaking her so hard her head was lolling from side to side like a rag doll's. Fearing for May's safety, she caught hold of the woman's habit from behind and yanked at it.

'Leave her alone,' she screamed out. 'You're hurting her.'

The nun slapped May hard on the side of her head, sending her sprawling to the floor. With her hands now free she reached round for Dulcie too and hit her with such force that she knocked her back up the passage. As the floor was polished, Dulcie's feet went from under her and she skidded some five or six feet on her back.

Suddenly there were Sisters everywhere, swarming like black beetles between the children, all shouting at once. Dulcie found herself hauled to her feet by two of them, and as she glanced round she saw Sister Teresa snatch May up under her arm and disappear down the stairs with her.

Before Dulcie could catch her breath she was thrust into a room and the door locked behind her. She was just about to scream out and hammer on the door when she saw she was in the chapel, and that immediately brought her to her senses. Even in her anger and fear for her sister she didn't feel able to make a scene in a holy place, so instead she genuflected in front of the altar and slumped down on one of the pews.

The large window was shrouded in white draped muslin, the walls were white too, and the altar was covered with a white cloth embroidered with gold thread. The only light came from a dozen or so small candles burning in little glasses under holy pictures.

Getting down on her knees, she began to pray. 'Holy Mary, Mother of God,' she began, 'please protect May and don't let her do anything worse. I'm sorry I pulled at Sister Teresa, but she shouldn't have shaken May like that.'

Suddenly all the events of the entire day caught up with her at once. There was no granny to run to, no friendly neighbours, she and May had been cast off, abandoned in a harsh, cruel place where no one cared about them. Wasn't it already bad enough that Mummy was dead and Daddy in prison? Did she and May have to be punished even more by being taken away from Granny and shoved in a nasty place like this? It wasn't fair! They hadn't done anything bad.

She leaned her arms on the pew in front and wept out her despair.

Sister Teresa was wild with fury at May's cheek and the ensuing tantrum. Although she and all the other Sisters had been told by Mother Superior to be extra gentle with the two new girls because they had just been torn away from their grandmother, she saw no reason why this should mean they should get away with such shocking behaviour.

Mother Superior might be officially in charge at the Sacred Heart, but in reality she was too old and frail to be anything more than a figure-head. Sister Teresa ran the convent and had done so since the end of the war. It was she who controlled the housekeeping, supervised the other Sisters and kept the children in line. In Teresa's opinion some of the younger Sisters like Grace were far too soft; she knew if they had their way the girls would be allowed all over the grounds, in and out of the house as they pleased, given toys and books, pampered with luxurious food, and before long the convent would be a shambles. As only a handful of the children had their keep paid for by a relative, the rest had to be kept by Church funds, so Sister Teresa saw it as her duty to the Church to keep expenditure to a minimum. As she also believed that every child who arrived through the doors was already stained with the sins of their parents, she felt no compassion for any of them.

She knew the Taylor girls' father was in prison for killing his wife, she'd read a report on the family. Clearly, judging by the scene tonight, their children were cast from the same mould. But she had her own way of breaking that mould and recasting children in a fit and proper manner.

As she carried the screaming, struggling child downstairs, tucked firmly beneath her arm, she decided on her most successful punishment. The girls whisperingly called it *the Dark Place* and quaked as they spoke of it, for those wilful girls who had been put in there were never the same again.

Sister Teresa couldn't use it very often, for Mother Superior claimed it was cruel and had banned its use, yet just the threat of it was usually enough. But Teresa had been observing May Taylor ever since her arrival, and she knew she wasn't likely to be intimidated by mere threats. Just the way she turned on beaming smiles and got others to return them was evidence she'd been spoiled and adored all her short life. Unless she wiped out her confidence now before she had a chance to worm her way into some of the weaker Sisters' affections, she would always be trouble. No one came out of the Dark Place with their confidence intact.

Sister Teresa put her hand over May's mouth as she went past Mother Superior's sitting-room. The old lady was a little hard of hearing so she probably hadn't heard the din from upstairs, and Sister Teresa didn't want her hearing anything now. Down the stairs to the basement she went, still keeping the struggling child gagged, and through the dining-room, where she paused to grab the cane from its permanent position beneath the large wooden cross on the wall.

May let out another shriek as she released her mouth, and struggled even harder to get free when she saw the cane.

'Scream all you like,' Sister Teresa said through half-clenched lips. 'No one is going to hear you.'

The basement was eerie at night, four long tables set for breakfast, and the only light a small red lamp beneath a picture of the Sacred Heart. The kitchen beyond was in total darkness, except for a very faint glow from the stove, and that made sinister rustling and stirring noises. Sister Teresa went through the kitchen and on through the door to the passage which led to steps up to the laundry rooms in the outhouses. It was very cold out here, and pitch dark. She kicked the door shut behind her before dropping May to the stone floor, and waited a second or two before flicking on the light.

The child was stunned momentarily into silence, not only by suddenly finding herself sprawled on the floor, but by the extreme cold. Her wide blue eyes were frightened, her nose was running, yet she still stuck her chin out in defiance.

'I am in charge here,' Sister Teresa said, lifting the cane threateningly above her head. 'You will never answer me back, question anything I say or do. Do I make myself clear?'

The child cowered on the floor, eyes on the cane. 'I only wanted my dolly,' she whimpered.

With that the nun brought down the cane, striking May hard on her legs. She screamed in pain, half turned to get up and run, but in doing so presented her bottom. The Sister struck her three more times in quick succession, then tossed the cane aside. Reaching down, she caught May by the shoulders of her pinafore dress, hauled her to her feet, then, holding her with one hand, opened the small door in the wall behind her with the other.

This was the Dark Place. Not a cellar, or a cupboard, but a place used to store ice in the days when the building was a private house. Two steps went down to an area of around six square feet, and as it was built alongside the well-shaft which once supplied the water, it was always very cold even in high summer, the thick stone walls slimy and wet.

'Get in there,' the nun said, pushing the child hard. 'You can scream as loud as you like because no one will hear you. When you are through with screaming, think on why you were put there. By morning I expect you will have seen the error of your ways.'

May did scream as she stumbled down the two steps into the pitch darkness below. But as Sister shut the heavy, lead-lined door and locked it, it was silent again in the basement, for the door made it completely soundproof.

Dulcie cowered away from Sister Teresa as she came into the chapel some time later. 'I'm sorry, Sister,' she bleated out. 'I didn't mean to pull at you and shout, I was just trying to help May.'

Sister looked down at the girl and took sadistic pleasure in the abject terror in her eyes. During the course of the day she had already observed the new girls were not alike in disposition. May was full of herself, bold as brass, but this older one was fearful, docile and sensitive. There was no need to punish her physically, the anxiety she'd feel by not being told where her sister was would make her suffer enough.

'Your sister was responsible for what happened tonight,' Sister Teresa said in a quiet, even voice. 'Not you. So in future don't interfere. Now go and see Sister Grace for your bath. I will get you your clean clothes and bring them to you and escort you down to the dormitory. I don't want to hear another word from you tonight. Is that understood?'

Dulcie was astounded by the gentleness in the woman's voice and by the knowledge that she wasn't going to be punished further. Maybe she'd let her imagination run away with her because the other girls said this nun was so nasty. Yet she didn't quite dare to ask where May was, that might be seen as insolence. Besides, May was probably in bed by now, and she'd find out what happened to her then. 'Yes, Sister Teresa,' she said gratefully. 'I'm very sorry about what happened.'

Half an hour later Dulcie was walking down the stairs behind Sister Teresa to the Juniors' dormitory on the ground floor. She could barely manage to genuflect at the statue of Mary on the turn of the stairs for she was wearing a flannel nightdress that was too large for her and carrying a bundle of clothes. Her hair was brushed free of its plaits and she had wound the rubber bands from the ends securely around her wrist so she wouldn't lose them. One set of clothes was the everyday uniform of a maroon jumper and grey skirt, along with clean underwear and grey socks. The other was a worn navy blue kilt and a matted Fair Isle jumper to wear tomorrow.

As she understood it, hers and May's clothes would go into that cupboard and get dished out next Saturday night to someone, not necessarily them. But right now she didn't care that she would be seen tomorrow in clothes that were far shabbier than her own. All she was concerned about was May.

Most of the other girls had had their baths by the time she got to the bathroom, for there were three baths in the room and the girls all used the same water. But Carol was still in there, and while Sister Grace turned away for a moment, she whispered that she thought May had been taken to something she called 'the Dark Place'. She couldn't elaborate on this, but just the way her eyes had rolled implied it was a terrible punishment.

'This is your dormitory,' Sister Teresa said, pointing to the room on her left at the front of the house. 'The lavatories and washroom are there,' she went on, indicating the door directly ahead of Dulcie. 'Put your clothes in the locker beside the bed and you will find your rosary hanging on the bed-head. I shall be back in a few moments for prayers.'

All the beds except one nearest to the window were occupied, the girls burrowed down because it was so cold.

Dulcie glanced around her as she made her way to the vacant bed, but as she saw May wasn't already in one of the other beds, her heart began to flutter with fright. She had been told earlier today there were two Junior dormitories, eight girls in each, so maybe May was in the other one, behind the third door she'd seen by the washroom.

By the time Dulcie had put her clothes away, Sister Teresa was back, ordering all the girls out of bed to kneel for prayers, so there was no time to go and investigate. Dulcie dropped to her knees on the cold lino and closed her eyes, but peeped through her lashes at the other girls. Carol, Helen, Janet, Ruth, Susan and Margaret were there, and another girl with freckles whose name she'd forgotten. All their heads were bent, their fingers flicking along the beads as they devoutly chanted the Rosary.

The girls leaped back into bed afterwards. Sister Teresa turned off the light and left after a stern warning that there must be no talking. Dulcie waited a moment or two, expecting someone to speak, but no one did, so, too scared to be the one to start it by asking where May was, she just lay there. She could hear the soft sounds of thumbs being sucked, the odd cough or the rustle of bedcovers as someone turned over, and she didn't think she'd ever felt so desperately lonely in her whole life.

She had shared a bed with May for as long as she could remember, and without that small soft body curled up to her back, the bed felt too big, and cold. Since November when it turned cold, they'd shared with Granny too, and though Dulcie had often been irritated by the sound of her snoring and smacking her gums, she'd give anything to hear it now. She turned her face into the hard pillow and cried. She couldn't even bring herself to say her own private prayers the way Granny always said she must, for she felt God had deserted her.

Sister Teresa waited until after midnight when all the Sisters were sleeping soundly before releasing May. The other Sisters believed she had merely given the girl a couple of strokes with the cane, then put her to bed, and as long as May was found there in bed in the morning, anything she said would be put down to a nightmare.

She had to go right in and haul May out bodily, for she was rigid with cold and terror and incapable of moving unaided. Sister Teresa lifted her out, shut and locked the door again, then sat May on a stool in the kitchen to look at her. She was in a disgusting state – hysteria had made her vomit down her clothes, and she'd wet herself, but that happened to everyone imprisoned in there.

'Are you sorry now?' Sister Teresa asked, looked dispassionately at the drawn, dirty face in front of her. May's eyelids were red and swollen, a clean white track down each cheek from tears, knuckles skinned from banging on the walls and door.

'Yes, Sister,' May hiccuped, and tears filled her eyes again as the warmth of the kitchen crept into her frozen body. 'Very sorry.'

'You will never answer me back again or question anything I say to you?'

'No, Sister,' she whispered, her eyes cast down on the floor.

'That's good, because you know if you do where I'll put you, don't you?'

May nodded.

The nun turned to the big kitchen sink and began to fill it with warm water. She always bathed the children down here after their punishment – to take them upstairs would attract attention. 'Take off your clothes,' she said. 'You're in a disgusting state.'

When the child was down to her vest she picked her up and sat her in the sink, using the opportunity to explain that she should never be naked in the sight of the Lord. May said nothing, all the fight had gone out of her, her eyes were vacant, she didn't even wince as the sponge passed over the weals on her legs and bottom.

Sister dried her afterwards, wrapping her in the towel

122

while she removed the wet vest and replaced it with a dry one. Then she produced May's own nightdress and put it over her head.

A tiny spark came back into the child's eyes then. She touched the soft warm material and looked up at Sister with gratitude.

'You don't deserve to have that back of course,' Sister Teresa said in a dry tone. 'But when I opened your suitcase a while ago and found your doll was broken, I thought it might make you feel better.'

'Belinda's broken?' May's eyes widened in horror.

'Yes, my dear, into pieces I'm afraid. But it was very foolish of your grandmother to pack a china doll in a suitcase.'

She went over to the kitchen table and opened a newspaper bundle. There lay the remains of Belinda, her china head caved in. A gaping hole in her skull revealed in a macabre manner the sockets and mechanism which made her eyes open and close. One crushed leg lay beside the trunk, which also had a gaping hole, and the two arms and other leg, all broken in two, were scattered about her.

May just stared open-mouthed at it, her eyes blinking very fast. Young as she was, she knew it was no accident. 'You smashed her,' she whispered finally.

Sister Teresa laughed, a cold, evil laugh which echoed round the kitchen.

'What a terrible mind you have,' she said. 'Say that again to anyone and you'll be right back in the Dark Place.'

On Sunday afternoon Dulcie stood at the playroom window staring bleakly out at the front garden. It had been sunny this morning when they walked to church for Mass, but since dinner the sky had grown darker and darker and it was so cold that one of the Sisters said she thought it might snow.

It was lovely and warm up here in the playroom. Dulcie's belly felt full from the dinner, behind her all the other girls were talking and laughing, but she was so worried about May she didn't feel able to join them.

When the bell rang this morning to get up, Dulcie ran straight into the other dormitory to check May was there. She was, but right away Dulcie knew something was badly wrong. Her face was just white and blank, and she was struggling into her clothes faster than Dulcie had ever seen her do before.

'Go away and get dressed yourself,' was all she said.

Dulcie did, after a brief warning 'she'd be in for it' from another girl. By the time she got into the washroom May was already there, trying to brush her own hair. Dulcie took over, brushed it, plaited it and fastened the ends securely with rubber bands, but as she worked on it, she asked May in whispers what had happened to her.

'Nothing,' May said, her face like a blank piece of paper. 'But she killed Belinda.'

She could see May's knuckles were skinned, and there was a red welt on the back of her leg just above her knee, but Dulcie couldn't question her sister further because all the other girls were warning her to get her own hair done before Sister Teresa came in. As it was, she was still cleaning her teeth when the nun entered, and everyone else was already lined up at the door to go to the chapel.

One small girl in May's dormitory had wet her bed, and Dulcie was so shocked by the way Sister grabbed the wet sheet, draped it over the child's head and shoulders and ordered her to go and stand in the hall, that any further questioning of May was put aside.

There was no chance to speak in the chapel, or over breakfast, which was porridge and a boiled egg. May had never liked porridge, but she gobbled it down so fast she spilled some of it on her jumper. Immediately afterwards, some of the girls from Dulcie's dormitory were ordered to go and make all the Junior beds. Carol was told to supervise Dulcie so she'd know how they had to be done.

The beds had to be made just so, the undersheet pulled tightly and tucked in, the top sheet folded back exactly ten inches over the blankets. Not one wrinkle was allowed to spoil the look of the white counterpanes, which had to hang exactly the same width on both sides of the bed.

Later that morning all the girls collected their rosaries and prayer books from their lockers, put on their coats, were handed a navy blue beret each, and then were led by four of the Sisters in a crocodile to church for Mass.

Once again Dulcie got no opportunity to speak to May as they were lined up in twos, the smallest at the front of the line. Janet, who was Dulcie's partner, told her to cheer up because Sunday was the best day of the week and the Sisters liked them to smile at people on the walk to church.

Dulcie liked Janet, she had pretty dark, curly hair and olive skin and her dark eyes danced with mischief as she whispered information about the school they all went to. 'It's good there,' she said. 'Hardly any of the teachers are nuns, and they aren't as strict with us as they are with the other kids. You'll be in Miss Heywood's class and she's lovely.'

If it hadn't been for May, Dulcie might even have felt happy. The walk was through pleasant roads with posh houses, the other girls all seemed nice, and when they got back from church the dinner was ready. It was almost as good as the dinners Granny made – roast beef, Yorkshire pudding and tasty gravy. Afterwards it was jam roly-poly and custard. She heard too that often on Sunday afternoons they went out to Chinbrook Meadows, but it was considered too cold for that today so they were sent up to the playroom instead.

Dulcie thought this would be the ideal opportunity to talk to her sister, but May just wouldn't tell her anything. Her little face was still very white and blank. She sat down beside Dulcie with her back against the pipes, but she kept a space between them.

'What happened? What did Sister do to you?' Dulcie begged her. 'Did she cane you?'

'I don't want to talk about it,' May said woodenly. 'Leave me alone.'

May had always been a great talker. When she told a story she embellished it for all she was worth. She could turn the most trivial incident into something important. Dulcie was fairly certain that if nothing much had happened other than a quick smack, she would have turned that into a beating, just for effect. So it stood to reason that Sister Teresa had found some way of knocking the very stuffing out of her.

'Just tell me if it was *the Dark Place*,' Dulcie whispered. 'Carol said she might have put you in there.'

At that May got up, so stiffly Dulcie knew she had been beaten and was aching. 'Don't ask me,' was all she said. 'She killed Belinda and she'll kill me too.'

'She can't kill you, I won't let her,' Dulcie retorted.

May just gave her a look, almost one of pity. 'Daddy killed Mummy,' she said, then turned away towards the crowd of Seniors who were just coming into the playroom.

During the next few weeks Dulcie tried to convince herself that the Dark Place was just a myth, like the bogeyman the children used to say lived in the coal cellar at Lee Manor School. It had to be a myth, no one seemed to know exactly where it was, and no one admitted to having been in there themselves.

Yet something had drastically changed May. She never spoke out of turn any more, she obeyed the rules, never argued when she was told to do something. She rarely giggled and even out in the playground she never had much to say for herself.

In many ways this had made things easier for Dulcie. She didn't have to watch May all the time, for she did what she was told by the Sisters without any back-chat. She ate everything that was put in front of her and swallowed the malt and castor oil the Sisters dished up once a week without a murmur. She stood in line for her clean clothes on Saturday nights and never said a word when she saw someone else being given her tartan pinafore dress to wear on Sunday. She didn't struggle while Dulcie plaited her hair in the mornings and she learned to tie her own shoe-laces.

But it was like having the sister she loved and knew so well replaced with a chilly stranger who just looked like her. The new May didn't want to be cuddled by Dulcie, she wouldn't even talk about Granny or the people they'd known in Hither Green. When Mother Superior called both her and May into her sitting-room a couple of days after their arrival and told them they were not, under any circumstances, to tell anyone their father was in prison, Dulcie was quite happy to agree for she didn't want to tell anyone anyway. But when Mother went on to say she couldn't allow them to receive or send letters either, Dulcie was horrified. Yet May didn't seem to care at all. She said she didn't want letters from him.

What hurt Dulcie most was that May didn't seem to need her or even like her any more. In the playground she played with the other smallest girls, in the playroom she was a pet of the Senior girls, even on the way to and from school she managed to avoid walking with her sister.

Granny had come to see them on the second Sunday they were there. Dulcie was desperate to tell her about everything, but one of the Sisters sat in the corner of the room for the whole visit, so she didn't dare. Granny had said she'd come again in four weeks, but she couldn't make it, her legs were too bad. Susan had been twice, and again a Sister sat in the corner listening, so Dulcie couldn't tell her anything either.

Dulcie was frantic to tell someone, anyone, how horrible it was here. That her sister was like a stranger, that she had to watch out for Sister Teresa all the time, and they were both terrified of getting on the wrong side of her. She wanted to speak of the children who wet the bed and had to stand in the hall with the wet sheet over their heads, how cold it was in bed at night, the long hours outside in the playground, the awful food, for Sunday dinner was the only good meal. How she hated having absolutely nothing of her own, not even her own vest and knickers. Even the little presents Granny and Susan bought them were snatched and broken as soon as they got back in to the playroom. Surely it wasn't right that small girls were forced to kneel in the chapel for two or three hours at a stretch just for getting into bed with each other to get warm, or severely caned for helping themselves to a slice of bread while laying up the tables for tea?

But there was no one to tell. The other girls said that if she told the teachers at school, they would just go straight to Mother Superior, and all she'd get for her trouble would be a punishment for telling lies. She had to be careful which girls she spoke about it to, for some of them would repeat what she'd said to the Sisters just to get in their good books. If she hadn't been going to school every day, Dulcie felt she might just shrivel up and die with misery.

Yet school was good. Some of the children there teased the ones from the convent, but they weren't really spiteful. She liked Miss Heywood, her teacher, and she could forget about the Sacred Heart while she was doing sums, reading books and writing essays. The only trouble was the hours at school went so fast, and the ones spent at the convent seemed interminable.

'Hello, my darlings,' Susan exclaimed, jumping up from her seat in the small visitors' sitting-room as Dulcie and May were brought in by Sister Grace. She held out her arms to them and they both ran headlong into them.

It was the first Sunday in April and Susan's third visit. She was excited, not only at seeing them, but because she'd just got a new job at a school in Eltham and would be starting there after the Easter holidays. She'd also met someone rather special a couple of weeks ago, and she was hoping it was going to grow into a romance.

'Do you think I could take them out for a walk?' Susan asked the Sister, who was just standing there smiling. 'It's such a nice spring day and I'm sure you are taking all the others out this afternoon.'

Sister Grace frowned. 'Mother Superior doesn't like the

girls leaving the grounds,' she said. 'We had an occasion once where a child didn't come back and the police had to be called to find her.'

'Surely you know I'm not going to run off with them?' Susan said with laughter in her voice. 'I've often wanted to, but as a teacher I couldn't do anything so irresponsible.'

'I'm sure you wouldn't, Miss Sims,' Sister said. 'But you know how it is. We have to have the same rule for everyone.'

'Well, may we go out in the garden then?' Susan asked. 'It really is too nice to stay indoors.'

It was agreed they could go into the front garden, so Susan led them out to the bench there. 'Doesn't it look a picture?' she exclaimed. 'Just look at those daffodils!'

She was impressed for it had looked so bleak on her last visit. The lawn was a deep lush green, and hundreds of daffodils had come up through it in one section. The trees around the garden were all just coming into leaf, and a large almond tree was in full blossom.

'Did you know we aren't allowed to go into the garden at the back?' Dulcie said suddenly. 'We have to stay in the old tennis court bit, and if we go out we get caned.'

Susan was surprised at this but said maybe that was just a winter-time rule so the children didn't bring mud indoors.

'No, it's all the year round,' Dulcie insisted. 'It's just another one of their mean rules because they want us to be unhappy. When it was really cold at half-term in February we still had to stay out there all day. It was horrible because there's nothing to play with. Not even a ball.'

Susan thought that Dulcie was just playing for sympathy. 'That does sound a bit grim,' she said lightly. 'But the weather's getting nicer now, feel how warm it is today.'

Dulcie went into a sulk, and May climbed on to Susan's lap, cuddled into her and began talking about her teacher in a baby's lisping voice.

'Did you know we aren't allowed to have letters from Daddy?' Dulcie said, cutting across what her sister was saying. 'And I can't write to him either.'

Susan was shocked by this news, but even more by Dulcie's belligerent tone. There was a challenging look in her eye and a tightness to her mouth that had never been there before. She also felt uncomfortable with May playing at being a baby, it was a bit sickening and quite out of character. Why were they being so strange?

'Did Mother Superior give you a reason?' she asked, her mind switching to Reg and imagining how upsetting it would be for him to get no letters.

'Not a sensible reason,' Dulcie said. 'Just that it wasn't nice for little girls to be having anything to do with a prison.'

Susan could well understand why Mother Superior felt that a prison visit might be harmful, but she could see absolutely nothing wrong with them receiving letters from their father. She thought she would have a word with Miss Denning about it and told Dulcie so.

'I don't want to get letters from him,' May said suddenly, sitting bolt upright on Susan's lap and dropping the baby's lisp. 'It's his fault we were sent here, and he isn't my father.'

'Of course he's your father,' Susan said. 'He couldn't help being put in prison either, he didn't do what they said he did.'

May shot off her lap and turned to face Susan, glowering at her. 'He isn't my father, I heard Mummy say so. Then he threw her down the stairs. He killed Mummy just like Sister killed Belinda.'

'May!' Susan exclaimed, reaching out for the child. 'This isn't like you!'

But May stepped away from her, big tears welling up in her eyes. 'I don't like you. You made that lady take us away from Granny.'

She turned and ran away, disappearing round the side of the convent.

'What on earth was all that about?' Susan asked Dulcie. She was astonished rather than hurt by the outburst. 'Who's Belinda?'

'Her doll. Will you just wait while I see where she's gone?' Dulcie said, jumping up. 'She might get into trouble if she's found indoors while all the other girls are out for a walk.'

Dulcie rushed off and Susan sat there feeling completely perplexed.

Miss Denning had warned her that she might find changes in the children in the first few months. She said Susan could expect them to be clingy, demanding, and perhaps a little aggressive at times. She had also said they might exaggerate about the kind of treatment they got from the Sisters. She said it was a normal reaction for children who'd just been taken into care. A kind of test to see if their visitor really cared about them.

But claiming Reg wasn't her father was such a peculiar thing for May to say. If she really had heard her mother say it, why hadn't she said something before?

Dulcie came running back. 'She's up in the playroom with a couple of the Senior girls,' she said breathlessly. 'Sister Anne knows she's up there, so it's all right.'

'Can you explain what she meant?' Susan asked, patting the seat beside her so Dulcie would sit down.

She listened carefully while Dulcie told her May had been different ever since she got punished on her first night here. 'I don't know what really happened,' Dulcie said, looking nervously about her as if imagining someone was eavesdropping. 'She won't talk about it. All she said was that Sister Teresa killed her doll. The other girls think Sister broke it purposely. May's been really funny ever since.'

'Is it bad here, Dulcie?' Susan asked. She felt close to tears, confused, hurt and so very disappointed. Yet she didn't know whether she was disappointed with herself for not winkling this out before, or with Maud, the children, the convent or even Reg.

131

'I'm getting used to it now,' Dulcie replied and gave a kind of sniffling sigh.

Susan sensed that Dulcie had intended earlier to spill out all kinds of hurts and injustices, but perhaps because May had been rude to Susan, she had decided that speaking out now would only bring further distress to everyone she cared about.

Was that the reason too why Reg never revealed what Anne had said to him that night?

Susan thought about it for a moment. Telling the court that May wasn't his child would have made little difference to the outcome of the trial, but if it was discussed in court, it would have been reported in the newspapers.

Suddenly Susan understood. Reg's love for May wasn't affected by discovering she wasn't his child. He wanted to protect her from slurs which might follow her into adulthood, and he also couldn't bear for the child to know how treacherous her mother really was. But how cruel fate could be – unknown to Reg the child had heard it straight from her mother's lips, and the very poison which Anne had sought to wound her husband with had found its way into her innocent child's heart.

'I'll speak to Miss Denning about the letters from your father,' Susan said, struggling to regain her composure. 'Is there anything else you want to tell me that she might be able to sort out for you?'

She saw something flicker across Dulcie's face. A hesitancy, and fear.

'You can trust me,' Susan said. 'I know how to deal with problems tactfully.'

But Dulcie's face closed up. 'No, there's nothing else,' she said. 'Just about Daddy's letters. I'd better go now and see what May's doing.'

Susan kissed her and gave her a bag that contained some sweets and a couple of books. 'Eat the sweets before the others get back,' she said with a smile. 'That's what I used to do when I was little so I didn't have to share them.

132

Say goodbye to May for me. I'll be back next month, maybe she'll have decided she does like me again by then.'

Dulcie ran off then and Susan went down to the gate. As she turned to close it behind her, she saw the child was standing at the side of the house, just watching her.

Dulcie didn't return her wave and Susan felt a cold chill run through her. A sixth sense told her that Dulcie's comprehension of the adult world had expanded since she'd been at the convent. She had lost her trust, knew that at just nine years old she was now on her own.

Susan's eyes swept over the convent, took in the stone cross above the front door, the beautiful front garden, the creeper just coming into bud which would soon cover the red brick with glossy leaves. It looked so serene and safe, yet was it just a facade? Were there dark, cruel things going on inside? Little minds being twisted by women who had no business to be caring for children?

'You can trust me, Dulcie,' she murmured to herself. 'I won't abandon you.'

Chapter Six

'Dulcie and May Taylor!' Sister Teresa barked out as all the girls were ready to file out of the dining-room after breakfast to get ready for school. 'You are to go straight up to see Mother Superior.'

The two girls looked at each other in alarm.

'Go now, don't just stand there,' Sister snapped at them. 'And pull your socks up, May.'

It was June, and the girls had been at the convent for six months. By obeying the rules implicitly they had managed to avoid punishment and even disapproval. But when any girl was ordered to go to Mother Superior it almost always meant trouble for her.

'I haven't done anything naughty,' May whispered to Dulcie as they left the dining-room to go up the stairs. 'Have you?'

Dulcie shook her head, yet she knew only too well that almost anything, from not getting out of bed quickly enough to giving one of the Sisters a surly glance or straying off the path going through the orchard on the way to and from school, was enough to be punished.

Both girls had come to accept that the convent was where they were to stay, and they'd learnt to make the best of it. Once the spring had come it was no longer an ordeal to be out in the playground, they'd grown used to the dull food, the strict discipline, they had their friends. But the distance between the girls which began after May's punishment on their first night had grown wider as the months passed. In different dormitories, each having their own group of friends, and with the age difference, there was little opportunity to regain their former closeness.

Dulcie still plaited May's hair for her every morning, she always kissed her goodnight at bedtime, and wrote letters to Granny for both of them, but they rarely spent any time together. Yet this summons was a sharp reminder that they were still sisters, and they instinctively clasped each other's hand for comfort.

Surprisingly, Mother Superior opened the door to them at their knock. They had heard that the reason she hardly ever came down for meals in the dining-room any more was because she was too frail to manage the stairs. But she looked sprightly enough to them, she wasn't even walking with a stick.

'Come in, my dears,' she said. Her tone was gentle and she took both their hands to draw them in, which suggested maybe they weren't in trouble after all.

She let go of them long enough to close the door behind them, then, putting one hand on each of their shoulders, looked from one anxious upturned face to the other. 'I'm afraid I have bad news for you,' she said. 'Your grandmother died late last night.'

Dulcie let out an involuntary wail of anguish. Susan had told them on her last visit that Granny was growing very frail, and the district nurse looked in on her every day, so they had been prepared. But it was still a shock.

Mother Superior slipped her arms around both their shoulders and drew them tightly to her. 'I am so very sorry, my dears. I know how much she meant to you both. But she was a very old lady and she'd been sick for some time. Now she's with Jesus in heaven, and all her troubles are over.'

It was the embrace more than anything else which made Dulcie sob, for in their entire time here no adult had ever held her, and as she saw Mother Superior as a similar age to her granny, it made her loss feel even sharper.

'I received this news from your grandmother's doctor this morning, by telephone,' the old lady went on, squeezing them tightly against her. 'He said to tell you she slipped away peacefully in her sleep while her friend

Nora was sitting with her. I believe this friend will contact all the family to tell them and arrange the funeral.'

Dulcie sniffed back her tears and nodded. Mrs Nora Walsh had lived next door to Granny for years, she and May had always called her Auntie Nora. She supposed Nora knew where all Granny's other children lived, her real aunts and uncles.

'Will she tell Daddy?' Dulcie asked.

'I'm sure she will,' Mother Superior said.

May began to cry then, and Dulcie extracted herself from the old lady's arm and went to comfort her sister. May had lost interest in Granny almost as soon as they got here, and when her funny little badly spelled letters came she could hardly be bothered to listen to them. But Dulcie supposed May was now remembering all the nice times they had had with her, and that skipping-rope she'd sent to her on her sixth birthday last month.

'We'll go up to the chapel together now,' Mother Superior said. 'We'll say some prayers, and you can each light a candle for her.'

As the girls followed the old lady across the hall and up the stairs, it was as if they were with Granny again, for Mother Superior clung to the banister, each step up as laboured as Maud's had been. The only difference was the long black habit which concealed her legs, the rustle of her starched wimple and the jingle of her crucifix at her waist.

Her wheezing breath sounded loud in the silence of the upper corridor – all the other Sisters were still down in the basement. The girls could hear the other children in the distance as they made their way through the orchard to the gate at the far end on their way to school. Dulcie wondered fleetingly if they would be expected to go on to school alone later.

Mother Superior was shaky from the climb up the stairs, but she still led the girls right up to the altar of the chapel, genuflected, then sank on to her knees on a hassock before it, indicating that they were to kneel beside her.

Her prayer was a simple one of her own making, asking God to take Maud Taylor straight to His bosom and thanking Him for giving her a long and fruitful life. She asked that he would comfort all Maud's children and grandchildren, and especially Dulcie and May.

After the girls had said the Lord's Prayer with her, Mother Superior moved back on to a pew and whispered to the girls that they must now light a candle each and say their own private prayers. Dulcie's hands were trembling so much she had difficulty in lighting a new one from the ones that were already burning, and the smell of the hot wax evoked many poignant memories of going with Granny to her church in Deptford and lighting candles for the grandfather who had died long before they were even born.

Out on the landing a little later, Mother Superior put both her hands on their shoulders again, looking down at them with concerned eyes. 'You will stay home today out of respect for your grandmother,' she said. 'As this is a special day of remembrance you may go anywhere in the garden and the orchard, but I ask that you behave with dignity. One of the Sisters will bring you sandwiches at dinner-time.'

Dulcie sensed that being allowed the freedom of the garden was offered out of sympathy for their loss, so she managed a watery smile, thanked Mother for her kindness, and taking May's hand led her back down the stairs.

From habit the two girls didn't speak until they were right out in the back garden. Although it was only nine in the morning, it was already very warm and sunny, with the promise of a hot day ahead. They stood for a moment by the fenced-in playground just looking at it, unsure of what to do with this unexpected freedom.

'It's nice that she let us miss school today,' Dulcie said eventually, just to break the silence. There had hardly been a day since they first came here that they hadn't looked longingly at the bushes beyond the playground, wishing

137

so much that they could take one of the little winding paths they could see between them. In winter when the foliage was sparse they had tantalizing glimpses of steps to sunken terraces, and in spring they could guess at the beauty of this forbidden place by the trugs of flowers the Sisters filled to decorate the hall and chapel. Yet now, even though they'd been given permission to explore, in their sadness they were hesitant and unsure of themselves.

May's hand tightened in Dulcie's. 'Do you think Sister Teresa knows Mother Superior said we can go anywhere?'

Dulcie heard the fear in her sister's voice and her protective instinct was aroused. 'I'll soon tell her if she doesn't,' she replied firmly. 'But let's go somewhere where she can't see us.'

The garden surpassed even their more fanciful imaginations. Once through the thick bushes by the playground they found a winding path leading to steps, and at the bottom of them a rose garden. Clumps of small flowers grew out of cracks in the paving-stones, and the ground beneath the rose bushes was barely visible through the weeds, yet the roses had withstood their neglect, and the air was sweet with their fragrance. They walked slowly, stopping every now and then to sniff the beautiful blooms, smiling at each other in delight. They found an arbour at the far end, built round a stone bench, more roses dripping from it, entwined with honeysuckle. They stayed there for some time, removing their cardigans, soothed by the warmth of the sun on their bare arms and legs. They spotted statues half hidden in bushes, Pan with his pipes, cherubs and a regal lady wearing a crown, and Dulcie made up stories about the happy family who had once played in this garden.

'Why don't they let us come down here?' May asked after a while. 'It's such a waste having a garden that no one sees. We'd all be so happy out here.'

Dulcie thought about this. 'I don't think they want us to be happy,' she said eventually.

'But why not?' May asked, her blue eyes wide with puzzlement.

'I don't know,' Dulcie sighed. 'I suppose just because they are mean.'

'Have you ever thought of running away?'

'Not really. There isn't anywhere to run to,' Dulcie replied. 'Why? Do you?'

'I used to when we first got here,' May admitted, chewing her lip thoughtfully. 'But I didn't know how to get to Granny's, or Susan's. Anyway, Sister Teresa said I was stained with my parents' sins, and everyone who looks at me can see it.'

Dulcie looked at May in alarm. Yet before she could reassure her sister it was rubbish, May began gabbling away nineteen to the dozen with other nasty and scary things Sister Teresa had said to other girls: they would die a painful death if they ever harboured bad thoughts about a nun, be struck down by God as they left the confessional if they had omitted to confess a sin, and in one case, when a child who had become ill after wolfing down a whole bar of chocolate a visitor had brought her, she was told that the chocolate would swell up inside her and make her burst.

Dulcie didn't interrupt her, not even to say it was all nonsense, because it was so good to hear May talking again in the animated way she always used to. She hoped that her sister was warming up to telling her what Sister Teresa had done to her on that first night.

But suddenly May changed tack. 'I wish I hadn't ever told the other girls I was glad to leave Granny's house because it smelled funny,' she said plaintively. 'It wasn't true. I liked living there.' Then, without drawing breath, she blurted out that she was ashamed because their father was in prison, and wished he was dead like their mother.

'It would be better to have nobody at all,' she said passionately, clenching her fists and looking angrily at Dulcie. 'Sometimes I've even been bad enough to wish you'd die too, Dulcie, so you couldn't keep looking at me and reminding me about Mummy. But now Granny has died I know it's because I'm wicked and to punish me.'

Dulcie was horrified to find that her sister had all this locked in her head. She'd never imagined May thought or cared about anything or anyone from the past. Yet shocked as she was, she sympathized. None of the girls here knew anything more than that their mother had died. One of the reasons they'd been given for not writing to their father was because the other girls might discover he was in prison. So the girls probably thought he'd abandoned them like most of theirs had. So many times when the subject of fathers came up, Dulcie would have given anything to be able to talk about hers, but she couldn't, she just had to squash down all her feelings about him and say nothing. May was often a kind of torture to her too, for every time she looked at her face, she'd see her mother's.

'Granny died because she was old and sick, not to punish you,' she said, putting her arm round May and cuddling her tightly. 'As for Sister Teresa saying you are stained by our parents' sins, that's a wicked lie just to make you scared.'

'Are you sure?' May asked, her voice trembling.

'Of course I am. Sister's nuts,' Dulcie said firmly. 'I bet she told you that something really bad would happen to you if you ever told me what she did to you on that first night we came here too! Didn't she?'

May nodded against Dulcie's shoulder.

'Tell me now then and that will prove she's a liar,' Dulcie said. 'We're stuck here, Mummy's dead, Daddy's in prison, and now Granny's dead. There isn't anything worse that could happen to us.'

Just saying that made Dulcie feel the loss so acutely that she began to cry. Granny was gone now, and they hadn't even been able to tell her again they loved her before she went.

'Please don't cry, Dulcie,' May said, squeezing her arm. 'I can't bear it. It makes me feel so bad and I don't really want you to die. Take a look at my front tooth, it feels all wobbly, do you think it's going to come out?'

It was so like the old May to find something trivial to distract her that Dulcie almost laughed. She was like a dragonfly, hovering over one place on the water, then shooting off again to something else.

She touched May's front tooth and sure enough, it was wobbly. 'I think it will be out before the day's over,' she agreed. 'But I don't think the Tooth Fairy visits here.'

'I never believed in Tooth Fairies,' May said airily. 'It's as silly as believing in Father Christmas. Now, let's go and explore the rest of the garden, before someone makes us go inside.'

Later that night, lying in bed watching the dormitory curtains fluttering in the soft breeze from the open windows, Dulcie thought over the events of the day. She never did manage to get May to tell her about what Sister Teresa did to her. Yet perhaps it didn't matter, for they had had such a lovely day together, and she had a feeling that if Granny was watching them she'd have taken pleasure in seeing them happier than they'd been for a long, long time.

Sister Grace brought them out corned beef sandwiches and an apple at dinner-time, and they'd taken them into the orchard and made a kind of den with some wooden apple boxes they found. It was so peaceful there, and warm in the sun, just insects buzzing and birds singing.

They both had sunburnt faces and arms when they came in for tea. Dulcie could feel her skin stinging a bit now. It was good to think she'd got her sister back as a friend. Granny had always said May needed her more than she made out, even if she was the more confident of the two of them.

The last thing Dulcie thought of as she began to drift off to sleep was May's words about feeling ashamed of their father. She should have told her sister firmly that was wrong, and that she must always keep her faith in him.

But she was guilty, too, of forgetting him: when she tried to imagine his face she couldn't really see it clearly any more. She wondered if he'd been told about Granny yet. He would be so sad, he'd loved her so much.

It seemed to Dulcie as the summer drifted by that she must be growing up because she didn't get so hurt and upset about anything any more.

She ought to have been upset when Mother Superior said she and May couldn't go to Granny's funeral, yet she wasn't. But then she didn't get upset either when Susan and Miss Denning did their best to try to change the Sisters' minds about writing to her father, and they still refused.

Susan came to see her and May the Sunday after Granny's funeral. She'd written to them immediately she got the news and said how sorry she was, and that she would be going to the funeral and would place some flowers from them on her grave.

It did make Dulcie cry when Susan told them about all the flowers that had been sent for Granny, and when she repeated all the lovely things her friends and neighbours had said about her at the service. Yet it wasn't really upsetting, it was kind of nice to think of Granny up in heaven without her bad legs, and all her problems over.

Later on that same afternoon Susan told them she was going to get married in August and that she'd be going to live in Yorkshire because her husband-to-be was a vet there. Dulcie found herself just listening to her explaining how she'd still write and visit, though not so often, and that they might even be able to come for a holiday in Yorkshire, and all the time she was thinking, *Well, that's Susan disappearing out of our lives too.*

'Trust me,' Susan said, perhaps guessing because Dulcie was quiet that she didn't really believe her. 'I won't forget you both, not even now I'm getting married.'

Dulcie just hugged her, said she was glad for her. How

could she say that so many people had urged her to trust them, and they'd all let her down?

Susan sent a little box with two pieces of wedding cake for them, each with a tiny silver horseshoe tucked into it. There was a lovely letter too telling them all about the wedding and her new home, and a photograph of herself and her new husband. Dulcie thought he looked nice, tall with dark hair, but a bit of a stern face. Susan said she would be writing to Mother Superior before long to ask when they could come to Yorkshire for a holiday, but as Dulcie wrote back she thought she would rather have a visit from Susan every month than wait all year to see her for a holiday. As she addressed the envelope to Mr and Mrs Ian Bankcroft, she had a nasty feeling that she might very well have lost Susan for good.

Chapter Seven

'This one's addressed to both of us,' Ian said to Susan as he came in through the kitchen door with a couple of letters in his hand. 'But I suspect it's really for you.'

She took the letter from his hand, glanced at the spidery writing, recognized it was from Mother Superior at the Sacred Heart, and put it down while she finished frying the eggs and bacon for his breakfast.

'This won't be a moment,' she called out. Ian had already gone into the living-room; through the door she could see him warming his backside in front of the fire. It gave her such ridiculous joy seeing him doing things like that, just as watching his intent expression when he was examining a sick animal, or hearing him chuckle to himself over a funny book did.

Ian wasn't handsome, he very likely wasn't even attractive to anyone else, or he'd probably have been snapped up years ago, for he was thirty-eight and had considered himself a confirmed bachelor until he met her. His forehead was too big, his nose too snub, and he was too thin for his six-foot height, but she had fallen for his soft grey eyes, the warmth of his smile, and his way with animals.

It was early December, they'd been married nearly four months and their marriage was all she had hoped for and more. She had never imagined herself capable of feeling so much passion and tenderness, or that she'd find such complete fulfilment in turning their little cottage into a real home. Every day brought fresh delights, whether it was helping Ian in the surgery, working out in the garden, or merely trying out a new recipe. When she looked out of the window and saw the beauty of the moors all around them, she wondered how she had ever tolerated brash, dirty London.

She quickly made a pot of fresh tea, slid the bacon and eggs on to a hot plate and carried them both into the living-room.

'That looks great,' he said, sitting down and attacking it with relish. 'Who's the letter from?'

'It's from the convent. I'll just pour the tea before I read it,' she said.

This was another part of being a vet's wife that she loved. The unpredictability of it. None of the regular meals at set times like her parents had. Ian could be in and out of the house twenty times in one day, away for twenty-four hours the next. It meant they appreciated each other's company and generally made the most of their time together.

Susan opened the letter.

Dear Mr and Mrs Bankcroft, she read. *I have given a great deal of thought to your invitation for Dulcie and May to spend Christmas with you. It was very kind of you, but sadly I must decline it for them. It is the most important religious festival of the year, and one I feel Catholic children should celebrate in their own church.*

I have recently been in discussion about the children's present and future welfare with our governing body here at the convent, and sadly we have come to the decision that in the children's best interests it would be advisable for you to gradually distance yourself from them.

We feel it is necessary to ask you to do this as it will of course come naturally anyway, as I hear you are expecting a child of your own, and given the great distance you live from London and the nature of Mr Bankcroft's work. But we would not wish your relationship with the children to come to a hurtful, abrupt end at that time, for it would be distressing for them. So we suggest your letters become gradually more infrequent as of now.

We are very aware how much you have done for the Taylor children in the past, and your affection for them, and so I feel sure you will agree to act in their best interests now.

Wishing you a joyous Christmas and a Happy New Year,
Mother

'I don't believe it,' Susan gasped, flinging down the letter in disgust. 'She not only won't let them come for Christmas, she wants me to abandon them too!'

Ian took the letter and read it.

'She has a point, Susie,' he said with a sigh. 'I mean about the baby, the distance and my work. It really won't be feasible to keep up visiting.'

'Not immediately after the baby is born of course,' Susan retorted. 'But I will be travelling down there every three or four months to see my parents anyway, and I explained that in my letter to Dulcie.'

'Maybe she got upset when she read it,' Ian said thoughtfully. 'You can never be certain how children will take such news.'

'Dulcie's very bright, brighter than that stupid woman who has the cheek to sign herself *Mother*. I knew she would understand. And I didn't upset them by telling them we were getting married either, they were pleased for me. I had no option but to tell them that day after Maud's funeral. If I'd left it till the next month it would've been just before the wedding, and how would that have looked? Like they were the least important people in my life!'

'It sounds to me as if the woman knows what she's talking about, Susie. She has had a great deal of experience of children in care.'

'That place is only one step up from the old workhouses,' Susan said angrily. 'They don't care tuppence about individual children, all they want is a docile flock of sheep they can finally herd into working in laundries, factories or even becoming nuns themselves when they are old enough. That's why they won't let Dulcie and May come here, and why they want me to stop writing and visiting,

146

because they know I'll put bigger ideas into their heads.'

Ian looked at his watch and got to his feet. 'Look, I've got to go, I've got a spaniel bitch to spay. Have a cup of tea, calm down, and we'll talk when I've finished.'

Susan felt crushed that Ian wasn't incensed by the letter, and by the speed at which he left the house. She remained brooding at the table for a few minutes, then loaded his breakfast things on to a tray and went into the kitchen. What could she do? She didn't have any rights because she wasn't a relative. Miss Denning couldn't intervene because Catholic orphanages were governed by their own people. It was pointless writing to Reg because he couldn't do anything, and it would only upset him. She had seen the rest of the Taylor brothers at Maud's funeral, and a sorry bunch they were too. All hard-faced, mean-spirited men, with harpies for wives. They hadn't even listened when she tried to tell them about Dulcie and May, they were far more interested in getting back to Maud's house to rifle through her stuff to see if there was anything of value. So she certainly wasn't going to get any help from them.

The only real option appeared to be to go along with what the nun said, or at least to seem to. But she wouldn't fade out completely, just bide her time, and maybe the situation would change. It was Dulcie's tenth birthday in a few days' time, she would post a present and a card, dutifully tell her how very busy she was at present, and that she might not be able to write so often for a while. With luck she'd be able to visit them again before the baby was due, and in private, away from any of the Sisters, she'd tell her the truth. Dulcie would understand. They might even be able to come up with some sneaky way of writing and receiving letters that Mother Superior would never find out about.

'I'm sorry I had to rush out this morning,' Ian said as he came in for some lunch at half past one. 'You must have thought I didn't care.'

'I was upset, but not by you,' she smiled, realizing that she mustn't try bulldozing Ian either. 'Anyway, I've sorted it out in my head now, I'll go along with what that silly old woman said, at least for the time being.'

The telephone ringing interrupted them. It was another emergency, a horse impaled on barbed wire several miles away. Susan quickly made Ian a sandwich and a flask of coffee to take with him, wrapped a warm scarf round his neck and handed him his bag.

'Don't spend the rest of the day brooding on the little Taylors,' he said as he kissed her goodbye. 'Just think about the little Bankcroft, and what colour we're going to paint the nursery.'

Dulcie sensed something different was going to happen, almost as soon as she woke up on New Year's Day of 1949. She couldn't imagine what, or why she should feel it, but she just knew. The feeling grew stronger still when she overheard Sister Grace speaking to Sister Teresa after breakfast. 'Of course it will be a wonderful opportunity,' she said. 'But it will be terribly sad for those children who can't go.'

Was it a pantomime or a circus? She'd heard other children at school talking of such things. But how would the Sisters decide who could go and those who couldn't?

As usual they were sent out into the playground, even though the temperature was below freezing with a biting wind. By half past ten some of the smaller girls were crying with the cold, so Dulcie organized a hopping game to warm them up.

Dulcie was now the second oldest in her dormitory. Carol, Helen and Janet had all had their eleventh birthdays during the year and moved up to the Seniors. Their places had been taken by Linda, Frances and Lily, from May's dormitory, and three new five-year-olds had arrived during September to take their places.

Ruth should have been the new leader as she was ten and a half, six months older than Dulcie, but she was a bit simple and a bed-wetter, so Dulcie had found herself in charge. Although not a leader by either choice or nature, she had a natural dignity and an air of calm that was admired by the other girls. During the summer holidays when the school governors had organized a short holiday in Dymchurch in Kent, the teachers there had noticed this quality and made her a team leader in many of the activities and games. By the time they returned to London all the children had grown used to Dulcie in this role and automatically deferred to her judgement in many areas. Dulcie felt she had to live up to their expectations, so she organized games in the playground, and up in the playroom helped the slower girls with their reading and learning their tables.

As her confidence grew, so teachers at school had begun to take more notice of her too, even to the extent of giving her the coveted part of Angel Gabriel in the Nativity play. She grew tougher too – if she fell over she didn't cry, if anyone called her names she laughed. She could now pull a face behind Sister Teresa's back without feeling that somehow the woman could see her. She always spoke after lights out when she felt like it. One day she'd even refused to eat her dinner, just to see what would happen, and to her amazement she didn't get it cold the following day after all, it seemed to have been forgotten. Daily she pushed the boundaries a little further back, a whisper as they went in for dinner, a quick run round the outside of the playground to collect some conkers, it felt good to be a little daring.

May, however, wasn't faring so well, and maybe it was this which prompted Mother Superior to blame Susan's influence. The arrival of the new five-year-olds had put May's nose out of joint, the Senior girls babied them now, not her, her front teeth had fallen out, giving her a less attractive appearance, and she was becoming known as a tell-tale amongst the other children. While the Sisters found little to punish her for, as May went out of her way to suck up to them, she wasn't keeping up with the rest of her class at school, and didn't appear to think it necessary to try.

New Year's Day dinner was toad-in-the-hole, Dulcie's favourite, followed by treacle tart which was May's. Then Sister Teresa announced that there would be no outside play that afternoon, but instead they were to go straight upstairs to the playroom, because someone was coming to speak to them. To Dulcie this was confirmation that the New Year ahead was definitely going to be better than last year.

Even the Senior girls had to join them, the washing up and clearing away left to the Sisters. They were all ordered to sit cross-legged in rows on the floor and warned that they were all to behave, and not to speak unless spoken to.

Sister Grace came in after they'd been waiting only a few minutes, accompanied by two women and a man. All at once the older girls started giggling, for it was extremely rare to see any man at the Sacred Heart.

'That's quite enough,' Sister Grace said, giving them a stern look. 'Anyone who misbehaves will be sent out to the playground.'

'Our visitors have come to talk to you today about Australia,' Sister Grace said, introducing Mr Stigwood, who put a large, thin black case on the table. 'Now, who can tell me where that is?'

No one put their hand up.

Mr Stigwood opened the case and drew out a map of the world which the two women held up for him. With a pencil he pointed to England. Then he moved the pencil to a much larger country down at the bottom of the map.

'This is Australia,' he said. 'Even if you didn't know where it was, I'm sure some of you know things Australia is famous for. Would you like to tell me?'

'Kangaroos,' one girl called out.

'Koala bears,' called another.

'Aborigines,' Dulcie said.

'Well done,' Mr Stigwood said, but he smiled only at

Dulcie as if that was the answer he'd hoped for. 'The Aborigines are the native people of Australia, as the Red Indians are the natives of America. But there is a great deal more to Australia than just its natives, the kangaroos and Koala bears, and today myself and my two assistants are going to tell you all about it.'

There were a couple of muffled groans from the Seniors as they clearly thought this was going to be a geography lesson.

Dulcie was entranced from the very first picture the ladies held up, which was of a long and beautiful sandy beach. As Mr Stigwood spoke of the warm water, palm trees, sand as soft as talcum powder and the heat of the sun, she was there in her imagination, splashing in the clear blue water.

He went on to show them pictures of sheep farms, only he called them stations. There were more of men cutting down pineapples, sheep-shearing, and chopping something he called sugar cane which towered above the men's heads. Then there were pictures of strange animals, yachts out at sea, fantastic-looking birds, men playing cricket, beautiful houses, jungles, horses, brilliantly coloured fish, and mountains.

By now all the girls were as immersed in the lovely coloured pictures as Dulcie was, the cold outside forgotten.

'Who would like to live in Australia?' Mr Stigwood asked as he put the last picture down.

Every single hand shot up.

'Well, that's a blessing,' he said, and laughed. 'Because we came here today hoping to find some children who wanted to come out there with us. You see, Australia is a very young country, there aren't many people there yet and there is so much space to fill.'

He went on then to show pictures of a school. A white-painted long low building with something he called a veranda all along the front of it. A group of girls in striped cotton dresses were sitting on the grass under a tree, they all looked very happy and smiley. Even the nuns who stood behind the group looked jolly. He said the school had its own farm and the girls helped with the animals, and that it was near a beach so they could go swimming.

To Dulcie, it appeared to be a place of freedom, warmth, fun and happiness. She wanted to go there so badly it almost hurt.

'So who would like to go to a school like this one?' Mr Stigwood asked.

Again every single hand shot up.

Mr Stigwood went on then to speak about how if they were chosen to go they would travel there on a huge ship and it would take six weeks to get there. He said that it was summer-time now in Australia, and in July it would be winter, but the winters were very mild, not a bit like England. One of the Senior girls asked what work prospects there were for girls at fifteen and Mr Stigwood said that they were better than in England with higher pay and usually shorter hours, and English girls were in very high demand by employers.

Dulcie was beside herself with excitement. When Mr Stigwood appeared to be about to depart with the two women, saying he'd leave them all to think about the wonderful opportunity he was offering them, she shot to her feet.

'My sister and I definitely want to go,' she said.

He looked at her and smiled. 'I'm glad to see such eagerness,' he said. 'But the Sisters will talk to you all in a little while about who is eligible to go, and who the life in Australia would be suitable for. What's your name?'

'Dulcie Taylor, sir,' she said.

'Well, I do hope you get selected, Dulcie,' he said. 'Good luck.'

For the rest of the afternoon all the girls could talk of nothing else. They sat in tight little groups, hope shining out of all their faces.

There were only two girls who didn't seem very enthusiastic, Janice and Maureen. But they were both nearly fifteen and due to leave soon anyway. They said they didn't fancy a country with so few people, they wanted to be near shops, cinemas and dance-halls. 'I shouldn't bank on you and May getting picked, Dulcie,' Janice said. 'They want orphans, and you've got a dad.'

After over a year of no contact with her father there were times when Dulcie almost forgot him. Guilt flooded through her and she looked at the older girl in dismay, not knowing what to say in response.

Janice grinned at her. 'Look on the bright side, Dulc, if they ship all the other kids off, they might have to close this place down. You might get fostered out somewhere. Anything's got to be better than here.'

But that wasn't a bright side, it looked even blacker to Dulcie. The other girls here were her friends now, she didn't want to be sent somewhere else which might turn out to be even worse. When Susan had written on her birthday and said she wouldn't be able to write so often now she was having the baby, she had slunk into the lavatories to cry about it. But later, when she'd calmed down, she'd read it again and decided Susan wasn't saying goodbye at all, just being honest. It was much the same situation with her father too, he couldn't write because they wouldn't let him. Yet it really wasn't fair that she and May were supposed just to sit and wait for people to write or see them! Why couldn't they go to Australia in the meantime?

At tea-time Mother Superior joined them in the dining-room for the first time in months apart from Christmas Day. After she'd said the grace, she spoke of Australia too.

'I'm sure most of you feel you would like to go,' she said. 'But before you build up your hopes, I must point out that not everyone will be eligible. In the next day or two I shall speak to each of you in turn, and I will submit the names of the girls I think will benefit most from the opportunity.'

The bread and marge seemed to stick in Dulcie's throat,

the tea had a bitter taste. When Janice caught her eye, she seemed to be saying, 'I told you so,' and it was all Dulcie could do not to burst into tears.

That evening as she said her prayers, she silently pleaded with the Virgin Mary to intervene on her behalf. She promised she wouldn't forget her father or Susan, that she would be really good and never ask for anything else for herself again.

On Monday morning it was even colder than the previous day, the sky was like lead, and Sister Grace said she thought it was going to snow. But they still had to go outside. May kept complaining that her inner thighs were sore, and when Dulcie looked at them she saw they were red raw, chapped with the cold. She felt very angry then that the Sisters could be so cruel as to send children outside in such weather – many of them had bad colds and coughs, their gabardine coats were so thin, even gloves, hats or scarves were denied them. That added even more fuel to her desire to go to Australia.

It was almost dinner-time when Dulcie and May were called in to see Mother Superior. Others had been called earlier and returned to the playground within ten minutes – none of them had any idea if they were going to be selected.

The old nun was sitting almost on top of her fire, and she didn't move when she called the sisters in, just told them to sit down.

'I believe you told Mr Stigwood you wanted to go to Australia,' she said, looking at Dulcie over her glasses.

'I do, Mother,' Dulcie said, quivering with tension. 'I want to go really badly.'

'Even if it means you won't be able to see Mrs Bankcroft any more, and you'd be leaving your father here?'

'Daddy won't be free till I'm at least sixteen, even with remission,' Dulcie said. 'And Mrs Bankcroft will be very busy with her own child.'

'What a sensible child you are,' Mother Superior said, smiling to reveal wobbly false teeth. She turned to look at

May. 'How about you, May, would you like to go to Australia?'

'Yes please,' May whispered. 'I want to be warm all the time. I've got really sore legs from the cold.'

The old lady half smiled. 'I'd like to be warm all the time too,' she admitted. 'But Australia isn't just warm, it's very hot. It's a very long way away too, you couldn't just hop on a train and come home.'

'There isn't any *home* here any more,' Dulcie said. 'None of our aunts or uncles write to us. Granny's gone, there's no reason to want to come back, except Daddy, and he could come there too when he gets out of prison.'

The nun looked very thoughtful, fingering the material of her habit. 'I'll see what I can do,' she said.

Dulcie knew the interview had come to an end, and to say anything more might even irritate the old lady. She knelt down, kissed the ring on her hand and thanked her.

'You are a bright and capable girl,' the old lady said, patting Dulcie's bent head. 'I believe you will do well in life, wherever that takes you. After dinner take May up to Sister Grace, she will give her some ointment for her sore legs. I will tell the other Sisters that there will be no outside play this afternoon.'

Dulcie's heart soared with happiness. To be praised and to be allowed to stay indoors was almost as good as being told they could definitely go to Australia.

'Thank you, Mother,' she said breathlessly.

Chapter Eight

'Carol Trueman, Janet Phillips, Dulcie and May Taylor, Pauline Dwight and Alice Field, all sit down and wait,' Sister Margaret announced after dinner. 'The rest of you will go outside as usual.'

It was the end of July, school had broken up for the summer holidays just the day before, no one had had any time yet to do anything wrong. The named girls all looked at each other in consternation, but they didn't dare speak, Sister Teresa was standing in the doorway just waiting to pounce.

Once all the other girls had gone upstairs, Sister Margaret told them they were to follow her up to Mother Superior's room. 'It's about Australia,' she said crisply, but whether this was intended to cheer or dismay them they couldn't tell, for her face was as blank as Sister Teresa's book of kindnesses.

Back at the end of January twelve girls had been selected by Mother Superior to go to Australia, including these six. In February they were all taken to Australia House in the Strand for an intelligence test and a medical. But since then they had been told nothing more, not even whether they'd passed the tests.

As they made their way up the stairs, Dulcie decided to herself that this group consisted of all the failures, for aside from her and May having a father, Pauline Dwight had a mother and Alice Field had a grandmother who visited her. None of the remaining six girls at present outside had anyone. She supposed Mother was going to break the bad news first, then call in the ones who were successful.

She wasn't really disappointed, not after all this time. Besides, just after the tests, Dulcie had written to Susan about what moving to Australia meant to her. Mother Superior tore the letter up and told her to rewrite it without the part about Australia. Her words were, *'There's no point in telling someone something which might not happen.'*

Mother Superior was sitting in her usual chair, a rug over her knees. She'd been poorly for months now, Dulcie couldn't remember when she last came down to the dining-room, or even into the playroom.

'Sit down on the floor,' she said. 'Sister Margaret, you take the chair by the window.'

The girls sat down and crossed their legs, pulling their summer dresses over their knees the way the Sisters always insisted on.

'I'm very pleased to be able to tell you girls that you will all be sailing on the SS *Maloja* to Australia on August the twelfth,' Mother Superior said.

For a moment there was a stunned silence. It was a subject they had talked about many, many times, before and after the selection of the twelve girls. But in recent months, because they'd been told nothing more, they'd put it aside. Dulcie knew that most of them, like her, were so used to being let down that they'd almost expected to be.

Carol broke the silence. 'Whoopee,' she shouted, and everyone joined in.

Mother Superior gave a faint smile. 'That's enough noise, I have important things to tell you.'

None of them could really believe what they were hearing. Sister Margaret was going to take them to the children's outfitters that very afternoon to buy them new clothes and shoes. On the morning of the twelfth they would be taken to Tilbury Docks in Essex by train, and the ship would be sailing on the evening tide, along with around another hundred boys and girls from orphanages around London. 'The voyage takes around six weeks,' Mother went on. 'None of the Sisters from the Sacred

Heart will be accompanying you, but there will be other Sisters to take care of you. Each one of you has been chosen because we believe you will benefit from this wonderful opportunity, so don't let me or yourselves down by behaving badly. Now, are there any questions?'

No one could think of anything to ask, all they could do was look at each other and grin. So Mother Superior dismissed them and told them to wait in the hall until Sister Margaret was ready to take them to the outfitters.

'Are we really going to get *new* clothes and shoes?' May whispered to Dulcie once they were out in the hall. Her eyes looked like two big glass marbles, almost popping out of her head.

'I think so,' Dulcie whispered back gleefully. She was so excited she felt she could burst, and even if she did feel sorry for the other six girls who presumably wouldn't be going, she couldn't think about them now. 'But just you behave yourself this afternoon, I wouldn't put it past them to suddenly say they've changed their minds if anyone plays up,' she said warningly.

It wasn't until they were going out through the orchard that Dulcie remembered Susan. She had written earlier in the month to say she had a baby boy called Edward, and she was hoping to come to stay with her parents in London at the end of August for a short holiday, during which she'd come to visit them. It was only the third letter they'd got this year, and it seemed forever since they had last seen her. Dulcie really wished they could see her before they left, for now she might never, ever see her again. Then there was her father.

Stricken with a sudden fear, Dulcie moved up to Sister Margaret's side. Next to Sister Grace she was the nicest of the nuns, and she didn't usually refuse to answer questions.

'Sister,' Dulcie asked hesitantly. 'Does our daddy know we are going?'

'Why, of course he does.' Sister pinched her cheek playfully. 'He'd have been asked for his permission.'

158

'He didn't mind, then?' Dulcie wasn't sure she liked the idea that he'd said they could go just like that.

Sister looked down at her. She had a red face, May had once said it looked like a tomato, and ever since 'Tomato Face' had been the nickname the girls called her in private. 'I expect he thinks you'll have a much better life out there,' she said, her blue eyes smiling. 'You will too, Dulcie. I wish I could go with you. Did you know they only chose the nicest, cleverest girls?'

Any lingering doubts or anxieties were soon swept away by the new clothes. Three cotton dresses, two nightdresses, a cardigan, shoes, socks, underwear and a swimsuit each. As they walked home again, each carrying their own bag of clothing, Sister Margaret told them that they each had a shiny new suitcase too, because they'd been delivered to the convent during the previous week.

Three weeks later Dulcie stood at the bows of the SS *Maloja*, her face turned up to the afternoon sun. She liked the warm wind pulling at her hair, the salty taste it left on her lips, but most of all she loved the emptiness of the ocean and the way that up in the bows she could hear nothing of the perpetual noise of the ship and its passengers, only the gentle sound of the water parting to let the ship glide through.

For the first few days the sea had frightened her, she had been nervous of going anywhere near the rails for fear a huge wave would sweep her away down into its depths. The vastness of it made her feel so very small and insignificant, the motion had made her queasy. But gradually she'd got used to it and now she loved it, for somehow that very vastness seemed to make the past seem less important.

The time had gone so fast after they knew they were leaving the convent for good – it seemed like a blink of an eye and they were on the ship. The tiny cabin she shared with her sister and four other girls was airless and cramped, yet she liked it. It was an adventure finding her way along narrow passageways and up steep polished wood companionways, never being entirely certain that she was going the right way. She adored all the jolly stewards who pinched her cheeks and said she had lovely eyes, they made her feel special. And never in her life had she had such huge meals, or even seen some of the things they dished up in the dining-room. She supposed this was how the rich lived all the time – snowy white tablecloths, silver cutlery, eating exotic things like prawns, curry, spaghetti and risotto. She tried almost everything, just to see what they were like, but her favourite things were chicken and fruit, and sometimes she ate so much she felt she might burst.

It was like a wonderful dream which just went on and on. Although there were over a hundred children on the ship, from all over England and Ireland too, there were very few grown-ups with them, just four nuns and a few young men and women who were going out to live in Australia too, and they didn't care much what the children got up to. So mostly they could do what they liked, haring around on the upper decks, playing quoits, cricket, or swimming in the small pool on the top deck. It was only when the other adult passengers complained about the noise they made that any effort was made to organize proper games or lessons.

On the last day, after nearly six weeks at sea, Dulcie had grown tired of playing hide-and-seek, chase and all those games which involved so much running around and shouting. She wanted to be quiet, to curl up with a book, or just watch the sea and the birds in solitude. That seemed funny to her, just as it had felt funny when she finally came to say goodbye to everyone at the Sacred Heart. She'd hated it there, yet when she went into the orchard for one last look around, she had begun to cry because it all looked so dear and beautiful. She had remembered how it looked back in the spring when the blossom was out. On the way to school they used to grab a handful and toss the petals over each other pretending it was confetti.

Then there had been all those wonderful days there last summer, when at last the Sisters let them go into the orchard to play, when they had lain on the warm grass, eating the fallen fruit, and telling each other stories about what they were going to do when they were grown up.

'I won't ever know what happens to them,' she said aloud.

'What happens to who?'

Dulcie turned sharply in surprise at hearing a boy's voice behind her. She would have been very embarrassed at being caught out talking to herself by any of the other boys, but it was only Duncan, one of the boys from Manchester, and she liked him. Like her he was small and blond, in fact one of the stewards had thought he was her brother. He was eleven, with the skinniest legs she'd ever seen, and a crop of freckles which seemed to grow every day.

She explained what she'd been thinking about.

'I don't much care about the other boys I knew,' Duncan said with a shrug. 'But sometimes I wonder what will happen if my mum comes back for me and I'm not there.'

The first day on ship, one of the young women who were supposed to keep an eye on them had encouraged each of them to tell the other children a bit about themselves. Duncan had been one of the first to speak, he said he didn't have a dad and his mum had put him in the home saying she'd be back for him, but she'd never come.

'They'd tell her where you'd gone and she'd come after you,' Dulcie said. 'But maybe we'll have such a great life in Australia that we won't care any more about the people who have made us sad.'

'I'm not so sure about that,' Duncan said forcefully. 'Grown-ups are so two-faced. They go on about being kind and generous, but they aren't, not to kids like us. We're told not to be bullies, yet they bully us. We're told we mustn't tell lies, but the nuns do it all the time. I've never met one grown-up who gave a toss about me, my feelings or even if I was hungry or cold. I don't suppose it's going to be much better in Australia either.'

'Of course it will,' Dulcie said quickly. 'They picked us all to go there because we were nice kids.'

'Did they?' He gave her a sharp look. 'I reckon they just wanted to get rid of us, like we were a load of rubbish that has to be dumped somewhere. No one wants rubbish on their own doorstep, so they send us to the other side of the world.'

'That's silly, Duncan.' She laughed. 'They were kind people who arranged all this, they want us to have a better life than we had in England.'

'I wish I could believe it the way you do. I reckon we're just like the convicts they used to send out there,' he said, and a lone tear trickled down his cheek.

The next day, as Dulcie and May waited in a queue in a tin shed at Fremantle Docks and saw the children up ahead were being fingerprinted, Duncan's words on the deck came back to Dulcie.

Everything had looked so wonderful just a couple of hours earlier. As the ship came in to dock, a band was playing, people were waving and cheering. Fremantle didn't look very special, just a lot of sheds and miles of concrete wharf, but the sea sparkled in the sunshine, and all those bright faces, the music and the cheering were very welcoming. The stewards and even the other passengers hugged and kissed all the children, wishing them all the best for the future. Dulcie felt so excited she could hardly manage to walk down the gangway.

But they'd only just set foot in Australia when the boys were separated from the girls and marched off in different directions. She felt bad enough that she wasn't even give a chance to say goodbye properly to her friends like Duncan, but far worse was to see brothers and sisters who had been together in orphanages back in England torn away from one another. No explanation was made, or any assurances given that they'd see one another again soon. All of them were crying, some even screaming, and a nun went amongst the girls and shook and slapped some of them to shut them up.

Dulcie held May's hand tightly as they waited in the queue. May had annoyed her a great deal on the journey, she'd been so full of herself, but just the thought of being separated from her permanently terrified her. It was so hot too, and there was no sign now of the nice younger men and women who'd taken care of them on the ship, just older, severe-looking people who spoke really strangely, to keep them in line.

'I'm so hot,' May bleated. 'I want a drink.'

'I expect they'll give us one in a minute,' Dulcie replied absentmindedly, busy connecting fingerprinting with convicts.

'If they don't get me a drink now I shall scream,' May retorted.

Dulcie was instantly alarmed. 'Don't you dare,' she said. 'You know what happened on the first night at the Sacred Heart, and that was all because you made a big fuss.'

When May whimpered with fright, Dulcie felt bad at reminding her of that night, for clearly whatever had happened to her nearly two years ago still had the power to frighten her. 'I'll ask someone nicely when I get a chance,' she said quickly and cuddled May. 'Now, just be patient.'

Through the open side of the shed Dulcie could see a hive of activity, men carting luggage on trolleys, huge wooden containers being unloaded from the ship's hold on to the wharf by cranes. There were so many families, not just the ones that had been on the *Maloja* but from other huge ships too. They stood in tight little bunches by their luggage, many of the women held small children and babies in their arms, with bigger children around them, and mostly they looked as anxious as she felt. She wondered where they were all going. Did they have places to stay? Or were they in much the same predicament as her and May, just waiting to be told where to go?

The queue shuffled forward very slowly, but at last it was their turn to approach the table at which sat two men and a woman.

'Names!' one of the men barked at them. Dulcie told him and he sifted through a pile of forms until he found theirs. The second man reached out to grab Dulcie's hand, pushed her index finger on to the ink pad, then squeezing it tightly rolled it carefully on to the bottom of the form, leaving a clear imprint. Then it was May's turn.

'May we have a drink of water, please?' Dulcie asked, her voice shaking with nervousness.

'You'll all get one before long,' the woman said, giving Dulcie a steely-eyed look as she handed her the form. 'Take that over there,' she added, pointing in the direction of another table at which two women sat.

Dulcie picked up her case and, telling May to come with her, did as she was told. Again they had to give their names, ages and which home they'd come from in England. Dulcie felt even more nervous as the two women had a whispered consultation as they looked at a large ledger. It seemed to Dulcie they were trying to decide where to send them, for there were several columns, some having just a few names, others far more. She thought she heard one of the women say 'only room for one there' and her heart nearly stopped with fright that they might separate them.

'St Vincent's in Perth,' the older of the two said finally, and to Dulcie's relief she put both their names in the same column. She wrote St Vincent's on their forms, and handed them back to Dulcie. 'You can go out to the refreshment stand now,' she said. 'That's out through the door at the side.' She pointed it out. 'Don't lose the forms, you'll need to hand them in to the Sister in charge.'

It was cooler outside the shed. A large table was laid out in the shade of the building with sandwiches, cakes and glasses of orange squash. Several smiling nuns were greeting each of the girls in turn, passing out refreshments. As Dulcie and May were directed to put their suitcases down and sit on a blanket, and saw the four girls from the

164

Sacred Heart were there already, along with several others from the ship, Dulcie's spirits lifted a little.

'Where are you two going?' Carol called out to her.

'St Vincent's,' Dulcie replied. 'What about you?'

Carol said she, Janet, Alice and Pauline were going to a place called St Joseph's, and they wished Dulcie and May were going there too. As more girls came to sit down on the blanket everyone chattered about where they were going, and although there were several girls still very upset at being separated from their brothers, the cold drinks, and finding themselves amongst friends, helped to cheer them all up.

A little later, all the girls were lined up for a photograph. The smallest ones, including May, were placed in front, and each one of them was given a teddy bear. The photographer told them jokes to make them laugh, and as the nuns watching were all smiling, the last of the children's anxieties were dispelled, and the happy moment was caught on film.

More cakes and squash were handed round before the girls were divided up into the groups for each home they were going to. As Carol, Janet, Pauline and Alice were led away with their quite large party to a bus, everyone cheered loudly.

It was the St Vincent's group that went next, just six in all – Dulcie, May, Susan, Mary and two seven-year-olds, Joan and Patty. As the nun led them round the side of the shed to where a car was waiting for them, another nun approached them and took the teddy bears from the three youngest girls' arms.

May let out a howl of rage and tried to snatch hers back.

'That's enough of that,' the nun said, slapping her hand. 'They were only lent to you, they will be needed again.'

Dulcie dropped her case and went to May, for once in complete agreement with her sister's anger. She looked up at the stern-faced nun and narrowed her eyes. 'That was a mean thing to do,' she hissed at her. 'They all thought they were a present.'

The incident cast a pall over the car ride. The nun who would be driving them introduced herself as Sister Ruth. Dulcie and Mary sat in the front with her, the other four smaller girls in the back, the three younger ones sniffling, two suitcases which there hadn't been room for in the boot stuffed down by their feet.

Sister Ruth seemed quite nice, she asked their names and told them it was just a short drive, but all the girls were so upset by the incident with the teddy bears that they didn't even whisper to one another.

The Sister kept pointing things out to them, the wide Swan River, which she said was famous for its black swans, King's Park which she said had beautiful exotic birds and huge old trees, but though Dulcie felt she ought to be looking out eagerly at the scenery, noting what was different to England, all she could think of was how hot it was and how dusty and strange the trees were. Even the pretty little bungalow-style houses with fancy lace-like iron work along the verandas and gardens crammed with strange-looking plants did nothing to cheer her, and all at once she felt tears welling up in her eyes.

It had been so wonderful on the ship that she had almost forgotten how horrible it could be at the Sacred Heart. Yet now as she looked down at her ink-stained finger and remembered how brothers and sisters had been cruelly separated and the teddy bears snatched back, she felt a sense of foreboding that maybe it was going to be even worse here.

Chapter Nine

'You haven't cleaned this, you lazy little beggar,' Sister
Anne said accusingly. She turned from examining a shelf
which was at her own eye level, but way above Dulcie's
head, and in the same movement swiped out at the child
with the thin leather strap she kept attached to her belt. It
licked across Dulcie's shoulder, the tip catching the back
of her neck which was already red raw with sunburn. 'Get
those pots down and scrub it.'

'Yes, Sister,' Dulcie said, not even daring to put her hand
on her neck to soothe the stinging. She certainly didn't
dare say she'd already scrubbed the shelf – in three months
at St Vincent's she had learnt never to answer back.

Dulcie's appearance had changed dramatically since
she got off the ship three months earlier. Plump rosy cheeks
were now hollow, her complexion rough from constant
burning and blistering in the sun. Her hair was cut exactly
the same as every other girl's here, straight across on a
level with her ear lobes, parted on the right and held back
from her forehead with a kirby grip. The green and white
striped uniform dress hung limply for she'd grown painfully thin, and her feet were bare, the soles callused
from the rough ground. Yet it was her eyes which exposed
how she felt inside. Fearful, demoralized, and so very
weary.

'I shall be back,' Sister Anne said ominously and
waddled out of the laundry room to check someone else's
work.

Dulcie poked out her tongue at the nun's retreating
back, then picked up a stool and carried it back to beneath
the shelf. The laundry room was little more than a shed

167

at the back of the convent, and she had been sent in here after dinner to clean it. This involved scrubbing not only the stone floor but the two large sinks, draining boards and the rollers on the huge wringer, polishing up the copper and every other surface too. As the laundry was used every morning and water and soap suds made a great deal of mess, it was a formidable task even for an adult. Dulcie had been cleaning for three hours, alone and without a break, and it was now spotless. The shelf she had been accused of not cleaning properly was one where heavy old cooking pots were kept for boiling up small amounts of washing, like handkerchiefs or soiled bandages. She knew that it was perfectly clean, she'd even gone right into the corners with a small brush, but she'd made the mistake of allowing it to dry before Sister Anne inspected.

Once again she clambered up on the stool, took the first pan and heaved it down, then the next. The stool wobbled precariously on the uneven floor, it was hard work getting up and down each time, sweat poured down her face, her damp dress and apron clung to her body, but finally she had all twelve pots down. Again she filled the bucket with water, picked up the bar of hard soap, and climbed back up to scrub.

Dulcie deeply regretted now that she'd ever expressed a desire to come to Australia. She hated St Vincent's, it made the Sacred Heart look like paradise. She'd had school to go to there, and on the walk to and from it she could see shops, buses, cars and ordinary people, so she still felt like a human being.

Since the day she'd arrived here she hadn't been out of the grounds once, and she had no idea what, if anything, lay beyond the scrubland they called 'the Bush' which surrounded St Vincent's. While she knew she couldn't be very far from Perth – she had after all seen for herself the big shops, the wide Swan River and King's Park, and recalled it only took another fifteen or twenty minutes to reach here – she wouldn't know in which direction to go once she'd reached the end of the dirt track which led to St Vincent's gates.

Even the nuns who weren't actually cruel couldn't be described as kind. They had sour faces, as though they had forgotten how to laugh, smile or say anything pleasant. But she supposed as there were a hundred girls here, and a great deal of land, they hadn't got much to smile about.

The heat was what wore her down – sometimes the intensity of the sunshine made her cross-eyed, and her head felt as if it might explode. Just ten minutes out in it, hanging up the washing, weeding or feeding the chickens, was enough to burn her fair skin – at night it was like trying to sleep lying on a hot stove. She might have been thoroughly miserable on icy days out in the playground at the Sacred Heart, and too cold in bed to sleep sometimes, but she found herself looking back on that longingly.

It was a lie that the food was better and more plentiful than in England. For breakfast they had something called Granuma which was horribly like semolina; at dinner they mostly got a kind of thick soup which didn't taste of anything, boiled grey fish on Fridays, and only bread and marge for tea. She was hungry almost all the time.

Along with the hunger and heat, there was the work too. The day started at six, and the cleaning of the dormitories and washrooms, and sweeping and washing the verandas had to be completed by breakfast-time at eight. Then there was a service in the chapel, followed by lessons. Some girls, Dulcie included, were often called out of these for other tasks – laundry, polishing floors or out on the farm. After dinner there were more lessons, or chores which could range from weeding the gardens and drive to mending clothes and household linen. They might get an hour or two to play between tea and evening prayers, but quite often still more jobs were found.

It was real school that Dulcie missed most of all. She had loved everything about it, the smell of milk, chalk and polish, the little desks, collecting things for the nature table. She loved to learn, and whether that was geography, history or just doing sums and writing essays, she had enjoyed it.

The two schoolrooms here had only wooden forms and rickety scarred tables. There were no pictures on the walls, few books, and such things as painting, handicrafts or playing percussion instruments were unheard of. The hundred girls from five to fifteen were divided into two groups, and even though Dulcie had been put in the Senior group as soon as she reached her eleventh birthday in December, only two of the other forty-nine girls were as advanced as she was, and they were fourteen-year-olds.

The Sisters weren't trained teachers, so the lessons were sketchy and very dull. Dulcie had been told by one of the oldest girls that no one in St Vincent's ever got to sit examinations, and they would all be sent out to do domestic work when they were old enough, so there was little point in trying hard.

All the sisters really cared about was neat handwriting, spelling and multiplication tables. They took the view that that, and being able to cook, clean and sew, was all a girl needed. As Dulcie could already read, write and spell well and knew her tables backwards, she was a prime candidate for any extra domestic work around the school.

This was why she was cleaning the laundry that afternoon while most of the girls were having spelling and multiplication tests. It seemed grossly unfair to her that she should be given a job that amounted to a punishment when through her own efforts she had mastered the skills the other girls lacked. But to voice such thoughts was unthinkable.

She rescrubbed the shelf, and after dampening a corner of her apron to hold against her burning neck, she sat down on the doorstep. From there she would be able to hear Sister Anne coming back along the gravel path from the school to the laundry, then she would jump back on the stool, dampen the shelf again, and be ready for the inspection.

In front of her was the kitchen garden where the Sisters

grew all kinds of vegetables, behind that was a chicken coop. They called them 'chooks' here, just another alien word she had to remember to use or risk getting a clout for being a Pom.

The soft clucking noises of the chooks, mingled with the chanting of tables coming from the schoolroom, was a peaceful, pleasant sound, and in the shade, a slight breeze fanning her, she was in danger of falling asleep.

But she fought against it, ears cocked for Sister Anne.

To her right was the orphanage, a series of four white-painted single-storey wooden buildings with a veranda along one side, linked to each other by covered walkways. Two of the buildings had two dormitories in each, twenty-five beds to a room with exactly two feet of space between each bed. Between the two dormitories was a small room where the Sister in charge slept and a bathroom and washroom. The Juniors were in one, the Seniors in another, and even sisters in the same age group were split up to discourage any closeness.

The schoolrooms took up another building and the fourth was used as an assembly hall and dining-room. Wire mesh covered all the windows to keep the flies out. Dulcie remembered how she'd thought they were prison bars the day they arrived. She didn't view that mesh with horror now, only gratitude, for the flies here were like nothing she'd ever seen in England. They tried to get moisture from your eyes, nose and mouth, and as fast as you flapped one lot away, another lot would appear. Then there were mosquitoes too, horrible things that made her arms and legs swell up in great itchy bumps. Thankfully she hadn't seen a snake yet, or any of the many poisonous spiders she'd heard about, but then she kept well clear of the places they were likely to be in.

Behind the laundry room and over to the left, out of her present line of vision, was the convent itself. It was a fine-looking stone-built, two-storey building with pointed eaves, grand chimneys, deep cool verandas and a chapel as splendid as any church she'd been into back in England.

There were dozens of nuns living there, many very old and sick and rarely seen outside. In front of the convent in the middle of the circular weed-free gravel drive was a large marble statue of St Vincent, the patron saint of orphans; beyond this, up to the heavy iron gates, were beautifully kept lawns shaded by pines and giant Moreton Bay fig trees. The irony that the Sisters who were supposed to live a life of humility and poverty should be housed in such a grand place, while the children who St Vincent vowed to take care of lived in little more than sheds, hadn't escaped Dulcie. She was often ordered into the convent to scrub and polish floors and she thought maybe this was why so many of the older girls thought they might become nuns themselves. As so many of the girls here, Australian or British, had never been in a real home, or even seen a film showing one, they probably thought the Sisters' life was like being a princess in a palace. The Sisters had wonderful food – real butter, fresh eggs, vegetables straight from the garden, a plentiful supply of meat and fish. Dulcie remembered bitterly how Mr Stigwood had told them back at the Sacred Heart that Australia was a land of plenty, a land that hadn't been torn apart by war. Yet she could recall Granny's neighbours dishing out far better meals even while the war was still going on, and afterwards in the terrible winter of 1947, than they ever got here.

She mopped her burning neck again with the damp apron and looked out beyond the vegetable garden to the paddocks. When they arrived here the grass had been lush and green, much like at home, and studded with wild flowers. Now it was just bare, dusty soil, the sun had scorched all the grass. The front lawns were watered nightly, but this was too vast an area to receive the same treatment. A flock of twenty or so sheep picked miserably around the lower paddock, and she wondered if they were as hungry as she was.

Yet for all the misery here, the Australian trees and wildlife enchanted Dulcie. When they first arrived there were bottle bushes in full bloom, scarlet flowers which did look exactly like a large bottle brush. She found the gum trees, with their curious misshapen trunks and papery barks, beautiful too; the grey-green leaves smelt heavily medicinal, wafting into the dormitories at night whenever there was a slight breeze. The huge Moreton Bay fig trees were lovely as well, creating such deep cool shade around their vast trunks. And the birds were an unfailing delight, ones called ringnecks, red wattles, Willy wagtails, grey fantails and singing honey-eaters, all so different to English birds and their songs so joyful.

At dusk they often saw kangaroos and emus too, though they rarely came close to the buildings. She wished they would, but Sister Ruth said they were too nervous as Father Murphy, who lived in the convent, regularly shot at them.

Overall, it seemed to Dulcie that Duncan had been right in thinking that British orphans were only sent out here to be got rid of. It wasn't a better life at all. They never got taken to the beaches, even though she'd learnt they were only a few miles from one. They learned nothing about the outside world.

Most of the girls were Australian, only ten British – six English and four Irish – and if any of them were caught together talking about home, they were always punished. Dulcie had thought the punishments were severe enough at the Sacred Heart, but they were nothing to the ones here. Like there, bed-wetting was punished by making the girl stand with the wet sheet over her head, but she also got the strap. Being forced to kneel on a gravel path for an hour or two could be used to punish anything from talking after lights out to not knowing multiplication tables. The strap was ever present, the Sisters used it in class, at mealtimes and while the girls were doing chores. Just being a bit slow scrubbing a floor was enough to get a couple of stripes on a bare leg.

There was absolutely no affection, or even recognition that the girls were individuals. Birthdays were only marked by having your name and new age called out. At Christmas each girl was given an orange, a small bag of sweets and a handkerchief. None of the British girls ever got any letters from home, not even ones who had come over a year ago, and every one of them was upset by this.

Dulcie suspected that letters did arrive but just weren't given out, for the Sisters were mistresses of deceit. Shoes, socks and hair ribbons were handed out for Mass on Sundays and when visitors called. Teddy bears and dolls were put on to beds then whisked away the moment the visitors had left. Lovely dinners were produced, the tables covered with a cloth, even sweets dished out at these times, but the moment the gates clanged shut again it was back to the normal sparse fare.

Dulcie could remember sobbing with the pain of blisters and cuts on her bare feet when she first arrived here, but she got no treatment, not even a shred of sympathy. Maybe her heart had now become as callused as her feet, because she'd even grown used to the Sisters' mania for breaking up close friendships between the girls.

Why anyone could consider friendship something sinister, or want to keep sisters apart, she didn't know. Perhaps they thought that mere orphans weren't entitled to any kind of affection, not even from their own kind. But when Dulcie was punished by having to crawl on all-fours up and down the gravel drive for two whole hours in blazing sunshine, just for being caught in May's dormitory giving her a goodnight kiss, she decided that the Sisters were mad as well as cruel and heartless. Try as they might, however, the Sisters couldn't stamp out friendship, it flourished ever more vigorously as the girls learned to be as deceitful as the nuns.

Dulcie had often felt angry at the strict and often senseless rules at the Sacred Heart, but here new rules were invented overnight and the severity of the punishment for breaking them was according to the whim of whoever caught the wrongdoer. The Sisters at the Scared Heart did at least respond if a child was ill or hurt. Here they ignored it.

If a girl got a splinter, an older girl dug it out. If anyone felt ill, she looked to friends for comfort. One girl had a bad stomach ache, and all the Sisters gave her was castor oil. Her pain got worse and worse over a week until she was screaming with it, and when they did eventually call the doctor he had to take her to hospital, having discovered that she had appendicitis.

So loyalty to one another thrived under cover. Tale-telling to the Sisters was almost unheard of, the older girls did their best to mother the little ones, the clever ones helped those who were slow, and when someone got a severe punishment, she had all the girls' sympathy.

Yet Dulcie found herself isolated, for she always seemed to fall between two stools: too bright to be in need of help with schoolwork, too well able to look after herself to need protection, too old to play with the little ones, too young to be included in the Senior girls' conversations. May had found a niche for herself in her Junior dormitory by being daring and funny, she even seemed to be able to charm a couple of the Sisters, but Dulcie couldn't turn to her for company, not without risking finding herself in trouble. She missed the London accents, girls like Beryl who had so many stories about her family and old neighbours. Almost all the girls here had nothing to talk about but St Vincent's, they knew nothing else.

So when Dulcie had free time, more often than not she spent it alone. She would find herself thinking about England, wondering how her father and Susan were. She'd written to them both as soon as she got here, but neither of them replied. Reverend Mother wouldn't allow her to write again, she said that it was a waste of a stamp to persist when it was clear people had lost interest in her.

Dulcie often thought about Duncan too. She hoped his orphanage was better than this one and that he still thought about her and all the good times they'd had together.

Hearing Sister Anne's footsteps on the gravel, she leaped

inside, took the wet cloth and jumped up on the stool to wipe the shelf over. As the Sister came into the laundry she was just lifting up a pot to put it back.

Sister Anne ran her finger along the shelf and nodded. 'That's better, why couldn't you have done it like that in the first place? Put the pots back now and then go and help in the kitchen.'

Dulcie waited until the woman had left, then poked out her tongue again. 'Miserable old crow,' she muttered. 'I hate you.'

It was just a few weeks later, in February, just before supper, that Reverend Mother called all the girls into the largest of the two schoolrooms. This was a very unusual occurrence as she rarely came over to the school buildings. Although her role in the convent was much the same as Mother Superior's at the Sacred Heart, she was much younger, the older girls reckoned only in her late forties. Stories about her abounded, she was said to be from a wealthy family in Perth, and she'd joined the Sisters of Mercy after being jilted by her fiancé. She intrigued all the older girls for there was a clearly defined difference between her and the rest of the Sisters. She had a cultured voice, a smooth, glowing complexion, and beautiful dark eyes. She had an elegant, brisk walk, and even if her body was shrouded by her black habit, it hinted at being a shapely one.

But this faint aura of glamour didn't strike any admiration into the girls' hearts, for they were all very afraid of her. She had a vicious temper and the sharpest tongue, and many of the older girls who had to help out inside the convent with the elderly and sick Sisters there had witnessed her striking these old women. She was known to have special favourites among the girls too, singling them out for piano lessons, trips into town and extra food. For some reason Dulcie couldn't quite understand, these favourites were never envied, but pitied.

Mother certainly had more contact with the outside

world than anyone else in the convent – almost every day the girls saw her drive off in her black Holden. Sometimes she stayed away for several days, and it was believed she went to supervise another orphanage and to give advice at the girls' reformatory.

When the girls were summoned, they immediately anticipated trouble, for if Mother just had some ordinary news for them, she would have come in and told them all over supper. So as they scurried into the schoolroom they were nervously smoothing down their hair and checking for unfastened buttons.

'Stand up in lines,' Mother shouted harshly as they came spilling in.

The tables were always stacked on top of each other every afternoon for the floor to be swept, and not being able to sit down on the floor was a further indication she was very angry about something. They quickly slipped into four rows, the youngest right at the front. Dulcie was in the third row, May in the second, the fourth being the oldest girls. Everyone was completely silent.

Mother folded her arms across her habit, tucking her hands into her sleeves, and walked back and forward for a few moments, her dark eyes scanning the girls. She certainly had a terrifying way about her – just one glance in a child's direction was enough to make them quake, and if her eyes lingered on them for more than a second or two they often began to cry.

'We have a thief in our midst,' she said at length. 'One of you has had the audacity to go into my office and steal a tin of toffees.'

A faint gasp from the girls broke the silence, for they all knew exactly what she was referring to. A visitor to St Vincent's had brought a big tin of toffees at Christmas. Everyone was given one in front of the visitor. The tin was then put in Mother's office on the ground floor of the convent. It had sat since then on a small table in clear view of anyone passing the window, and many of the bolder girls who were sent over to the convent to clean made jokes about slipping in there to help themselves to a handful.

Dulcie was astounded that anyone who had the daring to slip into that room should be stupid enough to take the whole tin, for it was obvious it would be missed. She glanced around at the other girls, looking for a guilty expression. But everyone she could see looked as surprised and innocent as herself.

'If the thief doesn't confess right now I shall punish you all,' Mother said. 'There will be no supper until this is cleared up.'

There was complete silence again, so quiet it sounded as if everyone was holding their breath. A minute passed, then another, still no one spoke out.

'Down on your knees then,' Mother said, her dark eyes glinting as if she was going to enjoy watching their discomfort. 'You will remain there until I have the culprit, even if I have to keep you here all night.'

A low groan from everyone was the only answer. The schoolroom floor was made of bare splintery boards, and even ten minutes of kneeling on it was a painful ordeal.

Dulcie had a graze on her knee and as soon as it came in contact with the floor it began to throb. She looked up at Reverend Mother's face, saw the malice in her eyes and knew that she meant what she said – however long it took, she would make them stay here.

The clock on the wall said half past five when they first came into the room, and as Dulcie knelt there she watched the second hand going round. After only fifteen minutes she felt she could scream with pain, but Reverend Mother sat down on a chair by the window, calmly watching them all, from time to time getting up and walking along the rows of girls, making sure no one had slumped back on to their heels. Small groans and sighs started, shuffling sounds as girls tried to pull their dresses down to kneel on, but thin cotton didn't act as a cushion, and by the time an hour had passed, many of them were in real distress.

Mother went out for a while, Sister Ruth relieving her. When she returned she asked if anyone was ready to own up, and pointed out that the longer they left it, the more severe the punishment would be.

It was just after half past six, when Angela, one of the five-year-olds, started to cry and everyone craned their necks to look at her, that Dulcie suddenly realized to her horror that May was the culprit.

She was only a few feet away from Dulcie, in the next row, two girls along. Dulcie had glanced at her right at the outset when Mother was speaking about the toffees, but then she'd had a wide-eyed, innocent look. Anyone else would have thought the present expression on her face was purely the result of discomfort, but Dulcie had seen that particular furtive expression too many times to be fooled. May was biting her lower lip and twiddling her hair, eyes darting around the room as if trying to weigh up if anyone could possibly know it was her.

It was Dulcie's guess she'd snatched the tin as an act of bravado to impress her friends. She'd probably hidden them away intending to share them out later, but she was a little pig for sweets, and had doubtless eaten them all. Had anyone else known about this, they would have accused her by now, for not even the most loyal friend would stay quiet under these circumstances.

While Dulcie thought May fully deserved punishing, she knew that this would be a caning offence – at least six strokes on a bare bottom. On top of that May would be punished further by the other girls afterwards for putting them through all this. That could involve anything from being burned with a hot iron, having her head held down the lavatory and the chain flushed, or being sent to Coventry indefinitely. Dulcie was certain that might very well push May back to the way she'd been at the Sacred Heart after Sister Teresa's cruelty.

When Reverend Mother slapped Angela for crying, Dulcie knew they really would be here all night, because May would never own up herself, no matter how much pain she put others through, she just wasn't made that way.

179

Dulcie felt she had to stop it all now. She was frightened of being caned, but it was the thought of what the older girls would do to her that really terrified her. Yet she couldn't let everyone else suffer now for something May had done.

Taking a deep breath, Dulcie stood up. 'It was me who took the toffees, Reverend Mother,' she said. 'I'm very sorry.'

There were gasps of surprise from everyone. Dulcie didn't dare look at them, but kept her eyes on the older woman who looked as if she was about to have a fit.

'You, Dulcie!' she exclaimed. 'Why?'

'Because I'm greedy, Mother,' Dulcie said, suddenly feeling her insides turning to jelly. 'I'm so very sorry. Can the others get up now? None of them had anything to do with it.'

Reverend Mother hesitated for a moment, her eyes narrowed in suspicion, but then made a gesture for them all to get up and said they were to go and get their supper. Some of the girls could barely stand, and they hobbled out, many of them looking back at Dulcie in puzzlement. May paused in the doorway, looking stricken with fear, but then she scampered quickly away.

Dulcie was trembling with fright, she had cramp in her legs and her back was aching from being so long in one position. Reverend Mother looked hard at her. 'I don't believe you,' she said. 'You are covering up for someone. Tell me who it is!'

Dulcie hadn't expected to be interrogated, she thought she'd just be caned and that would be it. Was she going to be forced to kneel again until Reverend Mother got the answers she wanted? Dulcie knew that would soon crack her.

'I did take them, Mother,' she insisted. 'I don't know why. I just did it on the spur of the moment without thinking. It was very bad and I'm sorry.'

'Would you swear on the Bible it was you?'

Dulcie gulped. She hadn't expected that either. Yet why

should she be afraid to swear it? God hadn't been looking after her so well, and she was only protecting her sister.

'Yes, I will,' she said defiantly.

Reverend Mother opened the cupboard under the blackboard and pulled out a Bible. 'Come here,' she said sharply. 'Put both hands on it and swear.'

Dulcie almost backed away. The big black Bible with its gold cross was sacred. She might be struck down by a stroke of lightning for lying even in its presence. How could she put her hands on it?

Yet she did, the leather felt cool and soft, and she just hoped God knew her motives were pure. 'I swear on this Bible I did steal the toffees,' she said.

'You will stay in purgatory for all time if you lied,' the woman reminded her. 'Is saving another girl punishment worth that?'

Dulcie pictured May's face as she had been that morning after Sister Teresa had finished with her, and decided she'd take the chance on purgatory. 'It was me, Mother,' she said.

Reverend Mother turned away for a moment and went over to a stool kept by the window. It was like a piano stool, with handles on both sides, but no padding on the seat. 'In that case take down your drawers and lean over this,' she said.

Dulcie bit her lip tightly as she slid her drawers down to her knees, and offered up a plea to God that he would understand, then bent forward, holding the two handles, and waited.

She heard Reverend Mother go to the cupboard under the blackboard, a faint rustle of something, then her footsteps on the wooden floor as she came towards her.

'It's not too late to admit who you are shielding,' she said.

'It was me, Mother,' Dulcie said once again.

The woman pushed her hands away from the handles, so she was bent double over the stool, then pulled up her dress, folding it back so it came right up over Dulcie's shoulders.

There was a swish through the air, bringing with it just a little breeze, then it hit her, and right away Dulcie knew this was no ordinary cane, but the switch she'd heard about from several of the older girls. They said it had about a dozen leather thongs fixed to it, and at the end of each one was a metal stud.

Her buttocks seemed to explode, as though the skin was already broken open, and she caught hold of the stool legs involuntarily. The second and third blows were even more painful, yet she forced herself not to scream. She lost count of the strokes after that, for the pain was so terrible there was no sensation of a pause between each one, it just seemed to go on and on, like being forced to sit on top of a fire. She tried to scream, but no sound came out, and it was only as she was on the point of passing out with the agony that she realized that was what the woman was waiting for, because she grabbed her by the hair, jerked her head back, and when she saw tears streaming down Dulcie's face she half smiled maliciously.

'I know you didn't take them,' she rasped, out of breath from her exertion. 'Don't think you can lie to me, Dulcie Taylor, and get away with it. I shall be watching you now till the day you leave here. One step out of place and I'll come down so hard on you that tonight's beating will seem like nothing.'

There was one more stroke, as a finishing touch, and she heard the woman walk away without another word.

Dulcie never knew how she managed to get up off that stool, pull her drawers up and get out of the classroom. When she reached the veranda, it was all she could do not to fall on to the floor and scream with pain, yet somehow she managed to fumble her way along the walkway to her dormitory. It wasn't just her bottom that hurt, but her whole body, each step like a hundred knives going into her. She concentrated all her effort on reaching the bathroom, but as she bent over to turn on the cold tap in the bath, she felt herself growing faint and her legs buckling beneath her.

She came round to find Sonia, one of the oldest girls, dabbing at her face with a cloth.

Sonia was very plain, with ginger hair and masses of freckles, but she was very tough and the undisputed leader here at St Vincent's. Abandoned as a baby, she'd never known anything but orphanages, yet they hadn't entirely subdued her fiery nature. She was the only one who dared answer the Sisters back, it was said she'd once punched Sister Anne for beating a five-year-old.

'Strewth, you're a brave kid,' she exclaimed. 'We all know it wasn't you that nicked the toffees. But your bum's gonna take a long time to get better, and tonight you'll think you're in hell.'

Sonia propped Dulcie up against the washbasin and first soaked her drawers with water to make their removal easier as they'd already stuck to her skin. 'Hold on tight while I whip them off,' she said. 'And don't you dare scream or Sister Anne will belt me for helping you.'

It was all hazy after that, for Dulcie was engulfed in such red-hot agony she could focus on nothing else. Yet even through that fiery haze she was aware of Sonia tenderly bathing her bottom, slipping a nightdress over her head, then putting an arm around her waist, leading her into the dormitory and laying her face down on the bed.

'You poor kid,' she heard the girl say as if from a long way off. 'Whatever did any of us do to get to end up in a place like this?'

Dulcie hurt too badly to be surprised to see May creeping into the dormitory later. While Dulcie often took a chance on being caught out in the Junior dormitory just to spend a few minutes with her sister, May never reciprocated. 'Does it hurt terribly?' she asked in a whisper. 'Look, I brought you an orange.'

An orange was like finding a lump of gold, and under any other circumstances Dulcie would not only have been wild with excitement, but curious as to where May got it.

'I don't want that,' Dulcie managed to say through her pain. 'The only thing that would make me feel better is if you were to admit to me that you stole the toffees.'

'But I didn't take them, Dulcie,' May said.

'You did, May,' Dulcie replied weakly. 'Admit it to me if no one else. I took this punishment to save your skin. Lift up my nightie and look!'

She heard May gasp as she lifted it, and knew it must look as terrible as it felt.

'I'm sorry she did that to you,' May whispered, putting one small hand on her cheek. 'But it wasn't me, I swear.'

Dulcie closed her eyes to dismiss her sister. Having sworn on the Bible herself, she knew that May swearing meant nothing either. Right then she wished she'd let her sister take her own punishment, she deserved it.

That night, once all the other girls had fallen asleep, Dulcie wept into her pillow. All the girls had been kind to her, each one had pledged to help her in any way they could. Dulcie felt some relief that they believed she didn't know who the real culprit was and that she'd taken the blame to save them all further punishment.

While their admiration and gratitude might make her future life here at St Vincent's better, that was no comfort now as she lay there in such agony. She wished she could just die in the night, for she knew that tomorrow she would be forced to get up and face all the usual jobs.

Yet she had another four years until she was fifteen and old enough to go to work. How was she going to survive that?

As Dulcie was crying in her bed, back in England Susan was just picking up the morning post from the doormat.

'Anything interesting?' Ian asked as she came back into the dining-room. Edward was sitting up in his high chair, his father spooning cereal into his mouth.

'All bills except one, that's from London,' Susan replied

as she flicked through them. 'I think it might be from the Sacred Heart. Let's hope they've found out where the girls are.'

She had been astounded, when she visited the convent at the end of August, to find Dulcie and May had been sent to Australia. Mother Superior had invited her in, given her tea, and said she was under the impression that Dulcie had written to inform her. The woman spoke in such glowing terms about what she called the Child Migration Scheme that by the time Susan left she was thinking that perhaps it was for the best.

But once she got home to Yorkshire and dug out Dulcie's old letters to read again, she began to have qualms about it. Dulcie liked writing letters and she was good at it, always putting in anything interesting or unusual which happened. So why hadn't she mentioned Australia if she'd been for a medical and an intelligence test?'

The most likely explanation was that she was told not to for some reason. But why?

The more Susan pondered on that, the fishier it became. Dulcie knew she was going to visit her at the end of August, and even if she was too excited about going away to write a sensible letter, she would have written something before she left. Unless of course she had and Mother Superior for some reason of her own had seen fit not to post it.

Susan gave her the benefit of the doubt at that point and waited patiently to get one from Australia. But Christmas came and went, January slipped past and still no letter, and it was at that point she wrote to Mother Superior asking if she knew the girls' new address.

Ian looked questioningly at his wife as she opened the envelope and took out a single sheet. 'It's from Sister Teresa,' Susan said, glancing up at him. 'Shall I read it aloud?'

Ian nodded, and spooned more cereal into Edward's mouth. He was nine months now, a sturdy little boy with his mother's soft brown eyes and his father's appetite, and his hair was finally growing, just a haze of light brown fluff.

> *Dear Mrs Bankcroft*, she read. *I am sorry to tell you that Mother Superior died in her sleep two weeks ago, here at the Sacred Heart. She was a good age at seventy-eight, but we all miss her very much. I am standing in for her until her replacement arrives. I am very sorry to hear that Dulcie and May haven't written to you, I know how fond you are of them, and they of you too. Sadly I have no address for them as they haven't written to us either. Also I haven't been able to find any name or address for the organization which arranged for the girls to go to Australia amongst Mother Superior's correspondence. I believe much of her contact with them was by telephone. When you do find the girls, as I'm sure you will, please remember me to them.*
> *Yours sincerely,*
> *Sister Teresa*

Susan put the letter down and looked helplessly at Ian. 'Can you believe they haven't even got any record of what organization the children went with? Doesn't that smack of incompetence?'

'Well, I suppose the old lady had it all in her head,' Ian replied, his tone a little chilly. 'But surely the father will know, Susan? He signed the papers to let them go.'

Susan noted the chill in his voice and knew she was going to get no further support or interest from him. 'Maybe I'll drop him a line then,' she said, then sat down at the table, and took over the feeding of Edward.

It was March before Reg received Susan's letter. When the warder handed him the envelope with the familiar, well-rounded handwriting at breakfast-time in the dining hall, he beamed in delight. It was the only letter to arrive since Christmastime when he got a very brief one from his brother Ernie.

Reg didn't even wait to get back to his cell, but ripped

open the envelope and read it as he went back up the metal staircase.

> Dear Reg, he read. *I expect you are surprised to hear from me again after all this time, but I felt compelled to write and ask if you have heard from Dulcie and May since they got to Australia. They didn't inform me they were going, and it was only when I called to visit at the Sacred Heart at the end of last August I learned of it.*
>
> *I'm quite sure their silence is only due to them having a busy and exciting time in their new school, but I am so anxious to hear how they are faring and wish to stay in contact with them.*

Reg stopped short on the staircase, unable to read on for he had a sudden sharp pain in his chest and his head felt as if it was about to explode.

'Australia!' he exclaimed. 'The bastards!'

Another prisoner coming up the staircase behind saw Reg stop in his tracks and clutch his chest and reached out to grab him, thinking he was having some sort of seizure. 'What's up, mate?' he asked. 'Shall I call a screw?'

Reg came round enough to see he was holding up the traffic on the staircase, brushed off the other man's hand, muttered something about getting bad news and went on to his cell.

Once inside, sitting on his bunk, he read the letter again, then slumped back to think it over.

It was bad enough when he was told that the convent wouldn't allow his children to write to him in prison, but he accepted it, thinking perhaps the Sisters were right and it would be a bad influence.

'The bastards,' he muttered again, white-hot anger rising inside him. 'Fucking evil bastards,' he ranted to himself, hitting the wall of the cell with his fist in the absence of any face to punch. 'How dare they pack my kids off to the other side of the world and never fucking tell me about it?'

Later that day Reg demanded an interview with the Governor. At five he presented himself at the office, and while he was waiting to be called in, he told himself he must control his temper or he'd get nowhere.

The Governor's name was Friday, a name that was sniggered about all around the prison. Yet 'Man Friday' as he was universally known was a decent sort. He did appear to care about the welfare of the men in his prison, he had been known to bend rules occasionally for deserving cases, he did actually listen properly to complaints, which according to the men who had been in many prisons was very unusual.

At the command to come in, Reg took a deep breath, gave his shoes a quick rub on the back of his trouser legs, and walked in.

'Taylor, three five four oh, sir,' he said, standing smartly to attention in front of Friday's desk.

Friday had the look of an accountant or a bank manager, rather than of a man who had worked his way up through the prison ranks, with his healthy, round shiny face, neatly trimmed moustache and horn-rimmed glasses.

'Well, Taylor, what can I do for you?' he asked. 'If it's a request for more building work I'm sorry, but there is nothing at present.'

'It wasn't that, sir,' Reg said. 'It's about my girls. You see, I've just found out they were sent to Australia.'

He took Susan's letter from his pocket and gave it to the man to read. 'She used to be my Dulcie's teacher,' he explained, then went on to add how much she'd done for both himself and the girls.

'Can they really send my girls away without my permission?' he asked, trying to control the anger rising inside him.

Friday read the letter through a second time, then sat back in his chair and folded his arms. 'Would you have given them permission to go if you had been asked?'

'I don't know,' Reg said. 'I'd have wanted to know a

great deal about where they were planning to take them before I made up my mind.'

'You would probably have wanted to know if you'd be eligible to join them there at the end of your sentence, I expect?' Friday said.

'Well, yes,' Reg said. 'All my plans for the future are with them in mind.'

'Maybe these people knew that, and also knew you would never be eligible to emigrate yourself,' Friday said. 'They might see that as a selfish reason, and not in the children's best interests. It is a land of great opportunity after all. Maybe they didn't want the children to be denied it?'

Reg began to feel irritated that Friday was twisting it to make these people sound right. 'I don't see it that way, sir,' he replied. 'I see a bunch of people stealing my children away from me. Surely getting twelve years and missing them growing up is enough of a punishment without whisking them away so far I'll never get to see them again when I get out.'

'Taylor, this is all me, me, me,' Friday exclaimed, then sighed deeply. 'You must forget your own feelings and think how good it is for them. Orphanages all over England are full to bursting point, there are not enough foster-parents to go round. By the time you are free they will be young women. Look at it logically for a moment – out there they will have a good education, they will have chances they'd never get in England. I can understand that you are upset because you weren't consulted, but surely you want what's best for them?'

'But I don't know that it is, do I?' Reg burst out. 'I wasn't asked or even told that they'd gone. No letters have come from them to me, or to their old teacher. What proof have I got that they are happy?'

'I expect they have been discouraged from writing to you and this Mrs Bankcroft,' Friday said, touching the letter on his desk. 'To save them the pangs of homesickness.

189

I am quite certain that even as we speak they are enjoying a far better life than they ever knew before, and without painful reminders from home they can grow up to be well-adjusted young ladies.'

Reg knew he was on a loser. It was quite clear Man Friday had no idea what it felt like to be banged up in a cell night after night, year after year, without any news of those he loved outside.

'Can I ask then that you just try to find out exactly where they are, and how they are?' Reg asked, trying very hard not to let any aggressiveness come into his voice. 'Surely in God's name as their father I'm entitled to that information?'

'How old are the girls now?' Friday asked.

'Dulcie's eleven, May's coming up for eight.'

The Governor looked thoughtful. 'Well, Taylor, I'll make some inquiries. But stop worrying about your children, I'm sure they are in good hands.'

Reg had a strong urge to thump the man for talking down to him, but knowing that would only get him a spell in solitary confinement and that would kiss goodbye to all chance of getting any help, he suppressed it, thanked the man, and allowed himself to be dismissed.

Back in his cell after supper, Reg planned his letter back to Susan. He knew he would have to word it carefully, without one word of criticism of the Welfare workers or the prison, as it would be censored. Yet at the same time he had to be able to show her subtly how distressed he was, for he thought she was the only person who was likely to help him.

Yet as he read her letter again, including the part he had ignored first thing this morning, when she spoke of her husband, baby and new home, he sensed that she was trying to tell him she wanted no further involvement with him personally.

He wrote two letters and tore them up, unable to get the tone right, and finally slumped down on to his bed, thinking bitter thoughts of Anne. He ought to have killed her, she deserved it for telling him May wasn't his. In those early days after her death he'd tried to convince himself it was her one last lie, and she'd only said it to make him mad enough to throw her out. But once he knew it was Tosh she was having it off with, somehow he knew it was true. If she could let such a maggot screw her in the afternoons and come home again to him, she was capable of anything.

Yet it didn't make him love May any less, knowing he had no part in her creation. He felt no differently about her than he did about Dulcie. He wished he could wipe all that love he felt for the pair of them out of his heart, it would be so much less painful to be locked in here without it. They were so young when he was taken away from them, they'd probably almost forgotten him by now. By the time they were young women and he was free, he'd be nothing but a man with a name the same as theirs, the man responsible for taking their mother away from them.

It was weeks before Dulcie recovered. For the first fortnight she hobbled about, unable to sit down. Yet courage, she found, was admired above all else in Australia, even by the Sisters. They were far kinder than they had been previously, giving her easy jobs which required no bending or stretching, patting her shoulder when they saw her wince with pain. Sister Ruth, one of the gentlest of the nuns, came into the dormitory each night to smooth some ointment over the weals. Even crusty Sister Anne found a cushion for Dulcie to sit on at mealtimes.

Nothing was said, not a word to indicate that they didn't think she deserved such a brutal punishment, but their silent kindness made Dulcie realize they approved of her nobility in taking such a beating for a crime she hadn't committed.

The other girls were sweet to her too, offering to help her dress, supporting her as she limped to the schoolroom. Sometimes she ached to be left alone, to be allowed just to think, for she felt so bruised inside, their compassion made her want to cry. But slowly the wounds healed, and it was good to find she now had a niche in the school, if only as a martyr.

It was May she had the most difficulty with. Dulcie wanted to reject her sister entirely, but she couldn't do that in case that made the other girls realize she was the real culprit. So when May came fawning round her, Dulcie had to be nice to her, and May was smart enough to make sure she was never on her own with her, for fear of getting an earful.

The weeks and months passed, punctuated by Holy Days when at least the food was better. It was good to stand at the window in the dormitory watching rain after so many months of drought, to sleep at night without the intense heat, to see the grass grow again, and plants suddenly shoot up almost overnight. On May's eighth birthday it poured incessantly, and the ground around the dormitories became a lake. One of the girls saw a big snake out on the veranda one morning and screamed so loudly that all the old nuns in the convent opened their windows to see what was going on. The snake slithered away in all the confusion, and for days afterwards all the girls lived in fear that it would come into the dormitory at night.

The kangaroos came closer as the vegetables grew in the garden, they stood by the fence like a group of old men considering if they were brave enough to jump it and get in to have a feast. More and more beautiful birds came down into the garden too, and some of the smallest girls were given the job of acting as human scarecrows to save the vegetables from being eaten.

It seemed no time at all before it was summer again, Dulcie's twelfth birthday, and then Christmas. She could hardly believe they'd been here for fifteen months now, and when she went to Mass and offered up her usual prayer that a letter would come from Susan or her father, she found that this time the thought of them didn't make her cry.

In January of 1951, Sonia was due to leave St Vincent's to work on a sheep station. She and Dulcie had become good friends ever since Sonia's kindness after her beating, and Dulcie felt terribly sad to be losing her. She knew now why the Sisters did their best to break up friendships, for happy children dared to get up to mischief, they plotted against the nuns. Dulcie's keen mind, blended with Sonia's daring and a strong desire to rise above their oppressive life, made the perfect partnership. While outwardly appearing to be subdued, willing and sweet-natured, they won trust. Once they had that they were unstoppable.

Through careful observation the girls discovered that the Sisters over in the convent all went to the chapel at seven in the evening, and it was easy to slip through the back door into their storeroom and help themselves to bread, fruit and cheese, which they smuggled into the dormitory to share with the other girls. No suspicion fell on any of the girls' heads as there was so much food there, and they were careful not to take too much at any one time.

Together they found ways of making the cleaning work easier and even fun, and after supper they organized games out in the paddock which lifted everyone's spirits. In more thoughtful moments Dulcie felt a little ashamed that she was constantly using her mind to outwit the Sisters, when perhaps she should be helping the younger girls with reading and spelling. But as Sonia pointed out on these occasions, a bit of extra food, affection and happiness went a great deal further than a reading lesson.

But on Sonia's last evening at St Vincent's all Dulcie could think about was how she was going to fill the hole in her life that her friend would leave. Suppertime tonight had been bittersweet, for although Sister Ruth had made a special cake and shared it out among the girls, and Sonia had received some little presents from the Sisters, making it almost like a party, there were many sad faces.

Dulcie was waiting out on the veranda by the school-room when Sonia joined her. She had been sent over to the convent after supper to say goodbye to Father Murphy and receive his blessing. The Junior girls had just been sent to bed, and the rest of the girls were playing rounders in the paddock.

'What was the blessing like?' Dulcie asked, trying hard to sound jolly.

'Hardly worth going for,' Sonia grinned. 'The old bastard made me kneel down, put his fat hand on my head and prayed that I'd keep my faith, work hard and remember all the kindness showed to me here. I thought to myself that I could put all the kindness showed to me in this bag and still have room.'

Sonia was holding in her hands a small calico bag, embroidered with poppies, which Sister Ruth had made for her as a going-away present.

Dulcie laughed. Such cynicism was typical of her friend. 'Well, it is a very pretty bag,' she said appreciatively. 'I hope she makes me one when I leave.'

'It's the only present I want to keep,' Sonia said, pulling a face. 'Everything else reminds me of things I'd sooner forget.' She upturned the bag beside Dulcie and spilled out the contents. 'Look!' she said, holding up a small square of towelling. 'That's from Sister Anne, it's a sanitary towel, and she's damn well done such huge blanket stitch round it that it's going to be like wearing sackcloth.'

Dulcie had no real idea what a sanitary towel was. The older girls often mentioned them, but she'd never liked to ask what they were for.

'This one,' Sonia went on, holding up a pin cushion, 'is from Sister Joan, that's going to remind me of all the times she hit me with a hairbrush.'

'What on earth's that?' Dulcie pointed to a tiny cone made of card and decorated with ribbons.

Sonia put it on her head. 'A very small dunce's cap,' she giggled. 'That's from Sister Agatha, she's been telling me I'm stupid since I was five. The old crow said it is for hanging on a dressing table and putting hairpins in. It's going to make me feel dumb for the rest of my life.'

Dulcie laughed, because she sensed that Sonia was actually touched to be given presents and all the scoffing was just bravado.

'Are you glad to be going?' she asked.

'Don't know really.' Sonia's grin vanished. 'I've hated it here for so long, but now I really can go it's scary. They might be even meaner to me at the sheep station.'

'But you can always leave if they are,' Dulcie said. 'You could go to Perth and get a job there.'

Sonia gave her a strange look. 'Do you know how far away things are from one another in Australia?' she asked.

'It's only about twenty miles to Perth from here,' Dulcie said. She'd picked that up from Sister Ruth.

'Well, the sheep station is five hundred miles from here,' Sonia said. 'That's a long way to walk. Besides, you have to stay until you are eighteen, or you get picked up by the police and taken to the reformatory.'

Dulcie's eyes widened. The reformatory was the Sisters' favourite threat and she knew the girls that got sent there had to work in a laundry which was like hell.

'I didn't know you couldn't leave until you were eighteen,' she gasped.

'Neither did I, not until Mother told me. Evil cow, she said it like she hoped I'd run away and get taken there. Anyway, even if I could get to Perth, what sort of job could I do there? I don't read good like you do.'

'You could work in a shop or a factory,' Dulcie said, thinking of jobs she remembered girls and women doing back home in England. 'You could be a nurse, you're good when people feel poorly.'

'I hardly know what a shop is. I've never been in one,' Sonia replied, her face darkening. 'Don't even know what a factory is, 'cept they make things. I don't wanna be a nurse, that's like being a nun. It's different for you, Dulcie, you know about stuff like that, you've seen it. I haven't. The only two places I've ever been to is here, and the place before I was five. I've never been on a train, a bus, I don't know anything.'

'I don't even know about men,' Sonia went on. 'All we get to see here is the priest and the Abo that cuts the grass. Sister Ruth tried to explain stuff to me about men, 'cos there'll be lots on the station, but I reckon she don't know much herself, she said I wasn't to let them try on any funny stuff, whatcha think that means?'

Dulcie didn't answer immediately. Gus, the Aborigine man who cut the grass, was nice, he often brought a few sweets in to give to the kids, he smiled all the time, even the Sisters liked him because he was so helpful. Yet she knew perfectly well he wasn't representative of all males. She remembered her granny's sarcastic comments about men – she had mostly felt they weren't to be trusted.

Aside from her own father and Duncan, Dulcie had hardly given the male sex a thought since she'd been here, and she racked her brain to think of what Sister Ruth might have meant by 'funny stuff'.

'Well, men can give you babies,' she said eventually.

'I know that, but that's when you're married,' Sonia giggled.

'You can have babies without being married,' Dulcie said, remembering what a girl back at the Sacred Heart had told her not long before she left for Australia. 'But if you do it when you aren't married you get called a tart or a whore.'

Sonia giggled at Dulcie using such words. 'You know everything,' she said admiringly. 'I won't try and find out then. But come on now, let's go and see who's winning at the rounders.'

It was much later that night, when once again Dulcie couldn't sleep for the heat, that she remembered she and Sonia hadn't even talked about whether they'd ever see each other again. Perhaps that was because they knew they wouldn't. It was bad enough here sometimes, but at least they all had one another. What would it be like to be sent out to work and not know one person anywhere?

Dulcie imagined the map of Australia hanging up in the schoolroom, and recalled that Sister Ruth had made a dot on it to show them all where Sonia was going. It looked such a little way away, but if it was five hundred miles, just how big was the whole country?

Her last thought before she fell asleep was how ignorant she was. All the other girls thought she knew so much, but she didn't, not really. Her world was limited to the area inside the fences of St Vincent's, what the Sisters told her, the few books she'd read, and the voyage from England to here. It didn't amount to much.

Chapter Ten

1954

'It doesn't seem possible that you've been here four years,' Sister Ruth said as she took the last pin from her lips and put it in the hem of Dulcie's dress.

Dulcie was standing on a chair, out on the veranda by the schoolroom. She'd made the blue cotton dress herself with instruction from Sister, in preparation for leaving to work on a farm in a place called Salmon Gums, hundreds of miles away down at the bottom of Western Australia.

Although the dress was only a simple short-sleeved style with a full gathered skirt, very like the St Vincent uniform, Dulcie was just pleased to have a new dress that wasn't green, and the white ricrac trimming on the neckline and sleeves made it look a bit more grown-up.

In four years the only real change in her appearance was that she'd grown to five feet four. She was still thin, still had the same uniform hair-style as all the girls, and the childish dress hid that she was developing a young woman's body. Yet despite the unflattering hair-style and clothes, she was pretty. Her big blue eyes, peaches-and-cream complexion, and the warmth of her wide smile made her so. Yet even though some of the kindlier Sisters often remarked between themselves that she would grow into a beauty, such things never reached Dulcie's ears, and she considered herself plain.

'I'm going to miss you,' Dulcie said hesitantly. Sister Ruth had always been the most decent of the Sisters, and in the last eighteen months she'd come to see her as a woman rather than just a nun, and discovered she was as much a victim of circumstance as she was herself.

Sister Ruth's dark eyes twinkled as she took Dulcie's hand to help her down from the chair. 'I shall miss you too,' she said. 'There isn't anyone else I can talk to about books or England. May isn't made of the same stuff as you at all.'

Dulcie hadn't realized for some time that Sister Ruth was English, for she'd been sent out to Australia with the Sisters of Mercy back in the thirties, and she'd picked up the Australian accent. One day when they were working alone together in the kitchen, Sister Ruth had spoken of London, and it transpired that she'd spent her childhood in Lewisham.

To find they were both from South London created a bond between them and they enjoyed sharing memories of places like Blackheath and Greenwich Park. As their friendship became closer, Sister Ruth admitted that becoming a nun wasn't so much her choice or a true calling as the result of a fear of the outside world.

Her father was killed in the Great War, and her mother, unable to cope alone with six children, put Ruth and her two sisters in a Catholic orphanage, keeping only the boys. Ruth said she was twelve at the time, a timid, sickly child, and when she reached fourteen and had the choice of either leaving to go into service or staying at the orphanage to help with the younger children, she chose the latter because it seemed safer. Eventually she was persuaded by her Mother Superior to take Holy Orders herself.

'Will you keep an eye on May for me?' Dulcie asked. She was due to leave in three days' time, and although she had a great many fears about leaving St Vincent's, losing touch with May was the biggest. Maybe she and her sister weren't as close as they had been when they were little, but all they had in the world was each other. Just the thought of not seeing May each day made Dulcie's stomach churn with anxiety.

She had made May promise that in three years' time,

when she was fifteen, she would let Dulcie know where she was being sent to work. Dulcie would be free to move on from her job then, and it was her hope that she could find a new one somewhere near May, and that eventually they could make a home somewhere together.

'You just stop fretting about your sister,' Sister Ruth chuckled. 'You know as well as I do that she's more than capable of looking after herself, she can charm the birds out of the trees.'

Dulcie frowned. Everyone had always said that about May right since she was tiny. She *was* charming, funny, vivacious and self-confident, but there was a dark side to her that few people were aware of. She was deceitful, cunning, greedy and wilful, and Dulcie was afraid that free from her restraining influence, and without her to cover up some of her misdeeds, she might get herself into serious trouble. There had been many more incidents like the one with the tin of toffees over the years and someone was always punished, but Dulcie had been certain in most cases that May was the real culprit.

May led a charmed life at St Vincent's, for she'd learnt to wind most of the Sisters around her little finger. Her cheeky, expressive face with those big, innocent-looking blue eyes had even captivated Reverend Mother, and she often took May to town with her in her car.

Almost every time May returned from one of these trips, she had something – a toy, a book, a bottle of scent – and though she always claimed they'd been given to her, Dulcie was sure she'd stolen them. Yet even more worrying was the way her sister played people off against one another. She started whispers to smear someone's character or cause trouble so cleverly that no one but Dulcie ever realized she was the perpetrator. It was as though she had to be the top dog at all costs, and if she couldn't be that with just her natural charm, she'd destroy the competition.

'What is it about May that worries you so much, Dulcie?' Sister Ruth asked, concerned by her frown.

'Because I know she isn't all she seems,' Dulcie blurted

out. Out of loyalty she would never have admitted such a thing to anyone else, but she had learnt she could trust Sister Ruth with confidences.

The nun put a comforting hand on her shoulder. 'I know she isn't,' she said softly. 'May is one of those people who will go through life taking exactly what she wants, by fair means or foul. I know you love her, but you are not responsible for her, and my advice to you now is that you should forget about her, do the best you can at your job, make a life for yourself.'

Dulcie was shocked to hear gentle Sister Ruth say such a thing. 'I can't forget her, she's my sister!'

'I know I'm right, Dulcie,' Sister Ruth insisted. 'So take my advice, dear, and look out for yourself. That's what May will do.'

On Dulcie's last afternoon at St Vincent's she was excused schoolwork and chores, and while the other girls were still in the classrooms she wandered around mentally saying goodbye to everything. She was surprised that she felt a little sad, for almost everywhere she looked there were far more bad memories than good. The gravel path where she was forced to crawl, the laundry room, schoolroom, convent and indeed the dormitories, were all tainted with recollections of pain, humiliation and cruelty. As she walked along the verandas she couldn't even count the splinters she'd got in her feet before they became as hard as car tyres. She could almost hear herself crying at night with fear, hunger and loneliness. Yet she had survived it, learnt to outwit the meaner Sisters, and even managed to find some happiness.

St Vincent's wasn't quite such a harsh place now, not compared with how it had been for her as a new girl. The food had improved in the last two years, new books and equipment had been bought for the school, the Sisters weren't quite so obsessed with breaking up friendships, and on several occasions the girls had even been taken in a truck to a beach for a picnic. Yet the punishments were every bit as cruel. Only a few days ago two eight-year-olds who had recently arrived from England had tried to run away. They were picked up within a few hours and brought back to be caned and have their heads shaved. Dulcie couldn't understand how anyone could treat homesick children so badly.

Yet now that she was leaving she found herself getting a little sentimental. The painted mural of the Virgin Mary on the veranda outside the schoolroom, the balustrade they dared each other to balance on like tightrope-walkers, both looked dear to her. She would never again hear the sound of chanted multiplication tables or run out into the paddock when the first autumn rain came.

She smiled to herself, amused that she had found anything she'd miss. Soon she would be seeing ordinary people, quite different to the patronizing do-gooders who came here to tut over the poor motherless children and hand out a few sweets. Her new life wouldn't be dominated by prayers and the constant reminders of sin. She would see pubs on her way through Perth, ordinary houses where families lived. There would be shops, ladies wearing makeup and high heels, mothers pushing prams, all that stuff she remembered from England.

Yet as Sonia had said three years ago, it was scary to leave. There was no way of knowing if this job was going to be a good one, or a worse nightmare, for Reverend Mother had picked it for her, and however nice she was to May, she'd always been mean to Dulcie.

Just last September an old girl called Mary came back to visit St Vincent's. Dulcie hadn't known her, for Mary had left here before she arrived. But because Dulcie was the oldest girl they had talked, and Mary told her that the sheep station she was sent to when she was fifteen worked her so hard she thought she would die of it. She warned Dulcie that Australians in the main ridiculed Poms, and saw all kids from orphanages as slave labour, there to be abused in every way. She talked about one of the station hands trying to have his way with her all the time. She warned Dulcie never to allow herself to be alone with any man, and to scream loudly and keep her legs clamped tight together if one caught hold of her. That had frightened Dulcie badly for a while, and it was still in her mind now. She wondered if just clamping your legs together was enough to prevent a man from raping you.

Dulcie tried not to think about her mother, father or Susan now, yet now and again she would have a vivid flash of them, as clear as if it had all happened last year. She often wondered if her father and Susan ever thought about her and May, and why they had just abandoned them. But it was only Granny she liked to remember, imagining her sitting on her stool on the doorstep when it was hot, chatting to her neighbours, the way she used to smack her lips when she had her nightly glass of stout. Funny, unimportant little pictures that came out of nowhere, and she'd hear her voice, smell that old lady smell, and feel the warmth and comfort of her arms.

May never spoke of any of them any more, she seemed to have forgotten it all entirely. Dulcie wished it could be that way with her too, but those teasing memories remained, often catching her unawares. Maybe they always would.

Dulcie looked through the gates for old times' sake. When she first came here she used to do this every time she was sent out on weeding duty, sometimes even considering running away. There had been nothing but St Vincent's in the lane then, but a year ago they'd started to build houses along it. She thought they looked very grand, with their posh verandas and big gardens, even if they were all on one floor, not proper two-storey ones like back home. Sister Ruth confessed she'd chatted to one of the new owners and got a tour of inspection, and had been astounded that they had two bathrooms, a washing-machine with an electric wringer, and the first television she'd ever seen.

Dulcie sighed as she turned away to go back and find the other girls. She hadn't ever seen a television either, but she imagined it was a bit like going to the pictures in your own living-room. She wondered if there would be a cinema in Salmon Gums.

There was a hotel in Salmon Gums, a big, quite splendid-looking building, but it was closed, along with the post office and two shops. The road going through Salmon Gums was just a gravel one, and when Dulcie found no one waiting to meet her she had walked a little way along it to see a school, still closed for the holidays, a yard with a couple of grain silos and a hall which appeared to be used for film shows, but she hadn't seen a single person apart from the station master when she got off the train, and even he had disappeared now.

It was late afternoon and swelteringly hot even in the shade of a tree, and the clock viewed through the post-office window showed she had been waiting for over an hour. Her feet were throbbing in the tight new shoes she'd been given when she left St Vincent's and she was hungry, thirsty, dirty and exhausted.

She idly picked at the SS *Maloja* luggage label stuck on the suitcase beside her. While the label itself brought back many good memories of the long, exciting voyage, it was also a sharp reminder that she and all the children who set out so eagerly from England had been cheated and lied to. The case held even less than she'd left England with – her old St Vincent's striped uniform dress, a cardigan, two nightdresses and two sets of underwear. There were a few presents from the Sisters, an embroidered bag from Sister Ruth, very like the one she had made Sonia, a tablet of scented soap from Sister Grace, and little handmade presents from some of her friends. Yet two days ago as she packed these little treasures and the five shillings she'd been given as pocket money for the trip into the embroidered bag, she had been so confident about her future. Even when Sister Ruth left her on Perth station after buying her a ticket to Salmon Gums, she'd felt excited and happy just to be let out of St Vincent's.

But all that confidence and excitement soon left her during the long and awful journey here. She had nothing but a shilling left now, and no one anywhere to turn to. If Mr Masters didn't arrive to collect her, she had no idea what she was going to do. She hunched her knees up under her dress, leaned forward on to them and sobbed.

The train had left Perth at seven in the evening and travelled on through that night to Coolgardie, for the connection to Salmon Gums. It was impossible to sleep on the hard seats and she had spent most of the time scared out of her wits by the other passengers, mostly male and many of them very drunk.

She had had the idea that once beyond Coolgardie the countryside would lose its desert-like appearance and become green and lush, like farmland she remembered in England. It was a bitter disappointment to see nothing more than miles and miles of stony, dry ground with sparse clumps of scorched grass and weary-looking gum trees. Whenever the train stopped at a small halt she would see a few houses, but they were mainly little more than wooden huts with tin roofs, at best like the prefabs she remembered back home after the war. Chickens pecked about by some of them, and now and again she saw a few sheep. In one place called Norseman she saw a man on a tractor hauling a heavy-looking chain across ground close to the railway. It appeared to be a way of clearing the ground of the big stones and old tree stumps, and just the vast area he had yet to clear made her heart sink further because it looked such an impossible place to attempt to grow anything.

When finally she got to Salmon Gums, there was no one waiting for her.

The sound of a car engine made Dulcie look up. A black pick-up truck was coming up the road, a cloud of red dust billowing around it. She hoped this was Mr Masters, so she gave her face a quick wipe with her hanky and stood up.

The truck stopped right by her. The driver had protruding teeth and a broad-brimmed leather hat. He didn't get out, and looked her up and down before speaking.

'You the kid from the orphanage?' he asked.

'Yes,' she said, picking up her case. 'Dulcie Taylor. Are you Mr Masters?'

'Nope,' he said. 'Just come to get you. Get in.'

Dulcie was hardly seated before he swung the truck round in the middle of the road and drove off in the direction he'd come.

The road was a wide gravel one, but before long the man turned off it into a narrower, far more pitted one lined with gum trees. Between the trees Dulcie could see sheep grazing.

'How far is it?' she ventured. The land was so flat and the sun so bright she felt she was viewing infinity and she couldn't see a house anywhere.

'Twenty miles maybe,' came the grunted reply.

The man stank, not just of sweat but as though he'd been wearing his checked shirt and stained trousers for years without washing them, and he smoked continuously. Dulcie sensed he didn't like women, so she didn't dare ask him anything else.

As they drove along in silence Dulcie felt panic rising inside her. Back at St Vincent's she'd been the cleverest girl there. Even Reverend Mother in one of her rare nice moments had complimented her on her thirst for knowledge and allowed her to borrow books from the convent library, an honour it was said that few other girls had been given. But now, alone with this smelly, sullen man, she could see that the works of Jane Austen, Charlotte Brontë and Charles Dickens had neither prepared her nor would help her in any way in this vast empty place. Even *A Town Like Alice* by Nevil Shute, which was at least contemporary and set mainly in Australia, had given her a false impression of the outback. She had devoured that book, imagining herself as the English girl who meets the brave Australian soldier out in Malaya and subsequently tracks him down to Australia. But now as they bumped along this hot, dusty road, she was reminded that the English girl in the book had been rich and middle-class, not a little penniless ex-orphanage girl, and she began to cry again.

'Christ almighty, don't start blubbing on me,' the man said suddenly, making her start.

'I'm sorry,' she said and sniffed back her tears. 'I'm just scared.'

He gave her a sideways glance. 'You're a bit small and skinny,' he said. 'You'll have to stand up for yerself with the Masters or they'll work you to death.'

That was the last thing Dulcie wanted to hear but she bit back further tears. 'How many other people work for them?' she asked, trying to control the quiver in her voice.

'Three of us clearing the ground right now.'

Dulcie remembered the man on the tractor and her heart sank even further. She had imagined a farm to be like the ones back in England, pretty orchards with sheep grazing under the trees, fields of waving golden wheat and a pond with ducks. 'You mean it's not a real farm yet?'

'They only got the land a couple of years ago,' he said, swatting away a fly from his eyes. 'We got a mob of sheep, and chooks, but can't grow nothing till we've got the land cleared and dug the dams.'

Dulcie was puzzled. You *built* dams across rivers, not dug them. What did he mean?

She took a chance and asked him.

'To catch the rain of course,' he said, looking sideways at her as if she was stupid.

Dulcie explained what a dam was to her.

'Oh, we ain't got no rivers or wells out here,' he said. 'All we get is the rain, and there ain't much of that, so we have to save what we can.'

He went on to say how they dug a big hole then waited for rain to fill it up.

Dulcie couldn't possibly imagine how that would serve any useful purpose, for surely all the water would evaporate in the sun, or disappear back into the ground. But she said nothing, after all she knew nothing of farming.

He turned off the long straight track later, and then she saw a sign with a name on it as if it led to a farm. This happened again later too, but in neither case did she see a house. Then they slowed down and turned at a sign which said 'Masters'.

'Is this it?' she asked. All the way here, behind the gum trees which lined the track, the land had been at least partially cleared. But this part was real bush – trees, boulders and sparse clumps of grass just like she'd seen earlier today from the train window.

'Yup, this is Masters' place,' he said, tipping his hat back and lighting up yet another cigarette. 'Four thousand acres.'

Acres meant little to Dulcie, but she remembered being told once that the big cattle stations up in the Northern Territory could be 200,000 acres or more, so she supposed this was small by Australian standards.

Finally she saw a barn in the distance and she assumed the house was there too, though hidden by the trees surrounding it. Dejected as she was, she leaned forward to catch her first sight of it, but as the man drove the truck in between two dense bushes, and she saw it, her heart plummeted.

The house wasn't much better than a shack made of wooden shingle, with a veranda all around it and a tin roof. The shingles were just grey wood, so old and weatherbeaten that many of them were warped. The veranda posts looked as though you could lean on them and they'd collapse. But for a washing-line with a few shirts and trousers hanging on it to dry at the side of the house, she might have thought it had been abandoned.

'Go on round the back and knock on the door,' the man said. 'Don't mind the dogs, they won't hurt you.' He leaped out of the truck and disappeared into thick bushes before she could say anything.

The dogs he mentioned came running round from the back of the house as Dulcie got out gingerly. One was a dark russet colour, the other black, and they looked capable of eating her alive. But they didn't bark or come running up to her, just stood there looking curiously at her.

Dulcie's whole being wanted to walk away from there, she knew without even setting foot in the house or meeting the owners that this was going to be misery far beyond the level of St Vincent's. Worse still, she had a feeling that Mother had known what it would be like and had sent her purposely.

But she couldn't walk away. It would be dark within a couple of hours, she'd never find her way back over twenty miles to Salmon Gums, and even if she got there, a few shillings wouldn't even buy a ticket to the next halt, let alone a real town. So there was nothing for it but to stay.

The dogs just looked at her as she skirted around the house and went up the steps to the veranda to knock on the back. The door was just a fly-screen, so Dulcie saw the tall, very thin woman coming even before she opened it.

'You'll be the girl from the orphanage,' she said. Her hands were floury and she wiped at her sweaty forehead with her forearm.

Dulcie nodded, intimidated even further by the woman's harsh voice. 'I'm Dulcie Taylor.'

'Well, don't stand there looking like a great galah,' the woman snapped. 'I'm Pat Masters, and there's spuds waiting to be peeled. Got an apron?'

'Yes, Mrs Masters, in my case,' Dulcie said. She couldn't believe the woman wouldn't ask her in and offer her a drink before ordering her to get out her apron.

'Well, get it out and put it on,' the woman said impatiently. 'And for Christ's sakes don't bloody well call me Mrs Masters. It's Pat.'

Dulcie was shocked to hear such profanity, that was a caning offence back in St Vincent's.

She put her case down and took out her apron and she was just putting it on when Pat came out with an enamel bowl with some potatoes and a saucepan filled with water to put them in once peeled. She dumped them on the ground and pulled out a knife from her pocket. 'Do them here, it's cooler than the kitchen. Don't go hacking off great lumps either,' she said curtly. 'And do them fast.' With that she went back inside, the screen door slamming behind her.

Dulcie's throat was so dry she could easily have drunk the whole saucepan full of water before her, yet she didn't dare do that or go and ask for a drink, not until she'd finished the potatoes. They didn't take her very long as she was well used to doing this chore, but because of her thirst it seemed forever. When she had finished she took courage in both hands and walked into the kitchen without knocking first. Pat merely glanced at the potatoes and told her to put them on the stove to boil.

It was incredibly hot and gloomy in the kitchen, and as the temperature outside had to be in the nineties, Dulcie reckoned it must be over 110 inside. She felt she might just faint if she didn't get a drink quickly.

'May I have a drink of water, please?' she blurted out.

'You can see where the tap is,' Pat snapped.

Dulcie filled a cup standing on the draining board and as she drank deeply she watched Pat rolling out pastry on the table. She made her think of Olive Oyl, Popeye's girlfriend, for she was so thin her hip-bones protruded through her thin sleeveless dress, and she had her dark hair pulled up tightly into a straggly bun. It was impossible to guess her age, she could have been anything between thirty and forty-five, but as her leathery skin was unlined, appearing to be stretched too tight over angular cheek-bones, Dulcie thought she was on the younger end of the scale and her worn look was due to a very hard life.

'You can wash up those dishes now,' Pat barked at her, the moment she'd put the cup down. She indicated a pile of dirty pots and pans on the draining board. 'There's hot water on the stove, and mind you don't waste it, water's precious out here.'

'May I take my shoes off?' Dulcie asked timidly. Pat had bare feet, or she wouldn't have dared ask.

Pat nodded, looking her up and down. 'You'll need to wear them outside though, there's snakes.'

The relief of taking them off was so great Dulcie didn't care about the snake warning, but she was put off by the filthy floor. It didn't appear to have been washed or even swept for weeks – as she went back to the sink she could feel crumbs and bits of meat under her feet.

In fact, once she felt brave enough to look around her, she saw that the whole kitchen was filthy. The walls and windows were thick with grease and dust and when she put the clean pots and pans away in the cupboard she noticed the newspaper lining the shelves was choc-olate-brown with age. Yet even more depressing was the sight of a row of hurricane lamps on a shelf, for that meant no electricity, and therefore the stove must be fuelled by wood. Yet they had a refrigerator – she saw Pat opening it – and she wondered what it ran on, but didn't like to ask for fear of looking stupid.

Pat spoke only once as Dulcie washed up, and that was first to inform her where the 'dunny' was, down the path by the back door and tucked behind a bush, then she said the pie she was making was rabbit, and the three men and her husband Bill came in for their meal at six.

Pat disappeared into a room off the kitchen the minute she'd put the pie into the oven, so Dulcie took it that she was to clean the table, because the men would be eating there.

She had been very hungry earlier, but the heat, dirt and exhaustion were making her feel queasy. She wiped the surplus flour off the table, then set to work to give it a good scrub.

Pat returned just as the table was drying. She merely glanced at it, making no comment. 'Lay it up for supper,' she ordered.

'How many for?' Dulcie asked.

'I've already told you once,' Pat barked. 'Three men and Bill, that's four, or can't you count?'

Dulcie wanted to cry then, but she was determined not

to. 'What about you?' she asked, thinking what about me too, but not daring to go that far.

'I can't eat a cooked meal in this heat,' Pat replied, as if that was Dulcie's fault. 'I eat later, and you'll get yours after the men finish.'

It was nine o'clock when Dulcie was finally shown where she was to sleep, and by then she could hardly move with exhaustion.

The men had come in at six, at which time Pat had curtly introduced her as 'the girl'. But she might just as well not have bothered because none of them responded, they didn't even look directly at her.

They were a sorry-looking bunch, they stank of sweat, they were unshaven and filthy. They didn't even wash their hands, just sat down, grabbed their knives and forks and began eating. Never in her life had Dulcie seen people eat in such a disgusting manner – they shovelled the food in, chewed it noisily with their mouths wide open, speared potatoes with their knives, and mopped up gravy with their bread.

Fortunately it was over very quickly, four plates mopped as clean as if they'd already been washed. Then they went out on to the back veranda for beer and cigarettes.

Not one of them spoke to Dulcie or to Pat, not even to thank her when she gave them second helpings. Perhaps they believed that their loud belches as they finished were enough appreciation for her cooking.

Dulcie gathered that the big dark-haired man was Bill Masters, as he was the one who did most of the talking about the next day's work. He looked about forty, and slightly ape-like, with a narrow brow, thick lips, swarthy skin and disproportionally long arms.

Jake was the name of the man with the protruding teeth who had picked her up from the station. When he'd removed his hat she saw he had little hair and some horrible red scabs on his scalp that made her feel even more queasy. He appeared to have no status amongst the group, keeping his eyes down at all times.

The other two men were so alike, heavy built, with red hair and beards to match that she thought they must be brothers, but she didn't catch their names. She wondered if they were relatives of Bill because he wasn't as curt with them as he was with Jake. Yet whatever their own peculiarities in appearance, to a man they were all coarse types with cold humourless eyes, sun-baked faces and bad teeth, their Australian accents far more pronounced than any she'd heard back at St Vincent's.

Then Pat dished up her meal. It was the scrapings of the pie crust from around the dish, about a tablespoon full of rabbit filling, two small potatoes, nothing more. 'Wash up afterwards,' was all she said, and disappeared into the other room again, taking one of the lamps with her.

Dulcie just looked at the plate and tears ran down her cheeks. It was probably better-quality food than she'd had at St Vincent's, and around the same amount, yet it was the insult behind it which hurt. It was just the leftovers, and cold now, and it stated that Pat regarded her as on a level with the dogs outside.

The men left the veranda while Dulcie was washing up, she heard the sound of a car starting up and moving away. She looked out of the back door, trying to summon up the courage to run across to the 'dunny', as Pat had called it, but it was pitch-black outside and so quiet she was too scared to go without a torch and she didn't dare take a lamp in case she tripped and broke it. As Pat hadn't reappeared to give her any further instructions, she swept and scrubbed the kitchen floor.

Pat came back to her just as she'd finished, looked down at the floor but made no comment. 'I'll show you where your bed is,' she said, yawning as if even that was really too much trouble. 'You'll remember the way to the dunny, follow the smell.'

That appeared to be an attempt at humour, but in

Dulcie's exhausted state she couldn't find it funny, and as Pat led the way out through the back door, carrying the lamp, her heart almost stopped in terror.

'Have I got to sleep outside?' she exclaimed.

Pat turned to her. In the yellowish glow of the hurricane lamp, her thin taut face looked sinister. Big moths, attracted to the light, swooped around her head, making her even more frightening.

'You ain't a guest,' she said. 'You're here to work. Workers sleep outside.'

Dulcie's case was still where she'd left it on her arrival and she picked it up and meekly followed Pat along the veranda round to the far side of the house. It was too dark now to see whether there were more outbuildings beyond the faint beam of light, or just bush. But as they turned the corner of the house, Dulcie saw a kind of lean-to shed built right on the veranda.

'This is your room,' Pat said, pulling open the door. 'When you hear the bell in the morning get up sharpish. There's a sink to wash in on the other side.'

Pat was gone before Dulcie could say a word, but she'd had enough time to see a windowless area no bigger than eight by seven containing nothing more than a truckle-bed, a stained mattress, a pillow and a lone blanket.

As Pat retreated back along the veranda, taking the only light with her, Dulcie was too stunned even to cry. She'd been fed scraps like the dogs, now she was expected to sleep like one too, to fumble her way in the dark into a bed that didn't even have sheets. What had she ever done to deserve such callous treatment?

She stood there for some little time in the darkness, reluctant to go into the shed for fear of spiders or other nasty creepy crawlies, yet afraid to stay outside too. Swaying on her feet with exhaustion, she finally succumbed to the bed, lying down on it fully clothed, but as the smell of stale urine wafted out of the mattress she began to sob.

*

By the end of February, after seven weeks with the Masters, Dulcie had only one constant thought, and that was how to make her escape. Each time she heard the sound of a motor her heart would quicken. Yet it was always only Bill Masters' truck or Ted's or Jake's motorbike, never a stranger who might be distracted long enough for her to slip on to the back of the truck and be taken back as far as Salmon Gums and the train.

No one came here, it was like being marooned on a desert island.

Never before had she seen such vast, intimidating emptiness. She could walk in any direction from the house and see nothing but miles and miles of land stretching right to the horizon where it met the harsh blue cloudless sky. Even the gum trees had a melancholy, stunted appearance, as if they'd struggled to survive but had almost lost the will to do so.

She'd worked hard enough at the orphanage, but looking back at that was like viewing a blissful holiday compared with what she was expected to do here. From six in the morning until nine or ten at night she never had a moment's respite from heavy labour, or one kind word.

By the end of the second day here she had found out why the house was so dirty and neglected. Pat didn't only do the cooking, cleaning and washing, she had to work outside too, as hard as any of the men, and Dulcie had to join her.

Dulcie didn't count feeding the chooks or milking the two rather scrawny cows as real work, she liked both jobs, and milking the cows was remarkably soothing and satisfying once she'd got the hang of it. She didn't mind cleaning the house either, for there was some satisfaction to be had in making windows sparkle and floors shine.

The wood-chopping was exhausting, every day a huge basket had to be filled, and as the stove would only take small pieces of around six or seven inches in length, the trees and roots the men had cleared on the land had to be

215

chopped or sawn into small pieces. That was hard, but it was the work on the vegetable patch which she hated.

There were no vegetables yet. Bill had cut down the trees and fenced in a plot of land close to the house for this purpose. Pat and Dulcie were expected to prepare it for planting.

It was only about the size of a tennis court, but it was full of stones and old tree roots. After the wood-chopping they worked on it until around mid-afternoon, with only a short break to prepare something cold for the men's midday meal. The ground was like concrete, they had to break it up with a pick-axe before digging it, then rake it, carting the stones in a wheelbarrow to make a drive in front of the house. The roots went for burning on the stove.

Huge blisters came up on Dulcie's hands, dirt got into them once they burst and they wouldn't heal. The constant bent position made her back ache intolerably and most days the temperature went over 100 degrees. Pat had given Dulcie a pair of old trousers and a long-sleeved shirt to wear, and an old-fashioned cotton sunbonnet to protect the back of her neck, but there was no sympathy for her aching muscles, sore hands and the infernal barrage of flies in her eyes and mouth.

Many times in the first few days Dulcie had looked at Pat's cold, dead eyes, mean, narrow lips and skinny body and hated her in a way she'd never thought herself capable of.

It was easy to put all the blame on Pat, for she was the one she had to spend all the time with, and Dulcie knew nothing about men anyway. But by the end of the second week, Dulcie had made observations about the whole group, and by listening to their conversations at mealtimes, and asking one or other of them the occasional carefully worded question, she had begun to see a bigger picture.

She gathered that the two red-headed men, Bert and Ted, were Bill's cousins and were in the throes of claiming the adjoining lot of land to his. While for now they were helping Bill clear his land, the long-term intention was to work the two parcels of land as one, machinery, labour and profits shared.

The Masters' land had once been owned by a veteran of the First World War. He had built the homestead, cleared a small portion of the land, then the Depression in the thirties came and like so many other farmers at that time, he just gave up and went back to the city to find work to feed his family. It had lain idle right up until 1952 when Bill had bought it on a conditional purchase at 1s 6d an acre because he was an ex-serviceman. From what Dulcie could gather from overheard conversations, money was very tight now, for Bill had borrowed the money for sheep, machinery, water tanks, and seed and fertilizer for the autumn planting. He was banking on the sheep producing many lambs this year, and a good harvest in the spring, but if there was little rain during the winter, the sheep would starve, the wheat and barley wouldn't grow and he would be bankrupt.

On the land Bert and Ted were after there was another homestead, though by all accounts it was in a worse condition than this one. They slept there, doing a little work on it from time to time, but they had all their meals with Bill and Pat, and brought their laundry to the house to be washed. Jake lived somewhere else again, Dulcie got the idea he had some family around here and went back to them at night. She also thought his lowly status in the group was the result of his owning no land of his own.

There was no doubt that Bill Masters was a brute. He treated his wife with utter contempt – it seemed to Dulcie that he'd only married her to have an unpaid housekeeper, and a whipping boy when things went wrong. After his evening meal he drove off with the men to the hotel at Salmon Gums, or to Bert and Ted's place where they played cards. When he came home late at night, drunk, Dulcie often heard him shouting at Pat, and the sound of slaps. Yet worst of all was hearing him raping her.

The first time she heard the loud squeaking noise and

Pat sobbing, she hadn't understood what was going on. She had strained her ears in the darkness of the lean-to, wondering what Bill was doing to his wife. But just a couple of days later she had been turning the mattress on the couple's old iron bed and she had heard the same squeaking noise again, and like a bolt of lightning it came to her.

Even in her ignorance of married love and all that entailed, she knew all too well that Pat was being taken by force, for the heart-rending sobs continued long after the squeaking ended. She began to notice the bruising on Pat more and more, sometimes livid red marks on her throat the next day, or a swollen eye. She wondered why Pat didn't run away and leave him.

It wasn't as if there was any comfort in the house. When Dulcie had got to see the rest of it on her first morning she was shocked by the starkness of it. Pat and Bill's bedroom held the bed, a large chest of drawers and a wardrobe, nothing more, not a rug on the bare boards, a bedside light, a picture or any feminine fripperies like she remembered her mother and granny having. Even the blankets on the bed were the harsh grey army kind, with no counterpane to cover them. The other bedroom was empty but for another iron bedstead.

The main room was large, taking up most of the front of the house, and the coolest room of all as the veranda kept it in deep shade and the screen door stood open all day to catch any breeze. There were two couches and three armchairs, all of them extremely shabby and she suspected left by the previous owners, a table and chairs which didn't match, a bookcase containing nothing but farming books, and a desk littered with papers. A wood-burning stove stood in one corner, a small rug before it, and a box for wood. Not a photograph, an ornament, or even a clock, and as in all the rooms the wood walls were whitewashed, but so long ago that they had turned yellow, sprinkled with the crushed bodies of insects.

Between the kitchen, and the outside wall where Dulcie's lean-to was, was what passed for a bathroom. Like the kitchen, it was filthy until she cleaned it, and held nothing but a primitive cold-water shower set above an old china sink. The procedure for showering was to take a basin of water warmed on the stove, wash all over, then shower it off with cold. While this was no hardship while it was so hot, Dulcie wondered what it would be like in the winter. All the waste water from here ran through a pipe into another tank outside, where it was reused for washing clothes.

Water, or the lack of it, was the real enemy here, Dulcie soon found, and she was impressed by Bill's devices to save every drop of rain that fell. The house, barns, sheds and even the dunny roof had tanks attached to guttering and downpipes. His 'dams', as Jake had described them, were effective, for Bill worked out how much would evaporate a year and adjusted the catchment area to compensate. That water was used for animals and crops, but the rainwater from the roof of the house went through a filtering system for drinking.

However impressed Dulcie might be that people had the stamina and the tenacity to take on a huge area of bush and turn it into farmland, she could find absolutely nothing to like about these people. They had hearts as stony as the ground, they ate and lived like animals, without one speck of tenderness for anything or anyone. The men had only one topic of conversation between them and that was farming, their tractors, sheep and the work in progress on the land to put in crops. In all the time she'd been here she hadn't heard one of them tell a joke, pass on a bit of gossip, or once turn to Pat and compliment her on her cooking.

There was no doubt Pat's life was grim – she couldn't drive, she appeared to have no friends or family, and all the provisions, kerosene for the lamps and refrigerator, mail and other essentials were mostly picked up by one of the men, usually Jake. That was the only sympathy Dulcie had for her though, because Pat seemed every bit as marooned here as herself.

Yet she did admire Pat's cooking skills, for even though all that was available was mutton, killed by the men, and the occasional rabbit they'd shot or snared, and even more infrequently, a chicken, Pat had a knack of making it seem more varied. Fresh vegetables were rare, mostly it was tinned peas, beans or carrots. Pat made all the bread, the yeast kept on a shelf above the stove where it would stay warm. Her pastry was rich and crumbly, she could make delicious dumplings, and she used dried vegetables in tasty stews. But because Dulcie still only got the leftovers, she refused to compliment Pat either. Sometimes she wondered whether if she was forced to stay here for a full three years she might end up as sullen and uncommunicative as the rest of them.

But she had no intention of staying here. While she was terrified of the prospect of being picked up by the police and taken back to the reformatory to work in the laundry, she was sure this was worse. So she did all that was asked of her and more, without complaint. When Pat gave her a ten-shilling note on Saturdays for her wages, she tucked it away in the little bag Sister Ruth had given her, and reminded herself that every week she stayed she'd have another to add to it.

On the eighth Monday, Dulcie woke in a sweat as usual, for the early morning sun came straight on to her lean-to and turned it into an oven. Pat hadn't rung the bell yet, but she guessed it wouldn't be long as the rooster was crowing. After a trip along to the dunny, which always filled her with foreboding about spiders, she washed in the sink outside on the veranda. She was only allowed into the inside bathroom twice a week to take a shower, and she got the impression Pat thought once was enough.

The washing had to be done on Monday mornings, in the sink outside. It was a formidable job as the men's clothes were always caked in dirt and needed a great deal of scrubbing to get them clean. Pat only ever used cold water, and to Dulcie who had been given endless lessons in laundry by the Sisters, this was crazy, so she adapted what she had learned at St Vincent's to make the job quicker and easier. On Sunday nights she collected up all the dirty washing and put it to soak overnight in cold water, then gave it a bit of a swill through the next morning before emptying out the water.

While the men were having breakfast she heated up a couple of pans of hot water, then once they had gone she carried it round to the side of the house and refilled the sink. She didn't know whether Pat had ever noticed what she did, she certainly didn't remark that Dulcie seemed to be getting the job done quicker than she had, or that the washing looked cleaner. But Dulcie had come to accept that she only spoke out to complain – praise was beyond her.

Early mornings were the best time of the day for Dulcie. She might ache from the previous one, she might be dreading the day ahead, but for just five or ten minutes before she was summoned to the kitchen, she felt something that approached happiness. She would sit on the steps of the veranda, the sun was just warm, the sound of birdsong all around her. There were always kangaroos hopping around amongst the bushes and gums. It made her smile when the little joeys jumped out of their mother's pouch, took a few hops about, then dived back in head-first. She always hoped they would clear off before Bill got up because he would shoot them immediately as he got two pounds for every kangaroo scalp and saw them as a valuable source of pocket money.

Sometimes she'd see an echidna feasting at an ants' nest and they reminded her of hedgehogs back in England. She remembered that someone had once brought one to school in a box, wanting to put it on the nature table, and her teacher had explained that even if it was all tightly curled up like a ball now, the minute the children left the class it would take off to look for slugs, so she thought it was kinder to take it and put it in someone's garden where it could find some.

There were always so many birds too at this time of day, and the pink and grey galahs were her favourite. When a whole flock of them took off together they looked like pink candy-floss. Emus would scuttle by, making her think of gormless ballerinas in their tutus, rushing late to a rehearsal. They too were in danger from Bill as they were worth five shillings a beak dead. Bob-tailed goannas came out from under rocks to sun themselves, and just occasionally she'd see a snake.

But all too soon Pat would ring the bell and she'd have to go in and face another gruelling day. Within twenty minutes the men would be here for their breakfast, bringing with them the stink of their unwashed bodies and their beery and tobacco-tainted breath. She always went and made Pat and Bill's bed now while they were eating, for seeing all that food going round in open mouths was too disgusting for words.

Dulcie was carrying one of the pans of hot water round to do the washing when Sly, the black dog, came rushing round the corner of the house. Dulcie thought he was going to jump up at her, as he often did because she petted him a great deal, so she swerved, afraid both of them would be scalded by the hot water.

But she stepped on a sharp stone, lost her balance and the water tipped out on to the ground. Sly was unhurt, he'd gone straight past her chasing something. She wasn't scalded either, but she'd lost the hot water.

'You stupid little bitch!' Pat yelled from the kitchen door. 'What the hell do you think you're doing?'

Dulcie turned to see Pat standing there, hands on hips, glowering at her.

'I'm sorry,' Dulcie said. 'Sly startled me. I thought he was going to jump up at me.'

She went back towards Pat, intending to fill the pan again and leave it to boil. But as she came up the steps of

222

the veranda and reached Pat, the woman slapped her hard across the face, making her reel back and drop the pan.

'That's right, blame the dog, you bloody drongo! Where were you going with hot water anyway?'

'To do the washing of course,' Dulcie said, putting her hand up to her stinging cheek.

'What's wrong with cold water?'

'Hot water gets it cleaner,' Dulcie said harshly.

Clearly Pat didn't miss the tone for her face went red with anger. 'You think you're so smart, don't you?' she hissed at Dulcie. Her face was almost reptilian with spite. 'I bet you think you could run this place better than me?'

Dulcie's only thoughts about this place were what a blessing it would be if a bush fire burned it and its occupants down. She couldn't say that, but she did let forth another version.

'The only running I'd like to do is running away from here. And you're the drongo if you don't know hot water washes better than cold.'

Pat leaped at her, fingers outstretched like claws to scratch her. Dulcie moved smartly to one side and Pat bumped into the veranda balustrade.

Dulcie was no fighter, she hated any kind of violence. But in the brief second before Pat sprang at her again, she knew this was an occasion when she must assert herself, or she'd be a victim for evermore. As the woman's hands caught her shoulders, Dulcie pulled her knee up sharply and kneed her hard in the stomach.

Pat reeled back, winded, hitting the balustrade with such force that it shook. 'How dare you!' she gasped, clutching her stomach. 'I'll get Bill to whip you tonight.'

'You struck me first,' Dulcie said, suddenly so angry she felt like kicking the woman again. 'You treat me like a slave, you make me sleep in a shed, feed me leftovers, then you wonder why I hit you back? You're a brick short of a full load.'

'No one gets away with speaking to me like that,' Pat yelled at her.

Dulcie was beyond fear now. If she had to walk all the twenty miles to Salmon Gums, she would. 'Oh really?' she said with sarcasm, walking away from her. 'What about Bill? He says far worse things than that to you almost every night.'

She braced herself for Pat to run after her and hit her, but as she glanced over her shoulder, the woman was hobbling back round towards the kitchen, almost certainly to get a weapon.

Dulcie panicked then. From what she knew of Pat and Bill they would punish her severely for what she'd said and done. There was really no choice but to run for it while she had the chance. She darted into her room, snatched her case from under the bed, threw her few belongings into it, and seconds later made off around the side of the house towards the road.

Surprisingly Pat was neither there to head her off nor coming behind her, and the fact that no one was chasing her quickly brought her to her senses. The road was long and straight, the men could very well be working some-where alongside it, and if they were they would spot her. On the other hand they could be somewhere over behind the house, and maybe this was why Pat hadn't come after her, because she'd gone straight to tell them what happened.

All at once she was really scared. Facing up to Pat was one thing, but she wouldn't stand a chance with Bill. What if he came after her in the truck and took her back to whip her?

She broke into a trot, holding the small case under her arm. The stones on the dirt road were already getting warm and she knew that within an hour or so it would be too hot for bare feet, even ones as tough as hers. But she doubted she could walk very far in her shoes either, they were too tight, so she had to get as far away as possible now.

Dulcie kept looking back, ears straining for the sound of the truck, and wondering if she dared jump into the bushes to hide if it did come. She'd learnt the habits of snakes now, they rarely came out on to open ground, and were more likely to shy away from a human than to strike. But jumping into bushes was folly – if they were surprised they would attack.

But the truck didn't come, and once she was past the end of the Masters' land she felt a little easier. All the same, the next road stretched on in front of her for miles and that daunted her. She looked up at the sky, it was its usual harsh bright blue, not even a hint of cloud. She thought back to that January day five years ago now when Mr Stigwood had talked about Australia's sunshine, it had sounded so wonderful then! But a ten-year-old child couldn't possibly know the difference between English summer sunshine and the remorseless, punishing heat here.

England and its changeable weather seemed so idyllic in retrospect. She remembered summer mornings when it had been raining all night, and getting up to find the sun shining and everything sparkling again. Just thinking of it brought back the smells of wet soil and flowers. She thought longingly of rainwater dripping from over-hanging trees, and could almost taste the freshness in the air. Then there was autumn, the leaves turning gold, yellow and red before falling to the ground. She could remember walking to Mass on Sundays with her father, kicking through them, delighting in the crackly noise they made. She had loved the first frosty mornings too, making slides on the pavement, seeing her breath coming out like smoke. She had seen mild frost a couple of times in Perth, but not enough to turn water to ice, and when the leaves stayed on the trees, autumn didn't have the same appeal. Would she ever get back to England, she wondered.

By the time she got to the next farm sign, Dulcie needed a drink badly and she wished she'd had the sense to fill up a bottle from her washing bucket before she'd run off. But she couldn't go up the track to the farmhouse – for one thing it was probably several more miles away and besides, the people here might be friends of the Masters. So she put her shoes and socks on, and on she plodded, trying hard not to think of thirst, or how far it was, and offered up a little prayer that a car or truck would come along and stop for her.

Dulcie knew it was midday when she saw she was casting no shadow on to the ground. It was now so hot she felt as if her head was frying. Was it better to stop in the shade of a tree for a while? Or to press on? She decided going on was the only real option, she would only be twice as thirsty after a rest. She passed the second farm sign and hesitated at the bottom of their track.

Suddenly in the distance she heard the sound of a truck rattling down the road in the direction she had come from. Her first thought was to dive behind some bushes in case it was Jake or one of the other men, but just before she made a move she saw it was red, not black like theirs, so she stepped out into the road to flag it down.

The sun was in her eyes so it wasn't until it was nearly up to her that she saw there were two male occupants.

'G'day! Where you headin' for?' the driver called out of his window. He had fair hair cut so short it stood up on end, and thick blond eyebrows.

'To Salmon Gums,' she said, suddenly scared. Sister Ruth had lectured her on the way to Perth station about never accepting a lift from a stranger. 'I'm fine walking,' she said, backing away a bit. 'But have you got any water to spare with you?'

'Strewth, girl, I'm not leaving you out here. You'll flake out before you even get there,' the driver retorted. His face broke into a wide grin, perhaps realizing she was scared, and suddenly he didn't look threatening any more. 'We're harmless as a couple of lambs. Now, hop on in, we're not going to hurt you.'

Dulcie hadn't looked at the passenger until then, and she saw he was half the other man's age, probably only seventeen or eighteen. She thought perhaps they were father and son, though they weren't alike. He moved closer to the driver to make room for her, and so Dulcie got in, squeezing her case between her feet. The lad handed her a half-full bottle of water and looked curiously at her as she guzzled it down greedily.

'No drink with you!' the driver said as he started up the truck again. 'No hat either! Where've you come from?'

Dulcie's instinct told her to say nothing, but the man had been kind enough to stop, he sounded friendly, and he didn't look a brute like Bill Masters and his men. 'A few miles up the road,' she said vaguely.

'And what's in Salmon Gums?' he asked.

'The train,' she said.

'Ah!' he said, and gave a little chuckle. 'So you're running away! Now, there's only two places on that road you could've come from, and my guess it's the Masters' place. Am I right?'

The driver wasn't looking round at her, he had his eyes on the road ahead, but the lad was looking sideways at her very intently. He was wiry, with dark auburn curly hair and freckles across his nose. 'Did they treat you bad?' he asked in little more than a whisper.

'Now, Ross, I'm the one that asks the questions,' the driver said, with laughter in his voice. 'Come on, love, tell me the score. You can trust me.'

Nervous as Dulcie was, her need for a sympathetic ear was greater. So she took a deep breath, then blurted it all out, the nastiness of the Masters, the stone-clearing, the leftover food, and finally what had happened this morning. The only thing she didn't say was that she had been sent from an orphanage to work there.

'I wasn't going to hang about and get a beating from Bill,' she said. 'So I ran.'

'Can't say I blame you running off,' the older man said, this time looking round at her. He was handsome, with smooth, tanned skin and sparkly blue eyes. 'Fair dinkum, I would've done too. But where're you heading for?'

'Is Esperance a big town?' she asked.

Both the man and the boy sniggered. 'If you blink you'll

miss it,' the man said. 'There's more life in Norseman or Salmon Gums. Know anyone in Esperance?'

Dulcie shook her head. 'I just thought it would be a better place to get another job than Kalgoorlie.'

'It's a beaut place,' the man replied, looking thoughtful. 'But work's hard to find for sheilas. You'd be better gettin' on home to your folks. Are they in Kalgoorlie?'

'I haven't got any,' Dulcie said, but she felt the boy nudge her with his elbow as if trying to stop her saying anything more. She hesitated for a second. 'I was brought up by my aunt there,' she lied. 'I can go back to her.'

Suddenly they were turning off the smaller road on to the wider one where the station was. She was surprised it had taken such a short time – clearly she'd walked a great deal further than she'd imagined.

The man pulled in at the post office, saying he had to pick up something. 'You two get out and wait in the shade,' he said to both Dulcie and the boy. 'I'll get some lemonade for you and I'll ask what time the train is.'

They all got out, the man went into the post office and Ross suddenly caught hold of Dulcie's arm. 'You're from an orphanage, aren't you?' he said. Dulcie was taken aback by the intensity in his voice and his eyes – they were a strange tawny colour, reminding her of a cat's.

Dulcie had always found it hard to lie to a direct question, but her hesitation answered the question for her.

'I guessed you were as soon as I saw you. But you'll be in big trouble if the police catch you,' he said.

'They won't catch me,' she said more confidently than she felt. 'Unless you're going to tell them where I am?'

'I don't dob people in. But there's plenty of bastards who will,' he said, looking deeply troubled. 'But I ain't happy about a young sheila out on her own, I'll be worried about you.'

To Dulcie that was as good as being hugged. Aside from Sister Ruth who'd expressed a little anxiety when she left her on Perth station, he was the first person to show any concern about her well-being for many years.

At that point the man came back out of the post office with three bottles of lemonade. Dulcie felt Ross stiffen, and it seemed to her it was a warning she shouldn't be too frank with the older man.

'There's no train today,' he said, 'but there's a bus to Kalgoorlie at six. You just wait here for it.'

The man introduced himself as John Withers and said he and Ross worked on a property down at Esperance. Ross stood back slightly, just looking at her. Dulcie had a feeling there was a great deal more he'd like to say to her but he couldn't in front of John.

'Don't suppose they need a cook, cleaner or even someone to look after their children?' Dulcie said, looking up at John hopefully. He had such a nice face, a wide smiley mouth and a direct way of looking at her, so very different to Bill Masters and his men.

'Sorry love, nothing doing. You go on home to your aunt, and next time make sure you find out about a place afore you get there. A sheila as young and pretty as you shouldn't be stuck out in the middle of nowhere.'

Dulcie blushed at the compliment, she thought she must look a fright in her old striped St Vincent's dress. But it could have been worse, she might have been wearing the men's trousers and shirt she put on for working outside.

'You got enough money for the bus?' John asked.

Dulcie nodded.

'Well, we'd better be off then,' he said. 'Look after yourself, Dulcie. You seem a smart girl, try and get a better job, in a shop or sommat. You got to be born to farming to really like it.'

As they got back into the truck, Ross was waving his arm, not like he was waving goodbye, but as if he was trying to tell her something. She looked towards the post office and saw that it closed at two. She thought perhaps he was warning her to get another drink and something to eat before it was too late.

After the hard work of the last weeks Dulcie didn't mind waiting for the bus one bit. She bought a magazine in the post office, a bar of chocolate and a big bottle of lemonade, then went and sat in the shade over by the station with her back to the wall, and took her shoes off.

She dozed a little, jerking her head up nervously whenever a car or truck went past. But she must have fallen dead asleep because she didn't hear the man walk up to her and only woke when he spoke.

'Wake up, little girl,' he said. 'I've got to talk to you.'

Her eyes flew open to see a policeman crouching in front of her. Panic made her curl into a defensive ball, her arms covering her head.

'I'm not going to hit you,' he said gently. 'Now, just sit up and we'll have a little talk.'

It was he who did the talking, not her. He said that John Withers, the man driving the truck, had become concerned on the drive back to Esperance because he sensed his young workmate had something on his mind. After some persuasion Ross finally admitted he doubted Dulcie had an aunt in Kalgoorlie and he was scared she'd come to harm.

'John's a good man,' the policeman said. 'He didn't call on me to try and make trouble for you, he just didn't like the thought of someone as young as you wandering around looking for work. Now, suppose you tell me all about it?'

Dulcie took a good look at the man. John had said she could trust him, he looked like she could too, but then he'd told on her. This man looked as if he could be trusted too, middle-aged, chubby, a round unlined face and soft brown eyes that were looking intently at her. His blue uniform shirt was clean and well ironed, his trousers had a sharp crease down the front. He even had a nice voice, she had heard the lilt of Irish in it. She didn't have any choice but to trust him, but maybe if she told him the whole truth he'd help her get a job.

So she told him everything, in far more detail than she'd told John and Ross. 'No one should get away with treating me like that,' she said. 'I had to leave, those people are pigs.'

He took her hand and helped her up, then led her over to a low wall for them both to sit down. 'The question is, what am I going to do with you?' he said. 'By rights I ought to take you up to Norseman and hand you over to the police there, because this isn't my patch. I'm stationed in Esperance, see.' He paused for a moment as if in deep thought. 'You must have been told by the Sisters what happens if girls like you leave a job before they are eighteen?'

'The reformatory,' she said. But even as she said the word she felt angry. 'But why should I be punished? I haven't done a thing wrong. It was them who treated me like a slave. That isn't fair!'

He nodded as if in agreement. 'The trouble is, you are a ward of the Australian government, and it's their rule that orphaned children must stay where they are sent. Now, suppose you put yourself in my boots for a moment. Suppose I was to let you get on that bus to Kalgoorlie. You'd get there well after eleven o'clock tonight. I know there are bad men who hang around the bus station waiting for young unprotected girls just like you to get off. Would you think, knowing this, that it would be a kind thing for me to let you do?'

'I suppose not,' she said reluctantly. 'But I'm not stupid. I wouldn't let anyone take me off somewhere.'

The policeman sighed. 'These bad men aren't stupid either. They have dozens of different ways of persuading girls,' he said. 'Sometimes they work with a woman, she might offer you lodgings or a meal. There's a street called Hay Street, that's where girls end up, and almost everyone of them started out just like you, a little innocent sucked into something evil.'

'Well, can't I go somewhere else then?' she asked. 'Somewhere there aren't bad people.'

The policeman sighed deeply. 'The way I see it, there's

really only one solution and that's to go back to the Masters.'

'Oh no,' Dulcie exclaimed. She clutched hold of his arm in her fear. 'Please don't make me do that, they'll be twice as nasty because I ran away.'

'Hear me out first,' he said, patting her hand. 'I take you back there, and I talk to them, give them a warning they've got to treat you better. Then you write a letter to St Vincent's, explain how unhappy you are and ask that they give you permission to find another job or that they find one for you. That way no one can punish you by sending you to the reformatory.'

'But I can't bear to go back there, I'd sooner die,' Dulcie said, beginning to cry.

The policeman put his arm around her shoulders. 'I'm sorry, love, I wish I could think of some alternative, I really do. If I take you up to Norseman as I really should, it will be taken out of my hands, they're tough bastards up there, used to troublemakers from the gold mines in Kalgoorlie, so I don't want to do that. But I'll ask around in Esperance, see if I can find someone who needs a bright girl like you. I'll come by from time to time too and check you're all right. Bill Masters will go easier on you after I've spoken to him.'

Dulcie could see she had no choice. Although the policeman hadn't said as much, she knew that if she refused to do as he said, he'd have no alternative but to take her to the police station in Norseman.

Sergeant Sean Collins kept stealing glances at the girl as he drove her back to the Masters' place. Her expression was one of abject misery, and judging by the way she wasn't crying or pleading with him, he suspected it was a state she'd been in all too often before. On his last trip to Perth a few months ago a policeman friend had spoken about hearing rumours of cruelty in orphanages run by both the Christian Brothers and the Sisters of Mercy. He said he had tried to get senior police to investigate, but was told in no uncertain terms that the Catholic Church was outside police jurisdiction. As a Catholic himself Collins found it hard to believe that nuns and priests should treat children badly, but now he knew that Dulcie, a completely inexperienced child, had been sent out to work on such a remote farm, without checks being made on the prospective employers, he wasn't quite so sure they were all they seemed.

Collins knew all about back-breaking land-clearing, he'd come over from Ireland at eighteen in 1920, and it was the only work he could get until he eventually got into the police force. He felt sorry for Dulcie and believed everything she had said, but he couldn't do anything more for her than he'd already offered. Hundreds of immigrants arrived every day in the big ports, not just from England but from all over Europe, and the migrant camps set up for them were bursting at the seams. People with a trade or profession had little trouble finding work. For willing, strong young men who were prepared to go wherever work was available, there was more than enough too. But for the rest, Australia often proved a great disappointment, a harsh, strange land of vast distances, extremes of temperature, prejudice and hardship. For a young, pretty girl like Dulcie it could also be very dangerous.

'You stay in the car while I go in and speak to them,' Collins said as they drove up to the Masters' homestead. It was almost six now and he could see the black truck parked up outside. 'Don't take it into your head to start running again. If they refuse to be reasonable I'll take you back with me.'

She gave him a look which said she hoped that would be the case, and it made a lump come up in his throat.

Collins went straight round the back – people in the outback didn't stand on ceremony, even the two dogs barely glanced his way. He rapped on the screen door and it was opened by Jake, whom he'd known for some years.

'G'day, Jake,' he said. 'Can I have a word with Bill?'

'How yer doin', Sean?' Jake said, grinning and showing

off his protruding teeth. 'You're a long way off your patch! Come on in.'

'When you hear about a runaway kid you don't care if it isn't your patch,' Collins said as he followed him in.

He was almost overcome by the heat in the kitchen, and by Pat when she turned at the stove to face him.

Her baleful look was enough to turn milk sour, but what really shocked him was her appearance. He'd only met her once before, that was just after Bill married her and was working up at Norseman. She wouldn't have been described as a pretty woman even then, but she was attractive and stylish with a good figure. She looked like a skeleton now, her face gaunt and her eyes dead.

'G'day, Pat,' he said, trying to disarm her with a wide smile. 'Sorry to call when you're having your meal.'

Bill was surprisingly courteous. He got Collins a chair, introduced his cousins Bert and Ted, and asked if he wanted a beer. He said their meal could wait a little longer.

Collins had met Bill on innumerable occasions. Before the war when he worked on several different properties all around this area he was known to be something of a larrikin. A bit boastful, too hot-headed sometimes, getting himself into fights when he got drunk. When he returned after the war, that seemed to have gone, he was quieter, didn't seem to laugh any more the way he used to. He once told Collins that all he wanted was a farm of his own, a wife and a few kids, so when he married Pat, Collins was glad for him. Then he got this place, and everyone predicted he'd fail as so many others had around here. Yet Collins hoped they were wrong. Bill was a hard worker, he was determined too, but perhaps if things were going badly, that was why he was taking it out on Pat.

Collins took the bottle of beer gratefully and launched straight into his reason for calling.

'It's about young Dulcie,' he said. 'I picked her up waiting for the bus to Kalgoorlie. I want to hear your side of what happened today.'

'She said the kid got into a blue and kneed her in the

belly,' Bill said, looking round at his wife. 'Didn't strike me as the kind that had it in her!'

Collins picked up that Bill didn't believe his wife. 'That's exactly what she told me she did do,' he said. 'But she only did it because your wife struck her first.'

'You hit her?' Bill turned towards his wife and scowled. 'Whatcha do that for? She's a good kid, never gives any lip, works like a dog.'

'She had it coming to her. She spilt a pan of water outside and then blamed Sly,' Pat retorted. 'You say she never gives any lip, you should've heard what she said this morning.'

Collins didn't know who was worse, a man who thought a fifteen-year-old should work like a dog, or a woman who would clout someone for something so trivial. It was also shocking that they clearly hadn't made any attempt to find the girl after she ran away – a twenty-mile walk in hot sun for someone without a hat or water could have proved fatal. In carefully chosen words Collins pointed this out to them.

'She's a good kid,' he finished up. 'You know that orphanage kids who run away have to be taken in. I don't want to do that to her, she doesn't deserve it. Now, how about taking her back and treating her right?'

'Whatcha mean? Treating her right!' Bill said, his low brow furrowed with a frown. 'We pay her ten bob a week, she gets her bed and board. What else does she expect, bloody French lessons, tennis in the afternoon?'

'No, of course she doesn't,' Collins retorted. 'She just wants what is fair, a proper meal, not leftovers, a decent room to sleep in, not a shed, to be treated kindly.'

'I had it a darn sight worse than her on the property they sent me to,' Pat burst out. 'I was only fourteen and I had to milk twenty cows at five in the morning. In the winter it was so cold I couldn't bend my fingers.'

At that outburst Collins understood Pat a little better. Maybe she was an orphan herself, and while anyone would expect that would make her more compassionate to someone in the same position, he knew all too well this wasn't so. Brutality begets brutality, children who receive cruelty will often be crueller still themselves.

'You give her leftovers?' Bill looked at his wife in astonishment. 'You said you put her dinner and yours back till we'd finished.'

'I do. She's lying,' Pat said but she gave the game away by blushing and looking away.

Bill looked at his wife, then back at Collins. 'I'll see she gets decent meals. She can sleep in the house too. But I can't make the work easier, farm work is hard, you know that.'

'There's such things as a rest at midday,' Collins said persuasively. 'Taking her into town with you once in a while. She's just a kid, a bright one at that. I reckon if you treat her better, she'll repay you over and over.' He looked up at Pat who was still glowering at him. 'Come on, Pat, give it a go, she could be company for you, a mate. I know you're sore at her for kneeing you, but at least it shows she's got a bit of spirit. I reckon if you took the trouble to talk to her you'd like her. I haven't been with her for long, but I do.'

Ted leaned forward and put his elbows on the table. 'Give it another go, Pat,' he said. 'It's lonely for you out here, and hell, things have been better since she came. Look at the floor! The windows! All clean and nice. You've nearly got the vegetable patch ready for planting now. You always say you haven't got time to go into town, but you will have if she stays.'

Collins thought it was sad that a relative of Bill's had to say the kind of things a husband should. But then he supposed if he'd married a woman as sour as Pat, perhaps he wouldn't have much time for her either. Yet even though it was clear the men all agreed Dulcie should stay, and perhaps Pat might come round too, he knew in reality he wouldn't be leaving the poor kid with a much better deal. The truth of the matter was that this job stank as much as the men did.

'Fair enough,' Pat said with a weary sigh. 'She can come back. But I'm warning you all, any lip from her and I'll kick her to hell and back. Now, get her back in here so I can dish up this meal.'

Dulcie was in bed by eight that evening. In the second bedroom, with sheets on the bed too. Yet it was only a minor victory, as was the plateful of mutton stew, she reminded herself. Pat hadn't apologized for anything, she hadn't even said anything that sounded as though she intended to be nicer. But at least she didn't feel quite so alone now. Sergeant Collins had said he would be calling in again. She would write to Mother at St Vincent's and ask permission to find another job. Bill had even slapped her on the back and said she was a good kid. She felt she had to try to like it here, at least for a bit.

Chapter Eleven

'Jake's just brought the post up, there's a letter for you,' Pat said as Dulcie came in with a load of wood for the stove. 'I've made you a cup of tea too.'

It was the first week in April, but it had suddenly turned cold, with a heavy grey sky. Dulcie put the box of wood down and warmed her hands on the stove.

'Cold?' Pat asked.

'Ummm,' Dulcie said. 'I was hot while I was chopping the wood, but by the time I'd got the chooks in their house I felt like a block of ice. But at least there aren't so many flies about now.'

She sat down at the kitchen table and Pat silently handed her a mug of tea and the letter. Dulcie knew immediately it was from Reverend Mother, her sloping handwriting was very distinctive.

Dear Dulcie, she read. *I am disappointed to hear that the job in Salmon Gums is not to your liking, but few of us find our first job exactly what we hoped it to be. You have to remember that positions for untrained girls are few and far between. I do not know at present of any other suitable for you, and advise you that you must just accept what you have and learn as much as you can. I am afraid that I cannot give you permission to seek another one yourself either. It is our duty to St Vincent's girls to deter them from foolhardy changes which could damage their future prospects. I am quite sure that you wrote to me in a moment of despondency and that it's passed now anyway.*

    Sincerely yours,
    Reverend Mother

Dulcie dolefully put the letter back in its envelope. She hadn't really expected the woman to show any real concern, but she was disappointed that she couldn't find herself another job. She picked up her tea and wrapped her hands round the mug to warm them.

'It wasn't what you hoped for, was it?' Pat said suddenly.

Dulcie looked at the older woman in surprise. Firstly, her tone had none of its usual brusqueness and secondly, she rarely asked questions about anything which might lead into a conversation. Had Pat guessed that she'd written to Reverend Mother asking to be moved, and that this was the reply?

'Come on! I'm not bloody stupid,' Pat said. 'It's from St Vincent's, isn't it? They won't let you leave, will they?'

Dulcie felt very embarrassed. 'No, they won't.' She hung her head expecting Pat to say something nasty.

Pat didn't come back with a sharp reply and when Dulcie looked up, to her astonishment the woman had a sympathetic expression. 'I wish she had said you could, for your sake,' she said. 'I'd miss your help. But it's no life here for you.'

Dulcie just gawped stupidly. In the three months she'd been here this was the first time Pat had ever said anything which implied she had even the slightest concern for her.

It had got a little better after she ran away, though only in as much as she got better food and slept inside, but Pat had remained just as surly, right until the hot weather broke in mid-March and it finally rained. That day was memorable because it was as though someone had given Pat a miraculous pill which instantly cheered her. She had called Dulcie out on to the veranda, smiling at the rain. 'We'll be able to plant the veg now,' she said. 'When the lambs are born there'll be new grass for the ewes.'

Dulcie came to the conclusion that it was the prospect of new grass for the ewes which had worked the magic, and that in itself suggested Pat wasn't quite as stony-hearted as she seemed.

She hadn't stayed smiling and cheerful of course, that

would have been too much to hope for, yet she was less harsh, like today, offering a cup of tea and a sit-down during the day. Sometimes she actually *asked* Dulcie to do something rather than just barking orders at her.

But then the rain and cooler weather made everything easier for everyone. There was more wood-chopping than before, but it wasn't as tiring to cook and clean, and the men were less grumpy at the end of the day. Bill was overjoyed to have full tanks and his dams full of water, and he too was eagerly awaiting the first lambs. The rain had softened the ground in the vegetable patch, so the last bit of digging and raking wasn't hard work.

Yet Dulcie still couldn't claim to be happy or even content. It was just less miserable. Sergeant Collins had been as good as his word and dropped in from time to time bringing her books and magazines to read, but she felt so very lonely, longing for the company of other girls. Pat had said there was a cinema in Salmon Gums, they even had dances in the hall once a fortnight, but without anyone to take her there, and no one there she knew, she couldn't go. She felt terribly isolated too, as Pat and Bill never had newspapers and did not even possess a radio. Even at St Vincent's they'd been told when King George VI died, and last year they'd been told a great deal about the Coronation of Princess Elizabeth and shown pictures of it. But she had no idea what was going on in the world now.

Sleeping inside the house was much more comfortable, but when Bill picked a fight with Pat late at night it was horrible to listen to. It wasn't just slaps he gave her, but punches, and when he was really mad he thrashed her with his belt. He didn't always rape her afterwards, but he did it often enough for Dulcie to come to expect the bestial sounds, even clearer now through the thin partition wall. He grunted out filthy words as he did it, and Pat's whimpering and pleas for him to stop made Dulcie's stomach heave with fright and nausea. After these attacks Pat would limp into the kitchen in the morning, her thin face grey and drawn with pain, and though Dulcie was often tempted to say something, just to show she was concerned, Pat's hostility prevented it. She often took it out on Dulcie by making her do the very worst jobs, like scrubbing out the dunny.

'So what did Reverend Mother actually say then?' Pat asked, breaking into Dulcie's reverie.

Dulcie didn't think there was any point in attempting to hide the contents of the letter, so she read it to Pat.

The woman's odd expression made Dulcie afraid she'd hurt her feelings. 'She's right really, I did only write to her when I was upset,' she said quickly.

'She's not right,' Pat said forcefully, pursing her lips. 'Don't you ever start believing nuns care tuppence about the children put in their care. They've done to you exactly what they did to me, packed you off without a thought for your safety or your future.'

'They did it to you? Were you in an orphanage too?'

Pat nodded grimly. 'In Adelaide. My mother died having my youngest brother, and all five of us were put in an orphanage. I was ten, the oldest, we had a little farm a way out of the town, but it was the thirties and the Depression and our dad had gone off to look for work.'

Pat paused, her lower lip quivering. 'He never came back for us. Or if he did no one ever told me,' she went on. 'We weren't even kept together, the baby went to one place, the two little boys to another and me and my sister to another.'

Dulcie gasped. 'That's dreadful, did you find them again later?'

Pat's face seemed to close up. 'That's not important. All I wanted to say was that the nuns did the same to me. They sent me off to a big cattle station when I was only fourteen. It was hell. Things happened to me there that I can't even bear to think about. It ruined my life.'

'But you met Bill and got married,' Dulcie said, hoping this would prompt further confidences. 'You've got a place of your own now.'

Pat gave her a withering look. 'I just swapped one kind of hell for another.'

She got up from the table and stood at the sink with her back to Dulcie. Her tense stance, the way she was gripping on to the sink, was evidence she had a lot more on her mind.

She turned round suddenly, her plain, thin face full of anxiety. 'I wish I could get you out of this,' she exclaimed. 'Oh, I know you think I'm the meanest person on this earth, I can't blame you for that, not after the way I treated you when you first came here, but I had my reasons. I didn't get the men to come after you that day you ran away because I wanted you to get right away, for your sake. If Sergeant Collins had come when I was on my own I'd have refused to take you back, that way he'd have looked out for you. I know you aren't in the kind of danger here like I was at the cattle station. But you deserve something better.'

Dulcie was astounded. She had never imagined this strange, cold woman was capable of any concern for anyone. While she couldn't totally forgive her for the past humiliations, it did seem as if Pat was attempting an explanation, even an apology, and that in itself was enough for now.

'Well, I can't go, Pat, not now,' she replied. 'So it looks like we're in this together.'

Pat gave her a long, cool stare. 'Don't you go looking for a mother in me,' she said with her more customary brusqueness. 'I'm not the person for that. But I'll try to do right by you.'

It was just a few weeks later when Dulcie woke up one morning to find blood on her nightdress and smears on her inner thighs. She looked at it in horror, convinced it was some serious and maybe even terminal disease, and wondered how on earth she was going to explain it to Pat so she'd get her to a doctor.

She waited till breakfast was over and the men had gone

off to work. The lambing had begun and they had to be vigilant for dingoes, shooting them to get the five-shilling bounty for their scalps.

Pat was putting some chicken feed into a pail, and when she saw Dulcie hovering in the doorway she snapped a reminder that cows couldn't wait forever to be milked.

'I just wanted to ask you something,' Dulcie said, struggling not to cry. 'You see, I'm bleeding.'

'Bleeding!' Pat exclaimed. 'Where from?'

Dulcie made a gesture towards her private parts.

'That's just the monthlies. I would've thought you'd started those a year or two back,' Pat said curtly.

Dulcie had no idea what she meant and the harsh tone made her eyes fill with tears.

'Oh, for Christ's sake!' Pat exclaimed. 'Didn't the Sisters tell you about that?' All at once her face softened, she put down the pail and came over to Dulcie, laying one hand on her shoulder. 'They didn't, did they? Those Sisters need shooting, the whole bloody lot of them.'

She made Dulcie sit down at the table and explained that it meant she had now stepped into womanhood and would be capable of having babies. As Dulcie listened, it suddenly dawned on her that this had to be what some of the older girls used to whisper about together, and why she'd seen them in the laundry in the evenings sometimes. She had always felt hurt that she was excluded from whatever it was, now she understood. Furthermore, it also explained the two small towels Sister Grace had given her on leaving. She had thought they were face flannels.

When she told Pat this, the older woman grimaced. 'That's typical of those sadistic old bitches,' she said. 'The place I was in, they made us scrub and scrub them till they were lily-white again, and made us feel like lepers. But you don't have to use those towels, they make pads especially for this, and you don't have to wash them, just burn them. I'll give you a packet and a belt to hold them in place. Next time I go into town I'll get a supply of them for you.'

It was such a relief to find she wasn't suffering from some disease or serious internal complaint that Dulcie burst into tears.

'There's nothing to cry about,' Pat said sharply. 'There'll come a time when you'll be glad to see it happen every month. You see, if you go with a man, and it doesn't come, it means you're pregnant. So just you be careful if you meet someone you really like, don't you go letting him sweet-talk you into doing it. Having a baby when you aren't married is a terrible thing.'

Pat had been marginally more talkative since the day the letter came from Reverend Mother, she had told Dulcie a little about the orphanage she was in, and about her brothers and sisters. Dulcie had reciprocated in part, she said that her mother died and her father put her and May into care because he couldn't look after them himself. She didn't trust Pat quite enough to tell her the whole truth.

Talking together had made things more comfortable, and Dulcie was no longer afraid of Pat for she had come to see the anger in the woman wasn't directed at her. Yet there was something about the way she imparted that bit of information about babies which sounded very much like personal experience, her dark eyes were full of pain and her lower lip was quivering.

'Did that happen to you?' Dulcie whispered.

Pat didn't answer immediately, but she put her elbow on the table and leaned her head against her hand, half-covering her eyes.

'Yes. But he didn't sweet-talk me, it was rape, and I was too young and stupid to even know that at the time,' Pat said, her voice rasping. 'I didn't know I was pregnant either, not until the pains came. I had it squatting behind a shed, like an animal.'

Young and innocent as Dulcie was, instinct told her that this was something Pat had never revealed to anyone before, and it was the very core of her deep melancholy. She reacted in the only way she knew to comfort, and that was to take the older woman in her arms and rock her against her chest, like a child.

She half expected to be rebuffed, for Pat to lash out with sarcasm, but instead Pat clung to her and sobbed.

'What happened to the baby?' Dulcie whispered, caressing the woman's bony back and shoulders. There was no reply, just deeper strangled sobs.

'He was born dead,' she said eventually, her voice muffled as Dulcie was holding her so tightly. 'I expect he was too early or that I never had enough food for the both of us. I dug a hole in the ground and buried his body, then I went back into the house and carried on with my work.'

For a moment Dulcie was speechless with shock. The mental picture of a young girl digging a hole and putting a dead baby into it was just too dreadful to contemplate. Yet however shocking it was, Dulcie could feel the pain, terror, guilt and shame that lay beneath the abrupt words. Pat was just a child herself at the time, with no one to turn to, and it was understandable that keeping such a hideous secret to herself, the guilt and shame multiplying over the years, had become an impossible burden.

Tears ran down Dulcie's cheeks as she rocked the woman. She wished she had the right words to comfort her and show her that she shared her anguish.

Pat suddenly jerked herself out of her arms. 'You must never tell anyone,' she pleaded, looking up at Dulcie with tear-filled eyes. 'I shouldn't have told you, it's so terrible. I don't know why I did, 'cept I wanted to warn you how bad things can be for young girls. Promise me you won't ever tell anyone?'

'Of course I'll never tell anyone,' Dulcie sobbed. 'It's the saddest thing I ever heard.'

'It would have been even sadder if the baby lived,' Pat said grimly. 'I wasn't even fifteen, the Sisters would have taken him from me, and he'd have had to go through the misery of an orphanage too. But I wish I hadn't told you now. I don't know why I did.'

Dulcie put her hand on Pat's cheek and stroked it. 'Don't

be sorry, Pat, maybe it will soothe the pain for you a bit.'

Pat just looked up at her, dark eyes still swimming with tears, her thin lips quivering. 'You're made of the right stuff,' she said, her voice wobbling with emotion. 'There's so much kindness in you, you're bright and plucky too. I reckon you'll turn out all right.'

The ploughing and the seeding of wheat and barley was done during the winter months, and the lambs were born too in June. Dulcie was shocked to find that here in Australia there was no such thing as a shepherd tending the flock as they had their young. The extent of the farmer's care didn't go any further than watching out for dingoes and shooting them.

Pat and Dulcie had to pitch in too, they were expected to help with everything from firing scrub on land Bill wanted cleared, putting up new fencing and keeping the fire breaks around the paddocks clear, to helping out in the shearing shed in August when the shearers came to do their job.

While involved in all this hard work, Dulcie began to understand why Bill and his men were like they were. To farm in the outback, a man had to become like the landscape, harsh and arid, for they couldn't afford to be weak, faint-hearted or sentimental. Whilst it didn't make Dulcie like them any better, she could at least respect their dogged perseverance.

Then all at once it was October and spring. Rainfall turned the paddocks of wheat and barley green and lush, and around the edges of the cultivated land, amongst the gums, patches of brilliantly coloured wild flowers sprang up. Dulcie was enchanted by them and was only too glad when Pat sent her off to take sandwiches for the men as it gave her an excuse to examine them. To see the Banksia trees alight with their red, yellow and orange flowers like prickly candles gladdened her heart, she got a thrill from seeing Kangaroo paws, delicate wild orchids, bright pink cone flowers, feather flowers, the yellow blossom on the wattle and pretty white myrtle. She picked bunches of everlastings and brought them home, gleeful when she found the colours wouldn't fade even after weeks.

Pat smiled at her enthusiasm and said she was in danger of falling in love with Australia and the outback, when most girls fast approaching sixteen were more interested in falling in love with a man. But Dulcie didn't ever see any young men, and if all farmers had personalities like Bill and his men, she didn't think she wanted a boyfriend.

It began to get hot during the day again and the flies came back with a vengeance. Sheep had to be checked for fly-blow, maggots breeding on their rear ends, and treated promptly with insecticide, and all the sheep had to be dipped to rid them of parasites. Each evening, no matter how tired Dulcie was, she had to lug pails of water from the tank on the barn to water the vegetables to keep them growing. Yet as soon as the sun went down, the nights were cold, and she and Pat would huddle around the fire in the living-room after the evening meal was cleared away.

Pat still often retreated into dark moods when she snapped at anything Dulcie might say or do. But Dulcie had learnt to accept that was just the way she was, just as she had come to accept that it was her lot in life to stay here till she was eighteen, to work a seven-day week without complaint.

Yet there were some good moments. Jake occasionally drove her and Pat to Esperance, and for a couple of hours they had a break from work, looking at the sea and the shops. Dulcie's savings were growing fast with nothing to spend her wages on, and Sergeant Collins still often dropped by to bring her new books and magazines to read. Bill taught her to drive the tractor, something she loved, on odd occasions he even let her drive the truck too, and she could cook nearly as well as Pat now.

May was her main anxiety, for she rarely wrote, and when she did it was never more than a few stilted lines.

Dulcie worried that Reverend Mother would send her sister to somewhere like this when she was fifteen. She knew May would never placidly accept the grinding hard work, the lack of company, or wearing clothes that were little better than rags.

Dulcie still wore her old green St Vincent's uniform dress most days. It was worn and faded, but she kept the blue one she'd made herself for best, which really meant she only wore it when she went to Esperance. When she was working outside on the farm she put on the old trousers Pat gave her, so there was really no need for anything else. Yet when she looked at the magazines and saw pictures of girls in pretty dresses, high-heeled shoes and stockings, wearing makeup with their hair all permed and glamorous, her heart ached to look like that too. Her hair had grown now, right to her shoulders, but the only attention it had was washing and brushing and tying it back just the way Pat wore hers. Her hands were callused, her nails all broken, the only care her complexion got was Ponds Cold Creme every night.

Pat said the spring weather was just right for a good harvest. They had light rain a couple of times a week right up until the crop began to turn golden, then nothing but sunshine from the end of October as it fully ripened. Bill was like a cat on hot bricks as he waited for it to be ready, any rain now would lower its value. But no rain came and in the third week in November Bill decided it was time, and he and his men began work with the combine at first light. Dulcie and Pat were pressed into service too, driving the tractor that pulled the machine. The grain came out of a funnel which filled sacks, then the sacks had to be loaded on to a flat-bed truck to be taken off to the bulkhead down by the station in Salmon Gums. There was no question of anyone stopping for a rest now, every minute counted at this crucial time and the men were often more bad-tempered than usual. Day after day the work went on, and still the weather held. Dulcie's face and arms were blistered by the sun, every bone in her body ached, but she found deep satisfaction in seeing one huge paddock after another left with nothing but the prickly stubble.

On the evening of Dulcie's sixteenth birthday in December she sat out on the veranda looking up at the star-studded sky and petting the two dogs. Sly, the older, dark one, was her favourite, he appeared to understand every word said to him. Prince, the russet one, was equally intelligent, but more aloof.

'It's my birthday today,' she whispered to them. 'But May hasn't written or sent me a card.'

Although the Sisters had never made anything of birthdays at St Vincent's, she and May had always made each other little cards and the other girls had sung 'Happy Birthday' and given the birthday girl the bumps. No one here knew it was her special day, and she hadn't liked to announce it. It hadn't seem to matter much during the day, they'd all been too busy for her even to think of it, but now in the still, warm darkness Dulcie ached to see her sister, and tears trickled down her cheeks.

Sly made a funny little whining noise and moved closer to lick her cheeks as if sensing her sadness. Dulcie hugged him to her, getting a little comfort from his affection for her.

The same evening, at St Vincent's in Perth, Reverend Mother was visiting one of the very old Sisters up in her cell on the first floor of the convent, when she happened to glance out of the window. The cell was on the side of the convent overlooking the orphanage, and she spotted May sitting alone on the steps of the veranda by the schoolroom.

Just the way the girl sat, her elbows on her knees, head in hands, told Mother the child was worried or upset by something. All the other girls were playing rounders in the playing field, she could hear their voices in the distance.

This small, pretty blonde with her big blue eyes and her winning ways had captivated her almost as soon as she set foot in St Vincent's. She felt no guilt that she singled this one child out for special treatment, or that her attachment to her in five years had grown far beyond mere affection. In her view May was special.

She turned back to look at the old lady lying in bed. 'I'll come back later, Sister, there's something I must deal with immediately.'

Reverend Mother let herself out through the side door of the convent and walked swiftly across the gravelled area which led to the covered walkways that connected the four buildings.

May looked startled when she suddenly appeared in front of her, and jumped guiltily to her feet. Although she was only twelve and a half, her body was rapidly developing. Only a few weeks earlier Mother had taken her to be fitted for a brassiere, and her first thought when she saw the girl sitting alone was that maybe she had began menstruation and hadn't been able to tell anyone.

'Well, May, why are you sitting here all alone?' she asked. 'Is there something troubling you?'

She took hold of May's hand and led her to walk with her away from the building down towards the kitchen garden.

'I was just thinking about Dulcie,' May said, looking up at her with an anxious expression. 'It's her birthday today. I hope she got the card I made for her in time.'

'I'm sure she did, I posted it myself,' the nun said, feeling absolutely no guilt that she had in fact destroyed it, just as she did all the letters to and from the sisters.

'I wish she would write to me,' May said, her voice quavering. 'I think she's forgotten me.'

It wasn't the first time May had made this remark, and as always Reverend Mother had a reply ready.

'When girls become old enough to work they often get their heads turned by their new way of life and lose interest in their siblings,' she said. 'I expect you'll find the same thing will happen to you too, May.'

'But she said she'd never forget me,' May pouted. 'She made me promise to write, she said when I was old enough to leave she'd find a job near where I get sent, and that one day we'd get a place together.'

This was something May hadn't revealed before, and it only served to make the nun feel she was right in intercepting their mail. She had long-term plans for May and they didn't include an older sister clinging on.

'Young girls say that kind of thing all the time,' she said, and caressed May's shoulder. 'But things happen, they make new friends, and they just move on. But you mustn't brood about it, you see, I intend to find you a much better job than just working on a farm in the outback, that wouldn't be suitable for you at all.'

'What kind of work would I do then?' May asked. Everyone who left here seemed to go to stations or farms.

'Well, there's positions in offices, department stores, all kinds of nice jobs for girls who are pretty, confident and well-spoken.'

'Am I pretty?' May asked, looking up at the older woman with wide eyes.

Reverend Mother laughed. 'You know you are, you vain little minx, and delightful with it. Now, run along back to the other girls and forget about Dulcie.'

She watched fondly as the girl ran back towards the playing field. May was pretty now, but Mother knew that in a few years' time she would be beautiful. She liked to imagine May at eighteen, her lovely blonde hair longer, styled by a real hairdresser, wearing one of those elegant sheath dresses that were all the fashion and dainty high heels and stockings. She felt that if she patiently continued to nurture her carefully through to womanhood, May would be hers for all time.

She felt absolutely no guilt at her guile in breaking down the bond between May and her sister, they had nothing but a dead mother in common after all. So she destroyed all the letters which came for May, and simply forged an occasional one back to Dulcie, making them as dull and disinterested as possible, to weaken the link still further.

May's handwriting was so childish it was very easy to forge, and if she was upset at getting nothing back from her sister, then that was an excellent opportunity to give her extra petting. May would thank her for it one day.

May was not comforted by Reverend Mother's opinions as to why Dulcie hadn't written to her. All she'd done was stir up all those contradictory feelings about her sister still more.

Mostly when she was feeling happy she didn't care about Dulcie. She had it good here, better than anyone else. If Mother did as she said she was going to do and got her a good job when she left, she certainly didn't want her sister turning up and telling her what to do. She'd had enough of that in the past.

Today, though, she'd been thinking about the good memories from the past, how Dulcie always stuck up for her, how she used to creep into the dormitory to kiss her goodnight, the way she always cared when no one else did. It was scary to think that in a couple of years she'd have to go to work, she wouldn't know anyone, they might be mean to her, and it would be nice to think Dulcie was nearby.

When she was feeling sad and alone she got frightened Dulcie had abandoned her because of that thing she'd heard her mother say the night she was killed. May had confided that to Mother once and she'd explained it meant she and Dulcie weren't real sisters. Maybe Dulcie didn't love her any more now she knew that.

But still more often she felt that her sister didn't write because God was punishing her for being so glad when Dulcie left here a year ago.

Dulcie's presence had inhibited her, even though May was popular with the other girls and the Sisters, and a particular pet of Reverend Mother's. Dulcie had always been greatly admired for her intelligence, kindness and ability to do any task quicker and more thoroughly than any other girl. She was honest and noble, and the story about her taking a terrible beating for something she hadn't done, just to save everyone being punished, was one of St Vincent's often repeated legends.

For the four years Dulcie was with her, May had squirmed every time the story was related to a new girl. She hated Dulcie for making her feel bad about herself. But more than that she despised her sister for not seeking revenge on anyone who ill-treated her. May never let anyone get away with anything – just a sharp word, criticism, a slap, someone leaving her out of something, and she found subtle ways of getting back at them. Even before Dulcie left there had been many girls who had to suffer the indignity of being punished as a bed-wetter because May had slipped out of the washroom and into the dormitory while the others were washing, to take a pee on the bed of the girl she wanted humiliated. She would steal and destroy any personal belongings, especially photographs of relatives or old letters, because she knew how much comfort and pride these gave to the owner. It pleased her to slip nasty things into a mean Sister's dinner, a few maggots from the compost heap weren't noticed amongst the pearl barley in soup, and when Sister Anne was ill for several days after eating one of the meals May had prepared, she was even more delighted.

Once Dulcie was gone, it was a great deal easier to creep around the Sisters and make them idolize her. She studied them, discovered their weaknesses, loves and hates, and used them to her own advantage. Sister Ruth loved flowers, so she pretended to have the same passion, helping her water them, asking her their names. Sister Agatha suffered from headaches, and when she sat down holding her head, May would go over to her and massage her forehead. But getting Reverend Mother's affection and keeping it had been the biggest triumph of all.

Yet May didn't want to be Mother's pet any longer. That was her real problem and there was no one she could go to for help or advice. Tonight she would give anything to have Dulcie here, for she knew that her sister would know what to do.

It had seemed so smart to suck up to Mother and become her special girl. To get to go out in the car with her, to be allowed to wear her hair longer, to have piano lessons with her. It was glorious getting taken into a tea shop and having a cream horn and hot buttered crumpets when they were out, a bar of chocolate here, an ice-cream there. Then there were all those little things May had stolen from shops while she was with her – chocolate, hair slides, sachets of shampoo, little toys and costume jewellery. No one watched a child with a nun, it was like suspecting a priest of dipping into the collection plate. She used those little goodies to buy friends, because suddenly she'd found she didn't have any real ones any more, except for those dags whom no one else wanted to play with.

She thought she was so clever, right up till about three months ago. She was out on the playing field with the other girls for gym exercises when she suddenly felt Mother looking at her in a special and unnerving way. All the girls were wearing just their knickers and vests, and many of them, like May, had budding breasts that jiggled up and down. Yet when it came to May's turn to do handstands, Mother moved forward to assist her by holding her legs, and her hand slid right down on to her bottom.

May had been patted on the bottom many times by other Sisters, but she knew this wasn't the same, and the very next time she had to go over to the convent for her piano lesson, Mother caressed her breasts and said she thought it was time she bought her a brassiere. A month earlier May would have killed to have such a thing. The girls who already wore them only got dished out with a secondhand one once their breasts were becoming an embarrassment. Yet she would rather have had the most worn, stretched one in the box than the humiliation of having Mother coming into the cubicle with her in the shop and insisting on fitting it herself, and her hands touching her bare skin.

Sometimes May tried to tell herself that this sort of touch was one that any mother would give her daughter, but even if she could only barely remember her own mother now, her heart told her that wasn't so. Reverend Mother kissed her on the mouth too when they were alone, and the last time she'd done it she put her tongue in and held her very tightly. It made May feel really sick.

The worst of it was, she knew it wasn't going to stop either, not unless she hit Mother or made a huge fuss. But what would that bring her? A beating like the one Dulcie got? She could still see those weals on her sister's bottom now and her face contorted with pain. She didn't think she could bear that.

Tears trickled down May's cheeks as she made her way on to the playing field. She had always held up that night Sister Teresa had put her in the Dark Place as the worst thing that could ever happen to her, she still had occasional nightmares about it. But this was equally bad in a different way because she felt a kind of evil presence with her at all times, knowing deep down that she was being sucked into something that was horribly wrong. Dulcie had once said before she left here that creeping around Mother wasn't a smart thing to do. At the time May just thought she was jealous of the treats she got. But maybe Dulcie knew what she was like, perhaps Mother had even touched *her*.

'You should have warned me, Dulcie,' she thought indignantly. 'And if you don't write to me soon I'll forget all about you too.'

The harvest was finally finished on Boxing Day. Apart from a roast chicken dinner, Christmas had passed like any other day, and Dulcie was glad of that. She was too exhausted when she crawled into bed on Christmas Eve to remember the time when she and May had hung their stockings on the end of the bed and lain awake for ages trying to see Santa Claus coming in to fill them.

She was up and out into the fields too early the following morning to dwell on how she and May would take their stockings along to their parents' room and get into bed with them. Daddy always put a silly hat on, and he'd make a tinsel crown for Mummy, and sing them 'Rudolph the Red Nose Reindeer' while they unwrapped the little parcels.

Occasionally during the day her mind slipped back to remembering the smell of the Christmas tree, the taste of sugar mice, or the sound of church bells and carols. But with the sun burning down on her as she drove the tractor, it was difficult to picture the frosty, foggy December nights back in England, seeing piles of tangerines in the greengrocer's, and turkeys and chickens hanging up in the butcher's shop window. Even if there was a slight sense of guilt that for the first time in her life she hadn't attended Christmas Mass, surely gathering in the harvest which would help feed so many people was really a better thing to be doing?

Then finally it was finished, the paddocks left with only short stubble, the grain all gone down to the bulkhead, and Dulcie shared Bill's jubilation.

'They said I'd never grow cereals out here,' he crowed, grinning from ear to ear. 'They said I'd go bust like all the others that tried, but I knew it could be done. I knew it.'

Dulcie could understand his elation. Sergeant Collins had told her on one of his visits that this area had defeated farmers again and again, the soil was too salty, the rainfall too low. Even though thanks to the experimental station at Salmon Gums it had been proved that by putting superphosphate on to the soil it would improve conditions, few men who hadn't been born and raised in this area were brave enough to risk breaking their backs clearing land and planting seed with no guarantee they would succeed where others had failed.

Many times during the harvesting Dulcie had found herself admiring Bill and his men. She might be appalled by their crudeness and lack of respect or understanding of women, but it took real men to take such vast areas of this arid, barren land, clear it and make crops grow. She felt they had every right to be pleased with themselves for it was a magnificent achievement.

Yet as she smiled at the men cavorting around like over-excited schoolboys and shared their joy, she glanced over at Pat, and the smile on her face froze. Pat was gazing at her husband with absolute hatred.

It not only chilled Dulcie but made no sense either. Bill might be hateful to Pat – in all the months she'd been here Dulcie had never heard him say a kind or tender word to her – but surely a good harvest meant security for both of them, in time a better home, and money in the bank? She wondered where the woman's mind was.

Later that same night, she found out. The men wolfed down their evening meal and went straight off to the pub. As Dulcie washed up the dishes she heard a faint sound from the living-room and went in there to find Pat crying.

She was sitting at the desk, her head down on a bed of paperwork. She still had bits of straw in her lank, greasy hair and was wearing the same cotton trousers and man's shirt she'd had on all week.

'What is it?' Dulcie asked, putting her hand on her shoulder. 'Are you feeling poorly? Why don't you go and get into bed and I'll make you some hot milk.'

'It will take more than rest and hot milk to make me feel better,' Pat sniffed. 'You don't know how hard I prayed for a storm, a bush fire, anything but to see that harvest gathered in.'

Dulcie was bewildered. She perched on the arm of the couch next to Pat. 'I don't understand. Surely a good harvest is good for you too,' she said. The woman badly needed a bath, she stank to high heaven and her hair looked as though she hadn't washed it for weeks. 'Tell me why you didn't want it, Pat, please.'

Pat sat up and looked at Dulcie. Her eyes were swollen and she looked pale despite her sun-burnt skin. 'He'll be unstoppable now,' she said with a shrug. 'He'll get more and more land, borrow more and more money, and he'll expect me to take the brunt of his bad temper when he's worried. I won't ever see a penny of anything he makes, but he'll have me working every waking hour. What sort of life is that?'

Dulcie had learnt from Jake that as far as the hard work was concerned Pat was no different to any other farmer's wife in the area, they all worked like dogs. Yet according to Jake, mostly they revelled in it, but of course they probably had husbands who treated them kindly.

'It might not be that way.' Dulcie thought Pat was being overly pessimistic. Bill might be a pig to her, but he wasn't a fool. 'Besides, if the harvest had failed you'd have been far worse off.'

Pat shook her head. 'I wouldn't, you see I had it planned. First I was going to say we couldn't afford to keep you any more. He would've agreed with that immediately and I could have found you a job in a decent place down in Esperance. Then I was going to go too, go on back to Adelaide and get work as a housekeeper or something.'

Dulcie's eyes widened with shock. 'You were going to leave him?'

'Surely you don't imagine I love him?' Pat snapped. 'You've seen how he treats me. Could any woman love a man like that?'

Dulcie didn't know what to say. Bad as Bill was, she'd got the idea Pat was totally resigned to it.

'You'll see why I have to leave him in the next few days,' Pat said darkly. 'He'll go on a bender now, drinking till he's got no cash left. He'll come home and hit me when I'm not dazzled by all his wild plans. It's going to be hell.'

Dulcie persuaded her to go and have a shower and wash her hair while she made her a drink. Then once Pat was in bed, she came and sat by her. She had no advice to offer her, part of her thought she was over-reacting because she was exhausted, she even thought that maybe if Pat showed a bit more enthusiasm towards Bill's plans he might be nicer to her.

Yet she was touched that this woman with troubles

enough of her own had wished to help her leave before she did. For that kind thought she was prepared to sit here all night if necessary.

'I was working in a pub in Kalgoorlie when I met Bill,' Pat said suddenly, her sun-tanned face very dark against the white pillow. 'I was twenty-two and I'd already been to hell and back several times. He came into the pub one night and talking to him was like having a breath of fresh, sweet air. He'd just been demobbed from the army but he came from a farming background – when he spoke of it he brought back good memories from when I was just a little kid. He said he was after a place down this way, and some blokes in the pub took the rise out of him and said he'd be wasting his time and energy. But it was that energy about him I liked, Dulcie, I'd known too many dead-beats. He stayed in Kalgoorlie for about a week before he got a job on a farm around Norseman, and in that time he asked me to marry him. He said I was everything he wanted.'

Pat broke off then and began to cry again. 'I might have known a man couldn't want me in a romantic way, all my life until then every man I ever met used me, then walked away. But I thought Bill was different,' she sobbed.

Dulcie stroked back her damp hair and wondered how anyone could imagine ape-like Bill to be a romantic hero – she knew nothing of men, but just one look at him had told her what he was.

'Well, I married him and right off I saw what he meant by "I was everything he ever wanted". A good cook, a slave, someone to kick about when he felt miserable. A woman who wouldn't complain when he spent every spare hour with his mates. I was a dream to him, but it was a bloody nightmare for me. Once we got this place it got even worse. I'm a prisoner, Dulcie, I'm only thirty-one and I look forty. Unless I make a break for it soon, that's my life for ever. All I can say is, thank God I never had a child by him.'

'Go to sleep now, Pat,' Dulcie urged her. 'You might be wrong about him, he might be so happy now that everything will change. I'll say my prayers for him and you tonight.'

Pat's dark eyes opened wide and she jerked her head off the pillow. 'Surely you don't believe in any of that claptrap any longer?'

Dulcie hadn't seen a priest or been anywhere near a church since she arrived here and she had no intention of ever doing so. She had turned her back quite firmly on all that 'claptrap' as Pat called it. But that was the Catholic Church, they'd lied and cheated her, she'd found what they did in the name of God was evil. But the God her granny had taught her to pray to was still there, she saw His handiwork every day out in the bush, felt His comforting presence all around her. She hadn't quite given up on Him.

'I still believe someone watches over us,' she said softly. 'I have to otherwise I'd just give up.'

But if God heard her prayers that night, he didn't intervene on Pat's behalf. Bill did come home drunk, vomited all over the kitchen floor, then forced his attentions on Pat in the most brutal manner. Dulcie lay quivering in her bed, listening to Bill's crazed lust and Pat's distressed whimpers, and promised herself she would never marry.

Pat was right in all her predictions. Bill kept up drinking both day and night for around a fortnight. Sometimes he didn't come home at all, and when he did, he hit her. The other men joined him in his bender at first, but by the end of the first week they were back to work again without him. There was an uneasy atmosphere when they came in to eat, as if they felt uncomfortable being in the house while Bill wasn't there. Yet all of them were nicer to Pat. Ted and Bert came in with wood they'd chopped for her, Jake often stacked up the dishes or took the chook-food pail from her hands and said he'd feed them. But then this time Bill had marked her face with his blows, and to see a woman with a half-closed eye was evidence of his cruelty to her, and perhaps they felt that Bill was going too far now.

Then suddenly Bill came back to work and took up the reins again, acting as if he'd just been away on a short holiday. Pat was right too about him wanting to get more land and new machinery – every evening over dinner he talked of little else.

Sometimes Pat would catch Dulcie's eye and gave her an 'I-told-you-so' look. But she had sunk back into one of her morose moods again and made no further confidences.

Chapter Twelve

'Where's Pat?' Bill asked as he came into the kitchen for supper. It was May, the lambing just over, and it was cold. Bill was scowling as usual and rubbing his dirty hands together to warm them.

'Mucking out the pigs,' Dulcie replied. Bill had bought three piglets back in January in the hopes they could breed from them. Pat had gone out a couple of hours ago, telling Dulcie to make the supper, and it was only now that Bill asked where she was that Dulcie noticed it was dark outside.

'Those bloody pigs get better treatment than us,' Ted said. 'What's for supper, Dulc?'

'Lancashire hot-pot,' Dulcie replied and half smiled at Ted's face lighting up. She had found the recipe in a magazine and it had become one of the men's favourite meals. The men sat down at the table and she put their plates of food in front of them.

Bill began to wolf down his, but stopped suddenly to look round at the window. 'Get Pat in,' he said sharply. 'All I need now is for her to get bitten by a snake and have to drive down to the hospital.'

Dulcie went straight away, only stopping to put on a pair of wellingtons and light a lantern. By day she never thought about snakes and hardly ever wore shoes outside, but it was different when she couldn't see what was on the ground.

She called Sly and Prince to come with her as the pigs' enclosure was on the far side of the barn. Many times in the past they'd barked a warning when there were snakes about, and their presence was comforting.

As she made her way over towards the pig sty, Dulcie was thinking about going to Esperance with Jake later in the week. Bill often let her go with Jake on his monthly trips into town, and during the summer months she'd been able to get to the beach while he collected spare parts for the machinery and provisions.

Dulcie thought sleepy little Esperance was heaven on earth. She loved the pine trees, the clear blue sea, the fishing boats and the little wooden-fronted shops. It wasn't as stiflingly hot in summer as Salmon Gums, there was no bother from flies, and the residents and holidaymakers seemed so jolly and friendly. When she sat on the beach with an ice-cream, looking at the sea, she didn't feel she'd been cheated by Australia, for it was like the pictures she'd seen all those years ago at the Sacred Heart. She was determined that when she was eighteen she would find a job here, and one day explore all along the coastline which Jake said was very rugged and beautiful.

'Pat!' she called, well before she got to the barn. 'Supper's ready.'

There was no reply, only a scuffle to her right. Sly barked, and Dulcie lifted the lantern to see a kangaroo just a few feet away from her. 'Shoo,' she said. She loved to see kangaroos, but not up close in the dark. Prince barked then and the kangaroo hopped away. Dulcie went on behind the barn.

Pat wasn't at the sty, and it didn't look or smell as if she'd mucked the pigs out. Mystified, Dulcie took the longer way back to the house, calling out her name. Just recently Pat had taken to going for a walk in the afternoons, she said it relaxed her, but she was always back well before the men came home.

Dulcie went back into the house. The men were just finishing their meal and they all looked up as she came in.

'She's not there,' Dulcie said, feeling a little worried now.

'What time did she go out?' Bill asked.

'About threeish. She said she was going to muck out the pigs, and for me to get the supper ready.'

'It doesn't take three hours to muck out three bloody pigs,' Bill said curtly. 'Anyone come by today?'

'No,' Dulcie said. 'Well, I didn't hear a truck or anything.'

Bill turned away from her and looked at the men. Suddenly they all looked concerned, not irritated as she would have expected.

'Shall I go out looking?' Jake asked.

Bill nodded. 'Take the truck, call in at the Petersons as you pass and see if she's there. I'll go over the back on the tractor.'

Ted got up. 'Bert and me will look over towards our place. She could've walked that way.'

Now that Dulcie saw they were worried, she became frightened.

'What shall I do?' she asked.

'Stay here,' Bill said. 'I'll leave Prince with you and take Sly.'

Dulcie sat down to eat her supper, but she had only taken a couple of mouthfuls when a thought struck her. Could Pat have chosen today to leave?

It seemed an absurd thought, for since that night when they finished the harvest last year, she hadn't said anything at all to indicate she ever thought of it. Yet she had been even more morose than usual in the past few weeks.

Dulcie put her supper back into the oven and went into Pat and Bill's room. Pat's hairbrush and comb still sat on the top of the chest of drawers. Her nightdress was folded under the pillow where Dulcie had put it that morning too. Feeling a sense of relief, Dulcie was just about to turn round and return to the kitchen and her supper, when she felt compelled to check the wardrobe too.

At first glance nothing was missing. Pat's best blue coat was still hanging there, and the usual four or five dresses, her two pairs of shoes, one with high heels, the other flat ordinary ones sitting beneath them. But then she remembered the two-piece navy blue costume Pat had bought in Esperance the last time they went there, and the new shoes. They were gone.

Pat had asked her not to mention them to the men. Dulcie hadn't thought that was odd at the time, in fact it had prompted her to tell Pat that her mother used to buy new clothes and never admitted it to her father.

Returning to the kitchen, Dulcie found she no longer had any appetite for her supper and gave it to Prince. As she cleared the table and washed up, all she could think of was Pat. She had been in one of her silent moods this morning, and Dulcie remembered that when she went out to feed the chooks and the pigs, Pat had been sitting at the table with a cup of tea. When Dulcie returned half an hour later, Pat was still sitting there, the tea cold in front of her. That was unusual – even in a sullen mood Pat never sat still for more than a few minutes. So she must've been brooding about something.

That navy costume and shoes were too smart to wear anywhere except in town – had she packed them in a small bag knowing that someone was coming by today who would give her a lift away from here?

The more Dulcie thought about it, the more certain she became that was what Pat had done. Without a suitcase and wearing her old work-clothes, a neighbour picking her up would think nothing of it if she said she needed something urgently from the shop, and that she'd wait there to get a lift back later.

The bus left at six for Kalgoorlie. Was she on it?

Part of her was glad for Pat, she even silently applauded her for finding the courage to go, yet she couldn't help but be horrorstruck by what this would mean for her. Bill would be furious when he discovered the truth, he might even take it out on her. How could she possibly stay in this house alone at nights with him?

The more she dwelt on that, the more scared she became. Yet at the same time she knew she mustn't tell Bill about the missing costume and shoes, or he might drive up to

Kalgoorlie and catch Pat before she could get on the train to Adelaide.

As the evening progressed Dulcie became even more confused, for each time the men came back in they looked more and more worried, and their questions ever more frantic. For the first time in the year and a half she'd lived in this house she saw these men did actually care about Pat. Bill certainly deserved to lose her, yet Dulcie felt very sorry that it was only now when he believed she was hurt or in danger that he was able to show his feelings.

'You should have gone out to look for her before it got dark,' he said to Dulcie, running his hands through his hair. His dark eyes were deeply troubled, yet he didn't sound as if he was blaming her, only himself for not coming home earlier. 'She could've been bitten by a bloody snake. She's so thin the poison would work twice as fast as it would in a man of my weight. But if she's lying out around here somewhere I can't understand why the dogs haven't found her.'

He checked their room and found nothing missing. He questioned Dulcie about what Pat was wearing and if anyone had come to the house in the last week.

Bert was the only one who dared voice the possibility that Pat might have left him. 'She could've, Bill! A snake bite don't knock you out right away, she'd have shouted for help or got back here. You've been saying for weeks that she's been acting weird. I reckon she's got another bloke and she's gone off with him.'

Bill took a threatening step towards him, but Ted intervened.

'You stupid bastard,' he said to his brother, making sure he was between the two men. 'We ain't exactly in the middle of Perth where blokes come and go without being noticed. I always said you think with yer dick not yer head.'

Jake cooled things down. 'Pat ain't the kind to go off with another bloke. We all know that, so shut yer gob, Bert. I reckon she just wandered off for a bit of a walk, went too far and got lost in the dark. Dulcie said she was wearing her old trousers, boots and that jacket with the rips in it. So she weren't planning to go out dancing!'

He froze Bert with a say-anything-more-and-I'll-break-your-neck look. 'She won't freeze in that lot, and we'll soon find her in the morning. Best thing we can do is get our heads down for a bit and be out looking for her as soon as it's light.'

It was after eleven when Ted and Bert left to go to their house. Jake went off on his motorbike, but Bill went out again with Sly. Dulcie stood out on the veranda for some time; she could hear Bill calling to Pat and saw the flash of his lantern through the bushes. She felt wicked allowing him to worry when by now Pat might be boarding the train to Adelaide.

It was after one when Bill finally came back in. Dulcie made him tea and put it in front of him.

'Go to bed now, Bill,' she said, touching his shoulder. 'You can't do anything more tonight.'

'Did she say *anything* to you?' he asked, looking beseechingly at her. 'Women talk about stuff when they're on their own, don't they?'

Dulcie sensed he was beginning to think Pat might have actually walked out on him. Perhaps while he was searching outside he'd come to see how badly he had treated her. Yet the surprising part of it all was that he wasn't angry, he just looked like a kid who'd been whipped.

'She's been very quiet for some weeks,' Dulcie said truthfully. She didn't understand why she felt sorry for him now, after all the times she'd heard him hitting Pat and calling her foul names. She looked down at his two big fists clenched on the table and could imagine clearly what damage they must have inflicted on his wife. 'But she didn't talk about personal things to me, Bill.'

'I treated her so bad sometimes,' he said, holding his head between his two hands. 'I wish I hadn't. When I get her back I'll get this place fixed up better for her.'

As Dulcie got into her bed, leaving Bill slumped on the couch in the living-room, she felt a piece of paper between the two sheets. She pulled it out, quickly lit the candle again, and saw it was a brief note from Pat.

Dear Dulcie, she read. *I've left. I couldn't stand it any more. The only thing I feel bad about is leaving you there to face the music. I reckon you won't find this until you go to bed, by then I'll be well away, but don't show it to Bill. I've left a note for him in our post-office box. Tomorrow you go down to the Petersons and ask them to ring Sergeant Collins, you can't stay there without me and I know he'll come and get you. You're a good kid, and I hope you'll get a better deal in your next job. Pat.*

Dulcie tore the note into tiny pieces and burned them one by one with the candle until it was nothing more than a sprinkling of ash. She didn't know how she felt: there was relief that Pat was safe, that she'd cared enough to worry about Dulcie's safety, and even delight that now she could get away from here too. But she knew too that when Bill discovered that Pat had left him, all hell would break loose.

She must have slept eventually because she woke with a start to hear the truck starting up. She pulled back the curtain and saw the first weak rays of daylight in the sky.

The fire was lit and the kettle boiling when Jake came in. He looked rougher than usual, clearly he hadn't slept much either. 'Bill out looking already?' he said.

Dulcie nodded. 'He was out at first light. Are the others with you? Shall I make your breakfast now?'

'They've gone off in their truck down towards Salmon Gums again. I'll take my bike and help Bill look around here. Don't start breakfast till they all get back.'

He was gone in a flash, and she heard the sound of his motorbike roar off around the back of the farm.

She busied herself getting the food ready for the chickens and pigs, trying to keep her mind blank. But she couldn't. If Bert and Ted picked up the mail while they were in Salmon Gums, Pat's letter with it, Bill would go mad with anger. Yet if they didn't collect the mail, how long would Bill go on searching out in the bush before he gave up? If he called the police, how could she go on pretending she knew nothing? What if they got other farmers to join in the search?

When Jake came back and said he'd called the police from the Petersons' farm, Dulcie felt sick with anxiety. She imagined them grilling her and eventually getting her to admit what she knew, then blaming her for wasting their time. What if Bill turned on her and hit her?

But then Bert and Ted arrived back, and by the angry expressions on their faces and the mail in Bert's hands, she knew it was all going to come out. Bill turned up moments later, wild-eyed and distraught, snatched the letter from their hands and ripped it open.

'The bitch,' he roared out as he read the letter. 'She's bloody well left me!'

Dulcie did what she always did when a row was brewing in the house, and rushed outside to do the chores. For once she was glad to milk the cows and chop wood, anything was better than going back inside and being drawn into the furore.

But even outside she could hear Bill's voice as he ranted and raved at his men and she wondered how long it would be before she was called in for more questioning and whether she dared make a break for it now and run down to the Petersons' farm.

She thought when a police car arrived at ten o'clock that her troubles would be over, but the two policemen from Norseman were very different from Sergeant Collins, more like Bill and his cousins in character – brusque, dismissive and arrogant. They made it very easy for her to do nothing more than show them into the house and offer them a cup of tea, as it was clear they thought a sixteen-year-old brought up in an orphanage had to be dense and wouldn't have been a confidante of a farmer's wife.

They stayed around half an hour, during which time Bill's voice roared out several times in anger and she heard glass breaking which suggested he was now drinking. Dulcie stayed outside, chopping wood for all she was worth, and it was only when the police came out, preparing to leave, that she plucked up her courage and asked them what she was supposed to do now.

'Carry on with your work,' the foxy-faced one said, as if he was surprised by the question.

'But I can't stay here alone with Bill,' Dulcie said, her eyes filling with tears at his harsh tone.

She saw them exchange glances. 'Why not?' the younger, fresh-faced one asked.

'It isn't right,' she retorted, wishing she dared ask if they would leave their daughter or young sister here with an angry man who was likely to go out and get rip-roaring drunk. 'Could you telephone Sergeant Collins in Esperance and tell him what's happened?' she asked.

'What's he to you?' the foxy-faced one asked.

'He was kind to me in the past when I ran away. He often comes by to bring me books. Please ring him,' she pleaded.

'Did you know Pat had left Bill?' the policeman asked brusquely, his eyes boring into hers as if blaming her for a fool's errand.

Dulcie shook her head. 'Please ring Sergeant Collins. I can't stay here, it's not safe.'

Perhaps it was the sound of something being hurled against the wall inside the house that made them take her seriously, for the foxy-faced one nodded and told her to keep out of the men's way.

It was quite the worst day she had ever had. Bill stayed in the living-room, only coming out now and then to go to the dunny. Ted went off in the truck, but he was soon back, a couple of bottles of whisky in his hands. Yet even though they stayed in the living-room getting drunk

270

together, a malevolent atmosphere seemed to permeate the entire house. Jake disappeared and Dulcie guessed he had enough affection for Pat to be unable to listen to Bill's drunken raving.

Even Sly and Prince looked apprehensive, curled up by their kennels out on the veranda. They never came into the house, but then their days were spent out with the men, and they were confused by their master's voice coming from the living-room.

Dulcie mucked out the pigs which Pat hadn't even begun yesterday, she weeded the vegetable garden, and only returned to the house when she knew she must make some bread and something for the men's supper. Yet all the time she was worrying that Sergeant Collins wouldn't come, or that if he did he'd say he couldn't help her. She didn't know if her savings were enough to get the train to Perth and rent a room until she could find a job there, and besides, she might be picked up by the police there.

She was just taking a loaf out of the oven when Sergeant Collins rapped on the door, and she had never been so pleased to see anyone. Before either of them could say a word, there was a loud bellow of laughter from the men in the living-room, and Sergeant Collins raised his eyebrows.

'They're drunk,' she said with a shrug. 'I can't stay here, Mr Collins, by tonight they'll be like madmen.'

For just one moment as he looked at her, she thought he was going to tell her to calm down and see how things went, but instead he put one hand on her shoulder. 'Go and get your things together and wait outside for me. I'll go and speak to Bill,' he said in a low voice.

Once Dulcie had run along to her room, Collins opened the living-room door, and almost recoiled from the smell of unwashed bodies, cigarettes and whisky.

Bill was sprawled out on the couch, a glass of whisky in his hand, the two red-headed cousins were slumped in chairs, equally drunk. There was another empty bottle on the cigarette ash-strewn floor, the hearth in front of the unlit wood stove littered with dog-ends they'd thrown in that direction.

'I heard about Pat,' he said. 'I'm sorry, Bill.' He felt that he ought to say more, but the words stuck in his throat.

'The bloody bitch walked out on me,' Bill said, his words so slurred they were almost unintelligible. 'How could she do that?'

Ted and Bert were both looking squint-eyed at Collins. He guessed they weren't so drunk they hadn't realized he'd come to do something more than to offer his condolences.

'I came about Dulcie,' he said quickly, seeing no point in beating about the bush. 'She can't stay here alone with you lot. It wouldn't be right. I'll take her home to my missus for the time being.'

'But who's going to cook for us?' Bert asked.

'You'll have to manage yourselves,' Collins said. 'By the smell out in the kitchen she's already made you something for today.'

Bill lurched to his feet scowling. 'She ain't leaving me now,' he said angrily. 'I need her.'

'She's just a child,' Collins said firmly, drawing himself up to his full height of five foot eleven, and hoping one of them wouldn't rush him. 'You are all drunk, and it isn't fair to expect her to cope with that, and looking after this place alone.'

As he looked around at the three men's belligerent expressions and sensed the menace seeping out of Bill, he had real sympathy for what Pat had put up with for so long. He had no doubt that Dulcie would be in real danger if he didn't get her out of here now. 'Don't even think of trying to stop me,' he said as he saw Bill lurch towards an empty bottle to use it as a weapon. 'Or you'll have far more on your hands than your wife leaving you to cope with.'

He left then, shutting the door behind him, and hoped that Dulcie was ready.

She was, waiting nervously out on the veranda, her suitcase in her hand. She had changed the faded dress she'd been wearing earlier to a blue one. It was too short, and tight around her chest, and the blue ribbon in her hair and her short white socks made her look about twelve, not sixteen.

'Come on,' he said. 'I'm taking you home with me.'

As Collins pulled away from the house he heard Bill yell something from the front door, and the sound of breaking glass as he threw the empty bottle at his car. When he glanced sideways at Dulcie he saw she was crying.

'You're quite safe now,' he said. 'I'm taking you home with me. My wife will take care of you.'

She cried for some little time, and Collins let her, for he could imagine what she'd been through today. The police at Norseman weren't noted for their gentleness, they had to be tough, their usual customers were the gold miners, whores and other itinerants who ended up in Kalgoorlie. Breaking up fights, two-up games, dealing with drunkenness, theft and prostitution was what they knew, and one little kid caught up in what was no more than a domestic row wouldn't trouble them. But it did trouble him. He wouldn't mind betting that most of the whores up there had started out much like Dulcie, nudged into that way of life because they had no one to guide them.

The saddest thing about it to him was that a girl on the threshold of womanhood should see such ugly things. Would she grow up to think Bill's behaviour to his wife was normal? If a man treated her marginally better than Bill did Pat, would she imagine she was lucky?

Dulcie fell asleep on the journey. Her head lolled against the window, her dress had ridden up above her knees, and her hands lay relaxed in her lap. Collins thought he ought to feel pleased she felt safe enough to drop off to sleep, but as he looked down at the many bruises and small scabs on her legs and knees, the calluses on her hands and the broken nails and lack-lustre hair, instead he felt only shame that this should happen to someone so alone in the world.

Chapter Thirteen

'You aren't going anywhere just yet, Dulcie,' Molly Collins said in answer to Dulcie's question about finding a new job. 'Sean and I have decided that you need a little holiday before you even start to think about that. Today I'm going to take you to have your hair cut. After that we'll take a walk along the beach, then maybe we'll buy some material so you can make yourself a new dress. That's enough for one day.'

Dulcie's eyes welled up with emotional tears. Since Sergeant Collins brought her to his home three days ago, she had been overwhelmed by his and Molly's kindness. They considered it a quite ordinary police house, but as it had electricity, a refrigerator and wireless and stood on the corner of Pink Lake Road, just a short walk to the sea-front and shops, Dulcie thought it was the height of luxury.

Mrs Collins wouldn't even let her do anything to help her, and she fed her food that Dulcie'd never even seen before. She slept in the bedroom of their daughter who was away at university, surrounded by dolls, teddy bears and pictures of film stars, and yet as she lay in the comfortable bed, Alfie their cat curled up beside her, she kept thinking it was only a matter of time before she would be plunged back somewhere awful again.

'Don't cry, my dear.' Mrs Collins came closer and enveloped her in her arms. She was a small, stout lady in her late forties, with a youthful face and gentle brown eyes. 'You've had a miserable time up there with the Masters, but it's all over now.'

Dulcie sobbed. It was a strange thing that while she

loved the hugs and cuddles Mrs Collins gave so readily they always made her cry even more.

Mrs Collins tipped up Dulcie's face to look at her and smiled. 'Now, come on, wash your face, brush your hair and we'll go out, get your hair done and buy some dress material. I've got a nice pattern I bought to make a couple of dresses for our Wendy before she went off to Sydney. I thought you'd look real beaut in pink, what do you think?'

Three weeks later Dulcie was in the kitchen helping Mrs Collins by laying the table for the evening meal when Sergeant Collins came home from work. He 'cooeed' from the front door, which Dulcie had come to notice meant he had exciting or interesting news.

Mrs Collins turned from her position at the stove where she was making gravy, and looked expectant. 'Want a beer, love?' she called out. 'Or can it wait till you've told us?'

He came into the kitchen. 'Told you what?' he asked with a wide grin.

'Whatever it is that's brought you home so perky,' she laughed.

'I've got the perfect job for Dulcie,' he said. 'At least I hope she'll think it is.'

'I'm sure if you think it's a good one, I'll love it,' Dulcie said.

She had come to trust his and his wife's judgement in everything. They insisted that they would contact Reverend Mother at St Vincent's by telephone rather than let Dulcie write a letter which might be ignored. The nun, finding herself speaking to a policeman, who in no uncertain terms pointed out that no inexperienced young girl should ever have been sent to the Masters' place to work, had little option but to agree that he should now find a suitable position for Dulcie. It was their suggestion too that she should have her hair cut and styled, and that she should make herself some dresses to go with her fashionable new hair-style.

The Collins' advice and care had made Dulcie blossom

in every way. She had managed to stop tormenting herself about Pat, she had after all found peace now.

Rested and well fed, Dulcie had put on a little weight, her complexion was almost as smooth now as it had been when she was a child. Her hands were softer and her nails cared for. Yet it was her hair which Dulcie prized most, for in the hands of an experienced hairdresser it looked beautiful. Because of the long-term neglect, several inches had to be cut off, but not in the brutal manner of St Vincent's. She had what they called a 'feather cut', short and bouncy, that brought back the natural wave and enhanced the pure blonde colour. When she looked in the mirror, for the first time in her life she saw a pretty girl staring back, the feathery effect framing her face, emphasizing features she'd never known were dainty until now.

So if Sergeant Collins was to tell her he had a job on a fishing boat, or even in the gold mine at Kalgoorlie, she would believe it would be right for her.

'It's with the Frenches,' he said, pulling up a kitchen chair and sitting astride it, leaning his arms on the back. 'You'll remember John Withers and young Ross that picked you up? Well, they work there too.'

'I couldn't forget them,' Dulcie smiled ruefully. 'They're the ones that dobbed me in.'

'Now, you know they meant it kindly,' he reproved her. 'Anyway, it's a real good farm, Dulcie, only a few miles out of Esperance. They've got all the modern amenities, not like the Masters' place. Bruce French and his wife Betty are getting on now, and they are good people, anyone will tell you that. Young Ross has come on a treat since he got taken on by them, and heaven knows what he'd been through before he turned up at their place.'

Dulcie's mind shot back to that day at Salmon Gums, and the brief conversation she and Ross had had. 'Was he in an orphanage too?' she asked curiously.

'I wouldn't be surprised, though no one's ever been able to get a word out of him about it. Bruce found him sleeping in his barn a couple of years ago. The poor kid was starving and sick, they took care of him until he was better, then decided to give him a job and see how he shaped up. Bruce reckons it was the best gamble he'd ever taken. Anyway, what d'you think, want me to take you out there tomorrow to meet them?'

It was another new experience for Dulcie to be asked if she wanted to do something rather than being ordered. 'Yes please,' she said. 'Would I be doing the same work as for Pat and Bill?'

'Much the same. Land-clearing, wood-chopping, cleaning out the dunny. Milking the cows. Cooking, cleaning and waiting on the table.'

Dulcie's eyes flew open in horror involuntarily, she'd thought it was going to be a better job.

'Don't tease her, you great galah,' Mrs Collins said sharply, smacking her husband on the shoulder. 'Don't pay no mind to him, Dulcie,' she said, and turning to the girl she tweaked her cheek affectionately. 'Betty French is a lovely lady, if she wants a girl to help out, it will be around the house, and you just wait till you see it, it's as lovely as she is.'

Sergeant Collins grinned at Dulcie. 'Yes, it's like Molly says, Betty's getting on, and a bit shaky on her pins. You'll have a nice room in the house, good food and a pound a week wages, how does that sound?'

'Wonderful,' she smiled. 'I just hope they like me.'

'They do already just from what I've told them about you,' he said. 'Now, didn't someone mention a beer?'

Dulcie's first impression of the Frenches' place as Sergeant Collins turned up the dirt track towards it the following afternoon was that it could be a farm in England, for the rainfall was much higher here than in Salmon Gums and the grass was thick and lush. Brown and white cows were standing almost knee-deep in clover either side of the track, there were English trees too, not just gums. As they approached the homestead, her heart quickened, for though it was similar in style to most Australian homes she'd seen, a single storey surrounded by a wide veranda, it was new, brick-built, the veranda painted a glossy green, and with a carefully tended garden in front of it.

She remembered how her heart had sunk when she arrived at the Masters' place, yet in the eighteen months she'd been there she'd grown so used to the dilapidated state of it, the empty kerosene and oil cans and other refuse that hung around it, she'd stopped seeing the ugliness of it. But care shone out of the whole of this place. As Sergeant Collins pulled round on to a gravelled area at the side, she noticed that even the tractor left there was shiny red and new-looking.

Before they had even got out of the car the front door opened and a lady came out to greet them. She was short, white-haired, very plump, and supported herself on a stick. She looked about sixty. Her cotton dress was lavender-coloured with a white lacy collar, and she had a very warm smile.

'G'day,' she said. 'I've just made a pot of tea and some scones. Do you want to go and have a chat with Bruce, Sean? He's over in the barn. Dulcie and I can get to know one another on our own.'

'Righto, Betty.' Sergeant Collins made a sort of mock salute. 'I can see when I'm not wanted.'

She laughed. 'I'll save you some tea and scones. Come back in half an hour.'

As Dulcie stepped into the big main room of the house she had the strangest sensation of belonging there. She couldn't have found one reason to support this feeling, for apart from Susan's parents' home in Blackheath, she'd never seen anywhere so nice.

Susan's home had been traditionally English with beautiful furniture that had been passed down through generations, its thick curtains and carpets designed for comfort and warmth in cold winters. The Frenches' was the exact opposite, modern, spacious, cool and uncluttered. Not a bit what she would have expected of an elderly farming couple.

The room was very large, with windows on three sides, a polished wood floor with a couple of animal-skin rugs, comfortable-looking armchairs and a couch, and a dining table and chairs by one of the windows. There was nothing old or shabby, the walls were cream, the table gleamed with polish, and there were lots of pictures on the walls.

'It's so lovely,' Dulcie gasped, looking all around her.

'Not what you expected?' the woman asked with laughter in her voice. 'When Ross came in here the first time he was afraid to sit down. I hope it doesn't affect you like that!'

She asked Dulcie to go into the kitchen and bring out the tray she'd got ready, explaining she found carrying things difficult as she needed her stick. The kitchen was every bit as nice as the living-room, all painted pale lemon and very modern-looking like pictures she had seen in magazines.

Dulcie carried in the tray and put it down on the table where Mrs French was already sitting.

'Now, dear,' she said as she placed the cups in their saucers and poured the tea. 'I know you had an awful time at the Masters', and I'm quite sure you want to forget it, so why don't you tell me about you?'

Dulcie didn't know what she meant by that.

Mrs French must have understood for she reached out and patted her hand. 'I mean, like your interests, hobbies and things,' she said. 'I don't suppose you got much time for anything like that with the Masters, but Sergeant Collins said you are very good at needlework and like reading.'

Dulcie pulled herself up sharply, she didn't want the woman to think she was stupid. 'Yes, I love reading, and I like needlework when I'm making something, but mostly at the convent I only got to do mending. I used to love painting and drawing too, but we didn't get a chance to do that either.'

Mrs French nodded in understanding, handing her tea

and suggesting she helped herself to a scone. 'How did you do at school? In your lessons, I mean.'

Dulcie explained that she had always been top of the class, but hastily added that she didn't think that meant a great deal as the Sisters were prone to taking her out of class to do domestic work. 'I don't know anything about science, history, geography or current affairs,' she explained. 'All the Sisters cared about was neat writing, good spelling, knowing your tables and the Scriptures.'

'That's about all I learned at school too,' Mrs French said with a shrug. 'I suppose they think that's all girls need to know as they'll just get married and have a family. Do you have ambitions beyond that?'

'I don't ever want to get married,' Dulcie replied hastily. 'I used to want to be a teacher, but I don't suppose that's possible without any school exams.'

'I'm sure you'll change your mind about getting married if the right young man comes along,' Mrs French said with a little chuckle. 'But I believe you can be anything you want to be, if you are determined enough. My husband's an expert on that.

'He was born in a humpy in the Karri forests near Manjimup, that's over Albany way, his father was a tree feller. Right from a little boy he drove bullock trains that hauled the timber out of the forest, desperate hard work, but he was a battler, like his parents before him.' The older woman paused for a second.

Dulcie nodded, fascinated, and she carried on.

'He was just twenty when he joined up for the First War, but by then he'd done all sorts, on a whaling ship out of Albany, and as a drover up near Geraldton. I met him in Perth in 1919, my father worked on the railways, and when he saw we were set on getting married he tried to persuade Bruce to join him. But Bruce had his heart set on farming, the government were offering land to old soldiers, so off we came down this way, and got a place north of here. We had some real hard times, Dulcie. During the thirties I thought we were going to starve to death. I used to beg Bruce to take me back to Perth, but he wouldn't have it, he was determined to be a farmer, you see.' She paused for breath again and to butter a scone.

'Now, Sam Oldenshaw had this place then,' she went on, waving the butter knife at the view of the farm outside the window. 'Bruce used to come and work for him sometimes. Sam couldn't pay him anything, like everyone else then he was struggling to keep going himself, but he'd give us some mutton and milk from his cows. Things got so bad for us we had to leave our place, and Sam let us come here. We were so grateful we worked like demons for him. Then when Sam died in 1938, he left the farm to us. We couldn't believe it. He was such a grumpy old devil. We never thought he appreciated anything we'd done for him.'

Dulcie smiled. Mrs French was clearly one of those people who had a great many stories to tell.

'Reckon Sam would be right proud of what Bruce has done since,' Mrs French said with more than a touch of pride herself. 'Sam only had seven hundred acres, and mostly everyone in farming failed round here because the soil was so bad. But my Bruce was one of the first to try the modern fertilizers that put stuff like copper and zinc into the soil – it worked too! Bruce turned it around and made it pay, he bought more land as well, we've got nigh on two thousand acres now. When we got to pull down Sam's old tumble-down shack and built this place, I was the happiest woman on earth. But like I said, if you want something badly enough, you can get it, providing you're prepared to work hard for it.'

By now Dulcie was pretty certain that she could be happy here. 'What sort of help do you need, Mrs French?' she said, anxious to bring the conversation back to the job.

'Oh, I don't know,' the woman sighed. 'Just general stuff, I reckon. I've never had anyone to help me before.'

Having heard how hard both Mr and Mrs French had worked all their lives, Dulcie sensed Mrs French felt a little embarrassed at finding herself in the position where she needed help with chores she'd always done herself.

'I expect polishing the floor, cleaning the windows and that kind of thing is hardest, isn't it?' Dulcie said, feeling she needed the woman to see she was keen to work. 'I'm really good at cleaning, the Sisters made us do it all. But I'm all right at cooking too, and doing the washing.'

'If you do all that there won't be anything much left for me to do,' Mrs French said with a smile. 'Well, let me show you round and I expect by then the men will be coming in.'

The whole house was as lovely as the living-room, and Dulcie was astonished to see a beautiful patchwork quilt on Mrs French's bed, each square embroidered with a different flower. 'That's my hobby,' she said a little shyly when Dulcie exclaimed over it. 'Maybe you'd like to make one too.' She went on then to show Dulcie her sewing-room, with the first electric sewing-machine Dulcie had ever seen. 'Of course the embroidery is all done by hand, but I join the squares by machine.' To illustrate this she showed her a baby's quilt she was working on, at present only the four central squares completed, each with an embroidered animal.

She showed her how she traced designs from books, and said she wished she could draw as she had ideas in her head she couldn't find pictures of. 'Maybe you'll be able to draw some for me,' she remarked, going on to show Dulcie samples of another kind of work she called collage, where small pieces of contrasting fabric were sewn on with embroidery stitches to make even more complicated designs.

After that she showed Dulcie the smaller of the two spare rooms, which would be hers, and it was all Dulcie could do not to burst into tears because it was so pretty. Pink curtains, another lovely quilt on the single bed, even a bedside light for reading and a white sheepskin rug on the floor.

'Was this your daughter's room?' she asked curiously,

unable to believe anyone would have such a lovely spare bedroom and be prepared to let her sleep in it.

'We don't have any children,' Mrs French replied, a wistful look in her eyes, then she cocked her head on one side and said she heard the men coming in.

Mr French was a big man. Not just in size, though he was over six foot and well built, but because he had a personality that filled the room. Dulcie's first impression was that he couldn't possibly be over sixty, even if his thick hair was snowy white, for his bright blue eyes twinkled like a young man's and his voice was deep and vibrant. It was only much later that she noticed he had baggy skin beneath his eyes, and he walked with a slight limp as if his knees were stiff.

The men at the Masters' place had done nothing to ease Dulcie's timidity with the male sex. Even alone with Sergeant Collins she was often tongue-tied. Yet there was something about the way Mr French spoke to her that made her feel as if she'd known him all her life. His gentle questions such as did she like the house, and did she think she could be happy working for him and his wife, were so unexpected it made a lump come up in her throat. She hadn't thought it was possible that any employer would care about her happiness.

'I know I'll be happy here,' she said eagerly. 'The only thing I'm worried about is that there won't be enough work for me in the house. I could do chores outside too, I can see to the chickens, milk cows, and I can drive a tractor.'

Sergeant Collins gave her a sharp look as if to warn her she was talking herself back into the same kind of work she did with the Masters.

Yet Bruce just laughed. 'Beaut!' he exclaimed. 'If you can manage a tractor, you'll soon pick up driving my car. Betty gets in a blue every time I keep her waiting to take her into town or to visit friends, so you'll be able to take her. Now, you're not scared of snakes, are you? There's more here than up at Salmon Gums on account of the lake.'

Dulcie gulped. She had learnt to put them out of her mind while with the Masters as she rarely saw one. But she couldn't say she wasn't scared of them.

'Now, don't go frightening her,' his wife reproved him. 'They hardly ever come near the house. Don't worry, Dulcie!'

By the time Dulcie and Sergeant Collins left about an hour and a half later, after a tour around the property in Mr French's farm truck, Dulcie felt as though she was floating on a cloud, and couldn't wait to get back the following day to start work.

Both Mr and Mrs French, who insisted she was to call them Bruce and Betty, were great talkers. After months of mostly being ignored by the Masters, it was thrilling to be with people who wanted to share their life and their passion for farming with her.

Dulcie supposed that Bill had had a similar passion too, yet he certainly hadn't shown joy in it as Bruce did. As they were driving around the edge of one paddock where clover was growing, towards the lake on the property, Bruce had suddenly made a statement which almost made her cry.

'I'm such a lucky man,' he said, looking round at her and grinning broadly. 'I might have been born poor, but I've been given such riches. I'm never sick, I'm strong and healthy. My parents loved me, my mother, bless her, couldn't read or write, but she somehow always found someone around who was willing to teach me. My father taught me respect for living things, he loved his trees and animals. I came through the First World War unharmed when so many of my mates copped it. Then I met Betty. She enriched my life then, and she still does. She's stuck by me through thick and thin, and we certainly had plenty of the thin in the past. Then old Sam leaves us this place! That was like being given the sun, the moon and the stars! Sometimes I wonder what I ever did to deserve such good luck!'

Dulcie knew the answer to that, even if she was too shy to say it. His luck came to him because he was a kind, good man and because he looked at everything with delight and optimism.

She had only seen Ross and John Withers at a distance across a paddock, but they'd waved, and she'd felt they were glad she was here too now. Betty said there was also a third man called Bob and they all lived in the bunkhouse on the far side of the farm, but took their meals in the house as she and Bruce saw them as family. Just that word *family* sent delicious shivers down Dulcie's spine – she'd had a taste of that with the Collins and she'd come to love it.

'I knew you'd like them and they'd like you,' Sergeant Collins said with great pleasure as they drove back into Esperance. 'Having no kids of their own has been their one sadness, Betty lost three babies during the Depression, you know. But she's never let it turn her sour. Did she tell you about old Sam who gave them the farm?'

Dulcie nodded.

'But what neither of them will ever tell you is that he was the meanest, most cantankerous bastard God ever created,' he said with some feeling. 'He'd take a horsewhip to a man for spilling a pail of milk, he treated women like dirt. But he took them in when their farm failed, and that was enough for Bruce and Betty. They slaved for him, nursed him when he was sick, treated him like he was their father even though he put them through hell sometimes.' Collins broke off to grin at Dulcie.

'That wily old fox got me to witness his will, but he kept his hands over the words so I wouldn't know what was in it. I was only a young copper then, too wrapped up in my own family and career to care much about anyone else, but I liked Bruce and Betty a lot and I sweated blood when I knew Sam was dying, imagining them turned out of the farm after all they'd done. But I reckon Sam had more upstairs than any of us guessed. It was like I'd won the Melbourne Cup the day I heard the good news. I never was so glad for anyone.'

Dulcie could only smile. In the same year Bruce and Betty got the farm she was born 12,000 miles away. Who would have thought that sixteen years later they would be brought together by the same policeman who witnessed that will?

Bruce had told her that the war, which came so soon after getting the farm, was the turn in his and Betty's fortunes, for suddenly the prices for beef, lamb, wool and cereals shot up. He had said jubilantly that he'd never looked back, and when he finally got the new house finished three years ago, all his dreams were fulfilled. Dulcie couldn't help but feel her dreams were about to come true too.

The following morning at eight Dulcie was ready to leave, her suitcase in the car, Sergeant Collins behind the wheel, but Mrs Collins was delaying them setting off by fussing around Dulcie and giving her advice.

'Now, make sure you come and visit us whenever you come into town,' she said yet again. 'Once you can drive Bruce's car, you bring Betty down here too. And look after that pretty hair and your lovely English skin. Now, are you sure you've got everything?'

'I've got an awful lot more than I came with,' Dulcie giggled. Her suitcase barely closed over the two new dresses she and Molly had made together, and some old clothes of their daughters they'd given her to work in. There was a box of books on the back seat of the car, a bag of oddments of fabric to give to Betty for her patchwork, and now Mrs Collins was pressing a box of sweets into her hands too.

Molly caught Dulcie's face between her two chubby hands. 'I wish I could keep you here,' she said, her eyes brimming with tears. 'It will be lonely without you. But there'll always be a place for you here if you need it, and don't you be a stranger to us.'

'She's only going a few miles up the road, Molly,' Sergeant Collins said impatiently from inside the car. 'Anyone would think she was going to Queensland.'

Dulcie hurriedly kissed Mrs Collins and got into the car. She felt choked up with all the kindness and affection, and somehow just thanking them for letting her stay with them didn't cover what she truly felt.

A month later Betty stood watching Dulcie take a beef and onion pie out of the oven.

'You're a good little cook,' Betty said, looking appreciatively at the golden-brown pastry. Dulcie had decorated it with leaves the way she'd seen her granny do. 'I'll be able to be a lady of leisure soon, just sit in my chair and ring a bell when I want something.'

Dulcie laughed. Betty's legs might be bad but she had an energetic spirit that wouldn't allow her to sit down all day. 'I can't see you doing that for long,' she said. 'Besides, you've still got a lot to teach me, I still can't make gravy like you do.'

Dulcie could hardly believe her change in fortune. Working for Bruce and Betty wasn't a job to her, but a joy, for they appreciated everything she did for them. It wasn't even hard work. The house was easy to clean, they had constant hot water, and even a washing-machine with an electric wringer. Preparing and cooking meals was a delight, for the men's eyes lit up when she put the food in front of them and they savoured every mouthful.

But best of all was that she was treated like one of their family. For the first few mealtimes Dulcie had suffered agonies of shyness, and she could barely eat her own meal with so many eyes upon her, let alone speak. But maybe Bruce and Betty sensed this, for they gradually drew her into conversations, and bit by bit she found herself less self-conscious.

Bruce, John, Ross and the third hand, Bob, were as different to the men at the Masters' place as cows to sheep. None of them viewed women as lesser beings, if anything they placed them on a pedestal as amazing creatures who had skills they could never master.

Bruce and John were the talkers. Reminiscences, gossip, discussions on current affairs flowed effortlessly from them. Ross and Bob were naturally quiet men who enjoyed listening rather than taking an active part in conversation.

John Withers, the man who had picked her up the day she ran away, was in his late thirties. She had remembered him as being handsome, but now she'd got to know him better it wasn't just his looks, the sparkly blue eyes, strong features and blond hair which appealed to her, she found he had a lovely easy-going nature too. He had vast experience gleaned from work on cattle and sheep stations all over Australia and told stories about characters he'd met that had them all laughing. He had been on active service in Burma during the war, and on his discharge in Sydney it was his intention to go up to Kimberley to find work as a stockman. One of his favourite anecdotes was how at that time he'd fallen in with a bunch of other men who had the idea of pooling their resources and buying a jeep, so they could travel all over Australia picking up work as they went. Two of them were insistent on heading towards Western Australia, and by the time they'd broken down twice in the middle of the Nullarbor Plain, John had had enough of their bright ideas, and parted company with them at Kalgoorlie. Bruce was in town collecting some spare parts for his tractor, and they met and got talking in a pub. Bruce offered him a few weeks' work clearing land, and John accepted it because he was broke. That was in 1946 and he was still here ten years later.

Betty told Dulcie in confidence that John was a bit of a ladies' man, with two or three different ones scattered around. She laughingly said she thought he'd only leave now if they found out about one another and it got too hot for him.

Bob Banks was forty-five, and until his mother died a couple of years ago, had remained living with her in Esperance. He had never married, and Dulcie thought this was probably because of his unprepossessing appearance. He had bad teeth, sticking-out ears, scarcely any hair, pitted skin and very bandy legs. His father had been the town blacksmith, and from what Bruce told her, a giant brute of a man who made his only son's life a misery because of his gentle nature and weaker constitution. Bob shut down the forge when his father died, and scraped a living for himself and his mother by being the town's odd-job man and mechanic. Turned down for active service during the war, he came to work for Bruce who was finding it hard to get any help, then when his mother died, finally came here to live.

Ross intrigued Dulcie the most. If she hadn't felt his sympathy to her that day a year earlier in Salmon Gums, or got to know the story of how he was found here in the barn sick and starving, she might have thought him snooty. When he did speak to her it was usually to make rather boastful statements about all the things he could do. He *was* a bit of a marvel for someone of only nineteen – he could bricklay, mend vehicles and knew a great deal about animals – but it was very odd that he never spoke of where he learned all these things, and she knew from Bruce it wasn't all from here.

She remembered him as being just a gangly, thin boy on that first meeting, but he had become a man and, although still slender, his body rippled with muscle. While he had lovely tawny eyes, good features and curly dark auburn hair, he couldn't be described as handsome, for there seemed to be something missing. It struck Dulcie one day that he had a great deal in common with the half-wild cats that hung around the barns. They were very apprecia-tive when she took them out a few scraps of meat, some-times they even let her stroke them. But mostly they were on their guard, watching her from a distance, aloof and perhaps a little afraid.

Bruce couldn't praise Ross enough, he said he worked tirelessly, he had an instinctive way with animals and he was hungry for knowledge. But even he said that he couldn't quite reach the lad, adding that unless someone managed that, he felt Ross was destined to end up like Bob, a man who had nothing in his life but work.

It was one of Dulcie's jobs to clean out the men's bunkhouse once a week and change the sheets on their beds. The bunkhouse had been purpose-built for the men and consisted of one large room with their three beds, a smaller one which was only used by shearers when they were called in, a minuscule kitchen where they could make tea and coffee and a shower room.

The first time Dulcie went to clean it, she was surprised by how few personal possessions the men had. Bob had the most – framed family photographs, a piano accordion, a rack of pipes, books and a couple of old blue and white ginger jars he said his grandfather had brought back from China. John had a beautiful saddle, one picture of his family up in North Queensland tacked to the wall, a biscuit tin with horses on the lid which she assumed held old letters and sentimental souvenirs, and a couple of guns, but Ross had nothing other than his clothes.

Ross's lack of personal possessions baffled Dulcie. It was quite understandable that he'd had nothing from his childhood on his arrival here – after all she had nothing more than the now crumpled wedding photograph of Susan and her husband and the little keepsakes from the Sisters when she left St Vincent's. Yet Ross had been living here for three years, and she would have thought in that time he would have acquired a few items, if only to give him some feeling of homeliness and permanence. With the money she'd earned up at the Masters' place she had bought herself a little needlework box, a diary, a frame to put Susan's picture in, and a teddy-bear nightdress case to put on her bed. But then maybe men didn't have the same nest-building instincts.

She had been told by John that having sheets on their beds was a luxury he'd never come across until he came here to work. He said in most places the bunkhouse was a filthy tin shed, the shower a tank outside you stood underneath and pulled a bit of string to get sluiced down. 'I must be getting old,' he said, his blue eyes twinkling. 'I've got to like a decent place to kip, the good tucker, and a boss that don't drive you into the ground.'

John was as easy to understand as he was to talk to. He held nothing back, he laughed at himself and the world, a happy man who had been something of an adventurer right from a young lad, eager to see the world and embrace new experience. Dulcie suspected he'd never saved a penny in his entire life and had been something of a hell-raiser too. He was good to be near, for despite his rough edges he had the soul of a gentleman, he never cursed in front of her and Betty, he wouldn't come into the house when he was dirty or drunk, and he kept everyone entertained with his stories.

Dulcie would watch Ross sometimes when Bruce and John were talking, and saw that he idolized them both as he hung on their every word, his tawny eyes full of admiration. Yet he got on well with Bob too, she had observed them working together on an engine. Bob only spoke to instruct or point out things, and Ross said even less, but it was a companionable silence. Dulcie felt they had bonded together because they had miserable childhoods in common. She was determined that she was going to find out everything about Ross before long.

Bruce came in just as Dulcie was putting the vegetables in a dish. 'Umm,' he sniffed just outside the kitchen. 'That smells beaut. I'm so hungry I could eat a raw kangaroo.'

'That's what you'll get if you don't hurry and clean up,' Betty said, turning her head towards him and smiling. 'I'll be banging the gong any minute.'

Dulcie had discovered that the men's habit of coming in to eat their meals all washed and in clean clothes was Betty's doing and not typical of any other farm or station. She said that in most places the stockmen ate in a shed or outside. But although Betty had come from a poor family herself back in Perth, her mother had high standards, and Betty had taken them with her into her marriage. She was too caring and interested in her employees ever to contemplate feeding them outside her house, so she found her compromise by insisting on the code of cleanliness, and that they minded their manners. Bruce had laughingly told Dulcie that if they had no manners when they arrived, they soon learned them – for all her sweetness, Betty was a force to be reckoned with.

Ten minutes later everyone was sitting at the table tucking into the beef and onion pie with obvious delight.

'You made this?' John said, looking at Dulcie. 'It's beaut!'

'It certainly is,' Bruce said, grinning. 'She's not just a pretty face, is she?'

Dulcie blushed scarlet.

'Did you learn to cook at the convent?' Ross asked shyly.

Dulcie giggled. 'Not really, that was like lessons in how *not* to cook, soup that was nearly all water, pastry like cardboard. I learned some good stuff from Pat, she was a good cook, then I tried recipes out of magazines. But pastry I suppose I learned from my gran back in England. She used to tell me stuff while she was making it.'

'What's England like?' John asked. 'I always wanted to go there.'

'I only really know about London,' Dulcie replied. 'I don't think you'd like that much, John, it's just streets and streets full of houses. The roads are really busy with cars and buses. It's noisy and dirty.'

'But I've seen pictures of castles, quaint little villages, big lakes and mountains,' he said in some surprise.

'There is all that too,' Dulcie said. 'But I never got to see it, apart from a few pretty villages when we went out with Dad for the day sometimes. There's lovely parks in London, though, we used to have one right near where I lived. That had a lake with lots of ducks.'

'What's a park?' Ross said.

'It's like a huge garden that belongs to everyone,' Dulcie said, shocked that he didn't know about such an ordinary thing. 'You must have them in the cities here too, there was King's Park in Perth. Not that we ever got taken there.'

'King's Park is glorious,' Betty chimed in. 'We used to have picnics there when I was a child. Bruce and I used to go there too when we were courting.'

The couple looked at each other and smiled.

'So parks are a good place to go with a sheila then?' John said, raising one eyebrow suggestively.

Dulcie laughed. 'Yes, I suppose they are, but where do men take their girlfriends down here?'

John leaned his elbow on the table and wiggled his fork at her, his eyes twinkling. 'Well, it all depends what kind of sheila she is, Dulc. There's some you might take in the saloon bar for a few bevies, there's some you have to take dancing. I reckon with a sheila like you, though, a bloke would be best to think of a walk along the sea-front holding her hand.'

'She won't be walking along the sea-front with anyone as dangerous as you,' Betty said indignantly. 'Not if I can help it.'

'Don't get all bristly with me, Betty,' John grinned. 'Dulcie's got to learn these things.'

'I think what John was trying to tell you,' Bruce said, his lips quivering as if he wanted to laugh aloud, 'is that men put girls into groups, and depending on what group she goes into, that's what decides what they do on a date.'

Betty changed the subject sharply, and it wasn't until the men had gone outside, and she and Dulcie were washing up, that Dulcie brought it up again.

'Explain to me what Bruce and John were talking about?' she asked.

'Well, dear, there *are* different sorts of girls.' Betty looked a bit embarrassed, drying the dishes very fast. 'There's the nice girls, the bad ones, and the in-betweens. Nice girls are the ones they all want to marry, and they don't take liberties with them. They'll take the bad ones drinking, knowing they can get their way with them, the in-betweens, well, they're in-between, they might be bad with the right bloke, and if he gives her a good enough time. That's the ones John said he'd take dancing.'

'So the nice girls only go for walks?' Dulcie said. 'That sounds a bit dull!'

Betty gave her a sharp look. 'Better to be a bit dull than end up getting a reputation for being fast,' she said. 'Young men have very strong urges, you go off somewhere smooching with one and there's no one about, anything can happen.'

'You mean they might rape a girl?'

Betty looked deeply shocked. 'Who told you that nasty word?'

Dulcie shrugged, she wasn't going to tell her it was Pat. 'I can't remember. But is that what you meant?'

Betty seemed to come over all wobbly and she sat down heavily on a kitchen stool. 'Rape is when a man forces a girl against her will, Dulcie. It's a very wicked thing and I don't believe many men would do it. But kissing and canoodling can make a girl lose her head, especially if she really likes the man and thinks he really likes her. Young men can be very persuasive, they all want the same thing, and they go all out to get it. So when you meet a young man, you keep to places where there's people. If he really cares for you, he won't push you, do you understand?'

Dulcie nodded.

Betty seemed relieved and got up off her stool to finish the drying. Daylight was fading now, but through the window in front of the sink they could see Ross and John perched on a couple of boxes by the barn having a cigarette.

'John's the kind of bloke you want to be wary of,' Betty said thoughtfully. 'I don't mean him exactly, he's too old for you and anyway he wouldn't try and sweet-talk you or he'd be out on his ear. But he's got charm, he's handsome and worldly, he knows what he's doing. Ross might end up like him in ten years, but right now he's shy, nervous of girls, he doesn't know anything. Yet don't let that fool you either, Dulcie, you never know with men how they are going to be when you're alone with them. When I was your age in Perth I met a young lad at church, sweet as pie, with lovely manners, then blow me if I didn't let him walk me home one night and he changed into a beast.'

'He didn't force you, did he?' Dulcie exclaimed.

Betty laughed. 'Never got a chance with me, I kneed him in the crotch and I was off up those back lanes like a rabbit.'

'So how do you know when the boy's perfect for you?' Dulcie asked.

Betty gave her a tender look. 'You'll just know. That sounds vague, I know, but it's true.'

'How long does it take?' Dulcie asked.

Betty blushed. 'It took me five minutes from meeting Bruce to know he was the one. But the secret is not to let on straight away, keep them dangling a while, wait and make sure.'

Dulcie sighed. 'It sounds so complicated.'

Betty laughed. 'It's not really, not if you keep your head. Besides, you're not ready for that sort of thing yet.'

It wasn't until October that Dulcie made any real headway with getting to know Ross better. They had brief conversations when she took tea out for the men's smoko, the Australian word for tea-break, and sometimes after supper, but these were always centred on the farm work. On this particular day, however, the men were mending fences on the far side of the lake, and to save them coming all the way back for their lunch-time sandwiches, she'd driven out with them on the tractor. Bruce, Bob and John were all together and she left the food with them.

'Have a look at the wild flowers while you're out here,' Bruce said. 'They're all just coming out by the lake. Ross is over there, he'll show you, but watch out for snakes.'

Dulcie always wore shoes outside now. She'd only been here a few days when she almost stepped on a brown snake. She jumped back and it slithered away, but the memory of the way it reared up momentarily as if to strike out at her had stayed with her.

She left the tractor and walked over to the lake. Fred, one of Bruce's three dogs, came bounding out of the gums surrounding it to greet her, showering water as he came.

Ross came through the bushes and looked suspiciously at her.

'Bruce said to come and look at the flowers.' She thought he was jealous because Fred the dog was making a fuss of her. 'Will you show me them?'

He merely nodded and strode off ahead of her down the edge of the track.

The sun was really warm now at midday, but by four or five it turned very chilly again. There had been a great deal of rain during the winter and the lake was almost twice the size it would be in summer. Dulcie thought the gum trees growing out of the water looked a bit sinister – she had come down here early one morning and there was a low-lying mist swirling around them, and she half expected to see some apparition rise out of it.

Suddenly Ross stopped. 'There you are,' he said.

The sight took her by surprise. There, sheltered by a semi-circle of thick bushes, was the most incredible array of flowers. Red, blue, purple, yellow and white, all jostling for attention, as beautiful as any display she'd seen in parks as a child.

'Gosh!' was all she could say, for the sight made a lump come up in her throat. She had thought the spring flowers up at Salmon Gums lovely, but there were only small clumps there, not this huge variety or so many of them.

'The Kangaroo paws are my favourite,' Ross said and sidled round the edge of the patch to pick one of the larger species at the back. There was something about the reverent way he was avoiding trampling the flowers that made tears spring into her eyes.

'Look, feel it,' he said, coming back to her. 'It's all furry on the stem.'

Dulcie touched it, keeping her eyes down.

'Why are you crying?' he asked. His voice was gentle – normally he adopted a curt tone with her.

'I don't know, I guess because they are so lovely, and unexpected,' she said, wiping her eyes with the back of her hand. 'Beautiful things always make me go all silly.'

'They do me too,' he said. 'New lambs, puppies and kittens. A calf was born when I first came here, and I cried like a baby.'

This was a major breakthrough as far as Dulcie was concerned, and she felt compelled to keep his attention. 'It was the careful way you went to pick that flower that really made me cry,' she admitted. 'Most men wouldn't have even noticed them being beautiful.'

'I expect I would have been like that if I hadn't come here,' he said. 'It's Bruce, you see, he loves the land and everything that's on it.'

'You were in some terrible place too, weren't you?' she said very softly, frightened he would rebuff her.

But to her surprise he nodded. 'I ran away three times, but they always caught me. The next time I made up my mind I wasn't going to be dragged back, beaten and have my head shaved, and I made it.'

'Where was this place?' she asked.

A fearful look came into his eyes and Dulcie instinctively put her hand on his arm. 'You're a man now, Ross, they can't make you go back there,' she said. 'You have to talk about it some day. You can tell me, I know what it's like to be ill-treated too.'

He just stood there for a moment, looking at her hand on his arm, but not shaking it off. 'It was Bindoon, about eighty miles north of Perth,' he blurted out. 'I got away at night, kept walking all through it, and next day, every time I heard a car or a truck I hid. I'd got some boots but no socks and my feet were bleeding and blistered. I was so hungry too, but I kept going all that day. I got lucky just as it was nearly dark, I saw a truck outside a house, with its engine running, there was nothing on the back but a few sacks. I reckoned the driver had delivered something to the house and he'd be out and on his way in a minute. So I got under the sacks and hid. He drove all the way into Perth.'

'But how did you get from there to here?' she asked, imagining herself hungry and with bleeding feet – at least when she'd run away she had a little money.

'I got on the train,' he said, still holding his head down. 'Of course I didn't have a ticket, and I had to keep ducking into the toilet when the guard came along. But I reckon he must've known I was there all along and felt sorry for me because just before we got into Kalgoorlie, he turned up unexpectedly and told me to try looking for a job there.'

'Then you came here?' she asked.

He half smiled. 'Yeah, someone told me I might get a job on a fishing boat. But it took a long time to walk it, I was too scared to try and thumb a lift, and the sole of my boot came off so I threw them away. I can't even remember the last part of the way, I was so weak and hungry. Bruce found me in the barn.'

'Why didn't you ever tell him and Betty about it?' she asked.

He shrugged. 'I suppose I thought they'd make me go back to Bindoon, so I kind of made up I didn't know where I'd come from. Every time they asked me something I just looked all stupid at them.'

Dulcie giggled. 'I bet that didn't fool them!'

He grimaced. 'No, I suppose it didn't. Betty once said when you find an animal that's hurt you don't try to find out how it got hurt, all you do is nurse it. So I got the idea they didn't really want to know where I'd come from, so I never did tell them. I still don't want to.' He paused, giving her a cold look. 'I don't know why I've told you. I bet you'll go straight back and blab it all out.'

'No I won't,' she said indignantly. 'Why should I? Just to get back at you because you let out about me to John before?'

'I didn't mean to give you away,' Ross said quickly. 'But I was scared for you. John saw me waving for you to hide off the road, and he kept on asking what was I trying to tell you. I didn't really even tell him. He guessed.'

Dulcie remembered then that wave which she thought was to remind her the post office was closing. She nodded. 'Okay, I was mad at you then, but as it turned out it was better to go back, or I wouldn't have ended up here. But for your information I'm not a blabbermouth or a tale-teller. I can't see why you can't tell Bruce now, he's fond of you and he'd like to know all about you. But I'm glad you told me, it feels nice to share a secret with you.'

His face had suddenly softened dramatically, almost as if by the telling of his story he'd shed a burden. The wary look was gone from his eyes, and his grin was a really happy one, turning up the corners of his mouth in a way that made him suddenly handsome.

'You got any secrets to trade?' he said. 'A pact so we don't tell on one another!'

She nodded. Something told her the only way to become friends with him was to show she too had a past.

Dulcie had told Betty and Bruce the same simple story she'd told Pat, that her mother had died and her father put her and May in the convent because he couldn't look after them. While she had talked about her gran and Susan on occasions to Betty, she had never felt able to say anything more, and Betty had never asked.

'My father is in prison in England, for the manslaughter of my mother,' she said.

Ross's mouth dropped open. 'Really!' he exclaimed, then his face hardened. 'No, you just made that up to be big!'

'I don't see anything big in saying something like that,' she said, hurt that he should see this as a lie, when to her it was offering him something very important. She turned her back on him and began to walk away.

He came after her and caught her arm. 'I'm sorry. I find it hard to trust anyone to tell the truth.'

'I don't tell lies,' she said, looking right into his eyes. 'I might leave things out, but I don't make things up.'

'Is it a real secret, or do Bruce and Betty know?' he asked.

'I've never told anyone.'

It was clear Ross didn't know what to say either. His mouth opened and closed and he was looking furtively around him as if wanting to run off.

Dulcie was still angry with him but she pulled herself together. 'I forgot to say I brought tea and sandwiches over. I'd better get back to the house, Betty will be wondering where I am. Thank you for showing me the flowers.'

She strode off back to the tractor, jumped on it and drove off back to the house, not even stopping to speak to Bruce. It wasn't until she was back in the kitchen that she found tears were streaming down her cheeks.

Fortunately Betty was in her sewing-room, engrossed in her patchwork. Dulcie washed her face with cold water and went back outside to do some weeding in the front garden. Yet even though she had outwardly composed herself, speaking of her mother and father had churned her up inside.

She had felt that the kindness shown to her by Bruce and Betty had wiped out all the misery of the past, that the unfair, cruel and humiliating things which had been done to her didn't matter any more. But that clearly wasn't so, or why would she feel so upset now? Pat had never got over the past, Ross clearly hadn't either, so why had she thought it would be any different for herself? She must have been stupid to think that just because she had a job she liked, a few pounds saved and a few new personal belongings, a happy future was assured.

The harsh truth was that she was still a ward of the Australian government, with no rights. She had a father back in an English gaol whom she had been prevented from keeping in touch with, and a sister back in St Vincent's whom she hadn't heard from since she left Salmon Gums. In all the excitement and happiness of the past months that hadn't seemed anything more than May just being too lazy to write, but maybe she was fooling herself about that, in just the same way she'd fooled herself into thinking the past didn't matter.

All at once the terrible beating Dulcie had received from Reverend Mother so long ago came back to her as though it was yesterday. She remembered only too well from her own experiences, and those of other girls, that the woman was cruel and vengeful. She'd often thought the main reason she'd singled out May as her little pet was to make a rift between them. Perhaps when Sergeant Collins telephoned her it made her really angry and so she had taken her revenge by holding back her letters.

The more Dulcie thought about it, the more likely this became. Letters were the only link between the sisters, and if they stopped completely, when May left St Vincent's, she wouldn't know where to find Dulcie.

But what could she do? She doubted getting Sergeant Collins to intervene on her behalf would achieve anything. Reverend Mother might even take it out on May. Dulcie shuddered, she knew there were a hundred and one ways the Sisters could make May's remaining time with them a misery.

Over the following few days Dulcie kept mulling this problem over in her mind. She thought of telling Ross about it and asking if he had any ideas what to do, but he seemed to be going out of his way to avoid being alone with her. This worried her too, she thought by sharing secrets that they'd become friends, but maybe he was wishing he'd never told her anything.

All the talk around the table at dinner was now of the approaching harvest. Like last year with the Masters, Bruce and his men were watching the weather, hoping there'd be no more rain while the wheat and barley fully ripened. Their crops looked good, the machinery had all been overhauled ready to start, it was just a case of waiting until it was ready.

Bruce and Betty went into Esperance to visit some friends late one afternoon, leaving Dulcie to see to the evening meal for John, Bob and Ross. It was a very subdued meal without Bruce to lead the conversation, and as soon as the men had finished eating they left the house, John saying he thought he might go down to the pub.

Dulcie saw him drive off in his battered old car, and she thought she saw Ross in the passenger seat. Once she'd finished the washing up she went to sit out on the veranda to watch the sun go down. So it was a surprise to see Ross suddenly appear in front of her.

'I thought you went with John,' she said.

'That was Bob,' he said. 'I said I'd stay and look after things.'

She knew he really meant her and this made her smile because it wasn't scary to be here alone, the dogs were in the yard and she felt perfectly safe. 'Would you like a cup of tea?' she asked. 'I was just going to make some.'

'Okay.' He nodded and sat down on the veranda steps.

When Dulcie came out with the tea he was gazing intently up at the sky. The sun was just about to disappear over the horizon and the sky was pink and orange. 'It's lovely, isn't it?' she said, handing him his tea and sitting down beside him.

'Umm,' he said thoughtfully. 'It's going to be a hot day tomorrow.'

'I'm glad you came over,' she said after a little while. 'I was afraid you were wishing you hadn't told me all that the other day.'

'I'm not very good at talking, especially to sheilas,' he said gruffly, looking straight ahead. 'Anyway, I thought you'd gone into a blue 'cos you told me that about your dad.'

Dulcie explained a little of how it had churned her all up. Ross went on to tell her he had been in another orphanage, called Clontarf, in Perth, since he was seven, and he remembered a lot of British migrant children being brought there. 'I suppose we were cruel, 'cos we used to laugh at the Pom kids whinging when they got burnt in the sun and 'cos they'd had their shoes taken away. But we were used to it and anyway that's the way it was there.'

Dulcie knew exactly what he meant. She hadn't forgotten the names the Australian orphans called her and the other English children at first, or the lack of sympathy from everyone. But she also remembered a year or so later watching more English girls arrive and thinking how drippy they were. She didn't think she was very sympathetic either.

'Was Clontarf a bad place too?' she asked.

He gave her a sideways odd sort of look. 'Yeah, and Castledare, the place before that, but I'd never known there was a different way of treating kids. The Brothers told us we were worthless lumps of shit right from when we were old enough to know what that meant. The work, punishments, horrible food, being cold in the winter and burning in the summer, that was just the way it was. It's only since I got here that I found out that not all kids get treated like that. But if Clontarf was bad, Bindoon was a hundred times worse. They told us we were going to a farm, packed us off on a truck like they was taking us off for a holiday. When we got there all we could see for miles and miles was bush, and in the middle of it, an orphanage only half completed. We'd been taken there to finish building it.'

'Young boys! Building an orphanage!' Dulcie said incredulously. 'I can't believe it!'

'We couldn't believe it either,' he said shaking his head. 'We'd always done bush-clearing, building and farm work at Clontarf, but not on such a vast scale as this. Boys built the whole of Bindoon, right from scratch, dug the foundations, mixed the mortar, hauled up the bricks, the lot. I was told the huge underground water tank was dug out and built by the first boys that went there, they were conned into thinking it was a swimming pool! Those poor devils had to sleep in tents too.'

He paused for a moment, and when Dulcie looked at him she could see he was trembling with rage. 'We had to shin up and down scaffolding, push wheelbarrows nearly as big as us, we got burns on our bare feet from the lime in it, but the Brothers didn't sodding well care, they had boots. The stones for the building came out of the bush, ruddy great boulders dug and hauled out by us. There was a Spanish architect, the Brothers were the overseers, but we were the labourers, like little ants building a nest, and if we stopped work for a minute, complained or did anything wrong, we got beaten.'

He paused briefly, and Dulcie noticed he was clenching and unclenching his fists.

'Bruce showed me a book once about how the Japs treated the soldiers in the prison camps over there,' he went on. 'I guess he was shocked I didn't react, but why should I? That's how it was for us too, only we were just kids. We had to learn to live with torn, bruised and burnt feet, with being hungry all the time. I've seen boys fall off scaffolding and even envied them when they got thrown on to the back of a truck to be taken to hospital because however much pain they were in, for a few days they'd get looked after and fed.'

Dulcie was astounded at this sudden and lengthy outpouring of his rage. It was difficult to believe him, but then surely no one could make up something quite so outrageous.

Yet once Ross started he couldn't stop, the humiliations and cruelty flowed out in a torrent. He told her about the top man, Brother Keaney, who hit them over the head with his stick for the slightest misdemeanour, how he humiliated the boys by giving them Irish girls' names, Bridget and Biddy-Anne. Of Brothers armed with leather straps, sometimes with metal slotted into them, who went among the boys as they were working, hitting them. There was no school, just work all the time. He said how they had no underclothes, just shorts and a shirt, how boys would rummage through the pig swill because they were so hungry. The boys who wet their beds were forced to wear a kind of sacking dress to shame them further. He described the main administration building as looking like a palace with mock marble floors and columns, domes and spires, how they'd built Stations of the Cross along the main drive, and how in his opinion Brother Keaney was a madman.

Dulcie watched Ross as he was talking. It was growing dark, but his eyes burned with rage and his mouth kept twisting up in a sinister sneer as he recalled it all.

She began to cry then and Ross put his hand on her arm. 'I wish I hadn't told you about all this now,' he said. He fell silent for a minute or two, his hand still on her arm. Then all at once his free hand gently touched her cheek with the softest of caresses. 'Still, I reckon knowing you were crying over me makes it worth it.'

Dulcie went inside after that, but Ross's words stayed with her. In some strange way they seemed to illustrate everything he'd lacked in his miserable childhood. However bad it was at the Sacred Heart, St Vincent's, and at the Masters', however forlorn and abandoned she'd felt, she had the knowledge of what love was inside her, clear pictures of family life tucked away in her mind. She knew what kisses, hugs and endearments were, but for Ross they must be as unfamiliar as a park had been to him. Yet he knew what tears were, he'd just never experienced anyone crying for him.

The day before they started harvesting all the men lingered longer over supper and Betty and Dulcie had finished washing up by the time they got up from the table. Betty asked if anyone would like a cup of tea, and when Dulcie said she fancied taking hers out on the veranda, Ross asked if she'd mind if he joined her. Since their last talk he'd been much less curt with her, he'd even brought a bunch of wild flowers round for her which made Betty claim he was sweet on her, and perhaps this was why everyone else opted for having their tea inside.

Dulcie was a bit embarrassed that they were outside while everyone else was indoors, but she enjoyed watching the sun go down, and besides, she still wanted to ask Ross's opinion about May and the letters.

'I was just thinking the other night, you must have been sixteen when you ran away from Bindoon,' she said after some brief general conversation. 'Why were you still there? Surely you could have left for a job somewhere at fifteen?'

He looked a bit embarrassed. 'On the time I ran away previous to that, I got hauled up in court,' he said. 'By that time they'd started sending delinquent boys to Bindoon, not just orphans, to, like, give them farm training and stuff. Just another way for the Brothers to get slave labour. Anyway, they sent me back there to stay till I was eighteen.'

'What, just for running away?'

He looked a bit shifty. 'I got caught stealing some food. Well, I had to, I was starving.'

Dulcie smiled and told him how she and Sonia used to steal from the Sisters' storeroom.

'Good job you didn't get caught,' he grinned. 'I don't suppose they go much easier on girls than boys. By the time I left Bindoon we had some blokes there that were twenty. If they were any good at carpentry, plastering or anything useful, they didn't let them go.'

Suddenly Dulcie understood better why Ross was so reluctant to talk about where he'd come from. If he'd been ordered by the court to stay at Bindoon till he was eighteen, running away again amounted to much the same as breaking out of prison. Under the circumstances she thought she might have remained silent too.

So she changed the subject and told him about May, and her anxiety about the letters. 'Do you think Reverend Mother isn't giving them to her to spite me?'

He nodded. 'I wouldn't put it past any nun. The Sisters of Mercy are just as bad as the Christian Brothers in my book. There were some of them at Castledare where I started off. I was only a baby, about a year old, when I was sent there with my two older brothers. I was six when they were sent off somewhere else. No one would ever tell me

306

where they went, they spanked me every time I asked. To this day I don't know where my brothers are, or why we got put in an orphanage in the first place. That's how much they care about families.'

'But someone must know,' Dulcie said. 'They do keep records. I used to sneak a look at Reverend Mother's papers on her desk and whenever a new girl came there was always a file with stuff about where she came from. I tried to find mine once, but I didn't have any luck, I think it must have been in the cabinet which was always locked.'

'I tried all that sniffing around too,' Ross said with a grin. 'If I was sent in to clean Brother Keaney's study I used to give it a right going over.'

'Did you find anything?'

'Not about me. But I saw some letters for other boys once, a big pile of them, mostly for the Maltese boys that came to Australia like you did. I didn't dare nick them, but I wished I had afterwards, 'cos those poor little sods never got them.'

He told her how sorry he felt for those poor kids. He said they weren't orphans and that their parents had sent them willingly, believing they were going to get a good education and go on to be engineers and craftsmen. 'They never had one lesson after they got there,' he said. 'I just hope some of them get back to Malta one day and tell their families what went on.'

Dulcie felt crushed now. All the time she'd been at St Vincent's she'd imagined that she was just unlucky to end up in a bad place. But Pat had suffered, and Ross too, and it seemed most, if not all, orphanages were run in much the same way. If this was the case there must be thousands of girls like her and boys like Ross, all with questions about their background or relatives that no one would answer.

'What can I do about May?' she asked.

'Maybe you could go back and visit St Vincent's,' he suggested. 'Bruce and Betty drive up there sometimes to visit her family, they'd take you with them. The Sisters couldn't very well refuse to let you see May, not if Betty was with you.'

Dulcie beamed. 'That's a brilliant idea.'

That night as she lay in bed she felt elated. The harvest wouldn't be completed until nearly Christmas. She doubted Bruce and Betty would want to make such a long drive during the hot months, but maybe in March or April they'd feel like going. That wasn't so very long to wait. Then it would be only a year until May was fifteen and able to leave St Vincent's.

Her last thoughts as she fell asleep were of the reunion with her sister. She imagined walking up the drive to the convent and May coming running to meet her. She was asleep even before the imagined embrace.

Part Two

1956–1963

Chapter Fourteen

It was April of 1956 when Bruce and Betty took Dulcie with them to Perth to stay with Joan, Betty's younger sister, for a short holiday. Joan's home was in Subiaco, quite close to the city centre, and Betty's other sister and brother and their families lived nearby too.

In the ten months Dulcie had worked for them she had blossomed. With Betty's encouragement in all things from cooking to gardening, her confidence had grown. Reading newspapers and books and listening to the wireless had given her a far better idea of what was going on in the world. Yet after sleepy little Esperance with its gravel roads, Perth was huge, bewildering and very exciting.

The streets were so busy with cars and buses, so many people jostling in the wonderful department stores, and such a huge array of clothes to spend her money on. Yet it was the phenomenon dubbed 'teenagers' she'd read about in the press that impressed her most. Back in Esperance, girls and boys of that age were called 'young people' or 'kids' and there was no sign that anyone considered them to be an important group. Here in Perth there were milk bars with juke-boxes, something she'd only ever seen in American films at the picture house in Esperance, and these places appeared to have been designed purely for these 'teenagers'.

She was too bashful to go into one, but she loitered by the windows as if waiting for someone and just looked. The girls had mid-calf-length dresses, wide belts cinching in their waistline, and wedge-heeled shoes. Most had far longer hair than hers, waving on to their shoulders, they

311

all seemed to be smoking, and the few that wore hats favoured the kind that looked like a wide band of feathers. Later she heard 'Blue Suede Shoes' by Carl Perkins wafting out of the doorway of a record shop, and looking inside she saw dozens of teenagers just hanging around tapping their feet as they listened to the music.

She had of course heard rock and roll music on the wireless, and read about Elvis Presley in magazines because many churchmen were saying he was a bad influence on the young. But none of that had appeared relevant to her until now. All at once it took on a new light – this was her generation, one that didn't dress or behave like their parents and had an entirely new taste in music. The more she looked around her, the more evidence she got that her age group were valued consumers. She saw teen bras, teen handbags, dress shops exclusively for the young where they sold Capri pants, pin-up girl sweaters and the wide belts she'd seen so many girls wearing.

She bought herself a pink spotted dress with a wide white piqué collar and a fashionable longer-length gored skirt, and a belt to go with it. She would have been happy to spend her entire holiday just looking in shops and watching people, but Bruce and Betty wanted to show her the sights of Perth.

They took her to vast King's Park, reminiscing about their courtship, for a boat ride down the wide Swan River, and to Cottesloe beach where Betty had spent so much time as a young girl. But today they were on their way to St Vincent's to see May.

Since early this morning Dulcie had been suffering from butterflies in her stomach. However much she wanted to see May, she was nervous of what this impromptu visit might throw up. May might not be pleased to see her, Reverend Mother could be nasty, and she was afraid that all the ghosts of the past would come back to haunt her again.

As they turned into the road approaching the convent, Dulcie leaned forward from her position in the back seat.

'That's it,' she exclaimed, pointing to the building at the far end of the road.

'But it's lovely,' Betty said in some surprise.

As Dulcie had so seldom come out of St Vincent's during her time there, the outside view of it now took her back to the first time she saw it on her arrival. It *was* lovely, with the golden-red of the brickwork, the fancy design around each of the gothic arches on the ground floor, and the matching windows on the chapel attached to it. Recent rain had revived the lawn after the hot summer, the pines and the Moreton Bay fig tree looked even taller and more majestic than she remembered. To anyone approaching it for the first time it looked so serene. Only the arched sign above the gate which said St Vincent's Orphanage gave any hint that children lived here too.

'That's only the convent and the chapel,' Dulcie said quickly. 'The orphanage buildings are all hidden, they aren't so lovely.'

Her heart was racing faster as Bruce got out of the car to open the gate. He looked almost comic wearing a suit and tie, for the jacket was too tight across his shoulders, the sleeves and trouser legs just a little too short. There was no mistaking what he was, city men didn't have such craggy, weather-beaten faces, or such broad shoulders. Yet if the Sisters jumped to the conclusion that he was just another ignorant bushman who held nuns in awe, they'd be in for a shock. Bruce was nobody's fool.

Dulcie took a small mirror out of her handbag to check her appearance as Bruce drove in up the drive. She'd had her hair cut again just before leaving Esperance, and with her new dress and white court shoes with a two-inch heel she felt she looked sophisticated enough to impress May. She was tempted to put on the lipstick she'd bought just yesterday, but Reverend Mother might just see it as a sign she had become fast.

'We'll stay with you for as long as you want us to,' Betty said as they all got out of the car. She looked very attractive too in a pale green dress and a matching hat, but then

Betty always dressed well, even at home. 'If you want us to disappear, ask me what time we are expected back for tea. We'll make some excuse then and wait out here for you.'

Bruce moved closer to Dulcie and picked a loose hair off her collar. 'Don't let Reverend Mother make you nervous,' he said, his blue eyes gentle with understanding about what this visit meant to her. 'We won't stand any nonsense from her, so neither must you.'

Dulcie rang the convent bell, glancing over towards the orphanage building as she waited. They had timed their arrival purposely, so they couldn't be fobbed off with excuses like May was in school and couldn't be brought out to see them. It was almost four now, and the bell for the end of lessons would ring any minute.

The door was opened by Sister Agatha and her eyes widened in surprise. 'Dulcie!' she exclaimed. 'Oh my goodness, how grown-up you look!'

Dulcie had no bitter memories of this Sister – while she was never exactly kind, she wasn't cruel either, just a fat old nun who wheezed when she tried to hurry. Yet all the same she immediately felt very small and cowed, just the way she'd always been in any Sister's presence.

'May I see May?' she asked. 'This is Mr and Mrs French who I work for. We came to Perth unexpectedly, so we couldn't arrange a visit in advance.'

As she nervously introduced Bruce and Betty to the Sister, she saw the old nun looked flustered. Dulcie guessed what was running through the woman's mind. Whenever visitors were expected the shoes and hair ribbons were dished out, soft toys and dolls placed on the children's beds, even special food put out in the kitchen. Sister Agatha probably realized there was no time now for such preparations.

The school bell rang loudly, instantly breaking the tranquillity of the place. There was the sound of a hundred chairs scraping backwards, and footsteps on the wooden boards outside the classrooms.

'Dulcie knows the way, we'll just go and find May ourselves,' Bruce said. 'No need to trouble yourself.'

'I'm afraid I can't let you do that.' Sister Agatha began to wring her hands. 'Reverend Mother is most particular that she sees all visitors first.'

'That's fine,' Bruce grinned. 'Just take us to her then. My wife and I have been longing to meet May, Dulcie's told us so much about her, and this place.'

A look of consternation flitted across the old nun's face. Dulcie thought it was lucky she had opened the door rather than one of the others. Sister Agatha was slow-witted, any of the others were capable of coming up with a first-class excuse for why it wasn't convenient now.

Bruce was across the threshold immediately without waiting to be asked in, Dulcie and Betty stepped after him and they followed the nun down the corridor. Once Sister Agatha had knocked on Reverend Mother's study door and got a reply, she couldn't make out the woman wasn't there because they'd hear everything.

'Wait here,' Agatha said in a trembling voice. 'I'll just see if she's available.'

The moment Agatha was at the study door, Bruce began to walk down the corridor too, beckoning for Betty and Dulcie to follow.

Agatha looked panic-stricken when she saw them coming, but by then Reverend Mother had called out for her to come in.

'It's Dulcie Taylor and Mr and Mrs French, they want to see May,' she said.

Before Reverend Mother got a chance to make any reply, Bruce was at the door and walking in.

'G'day, Reverend Mother,' he said. 'My wife and I are just up from Esperance for a visit and we've brought young Dulcie to see her sister. We thought it would be a good time now, school's over and it's not tea-time yet.'

If Dulcie hadn't been so scared she might have burst into laughter. Bruce was nothing like the usual male visitors here. They were always fawning little men, dragged

315

reluctantly along by their do-gooding wives. The force of Bruce's expansive personality filled the small room, just as his shoulders filled the doorway, and although Reverend Mother was tall, she had to look up to him.

'It is usual, Mr French, to make an appointment first,' she said, her voice like ice.

'I'm not a usual sort of bloke,' Bruce grinned. 'Farmers don't go in for appointments, and anyway one little girl seeing her sister can't interfere with anything, can it?'

The head nun looked shaken, but she composed herself quickly.

'Dulcie!' she exclaimed, as if seeing the prodigal daughter in front of her. 'How lovely to see you again. What a young lady of fashion you've become!'

'She's as bright as a button too,' Bruce butted in. 'Best thing we ever did was take her on. Don't know what we'd do without her now.'

'I'm very glad to hear that,' Reverend Mother said. 'I hope your wife agrees with that glowing testimony?'

Dulcie had a sharp and sudden memory of this same woman beating her until she thought she was going to die. She'd looked at her then with child's eyes, seeing a tall, handsome woman, and often pondered on why if she was cruel she wasn't ugly too, for those things went together in her mind.

Now, as an adult, Dulcie found she was neither as tall nor as handsome as she remembered. She was just another nun on the wrong side of forty with piercing dark eyes and a sallow skin. Yet even more pleasing was to see that this time it was she who looked frightened. Not of Dulcie maybe, she still looked at her in the same disdainful way she always had, but of Bruce.

'I more than agree with my husband's views,' Betty said. 'I can't begin to tell you what Dulcie means to us both. You must have been very sorry when she left here?'

'She was always one of my smarter ones,' Reverend Mother replied. 'Yes, I was sorry when she left, but then it was time she took her place in the world.'

'We'll just go and find May now,' Bruce said in a firm tone. 'Don't trouble yourself to come out, Reverend Mother, I'm sure Dulcie knows the way.'

'I cannot allow that,' Mother said, her voice rising slightly as if panicked. 'I'll have May brought in here, you can talk to her with me.'

This was exactly what Dulcie had been afraid of. To be forced to talk to May in front of the head nun would make the visit almost pointless. She shot a look of appeal to Bruce.

He half smiled and lifted one bushy eyebrow. 'To me that smacks a little of a prison visit! Are you afraid she might tell us something you don't wish let out?'

'No, of course not, but we have rules,' she said hastily, clearly unable to come up with anything stronger.

'Rules are made to be broken,' Bruce smiled. 'Don't worry, we'll come and speak to you when we're through. Thank you so much!'

He had taken his wife's and Dulcie's arms, nudged them out the door and followed before the woman could come back with anything further.

They found May out in the playing-field beyond the dormitories. She could have been about to join the other girls who were engaged in starting a game of rounders, but Dulcie knew by the way she was standing with her back against one of the dormitory walls that this was unlikely.

As Dulcie called her name, May first stared in disbelief, then once she realized her eyes weren't deceiving her, she hared across the grass to them and threw herself into Dulcie's arms.

'Is it really you?' she said incredulously. 'I never thought I was ever going to see you again.'

'I didn't dare put that we were coming visiting in my last letter in case Mother found some excuse to stop me coming,' Dulcie said, and quickly introduced Bruce and Betty.

May shook both Bruce and Betty's hands but turned

again to Dulcie looking puzzled. 'Last letter?' she said. 'You haven't written once since you left.'

'Don't be silly, May,' Dulcie said a little sharply, imagining her sister wanted to make herself look hard done by in front of Bruce and Betty. 'I've written dozens of letters to you. Before I changed jobs you always wrote back too.'

May looked bewildered now. 'I kept on writing to you for ages, but you didn't reply. What do you mean, changed jobs? When was that?'

Betty said how often she'd seen Dulcie writing letters to May, Bruce joined in and said he'd taken them to the post office. While Dulcie was quite prepared to believe May hadn't got any of these, she couldn't accept that her sister hadn't got the ones she sent from Salmon Gums. She mentioned specific things she'd written to May, including her descriptions of the lambing and the harvest, but May only looked blank and remained adamant she knew nothing of this.

Fortunately Dulcie had the last two letters she'd received from May in her new handbag. She had brought them with her to prove to Reverend Mother how long it was since she'd heard from her sister. She pulled them out and gave them to May. 'Look, you sent me these, but you didn't say in either of them that you hadn't heard from me,' she pointed out.

May read one of them and looked puzzled. 'I didn't write this,' she said. 'It looks a bit like my writing, but it isn't.'

Bruce, who had been listening carefully to all this, moved closer. 'Do you swear you haven't had one letter from Dulcie, not in over two years?' he asked. 'This is really important, May, we can't make a complaint until we're absolutely certain.'

May looked up at him with wide eyes. 'No, not one. I gave up writing in the end,' she said. 'Mother said it was pointless as it was plain Dulcie had lost interest in me.'

That statement rang true to Dulcie. They were almost

exactly the same words Mother had used to her when she kept writing to Susan soon after her arrival here. She knew how hurtful it must have been to May.

With tears in her eyes she hugged her sister tightly. 'I could never, ever lose interest in you, May. I think Mother must have destroyed my letters because she wants to keep us apart.'

Aware that this visit could come to an abrupt end at any moment, Dulcie hastily explained that she wasn't at the same place she'd started out and that Bruce and Betty were her new employers. She took a scrap of paper from her bag and wrote down the address. 'Keep it safe, May,' she said. 'Even if Mother doesn't give you any further letters from me, it's only a year till you leave here. Write and tell me the minute you've got a job.'

Bruce assured them both that he would make certain Reverend Mother wouldn't intercept any further mail and said he thought he and Betty would go back to her now and have it out with her and leave the girls to talk alone.

May looked fearful. 'Be careful what you say to her,' she said in a quivering voice. 'She can be so horrible if anyone upsets her.'

'So can I,' Bruce laughed. 'Now, you and Dulcie have a chat and we'll come back in a while.'

The two girls sat on the veranda steps, just the way they used to in the past. Yet it wasn't comfortable the way it had been then. May was pleased with the sweets Dulcie had bought her, she admired Dulcie's new hair-style, her dress and shoes, and said she thought Betty and Bruce seemed very nice, but it was almost like trying to start up a conversation with a stranger. May was willing enough to gossip about the other girls, many of whom Dulcie didn't even know, yet every time Dulcie tried to steer her into more personal things, May veered off in another direction.

Always a keen observer, Dulcie noticed that May's hair had been allowed to grow much longer than the other girls'. Her uniform striped dress was newer than anyone else's and it fitted her properly too. She hadn't expected that her little sister would have developed a woman's body when she wasn't even quite fourteen yet, but she had, her breasts were bigger than Dulcie's, and she had real curves, while Dulcie still had a very boyish shape.

The once strong similarity between them wasn't so marked now, except for the blonde hair and blue eyes. It was as though each facial feature of May's, which had once been identical to her own, had been altered slightly in the last two years to make her more outstanding. Her mouth was wider, her lips fuller than Dulcie's, her nose had a slight flare to the nostrils, her eyes were a more intense blue. Although Dulcie normally found it hard to picture her mother any more, when she looked at May it all came back to her. She could see that in a few years her sister was going to be even more beautiful.

Most of Dulcie's old friends had left here now, so she didn't find it odd at first that none of the other girls broke off from their game to come over to speak to her. Yet after a little while she sensed that both she and May were being watched closely, and seeing several familiar faces, Dulcie waved. Two girls came over briefly to admire her dress, hair and shoes, and ask what her job was like, but they didn't speak to May at all, and soon returned to their game.

'Have you upset them?' Dulcie asked curiously. In her time here any old girl turning up was an event, everyone wanted to speak to her to find out what life was like away from the convent.

'I expect so,' May said airily. 'They've always been jealous of me, they were even when you were here. I have piano lessons, you see. Mother gives me them, they don't like it.'

'You're still her pet then?'

'Yeah,' May said with a non-committal shrug.

Two years earlier May would have elaborated, boasting about her special treatment, but the way she said nothing more made Dulcie suspect her sister had come to see the downside of being a pet. Treats and the absence of severe punishments couldn't really compensate for being alienated from the other girls. As she remembered, it was only them who made this place tolerable.

'I have to keep in with Mother,' May blurted out. 'I don't like it, I hate her mostly. But I don't want to be sent out to some sheep station way beyond the black stump. I want to work in an office or a shop, here in Perth.'

Having discovered for herself what could happen if a girl got into Mother's bad books, Dulcie sympathized in part, but it also reminded her that May hadn't asked her anything about her job, or even if she was happy. It saddened her to find May had grown even more self-centred and calculating than she'd been as a little girl.

When she tried to talk about the farm a little later, May cut her short. 'How can you stand being somewhere like that?' she said with a horrified expression. 'If Mother sent me somewhere like that I'd run off to Sydney or somewhere lively.'

'Have you got any real idea how big Australia is?' Dulcie asked, smiling at her sister's naivety. 'You can't *run* off to anywhere, you need money for fares, food and somewhere to sleep. I really do hope Mother gets you work in an office or a shop, but don't bank on it, May. Be careful, you put one foot wrong with her and she'll make you pay.'

May looked up at her, perhaps sensing that Dulcie really knew what she was talking about. 'Why did you leave your first job?' she asked at last.

Dulcie had no intention of telling her about the misery she experienced there, but at the same time it was a good opportunity to slam home the message that Mother couldn't be trusted. 'Because the farmer's wife ran off,' she said. 'It wasn't very nice there, May, and I'm pretty certain Mother knew it and sent me there purposely.'

All at once May snuggled up to her the way she'd done as a little girl. 'I've missed you so much,' she said in a croaky voice. 'I told myself I hated you when no letters came, but it didn't really work. I just felt sad.'

'I always think about you every night,' Dulcie said truthfully. 'I pray for you to be kept safe and that the Sisters are kind to you. I don't go to church any more, but it looks as if God answered my prayers because I can see they feed you better here now.' She playfully pinched her sister's plump cheeks.

'Someone said they had an inspector round,' May smirked. 'It must be true because the food did get better suddenly. We get an orange or an apple most days now. At Christmas we even got a little tin of sweets each.'

'I sent you a manicure set,' Dulcie said.

May sat upright. 'Was it a pale blue leather case?'

Dulcie nodded. 'She passed it on to you?'

May grinned. 'No, but I saw it in Mother's study, and I pinched it. I've got it hidden away.'

Dulcie hardly knew what to say. 'You mustn't steal things,' she said, more out of habit than real conviction.

'It's not stealing when it belonged to you in the first place.' May shrugged. 'Mother's the thief, not me.'

From then on May did begin to show some interest in Dulcie, if only to ask if she went out dancing. Dulcie told her that she'd been to two dances, one on her seventeenth birthday in December and again on New Year's Eve. She described the new turquoise shantung dress she wore, and said how Bruce and Betty had taught her to waltz.

'Did anyone ask you to dance?' May asked, wide-eyed.

'A few boys,' Dulcie said. 'But they were a bit funny, none of them came to talk to me later, Betty said she thought it was because they thought I was Ross's girl.'

She had to explain then who Ross was, and how she, Betty, Bruce, John and Ross had all gone to the dance together.

'Isn't Ross your boyfriend then?' May asked.

Dulcie smiled. 'I think I'd like him to be, but I don't think he likes me as anything but a friend. He didn't even dance with me once, he kept disappearing to go and get a beer.'

She was just telling May that Bruce let her drive his Holden now and she often took Betty into town to drop her off at her friends, when Bruce came back and interrupted her.

'We'd better go now, Dulcie,' he said, and she thought he was cross about something because his face was all tight and set.

'It was nice to meet you, May,' he said, coming a few steps nearer and kissing her cheek. 'If you ever want a holiday with Dulcie we'll be more than happy to put you up. I'm sorry I've got to drag her away now, but you make sure you hold on to our address.'

Dulcie waved back to May right until the car turned the corner at the end of the road and she couldn't see her any more. 'What happened between you and Mother?' she asked. Bruce and Betty had both seemed strained and anxious to get away in a hurry.

'She denied that any letters had come from you, she tried to say that you were too lazy to write any, and that you'd told us a pack of lies to make us feel sorry for you,' Bruce said, half turning his head as he spoke to Dulcie in the back. 'I said she was the liar as I'd personally posted letters written by you to May. It was all very nasty.'

'I'm sorry,' Dulcie said. She thought Bruce and Betty were cross with her now.

Betty turned in her seat to look round at Dulcie. 'Why didn't you tell us your father was in prison?' she asked.

Dulcie felt as if she'd been given a sudden and hefty jolt. 'She told you that?' she asked incredulously, her eyes instantly filling with tears. 'I didn't think she knew!'

'Oh, she knew all right, it was like the hidden card up the sleeve,' Betty said with a deep sigh. 'It took the wind out of our sails. We'd already said how well we knew you, and how honest we'd found you.'

Dulcie hung her head in shame. There had been many

times she'd almost told Betty, but she always lost her nerve at the last minute. The longer she kept it to herself, the more difficult it became to admit it. Now she'd messed everything up and they distrusted her.

'I didn't tell you any lies,' she whispered. 'I only left it out.'

'Look at me, Dulcie!' Betty said.

Dulcie lifted up her head and she saw no anger in Betty's face, or disgust, only bewilderment. 'She said your father murdered your mother. Is that true?' Betty asked.

'No,' Dulcie said, shaking her head. 'He was convicted of manslaughter, but he didn't even do that.'

Bruce drove to a quiet road and pulled up. 'Why don't you tell us the whole story now?' he suggested.

It was a lovely tree-lined suburban street with pretty houses and neat gardens. As Dulcie started to tell the story she was reminded of how her father had loved the equivalent kind of street back in London, how he'd choose a walk through them in preference to a quicker main road. He always used to say they'd live somewhere like it one day.

She told them everything, not the abbreviated version she'd given Ross. It was surprisingly clear in her head for over the years she had mentally sifted through the views and facts which Susan and her granny had so often discussed in front of her, both before and after the trial, and added that information to what she had witnessed herself.

'Mum and Dad used to fight all the time,' she said finally. 'But Dad would never have hurt her. Gran used to say "she'd try the patience of a saint", and she was right because even though I was only little then, I used to wonder why Mum kept doing the things she did to upset him.'

Bruce and Betty were both silent for a few minutes after she finished, both turned in their seats looking at her in the back of the car. Bruce appeared older suddenly, the bags under his eyes more pronounced, his eyes grave.

Betty looked as if she might cry, her sweet face puckered as if trying to control her emotions.

'I got you to tell us about your father, Dulcie, because I wanted to know how you really felt about him,' she said. 'You see, when you said he just left you and May at the orphanage because he couldn't look after you, both Bruce and I got the impression he'd abandoned you. I'm sorry to say we couldn't help but see him as a heartless man. Then of course when Reverend Mother told us he killed your mother – ' She broke off as if unable to finish.

Dulcie understood completely. Under those circumstances they couldn't be blamed for imagining Reg Taylor was a brutal, black-hearted murderer.

'He wasn't like that at all,' Dulcie said sadly. It was awful to think that by keeping her past from them her father's character could be so distorted. 'I always felt bad about saying he'd put us in the orphanage, because if he'd been free he would have looked after us better than most women could.'

'I can see that now,' Bruce said. 'And it makes it even harder to tell you what Reverend Mother told us.' He paused, looking at his wife as if for support. 'You see, your father died in prison six months ago.'

There was complete silence for a moment, Dulcie looking at them as if she hadn't or couldn't take it in.

'Daddy's dead?' she gasped eventually. 'No, he can't be! Mother just told you that to hurt me.'

'I'm so sorry, Dulcie, but it *is* true,' Bruce said. 'Reverend Mother showed us the letter she received from England. He had a fall while working on a prison building and he died as a result of his accident. There was a copy of his death certificate too.'

Dulcie looked at them bleakly. It was such a shock she couldn't even think, much less speak.

'I asked why she didn't write and tell you,' Betty said, reaching out for Dulcie's hand. 'Her words were, "Dulcie isn't my responsibility any longer." I don't know how I controlled myself. I wanted to slap her.'

'But she can't have told May either!' Dulcie said, looking from one to the other of them. 'She would have said something if she knew.'

Betty nodded, but said nothing.

'We're so terribly sorry, Dulcie,' Bruce said gently. 'If only you'd told us about him, we would have encouraged you to write to him once you got to our place. If you didn't know that Reverend Mother knew about him, does that mean you were unable to write to him ever since you got to Australia?'

Dulcie nodded, and said how they weren't allowed to write back at the Sacred Heart either. 'They told me I wasn't to tell anyone about where he was, and I didn't. So when we got here I just carried on that way. So did May.'

'She didn't,' Betty said. 'She had said a great deal about it to Reverend Mother. All of which that woman took great pleasure in throwing at us. We got the impression May spends a good deal of time with her.'

'May's her pet,' Dulcie said with a sigh.

Bruce and Betty exchanged glances which Dulcie noticed immediately. 'Why? Is there something wrong with that?' she asked.

'No, my dear,' Betty said soothingly. 'But I think we'd better go home to my sister's now and have a cup of tea. Perhaps we should have done that before we told you, but we thought it might be easier to break the news in here, I didn't want my sister listening in.'

Dulcie slumped back on to the seat for the rest of the drive home and didn't say a word. For nine years, ever since her mother died, she had clung to the idea that one day she and May would be reunited with their father. Her faith in this had been shaken when he signed the paper to send them to Australia, yet as time had passed she'd come to see that he couldn't have known how things would turn out and he must have thought it would be the best thing for them. So many nights she'd lain awake comforting herself with a dream of meeting him off a ship and running into his arms. But that dream was gone now. After being called an orphan for so many years, she really was one now.

Much later that same night, Bruce and Betty lay wide awake in the spare bedroom at Betty's sister's, both unable to sleep.

They hadn't slept well since they got here five days earlier. They found the city with its cars, buses and people shouting too noisy. The bed was lumpy and the room too cramped.

'We'll go home tomorrow,' Bruce said, drawing Betty into his arms. 'We don't belong here.'

Betty didn't reply for a moment, remembering how often after she first married Bruce and went to live in the outback with him, she'd longed to be back here. She had missed her old friends from school and the ones she went dancing with. She missed street lighting, shops, cinemas and hot baths. She thought the bush was ugly, nothing but miles of scrubby, arid land, where everything from cooking a meal or getting water was just so very hard. But she loved Bruce, she trusted him, and even through all the disasters, hardships and the grief of losing three babies, that love had sustained her, and finally she'd come to love the bush and farming as much as he did.

'No, we don't belong here,' she murmured. 'I don't think we belong in the same world as people like that woman either! You know, when we first got to St Vincent's, I actually thought Dulcie had made up a lot of the stuff she told us. Now I reckon it was even worse than she said. That woman didn't have a shred of sympathy for Dulcie, did she? She took an almost malicious delight in passing on the news her father was dead. It was just as if she wanted to destroy the last few good memories Dulcie had of her early childhood. And I didn't like the way she talked about May either.'

'Something slimy there,' Bruce agreed. He couldn't put

his finger on what it was, but he knew it wasn't right. Yet on the face of it May was doing all right. She was a very pretty girl, healthy and apparently well cared for. So perhaps he was over-reacting.

'Dulcie's a little marvel, the way she handles things,' Betty said. 'I would have expected her to have been really weepy and down this evening, but there she was, helping with the tea, doing the washing up, almost as if nothing had happened. If I didn't know her so well I'd think she didn't care.'

'Oh, she cares all right, make no mistake about that,' Bruce said with feeling. 'But she's been conditioned by those bloody Sisters to hide what she feels. On top of that she'll be thinking of us, not wanting to spoil our holiday. Look at that business with Pat Masters, she was evil to Dulcie, yet I've never heard her say a nasty thing about her.'

'I've always suspected she found out something about Pat and came to sympathize with her,' Betty confided. 'I'd give anything to know what it was, but you can bet Dulcie will take it to the grave with her. I expect right now she's lying awake fretting about her sister!'

'I got the idea that kid can look after herself,' Bruce replied. 'But I don't suppose that will stop Dulcie showering her with ten times more love and care than May will ever give back. There's a touch of the martyr in Dulcie. I just hope she never falls for some bastard who'll make use of it.'

'I wonder if her father really did push her mother?' Betty said thoughtfully.

'I would have, if everything Dulcie said about her is true,' Bruce replied. 'But somehow I don't think he killed her, Dulcie got that gentle nature of hers from someone, and it surely wasn't her mother.'

'May was very pretty, wasn't she?' Betty said.

'Too pretty for her own good.' Bruce sighed. 'I wish we'd had longer with her, I sensed something about her, but I don't know what it is.'

'Me too,' Betty agreed. 'Sort of calculating. I don't think I'd trust her the way I do Dulcie.'

'My wish for our little Dulcie is that she falls in love with a really decent bloke very soon, gets married, has a whole lot of kids and stays near us for ever,' Bruce said. 'Wouldn't that be nice?'

'Umm,' Betty agreed. 'Maybe it will be Ross. They like one another.'

'Maybe, but Ross is another one who has a few dark corners, something's not quite right there.'

'I wouldn't mind taking a bet on Dulcie getting it all out of him,' Betty murmured. She was getting sleepy now.

'I wouldn't want her to confuse love with pity,' Bruce said. 'That's a dangerous area for someone to get in that's already a bit of a martyr. I'd like her to fall for someone like John, uncomplicated, full of life and passion. She'd really blossom then.'

Betty was too sleepy to reply, but she squeezed her husband's hand in agreement.

After Dulcie told Ross told about her parents they had become friends, but it wasn't an easy or comfortable relationship. Ross had little real conversation and he was prickly and moody – if she asked too many questions, teased him or argued with his opinions, he often didn't speak to her for days afterwards. When this happened she felt hurt and always promised herself she would ignore him when he finally came round again, but she never did. This was partly because she felt sorry for him and imagined all young men were equally moody, but mostly because she felt inexplicably drawn to him.

They got on best when they worked alongside one another outside. The previous August when the men came to shear the sheep Dulcie had helped out in the shearing shed, and it was Ross who'd shown her how to sort and grade the fleeces, helping her so she kept up with the shearers. During the harvest it was much the same, and so she got the idea that he felt more relaxed with her when there were lots of other people around, and stopped trying to seek him out alone.

Yet he wasn't happy at either of the two dances when they went with Bruce, Betty and John. When he was actually in the hall he spent the time leaning against the wall with his hands in his pockets. She blamed herself for that, because she'd seen girls looking admiringly at him and thought maybe she was cramping his style by being there. Yet he'd been so kind when they got back from Perth and she told him about her father's death.

Bruce and Betty were very kind too, but they didn't understand how she really felt, not the way Ross did. He hadn't sneered when she explained to him that she had always felt as if she had this little box tucked away inside her. A place where she kept all the good memories of her childhood. She told him that until she was informed her father was dead, she found it comforting to open that box and examine the contents.

Walks in Manor House Gardens, going to Mass with her father, seeing the Christmas lights in Regent Street with both her parents at Christmas, days out at the seaside, listening to *Children's Hour* on the wireless and making toast on the fire. When she opened her box she could hear London accents, see the blossom on the trees in spring, hear the crackle of leaves underfoot in autumn, smell fog, the River Thames, lilac and roses. There was the taste of fish and chips, she could almost feel the heat through the newspaper bundle as she carried it home, pork pies, shrimps from the stall in Greenwich on Sunday afternoons.

All the nice memories of her parents were there, the silky feel of her mother's hair, the smell of the scent she wore on special occasions, her laughter and the songs she used to sing to her and May.

But the memories of her father were the best of all, the bristles on his chin when he needed a shave, the way he used to throw her up in the air and catch her. How it felt to ride home on his shoulders when she was tired, and how snug she felt when she sat on his lap for a cuddle.

She told Ross how in all the time at St Vincent's this collection of memories had given her a clear identity. She wasn't just one of those Pom child migrants, but English Dulcie Taylor, with a father called Reg who was a builder. Her dreams of being with him again one day and perhaps returning to England had sustained her when things were blackest.

Ross had put his arm around her and wiped away her tears when she told him she felt as if her box with all those precious things inside it had been smashed now her father was dead. She said that she was left with an empty space inside her that nothing would ever fill.

When he told her that he knew how she felt because he lived with an empty space inside him too, she believed him. She could see the bleakness in his eyes, hear the break in his voice, and knew they were two of a kind.

Neither of them had ever spoken of that since, but it had created a bond between them. Back in April when the lambs were being born they had shared the responsibility of hand-feeding two motherless ones. One day when they were sitting together playing with them, he'd said, '*Maybe we can both start a new box of memories. This one could go into it.*' Then he asked her if she wanted to go to the pictures the following night to see James Dean in *Rebel Without a Cause*.

She wasn't sure if he was actually asking her for a date. Or if he was going to the pictures anyway and didn't fancy going on his own. There was no way she could ask without embarrassing herself so she just nodded and left it at that.

As Dulcie went about her chores that day, she came to the conclusion Ross *had* been suggesting a real date. She wondered whether he would kiss her, and just the thought of that made her feel shaky and excited.

There had been a great deal in the news about James Dean's death in a car crash the previous year, and the little cinema in Esperance was packed to capacity.

Despite thinking James Dean was the biggest dreamboat

ever with his chiselled features and his sexy eyes, Jim, the character he played in this film, made Dulcie feel strangely uneasy. Maybe it was just because Ross hadn't moved a muscle since the film started, not even attempting to hold her hand or put his arm around her the way all the other young couples were doing. Each time she glanced sideways at him he was completely entranced, drinking it in as though he wanted to be just like Jim.

She was entirely engrossed by seeing how American teenagers lived, for the glimpse she'd had of their Perth counterparts had stayed with her when she returned home. Yet envious as she was of their seemingly far more exciting lives, more money and nicer clothes than she could ever expect to have, she couldn't really understand why a film should glorify them causing their parents so much trouble.

'That was fantastic,' Ross exclaimed as they came out of the cinema. 'Best film I've ever seen.'

'I liked *East of Eden* better,' she said.

He looked at her in surprise. 'That was old-fashioned,' he said dismissively.

'Not that old-fashioned,' Dulcie said as they began walking towards Bruce's car. 'Anyway, I like to be away from it all when I watch a film.'

'But this film did that to me!' he said, a note of intensity coming into his voice. 'It made me want to rebel against stuff.'

'What have you got to rebel against?' she giggled. 'Getting up at five, milking cows, ploughing! I thought you liked all that.'

He seemed stuck for an answer and didn't reply until they were in the car heading home. 'I would have thought you'd want to rebel too,' he said. 'We had our childhoods snatched away from us, we've been treated worse than animals. We should make a protest.'

Dulcie laughed. 'Oh, don't be silly, Ross! What are we going to do, smash a few shop windows in, ride motorbikes around Esperance frightening old ladies? All that film showed me was how spoilt those American teenagers were. What did they have to grouse about? I didn't admire them, not one little bit.'

'You don't get it, do you?' he said, turning towards her, his face full of anger. 'We've got nothing, you and I. We'll probably never have anything either. Our lives are nothing but work and more work. We don't earn enough to ever think of having a place of our own, we can't break away and go to the city because farming is all we know. You and I are only one step up from the Aborigines.'

Dulcie was bewildered. She had always sympathized with the Aborigines around Esperance because even though they were warm, friendly people and the men were excellent stockmen, they appeared to be very much on the fringe of Australian life. But she'd never seen herself in the same light as them. 'But I'm happy with Bruce and Betty. I thought you were too?'

He banged one hand hard on the steering-wheel. 'Don't you see it's a trap? I know they are good people, but do we have to spend the rest of our lives being grateful, working our arses off just because someone was kind to us?'

'You're free to go whenever you want to,' she said. This wasn't how she expected a date to be. She thought he might have said how pretty she looked, held her hand, even tried to kiss her. She didn't understand why he'd suddenly become so bitter.

'I *know* I'm free to leave,' he sounded exasperated. 'But what else is out there for someone like me?'

'Leave and find out,' she said. She was getting cross now.

A kangaroo jumped out of the bushes right into the car's path. Dulcie screamed, Ross braked hard, the car went into a skid and Dulcie hit her forehead on the wind-screen.

'Stupid fucking animal!' Ross yelled, but managed to control the car before they hit a tree. He stopped, and put his head down on the steering-wheel.

'Are you all right, Dulcie?' Dulcie asked herself in sarcasm because she thought that should have been his first thought. 'Well, actually I did bang my head quite hard, Ross, in fact I think I'll have a great big lump there by the time we get home, but don't worry about me. You look just like James Dean in one of his sulks.'

Ross lifted his head up and looked at her. 'I wasn't sulking, it just gave me a shock, that's all. If we'd hit him it would have buggered the car up good and proper.'

Dulcie felt her forehead, it was already swelling and it hurt. She wanted to cry with disappointment that her first date had gone so badly wrong. 'Let's go home,' she said wearily.

Ross didn't say another word for the rest of the way home. Bruce and Betty must have gone to bed because the living-room light was turned off. Ross parked the car and Dulcie hopped out immediately, making for the house. She had got to the back porch when Ross caught up with her.

'I'm sorry,' he said, catching hold of her arm. 'Let me look at your head?'

The porch light was on and he pulled her beneath it. 'It looks bad,' he said. 'Shall I come in with you and bathe it?'

'I can do it,' she said wearily. 'Betty would only get up if she heard you. Thank you for taking me to the pictures.'

But as she went to walk in, he caught her arm again. 'You wish you'd never come out with me, don't you?'

Dulcie was tempted to say yes, but he looked so crest-fallen she couldn't. 'No I don't.'

'I'm sorry I made you hurt your head,' he said. 'I'll make it up to you.'

In the yellowish light his eyes looked even more cat-like than usual. There was a kind of begging look to them, the way the cats in the barn looked at her when they were hungry.

'I've got to go in now and put some ice on this bump,' she said. 'I'll see you in the morning.'

He lunged at her, caught her up in his arms and kissed her passionately, just the way she'd hoped for for so long, then to her surprise and dismay, he turned and loped away across the yard without another word.

When Dulcie got up the following morning Betty was already in the kitchen making some tea. As she turned to speak to Dulcie, her hands flew up in horror. 'My goodness, what's happened to you?' she asked.

Dulcie explained. 'We didn't hit the kangaroo,' she finished up. 'The car's fine.'

'I'd rather see a bump in the car than one on you,' Betty said. 'Let me put some ice on it.'

Dulcie had done that before she'd gone to bed, but it hadn't helped much, she had woken to find a lump on her forehead like a small purple egg. Betty nudged her to sit down and holding a couple of ice cubes in a tea-towel she held it to her head. 'So how was the date until this happened?' she asked.

'Fine,' Dulcie lied. She had no intention of letting on that Ross felt they ought to become a pair of rebels. 'But it gave us both a bit of a shock.'

'I should think it did.' Betty tutted in sympathy. 'Bruce has hit so many of those wretched 'roos over the years, he says it's better not to try and avoid them because they invariably jump out of the way anyway. What was the film like?'

'Great!' Dulcie tried to smile and look enthusiastic. If she didn't Betty would be probing all day. 'Do you think they sell jeans for girls in the shop in town? I fancy a pair.'

Betty looked horrified. 'Surely you don't want to dress like a boy?'

The one impact that the film had made on Dulcie was girls in jeans. She thought they looked sexy and wonderful. When she couldn't sleep during the night because her head hurt, and she couldn't stop recalling that kiss from Ross, she'd decided that she was going to get a pair of jeans and be the first girl in Esperance with them.

'I won't look like a boy in them,' Dulcie grinned. 'Just you wait.'

'Ross might not like it,' Betty said darkly. 'Men are funny about things like that.'

'Too bad,' Dulcie said with a toss of her head. Maybe she would rebel in her own little way. Her wages had been put up to two pounds a week since her seventeenth birthday, so she could afford to buy a few new clothes that would make Ross's eyes pop out of his head. She wasn't going to creep round him any more either. He'd have to come begging for kisses.

Chapter Fifteen

'A *maid*!' May exclaimed in horror. 'You said you'd find me a job in an office!'

May's fifteenth birthday was only one week away and for the last couple of months she'd spent every waking hour in daydreams of swanning around a city centre office being admired by all the male staff. When she was called over this afternoon to Mother's study she imagined she was going to be told the location of this place.

'With an office job you would have no accommodation, May,' Mother said sharply. 'Rooms are too expensive for a young girl just starting out and I don't believe you would be able to deal with living alone anyway. Besides, you need to learn to type and do shorthand to get a good office job, you can do that at night school with this job.'

'Where is it?' May asked suspiciously. 'If it's out in the bush I'm not going.'

'It isn't out in the bush, it's here in Perth, in Peppermint Grove, and Mrs Wilberforce is a relative of mine.'

May was slightly cheered by Peppermint Grove. She had been there several times with Mother and it was a nice area with beautiful houses, set beside the River Swan, with Cottesloe beach only a twenty-minute walk away. But she didn't like the idea one bit that it was to work for a relative of Mother's. Everything she said and did would be reported back, not to mention Mother dropping in all the time.

But of course she couldn't say that. 'What does a maid do?' she asked.

'Answer the door and telephone. Washing, ironing, helping with the cooking, cleaning. Mrs Wilberforce entertains a great deal and when she has guests she'd expect you to wait at the table. But it is not a hard job, May, and the experience could be invaluable to you as Mrs Wilberforce is a real lady and likes everything done as it should be, you can learn a great deal from her. You can attend night school twice a week, and she'll give you a whole day off, plus four pounds a week wages.'

The thought of four pounds a week almost wiped out May's reservations. That was a pound more than Dulcie got at eighteen! 'Can I meet Mrs Wilberforce first?' she asked.

'I shall be taking you there for an interview tomorrow,' Mother said. 'Now, just be sweet and willing like you can be when you want to, and I'm sure Mrs Wilberforce will take you on. You see, she particularly wants an English girl, and one who speaks well. She is English herself, her husband is Australian of course, he's my second cousin. He is a banker, and they have two married sons.'

May didn't entirely believe that this job would be a good one, she had stopped believing anything the woman said after she'd discovered she'd lied about Dulcie's letters. She hadn't forgotten either that she would probably never have been told about her father dying back in England but for Mr and Mrs French coming to the convent. Not that either of those things mattered too much now, all May wanted to do was get out of this place and away from Mother.

After being dismissed, May didn't go back to the school-room as she should have, but skirted round the side of the chapel and sat down on a secluded bench. She'd missed many a morning or afternoon of school this way, the Sisters just assumed she was still with Reverend Mother. She put her arm down through the back of the bench and rescued her cigarette tin from its hiding place. While in Perth with Mother about a year ago, she'd gone into a sweet shop owned by an old lady and made conversation with her. By her second visit she'd made the old girl trust her so much she asked May to mind the shop while she went and put her kettle on for a cup of tea. It was so easy to steal a couple of packets of cigarettes and slip them up the elastic of her knicker legs. She did the same again every time she went to Perth, and it was doubly rewarding as the old lady always gave her a bar of chocolate just for coming to see her.

May would've liked to share the cigarettes with another girl, but there was no one here she could trust. All the girls were jealous of her, they would do or say anything to get her into trouble, and it wasn't worth taking that risk now she had so little time left here.

Opening up the tin, she took one cigarette from the packet of Craven A inside and lit it, hiding the tin again afterwards. As she leaned back to enjoy it, her mind turned to all her other hiding places. There was a tin in the woodshed holding nylon stockings, lipsticks, nail varnish and other cosmetics. Down at the pig sty a small tin holding almost ten pounds was tucked away behind a broken brick. In the boiler-room was a cardboard box containing a tight pale blue skirt, a white blouse, some underwear and a pair of high-heeled shoes.

Clothes were so easy to steal, she'd got them on two separate occasions when she'd been in Boan's department store with Mother. As she was already carrying a large store bag holding purchases Mother had made, it was a cinch to slip something else in. The real difficulty was getting it out of the bag when she got back here without Mother noticing anything. Fortunately both times Mother had sent her into the convent ahead of her, and she'd slipped her items into the broom cupboard a couple of doors away from Mother's study, then retrieved them later, hiding them under her cardigan.

Stealing the shoes was her biggest triumph, for she'd done it right under Mother's nose. Mother was buying a new pair for herself, horrible black heavy lace-ups, but another woman sitting just one chair away was trying on pair after pair of beautiful shoes. Maybe if they hadn't been size fours, the same size May took, she wouldn't have thought of it. But the dainty white ones with the peep-toes that the woman had already discarded as too young for her seemed to be saying, *Take me, take me*, so she did, slipping them into the shopping bag beneath the length of flannelette Mother had bought for the Sisters to make new nightgowns.

But now as she sat here thinking about all these goods and how she was going to retrieve them, it occurred to her that if Mrs Wilberforce was a relative of Mother's and on good terms with her, she couldn't start wearing all these things right off without drawing suspicion on herself.

'You evil old witch,' she murmured. 'You're still going to try and keep me in your web, aren't you? You won't succeed though, I'll do it your way for a while, but only till I've got some money behind me.'

May had remembered Dulcie's words about needing money to get anywhere, and although she'd managed to steal some change from the donation box in the chapel every time she was sent in there to do some cleaning, the visitors were mean and the most she'd ever got at one time was two shillings.

But it mounted up, she had almost ten pounds now, and maybe at this job she'd find some way of adding to it, on top of her wages.

She'd been stealing things for so long now that it was second nature to her. If she saw something she wanted, she took it. It was her way of getting back at all those who had so much and didn't care that girls like her were shoved into orphanages and forgotten. Although she wasn't clever in the classroom, she felt she could outwit almost anyone, and she'd had considerable practice.

A thought sprang into her mind and she smiled at its cunning. As soon as she got to this new job, she'd make up a parcel of the things she couldn't explain, and post them to herself. Then she could tell Mrs Wilberforce that Dulcie had sent her them as a present. She might even be able to get the woman's sympathy by hinting that Mother had intercepted their letters in the past.

Suddenly she felt optimistic again. She dogged out her cigarette, pulled the tip apart and scattered it in a flowerbed, then made her way round the back of the convent to the schoolroom.

Eunice Wilberforce kept glancing out of the window the following afternoon. She was nervous because she didn't want one of Miranda's girls, she'd hadn't liked Edward's cousin even before she became a nun, and she liked her even less now.

'What possessed you, Edward, to tell her I needed help?' she murmured to herself. 'I'd have been much happier with a girl I'd found myself. I don't want some cowed, frightened little thing. I want someone with a bit of personality, a pretty, fresh-faced girl I can have some rapport with.'

Edward didn't like Miranda much either, he'd spent a great deal of his early childhood with her and even though he was six years older than her, she had continually got him into trouble. But being a strong Catholic he felt proud she'd taken her vows and risen to become a Reverend Mother. He got his bank to make donations to St Vincent's, and every year at Christmas he always sent out a huge hamper of treats for the girls.

Mrs Wilberforce glanced around her very English drawing-room with pride. There were oriental rugs on the polished floor, a sumptuous couch and armchairs, and an antique china cabinet filled with old Worcester porcelain that had been in her family for generations. The older she got, the more important maintaining her Englishness seemed to be, though she couldn't for the life of her explain why.

She had lived in Australia for thirty-eight years and whilst she was happy and considered herself very fortunate, she still ached for all things English. That was why they bought this two-storey-house in View Road. She fell immediately for its English Edwardian grey stone, its bay windows and cast-iron railings surrounding the overgrown front garden. It bowed to Australian style in as much as the original house had been extended to one side with all the new upstairs rooms opening up on to a veranda, but it had a tiled roof, not the usual tin, and the downstairs rooms had all the elegance and graciousness of the Edwardian period.

Before and during the war they'd had both a live-in maid and a daily woman to do the rough work. Mrs Wilberforce had dispensed with the maid once the boys got married and moved into their own homes, and her daily gradually dropped first to three days a week, then two, and finally retired a year ago, since when she had had to struggle on alone.

It was now too much for her to manage, she did need help, but she regretted telling Edward that, for she might have guessed that he would immediately see St Vincent's as an ideal source. It wasn't that she was averse to taking on an inexperienced orphan, heaven knows they needed a start in life more than anyone. It was just that Edward had cooked this up with Miranda without first consulting her, and she felt she would have to take whoever was offered, whether she liked them or not.

She heard a car draw up and peeped through the lace curtains. It was Miranda. Just the sight of that tight wimple round her face made her own face tighten with irritation.

But as she watched the girl got out of the car, and Mrs Wilberforce had to blink to make sure she was seeing right. A very pretty blonde girl, not the kind of mouse she'd expected.

'If I've got to have her, it will be on my terms,' she said aloud to make herself feel stronger, and glanced at herself in the mirror over the mantel before going to open the front door.

Mrs Wilberforce was fifty-seven, but no one thought she looked it. Her hair was a deep auburn, only slightly grey at the temples, and she'd retained her slender figure, unlike most of her girlfriends. Why should she be intimidated by a nun?

The bell rang and she made her herself walk slowly to answer it.

'Good afternoon, Mrs Wilberforce,' Miranda said. 'This is May Taylor. May, this is Mrs Wilberforce.'

'I'm very pleased to meet you, mam,' May said, and smiled.

Mrs Wilberforce was taken aback by the girl's looks. Her hair gleamed like gold satin, her eyes were wide and almost turquoise blue, her skin was peachy toned, with not a blemish in sight, she even had straight, white teeth.

Mrs Wilberforce took them through to the dining-room at the back of the house. She had already laid out tea things there, and as the afternoon sun came through the French windows, it was far more pleasant at this time of year than the drawing-room.

Half an hour later, the tea drunk, biscuits and cake eaten, Mrs Wilberforce had heard only Miranda speak, the poor girl had hardly been able to say a word for herself.

'Reverend Mother,' Mrs Wilberforce said – she had to use the woman's right title in front of the girl – 'would you mind waiting in my drawing-room while I speak to May alone? We won't be long.'

'Of course, Mrs Wilberforce,' Miranda said politely, but as she got up, the stiffness of her stance and facial expression showed her displeasure.

Mrs Wilberforce waited until the door was shut and she'd heard Miranda go into the other room. 'Would you like to be my maid?' she asked point-blank. 'Or have you been pushed into this?'

She liked what she'd seen of this girl, she spoke well, she appeared to have good manners, but she was almost *too* pretty, those big blue eyes looked so hungry for affection.

'Yes, I do want to be your maid,' May said, but hesitated, as if there was a 'but'.

'You can say anything you like. I'd like to know what is on your mind,' Mrs Wilberforce said firmly.

343

May shot a look at her as if trying to summon up the courage to say something.

'Reverend Mother can't hear you,' Mrs Wilberforce prompted. 'I don't want to take someone on who isn't really happy about it.'

'Well, it's just that I'm scared she'll always be coming round here,' May said, looking down at her hands. 'I know she is your relative, but I want to forget St Vincent's, I haven't been very happy there.'

Mrs Wilberforce smiled inwardly. She had got the initial impression that Miranda and the girl were equally fond of one another. Clearly this wasn't so.

'Reverend Mother rarely calls here,' Mrs Wilberforce said. 'She's my husband's cousin, not mine. I wouldn't be encouraging her to visit, not unless you want me to.'

May suddenly beamed. 'Then I'd like to come if you'll have me,' she said. 'But please don't tell her what I said.'

'Of course not, May.' Mrs Wilberforce felt a weight lifted from her shoulders. 'Now, is there anything else you want to ask me before I show you round?'

'Will I be able to go to the beach on my day off in the summer?' May asked.

'Of course, and you can often take a walk down to Keane's Point on the river too in the afternoons when there's nothing to do.' Mrs Wilberforce smiled. 'As long as you do the work I ask you to do, and do it well, be polite to my guests when they call and come straight home from your evening classes, I'm sure we'll get on just fine.'

'Mother said you are English too?' May said. 'It's so nice to hear your voice. It makes me think of home.'

That pleased Mrs Wilberforce – after all her years in Australia she was often afraid she might have inadvertently developed the ugly native drawl. May had partially retained her English accent too, and she thought that with a little coaching she could bring it back completely. 'I come from a place called Worcester,' she said. 'I can't imagine you'd know where that is if you were only seven when you were sent out here, but I could show you pictures of it. But tell me, May, do you like Australia?'

'I don't know yet, mam,' May said, looking at her with wide, appealing eyes. 'I haven't liked it much so far. But maybe it will be different once I leave St Vincent's.'

Mrs Wilberforce felt a lump come up in her throat. She had been out to St Vincent's twice with Edward, and on both times she'd come away feeling tearful. She had seen nothing to alarm her, yet she had the feeling that unpleasant things did go on there. Perhaps she'd discover the truth once May settled in.

'Come along then,' she said, getting up. 'I'll show you the rest of the house.'

As Mother drove May back to St Vincent's half an hour later, May knew she was cross about something, almost certainly because she'd been sent out of the room. But May didn't care. She liked Mrs Wilberforce and felt she liked her too. The house and garden were lovely, and even if her bedroom was very small, it was much nicer than she'd expected. But best of all was the certainty that Mrs Wilberforce didn't like Mother, she hadn't said so of course, but May had felt it, and maybe with her help she could break free of the woman for good.

'I'm going to miss you,' May said, forcing herself to sound really sad, because it wouldn't do to show she was delighted with this job. 'Mrs Wilberforce wants me to start on Saturday, I won't even be at St Vincent's for my birthday on the Tuesday afterwards.'

'I'll pop in to see you that day and bring any mail from your sister,' Mother said, glancing at her sideways. 'We can meet for lunch sometimes on your day off too.'

'That would be nice,' May lied. 'Mrs Wilberforce said I could keep up my piano practice too.'

Mother put her hand on May's knee. 'You'll always be my special girl,' she said. 'That's why I found you such a nice job. I hope you appreciate it?'

May looked down at the hand on her knee and

shuddered. In the last year that same nasty veiny hand had been right up her knicker legs, prodding, poking, stroking, making her feel sick, and she wished she dared brush it off now and tell the dirty bitch to leave her alone. But she couldn't, not yet. It wasn't safe. She knew too she would have to submit to even more fondling before she got away.

But one day she'd make her pay.

Dulcie was kneeling down in the garden planting out some petunias as Bruce and Betty arrived home one afternoon from a shopping trip up in Kalgoorlie.

'There's a letter for you, Dulcie!' Betty called out as she got out of the car. She had picked up the post on the way home and she recognized the handwriting as May's, the first letter to come from her in over three months.

Dulcie leaped up and came running over. As Betty handed her the envelope she let out a whoop of delight.

'You sit down and read it,' Betty suggested. Dulcie's shoes were covered in mud, as were her hands. 'I'll make us a cup of tea and bring it out on the veranda.'

Dulcie was so excited she couldn't even wait until she was sitting down, but ripped open the envelope and began reading it as she walked back to the house.

The address was View Road, Peppermint Grove, in Perth and it was dated 22 May, a month ago.

Dear Dulcie, she read, *As you can see I've left St Vincent's now and I'm working as a maid here in Peppermint Grove for Mrs and Mrs Wilberforce. It's a nice house, a real one like back in England with an upstairs. It reminds me of the posh ones by the park back in England. The river is just two minutes away down the hill, but it's more like a beach because people swim there in the summer. Cottesloe beach is a walk away in the other direction. There's lots of shops, buses and trains. I have to do cleaning, washing and ironing, and when Mrs Wilberforce has guests I wait at the table and all that stuff. She's very fussy, everything has to be just so, sometimes I get*

*really fed up, it's so quiet and lonely too. I go to night school
now, I'm learning to type and do shorthand. I'm not very good
at shorthand, I can't remember it for more than a minute! Oh,
and I get four pounds a week! Last week I bought a dress, it's
pink with one of those bell-shaped skirts that are in fashion.
Have you seen them? I'm going to let my hair grow now. Mr
W. is a cousin of Rev. Mother, he works in a bank. She keeps
coming round and Mrs W. is getting cross about it, I don't
think she likes her much. I often tell Mrs W. about you. Is
Ross your boyfriend now? I can't believe you are eighteen and
I'm fifteen, we used to talk so much about what we'd do then,
and how it would be when Daddy came for us. But it's all
different now, isn't it? Are you going to stay there now? Do
you love Ross?*

Write soon and try and send me a picture of you.

Love and kisses,

May

Betty came out with the tea just as Dulcie had finished
reading the letter for the second time. They sat down on
the two chairs on the back porch, and Dulcie told her the
gist of what May had to say. She wasn't going to give
the letter to her to read as she was embarrassed at the
references to Ross.

Dulcie supposed he was her boyfriend. They went to
the pictures almost every week and he took her out on the
motorbike he'd bought, but although he held her hand in
the pictures and kissed her goodnight, it didn't seem like
a real romance.

'It sounds like she's fallen on her feet,' Betty said. 'Peppermint Grove is the nicest place to live in Perth. My sister
and I used to go and look around there all the time when
we were girls. I used to dream of living in one of the
houses overlooking the river.'

'May's a funny girl,' Dulcie said thoughtfully. 'She
hasn't said that she likes it there. If I'd been sent somewhere
like that and got paid so much I'd have thought I was the
luckiest girl in the world.'

'Some people don't know when they are well off,' Betty replied. 'But I suppose it must be a bit lonely if she's only got Mrs Wilberforce for company all day.'

'I wish she'd told me what the people were like, what she thinks about and what she does in her spare time,' Dulcie said wistfully. She went on to read out that sentence about their father. 'That's the closest she can get to saying she's sad it didn't turn out the way we hoped it would. But then she isn't much good at letter-writing.'

'She's very young,' Betty reminded her. 'When I was fifteen all I thought about was boys and wishing I had some pretty clothes.' She wished Dulcie would think about herself and not others so much. But she decided she would change the subject.

'How is it going with Ross anyway? Can we expect the sound of wedding bells one day?'

Bruce and Betty teased her a great deal about Ross, yet even if it was always light-hearted, Dulcie sensed they hoped they might have a future together.

'I don't think Ross thinks along those lines.' Dulcie sighed. She could see him over by the barn working on a repair to the tractor with Bob. The winter sun was warm today and he'd taken off his shirt. Just the sight of his muscular chest and arms made her tingle, but she didn't think he felt the same way about her.

'Of course he does,' Betty scoffed. 'Why else would he spend all his spare time with you?'

Dulcie got up from her seat, it was time to get the supper on. 'Maybe it's because he's too shy to look for anyone else,' she said. 'I'm what you might call convenient.'

Betty said nothing more as they both went indoors. Dulcie had made a mutton stew in the morning and it had been cooking slowly all day, she only had to make some dumplings to add to it and peel some potatoes.

As she laid the table for supper Betty came back into the living-room. 'What did you mean exactly by "convenient"?' she asked.

Dulcie blushed. Betty hardly ever let a chance remark

pass by, and obviously she'd been brooding on that one. 'Well, I'm just here, aren't I? He doesn't have to make any effort,' she said.

Betty put her hands on her hips and glowered at her. 'Don't you ever put so little value on yourself,' she scolded. 'I never heard anything like it. I *know* that if you lived fifty miles away in the bush, Ross would still want to see you. I daresay he'd walk there barefoot if necessary.'

'That's not the impression he gives me,' Dulcie retorted.

'He's never told me about his life before here,' Betty said. 'But I nursed him when he first arrived and I learned a great deal about how it had been from the way he reacted to me. There were deep scars on his body from whips and canes, there were marks from boils that had never been treated, and he wasn't just thin from a long journey without food, but from long-term undernourishment. I don't think he'd ever known any love and affection, he didn't trust anyone. It took months before we got any kind of normal response from him, he was brusque, know-it-all, shifty and quite frightening really. I have to admit there were times when both Bruce and I felt like chucking him off the place.' She paused for a moment, looking at Dulcie.

'We healed his body completely, we taught him how to behave so he could fit in with us, and he showed his appreciation not in words, but by working like a demon for us. We've grown very fond of him and I believe he feels the same about us, but we know there is a part of him we'll never reach. I believe you could, Dulcie, that is if you want to. The question is, do you?'

Dulcie nodded. She had been in a state of permanent wanting for months now. She wanted to be held in Ross's arms, kissed properly like people did on films, she wanted to know what he was thinking and what he felt for her. But she couldn't say that to Betty.

'He's just so difficult and moody sometimes,' she blurted out. 'Every time I think he's about to open up to me, he suddenly clams up.'

'Does he ever . . .' Betty paused. 'You know, try it on?'

Dulcie was equally embarrassed. She shook her head.

Betty looked relieved. 'Well, he must think you are special. John took him up to Kalgoorlie once before you came here, he told me Ross was like a mad thing with a girl he met up there.'

Dulcie smarted. 'I didn't know he'd had any other girlfriends,' she said.

Betty winced. 'She wasn't a girlfriend, just a girl in a pub. You know what I mean.'

Dulcie realized that was Betty's polite way of saying the girl was a whore.

'Anyway,' Betty went on, 'men behave differently with nice girls. Like I told you before, they're the ones they want to marry.'

Dulcie wasn't convinced that it was normal for a man to take a girl out for over a year and never attempt to do anything more than give her the most chaste of goodnight kisses. In the magazines she read girls were always complaining that their boyfriends spent every minute of a date trying to lure them into sex. But she couldn't say any of that to Betty.

Over supper that evening Dulcie was still thinking about what Betty had said earlier, and she found herself only half listening to the conversation around the table, and watching Ross. She liked the boyish way he looked, his unruly dark auburn curls, the freckles across his nose, and his shy, lopsided smile. Yet it was more than his appearance which fascinated her, for he had a curious blend of almost bombastic confidence in some areas, yet chronic timidity in others. Bruce often remarked on his remarkable gentleness and patience with animals, whilst John complained of his explosive temper. He had great physical strength and stamina, working tirelessly without complaint, yet sometimes he was incredibly stubborn, refusing to budge an inch when a principle was at stake.

The conversation was all centred on the cows. In the last week fifteen calves had been born, and eight more were expected in the next day or so. Two days earlier

Bruce had been forced to do an emergency Caesarean section on one of them. Although he had assisted a vet with the same operation many times before, this time he couldn't get hold of him, so he was forced to tackle it himself or he would have lost both mother and calf. Fortunately he was successful, a fine, healthy little heifer was delivered, the cow was stitched up again and now she was recovering.

'Put her and the calf back in the paddock with the others tomorrow, Ross,' Bruce said. 'I'll need that pen free.'

'Leave her another day, boss,' Ross said. 'She's not right yet.'

Although Dulcie had only been half listening up until then, she felt a sudden charge in the atmosphere. John and Bob looked at Ross in surprise. Bruce was staring at him as if unable to believe what he'd just heard.

Dulcie knew Bruce was very experienced with cattle, but even if he hadn't been it wasn't done for the youngest hand to challenge any instruction given by the owner. Ross coloured up when he saw the expressions on everyone's faces.

'I was with her just now,' he said quickly. 'I tell you, she's not right.'

'Bit cocky, aren't you?' John said in a sharp tone.

Ross merely shrugged, but his belligerent expression showed he had no intention of backing down.

Dulcie suddenly felt anxious. Bruce was a very amiable man. He never threw his weight around, and allowed his men to use their initiative. But even so she sensed Ross had really annoyed him. 'Since when did you know better than me? You'll do as I said,' he growled at him. 'Put her in the paddock tomorrow.'

'No. She's not up to it.'

Utter silence descended in the room, not the scrape of a knife and fork or the faintest sound of chewing. All eyes were on Bruce, like they were waiting for a firework to go off.

'Do it tomorrow morning or get off my property,' Bruce

said, and even though he hadn't raised his voice it had an icy quality.

Dulcie held her breath, willing Ross to apologize – even an 'Okay, boss' would have done. But he just sat there, staring woodenly at his half-eaten dinner.

No one spoke again and as Bob and John finished their meal and got up to leave, Ross hurried out with them. Seconds later Dulcie heard the sound of his motorbike starting up.

Bruce got up from the table and flopped down in an armchair. It was quite clear he was very rattled, and perhaps tonight's incident wasn't the only one on his mind, for Ross was often very cocky. Dulcie hastily stacked the dishes on to a tray and was out into the kitchen to start the washing up in seconds. Betty brought a couple of things through in her hands, and although she didn't speak, she made a face and rolled her eyes back to the living-room as if to say she ought to get back there with her husband and try to calm him down.

'Cocky little bastard!' Bruce roared out a few seconds later. 'I should have knocked him off his seat.'

Dulcie winced. Back at the Masters' place she heard so many angry remarks bandied around that she barely noticed them after a time. But she'd never seen Bruce angry before and it scared her.

'Now now, Brucey,' Betty said soothingly. 'It was all a storm in a tea-cup, he just forgot himself, that's all.'

'He forgets himself too often, last week he argued with me about fertilizer, a few days before that he tried to tell me I ought to put the paddock down by the lake down to clover.' Bruce snarled. 'The drongo's only twenty. I've got over forty years' experience of farming on him. He'd never even seen anyone do a Caesarean until that one, and he dares suggest he knows more about the aftercare than I do!'

Standing at the kitchen sink, Dulcie felt a cold shiver run down her spine. Maybe there was something wrong with the cow, but if Ross thought so he should have asked

Bruce to go with him to look at her before supper, not just trotted it out as if he were an expert.

One thing was certain, Ross wouldn't apologize, and neither would he move the cow, he was much too stubborn. Nor would he plead to be kept on. He'd pack his few things and he'd be off without a single backward glance or a goodbye. Yet she knew how he'd feel inside – devastated.

There might be some parts of Ross's character which she didn't understand, but she knew what Bruce and Betty meant to him. In their home he'd found happiness and security, through the work they'd given him he'd found self-esteem and fulfilment. To be cast out from here would strip him of all these things. He'd find another job soon enough, but he'd take resentment with him, and before long he'd be on the move again, and with each successive move he'd become more bitter and resentful.

She couldn't bear the thought of that. She'd heard so many of John and Bruce's tales about the hard stockmen who went from one property to another, never staying anywhere long enough to form any attachments. They worked, then drank and gambled their money away, then went back to work again. No real friends, no love, family or possessions. A life as arid as a desert.

And if Ross left who would be her friend then? She had gone into the ice-cream shop in Esperance where all the young people gathered dozens of times, but no one had ever spoken to her. Since her first dance on her seventeenth birthday she'd been to at least eight or nine more, but although people nodded and smiled at her and boys asked her to dance, she still didn't know anyone any better than she did a year ago. They called her *The Pom girl out at French's*. They weren't even interested enough to find out her name. But then they made jokes that a person had to live around these parts for twenty years before they were considered a local.

Dulcie went to bed early and read a book for a while, but the words just danced about in front of her eyes, and finally she turned off the light and tried to sleep. But she couldn't, instead she began to cry, both for herself and Ross. There were many times when she wished she could leave here, go to the city and find a job where she could use her brain, wear nice clothes and rise to be somebody, rather than just a skivvy. Yet in her heart she knew she wasn't ready for the outside world yet. She was scared of being on her own, distrustful of strangers, and didn't think she could make rational decisions for herself yet. She guessed that Ross was much the same. He was even more awkward with people than she was.

Just the thought of him riding around on his motorbike tonight chilled her. He had bought it soon after they saw *Rebel Without a Cause*, and a denim jacket and cowboy boots to complete the image. She'd teased him about it so often, calling him Rebel Ross as she tipped up his leather stockman's hat and made him do the sneer like James Dean's. She had always found it funny that he liked to project a rebellious image, but if he was out there seething with anger, maybe with a few schooners of beer inside him, he could pick a fight with someone a great deal tougher than him and he might be badly hurt.

As she lay there crying and thinking about what losing Ross would mean to her, she suddenly saw she loved him. Maybe their friendship had sprung from sympathy, but it was a great deal more than pity she felt for him now, or why else would she feel so torn apart?

The next morning she got up reluctantly as she heard Bruce go out. She had hardly slept at all, and she felt drained from spending most of the night wondering if she should try to plead with Bruce on his behalf.

She was washed and dressed and making a cup of tea for Betty when Bruce came back in. He didn't speak but went over to the bookcase in the living-room to pull a book down.

Dulcie poured him a cup too, and took it in to him. He nodded thanks but didn't speak or even look up, and she took it that he was in a bad mood and it wouldn't be advisable to add to it.

When she took a cup of tea to Betty, and Betty asked her to cook the breakfast because she was feeling crook, Dulcie became even more anxious. Betty didn't look ill, and she never stayed in bed even when she was, so it appeared she just didn't want to witness any ugly or upsetting scenes.

Bruce went out again, but he hadn't touched his tea, and as Dulcie laid the table for breakfast she kept glancing out of the window. She saw John and Bob herding the cows from the milking shed back into their paddock, but there was no sign of Ross. Yet his motorbike was there by the barn, so she decided she would cook him breakfast anyway, and she'd take it to Betty if he didn't come in for it.

John and Bob arrived right on seven-thirty as usual, both looking a little strained, without their usual cheery greetings. Bruce arrived a few minutes later.

'Where is he?' Bruce asked from the doorway, bending down to take off his boots.

'In the bunkhouse packing,' John said. 'He'd already got the cows in the shed and started on the milking before Bob and I woke. He's just about to leave.'

'Get him,' Bruce said curtly and padded into the bath-room in his socks to wash his hands.

Dulcie wished she could go outside so she didn't have to witness anything further. But there was toast to be made, tea to be poured, and she had no good reason to go out.

John brought Ross in just as Bruce was coming out of the bathroom. Ross looked defeated, his eyes cast down, shoulders hunched. 'Sit down, you two,' Bruce said to the men. He stood behind his own chair looking down at Ross.

'Seems you were right after all about that cow, Ross. She's not too good. Got a bit of an infection I'd say. I've bathed the wound and given her a shot. We'll leave her where she is for a few more days.'

Dulcie gulped back a gasp, put the breakfasts down on the table and hurried out again to get the others.

She was staggered, not just that Ross had been right,

but that Bruce was big enough to admit it. She didn't think that many men would be so honest. She waited breathlessly, half expecting Ross to come back with some smug remark, but he didn't.

'Next time you feel there's something wrong with one of my animals, just tell me,' Bruce said, his voice softer now. 'There's a right and a wrong way to go about everything, and you've got a knack of getting up anyone's nose. After you've finished your breakfast you can unpack your stuff, unless you really want to go. You've got the makings of a good stockman, and I don't want to lose you.'

'Thanks, boss,' Ross replied. 'I didn't want to have to go.'

'Men!' Betty exclaimed a little later when she got up. 'They're all as stubborn as mules. I had to make Bruce go and check the cow himself this morning, just in case Ross was right. He didn't want to, and the lad would have shot off without even a goodbye. Still, it's all over now. Let's hope we don't have any more nastiness like that again, it twists me up inside.'

'Me too,' Dulcie agreed, hoping this wouldn't make Ross even more big-headed now. 'Are you feeling better now?'

Betty smiled. 'There wasn't much the matter with me, I just thought it best to keep out the way. I hope Ross has learned his lesson though, my Bruce won't stand for anyone trying to tell him how to run his farm, not even me.'

Late in the afternoon Dulcie went over to the cattle pens because another calf had been born during the morning. Ross was there, raking out dirty straw, so she admired the new calf, watched it for a little while, then went over to see the cow that had caused the trouble.

Her stitched wound was a bit puffy and red in one small area, yet when Dulcie had looked at her the previous day she didn't think it was like that then, or Bruce would have noticed it himself. She asked Ross what made him think something was wrong. 'I don't know,' he shrugged. 'Just a feeling, but the same feeling tells me she's on the mend now too.'

'It wasn't very smart to be such a know-all with Bruce,' she reproved him gently. 'If you hadn't turned out to be right, you'd have been gone by now.'

'Would you have cared?' he asked, his head down.

'Of course I would,' she said.

'But does that mean you'd still be my girl?'

Dulcie blushed, he had never referred to her as *his girl* before. 'It would be difficult to be that if you went miles away,' she said.

'So you wouldn't have left with me then?'

Dulcie was about to retort that of course she wouldn't have, but she stopped herself just in time, realizing that implied she didn't care, which wasn't so. 'Would you have wanted me to?' she asked.

He blushed then and turned his head away. 'Yeah, I reckon so,' he mumbled.

A sweet, warm feeling ran through her, she moved closer to him and put her hand on his arm. 'I didn't know you felt that way,' she said in a low voice.

He lifted one hand and touched her cheek very softly, his eyes meeting hers. 'I don't know how to say stuff like that,' he said. 'I thought you'd just feel it.'

She needed that clarified. Was he trying to say he loved her? 'I thought you saw me as just a friend,' she said.

'You are that too,' he replied, then paused as if searching for the right words to explain what he meant. 'But you're special. I want you with me for ever,' he finally blurted out.

'You mean, like, getting married?' she asked, her voice hardly more than a whisper.

He nodded. 'But I don't know how, we wouldn't have anywhere to live, would we? Not unless we moved away from here.'

Dulcie was thrown into confusion. Not only was that

the last thing she expected to hear today, but in her mind proposals were supposed to be made by moonlight, with all problems swept away by the couple's desire for one another. Yet here they were on a grey June day, by a stinking cow pen, and Ross hadn't even taken her in his arms to show her this was an important moment.

'Other couples get round that sort of thing,' she stammered out.

'You mean you would marry me?' he asked, his tawny eyes full of surprise and delight. 'Really, Dulcie? You aren't kidding me?'

His face was suddenly transformed. A smile was spreading from ear to ear, that wary look she was so used to, gone. He was handsome now, every feature softened, his eyes sparkling. 'I can't believe it,' he gasped. 'I want to hug you but I can't 'cos I'm so dirty.'

It was only then that Dulcie noticed he was filthy, his hands, forearms and clothes all daubed with dirt and cow manure, he even had bits of straw in his hair. 'Maybe we ought to wait then until you're cleaned up,' she said laughingly. 'I don't expect you smell so good either.'

'I'll take you out after supper tonight,' he said eagerly. 'We'll go to the Pier Hotel.'

Dulcie leaned forward and kissed his grubby cheek. She felt as though a million bubbles were bursting inside her, and she didn't know how she was going to go back to the house and prepare a meal as if nothing had happened.

'After supper then,' she said, smiling with her mouth, eyes and her whole body. 'I can't wait.'

'What is this?' Dulcie looked suspiciously at the dark red liquid in the glass Ross had just brought her. It was half past eight and they were in the private bar of the Pier Hotel. There was no more than a handful of people in there, mostly middle-aged couples talking quietly, but the main bar next door was very busy and noisy with men only.

'It's port and lemon,' Ross whispered. 'That's what ladies drink.'

Dulcie had never tried any kind of alcohol before, and she thought this drink smelled like cough mixture, but if Ross thought she should be trying a grown-up drink then she was prepared to like it. She sipped it cautiously and found it wasn't that bad.

They sat for a while in awkward silence, neither of them knowing what they should say now they were here. Ross was wearing a hairy, badly fitting grey suit, a white shirt and tie, his auburn curls suppressed with some kind of oil. But although Dulcie was touched that he'd dressed himself up like this for her, rather than wearing the denim jacket and open-necked shirt he normally wore when they went out, he looked awkward and uncomfortable.

'Did you say anything to Betty?' he asked eventually.

Dulcie said she hadn't, but that she didn't know how she kept it to herself as she was so excited.

'I reckon we'll have to tell them together,' Ross said. 'Maybe tomorrow night after John and Bob have gone off to the pub. I can't say anything in front of them or they'll start ribbing me.'

'You want to tell them?' Dulcie said in surprise. As he was so secretive in most things she'd half expected he'd insist they kept it to themselves at least for a while. But it pleased her, it meant he really was serious.

'When will we say we're going to get married, Ross? They'll want to have some rough idea.'

He shrugged. 'I suppose when we've found somewhere to live. Maybe there might be something here in Esperance.'

Dulcie liked that idea, a dear little house of her own to come home to every night. But when she said that, Ross looked at her really oddly. 'You can't carry on working once we're married,' he said. 'That isn't right.'

'But what about Betty? She needs me.' Dulcie frowned. She hadn't expected that. 'Besides, the money would be useful and what would I do all day alone?'

'You'd look after our home of course,' he said.

Dulcie thought she'd let that slide by, it wasn't important now. She wanted to talk about weddings, May being her bridesmaid, and for Ross to hold her hand and tell her he loved her.

After two drinks in the hotel they went down on to the pier to look at the sea. It was cold, windy and very dark, but the sky was studded with stars, and the port and lemon had given Dulcie a rosy glow inside.

'Ask me properly?' she said when they reached the end of the pier, turning to him and putting her arms around his middle.

He grinned sheepishly and cupped her face in his hands. 'Will you marry me?' he asked, kissing her nose.

'Yes, I think I will,' she giggled. 'But only after you've said the other bit.'

'What other bit?'

'Well, men usually say it before they ask a girl to marry her,' she prompted. 'It's the reason they ask.'

He frowned, dropping his hand from her face to her shoulders. 'I don't know what you mean,' he insisted and she didn't think he was joking.

'I love you?' she said questioningly. 'Or don't you? Maybe you only want a wife to cook and clean for you?'

'Of course not,' he said, looking shocked she would say such a thing.

'Well, maybe you don't love me then?' she teased.

'I do, I wouldn't want to marry you otherwise.'

Dulcie had to be satisfied with that, because it was clear he wasn't going to say the words. So she pulled him closer to her and waited to be kissed. His lips brushed hers lightly and moved away to her cheek, but Dulcie held on to him tightly until his lips came back to hers, and at last he kissed her with some feeling.

'I love you, Ross,' she said, when they finally broke away. 'We're going to be so happy.'

*

'Married?' Bruce looked at Ross in astonishment. He had wondered why Ross had told John and Bob he wouldn't go down the pub with them tonight, and why he had hung around until they left the house. Then Dulcie had come into the room too, and Ross had blurted out that he wanted to marry her.

'Oh, I didn't mean right now,' Ross said hurriedly, taking Bruce's astonishment for disapproval. 'We don't have enough money, or anywhere to live. We just wanted to tell you, that's all.'

Betty smiled warmly. 'We're really happy for you, it's wonderful news, isn't it, Bruce?'

Bruce got out of his chair and beamed at them. 'Of course it is.' He kissed Dulcie's cheek and shook Ross's hand. 'You just took me by surprise, that's all.'

Betty got Ross and Bruce a beer, while she and Dulcie settled for tea. They chatted awhile about all the difficulties about where they would live, then Bruce suggested getting a caravan for them.

'If we put it close to the bunkhouse or the barn we could link up the electricity and the water,' he said eagerly. 'That would be far easier for you than driving back and forth into town.'

Dulcie was thrilled at this suggestion and looked at Ross to see his reaction. He looked guarded, but he said nothing, so by that she took it that he wasn't going to make an issue of her not working.

'January would be a good time to take the plunge,' Betty said. 'With the harvest over and all. Or is that too soon?'

Ross smiled. 'Not too soon for me. What do you think, Dulcie?'

'Just perfect,' she said dreamily.

Chapter Sixteen

May took off her sandals and in bare feet walked along Cottesloe beach to where a group of young men were playing ball in the sea. She'd seen this same group on her day off the previous week, and although none of them had spoken to her, the tall, dark-haired one who had appeared to be their leader had looked at her with interest. She hoped that today he might speak.

It was January and already very hot even though it was only ten in the morning. Mrs Wilberforce had given her a lecture this morning about not getting burnt, but May felt she was already sufficiently tanned to stay there at least until midday, by which time she hoped she might be invited to go for a drink somewhere in the shade.

As she got closer to the men, she felt their eyes on her, but she pretended not to notice and stopped to lay her towel down on the sand. Then, unzipping her dress, she let it slither down her body to reveal her new turquoise swimsuit. It was the most gorgeous one she had ever seen, not the cheap ruched and elasticized kind like most women wore, but smooth, thick satinized cotton, and boned to give her a glamour-girl appearance. She had stolen it from Boan's department store, wearing it out under her clothes, for there was no way she was going to pay eight guineas for a swimsuit, however lovely it was.

She stood for some little time, sweeping her hair up into a pony-tail, perfectly aware the men were watching her. Finally she sat down and took a magazine out of her bag to read.

May knew she was as close to physical perfection as it was possible for a girl to be, her figure was the ideal, her legs were long and shapely, her face and hair were flawless. But in the eight months since she'd left St Vincent's, she'd come to see that looks weren't all she needed to get on in life. Mrs Wilberforce's friends had made her very aware of this, for though they were always pleasant to her face, she had heard them refer to her as *the St Vincent's girl*, and *the poor wee thing*, as if she had some terrible affliction.

May had imagined, too, that there was nothing very difficult about being a maid, yet she'd soon discovered that wasn't so. Domestic work at St Vincent's was of the most basic kind, scrubbing and polishing floors, washing up and laundering ordinary cotton dresses. She had never been taught to cut bread thin enough for the kind of dainty sandwiches Mrs Wilberforce expected when her friends came to tea, or how to iron the kind of delicate garments she owned. Laying a table, cooking and even answering the telephone were all traps to show her ignorance. Many times she had in fact seen herself as *the poor wee thing*, and cried as she worked because however hard she tried to remember all the instructions she was given, she always seemed to blunder. She mustn't slop tea into a saucer as she handed it to someone, there was one cloth for cleaning the toilet seat, another one for cleaning the bath. She had never answered a telephone before, yet not only was she expected to ask who was calling, but take down any message too if Mrs Wilberforce was out. Spelling had never been her strong point, and so many of the callers had strange names she couldn't even pronounce, let alone spell correctly.

She could still recall with dismay the lunch party Mrs Wilberforce had thrown just after she arrived. Two of the ladies winced as they put their forks in their mouths because they tasted the silver polish. How was she supposed to know that cutlery had to be washed in hot soapy water after cleaning? When Mrs Wilberforce said she thought that was obvious, May had burst into tears. It wasn't obvious to her, she'd never cleaned silver in her life before.

The days were endless drudgery, clean this, prepare that, why haven't you dusted that lampshade, why have you forgotten the butter knives again? Her head reeled with trying to remember jam spoons, napkins, pickle forks, to put soda crystals down the sink after washing up, to plump up cushions and never put anything hot or wet on the dining-room table.

Yet the hardest thing of all to adjust to was the idea that a maid should be silent and almost invisible. She'd had the idea that she would be almost like the daughter of the house, that in return for doing their housework she would watch their television, read Mrs Wilberforce's magazines, eat with the family, sit out in the garden and be included in conversations. This wasn't so. She was just a servant, and when she wasn't working, her own room was where she had to be, and she ate her meals alone in the kitchen.

For the first few weeks Mrs Wilberforce was constantly ringing her little silver bell and asking where the marmalade or the butter was. May often wanted to snap at her and say breakfast to her was a bowl of lukewarm Granuma, and how on earth did they think she could make three-minute boiled eggs, a pot of tea and all that toast, all at the same time!

She had to rush her own breakfast and be at the front door to hand Mr Wilberforce his briefcase and hat, and brush down his jacket before he left the house. She couldn't think for the life of her why a man expected anyone to do that for him.

Maybe it wasn't quite so hard now she'd learnt what was expected of her, but she still resented that except for going to night school twice a week, she was kept busy all day until around eight in the evening. Granted, on days when no one came to tea, or Mrs Wilberforce went out, she had a couple of hours in the afternoon when she could go out, to the shops or down to the river to sit in the sun, but almost every week they had guests for dinner on one night, and she had to be there, waiting on them until they'd left the dining-room, sometimes till as late as ten.

Yet however hard May thought her job was, she had learnt from the other girls at night school that she would be a fool to run away before she'd got her diploma in shorthand and typing. Girls who worked in shops or as office juniors were paid less than her, and they said it was difficult to find somewhere affordable to live. Yet May envied them so much when they talked of going dancing at the Embassy or the Calypso on Saturday nights. Mrs Wilberforce said she was much too young for such things, and pointed out that coming in at nine-thirty twice a week from night school was late enough to be out at her age.

Yet fed up as May often was, she always woke on her day off feeling joyful and expectant. Sometimes she even thought fleetingly she was lucky. She had after all, with Mrs Wilberforce's help, managed to distance herself from Mother. She called twice in the first month May started the job, but Mrs Wilberforce made it plain she didn't like unexpected visitors, and since then she'd only telephoned occasionally. May could cope with telephone conversations and it was easy enough to wriggle out of any invitations to lunch by saying Mrs Wilberforce needed her that day. As long as Mother knew she was doing her job properly, attending night school and going to Mass every Sunday, she had no excuse to call round. The relief May felt that she would never again have to submit to her degrading, perverted embraces, was enough to make her feel affection for the woman who stood between herself and Mother. Maybe this was only on good days, when she hadn't burnt, broken or spoilt something and Mrs Wilberforce praised her. Yet deep down she knew her mistress was a fair, good-hearted woman who really did have May's future at heart, and even if not entirely happy with her lot, she knew she could be considerably worse off.

May lay down on her towel. The sun was growing hotter by the minute, but for now she was happy to feel it searing into her skin until she was so hot she'd be forced to go in for a swim. She wondered if Dulcie went to the beach much where she was, and if there was more than she'd said to the postponing of the wedding.

May was really surprised when Dulcie wrote last July to say she was marrying Ross in January. She had enclosed a photograph of them together and May's first thought on seeing the face of her future brother-in-law was that he looked so very ordinary and had nothing in common with James Dean as Dulcie claimed, apart from a lopsided smile. The letter was full of Dulcie-isms, going on about how excited she was at the prospect of having her own home, even if it was only to be a caravan, how she didn't even know Ross loved her until he proposed, and how much she hoped May would be her bridesmaid, and she thought she'd look gorgeous in pale blue satin, and she must send her exact measurements to her so she could get the dress made.

On the strength of this May had asked Mrs Wilberforce if she could have a week's holiday in January, and it was agreed she could.

It was nearly the end of November when Dulcie wrote to say Betty French was very ill, and under the circumstances she and Ross didn't feel they could go ahead with the wedding in January. May couldn't imagine why Betty being ill should upset plans for a wedding, but Mrs Wilberforce said it might be because Dulcie was actually nursing her, along with all her other duties, and she was just too harassed to cope with a wedding too.

'You wouldn't catch me nursing some old farmer's wife,' May thought as she lay in the sun.

The heat of the sun suddenly lessened. May's eyes shot open to find the tall, dark-haired man was standing beside her casting a shadow over her face.

'Sorry to disturb you, love,' he said. 'Got a light?'

May guessed this had to be an excuse to talk to her. She didn't believe that none of his friends had a box of matches or a lighter. He was even better-looking close up than he'd been from a distance, dark, sleepy-looking eyes, a golden tan and a muscular physique. 'I think so,' she said, sitting up and reaching for her bag. She rummaged in it and pulled out a box of matches.

'Want one?' he said, holding out a packet of cigarettes to her.

'Thanks,' she replied, taking one, but handed the matches to him.

He knelt down on the sand beside her and struck a match, lighting first her cigarette, then his own. 'Do you live round here?' he asked after taking a puff.

'Nearby, in Peppermint Grove,' she said.

He settled back on his heels, looking at her appraisingly. 'Rich dad, huh?'

May just shrugged. It wasn't her intention for him to take that as confirmation, she just wasn't used to talking to men, and this one was at least twenty-four, with the skimpiest red bathers she'd ever seen, and the huge bulge inside them was unavoidable.

'I said to my mates that's a rich sheila if ever I saw one,' he said with a wide grin, showing very white teeth. 'But you're a Pom, aren't you? I didn't expect that. You just here for a holiday?'

She nodded, delighted that he thought she looked like a rich girl. She couldn't disillusion him now by telling him she was a maid. His voice was rough, and judging by his muscles he did a labouring job of some kind, maybe he didn't even have one if he could spend a Wednesday on a beach.

'I'm May,' she said, feeling she had to try to act sophisticated and confident. 'What's your name?'

'Nev,' he said. 'So how long are you here for?'

May's brain always seemed to work faster when she was intending to make something up. She'd only seen him once before, but for all she knew he might have seen her dozens of times since November when she first came down to this beach. 'I've been here a while already, I don't know how much longer we're staying, Daddy's here on business.'

He nodded. 'How old are you, May?'

'Seventeen,' she lied.

He stayed after he'd finished his cigarette, firing questions at her, and May lied to all of them. They were staying with her aunt and uncle, her mother was back home in England, and her father had taken her along on the trip so she'd see something of the world before going back home to a finishing school. Effortlessly she drew upon things Mrs Wilberforce had told her and painted a picture of a spoilt little darling who had wanted for nothing in her entire life.

Nev didn't give much of himself away. He said he was taking a holiday before going over to the East Coast to work. He used the expression 'Subbie's' when he referred to his friends, so she took it that they all came from Subiaco, an older part of Perth she'd been through on the train while going into town.

They went for a swim together, had several more cigarettes, and still he didn't go back to join his mates.

'I'd better get out of the sun now,' she said eventually. She could feel her shoulders getting very hot. 'I was thinking of going along to that café further down the beach.'

'I'd like to go with you and buy you a drink,' he said. 'But I didn't bring any money down here with me this time because the last time I came I had my wallet pinched while I was in the sea.'

'I'll buy you one,' she offered. She thought he was lovely and she didn't want to take the chance he'd shoot off if she left.

'I don't like bludging off sheilas,' he said.

May grinned at him. 'I'm not a sheila, I'm May, and I wouldn't call accepting one drink "bludging". Anyway, I can't stay here, I'm burning.'

So he went with her, only returning to his mates long enough to pick up a pair of shorts and a shirt.

May went home to View Road at four. She hoped Mrs Wilberforce would be out so she could shower, change and get out again before she came back, but that wasn't to be. She was sitting on the upstairs veranda reading a book and saw May coming through the gate.

'You shouldn't have stayed out in the sun for so long,' she tutted disapprovingly as she met her at the top of the stairs.

'I wasn't out in it for very long,' May said. 'I met one of the girls from night school on the beach, we sat under the café awning and had a chat.'

'That was nice for you to have some company.' The older woman smiled with real warmth. 'What's her name?'

'Belinda,' May said, the first name that came into her head. 'She asked me to go to the pictures with her this evening. I just came home to ask you if that was all right.'

'Of course it's all right, it's your day off. I'm glad to hear you've made a friend.' Mrs Wilberforce beamed. 'I believe *Funny Face* with Audrey Hepburn is on at the Piccadilly. Is that what you're going to see?'

'I don't think Belinda knew what was on,' May said. 'I hope it's that. But I'd better rush, because she's waiting for me at the station.'

'Why didn't you bring her home for a cup of tea?' Mrs Wilberforce asked. 'I'd like to have met her.'

'I didn't like to, not without asking first,' May said.

She was off to her room in a flash, stripping off her dress and the still damp swimsuit beneath it. Nev was going to meet her at Perth station at half past six. Now she had to make herself look like the rich girl he took her for.

As she stood under the shower, letting the water wash away all the salt in her hair, she felt so happy she could burst. Nev was just what she wanted in a boyfriend, tall, dark and handsome, a bit tough so she felt protected, easy to talk to and not too smart, so she didn't feel inferior. She had met both of the Wilberforces' sons at Christmas, and though they were both nice-looking, and the kind of well-mannered, successful men she'd wanted to attract, she knew immediately by the way they kind of looked beyond her when they were introduced that she could never hope to find a boyfriend in that league, not while she was still a maid.

But she could cut her teeth on working-class Nev. He was impressed by her, maybe even a little intimidated too. Through him she might even meet someone else with a good job and a car. Besides, he made her feel all funny inside.

He had walked her home as far as the Cottesloe shops over the railway bridge from the beach and kissed her goodbye. She had been so afraid that when she was finally kissed by a man it would feel as repulsive as being kissed by Mother, but it wasn't a bit like that. It was sweet, heady, a taste of something utterly new and compelling. She couldn't wait for more.

'I bet you won't come tonight,' he said, his dark eyes all sorrowful. 'You'll go on into your posh house and think, what do I want with a bloke like that?'

'Of course I won't,' she said, tempted then to tell him she was only the maid. But she was enjoying the play-acting, and anyway he might not like her as much if he knew the truth.

An hour later she was ready. She wasn't entirely pleased with her hair, normally she washed it at night and set it with her new set of fat plastic rollers that made it go all slinky and wavy, but without a hair-dryer she couldn't get that effect in an hour, so she'd had no choice but to let it dry naturally. With her pink dress with the bell-shaped skirt, her white peep-toe shoes, gloves and handbag, she felt glamorous enough to knock anyone out, and she would put on more lipstick when she got out of the house.

'You look lovely, May,' Mrs Wilberforce said as she came down the stairs. 'Now, make sure you get home by ten, won't you?'

'Yes, Mrs Wilberforce.' May forced a dutiful smile. She hoped Nev wouldn't mind her having to go home so early. But she'd already told him her father was a bit strict.

'Make sure you don't spend your fare home either,' the

woman added. 'My boys were always doing that when they were your age. I can't count the times they had to walk home.'

May smirked. She had all her money in her handbag, over fifteen pounds. If she was playing at being a rich girl she needed the props to make it convincing.

May got to Perth station far too early, and so she went into the waiting-room and sat there till half past six rather than hanging around outside looking eager.

When she finally went out, there he was, wearing a white open-necked shirt and jeans, leaning against the wall. She was a little dismayed that he was dressed so casually, but he was so handsome that faded very quickly.

'I thought I'd take you to King's Park,' he said as he took her hand. 'It's too hot for the pictures.'

May was disappointed. King's Park made her think of Mother, because she often took her there. Her white shoes weren't comfortable for walking a long way, and besides, she'd got the idea this afternoon that Nev wanted to show her off to all his mates. But it *was* too hot for the pictures, and perhaps he thought the park would be more romantic, so she said nothing.

He asked her about England as they walked, and as May remembered so little about it, she just told him things Mrs Wilberforce had told her. How cold it was there in January, of tobogganing down hillsides and ice-skating on a frozen pond.

'What are the Teddy boys like?' he asked, throwing May completely. 'Do they really rip up the cinema seats and stuff?'

May had never even heard the name, let alone knew what they were like. 'Oh, there aren't any where I live,' she said.

'But I read in the paper that the craze had swept over the whole of England,' he insisted.

'Maybe it started after I left,' she ventured. She listened to his description of their long drape jackets, their hair pulled out in a quiff in front and long sideburns, and she was even more mystified.

'Bill Haley got it started,' he said. 'You know, with "Rock around the Clock".'

May remembered hearing that record at St Vincent's. It had been on the wireless once while she was in Mother's study. She'd switched it off almost immediately and made some remark about it being music of the Devil, but the tune had stayed in May's head. Mrs Wilberforce didn't put the wireless on unless it was for a play, *Woman's Hour* or the news, so she never heard popular music there either. All she knew of it were snatches of songs coming out of milk bars or pubs, never enough to get to know what song it was, or who sang it. In a flash May realized she had to find out about such things or look like an ignorant little country mouse.

'My family don't go for that kind of stuff,' she said apologetically. 'They listen to classical music.'

Nev talked about his friends, one of whom had a Ford Zephyr, and how they would ride up to Scarborough beach at the weekends, get blazing drunk, get into fights and sleep on the beach. To May that sounded dreadful, yet it was another pointer to how cloistered her life had been at St Vincent's and still was. Even as she made a coy remark about how exciting it sounded, she found it did give her a thrill. Maybe Nev was just what she needed to find a whole new kind of world.

'Me mates all want to go to England now,' he said. 'That's why we're going east to work, you can earn more on the buildings there, and save quicker.'

'Why d'you want to go to England?' she asked curiously.

He put his arm around her shoulders and hugged her to him. 'I've heard the sheilas are red-hot for one,' he said with a grin. 'A bloke I know just came back and he said Soho was beaut, loads of night-clubs and boozers. He reckoned Perth was a dump compared to London, all we've got is the sun and the sea.'

May was stumped for a reply to that. Her only clear memories of London were walking from the Sacred Heart to school, and that didn't set her heart beating any faster.

The sun was going down fast as they reached King's Park, and Nev took her to a seat where they could watch it sink over the River Swan. Everywhere May looked she could see courting couples, and she found she didn't mind being here after all, not with Nev's arm around her as she admired the view.

Once it was dark, the city took on a magical quality she'd never seen before, millions of twinkling lights, the street-lamps like strings of brilliant diamonds along the dark slick of the river. 'It's so beautiful,' she whispered. 'I've never seen it at night before.'

'Not as beaut as you,' he said, taking her in his arms to kiss her.

May felt as if she was rising up on a warm, fluffy cloud. Nev's lips were so soft yet so eager, his fingers running through her hair made her feel so wanted and special. At last she felt she understood all the feelings spoken of in romantic stories, for it was as if they were the only two people left in the world, two hearts and bodies wanting nothing but each other. His kiss this afternoon had been thrilling, but it was nothing compared to the ones now. She could feel his hand on her side, hot through her dress, his thumb stroking the side of her breast as he kissed her, and suddenly she wanted him to put his whole hand over it, squeeze her nipples. It didn't make sense to her, she'd hated it when Mother did it, but the need was so strong she found herself wriggling to make herself more available.

'Let's go further into the park,' he suggested, kissing her throat, his lips moving right down to her cleavage. 'Too many people come this way.'

She hadn't been aware of other people, but she was willing to go anywhere with him now. He led her a few yards into the bushes, and leaning her against a tree he kissed her again and again, fondling both her breasts, pushing them up till they almost came out of her bra, and insinuating his knee between her legs.

'Come on,' he said a little later, taking her hand and leading her still further into the bushes. 'Let's find somewhere we can lie down and I can unzip that dress.'

All at once May was scared. The zip on her dress was on the side seam, and she wasn't going to take it right off, not for anything. Sitting on a bench or even standing by a tree was one thing, lying down was quite another, and her instinct told her he wanted more than just kisses.

But she let him lead her, afraid of looking childish, though when he pulled her down on to the ground she panicked, from fear not just of what it might lead to, but of snakes and spiders, and her dress being spoilt.

'I don't like it here,' she said in alarm as she felt something creep along her bare arm. 'Take me back to where there's people and lights.'

'Aw, come on,' he said mockingly, pushing her down with his body and kissing her throat. 'This is where a bloke takes his best girl, I'll look after you.'

'But I'm hungry and thirsty, Nev,' she pleaded. 'I didn't have any tea before I came out.'

'I ain't got enough money to take you anywhere to eat,' he replied, nibbling at her neck. 'I just want to eat you.'

To May that sounded as if he would have taken her somewhere else but for money. 'I've got some,' she said, grabbing her bag lying on the ground beside them. 'I'll treat us both.'

He snatched the bag from her and tossed it aside. 'I told you I don't take money from sheilas. Now, give me a kiss,' he said, pushing her back on to the ground.

She submitted to his kiss, but without the earlier passion. He leaned up on one elbow and looked down at her. 'What's wrong? I really like you, May, half past six couldn't come fast enough for me to see you again.'

The greater part of her was appeased by his statement and she felt she had nothing to fear. She had liked the way he had made her feel earlier, she wanted to lose herself again. Yet a small voice inside her head was whispering that she knew nothing more of him than his name, and she didn't think it was right to be in such a secluded place on a first date.

'I'm scared,' she admitted in a whisper. 'I just don't like it here. There might be snakes.'

'The only snake around here is this one,' he said, taking hold of her hand and putting it on the bulge in his trousers. 'But he's not going to bite you.'

Just the touch of that hard thing brought all her fears sharply into focus.

'No,' she said pushing him away with both hands. 'I want to go.'

He moved so quickly it took her by surprise. One minute he lying beside her leaning up on one elbow, the next he was on top of her, and his hand was groping up her thigh.

'Stop it,' she shouted. But his mouth came down on hers and he thrust his tongue into her mouth at the same time as his fingers were pulling her knickers to one side.

The combination of the slug-like tongue and his finger insinuating its way inside brought back all the nauseating memories of Mother. She bucked under him, got her mouth free and screamed. But he clamped his hand over her mouth and stifled it.

'You know why you came up here with me,' he growled at her. 'And you're going to get it. Scream and I'll land you one.'

It was like being held in a vice, his whole body was pressing down on her, and even though she managed to get her hands free, she couldn't push him off. Worse still, she found he had opened his trousers at some point, for she could feel his penis hot, hard and smooth against her leg, and as she tried to buck under him, he thrust it hard against her.

'Open your legs, you bitch,' he muttered at her, and letting go of her mouth for a second, he grabbed her legs, pulling her knickers off, and then prised them apart, managed to force it inside her.

May did yell out, but only momentarily, for he clamped his hand back on her mouth and bit into her neck as if to remind her he'd hit her. It hurt so much, stones were digging in her back, she felt like she was being crushed by his weight, and still that gigantic thing of his was boring into her as if it was tearing her apart. 'Poms are all shit,' he hissed at her. 'The men are faggots, the women are slags. I knew you were a slag the moment I saw you, so I'm giving you what you wanted.'

May was so stunned by the rapid progression from loving attentiveness to this brutality that she stopped fighting him. She felt the same way she had done that night in the Dark Place, rigid with fear, hurting inside and out and unable to understand why her actions warranted such a brutal punishment.

He was making loud grunting noises that appeared to be getting louder all the time. Then he let out a kind of low bellow and was finally still. He rolled off her immediately, and May just lay there transfixed with horror at what had happened. She couldn't see his face in the darkness, just the white of his shirt and a flash of his teeth, which suggested he was grinning at her.

But in a second he was up on his feet and looking down at her, and in that moment she realized he had her handbag in his hand.

'So let's have the money you wanted to flash around,' he said, and she heard the clasp click open.

May tried to get up, but every bit of her hurt, and she wasn't fast enough. She saw him snatch something from her bag, then he flung it back at her.

'Pom slut,' he snarled, and with that loped off into the darkness.

May crawled on her knees to her bag, and as she moved she felt something wet and sticky run down her leg and all at once she fully understood what it was he had done to her.

It was that thing which made babies! She had heard the girls at St Vincent's giggling about it so often, smugly believing she knew so much more about it than they did because Mother had told her. But Mother hadn't said it was ugly and shameful, or that a man could force it into her against her will, she'd wrapped it all up with pretty stuff, like love, weddings and honeymoons.

Blinded by tears, May staggered back in the direction they'd come earlier and once she came to a path and a lamp she opened up her bag to look inside. He had taken the roll of pound notes, but the key of the front door was still there, and her small-change purse with about five shillings in it. Her cigarettes were there too, and she lit one immediately to try to stop shaking.

She looked down at her dress and saw it was badly crumpled and stained with grass and dirt. What was she going to do?

Slumping down on to a seat, she dragged desperately on the cigarette and tried to think. She was used to feeling very alone, she'd been that way since Dulcie left St Vincent's. But this was worse, much worse, and her mind was woolly, the way she felt the time she'd had a tooth taken out with gas. She sat there crying for some time, hoping that someone would come along and she could tell them she was hurt. But no one came and eventually she began to walk on down the path to the road.

Once she'd got there, she recognized it was the same road the buses ran along to and from town. She had also come to see that asking someone for help would only make her predicament worse. They would call the police, and what would they think of her if she said she went off into the park in the dark with a man she'd only met that day, and that the only thing she knew about him was his Christian name? They would want to take her home too, and once Mrs Wilberforce knew she had lied about where she was going that evening, she'd be bound to sack her. That was likely to mean she'd be sent to the reformatory, where they sent all troublesome girls. Or worse still, she'd be sent back to Mother.

It was lucky that a bus came along very quickly, and as

it was almost empty she slunk into the first seat, and using the small mirror in her bag checked her face. It surprised her to see it didn't look any different, she had expected the horror she'd been through would be reflected back at her. There was a mark on her neck where Nev had bitten into her, but her hair covered it for now, and she thought her uniform dress would come up high enough to conceal it.

But when she thought what that evil bastard had done to her, white-hot anger flowed through her. She'd trusted him, yet he'd humiliated her in the worst possible way and robbed her. And he'd got away with it.

As the bus got nearer to Peppermint Grove, she also remembered with horror that he might very well have made her pregnant too. 'I'll kill myself if that's the case,' she thought, tears starting up in her eyes again. 'It's bad enough being a little bastard myself, without giving birth to another one.'

It was four days later when May found that she wasn't pregnant. When she saw the usual monthly blood, she sat down on the toilet and cried with relief and even offered up a hasty prayer of thanks.

She had been through hell, trying to work and respond as normal to Mrs Wilberforce, while all she really wanted was to stay in bed and hide from the world. The fear of pregnancy had expanded in her mind till she couldn't think of anything else, and when she tried to go to sleep at night she would relive the ordeal over and over again.

The worst of it was the self-recriminations. Maybe if she hadn't lied to him about who she was, he might not have been that way. Or maybe he knew she was lying and he did it to teach her a lesson? Why wasn't she strong enough to say she didn't want to walk in the park? And surely she wasn't a slag just because she'd spoken to someone on the beach and bought him a couple of glasses of orange squash?

Yet even though she felt relieved that at least she wasn't

pregnant, the hurt inside her wouldn't go, it had cast a black shadow over everything. Everything seemed as soiled as her pink dress – her body, her mind, the view of the garden from her bedroom window, even food didn't taste or smell the same. Ugly thoughts kept popping into her head, she wanted to lash out at someone, and she felt even more alone than she had back at St Vincent's.

She found herself hoping something bad had happened between Dulcie and Ross, or that one of the Wilberforces' sons would meet with an accident, just so Mrs Wilberforce would look as miserable as she felt. She stole a five-pound note out of one of her friends' handbags one afternoon. The group of women came round every Monday afternoon to play whist in the dining-room, but they all went out in the garden for a while, leaving their bags by the table. May opened them all and looked inside, and a nice crocodile one contained so many notes she guessed it wouldn't even be noticed. It didn't wipe out the misery inside her, but at least she felt she was striking back in some way. She made up her mind that no man would ever hurt her again, and that in future she would always have the upper hand.

Chapter Seventeen

'You shouldn't have to be doing this for me,' Betty said as Dulcie prepared to give her a blanket bath. 'I could ask Bruce to get a nurse in, or get them to take me into hospital. I'm spoiling your life.'

Dulcie assumed Betty was thinking about her postponed wedding. 'Don't be so daft,' she laughed, as she folded back the towel covering Betty and began to wash her chest, neck and arms. 'We aren't in a tearing hurry to get married. I'm only just twenty-one, remember. Besides, you'd hate it in hospital, and I doubt we could get a nurse to stay out here. And I like taking care of you.'

Betty had become ill fifteen months earlier. At first it was just mild stomach pains, loss of appetite and listlessness, then the pains got worse and finally she was taken into hospital in November for tests, where they found she had cancer of the womb. A hysterectomy was performed immediately, and she returned home in December. Knowing she would need careful nursing for some time, Dulcie put off the wedding, and although Betty made a good recovery from the surgery, later in the year it was found the cancer had spread throughout her body. Now it was January again and there had been no celebrations for the New Year of 1959, because they all knew that she had only a couple more months to live.

Dulcie looked down at Betty lying on the bed, and her heart welled up with love and sympathy for her. She had lost so much weight, her once plump cheeks were hollow and flesh hung in folds around her neck and beneath her eyes. It was doubly hard for a woman who had always been strong and healthy to accept she couldn't beat this, and though for a very long time she had fought it, making herself get up and do little chores even when she was in severe pain, now she was too weak even to turn herself in bed. Yet her mind was still as active as it always had been, and she focused it on others, worrying that she was becoming a nuisance and a hindrance.

But she wasn't a nuisance, for she had retained her good humour, her interest in everything and everyone. She never complained, she was always delighted when anyone called to see her, and touchingly grateful for any little kindness.

When she and Dulcie talked about milestones in the last year, the one that always made them laugh most was their embarrassment when Betty first needed help with bathing. Dulcie had never seen an older woman naked before, and Betty admitted that even Bruce hadn't ever seen her that way in their entire married life.

Betty would laughingly remember how Dulcie once stuck a soapy flannel in her mouth because she had her eyes shut. Dulcie would tease her back with the reminder of the time she put both legs in one knicker leg because she wouldn't let Dulcie help her, and how she tried to hobble out of the bathroom like that.

Laughter had taught them how to cope, and they found the embarrassment disappeared. Now they were comfortable about it all, blanket baths and bedpans were just another part of the routine, like the medication and bed-making. But the one thing Betty could not accept was that Dulcie was overworked and she was spoiling her life.

Dulcie was speaking the absolute truth when she said she liked looking after Betty. She hated to see her so thin – her weight had dropped from around twelve stone to eight, and her legs and arms were like sticks. It grieved her to see a woman who had once loved her food unable to eat more than a few mouthfuls. But Betty hadn't lost her sweet nature or her patience, and she was always far more interested in hearing the gossip, talking over old times or discussing things in the news, than she was in herself.

If Dulcie hadn't grown to love Betty so much, perhaps she might think herself overworked, for she ran the house alone now, doing all the cooking, cleaning and laundry, and had to get up during the night to turn Betty, give her medication and bedpans. She couldn't have a day off, the only breaks were when Bruce sat with Betty, and then she had shopping and other errands to run. Yet she didn't feel hard done by in any way; for the first time in her life she felt needed, cared for and appreciated. What she did here seemed so very little in return for all the kindness that had been shown to her in the past.

Dulcie rinsed and dried Betty's top half and covered that up with a dry towel. 'The bottom bit now,' she said, moving the basin of warm water further down the bed and removing the lower towel. 'Now, suppose I move your bed over to the window afterwards?' she said as she put soap on the flannel. 'You'd be able to look at the garden and see Bruce and the men when they're over by the barn.'

'You are such a kind girl,' Betty said, her voice quivering with emotion. 'Too kind sometimes. You should think of yourself more often. I hear you singing along to that pop music sometimes and I think you ought to be off to Sydney, going to dances and parties, buying lovely clothes and being taken out by men who could give you all the things you deserve.'

'I don't want to go to dances and parties.' Dulcie smiled as she soaped the old lady. 'I've got everything I want right here.'

'That's just because you don't know what you're missing,' Betty said.

Dulcie rinsed out the flannel and wiped off all the soap. 'You haven't seen much of the world yourself, and you don't think you've missed anything,' she said reprovingly.

'It was different for my generation,' Betty said firmly. 'We had the two wars, and the Depression in between, and we didn't know what was happening elsewhere in the world. But you read, you watch the television, you listen to the wireless. You know so much more about what's on offer than I ever did.'

Dulcie dried her carefully, then massaged her legs and feet with some cream. 'I'm going to turn you over on your side now,' she said. 'Can you roll over if I give you a push?'

Once she'd exposed Betty's back and bottom she washed and dried it carefully, checking for bed sores, then fluffed talcum powder on it. 'No sore places,' she said. 'But once you've got a clean nightie on I think you ought to stay on your side for a bit.'

'You always change the subject when I get serious.' Betty wiggled a finger at her. 'You see, I worry about what will happen when I'm gone. You'll be all alone here with the men, they aren't much company, you know! You need women friends. I couldn't have survived out here without mine.'

Dulcie hated it when Betty spoke of *going*. It was she who asked the doctor point-blank how long she had left, she said she needed to know so that she could put her house in order. Her courage and lack of self-pity was admirable, maybe it was sensible to face it and get everything done or said that she found necessary, but Dulcie found it distressing.

'Maybe I'll join your Country Women's Association,' she said, slipping the clean nightgown over Betty's head and carefully easing it down over her.

'That's for older women,' Betty said. 'You need friends your own age, not a bunch of old biddies talking about jam and their grandchildren.'

'I've got Ross, remember,' Dulcie reminded her. 'We will get married before long.'

'I'm not so sure Ross is right for you any more,' Betty said with a sigh.

'Of course he is,' Dulcie said in surprise. She pulled up a chair by the bed and sat down so she could look right at Betty. 'What makes you say that?'

When lying on her side, the looseness of Betty's flesh on her face was most noticeable – she had joked one day that Dulcie ought to make a few tucks in it, the way you did with a too large garment. Even her eyes had faded to the colour of duck eggs, and there was never any sparkle in them any more.

'I don't think he's warm enough for you,' she said, reaching out and taking Dulcie's hand. 'You need warmth to blossom, Dulcie, without it you'll just shrivel up. You get it from me and Bruce now, but I'm afraid you'll find it suddenly colder when I'm gone.'

'But Ross loves me, I love him,' Dulcie insisted. 'He'll be different once we're married.'

'I don't think so, dear,' Betty said gently. 'He'll look after you all right, I don't think he'll ever become a boozer or a wife-beater, but there's no passion in him.'

Dulcie blushed. 'That comes after the wedding surely?'

'It should be there from the start, from the first kiss,' Betty said, her eyes suddenly damp. 'You've seen each other every day for over two years, yet I've never seem him kiss you impulsively, hug you, run to you. I put it down to shyness for a long time, but it's more than that.'

'He's different when we're alone together,' Dulcie said. Yet even as she said it, she knew that wasn't entirely true. He hadn't once tried to go any further than kissing, the way she had been told most men did. On several occasions she'd tried to instigate something more, and each time it had been him who backed away, saying that must wait until they were married.

She had always thought this was consideration for her, and fear they might go too far. But just sometimes it did feel like rejection.

'I'm only speaking out because I'm so fond of you, dear, and because there isn't anyone else to point these things out to you,' Betty said, squeezing her hand. 'I want you to think hard before you commit yourself to marriage, ask yourself if everything really is right. Think about Bill and Pat Masters, that was a marriage which went wrong because they weren't suited.'

'Bill was just a brute,' Dulcie protested. 'Poor Pat never had a chance with him.'

'He was, but you were still a child when you were there,' Betty said. 'You'd had no experience of life, or people. You could only have seen it from Pat's viewpoint. There are always two sides to every story.'

'I don't see that going over all that stuff will help in any way,' Dulcie exclaimed. 'I'm nothing like Pat, and Ross certainly isn't like Bill.'

'I didn't say they were like you and Ross. I just want you to think about what you saw there, in the light of what you know now. You may well find something there which strikes a chord within you.'

'It's time you took your medicine now,' Dulcie said, getting up and opening up the pill bottle and laying out the five different ones Betty had to take, and pouring a glass of water.

'Once again you're changing the subject,' Betty said with a smile. 'If you don't overcome that before you get married you're going to find yourself in serious trouble before long.'

Dulcie left Betty after that, smarting a little at what she'd said. She swept and dusted the living-room, filled up the washing-machine with water and switched on the heater, then once she saw that Betty had dropped off to sleep she went outside to sweep the veranda.

It was one of those swelteringly hot, still days where the sun made mirages of water across the paddocks, and the ground cracked open with the heat. The birds were silent, the sheep and cattle lying listlessly under what shade they could find, the only sound the buzzing of insects. Dulcie had planted pansies in the garden during the spring, but they were scorched with the heat now, only the geraniums still putting on a brave show.

She had found so much to love about Australia, she felt

she belonged here, yet every now and then she could feel dwarfed by its vastness, bruised by its harshness and saddened by its lack of history. At those times she would think longingly of the gentleness of England, the soft rain and breezes, ancient buildings, small fields surrounded by neat hedges, villages which had remained unchanged for centuries. She ached to see crowded, noisy markets again, to see throngs of children tumbling out of schools, to be in an old church, smelling the polish and incense, and listening to an organ playing.

As she swept up the dust, she remembered how scornful Ross had been when she told him that one day. She could understand it was impossible for him to share her memories, but she couldn't understand why he appeared to resent her having them. Did he want her to do what he'd done, erect a kind of screen on everything that had happened to her before she got here?

Dulcie stopped her sweeping for a minute, suddenly seeing that this was perhaps what Betty meant when she said Dulcie must think about Pat Masters.

She never dwelt on the miserable time she'd had at Salmon Gums, she'd put that behind her. If she ever thought momentarily about Pat it was only to hope she had a happier life now, wherever she was. Yet she remembered now that Pat hadn't ever spoken about her past, not until that letter from Reverend Mother came. That was the turning-point in their relationship, when she came to understand the woman a little better. Whatever Betty said, Dulcie couldn't see even a vague similarity between herself and Pat, other than they'd both been in orphanages, yet now she came to think about it, there were similarities between Pat and Ross. The bitterness, difficulty in talking about their feelings, and the moodiness.

Goose pimples popped up all over Dulcie, despite the heat she felt chilled. Betty was right, she was just a child while she was with the Masters', she'd been nervous of men, and her only knowledge of love and marriage came from romantic books and distant memories of her parents.

Now as she thought back to her view of Pat and Bill together as a couple, she realized that she'd just assumed Bill was the one entirely responsible for all Pat's unhappiness.

Dulcie shook herself. Whatever Betty said, it didn't do to dwell on all that again, people did do strange things to one another. Some people like Betty, Bruce and John could communicate easily, show affection and give praise, others like Ross and Bob couldn't. It didn't necessarily mean they were lesser people, they were just different. Look at her and May – the same parents, the same upbringing, but so very different.

Thinking of May reminded Dulcie that her sister's letters were getting further and further apart again. She had sent a card and a very pretty petticoat to Dulcie for her birthday in December, there had been a brooch too at Christmas, but not a letter, and the last one was way back in September.

'I'll write tonight,' Dulcie thought. 'Maybe she's got a boyfriend now, and anyway my letters have been very dull since Betty got ill.'

'How is your sister?' Mrs Wilberforce asked May as she came into the kitchen and found the girl sitting at the table reading the letter that came this morning. 'And is Mrs French any better?'

May looked up. Mrs Wilberforce was dressed to go out in a pink and white candy-striped shirtwaister dress and a white broad-brimmed hat. 'Dulcie's fine, but Mrs French is dying,' she said with a dramatic sigh. 'Dulcie doesn't think she's got more than a couple of months left.'

'Oh, how awfully sad,' Mrs Wilberforce exclaimed, her face clouding over. 'Dulcie must be very fond of her to stay and look after her.'

'That's the way Dulcie is,' May said, and unexpectedly her eyes began to prickle with tears. 'She's one of those people who cares more about others than she does about herself.'

Mrs Wilberforce picked up on the shake in May's voice,

saw the swimming eyes and felt a surge of tenderness for the girl, for clearly she cared far more for her sister than she'd ever let on. When the wedding was postponed, May hadn't showed much emotion, only some pique that she wouldn't get her holiday. Yet now Mrs Wilberforce recalled that later, a year ago, around the time the wedding should have taken place, May had become very withdrawn. She hadn't linked the two things before, but maybe May had been worrying about Dulcie.

'She sounds such a nice, kind girl,' Mrs Wilberforce said. 'I'm sure you are longing to see her again. Of course we can't really talk about weddings and holidays at the moment, but maybe they will come about later this year.'

Mrs Wilberforce was never quite sure exactly how she felt about May. Mostly she considered herself very fortunate to have such a polite, obedient, competent and willing maid. She was so bright and sunny, charming almost everyone who came to the house, and her interests – fashion, popular music, cosmetics and films – were all very normal for a teenage girl.

Yet for all that, now and again May made her feel uncomfortable. She couldn't put her finger on exactly what it was, yet she sensed something vaguely predatory about her. Often when Mrs Wilberforce returned home from an outing, she had a feeling the girl had been going through her things. Nothing was ever out of place or disturbed in any way, and she always told herself she was being silly. Yet the irrational fear persisted, and she found herself observing how silently May moved, the occasional resentful look, and wondered why it was that after twenty months with her she still felt she really didn't know her at all.

May told her about her friends at night school, the girl Angelina with whom she so often spent her day off, but she never revealed anything personal about herself.

She would watch May leaving the house on her day off and smile because she looked like a fashion model. Not a hair out of place, not a crease in her dress or a speck on her shoes, and she would have expected that anyone taking so much trouble with her appearance was intent on catching the eye of some young man. Yet May never spoke of boys, not even obliquely. She was seldom late home from night school, or on her day off, and even when Mrs Wilberforce had agreed that at sixteen and a half she was now old enough to go dancing on a Saturday night, and therefore could stay out till eleven, May had only asked to go twice since the New Year began.

It shamed Mrs Wilberforce to think that she'd searched the girl's bedroom a few weeks ago, looking for something that might throw some light on May's real character. But there was nothing unusual, except that it was remarkably tidy. Letters from her sister kept in a biscuit tin, the photograph of Dulcie and her intended by the bed, a few books and magazines and the usual range of cosmetics. She did seem to have rather a lot of clothes, but then of course her sister often sent her things. There was certainly nothing to be alarmed about there.

Now May had revealed her affection and admiration for her sister, Mrs Wilberforce felt a little guilty about her suspicions. Poor May had never known a real home, or parental love and affection, and it was sad that the two girls who clearly did love each other were so far apart.

'It's not long now till your seventeenth birthday,' Mrs Wilberforce said, feeling she had to change the subject or May might get really upset. 'You should be taking your secretarial diploma then too! How is that coming along? Do you think you'll get a distinction?'

May smiled weakly. 'I doubt it, I'm not so hot at spelling or shorthand,' she said. 'But I'm the fastest at copy-typing.'

Mrs Wilberforce knew this was so, she had telephoned the night school once around six months ago, afraid May wasn't attending. She was told her attendance was excellent and that her only failing was spelling.

'As I understand it, offices need far more copy typists than shorthand typists anyway,' Mrs Wilberforce said.

'With your smart appearance you'll get a good job anywhere. Not that I want to lose you,' she added quickly.

'I don't want to leave here either,' May said, giving Mrs Wilberforce one of her wide, melting smiles. 'You and Mr Wilberforce have been so good to me, and this house is so lovely. But I suppose I must think about a real career soon.'

Mrs Wilberforce's doubts about the girl vanished in the face of her gratitude. 'You're a good girl,' she said, and impulsively patted her hand. 'You have a home here for as long as you need it. I've got to go out today, but there's nothing pressing that needs doing, so why don't you take some time off and write back to Dulcie? I'm sure you've got a great deal you want to say to her.'

After Mrs Wilberforce had left the house, May took her writing paper and pen out on to the upstairs veranda, settled herself at the table and began a letter to Dulcie. Yet once she'd said how sorry she was about Betty, she couldn't think of another thing to say. Dulcie's letters to her were so vibrant, bits about the men at the farm, the animals, what she thought about, things she'd heard on the wireless and seen on the television. Always so interesting, making vivid pictures of her life down in Esperance.

May just couldn't write in that descriptive way. However hard she thought it all out first, it just came out like a lists of facts. She sat back in the chair, chewing distractedly on the end of the pen and looking around her for inspiration. The upstairs veranda was her favourite place. The trees at the side of the house made an umbrella of thick green shade, and there was a beautiful purple climbing plant tangled all along the balustrade. It was too hot now at midday for many birds, but in the morning the trees were full of noisy red wattlebirds, colourful ringnecks, and Willy wagtails. If she was to walk around the veranda to the part at the front of the house, she could see the River Swan though a gap in the houses. It was so wide and blue it looked more like the sea than a river, so serene with the huge Moreton Bay figs lining the fore-shore and glimpses of yachts and cruisers gliding past. She knew Dulcie would like to see that picture, if only she could write it.

When she was alone in the house, like now, May liked to pretend it was hers. She would imagine herself in a white evening gown, sitting out here in the evenings with her husband. They would have dozens of candles lit, music playing in the background, and drink champagne. It was funny really that she should think such things, for she had no intention of staying in Perth after she was eighteen. But then perhaps it was just habit, for in the months following her rape, this house had been a safe and soothing haven, and she had come to love it for its cool old elegance and the order and peace of it.

In the early morning she would often go out into the garden and just breathe in the cool fresh air, gaze at the old trees and bushes, and think what heaven it must have been for the Wilberforce boys to grow up here. Mrs Wilberforce laughingly said it was like a jungle, and really she should get someone in to be ruthless with it, but she didn't because she liked it just the way it was. May felt just the same, nature had accomplished something beautiful all on its own, and it should be left that way.

It was out there in the garden, too, that she'd finally come to terms with the rape. She still burned with shame about it sometimes, yet she could see she had been stupidly trusting, and she didn't intend to repeat that mistake. No man would ever humiliate her again, or get her for nothing. She wouldn't even kiss a man unless he was rich, well-mannered and well-dressed, and though such a man might be difficult to find – Perth was full of crude, loud-mouthed larrikins – in the last year she had come up with one or two more original hunting ploys.

It was just that which made it so hard to write to Dulcie. She was so saintly, noble and patient, believing that hard work and kindness brought their own rewards, that love came to those who deserved it. She would be horrified if

May was to tell her she scoured the poshest hotels in Perth looking for a likely man.

May giggled to herself. She thought it was very resourceful, she just went into the hotels and made out she was waiting for someone. Out of eight occasions she'd tried this, on five she'd struck up a conversation with a businessman who had offered her a drink. All but one of them had been old, at least forty, but from each of them she gained more confidence and a little knowledge of their businesses. The fifth, a South African lawyer, could have led to something more if he hadn't been just passing through Perth. He was thirty-two, tall and slender and although not handsome, extremely presentable in a beautiful cream linen suit. A drink with him had led to dinner, and she knew he was very taken with her.

May giggled again as she remembered his goodnight kiss before he put her in a taxi to go home. She liked his kiss, she liked him too, but he was leaving for Sydney the next day and he wasn't coming back. She took the five pounds he offered for her fare home, got out of the taxi on the next corner, caught the bus home and pocketed the money. That was a very good day!

Yet she couldn't continue to go into the same hotels, she was far too noticeable, so she also had to rely on Angelina. Angelina worked in her father's milk bar by the station, and they had become friendly because May always went in there for a drink before going to her night class. Sometimes if Angelina could persuade her father to let her have the same day off as May, they spent it together.

Angelina knew just about everyone in Perth, and through her May had met a teacher who took her to the pictures, a post office worker who did the same, and three times she'd been to the Saturday night dances at the Embassy on a double date with Angelina. None of these men were worth going out with a second time, the teacher was too earnest and dull, the post office worker too randy, sticking his hand up her skirt the first time he kissed her, and the two men at the dance almost as bad. What she wanted was another South African lawyer, a man of substance, who knew how to treat a lady.

She knew Dulcie thought that Perth was the most exciting, beautiful place. May thought it was beautiful too, just a walk out of the house down to Keane's Point on the river was enough to lift her spirits when she felt dejected, and there were many more lovely places too. But she couldn't find it exciting, St Vincent's was too close at hand with all its nasty memories. Mother kept telephoning, and now and then called round too. May wanted to be rid of all that, go to a new town where she could start again without anyone knowing anything about her. Mrs Wilberforce's friends were everywhere here too, she saw them on the bus, at the local shops and in town. She sometimes felt that if she sneezed while she was out, Mrs Wilberforce would know about it by the time she got home.

She had money saved now, over forty pounds in all, for she stole most of her clothes and only used her wages for bus fares, drinks and going to the cinema. Once she got her diploma she would be off.

'Have you made any more plans about your wedding?' she wrote. 'I'm longing to come and see you and meet Ross.'

She chewed on her pen again, unable to think of anything further to say. There were things she longed to ask Dulcie, like how it felt to be in love. Did she ever get that feeling of being haunted by St Vincent's, as though it was somehow their fault that they were put in an orphanage? She wanted to know if Dulcie still went to Mass. She never mentioned it in her letters. May had no intention of ever going again once she left this house, but while she was here Mr Wilberforce insisted she went. She hadn't really minded going up until she was raped, she'd even gone to confession then, determined to tell the priest. But she found she couldn't. She didn't trust the priest enough not to tell the Wilberforces.

Just thinking about that day when she'd stood inside the church trying to summon up the courage to go into the confessional brought back a sudden recollection of something Dulcie had once said. 'Trust me!' she'd spat out one day soon after they arrived at St Vincent's. 'As soon as someone says that you can be sure they are going to let you down or hurt you.'

At the time May hadn't understood what her sister meant. It had gone into the back of her mind and been forgotten till now. But it meant something now, she could see perfectly what Dulcie was getting at. There wasn't anyone out there you could put your trust in, least of all God, because he just appeared to look down and let the most terrible things happen to people. Look at the way the Sisters were, sheltering in their comfortable convents, praying all their pious prayers, while they beat and half starved the children they were supposed to be caring for!

May leaned back in her chair looking up at the tree which sheltered the veranda. Through small gaps in the foliage she could see patches of blue sky, and in a strange sort of way it seemed symbolic. The dense, dark green was like all that religious dogma they'd pushed down her throat for as long as she could remember, the blue sky beyond was a glimpse of the real truth.

It wasn't the meek who inherited the earth, as she'd always been told, it was the strong and the brave. In fact just about every little sanctimonious phrase the Sisters preached was just propaganda to keep girls like her humble and in their place.

May had an urge to share this inspiration with Dulcie, but as she put the pen to paper the thoughts which had been so clear just a moment earlier vanished like the sea rolling over writing in the sand. Angrily she pushed the half-written letter away, put her arms down on the table and rested her head on them, suddenly stricken by the knowledge she was unable to communicate anything more than trivia to her sister.

She began to cry then, it wasn't just Dulcie, she couldn't share her real thoughts with anyone, she never had been able to. She talked to Mrs Wilberforce about the house, the garden, what she'd seen at the pictures, but never anything deeper. It was the same with Angelina and the girls at night school, just gossip, nothing more. Was that why she felt so empty most of the time?

The saddest thing of all was she could see Dulcie's face in her mind's eye, and she knew in her heart her sister would give anything to get a letter like the one she wanted to write. She had always been one for believing talking things out made people happier. May could recall that day in the garden at the Sacred Heart, when they'd been told Granny was dead, and how Dulcie had tried to get her to speak about what Sister Teresa did to her. She should have told her, maybe it would have helped.

May remembered how it was after Dulcie left St Vincent's, hearing the other girls talking about her. '*She always understood*' was one remark she heard so many times. '*You could tell her anything and you knew she'd never pass it on*' was another. Dulcie had been badly missed when she left, there were many girls who'd cried, but yet she, her sister, had been glad to see the back of her.

What did that make her?

May got up then and went inside. She would rather tackle a pile of ironing or clean the silver than think too hard on that one.

Chapter Eighteen

'Wake up, Bruce,' Dulcie said as she shook him vigorously.

He awoke immediately, sitting bolt upright in the single bed of the spare room into which he'd moved when Betty became seriously ill. 'Is she worse?' he asked.

'I'm so sorry,' was all Dulcie could get out before she burst into tears.

She had been woken at two by the alarm she'd set to turn Betty over, and gone into her room. Betty was lying on her side just as she'd left her a four hours earlier, seemingly in deep sleep. Dulcie gently drew her bedcovers back and laid her hands on her side, intending to roll her over, if possible without waking her. When she encountered a slight chill and rigidity she switched on a brighter light to check. Betty was dead, she had ceased breathing and she had no pulse.

'She's dead!' Bruce looked at Dulcie as if he didn't believe her and leaped out of bed.

Dulcie followed him into the big bedroom. It was the end of May now, Betty had hung on far longer than the doctor expected and in the last few days had even seemed a little better. Bruce had spent a great deal of time with her in the past few months, leaving the other men to do the ploughing and seeding while he read to his wife or just sat talking to her.

Dulcie stood awkwardly at the door. Bruce was kneeling beside the bed, crying and covering Betty's face with kisses. She had felt their deep love for one another right from the first day she came here to work and she knew that even though Bruce believed he had prepared himself for this moment, he wasn't ever going to be the same again without her.

Bruce was like a water-mill, Betty the stream that kept him going. They had both liked people, yet they had everything they needed in one another. Even as she looked at the big man sobbing beside the bed, she could almost see him shrinking and she couldn't bear to see him in such pain.

'I must call the doctor,' she said gently, trying hard to control her own grief. She couldn't imagine a day without Betty either. She had been her mother, teacher and friend. She went over to him and bent down to embrace him. 'I'm so sorry, Bruce,' she whispered. 'She was the most lovely person in the whole world.'

'What do we do?' he asked, looking up at Dulcie, tears running down his big rugged face. 'How can we bear it?'

She held him again, drawing his face to her chest, and wished she knew the answer to his question.

'She died in her sleep without pain or she would have called out,' Dulcie said soothingly. 'I came in to turn her.'

'Will you call the doctor?' he whispered, his voice cracking. 'I'll just stay here with her.'

Dulcie fetched his dressing-gown and slippers, dressed him like a child, then moved the chair to the side of the bed and urged him to sit on it. 'I'll get you some brandy once I've called him,' she said softly. 'Do you think I should wake the men up too?'

Bruce looked at her vacantly. 'What can they do?' he asked.

'Nothing,' she replied. 'So I won't call them unless you want me to.'

Dr Freeman said he'd be over as soon as he could, and Dulcie poured Bruce a brandy and took it in to him. His head was bowed down on the bed, and he was still holding one of Betty's hands. She patted his head and told him she'd put the drink down beside him and that she'd be in the living-room if he wanted her.

It was cold, so she cleared out the stove and lit it, but as she knelt in front of it blowing on the flames she thought of all the times she'd seen Betty do the same thing. She had never been like Pat, relegating all the messy and difficult jobs to Dulcie. Before Betty became ill she was often up earlier than Dulcie, mixing up the chicken feed, laying the table for breakfast, and in winter lighting this stove. She liked fires, and she often told Dulcie about the time when she and Bruce lived in a tent out in the bush. She said she kept a fire burning all night then to keep the dingoes away and she would sit beside it for hours, planning the dream house she and Bruce would have some day.

Dulcie could imagine how hard Betty's life was in those early years, especially as a new bride straight from the city. Yet her stories of that time were all humorous ones, without a trace of self-pity or bitterness.

It didn't seem fair to Dulcie that she had been taken so early, that the years of comfort she'd had were so few in comparison to the tough ones. Yet it was only a few days ago that she'd said material things alone could never make you happy. She said she believed it was the ability to find joy in the simple things, the man you loved, the beauty of nature, sharing and building a home together that brought true happiness.

Through her Dulcie felt she had reconciled herself with her past. She no longer brooded on her mother's death or her father's conviction for her manslaughter, for Betty had taught her to accept what she couldn't change. She rarely gave a thought to the cruelty at the Sacred Heart or St Vincent's, and she'd lost her resentment of the Sisters for preventing her from writing to her father. Her mind often turned to England, but it was good memories she held on to, and as an adult now she could forgive those who she once felt had let her and May down. Her uncles and aunts on her father's side had never been close, and once Susan had married and had a child of her own she probably didn't have the time to keep in touch with two small children she knew she could never see again.

Instead, Dulcie thought how well her life had turned out. The affection Bruce and Betty had shown her had given her confidence and self-esteem, she had Ross and a lifetime of happiness with him to look forward to, May was settled and happy in Perth, and in time she hoped for children of her own. Betty had taught her that life was what you made it, and she was determined that she would never lose sight of that.

Yet Betty's death was going to change things, there was no doubt about that. While Dulcie felt confident she could continue to keep everything in the house going the way it always had been, she wasn't so sure Bruce would be able to cope.

At six o'clock Dulcie went over to the bunkhouse to tell the men the sad news. She thought it better to tell them before they got to the house, as she had persuaded Bruce to lie down after Dr Freeman called. It seemed Betty's heart had just given out and he assured both Bruce and Dulcie she would have felt nothing.

Dulcie stood at the door of the bunkhouse before knocking, trying to control herself so she could tell them without breaking down. She knocked, and a few seconds later John came to the door wearing nothing but his underpants.

As soon as he saw it was Dulcie, he partially hid himself behind the door. 'What's up, Dulc?' he asked.

'Betty died earlier this morning,' she blurted out. 'I thought I'd better let you know before you came over, so you were prepared.'

His handsome bronzed face just crumpled. 'Strewth, Dulc,' he gasped. 'How's the boss taking it?'

Dulcie just shrugged. Bruce wasn't hysterical but then he had known this was coming, yet she had found his utter silence since the doctor called more disturbing than hysterics. 'Will you tell Ross and Bob?' she asked. 'I'll go back and start breakfast.'

'You all right, Dulc?' he asked, perhaps surprised she was talking about breakfast.

She nodded, even though she certainly didn't feel *all right*. 'I'll put the kettle on, I expect you'll all need a cup of tea.'

As she walked back across the yard to the house she felt very strange. The birds seemed to be singing very loudly, she was icy cold and her vision seemed just a bit distorted, but she mentally brushed it aside, forcing herself to think of the job in hand, making tea and then breakfast.

She was just putting the pot of tea on the table when the men came in. All three faces were anxious and tense.

'Where's the boss?' John asked in a whisper.

'In his room,' Dulcie replied. 'Go in to him, John, I'll give you some tea to take to him.'

Neither Bob nor Ross spoke. They stood awkwardly, as if they were unused to the house. Dulcie poured the mugs of tea, wondering why Ross didn't come and put his arms around her, or even ask her any questions.

As John went into the bedroom, taking the tea with him, she told Ross and Bob to sit down. 'She died in her sleep,' she added. 'I found her at two this morning.'

'Why didn't you come and tell us?' Ross asked in a croak.

'There was nothing you could do,' she said, taking her tea and going over to the armchair by the stove because she was so cold.

It was Bob who came over to her. He knelt down in front of her and took her hand in his. 'You're like a block of ice,' he said, chafing her hand between his big ones. He turned his head towards Ross. 'Get a blanket for her.'

Ross rushed to her bedroom and came back with one. Bob tucked it around her and put her tea into her hands. 'You've had a bad shock, Dulcie, you just stay there and get warm. We can look after ourselves.'

His concerned tone made tears come to her eyes and Bob saw them. 'You cry if you want to,' he said in little more than a whisper. 'I know I feel like it, Betty was beaut, the kindest woman I ever knew. But you've been doing everything for her for a very long time, like you was her daughter.'

It was probably the most he'd ever said to her at one time, and the first time he'd expressed his feelings about anything.

'It's going to be so sad without her,' she said, looking into his plain face and seeing grief that mirrored her own in his pale brown eyes. 'What will we all do, Bob?'

'We have to remember she's got no pain now,' he said simply. 'We have to take care of Bruce and look after the place. That's what she would've wanted.'

John came back into the living-room. He looked down at Bob kneeling by Dulcie, across to Ross who was sitting at the table, then back to Dulcie. 'Bruce is doing okay, I think,' he said, his voice hushed and his eyes full of tears. 'He said he's relieved she's free of pain now, and he wants me to go with him later to arrange the funeral. It's you he's worried about, Dulcie, go in and talk to him, we'll get our own breakfast.'

Bob draped the blanket round her shoulders as she got up. 'Keep that round you,' he said, and patted her cheek gently.

Bruce was lying under the eiderdown, still in his dressing-gown and pyjamas. He gave her a watery smile as she came in. 'Are you cold too?' he asked, seeing the blanket. 'That's how I feel as well.'

Dulcie sat beside him on the bed and took his hand. He squeezed it appreciatively. 'Betty loved you,' he said simply. 'I just wanted you to know that. Only last night she said it again and told me to tell you when she was gone. I reckon I ought to have given you a hug earlier this morning, but I was only thinking then of how *I* felt. I'm sorry.'

Tears ran down her cheeks. 'You don't have to say you're sorry about anything,' she said. 'I loved Betty too, and even if we are all glad her pain is over, it's going to be so tough without her.'

Bruce nodded. 'Right now I don't want to live without her, but I guess I'll come round. We've got calves to be born, crops to sow. A farmer of all people knows life has to go on. How's Ross bearing up? You still want to marry him?' he asked. 'Only Betty wasn't convinced it was right.'

'I know,' Dulcie sighed. 'I do still want to marry him, but it's not a good time to talk about it now.'

Bruce shrugged. 'Maybe not. Reckon Ross will be as badly hit as the rest of us by Betty going, she's the nearest he ever got to a mother.'

Dulcie remembered Ross's silence back in the living-room.

'Grief is something that has to be talked about,' Bruce said, as if he knew what she was thinking. 'It isn't the male Australian way to talk about feelings, but Betty got me out of that way of thinking, she came from a family who weren't scared to show emotion. She said to me once when she was in a temper, "Look here, Bruce, there's nothing manly about behaving like a brick wall, that just makes you look empty-headed. Cry, scream, anything that shows me you've got something inside you, or I'll bloody well leave you."'

Dulcie smiled. She could almost hear Betty saying that. 'I'll pass it on to Ross,' she said. 'Now, could you eat a bit of breakfast? Just some scrambled egg or something light?'

'I'll try,' he said with a sigh. 'That's if you'll have some too. But we'll wait till the men have gone out if you don't mind. I can't face them just yet.'

'Is it okay if they go in to see Betty?' she asked tentatively.

He nodded, his eyes filling with tears. 'You do whatever you think best for now, Dulcie. My mind's all fuzzy.'

Later that afternoon Dulcie found her mind was all fuzzy too. The undertaker had called and taken Betty away, Bruce was outside somewhere, the house silent and empty. Her days had been so busy for so long that she didn't know how to fill the time now there was no nursing to be done. She'd already cleaned Betty's room, removed all the bottles of pills and medicine, changed the bed and put it back exactly how it was before she became ill.

She had a Lancashire hot-pot in the oven for supper. Everywhere was cleaned and dusted, and now there was nothing more to do she didn't know what to do with herself. She knew what she really wanted, for Ross to come in and talk to her, but he hadn't been near all day. By the time she'd finished talking to Bruce early this morning he had left to go and milk the cows.

Bruce and John were in town at midday, and it would have been an ideal opportunity for Ross to come over and speak to her, but instead Bob came to collect tea and sandwiches for them both. It felt very much as if Ross was purposely avoiding her, but she couldn't understand why. She knew he must be hurting about Betty, so why not speak to the one person who shared that same hurt?

She had cried on and off most of the day. Betty's personality was stamped on everything she touched or looked at, she needed to talk about her, to be held and comforted. If Ross truly loved her why didn't he know this? It wasn't as if he had to keep up a tough front with the other men – John had cried over his breakfast, and couldn't eat it, and Bob had shown her such concern when she was cold. Even if no one did any work at all today, Bruce wouldn't care. Dulcie knew he hadn't gone outside to work when he returned from town, it was only because the house felt so strange without Betty.

Ross didn't come into the house until six-thirty, and even then he didn't look at her or speak. He was pale-faced and tense, staring intently at the pattern on the tablecloth, and didn't even appear to be listening when Bruce told them all the funeral would be on Friday, three days away.

'Her sisters and brother and their families will be coming as soon as they can,' he said. 'They'll probably get here Thursday night. The women can all sleep in here, and the men with me out in the bunkhouse. They'll all give you a hand, Dulcie, we'll have to lay on a bit of a spread too for after the funeral.'

Dulcie was glad to know she had something to fill the

next two days. She had gone with Betty twice to help neighbours prepare food for such occasions, so she knew what was needed.

'If you write out a list of what you need, Dulcie,' John said. 'I'll get it all tomorrow. I'll sort out the bunkhouse too and make up the beds. You'll have enough to do in here.'

Dulcie shot him a look of gratitude.

'Have you got something black to wear?' Bob asked her, his lips trembling.

Dulcie shook her head.

'Reckon you can find something in town?' Bruce asked. 'Betty's got a nice black hat in the cupboard, I think she'd like you to wear it.' He glanced round at his men. 'You all got black ties?'

Dulcie dished up the supper, listening to Bruce talking about moving the sheep into a new paddock. She guessed he felt like her, thinking if he found enough jobs to do he'd feel better. She noticed he was forcing himself to eat, his movements were slow and deliberate, yet he gave up half-way through the plateful. 'It was good, Dulcie, but I don't feel like eating,' he said.

'It's okay,' she said gently. She couldn't eat her own either, and John was struggling.

But Ross kept on eating, silently and intently.

'Do you want to come down the pub?' John asked Bruce when the meal was finally over.

'Nice of you to ask, but no thanks,' Bruce said. 'I've got a heap of phone calls to make tonight. I'd best make a start on it.'

Dulcie began stacking the plates to take them into the kitchen. She hoped Ross might stay behind to help her. But he didn't, he followed John and Bob out and didn't even say goodnight.

By nine Dulcie was in bed. She could hear Bruce's voice in the living-room as he made yet another call. She guessed he was weary of explaining the same thing over and over again, of listening to all that sympathy. She had offered to make some of the calls for him, but he'd refused, simply saying, 'Betty was loved by a great many people. It wouldn't be right for me not to speak to them myself.'

Dulcie was exhausted. Since Betty became ill she'd never got to bed much before eleven-thirty, and then got up again in the night. Yet even though it was good to know she could sleep through uninterrupted till morning, she felt so empty. Why hadn't Ross spoken to her? Did he think she was to blame in some way? Maybe Betty had been right about him after all?

She cried then, long and hard, feeling even more alone than she had while she was at the Masters'. She had thought Betty's illness was the only obstacle in the way of getting married, now it seemed that Ross didn't even want her.

'You stinking dingo,' John hissed at Ross as he slung out a right hook and landed him squarely on the jaw, knocking him clean off his feet so he fell back into a puddle outside the pub. 'Call yourself a man! You're nothing but a heap of shit.'

'That's it, leave him,' Bob said, urgently trying to haul John away. 'Bruce won't like to hear you've been fighting.'

John had been seething with anger at Ross all day. He'd noticed how he'd ignored Dulcie and how he'd said not one word of condolence to Bruce. But he'd controlled himself, expecting the kid was waiting for the right moment to speak to both of them. Then when Ross followed him and Bob out of the house John's anger had risen again. By the time he'd had a couple of schooners of beer, he wanted to knock his block off.

Yet he suppressed the desire and tried to speak to the lad. He pointed out it was ignorant not to express sorrow when someone died, even if they weren't well known to you, but when it was someone like Betty, a woman who'd taken him in and cared for him, it was just plain insulting, callous and inhuman.

To his astonishment, Ross had belted him in the guts,

right there in the bar, and told him to mind his own business. As John was well known and well liked, a couple of blokes had grabbed Ross and hurled him outside. John and Bob had quickly followed and that was when John hit him.

'I won't hit him again,' John snarled. 'Let him slither off into the bush like the snake he is.' He glowered at Ross lying there on the ground. 'You aren't normal. You're like a block of bloody ice, you've got that lovely young Dulcie wanting to marry you, but you couldn't even give her a bit of comfort.'

Ross got to his feet, swaying from the blow and clutching at his jaw. 'It ain't your business what goes on between me and Dulcie,' he protested.

Bob held John back.

'That kid's been nursing Betty for well over a year,' John yelled at him. 'She's been getting up in the night to care for her, she does everything in the house, and I expect she's tired out. Are you so fucking dense you can't see that? Asking a girl to marry you means you love her, want to look after her. Or are you a poofter and you only want to get married so she'll cook for you?'

'Leave it, mate,' Bob said.

'I can't,' John said, turning to push Bob away. He took a couple of steps nearer Ross and stood legs astride, ready to hit him again if necessary. 'Dulcie's the best-looking sheila for miles around, God only knows why she chose you. You don't deserve a sweet thing like her, but if you don't start treating her proper, so help me, I'll kill you.'

With that he turned and made his way back to the truck, Bob running after him. 'We can't leave him here,' Bob said, realizing John intended to go.

'Oh yes we bloody can,' John said. 'By the time he's walked home maybe he'll have worked out what I mean.'

John drove in silence for a couple of miles, then suddenly slammed his fist down on the steering-wheel. 'I've done things to sheilas I'm not proud of,' he exclaimed. 'But I've never treated one as coldly as that. How can he be like that?'

'He never had anyone to care for him, that's why,' Bob said quietly. 'He don't know lots of things, wherever it was he was brought up, he had it tough.'

'You had it tough as a kid, so did I, so did Bruce and Betty,' John said angrily. 'As for Dulcie she had it even worse, shipped off over here like she was a side of beef. It hasn't turned us into chunks of ice!'

'I thought of killing my pa once when I was a kid,' Bob said. 'He came home from the pub and beat me black and blue for forgetting to get the wood in for the fire. I planned to whack him over the head with something and push him into the fire in the forge. I never tried it, he was too big and quick. I felt a failure because I didn't.'

John grinned. He'd heard stories about Bob's father, he was by repute the nastiest, most evil-tempered man that ever walked in Western Australia. 'Don't reckon you'd have lived to tell the tale if you had,' he said. 'But what's that got to do with Iceman?'

'Reckon he's been where I've been, and worse,' Bob said. 'I never had the confidence to get a girl, Pa knocked it out of me. Ross is lucky Dulcie took a shine to him otherwise I reckon he'd never find one either.'

'But he *has* got her, she's crazy about him,' John said in exasperation. 'What you've said doesn't explain why he's so weird. Look at you this morning, you wrapped Dulcie up in a blanket. You knew what to say to her. Explain that?'

'She looked like Ma did when Pa died,' Bob said simply.

John could say nothing more. He understood completely why Bob was timid, he was a weedy, bullied kid, and he'd grown into a man who saw himself as second-rate. But Ross was young and strong, decent-looking, a nice enough bloke most of the time. Dulcie with her looks and figure was enough to make any bloke's heart race faster, so why wasn't Ross with her tonight?

*

Ross got a lift part of the way home, but as he walked the last few miles he was sobbing. When John told him Betty had died this morning he felt his whole world had crumbled. He worshipped her, owed her so much, for he always knew it was her persuasion that had stopped Bruce calling the police when he found him in his barn.

He had never had a woman touch him before that day, well, not since he was around five, and that was never tenderly. Betty washed him all over, dressed the wounds on his feet, fed him soup and all the time kept whispering, *'My poor boy,'* and *'You're safe now, no one's going to hurt you.'*

Yet as he got better he sensed he ought to tell her how much he appreciated it, but he just couldn't – he felt the words in his heart, but they wouldn't come out. It was easier to show it, by working hard, harder even than John and Bob. That's all he knew, proving himself, just the way he used to with the Brothers, being harder, tougher than anyone else.

He had to learn so much in that first year at the farm. The work outside was no problem, he'd done all that and more back at Bindoon. It was how to behave in the house and around people he had problems with. He would eat till he was almost bursting, hide bread, cheese and fruit in his pockets, because he couldn't quite believe there would always be food for him. He didn't understand compliments, they sounded the same as sarcasm to him, and he didn't know how to make polite conversation. He tried to copy John in everything, but the teasing remarks John made to people came out like rudeness when he attempted them. John could down five or six schooners of beer and still be sober – when he tried to keep up with him he disgraced himself by being violently sick. He couldn't take criticism either, one sharp word and he smarted silently for days. He couldn't trust or show appreciation, and he thought he could do everything better than anyone else.

When he looked back at that time he blushed with shame. Maybe if he'd told the men how Bindoon really was and asked for their help and guidance, he might not have made such a fool of himself. But asking for help was another thing unknown to him. At Bindoon you did what you were told, never questioned anything the Brothers said, they were all-powerful and the boys were nothing but their slaves.

By the time Dulcie came to the farm, Ross believed he'd cracked it all and that he was the same as any other man. But Dulcie with her endless questioning had made everything resurface. She made him feel a whole lot better about himself on the one hand, but on the other he had blinding flashes of inadequacy that he hadn't until then been aware of. He couldn't say or show what he felt, physical contact was very hard for him. All his life he'd been told it was sinful, especially touching oneself, and however hard he tried to dismiss what he'd been taught, it remained. He was deeply ashamed whenever he succumbed to the temptation of masturbation, vowed he'd never do it again, and even blamed Dulcie for arousing all these perverted feelings inside him. He did truly love her, she had every quality any man would want in a wife, she was on his mind from morning till night, yet he sensed she wanted more from him than he could ever give.

When Betty got sick and they had to put off the wedding, he was both relieved and disappointed at the same time, but he couldn't pinpoint exactly why. Worse still, Betty's illness brought back problems he thought he'd overcome. He knew he ought to go into Betty's room and sit with her like John and Bob did so often, talk to her, try and make her laugh. He tried it once but he failed miserably. He panicked when he saw how ill she was. He couldn't take her hand or kiss her cheek because he thought that would alert her to how little time she had left. He sat there by her bedside squirming with embarrassment because he couldn't think of anything to say to her. He hated John because he could charm so effortlessly – even Bob who said little most of the time would look at magazines with her, talk about his mother, his childhood in Esperance, and ask about Betty's family in Perth.

The more Ross stayed away, the worse it got. Almost every day he'd tell himself that tomorrow he would go in there, tell her outright what she meant to him, how she'd turned his life around and that he loved her. Yet every day he made an excuse to himself – she would be sleeping, he had an important job to do, she didn't really want to see him or she would have asked for him. Sometimes he even felt angry that he wasn't summoned because it showed he meant nothing to her.

Finally he was too late. Betty had died without hearing how much he appreciated all she'd done for him.

He'd wanted to tell Bruce that today, and maybe he could have if only Bruce had asked him to go to town with him to make the funeral arrangements instead of John. He was jealous about that, just as he was always jealous when John made Dulcie laugh, or said how lovely she looked.

He knew when Bob wrapped Dulcie up in that blanket this morning that he should have thought of it, but he didn't because he was wrapped up in his own misery, and so he shot out to milk the cows. It was easy to show animals his feelings, no words were necessary, they just felt it all and responded. He supposed he imagined Dulcie would be the same way, that she would just know how he felt.

He had blown everything now. He had idolized John, seeing in him what he wanted to be, but John thought he was a worthless lump of shit just as the Brothers always had. *A dingo* he'd called him, and nothing came much lower than that.

How would he face Bruce tomorrow, knowing he had failed him by not speaking out and saying how sorry he was that he'd lost his lovely wife who was so very special to him? Why couldn't he see this morning that his own grief was no bigger than anyone else's? Every single person who met Betty had loved her.

And Dulcie. What could he say to her? Sorry that he

didn't think of her? Just admitting it proved his failure to act like a normal person.

He felt just the way he had back at Bindoon, a wretch with no purpose except to toil for the benefit of the Brothers, a lump of shit who could be abused in every possible way because he had no feelings and belonged to no one. He had tried to be like normal people, to learn their ways, trust again, but he would never be that way, a part of him was missing. Maybe John was right and he should just slither off into the bush like the snake he was. But he couldn't, he needed Dulcie.

'Now, Bruce, just remember that you have a big family up in Perth, and you can come and stay with us whenever you need us.'

Dulcie listened to Betty's diminutive sister Rose offering Bruce comfort and hugging him before she got into the car, and it was like seeing and hearing Betty all over again. Rose and the other sister Joan were so like Betty in looks and personalities that for the five days they'd been here she'd felt safe and secure. With them she'd been able to express her grief, to laugh at the things Betty said, to listen to childhood stories and applaud her many talents from her fine needlework to her gift with people. But now they had to go. Their grown-up children had left yesterday, along with Betty's brother Clive, his wife and daughter too. The house was going to be so empty and quiet again.

Rose finally got into the car and it rolled out down the track. Dulcie moved closer to Bruce, feeling his deep sadness at the parting. She slipped one arm through his and waved with the other.

People said it was the best attended funeral they'd ever known. The shops had closed out of respect in Esperance, and the mourners had come from a 150-mile radius. Dulcie had worn Betty's pert little black hat with a veil, and it was only much later that Rose had told her Betty hadn't bought it for a funeral as she supposed, but to wear on her honeymoon on Rottnest Island off the coast of Perth.

She'd scandalized her mother by choosing black instead of a pastel shade, because she said she wanted to look seductive, not pretty.

'Her family are all so kind,' Bruce said with a sigh as the car finally disappeared. 'For two pins I'd sell up and go and join them in Perth.'

'Why don't you then?' Dulcie asked as they walked back to the house.

Bruce stopped and tweaked her cheek. 'Because I'm a farmer, not a city boy. I'd like being near them for a while, but it's too confining, too noisy.'

'You could get a smaller farm somewhere near enough to visit whenever you felt like it,' she said.

'I could, but I won't,' he said with a smile. 'I can feel Betty here. I've got long roots that won't pull up easily. Just don't you leave me until I've got settled again.'

'I'm not planning on going anywhere,' she said.

For all the shock of Betty's death, the sadness of the funeral and the knowledge that life wasn't ever going to be quite the same again here, Dulcie felt optimistic. She knew there had been a bit of a fight between John and Ross on the night of Betty's death, Ross had come in the next morning with a bruise on his jaw. But he'd apologized to her, cuddled and kissed her and explained that he was too upset to think straight. He'd gone off with Bruce for a walk and a chat later that morning, and though neither of them had told her what had been said, the air was cleared.

While all the visitors were here, she hadn't seen very much of Ross, but that was just through circumstances. She was up to her ears in preparing and cooking food. Ross, John and Bob came in for their usual meals, then scurried out to work again to make room for the guests. But Ross had been at her side throughout the funeral, and although his face was set like concrete and he didn't allow himself the weakness of tears, she sensed that when he disappeared from the wake in the house later, it was because he wanted to cry in private.

He had come in after the evening milking, and he'd

made a great effort to be sociable. She was touched too how much he tried to help her, collecting up plates and cups, washing up and getting people drinks.

'Would you like to go up to Perth for a holiday?' Bruce said as they got to the house. 'You haven't had a day off in over a year, and you could stay with Rose or Joan. It would give you a chance to see May.'

Dulcie was taken aback by the offer. 'But you need me here!' she said.

Bruce smiled. 'I didn't mean for you to go right now. Maybe later, in the spring. We can manage okay, believe it or not I can cook and wash a few clothes. I'm not helpless.'

'It would be great to see May,' she said gratefully. May was seventeen now, she'd got her shorthand and typing diploma, and she'd hinted in both her last two letters that she wanted to go and work in Sydney. Once she was there Dulcie knew she'd never get to see her, it was just too far away.

'Then you must go,' Bruce said as they went indoors. 'I don't suppose Ross will be too pleased, but it will do you two good to have some time apart to think things out.'

Bruce stayed indoors that day. There were a hundred and one jobs outside to be done, but he felt drained, emotionally and physically. He pulled the armchair up close to the stove, put his feet on a stool and closed his eyes. He could hear Dulcie putting the bedrooms back to rights again, and it was a comforting, peaceful sound after all the noise and bustle of the last few days.

It had been Betty's idea that Dulcie should go to Perth for a while. She'd made the suggestion several months earlier, because she felt Dulcie should have a chance to compare life in a city with here in the bush. She hadn't been entirely happy about her marrying Ross, and although back then Bruce had scoffed at her reasons, he had come to understand them a great deal better in the last week or so.

When Ross came to him the day after Betty's death and

poured out how he'd felt about her, and how sorry he was he hadn't told her himself, Bruce felt deeply for him. He guessed Ross had opened up as a result of John laying into him, and it saddened him even more to think that it took violence to goad him into expressing his feelings. Dulcie was quite the reverse, all it took to gain her confidence was affection.

He'd watched the pair of them at the wake after the funeral and noted alarming differences in their manner. Dulcie liked people. She might be a little shy still, but she was interested, attentive and a natural diplomat. How she had managed to produce so much food in just a couple of days astounded him, and Rose and Joan both pronounced her a little wonder, yet she didn't once overstep the mark into familiarity but retained her position as housekeeper, making sure everyone had enough to eat and drink, that their beds were made and clean towels laid out for them, and she cleaned and tidied around everyone without anyone really noticing.

Ross, however, veered between ingratiating himself with the guests and ignoring them. Sometimes he was too familiar, almost as if he was part of the family, at other times so distant he could have been a newly arrived stockman. He drank too much, interrupted some of the men's conversations, and he was awkward with the women. It was true he helped Dulcie quite a bit, but in a flamboyant way that was irritating. The top and bottom of it was that he obviously felt like a fish out of water and he was trying far too hard.

Bruce couldn't help but look at John and admire his effortless charm. He paid the women gentle compliments, remembered their names and found them seats. He could talk to city-born Clive just as easily as he could to some of the old farmers. He curbed his drinking, introduced people to one another and managed to maintain just the right balance of solemnity fitting to the occasion without letting it sink to maudlin levels.

That night when Bruce went to bed over in the bunkhouse, he found himself wishing it was John Dulcie loved. He was too old for her, he had a long record of loving and leaving women, but he had a youthful spirit, and Bruce suspected that he'd left more women smiling than he'd ever left in tears. But it was the openness of his character that appealed most. There was something malignant inside Ross, some deep hurt he hadn't been able to overcome. He'd blurted out when they had their talk that the school he'd been to and run away from was Bindoon, and that it was the treatment he'd received there which made him different from other people. Yet Bruce remembered reading in the paper that Brother Keaney of the Christian Brothers who founded it received an MBE for his unselfish and efficient work with the youth of Australia. Keaney was a popular hero throughout Western Australia. Bruce couldn't imagine such a man condoning ill-treatment of the children in his care.

In view of all this, Bruce intended to encourage Dulcie to wait a little longer before marrying Ross. She would be twenty-two in December, old enough to marry anyone she chose. But there was no harm in introducing a little more variety and outside interest into her life. That's what Betty would have done if she hadn't become ill.

Just thinking of her made the sadness well up inside him again. He knew Dulcie had moved all his things back into their old bedroom today. Tonight he'd sleep under Betty's beautiful quilt, he'd look up at the curtains and remember how flushed with excitement Betty had been as they hung them together. It had meant so much to them both finally to have a real house of their own. They believed then that they still had another twenty years or so to enjoy it. The bed was going to be too big without her, the whole place seemed pointless without sharing it with her. They had no children to leave it to, perhaps he should sell up?

He sighed and opened his eyes. Dulcie was standing in the doorway looking at him. 'Would you like some tea?' she asked, her sweet face wreathed with concern.

'If you come and sit with me and have some too,' he said. 'I got into thinking sad thoughts.'

She came closer and ruffled his hair. 'It will be like that for quite a while,' she said. 'But you can share them with me if you want to.'

He half smiled. For someone so young she had so much understanding. 'No, you just boot me out to do some work,' he said. 'That's what Betty would have done.'

'I will when I think that's what you need. But right now you need rest, tea and sympathy.'

'I'll drive you up to Perth when you go,' Bruce said impulsively. 'I'll drop you off with Rose and Joan, then go on up to Geraldton and see some old mates. Then I can pick you up on the way back. Reckon we both need something to look forward to.'

Chapter Nineteen

Dulcie walked down View Road in Peppermint Grove with a light step, happily admiring all the nice houses and well-kept gardens. She had never really been able to imagine where May worked, what the house was like, or the neighbourhood. All she knew was that it was near the river on one side, and the sea on the other.

It was November, a warm spring afternoon without a cloud in the sky. She and Bruce had driven up from Esperance and arrived at Joan's yesterday. Tomorrow Bruce was going on up to Geraldton, and when Dulcie telephoned May this morning Mrs Wilberforce invited her over for tea.

Dulcie paused for just a second when she saw number 32, suddenly understanding what May had meant when she said it was an English house. It was perhaps the oldest in the street, and very like the Edwardian villas she remembered in Blackheath. Old grey stone, bay windows, and a tiled path up to the front door. She could remember such houses having a balcony upstairs too, but this one had been extended to a veranda right round the side of the house. The many climbing plants scrambling up to it and the bushes and trees shading it made her think of pictures she'd seen of homes in the tropics.

'Dulcie!' May exclaimed gleefully as she opened the door. 'It's so good to see you. Come on in, Mrs Wilberforce is really pleased she's going to meet you at last.'

'You can't imagine how excited I've been,' Dulcie said as she hugged her sister. 'But let me look at you! I can't believe it, you're so grown-up.'

She had never doubted that May would still be pretty,

but in the three years since they last saw one another May's looks had taken on a new dimension. Even in a plain navy blue dress and apron she looked polished, not a blemish on her perfect complexion, her hair fixed up in a sleek style Dulcie recognized as a French pleat. She was no longer just pretty, but beautiful.

'I feel like a country bumpkin next to you,' Dulcie admitted, suddenly wishing she'd made a little more effort with her appearance – putting her hair up in a pony-tail was hardly sophisticated.

'You look lovely to me.' May grinned, then moving closer went to whisper in her ear, 'Come on, let's get this tea over with. After that we'll go down to the river so we can talk. I've been saving my days off, so I've got three whole days to spend with you.'

Dulcie thought Mrs Wilberforce was the most elegant and gracious woman she'd ever met, beautifully dressed, her hair just so, and such a lovely English accent. But then she was spellbound by everything here in Peppermint Grove – Mrs Wilberforce, her house and garden, even her own sister's looks. She couldn't help but feel a little envy that May had landed a job like this, while she'd been packed off to Salmon Gums.

Yet seeing her little sister acting like a real lady, pouring tea into bone-china cups, passing round plates of dainty sandwiches and cakes, all prepared by herself, was so pleasing. She would have been very upset to find May in a position where she was treated like a drudge.

'Isn't farming rather a hard life?' Mrs Wilberforce asked at one point in the conversation. 'You look so very fragile, Dulcie. I expected a big strapping girl.'

Dulcie laughed. Both Joan and Rose had made similar remarks to her at the funeral. She supposed she didn't look like the stereotype farm girl. 'I'm tougher than I look,' she said. 'Besides, I don't actually work on the farm, except at harvest when I pitch in. I feed the chooks, look after the garden, but everything else is indoors.' She went on to describe a little of how it was at her first job and Mrs Wilberforce winced.

Mrs Wilberforce asked how Mr French was managing without his wife, and it was clear to Dulcie she was as kind-hearted as she was elegant. Then finally the tea was over, and she told the girls they could go on out, and that she would clear up.

'Just let me take these out.' Dulcie hastily began stacking up the plates and cups on to a tray. 'I wouldn't feel right leaving you to do it.'

'What a sweet girl you are, Dulcie,' Mrs Wilberforce said, smiling. But she took the tray from Dulcie's hands and shooed them both out. 'Go on with you. You've got a lot of catching up to do.'

May chattered non-stop all the way down to the river, pointing out her favourite houses and what she knew of the people who lived in them. Dulcie stopped listening when they came to the riverside, for it was breathtakingly beautiful. It was in fact a little curving bay, small boats moored at anchor, a narrow strip of sand along the water's edge and several children splashing in the shallows, which gave more of an impression of a seaside scene than a river.

'You aren't listening,' May said, her voice a little sharp.

'I'm sorry,' Dulcie said guiltily. 'I was just taken aback by this place. It's so lovely.'

'Umm,' May replied. 'A bit boring though, I always see the same people here. Anyway, I was telling you about the new can-can petticoat I bought, it's got about a mile of net.'

Maybe Dulcie looked blank, for May launched into telling her that net underskirts were the latest craze from America and some girls wore two or three under their dresses when they went dancing. It seemed she went dancing most Saturday nights with her friend Angelina. 'I love jiving,' she said rapturously. 'Can you do it?'

Dulcie had seen jiving on the television and on the news at the cinema, but it hadn't arrived at the Saturday dances in Esperance as far as she knew. But then she hadn't been to one for over a year. When she told May this her sister looked appalled.

'But what do you do then when you go out with Ross?' she asked.

'Mostly to the pictures, but we haven't been out anywhere for ages because of Betty being so ill,' Dulcie replied. 'He's not very keen on dancing anyway.'

May wrinkled her nose. 'I wouldn't marry a man who didn't like dancing, I like to get dressed up and be seen by everyone when I'm on a date. Are you still going to get married?'

Dulcie nodded. 'We haven't set a date yet, but I think it will be next January or February. It depends on Bruce really.'

'Why?'

'Well, he keeps trying to put me off. I don't mean in a nasty way, he isn't like that, but I suppose he thinks I'm still a bit young.'

'You're nearly twenty-two, that's old enough,' May shrugged. 'I expect it's because he wants you to stay in his house looking after him. Men are selfish like that.'

'It's not that, he doesn't think I've looked around enough yet.'

'Well, you could do better than a stockman,' May said bluntly. 'I don't understand why you've stayed on a farm anyway, it must be so boring.'

Dulcie didn't want to get into an argument about that so she asked May if she had a boyfriend.

'Two,' May said. 'There's Ken who lives just up the road from the Wilberforces, and Matt, he's an accountant with an office in the city.'

After much probing for more information about these two boyfriends, and a little astute guesswork, Dulcie established that Ken was the stand-in for when Matt wasn't available. It crossed her mind Matt might have another girl too, for it seemed odd that he could only find time to take May out once a fortnight. Ken on the other hand sounded very nice. He was twenty and at Perth University studying mathematics, and lodging with his aunt.

'I hope you aren't going to give me one of those *don't you get carried away* talks,' May said suddenly. 'Mrs Wilberforce did that one day, and it was so embarrassing.'

'Do you mean getting carried away about getting married?' Dulcie said innocently.

May burst into laughter. 'No, of course not. I meant sex, silly. Mrs W. thinks everyone is as dumb as she was when she got married. She started trying to tell me about French letters, as if I didn't know about them.'

Dulcie was lost now. 'What are French letters?' she asked.

May looked at her in astonishment, then giggled. 'You *must* know, Dulcie. You've been going out with Ross for ages. Or are you such a good girl you don't let him do anything?'

'Of course not, we'll wait till we're married,' Dulcie said indignantly. 'I'd be scared of having a baby.'

'That's what French letters are for, you chump!' She paused to look at Dulcie and perhaps saw real bewilderment. 'Don't tell me no one told you?'

Dulcie could hardly believe her ears as her little sister who she expected to come looking to her for advice proceeded to tell her about these rubber things men put over their penis to prevent a girl getting pregnant. But the worst of it was that May sounded as she was speaking from personal experience, not repeating something she'd just been told.

'Have you done it then?' Dulcie whispered.

'Of course not,' May said, but she didn't sound convincing. 'I'll wait until I meet the right man.'

During the course of the next three days Dulcie was to discover that May not only looked far more sophisticated than she did, but she really was. Gone were the days when Dulcie had to look after her little sister and explain things to her, May appeared to know everything. From the first of her three days off work when she met Dulcie at Perth station wearing stiletto heels, her hair teased up into a beehive, and her new net petticoat under a pink and white dress with a full circular skirt and her waist pulled into a handspan with a three-inch belt, Dulcie was in awe of her.

May took her into huge department stores and dismissed every item of clothing Dulcie wanted to buy as old-fashioned, insisting she let her choose something for her. Once Dulcie had actually tried a dress very similar to the one May was wearing, she did think her own plain shirtwaister looked a bit dowdy, but yards of net petticoat on a farm was hardly practical. May broke down her objections, saying there was no point in buying a dress that looked just like the ones available in the shop in Esperance, and besides, she'd be going out more now she hadn't got Betty to look after.

May knew her way round the cosmetics counter too, and insisted Dulcie should buy eyeliner and pale lipstick because that was the look of the moment and Dulcie's eyes were her best feature. She scoffed at the low-heeled shoes Dulcie wanted to buy and talked her into buying a pair of pointed-toe sling-backs with three-inch heels.

May led her into record shops where they listened to the Top Ten, and she seemed horrified Dulcie hadn't heard 'Till I Kissed You' by The Everley Brothers, or 'Poison Ivy' by The Coasters before. 'You've got to get hip,' she exclaimed. 'Don't you listen to John O'Keefe's Six O'Clock Rock? Even Mrs W. likes to hear it so she knows what's going on.'

Dulcie thought 'Till I Kissed You,' was the most wonderful song she'd ever heard. She wished she had one of the Portagram record-players that May said Mr and Mrs Wilberforce had bought her for her birthday, so she could buy the record and take it home and play it to Ross. But they were £66 3s, half a year's wages, and she couldn't even afford to buy one of the new transistor radios May showed her, though she thought it would be lovely to lie in bed at night and listen to music.

*

Being with May was like entering a whole new world. They went into smart milk bars which looked like something out of American films, all shiny plastic and chrome. They sat up on high stools and had frothy coffee, and May insisted she tried a cigarette. She knew how to work the juke-box too and selected 'Till I Kissed You' especially for Dulcie. So many people seemed to know May too, though more men than girls, and she watched in envious amazement as her sister flirted effortlessly with them.

That first afternoon they caught a bus up to King's Park and lay on the grass in the sun, just talking and looking at fashion magazines together. To Dulcie that was almost the best part of the day, for she felt the same closeness they'd had when they were little girls, looking at their mother's magazines together. Later they went back to Joan's house in Subiaco for tea, and afterwards May backcombed Dulcie's hair and put it up in a beehive and supervised her new makeup. It was thrilling and scary going out to the dance at the Embassy later. Scary because Dulcie didn't know how to jive, but thrilling to see how modern and even glamorous she looked in her new dress with a new hair-style.

The dances in Esperance parish hall were Old Time or ballroom style, the band could be anything from just a pianist or a pianist and drummer to almost a whole orchestra of local musicians on an important occasion, and young and old alike went to join in the Barn Dance, Pride of Erin and the Oxford Waltz.

The Embassy was quite different. Roy Jenkins's band were seasoned professionals, slick-looking men in dinner jackets and bow-ties, and they played all kinds of dance music. The lights were low, sparkly mirrored balls hung from the ceiling, there was even a bar which served alcohol, something unheard of back home. It wasn't so difficult to learn basic jive steps, not after she'd had a couple of port and lemons, and she and May had no shortage of enthusiastic partners.

Maybe the first day with May was the best one. It did

get a little bit repetitive when they kept looking in shops, going into milk bars and sitting around while May smoked and talked about clothes. She did seem a bit obsessive about how she looked and the impression she was making on other people, and not at all grateful that she'd been so fortunate in getting sent to the Wilberforces. She said airily that she was going to work in Sydney next year, and she scoffed at Dulcie's anxiety that maybe her new secretarial qualifications wouldn't be enough without experience to land a good enough job to be able to keep herself. Dulcie also thought she was a bit too forward with men. But all the same it was wonderful to be with her again, becoming friends along with being sisters. She so much hoped they could build on it and put all the sadness of the past behind them.

On their last day together it was overcast and a bit chilly and they spent the whole day in shops. May suggested they went into the Criterion Hotel which she said was very swish and think about what they wanted to do that evening. It was already nearly six, and Dulcie's feet were aching from wearing her new shoes, so she was grateful to be able to sit down somewhere warm and comfortable.

May ordered a pot of tea and toasted tea-cakes, and they'd hardly even poured the tea before the man at the next table started speaking to May. Within ten minutes, the man and his friend were sitting beside them, and all at once Dulcie became aware that May not only wanted their company, but she'd suggested coming in here for the sole purpose of picking someone up.

They were nice enough men, both in banking they said, mid-thirties, well-dressed and staying at the hotel while they completed their business in Perth. After the tray of tea was taken away the men insisted on buying them a drink and then asked them to have dinner with them. May agreed without even asking Dulcie if she would like it, and while the men went to the dining-room to book a table, Dulcie told her off.

'We don't know them, we can't,' she said flatly.

'Oh, don't be so stuffy,' May retorted, taking her compact out of her bag to powder her nose. 'I'm hungry and you must be too, it's our last night together and they are nice.'

'But I'm engaged to Ross,' Dulcie said. 'I don't feel right about having dinner with another man.' She wanted to say she'd never even been in a proper restaurant before, let alone to dinner in a smart hotel dining-room, and she was scared of showing herself up. But she couldn't bring herself to admit that.

'You don't have to do anything other than eat the dinner and chat,' May said quite calmly. 'Do it for me, I really like the look of Mike, he's my type.'

Dulcie had thought Mike was nice-looking, with dark hair, sharp brown eyes and olive skin, but she was sure he was married, single men didn't have the sort of confidence he had. Yet while she was thinking how she should say this, without sounding like a kill-joy, May told her to close her eyes and hold out her hand because she had something for her.

She did as she was told and heard May rustling her shopping bag. 'You can open your eyes now,' May said as she put something box-like and heavy into her hand.

Dulcie gasped when she saw it was a little red transistor radio, the very one she'd looked at earlier today. 'Oh, May,' she exclaimed, forgetting she was cross with her.

'Sorry I couldn't wrap it up, but I had enough trouble buying it without you seeing me,' May said, looking a bit anxious. 'I hope you like it.'

'Like it! It's wonderful, just what I always wanted, but you shouldn't have, it's much too expensive.'

'I earn more than you do,' May laughed, the tension fading from her face. 'I'd been saving up to buy you something special for your birthday next month, and it seemed so perfect. But it would be hard to post, so I want you to have it now.'

After that Dulcie didn't feel able to object to anything,

not even being picked up by two strangers. She had three port and lemons, and by the time they went into dinner she was too tiddly to be intimidated by the posh dining-room with its snowy tablecloths and candles. Mike and his friend James were nice, even if they did keep teasing her about living out in the bush, the steak dinner was one of the best she'd ever eaten, and she felt even more relaxed after a couple of glasses of wine too. It wasn't until she saw it was nearly ten that she grew anxious again. 'We must go now,' she said to May. 'Joan will be worried about me.'

She expected May to protest, but surprisingly she didn't and even asked James to get her a taxi. 'I can't come with you, your taxi goes the wrong way,' she said. 'But I'll get another one after you've gone.'

They said goodbye on the pavement of the hotel, Dulcie clutching her shopping bag holding the pair of tight denim jeans she'd brought that morning, and the radio, while the taxi James had paid for in advance waited. As they hugged each other, Dulcie was suddenly very aware that their time together had run out and there was no time left to say all the important things she'd planned to say tonight.

She looked out of the back window as the taxi drove off and saw May still standing there waving, looking like a model in her red sheath dress with her hair up in a beehive. Dulcie's last thought was that she shouldn't have left her little sister alone with two men, but the port and the wine numbed her anxiety and she was almost asleep by the time she got home.

'How was it being with May?' Bruce asked as they drove out of Perth three days later to return home. 'As good as you expected, or disappointing?'

'Different to how I expected,' Dulcie said thoughtfully. 'She's all grown-up, she seems older than me now.'

'Well, that's good news,' he chuckled. 'One less person for you to worry about.'

Dulcie smiled as if in agreement, but she wasn't so sure

in her mind. During the last three days relaxing at Joan's house, she'd had time to reflect on many things about her sister. She was worldly and very chic, confident and composed, all such admirable qualities. Yet Dulcie did feel disappointed that she hadn't once managed to break through her sophisticated veneer and catch a glimpse of what lay beneath.

Maybe it wasn't a veneer, it could be that was all there was to May – after all, even as children their temperaments were quite different. Yet it was strange to her that May gave so little away about herself. Every time Dulcie had drawn the conversation towards their childhood or even to what May really wanted for herself in the future, her sister had quickly turned it back to films, clothes, music or makeup. The way she'd talked so effortlessly to the two men in the hotel suggested she'd done it before. She had spoken of her friend Angelina, yet she hadn't taken her to meet her. Was it because she was afraid Angelina might let slip something May didn't want Dulcie to know about?

Yet it was so generous of May to buy her the radio, that proved she had a kind heart. It could be herself who was the strange one? Maybe she was at fault in wanting to dig up the past, and May could very well be so well adjusted she had no interest in it. As for Angelina, well, maybe May hadn't wanted a third party intruding on their time together – why did she have to find that suspicious?

By the time Dulcie and Bruce arrived back in Esperance two days later, having stopped overnight in a small boarding house, Dulcie's mind had moved away from May on to the forthcoming harvest, and Ross. She couldn't wait to see him and tell him everything she'd done and seen. It was going to be lovely working out in the fields with him again, for even though getting the harvest in was exhausting, it was fun too.

Eleven days away had made home seem so much more desirable than city life. While it was lovely to have some new, fashionable clothes and a little more experience of how others lived, going away had heightened her sense of belonging down here. As she saw the clear blue water of Esperance Bay, the pine trees, the fishing boats and the sleepy, safe little town, a lump came up in her throat for she loved it all.

Ross welcomed her back with real delight, picking her up in his arms and whirling her around. 'I missed you so much,' he said, his voice cracking with surprising emotion. 'It feels like you've been away for ever.'

John, Ross and Bob had cooked their meals themselves while she and Bruce had been gone, but though they'd washed up and watered the garden, that was all they'd done and the whole house looked dusty and uncared for. Yet that pleased Dulcie because it showed she was needed, and when John and Bob came bounding over to see her and Bruce, she felt their real affection.

That evening, over a hastily put together meal of corned beef, mashed potatoes and baked beans, there was so much to talk about. Bruce was invigorated by seeing his old friends up in Geraldton. He'd been out riding in the bush, something he never did here any longer, and had spent evenings in a pub swopping stories with stockmen. The old sparkle came back into his eyes when he spoke of buying a couple of horses because he'd got lazy driving around the farm all the time, and as John was equally enthusiastic, suggesting they might even do some breeding, Dulcie felt that the new decade of the sixties which would soon be here was going to bring some big changes to all their lives.

She told them all about May with pride, and showed them her new dress, jeans and the transistor radio. It was a little disappointing that the reception wasn't as clear as it had been in Perth, but it was a thing of wonder to John, Bob and Ross that it could run on such small batteries and be carried around. None of them had ever see one before.

Bruce had ordered a freezer while he was in Perth. He had first heard that they were being made for domestic use in 1957, but the cost had been prohibitive until quite recently. To be able to keep slaughtered meat for months on end was an exciting innovation, for though down here in Esperance they could buy fish and quite a variety of other foods, and didn't live entirely on mutton and corned beef as many bush farmers did, it would mean they could kill and store their own beef. Bruce said the salesman had claimed that within a year or two frozen vegetables would be available too.

'It's good to have you both back,' John said with a wide grin. 'I told Ross that once Dulcie got a taste of city life she'd be off.'

Dulcie looked at Ross, sensing just a tiny bit of malice in John's remark. Ross was grinning, but his eyes were cold.

'I liked it while I was there, but this is home to me,' she said quickly.

Bruce broke up the evening at nine o'clock by saying he was going to bed, the long drive had tired him out. Bob and John immediately got to their feet, but Ross stayed, making it plain he wanted to talk to Dulcie alone. This was a first, in the past he had always been awkward about their relationship and his position as junior stockman, so he mostly left the house with the other men, and Dulcie had to go outside and sit on the veranda so he would feel able to return and speak to her.

John and Bob were hardly out of the door, and Bruce was still in the bathroom, when Ross moved over to sit beside her on the couch. 'Can we get married now?' he asked.

Dulcie was often dismayed by Ross's lack of diplomacy. He appeared unable to grasp the concept that there was almost always a right and a wrong time to pass on a piece of information or to ask a question. While this wasn't the wrong time exactly, she felt he could have led up to it by asking about her holiday, was she tired, truly glad to be back, and had she missed him?

'Is the house on fire or something?' she asked sarcastically.

'Well, I need to know,' he said.

'Right this minute, before I've even had time to collect my thoughts?'

'You shouldn't need to think about it, it's either yes or no.'

'No it isn't, Ross,' she said a little impatiently. 'There's maybe too. I do want to marry you, but it might be better to wait for a year or so. That's what I need to think about, and so should you.'

'But we were going to do it last January and we couldn't because of Betty. Suppose I wait another year, then Bruce gets ill and you have to nurse him. Am I always going to be last in line for your time?'

'What's brought on this sudden impatience?' she asked, shocked at his selfishness. 'Has John been teasing you about me all the time I've been away?'

'No. But I missed you and I got to think you might be just stringing me along until someone better turned up.'

'If I was hoping for someone better this wouldn't be a very sensible place to wait.' She laughed mirthlessly. 'No one ever comes here.'

He kissed her suddenly without any warning, hugging her so fiercely he almost crushed the breath out of her. 'I love you, I need you and I can't wait any longer,' he blurted out.

The passion in his voice touched something deep inside her, and she kissed him back lingeringly. The warmth of his lips, his darting tongue meeting hers sent shivers of delight down her spine. As she heard Bruce go into his bedroom and close the door, she relaxed further, sinking back into the cushions on the couch, and drew Ross closer.

Maybe it was different just because it was the first opportunity they'd ever had to be here in the house together with no one around, but for the first time in their courtship, Dulcie felt that Ross really wanted her now. He wasn't stiff and holding back any longer, his hands were running along her sides and her back, making her tingle from head to foot. She could feel her breasts throbbing, a yearning deep down in her belly.

She could feel his excitement, hear his breath growing louder as his kisses became more intense, he was almost on top of her now and for the first time ever she could feel his penis hard against her. As he cupped his hand round her breast and the tingling feeling grew even stronger, all at once she understood that this was real love-making, a prelude to sex, and she knew she wanted it.

His hard, slender body felt so good. She ran her hands down his sides as he kissed her, delighting in sensing his immediate response. His fingers fumbled at the buttons on the front of her dress, but at last he had them open and his hands snaked in to touch her breasts. She felt his frustration as he had to find his way through her slip and then her bra, but suddenly he was fondling her breast, his fingers playing with her erect nipple, and nothing in her life had ever felt that good before.

Arching her back, breasts pushed at him, her hands ran over his buttocks as she undulated her lower body against his. 'I love you, Ross,' she whispered, knowing that now she felt this way he had to be the only man in the entire world for her. 'I will marry you, as soon as you want.'

One of his knees was between her legs now, pushing at her and making her lose all control. His breath was coming ever harder and more laboured, and his kisses deeper and more sensual, then suddenly he made a kind of deep moan in his throat, shuddered and became still.

Dulcie felt the change in him instantly, but didn't understand it. He sat up, ran his fingers through his hair and looked distinctly uncomfortable. 'I'd better go now,' he said gruffly. 'Bruce won't like me being here after he'd gone to bed. We'll talk to him about the wedding tomorrow.'

He was gone before Dulcie could say anything.

The following morning Ross stayed behind after breakfast to ask Bruce if he minded if they got married in January.

'If that's what you want,' Bruce said, looking from Dulcie to Ross with a slightly stunned expression. 'I know someone that's got a caravan for sale, I'll get in touch with him about it. I'd like to suggest you both stayed in the house with me, but I don't think that would work. I think you need a place of your own.'

Dulcie wondered why Bruce didn't look more pleased. She knew he really liked Ross, he'd said she ought to wait until she was sure, now she was, so what was the matter with him?

Ross went back out to go with John and see if the barley was ready for harvesting. 'Are you really sure, Dulcie?' Bruce said almost the minute the screen door had shut behind Ross. 'Has he railroaded you into it?'

'No, of course he hasn't,' Dulcie said indignantly. 'I love him, I want to marry him and be with him forever.'

Bruce sat down rather heavily by the table. He looked old suddenly and a little confused. 'I wish Betty was here,' he said. 'She could have told you things I can't.'

Dulcie blushed, she was sure he meant about sex. 'I do know about all that stuff,' she said softly. 'I know I still look very young but I'll be twenty-two in a week's time, and Betty wasn't even that when she married you.'

'Maybe I'm just jealous,' he tried to smile. 'You're both so young with your whole lives ahead of you, and I'm an old man.'

'Not so old,' she said, and walked over to him and lightly smoothed his cheek. 'And we'll still be here to help look after things, nothing much is going to change.'

He gave a soft little sigh. 'I wish you every happiness then,' he said, catching hold of her hand and kissing it. 'You both deserve it.'

At the registrar's words *I now pronounce you man and wife* Dulcie had expected that she would experience a rush of excitement and feel completely different. She didn't, all she felt was a sense of relief that she could soon have a cold drink and maybe slip out of her shoes which were killing her. Of course it was wonderful to be Mrs Rawlings at last, and have a gold ring on her finger to prove it, but she doubted the wisdom of coming to Kalgoorlie to get married, just because it was considered fashionable. It might be fun to be in a bustling, bigger town with shops, dozens of pubs and hotels in the winter, but she didn't think it was such a good idea in January when the temperature was close to 100 degrees. And if they'd married in Esperance many of their neighbours could have come. Two hundred miles deterred all but the closest friends.

'You may kiss the bride,' the registrar said. As Ross leaned closer to kiss her lightly on the lips, John made a kind of whooping noise behind them and everyone burst into laughter.

Dulcie turned and smiled. John looked very handsome in a white shirt and grey trousers, shoes polished like mirrors and with an ear-to-ear grin. Bob looked hot and uncomfortable in a suit and tie, he had borrowed the suit for the occasion, having little call for smart clothes, and it was a little too big, emphasizing his slight frame. Bruce looked distinguished in a cream linen jacket, a red carnation in his button-hole. But it was May who stole the show in a pink lace two-piece with matching picture hat. On the way to the town hall several people stopped her and wished her luck, clearly thinking she was the bride.

Ross slipped his arm around Dulcie's shoulder. 'Well, Mrs Rawlings,' he said. 'I think we have to sign the register before we can leave.'

Dulcie turned back to the desk with her new husband and watched him as he leaned forward to sign the book. He had a new grey suit, a red carnation and a rather severe new hair-cut. She wished he'd left it wild and curly, there was a very obvious band of white skin across his forehead and along the back of his neck showing the length it had been until two days ago.

She leaned over to sign her name too, forgetting for a brief second she had to use the new one, but she quickly changed the 'T' into an 'R', and the registrar winked at her.

Outside the town hall they paused for photographs. The landlady at the Old Australia Hotel had organized this for them, along with a wedding breakfast in the dining-room. Bruce had booked and paid for a room for three nights. May had used it last night as she'd come by train from Perth, Dulcie had gone there today to freshen up and change into her wedding finery after the drive up from Esperance with the men, and for the next two nights it would be the honeymoon room, as May was going back to Esperance tonight with the men.

It was blastingly hot and the flies bombarded them as they walked back up the street towards the hotel. Kalgoorlie was right out in the desert, a rough, tough place that had been thrown up at the turn of the century when gold was discovered. There was still a working gold mine here, and almost all the old vices still flourished too – prostitution, gambling and hard drinking.

It reminded Dulcie of cowboy towns in the Wild West, with huge old hotels, saloons on street level, wide verandas upstairs and wooden sidewalks beneath. All that was missing was a few horses tied to hitching posts. It did have a great deal of character, she almost expected to see a couple of cowboys burst out of one of the saloon doors and begin shooting at each other. But she knew now she shouldn't have listened to all those well-intentioned people who insisted this was *the* place to get married.

It would have been far more romantic by the sea, she and Ross could have walked out on the jetty in the moonlight tonight, there would have been no 'blowies', and tomorrow they could have swum and laid around on the beach. But she wasn't going to breathe a word of that as Bruce had generously paid for it all. Neither was she going to look enviously at May's outfit and wish hers was as stunning.

Dulcie had made hers herself, a pale blue shantung sleeveless dress with a matching bolero jacket. Her hat was a blue pill-box with a veil, and she wore a spray of white gardenias. Both Bruce and Ross had said she looked gorgeous – perhaps she did, and it was only the heat which was making her wilt.

Two hours later as the sun was going down, Dulcie was laughing fit to bust. She was a little tiddly after two glasses of champagne and a couple more of wine, and cool at last because the upstairs dining-room at the hotel opened out on to a wide, shady veranda. Sadie Wells, the landlady, had lent them her son's record-player and his record collection, and May was teaching John to jive.

John was an enthusiastic dancer rather than a good one, and although he quickly got the idea of the steps, he kept breaking off to do impersonations of Elvis Presley to 'Jail House Rock'. He had got the gyrating pelvic movements perfectly, and with a beer bottle in his hand as a microphone and a lock of his hair pulled down on his forehead, he really looked like Elvis. Bob was quite drunk and between records kept telling jokes – Dulcie had never heard him say so much in one day. Both Bruce and Ross seemed supremely happy too.

Dulcie felt she had to acknowledge that much of this merriment was May's doing. She had charmed them all, made a fuss of Bruce, warmly welcomed Ross as her new brother-in-law, clowned with John and drawn Bob out of his customary silence. It was she who dared approach Sadie and ask if there was a record-player. Considering she'd come such a long way for a wedding where she knew no one but her sister, to find that Kalgoorlie was a dusty, hot town set in the middle of a desert and that for the next two days she'd be stuck out in a farm in the middle of nowhere without even her sister for company, Dulcie had expected sulks. But there had been none, in fact she appeared overjoyed by everything.

Some of the other guests staying at the hotel had come out on the far end of the veranda, and when May saw their interest and amusement she danced down that way and urged them to join in. There was a tall, dark-haired man in a cream suit among them, and before long May was jiving with him.

'Are you happy?' Ross asked Dulcie, coming to sit beside her on an old couch.

'Extraordinarily happy,' she said, kissing his cheek.

He took her hand in his, and squeezed it. 'I can't believe you're really my wife now,' he said, his tawny eyes looking tenderly into hers. 'It's like a dream come true.'

'The best is yet to come,' she said, running one finger around his lips. There had been many more kissing and petting sessions since that first one after she'd come back from Perth, though rarely in the house, and they always ended as abruptly as that one had. It had become very frustrating for her, but when she finally plucked up the courage to speak of it, Ross said he was afraid of going too far. She couldn't wait now until they could go to their bedroom, even on the drive up here this morning she'd thought of little else.

'Your sister is lovely,' Ross said suddenly, looking down the veranda to where May was dancing with the dark-haired man. She was looking up into the man's eyes and flirting madly. John was also along there, dancing with a very fat lady. 'She isn't like I expected at all.'

'She isn't really like I expected either,' Dulcie said fondly. She was delighted May had fitted in so well, she felt proud of her, and hoped that from now on they could be closer. 'It's lovely to find your sister can be a friend too.'

'I wish I knew where my brothers are,' Ross said.

'If we go to Perth one day we could go to the orphanage where you were all sent first and ask to see their records,' she suggested.

'I couldn't do that,' he said, looking shocked.

'Why not?' she laughed lightly. 'I'd be with you, they couldn't hurt you in any way now.'

'I think I'd be sick just walking through the gates,' he said. 'Anyway, let's not talk about that. Let me get you another drink.'

*

It was nearly ten when Bruce said they really ought to go home, he'd got someone in to milk the cows this evening, but they'd have to be up early tomorrow morning and it was a long drive on a bad road. He looked over to where May was talking animatedly to the dark man and smiled. 'Besides, I'd better get May back to the farm before she gets into any mischief.'

Bruce rounded them all up and Ross went into the bedroom and collected May's suitcase and hat. 'We'll see you all in two days,' he said, shaking Bruce's hand. 'Thank you for everything, Bruce. It's been a beaut day.'

'It has that.' Bruce beamed and kissed Dulcie. 'I'll be at the station to pick you up. Don't worry about May, we'll look after her.'

It was suddenly quiet after they'd all gone. No traffic in the wide streets, just a murmur of music from the pub across the way. The man who had been dancing with May and his friends had disappeared. Sadie had removed all the food and drink from the dining-room and laid the tables up for breakfast, but she'd left some soft drinks and a bottle of wine in a tub of ice in their room, which was a few doors along on the veranda.

'I'll go and get us a drink,' Ross said. Now they were alone he seemed jittery.

'I'll just have lemonade,' Dulcie said, aware now that she was drunk.

When he came back with a bottle of whisky in his hand and her lemonade, she was a bit shocked because he'd already drunk far more than anyone else today. But he only poured himself a small glass, so she said nothing.

They sat side by side for some little time without speaking. It was still very warm, without even a hint of a breeze. 'It's been a beaut day,' Ross said after a while, his words slightly slurred.

'The best ever,' she said, turning towards him and kissing him lightly on the lips. 'But let's go to bed now?'

He looked at her for a brief second, then turned his head

away. 'I reckon the room will start spinning if I lie down. Maybe I'd better stay out here tonight, I might get sick.'

She laughed, imagining Sadie's shock to find a young bridegroom sleeping on a couch outside his room. She took the glass of whisky from his hand. 'You'll do nothing of the sort,' she said, and took hold of his arm to pull him up. 'Only dogs sleep outside.'

He shook off her hand. 'You go on in, I'll just sit here for a bit and sober up.'

Dulcie thought that meant he wanted to give her time to get undressed, and as this was something she was nervous about doing in front of him, she slipped away reminding him he wasn't to drink any more whisky. She undressed, washed, brushed her hair and climbed into bed to wait for him, turning off the light so the mosquitoes and moths wouldn't come in through the open door.

She must have fallen asleep, but she woke partially as he crept in beside her later, enough to be aware he'd shut the door on to the veranda and pulled the curtains across, but not enough to speak. Sleepily she turned to him, sliding one arm across his chest, but sleep overtook her again and the next thing she knew daylight was coming through cracks in the curtains.

It was some minutes before she realized Ross wasn't still in bed with her. She could feel a warm patch where his body had been, and imagining he'd just gone down the corridor to the bathroom, she drifted off again.

The sound of traffic woke her, but Ross wasn't in bed beside her. The door to the veranda was open, and she could smell cigarette smoke, so he had to be out there. Pulling on her housecoat, she went outside. He was sitting on the couch fully dressed, he'd even shaved as if he was ready to go out somewhere.

'What time is it?' she asked, imagining it was very late.

'Nearly eight,' he said. 'Time for breakfast. Are you going to get dressed now?'

As Dulcie had never stayed in a hotel before, she assumed they had to get up and have breakfast. Although disappointed that he was showing no inclination to come back into the room with her, or even give her a good-morning kiss, she put this down to embarrassment.

It seemed a very long day. They spent the morning exploring the town, but it was too hot to get much enjoyment from looking in the shops, and Ross admitted he wished they were down at the beach in Esperance. In the afternoon they went to see *The King and I* at the cinema, but Ross had a couple of beers before they went in and he fell asleep and missed most of it. They had a meal in a restaurant, huge steaks nearly as big as the plates, and feeling bloated they went back to the hotel.

'Let's go and have a lie-down,' Dulcie suggested after a pot of tea out on the veranda.

'We can't,' Ross said, inclining his head to a couple sitting about eight feet away from them. 'What will they think?'

Dulcie didn't care much what they thought, and said so, but Ross said if she wanted to lie down he'd stay outside. So she stayed outside with him and tried not to sulk. Later they went for a walk, stopping at a couple of pubs for a drink, and finally it was eleven o'clock.

Once again he insisted on staying outside their room with a glass of whisky and a cigarette, and Dulcie lay in bed alone wondering why he was being so strange. It was over an hour later that he eventually came creeping in, peeling off his clothes in the dark, perhaps thinking she was asleep. She said nothing and waited for him to get into bed.

He got in but made no attempt to cuddle up to her. She could smell the whisky on his breath and wondered if he was drunk again. After several minutes of lying there tense and hurt, she moved closer. 'Give me a cuddle,' she whispered.

His arms went round her quickly enough, and he drew

her on to his shoulder, yet his body was as stiff and uncomforting as a corpse and he didn't utter a word.

Finally it was too much for her for it felt as if there was an invisible barrier between them. She turned over, moved back to her side of the bed and began to cry silently. She felt abandoned, the way she had on her first night at the Sacred Heart.

'Don't cry, Dulcie,' Ross whispered in the dark. She felt him turn on to his side and his arm stole round her middle. 'I can't bear it when you cry.'

'What have I done?' she asked through her tears. 'It's our honeymoon, why are you being so peculiar with me? Don't you want me?'

'You haven't done anything,' he said. 'It's just so hot and kind of strange here. I'm not used to hotels.'

'Neither am I,' she retorted. 'But I could get used to it, it's nice being in a place where someone else does everything for you. It's not that hot now either, so kiss me properly and stop being silly.'

He did give her a kiss, but a perfunctory, dutiful one. That was the final straw for Dulcie and she began crying again. 'What have I done wrong? Tell me, for goodness sake, and get it over with.'

'You haven't done anything wrong,' he said. 'It's all me.'

She sensed anguish in his voice now and she turned towards him, deeply puzzled. 'Tell me what it is, Ross,' she whispered. 'I don't care how bad it is, just tell me.'

'I shouldn't have married you,' he said in a small voice.

She just lay there for a moment, too stunned to speak.

'Why?' she asked at length. 'Why shouldn't you have married me?'

'Because I can't be a real husband to you.'

His words seemed to hang in the darkness, flapping like a huge bat under the fan on the ceiling. 'I don't understand,' she gasped out. 'You said you loved me!'

'I do love you,' he whispered. 'I'd do anything in the

440

whole world for you. I'd die for you. But I'm not like other blokes.'

The first thing that popped into her head was that he meant he was a poofter.

John used that word all the time. She didn't know what it meant exactly, John used it scornfully, sometimes to describe a man who was a bit timid or soft, but mostly when he was talking of men who didn't like women. Ross wasn't soft or timid, not by even the toughest men's reckoning, so it had to be the latter. But why would he want to marry her if that was the case?

'But you've wanted me before,' she retorted. 'You did, you know you did. How can you say you're not like other blokes? I know you are.'

'You don't know,' he said, his voice cracking with emotion in the darkness. 'I can't do it, let it be at that. I made a mistake thinking I'd be all right once we were married, but it just isn't there. I'll push off tomorrow morning.'

Indignation took over from feeling abandoned or even shocked. Dulcie sat up and switched the light on. He was lying on his side, and tears were coursing down his cheeks. In his striped pyjamas he looked closer to twelve than twenty-four.

'What do you mean, you'll push off?' she asked incredulously. 'Are you saying you'll run out on me, two days after our wedding? You can't be serious.'

'I can't come back to Frenches' with you, that's for certain,' he said, covering his face with his hands. 'I'd be a laughing stock and everyone would feel sorry for you. It's best I just go. You can tell them what you like.'

Dulcie just sat there for a moment, unable to believe this was really happening. She had read in magazines about some women who were too frightened to consummate their marriage, but she'd never heard of a man being that way. She looked down at him, he was crying, curled up like a little boy expecting a good hiding, so it certainly wasn't a joke in poor taste. Did he mean that part of him didn't work? But how could he know that without trying?

'You aren't running out on me,' she said firmly. 'You should have told me if there was something wrong with you, but we're married now, for better or worse, so you'd better explain yourself.'

'I can be a good husband in every other way,' he said, peeping at her from behind his hands. 'I can build a house, feed you, clothe you, all that. But I can't – ' He stopped in mid-sentence.

'Make love to me?' she prompted. 'Is that what you mean?'

A faint nod and a sniff confirmed this.

'But you haven't even tried,' she said in bewilderment. 'You haven't even given me a real kiss since we got married.'

There was a long silence. 'I can't bring myself to,' he said eventually.

Dulcie slumped back on the pillow, utterly perplexed. Looking back, she could now see for herself that he'd never really ever wanted to indulge in anything physical, kissing and cuddling was always prompted by her. Betty had said that passion should be there from the first kiss, and it hadn't been, she'd just been too dumb or innocent not to recognize it wasn't. But he had been passionate that night she came back from Perth, and on other occasions since. She thought about that and remembered how he always stopped suddenly. Was that what he meant by *he couldn't bring himself to*?

'Are you a poofter?' she asked.

He sprang up in bed at that, his face purple with anger. 'You what! Strewth, Dulcie, what a thing to say!'

'Then what *are* you, Ross?' she said scornfully. 'I'll tell you what I think you are! A bloody liar. You made me believe this was going to be happy ever after. You begged me to marry you when I got back from Perth. You said you needed me and wanted me. Why did you say those things if you didn't mean them?'

'I do need you, Dulcie,' he said, his voice quivering. 'You don't know how much.'

Dulcie felt as if her whole world was falling apart. She'd known this man for over four years, she thought she really knew him. Was this what Betty had been afraid of when she spoke of his coldness?

She switched off the light, got out of bed, pulled on a housecoat over her nightdress and went outside on to the veranda. Ross's cigarettes and whisky were on the table. She pulled the stopper and took a long swig, she hated the taste and it made her throat burn, but she wanted to be anaesthetized. She took another, then another, and was just on the point of throwing the bottle back into the room at him when she stopped herself.

'You can't even do that,' she thought scornfully. 'Afraid of upsetting the landlady and even him. God, you are so bloody pathetic!'

She slumped back on the couch and defiantly lit one of his cigarettes. Images of Ross kept sweeping through her mind, on his motorbike, milking the cows, driving the combine harvester, heaving the sacks of grain on to the back of the truck. Everything about him was so masculine, he could build walls, dig dams, cut down trees, mend motors. She'd believed he could do anything, she thought he was just like Bruce, a kind, decent and hard-working man with whom she could be happy for ever.

What was she going to do now? If she left him here and went home on the train alone she would be forced to explain. But it wouldn't just be to Bruce, May was there too. She couldn't bear the thought of that. Besides, how would Bruce manage without Ross? He did the work of two other men, everyone had always said that. There really was no choice but to go home tomorrow as if everything was fine.

She cried for a little while but she was reasoning with herself. If she could just forget that she'd been cheated by Ross, looking at it logically, if she hadn't ever been made love to, how could she miss it? Ross would still be her friend, the only difference being married made to people's lives was that they lived under the same roof and slept in the same bed. She remembered one of Granny's sayings, *Time sorts out most things.* Perhaps it would sort this one out too.

She went back into the room. There was enough light to see he was still awake, lying there waiting for her, his eyes glimmering in the dark like a cat's.

'What have you decided?' he asked.

'That we stay together and try to work it out. So maybe you don't want to make love to me – '

'I do,' he interrupted her. 'I just can't.'

Dulcie sighed, took off her housecoat and got into bed. 'Maybe that will change. We'll just go along as we are now and see what happens.'

'But how can I expect you to live like that?' he asked. 'It isn't fair.'

'I don't know any different, do I?' she pointed out. All at once she was bone-weary, she didn't want to talk or think about it any more. 'Now, let's go to sleep because I'm tired.' She turned out the light and lay down to show this really was the end of the conversation.

But she could feel him lying there tense and unhappy and her sympathy was aroused. 'I love you, Ross, however you are,' she whispered to him in the darkness.

He let out a big sigh and his hand reached out for hers under the covers to squeeze it. 'I'm sorry, Dulcie,' he whispered. 'You deserve more.'

Ross fell asleep long before she did. She lay there listening to his breathing and to the sound of the fan spinning above their heads. *You deserve more.* She'd had that said to her almost as many times as *Trust me,* and it sounded just as insincere. Perhaps the truth of the matter was that she'd been singled out at birth for disappointment and sadness. She supposed she would just have to learn to live with it.

Chapter Twenty

'You crook, Dulcie?' Bruce asked, giving her a sharp look. 'You can go back to bed if you are. I'm sure May won't mind me taking her to the station on her own.'

It was Dulcie's fifth day back at the farm, and she had just finished clearing away the breakfast things. May was in her old bedroom packing her case.

'I'm fine,' Dulcie smiled weakly. She knew she looked pale and had dark circles under her eyes. 'It's just so hot at nights in the caravan, that's all.'

She had braved it out, managed to convince them all that she and Ross had had a wonderful time in Kalgoorlie and she hadn't a care in the world. May's presence helped in this deception for she tended to monopolize conversations at mealtimes, each afternoon she and Dulcie went to the beach together, and in the evenings they all went out to the pub.

May was a tonic for everyone, she was effervescent, chatty, fun and daring. She had one of the new bikini swimsuits, and the sight of her exposed tummy had raised the eyebrows of all the older people of Esperance. John had taken her to the Friday night dance while she and Ross were in Kalgoorlie, and by all accounts most of the single men were desperate to dance with her. Dulcie didn't feel the least bit jealous that her sister received so much attention, she took pride in it, and was delighted that old friends like Sergeant and Mrs Collins liked her too. By day, whether Dulcie was doing her routine chores or out with her sister, she could put aside the sadness inside her. It was only the nights that were torturous, for it was hot and cramped in the caravan, and so hard to sleep when every slight touch was a reminder Ross wasn't a real husband.

Yet he was so lovely in so many other ways. He got up in the morning and made her tea, he talked to her more now than he ever had before, he had fixed up the caravan so it was like a little palace, and he'd gone out of his way to be extra specially nice to May.

But May was going back to Perth today, and it might be months before they saw one another again. Although Dulcie couldn't confide in her sister about Ross, it had been so good to have some feminine company, and she understood now why Betty had set so much store by her women friends.

'I suppose the caravan would be much hotter than the house,' Bruce said anxiously. 'Maybe you ought to come back in the house till the end of the summer?'

'No, the caravan's our home now,' Dulcie replied. She knew if she was that close to Bruce he might work out for himself what was wrong. 'Don't worry, I'll get used to the heat.'

'I've been thinking of getting Ross to build a real house for you,' Bruce said. 'The site of Sam's old house the other side of the barn would be a good spot. The caravan will be no good once you start a family.'

Dulcie's heart plummeted. In all her efforts to make everyone think she and Ross were radiantly happy she hadn't actually considered that unless the situation changed there would be no children. 'A real house would be nice,' she forced herself to agree. 'But there's no hurry, Bruce, we're fine as we are.'

May came out of the bedroom wearing blue cotton slacks and a white broderie anglaise blouse, her hair tied up in a pony-tail with a blue ribbon. She had a deep suntan now and she looked very lovely.

'Do you think this is all right for travelling in?' she asked. 'It's going to be so hot and sticky.'

'I should think it's perfect,' Dulcie said, remembering

how awful she'd found the same journey. 'But have you got a cardigan handy? It might get cold overnight.'

May nodded, peering at herself in the mirror over the fireplace. 'I've left my hat for you, Dulcie,' she said. 'I doubt I'll get a chance to wear it again, and it's so awkward to carry, but you could wear it for the christening.'

Dulcie's skin prickled uncomfortably.

'Give her a chance,' Bruce said jovially. 'She hasn't been married five minutes.'

Dulcie watched the train leaving Esperance until it was just a speck in the distance, tears running down her cheeks. She had made May enough sandwiches to feed an army, she had drinks, magazines and books to read, and she was going back to a place where she was wanted and needed, yet Dulcie was still worried she'd be as miserable on the long journey as she herself had been five years earlier, and she knew she was going to miss her company.

Bruce put his arm around her and drew her to his shoulder. 'You will see her again soon,' he reassured her. 'For all that city talk she comes out with, she was taken with life down here, she'll be back.' He wiped her face dry with his handkerchief and kissed her comfortingly on the forehead.

'What if she does go to Sydney when she's eighteen?' Dulcie said as they walked back to the car. 'We won't be able to see one another then.'

'Yes you will.' Bruce grinned at her and tweaked her cheek. 'Haven't you noticed transport is improving all the time? I wouldn't be surprised if ordinary people like you and me couldn't fly across Australia before long. There might even come a time when you could fly from here to Perth! Look how many people are coming this way to live now!'

Dulcie nodded. He was right about that, Esperance was changing rapidly. She'd heard that in 1953 the population was only 700, yet by 1959 it had more than doubled, and more were coming every week. New shops had opened in the town, houses were being built, and all the little guest-houses were having a boom time. She knew too that all the farmers were doing really well, the prices for cereals, wool, beef and lamb rising steadily. Bruce had kept increasing both her wages and the men's each year – the twelve pounds a week she got now was a far cry from ten shillings at the Masters'.

'We'll go in the milk bar and have some coffee before we go home,' Bruce said. 'It's going to be a bit on the quiet side there without May around.'

May left on Thursday, and she was due back in Perth on Saturday morning. When the telephone rang around five o'clock on Saturday afternoon, Dulcie ran to it, expecting it was May saying she'd got home safely. But it was Mrs Wilberforce.

'I'm concerned because May hasn't arrived back,' she said, her tone worried. 'Did she leave you as arranged?'

'Well yes, Mrs Wilberforce,' Dulcie said. 'I saw her on to the train myself.'

'Where is she then?' the woman asked.

'I don't know. Maybe she's just gone to see a friend in town before returning home,' Dulcie suggested.

'I shouldn't think that's very likely. Not carrying two heavy suitcases – she would just get in a taxi.'

Dulcie was about to say that maids couldn't afford to *just get in a taxi*, when she remembered May had only one suitcase. It would certainly have stuck in her mind if there had been two. Who would go away for just a week's holiday with two?

The old habit of loyalty between May and herself was too deeply ingrained for Dulcie to blurt this out. She confirmed again that May had left, and said she would telephone later tonight to see if she had turned up.

But after she'd put the phone down, Dulcie's mind spun with other possibilities. If May had set off with two suitcases, she must have left one of them at Kalgoorlie station, or even with Sadie at the hotel. There was only one reason that she'd do such a thing, and that was because she hadn't ever had any intention of returning to Perth.

The day before May left Bruce had offered to drive her to Kalgoorlie because it was quicker by road, but she'd flatly refused, saying it was too long a drive for him. At the time Dulcie had been touched by her thoughtfulness, she certainly hadn't considered her sister might have a devious plan up her sleeve.

She looked up the telephone number for Kalgoorlie station and rang it. The ticket clerk confirmed a young woman with blonde hair had picked up a case she'd left with him for over a week, and said she had bought a ticket to Sydney, intending to catch the 11 p.m. train.

Dulcie put the phone down and walked outside on to the veranda. She was stunned that her sister could be so cunning. She thought it was stupid and reckless to run out on a good job, and wondered how May would manage without a reference.

Yet setting all the practical considerations aside, she couldn't help but feel a certain admiration for her sister's pluck. It was very brave to throw security out of the window and set off to the other side of Australia when she knew no one there. But May wasn't yet eighteen and she could be picked up by the police.

Deep concern and anxiety took over as she imagined her sister sitting on that endless train journey which took several days. She would be exhausted by the time she got there, and anything could happen to her. Did she have any money? Did she have the least idea of how to go about finding a place to stay?

Ross saw her standing on the veranda and came over from the barn where he'd been working on a repair to the plough. 'Something up?' he asked as he got closer. 'You look rattled.'

Dulcie explained, and slumped down on to a seat. 'What do I do, Ross? If I tell Mrs Wilberforce the truth about where she's gone, she might contact the police. They could pick May up on the train.'

He sat next to Dulcie and put his arm around her. 'Don't worry about her, she's a survivor. She'll charm someone into looking after her, you can be sure of that. Don't tell Mrs Wilberforce what you know, May will only blame you if she gets caught. Mind you, if that woman's got even half a brain she'll work it out for herself.'

'I'm surprised she hadn't already thought of it, if May took all her clothes with her,' Dulcie said.

Ross smiled. 'May's quite an actress. You can bet your boots she thought up some good reason to take them all. Don't be mad with her, Dulc, she might have been miserable there, you don't know.'

'If she was, she would've told me,' Dulcie said dourly. 'She isn't a martyr like me. But what am I going to say to Mrs Wilberforce when I phone her?'

'Nothing,' Ross said with a shrug. 'Just make out you are as mystified as she is.'

Dulcie had a difficult conversation with Mrs Wilberforce. The woman was upset and disappointed that May thought so little of her that she could just take off without a word. Out of loyalty to her sister Dulcie didn't say she knew May had gone to Sydney, and tried to soothe Mrs Wilberforce by saying she appreciated all she'd done for May, and she thought it was a spur of the moment decision on May's part, because she was burning to get an office job in a big city.

But once Dulcie had put the phone down she burst into tears. Bruce came into the room and took her in his arms to comfort her.

'There, there,' he murmured, holding her tightly. 'I know you are upset that May behaved so recklessly, but maybe she had good reason. I for one am glad that at least she's well away from that bloody Reverend Mother.'

Dulcie looked up at him in surprise. 'What's she got to do with it? May didn't suffer at her hands the way I did.'

'I'm not so sure about that, Dulcie,' he said gently. 'Maybe she wasn't beaten as you were, but I think she was and still is afraid of that woman. She mentioned her the day before you and Ross came home.'

'What did she say?'

'That the woman had kept on telephoning, and she felt she would try to manipulate her into another job of her choosing. I reckon that's why May chose to run away now. She probably thought if she left it until she was eighteen that might be too late.'

'She never said anything like that to me,' Dulcie said, a little hurt.

'Sometimes it's easier to tell an outsider. Perhaps, too, she told me so I would pass it on to you now.'

Dulcie thought about that for a moment. 'What can I do now, Bruce? I feel so scared for her.'

'You can't do anything but wait until she contacts you. But try to look at all May has got going for her. She's got secretarial qualifications, a good personality. She's very pretty and she's clued up about people. She's used to city life too, remember. If anyone can make it in Sydney, it's her.'

Dulcie realized she must go back to Ross in the caravan. It was after eleven now and she'd said she wouldn't be long making the phone call.

'You are quite right,' she said with a deep sigh. 'And I'd better go.'

'I'll have a talk with Ross about building the house tomorrow,' Bruce said, patting her shoulder. 'It's you and him you have to concern yourself with, Dulcie, your sister can make her own life.'

Ross was in bed when Dulcie got back to the caravan, listening to her radio. It was so hot and airless in there that her spirits fell even lower. She glanced about her, feeling irritated by how cramped it was, yet when Bruce and Ross towed it here she'd been thrilled and couldn't wait to make it into a real home.

They never bothered to put the bed away during the day, there was no point as they didn't use the caravan during that time. As the bed took up the whole living space, all that was left was the little kitchen area by the door. Ross had repainted the caravan all white inside, and the kitchen cupboards pale blue. She'd made blue and white gingham curtains, and a deep blue fitted bedcover, so even with the bed down it looked neat. But the reality was that the bed dominated everything, it was the only place to sit, they even had to crawl across it to get to the cupboards where their clothes were on the other side.

She sat on the end of it now, to tell Ross what had happened.

'She'll be right,' he said, lying back on the pillows, his arms behind his head. He was wearing only his pyjama bottoms and his chest was tanned and deep golden-brown. 'She's bound to write to you soon too. Maybe one day we can go there for a holiday. They say Sydney's beaut.'

Dulcie pulled her nightdress from under the pillow and took it into the kitchen area to change. The door of the cupboard opened back to shut off the other room for privacy, and she needed it, his rejection of her in a physical way had made her begin to believe her body was repulsive.

As she took off her clothes she told Ross about Bruce suggesting he built a house. 'He said he'll talk to you about it tomorrow,' she finished up as she came back into the bedroom part to get into bed.

His face was a picture, eyes shining with excitement and delight. He hadn't looked like that since the wedding breakfast, but instead of pleasing her it made her feel even sadder. What good was a fine house if the two people who had to live in it were only like brother and sister?

He turned off the light and the radio, and put his arm around her. 'Just think, Dulc, a real house of our own!' His voice was almost squeaking with glee. 'I'll make it so pretty, everything just where you want it. We could have a big window right down to the floor so we can sit there in the evening and watch the kangaroos and the birds from our easy-chairs.'

She wished she could join in his excitement, she had so many ideas in her head for her dream house, collected together over the last three years. But she thought she'd rather live in an old shack, cooking over an open fire, and have passion, than spend the rest of her life in luxury and feeling rejected.

'Goodnight,' she whispered, turning to kiss him, and to her surprise he kissed her back the way he had when she came back from Perth. It was lovely, sweet and lingering, and she got that churned-up feeling of longing inside her again.

'I love you so much,' he whispered in the darkness and he unbuttoned her nightdress and reached for her breast.

Dulcie hardly dared breathe, she was so afraid he would stop suddenly, but he didn't, he stroked her breast and kissed her again and again, his lips moving down her neck and throat until he reached her breast and sucked on her nipple.

It was like fireworks exploding inside her. She stroked his hair, his neck and shoulders, smoothing him, loving him, yet silently begging him not to disappoint her. His hand moved down her body, found the bottom of her nightdress and slowly moved up her leg and thigh.

Her heart was racing, her mouth dry, but she could hear him moaning softly and his breath becoming louder. Tentatively his fingers stroked at her pubic hair, she could almost feel his fright at having come so far, but he didn't pull away. She moaned involuntarily as at last his finger slipped inside her, and she gave herself up to the blissful sensation, her fear vanishing.

She had never felt anything like it before, each delicate probe sent spasms throughout her entire body. If he never went beyond doing just that she could be happy for the rest of her life. But she wanted to please him too, and she lifted his face from her breast to kiss him, at the same time arching her back so he could go further inside her. He wasn't just kissing her now, but devouring her, and it was wonderful. She ran her fingernails down his spine, and her pleasure was heightened still more by his shudder of delight.

He was half over her, his mouth so eager, moving between her lips and breasts. Dulcie slid her hands down his sides to push down his pyjamas. She could feel his penis hard against her thigh, near the source of her pleasure, she slid her hand towards it, and tentatively cupped her hand around it.

All at once it went limp and as it did he drew away from her like a startled cat. His reaction was so sudden, just like a light being switched off, and for Dulcie, a sick feeling of dread replaced the bliss there had been just moments before.

'It's all right,' she murmured instinctively, as she would to a frightened child. 'I love you, everything's all right.'

But it wasn't all right. He turned his face into the pillow and she knew he was crying. Bewildered as Dulcie was, she sensed that trying to question him would only make the situation worse. She curved herself along his side, put her arm around his back and just held him.

As she lay there in the darkness, holding him, she wished that she knew more about the mechanics of love-making in humans. She knew exactly how it worked for animals, living on a farm she'd seen it all dozens of times. Clearly it worked much the same way for humans, but perhaps there was a further dimension she didn't know about. She had thought that touching his penis would give him pleasure, but clearly it had repelled him. It was her fault.

The feeling that it was all her fault grew as the months passed. Ross could not be induced to talk about what had happened that night, and he didn't touch her again. She had received only a postcard from May with a picture of Sydney Harbour Bridge. No address to write back to, just a couple of lines saying she was safe and well. If her own sister thought so little of her that she couldn't write a proper letter, it stood to reason she was lacking in something.

She missed Betty so much too. No more cosy woman-to-woman chats during the day, discussion about recipes or a new design for a quilt. Dulcie felt she could have confided her worries about Ross to her, and she would have known what to do.

The summer ended with violent storms, bringing heavy rain that turned the paddocks into lakes. Ross had dug the foundations for their house during the hot weather and he was furious that the work he had done was now wasted, the holes filled again with mud. Dulcie could keep the mud out of Bruce's house, but it was impossible to keep it out of the caravan, just a walk over to the lavatory in the bunkhouse brought it in. Sometimes at night when she was tired, she'd sit on the end of the bed and weep with frustration to see the tiny floor in the kitchen area which she'd only cleaned that morning filthy again. However careful they were to remove their shoes the minute they got inside, the mud still seemed to get on their bare feet and ended up on the sheets.

Before the rain came she'd decided she should make the evening meals for herself and Ross in the caravan. She felt that if they pretended to be a happily married couple, perhaps they'd eventually become one. It was enough hard work putting the bed away so they had a table and benches to sit on, but the little stove was temperamental, flaring up suddenly for no reason, and the meat was often raw in the middle and burnt on the outside. She could hardly blame Ross for going off to the pub later, she was so tetchy after cooking a meal and serving it in the house, then rushing over here to do it all again. On top of that the caravan was often full of smoke.

She tried cooking their meal in Bruce's house while she made the men's, and bringing it over, but that was just as much of a palaver, running backwards and forwards for something she'd forgotten. Ross still went off to the pub, and so when the rain came she gave it up and they went back to the house for meals as before. But she felt such a failure.

Once it began to get cold, the caravan was like an icebox and so was the shower in the bunkhouse. Soon she was darting over to the house in the mornings in her dressing-gown, having a shower there and dressing. That made her feel guilty too for it was like rejecting the home Ross had worked so hard on. She would linger in the house with Bruce after supper, staying longer and longer with him. She told herself she was just keeping him company and what was the harm in that?

Yet she knew there was harm, for she and Ross were locked into a circle of destructive behaviour. She knew if she was to beg him to stop going to the pub, he would, but that would mean she'd have to stay with him in the caravan. While he was drinking he wasn't going to make any attempt to sort out their marital problems; if he kept away from her, she could pretend they didn't exist.

Sometimes Bruce would make a concerned remark about the way things were, but Dulcie didn't think he had any real idea of the gravity of the situation, for Ross going off to the pub wasn't unusual behaviour. Few Australian men were homebodies, drinking with their mates after work was considered quite normal.

Bruce had always liked a drink himself, but lack of money to spend on it for most of his marriage had meant that by the time he did have the money, he had lost the urge. He was glad of Dulcie's company too, sometimes they watched television, sometimes she helped him with the accounts, or they just talked. He still missed Betty so much, and as time passed, Dulcie was becoming more and more the daughter he'd never had, and she looked upon him as a father.

Towards the end of the winter, Ross began working on their house in earnest. He would get up an hour earlier to lay a row of bricks before starting the milking, any spare time during the day and he was back to it. He lost interest in going to the pub, after supper he would take a couple of kerosene lamps out there with him to continue, his bedtime reading was books on building.

These were times of happiness between Dulcie and him. By day she would help him when she could, passing bricks, mixing concrete, and the shared project pushed their problems aside. Ross was never more content than when he had hard work to do – he flourished on it, smiling and whistling all day. He was more demonstrative with his affection for her, he talked and laughed readily. Dulcie could pretend then that everything was fine, she didn't attempt to try to coerce him into love-making any longer, and quite often days would pass without her even thinking about it.

Yet it was around early October that she began to see he was driven in a way other men weren't. She studied John, Bob, Bruce and other men who called at the farm, and noted that although their work was very important to them, it wasn't their whole life the way it was with Ross. They looked forward to the fortnightly Friday night dances, the annual ball at the Bijou theatre was eagerly anticipated, as were picnics at the beach, parties and barbecues. In winter football was the sole topic of conversation, for every small town had its team and every single man went to see the Saturday matches even if it meant driving 100 miles or more. But Ross showed little or no interest in any of these things. His love was work, and the harder he drove himself the happier he was.

And so Dulcie wrote to a problem page in a women's magazine, asking for their advice. Even if she'd been able to get over her embarrassment at talking about such an intimate subject with someone she knew, she felt she couldn't admit such things to anyone who also knew Ross. So she poured it all out in a letter and enclosed a stamped addressed envelope for a personal reply.

The harvest, her birthday, Christmas, the new year of 1961 and their first wedding anniversary on 8 January passed before the reply came. Bruce came in with the post while Dulcie was doing some ironing. 'Have we resorted to writing letters to ourselves now?' he joked as he handed her the envelope addressed by herself.

'I wrote to a magazine in Sydney,' she said, blushing furiously. 'I hoped they might be able to help me find out where May is.'

She felt ashamed of telling him a lie, and it shocked her she could think one up so fast. Perhaps she getting more like May.

Bruce laid his hand on her shoulder. 'She'll get in touch when she's ready,' he said. 'The truth of the matter is that she's probably having such a bloody good time she's forgotten her big sister will be worried.'

'But it's a whole year now,' Dulcie said, glad to unburden this anxiety, if not her main one.

'A year goes past very quickly when you're having fun. You and Ross should get out and enjoy yourselves more. I've just been talking to him, he's almost ready to put the roof on. I think we ought to throw a roof-raising party like we used to do in the old days.'

Dulcie smiled. 'That sounds good. Do we have it in the house?'

Bruce chuckled. 'No, of course not. We have a picnic or a barbecue, all the men help put the roof on, the women sit about and chat. Once it's done we all celebrate with drinking and dancing.'

'That would be fun,' she said with enthusiasm, thinking of how many of Bruce and Betty's old friends she could invite.

'I'd better get going,' Bruce said, leaving her letter on the ironing board. 'We'll talk about it over supper tonight, and get a list of guests together.'

The minute Bruce went out, Dulcie snatched up the letter and took it into the bathroom in case anyone came in while she was reading it. She perched on the lavatory and pulled out the letter.

Dear Mrs Rawlings, she read. *Thank you for your letter, I'm sorry I have taken so long to reply. It must be very distressing*

*that you have been unable to consummate your marriage, but
far more so for your husband. You say he is driven by work,
and I would say this is caused purely by what he perceives to
be his sexual failure.*

*My advice to you is to just be patient and loving. Never
belittle or nag him, and let him feel the constancy of your
love for him. When he does appear to wish for some kind of
lovemaking, make no demands on him, just accept what he
offers and don't question him if he is unable to complete the
act. You said that he lost his erection when you touched it. It
may be that you were too rough, or hasty. It is quite usual for
men to dislike women taking the dominant role. As for him
refusing to talk about all of this, I am surprised you imagine
other men could! By asking him to speak of it you are giving
him the message that you find him disappointing, and therefore
he is even less likely to try again for fear of further failure.*

*You have only been married a year, and it seems to me you
have been blessed in other directions in that your husband is
hardworking and kind to you. Be patient, show him how much
you love him, allow yourself to cuddle up to him without any
expectations, and I am sure in time his problem will disappear.*

I hope my advice is helpful,
Yours sincerely, Aunt Angela

Dulcie read the letter through several times, then tore it
into pieces and flushed it down the lavatory. She was very
disappointed, and she knew without being an expert that
all Aunt Angela had done was make her feel even more
guilty and responsible than she did before. She sat there
for some little time thinking about it. She was patient
and loving, she never belittled Ross or nagged him, but
whatever this woman said, she didn't feel she could keep
it up indefinitely.

Surely she had a right to be happy? To have children,
and to look to the future with optimism?

'I should never have married him,' she whispered to
herself. 'Now I'm trapped because he's building that house
and I'll have to stay for ever.'

But you love him, a little voice in her head reminded her. *There must be some reason why he's the way he is.*

'What did the magazine suggest about finding May?' Bruce asked at supper.

Dulcie gulped. She had forgotten about that. 'Um, nothing much,' she said, searching desperately for something sensible to say. 'They said I could try putting an advert in the Sydney paper asking her to come forward,' she added hastily.

'Why don't you try it?' Ross asked, putting one hand over hers. 'I hate to see you so worried about her.'

'I doubt May ever read a newspaper in her life,' John said. 'But someone else might write and tell you where she is.'

'Perhaps I'll try it then,' Dulcie said. 'Now, what about this roof-raising party? Are we going to organize something?'

Dulcie came out of the house carrying two large pitchers of orange squash and smiled at the scene in front of her. Around fifteen couples and their children were scattered around the front garden. The older ladies were sitting on chairs under the shade of the tree, plates of sandwiches, flans and cake on their laps, the younger ones in groups on the grass, the men gathered around another tree by the side of the track up to the house where they had set up the beer on a table. Children were scooting around everywhere and a couple of prams holding babies were being rocked by their mothers as they chatted. Everyone looked very happy to be there.

'This chicken is beaut!' old Mrs Scarsdale, a close friend of Betty's, called out to Dulcie, waving a drumstick in her hand. 'I'd say it's as good as Betty used to make.'

'Well, thank you, Mrs Scarsdale,' Dulcie said as she went over to top up empty glasses for the children and the women who weren't drinking beer. 'I wish she was here today with us, she loved parties.'

The roof had been put on the house over three hours ago, amidst much laughter from the women and subdued cursing from the men. It was a tin one, as almost all roofs were here, and once it was on and secured, everyone had cheered, toasts had been made, then Ross picked Dulcie up in his arms and carried her inside. 'Well, Mrs Rawlings?' he joked. 'Does it meet with your approval?'

It wasn't anywhere near finished inside of course. The windows had to go in, the walls had to be plastered, but the floor was in, and the veranda outside, and at last it was beginning to look like a real house rather than a pen for animals.

There were two bedrooms, a bathroom and a large living-room, with the kitchen opening off from it. The windows in the living-room went right down to the floor just as Ross had said, so they could sit and watch the kangaroos at night.

'It's almost perfect, Mr Rawlings,' she said, kissing him on the lips. 'So just go on to perfect it, and make it snappy!'

'Great tucker, Dulcie!' Steve, a stockman from a neighbouring farm, called out. 'If Ross ever gets tired of you I'll take you on, cooks like you are hard to find.'

Dulcie laughed. She'd had so many compliments like that today, and ones from men who said how pretty she was. She was wearing the dress May had insisted she bought in Perth, with the net petticoat underneath, and she had put her hair up the way May used to do hers. It was lovely to be the centre of attention for once.

Bruce was sitting with the older ladies and she went to ask him if he wanted another beer. It was good to see him looking happy again, and Betty's old friends were all making a fuss of him. 'I'll just have some of that squash,' he said. 'You know when you're getting old when you can't hold the beer any more.'

'Old age brings its own rewards,' she teased him. 'At least you get a seat in the shade and don't have to stand about with all the younger men boasting about your car or your dog.'

Bruce beckoned to her to come closer. 'Have you talked to the English bloke yet?'

'Yes, he's nice,' Dulcie replied. 'He and his wife were very touched we invited them because they don't know many people.'

Doreen and Mike Perkins and their children were one of the many new families to the area. Dulcie had met Doreen in the shop in town, and when she heard her English accent she stopped to talk and introduce herself. Doreen and Mike had only been in Australia two years, and they'd bought a farm up at Gibson.

'He's a damn fool,' Bruce whispered. 'Talking about putting a swimming-pool in.'

Dulcie laughed, she had heard Mike talking about it to the other men, but they'd soon put him straight that water around here couldn't be wasted on something so frivolous. Yet she sympathized with the man, it was so hot in the summer, and it took English people a long time to really value water. Just thinking that reminded her she no longer thought of herself as English. Doreen and Mike had been surprised to discover that she was, she sounded and acted so Australian.

'Maybe the swimming-pools will come when the planes do,' she teased Bruce, and playfully tipped his cotton hat right over his eyes. 'Or maybe hell will freeze over first!'

'You look and sound happier today,' he said suddenly. 'Is that because the house is nearly ready? Or just because you've got some company?'

'Both, I expect,' she said lightly.

'You make sure you arrange to meet some of these young wives again,' he said, looking sharply at her. 'The house alone won't give you what you need.'

She wondered how much he'd picked up about her and Ross. A man as astute as Bruce who had had such a long and loving marriage wasn't likely to be fooled for long. But she was saved from making any further comment because one of the babies in a pram started to cry. It was Doreen's youngest, born here in Esperance, and knowing Doreen had gone into the house with another child to use the bathroom, Dulcie went to the pram and picked the baby up.

She had never held a small baby before, not since May was tiny anyway, yet she instinctively supported its tiny head and laid it gently against her shoulder, patting its back soothingly. 'There, there, Mummy will be back soon.'

Dulcie had no idea if it was what she said that triggered her tears, a reminder of her own mother, or the desire for a baby of her own. But all at once she was crying and she couldn't stop.

Bruce got out of his seat and came to her. 'Whatever's the matter?' he asked.

'I don't know,' she sobbed, trying to hide her face against the baby's back.

'Come inside with me,' he said, and taking her elbow he led her away. Doreen was just coming out as they got to the door. She was a small, plump woman with short dark hair and kind eyes. 'Has she been playing up?' she asked, then seeing Dulcie's tears, she moved closer. 'Shall I take her, or was it her made you cry?'

Dulcie nodded. 'She's so beautiful. It's so good to hold her.'

Bruce was just standing there saying nothing, but taking the scene in. 'Can she borrow her for a bit?' he asked Doreen.

'By all means,' she said. 'But call me if she starts yelling.'

'Come in my room,' Bruce said once they were indoors. 'We can talk privately there.'

Dulcie sat down on the chair by the window, and she remembered how often she'd sat right here when Betty was ill. She'd learnt so much in this room, not just about Betty's life, but herself too. She'd put away the sadness of her childhood, grown into an adult as she bathed and cared for her friend. She thought the self-esteem she found within these walls would stay with her for ever, but she knew it was crumbling now.

'I've seen that look on Betty's face so often when she held a baby,' Bruce said as he closed the door. 'But you are young, Dulcie, you can have one of your own. So I can only think you are crying because you don't believe that.'

Dulcie lowered the baby girl to her knees and held the two tiny hands in her own, looking down at the sweet little face with its rosebud mouth and button nose.

'I suppose so,' she said reluctantly.

'You've only been married a year,' Bruce said, sitting down on his bed and looking at her. 'Now, I know I've no right to pry, you don't have to tell me anything if you don't want to, but I've known for a long time there was something badly wrong between you and Ross, and you might feel better if you confide in me.'

Dulcie glanced up at him. He was so big, he made her think of a saggy, baggy, well-loved old teddy bear sometimes – the way his stomach crept over his belt, the bags under his eyes and the brown liver spots on his hands and face. All so dear and familiar, and such a wealth of understanding in his fading blue eyes. She enjoyed so much looking at old pictures of him when he was young and handsome, dashing astride a horse, wearing long boots and a slouch hat. The ones of him in uniform showed a man who would have died cheerfully for the country he loved. He had done so much, seen so much, he'd taken tragedy and poverty in his stride and worked his way through them. She knew that whatever she told him today would go no further than these four walls. She felt too that he'd understand both her and Ross.

'I want to, Bruce,' she whispered. 'But it's not easy to talk to a man about things like this.'

'I was married a very long time,' he said gently. 'Betty and I shared everything, I'm sure you could have confided in her if she was still with us, so pretend I'm her, and maybe that will make it easier.'

'We can't have a baby,' she blurted out. 'Because we don't do it.' She blushed furiously, bending her face over the baby.

'Is it you who doesn't want to, or Ross?' he asked quietly.

'It's not that he doesn't want to, he's not a poofter,' she said quickly. 'He just can't.'

'I see,' he said, his voice grave. 'Can he talk about it to you?'

He had opened the floodgates for her and it all came tumbling out in a torrent. She didn't say much about the mechanics of it, only that Ross got to a point when he just froze and cried. Most of what she said centred on her own guilty feelings that it was all her fault. She even told Bruce about the letter from Aunt Angela and her advice.

'But how long can I go on being patient for?' she implored him. 'He works all hours to avoid being with me. Once the house is finished, what will he do then? I feel so wretched and ugly because of it.'

Bruce lifted the baby, who had now dropped off to sleep again, on to the bed. Then, taking Dulcie's hand, he pulled her up and hugged her tightly.

'You poor love,' he murmured by her ear. 'I never guessed it was that, I just thought you were fighting. But I think your Aunt Angela is living in the last century, you mustn't take the blame for this.'

'But what do I do, Bruce? I do love him, we've got so much in common, he's my friend.'

'I don't know,' Bruce said thoughtfully. He sat down on the chair and let her sit on the bed. 'It's not anything I've come across before. I've heard of men not be able to do it when they're drunk, but that's different. It strikes me he needs a doctor, one of those who goes into what happens in your head.'

'A psychiatrist?' she said in alarm. 'They only deal with barmy people.'

Bruce half smiled. 'Well, there's plenty of men would say he is barmy if he can't make love to you!'

Dulcie blushed. 'He had a terrible time at Bindoon, the orphanage he was in,' she said. 'Could that be something to do with it?'

'Maybe,' Bruce said. 'But it strikes me that if he really loves you, it should be him who tries to find out what's wrong with him, not you. No one should have to be responsible for someone's else's happiness.'

'Not even when they are married?'

Bruce shook his head. 'I agree if one of you is ill or injured the other one should take care of you, that's part of the deal. But if he won't talk about this, won't get help, he isn't being fair to you.'

'I can't leave him, Bruce,' she said, tears starting up in her eyes. 'He needs me too much.'

Bruce sighed. 'You've got to make him talk about it then. There's no other way. Be firm and say unless he does, you have no choice but to end the marriage. It wouldn't even be divorce, in cases like this the marriage is just annulled.'

'I can't threaten him!'

'Sometimes it's the only way to deal with certain problems,' Bruce said sadly. 'I know he loves you. I don't think he'd stand by and let you go.'

'But I might make him worse,' she argued.

'He's got to face whatever demons are inside him some day. But let's go and have a cup of tea now – put all this aside and enjoy yourself. Who knows, putting the roof on the house might even bring him right!'

Dulcie smiled. Bruce was ever the optimist, that was almost certainly what had brought him through to where he was today.

'You won't be tempted to say anything to him?' she asked.

He tightened his lips together. 'My lips are sealed,' he muttered through them.

Dulcie laughed. 'I'd better take this baby back to her mum.'

'Just a minute.' Bruce caught her face between his two hands, and kissed her on the forehead.

'What's that for?' she asked.

'You're a special girl, Dulcie. Don't forget that.'

Chapter Twenty-one

Pale winter sunshine slanted through the end window of the living-room, casting a beam across the part of the floor Dulcie was polishing. She sat back on her heels for a moment, looking at the room with pride.

Ross had finished the house at the end of March, and they'd moved in immediately. With money they had saved, they bought a bed, cooker and refrigerator. But since then they had added other bits and pieces, hand-me-downs from neighbours, including a three-piece suite, and a couple of rugs.

It was like heaven to Dulcie, and she knew it was to Ross too. Everywhere was painted cream, the three-piece suite was mossy green, and one of the neighbours had given them a beautiful old jarrah wood coffee table, which Ross had lovingly sanded down and revarnished. The table and chairs didn't match and they were poor quality, but Ross had varnished them, and Dulcie had made smart piped cushions for the chair seats. When the sun came in during the late afternoon the small side window, with a view across the paddocks, was a good place to sit. The big window Ross had promised had turned into glazed doors, so they could open them right up in the summer. The view there was of the lake in the distance, and just as Ross had predicted, it was a perfect place from which to view wildlife.

Dulcie had turned to painting and drawing since they moved in, and Ross had framed one of her pictures and hung it on the wall above the fireplace. It was of the lake in winter when the gum trees grew right out of the water. Everyone who had seen it remarked on how she'd captured the eeriness of it. While Dulcie didn't really think it was as good as they claimed, she was pleased with it.

It was late August now, and a very chilly afternoon. She would have to go over to Bruce's in a moment and start cooking the supper, but she just wanted to get the floor finished first. Ross had sanded the floorboards, sealed and varnished them. They really didn't need polishing, only wiping over, but she liked the smell of polish and the feeling she was taking good care of the house.

She and Ross ate with Bruce, John and Bob most nights, because it was easier for her to cook only once. But on Sundays they all came here, and she loved preparing a big roast, with a special pudding too.

The excitement of moving into the house and turning it into a real home had taken Dulcie's mind off the problem with Ross. At times she could even forget there was one. Yet sadly it *was* still there.

She had taken Bruce's advice and tried to make Ross talk about it, but it was hopeless, he just walked away from her, or if they were in bed, turned his back on her. The suggestion he spoke to a doctor about it sent him into a dark sullen rage for days. So Dulcie had fallen back on Aunt Angela's suggestions, remaining calm, passive and non-confrontational. On the rare times Ross instigated love-making and froze half-way through, she found herself resigned rather than tortured. While she hadn't given up all hope that one day things might change for the better, she tended to look at all the good parts of their marriage, and ignore the rest. They didn't fight or argue, Ross was appreciative of everything she did for him, and it was he who encouraged her to start painting and to become friends with Doreen, the woman she'd met on the day of the roof-raising. Dulcie often drove over to visit her in the afternoon and played with her children. In the evenings she painted or sewed, and Ross busied himself making something.

He was a marvel, he could make anything. She only had to say she wanted a bedside cabinet, a chest of drawers or some shelves, and he produced it. He worked in the spare bedroom mainly, as they had no furniture to put in there. But he had plans for building a shed on the side of the house next January when there wasn't so much work to do on the farm.

On finishing the floor, Dulcie set the rugs straight, then slipped on a jumper before going over to Bruce's. As she walked in, Bruce looked up from the table where he was doing some paperwork.

'So what choice morsels have you got in store for us tonight?' he asked. 'Is it mutton or corned beef?'

This was his favourite joke, based on the time when that was all farmers ate. They could buy almost anything in Esperance now, including, at a price, the ready prepared frozen food which had once seemed a million light years away. Dulcie didn't buy it, she thought it was too extravagant, and besides, there was a good variety of fresh food available now.

'Toad-in-the-hole,' she said. Bruce used to laugh every time she said that name. She supposed sausages baked in a Yorkshire pudding was an English dish, as Granny had often made it. Bruce teased her now by calling it Dingo-in-the-well, or Rabbit-in-the-trap, but whatever it was called, all the men liked it.

'Beaut,' he said, rubbing his stomach. 'I've been thinking about food all day. I always do when I've got paperwork to catch up on. By the way, there's a letter for you. John brought the post in a while ago, I didn't see there was one for you immediately or I'd have brought it over.'

He rummaged under some papers and pulled it out. 'From someone who doesn't know you've got married, it's addressed to Miss Taylor.'

The only post Dulcie ever got was from mail order companies, but seeing this envelope was handwritten she almost snatched it from his hand and ripped it open.

The address at the top was from someone in Sydney.

Dear Dulcie, she read. *I find myself in a difficult predicament, a part of me tells me to mind my own business, but the other keeps telling me I must write to you. This is a difficult letter for me to write, for reasons I will explain as I go along, but finally I decided to follow my hunch, and contact you with regard to your sister May. Firstly please excuse me addressing you as Dulcie alone, but I do not know your married name. Though in fact I saw you once at your wedding in Kalgoorlie . . .*

'It's from someone who knows May, he met me too in Kalgoorlie,' she burst out to Bruce.

He looked up at her in surprise. 'Stone the crows,' he exclaimed. 'Well, hurry up and read it. Don't keep me in suspense!'

Dulcie fumbled for a chair as she read on.

I was the man in a cream suit May danced with out on the veranda at the Old Australia.

I didn't expect at that time to ever see your sister again, but to my surprise when I was waiting for the Sydney train a few days later, there she was complete with luggage. To cut a long story short, we travelled together, and when we arrived in Sydney, I offered her a bed at my house as she hadn't got anything organized.

She stayed with me for most of that year, during which time she found secretarial work in the city. I have to admit at this point I had fallen in love with her, and would have married her at any time, but in November she disappeared, without any prior warning, not even an explanatory note.

I called where she worked, to find she'd left there some weeks earlier. I went to everyone she knew, but could find no trace of her.

Clearly she didn't return my affections, so I eventually decided to cut my losses and stop looking for her. But then in July of this year, a friend told me he'd seen her in the King's Cross area of Sydney. The strangest thing was that he said she was pushing a pram!

I am an artist, and not the most organized, conventional or smart man. But even I could work out that if the baby she was pushing was hers (I have since ascertained it most definitely is), then I could be the father. But at that time, without any proof it was her child, only surprised, and somewhat hopeful because she was still here in the city, I searched around my house looking for anything she might have left behind. I was looking for a diary, an address book, anything that might give me a new lead.

What I did find shocked me to the core. A small bundle of letters fallen behind a chest of drawers, all addressed to May, from you, most to an address in Perth, but a few in her last year at St Vincent's orphanage.

Their contents turned everything May had told me about herself upside down. She said that you both came from a well-to-do family in Worcestershire, that you'd left first to come to Australia, and May had followed you later once you became engaged to the farmer whom I'd seen in Kalgoorlie. She told me a great deal more too, depicting you as some kind of evil fiend. But as I read your lovely and often poignant letters to May I saw the truth.

Any sensible man would have dismissed her from his mind entirely at that point, but I found I couldn't. Which is why I checked hospital records to discover if she had given birth. She had, a little boy on 5 May of this year.

It transpires May is far younger than I believed, she is cunning and I suspect more than a little unbalanced. I do not say this to hurt your feelings, Dulcie, but to lay my cards on the table. I hope that you share my conviction that any child should be protected and brought up in a secure and loving home.

Maybe this baby isn't mine. But that is almost immaterial, because there is still a little mite out there with her in King's Cross, a dubious place at best, and I fear for its safety. I have recently managed to discover May's address, and how she is supporting herself, but that leaves me with even more anxiety. I believe that if I go there, it is very likely she will just vanish again. A letter either from me or you will probably have the same effect. The only thing I can think of which would work *is for you to take her by surprise and call on her. I believe if she was confronted by you in person, she would not only let you see the baby, but she might be persuaded to think of its future welfare.*

I know it is asking a great deal of you to come all the way to Sydney. But the love you show for her in your letters prompts me to ask this, and I am quite certain you have been very anxious about her since the day she left your farm. There is of course a small chance that she has already contacted you, if so please forgive me for spilling out information which you might find distressing. But my hunch is that May is much too ashamed to write to you, just as she is to me.

Yours sincerely,
Rudolph Jameson

Dulcie was shaking by the time she finished the letter. Silently she passed it over to Bruce, sank down on a chair and held her head in her hands.

The man in the cream suit. She remembered him so clearly. Well over six foot tall, and she thought in his middle thirties. A trifle overweight, strong features and a booming laugh. He sounded English in his letter, well educated, and by the tone of it, a decent man. She thought it was likely that May had latched on to him, assuming he was rich.

But artists weren't rich, and if it took him months to find those letters he probably lived in squalor. Was that why May had left him?

Bruce finished reading the letter and put it down. 'Strewth!' he exclaimed, running his hands through his white hair. 'What on earth can I say, Dulcie?'

'Do you believe him?' she asked. 'It couldn't be a hoax, could it?'

Bruce looked perplexed. 'It sounds dinkum to me. He looked like a real gent that day in Kalgoorlie, and he's an educated bloke by the sound of it. But putting the baby aside for a moment. Has May made up whoppers like that before?'

'Not as far as I know,' Dulcie said. 'She was always a bit deceitful and cunning. But she wasn't like it here or in Perth. I thought she'd grown out of it.'

'There was no reason for her to tell any lies here, we all knew the truth about her situation,' Bruce said evenly.

Dulcie's mind felt fuzzy, she couldn't take it all in. 'A little boy, he'll be nearly four months old now!' she exclaimed. 'He can't have made that up, we could check it. But I just can't imagine May having a baby, everything she ever said made me think she'd be too set on having a good time to risk getting herself into trouble.'

Bruce put his hand on her shoulder and squeezed it in silent understanding at her shock. 'Accidents can happen, even to people who think they know how to avoid them. The man's put his phone number on here. How about I phone him after supper and have a man-to-man talk with him?' he suggested.

Dulcie agreed this was a good idea.

'But before I do that maybe we could find out a little more about him. There's that artist woman in town who showed her stuff in the summer. She comes from Sydney, doesn't she?'

'Jennifer Alcott,' Dulcie said, she'd spoken to her herself when she first took up painting. She picked up Rudolph's letter again, looking at the address. 'She might have heard of him, if nothing else she might be able to tell you what Watson's Bay where he lives is like, and about King's Cross.'

They had a cup of tea together and then Dulcie said she would get on with making the supper. Bruce said he'd phone Jennifer.

As Dulcie whipped up the batter for the Toad-in-the-hole, she cried. While she had worried about May when she first disappeared, she had believed she was level-headed enough to manage on her own. And now a baby!

But why had May told all those lies about her? What possible reason could she have for betraying her only

473

sister in such a way? She wondered too what Rudolph meant by King's Cross being a dubious place. Did he think May was in some kind of danger?

Bruce came into the kitchen just as she was starting to peel some potatoes. 'Rudolph Jameson is a very well-known and respected artist,' he said, putting one hand on Dulcie's shoulder. 'Jennifer said she'd been to one of his exhibitions but never met him personally. He is English. Watson's Bay where he lives is a small, rather select place at the end of Sydney Bay. Jennifer said it's the kind of place any artist would want to live, but few do because they couldn't afford it.'

Dulcie was relieved to hear that. 'King's Cross?'

Bruce frowned. 'A red light district.'

Dulcie looked puzzled.

'Prostitutes, strip clubs, that kind of thing,' Bruce said sheepishly.

'May's living somewhere like that, with a baby!' Dulcie's voice rose in horror and she turned deathly pale. 'She wouldn't, she couldn't do that, could she?' she asked in a whisper.

'You can live in a place without being part of what goes on there,' Bruce said quickly. 'It's probably a cheap place to live where people don't ask too many questions.'

Bruce's explanation made sense. Dulcie imagined that an unmarried mother wouldn't find it easy to find a decent place to live, yet as she continued with cooking the supper, her mind turned back to that evening in Perth when May had taken her to the hotel. May had been so relaxed with those men, it was as though she'd done it dozens of times before. Even down here Dulcie had seen the ease with which she flirted with men, and thinking back to odd knowledgeable remarks she had made on both occasions, it was very unlikely she had been a virgin then.

'That doesn't mean she could sell herself to men,' she told herself firmly.

Dulcie and Bruce told Ross and the other two men about

the letter over supper. All three men read it in turn. John remembered more than anyone about the man at the wedding because he'd been dancing up at that end of the veranda.

'May was coming on to him,' he admitted. 'It was like none of us existed the moment she saw him. If you remember, she hadn't set the date for her return journey at that point either. It was only when she got back here she said she was going to catch the Thursday train.'

'You mean she intended to see him again?' Dulcie said.

John shrugged. 'It looks that way to me. Of course, she must have been planning to go anyway, or she wouldn't have left the case at Kalgoorlie. But I don't reckon it was coincidence she bumped into him.'

'What was the bloke doing in Kalgoorlie anyway?' Ross said. 'Weird place for an artist to be!'

'He'd been up to Alice Springs,' John said. 'I heard him talking about the "Rattler".'

Dulcie nodded. The 'Rattler' was the train from Kalgoorlie to Alice Springs. It wasn't a journey for the faint-hearted, but she had read somewhere that artists were always going out there to see Ayers Rock and the Aboriginal people who lived around it.

'I reckon the bloke's a brick short of a full load,' Ross said suddenly. 'You can bet your life May's shacked up with another younger bloke and he's just hopping mad and wants to make trouble for her.'

Dulcie looked at Ross. His eyes were narrowed, his mouth set in a straight line. She had expected him to be as shocked as she was, but he sounded furious and that was puzzling.

'I don't believe anyone intent on causing trouble would write a letter like that,' she said. 'He'd just say all the nasty things and leave it at that. He sounds really worried about the baby. I think there's something more he knows about May which he hasn't said too.'

'I agree with you there, Dulc,' John said. 'Look, I liked

May, but if she hadn't been your sister, I reckon I'd have been wary of her.'

'Why, John?' Dulcie asked.

He looked a little sheepish.

'Go on,' she urged him, knowing his experience with women. 'Say what you think, I won't be offended.'

John sighed. 'Well, she ain't sweet and kind like you, Dulc. I put her down as a girl on the make.'

'If she's like that, then surely she would have stayed with this bloody Rudolph?' Ross interrupted. 'I reckon him and you lot are all a mob of sticky beaks. It's her life and she can live it how she chooses.'

'She's just a kid still,' Bob said unexpectedly – he hadn't said one word up until now. 'I think you ought to go there, Dulcie, and find her.'

'Oh no,' Ross roared out, slapping his hand hard on the table. 'Dulcie's not going traipsing all the way to Sydney just because some ponce writes to her. If May's got herself in a mess, it's up to her to get herself out of it, and I don't believe she has or she would have got in touch with Dulcie.'

'She might be too ashamed to.' Dulcie frowned at Ross, she couldn't understand why he was being so nasty. 'Why are you being so hard? You're getting muddled!'

'I'm not muddled,' he yelled, making everyone look at him askance. 'It's perfectly clear to me. I'm not having my wife going thousands of miles to check on some bloody selfish little tart.'

'Don't you *dare* speak to me like that,' Dulcie shouted back.

'Calm down, both of you,' Bruce said, his eyes full of concern. 'I want you both to think of the real issue here.'

'The baby,' Bob said quietly. 'That's the real issue. Is May looking after it properly?'

'Bob's hit the nail right on the head,' Bruce said. 'We don't know Rudolph, and he's a grown man so he's hardly our concern. May *has* been selfish and reckless, and there's a certain truth in what Ross says that if she's made her bed, she must lie in it. But a baby is a small, helpless little thing, and you of all people, Ross, should know what can happen to children whose mothers for some reason or another can't look after them. Now tell me, Ross, are you really prepared to refuse to let your wife travel to Sydney to check that her nephew is safe and well cared for?'

There was complete silence as everyone waited for Ross to answer, not a click of a knife and fork, hardly a breath.

He was struggling internally, Dulcie could see a tick under his right eye, his brow furrowing, his lower lip quivering. She guessed he was thinking how different it might have been for himself and his brothers if there had been some relative who cared.

'But Dulcie's not used to cities,' he blurted out eventually. 'May could be living with some ape who won't like Dulcie turning up, it could be dangerous.'

'You're forgetting I was brought up in one of the biggest cities in the world,' Dulcie said indignantly. 'I know how to be tactful, so why should anyone resent me turning up? All I need to know is if May and the baby are safe and well. Once I've established that I'll come on home.'

Bruce got up from the table and looked down at Ross. 'I'll telephone Jameson now. Will you trust my judgement to work out whether the bloke is okay? None of us can go with her, we're all needed here.'

Ross's lip curled and Dulcie knew he was never going to let her go with his approval, but suddenly she didn't care.

'I trust your judgement, Bruce,' she said, looking right into the older man's eyes. 'You phone him.'

Two nights later Dulcie was standing on the platform at Kalgoorlie station with Bruce beside her, waiting for the eleven o'clock train. As they looked down the track towards the east, there was complete darkness, not a flicker of light beyond the station sheds. She knew the journey would take her right across the vast Nullarbor Plain, almost 2,000 miles of desert-like emptiness before she saw any farmland again.

It was biting cold, and she shivered and pulled the collar of her coat up around her neck. Bruce had bought her a first-class ticket so she would have a sleeping berth and three meals a day. She might have been excited if it hadn't been for the thought of Ross sulking at home.

'Don't worry about Ross,' Bruce said, as if he'd picked up on her thoughts. 'He's being childish and it will do you both good to be parted for a while. He's got to learn to give, and you've got to learn that you are entitled to take.'

A whistle blew down the track and the train drew into the station. 'I'll phone you,' she said, standing on tiptoe to kiss his cheek. 'Don't you worry about me. I'll be fine.'

Bruce got on to the train with her, for it wouldn't be leaving for an hour. The steward checked her ticket, took her case from Bruce and led them down a narrow corridor to the sleeping compartment.

'You've got a double all to yourself,' he said with a wide and friendly grin. 'The first class is half empty on this trip, so there's only one sitting for meals. Would you like early morning tea?'

Bruce spoke for her, saying she would, and the steward opened the cabin door. The bottom bunk was pulled down and made up ready for her, and the steward showed her the washbasin and toilet which ingeniously pulled down from the wall.

Bruce sat down on the bunk.

'It's comfy,' he grinned. 'Reckon you'll be as snug as a bug in here.'

Dulcie was impressed by the starched sheets, the shiny wood panelling and the many little cupboards. 'It's like being back in the caravan,' she said gleefully.

'I really ought to go,' Bruce said. 'Why don't you put your stuff away and wander down to get yourself a drink before you turn in?'

'Okay,' she said, remembering he had a long drive back.

Bruce got up from the bunk, filling the confined space. He held out his arms for one last hug. 'Whatever happens in Sydney, and I mean whatever,' he said gruffly against her hair, 'just remember we are friends. You can tell me anything, I'll support any decision you make, even if that turns out to be that you don't want to come back.'

'Of course I'll come back, silly,' she said, moving back from him a little to look at his face.

He had an expression she couldn't quite read.

'Situations can change us,' he said, patting her cheek tenderly.

'Go on with you now,' she laughed, giving him a playful nudge towards the door. 'Sydney won't change me, I'll sort out May and be back before you know it.'

He kissed her on the cheek, pressed her silently to him one last time and left. She watched as he walked along the narrow corridor, his shoulders were so wide he had to half turn in places. She knew just by the slump of his shoulders that he was afraid she wasn't going to come back, and that mystified her.

Dulcie loved the train ride. It was wonderful to wake up in the morning, pull up the blind and watch the scenery, knowing she didn't have to get up unless she wanted to. But the thought of a breakfast cooked for her was too appealing, and off she'd go to the dining car. She found herself meeting and chatting to people from all over. Many were Australians, but she met English, Americans and New Zealanders too. Some were going to visit relatives, others had business in Melbourne, Adelaide or Sydney, some were just travelling around Australia. Because she was on her own many of them were especially kind, asking her to join them for meals, or to go into the saloon and have a chat. She didn't spend half as much time reading as she'd expected to.

The dreary wasteland of the Nullarbor Plain eventually gave way to farmland, and she laughed with delight as kangaroos hopped along beside the train. She saw so many birds, flocks of galahs, pretty little parakeets, and dozens of other varieties unknown to her. After the big lunch she would lie down in her cabin to read, for she often fell asleep, and as the days crept by she realized this was the first time in her life she'd been able just to relax and please herself.

Often she sat staring mindlessly out of the window at the vast, empty spaces, and she would remember how she'd loved to look at the map of Australia back at St Vincent's. Yet that map had given her no idea of the huge distances. The whole of England could fit in between Perth and Esperance, but that was just a small hop compared with the distance between Perth and Sydney. She would wake in the morning to see the scenery hadn't changed from the night before, although they might have travelled another 400 miles. And still the train kept going.

She found it odd that she thought so little about home, but perhaps that was intentional. Ross had been sulky and nasty right from the moment he'd read the letter from Rudolph, growing nastier still after Bruce had spoken to the man on the telephone. But the night before she left he came into the bedroom where she was packing her case and tipped the contents on the floor.

'I forbid you to go,' he shouted at her, his face contorted with anger.

'I have to,' was all she said, and bent to pick up the clothes. He caught her by the hair, swung her back and slapped her face.

'If I say you aren't going, then you fucking well won't,' he screamed at her.

He stormed out to the pub after that, returning so drunk he could barely stand, and collapsed on to the couch, where he stayed all night. He didn't speak in the morning, not a word all day, and when Dulcie finally left for Kalgoorlie with Bruce he had gone off somewhere on his motorbike.

Dulcie guessed he was jealous because she was putting May and a man she didn't even know before him. Yet even if she understood his reasoning, by hitting her he had lost her sympathy. She had no choice but to go, it wasn't a question of who held the larger slice of her heart. She was in fact just as angry with May for making up nasty stories about her as she was with Ross. Only the baby's welfare concerned her, and she wasn't sure she would ever forgive Ross for not finding it within him to see that and let her go with his blessing. Perhaps that was why Bruce was afraid she wouldn't come back, maybe he thought that once she was away from Esperance she'd see nothing to go back for. But Bruce was mistaken, there was a great deal there to bring her back, Ross was her husband, and she wasn't ready to give up on him yet.

Finally it was the last night, tomorrow morning she would arrive in Sydney and meet Rudolph. She packed her case again before dinner and joined all the friends she'd made for drinks before the meal. She was no longer scared of what lay ahead, she felt rested and calm.

The train stopped and started a great deal that last night, and when she woke the next morning she found the scenery had changed dramatically. They were in the Blue Mountains now, thick pine forests, with sheer drops at the side of the track, like nothing she'd ever seen before.

Sydney was huge, they were chugging through suburbs for a couple of hours before they finally reached the station. She saw rows of Victorian terraced houses that took her straight back to England, and something inside her told her she was going to like it here, whatever she might find when she confronted May.

Rudolph was waiting for her on the platform, and she recognized him immediately, even though he looked so different to how she remembered. Maybe it was only his height and the strong features, for without the flamboyant cream suit, Panama hat and bronzed face, he blended in with all the other businessmen in their sober dark suits.

His hair was thicker and blacker than she remembered, his skin pale now, and he looked thinner. Yet as he came towards her, dark eyes smiling, she felt the oddest kind of kinship with him, as if they already knew one another well.

'Dulcie!' he said, his voice a rich, deep growl. 'I am *so* pleased to see you. Was the journey appalling? Are you exhausted?'

He had such nice eyes, slightly hooded, and his handshake was firm and warm.

'The journey was lovely.' She smiled up at him. 'I'm not a bit tired, I slept like a log the whole way.'

He snatched up the case she'd put down on the ground. 'I'm glad to hear that, and if it's all right with you I'll take you straight to the hotel I told Bruce about,' he said. 'It's a small family one, an English couple who are friends of mine run it. As you aren't tired, maybe we can have coffee there. Later, if you feel up to it, we'll have a walk around down by the harbour and have some lunch.'

They went in a taxi to the hotel, Rudolph pointing out places of interest as they went. Perth, the only other Australian city Dulcie'd seen, was mostly new buildings. Sydney evoked half-forgotten memories of the West End of London with its old and imposing grey stone office buildings, narrower streets, smart shops and the vast amount of traffic.

'The place I'm taking you to is called The Rocks,' he said. 'You'll see why when we get there. It was where the first convicts settled, and most of the houses are tiny and very old. It's become very smart to live there now, a bit like Chelsea or Hampstead in London. The hotel is called the Sirius, named after the first ship that came to Sydney. The upstairs rooms have lovely views of the bay. I asked Nancy, that's the landlady, to give you a good one.'

They were there in no time at all, an area of narrow cobbled streets winding up through the huge grey rocky cliff. The taxi stopped at the bottom of some steps, and Rudolph picked up her case and led the way to the house at the top. Dulcie had caught glimpses of the harbour in several places on the route, but as she got to the top of the steps and turned to look, she gasped, for the entire harbour lay before her in one huge glorious sweep. Although it was chilly and windy, the sun was shining and the sea was as blue as the sky above. Sydney Harbour Bridge which she'd seen so often in pictures began right here on top of the rocks, overshadowing the back of the hotel.

'That's the famed Opera House.' Rudolph pointed out a strange-looking half-completed structure further along the harbour. 'It looks appalling now, and heaven only knows when it will be finished. But I'm of the opinion it will be very beautiful once it is. Before we go in and meet Nancy, I thought I'd better tell you she has met May on many occasions, and she knows something of our predicament. I hope you won't be embarrassed by this, it was my hope you'd feel more secure in a strange city with English people who know May and myself.'

Dulcie thought then what a gentleman he was, and that May was a fool to walk out on him.

'It's very kind of you,' she said. 'And I'm not embarrassed. Thank you, Rudolph.'

He smiled and his eyes sparkled. 'Call me Rudie, Rudolph is only good for Christmas parties. I can't imagine why my parents saddled me with it.'

Two hours later they were still in the small dining-room at the front of the house overlooking the bay, on their second pot of tea. Dulcie's room was delightful, on the top floor with a view that left her breathless. The whole hotel was very English and chintzy, she even had an eiderdown on her bed, the first she'd seen since she was a child. Nancy was a Londoner, a pretty woman in her mid-thirties with curly auburn hair and freckles.

But the hotel and the view had been forgotten as Dulcie listened to Rudie's story about himself and May. He began by telling her how it all started, that he was still in the Old Australia Hotel when May turned up in the late afternoon, looking for him.

'I was astounded,' he said with a wry smile. 'She'd made a big impression on me on the day of your wedding, but I hadn't expected to see her ever again. She said she was off to Sydney too and we spent the evening together while waiting for the train. I had booked a first-class sleeper cabin on the train, so when I discovered May was intending to travel second-class, without even a couchette, I said she could share my cabin if she liked and I would pay the extra fare for her.'

'And she agreed, just like that?' Dulcie asked.

'I kind of insisted,' he said, looking faintly embarrassed. 'You see, by then she had already started to make things up, and I felt sorry for her, she seemed shaky, upset and exhausted. I really couldn't bear to think of her suffering the discomfort of second class.'

Rudie glossed over the rest of the journey, but Dulcie felt they must have become lovers on the way, because he said he took May straight to his house when they arrived in Sydney and said she could stay until she found herself a job.

Dulcie didn't much care that it appeared May had cold-bloodedly traded sex for a cabin on the train and a place to stay in Sydney. But she was shocked to the core by the magnitude of the lies she told Rudie to gain his sympathy.

'Devilish strict, that's how she described her parents back in England,' he said. 'She said they were furious when you left for Australia three years ago and they took it out on her. So when you wrote and begged her to come out and join you, and painted a blissful picture of golden beaches, parties and barbecues, she blew her last savings on a ticket and out she came too.'

'We came in 1949!' Dulcie exclaimed.

'As long ago as that!' He shook his head almost in disbelief. 'Well, she said that you were already engaged to Ross then, and that his father, Bruce, had the biggest farm in the South West. According to May, you were the farm secretary, but the job was really beyond you, and you needed her help. But once she got to the farm, she found that she was expected not only to type the farm letters but to cook, clean the house, tend the vegetable garden and nurse Bruce's terminally ill wife.'

He paused for a moment, half smiling at Dulcie's horrified expression. 'It all sounded so ghastly, yet utterly plausible,' he went on. 'She described Betty messing the bed, calling her at all hours of the night, working her fingers to the bone while you did nothing but swan off out to lunch with friends and neighbours. She cried about Betty, saying how much she suffered, and how she felt she couldn't go off and leave her with you because you were so nasty to her. I swallowed it all, hook, line and sinker. That she was paid no wages, that she'd used up all her savings so she couldn't even get to Perth to find the kind of secretarial job she'd been trained for. She even told me she'd been raped by one of the stockmen, and you knew but didn't lift a finger.'

'So how did she explain away her jollity at our wedding?' Dulcie asked with a smirk. 'Or why she had a more expensive outfit than me, and indeed how she came to escape my evil clutches?'

'The jollity was put down to drink. She said it was your intention to marry her off to Bob, I think his name was. The smaller, weedy chap in your party with bad teeth. She said he had a big property down near you, which Ross and Bruce wanted to amalgamate with theirs, and you'd only bought her that outfit for her to impress him.

'As for her escaping, she said that you and Ross had gone off on a honeymoon further down the coast, and as Bruce wasn't taking too much notice of her, she helped herself to a few pounds you'd left for housekeeping, and she managed to get a lift down to the station with a delivery man, and got on the train before anyone knew she'd gone.'

Dulcie shook her head in despair. 'But you saw me that day! Did I look capable of being that wicked?'

'Well, of course I only heard all this several days after seeing you,' he said. 'By then I could only remember you vaguely, and we didn't speak, did we? May said you'd always been jealous of her because she was prettier, your parents favoured her, and that part of the reason you

485

turned so nasty was because you suspected Ross liked her better than you. The picture I got of you was of this neurotic, slightly demented English rose, who was manipulated first by severe parents, then by Ross and his father, whom May described as brutes. She said money and position was everything to you, you were so determined to have a life comparable with the one you'd had back in England that you'd set your cap at the first man with money who came along.'

Dulcie began to laugh then. It was just so far from the truth that all she could do was laugh.

'She was a good storyteller.' Rudie grinned sheepishly. 'I'm glad you can laugh about it because she almost had me in tears when she told me. Her descriptions of Betty's painful death, the clearing up, her grief at losing the old dear, it was all so real. Can you imagine how I felt when I read those letters of yours and found that it was you who was nursing Betty, and that she'd never even been to the farm at that time?'

'Didn't she ever slip up somewhere and make you wonder about her?' Dulcie asked. 'You said she was with you for a long time.'

'No, never,' Rudie said emphatically. 'You see, she had this way about her. Always so well-groomed and poised. She laid the table just so, she knew about wines, the right glasses, how to entertain. Her accent was so English, it all fitted in with what she'd told me about her home in England and what I remember of "ladies" back there. Of course once I knew she'd been a maid, trained by an Englishwoman, I knew where all that had come from.'

'But surely you sometimes saw another side of her?' Dulcie asked. 'Right from a toddler May could charm, act so sweet, make people laugh. But there was always a darker side, and most people saw it before long.'

Rudie nodded. 'Oh yes, I saw that, deep melancholy, insecurity, tantrums too, but that all fitted with your over-bearing parents, the traumas she was supposed to have suffered in Esperance. She even had nightmares about the rape.'

He paused for a short while and lit a cigarette. 'I think what convinced me *most* that it was all true was the way she wanted to put it behind her. Soon after she came to live with me she said, "I'm going to forget it all now, it's happened and it was horrible, but I've got a new start now." She didn't like me to speak of it to anyone else, she would just make jokes about "There you go reminding me again" sort of thing. It seemed so plucky, so rational.'

'She was always an actress even as a little girl,' Dulcie said. 'What I don't understand though is why if you wanted to marry her, she didn't take you up on it? I mean, if she'd only used you to get to Sydney, and didn't really care about you, surely she'd have been off immediately?'

He smiled ruefully. 'That was the biggest puzzle when she first left. But now I know the truth about her, it strikes me she realized it would all come out in a wedding ceremony. You have to show documents, birth certificate, etc. I was talking too of taking her to Siam for a honeymoon, how could she explain that she didn't have a passport?'

'So you think she panicked?'

'Well, I did keep pressing her, I thought she was twenty-one you, see, so she wouldn't need her parents' permission.'

Dulcie thought on this for a bit. 'I can understand her running off because she didn't want to be found to be a liar, or because she found someone she liked better. But why go if she was expecting a baby? That's a time when any woman would want the security of a man who loves her. You'd think she'd have hung on at least until it was born, stringing you along about getting married.'

'That's the part I still can't figure out,' he said woefully. 'Let's go for a walk round, have some lunch, and it might come to us.'

Dulcie was entranced by Sydney. She thought it had every-thing, the beautiful harbour, glorious parks, fantastic shops, the hustle and bustle of London yet with clean air and sunshine. Perth was so new and flat that even if it was clean and admirable in almost every way, it was dull compared with Sydney. The city butted right on to the Circular Quay and there were winding, quite steep hills to take you away from the water front. The Botanical Gardens rivalled even Greenwich Park back home for its formal flowerbeds and exquisite trees and shrubs. Here at last there was history, maybe less than a couple of hundred years of it, and much of that very shameful, but it was astounding to think that a city of such beauty had been built by prisoners.

Rudie clearly loved it too, for he pointed out the marvels of engineering in the bridge, the volume of ships coming into the harbour, the many trees, the new tall buildings which he said would probably rival New York's sky-scrapers in time. He showed her pretty Victorian terraces with delicate lacy iron balconies, and spoke of the splendid museum, art gallery and theatres he hoped her could take her to while she was here.

Dulcie already liked Rudie. He was easy to be with, conversation flowed between them effortlessly. She thought maybe it was his artistic temperament which made him so different to other men she had met, he liked women's company, he spoke of them affectionately, as equals. Yet one of the nicest things about him was his lack of ego. It was obvious from his clothes, quiet confidence and bearing that he was as successful as Jennifer Alcott had said, but he called himself a *painter*, rather than an artist, and referred to his work disparagingly as *daubs*. She had also learnt from Nancy that he intended to pay the entire hotel bill for as long as it was necessary for her to stay here. Though she felt a little embarrassed by such generosity, it was something of a relief for she'd been worried about the cost.

It was while they walked in the Botanical Gardens after lunch that he rather abruptly said he must talk now about what he knew of May's present circumstances.

'I didn't want to launch into it as soon as you got here,' he said with a big sigh. 'I wanted to give you time to acclimatize and for us to get to know one another first. But I can see now it's not going to get any easier through waiting.'

'I'd rather know everything now,' she said, thinking she felt so utterly at ease with him, nothing he could say would shock or embarrass her. 'So fire away.'

'It's not too good,' he said warningly. 'You see, when I wrote to you, all I knew then was roughly where May was, and though I had some thoughts on how she was supporting herself, there was no proof. But I have tracked her down now and got that proof.'

'Go on,' Dulcie insisted. 'Just spit it out.'

'She's working as a prostitute.'

Dulcie blanched, looking up at him in horror. It had been at the back of her mind, but she had dismissed it as over-active imagination. 'How could she do that?' she said in little more than a whisper. 'Are you absolutely sure?'

He nodded. 'She's not working the streets,' he said quickly. 'My source told me she's at the top end of the market, calling on men in hotels. But in a way that makes it worse, because she's undoubtedly got a pimp.'

'What's that?' Dulcie asked.

'A thug who looks after her, arranges it all and takes a huge part of her earnings,' he said. 'He controls her.'

'I can't imagine May letting anyone do that,' Dulcie said.

'I don't suppose she's got much choice. Girls don't usually seek them out, they muscle in, they are dingoes, just about as low as you get. Often they run a whole mob of girls.'

A cold chill went down Dulcie's spine. 'What about the baby? Is he there with her? Have you found out his name and if he's well cared for?'

'She registered him as Noël Mark Taylor, father unknown. She was staying at an address in Surry Hills at

489

the time of his birth. I went round there and asked about her. A neighbour said she had moved in around Christmastime with an older man, but they moved out around six weeks after the baby was born. The baby is still with her, but I have no way of discovering if she is looking after him properly.'

They continued to walk silently, Dulcie's mind churning over what Rudie had told her. She was utterly appalled that her sister could stoop so low, yet she knew she must find her for the baby's sake. He was her nephew after all.

'Noël,' Dulcie mused. 'I wonder why she called him that, it's usually a name for boys born at Christmas.'

'My first thought was that it was the closest she could come to Rudolph without giving the game away,' he said with a humourless laugh. 'But maybe that's wishful thinking.'

Dulcie counted back. 'So he would have been conceived around August last year. How were things between you then?'

'Perfect,' he said. 'I can't see how she got up to anything then, I had a big exhibition on at that time, here in the city just around the corner from her office. She used to join me there as soon as she got out of work, she was excited by how many paintings I was selling, and all the stuff about me in the press. I might be a blind fool, but I really can't believe she was two-timing me then. Later, yes, in October she became very moody and withdrawn, and just before she went in November she was impossible. But not then. She was the most loving in our whole time together.'

Dulcie heard the crack in his voice. 'You still love her, don't you?'

'I don't think you can love someone you never really knew,' he said glumly. 'All day today I've been so conscious of how I felt about her, because you are so alike physically. Your hair, eyes, even your voices have the same tone. But when you talk, and listen, I see the real difference. You only speak when you have something that needs saying, I think you prefer to listen. May chattered constantly, she was bright, breezy, often very funny too, but there was no depth to what she said. She didn't ever listen, she was just waiting for a chance to give her views. Of course I didn't see that at first, I suppose she cast a spell over me.'

Dulcie could understand that. For months after May left Esperance men were still asking after her, she'd made her mark there too.

'Tell me where she lives now,' she asked.

'On the edge of King's Cross in Darlinghurst. King's Cross has the reputation of being the red light district, but in fact the real action takes place in Darlinghurst. In reality King's Cross is a very bohemian community, a rich mixture of artists of all kinds, single people in flats and bed-sits, families and old people. It's because of the bars, the strip clubs and night-clubs that it's got a tawdry image. All the visitors to Sydney and the young people charge up there over the weekend, it does get a bit wild.'

'So she's between the two?' Dulcie raised an eyebrow.

'She's got a flat in one of the big old terraced houses. All the girls living there are on the game. But I don't think she's lived there ever since she left Surry Hills. My guess is that she lived somewhere smarter for a while, perhaps still with the same older man, then he left her, so she had to find somewhere cheaper. Maybe she was forced into prostitution because I still can't believe she'd choose such a life.'

Dulcie was touched that he still cared enough to find excuses for May. She remembered too how Sergeant Collins had spoken of young girls being lured into that way of life. 'I'll go there tonight,' she said impulsively.

'You'll do no such thing,' Rudie said quickly, looking alarmed. 'It's no place to go at night. I think morning, around nine, would be the best time, you'd catch her unawares, when the other girls are sleeping.'

'Tomorrow then?'

Rudie sighed. 'I was going to suggest that you came to visit me. It's only a ferry ride from the circular quay. I thought it would be best if you got used to Sydney before steaming in there.'

Dulcie shook her head. 'I need to see her straight away, I can't wait,' she said. 'Apart from anything else she might get wind I'm in town and vanish again. Besides, I have to see Noël is all right.'

Rudie made a defeated gesture with his hands. 'Okay, for the baby's sake. But I don't like the thought of you going there alone.'

'I shouldn't think she'd let me in unless I was alone.'

'I could come with you and wait around the corner. At least I'd be close if anything happened.'

'What can happen in broad daylight?' she asked, and smiled at him. 'The worst she can do is tell me to push off. If she senses you're close she'll just be more tense.'

'We'll get a taxi up there now then,' he said, taking her elbow and leading her towards the park gates. 'Just so you can see where it is.'

Rudie asked the taxi driver to slow right down as they went down Forbes Street. The first thing that struck Dulcie was that it looked much like any ordinary working-class area, nothing at all to suggest it was a nest of vice. The tall, almost barrack-style terraced houses were grimy and lacking in paint, and there were no trees or window-boxes to soften the greyness of it. But it was quiet, the few people walking along it looked harmless, there were even a few children playing cricket.

'That's it, number 52,' Rudie said, pointing to a house where the door was open, revealing a dark and grubby-looking hall. 'The person who gave me the information thinks she's on the top floor at the back.'

They drove straight back to the hotel afterwards as they were both expected for the evening meal. Rudie left immediately afterwards because Dulcie was so tired, but as he left he stopped for a moment and took both her hands.

'Good luck for tomorrow,' he said, his dark eyes full of concern. 'Ring me as soon as you've seen her.'

Dulcie woke up before six the following morning, and unable to drift off again, she got up and sat by the window looking at the view of Sydney Harbour. There was a haze of mist just above the water, and the air was full of circling gulls. She could look right down on to the quay where she'd walked yesterday with Rudie, it had been crowded with people then, but now the birds had it all to themselves. A couple of pelicans sat like two old men on two capstans, egrets with their long thin beaks pecked at litter left from the night before. It was such a beautiful and peaceful scene she felt her eyes prickle with tears.

Just twenty-four hours ago she was still on the train, opening the blind to see the Blue Mountains. Who would have thought that in such a short time she could have experienced so much? It was as if she'd been turned upside down and shaken, loosening up all her ideals and principles, and injected with a whole new morality.

A couple of weeks ago she would have been shocked rigid to hear of anyone living with a man they weren't married to. Now she knew her own sister had done that, had a baby, was selling her body and was almost certainly under the control of a pimp. And all this knowledge had come from a man she barely knew! A short while ago she would have wanted to believe that May's downfall was entirely Rudie's doing, but she knew better now. Rudie, with his almost transparent honesty, had shown her a side of May she could never even have dreamt of.

How odd it was too that she could talk of such shocking things, almost effortlessly, to a stranger, yet she couldn't talk to her own husband about their problems within their marriage.

Now she was intending to go alone to that house in Forbes Street, to face her sister who would very likely be hostile. Yet she wasn't really scared. Why was that?

It seemed to be something in the air in Sydney. All day yesterday she'd felt a kind of fizz inside her that she'd never experienced back in Esperance. She liked the crowds, the traffic, the noise and bustle. She wanted to walk alone around the streets and make this city her own. Was that why Bruce seemed afraid she wouldn't want to come home?

'You've got to go back,' she reminded herself aloud. 'You can't run out on Ross.'

Yet just thinking of him made the fizz die within her. She had telephoned Bruce briefly last night just to say she was safe and Rudie was even nicer than they'd both expected. Bruce asked if he should run over and call Ross, but she'd said she was running out of change. A poor excuse, but she didn't want to hear that bleakness in his voice.

Nancy had thoughtfully left an electric kettle in the room and a tray of tea things. She made some tea and took it back to the window, thinking about what she should wear today. She supposed just jeans and a jumper would be fine, casual enough not to draw attention to herself, and comfortable too if she ended up walking a long way.

At half past seven she went downstairs to have her breakfast. Nancy gave her a wide smile as she saw her coming down the stairs. 'Did you sleep well?' she asked.

Dulcie had taken to freckle-faced Nancy immediately, her London voice held good memories of her granny, the warmth with which she'd welcomed her to her hotel made her feel safe, and there was something about the woman's bright eyes, a kind of happy glow from within her, which made her feel that before long they'd be firm friends.

'Like a log,' Dulcie replied. 'It's a very comfy bed. But I don't think I really want any breakfast, thank you.'

'Oh yes, you must, just have some cereal and see how that goes down. I've found a little map of the city so you don't get lost, go on in the dining-room and sit down, I'll bring it with the tea in a minute.'

*

Dulcie got the taxi driver to stop in William Street at the end of Forbes Street and after paying him, walked to number 52, her heart thumping like a steam engine. What was she going to do if May slammed the door in her face? What if there was a man with her?

There were several bells on the door, but May's name wasn't on any of them, so she rang the bottom one which had no name on it. No one answered, and she was just going to try another one when suddenly the door opened and a woman of around forty clutching a dressing-gown round her glowered at her.

'Yes?' she said.

'I'm so sorry to wake you,' Dulcie said. 'I wanted May Taylor, but her name isn't on any of the bells.'

'Doubt if she'd answer it if it was,' the woman snapped. 'You'd better go on up.'

'Which room is it?' Dulcie said once she was half-way up the dirty hall.

'Follow the screaming,' the woman grunted before disappearing through a door at the back of the house.

Dulcie could hear a baby crying and she covered her nose as she started up the stairs. The smell was awful – stale cooking, lavatories and mildew all mixed up. She had smelt this before but it wasn't until she reached the very top of the stairs and saw a large white sink on the landing that she remembered where. It was the house they lived in at New Cross during the war.

The crying baby was another reminder, May used to cry a great deal in those days. Dulcie could see herself rocking the pram because Mum was trying to have a rest. It was almost like going round in a circle and finding yourself back where you started, only she and May were grown-up now, and the crying baby was her sister's.

Bracing herself, Dulcie knocked on the door.

'Oh, for God's sake, I can't help him crying,' came May's yell from within. There was a sound of feet stamping angrily across the floor and the door flew open.

'Dulcie!' May gasped, her hands flying up to her mouth. 'Oh my God!'

She looked terrible, wearing a stained nightdress and with her hair like a bird's nest. There were dark shadows under her eyes and her complexion was muddy.

'Hello, May,' Dulcie said, walking in before May could gather her wits to stop her.

She took in the room with one horrified glance. It was untidy, dirty, it stank of soiled nappies and vomit and it was very cold. But she barely took in the unmade bed, the piles of strewn clothes and unwashed dishes. Her eyes went straight to the pram, a navy-blue carry-cot on wheels. Two little fists and bare feet were just visible. Dulcie was over to it in a trice.

He had dark hair, and he was red in the face from screaming. A half-empty bottle was propped up beside him, which had clearly fallen out of his mouth, and his little nightdress was sodden.

Dulcie picked him up. 'He's soaking wet,' she exclaimed.

May was just standing there, so taken aback she hadn't even shut the door.

'And you mustn't leave a baby with a bottle like that, it's dangerous,' Dulcie said.

May recovered herself. 'Same old Dulcie, always knows everything,' she jeered at her, moving nearer to her. 'Put him back and piss off.'

'I won't,' Dulcie said more calmly than she felt. 'Shut that door. Give me a clean nappy and some dry clothes, and while I'm changing him you warm up that bottle.'

'Now look here,' May said, but she shut the door anyway. 'Don't you think you can come marching in here telling me what to do.'

Dulcie ignored her, swept the clothes off the chair, and sat down with the baby on her lap. She had often changed Doreen's baby since they became friends, but she hadn't expected that the training would come in useful so soon. But as she unpinned Noël's nappy she saw his bottom was red raw. She could tell May hardly ever changed him. No wonder he was so angry!

'He's got awful nappy rash,' she shouted above the screaming. 'Have you got any cream for him?'

'There's some over there,' May snapped. 'On the dressing table.' She had moved over to the sink and she was fiddling with some kind of water heater on the wall above it.

Holding Noël under one arm, Dulcie got the cream. She smeared it all over the red area, then folded the clean nappy May had slapped at her. It was badly stained, but it would do for now. Then she got him a dry vest and another little nightgown and he began to stop crying. May brought over the bottle in a jug of hot water. After testing the temperature, Dulcie wrapped a blanket round him to keep him warm and began feeding him.

'Right,' she said finally. 'Looks like I came at the right time. Now, while I'm feeding him, why don't you tidy up?'

From her position in the corner close to the window, Dulcie could take in the whole room. The kitchen part was sectioned off with a high counter and contained a sink, cooker and fridge. The main part of the room held a double bed, two armchairs and a large wardrobe which covered one wall, plus the dressing-table. The stained wallpaper was hanging off the walls in some places, the furniture was battered and ancient. Like the sink out on the landing, it took Dulcie right back to New Cross and brought back unpleasant early memories of her mother lying in bed most of the day.

'How did you find out where I was?' May said, standing in front of Dulcie with her hands on her hips.

'Through Rudie,' Dulcie said, trying not to get angry at May's indifference to her and the baby. 'I wouldn't have come after all the wicked lies you've told him about me, if it wasn't for finding out about this little one. But get on with the clearing up while we talk. I don't want to sit in a dunny all day, even if you don't mind.'

'Who the fuck do you think you are?' May snarled at her. 'I don't need you around, bugger off.'

'You were once such a lady,' Dulcie said, looking right into her sister's eyes. 'Don't swear at me, May. It doesn't impress me.'

Their eyes remained locked for a few moments, and Dulcie was determined she wasn't going to look away first. She knew her only chance with May was to keep the superior position, to give her no opportunity to lie, manipulate her, or to make her cry.

'Clear up now,' she commanded.

Surprisingly, May got on with it. She made the bed, then folded it back into a settee, picked up all the dirty dishes and took them into the kitchen, then she came back to collect up all the clothes. Dulcie realized it had also given May a chance to collect herself and she guessed she would go on the attack before long.

'You've already made up your mind that I'm in the wrong, haven't you?' May said as she hung dresses on hangers and shoved sweaters into drawers. 'You've listened to Mr Fancy Pants and taken his word for everything.'

Noël finished his bottle and Dulcie lifted him up to wind him. He was the sweetest little thing, dark brown hair, his eyes still blue, but they looked as if they were turning brown. He didn't look like May had as a baby. She knew she mustn't show that her emotions were being tugged by this tiny, helpless little chap.

'Rudie wrote to me after finding the letters I wrote to you at St Vincent's and at Peppermint Grove. You hung yourself by leaving them at his house because through them he realized everything you'd told him about both of us was lies. But he didn't find them till after someone he knew saw you with a baby. The reason he wrote to me was because he feared for Noël. From what I've seen this morning he was right to be afraid.'

She saw May's face contort, perhaps because of the

reference to the letters and because she knew she had been well and truly found out.

'I'm not usually like this. I had a bad night,' May said, moving over to the kitchen area to fill the sink with hot water. She suddenly spun round to look at Dulcie, her brow furrowing. 'Hey, how did you get that good with babies? Have you got one of your own now?'

'No,' Dulcie said. 'And don't try to change the subject. I'm not leaving here until you've told me the truth. Why did you tell such wicked lies about me, and turn your back on me, May? Why did you leave Rudie when you were already pregnant, and how have you ended up as a prostitute?'

'You've always been on my back.' May glowered at her. 'Always the goodie-goodie, aren't you? Why can't you face it that we've got nothing in common, apart from the same mother? Get out of my life, and stay out of it. I don't want you or need you. I never have. You make me sick.'

Dulcie felt as if she'd been punched in the stomach, and if it hadn't been for the baby in her arms, so warm against her shoulder, she might have walked out.

'You're right, we've got nothing in common,' she agreed. 'You're a dirty slut now and I don't relish the thought that you are my sister. But this is my nephew, and until I discover that you love him and will protect him and take care of him properly, and answer my questions, I'm not leaving. Have you got that?' she finished up. 'You've got one chance, that's all. Tell me the truth!'

May looked winded now. 'I didn't mean to tell a lot of lies about you,' she said in a softer tone, as she made two cups of instant coffee and lit up a cigarette. 'Yeah, I did plan leaving Esperance on that day knowing I'd see Rudie again, I knew he liked me and I guessed he had money, so I said what I did to get his sympathy. Then we got here and he took me to his house, well, it took my breath away it was so nice, I wanted to stay with him, for the first time ever I felt secure and happy. So I had to stick with the story I'd told him. That's why I couldn't write to you.'

'So you would have cut me out of your life for ever rather than own up you'd told a lot of lies?'

May shrugged. 'We got by before when Mother wasn't giving me your letters.'

Dulcie assumed that meant May would have been prepared to lose her for ever.

'Did you love Rudie?' she asked.

May gave her a cold stare. 'What's that got to do with anything?'

'I would have thought it had everything to do with it. You lived with him, you slept with him. Did you love him?'

'I sleep with men to get what I want,' May said. 'I don't wrap it up in all that stupid soppy stuff, only creeps like you need to do that to justify it.'

Dulcie was shaken by the venom in her voice.

'What made you feel that way?' she asked in bewilderment.

'If you were to live around here for a while you'd soon find out,' May said, stubbing out her cigarette and immediately lighting another one. 'Sex is just another commodity. Wives trade it for being looked after, tarts take money for it.'

'But you haven't been here that long,' Dulcie reminded her. 'You weren't a prostitute when you first met Rudie.'

'You think you know me so well, but you know nothing,' May shouted at her. 'Even back in the Sacred Heart I learned to get an easy time of it I had to suck up to the Sisters and the older girls. By the time I was twelve I had to let Mother kiss me on the mouth, rub my tits and stick her fingers up my knicker legs. It's much the same with the punters who pay me now. I don't have to like it, I just trade it.'

Dulcie involuntarily clutched Noël tighter. 'The Reverend Mother did that to you?'

May gave a mirthless laugh. 'Oh, you'd like to think I was lying, wouldn't you? Well, I'm not. Why do you think

I got the treats, piano lessons, extra food, didn't have my hair hacked off? It was a trade-off, I sat on her lap and let her fiddle with me and in return I got all that and didn't get beaten.'

Dulcie was winded, so shocked she hardly knew what to say. 'I knew you were her pet, but I didn't think – '

'Think!' May interrupted her. 'You couldn't think of things like that, you're too bloody holy. Look at that time you took the beating instead of saying I'd taken those toffees. You were a mug, a bloody drongo. It didn't teach me anything except that I'd got to be a bit more devious next time I swiped something!'

'Didn't you even feel ashamed?' Dulcie gasped.

'Ashamed of what? For nicking some sweets that were ours by rights? No, I bloody wasn't. You traded yourself too, by taking that beating without telling Mother it was me, you became a bloody heroine. You got your reward, everyone sniffed round you and loved you for ever more.'

'I did it to save you being hurt,' Dulcie said shakily. 'Not to be a heroine.'

'But you didn't mind hurting me by ignoring me for weeks after,' May spat back. 'I felt cast out, like a bloody leper. Was it any wonder I crept round Mother for a bit of comfort and affection?'

'I ignored you because I wanted you to apologize to me,' Dulcie said indignantly. 'Don't try to push the blame on to me for what happened between you and Mother.'

'You've got no idea what it was like, have you?' May's face was contorted, her eyes wild and crazy-looking. 'Do you know how it feels to be kissed by someone like her, to feel her hands creeping up my legs, her breath rasping in my ear as she gets off on it? It's shameful, creepy, so horrible it makes you feel sick.' Her voice rose to a shriek. 'I couldn't blow the whistle on her, who would have believed me? I couldn't even avoid her because she used to send for me. You've no idea what hell it was sometimes. I didn't have a friend in the place come the end. And then she sent me to the Wilberforces so she could still come creeping around.'

Dulcie had told herself before she got here that May was bound to tell her lies, but she instinctively knew this was the truth. Mother had always made her flesh crawl, though she couldn't ever put her finger on why.

'Why didn't you ever tell me this?' she asked.

'How was I supposed to tell you?' May grimaced. 'Mother read all the letters I wrote to you, and what could you have done anyway?'

'It might have just been better for you if we could have shared it,' Dulcie said sadly, knowing that in reality there was nothing she could have done.

'I suppose you'd have liked to have known when a man raped me in King's Park too,' May blurted out. 'You couldn't have done anything about that either. I didn't even confess it to the priest because I was afraid he'd tell Mrs Wilberforce. You see, I learned very early I couldn't trust anyone.'

Dulcie made her tell her exactly what had happened, and as May haltingly related it, she could see the pain in her eyes and guessed this was why she'd told Rudie she was raped by a stockman – she had to unburden herself somehow.

Dulcie felt the pain herself. Maybe May was foolish to go into the park after dark with a man she'd only met that day, but she was so very young then, looking for the love that had been denied her. Sadly it seemed he'd smashed it out of her for good.

'I'm so sorry, May,' was all she could say.

'You don't have to be sorry,' May said with a shrug. 'It happened and I made up my mind then that no one would ever get me for nothing again. I reckon in some ways it's better to be the way I am than the way you are.'

'What do you mean?' Dulcie asked. 'What have I done?'

'Nothing, that's my point, you just dote on that mental cripple of a husband.'

Dulcie bristled. 'How dare you! Ross isn't a mental cripple!'

'No?' May smirked. 'He's like a box of ice. Oh, don't bother to deny it. I know things about men, you see. I've made it my business.'

Dulcie looked down at the sleeping baby in her arms and felt bitterly ashamed that his mother should be admitting to such things. Yet even worse was that her sister of all people should have worked out that her marriage to Ross was a sham.

'Put a clean sheet in the pram and I'll put him back to sleep,' Dulcie said to hide her confusion.

'I haven't got any clean ones,' May snapped at her. 'Do you see a washing-machine in here, a line outside to dry stuff on?'

'Then take one of the pillow-cases off your bed,' Dulcie said. 'They might not be clean either, but at least they are dry.'

Once Noël was back in the pram, Dulcie drank her coffee and dried up the dishes May was washing. Beneath the sink was a bucket of soiled nappies, there was a mountain of dirty washing too in a cardboard box.

'You can't bring a baby up here,' she said to May. The nappies still had lumps of faeces in them, and it turned her stomach to think her sister hadn't sluiced them off in the lavatory before putting them to soak. She pointed this out to her, and asked if she boiled Noël's bottles and teats to sterilize them. May said she did, but Dulcie didn't believe her.

'You might get away with it now while the weather's cold,' she said. 'But when the summer comes he could get seriously ill if you carry on that way.'

May walked a little way away from her, then turned, a sneer on her lips. 'I won't have him in the summer, I'm taking him to the Sisters. They can take care of him.'

Something just snapped inside Dulcie, she leaped towards her sister and slapped her hard across the face.

May reeled back and fell against the wardrobe.

'You cold-hearted bitch!' Dulcie roared at her, all restraint gone. 'After all we suffered at the hands of those women, you'd take your baby and give it to them?'

'They aren't all like that,' May said, but she was scared, shuffling along on the floor trying to get away from Dulcie.

'Maybe they aren't all like that. But there's enough rotten apples in the barrel to spoil the good ones. A few minutes ago you were telling me what that witch of a woman at St Vincent's did to you! How can you even consider putting Noël through that?'

'I haven't got any choice,' May said, scrambling to her feet. 'Look at this place! Look at what I am now!'

'I'm looking at it and it makes me sick,' Dulcie roared at her. 'But if you think I'm going to let you hand over Noël to an orphanage you're sadly mistaken. Who is his father? Is it Rudolph?'

She advanced on her sister, quite prepared to strangle the truth out of her if necessary. May backed further away, her eyes wide with fright.

'Yes,' she whimpered.

That answer momentarily stunned Dulcie. 'But why did you leave him then?' she asked after a moment or two.

'Because he would have insisted on getting married right away.' May began to cry. 'It would have all come out then. I tried everywhere to get an abortion, but the doctor I went to in the Cross said I was too far gone.'

'But Rudie's a decent bloke,' Dulcie said in bewilderment. 'Why couldn't you just tell him the truth? He might have been upset about the lies for a while, but he'd have got over it.'

'You don't see it, do you?' May said, tears running down her cheeks. 'I don't love him, every time he touched me it made my skin crawl. It was as bad as Mother touching me. Was I supposed to live with that for ever, just because of him?' She thumbed towards Noël.

Dulcie was at a loss now.

'Didn't you feel anything for him? Not even at the beginning?'

May shook her head. 'I just used him, same as I've always done with men. I don't feel anything but nausea with any of them. It was even worse with him, because he wanted the whole love thing. I can stand being fucked by almost anyone, providing they make it worth my while, but I can't bear someone wanting to own me.'

Dulcie began to cry, even though she'd told herself she wouldn't under any circumstances. May had to be mad, surely every girl wanted what Rudie was offering?

'Don't start crying on me for God's sake,' May said, grabbing a cigarette. 'It's bad enough having him doing it all the time.' Again she thumbed towards the pram. 'Go away, leave me alone. I can't take all this emotional stuff, I never could.'

'Do you love Noël?' Dulcie asked, through her tears.

'Not in the way you'd like me to,' May said, her voice cool and measured. 'I wouldn't harm him, but I'm no good to him. Guess I'm just like our mother. History repeating itself.'

Dulcie could only stare at her sister in horror. Vivid images of their mother danced before her eyes, May was just like her in almost every way, looks and character. That bold, cold stare, the inability to put anyone before her own selfish needs.

'I understand now why Dad killed her,' May said. 'I push men to the edge like that too.'

'He didn't kill her, she fell,' Dulcie said.

'He did, Dulcie, and you know it,' May said. She tapped her forehead. 'It's all up here, I can remember everything about that night, only it took years to understand what I'd heard.'

Chapter Twenty-two

May's words brought that terrible night so many years ago into sharp focus for Dulcie. She could feel May's small, warm body next to her in the darkness, see the chink of light around the bedroom door and hear her own heart thumping too loudly as she listened to her parents shouting at each other out on the landing.

She was thrown into confusion at reliving the scene. She had always firmly believed May was asleep at that point of the argument between her parents, yet as she had claimed so many times to have heard *May's not your child*, it was feasible she had heard the rest too. But Dulcie had kept her father's words to herself for so long she had no intention of admitting them now. 'You didn't hear anything that night. You were asleep,' she retorted defensively.

'Oh yes I did. Dad said he was going to kill Mum. I heard him perfectly clearly, just like you did.'

'Rubbish,' Dulcie snapped. 'You've just invented that. The only thing you ought to remember about that night was that because of it two small children ended up in an orphanage. That must never happen to Noël.'

May shot her a defiant look. 'I can't give him anything but misery. So if you think you can improve on that, you take him!'

'You can't just give him away,' Dulcie said in horror.

'I'll take him to the Sisters then.'

Dulcie slumped down on to the chair, unable to believe anyone could be so callous. 'But you're his mother!' she exclaimed after a moment or two's thought. 'He isn't a stray dog or a bit of unwanted furniture, he's your own child! How can you be so unfeeling?'

'Our mother was unfeeling too. She didn't give a toss about us,' May said, tossing her untidy hair out of her eyes. 'You were more of a mother to me than she ever was.'

'Never mind about our mother and trying to put the blame on her,' Dulcie snapped. 'Just tell me, if Noël was to be taken away from you, what would you do then?'

'What would I do?' May looked fleetingly puzzled at the question. 'I'd get out of this flea-pit for a start.'

'I meant with your life,' Dulcie said impatiently. 'What sort of work would you get?'

May sniggered. 'What I'm best at. Only I'd be a bit more selective and pick the men myself.'

Dulcie's jaw dropped. 'May, you couldn't! Surely you'd want to get a decent job?'

May just laughed. 'What, bang away at a typewriter all day and earn ten quid a week if I'm lucky? I could earn more than that from just one screw.'

Dulcie looked at her sister in utter horror. Maybe Reverend Mother and the rapist had been responsible for twisting her morality in the first place, she could very well have been forced into prostitution after Noël's birth, but her attitude wasn't one of a victim, it sounded very much as if this was her chosen path.

She asked May point-blank when she'd first taken money from a man.

'Back in Perth,' May said airily. 'Remember those two men we had dinner with? I got fifteen quid off one of them after you'd gone, and my taxi fare home. He wasn't the first either.'

Dulcie turned from her. She wanted to rage, tell her she didn't want to spend another minute with her. Yet a tiny part of her still clung to the hope that it was all bravado and soon May would admit as much and ask for help. 'I wondered how you could afford such nice clothes,' she said weakly.

'I didn't buy many of those, I used to nick them,' May said, shocking her still further. 'Remember the radio I gave you? I took that and put it in my bag right in front of you.'

Dulcie's eyes widened, she felt she couldn't take any more shocks. 'Why?' she gasped, remembering how touched she'd been by May's generosity, and how much pleasure she'd had from the gift.

'Why?' May repeated. 'Because I wanted to give it to you.'

'But I'd have hated it if I'd known you'd stolen it,' Dulcie retorted. 'How could you? If you'd been caught you'd have been sent to the reformatory.'

'I didn't get caught because I was so good at it,' May smirked. 'Anyway I was just taking back what was owed to me.'

'Owed to you?' Dulcie held her head in her hands despairingly.

'Yes, owed. I was deprived of everything as a kid. They took my toys and clothes, half starved and beat me too. I see taking money from men as evening up the score with everyone in those orphanages who hurt me, including Mother and the man who raped me. But for them I might not be the way I am now.'

'They might be responsible in part, but you can't spend your whole life taking revenge on innocent people,' Dulcie implored her. 'I had just as tough a time as you. You can't imagine what I went through at my first job. But I haven't let it make me hate everyone.'

'No, but you've become a martyr,' May laughed scornfully. 'I think that's worse. You've married that dag Ross because you felt sorry for him and because you think that's all you deserve. You work like a crazy woman on that farm, bend over backwards for them all. What do you get out of it?'

'My self-respect for one thing,' Dulcie said hotly. 'And I didn't marry Ross because I felt sorry for him.'

'Oh yes you did,' May said with laughter in her voice. 'You know you're a worse liar than me! You might not spin yarns to other people, but you lie to yourself. I reckon that's even worse.'

'I don't, I don't,' Dulcie insisted, beginning to cry. 'How can you be so nasty to me?'

'Because you ask for it,' May said, insolently folding her arms across her chest. 'I bet you would take Noël too, and look after him until your dying day as another act of martyrdom. You'd expect to get your reward in heaven, no matter what hell your life on earth was because of it.' She paused, giving her sister a knowing look. 'Ross would give you the hell, because Noël would be another reminder of his own failure in that department. Don't try to deny it either, I knew your little honeymoon was a failure. I could see it both in your eyes and by the way you were with each other.'

'That's not true.'

May laughed again. 'See what I mean about you believing your own lies? I reckon you're still a virgin.'

Dulcie jumped to her feet, intending to run out, never to see May again and leave her to face what was coming to her. But as she glanced down at Noël in his pram her heart contracted painfully. He was sound asleep sucking his thumb, one finger curled round his tiny nose. All at once she knew she would carry that picture with her in her mind, she wouldn't be able to forget the propped-up bottle, his red-raw bottom, and she'd be haunted by imagining him alone and crying while May was out looking for men.

'Go,' May said, seeing her hesitation. She moved to a position between Dulcie and the pram. 'For God's sake get out of here and forget us. He'll be all right, I'm going to put him in care and they'll put him up for adoption.' Her voice was harsh in the stillness of the room. 'I'm a thieving, lying tart, rotten through and through, but there's just a little bit of me that's decent enough to want a real mother for him.'

'Couldn't you *try* to be a real mother?' Dulcie took a step nearer her sister, suddenly wanting to embrace her and try to love her out of all this wickedness, yet knowing full well she'd be rebuffed. 'You could get help from a

Welfare worker, they'd move you somewhere, get you money. Rudie would help too, I know he would.'

May shook her head. 'There's always strings attached to help from Welfare workers, we of all people know that. You can't trust them. As for Rudie, I couldn't bear to even see him again, let alone accept help from him. But I don't know why you are bothering to argue. You know I'm no good, you know it's better for him to be taken from me.'

Dulcie heard the truth in what May was saying, but her honesty suggested her sister cared for Noël a little more than she was letting on.

'What if I took him with me, just for a few days, to see how you feel?' Dulcie said impulsively. 'A little break so you could think it over.'

Surprisingly May's eyes welled up, it was the first time she'd shown any sign of emotion. She took a step nearer to the pram and looked down at Noël.

Dulcie held her breath, waiting for May's reply. She was sure that if she could get her to agree to this she would soon come to her senses.

A tear ran down May's cheek and she reached out and smoothed Noël's head, her lips quivering. 'Okay,' she sighed. 'But don't expect it to make me feel any different.'

Dulcie slowly exhaled. She felt she'd won the first round. 'I'll have to go and ring the hotel and make sure they don't mind,' she said. 'Why don't you get washed and dressed while I'm gone?'

An hour later Noël was ready in his pram to go with Dulcie.

'He likes to snuggle this cloth to get to sleep,' May said, showing Dulcie a piece of terry towelling which she then put in the pram beside Noël. She had already packed a bag with some clothes, nappies, bottles and his milk powder. 'If you give him his last feed about nine tonight, he should sleep through the night.'

Dulcie had rung Nancy and asked if it was all right to bring Noël to the hotel, and even though she'd sounded very surprised, she said he would be very welcome. But now the moment had come, Dulcie was a little nervous. 'Do you give him any solid food yet?' she asked, all at once aware she didn't know much about looking after babies.

'I haven't tried it yet,' May said. 'But you can try if you want to.'

'I'll ask Nancy, she's got two children so I expect she'll know what's best,' Dulcie said. 'But you do realize Rudie will come to see him? How do you feel about that?'

May was dressed now, in jeans and a sweater. She'd brushed her hair and she looked more like her old self. 'I don't know,' she said thoughtfully as she looked down at Noël in his pram. She sighed deeply. 'I can't think straight at the moment. I'm still trying to get used to the idea of seeing you again.'

'Is it so awful?' Dulcie asked, moving nearer to her sister. 'There was a time you always wanted me around.'

May turned, her eyes brimming with sudden tears. 'No, it's not awful, I just didn't want you to see me like this.'

'I couldn't stop loving you just because you are in a mess,' Dulcie said gently. She tentatively held out her arms.

May rushed to them, just the way she had as a little girl. 'I'm sorry, Dulcie,' she whispered against Dulcie's neck. 'I wish . . .' She broke off suddenly.

'You wish you could turn the clock back and start again?' Dulcie suggested. 'That's impossible, but I'm here now, you'll have time on your own to think things through, and I'll help you however I can. But let me take Noël now, so I'm back at the hotel before he needs another feed. Ring me tomorrow morning, I've left the phone number and address by the kettle.'

May still clung to her, and it proved to Dulcie that she wasn't as callous as she had made out earlier. She had watched May getting Noël dressed and the gentle way she handled him was evidence she did love him. 'We'll get through this together,' Dulcie whispered, stroking May's neck tenderly. 'You aren't on your own any more.'

May lifted her head and stroked Dulcie's face, her full lips trembling with emotion. 'I'm glad you came now,' she said, her eyes glistening with tears. 'I'm so sorry I said such wicked things about you. I always felt bad about it.'

As Dulcie pushed the pram down William Street her mind was in turmoil. She knew perfectly well she'd been much too hasty in offering to take Noël away, yet the alternatives, leaving him to be neglected, or going to a Welfare worker and expressing her fears about her nephew's safety were unthinkable. May could well have bolted with him the moment her back was turned, and if the Child Welfare Department got there first they'd whisk him away immediately, and the chances were she'd find herself having no say in Noël's future.

Even her thoughts about May were jumbled and confused. She felt desperately sorry for her on one hand, yet also furious at her lack of regard for her baby, and upset that she intended to continue in her life of vice. Yet how could she really blame May for her lack of maternal feelings when she'd been set such bad examples by both her own mother and the Sisters?

Dulcie remembered only too well how she'd craved love and affection both at St Vincent's and while she worked for the Masters. If someone had come along who appeared to care for her, she might very well have fallen into the same trap as May.

Yet May had softened when Dulcie returned from making the telephone call. She had held Noël lovingly, she'd even asked how Ross had reacted to his wife coming all the way to Sydney, and how long she was intending to stay.

But it was those last few tearful words before Dulcie left with Noël that really gave her hope that May wasn't a lost cause. May was aware now of how far she'd fallen, she had shown some remorse. It was a start, and they had parted as friends.

Yet that couldn't quite take the sting out of May's cruel remarks about her. She didn't really believe she was a martyr, that she lied to herself, or that she'd married Ross out of pity, yet a small voice inside her kept whispering that May might be right.

As she walked, she looked down at Noël sleeping and an almost unbearable pang of tenderness went through her. She'd wrapped him up like a cocoon in a blanket so all that was visible was his little face and a tuft of dark hair sticking up. It wasn't fair that she had been denied a normal marriage, and a baby of her own, yet May, who cared for nothing and no one, should get this little treasure and then want to abandon him.

'He *is* mine. I know he is,' Rudie said gleefully, looking down at Noël kicking on a rug. 'He looks just like the photos of me at the same age.'

They were in Nancy's sitting-room, a small room leading off the kitchen at the back of the house. It had the same very English quality as the rest of the house, but shabbier, with Nancy's two school-age children's toys and books strewn everywhere.

Dulcie had taken off Noël's nappy to let the air heal his sore bottom, and he was lying there gurgling delightedly at the freedom to kick his legs, and the attention he was getting from three strange adults.

'I'm absolutely certain May was telling the truth about that,' Dulcie said. 'But blood tests can confirm it, can't they?'

Nancy sat down on the floor by Noël to tickle him, and he returned her smile with a chuckle of glee. 'I don't have any doubt Rudie is his daddy,' she said thoughtfully. 'But I'm not sure that gives him any rights, not when he wasn't registered as the father at birth.'

'I think I should get some legal advice right away,' Rudie said.

When Dulcie arrived back here over an hour ago, Rudie was already waiting for her, rushing down the steps to carry the pram up into the house. Nancy had brought them into this room so they could talk privately, and over a cup of tea Dulcie had told both of them why she felt compelled to take Noël away with her.

She broke down several times as she described the awful room May lived in, her callousness in her intention to put Noël into care, and the fact that she showed no shame at her sordid occupation. Yet she couldn't reveal all that May had said about her, their parents and Reverend Mother, that was just too embarrassing to talk about to people she'd only known for such a short time.

Nancy agreed she would have done exactly what Dulcie had done. She also shared the view that May might come to her senses after a couple of days away from her baby, and possibly want to reform. But Rudie was more pessimistic, he took the view that May would take the opportunity to call on an adoption society, and he wanted legal advice to discover if he could have any say in the matter.

'Hold on,' Dulcie begged him. 'I only told May I was going to look after him for a few days, we must give her a chance to think about what Noël means to her. You go speaking to a lawyer about this and the next thing we know there'll be Welfare workers rushing round here to snatch him away.'

'You're over-reacting,' he said, giving her a sharp look.

'I'm not,' she insisted. 'I'm speaking from experience. That's what happened to May and me, remember. You can't trust those people, they say one thing and do something else.'

'But what if May promises to look after him properly, just to get you off her back, and then reneges on it later?' Rudie argued. 'She could disappear with him, even abandon him in another state. How would we know? We are his next of kin for goodness' sake, so we need help to put the screws on her so she becomes accountable for his

514

welfare. I think we should stake a claim to him now, so we have a legal right to have some say in his future.'

'You are both right, but calm down,' Nancy said. 'It must have been quite a shock for May having Dulcie turn up out of the blue this morning. I think if I'd been caught on the hop like that I might have said all kinds of things I didn't really mean. She could be missing him already, feeling ashamed of the things she said to Dulcie. Give her a chance to prove herself, and meanwhile you two can get to know little Noël.'

She paused and looked at Rudie. 'If you do something now that upsets May, she might just deny he's your baby out of spite, then where will you be? Also, before you start demanding rights as his father, you've got to think whether you are really prepared for the long-term commitments which come with that.'

Rudie and Dulcie looked at one another, but neither spoke. Nancy laughed and picked Noël up off the floor to cuddle him. 'You've got them wrapped around your little fingers already,' she said to him, kissing his nose. 'I think it's time you showed them the downside of babies, a nice bit of screaming should do it.'

Dulcie giggled and Rudie smiled.

'Okay,' Rudie said, putting his hands in the air as a gesture of surrender. 'No legal advice until we see how the wind is going to blow. But let me have a cuddle with him, you two have been monopolizing him.'

'I'd better put a nappy back on him then before he pees all over you,' Dulcie laughed. 'That's another downside of babies!'

Nancy got up, plonking Noël into Dulcie's lap. 'I've got some work to do,' she said. 'You stay in here as long as you want to, my kids won't be back till about five. I'd better see if I can find some of my old nappies and clothes for him, there wasn't much in that bag you brought with you, Dulcie. I'll dig out the nappy bucket too and put it in the kitchen. Come on through when you want to make up his bottle.'

Dulcie dressed Noël again and passed him over to Rudie. As she watched him tickling and chatting to him she felt a lump come up in her throat. She couldn't remember ever seeing another man playing with a baby, and it was very touching.

'Things have all moved a bit too fast, haven't they?' she said after a little while. 'I certainly didn't expect to be baby-sitting quite so soon.'

'Nor me,' he said, his face suddenly very serious. 'Now, are you going to tell me what May said about me?'

Dulcie studied him for a moment while she chose her words. He didn't fit into a 'type' as most men she'd met did, and it made him confusing. He was neither a manual worker nor a businessman, nor of the professional classes, yet he had some of each of their characteristics.

She would have expected an artist to be more unkempt, perhaps eccentrically dressed, but he was wearing a tweed jacket and carefully pressed casual trousers. His hands were slender and beautifully shaped, yet his shoulders were wide and both his upper arms and thighs appeared muscular as if he'd done manual work. His face was intriguing too, such very smooth, pale skin, perfectly shaped dark eyebrows, a classic nose and slightly hooded eyes. She would have expected such refined looks to indicate a reserved man, yet he was quite the reverse. He wasn't exactly handsome, but he was certainly attractive. Especially when he smiled. She also found his sensitivity very attractive. Maybe it was intelligence. The way he came straight to the point about things and seemed to understand people's feelings and motives instinctively.

'Was May so nasty about me that you can't bear to tell me?' he asked, when she didn't answer his question immediately.

'No, she wasn't nasty,' she lied. 'But I think you've got to accept she just strung you along right from the beginning. She doesn't seem to understand love in the way the rest of the world does.'

He grimaced. 'Okay. I'll try not to ask for her exact words. Obviously I wouldn't like them.'

'I didn't press her for an explanation about you,' she said. 'I'd tell you if I'd learnt anything which would help you to understand better.'

Neither of them spoke for a little while. Rudie continued to play with Noël and Dulcie watched.

'She did tell you something which has disturbed you though,' Rudie said suddenly, breaking the silence. 'I can tell. Come on, try and tell me, Dulcie, even if it's embarrassing for you. You know what they say, a problem shared and all that.'

Dulcie thought for a moment. Even before she met him here in Sydney she felt she knew this man, and that feeling had grown stronger ever since. Yet he didn't know the influences which had moulded and shaped her and her sister. As it looked as if their futures were going to be linked through Noël, perhaps it would be better to go right back to the beginning and tell him about their parents, that way he might understand them both better.

'I can't just tell you what was said today, not without explaining the past first,' she said hesitantly. 'You see, it's all connected, both May and I are how we are because of it.'

Rudie tucked Noël into the crook of his arm. 'Go on then, fire away,' he said.

'It all began back in London in 1947.'

As Dulcie was telling the story about their mother's death and the aftermath, May was packing her suitcase, tears running down her cheeks.

She had never for one moment ever thought Dulcie would turn up in Sydney. She had often worried that Rudie or one of his friends would spot her, but she'd lessened the likelihood of that by keeping well away from places they frequented. But Dulcie had never posed any threat, she lived too far away.

When she opened the door and found Dulcie there she was so severely shocked that her senses left her completely.

She was angry with herself now for forgetting she'd left those letters behind at Rudie's, for not anticipating he would go to such lengths to find her, and for allowing Dulcie to provoke confessions from her. But above all else, she felt completely broken because she could see herself now as she really was, through Dulcie's eyes.

Yet angry as she was at being caught unawares, Dulcie had given her the chance of escape she'd dreamed of for so long, and she knew she had to take it.

'If only!' she sighed, remembering the plan she'd made before Noël was born, and hastily forced a pair of shoes down the side of the case.

She had intended to give a false name when she was admitted to hospital, then after the birth slip out and abandon Noël there. Yet for some reason she still didn't understand, she couldn't go through with it. She wished to God she had! There would have been a hue and cry, but she'd have been safely off up on the Gold Coast, free of Arnie and the hell she'd ended up in. Eventually Noël would have been offered for adoption. Rudie and Dulcie would never have found out about him, or how low she'd sunk.

She had had everything anyone could possibly want when she first arrived in Sydney. Rudie's cottage in Watson's Bay was heaven come to earth, long blissful days on the little beach, by night he'd taken her out to parties, dinners and night-clubs. He knew everyone who was anyone, he was fun, generous and loving. The only thing missing was that she couldn't return his love.

If only she could have admitted it to him, she could have kept his friendship if nothing else. But she couldn't, and she wasn't brave enough to find a place of her own either, and in continuing to lie to him, she found she had a noose around her neck which was slowly strangling her.

When she realized she was pregnant it was like being plunged back into the Dark Place. She felt the exact same terror she'd felt that night, the same sense of hopelessness. Even if she wasn't locked up in darkness, evil images flashed through her mind constantly, making her sick and shaky. The baby inside her and Belinda, her doll, became one and the same. She had nightmare visions of Sister Teresa taking a hammer to her baby's skull and visualized brain and blood spilling out on to the floor. The snake she'd felt wound round her that night came back, constricting her so tightly she couldn't breathe. She vomited every time she ate, and at night she was afraid to close her eyes for the relentless nightmares. Sometimes it was Reverend Mother who came to her, she'd feel that slug-like tongue in her mouth, her fingers pushing up inside her. Other times it was Nev, pushing her down into a pit of snakes and spiders which slithered and crept all over her.

How could she tell anyone how she felt? Certainly not Rudie. To admit to such appalling visions would surely get her locked up in a lunatic asylum, and she knew he could never begin to understand her horror at bearing his child. It was in utter desperation that she ran to Arnie Guthrey, a man she had met in King's Cross at a party not long after she arrived in Sydney. He was the only person she knew who could help her to get rid of this loathsome thing growing inside her, and she'd believed once that was done she'd be her old self again.

Arnie, whom Rudie knew only by reputation, had casually mentioned that he owned a strip club in The Cross, drove a flashy pink and white Cadillac and managed a rock and roll band, all of which made him interesting to her. She wasn't physically attracted to Arnie, he was small and wiry, with sallow skin and slicked-back hair, given to wearing sharp suits and chunky gold jewellery, but they struck up an instant friendship.

At weekends May often went to King's Cross and while Rudie was talking to his arty friends she'd explore and go into some of the coffee bars where she often ran into Arnie. Maybe it was because he was something of a rogue and wasn't part of the set Rudie mixed with that she found herself confiding in him. Long before she became pregnant she told him how she'd only picked Rudie up at Kalgoorlie because she thought he was rich. It felt good to have someone with whom she could be herself. Arnie laughed when she admitted the lies she had told Rudie, about how she used to shop-lift and take money from men in hotels. He said that if she ever left Rudie he'd take care of her, and she believed him.

Arnie did try to get her an abortion, but her pregnancy was already too advanced. He made good his promise to her at first, he let her stay in his flat in The Cross, and later on they moved to a larger one in Surry Hills so Rudie wouldn't find her. She already knew by then that Arnie's main income came from vice and drugs and she had also heard he was a very dangerous man to cross, but she stupidly believed he cared too much for her ever to hurt her in any way, and that he'd support her until she could get the baby adopted.

But she was quite wrong. Within just a few weeks he blackmailed her into prostitution by saying he'd go to Rudie and tell him the truth about her if she didn't comply.

She soon discovered there was a whole world of difference between having sex with a man she'd selected herself and being forced into it with men Arnie found. Right up to her eighth month she had to endure a living nightmare of perversion and cruelty, for Arnie found disgusting men who got a kick out of kinky sex with pregnant women. He beat her up when she complained, and she couldn't run away because he took all the money she made.

'If only you'd stuck to your plan,' she murmured to herself as she forced the lid of the case shut. When she held Noël in her arms for the first time she was completely overwhelmed by emotion, and like a fool she'd allowed herself to believe in happy ever after. But Arnie had her back with men within three weeks. He'd get some young girl to mind Noël, then drive her to the hotels where he'd made arrangements with a punter, sometimes as many as four or five in one night.

The landlord in Surry Hills got wind of what was going on, and they were thrown out. The same thing happened in the next place, and finally Arnie dumped her in this rat-hole in Forbes Street, and it was there she met the other girls he managed. Almost all of them had started out as she had, imagining he cared for them. He didn't need to keep her in a decent place any more, he even let her keep some of the money she earned, for she couldn't run from him easily with a baby in tow.

But now Noël was safe with Dulcie, and Rudie knew everything, there was nothing to stop her fleeing. By the time Arnie called round here at eight tonight, to give her the orders for the evening, she would be on the train for Brisbane.

May humped the case down on to the floor and looked around the room. She had washed all Noël's remaining clothes and nappies and hung them up to dry, she'd even cleaned the room thoroughly. One of the most shameful things about today had been Dulcie seeing her living in such squalor, May hoped that when she came back to look for her, at least that one image would be wiped out.

She glanced at herself in the mirror, wishing that Dulcie could have seen her like this too, instead of looking like a dirty slut. Her hair was washed now, hanging in soft silky waves to the shoulders of a smart black suit Rudie had bought her when she got her first job in Sydney. With stockings, high heels and just a touch of makeup she looked like an elegant secretary. Maybe her eyes had lost the sparkle they once had, and her body wasn't quite so firm, but no one would take her for a prostitute.

Going over to the kitchen counter she leaned on it to write a letter.

Dear Dulcie, I've gone. It's the only thing I can do. You do what you think is best for Noël, because he'd have no chance of a decent life with me. I was telling the truth when I said he was Rudie's son, and please tell him I'm sorry that I wasn't what he believed I was. I've got our mother's bad blood, I can't

521

*help it. I expect I'll come to a sticky end too. I hope you get to
be happy, you deserve to be. I said some cruel things today,
and I won't take them back because they were all true. But I
said them because I love you and I hoped they would make you
stop and think before you ruin your life for other people.*

   May XX

She looked at the letter for a few seconds, suddenly
realizing it was the first time she'd ever managed to write
exactly what she really thought to Dulcie. There was a
whole lot more she wanted to say, especially as she knew
this would be her very last letter to her. But if she wrote
what was in her heart, Dulcie would move heaven and
earth to find her, believing she was worth saving, and she
didn't want that.

   Chewing on the pen for a few moments, she realized
she had to formalize her sister's position about Noël.

P. S., she wrote. *I wish to make it known I want you, Dulcie
Rawlings, née Taylor, to be legal guardian to my son Noël
Taylor. All decisions about his future must be made by you.
Dated 2 September 1961.*

   Signed May Taylor

May first propped up the note on the counter-top, but
then, realizing Arnie had a key and might very well come
in and take it, she added another postscript:

*Noël's clothes are clean and dry back in the flat, I'm enclosing
a key for you to collect them. Kiss him for me.*

Then she folded it up, slipped it into an envelope with
her key and Noël's birth certificate, and addressed it to
Dulcie c/o the Sirius Hotel, The Rocks, Sydney, and put it
in her pocket to post on the way to the station.

   She paused at the doorway, looking back. She noted the
threadbare curtains, the bed settee that never closed up
properly, and her eyes welled up at the sight of Noël's

little matinee jackets, bootees and romper suits on the clothes-horse. Dulcie would never know she'd chosen those things with care and love. Or that on so many nights she'd come back here and taken him into bed with her, just to smell his baby smell, touch his smooth skin. He had been her downfall, yet maybe if things had been different he could have been her saviour. She felt ashamed now that his name had sprung from a drunken joke: *There's no 'ell on earth like a new baby*. She should have given him a proud name, James, Edward or even Rudolph. But it was too late for that now.

Dulcie was giving Noël his bottle at eight the following morning when she heard Nancy coming up the stairs. Tucking the baby under her arm, she opened the door to see the older woman bringing her a breakfast tray.

'I thought I'd bring it up,' Nancy said, looking anxious. 'How was he during the night?'

'Slept right through from the last feed.' Dulcie smiled.

Nancy put the tray down on the table by the window. 'Let me finish with the bottle and wind him,' she said, holding out her arms for him. 'You eat your breakfast and read the letter that's just come for you.'

'A letter?' Dulcie exclaimed, handing over Noël and the bottle. 'It can't be from Ross, I only gave Bruce the address the first night I was here.'

As soon as she saw May's writing she instinctively knew it was trouble. She ripped open the envelope and blanched as she saw the key and Noël's birth certificate and read the note hurriedly.

'Oh no!' she exclaimed. 'She's gone.'

The room began to spin. All those small anxieties yesterday and Rudie's doubts about May's intentions whirled about her in a mad dance.

'She's gone?' Nancy repeated. 'Gone where?'

Silently Dulcie handed her the letter, but held the key in her hand staring at it. She couldn't believe May would do this to her. Looking after Noël for a few days was one thing, but just to dump him on her and run off was something else altogether.

'I played right into her hands, didn't I?' she said glumly as Nancy gasped and let the letter fall to the floor in shock.

Dulcie slumped down at the table and with trembling hands poured herself some tea. 'What am I going to do, Nancy? I can't just keep him. Did she really think by writing that stuff on the end of the letter she would make it right? Am I supposed to just take him back to Esperance and expect Ross to be delighted?'

Both women fell silent, overcome by the seriousness of the situation.

'She must have been desperate,' Nancy said at length. 'You said yesterday she talked about taking him to the Sisters, well, maybe she was afraid to do that herself. I suppose we ought to be grateful she didn't just abandon him somewhere. Also, if she'd run off without a word the police would have had to try and find her before they could allow anyone to make any decisions about him. At least she's given you the authority to act on his behalf.'

'But I don't *know* what to do, and I can't understand how she can be so callous!' Dulcie exclaimed, beginning to cry.

'She did leave him with the one person who could be trusted to care for him,' Nancy said gently. 'Don't judge her too harshly, Dulcie. We don't know what she's been through since she left Rudie. My mother always used to say you have to walk a mile in someone's else's boots before you can judge them.'

But Dulcie continued to cry. She was stunned, frightened and overawed by the enormity of the responsibility her sister had thrust on her. Yet as Nancy's words began to sink in, and as she looked at her sitting there calmly feeding Noël, she realized the woman was quite right. They didn't know what May had been through in the past months – much of what she'd said yesterday could have been bravado. No one would live in such squalor out of choice, and when she thought back to that room she realized there had been no comforts there, no sign of any wealth.

'What did you think of May when you first met her?' she asked through her tears.

'I liked her,' Nancy said evenly. 'Rudie asked all of us over to his house one Sunday, not long after they got back from WA. We spent the afternoon on the beach swimming with the kids, then went back for an early supper at Rudie's place. I thought she was a bit secretive, she didn't say anything about her past, but she was a good hostess, looking after us all, making us laugh a great deal. Of course she was very beautiful too, and I think most of us are drawn to attractive people.'

'You didn't suspect her of anything odd then?'

Nancy shook her head. 'She seemed to be everything Rudie had said – ladylike, amusing, sweet-natured. If we did have a worry it was only because of the age difference between them. Later on, nearer to the time she disappeared, I had a few niggling anxieties: she appeared distant, kind of preoccupied and snappy with Rudie. But then everyone has their moments like that.'

In some way it made Dulcie feel a little better that Nancy had liked May, and she dried her eyes.

'Tell me what Rudie was like when she went,' she asked. He had made light of that so far, and Dulcie wanted to see the whole picture.

'He was devastated. He didn't eat, sleep or work, he lost a great deal of weight,' Nancy said.

Noël began making a loud slurping noise as he reached the end of the milk in his bottle, and the sound made both women smile despite everything.

'Well, *he* isn't bothered by anything,' Nancy said, hoisting him up on to her shoulder to wind him. 'Now, try and eat your breakfast, Dulcie. It's going to be a difficult day for you, and you can't handle it on an empty tum. Would it help if I rang Rudie and told him what's happened?'

you be his legal guardian, that's something. Of course I'm not sure that an unwitnessed letter like this is legally binding, but it's better than nothing.'

'Aren't you angry with her?' Dulcie asked.

'Yes and no. I think it's like Nancy said, she must have been at breaking-point, and once she knew Noël was safe with you she just took off.'

'But it isn't fair to do this to me.' Dulcie sighed. 'I don't know much about babies, and it's not as if I'm even in a home of my own. How on earth did she expect me to manage?'

'I'm sure she knew you'd find a way.' Rudie half smiled, looking down at Noël in his arms. 'You have that air of utter dependability. The question is, are you prepared to take care of him until we can come up with a more permanent solution?'

'Of course I am.'

A look of relief swept across his face. 'Thank heavens for that. I was afraid you'd blame me for getting you into this.'

'How could I blame you? It was me who brought him home with me. Besides, he is a lovely baby, and my nephew, I want to take care of him.'

'You won't have to do it alone, I'll help,' he said.

His words soothed Dulcie's anxiety. She had already decided in her own mind that the only way to prevent Noël ending up in a grim orphanage was to hang on to him for as long as possible. That way she could make sure the Welfare Department found the right foster-home for him. Clearly Rudie was of the same mind as her, and with his support and his knowledge of the legal system here in Sydney she knew that task would be a whole lot easier.

'I feel better now,' she said with a shy smile. 'I suppose I just panicked.'

He beamed at her. 'We'll share everything. I'll even learn to change nappies too. Now, let's take this little tike to see Frank Wetherall.'

*

527

Mr Frank Wetherall, Rudie's lawyer, was a funny little dried-up old stick of a man, less than five feet five, with a few strands of white hair spread across a large bald patch, a heavily lined face and a dark suit which looked too big. But his eyes were bright and piercing, and his voice was deep and resonant. He sat behind his desk with his hands clasped together as they told him the story, only stopping them now and then to clarify a point.

He studied the letter from May intently for several minutes without speaking. Then he looked up at them with an expression of deep sympathy and understanding.

'I am very sorry you have been thrown into such an unenviable situation.' He sighed. 'Now, under normal circumstances, say in the sudden death of the mother, Mrs Rawlings would be granted automatic guardianship of her nephew, but as Miss Taylor is only nineteen, a minor still, and a ward of the Australian government, and she is still living, having abandoned her child, the situation is much more complicated. In law Noël has now become a ward of the government too, and while the Child Welfare Department may eventually pass judgement that you become his legal guardian, they do have powers to take him away from you into care, and they certainly wouldn't allow you to take him out of New South Wales until they had reached a decision.'

'But I couldn't just take him home with me anyway,' Dulcie said quickly, alarmed that he even thought that was her intention. 'Not without first getting my husband's agreement.'

The lawyer nodded in understanding. 'Of course not, Mrs Rawlings. It is a delicate situation and one that needs careful thought and discussion with all parties involved. I would make the suggestion that you find a temporary home here while the authorities make their checks, for they are unlikely to see a hotel as suitable even as a temporary home for a baby.'

Dulcie's heart sank, she had no money for that. She looked at Rudie helplessly.

'Mrs Rawlings could stay with me,' he said hastily. 'That is if, of course, if she is agreeable. Then we could provide a united front as father and aunt together.'

'Umm,' Mr Wetherall murmured thoughtfully. 'I'm not sure that they'll approve of such an arrangement. These officials can be sticklers for propriety.'

Dulcie got up, hugging Noël tightly to her chest. 'We'll convince them it's the best arrangement,' she said firmly. 'But before we go any further, I want to make something quite clear. I can cope with the Welfare taking him away from me to a foster-home if they think that's in his best interests, but I will not stand for him being sent to any place run by the Sisters of Mercy, or the Christian Brothers.'

'Why?' Mr Wetherall asked, looking extremely shocked.

'Because his mother would not have ended up the way she is now had she been spared the Sisters' cruelty. My husband was equally badly treated by the Brothers. Just remember that is not an option.'

'I hope Wetherall isn't a Catholic,' Rudie said as they got into a taxi to go back to the hotel. 'They all idolize the Sisters of Mercy, and the Christian Brothers even more so.'

'Do you approve of the Sisters of Mercy now you know what happened to May and me with them?' Dulcie asked. She hadn't said anything about May's treatment at the hands of the Reverend Mother yesterday, but she had told him about the Sisters' awful cruelty.

'No, I don't,' he said.

'Well, when I get around to telling you what the Christian Brothers did to Ross, you'll see them in the same light as the Sisters,' Dulcie said tightly.

'Some of the best schools in Australia are run by the Christian Brothers,' he said reproachfully. 'Many of my friends have them to thank for a first-class education.'

'I daresay that children who have parents looking out for them have nothing to fear from them,' she said tartly. 'It's orphans that concern me, and if we can't get guardianship of Noël, that's just what he'll be.'

Rudie suggested that they should go to his place for the rest of the day so Dulcie could decide if she'd like to stay there. After a brief talk with Nancy, they collected the pram, Noël's things and a coat for Dulcie and set off for the ferry which left from the Circular Quay, just a short walk from the hotel.

Dulcie suddenly felt very ill at ease as she manoeuvred the pram through the crowds along the quay. It was her hasty actions which had started this, she was in a strange town, with a man she only barely knew, totally unprepared to look after a baby, and in a few days' time she was going to be taken to task by Welfare workers. On top of that she had to make decisions about Noël which would affect his whole life. It was like one of those weird dreams where she was running as hard as she could but getting nowhere, and in this case she knew she wasn't going to wake up suddenly and find it wasn't real.

'Don't look so worried,' Rudie said, clearly sensing part of what she was feeling. 'It isn't all on your shoulders, Dulcie, we're in this together. You don't have to stay at my place if you don't like the idea. Let's just pretend we're borrowing Noël for now, and see how it goes today.'

Her smile was weak, but she felt grateful he seemed to understand how she felt, she supposed he was just as nervous too.

'I have got a car,' Rudie said as they waited in the queue for the boat. 'But it's far more pleasant to come into the city this way. Of course until you arrived I didn't do the trip so often, I stayed at home and painted.'

'You mustn't let me and Noël interfere with your work,' Dulcie said quickly. 'I don't need escorting everywhere or being fussed over.'

He patted her shoulder affectionately. 'It's a pleasure having someone to look after. I work far too much most of the time.'

Dulcie hadn't been on a boat since her arrival in Australia, and though when the ferry arrived it was like a toy boat compared with that huge ship, her spirits lifted as soon as it got underway and chugged off down the harbour.

Leaving Noël in his pram in the warmth of the cabin, she went up to the bows so she could see everything. The wind was so strong it soon whipped strands of her hair out of the neat French pleat, and Rudie came up beside her to point out the places of interest on either side of the bay.

'You should see it in summer,' he said, the strong wind making his eyes water. 'Hundreds of sail-boats scudding along, flash blokes showing off in motor-boats, water-skiers, divers, all sorts. Sometimes I tell myself I should go back to England and find new subjects to paint, but each time summer comes round and I see that azure sea, those billowing sails, I fall in love with it all over again.'

'So you mainly paint this?' she asked, suddenly realizing she hadn't even asked him about his painting.

He nodded. 'Oh, I do the odd trips to other places, the Blue Mountains, the outback, like the time I ended up at your wedding party in Kalgoorlie, but it's the sea and boats I love, and that's what sells for me too. I grew up in Cornwall, you see, so the sea, fishing boats and all that stuff are in my blood. Even when I got sent away to school I always painted that in art classes.'

'Did you earn a living as an artist right from when you first came here?' she asked, glad to be talking about something other than Noël for a while.

He laughed. 'I tried, but it was a no-hoper then. Fourteen years ago, the war had only just ended and Australians weren't interested in art. I worked on building sites, waited on tables, and kept telling myself I'd push off to some country where they did care. But then in 1953 I got a job in the Sheraton Hotel as a cocktail waiter and I got chatting to a couple of blokes one evening – they were English too, a right pair of pansies. They were opening a restaurant in The Cross, and they asked me where they could go to buy some pictures to give the place a bit of colour. I thought

531

on my feet and said I'd be round the next day to show them some, didn't tell 'em I'd painted them. The upshot was that they loved them, hung them in their restaurant, put prices on them and took a small percentage whenever they sold one.'

'And you gave up being a cocktail waiter?'

'Not straight away,' he smiled. 'I had another couple of years at the Sheraton, but Clive and Tony became very influential amongst the arty set in The Cross, and they carried me along with them. If we can get a baby-sitter one night, I'll take you for a meal at their place. They are lovely people.'

'Look, we're nearly there,' he said suddenly, pointing ahead to a small cluster of houses on the right of Sydney Bay. Just beyond it the harbour opened up into the open sea and Dulcie could see huge waves crashing against the rocks either side of the opening.

Dulcie fell silent as they got to Rudie's house. She had chattered most of the short walk from the ferry, admiring the little harbour, the small sandy beach, the dear little houses and the peace of the place. But she hadn't expected his house to be the way it was.

It was wooden clapboard, painted pale blue with white shutters, the prettiest house she'd ever seen. It had no front garden, apart from a low hedge, and the street wasn't paved. It looked like a dolls' house to her, or the kind children drew, two windows up, two below and the door in the middle.

Perhaps it was just because Rudie was an artist that she'd expected it to be a bit dilapidated, and she paused in surprise, still holding the pram. The paint was pristine, even the hedge was neatly trimmed. Three panels on the front door were painted white like the window-frames, but the surrounds were picked out in the same blue as the house.

'What do you think?' he asked, grinning boyishly. 'A suitable place to be inspected by Town Hall officials?'

'If the inside is as lovely as the outside, they'll be wanting to rent rooms here themselves,' she laughed.

Noël woke up as Rudie lifted the pram in through the door. His eyes opened wide as if he was astonished, and Dulcie thought he had good reason to be. It was one very large room, the front door opening into it. All the walls except the one with the fireplace were white, the other vivid yellow. The floor was timber, varnished a pale honey, with brilliantly coloured rugs, and there was little furniture, just a couple of low couches by the fire and a table and chairs painted turquoise blue.

But it was the ceiling Noel was staring up at. Mobiles of fishes, sailing boats and aeroplanes hung from it, all dancing in the breeze from the open door. Dulcie had never seen anything like them in her life.

Then there were the paintings on the walls. She stared at them in awe, for they had an almost childlike simplicity, boats on the sea, waves showering over rocks, some of children on the beach. There were several of the outback too, the red soil, stark gum trees and the harsh blue sky.

'They are so vivid and marvellous,' she finally managed to get out. 'But they aren't a bit how I imagined you'd paint.' Back in Esperance she was always borrowing art books from the library, but Rudie's work didn't compare with any of the famous artists she knew, it was quite unique.

'I suppose I'd be called a *primitive* back in England,' he chuckled. 'That's posh Bond Street art gallery lingo for childish and lacking in technique.'

When Dulcie finally managed to tear herself away from the paintings she was struck by how neat and clean everything was. It didn't look one bit how she imagined a bachelor would live.

'Go and inspect the kitchen,' Rudie urged her with a smile playing around his lips.

Dulcie opened the door he pointed at, and cried out with delight. It was long and narrow, painted yellow and turquoise too, jolly ceramic fish decorating the walls above the modern work surfaces, and at the far end French doors giving on to a small garden.

'It's so pretty,' she exclaimed. 'And you keep it so nice. I can't believe it.'

'I make all the mess upstairs in my studio,' he said. 'I've got someone who comes in to clean too. Boarding school, and the couple of years I spent in the airforce before I ended up here, taught me to be tidy. Besides, there's something very calming about order. I like everything in my life to be beautiful.'

He hiked Noël out of the pram and blew on the mobiles to make them turn faster. Noël squealed with delight and reached out his little hands to try to touch them.

'You can't play with them, Daddy took a long time to make those,' he said.

Dulcie's eyes suddenly filled with tears at hearing the word *Daddy*. It had been clear to her from the outset, in the way Rudie tracked May down because he suspected she had his child, that he had an unusually strong sense of duty. Now the way he called himself *Daddy* told her he had already passed the point of mere duty, she knew in that moment that he would stand his corner and fight for the right to give Noël his name, his care and love.

It was later, after Noël had been fed and was lying down on the rug kicking his legs while they had a cup of tea and a sandwich, that Dulcie's earlier fears came back with a vengeance.

She might have felt a bit awkward and strange while they were down on the quay an hour or so ago, but now reality had hit her with a sickening thud.

Over the last forty-eight hours she'd had one shock after another, and she thought she'd weathered them all pretty well, but now here she was in another new place, a baby on the floor in front of her, Rudie sitting beside her, and she was blithely speaking of coming to stay here with him.

What on earth would Ross say about it? She'd barely given him a thought. Was she going mad?

'I'm scared, Rudie,' she blurted out, and began to cry.

'I am too, if that makes you feel any better,' he admitted ruefully. 'But we had no choice, did we? It was an emergency.'

'But while we've been acting like two kids playing mummies and daddies, I'd almost forgotten I've got a husband. How can I explain how it came to this? I haven't got much money and I can't even tell him when I'm coming home.'

Rudie took her hand and squeezed it. 'I suppose he's your typical Australian male? Expects his wife to do exactly as he wants?'

'I wouldn't call him typical,' she sniffed. 'He's not one of those hard-drinking, out-with-his-mates-type men. But he's jealous, and I've already told you he didn't want me to come here.'

In her head she could already imagine the telephone conversation, Ross's voice tight with anger, asking her far more about Rudie than about the baby, blaming her for sticking her nose in, reminding her where she belonged.

'Maybe I should speak to him,' Rudie suggested.

'That would make him even more suspicious,' Dulcie said.

'Then you must tell him what you intend to do,' Rudie said after a moment or two's thought. 'Don't ask for his approval, or what he wants, just tell him how it is, that you need to stay here until the Welfare people have been to see us. They might not let us keep Noël anyway, Dulcie, you know that.'

'But even if they insist on taking him to a foster-home I couldn't just go back home and leave him,' Dulcie sobbed. 'I'd have to stay a while and make sure everything was all right.'

'Just say you need time to work things out,' Rudie said calmly. 'As for you not having much money, you don't need any. You don't think I won't feed you while you're here, do you?'

'No, I suppose not. But it's embarrassing.'

'Don't forget the arrangement I made with you originally was that I would pay the hotel bill while you were here,' he said pointedly. 'I shall save a good deal if you are here, and it leaves me more time to work too. Now, why don't you come upstairs and look around, maybe you'll feel less scared once you know where you'll sleep.'

Rudie picked Noël up and led the way up the stairs which were behind a door by the kitchen. They were narrow cottagey ones that twisted slightly, bringing them up on to a tiny landing. 'This is the studio,' he said, taking her into the first of the two rooms at the front.

An easel, a stool and beside it an old tea trolley stacked with tubes of paint and pots of brushes were the only furniture. Paintings and canvases were stacked all around the walls. Pencil sketches were tacked to the walls with drawing-pins. The floor was bare boards, speckled with paint.

Dulcie went over to the window, the sea was visible over the roofs of the houses along the harbourside and in the far distance she could see Sydney Harbour Bridge.

'It's not as messy as I expected,' she said, glancing round the room.

'I tidied it the day before you arrived in Sydney,' he said with a smile. 'I'd just finished a picture then, and I haven't started anything else yet.'

'Can I look at these?' she said, moving over to the pictures stacked against the walls.

'Those ones are for my next exhibition,' he said, pointing out ones against the chimney-breast wall. 'These are all old ones, some too bad to sell, others I'm too fond of to part with. But don't look now. I brought you up here to see the bedrooms.'

He walked out and Dulcie followed him on to the landing. 'That's my room.' He waved his hand to the other one at the front. Through the open door Dulcie could see an old-fashioned double bed, the wooden headboard painted purple.

The bathroom was opposite his room, but Dulcie only saw that fleetingly as Rudie opened the last door on the landing and walked right in. 'I've made this into a guest bedroom, and I'd intended to turn the room leading off it into a bathroom,' he said. 'Lucky I didn't get around to that as it's turned out.'

Dulcie gasped in surprise. The room was painted a duck-egg blue, carpeted in the same colour. Another old wooden bed and the rest of the furniture were painted white but beautifully decorated with sprays of hand-painted flowers and leaves.

'Did you do this?' she asked, stunned by its beauty and originality.

He nodded. 'Doing up old furniture is a bit of a hobby,' he said. 'But do you think you could be happy staying in this room for a bit?'

'I could be happy here for ever,' she exclaimed impulsively, then suddenly aware she sounded far too effusive, she blushed scarlet.

Rudie just laughed. 'I'm glad you feel that way, it makes me feel easier. I did it all after May left.' He pointed to the tiny room leading off it. 'That, as I said, would've been the bathroom. I'm glad now I didn't make a start on it. It will be perfect for Noël.'

It was bare aside from the carpet, the walls plain white. 'I could go to town on decorating it, buy him a cot, put some mobiles up here. What do you think?'

Dulcie took Noël from his arms and smiled with delight. 'I'm sure Noël will be thrilled by it.'

'I hope so,' he said. 'Now, I reckon it's about time we got in the car, drove to get some nappies and perhaps collected your things from the Sirius and the rest of Noël's stuff from Darlinghurst. That's if you haven't gone off the idea of staying here?'

She looked up at him, saw his eyes twinkling and suddenly felt far more secure. 'No, I haven't gone off the idea,' she said. 'Let's go.'

*

It was cold that evening and Rudie lit the fire as soon as they got back in. He had bought so much in the baby shop – nappies, a bucket with a lid, a couple of blankets, a warm coat and leggings, two little jumpers and some tiny dungarees, and he'd got the phone number of someone who had a second-hand cot for sale.

Dulcie had gone up into May's old room in Darlinghurst alone, leaving Rudie in the car to mind Noël, mainly because she didn't want Rudie to see the squalor. But she was astounded to find the room neat and clean, the washed baby clothes hanging on an airer. It seemed like a message from her sister that she wasn't all bad, and in some strange way it soothed Dulcie's anger towards her.

Noël was now tucked fast asleep into his carry-cot upstairs, and they had just finished eating the fish and chips Rudie had slipped out to buy from the shop down on the harbour.

'That was delicious,' Dulcie said with a smile as she sat down on the settee. 'It took me right back to the ones we used to get back home in England. When I was at St Vincent's I used to dream about fish and chips, so much so I could even smell the vinegar.'

'I didn't ever have them from a shop until I was in the airforce,' Rudie said. 'My folks thought they were common. I can remember walking back from the pub to the base in the blackout, half cut, a great steaming parcel in my hands. Nothing ever tasted or smelled that good.'

'Did you fly planes?' she asked, curling her legs up under her and leaning back on a cushion.

He laughed. 'Who, me? Do I look like a hero?'

'You do actually,' she said with a giggle. 'I can just imagine you with a little moustache and Brylcreemed hair, saying all that "Chocks away" stuff and "Jolly good show!"'

'I'm sorry to disappoint you, I was just a pen-pusher, and anyway I was only in for the last two years of the war,' he said. 'I missed the Battle of Britain and all that. I was supposed to go to university then, but I came out here instead.'

'Tell me about your family,' she asked.

'Dull stuff,' he grinned. 'Dad was an accountant with an office in Truro, our home was in Falmouth. Two older sisters and a grandmother who Dad said turned me into a pansy. That's how he perceives artists, musicians, anyone who doesn't do what he calls a "real" job. If he'd had his way I'd have been strapped to a desk like him.'

'Was it a happy childhood?'

'Pretty much so, nice house, lovely garden, we weren't rich, but comfortable as they say. Only blot was being sent away to school, I loathed it for the first four years. Boys can be cruel bastards, always looking for someone smaller and weaker to thump. I had more than my share of that.'

Dulcie smiled. The way Rudie spoke reminded her of actors in English films, the same crisp short sentences, the well-rounded vowels and the deepness of his voice. She liked the way he understated everything, no boasting, or using some device to make himself appear cleverer or braver than others. The exact opposite to Ross.

'Why don't you tell me about Ross now?' he said, as if he'd picked up her thoughts. 'You said you would when you got around to it.'

Dulcie told him first how she met him the day she ran away from the Masters, then went on to tell him Betty's story of how she and Bruce had found him in the barn on their farm.

'I suppose I was drawn to him at first because of that,' she said. 'It was obvious to me he'd had a very unhappy childhood, and it made us equal. I suppose I was touched too because he confided in me about it and not in Bruce or Betty.'

She went on to relate all the awful things Ross had told her about Bindoon, tears starting up in her eyes as she spoke.

'So he never had anything to do with women until he arrived in Esperance, then?' Rudie asked.

'No. Well, I think he said there were a few Spanish nuns who did the laundry, but he didn't have any contact with them.'

'That must have made it difficult for him to relate to women then?'

Dulcie nodded.

'But you broke through that?'

Dulcie suddenly felt this was getting a little too personal. 'I suppose so, but he's still not easy to talk to, not like you, Bruce or John.'

'May described him as a brick wall,' Rudie said with a little smirk. 'Was she just being cruel, or is that how he is?'

Dulcie thought for a moment. 'No, he isn't like that, saying he's like a brick wall implies he's an empty sort of person, which he isn't,' she said at length. 'He just isn't what you'd call a conversationalist.'

Rudie looked at her. 'Tell me, Dulcie, why do I keep getting the impression that there is something very big holding you two apart? I know I've been swayed by things May said, which might not have been true, but you haven't said anything that convinces me you are truly happy together. Have you got some some real anxiety about it?'

'What exactly did May say?' Dulcie asked. She didn't want to know, yet she had to, she wanted to turn this conversation in another direction, yet she couldn't.

'To put it bluntly, she didn't think Ross was capable of love-making.' He looked embarrassed.

Dulcie dropped her eyes from his. She wanted to deny it, but her sister's charge that she lied to herself was stuck in the forefront of her brain, and she couldn't bring herself to prove her right.

'She was correct then?' Rudie said softly. 'Oh Dulcie,' he sighed. 'I was really hoping that would prove to be another malicious lie.'

Dulcie looked up defiantly. 'What would she know about married love? She only had sex with men for money.'

Rudie nodded, not so much in agreement as acknowledgement that he understood why she had to reply with such bitterness.

'It seems to me that May, you and Ross have all been badly damaged by your upbringings,' he said very gently. 'Each one of you has found a different way to cope with it, and I really don't know which is the saddest.'

'There's nothing sad about me,' Dulcie said indignantly.

'Self-sacrifice is sad,' he said, his hand stealing across the arm of his chair to touch her arm lightly. 'It's rather beautiful, it's good for those on the receiving end of your boundless compassion, but not good for you personally.'

'You're as bad as May, she said I was a martyr yesterday, but then I suppose she put this idea into your head.'

'The only idea she put into my head was that you were a cruel fiend,' Rudie reminded her. 'I believed it implicitly until I read those letters from you. I certainly didn't see a martyr there either, only a young girl who took her role as big sister very seriously. What I think now comes from you, no one else. I think, Dulcie, that you have taken all the blame on to your shoulders for everything that happened to you and May.'

'I haven't!'

'Oh, I think you have, my dear. And when you met Ross you took him on board too. I daresay if I was weak and vulnerable you'd do the same for me.'

'I wouldn't,' she said, getting flushed with indignation. 'That's a ridiculous thing to say.'

He smiled. 'How much of what May said about me have you kept back?' he asked tauntingly. 'All you said was *she doesn't see love in quite the same way as other people.* I wouldn't mind betting she said I made her skin crawl, but you wouldn't tell me that, you'd be too afraid of wounding me.'

Dulcie couldn't answer because she knew he was right in that instance.

'May's way of coping with her wounds was with cunning,' Rudie went on. 'I suspect Ross's way is denial. Strangely enough, I suspect that cunning and denial are easier to jettison overboard in the long run than self-sacrifice.'

'What do you mean by denial?' Dulcie asked.

Rudie laughed.

'What's funny about that?' Dulcie felt irritated now.

'Anyone else would want to talk about their own problem.' He grinned. 'But not you, shove that to one side, let's help someone else first.'

Dulcie frowned. 'I don't believe I have a problem, but I'm curious about Ross. Is that so extraordinary?'

'Not for you, it's all part of your character. By denial I mean he won't admit to himself there is anything wrong with him, I expect he's even blanked out whatever it was which started it. But you've taken the blame, haven't you? I bet you feel you aren't pretty or sexy enough, or maybe too that you are just plain wicked for desiring sex.'

Dulcie blushed to the roots of her hair and Rudie laughed again.

'Dulcie, you are absolutely delectable, any red-blooded man would want you. Believe that if nothing else. Whatever is wrong with Ross is tucked away in his past, some bad experience he can't face up to. I expect he does love you, in fact I'm positive he does, but until he accepts that he has a problem, it isn't going to be cured.'

'We shouldn't be talking about Ross like this,' Dulcie insisted. 'It's not right.'

Rudie leaned closer to her and took her hand in his. 'No, perhaps we shouldn't,' he said in a far gentler tone. 'I've embarrassed you, put you on a spot, and I had no right to do that, but believe me, if I have overstepped the mark, it's only because I want to help.'

Dulcie glanced nervously at him but was moved to see merely tenderness and concern in his dark eyes. 'I can see that,' she said. 'I'm just not used to men who talk about feelings, emotions and such things. Just before Betty died, she tried to warn me off Ross, but I was too stubborn to really take on what she was saying. But we're all guilty sometimes of only listening to what we want to hear.'

'There's nobody worse than me at that,' Rudie laughed. 'In the next day or so I'll have dozens of friends ringing me advising me against trying to keep little Noël. But I won't listen.'

'You don't mean permanently, do you?' she asked, for there was something in the way he'd made that remark which sounded as if he was thinking long-term.

Rudie leaned back in his chair and smiled at her. 'Yes, I guess I do, though it's a bit soon to put my hand on my heart and swear to it. How can I possibly sit back and watch my own son go to a foster-home or be adopted?'

'But Rudie, a man can't bring up a child on his own.'

'Why not?' he said, giving her a sharp look. 'Men have to manage when they are widowed or their wife walks out on them. You told me yourself that your father was the more capable parent. Look, I'm thirty-five, Dulcie. I have a decent home, I earn enough from my painting to live very comfortably, I've sowed all the wild oats I want to. I didn't actively ever think I wanted children, I doubt many men do, but when I picked little Noël up in my arms today I felt something special, and it's grown throughout the day.'

'Aren't you getting a bit carried away?' she said anxiously.

He laughed softly. 'Maybe I'm being a little idealistic, I have to admit I know absolutely nothing about babies and small children. But I do know how to love, isn't that enough to be getting along with for now while I learn the rest?'

A vision of Noël in a bleak nursery filled with dozens of other unwanted babies all crying piteously came into her mind, and she knew he was right. She nodded.

He reached out and took her hand, squeezing it tightly. 'A small really selfish part of me can't help wishing that you won't ever want to go home and that we can bring Noël up between us.'

*

Later that night as Dulcie lay in the guest bedroom, Noël in his carry-cot beside her, she thought about that remark of Rudie's again. He'd said it lightly and later he'd even apologized and said he was being quixotic, for it seemed to him whichever way the authorities went, one of them was going to be hurt.

She might not have had much experience with men, but she sensed Rudie was attracted to her. It was of course only because of her strong similarity to May, but she reminded herself that in future she must stress how much her marriage to Ross meant to her, and steer conversations away from personal subjects.

Yet she couldn't help but think a little wistfully how different it would be if she weren't married. Since arriving in Sydney she'd seen how narrow her life had been so far, so little fun, so much hard work. Just these few days had expanded her horizons enormously, it was good to see crowds of people, to feel the pulse of a big city and it had made her think of the ambition she once had to become a teacher and to travel. She knew she was going to find it hard to accept the limitations of life back in Esperance.

But she couldn't allow herself to think along those lines. Tomorrow she would have to ring Ross and tell him everything. It was that she should be thinking about, preparing what she was going to say to reassure him, not day-dreaming of something that could never be.

Noël made a funny little squeaky noise and she leaned up on one elbow to look at him. He was sound asleep, thumb in mouth, the covers tucked firmly round him, and the sight brought tears to her eyes. Where was May tonight? Was she thinking of him and regretting her actions? Or did she in fact know Rudie so well that she knew Noël would be here safe in his house?

'Oh, May,' Dulcie whispered to herself. 'Why wasn't all this enough for you? A good man, a nice home by the sea, it's so much more than most women get.'

She lay back on the pillow, remembering what Rudie had said about her, May and Ross all being damaged and coping with it in different ways. She didn't agree, in her opinion she and May had always been much the same way they were now. She had always been a carer, the one that held back, observing and listening. May had always fought for a centre-stage role, whether that was through charm or cunning. As for Ross, she couldn't for the life of her see what Rudie meant by saying he was in denial, after all he'd told her everything that had happened to him as a child. Besides, surely a child brought up without love and affection would want much more than a normal person? So why would he turn away from her all the time?

Dulcie took the bull by the horns and rang Ross the following morning when she knew he would be in Bruce's house having breakfast. She had left Rudie upstairs giving Noël his bottle and she had thought until she heard Ross's voice that she was totally prepared. But his first question, when was she coming home, threw her, not by the content – she had expected that – but by the sullen aggression of his tone.

'Not for a while,' she began, then without giving him a chance to say anything more she launched into what had happened.

He didn't interrupt at all, not until the part where she came here to Rudie's house, and then he let rip. 'You can leave there right now and get the train home tonight,' he barked at her. 'It's his kid, let him bloody well look after it.'

'I can't do that,' she said. 'May asked that I be Noël's guardian, I have to stay and see it through.'

'Your sister is a tart, and her little bastard is nothing to you,' he shouted. 'I'm your husband, I have rights.'

'Not to tell me to ignore my own nephew,' she retorted. 'I thought you of all people would have a little compassion for Noël. I even hoped you would tell me to bring him home so we could bring him up.'

'I don't want another man's kid in my house,' he roared at her. 'Especially the leavings of a slut and a bloody artist.'

She gasped at his cruel words, and her anger flared up

545

and spilled over. 'Then I may never come home,' she snapped. 'Seeing as I'm not likely to ever have a child of my own. Or even a normal marriage.' To make her point even clearer she slammed the phone down.

Seething with rage, she stamped out of the house and down the road and turned down to the little beach. The sand was damp from a shower during the night, and aside from a couple of fishermen unloading their catch at the far end, there was no one else around.

She stood still for a moment or two taking deep breaths to calm herself. The sun was shining, the sea very calm and blue, and the only sound the gentle swish of the sea over the sand and birds singing in the trees. Sydney Harbour Bridge in the distance looked so graceful, and she was reminded by the many tall buildings near it that there must be hundreds of people there in the city with problems even larger than hers. A squawking noise behind her made her turn, and there on a small tree in one of the gardens of the cottages by the harbour were a couple of sulphur-crested cockatoos.

They were so beautiful and unexpected, both had their beady eyes fixed on her and they sounded as if they were scolding her, that she was forced to smile, and immediately she regretted saying something so cruel to Ross.

'He'll come round in a day or two,' Rudie said encouragingly when she told him about her conversation with Ross. 'I expect he'll go down the pub tonight, drink himself senseless and wake up tomorrow morning feeling like hell and missing you. That's the point when common sense takes over, because he'll see if he carries on like that he will lose you.'

'But I'm ashamed that I said that about not having a child of my own,' she said, blushing furiously.

Rudie shrugged. 'It's better said than left to fester,' he said. 'He might just think on it enough to try and get some help.'

'Where would anyone go for help like that?' she asked,

thinking of the time she wrote to the Agony Aunt in a magazine.

'A psychiatrist,' he said, then seeing her anxious expression he put his arm around her shoulder and squeezed her. 'I know from what you've told me about him he isn't likely to go for that, but I've got a friend who is one, you could try talking to him while you're here, he might be able to give you some advice.'

'I doubt I could bring myself to talk about something like that to anyone,' she said sadly.

'You managed to tell me, even if it was more me digging it out,' he replied. 'But let's take Noël for a walk now, and let me show you the sights. We'll drop in at the doctor's on the way too and get him to check our little man out.'

Chapter Twenty-three

The next nine days were a time of discovery and joy for both Rudie and Dulcie as they shared caring for Noël. He appeared to them to be an exceptionally placid baby, only crying when hungry, and sleeping solidly from seven in the evening round to eight the next morning. The local doctor had weighed and checked him out, pronouncing him a fine healthy baby, and suggested they started him on some solid food. He was sympathetic and supportive when they explained the predicament they were in, giving them a couple of child care books to study. He had already made a home visit and filed a report with the Child Welfare Department in their favour. His advice to them at that time was just to enjoy Noël and not to worry about the officials.

They had been enjoying everything, even the shared domestic chores. Rudie liked to bath Noël, push the pram and change nappies, and for Dulcie who had never before seen a man doing traditionally female jobs, it was a source of wonder. But then Rudie was happy for her to take over male roles, it was she who put the second-hand cot he'd bought together, and while she was painting it pale blue, he hung the curtains at the window in Noël's room. When she admitted on her third day there that she liked to draw and paint too, he put a canvas on his easel and said she was to paint something for Noël while he took him out for a walk.

Dulcie was nervous about painting anything when Rudie was such an expert, but inspired by a large white floppy rabbit he had bought for Noël, she painted him propped up on a couple of books on the window-sill.

When she finally finished it two days ago, Rudie was genuinely admiring, saying he thought she could easily become a children's book illustrator. While she didn't entirely believe this, it had given her a warm glow.

It occurred to Dulcie on around the sixth night, as they bathed Noël together, that this was how married life should be. Togetherness, a great deal of laughter, neither one trying to out-do the other. They discussed what they would eat, and when, for Rudie didn't have a set timetable. Some days she got up at seven to find he'd been painting since first light, others he was still in bed at nine. Sometimes he ate like a horse, other times he only wanted a sandwich. She found this pleasing, for her life so far had been set in strict lines from which there was no deviation. It was so nice to be asked to go to the beach with him to watch the sun go down, taking turns in carrying Noël. To have her opinion asked about a new plant for the garden, or just to sit over a bottle of wine in the evenings and talk about books, or listen to his records. Rudie loved pop music, he said some of his more dignified friends despaired of him for not listening to classical music or jazz, and he would turn up his radiogram to blast out Del Shannon's 'Hey Little Girl', or Billy Fury's 'Last Night Was Made for Love' and sing along with them too.

Dulcie kept having to remind herself how easy it was for Rudie to be young at heart and happy, for he had everything anyone could want. A comfortable childhood, loving parents, success in his chosen career, dozens of good friends. She knew she shouldn't be comparing him with Ross and wishing he was less rigid and staid. Ross had never had a chance to see rock and roll bands, or the opportunity to listen to English records. He'd never lived in a city, he'd never had much chance to make friends.

Yet she knew in her heart that even if Ross was to come to Sydney, he would sneer at the kind of bohemian people Rudie knew, he wouldn't want to try foreign food, he'd find fault with everything. Sadly, his idea of a good time only stretched to downing around eight schooners of beer. He would never dream of using his talent at carpentry or building to make a living, even though she knew it satisfied him far more than farm work. In truth she had come to see he had a deeply engrained notion that he deserved nothing better than being a farm labourer.

Nine days after Dulcie had come to stay at Watson's Bay, Rudie took Noël out for a walk in his pram after lunch, leaving Dulcie to write a letter to Ross. As he pushed the pram out through the front door, he glanced round at Dulcie sitting at the table, pen in hand, but resisted the temptation to say anything which might confuse her further.

Two Child Welfare officers had called that morning to check on Noël and to assess the situation. Dulcie had told them that she wanted joint guardianship with Rudie, and that she believed it to be in Noël's best interests to stay in Sydney with his father, where the schools and medical facilities were better, and that she would see Noël in the holidays.

Rudie had stated he intended to employ a part-time nanny, and as he worked from home and had a cleaner too, Noël would be well looked after. Everything was going well, both he and Dulcie could see the officers had overcome their initial suspicion that a bachelor couldn't take care of a small baby alone. They seemed relieved too that there was no question of Dulcie demanding to take Noël permanently out of the state and away from their supervision. Once Rudie had agreed to take a blood test to prove he was Noël's father, it looked as if they were home and dry. But then suddenly one of the officers turned on Dulcie and began questioning her.

Rudie knew very well that what Dulcie really wanted was to take Noël home with her, but Ross had refused even to consider it. Rudie guessed too that the holiday arrangements which Dulcie had spoken of so convincingly would be unlikely to materialize either, because of Ross's jealousy. Yet Dulcie hadn't allowed the officers to get even a glimpse of this. She courageously answered their probing questions about her husband and home life, creating an impression with the officers that Ross was in complete agreement with everything she said. Her only concern was that the officers should find no grounds to take Noël into their care.

Then, right at the end of the visit, the officers said they would need a written testimony from Ross that he shared his wife's views. They left then, leaving Dulcie and Rudie completely stunned.

Dulcie recovered quicker than Rudie did. She said she would have to resort to blackmail – either Ross wrote that testimony, or she'd refuse to come home.

Rudie took the path up to the headland, stopping for a moment when he reached the top to look down at the Pacific Ocean pounding on the rocks far below. It was a sight that never failed to inspire him, a reminder of how it must have been for the first sailors who came to Australia, seeing all those daunting cliffs, then discovering the inlet into one of the safest natural harbours in the world. In the past he had stood in this spot and imagined himself as captain of one of those ships, or one of the felons aboard, and thought of their feelings as they approached the end of their voyage.

But today Rudie barely noticed the wheeling gulls or tasted the salt spray on his lips. His mind was centred on his past and what the future might hold.

He had loved two women before May, one was back in England, a young WRAC at the camp in Lincolnshire during the war, the second here in Australia. Like May, they'd both been pretty, blue-eyed blondes. Julie, the first, had jilted him for a dashing pilot; Claudine, the second, had thrown him over for a doctor. But he couldn't say all blondes were bad news to him, for there had been many others over the years, brunettes and red-heads too – he'd had a great deal of fun and happiness with many women.

But until he met May, marriage had barely entered his head, his art was all-consuming.

Looking back at that relationship now, with the benefit of so much more knowledge about May, he could see he had fallen for a mirage. It had been so thrilling to find someone so young, beautiful, charming and refined, yet so hot in bed. What a pathetic fool he'd been to imagine he'd taught her all she knew, or that the passion she responded with was real.

Yet the hurting was over now. By meeting Dulcie and discovering the whole truth about May, including the appalling business of that perverted Reverend Mother, he saw May quite differently. When he thought about her now it was not with regret, or love, only with concern she might be in danger, and sadness that she was such a troubled girl.

He had no real anxiety about Noël either, for in his heart he knew the authorities wouldn't oppose a man's right to keep his own son, not when he was so well known and respected. They might string him along for months, put him through every kind of test, but he'd win in the end, for the longer Noël stayed under his roof, the less easy they'd find it to remove him without a public outcry.

Dulcie was his real concern, for she was the one who was going to lose in all directions, and his heart bled for her. She had such a huge capacity for love, she gave it willingly and joyfully, expecting nothing in return.

As he stood there gazing out to sea and thinking of her writing the letter that would in effect destroy any possibility of her being free to return to Sydney to see Noël, or even to have him with her for holidays, tears came to his eyes. It wasn't right, she had already lost so much – both her parents dead, a husband who was one in name only – and now her own sister had brought further heartache to her door.

But as the tears trickled down his cheeks, a sudden realization came to him.

He had fallen in love with her!

All at once he was trembling, he had to grip on to the pram handle to support himself. Why hadn't he seen it coming? He'd liked her from the very first, admired her kindness, honesty and inner strength. Since then he'd found dozens of other attributes that were usually lacking in his women friends. Dulcie was capable, artistic, a deep thinker, and someone who got things done.

'Oh God,' he gasped, turning his eyes up to the sky. 'Why have you done this to me? She's perfect, but she's not free to love me back.'

Now he could understand why his blood had almost boiled each time she'd put the phone down on Ross and burst into tears. Maybe it wasn't the man's fault that he couldn't consummate the marriage, but that didn't excuse him showing so little concern for his wife's feelings about her nephew, or for behaving in such a cruel, dictatorial manner. Rudie knew that Dulcie's love for Noël had grown day by day, just as his had, he saw the joy and delight in her eyes when she held him, felt the ache in her heart when she contemplated parting from him, and sensed how empty her life would be when she did go home.

At times he'd even been tempted to persuade her to fight for her right to take Noël back to Esperance, for she was an ideal mother. But he couldn't do that, for the same reason she never voiced that this was what she wanted. They both knew it was unlikely Ross would ever accept him, let alone grow to love him, and that wasn't fair to Noël.

Dulcie had often said how she would have thought a damaged child once grown up would actively seek to protect other children, but it didn't always seem to work that way. Rudie guessed that most of the cruel nuns, and the Brothers at Bindoon, had been victims of cruelty themselves as children. They did what they'd been taught and saw no wrong in it, and that was the real horror of it, for unless someone stepped in and broke this hideous chain, it would go on into perpetuity.

But he didn't want to think of such sad things, he would

rather picture Dulcie's sweet face. Now he could see why these last few days had been so happy, why he'd woken each morning full of excitement. He wished he could go home and tell her so, that he wanted to share everything, his success, home, wealth and Noël, with her for evermore.

A cloud slipped over the sun, and the sudden chill reminded him he couldn't have her. It was no good. Her religious convictions and the vows she'd made to Ross wouldn't allow her to accept his love, or return it. All he could do when the time came for her to return home was to let her go without the burden of guilt. Maybe he could tell her there was a home waiting here for her if she ever needed it, but he knew she wouldn't take him up on it, she was far too noble to give up on Ross.

Noël yawned, stretched and opened his eyes. He saw Rudie looking down at him and gave a gummy smile.

'You persuade her, little man,' Rudie whispered, bending over to tickle him. 'You've got more charm than me.'

September faded into October, and Dulcie and Rudie had several more visits from the authorities, and a great many letters passed between them, Mr Wetherall and the Welfare Department. Ross had written the letter to them, as instructed by Dulcie, agreeing that he fully supported his wife's and Rudie's plans for Noël, and there was no doubt now that in due course the joint guardianship would be formally approved.

But the letter Ross wrote to Dulcie at the same time he sent the one to the Child Welfare Department had a quite different content. He said that if she wasn't back home by mid-November to help out with the harvest he would write again to the Welfare people and state that he'd only written the first one because his wife had pressured him into it, and that he was totally against her having any connection with the child. He said he considered Rudolph Jameson to be an immoral man, totally unfit to bring up a child because he had abducted a young girl and taken her to live with him, and in his opinion May fled from him because he ill-treated her. He finished up this letter by saying Dulcie had a duty to him and Bruce which she had neglected, but that he would put that aside if she came home and spoke no more about this child.

Dulcie cried bitterly as she read the letter, knowing Ross was quite capable of carrying out his threats if she didn't comply with his wishes. The most tragic thing to her was that Ross had learnt nothing from his own harsh upbringing but personal survival, and he was prepared to let a child suffer to gain what he wanted.

Yet however unhappy Dulcie felt about the future of her marriage, and indeed returning to Esperance, she couldn't help but feel joyful when she looked at Rudie and Noël together. Rudie was a superb father, deeply committed, loving and full of fun. Watching him spoon-feed Noël was a delight. Noël was as greedy as a baby bird, eager to try almost anything, and as Rudie fed him he would keep up a running commentary on the benefits of iron in spinach or protein in chicken, as opposed to the negative value of chocolate pudding which was Noël's favourite. It seemed to Dulcie, too, that Noël was growing far more like Rudie, he had his long, slender fingers, and when Dulcie smoothed down his dark hair after a bath and parted it to one side, it made her laugh to see the similarity.

Their days together had fallen into a pattern. Rudie painted in the mornings, while Dulcie either did chores or took Noël out while Mrs Curston was cleaning. After lunch sometimes Rudie took Noël out alone, leaving Dulcie to paint or read, or they went out together. It was getting warm now, sometimes hot enough to have a swim in the sea, and they often took the ferry into Sydney to walk in the Botanical Gardens, dropping in later to see Nancy at the Sirius.

Rudie had found a nanny for Noël, Sarah, the nineteen-year-old daughter of a neighbour, who was at college studying languages. At present she only minded Noël occasionally for an hour or two to get them used to one another, but the plan was that once Dulcie had gone home Sarah would fit her hours with Noël around her lectures, an afternoon a couple of days a week, or evenings when Rudie needed to go out, and most of the day during the college holidays so that Rudie could paint. With Mrs Curston's help too, Dulcie could see that there was really no need for her to stay on now. Rudie was perfectly capable of handling everything, and any forms which needed to be signed could be sent through the post. But neither of them spoke of this, and Dulcie knew Rudie was as reluctant for her to leave as she was.

On the morning of 20 October, Wetherall sent a letter confirming the blood tests Rudie had taken proved he was Noël's father, and jubilantly pointed out that this meant there was no fear of any further interference from the Welfare Department, aside from routine visits from a health visitor. His only real concern was that May might suddenly turn up again and claim her child back. Since this was unlikely, as the police had failed to find her, they took the ferry into town for a celebratory lunch.

They got home at four in the afternoon, slightly merry after a bottle of wine, and left the front door propped open as it was a very warm day. Dulcie was changing Noël's nappy on the floor and Rudie was making a cup of tea, when a male voice called out, 'G'day, Mrs Rawlings, it's the police. May we come in to speak to you?'

Dulcie looked up and saw a big man in a grey suit, with a smaller uniformed man just behind him. 'Of course,' she said, assuming they just wanted to report another line of inquiry about May which had led nowhere. There had been around five or six such visits in the past six weeks, though not by these two men. 'Rudie!' she called out. 'It's the police, will you make another two cups of tea?'

She picked Noël up in her arms, asked the men to sit down, and sat down herself to fasten up Noël's romper suit. 'What is it this time?' she asked. 'A new lead on May?'

It was only when the two men exchanged glances before speaking that she felt nervous. 'Have you found her? Where is she?' she said.

Rudie came out of the kitchen then carrying a tea tray and stopped short, perhaps sensing this wasn't like all the other visits.

'I'm very sorry to bring bad news,' the plain-clothes man said, looking up at Rudie, then back at Dulcie. 'But a young woman was found dead this morning on the Gold Coast, and we think it is your sister.'

Dulcie just stared blankly at him. She took in his red and black striped tie, the way the starched collar of his shirt appeared to be digging into his thick neck, even that he had very pale blue eyes and a sun-blistered face, but she couldn't take his words in.

Rudie put the tray down on the coffee table with a clatter and took Noël from her arms. 'You only *think* it's May?' he asked. 'Don't you know for certain?'

'These things can never be exactly certain until the body has been identified,' the man said. 'But her description, what we know of her, all fits May Taylor. I'm so sorry to be the one to bear such sad news. I wish there was a gentler way.'

'She's dead?' Dulcie said in a hoarse whisper. 'How did she die?'

Rudie put Noël in his pram and wheeled him out through the kitchen to the garden. It was only then that Dulcie realized this wasn't some quirk of her imagination but real. Rudie was wheeling Noël away because his sensibility wouldn't allow anyone to speak of something so awful in his son's presence.

'She was drowned,' the policeman said, wiping sweat away from his forehead with a handkerchief. 'Her body was found at daybreak today on the beach by a man walking his dog. The local police hadn't established her

557

time of death when they contacted us, but it seems likely she went in for a swim the previous evening when the surf was high.'

The uniformed man began pouring the tea, aware Rudie and Dulcie were too shocked to do it. He put two sugars in Dulcie's, stirred it and took it over to her. 'Drink it up,' he urged her.

It was Rudie who asked all the questions, all Dulcie could do was just sit and let it wash over her head.

'But you centred your search for her on the Gold Coast,' he said. In a previous visit the police had reported that a guard on a train to Brisbane had recognized May as having been on his train from a photograph he was shown, and later a taxi driver had said he drove her to the Gold Coast. 'Why couldn't you find her?'

'It's a big area to cover,' the plain-clothes man said. 'The police concentrated their search amongst – ' He broke off, clearly embarrassed.

'Amongst prostitutes?' Rudie finished it for him.

He nodded. 'I really can't tell you much more,' he said. 'All I know is they haven't found out what she was doing or where she was living yet. My job was just to break the news to you and ask that you go up to Brisbane to identify the body. Maybe by the time you get there, there'll be more information.'

It was then that Dulcie began to cry, remembering how May had said in that last letter to her she expected she'd come to a sticky end.

The police left soon after, asking that Rudie ring them later to make the arrangements. Dulcie vaguely heard them speaking of a small plane, and the need for urgency.

Rudie sat down next to her after they'd gone, and took her into his arms. 'There's nothing I can say,' he said mournfully, smoothing her hair. 'She was your sister and you loved her, it's so, so sad.'

Dulcie sobbed into his chest. She knew he was right, there was nothing he could say. After the initial hope that

May would return penitent and wanting to take care of Noël herself, they had begun to want her to stay away for ever. Had she drowned by accident? Or had she committed suicide because of what she'd done? Dulcie couldn't bear to think it might be that.

By noon the following day, Dulcie and Rudie were at the mortuary. They had left Noël with Mrs Curston and flown up to Brisbane on the plane the police had recommended and would return at six in the evening. Both of them were still in a state of shock – on the journey here they'd barely spoken, both locked into their own private thoughts.

They were met at the mortuary by a local police inspector who introduced himself as Mike Haggetty. He said little other than offering his condolences and suggested they got it over with straight away and talked later.

The white tiled room he took them into was as cold as a refrigerator after the heat outside and smelled strongly of chemicals. The body was laid out on a marble table covered in a sheet. Haggetty waited only a second or two to make sure they were ready, then folded back the sheet to expose just her face and neck.

Dulcie gave a little cry and covered her mouth with her hands. She had spent the whole journey here trying to tell herself it wouldn't, couldn't be May, but of course it was. Her skin looked so pale and waxy, someone must have brushed her hair carefully for it gleamed under the bright light, the only colour in the white room, but in every other way she looked little different to how she'd been the last time Dulcie saw her over seven weeks earlier.

'Is it May Taylor?' the policeman asked formally.

'Yes, it's May,' she whispered, reaching out to touch her hair, remembering how she used to plait it for her at the Sacred Heart. It was as long now as it had been then, and just as silky, tumbling down over the end of the table. She leaned over and kissed her sister's cheek, but her skin was cold and unyielding. She turned away, overcome by emotion, and felt Haggetty catch her arm to steady her.

'She was a very beautiful girl,' he said softly. 'You are very like her, Mrs Rawlings, and I'm so sorry she met her death so very young.'

Dulcie sensed Rudie was looking at May, but she didn't turn to watch him, just walked blindly to the door, tears streaming down her face, suddenly chilled to the bone, for she'd promised her father and granny to look after May, and she'd failed.

Rudie stayed for just a moment or two longer, then Haggetty took them both to a small office up a flight of stairs. 'I'll get you both a cup of coffee,' he said. 'I expect you'd like to be alone for a little while.'

Dulcie walked over to the window. It had frosted glass on the lower half, but the top part, at eye level, was clear. It overlooked a small side street, and as she looked out, a young woman in a pink sundress and sun-glasses walked by pushing a pram. She could hear the rumble of traffic in the distance too.

'Everything's ordinary out there,' she said in a hushed voice. 'People going about their daily lives. I want everything to stop, if only for a minute. It doesn't seem right that it's only you and I mourning her.'

Rudie came up behind her, put his hands on her shoulders and leaned his head against hers. 'I wanted to paint her,' he whispered. 'She never let me. I don't know why.'

'Maybe she thought you would make her keep still for hours,' Dulcie whispered back. 'She could never stand that.'

'I wish I'd known the real May,' he said, his voice strangled as if fighting back tears. 'Like you did.'

Dulcie turned round and took his face in her two hands, his eyes were brimming now. 'I think you knew her far better than me, Rudie. I've got the image of the little May stuck in my head. But does it matter if we've got false images? Let's just try and keep the good ones, and forget the rest.'

Dulcie was suddenly aware how close they were, their bodies almost touching. He was gazing down at her, and she couldn't draw back or even look away from him, for his eyes held her.

All at once she wanted him to kiss her, for his eyes told her that's what he wanted to do, but just as his lips came down to meet hers, the door opened and Haggetty came in with their coffee.

'I put sugar in, I thought you'd need it,' he said.

It was Dulcie who moved, drawing back from Rudie as if she'd been stung.

'Thank you, inspector,' she said, blushing furiously. 'Can we ask if you have any more information about May's death now?'

'If you're sure you're ready for it,' he said, looking from one to the other, perhaps sensing an unusual atmosphere. 'I could go away and come back later.'

'We're as ready as we'll ever be,' Rudie said with a sigh, and sat down at the small table where Haggetty had placed their coffee.

Haggetty waited until Dulcie had sat down, then he followed suit and offered them each a cigarette. When they refused, he lit one up himself.

'May was last seen at about six-thirty in the evening walking along the beach, alone. We believe she went into the sea soon after, despite the warning flag flying.'

'Are you saying it was suicide?' Rudie asked quietly.

'We can't say that,' Haggetty said. 'People often swim when it isn't safe, especially the young. But it *is* very unusual for girls to go in alone, especially when it's getting dark.'

Rudie and Dulcie looked at each other helplessly.

'Did you find where she was living?' Rudie asked.

Haggetty nodded. 'She'd taken a room in a boarding house under the name of Belinda Smith. We checked that out, but there was nothing there other than her clothes.'

Dulcie gulped at May's assumed name. It was so very poignant that she'd used the one of her old doll.

'There was no note then?' Rudie said. 'Doesn't that confirm it was an accident?'

561

Haggetty dropped his eyes. 'Maybe. But we didn't find a towel, bag or even shoes on the beach. Only a cotton dress.'

'What about her landlady? Did she tell you anything about May?'

'Not much,' Haggetty said. 'Just that May had turned up one morning about six weeks ago with a suitcase and asked for a room. She thought she must work in a bar somewhere because she spent her days on the beach and came home late at night.'

'If she was there all along, why didn't you find her before?' Rudie asked. 'After all, she's not the kind of girl not to be noticed.'

'We weren't looking in the right places,' Haggetty said. 'I don't want to offend you at such a time, but we were told to look for her amongst the working girls. I wish to God we had asked around more generally, maybe we could've prevented this.'

'Do you mean she hadn't worked up here as a prostitute?' Dulcie whispered.

'Not so far as we know,' Haggetty said. 'An elderly man who lives across the road from the boarding house said he met her on her second day on the Gold Coast, she had fallen asleep on a bench, her suitcase beside her. He felt sorry for her, guessed she hadn't got anywhere to stay, and so he woke her up and spoke to her. He sent her to the boarding house.'

'Sounds familiar,' Rudie said, with a trace of harshness in his voice.

Haggetty raised one bushy blond eyebrow inquiringly.

'She'd done that before,' Rudie said by way of explanation. 'But go on, did this man know what she'd been doing in Sydney?'

Haggetty shook his head. 'She told him she'd run away from a violent boyfriend.'

'Maybe it was true,' Rudie said. 'We always assumed she only ran away because of the baby, but there could have been a man behind it.'

'I daresay there was,' the policeman said. 'She certainly kept herself to herself. We asked questions in all the bars, she hadn't made any friends that we can find.'

'Was she working in one of them?' Dulcie asked.

Haggetty shook his head.

'Then how was she paying for her room?' Rudie asked.

Haggetty shrugged. 'We don't know, maybe she had savings.'

Dulcie knew this was unlikely, but she wasn't going to voice that or even consider how May might have supported herself in her time at the Gold Coast. May was dead now, whether it was accidental or intentional didn't really matter. Nothing could bring her back.

'What about the funeral?' Rudie asked. 'Should we arrange it now?'

'We won't be able to release her body for a few days,' Haggetty said. 'We'll let you know as soon as possible.'

'May's dead, Ross.' Dulcie said when she reached him on the telephone later that night.

'Speak up,' he said. 'I can't hear you.'

Dulcie repeated it, louder this time, and her voice seemed to echo around Rudie's living-room. 'I've just got back from Brisbane identifying her body.'

'Oh no,' he gasped. 'What happened to her? Are you okay?'

It wasn't much, but it sounded to Dulcie as if he was receptive for once, and trying to control her tears, she told him about it.

'Strewth, Dulc,' he exclaimed as she finished. 'You've fairly laid me out! I don't know what to say. I'm so bloody sorry, you know I liked May, we all did here. She might have gone wrong, but she didn't deserve that.'

It wasn't the most tender of condolences, but there was real sincerity in what he said, and it made Dulcie cry.

'D'you want me to come up there for the funeral?' he said. 'I could jump on the train.'

Later she was to see the bitter irony that he was prepared

to jump on a train for a funeral, but not to help an abandoned baby, yet right then she was touched that he had found his heart again. 'I don't think there's much point in that,' she said. 'We don't know when the body will be released yet, it could be as early as tomorrow or the day after, and we'll have to have the funeral immediately. You stay there, I can manage.'

'You'll be right home afterwards then?' he asked.

'Yes, Ross,' she sighed, knowing she really had no excuse to delay it any longer. 'Rudie's blood tests have proved he is Noël's father, so he's safe now.'

'I can't wait to have you home again,' he said with real warmth. 'I've made a few surprises for you while you've been away. We've all missed you.'

'I've missed you too,' she sobbed, suddenly wanting to be back in her own little house, seeing the animals, cooking for everyone, tending her garden and away from all this heartache. 'I'll ring again and tell you when I'm coming back.'

'I love you,' he said, then put the phone down.

Rudie came over to her as she stood there sobbing, the receiver still in her hand. He took it from her and replaced it, then put his arms around her and held her.

'Was he nasty again?' he whispered.

'No, not at all,' she said through her tears, leaning into his big chest. 'I don't know why I'm crying.'

'You have every reason to cry,' he said soothingly. 'Your sister's dead. You've got the funeral to go through, and you've got to leave Noël. I think that would make even the most tough person crack.'

He led her over to the settee, then fetched her a glass of brandy. She drank it in one gulp, shuddering as it burned its way down her throat. 'I promised Dad and Gran I'd take care of May, but I failed them,' she said.

Rudie turned to her, took her by the shoulders and shook her. 'You haven't failed anyone,' he said angrily. 'You were just a little girl when your mother died, and you did more than most adults would do to protect her.

You've got to stop this thinking you are responsible for other people, Dulcie. The only person you are responsible for is yourself. Part of that responsibility is finding personal happiness too. Promise me you'll strive to find it?'

She looked at him bleakly. 'I'll be happy once this is all over and I'm home again.'

'There you go again, lying to yourself, just like May said,' he snapped. 'You know you won't be. You'll do what everyone else wants, make them happy, but forget yourself. You've got to learn to take, Dulcie, or stay a damned doormat all your life!'

'What do you suggest I do when I get home?' she snapped back at him. 'Demand that I go to college and get a few qualifications, refuse to feed the chickens because it's beneath me? It's all right for you, you can do exactly as you please, on a farm there's boring routine work which has to be done day after day. I'm Ross's wife, I have to do it.'

'I'm not talking about work and you know it,' he retorted. 'You've got to make Ross get help to sort out his problems, and if he won't, then for God's sake leave him.'

'I can't do that.' She was shocked at him being so brutal.

'Go and see my friend Stephan the psychiatrist tomorrow,' he said forcefully. 'At least go home armed with his advice if nothing else. I can't bear to think of you living the rest of your life unfulfilled and neglected, that's a worse punishment than anything those nuns did to you.'

'Sex isn't everything,' she said defiantly. 'It's companionship that counts.'

'Rubbish,' he roared at her. 'You are a beautiful, desirable woman, Dulcie, sex might not be everything, but it's a wonderful, splendid thing given to us to make sure we stay together as couples and make babies. What you call companionship will wither and die without it, you'll end up a bitter old lady with nothing in your past but sad memories.'

'Having sex didn't do May any good,' she said, wanting to hurt him. 'She didn't really like it, you know, not even with you.'

His face crumpled. 'If she'd only been honest with me I could have helped her,' he said. 'Don't you think it hurts me now to know she only endured it for what she could get from me? If I'd known then about what that evil nun had done to her, I would have acted quite differently. She hid her real problems, used her cunning and charm to get round them. But you are worse in many ways, Dulcie, you're prepared to let anyone do almost anything to you, take any amount of humiliation, in the mistaken belief this will make them love you more.'

'I don't,' she roared at him, jumping up and making towards the stairs.

He ran after her and caught hold of her wrists. 'You do,' he insisted. 'I haven't known you that long but I can see how you ended up like this. Right from a little girl you were caught in the cross-fire between your parents. On one hand you tried to cover up for your mother's neglect to you and May by doing things she should have been doing, and you were rewarded for this by praise from your father. When she died, you protected your father, never knowing for certain whether he really pushed her or not.'

'He didn't push her,' she retorted. 'She fell.'

'Maybe so, but that hardly matters in the face of the confusion and guilt you must have felt. Then you felt even more guilty while you were with your granny because you thought you and May were the reason she became poorly. From then on it's my guess you took the blame for every last thing that happened to you and May, including being sent here to Australia.'

'I didn't,' she said, but a vision of her getting the beating at St Vincent's for stealing the toffees came into her head.

'You did, and you've got to stop blaming yourself, and put that blame firmly on the shoulders of those who were responsible. It wasn't anything you did that made May go wrong, it was the treatment she had at the hands of the Sisters. You did the right thing when you took Noël away from her, you are not in some way responsible for her death. But most of all you've got to stop thinking you are to blame for your husband not making love to you. It's his problem, try and get him to share it with you by all means. But don't take it on your own shoulders.'

'I can't help the way I am,' she cried.

'You can't do anything about the past,' he said firmly. 'It's done and it can't be mended. But the future is different, you can be in control of that, if you just think what you really want and reach out and take it.'

'But I don't know what I really want,' she sobbed.

Rudie put his arms round her and drew her to his chest. 'I know, you've spent so long thinking what everyone else wants, including Noël and me, that your own desires and needs have been forgotten. For now all you need to do is take one day at a time, visit Stephan, get the funeral over, then go back home. Somewhere along the line what you want and need will come to you.'

She sobbed against his chest, wishing she dared say she wasn't entirely sure she wanted to go home.

'Don't forget I'm your friend, for ever,' he said softly against her hair. 'We're related through Noël, and there will always be a home here for you if you need it. Even if Ross doesn't want Noël visiting you at the farm, I shall come to Esperance every summer and stay in a hotel so you can see him. I'm not going to let you slip out of our lives.'

She lifted her head up. Rudie was looking down at her, his dark eyes glistening with unshed tears, lips quivering, and suddenly she was kissing him.

It seemed to Dulcie that she was falling through space locked in his arms. Nothing mattered any more but the bliss of his lips on hers, the delicious sensations coursing through her body. Never before had she felt anything quite like it, her reason was gone, she had no will to control herself. To be in his arms, feeling the sensual delights of his probing tongue, was all that counted.

Rudie broke away first. 'We mustn't do this, Dulcie,' he whispered, leaning his forehead against hers. 'It will only make it harder for us to part.'

All at once she came back to reality, blushing as she realized what she had unwittingly started. 'I'm so sorry,' she said.

He just looked at her wistfully. 'There you go again, taking all the blame. I've wanted to kiss you from the first moment I met you. Go to bed, Dulcie, don't tempt me any more, I might start to think there's hope for me.'

She ran up the stairs like a startled rabbit, not even stopping to say goodnight.

Chapter Twenty-four

'Just sit back and relax, Dulcie,' Dr Stephan Heinne said gently. 'You've been through so much emotional upheaval in the last few days that I expect you think seeing me will be some sort of inquisition, but it won't be, you can tell me as little or as much as you like, in your own time.'

Stephan was Rudie's psychiatrist friend, and Dulcie had been a little taken aback that he had made this appointment so quickly. It was only yesterday that they returned from Brisbane, and after what happened between them, this seemed to her to be his way of avoiding any discussion about it.

Rudie needn't have worried, she had no intention of asking him why he had kissed her like that, she certainly wasn't going to admit it had shaken her to the core and left her more confused than ever. But she couldn't refuse this appointment, however badly timed it was, she did after all need advice about Ross. So she had come, reluctant and scared stiff.

Yet the moment she stepped into Stephan's consulting room and saw him for the first time, her fear suddenly vanished for he didn't look the least intimidating. He was as short as her, his round, well-scrubbed face boyish and appealing. She couldn't help wondering if he wore those thick-rimmed glasses to try to make himself look more intellectual, but in fact all they did was emphasize his large grey eyes.

She knew he was born in Austria, educated in England and was considered one of the most eminent men in his field, but like Rudie he'd struggled when he'd first arrived in Australia, for they'd become friends while they were both waiting on tables.

Stephan's consulting room in Rose Bay was more like a study, the walls lined with books, and a view of the harbour from the window. She felt she might be able to open up to him.

'First may I offer my condolences about your sister,' Stephan began, his grey eyes soft with sympathy. 'Rudie told me about her when she disappeared last year and has kept me up to date since then.'

'It was only yesterday that we went to identify her body,' Dulcie blurted out, tears springing into her eyes. 'I kept hoping it wouldn't be her, but of course it was.'

'So very distressing for you,' he said softly. 'One always expects a younger sibling to outlive you. I'm sure it brought back poignant memories from your childhood.'

Dulcie nodded. 'I still can't really believe she's dead,' she said, her voice trembling. 'There's so much I wish I'd said to her, and stuff I wish I hadn't.'

'Would you like to talk over any of that with me?' he asked.

'I don't think I could,' she said. 'It's too raw right now, I guess I'll sort it out for myself once the funeral's over. But then I have to go home to my husband in WA. It was Ross I really wanted to talk to you about. You see, we have a problem.'

Stephan nodded. 'I hope I can be of some help. Giving advice about someone I've never met can be difficult, but I'll try. Now, suppose you tell me what the problem is.'

Dulcie thought Rudie might have already told him this, if so there was little point in being coy about it. She took a deep breath and blurted out that Ross seemed unable to make love to her.

'Do you mean never, or just infrequently?' he asked.

'Never,' she said. 'We've been married for almost two years now and I don't know what to do.'

He probed a little, asking her questions about Ross's general health, what kind of man he was and what line of work he was in, then moved on to ask about their honeymoon. Dulcie wanted to run out of the door at that point. She hung her head with embarrassment as he probed to find out how far they had got, and what Ross's reaction was to his failure.

'I confided in Rudie and he said Ross is in denial, whatever that means. Something from his past that he can't get over,' she said hastily, anxious to move on from the physical questions to something she felt more comfortable with.

Stephan asked her to tell him all she knew about Ross's childhood, and listened very closely as she related it. 'Appalling,' he agreed, wincing with horror. 'Almost unbe-lievable. Yet I have recently heard several similar stories about that place, and I don't doubt a word of it. I think that Rudie is probably spot on with his opinion, I would say Ross has been deeply scarred by his experiences there, and what Rudie said about denial means that Ross has never attempted to look at it or deal with it, he's locked it away inside him.'

'But he hasn't, he told me about it,' she said.

Stephan half smiled. 'He's told you the bits he can look at, but I suspect there's a great deal more tucked away. Tell me, Dulcie, is there anything about your childhood which you can't or won't talk about?'

Dulcie thought for a moment. 'I suppose I don't talk about how the Sisters made me feel about myself.'

'Why not?'

'It's not very nice to admit that someone made you feel utterly worthless, is it?'

'It certainly isn't. Do you still feel that way sometimes?'

'Yes. This thing with Ross makes me feel that way.'

'When he rejects you?'

She blushed. 'Yes. It's like there's something wrong with me.'

Stephan nodded. 'Have you thought he might do this because he's afraid any intimacy with you might break down his own defences?'

Dulcie looked baffled.

Stephan smiled. 'Let me put it this way, suppose you had a secret, something which made you feel disgusted and ashamed, would you put yourself into a situation where you might inadvertently let it slip?'

Dulcie could only think of how she used to hide the truth about her father being in prison. 'No, I don't suppose I would. But I don't believe Ross has done something bad.'

'I think it's far more likely something bad was done to him,' Stephan said evenly. 'But when bad things are done to children, quite often they think they are the one to blame, especially if that adult was in a position of authority or trust. A great deal of my work with troubled adults is caused by this. I can only begin to help to heal them once they tell me what happened to them. I can go through it then, showing them that it wasn't their fault. Eventually I come around to showing them how to shift the burden of guilt back to the person who is responsible.'

'But I know Ross wouldn't talk to someone like you about it,' she said bleakly. 'He wouldn't go to an ordinary doctor unless he was nearly dying, he thinks men have to be tough all the time. Psychiatrists to him are for mad people, if I even hinted that I'd told someone about this he'd be furious with me.'

'That's a common Australian male attitude.' Stephan grinned. 'It will probably take decades before it changes. But you can help him, Dulcie. You can find out what his secret is.'

'But how?' she asked. 'If he's afraid of making love in case he lets something slip, he isn't just going to come out with it, is he?'

'He might if you press the right buttons.'

'What would they be?' Dulcie asked in bewilderment.

'I think it might be a start to get him back to Bindoon. It's almost certain that whatever happened to him took place there.'

'He wouldn't go there again!' she exclaimed.

Stephan looked at her, his grey eyes studying her carefully. 'Dulcie, you're intelligent, you're compassionate, and I don't doubt resourceful too. You'll need a challenge when you get home, because from what I hear it's going to be hard for you to leave Noël.'

'It is,' she agreed sorrowfully. 'But getting Ross to Bindoon will be impossible.'

'Nothing's impossible if you are determined. Use your love for Noël, that indignation you have that anyone could hurt a child, to light a fire under Ross,' he said with urgency in his voice. 'Make him see you aren't prepared to just go on the way you have been. Be strong and forthright.'

'I'm not good at that,' she said helplessly.

'You are, you came here to talk to me didn't you? You had the courage to take Noël away from May, and the persistence to take care of him. You can do anything, Dulcie. Just believe it.'

'But what if I fail?' she said. 'What then?'

'You won't fail, it's only Ross who can do that. He's the one who has to face up to his demons and agree to get help. If he won't, you must walk away.'

'I can't do that,' she gasped. 'He's my husband.'

'Even in the eyes of the law an unconsummated marriage is grounds for annulment,' he said firmly. 'In the eyes of God I'd call it a travesty. You deserve happiness, Dulcie, you owe it to yourself to find it.'

Three days after Dulcie's talk with Stephan, she and Rudie were back in Brisbane for May's funeral, waiting in a sombre room for the undertakers to arrive.

It had been a very strained three days. They had shared the chores and looked after Noël just as they always had, but there was a distance between them. Dulcie was deeply upset by May's death, disturbed by the feelings Rudie's passionate kiss had stirred up, dreading the moment she had to leave Sydney, and Stephan's advice about Ross kept going round and round in her head until it made her feel dizzy with anxiety.

She guessed that Rudie was feeling just as wretched.

Several times in the past couple of days he had shut himself in his studio, or taken Noël out for a walk alone. She guessed he was brooding about May, looking back to the good times with her and perhaps blaming himself for the way things turned out. He was probably anxious about coping with Noël alone once she went home, perhaps regretting that kiss too. Dulcie sensed he was keeping his personal worries to himself in deference to her feelings, but she wished he would speak of them, just to clear the air.

She glanced sideways at him. He looked very severe in a black suit. Even though his face was tanned and he claimed to have put on several pounds in weight in the past few weeks, she thought he looked gaunt and hollow-eyed.

Yet even though they had barely spoken on the plane coming here, now that the time for leaving was so close, she was becoming ever more aware of how much she was going to miss him. He was so comfortable to be with, so interesting and funny. That kiss hadn't helped either, she had tried to banish it from her mind, but it kept coming back, making her stomach contract and her skin tingle. She supposed it was nothing much to him, he'd kissed so many women in his life, but she wasn't going to be able to forget it in a hurry.

As for Noël, she could hardly bear the thought of leaving him. A day without his merry chuckles was impossible to contemplate. Even leaving him today with Mrs Curston, knowing they wouldn't be back until tomorrow night, was a wrench. How could she hope that Ross would come to see what Noël meant to her? She couldn't even put it into words herself.

The undertaker came to the door to see if they were ready to leave, and they filed out. As there were only the two of them as mourners and a handful of people who had clearly only come out of curiosity because they'd learnt the deceased had been drowned and had been a prostitute, it was fortunate that the church was such a tiny one, but Dulcie was touched that the priest conducted the service with as much reverence as he would have done for a well-loved member of his own congregation.

The smell of the incense took Dulcie right back to the church she went to with her father in London. She could almost feel five-year-old May wriggling in the pew beside her, and see their father giving her a warning look to behave herself. She barely heard the priest's words, for images of May were coming thick and fast. Pushing her on the swing in the park, May's thick blonde plaits jumping up and down. Watching her trying to dress herself, getting all her cardigan buttons mixed up. Seeing her little face alight with glee as she carried a goldfish home in a jam jar from the fair on Blackheath.

Her heart ached for her sister, it wasn't May's fault she went wrong. She was just an innocent, sweet little girl when their mother died, and it was adults supposed to be caring for her who corrupted her. Dulcie looked up at the priest and remembered how once she truly believed all priests were men of God. Perhaps this one really was, but she knew now that there were more evil people hiding under the protective mantle of the Catholic Church than there were outside it. People like them had stolen May's childhood, without them she might have been a happy young bride now, on the threshold of a new life.

'Rest in peace, May,' she prayed silently, tears streaming down her face. 'I loved you even if I didn't fully understand you. Rudie and I will see no harm comes to Noël.'

Four days later, at seven in the morning, Dulcie prepared to bath and dress Noël for the last time. Her train was leaving at ten-thirty and Sarah would be here later to mind him while Rudie took her to the station. She stripped off his little sleep-suit and nappy, holding him on her lap, then took her time soaping his body, impressing everything about him on her mind for all time.

He was plumper now than when she first took him from May. He'd gained five pounds, he had one tooth, and he was far stronger, able to lift his head right up when they'd laid him on his tummy. She noted the two small dimples just above his fat little buttocks, the spare chin, the way his tummy stuck out like a little Buddha's, and a small brown birthmark on his right ankle. He had Rudie's dark eyes, and as she looked intently into them he gave her a wide gummy smile which made her laugh.

He loved the water, splashing as though he was born to be a life-saver. She felt a pang of longing at the thought she wouldn't see him in the sea for the first time, sitting up alone, crawling or taking his first steps. Rudie had said that he'd bring him to Esperance next spring for a holiday, but that was such a long way off.

Her case was packed, waiting downstairs by the front door. It seemed in so many ways that she'd been here for years, not just a couple of months. She didn't even feel like the same person any more. She'd learnt to cook Italian and French food while she'd been here, drunk wine and brandy, seen elegant dress shops and visited art galleries and museums which had given her such a different perspective on everything she knew before. She knew she wouldn't be able to share it all with Ross, one word of any of that and he'd be seething with jealousy because another man had introduced her to it all. But as she lifted Noël out of the bath and wrapped him in a towel to dry him, she realized this was the one experience above all which had changed her. She would be wanting a baby of her own more than anything else, and once Ross got wind of that he'd probably shy even further away from her.

'You've got to do what Stephan said,' she murmured against Noël's wet hair. 'Be strong and forthright.'

Noël began pulling at her hair and laughing up at her, and her gloom lifted. She would find a way to get through to Ross, she was determined.

*

'Please go,' Dulcie begged Rudie once he'd escorted to her sleeper compartment on the train. 'It will just prolong the agony if you stay, the train isn't going for a while.'

'Agony is it!' he said with a smile. 'A nice thing to say after all this time.'

'You know what I mean. It was terrible saying goodbye to Noël, and now to have it all over again in slow motion is even worse.'

She thought her heart was breaking as she kissed Noël one last time. She had cried half-way into Sydney and it wouldn't take much to start her off again. Everything she glimpsed on the journey – the last view of Watson's Bay, Sydney Harbour Bridge, the Botanical Gardens, the half-built Opera House – all made her choke up. She wanted to hide in this cabin now, cry her heart out alone, and try to put it behind her before she got home.

'Okay, I'll go,' he agreed reluctantly. He rifled through the books and magazines he'd bought for her on the station. 'Are you sure you've got enough to read?'

'You know I have,' she said.

'Well, can I give you a hug then?'

He looked so boyish and unsure of himself she had to smile. She stood up and put her arms around him, leaning her face into his big chest. He hugged her tightly for several minutes, and she sensed he was crying. 'Always remember I'm your friend,' he whispered eventually. 'If anything goes wrong, if you need anything, just pick up the phone and call me. Whatever it is, I'll help you.'

'Thank you,' she murmured into his chest, wishing she dared say how much he meant to her. 'Ring me sometimes at mid-morning, I'm usually in the house alone then.'

He put his hand under her chin and lifted it. 'I wish you well with Ross,' he said with tears rolling down his cheeks. 'But if it doesn't go well, come back.'

Dropping a brief kiss on her lips he hurried off, and as she watched him go, half-turned sideways in the narrow passage, she was reminded of Bruce when he'd seen her off at Kalgoorlie, for he had the same despondent slump to his shoulders. She could still feel the warm imprint of his lips on hers, his last words rang in her ears, and in a flash of insight she realized he loved her.

She wavered in the doorway of the cabin, sorely tempted to run after him. But there were other people coming down the corridor now. Besides, what would she say to him?

As the train chugged out through the Blue Mountains she barely saw them through her tears. It was as though her mind was split in two. On one side she could see Rudie with Noël on his knee, her pretty little bedroom, the sights of Sydney. On the other side was Ross, Bruce, the farm, and her house with its polished wood floor and the window overlooking the lake. She knew she had got to let the second part slide over the first and obliterate it, yet it stubbornly stayed there, taunting her.

Looking back on all that had happened in Sydney she could see now that what she had mistaken for friendship was in fact love, on both sides. She could liken it to farming – the ground had already been prepared with their shared anxiety for May, even before she arrived in Sydney. Both being alone and bruised acted as a fertilizer, then the seeds of love were sown when Noël entered their lives. The worry about whether he might be taken from them was like rain, the happiness they shared with him the sunshine. It was hardly surprising that the seeds began to sprout and grow.

It could have escalated into an affair too when Rudie kissed her, for she knew in her own heart she was so needy that night that one more kiss would have torn away all her resistance. Now at last she understood why Rudie had kept his distance since that night, why in the last four days since the funeral he hadn't put his arms around her the way he used to when she was upset. How honourable he was, how sensitive and strong.

'You've got three days to put him out of your mind,' she told herself firmly. 'You can't have him and Noël. Ross, the farm and Bruce is your life, that's where you belong.'

Dulcie heard Ross jubilantly shout her name as she stepped down from the train at Kalgoorlie, but in the mêlée of passengers getting off the train and those trying to board it, she couldn't see him for a moment.

It was ten at night and the four-day journey had seemed interminable. The food on the train had been as good as on the way out, the other passengers probably just as interesting, but she'd found herself unable to eat or talk to anyone. She had tried to read, but the words danced in front of her eyes. She had tried to sleep too, but it had evaded her. Hour after hour of just lying flat on her back staring up at the ceiling and listening to the chugging of the train seemed only to stimulate memories. Her mind clung stubbornly to pictures of Rudie and Noël.

'Dulcie!'

She turned her head to see Ross pushing his way through the crowd. He was grinning from ear to ear and even though the platform was dimly lit, she could see his eyes shining.

He was upon her before she could even catch her breath, he snatched her up in his arms and spun her round. 'I thought the bloody train would never get here,' he said breathlessly. 'It's beaut to have you back.'

His excitement was infectious. Dulcie banished her melancholy and hugged him back with equal enthusiasm, suddenly genuinely pleased to be back. He looked so handsome, his forearms and face were deeply tanned, set off with a white open-necked shirt, and his tawny eyes sparkled. His hair had grown considerably in the two and a half months she'd been away, it was now curly and tousled the way she liked it best, glinting pure copper under the station lights.

'You just wait till you see the surprise I've got for you,' he said as he led her out of the station to Bruce's car.

'Are you going to kiss me?' she said once he'd put her case in the boot.

'What, out here?' he said, looking around him at the many people milling around.

'Yes, out here,' she insisted, thinking she might as well test the water right now.

He put his arms around her and kissed her lightly on the lips.

'No, a real one,' she said, holding him tightly.

To her surprise he didn't wriggle away, but gave her a lingering kiss which sent tremors down her spine. 'That's better,' she said with a smile once he'd eventually let her go.

She had forgotten how dark the bush was at night, and how scary the rough road to Esperance was. Ross chattered like she'd never known him do before, telling her that the crops were nearly ready now for harvesting, how Bruce had bought a couple of baby pigs, and that lightning had caused a small bush fire. Dulcie listened, but she was on the edge of the seat watching out for kangaroos as Ross didn't seem to be paying much attention to the road.

There were a great many kangaroos, but fortunately none chose to leap in the path of the car, and finally they came to the track that led up to the farm.

The familiar smell through the open window made her heart suddenly leap with joy. It took her back to when she first came here. On so many evenings she'd gone out on to the porch, and the warm breeze had brought the rich aromas of the animals, the hay and grass to her. She would listen to the sounds of the night, rustlings of small nocturnal animals, cicadas chirruping, the lowing of cows, and feel a peace and happiness she'd never known before.

Ahead she could see the shape of Bruce's house and the tall pine trees close by, silhouetted against the night sky. It was in darkness now, but she would see him in the morning. She turned in her seat and smiled at Ross. 'It's good to be back,' she sighed.

The dogs barked a welcome as Ross drove up to the barn. Dulcie jumped out of the car and they came running to her, whining with delight and wagging their tails. 'Good boys,' she whispered, fondling each of them. 'Now be quiet or you'll wake everyone.'

Ross took her case in one hand and holding her hand with the other, led her towards their house. At the door he ordered her to close her eyes, then picked her up in his arms and carried her in.

'You can open them now,' he said, and put her down.

He had left a table-lamp alight, and Dulcie gasped when she saw the room. Not the untidy mess she was expecting, but the floor mirror-bright with polish, a vase of marigolds on the table, and a desk against the wall where previously there had been nothing.

She moved over to it, laying her hands on the smooth golden jarrah wood, and gasped with wonder. 'You made this?' she asked.

'Yeah.' He shuffled his feet and looked boyishly uncertain. 'I got the wood before you went away, and it took my mind off missing you while I was making it.'

'I can't believe it,' she exclaimed, opening each of the four drawers on either side of the knee hole. 'It's a work of art!'

She wasn't exaggerating, it really was. It felt as smooth as silk under her hands – the edges were rounded and the drawers glided in and out silently. The legs were turned and shaped in Queen Anne style, graceful and perfectly proportioned.

'This is what you should be doing all the time, not farming,' she said, going over to him and hugging him. 'You are a craftsman, Ross, in Sydney people would pay a fortune for such a piece.'

'I made it for you,' he said, his eyes shining. 'I liked to think of you sitting there writing letters while I was making it. I wouldn't like making things for anyone else.'

'Thank you, thank you, thank you,' she said, covering his face with kisses, knowing this was no time to plan a new future for him. 'It's the most wonderful surprise, such a lovely welcome home.'

'I did some other small things too,' he said, taking her hand and leading her into the kitchen to show her a wooden rack he'd made for mugs to hang on, and a rail for tea-towels. 'Tomorrow you'll see I've dug over a bit of ground outside the French windows, so you can plant some flowers there.'

She knew this was his way of apologizing for his hard attitude about Noël. While she would have preferred sympathy and understanding about what she'd been through, and questions as to how Noël was, it was perhaps the best he could do for now.

'You are wonderful,' she said with a warm smile. 'And you've kept everywhere so nice too.'

'It wasn't like this two days ago,' he admitted, looking a little shamefaced. 'I had to beaver around and make it look good again.'

'Can we go to bed now?' she said, suddenly feeling exhausted. 'I couldn't sleep on the train.'

There were flowers in the bedroom too, and the bed was made up with clean sheets. By the time Dulcie had washed and cleaned her teeth, Ross was in bed, his chest and arms deep brown against the linen.

He pulled her into his arms the moment she got in beside him, and kissed her with such tenderness it brought tears to her eyes. But that was all, a few minutes later he turned out the light, said goodnight, then turned over to go to sleep.

Dulcie lay there for some little time. She wasn't upset, he could after all have harangued her all the way home with suspicious questions about Rudie, and until she got him right out of her mind she wasn't sure she wanted more from Ross. The desk and the other things he'd made were evidence of his love for her, and anyway she hadn't expected that her long absence would bring on a miracle.

Yet now she was back here, it didn't look so easy to make him confront his past in the way Stephan had said she must. Suppose she did manage to get Ross back to Bindoon, but whatever happened there came out and pushed him over the edge? Right now he was able to function well in every aspect of his life, except in making love. He was an excellent stockman, he could repair vehicles, build things, knew all about crops, he worked well with other men. Did she have the right to threaten that?

The old habit of closing her eyes and praying took over. Silently she asked for God's guidance in this matter and asked if He would give her a sign when the time was right to tackle it. Yet even as she drifted off towards sleep, she thought how often in the past she'd waited for help from above which never came.

Early the following morning, Bruce came bounding out of his bedroom as Dulcie opened his front door. He was still in his pyjamas, but he threw his arms wide in welcome and his smile lit up the still dark room. 'Dulcie! Welcome home,' he roared. 'I didn't hear the car last night, so I was afraid you'd missed the train.'

Dulcie ran into his warm hug with delight. 'It's so good to see you again, I missed you,' she said.

'You look different,' he said, holding her shoulders and pushing her back so he could look at her. 'Can't put my finger on what it is, your hair's the same, so are the clothes.'

'Too many shocks in a short space of time, I expect,' she laughed. Yet she knew what he meant, she'd seen it in her own face during the journey home. The girlishness had vanished, it was an adult face which looked back at her in the mirror.

'I'm so very sorry about May,' he said, his smile fading. 'That wasn't something any of us could have foreseen.'

'I know,' she agreed. 'I still find it hard to believe. Even at the funeral I don't think I really took it in completely. I spent an awful lot of the journey home crying.'

Bruce put his hand on her shoulder and squeezed it in understanding. 'If you want to talk about it any time, you just say so.'

'I expect I'll tell you every last thing in the next few days,' she said. 'But right now I want to know how you are, and what's been going on here.'

She thought he looked thinner, the baggy skin on his

face was more noticeable. But unshaven, hair uncombed and wearing pyjamas, he wasn't at his best.

Over a cup of tea he gave her a quick rundown on the same things Ross had told her about the previous night. 'The bush fire could have ruined me, the crops were almost ready for harvesting, but Ross was a marvel, he contained it in a very small area,' he said with a broad smile. 'Your old man might be a bit of a drongo in some ways, but my God he was like bloody superman that night. He drove the tractor with the scraper like a bat out of hell right up alongside the line of fire, so close I thought he'd burn to death. But he made the bloody fire break, and it held. Thanks to him we only lost around five acres of crops, it could have been the lot.'

'When are you going to start the harvest?' she asked. Although it was only daybreak, from the window in her house she'd seen the wheat waving in the breeze, thick and golden.

'We'll go out after breakfast to check it,' Bruce said. 'Reckon it might be tomorrow or the next day.'

'I'd better get the breakfast started,' Dulcie said, looking at the clock. 'They'll be finishing the milking soon.'

'I'll go and get myself dressed,' Bruce said. 'Don't lay into me if you can't find things in the kitchen. I tried to keep it right, and Doreen came in and gave everything a good clean yesterday, but it sure ain't the way you used to keep it.'

Dulcie smiled. 'That's good, it will make me feel indispensable.'

'You are,' he said, his face suddenly serious. 'Not just for your cooking either. We all missed you.'

Breakfast lingered on for over two hours, for everyone had so much they wanted to ask. John's questions were mainly about Sydney, and the surf beaches he'd heard so much about, Ross was more interested in May's death, even Bob who was usually so silent asked about Noël and Rudie.

584

Bruce seemed quite content just to sit and listen, but now and again Dulcie caught him looking at her with the oddest expression. She didn't know why, she'd been very careful in what she said. Although she waxed lyrical about the sights of Sydney, she'd tried to be matter of fact about Rudie, his home and Noël so as not to antagonize Ross.

Eventually the men went out, they were going to drive round to check the crops. Bruce stayed behind and helped Dulcie clear the table. At first he talked about domestic things, like the freezer was nearly empty and the garden needed tidying up as Betty would be appalled at its neglect, but then he suddenly asked her point-blank about how she felt at leaving Noël behind.

'Don't try to kid me,' he said, his big face very stern. 'I know you better than you think I do, and I can bet you felt you'd had your heart torn out, especially it coming so quick after May's funeral.'

Dulcie sighed. She had hoped he had been taken in by all her bright chatter over breakfast. 'Okay, it was like that,' she said, her eyes filling up. 'I wanted that little boy more than anything else in the world.'

'I didn't think you'd come back,' he admitted. 'And much as I knew I'd miss you – for your sake I hoped you'd stay in Sydney.'

'How could I do that?' she asked. 'I'm married to Ross.'

He just gave her a look which said reams. 'It's your life, sweetheart, but I know Betty would never have forgiven me if I'd refused to take in one of her sister's children.'

'I might have felt like that if Noël had to go to an orphanage, but he's with his father, and Rudie can do far more for him than I could.'

'Maybe that's so, but I just hope you don't find your life here is empty now,' he said, reaching out and fondling her hair.

At his gentle, caring touches, Dulcie felt like bursting into tears, but she was determined not to. 'How can it be empty when I've got you lot to look after? With all the washing and cleaning to catch up on, and the harvest about to start, it will be Christmas before I even have a chance to catch my breath.'

Bruce picked up his hat and walked towards the door, but as he reached it he turned and looked back. 'Just for the record, John, Bob and me all wanted you to bring Noël back, and if Rudie wants to bring him here anytime, as far as we're concerned he's family and very welcome.'

He went out then, the screen door slamming behind him, and Dulcie burst into tears.

In the following weeks Dulcie found it was much as she said, there was so much work to do she had little time to dwell on Noël, May, Rudie or even Ross. From first light till late in the evening she kept busy, cooking, cleaning, helping with the harvest and other jobs around the farm. Rudie telephoned once a fortnight, only a brief call, but he kept her up to date with Noël's development and reassured her he was managing.

From time to time Dulcie would find herself crying as she went about her chores. Sometimes it was for May, sometimes for Noël, and now and then for herself. Memories of the happy days with Rudie in his cottage taunted her, she would think about that kiss he'd given her and get a pain of longing inside her. It seemed grossly unfair that she'd been shown a whole new world on the other side of Australia, yet she had to return to the old one and try to forget what she'd seen.

For the first time ever she was resentful of the tedious work she had to do, bored with conversations about farming, fed up with being at everyone's beck and call. After Ross's initial pleasure at her return had worn off, Dulcie realized that he had learnt nothing while she'd been gone, in fact he was downright smug that he'd got his way in getting her back home without Noël. He didn't want to hear anything about her experiences, he hadn't asked her how she felt about May's death, and about Noël, or even considered she might still be thinking sadly about them both. She wanted to be reassured by him that May's death had been an accident, but the one and only time she tried to talk about it to him, all he did was shrug and say, *Well, she wasn't much of a swimmer, and she'd cocked her life up too.* Didn't he realize how much that hurt? It sounded as if he thought May's death was almost a blessing.

Every Saturday night he would go down to the pub and return home blinding drunk. While she didn't begrudge him going out once a week, she was quite happy to go into Bruce's and watch TV, paint or sew, what did hurt was that he went out to avoid talking to her. On weekday evenings he worked outside until it was dark, often carrying on later working on farm equipment in the barn. When he eventually came in he used tiredness as an excuse and went straight to bed.

She was dog-tired mostly herself, but she ached for the kind of evenings she'd had with Rudie. Eating a meal together, listening to records or the radio, talking about anything and everything. Day by day she could feel her spirit slowly seeping away.

The day they finished the harvest, Dulcie had cooked a special Italian meal as a surprise for everyone. She made pasta with a rich mushroom, ham and cream sauce, salad, home-baked rolls with garlic butter, and she got some bottles of Chianti and laid the table with candles and flowers. Bruce, Bob and John entered into the spirit of it, speaking in ridiculous Italian accents, Bruce even put on some opera music on the radiogram, but Ross merely pushed the food about on his plate and said he didn't like 'foreign muck'. He disappeared out the door while the rest of them were eating ice-cream and strawberries from the garden, and seconds later they heard him roaring off into town on his motorbike.

It was on her twenty-third birthday in December that Dulcie found she'd had enough. She had said all week that she wanted to go to see *The L-Shaped Room* with Leslie Caron at the pictures. On Friday evening, her birthday, she got all dressed up, as did Ross, and he drove her into town in Bruce's car. But when they got to the cinema Ross shoved a pound note in her hand, said he was going to the pub and he'd meet her later.

He ran off across the road to the pub before she could even say anything, leaving her speechless with rage. She couldn't bear the thought of going into the cinema alone, and she didn't feel able to follow him into the public bar and insist he took her either, for women just didn't go in there. As he'd left the car keys with her, she got back into it and drove home.

The drive home did nothing to cool her anger, in fact when she got indoors she was so mad she was tempted to take an axe to the desk he'd made her. It was a sweltering hot night, not even the faintest breeze coming in through the fly-screens on the windows. She was too angry to read or paint, and the sound of moths and other insects battering themselves against the windows, attracted to the light, irritated her beyond reason.

Suddenly she felt as if she were in a prison. It might be a pretty comfortable one, and the door was unlocked, but all the same that was how it felt. All she did was work, she had no real friends, and even her husband thought so little of her that he'd rather spend her birthday night in the pub with his mates.

She could imagine Rudie's little house so clearly. If she'd been there now he would have invited a few friends round, maybe they'd have had a barbecue in the garden. He'd have his rock and roll records on, and later everyone would dance. He would have brought her a present too, and probably one from Noël. Ross hadn't even given her a card, let alone a present. He was going to come home later drunk as a lord, flop into bed and spend the night snoring. Why on earth was she staying with him? What did she get out of it?

This house was the only tangible thing she could think of, and he never stopped boasting about it either. The truth was she'd rather be in her old bedroom in Bruce's house than living with a man who was like a brick wall.

She suddenly recalled that was May's description of him to Rudie, and she'd actually denied it. Yet that was exactly what he was like! She was sure if she managed to climb to the top of it she'd find nothing on the other side either.

It was after one in the morning when Ross finally came in. She had gone to bed, but she was too angry to sleep and so she was sitting up in bed looking at a magazine.

'What the bloody hell did you take the car for?' he said, staggering into the bedroom.

'To get home of course,' she snapped.

'I had to bludge a lift,' he said. 'I looked a bloody drongo 'cos I'd already told the blokes you were at the pictures.'

'Did you tell them it was my birthday and that you couldn't even bear to spend one evening with me?' she said, her anger rising even more. 'No, I don't suppose you did, you'd be too busy bragging about how big the harvest was here, and how you look after all the machinery and stopped the bush fire. Do they all look up to you in there? I wonder what they'd think if they knew you couldn't even fuck your wife.'

He just stood there staring at her. He had a beer-stain down the front of his shirt, and his eyes were all wild and bloodshot. He looked as if he couldn't believe what he'd heard. She had never used that word before, and it even shocked her.

'You bitch,' he said eventually. 'Take that back or else.'

'Or else what?' she taunted him, getting out of the bed. 'You'll hit me? Go on then, make me really proud of you.'

'I don't hit women,' he said.

'You do, you hit me before I went to Sydney,' she shouted back at him. 'But you can't touch me like a normal man. What are you, a bloody queer?'

She knew this wasn't the right way to be with him, it was cruel to ridicule him, but she didn't care. Maybe she even wanted him to attack her, at least then she'd be justified in walking out for good.

'I'm not queer,' he shouted and punched his fist so hard against the wall that he made a dent in the plaster.

'Well, tell me why we've been married nearly two years and I'm still a virgin,' she said vindictively. 'I could get our so called "marriage" annulled tomorrow. I might as well, there's nothing in it for me.'

All the pent-up frustration and bitterness poured out then. She raged at him for being so callous about Noël, she pointed out he hadn't once asked her anything about May's funeral, or even asked who took those lovely pictures of her.

'I want a husband I can talk to, share my feelings with,' she screamed at him. 'Not a bloody brick wall.'

'Be quiet, the men will hear you,' he said, and sank down on to the bed.

'I don't care who hears,' she raged. 'I've lived a bloody lie for two years, making out we were happy. May knew the truth, she taunted me with it the last time I saw her alive.'

'She was a lying tart,' he said.

'Maybe she was, but she knew what was what. She said I only married you because I felt sorry for you.'

'Did you?' He looked up at her, his eyes suddenly brimming with tears.

'Yes,' she said defiantly. 'And I've stayed with you for the same reason. But I don't feel sorry for you any longer. I just feel sorry for me because I've got nothing.'

'But I built this house. I've worked so hard for you,' he whimpered.

He looked pathetic to her, sitting there hanging his head. The fumes of the beer he'd drunk were gradually filling the bedroom.

'You built this house so you could boast about it,' she snapped. 'You work hard so you don't have time to think about what's really wrong with you. That's the truth, so don't get on your high horse and say I'm ungrateful.'

'Are you going to leave me now?' he asked, his voice hardly more than a whisper.

That plaintive question cut through her anger, and all at once she remembered that she had intended to cure him a few weeks ago, not crush him.

'Only if you refuse to do what I say,' she said.

'I'll do anything,' he whispered. 'Just don't leave me.'

She took a deep breath. 'Well, the first thing is that you stop avoiding having to talk to me. You won't work every evening any more.'

'Okay,' he said.

'The second thing is that you've got to try and overcome whatever it is that stops you making love to me.'

'But I don't know what it is,' he said.

'Then we have to find out,' she said firmly. 'After Christmas we're going to take a trip up to Perth. You're going to take me to Bindoon.'

He visibly shuddered and shook his head. 'I can't do that. I don't ever want to go back there.'

'You might not want to, but you're going to,' she said. 'If not, I'm leaving.'

She couldn't believe she could be so hard. Most of her wanted to put her arms around him and comfort him, but a small steely part insisted she had to hold her ground.

Nothing was said for some minutes, he continued to sit on the bed, his head in his hands, she stood by the window, hands on hips, glowering down at him. Yet the longer she stood there, the stronger she felt. Saying her piece tonight had brought her spirit back, she wasn't going to lose it again.

'Well?' she asked eventually. 'Do I get a promise, or do I leave? It's up to you.'

'You don't know what it's like up there,' he said.

'If you take me there I will,' she said.

'Okay,' he sighed. 'I'll go.'

'If you back down when the time comes, it's over,' she reminded him. 'There won't be any second chances.'

He looked up at her, his eyes full of tears. 'Why are you being so hard?'

591

'For your own good,' she said tartly. 'And for mine, because this isn't a marriage, Ross, it's misery. I don't intend to spend the rest of my life living this way.'

Chapter Twenty-five

'There it is!' Ross exclaimed, slowing down and pointing to a track off the road they were on. 'That's it, bloody Bindoon Boys' Town.'

His voice held a curious mixture of dread and excitement, and as Dulcie looked at him, rather than towards where he was pointing, she saw his face was flushed and his lips trembling.

'I can't see anything but trees,' she said.

'It's a bloody long way down the drive,' he said sharply. 'You should try walking it in bare feet.'

It was the first week in February and they'd left Esperance eight days ago, driving up the coast to Perth making two overnight stops on the way. Since then they'd been staying with Joan, Bruce's sister-in-law, in Subiaco. So far the holiday had been a dismal failure, however hard Dulcie tried to please Ross. She knew of course that he didn't want to go in the first place, but she'd had high hopes that once they were on their way he'd enter into the spirit of it. Yet it seemed he was determined to be difficult. It was too hot to go on the beach, he didn't like the city, food was too expensive, the beer was flat, he saw no point in looking in shops without money to spend. Parks were boring, he had nothing to talk about to Joan and her relatives, he snapped and grumbled at Dulcie constantly.

She knew the root cause of this was because the trip to Bindoon was to be part of the holiday, and perhaps he hoped if he made her mad enough she'd want to go home. Yet Dulcie had seen for herself right from Christmas that Ross was in fact incapable of enjoying himself.

She didn't know why she'd only just woken up to this, for he was no different to how he'd always been; awkward with new people, too bombastic with those he knew well, he had no conversation aside from farming and he wasn't curious about other people. Yet now she had noticed he never relaxed, he always had to be doing something all the time, and he was at his happiest when it was hard physical work. But saddest of all to her was that he had no sense of fun.

At Christmas they'd gone to the beach for a picnic with Bruce, Bob and John. Ross got cross with her because she larked around in the sea with the men. Maybe it was childish that John kept pretending to be a shark, diving under the water and grabbing her legs, or that John and Bob made a human pyramid with her on the top, only to be thrown off when John lost his balance, but it was fun. She kept urging Ross to join in, but he stood in the shallow water glowering like a petulant six-year-old and later told her she'd made a fool of herself.

Drinking was his only relaxant, two or three beers and he became mellow, but he rarely stopped at that. He would go on downing them, becoming argumentative and ready to start a fight with anyone.

The more she saw all these flaws in his character, the more she found herself thinking of Rudie and comparing them. Rudie knew how to relax, he just flung himself on the couch with a book or listened to music and was sublimely happy. He made fun happen, whether it was ringing round a few friends to invite them to supper, suddenly downing his paint-brushes and suggesting a walk, a ride on the ferry to Sydney, or some fish and chips down by the beach. To him a roomful of strangers was a roomful of potential friends, talking, dancing and laughing were completely natural to him.

She was very careful to keep in mind Ross's talents. Rudie couldn't have built her a house, he couldn't toil tirelessly the way Ross did. She doubted very much that he was brave enough to drive a tractor right up to a bush fire, to hunt down a snake she'd seen and kill it for her, or to stay up all night with a cow in labour.

But it was fun, affection and laughter Dulcie hankered for. She was alone most of the day while the men were outside working, with only an hour of cheerful company with the men at supper, then back to her house for an evening of silence. If this trip didn't bring some change or response from Ross, she knew in her heart she'd have to walk away for good for it was slowly destroying her.

'Come on, drive in,' she said, for Ross was just sitting there with the engine running, staring at the sign that read 'Bindoon Boys' Home'.

'We can't go in,' he said. 'The Brothers won't like it.'

'They can't turn an old boy away from his school,' she said firmly. 'Besides, this is what this trip is all about, you are going to show it to me and defy the Brothers. They can't hit you now, remember.'

Slowly and reluctantly he edged the car into the drive, which was just dry gravel, flanked on either side by scrubby land with a few sparse trees. 'This was all thick woods,' he said. 'We chopped the trees down and cleared the ground of stones for the building work.'

The track kept going and going, then it began to dip downwards and curve to the right. Ross stopped sharply on the bend. 'There it is,' he said, nodding his head to the buildings below.

Dulcie gasped, not in horror, but at its beauty. To her it looked like an Italian domed palace stuck in the middle of the bush. Bathed in strong sunshine, its red tiled roofs, the porticoes and stone balustrades along both floors of the main building were incredibly impressive.

'All built by children,' he muttered grimly. 'See those golden-coloured stones used on the end walls, those are the ones we collected from back up where we passed just now. Bloody great boulders, most of them, I dropped one on my bare foot one day, it swelled up and went all black, but Keaney made me go on working.'

He opened the car door and got out. Dulcie followed

him. 'See that,' he said, stopping by a wire fence and pointing to a large stone cross on a plinth in front of them. 'That's one of the bloody Stations of the Cross, we built those too. Hauled them up here, breaking our backs.'

He pointed out the other twelve all along the drive. 'Take your shoes off,' he ordered her. 'Feel how hot it is!'

Dulcie slipped one foot out of her shoes, but as she put it down on the ground she winced at the heat and the sharpness of the stones, quickly lifting it up again.

'Walk on it!' Ross insisted. 'You wanted to know what it was like here, try that!'

Hardened as Dulcie's feet were, she could only take a few hobbling steps before putting her shoes back on. It was almost inconceivable that young children with tender feet had been forced to endure it day after day.

They got back into the car and Ross drove on down to the school. His face was grim, but he drove faster now, pointing out the Technical Building which had been the first project he worked on when he got here in 1947. He described how a ramp had been built which went from the first-floor level to the top of the walls at an angle of eighteen degrees, and how all the materials to lay two giant slabs of concrete which would roof in the two wing ends of the building were put in hessian bags on wheelbarrows, which two boys would haul it up like coolies. He said railway lines were used to reinforce the massive concrete beams, weighing forty-five pounds to the foot, and that they too were manhandled up this ramp by a line of boys on each side.

'It was bloody dangerous, if just one boy lost his footing, a half ton of steel out of control could cut off their legs, knock them off the ramp or even kill them if it landed on top of them. I reckon it was like building the pyramids or the Burma railroad.'

Ross stopped the car suddenly in front of a large bronze statue up on a plinth which stood right in front of the school. It was of a Brother, his arm paternally around a small boy's shoulder.

'That's him, the bastard,' Ross hissed. 'Fucking Brother Keaney. So-called friend of orphans. See, he's got boots on, but the boy's got none, at least they got that right. But how dare they honour him with a statue!'

Dulcie had heard a great deal about this Irishman Keaney from Ross. He got his first blow from him as a six-year-old at Clontarf orphanage in Perth, where Keaney was once the Superior. Even there this six-foot-two, eighteen-stone man was building, using children as labourers – in that case his construction work was a large chapel. Then he went on to Tardun, yet another orphanage where he played a part in settling boys on their own farms.

'Park up the car,' Dulcie said, anxious to get out and look around. 'You can look at that again later.'

Ross drove on and they left the car by some outbuildings. It was very quiet, the current boys at the school were clearly in class or out working on the vast area of farmland surrounding it. Flies bombarded both of them, a sharp reminder to Dulcie of her time at the Masters' place in Salmon Gums. There were of course a great many flies at Esperance too at this time of year, but not in this quantity because of its position near the coast.

'They were more torture,' Ross said as he flapped them away. 'They'd cling to your eyes, nose and mouth, and feed on sores or broken skin. But you got used to it.'

Dulcie didn't think she could ever get used to it, but she was distracted then by a Brother coming towards them, out of the building Ross had said was the dairy. He wore a long black soutane, his head bare. Ross stiffened, his face blanching, clenching and unclenching his hands.

'Do you know him?' she whispered.

'Yes, it's Brother Casey,' he whispered back.

Dulcie knew instinctively that Ross was unlikely to be able to speak coherently to this man, so she stepped forward. 'G'day. I'm Dulcie Rawlings,' she said, 'Ross's wife, he's just brought me here to show me round his old school.'

Brother Casey did not look frightening, he was well

over sixty, slender with white hair, walking with a stick, and his smile was welcoming. 'I'm pleased to meet you, Mrs Rawlings,' he said, shaking her hand. 'And how are you doing, Ross?'

'Fine, sir,' Ross said, his voice cracking with nervousness. 'Just up from Esperance on a holiday.'

'Are you farming?' Brother Casey asked. His sharp blue eyes kept darting to Dulcie. She wondered if he had been cruel to Ross, and if he was going to say anything about him absconding.

Ross nodded. 'A big spread down on the coast. I manage it now.'

This wasn't strictly true, but Dulcie could perfectly well understand his need to boost his image.

'I've got some chores to do,' Brother Casey said. 'But you can show your wife around. You'll find some changes since you were here.'

'Where are all the boys?' Dulcie asked. 'It's very quiet.'

'Some are in class, some out working. But a bunch of them have gone out camping in the bush, they won't be back till tomorrow.'

He abruptly turned and walked away, and it was only then that Dulcie realized he wasn't in the habit of welcoming old boys, and hoped they'd leave quickly.

'Was he one of the cruel ones?' Dulcie asked as the man disappeared back into the dairy.

Ross shrugged. 'They all were, but he never laid into me. He only came here in my last year. But I want to go now, there's nothing I want to see.'

He was still very pale, and Dulcie was astounded that a man who could stand up to anyone normally should be made so fearful by one old man.

'But there's a lot *I* want to see,' she said firmly. 'So come on, show me around.'

He took her over to the Technical Building and she peered through the windows. In one room there were some boys doing woodwork, but most of the other rooms were rather bare classrooms, much like the ones at St

Vincent's. He took her up the flight of steps into the impressive two-storey main administrative building, pausing nervously under the arched entrance.

'See that,' he pointed to a mosaic ahead of them on the marble floor. 'I lost most of the skin on my fingers doing that.'

It was cool after the searing heat outside, the yellowish-gold floor so clean and shiny it looked wet. The mosaic was a circle of pale blue, *Fratres Scolarum Christianarum De Hibernia* in red lettering inside it. A green cross with a white star at its centre took up the space in the circle. Beneath this was a design like a blue ribbon, *Boys' Town* in red set into it.

'What does the Latin mean?' she asked.

'Buggered if I know,' he shrugged. 'To me it means *Welcome to Hell*.'

She bent over to feel the mosaic. It was so smooth that it was difficult to imagine that each tiny piece of marble had been placed there by the hand of a small boy.

Yet as Ross took her into the building she saw for herself how he came to know so much about building, and indeed was such a perfectionist in his work. Marble pillars, graceful arches in blues, creams and greens, it was all so incredible. He had previously told her there were two Italian stonemasons working under Father Urbano, the architect who directed the boys in their work. For these men he had some affection, for they had been kindly towards the boys, yet all the labouring – and Dulcie was overwhelmed by the sheer size of the place – was done by the boys, the Brothers working merely as overseers.

There was so much she wanted to know, what the rooms upstairs in the building were used for, how many Brothers were there in Ross's time, and how many now. She wanted to know if it was still a cruel place, to see close up, perhaps even speak to some of the boys, but Ross was growing more and more agitated. He kept speaking of other boys by name, describing atrocities that were done to them as if it had all happened yesterday, and he barely let her see the beautiful chapel before dragging her outside again.

'John had a wheelbarrow full of cement fall on top of him,' he said, pointing up to the dome on the roof. 'He was badly hurt, the lime was burning his eyes, and all the Brothers did was stick him head-first into a tank of water.'

'Show me where you slept,' she said. It was hard for her to believe this peaceful and beautiful place had so much horror attached to it. There were flowerbeds, palms, well-kept lawns. Beyond the school buildings were vine-yards, paddocks with cows and sheep, others planted with crops. The shady verandas in front of the dormitories and the Brothers' rooms had all the serenity of cloisters in a monastery.

Yet as Ross led her along them he was trembling. He spoke of bed-wetters being forced to stand there for hours wearing a sack-like dress to humiliate them, of Dawe, the Brother he mentioned most frequently, whacking them over the head with a strap to wake them in the mornings. Dulcie couldn't imagine it ever being cold here, but Ross talked of the winters when they shivered under one blanket, of walking in bare feet on frosty ground to milk the cows, of the hunger pains they suffered continually.

He paused outside one room, glancing fearfully at it. She caught hold of his arm and found it was stiff with terror, his hand icy cold. 'What happened there, Ross?' she asked gently. 'Tell me.'

He kind of shook himself and strode on away from the place. Dulcie ran after him, knowing in her heart his secret lay there. But he wouldn't stop or speak to her.

She saw a few Brothers, mostly younger than the one they'd spoken to earlier, and she guessed they had come here since Ross's time as they showed no recognition, only faint curiosity. A young boy of about fourteen was weeding a flowerbed, he looked up and smiled as they rushed past him, and though Dulcie wanted to stop and speak to him, she had to follow Ross.

Ross didn't stop until he came to a huge tomb, close to the statue of Keaney. His face was purple with indignation and his eyes almost popping out of his head as he saw the inscription on it. 'They've even buried the bastard here! I don't believe it!'

He struck the tomb with his clenched fist, skinning his knuckles, then turned to Dulcie, so agitated he was shaking. 'Look, they gave him an MBE. Can you believe the Queen would award that to a man who beat and starved little kids! He ought to burn in hell.'

Dulcie knew that Ross had run away from here in 1953, and as she'd seen a plaque in the grounds commemorating the day the school was officially opened in October of that year, she'd assumed Keaney died before then. On his tomb the date of his death was given as 1954, and perhaps as Ross never read newspapers, he'd never known the man had died.

She looked up at the statue of Keaney and tears ran down her cheeks as she remembered Ross's tales of how this big bully of a man and his friends would have drunken parties, and he would get some of the boys in to sing to them. How shameful that a bunch of grown men of the cloth and local dignitaries should eat and drink the profit made from foodstuffs grown by boys who never received anything more than watery soup, bread and porridge.

She too felt it was disgusting that he'd been honoured by the Queen, especially as she knew the kind of trickery Keaney had used to convince the majority of Australian people he was some kind of saint.

The whole property had been called Mount Pleasant, and the benevolent owner, a widow called Catherine Musk, gave it to the Christian Brothers with the intention that the Brothers were to use it to place needy boys and orphans on their own farms. She undoubtedly gave Keaney the responsibility for clearing the land and building a school because she believed him to have all the qualifications and heart for the formidable task.

The Brother became a living legend known as *Friend to the Orphans*, for his charismatic, expansive personality had endeared him to the Australian public and he wasted no time in plucking their heart-strings to make them dip into their wallets to give generous donations for this new project. It was truly remarkable what he achieved, Dulcie could see that just by looking around her. She could well imagine why people called him a genius. But then they didn't know that he achieved it purely through brutality and terror.

Perhaps now Bindoon did live up to what it was intended to be, a college to train boys in agricultural work. But for those boys like Ross who came in the early days there was no real schooling, many never learned to read and write. It was like a concentration camp where the only real skill they learned was survival. Yet some hadn't even learnt that, for she knew some boys had died here, and she suspected that most of the old boys, like Ross, were haunted by the cruelty they'd experienced at the hands of the Brothers.

An odd sound from Ross brought her mind back from Keaney to her husband. She saw he was now sitting on the grass, his legs up tight to his chest, arms clasped round them.

She sat down on the grass beside him and tried to comfort him, but he was as stiff as a board, as though every muscle in his body had seized up. 'Tell me what's wrong,' she asked, but there was no reply, just plaintive sobs, and she realized she must get him away from here before someone came over to them.

'Can you walk to the car?' she asked, standing up and pulling at his arm. There was no response, it was as if he'd been struck deaf, dumb and blind.

'I'll go and get it and bring it here,' she said, thinking the sight of the car might bring him round, and she ran off to get it.

He was still in the same position when she drove back, he didn't even turn his head to look at her.

'Ross, get up and get in the car,' she ordered him sharply, pulling at his arm again. But his hands were still locked round his knees and he appeared to be almost in a trance.

She was scared now, very aware this was all her doing. 'Get up, Ross, or I'll have to get one of the Brothers,' she said, and slapped him lightly on the shoulder. Again no response.

'Brother Dawe's coming to get you,' she said in desperation. 'Look, he's coming now.'

To her surprise it worked, he leaped to his feet, jumped into the passenger seat of the car and slid down in the seat as if trying to hide himself.

She drove away quickly, her heart pounding with fright. Bruce had been apprehensive about this trip, he'd even suggested it might knock Ross off his rocker, but she hadn't believed that. Now she wondered if it had – he was still crying, but he'd bent his head down on to his knees and she couldn't see his face. She drove until she was right out of the drive and on to the road back to Perth, and only stopped again when she saw a small parking place covered with shady trees.

Turning off the engine, she turned to him and made him sit upright. 'It's okay now, we're well away from there,' she said.

He let her hold him tightly, leaning his head on to her shoulder, but he continued to cry.

'Tell me what happened,' she begged him, caressing his hair and winding the auburn curls around her fingers.

It was a long while before he began to speak in a whisper, and at first it made no sense to her. There was something about making butter in the dairy. But as he began to make a turning motion with his hand, she realized he was talking through something that had happened a long time ago.

Ross was unaware that he was now a grown man, or that he was in a car with his wife. He had slipped back to when he was twelve, his stomach ached with hunger, his arm almost dropping off with turning and turning the churn handle, but until he had made the butter he knew he couldn't hope for any supper.

He had a painful stone bruise on the sole of his foot,

and he could barely put it down on the cold stone-flagged floor, his hands were red raw from making bricks all day. Keaney had caught him with some stolen grapes from the vineyard an hour ago, whacked him over the head with his big heavy stick, and ordered him in here to make the butter as a further punishment.

Yet dejected as Ross felt, there was nothing particularly unusual about his situation. From as far back as he could remember he had never received any real kindness from any adult, and he didn't expect it. He counted himself more fortunate than the English boys who had arrived recently. They had turned up in smart little suits, socks, shoes, even caps and ties, and looked in horror at the Australian boys with their ragged shorts and shirts and bare feet. It made him smile to see them hopping around on the hot ground once they'd been stripped of their good clothes, and he even enjoyed their shock at discovering they wouldn't be getting lessons, only doing building work.

He would listen to their tales about how they'd been treated like princes coming over here on the ship, and he supposed it would be hard to bear hunger and ill treatment after that. Maybe that's why so many of them cried in bed at night, and wet the bed.

Ross was used to working day in, day out, first light until dusk. He was used to hot summers and he supposed he'd eventually grow used to the cold winters, though it had been something of a shock when he first got here because it had never been so cold at Clontarf. He didn't expect wounds and injuries to be treated, he'd learnt a long time ago to live with hunger and the absence of any kind of affection from adults. He stiffened when the dairy door opened, expecting that it was Brother Keaney checking up on him, but it was Brother Dawe, known to all the boys as 'Honk' because of his large nose.

'Put some beef into it,' Dawe said after a moment or two of watching him turn the handle of the churn. 'Or you'll be here all night.'

'I think it's nearly there,' Ross said, not daring to turn his head to look at Brother Dawe.

There was no reply to this, and it unnerved Ross to be watched in silence. A few minutes passed with Ross trying desperately to turn the handle faster, and then in desperation he glanced round, and to his horror saw the man was standing there with his soutane unbuttoned, fondling his penis, looking right at Ross.

Ross couldn't run out – Dawe was standing against the closed door – he didn't dare say anything either. So he just turned back to his churn and turned the handle even faster.

'Come here and make some cream for me,' Dawe said in a low voice.

Ross said nothing, but his heart was pounding in terror. He heard the man step closer, and sweat began to run down Ross's face. Dawe was so close to his back now that Ross could feel his breath warm on the back of his neck, and he tensed, knowing something terrible was going to happen.

Dawe put his hand on to Ross's thigh and slowly slid it up beneath the leg of his shorts. The boys at Bindoon were not issued with underpants, so it was only a second before he had his hand on Ross's penis.

'Please don't, Brother Dawe,' Ross whimpered, his bowels loosening with terror.

'It's your duty to obey me, you little maggot,' Dawe said, and squeezed his penis tightly, making Ross squeal with pain. 'One more word out of you and I'll see you are up for a thrashing on Sunday morning.'

On Sunday mornings Brother Keaney always called boys out for a public thrashing after church – sometimes his victims didn't even know what they'd done wrong. Ross had already received two such beatings, which had left him hardly able to walk, and he wasn't anxious to get a third.

But all at once, before Ross could make any further protest, Dawe had the buttons on Ross's shorts undone, and they fell down to his knees. Before he could even cry out, Dawe was bending him over a stool and parting his buttocks.

Ross knew it was a sin to play with yourself, Dawe himself was always ranting about this and accusing boys of doing it. He had heard older boys talking of fucking girls too, and of queer men doing it to other men, but until that moment when he felt Dawe push his erect penis against his anus, he hadn't really believed any of it.

He screamed out with pain, for it felt as though he was being torn apart, but Dawe put one hand across his mouth, and with the other pressed down on his neck.

The effect was like being strangled, and the more he tried to move, the harder Dawe's hold became on him. But aside from the agony of being penetrated, the fear of dying from strangulation, there was also the man's verbal abuse.

'This is all you're good for, you dirty little shit,' he said. 'A good shagging will sort you out. You came from the gutter and you'll end up there too.'

Ross was close to passing out with the pain, and the animal grunting noise Dawe was making grew louder and louder as he forced himself harder and harder into Ross. Then suddenly the grunting stopped, he was released and pushed to the floor like a pile of rubbish.

Dawe wiped himself on a cloth which he then flung down on top of Ross. 'Get up and get that butter made, or you will be up for the Sunday thrashing,' he said as he strode out the door.

Dulcie could hardly believe what she'd been hearing, and the sight of her tough husband pouring it out with tears streaming down his face like a six-year-old was too terrible for words. There had been moments when she was confused by what he said, especially at the beginning when he was speaking of his sore hands, the stone bruise on his foot and the English boys. But by the end of the story she realized why all that was important, he thought he was worth nothing in the first place, he accepted everything that was done to him as his due. Yet that brutal, criminal act had pushed him into utter darkness where there could be no hope of salvation.

She tried to comfort him, but he kept on talking and crying and she heard how in the next few years he lived in constant fear of Dawe. He would be ordered to clean his room, and it always resulted in either forced anal or oral sex. Dulcie didn't even know what the latter meant, but Ross told her graphically that Dawe forced him to take him in his mouth. He said that he bled from his back passage all the time, that once a part of his bowel had started to come out and Dawe pushed it back in with a stick.

Sadder still was that Ross told her that however disgusting he found it, he tried to make himself believe the man loved him because he sometimes gave him cake, fruit, sweets or cigarettes afterwards.

Dulcie had never been so afraid. Stephan had said if she pushed the right buttons the truth would come out, but she wished now she hadn't. They were on a lonely road some eighty miles from Perth, and she didn't know what she was going to do. Ross was distraught, how could she take him back to Joan's like that?

She had water in the car, warm now from being in the sun all day, but that was all she could offer him.

'I'm so sorry, Ross,' she said. 'I wanted to know what happened to you there, but I never dreamed it was anything like that.'

He gulped the water down, but a few moments later he opened the car door, leaned out and was violently sick. She knew then there was nothing for it but to drive him home to Esperance, for there was no hope of continuing their holiday.

After all that talking and crying he went completely silent. He got out of the car, urinated and climbed into the back and lay down. Dulcie took that as a signal she had to make all the decisions, and she drove off back to Perth.

It was five in the afternoon when she got back to Subiaco,

leaving him in the car. She hastily explained that Ross was ill and she was taking him home, packed their cases and left hurriedly.

At eleven o'clock the following night, Dulcie drove into the farmyard. Ross was still curled up in the back of the car where he had remained for the whole journey, only getting out to relieve himself a couple of times. He had refused to eat anything, drank nothing but odd sips of water, and he hadn't spoken at all.

John came running out of the bunkhouse at the sound of the car and the dogs barking. 'You're home early,' he said. 'Something wrong?'

It was such a relief to know she wasn't alone with this problem any longer and she hoped that familiar surroundings might bring Ross quickly back to normal.

'Ross is ill,' she said, nodding towards the back seat, willing John not to ask too many questions. 'Can you help him into the house?'

'What's wrong with him?' John asked, peering curiously into the back where Ross still lay curled up and seemingly unaware he was home.

'I don't know exactly,' she said, putting her finger to her lips to silence any further questions. 'I'm dog-tired. I drove all through the night and today. Let's just get him to bed for now.'

John was marvellous. He leaned into the car, hooked Ross over his shoulder and pulled him out. Then he carried him over to the house and into the bedroom.

'Shall I take his clothes off?' he asked, looking at Ross lying on the bed staring blankly at the ceiling and back to Dulcie in bewilderment. 'He smells a bit high!'

'I expect I do too,' she said wearily. 'You go, I'll see to him.'

It was another hour before Dulcie finally got into bed beside Ross. She'd stripped off his clothes, washed him and put clean pyjamas on him, but he still had said nothing. He didn't even seem to know her, or where he was.

The last thing she thought before sleep overtook her was that if he didn't come out of this, she'd be responsible.

'He's still in bed!' Bruce exclaimed the following evening when Dulcie went over to his house briefly. She had slept right through until nine that morning, then once she saw Bruce going into his house alone, she'd slipped out to tell him what had happened. She didn't give him any detail, only that Ross had been severely upset by going back to Bindoon, and he appeared to be in shock. She collected some eggs, milk and bread, then went straight back for she was afraid to leave Ross alone. But although he'd drunk a cup of tea later, and asked how they got home, he had lapsed back into silence since.

'I don't know what to do, Bruce,' she said, beginning to cry. 'He isn't speaking, he won't eat. He's just lying there.'

'Should I call the doctor?' Bruce asked. 'This is a new one on me, I've never known Ross to have anything wrong with him.'

'Maybe he's making up for all the time he was sick as a boy and he still had to work,' she said. 'We can't call the doctor out now, it's not as if he's got a temperature or he's vomiting or anything.'

She couldn't tell Bruce what had really caused it, it was too horrible and sickening. Throughout the long drive home her mind had churned it over and over, just like that butter Ross had been making, and she fully understood now why he couldn't make love, and she blamed herself for forcing it out of him.

'Couldn't you call that shrink in Sydney that had the bright idea of taking him back there?' Bruce said.

'It's too late to call now,' she said. 'Besides, the number's back in our house.'

'It's not too late when it's an emergency,' Bruce said, looking sharply at her as if suspecting she was holding something back from him. 'I'll come over with you while you get it, I'll stay with Ross while you make the call. You never know, he might respond to me. I was the one who found him in the barn after all.'

Dulcie felt she had no choice but to make the call then, and Stephan didn't sound the least annoyed to be called so late. He said he'd just returned home from visiting friends. Haltingly Dulcie explained about the trip to Bindoon, and the state Ross was in now.

'What happened, Dulcie?' he asked. 'Something did happen, didn't it? Or he told you something. Please tell me, I can't help unless you do.'

Dulcie began to cry. 'He was raped by one of the Brothers,' she blurted out before she could lose her nerve. 'It went on for several years.'

There was absolute silence for a moment, then Stephan sighed deeply. 'Oh Dulcie, I feared it might be something like that. I wish I had been wrong.'

She felt just a slight sense of relief at telling him. 'What do I do now? Should I call a doctor?'

'Wait a couple of days, sleep is a great healer,' he said soothingly. 'If he's lying awake, try and get him up, encourage him to eat. It's quite likely he doesn't remember he's told you about it, to him it will almost certainly seem like he's had a mere mental flashback, and I expect he's had those before. Once he begins to talk again, tell him that he told you, try and get him to speak of it again. Admitting such terrible things happened is half the battle.'

'What's the other half?' she asked.

'Dealing with it. You will remember I told you he has to learn to put the blame for it on to that Brother, and let go of his guilt and shame. Sadly that's often the hardest part. You might find he has bursts of extreme anger, he may become clinically depressed. His local doctor will be able to help with that, though I can't recommend you tell him the whole story, not unless you are very sure of him, for if Ross comes up against disbelief, it could set him back badly.'

Dulcie had no intention of telling the local doctor, but she felt indignant that Stephan should suggest Ross wouldn't be believed, and said so. 'Surely anyone who had heard what I heard would want to string that Brother up?'

'I'm afraid when there is a choice between believing an orphan boy and a man of the cloth, the cleric wins hands down,' Stephan said quietly. 'The Christian Brothers have a unique place in the history of the country and in the affections of its people. I personally would like to see this Brother prosecuted and sent to prison. Ideally I'd like that orphanage and all others thoroughly investigated, so that no other child has to suffer cruelty or abuse. But it would have to be a very brave man to start that particular ball rolling, he'd need a great deal of back-up from other old boys too. I don't somehow see Ross, from what you've told me about him, as that man.'

'No, nor do I,' she said regretfully. 'But it's a terrible thought that even as we speak it might be happening to other helpless children.'

'Look after Ross for now,' he said gently. 'I will pass a discreet word around to people I know who do have influence in such matters. Ring me again in a few days to tell me how things are progressing.'

The next few weeks were agonizing for Dulcie. She was run ragged with all her usual duties, and needing to keep going over to check on Ross. She did eventually manage to bully him into getting up and dressed to sit in a chair, but he just stared out of the window vacantly. The doctor wasn't a great deal of help, he gave him some pills and a tonic, but that was all. Bruce, John and Bob were all sympathetic towards him up to a point, but mental illness was way out of their comprehension. Dulcie sensed that their sympathy was slowly turning to resentment as they struggled to do Ross's work too, and if he didn't snap out of it, the way they expected he should, then a mental institution would be the next step.

She felt as if the weight of it all was solely upon her shoulders. She was responsible for taking him to Bindoon. She had the hideous images in her mind she couldn't share with anyone else. She took on the guilt that the other men were doing his work, and lived with the fear that if he was taken to an institution, he'd never get out. Yet over and above everything else a small voice at the back of her head kept whispering that this was her punishment for allowing herself to dream of a life with Rudie and Noël.

It was that last thing which plagued her the most, for even if she hadn't been physically unfaithful to Ross, she had had it in mind a hundred times. So all she could do was try to bring him out of it.

She sat in front of him and repeated everything he'd told her, but there was no reaction. She tried just holding him and stroking his hair, pleading with him to talk to her, but that didn't work either. Once she even slapped him, but felt so ashamed when he looked at her in shocked surprise that she burst into tears. Reading to him, playing music and giving him his favourite meals didn't help either. He ate some of whatever she put in front of him, but with no enjoyment. When he did speak it was usually something about the farm. Just questions like had the cows been milked, or had Bruce decided on which paddock was to be ploughed next. He didn't appear even to know what season it was, for he asked about lambing one day, and that would be months ahead.

The nights were the worst time for her. During the day she had so much to do that sometimes she could switch off her anxiety and guilt. But the moment she turned off the light and lay next to him, it came back with a vengeance. On one hand she had the terrible images Ross had given her flashing through her mind, on the other she had the lovely ones of Noël and Rudie, the cottage in Watson's Bay. At least before they went to Bindoon she had a straight choice, stay or go. Yet she couldn't possibly leave Ross like this, there would be no one to look after him. But how long could anyone be expected to take care of someone in his condition?

The answer of course, was for ever. That was the deal in marriage, for better or worse, in sickness and in health.

She had to ring Rudie and ask him not to contact her any more. It was too painful to listen to him talking about Noël sitting up on his own, and his first attempts at crawling. She didn't want to visualize the new painting Rudie was working on, or hear news about people she'd met and liked.

He said he understood, but all that did was make her feel more hopeless, for no one could really understand the torment she was going through.

One afternoon Dulcie was washing over the floor in her living-room and Ross kept walking on to the wet parts. She had been pleased when he first began getting out of his chair and walking about, even though he was still silent, but the pleasure had soon turned to irritation. At least when he was sitting she could work round him, in the evenings she could paint or read. But his pacing up and down was too distracting to concentrate on anything.

She was tired, longing for real company, and the sight of Ross still unwashed and unshaven, still wearing his pyjamas because she'd forgotten to order him to get washed and dressed this morning, was too much to bear.

'For heaven's sake, stop that pacing and go and get dressed,' she yelled at him. 'I've got enough to do without you getting in my way. It's just not fair!'

He didn't appear to have heard her because he continued to pace up and down. Dulcie hastily finished the floor around him, and was just getting up off her hands and knees when he finally spoke.

'Nothing's fair in this life,' he said, his speech slow and slightly slurred.

'You're right there,' she said tartly. 'I've been taking care of you for over four weeks now and you don't even seem to know I'm here.'

'You shouldn't have made me go back there,' he retorted.

Maybe she ought to have been delighted that he was answering her back, yet all she heard was him putting the blame on to her.

She threw the wet cloth down on to the floor. 'Is that what this is all about then? You're punishing me for making you remember?'

He shook his head.

'It seems that way to me, Ross,' she said. 'You've got to put the blame on Brother Dawe, nobody else. You've got to try and get back to normal too. Bruce needs you, I need you.'

'You don't need me,' he said. 'Neither does Bruce, both of you could easily get someone else.'

Something snapped inside Dulcie. 'You feel so bloody sorry for yourself it makes me sick,' she hissed at him. 'It was awful what happened to you, but you can't just sit there dwelling on it. Sure I could get someone else, I'd probably get a far better deal than you, too. Bruce could fill your job tomorrow, but he won't do that because he's an honourable man, and I won't go because I'm married to you. But don't tempt us too far, Ross. We have a breaking-point too.'

She rushed towards the door, stopping only as she reached it. 'For heaven's sake get yourself washed and dressed,' she shouted at him. 'It makes me sick to see you shuffling about like that.'

Outside the house she felt bitterly ashamed of herself, and instead of going into Bruce's she skirted round his house and sat on the bench under a tree at the back of it. This had been Betty's favourite spot to sit outside in the spring. She said it was a good place to survey the farm and think how lucky she'd been to end up owning it.

It was a good place. Behind her was a paddock with grazing sheep, to her right she could see right down the track to the road, and the paddocks on either side. On her side of the track there were more sheep, across it, heifers and the two horses Bruce had bought a while back. Straight in front was Bruce's house, and beyond that his land stretched on for ever. To her left was the barn, the bunkhouse and her own house, and all around them were pine trees, and an English oak, planted in the early part of this century. Beyond that was more pasture and the lake, and even if the summer sun had dried up the grass, there was still plenty of grazing left, for they had many short showers here, even in the hottest months.

She wondered where Bruce, Bob and John were working today, they hadn't said this morning at breakfast. She guessed they probably talked among themselves about Ross while they were out, wondering what on earth they were going to do about him. They couldn't manage for much longer without him, he had always done such a huge share of the work. Bruce was too old to be attempting young men's work, and neither Bob nor John had Ross's patience and empathy with animals. They would have to find a replacement for him soon.

She was still sitting there when she saw John and Bruce driving back up the track in the Ute. John waved his hat out of the window when he saw her, and there was something about the gesture that told her he had something to say to her.

Running over to meet them, she saw Bruce get out of the driving seat and open the passenger side for John. He appeared to have something in his arms.

As she got closer she realized it was a puppy. John was holding it against his chest like a baby and it was licking his face.

'A puppy!' she said gleefully, putting aside her earlier gloom. 'Oh, let me hold him! Where did you get him?'

John put the black and white pup into her arms. 'We went to Condingup, to see a bloke about some fencing. His bitch had puppies about eight weeks ago, this one needed a home.'

Dulcie held the puppy up to get a good look at him, he

had a look of a Border collie, with floppy, fluffy ears. 'He's beautiful,' she exclaimed. 'What're you going to call him?'

'That's up to Ross,' Bruce said. 'We got him for him, thought it might bring him round a bit.'

A lump came up in Dulcie's throat. Ross loved dogs, she knew he had always wanted one of his own. But it was Bruce's big-heartedness which choked her up, he had thought of the one thing which really might help Ross.

'Come over now and show it to him,' she suggested. 'We had some sharp words earlier, he could do with seeing that you two care about him.'

The two men exchanged glances, they'd both been in and out to see Ross many times just after Dulcie brought him back from Bindoon, but she knew they'd stopped coming because they both felt embarrassed and ill at ease that he didn't respond to them.

'He was talking earlier,' she said. 'I was nasty to him too.'

John half smiled. 'You couldn't be nasty if you tried,' he said gallantly.

'You'll see just how nasty if you don't come,' she said with a smile. 'Go on, he's not so scary now. I ordered him to get washed, shaved and dressed. If he's done that without me standing over him, that's an improvement.'

Ross was washed and dressed when Dulcie went in. He was sitting in the chair looking out of the window at the lake in the distance.

'Bruce and John have come to see you, Ross,' she said.

He kind of nodded, but didn't turn his head to look at them.

'We brought something for you, Ross,' Bruce said and stepping forward he held out the puppy and put him into Ross's lap.

Dulcie held her breath and watched as Ross's hand instinctively moved to prevent the pup falling on to the floor. As his fingers made contact with its fur, the pup wriggled closer to him and began licking his hand.

There was utter silence, three pairs of eyes all centred on Ross and the puppy. Slowly Ross's hand moved to its back to stroke it, he fondled its ears and drew it closer still to him till it nestled in his arms. Dulcie almost felt a pang of jealousy that she had stroked and caressed Ross so many times in the past couple of weeks, yet never once had he reciprocated. But this puppy had managed to get through to him.

'He's yours, Ross,' Bruce said, his voice croaky with emotion. 'You'll have to give him a name.'

Ross's head turned towards Bruce and for the first time since they arrived home there was a light in his eyes. 'He's for me?' he whispered.

John stood awkwardly, his hat in his hand, but Bruce moved closer and knelt down beside Ross to pet the puppy. 'Yeah, he's yours, for keeps. His ma's a first-class sheep dog, so mind you train him well. I had a dog just like him when I was your age, best dog I ever had.'

'What was his name?' Ross asked.

'Jigger,' Bruce said, and chuckled. 'Bloody silly name. Don't know why I picked on that one, but it suited him.'

Ross looked down at the puppy falling asleep in the crook of his arm and half smiled. 'I'll call him Jigger then.'

Dulcie made a cup of tea for everyone and though Ross said little more, she felt a new lightness in the room, where before there had been only gloom. Later, when Bruce and John left, she followed them outside, leaving Ross still petting Jigger in his lap.

'Thank you so much, both of you,' she said, looking from Bruce's old baggy face to John's still handsome smooth one. 'How did you know?'

'We didn't, not for sure,' Bruce smiled. 'But I remembered how Ross told me he caught a baby rabbit once and kept it as a pet tucked into his shirt. 'Course I didn't know then what it must've meant to him to have something of his own to love, but when I saw that pup, I just had a feeling.'

'Guess it will mean more work for you,' John grinned. 'Puddles and stuff.'

'I don't mind that,' Dulcie said. 'Not if it helps to get him better.'

Bruce patted her shoulder. 'I wish I could have found something to bring a smile back on to your face too.'

'You have,' she said, breaking into a grin. 'It's called hope.'

Chapter Twenty-six

'Bad dog,' Dulcie said, snatching away a shoe Jigger had been chewing at. 'If you keep on doing that you'll have to stay outside like the other dogs.'

Jigger looked up at her with mournful eyes, and she had to smile. He was naughty, always into some mischief, but he *had* brought about Ross's recovery and for that she could stand the odd chewed shoe.

It was now October, eight months since Ross had the breakdown. He had been back at work for six months now, and on the surface he was his old self again. Yet the experience had changed him in many ways which only Dulcie saw. He was more appreciative, less of a braggart, and he could talk to her about things he once would never have discussed.

Yet it was undoubtedly Jigger who saved him, not her attention or the pills the doctor gave him. Jigger made him go outside again, for he was too afraid the puppy would get bitten by a snake to allow him out alone. He had to build him an outside pen too, and that brought back his old pleasure in making things. Playing with the dog, training him and sensing the animal's unconditional love for him gave him back some self-worth, and as he gradually took up smaller jobs around the farm and re-established familiarity with the other men, so he truly began to recover.

'What's he done now?' Ross came out of the bathroom and looked at Jigger standing there with his tail between his legs.

'A shoe again,' Dulcie said. 'Funny it's always mine he takes.'

'I expect they smell better,' Ross joked. 'I'll buy you a new pair.'

'He ought to be kept outside like the other dogs,' she said. Bruce's dogs never went in the house. They were with him all day outside, but in the evenings they went in their kennels.

'Could you really shut him out?' Ross said, bending to pet the dog. 'I bet you'd lie awake all night worrying in case a snake got him.'

Dulcie sighed. That was true, she would. Yet sometimes when Jigger brought in mud all over her floor she got so mad she felt she might explode.

'They are only puppies for such a short time,' Ross said, a note of pleading in his voice. 'A year from now he'll be all grown-up and he'll be out working with me all day.'

'Okay, he can stay inside,' she said. She did in fact love his company when Ross went out in the evenings. He would curl up at her feet, making comforting little snoring noises, and she loved him just as much as Ross did.

Ross put his arms around her and held her tightly. This was one of the new developments too, he was far more affectionate and demonstrative. Yet sadly kisses and cuddles were as far as he went, he still hadn't made any attempt at love-making and now she doubted he ever would.

Strangely it no longer bothered Dulcie, all desire for him had vanished during the time he was ill. Their relationship had become a comfortable one of brother and sister since, and although she thought she ought to be protesting, since the whole point of going to Bindoon was intended to bring back his sexuality, she had lost the inclination to make an issue of it.

'When is it that Rudie's coming?' he asked, a note of tension in his voice.

This was only a partial breakthrough. Ross had finally accepted that he couldn't prevent Dulcie's interest in her nephew, yet he was still extremely guarded about his father. Despite all Bruce's efforts to encourage him to invite

Rudie to stay here with Noël for his holiday, Ross wouldn't relent. But when Dulcie had found a small house in Esperance for Rudie to rent, he softened, and agreed she could bring Noël here during the day while his father painted.

'Next Tuesday,' she said. 'He's flying to Perth on Monday, staying the night there, then on to here the next day.'

'The man must have more money than sense, coming all that way,' Ross said churlishly.

'More heart than sense,' Dulcie corrected him. 'He wants me to see Noël, he thinks it's more important than the time or money involved. I can't wait to see Noël, I hope it will be warm enough to go on the beach.'

Ross just sniffed. 'Well, I'm going up to Kalgoorlie this weekend.'

He had been going to Kalgoorlie with some of his drinking mates from the pub every month for some time, leaving early Saturday evening and coming back on Sunday. Dulcie didn't mind, she enjoyed an evening all to herself and a lazy Sunday. Besides, he was always nicer when he returned, jollier and chatty. But the way he announced it this time was a bit irritating, as though he wanted to prove he too could have friends outside their marriage.

'Just don't get into any fights,' she said. 'And sober up before you drive home.'

'I don't get in blues any more,' he said, grinning down at her. 'You cured me of that.'

Once Dulcie would have used that as an opener for discussion on the effects of his breakdown. But as her need and desire for love-making had faded, so had the compulsion to try to dig more out of him. He had said once, when he was making the first steps towards recovery, that telling her what had happened to him was like putting oil on rusty hinges on a door.

He said he'd always been aware of what was behind the door, the only difference now was that he was able to open it and look at it, and close it again easily. And then said that he saw her as the only purity in his life, and that by attempting to make love to her, it would soil the image he had of her.

By that Dulcie could only surmise this meant the hideous memories of Doyle came back whenever he became aroused. As she felt she was responsible for bringing on his breakdown, she wasn't anxious to do anything more to him that might result in a relapse. Ross seemed happy now, even playful and joyous sometimes. They got on well together, there were few rows, and that was enough for her.

Stephan seemed concerned at her attitude the last time she spoke to him on the telephone. He said such a view might be okay when a couple were in their fifties or so, but not at her age. She had been a bit sharp with him, indeed she'd implied it was none of his business, and she hadn't spoken to him since.

'You have a good time up there,' she said with a smile. John said he couldn't imagine what the attraction of Kalgoorlie was. Dulcie didn't much care, as long as Ross came home in a good mood. She hoped it would last right through the time Rudie and Noël were here. Besides, it meant she could go down to the house Rudie was renting on Sunday morning. She wanted to make sure it was clean, make up the bed and cot with aired bedding, leave the toys she'd borrowed for Noël in there, and put some food in the fridge.

'What will you do while I'm away?' he asked, then grinned broadly as she glanced across the room to a half-finished painting on the easel she'd bought just recently. 'That's a daft question, you'll be finishing that off, won't you?'

Dulcie smiled, for even the thought of painting made her happy. It had become her passion, and she could hardly wait to show Rudie her work. Inspired by his remark that she could maybe illustrate children's books, her pictures now were all fantasy – fairy-tale castles, princesses on white horses, wicked witches, goblins and fairies. As she painted she often made up the story in her head too, and it lifted her away from the farm, memories of her own bleak childhood, the death of her sister, and Ross's troubles.

'Yes, I'll be painting,' she said, even though for this once it was a lie.

As Dulcie waited for Rudie's plane to arrive on Tuesday morning she reflected on how Bruce had predicted several years ago that one day there would be regular planes coming into Esperance. Maybe it wasn't much of a service yet, just a Douglas DC3 seating around eight people, twice a week, but Esperance was growing fast. At the last count the population had risen to 4,500, so it was conceivable that in a few years there would be a daily service.

She wondered too as she stood there looking up at the sky, waiting for the plane to come into view, how it was going to be to see Rudie again. A year had passed since they said goodbye on the train in Sydney, and though she thought at that time he was in love with her, maybe it was only all the emotional pressure at that time, the worry about Noël, the shared grief for May and living in such close proximity to one another, for in his many phone calls since, he had said nothing to make her think he thought of her as anything other than a friend.

Yet even so, she had still felt compelled to get her hair done yesterday, to wear her newest dress, a figure-hugging pale blue one that John claimed she looked like a pin-up girl in. And her pulse was racing.

At last she saw the small plane descending, its wheels lowered for landing. It hit the dirt runway, bounced up again once, then down again, ran for a few hundred feet then gradually came to a halt.

A man and woman got off first, followed by two young men and another couple, then suddenly Dulcie saw Rudie bending slightly to get through the plane doorway, Noël in his arms.

She couldn't contain her excitement a moment longer, and ran to them regardless of the curious looks from the other passengers she passed.

'There's Auntie Dulcie,' she heard Rudie say, and he began to run to her too, making the child laugh.

'Oh, Rudie,' she gasped as she reached him. 'It's so good to see you both again. Let me look at Noël!' She held out her arms and he went to her eagerly, even though he was far too young to know who she was.

At almost eighteen months he was a real little boy now, and very much like Rudie, black hair curling at the back of his neck, with soulful dark brown eyes. Yet there was a glimpse of May too, he had her delicate little nose and the same wide mouth. 'Was he good on the plane?' she asked.

'Extremely,' Rudie grinned. 'Though he did stand on the seat and yank the man in front's hat off. From Sydney to Perth he slept nearly all the way, so I had a pretty easy time of it.'

They just stood there for a moment or two smiling at one another, Noël sitting astride Dulcie's hip, and in that moment she knew that nothing had changed between them.

'I've got the car out front.' She pointed to beyond the airport building. 'I checked out the house I got for you on Sunday, and everything's fine. I hope you're going to like it here.'

'With you here, how could I fail to?' he said, pulling a silly face. 'I don't know this part of Australia and I'm looking forward to exploring it and doing some sketches.'

By the time Rudie had collected his luggage and Noël's pushchair and loaded them into the car, and they had taken off to the rented house, they were chatting and laughing as easily as they had a year earlier. The only difference now was that Noël wasn't a helpless baby but a bright toddler who sat up on his father's lap commenting on just about everything he could see out of the car windows, albeit in baby language.

The house was an old-style clapboard one, similar to

Rudie's own, just a two-minute walk from the Pier Hotel, overlooking Esperance Bay. The owners, acquaintances of Bruce, had a farm up in Norseman and used it for holidays. It was a bit post-war austerity standard, with a Rexeen-covered three-piece suite, a chunky sideboard and a poky kitchen, but Rudie was delighted with it.

'Nothing much for that little pickle to damage,' he said laughingly as Noël ran around exploring. 'I had visions of one of those places packed with ornaments and spindly furniture. That could have been hell.'

'It reminds me of homes back in England,' Dulcie said, looking at the old drop-front kitchen cabinet and a cooker on legs. 'But the hot-water system works properly, and it's not cold or damp. Mrs Collins – that's the policeman's wife I told you about – offered to baby-sit for you too, if you want to go out to the pub one evening.'

'I wasn't aiming on going out boozing while I was here,' he grinned. 'But it might be nice to take in a bit of the local colour one night.'

Dulcie gave him the Collins' address and telephone number, and said they'd hoped he would call round anyway for a drink and a chat. 'You'll find people very friendly round here, they love to meet anyone from the big cities, and of course they met May when she was here, so they are dying to see Noël.'

There was a shriek of delight from Noël, who had just gone into the dining-room and seen the box of toys there. He came hurtling out on a wooden-wheeled horse to show it to them.

'I wish you could have stayed at the farm,' she said wistfully. 'We could've spent so much more time together.'

'That's exactly what Ross didn't want,' Rudie said. 'I can't say I blame him either. You're quite a prize!'

Dulcie blushed. 'He's being stupid then,' she said quickly. 'After all, Noël is the one who's likely to capture my heart, and Ross doesn't mind me having him up there.'

After she'd made tea she took Noël on her lap to feed him a drink from a cup. He was very good with it, not spilling a drop, and Rudie said the only time he had a bottle now was before bed. Dulcie thought he was advanced in his speech too, for he could say quite a lot of words clearly. She thought he was the most handsome little boy, his dark lashes were so thick and long, his skin peach-coloured, and when he nestled back into her arms sleepily after his drink she felt a surge of love for him.

'He's got May's nose and mouth,' she said as he began to drop off as she stroked his forehead.

'I only ever see your face in his,' Rudie said with a smile. 'But tell me how you are. And how things are between you and Ross. You've never said when I phoned. I know too that you don't call Stephan any more.'

Dulcie had never told Rudie what caused Ross's break-down, and she knew Stephan had far too much integrity to divulge it.

'Ross is well and happy again,' she said. 'Everything's fine between us. But you'll see for yourself on Sunday, Bruce has invited you up for the day.'

Quickly she changed the subject to her painting, and pointed to the folder she'd brought with her and left on the table. 'Please look at them, I really want your opinion.'

Noël was now fast asleep, his little body curled right up against hers. Rudie took the folder and began slowly turning the pages. When after a few minutes he still hadn't made any comment Dulcie felt foolish. 'You don't have to go right through them, I don't want to bore you,' she said.

He looked up at her, a puzzled expression on his face. 'Bore me? Dulcie, a man would have to be in a coma not to want to look at this work. It's fantastic! If I'm silent it's only because I'm stunned.'

'They aren't too bad then?' she asked timidly.

He threw back his head and roared with laughter. 'That's a real English understatement. "Not too bad!" It's stupendous work, absolutely brilliant. I just can't believe that you've progressed so far since Noël's rabbit painting. That was good, but not in the same league as all these.'

'You're just humouring me,' she giggled.

626

'I'm certainly not,' he said, continuing to turn the pages. 'All I can say is, if all this came out of Ross's breakdown, then I'm glad he had one.'

'That's a terrible thing to say!' she exclaimed. 'You should be ashamed of yourself.'

He just looked at her and shrugged. 'No, I shouldn't. It's the truth. I can see from this work that you escape while painting. As your ability grows, so your imagination grows wings and flies to places you never could have reached if your life had been untroubled. I'm frankly envious, my work is banal compared to this.'

'Rubbish,' she retorted. 'Your paintings are uplifting, so vivid and compelling.'

He smiled. 'They're a good substitute for a view, that's all. The people who buy them take home a bit of Sydney Harbour on a sunny day. I'm not a *great* painter. Mine isn't work of imagination, I just sketch and paint what I see. If I was to be locked into a room with enough paint and canvases for a year or two, I'd run out of ideas in no time. But this has all come out of your head, unless of course there's a few goblins and fairies up at the farm you haven't told me about.'

Dulcie laughed. 'A few kangaroos, emus and snakes, that's all. Do you think I could get some work illustrating children's books now?'

'I'm absolutely certain of that,' he said, his eyes sparkling. 'May I take a few of these back home with me? I've done a couple of designs for book covers recently, so I know a few people in the publishing world and I'd like to show these to them and get their opinion.'

Dulcie glowed. 'That would be wonderful.'

Rudie went off upstairs to unpack, and Dulcie continued to sit with Noël asleep in her arms, happily day-dreaming of a day when she'd get paid for doing what she liked most. While she thought Rudie was being over-effusive, and perhaps biased about her ability, he was famous back in Sydney and he did have good connections.

She looked down at Noël and smiled, imagining a new series of pictures with a little boy like him and farm animals. She could hardly wait to take him to the farm and show him lambs, calves and horses.

Glancing at her watch, she saw it was already one o'clock. She had made sandwiches for the men's lunch this morning before she left, but she thought she'd better get back soon, or Ross might be grumpy. Fortunately he'd come back from Kalgoorlie in high spirits, he'd even brought her a present, a pair of gold earrings. She wondered what it was that he liked so much about Kalgoorlie. Was it just the wildness of the place, that you could get as drunk as you pleased without anyone caring? Or something more? She hoped he wasn't getting caught up gambling at Two Up, she'd heard so many women complaining that their husbands lost a small fortune that way.

'So how is the little man?' Bruce asked eagerly when she got back around four that afternoon.

'Oh, he's so beautiful I could eat him,' Dulcie enthused. 'But I'm going to collect him tomorrow at eleven and bring him back here, so you'll see him for yourself.'

'Everything all right with the cottage?' Bruce asked.

'Rudie's delighted with it. Noël fell asleep on my lap not long after we got there, then we took him out, had some lunch in the café and I showed them about. The man was coming with the car at four, so I left them to it then.'

'It's a bit lonely for Rudie alone with a kid,' Bruce said, looking a bit anxious. 'What's he going to do with himself in the evenings?'

'There's the television, he reads a lot, he'll be fine. He makes friends easily, I wouldn't be surprised if he doesn't know half the town by the end of the week.'

'Maybe I'll go down there tomorrow night, take a few beers and have a chat,' Bruce suggested. 'I'd like to get to know him. Besides, it might shame Ross into being a little more hospitable too.'

*

Dulcie had a lovely time with Noël the following day. From the moment he got out of the car and toddled across to see the dogs, he was happy. She showed him the new calves, the pigs and horses, and he laughed so much when she put a sugar lump in his hand and the horse nuzzled it up off his palm.

He was a great hit with all the men, including Ross, for at midday he trotted behind her as she took tea and sandwiches over to the barn for them, then promptly perched himself on Ross's lap and demanded some of his sandwich.

John gave him aeroplane rides, swinging him round and round. Bob let him sit up on the tractor, and Ross took him off to feed the last bits of sandwiches to the pigs. Bruce wasn't going to be outdone and saddled up his horse, put Noël in front of him and they cantered round the paddock. Dulcie stood and watched, her heart overflowing with joy to hear their laughter.

Later she put Noël down for a sleep in her old bed while she began preparations for the evening meal. As she peeled the potatoes she glanced out of the window, and to her surprise Ross was shinning up the oak tree with a rope slung across his shoulders. She watched, puzzled. John was standing on the ground looking up at Ross, who was now astride a thick branch and shuffling along. John appeared to be shouting some instructions.

Ross fastened the rope around the branch with a clove-hitch, then promptly slid back down it to the ground. Finally she saw what they were doing. They were making a swing from an old tyre.

She laughed aloud as she saw them testing it out, both clinging on to it together at one point, then suddenly she found herself irrationally tearful that the arrival of one small boy could bring back the child in both these grown men.

But Noël brought back the child in her too, for when he woke up from his nap she took him outside to test the swing and before long she was inside the tyre herself, with Noël on her lap, swinging to her heart's content.

He got filthy outside that afternoon. He chased Jigger around the yard, he was on and off the swing a hundred and one times, climbed on some wooden boxes, jumped down into her waiting arms, and dug in some sand with a little spade. She had to strip him off and put him in the bath before supper, his little shorts, tee-shirt and socks so dirty she had to put them to soak before attempting to wash them. But fortunately Rudie had put a spare set of clothes in a bag, so she guessed he must go through this most days himself.

Bruce said he would take him home after supper, and even though Dulcie wanted to go herself, she said nothing. Ross had sat Noël up on a cushion on a chair beside him at the table and helped him feed himself, and as Ross seemed relaxed and happy, perhaps it was best not to push anything. She would see Rudie and Noël the following afternoon anyway – maybe by then Ross would be suggesting she brought them both back for supper.

When Rudie heard the knock at the door of his rented cottage, he expected it to be Dulcie. But he was a little surprised to see the man he'd seen only fleetingly at Kalgoorlie three years earlier, with Noël in his arms.

'G'day, Rudie,' Bruce said. 'I offered to bring the little chap home so I could meet you, we can't really count that day at Kalgoorlie since we never even spoke.'

Rudie's face broke into a broad grin, and held out his arms for his son. 'Good to see you, Bruce. Come on in. I can't offer you much more than a cup of tea, I haven't got around to getting any booze in.'

Bruce waved a bag as he stepped inside the house. 'Good job I brought a few beers then! Noël's been a great hit with everyone today, but I reckon he's bushed now. Dulcie said to tell you he's had a bath and a good supper.'

Rudie kissed his son's cheek. Noël was already sleepily laying his head on his father's shoulder. 'You pour yourself a beer and I'll just get him ready for bed. I hope he's been good?'

'A real charmer,' Bruce said. 'He's been on a horse with me, on the tractor with Bob, and John and Ross made him a swing. Never seen Dulcie so happy.'

As Rudie stripped off Noël's clothes and put on his pyjamas, he watched Bruce go out into the kitchen and return with two glasses of beer. Dulcie had spoken of this man so often, Rudie felt as if he already knew him, yet strangely, the picture he had in his mind of their first meeting, things May had said and the conversations with Bruce on the phone, had given him the idea he was a much younger man.

He was big, muscular and seemingly fit, a warm, vibrant personality with a smile that would light up a room, yet despite all that Rudie sensed this was a man who was now close to the end of his life. He wondered if Bruce knew this himself, for it could explain why he showed such fatherly concern for Dulcie.

'Reckon he's got the makings of a country boy,' Bruce said jovially. 'He really likes animals.'

'I'll have to make sure he gets more contact with them then when I get home,' Rudie smiled. 'Maybe I'll get him a dog, and take him out horse-riding. I might be a city slicker myself now, but I was brought up in the country too.' With Noël in his arms he nipped out into the kitchen to get his bottle of milk. 'That's one of the drawbacks with bringing a child up on your own,' he said as he returned. 'You haven't got another person to suggest things you haven't thought of.'

'Maybe you should look around for a wife,' Bruce said.

Rudie laughed, the way Bruce spoke he made it sound like you went to the market and just picked one out. 'I'd be worried I might find the wicked stepmother,' he said. 'Maybe I'm a bit jaundiced but most of the women I meet are more interested in what I've got than the real me and Noël.'

Noël drank his bottle in double-quick time, then Rudie carried him up to bed.

'I have to hand it to you,' Bruce said as he came back

down again, 'you've done a fine job with that little lad. He's a credit to you. And it was real good of you to bring him all this way so Dulcie could see him.'

'It's important Noël keeps in contact with her,' Rudie said, picking up the drink Bruce had poured for him. 'As he grows up I want the picture in his head of his mother to be a positive one. I know there's a likelihood that someone, someday, will spill the beans about May, but if he's got his aunt about, it won't hurt him.'

Bruce nodded in agreement. 'Dulcie needs him too. It choked me up seeing how happy she was with him today. She's had such a bloody raw deal in life, and fond as I am of her, if she told me she wanted to take off to Sydney for good, I'd be happy for her. She deserves something better than she's got now.'

Rudie hadn't expected such a statement from a man who clearly saw Dulcie as an adopted daughter. 'Are you saying she isn't happy?' he asked. 'She gave me the impression everything was fine now.'

Bruce sighed. 'She would. But then her idea of personal happiness is when everyone else around her is content and comfortable. My Betty was a bit like that too, but then we had the foundation of a strong, loving marriage, and we weathered the storms together. I don't see Dulcie's and Ross's marriage in the same way, it's all her giving, and him taking.'

Rudie realized then this was precisely why Bruce had called on him tonight, he was worried about Dulcie and he needed to share it with someone else.

They talked for a while about Ross's breakdown, and it became clear to Rudie that Bruce was as much in the dark about what happened up at Bindoon as he was.

'How is he now?' Rudie asked.

Bruce shrugged. 'His old self in most ways. Competent, hard-working, the perfect stockman, you could say. Bob and John, my two other stockmen, are good men too, but not in the same class as Ross because he can do almost anything, twice as quickly, more thoroughly. Yet I know

John and Bob inside out. Not Ross though, he's a dark horse, you can't get close to him.'

'Dulcie said something today about him going up to Kalgoorlie once a month. Do Bob and John do this too?'

'Not Bob,' Bruce grinned. 'He's a bit of a mother's boy. He doesn't go much on hard drinking and throwing his money away on sheilas. John used to when he was younger, he was a wild one then, but he's calmed down, still likes a few beers and the sheilas, but he wouldn't drive a hundred and fifty miles for it now.'

'Is it beer or women Ross goes to Kalgoorlie for then?' Rudie asked.

Bruce hesitated.

That hesitation said reams to Rudie. 'You think it's women, don't you?' he said.

Bruce suddenly looked anxious. 'Look, mate. I don't know anything for certain. But the bloke comes back from there looking like the cat that's been in the cream. The two blokes he goes with are both womanizers. If it was just beer he wanted he could get that here.'

Rudie thought about it for a moment. He knew Kalgoorlie's reputation, it was the one place in Australia where prostitution was, if not legal, accepted. The thought of Ross going with women like that and then coming home to Dulcie filled him with horror.

He might have only just met Bruce, but he knew the man was worldly, intuitive and fair. He wouldn't have come here to speak about this unless he was completely certain in his own mind that was what Ross was up to.

Rudie thought it was time he laid his cards on the table. 'Dulcie confided in me in Sydney that Ross had never consummated their marriage,' he blurted out. 'It was a shrink friend of mine who suggested to her this might be because of something which happened to Ross at Bindoon.'

'I know all that,' Bruce nodded. 'Dulcie told me.'

Rudie looked relieved.

'So did Ross get cured?' Rudie asked him.

'I don't know.' Bruce shook his head. 'You can't ask something like that. Dulcie never told me what happened at Bindoon, but it had to be pretty bloody bad or Ross wouldn't have gone off his rocker, and she looked as if she'd been to hell and back too. She was so relieved when he got better that I couldn't bring myself to ask anything that might embarrass her.'

'Stephan would know,' Rudie said thoughtfully. 'But he wouldn't tell me! The only thing he told me was that Dulcie finally got a bit snotty with him and she hadn't rung him since. Oh shit, Bruce! We can't interfere, can we?'

The two men sat drinking their beer for several minutes in silence. Rudie was thinking that whether or not Ross was making love to Dulcie now, the end-result either way was likely to end in more misery for her. He guessed Bruce's thoughts were running along the same lines.

'Maybe I should tackle Ross about it,' Bruce said. 'I mean, about what he does up in Kalgoorlie.'

'He's not going to admit to going with tarts, is he?' Rudie said dejectedly.

'What if we could get some proof?' Bruce said thoughtfully. 'Mind you, I can't imagine how we'd get that.'

'Those girls talk if you make it worth their while,' Rudie said. 'That's how I found out where May was.'

'Could you go up there and ask around?' Bruce asked.

Rudie was horrified. 'Oh, come on, mate!' he exclaimed. 'How would it look if I started trouble for Ross? People would think I was after his wife!'

'But you do want her, don't you?' Bruce said in a low voice, his blue eyes looking straight into Rudie's dark ones. 'Let's cut all the crap, Rudie, I'm getting old, I love Dulcie like she was my kid, I want happiness for her while I'm still around to see it. When she came back from Sydney I knew she wasn't only grieving for Noël and her sister, but you too. I used to see a brightness in her face whenever you phoned, the way she spoke of you. And I've been around long enough to know a man doesn't fly right across

Australia purely because he wants his son to see his aunt.'

'There's been nothing between us but friendship,' Rudie said hastily, but he felt himself blushing under the older man's intense gaze.

Bruce nodded. 'I know that too. Dulcie wouldn't have come home if she'd been up to any hanky-panky.' He sighed and ran his fingers through his hair. 'I hold myself responsible for her marrying Ross. I care about him too, you see, and when Dulcie came along I guess I thought they had enough in common to find real happiness together. I should have looked closer like Betty did, but I got carried away with the idea they'd stay with us into our old age, maybe with a whole bunch of kids for us to enjoy like grandchildren. I planned to leave the farm to them too.'

'You mustn't feel responsible, they must have fallen in love with one another.'

'How can two kids brought up in cruel institutions without anyone of the opposite sex know anything?' Bruce said fiercely. 'They were thrown together, they sensed my approval. Ross was bowled over by her pretty face, kindness and cooking, and Dulcie, being the way she is, thought her pity for him was love. Betty and me knew there was no passion between them, they were like two kids at Sunday school. I know now that when Betty died I should have talked them out of it.'

'But you were grieving,' Rudie said.

'I was, but that's no excuse. It was self-interest, I wanted them to stay around for ever, Ross was too good a stockman to lose, Dulcie was too good a housekeeper.'

'You also loved them both,' Rudie said quietly, knowing this was true.

'Yes, I do, Ross as much as Dulcie. But that's the real bugger of it all, Rudie. If they stay together Dulcie is going to spend the rest of her life unhappy. If I encourage, or force her hand to leave Ross, then he will be unhappy. It's like the bloody judgement of Solomon.'

A tear trickled down Bruce's cheek, he wiped it away

and stood up. 'I'd best be going now. I've said more than enough.'

Rudie stood up too and impulsively embraced the older man. He understood now why Dulcie loved Bruce so much, and he was humbled by the man's honesty and courage. 'I'm glad you came tonight,' he said, his voice cracking with emotion. 'But Bruce, you've got nothing to reproach yourself for, you've been a real father to both Ross and Dulcie, you've redressed a great many of the wrongs done to them. Whatever happens, you've been the best and greatest influence in their lives.'

Bruce took a step back from him, looking shamefaced. 'Strewth, Rudie,' he said wiping his eyes. 'I only came down here for a beer!'

The following afternoon Dulcie came to meet Rudie and Noël as promised and she was excited because Ross had asked Rudie back for supper. 'It was him who suggested it, not Bruce,' she insisted. 'I suppose he's realized he was being stupid.'

Rudie held his counsel. He didn't think Ross was stupid, far from it. He guessed today's unexpected invitation was because the man wanted to weigh up the enemy so he could plan a strategy to destroy him. Clearly Ross knew if he waited until Sunday to meet him, he might run out of time.

They took a walk along the esplanade, and let Noël run around on the beach and go on the swings. Then they left for the farm at four-thirty, Rudie following Dulcie in his car so he could drive himself back later.

Rudie had been to several sheep and cattle stations up in Queensland and in Victoria, he was familiar with vast acreage, the dust-dry soil and the tough, lean stockmen who made their living there. So he felt some surprise as he drove up the track at Frenches', to see it was far more like an English farm. The grass was thick and lush, the cows in the paddock plump, even the trees clustered around the yard weren't native Australian ones.

Noël had sat quite still on the back seat until he realized this was a place he'd been before. He stood up and waved his arms excitedly, saying 'Doodo', his word for dog.

Dulcie came running over as Rudie stopped, opened the door and let Noël out. He ran straight towards the dogs, giving Rudie a moment of panic.

'They are okay with children,' she reassured him. 'I always feel safer near them, they sense snakes before we can, and bark.'

Rudie found himself nervous, glancing this way and that – Dulcie hadn't ever mentioned snakes before. She laughed at him. 'I used to do that all the time,' she admitted. 'But I learned where they're likely to be and avoid those places. They never come into the yard.'

When a man came riding into the yard on a horse, Rudie knew immediately by his youth that he had to be Ross, even though he had no real recollection of him from the evening in Kalgoorlie. He suspected too that his arrival on a horse was staged, for it immediately put Rudie at a disadvantage.

'G'day,' Ross said, tipping back his hat and looking down at him with a hint of a sneer. 'So you're Rudolph! The bloke up at Kalgoorlie.'

Rudie had expected Ross to be hostile, but he hadn't been prepared for such a good-looking man. The impression he had in his head from their brief meeting three years earlier was of a mere boy with a freckly face and short cropped hair.

Ross looked like a Hollywood-style cowboy with his checked shirt, jeans and leather hat, broad-shouldered and lean-hipped. Beneath the tipped back hat was a mop of dark auburn curly hair, his skin was lightly tanned and his eyes a curious amber colour. He did have a sprinkling of freckles, but they only served to enhance his neat, regular features.

Noël came running back to Rudie. 'Gee gee,' he said, holding his arms up to Ross.

'Wanna come for a ride with me?' Ross asked, and before

Rudie could say anything, he reached down, grabbed Noël by his outstretched hands and pulled him up, settling him in the saddle in front of him.

Rudie watched, his heart in his mouth, as Ross cantered down the track, turned into the paddock and rode off across it. He would have trusted Bruce implicitly with a child, but he didn't feel the same about this man.

Dulcie came up beside him. 'Don't look so scared,' she said with a giggle. 'Ross won't let him come to any harm, though he is showing off a bit.'

In the next three hours Rudie saw a great deal more of Ross showing off. Before supper the rope on the swing became twisted, and Ross shinned up the tree to sort it out, then climbed down the rope like a monkey. He took Rudie and Noël in to see the cows being milked, asked Rudie if he wanted to try it, then ridiculed him when he couldn't produce even a drop of milk. He chased and caught a chicken for Noël to look at and touch.

It didn't help at supper when Noël wanted to sit next to Ross, and instead of eating his own food kept pointing to Ross's plate. Ross of course played up to it and fed him, giving Rudie sly glances.

John wanted to know a great deal more about Sydney, and Rudie said if he ever came he'd be welcome to stay at his place.

'You won't like it there, John,' Ross guffawed. 'It's all nancy boys, blokes in suits and posh sheilas.'

Rudie looked at Dulcie and saw she was blushing.

'Don't be a drongo, mate,' John said to Ross, perhaps sensing her embarrassment. 'You've never been to Sydney.'

'Don't want to either,' Ross retorted. 'Bloody cities do nothing for me.'

So it went on, and however hard Bruce or John tried to speak directly to Rudie about his work, and Sydney, Ross kept butting in with sarcastic remarks or jokes which were always about Englishmen.

Rudie didn't care that much, it was interesting to observe

all the men Dulcie had spoken of with such warmth at close quarters. John was the one he remembered the best from Kalgoorlie, he had been nervous of him then because he thought he was May's boyfriend and half expected him to get into a strop when he danced with her. He felt drawn to him now, he liked the man's directness and good humour, and his lazy drawl was as attractive as his face.

Bob was so silent it was difficult to draw any conclusions about him. Rudie remembered Dulcie telling him he had been bullied by his blacksmith father, and guessed he was always shy with strangers. His sticking-out ears, thinning hair and brown buck teeth didn't do him any favours either, and he thought Bob had drawn the short straw in life.

Bruce's manner here at his own table was interesting too. He could easily have rebuked Ross, Rudie was sure under normal circumstances he did, but at times it was almost as if he was egging Ross on to be rude. Was his hope that Rudie wouldn't feel sorry for Ross if he made himself unpleasant enough? Or did he want Dulcie to see her husband in his worst light?

But it was Dulcie Rudie's eyes were drawn to most of all. Her face was very pink, a combination of being by the hot stove earlier, and embarrassment. She had her hair up in a pony-tail and was wearing a pink checked shirt and jeans. Each time she got up to fill the gravy boat or help someone to more vegetables, he noted her tiny waist and pert bottom and wished he could help the way he felt about her.

Yet for all Ross's arrogance and loutish bad manners, Rudie could sense that under normal circumstances this was a harmonious group of people who cared deeply about one another. He noted how often John and Bob went to help Dulcie, the way all the younger members looked up to Bruce. He was touched too how every one of them, including Ross, was so warm towards Noël. They clearly liked having a child in their midst.

But above all the things he observed, the one thing which

struck him was the lack of anything physical between Ross and Dulcie. Most men, he thought, if they felt they had a rival in their midst, would touch their wife. A familiar pat on the bottom as she poured him gravy, perhaps a tweak of her cheek when she gave him more potatoes. That was a standard way of saying, *This woman is mine*. Rudie had seen it played out in every kind of social circle. A woman too would put her hand on her husband's shoulder, serve him first, get him to tell a story which showed him in a good light. There was none of that.

Rudie felt sure now that there was no intimacy between them whatsoever.

As Ross began to tell a story about a kangaroo hunt, which it appeared would also illustrate he was a crack shot, Rudie's mind turned back to what Bruce had said about the women in Kalgoorlie, and he wondered if it was possible for a man to be impotent with his wife and yet function perfectly normally with a whore. Although it struck him as bizarre, he wished he was in a position to stay far longer in Esperance, to get to know this man better.

Yet however fascinating Ross would be to study, his constant jibes were wearing and it was something of a relief to see Noël's eyes drooping after he'd eaten his pudding. 'I hope you won't think me rude if I take him home now,' he said to Bruce.

Bruce's eyes met his and a spark of understanding flitted between them. 'No, of course not, but drive carefully and watch out for roos.'

Dulcie got up from the table, went to Noël, wiped his mouth and lifted him into her arms. His head went down on her shoulder almost immediately. 'May I have him for the day tomorrow?' she asked.

'If you'd like to. I had a mind to go to Albany and look around,' Rudie said.

'Shall I keep him overnight, then you won't have to rush back?' she said eagerly.

'Watch out, she's trying to steal him from you,' Ross crowed.

Rudie ignored him. 'That's a nice idea if you really don't mind. I'll bring all his stuff in the morning.'

Rudie took the child from Dulcie's arms and laid him up over his shoulder. He thanked them for the supper, said goodbye and Bruce said he would walk out with him to the car.

'Watch out for snakes,' Ross yelled out as they got to the door.

'Sorry about Ross,' Bruce said as they walked across to the car. 'He isn't normally like that.'

'It was understandable,' Rudie said. 'I'm English, from a city, I can't ride a horse or shoot a gun.'

Bruce chuckled. 'You're a tolerant man, Rudie. I would have wanted to whack him.'

Rudie smiled. 'I think I'd have come off worst!'

It was six o'clock the following evening when Rudie drove into Kalgoorlie and parked outside the Old Australia. He got out of the car and stood for a moment looking up at the veranda, remembering the night he first met May and danced with her up there.

She had looked so beautiful in that pink costume. He'd barely noticed the bride or the groom. What a shame he hadn't got to know the rest of the group that night, he might have saved himself so much pain. And now he was back here again, this time looking for information which might hurt all of them.

Was it right to do that?

He sighed. He had to know, Bruce needed to know too.

He checked in, had a chat with Sadie the landlady who greeted him like a long-lost son, washed and put on a clean shirt. It was so hot compared with down at Esperance, the ceiling fan merely stirred the warm air around and the room looked even seedier than he remembered it.

Going out on to the veranda later, he looked down towards the room Dulcie and Ross had been in. He recalled now that at breakfast the morning after the wedding Sadie had been making jokes about the newlyweds. She had said the groom was up early, having a smoke outside. She wondered if he'd left the bride smoking from passion in bed.

He had laughed with everyone else that morning, but now he knew the truth it wasn't funny any more. He wondered how Dulcie felt that morning, and on all the subsequent ones. He expected she thought she was to blame. He took out his wallet and removed the newspaper clipping inside it. It was of Dulcie and Ross, taken at their wedding. He'd gone into the newspaper office this morning to look at the old papers from that time, and when he found what he was looking for, he'd asked for a copy. He carefully tore off Dulcie's face – he only needed a picture of Ross to prompt the girls' memories.

Rudie waited until nine before going down to Hay Street. He'd had a few scotches to make him feel less conspicuous, but not enough to dull his mind. Yet he did still feel conspicuous as he turned into the street – the girls were all out in force as it was a warm night, and as it was a Thursday, there weren't the crowds of men milling around as there would be at the weekend.

He picked on a young blonde girl first, thinking Ross was likely to make for someone similar to Dulcie.

'Do you know this man?' he asked, showing her the photograph.

'Whatcha want to know that for, mate?' she asked.

She looked tired and worn, even if she was only about seventeen. 'He's an old friend of mine and I've lost touch with him,' Rudie said. 'Someone told me they saw him up here one weekend. I hoped one of you girls might have met him.'

She looked at the picture again. 'No, mate, I ain't seen him. He's young, ain't he, they mostly go for the older girls.'

Rudie tried a blonde woman of about thirty-five next. She looked raddled, her hair like a bird's nest, and makeup so thick it could have been put on with a trowel.

'I might've seen him,' she said, squinting up at Rudie speculatively. 'But it'll cost yer.'

Rudie pulled out a ten-shilling note. She looked at it, and back at him as if weighing up whether it was worth trying for more.

Rudie grinned at her, not letting go of the note. 'I'll be fair if you've got some real information,' he said.

'I've seen 'im,' she said. 'But never done no business wif 'im.'

'You get this if you tell me who's done business with him,' he said.

'I'll need more than that to remember,' she said, but the sly way she looked at him suggested she really knew nothing.

Rudie put the note away, wished her a good evening and moved on. He spoke to many other women, a few were like the first girl and said they didn't know him, some were like the second one and tried to get the money for nothing. Many more of them tried to persuade him into trying their services.

He was beginning to feel dispirited, for he'd had this same problem with the girls around King's Cross and Darlinghurst while he was looking for May. He knew those who really knew something often needed quite a bit of persuasion to talk, and it wasn't always purely money which loosened their tongues.

By the time he'd got almost to the end of the street, over an hour later, he knew the girls would have whispered to one another what he was asking about. This was the point when someone might come forward of their own volition. By now they would have agreed he couldn't be a cop, or a private detective. The fact he was looking for a man, not a girl, would help too.

A striking-looking redhead in a very short, low-cut dress broke away from talking to another girl and came up to him. 'Let's have a look at that picture,' she said.

Rudie showed her, and she took it under a street light to see better. 'Yeah, I reckon it's the bloke I know,' she said, looking up at Rudie. 'But this ain't a good photo of him.'

Rudie knew then this one really was on the ball. 'No,

it's an old one taken three years ago,' he agreed. 'I expect his hair's longer than that now, it's a dark auburn and curly. Does that fit the bloke you know?'

She nodded, and Rudie gave her the ten shillings. 'There'll be more if you can tell me anything useful.'

Strangely enough, she shoved the note back into his pocket. 'I only did business with him once. He always makes for Mary, so offer her the money.'

'Which one's Mary?' he asked.

'She's got someone with her right now, but she'll be out soon,' the girl said. 'You a mate of this bloke?'

There was something about the way she asked that which made Rudie sense she hoped he wasn't.

'Not exactly. I just need to know a bit of stuff about him. Does that change your mind about introducing me to Mary?'

She grinned mischievously. 'Whatcha want to know, a bit of dirt on him?'

'Do you know some?' Rudie couldn't help but like this woman, her eyes sparkled, she radiated warmth and she was very attractive.

'You tell me why you want to know and Mary and me might help you,' she said, putting her head to one side like a cockatoo. 'It's a slow night tonight, you're better-looking than most of the blokes that come down here, you've got class and all. Bloody Nora, I'm just being a sticky beak.'

Rudie laughed. She had leapt up in his estimation by being so honest. 'How does a fiver between you both and a few drinks sound?' he asked. 'But I want straight talking, no making up fairy stories!'

She looked him up and down for a second. 'We don't want no fairy stories from you neither!'

'Done,' he said, holding out his hand to shake hers.

While they waited for Mary to appear, the woman introduced herself as Dolly, and told him that Mary was half Aboriginal. 'She was one of them kids taken away from her folks by the Holy Rollers,' she said. 'She tells me about

644

the mission they took her to, run by nuns it were, cruel bitches. They had this idea, see, that if they took the kids that weren't full blacks they could make them like whites. Bloody silly idea, but they did it to thousands of kids. Mary got raped at her first job as a maid, only fourteen she was, she told the woman she worked for, but all she did was kick her out. That's how she ended up here.'

Rudie wondered if the similarity in backgrounds was what attracted Ross to Mary. 'How about you, Dolly, how did you end up here?'

She just shrugged. 'Wrong choices of men, short of money, nowhere much else to go. Same as most of us here.'

Dolly shot off back up the road suddenly, and Rudie saw her talking animatedly to a dark woman who had just come out of one of the houses. She had all the Aboriginal features – the squat nose, the thick lips – but coffee-coloured skin and lovely long black curly hair worn loose on her shoulders. She looked round at Rudie, then turned back to Dolly. It looked to him as if she needed some persuasion.

But then just as he was beginning to think she was going to refuse, the two women came towards him. He guessed they were both in their late twenties, they still had good figures and skin, but the first flush of youth had gone.

'Thank you for agreeing to talk to me,' he said. 'Can we go to a bar to talk?'

It was apparent even before the girls took him to a bar just around the corner that the two women were very close friends, and had been for some years. Mary wasn't attractive, or striking like Dolly, she was also far less talkative, but he got the impression she was sharp-witted and kind.

Once in the bar, three glasses of scotch in front of them, the women lit up cigarettes and sat back waiting for him to explain himself.

'I want to know about this man because he is married to my sister-in-law,' he began. Calling Dulcie that wasn't so much a lie as needing to make the story simpler. 'I already knew they weren't really happy, but when I came over from Sydney with my son to visit her, I was told he comes up here regularly.'

He explained as briefly as he could about Ross and Dulcie's background. 'I am very fond of my sister-in-law, and I think she's got a real raw deal,' he went on. 'But she is so caring and loving that she'll put up with almost anything rather than leave her husband.'

'You want me to tell you something that will persuade her?' Mary said. Her voice was very unusual, for though she had a strong Australian accent, the sound of it was soft and melodic.

'I guess that's about the size of it.'

'Where's your wife?' Mary asked.

'She's dead, it happened a year ago in Sydney. My sister-in-law came over then to help me with my son. He was only a baby.'

'You want her to leave this man, then, for you?' she said, looking at him hard.

He hadn't thought of it that way, and he certainly hadn't meant it to sound like that. 'They've got a marriage in name only,' he said. 'There's nothing between us, we're just friends. We became close when May died. But yes, I suppose if I was really honest, I do want her myself. That isn't the issue, though, I only want to get to the bottom of what is wrong with her husband.'

The two women exchanged glances, they seemed faintly amused and he hoped to God they weren't playing him along for some kind of sport.

'What d'you mean by *a marriage in name only*?' Dolly asked. 'That he can't get it up with her?'

Rudie blushed. 'Yes, that's it.'

'He can't or he doesn't want to fuck her?' Dolly said crudely, her eyes glinting as if she was enjoying his discomfort.

'He couldn't when they got married, right up till he had a sort of breakdown back earlier this year. She hasn't said if there has been any improvement since then, but I doubt it somehow. That was why I was so surprised when I heard he was coming up here.'

'Lots of blokes who come to us can't get it on with their wives,' Mary said. 'To us there's nothing weird about that.'

'Why do you think that is?' he asked.

She shrugged. 'Sometimes they've married women they just don't fancy. Now and again the bloody fools have put their wife on such a pedestal they can't give her one. But most of the married men who come here either don't get enough at home, or they just get turned on by sex with a whore.'

'What do you think this man's problem is then?' he asked, pushing the newspaper picture over to her, so she would be absolutely clear who they were talking about.

She picked up the picture and looked at it for a few moments without speaking. 'He's a strange one all right,' she said eventually. 'I didn't know he was married, I got the idea he was a stockman way out in the bush somewhere.'

'He came to me the first time, I couldn't do anything with him,' Dolly said. 'We don't like that, they usually get nasty, but he cried and I felt sorry for him.'

Rudie saw that her face had softened. 'I knew something bad had happened to him,' she went on. 'He kept muttering something about his brother. I thought maybe he'd died, stuff like that does affect men and they often come to girls like us because they haven't got to sweet-talk us into sex. So I didn't chuck him out, I gave him a drink and just held him for a while.'

'I think he was talking about the Brothers, you know, the Christian Brothers,' Rudie said. 'He had a very bad time with them as a kid.'

'That's what I said when she told me,' Mary butted in. 'I know what some of them are capable of.'

'So what happened after that first night?' Rudie asked. 'How long was it before he came back, and why did he go for Mary.'

'It was exactly four weeks later in May when he came

back,' Dolly said. 'I remember because I never expected to see him again. He wasn't drunk either, they usually are on a Saturday night. He came right up to me and asked if I could recommend a girl for him. I got the idea he meant someone who would be kind to him if he failed again. So I suggested Mary.'

'You'd better tell him what the bloke said when he saw me,' Mary suggested.

'I don't want to tell him that,' Dolly said sharply, and for the first time in their conversation she looked embarrassed.

'Well I will then, 'cos I reckon it's important,' Mary said. 'He took one look at me and said, "I don't want a bloody Abo." Well I've heard that about a million times in my life, and it's like a challenge to me now. So I said he'd find it easier to get it on with me if he thought I was way beneath him, and I pointed out that I had more regulars on the street than anyone.'

'She does too,' Dolly chipped in. 'Anyway, he stood there wavering. I reckon he couldn't face going up to anyone else. Then suddenly he agreed. He went off with Mary and they were gone a long time.'

Rudie looked to Mary. 'Did he make it with you?'

She grinned. 'Oh yes. It was a matter of pride with me to make sure he did. Twice in fact. Since then he's been back every four weeks like clockwork.'

'Would you say it was his first time with a woman?' Rudie asked.

'Yeah, I'd say so, he was so thrilled and excited afterwards. Like a young boy.'

'Was he like any other man?' Rudie asked curiously. 'I mean, did he get straight into it, or what?'

'You're a bloody sticky beak, aren't you?' Mary said, but she laughed. 'No, he didn't get straight into it. I had to bully him. He seemed to respond to that. Still needs it now, or wants it, whichever way you want to look at it.'

Rudie got the women another drink, he didn't want them rushing off now. 'So what do you clever ladies reckon about my brother-in-law?' he asked, leaning over the table towards them conspiratorially. 'You must get like shrinks after a year or two at your game. Would he be going home to his wife after, and being the big stud?'

'I doubt it,' Dolly said. 'If that was the case and he was cured he'd have a different girl every time he came here.'

'It's like I said, he can do it with me because he thinks I'm lower than him,' Mary said bluntly. 'Want my opinion?'

Rudie nodded.

'He'd been buggered as a kid.'

Rudie's mouth dropped open. 'What makes you think that?'

She shrugged. 'I've met a couple more like him in the past. Same types, brag about how strong they are, how they can do this and that. The sort that get drunk and pick fights. They don't think much of themselves really, so they have to hide that with all the tough stuff. But you get glimpses of the frightened little boy underneath. This one, John he calls himself, but I don't suppose it's his real name, has come close to admitting it. He said he got crook after going back to his old school. He said stuff happened there that ruined his life.'

'It could have just been the beatings and the semi-starvation,' Rudie said.

Mary waved her hand impatiently. 'We all got that, every bloody kid who got stuck in an orphanage, whether it was the Fairbridge Schools, the Sisters, the Brothers, or a bloody mission like they stuck me in. We can get over that. But rape, that's something you can't forget, can't get over. It stays with you, it taints everything.'

'I'm sure it does,' Rudie said, wondering if she knew Dolly had told him that's what happened to her too.

'You think I like sex?' Mary said, her dark eyes flashing. 'I hate it. But sometimes, when I meet a man like this John, and I know how scared and sickened he is by it too, I don't mind it so much, it makes me feel a bit better to see him getting over that hurdle.'

Rudie saw then why he'd decided she was kind – she was. And his heart ached for her and all the other boys and girls who had had their lives tarnished by people who were supposed to care for them.

He'd heard enough, it was time to go. He stood up and pulled out his wallet, handing Mary a ten-pound note, far more than he'd intended to give her.

'I don't want that,' she said. 'I talked to you like a friend.'

'This comes from a friend,' he said quietly. 'You both buy yourselves something pretty from me. You've been a great help.'

'What are you going to do with what we told you?' Dolly asked.

'I really don't know,' Rudie sighed. 'My wife, her sister and her husband, all three of them, had been so badly scarred by their childhoods. My wife is dead, and the other two have no chance of finding real happiness if they stay together. You tell me, do I save one and let the other flounder in rage and bitterness? Or should I walk away and do nothing for either of them?'

The two women looked at one another.

'Save his wife,' Mary said, her dark eyes glistening with tears. 'He won't stop coming up here now. He can't, it's like a drug to him.'

'But do I tell his wife he comes here?' he said. 'That will hurt her so badly.'

Mary stood up and moved closer to Rudie. She was very short, barely reaching the middle of his chest. 'He's a decent bloke at heart,' she said. 'I've seen that side of him too. Talk to him alone, tell him what you know, and ask him to let her go free.'

'He won't do that!'

'He might,' she said, looking up at Rudie, her eyes full of compassion. 'He's trapped too, remember, she's a daily reminder of his failure. You never know what people will do for love.'

Rudie glanced around the pub. It was only half full, a grubby, sour-smelling place, and almost everyone in it – the whores, the miners from the gold field, stockmen from out of town – all looked like losers. Dolly and Mary belonged here, they were part of it, yet in all his life he'd never met anyone quite as astute and big-hearted as Mary. He bent down and kissed her cheek. 'Thank you, Mary, it was a privilege to meet you.'

He turned to say goodbye to Dolly, expecting to find her laughing at him, but instead she was looking at her friend with pride.

Rudie left the Old Australia at five in the morning, leaving a goodbye note and payment for his room for Sadie on her desk. He had tossed and turned all night, unable to sleep for the images which kept thrusting themselves at him. He had no plan made, he almost wished he'd minded his own business and hadn't found Mary. However, he looked at the problems ahead of him and he could only see them multiplying.

Any anger he'd felt at Ross had gone. He knew Mary was right about what had happened to him, for once he'd thought it all through, it all added up. Dulcie's lack of explanation to anyone about what had happened at Bindoon, Ross's breakdown, and her steely determination to pretend everything was fine. If he were Ross he might also have turned to a prostitute to comfort himself. He couldn't help feeling glad it was Mary he found, for she like her biblical namesake was 'blessed among women'.

The sun was coming up, flickering through the leaves of the gum trees, the dirt road ahead turning to gold. In all his years in Australia he'd believed it was a magical place where even those with the smallest of talent or ability could make a good life for themselves. His own life bore out this belief, for it had certainly been a charmed one. A successful artist, a lovely home, money and good friends. He would look out from Watson's Bay and marvel at Sydney Harbour and the bridge in all its majesty, and never once until he met Dulcie did he ever consider that his adopted country had any flaws.

But he was very aware of those flaws now – the government's policy towards its orphans and its native people, the Aborigines. He could remember meeting an old friend at the docks in Sydney who had escorted a group of boys to Australia under the Big Brother scheme. It never occurred to him to ask where those boys were bound for, or would anyone be watching over them.

He had heard many times about the Aboriginal children who were taken from their parents, and in his ignorance he had imagined they were being rescued from a terrible life and given a wonderful one.

Now he'd met Mary, and though she'd said so little about that Mission she'd been taken to, he knew it was appalling. He guessed those English schoolboys he'd seen on the docks were probably pressed into virtual slave labour on sheep and cattle stations. Thousands of Marys, Dulcies, Mays and Rosses. All casualties of a society which just let things happen, assuming someone else was taking responsibility.

There was a pain inside him, an anger he thought must be akin to that which Ross felt. He knew he couldn't just sit and paint pretty pictures any more. He had been given a son, and with that came a measure of responsibility for everyone's children. Noël had come very close to ending up in one of those orphanages and he had to keep that in his mind, and when he returned to Sydney he had to do something.

He didn't know quite what now. Maybe just rattle doors, insist on visiting institutions and reporting those who failed their charges. Or speak up publicly and make others listen.

He saw kangaroos up ahead going across the road and slowed right down, coming to a complete halt. One stopped in the middle of the road and looked back. At the side of the road was a tiny one; the mother made an impatient gesture to it, and it bounded towards her, jumping head-first into her pouch.

Rudie laughed aloud as he saw the joey struggling to turn himself round the right way inside, for he was almost too big to get in there now. The mother looked down at him, as if satisfied he was in there safely, then bounded off the road.

However comic the scene had been, coming so soon after he'd been thinking he must do something to protect children, it seemed to be a sign that he was to vow he would carry it out.

'Okay, God,' he said, in the same way he'd often made deals with his Maker during his time in the airforce during the war. 'I promise I'll do my best to carry it out. But you've got to help me out now with Ross.'

Chapter Twenty-seven

'So how was Albany?' Dulcie asked as she made Rudie a cup of tea. 'Did you make any sketches?'

It was nine in the morning. Rudie had gone home after returning from Kalgoorlie, made himself some breakfast and read the paper, then come on out to the farm to pick up Noël. Dulcie had been surprised that he'd arrived so early.

'I didn't go there after all,' Rudie said, afraid she'd start quizzing him about it. He picked Noël up and sat him on his knee. 'I drove out into the bush and looked around.'

'One place is much like another out there,' she smiled. 'You must have been bored stiff.'

'You might have seen it all before but I haven't,' he said. 'I looked at the wild flowers, the shape of the trees, I wasn't bored at all. Anyway, how has Noël been? Did he sleep all right last night?'

'Like a log. Ross let me have him in bed with me, he slept in the bunkhouse with John and Bob. I didn't sleep much though, I kept waking up and looking at Noël. He's too beautiful for words.'

Rudie smiled. Her face had a sort of shine to it this morning, like an inner light had been switched on. He could only hope that one day it would stay on permanently.

'I'd better get out of your hair,' he said. 'You must have a lot of chores to do. It's going to be a warm day today. I'll take Noël down to the beach.'

'You don't have to go,' she said.

Rudie picked up that she really meant perhaps he'd better – besides, he felt so troubled he knew he'd be better off alone. 'Oh yes, I must,' he said, putting Noël down on the floor and getting up. 'Thank you for having him, I know what hard work it is running around after him all day.'

'I loved having him,' she said, bending down to kiss Noël. 'Will I see you before Sunday?'

'I'm not sure.' Rudie felt flustered. His plane left on Tuesday morning, and sometime between now and then he had to tackle Ross. On the one hand he wanted to do it as quickly as possible as it was eating away at him. But he knew too that once he had done it, whatever the outcome, he really couldn't come here again, and Dulcie was going to find that very puzzling and hurtful.

'I'll leave it to you to ring me,' she said as she packed Noël's clothes into a bag. 'I'll be in town doing the shopping tomorrow afternoon, so I could pop round then.'

Rudie picked Noël up, took the bag from her and dropped a kiss on her cheek. 'Thanks for everything,' he said as he made for the door. He hesitated at the door, glancing back at her, wanting to say something more, but unable to find the words.

'What is it?' she asked, sensing he had something on his mind.

'Nothing,' he shrugged. 'Only that you look beautiful this morning.'

Dulcie watched Rudie cross the yard to his car and put Noël on the back seat. While his compliment had made her glow inside, she was puzzled because he'd been so odd. In the past he'd have told her every last thing about his trip out into the bush, any people he'd met, what he'd seen. He didn't seem very eager for them to do something with Noël together either. Was he afraid that she was getting too attached to Noël? Was it that he felt uneasy here because of Ross, or was he just plain bored being in such a quiet place?

She went into Bruce's room to make his bed, suddenly feeling deflated. She had been looking forward to Rudie's visit for weeks now, if she was entirely truthful with herself she'd spent the entire year waiting for it. What if he never wanted to come again?

All at once she saw the years stretching out ahead of her, empty and bleak. She had her painting, but how long would that sustain her for? There was the cooking, cleaning, laundry and gardening to keep her busy, but that did nothing to feed her soul and spirit. Was she destined to end up with nothing more to look forward to than the monthly meetings of the Country Women's Association, hearing her friends there speak of their children and grandchildren, when she didn't even know what it was like to make love, let alone hold her own child in her arms?

At eight that evening Rudie was in the Pier Hotel having a drink with Sergeant Sean Collins. When Rudie got back from the farm that morning Sean had pushed a note through the letter-box suggesting this and saying that Molly his wife would be happy to baby-sit.

Molly and Sean were just as Dulcie had described them, jolly, kind-hearted people with a keen interest in others. Noël was asleep by the time they came, but Molly went upstairs to look at him, enthused on how handsome he was, and insisted she'd be fine if he woke up, in fact she hoped he would. By the time Sean and Rudie left the house she was sitting knitting as comfortably as if she were in her own home, and Rudie had no qualms about leaving her to it.

Once in the pub, Sean, being a policeman, was very keen to hear about May's drowning, and they were still talking about it when Ross came into the bar.

Rudie's heart sank – he hadn't expected to run into him tonight – but Ross just nodded at him and Sean and went right down to the far end of the bar to join a group of men.

'What do you make of him?' Sean asked, nodding towards Ross.

'I haven't had enough time with him to judge,' Rudie said cautiously.

'I can't warm to the bloke,' Sean said, his round face breaking into a disapproving frown. 'Oh, I know he can do anything, that he's Bruce's right-hand man, but I can't be doing with all his bragging and showing off.'

'I was on the rough end of that on Wednesday night when I stayed out at the farm for supper,' Rudie said lightly. 'But I suppose I was fair game being a Pom and a city man.'

'Funny bloke,' Sean said with a grimace. 'You'd think having a boss like Bruce and marrying the best-looking girl for miles around would be enough, but he's still got a bloody great chip on his shoulder.'

'Well, he had a tough childhood by all accounts,' Rudie said, wishing he could think of a way of changing the subject.

'There's not many round here that didn't,' Sean said. 'Bob, the bloke with the sticking-out lug-holes up at Bruce's, he went through hell with his old man, yet you couldn't meet a nicer, straighter bloke.' He waved his hand towards the end of the bar to the group Ross was with. 'Most of them were born before and during the Depression, they knew near starvation, worked alongside their folks practically from birth. You won't hear any of them whinging though.'

'I don't think Ross whinges,' Rudie said in his defence.

'Maybe not, in so many words, but he's too bloody quick to take the piss out of anyone weaker than himself, and to start a fight over nothing. He got into a blue one night in here just because someone joked that he went off his rocker for a bit. Strewth, the bloke that said it was just being sympathetic, the same thing happened to him when his kid died of kidney failure.'

Luckily a friend of Sean's came and joined them at that point and the conversation moved from police work to sailing. Rudie was a keen sailor himself so he forgot about

Ross, downed a few schooners of ale, and before he knew it, it was after ten.

'We'd better get back to Molly,' Rudie said. 'We did say we'd only be a couple of hours.'

While Sean finished up his beer, Rudie went out the back to the toilet. The bar was packed now – it looked as if every man for fifty miles around had come here to drink – and on his way back through the bar someone grabbed his arm.

Rudie turned to see it was Ross but knew immediately the man wasn't about to offer him a drink or exchange pleasantries. His lips were curling back and his eyes were narrowed. 'I want to talk to you,' he snarled.

'I'm on my way home now,' Rudie said, trying to act as if he hadn't noticed the man was fighting mad. 'I'd be glad to talk to you any time, but not right now, Molly Collins is baby-sitting and she's expecting me back.'

Maybe the reminder that Rudie had been drinking with a policeman was enough to deter Ross for he let go of his arm. The entire group of men Ross had been with all evening had moved into a semi-circle around them during this exchange. There was no menace in their faces, only curiosity.

'When then?' Ross said.

Rudie shrugged. 'Tomorrow if you like. Or Sunday, I'll be up at your place then.'

'You bloody won't,' Ross said, the snarl in his voice back again. 'I'll sort you out before then.'

It was probably Sean Collins coming over that made him back off. 'Ready to go?' he called out through the crowd. Rudie hastily beat a retreat.

Once he and Sean were outside the pub, the policeman looked hard at him. 'What was going on there?'

'Nothing much,' Rudie said, though he was a little shaken. 'Ross was a bit stroppy, that's all.'

'Why?'

'Blowed if I know,' Rudie shrugged. 'He was drunk.'

*

Sean and Molly stayed for a while for a chat, and finally left just after eleven o'clock. Rudie made himself a cup of tea and was sitting on the couch reading, when someone knocked on the door.

He thought maybe Sean had left something behind and come back for it, so he opened the door immediately. To his shock it was Ross and before Rudie could say a word he barged past him into the living-room.

'Now look here, Ross,' Rudie said warningly. 'I'm happy to talk to you any time, but you're drunk, it's late, and there's a small child upstairs.'

'I'm not drunk,' Ross said indignantly, even though he was swaying on his feet. 'All I've come to say is that you'd better bloody well keep away from my wife.'

'I came here for a holiday so Dulcie could see Noël,' Rudie said, trying to keep calm. 'The only time I've seen your wife alone was when she drove me here from the airport.'

'You were up at the farm this morning with her,' Ross said.

'I called to collect Noël and I didn't stay more than half an hour.'

'You've arranged to see her tomorrow.'

Rudie shook his head. 'No, I haven't, and anyway, what would be wrong with that? She wants to see her nephew as much as she can.'

'I ought to lay you out,' Ross said, his lip curling back once again. 'You enticed her off to Sydney, turned her head with your city ways and that kid. No wonder she's always crying.'

'If she cries it would be because of you, not me.' Rudie felt his anger rising. 'I didn't entice her into anything, the things which happened, May running off and leaving her with Noël, couldn't have been foreseen. But you showed no understanding or sympathy. I haven't forgotten that letter you sent her blackmailing her into returning home, so I'm damned sure she hasn't.'

Ross stepped towards him his fists clenched.

'You hit me and I'll have the police after you so fast you won't know what's hit you,' Rudie warned him. 'Now, it just happens I've got some things to say to you too, though I'd intended to choose a better time than this. So bloody well sit down and listen.'

Maybe it was the authoritative tone, but to his surprise Ross did sit down, at least almost fell into an armchair. Having got the advantage Rudie remained standing, and looked down at him.

'I went up to Kalgoorlie yesterday and discovered what you go there for once a month. Don't bother to deny it either. I've got proof.'

Ross's mouth dropped open.

'What's more, I intend to tell Dulcie,' Rudie added.

'You can't do that, you bastard.' Ross tried to get up but fell back.

'I can and I will. A woman has a right to know if her husband is going with whores. You could be infecting her apart from anything else. You are the bastard, Ross, not me. Dulcie is a good woman, she deserves better than that.'

'I haven't infected her.' Ross was sullen.

'How do you know? Did you know the symptoms of syphilis can go unnoticed in a woman for a long time? That a child in her womb could be infected too?'

Ross looked at Rudie blankly, his mouth opening and closing. 'I haven't been with her, not since I started going up there.'

'So you prefer whores to Dulcie, do you?' Rudie asked. 'How do you think that would make her feel?'

All at once Rudie saw the fight go out of Ross. He sagged visibly and his lips began to tremble. 'Don't tell her, please. I won't go there again. I promise I won't.'

'I won't tell her if you let her go,' Rudie said quietly. 'Your marriage is a sham, Ross, you know it and so do I. So be a real man and do the right thing.'

Ross looked up at him and Rudie saw the face of a young,

frightened boy. His heart contracted with sympathy for him, yet he knew he had to carry on.

'I mean it, Ross, you have two choices. Either you tell Dulcie that you know your marriage has failed and you want your freedom, or I tell her what you've been doing. If you choose the first, she'll retain her affection for you. But if it's to be the second you'll hurt her so badly you're going to lose everything she ever felt for you.'

'You bastard,' Ross said, but his voice had lost its venom. 'You just want her for yourself.'

'Maybe I do want her, but believe it or not, that's not my reason for confronting you with this. Someone has to step in between you two, if they don't it's likely to end in tragedy. It's no good you saying you'll stop going to Kalgoorlie to get a woman, you won't. You need it, they give you something you can't get with Dulcie. You tell me what she gets out of being married to you.'

'Same as any other wife, a nice home, enough money,' Ross said sullenly.

'No, Ross, she doesn't get the same as other wives, does she? She might have the nice home and enough money, but then she works just as hard as you do, and her role is only housekeeper. What about love and children?'

Rudie had carefully avoided bringing up the subject of sex, he wanted to push the man, not crush him, and he didn't want Dulcie or Mary blamed for telling him.

'I do love her,' Ross insisted.

'How much do you love her? Enough to want her happiness above your own? That's what real love is about. Dulcie is like a caged bird with you, Ross. You think if you feed her, keep her warm and safe, that's enough. It isn't, not for someone like her.'

'We're the same,' Ross said, his voice rising. 'We've had terrible things done to us. We need each other.'

Ross shook his head. 'You don't, not any more. You both need to put all that behind you and start anew. What caused your breakdown, Ross?'

Ross's head jerked up and his eyes narrowed. 'What's she told you?'

'There you go, blaming Dulcie,' Rudie said. 'Is everything her fault? She didn't tell me one word, she wouldn't. She didn't tell Bruce either. But I can make educated guesses, Ross, I went to an all-boys boarding-school in England, they aren't places that are noted for their kindness to young boys either.'

'Nothing in England compares with how it was at Bindoon,' Ross shouted at Rudie. 'You got to wear a smart uniform, you got three real meals a day, you had lessons or you wouldn't be such a smart bastard now. Maybe you got the cane now and then, but that's all.'

'That's all you know,' Rudie said, remembering how one sixth-former had stripped off his shorts and underpants and held him against the fire in his study until his buttocks were singed. And how on many occasions he was held upside down with his head in the lavatory and the chain pulled. 'Maybe the things which happened to me weren't as bad as the things that you had to endure, but to me it was hell.'

There was silence for a moment, Ross sitting there looking at his hands in his lap. 'Do what I said and let her go, Ross,' Rudie said after a few minutes. 'You won't have to leave the farm, or your house.'

'D'you really think Bruce would keep me on if Dulcie went?' Ross snarled again. 'I'd be out on my ear the next day.'

'No, you wouldn't,' Rudie moved over to Ross and tentatively put his hand on the younger man's shoulder. 'Bruce cares as much for you as he does for Dulcie. He is as unhappy about how things are between you as I am. A man like him who had a long and happy marriage senses when something is wrong in other people's. You are even more indispensable to him than Dulcie, housekeepers are two a penny, good stockmen are rare. Besides, if you do as I said, you will keep Dulcie's friendship and affection, she'll stay in touch with you, and Bruce too.'

He paused, letting his words sink in. 'Do the right thing, Ross. Be a real man and let her go.'

Ross began to cry then, great shuddering sobs which came from deep within him, and Rudie could do nothing but just sit on the arm of his chair with his hand on Ross's back. He recalled a scene just like this one in his own past. It was him crying then, a twelve-year-old boy pleading with his father not to be sent back to school. He could hear his father's words still. 'You can't run from this, Rudie. If you do you'll be running all your life.'

His father was right of course, he went back to school and learned to cope with, and rise above, being called 'Pansy Jamsy', and the older boys' cruelty and jibes because he preferred to paint and draw than play rugby. Later, in the airforce, and when he first arrived in Australia he experienced more of the same, but by then he'd learnt to laugh with those who ridiculed him.

He gave Ross some brandy later and urged him not to attempt to drive home, but sleep in the spare bed upstairs. It wasn't made up, and there were no more sheets anyway, but Ross didn't appear to notice, just lay down like a beaten dog. Rudie removed his boots for him, covered him up with a blanket and felt ashamed that he'd inflicted this much pain on anyone.

Ross was gone when Rudie woke up the next morning. The blanket he'd covered him with was neatly folded, a poignant remnant of his training at Bindoon.

Dulcie had gone to bed early and fallen asleep straight away, so she didn't know that Ross hadn't come home until the following morning when she woke to see his side of the bed unruffled, his pyjamas still on the pillow. She sat up in bed and pulled the curtains back to find it was raining.

She was washing when she heard his motorbike, and a few seconds later he walked in.

'Where have you been?' she asked.

'I stayed at a mate's place,' he said. 'I had too much to drink to drive back.'

He had a closed expression on his face which warned her not to ask questions. So she made them both a cup of tea while he put on his work clothes.

At breakfast he was silent, but that was nothing unusual, especially when he'd been drunk the night before. She got on with her work once the men had gone out again, and she was doing some ironing and listening to the radio when Ross came in again about ten-thirty.

'Come over to our house,' he said. 'I want to talk to you.'

In their entire married life he had never said such a thing. When they had talks they were almost always precipitated by her. She turned off the iron and the radio, grabbed an oilskin to put over her head, and ran through the rain after him.

He told her to sit down, but he remained standing by the fireplace. His face was rigid, but he didn't look exactly angry. 'I've decided we have to get a divorce,' he said.

Dulcie could only stare at him in utter shock. 'A divorce!' she repeated. 'But why?'

'You know why, Dulcie,' he said. 'We haven't got a marriage, have we? It's not right.'

'But it's so sudden,' she said. 'Why now?' Then, remembering he hadn't come home, 'Is there someone else?'

'Don't be a bloody drongo, Dulc,' he said. 'Look, you go, clear off to Sydney if that's what you want. Just do it quickly.'

She got up from her seat. 'You can't just tell me to go like you're sacking me,' she said feeling hurt and angry too. 'You explain what brought this on. Is it because of Noël and Rudie being here?'

'No. Well, I suppose it is in a way. I've seen the way you are with that kid and I can't give you one.'

Dulcie felt bewildered and stunned that he could go out on Friday night seemingly perfectly happy, then return the following day and insist it was all over. 'But you could get help,' she said pleadingly.

'I don't want help from some shrink,' he snapped at her. 'Look, I want you to be happy and I know you never will be with me.'

She ran to him and put her arms around him, suddenly so afraid. 'But I love you, Ross, how can you send me away?'

He held her tight against him for a few minutes without speaking, and she could feel a kind of shuddering inside him. 'I love you too. I always will,' he said. 'But it's not a married love, is it? We're just two frightened kids clinging together. You'll be all right in Sydney. You can get a job in an office, make friends there with people like you. You might get to sell your paintings, you can buy nice clothes and all that stuff.'

'But what about you?' she cried. 'What will you do?'

'I'll be here, running the farm, same as always. It's what I like and what I do best. I couldn't live in a city.'

'No, Ross,' she cried out. 'We married for richer or poorer, better or worse. We're Catholics, we can't divorce.'

'We're not Catholics any more!' he shouted. 'That's one thing we did manage to chuck overboard. Besides, you once told me you can get a marriage annulled if you haven't done it. Even the Catholics go along with that one 'cos it means you don't get any kids.'

He put one hand on either side of her face and just held it. 'You've got the sweetest face I've ever seen. I want it to still be like that in twenty years, but it won't be if you stay with me. Go, leave me, but stay my friend, that's all I want.'

He let go of her suddenly and ran into the bedroom. Dulcie ran after him and saw he was pulling open drawers and taking out shirts and socks.

'Where are you going?' she said in panic.

'Away, until you've gone on Tuesday,' he said. His face was hidden from hers. 'I don't want you here when I get back. There's money in the desk drawer. Take all of it. Just write to me and phone me now and then.'

He shoved his things into a bag, grabbed his best jacket from behind the bedroom door, pausing only to pick up his shoes.

'But what will I tell Bruce?' she shouted after him as he pulled open the front door and went out.

He turned to look back at her in the doorway, the heavy rain was already soaking his shirt and jeans.

'That I wanted you to be happy for ever,' he said, then ran to his motorbike.

He stuffed the bag of clothes into the box on the back of the bike, leaped astride and jumped down hard on the starter, and it roared into life.

She saw him go hurtling down the track, and watched as he finally turned on to the road at the bottom and disappeared out of sight.

Bruce came over later and the door was open so he called through. 'Are you in there, Dulcie?' he yelled out. 'I can't find Ross. Has he gone into town for something?'

Dulcie had been lying on her bed crying. She sat up and called Bruce in. He came to the doorway of the bedroom, rain running off his oilskin coat.

'He's gone,' she said.

He saw her swollen eyes and the soggy handkerchief clutched in her hand.

'What do you mean, he's gone? Gone where? Why are you crying?'

Through her sobs Dulcie blurted out what had happened. 'He drove off without even a coat on,' she said. 'He said he wanted me gone by the time he gets back on Tuesday.'

'But why?'

'He said it was because he wanted me to be happy for ever,' she said, still crying.

Bruce took off his oilskin and hung it by the door, then went back to the bedroom, took her hand and led her into the living-room where he sat her down on the couch. Sitting beside her, he put his arms around her and held her tightly for a few minutes.

'Tell me again,' he said. 'It doesn't make any sense to me at all.'

She repeated it all, including that Ross had stayed out all night.

'Well, on the face of it it looks like he's done the very bravest thing,' Bruce said after a little thought. 'You haven't been happy, Dulcie, we all knew that. He's given you a chance for a whole new life.'

'But how can I just leave here?' she asked. 'What will I do without you? Who will look after you?'

'I can get another housekeeper,' he said. 'Maybe nowhere near as good as you, but I'll get by. Ross was right too when he said I'd rather see you happy. I would. So would John and Bob. You'll be fine without me too. We can write letters and phone each other. I'll come and visit you on the plane as well. It's not as if you've got to go off to somewhere you don't know either. Go to Sydney. You'll have Rudie and Noël and all those other people you met there.'

Dulcie sniffed and wiped her eyes on her handkerchief.

'I know you never wanted to leave there last year,' he said gently, stroking her hair. 'You came back out of duty and because Ross forced your hand. Well, you've fulfilled all that duty now. No one could have made more effort than you did, you nursed him through the breakdown, did your very best to make everything right. But you know in your heart it will never come right. I wouldn't try growing cabbages year after year if they kept failing, would I?'

'No, I suppose not,' she said.

'Well then, you can't keep trying at a marriage that hasn't got the right ingredients to start with.'

'But it had, it had,' she cried again.

'Dulcie, you know that's not true. It's like Ross himself

said, you were just two frightened kids clinging together. You thought because you had miserable childhoods in common that was enough. You're a battler by nature, Dulcie, but much as I admire that quality in people, there are times when battling alone can't pull things through. Look at Betty and me! We spent years trying to make our other farm work, but it just couldn't be done, so we had to walk away from it.'

'I did love him, I still do,' she sobbed. 'I can't bear to think of him all alone.'

'Yes, but the kind of love you feel for him isn't the kind good marriages are made of, it's sisterly, friendly love. And don't you worry about him being alone, you know perfectly well he's a loner by nature. I promise you in a week or two he'll be back down the pub, shooting off to Kalgoorlie with his mates, and you know he'll be happier too, because he won't be hurting you any more.'

Dulcie sank into silence for some time. Bruce went off to the kitchen and made her a cup of coffee, lacing it with some brandy.

'But what do I do?' she said, looking up at him as he handed her the coffee. 'I can't just tell Rudie I want to go to Sydney on Tuesday with him, and expect him to look after me.'

Bruce almost felt like laughing at her naivety. 'You know perfectly well Rudie will be only too pleased to put you up for a bit. But you don't need someone to look after you, you're the girl who looks after everyone else. Go to Sydney, find yourself a job and a place of your own.'

He stood up. 'I'm going to leave you on your own for a bit,' he said. 'You sit here and think it all out. Maybe have a little nap. I'll make the sandwiches for the boys, we can't work outside in this rain anyway. Then when you've got your head straight again, you come on over.'

'But what about the shopping!' she said.

'I can get that,' he said. 'I saw your list on the window-sill.'

He was gone before she could say anything else, the

door slamming behind him, and she lay down on the couch and burst into fresh tears.

A whining sound and a scratch on her arm made her open her eyes. Jigger was beside her, one paw on her arm, his brown eyes big and mournful. His coat was very wet, he must have slipped in as Bruce left.

'Did you chase after your dad?' she asked him, petting his silky ears. 'He'll be back, Jigger, he wouldn't leave you.'

She had to get up then and find a towel to dry him off, and just the act of rubbing him all over, feeling his tongue licking at her bare arms, made her feel a little better.

Moving over to the window which looked out on to the lake, she stared out. The rain was slowing down now, there were patches of blue sky among the dark clouds. She knew that within an hour it would be gone, the sun out again. To her right the paddocks of wheat were pale gold – as long as it didn't rain again now, it would be a bumper harvest this year.

'But you won't see it,' she whispered. 'You won't be here to make a celebration supper, not for your birthday, or for Christmas.'

But as she said this to herself she thought of the sun shining on Sydney Harbour, felt the wind in her hair as she rode on the ferry, and saw the rose beds in the Botanical Gardens.

A strange feeling crept up her, starting from her feet, a warm, tingly feeling like lemonade bubbles bursting in her veins. It seemed to gather momentum as it went up her legs into her belly and beyond, and suddenly she felt lighter and full of hope.

She turned and looked at her living-room. It was as lovely to her as it had been when they first moved in, yet surprisingly it didn't hurt to think she would soon be saying goodbye to it. Walking over to the jarrah desk Ross had made her, she slid her hand along the smooth surface and felt a pang at leaving that behind. She could almost feel the love he'd made it with.

But Bruce was right, it was the wrong kind of love for marriage. Ross would be happier without her eventually, maybe one day he'd even meet a woman he could make love to.

It was nearly five when she went back over to Bruce's house. She had had a bath, washed her hair, and put on a pretty pink and white gingham dress she'd made herself.

The three men were sitting at the table talking. As she walked in they all moved to get up. Three anxious faces, each one so very dear to her.

'Stay where you are,' she said with a smile. 'I'll make us all a cup of tea.'

'I'm so sorry, Dulc!' John said, his handsome, usually smiling face glum and troubled. 'Strewth, I've got to admit there were dozens of times I wished something would happen to make you see Ross wasn't for you, but I never expected it to come so sudden.'

'It's better this way, John,' she said. 'I'm all right about it now. But I shall miss you all so much.'

'I didn't know whether to phone Rudie or not,' Bruce said. 'We'd just been discussing that, and if we ought to book a plane ticket for you.'

'I won't be going with him on the plane,' she said, looking to each of their faces in turn. 'I don't want Ross to be hurt still more when he comes back. I'll catch the train tomorrow night to Sydney.'

They all looked stunned. 'But it's such a long trip.' Bruce exclaimed.

'I think I need some breathing space,' she said simply. 'When I get to Sydney I'll find a room and a job. I won't be going to Watson's Bay except to visit Rudie and Noël.'

'Fair dinkum?' John said. 'You're gonna do it on your own?'

She laughed. 'I'm a big girl now, John, and I don't intend to jump from the frying pan into the fire. I can make it on my own.'

'Is there anything I can do for you?' Bruce asked. His

eyes were wide with surprise and his lips were trembling with emotion.

'You could ring up and book me a berth on the train,' she said. 'And lend me a suitcase too if you've got one spare. I've got an awful lot more stuff than I arrived with. Can I ask one of you to drive me to the station tomorrow evening too?'

All three of them simultaneously offered, and Bruce laughed. 'Reckon all three of us'll be taking you. We've got to give you the royal send-off.'

It was after supper that Dulcie phoned Rudie to tell him. She had considered every possible aspect of her move to Sydney during the afternoon, and she had it completely straight in her head now.

'I'm leaving Ross,' she began, after only the briefest of pleasantries about Noël, then launched into what she intended to do.

'You don't have to do that,' he began, but she cut him short before he could offer her a plane ticket or a room in his house.

'I know, but that's what I'm going to do. I know it's right.'

There was a brief pause. She supposed he was as shocked as Bruce and the men. 'How did this all come about, Dulcie?' he asked.

She told him the story as calmly as she could. 'Then he took off on his bike,' she finished up. 'The last thing he said was that he wanted me to be happy for evermore.'

Dulcie thought Rudie sounded very odd – when he questioned her more closely, his voice seemed a bit croaky. 'So you understand why I don't feel able to go on the same plane as you?' she said finally. 'I have to leave him some dignity.'

'Yes, of course,' he said. 'Would it be wrong for me to still come up there tomorrow?'

'No, of course not. We all want to see you and Noël. I'll be leaving in the evening, so come about ten so we can all have a nice long day together.'

*

Rudie wept when he put the receiver down. However he looked at it, whatever benefits his actions would have on the rest of Dulcie and Ross's lives, he would always feel ashamed that he'd blackmailed Ross and caused him such pain.

He hadn't expected the man to act so quickly or so honourably. Clearly there was a great deal more to him than a mere braggart. In his stupidity, too, he hadn't realized Dulcie had always known this, nor had it occurred to him that if she gained her freedom she wouldn't necessarily come running crying to him.

In fact he could see now that there was far more to Dulcie too than he'd ever imagined. He'd seen and admired her sweetness, compassion and stoic acceptance of whatever life threw at her. She was the perfect companion because she delighted in the simplest things – a sandwich made for her, a paddle in the sea, a ride on a ferry or bathing a baby. That night after May's funeral when he kissed her, everything had come together in his mind to tell him she was the woman he wanted to spend the rest of his life with.

But she had a steelier side that he'd never even guessed at. He ought to have seen it when she showed him her marvellous paintings, for she had advanced so far in her technique that it was obvious she had been persistently working night after night on them. Now she was intending to travel alone to Sydney, to find a job and a home all by herself, and though he admired her spirit and the pragmatic view she'd taken of Ross asking her to leave, he was afraid that there might not be much room in her new life for him.

He poured himself a stiff brandy and his thoughts went back to Ross. Tonight he would almost certainly have the longest, loneliest night of his adult life and it was bound to take him back to his childhood where he would relive again all the hurts, humiliations and shame.

'You poor bastard,' Rudie muttered to himself. 'But you can take some pride in doing the right thing by Dulcie.'

*

At six-thirty the following evening, John put Dulcie's two large suitcases and a smaller one containing the things she needed on the journey into the boot of Bruce's car, then got in the back with Bob. Bruce came out of the house next and got into the driving seat.

'I left her in there to say goodbye to Rudie and Noël in private,' he said over his shoulder. It had been a strange sort of day – he felt unbearably sad that Dulcie was going out of his life, yet joyful that she was finally going to get the kind of life she deserved.

It had been good to spend more time with Rudie, he liked the man so much, and Noël was a delight, anyone's dream grandson. Yet that was tinged with sadness too because although he might be able to get to Sydney once, perhaps twice, to see them, he knew in his heart that time was running out for him. Then over and above all that he was mystified as to why Ross suddenly let Dulcie go. Ross was many things, a complex and often contradictory man, but he wasn't known for putting other people's needs before his own. Why would the man shoot himself in the foot?

'Reckon Dulc and Rudie might make a go of it?' Bob said, tapping Bruce on the shoulder and ending his reverie.

'I hope so,' Bruce said, not trusting himself to turn to look at his men because he was close to tears. 'They are right for each other. But it's early days yet. Dulcie's doing the right thing going on her own. It will make it easier for Ross to bear.'

'I can't for the life of me understand why he suddenly told her to push off,' John said. 'One moment he was fighting mad about Rudie and Noël coming here, next moment he's throwing them together. I know he could be a weird bastard sometimes, but this ain't in character.'

'I reckon he'll be back tomorrow,' Bob said thoughtfully. 'Maybe he got all fired up and thought it was the right thing at the time, but hell, he's bound to have second thoughts. Sheilas like Dulc aren't thick on the ground round here. I bet he comes back fighting mad tomorrow.'

'Then it's a good thing Dulcie's going now,' Bruce said. 'I wouldn't want her to see him after a couple of days' hard boozing. I don't relish it myself.'

Silence fell in the car, each of them contemplating how Ross would be when he came back.

In the kitchen Dulcie had just finished stuffing a few last-minute odds and ends into her handbag. Rudie and Noël just stood there looking at her expectantly.

'One kissy for Auntie,' Dulcie said, sweeping Noël up in her arms. He obediently opened his mouth like a goldfish, making her laugh. 'Oh, a big wet one,' she exclaimed as he put his mouth to her cheek.

'Any chance that I get a kiss too?' Rudie said. 'One with a bit of hope attached to it?'

She put Noël down and went to him. Rudie took her head in both hands and tilted her face up to his, looking into her eyes. 'I wish you a safe journey,' he said, kissing her lightly on the lips. 'You ring me as soon as you get there, so I know you're safe. You're very precious to me,' he whispered. Then suddenly he put his arms around her and really kissed her. Like the kiss he'd given her on the night of May's funeral, it was tender and sensual, awakening every nerve ending in her body. His tongue flickered against hers, his hands caressing her back and neck, and she felt she was falling through space into a place where nothing mattered but him.

'Was there hope attached to that one?' she whispered huskily as they clung together.

'More than I dreamed of,' he whispered back. 'But you must go now. Call me!'

Dulcie hesitated before getting into the car, looking round her one last time, remembering how happy she felt the first time Bruce drove her around the farm. It looked so beautiful now, the sun sinking down behind the pines, the sky dark pink with a hint of purple.

Maybe she hadn't been happy for the entire six years

here, but she knew she would always look back on it with affection, remembering this was where she had been shown love and approval, a place she'd learnt to trust again and to find herself.

Jigger came bounding over to her, wagging his tail and making a whining noise as if he too was saying goodbye. She bent to pet him one last time. 'Good boy,' she whispered. 'Take good care of Ross for me.'

'See you in Sydney,' Rudie said, bending to kiss her cheek. 'Say bye-bye, Noël,' he said to the child in his arms.

'Bye-bye,' Noël said and began to wave furiously.

Dulcie turned to look back as Bruce drove off. Rudie was still standing there, Noël still waving. The fading sun behind them glinted on their dark hair, their faces in shadow.

Chapter Twenty-eight

'Dr Heinne will see you now, Mrs Proctor,' Dulcie said to the elegantly dressed middle-aged woman in the waiting room. She smiled encouragingly for it was Mrs Proctor's first appointment with Stephan, and she could see she was nervous. 'If you'd like to follow me.'

She led the way up the stairs to Stephan's consulting room on the first floor, and opened the door. 'This is Mrs Proctor, Dr Heinne,' she said.

Stephan got up from his desk and came to greet his patient. 'Good morning, Mrs Proctor, do come in.' He smiled briefly at Dulcie. 'Thank you, Miss Taylor. Hold all calls.'

Dulcie walked back downstairs again to her small office next to the waiting-room, smiling as she caught a glimpse of herself in the large mirror in the hall. She wore a plain white button-through uniform dress with a wide white belt, her hair swept back into a neat chignon. It was the kind of look she'd always admired since she was a small girl – sleek, understated yet glamorous.

A year had passed since she left the farm, and sometimes as she sat in her office making out bills, answering the telephone and keeping Stephan's books and files for him, she had almost to pinch herself to prove this wasn't a dream.

She had found a small room in Surry Hills on her arrival in Sydney, and as a temporary measure, until she found something better, she took a job as a waitress in a restaurant close to The Rocks. During her first month she was often filled with self-doubt, for the city she'd dreamed of so often back in Esperance seemed a lonely and frightening place. She would go and visit Rudie and Noël once a week on her day off, but she was determined not to rely on Rudie or any of his friends she'd met previously for company, she felt she had to make a life of her own. Telephoning Stephan was a matter of courtesy – she felt she owed it to him to tell him herself she'd left Ross, he had after all given her so much support and advice in the past.

Stephan was delighted to hear from her and insisted on taking her out to dinner to hear her news in more detail, and during the course of the evening he asked if she'd like to be his receptionist-cum-secretary.

Dulcie's first thought was that he'd invented the job purely out of sentimentality, or even pity, but as it turned out that wasn't the case. He really did need help, and as he explained, the very nature of his work meant he had to have someone entirely discreet and trustworthy, who would also empathize with his patients. He said he thought she was ideal for the job.

Within a week of working for him she knew it was her dream job. His system of filing was disorganized, he was very behind with sending out bills, and when he was with a patient he had to ignore the phone, which often upset the caller. It felt good to create order out of chaos, to work in a calm environment and to know she was making Stephan's life a great deal more comfortable.

It was a long journey from Surry Hills to Rose Bay, so she found a tiny self-contained flat nearby, and as her working hours were far shorter than in the restaurant, she had long evenings in which to paint. It was also much easier to visit Noël and Rudie as it was only one stop on the ferry or a short bus ride.

Her feelings about Rudie were very confused. She felt she loved him, he dominated her thoughts constantly, but she was afraid too. Was she just a substitute for May? Was she chasing a dream because of Noël? Was she fooling herself it was real love the way she had with Ross? Sometimes she felt that her feelings would be clarified if she let herself go and went to bed with Rudie, yet this too was a problem, for she still clung to the idea that sex outside of marriage was wrong.

In many ways her moral dilemma was solved when she started proceedings for an annulment of her marriage on the grounds of non-consummation. It began with a medical examination to establish that she was still a virgin, and her solicitor warned her that right up until the annulment had been granted, if Ross decided to challenge it, she could very well be called for yet another physical examination. So she couldn't let Rudie become her lover.

Rudie was so patient and understanding. He didn't put her under any pressure or make her feel guilty, he seemed happy just with kissing and cuddling, and before long they were spending all their spare time together at weekends. Gradually Dulcie was able to see for herself that she hadn't ever been a substitute for May, and big attraction as Noël was, it was his father she was falling deeper and deeper in love with.

Thankfully Ross made no protests about the annulment, agreeing completely with her statement and co-operating with the lawyers. Letters passed between them and although he didn't sound exactly happy, he appeared resigned to his single status. Bruce reported he had spent some months drinking heavily, with morose periods, but that by the time the lambing season began in May he had bucked up and had begun making furniture again in his spare time.

Bruce had a new housekeeper now, an Italian woman called Maria who came in six days a week. He said she was fat, and slovenly compared to Dulcie, but she was jolly and an excellent cook. John had a new lady in his life, Maggie, a widow of thirty-eight with three children. Bruce said they often came to the farm on Sundays and it was good to have some kids around. He hoped John might finally take the plunge and marry Maggie because she was a good sort. As for Bob, he went on just as he always had, happy that he had a job and a home, asking for nothing more.

Dulcie sat down at her desk and checked the appointment book. The next patient wasn't due for an hour. She had already filed all the patients' notes from the previous day and sent out bills, so she really had nothing much to do now but take calls. This was Stephan's home as well as his workplace, and she usually made them both sandwiches and coffee for lunch, which they ate in his kitchen at the back of the house. She always looked forward to that hour, Stephan was a fascinating man, and through him she had learnt a great deal about the long-term effects of an unhappy childhood.

This had helped her understand herself far better, to study and accept what had happened to her in the past, then put it away and look only to the future. Yet while learning all this, she could also see so clearly how for most emotionally scarred people this was almost an impossibility. Had May lived, it was unlikely she would ever have reached that understanding. Ross too would never be entirely cured. She often thought about the other girls she had known at St Vincent's, the boys at Clontarf, Bindoon and other orphanages, and knew that for the vast majority of them their lives would be lonely, deprived and fraught with personal problems.

'Dear Stephan,' she murmured to herself. 'What a lot I owe you!'

She would never forget the day in August when she came in to work and told him the annulment of her marriage had been approved. He was standing in the hall, and as she told him he came forward and hugged her, the first time he had ever done such a thing.

'This is the real start of your new life now,' he smiled, his eyes all sparkly through his glasses. 'You've shed your skin, now you can grow a new one.'

'What sort of skin shall I have?' she joked. 'Will it be sophisticated or arty, or maybe the skin of a serious-minded secretary?'

'You can be all of those at once,' he laughed. 'It can be mink, satin, silk or tweed, whatever you fancy. You've got so many talents you can even have ones you slip on and off to suit the moment.'

'I feel I ought to celebrate the shedding of my old skin,' she said. 'How would you recommend I do that?'

He looked at her for a couple of seconds. 'Well, Miss Taylor, in my capacity as a friend, employer and past "shrink", I'd recommend getting laid.'

Dulcie giggled. Like the hug, such personal remarks were out of character for Stephan. 'Oh really! Just like that!'

He smiled. 'You know Rudie's been waiting patiently for a very long time. I would imagine you'd make his day, or even his year, if you rang him and suggested a candle-lit dinner for two.'

'Maybe it would have happened anyway,' Dulcie murmured to herself. 'I'm sure I didn't really need Stephan's permission to go ahead.' But she smiled and sat back at her desk reliving that delicious, wonderful night.

She had arrived at his house at seven-thirty to find the living-room lit up with dozens of candles, the table laid with flowers and crystal glasses, fire lit, a wonderful garlicky smell wafting out of the kitchen and The Kinks' 'Tired of Waiting' playing.

'So you're tired of waiting!' she said with a grin, for though Rudie had a passion for English pop music, she guessed he had selected that one specially.

He only laughed and held out his arms to her. 'It's wonderful news that the annulment's gone through, I'm so happy for you that all the beastly stuff is over.'

She sighed happily and kissed him passionately.

'Umm,' he said when they eventually came up for air. 'That one had more than hope in it, more like a green light.'

Dulcie giggled. 'I'm starving, what's for dinner?'

'My most famous culinary masterpiece,' he said. 'Bœuf Bourguignonne, liberally laced with red wine and brandy. I have also made a pudding which I'm told is guaranteed to keep you in my clutches for ever.'

'Then I shall be wary of it,' she laughed. 'But I'll just nip upstairs and take a peek at Noël first.'

As she went through her old bedroom, Dulcie paused for a moment. She had stayed the night here many times since coming back to Sydney, and so often she had lain awake, wanting Rudie with all her heart, yet afraid to get up and go to him. Her idea that sex before marriage was wrong appeared to be so very old-fashioned now. Almost every day she read in the papers that young people in England and America were challenging the old rules of morality, they had sex casually with anyone they pleased, smoked pot, went to weekend-long pop concerts and wore outrageous clothes. A pill had been invented to prevent pregnancy, and though at the moment it was only for married women, soon single girls would be able to have it too.

Australia was catching up as well. Young people were flocking off to visit Europe, coming back with tales of hitchhiking across the entire continent, of the wild boutiques, discotheques and bed-sitter lands of London. It seemed strange to Dulcie that the parents of these youngsters had left Europe for Australia looking for a superior way of life, and now their children believed Europe was Utopia.

She went in to see Noël. He slept in a little bed of his own now, the once bare room full of toys of every description, the walls bright with jolly posters. She thought how different it was for children now, compared to how it had been for her generation. No war, no rationing, a huge variety of food, almost every family had a car. Things like television and washing-machines were no longer luxuries but essentials.

He was a real little boy now, he spoke as well as an adult, could count up to twenty, do simple jigsaws, and knew his books so well he pretended he could read them. She bent over him, stroking his dark hair out of his eyes, admired his peachy skin and his long eyelashes. When she thought about May now, it was never with sorrow or bitterness, only gratitude that she'd passed Noël over to her. He liked a centre-stage position just like his mother, and with his looks and happy disposition, he'd probably keep it.

'Sleep tight,' she whispered and kissed his cheek. 'I love you.'

The dinner was superb, and the pudding Rudie claimed would keep her in his clutches for ever was a pavlova filled with raspberries, passion-fruit and cream. They left the dishes on the table and lay on the rug in front of the fire, drinking wine and kissing with sweet soul music playing in the background.

Their clothes just seemed to come off by magic – one moment they were rolling together fully dressed, the next naked – and even though Dulcie had seen Rudie stripped to shorts dozens of times on the beach, it was a thrill to caress those broad shoulders, the firm muscles in his arms, and feel the smoothness of his skin at last.

It was the kind of love-making she'd imagined in her dreams for so many years, unrushed, sensual and so loving that she felt she just might die from ecstasy. He stroked, sucked and kissed her breasts so tenderly it brought tears to her eyes. His fingers explored her vagina with such delicacy that she cried out for more. He unleashed feelings she never knew existed, made her feel wanton and utterly desirable.

It seemed shocking that a man would want to kiss and lick her in such intimate places, but it was so wonderful she lost all her inhibitions and found herself reciprocating too, wanting him to feel the way she did. It did hurt a little when he finally entered her, and the moment was marred slightly by him stopping to put on a sheath. But the knowledge she was at last losing that virginity which had caused so much hurt and disappointment in the past more than made up for the discomfort.

'I love you, Dulcie,' he said, holding himself away from her marginally and looking right into her eyes. She could see his love for herself, those dark eyes soft with tenderness and adoration. 'Nothing will ever come between us now.'

He plunged into her, his hands holding on to her buttocks, his breath hot on her face. Dulcie gloried in it, rising to him to take him further and further into her. She felt complete now, a real woman.

Later, as they lay together in front of the fire, the candles gradually flickering out one by one, he spoke of how long he had loved her.

'I think it began when I read your letters to May,' he said. 'Angry as I was that she had lied to me about so much, I found a picture of you forming in my mind. The oldest letter was the one you sent after you'd been to visit May at St Vincent's and heard about your father's death. You were being cautious in what you said, and I guessed it was because your previous letters hadn't been passed to May and you knew that one would be read before it was given to her. Yet you managed to convey such concern for her. In the later letters sent to the address at Peppermint Grove I learned so much more about you, I knew you were generous, loving and with a great sense of humour too. There was a description in one of a football game you'd gone to with Bruce and John. I was almost there, hearing all the spectators honking their car horns when someone got a goal. You were obviously more interested in watching the crowd than the football!'

Dulcie laughed. 'I was always bored stiff by the men discussing football. That was the first and last game I ever went to. So what did you think of me when you met me off the train?' she asked.

'My first impression was that you were like Bambi, all big-eyed, sweet and fragile. I didn't expect that. I'd somehow built you up in my mind to be taller, stronger-looking, even a bit stern. I was nervous then, I thought I'd made a mistake enlisting your help, that you'd crumple when I told you what May was doing. But you proved me wrong.'

'What did you really think when you got the message May had skipped off?' she asked. This was something she'd never put to him, and it seemed important now.

He looked faintly sheepish. 'The very first thought was that I'd opened a can of worms I was never going to be able to close. I was as scared as you must have been. But what made it better was you. I hadn't expected you to be so practical and unhysterical. I knew then fate had stepped in for both of us.'

'Don't tell me you fell in love with me then, because I don't believe it,' she laughed.

'No, I didn't think that, but I knew within a day or two of you coming here with Noël that you were completely special. Everything from the past just seemed to fade. The more you told me about you and May, the more I saw you with Noël, the stronger the feeling became, but it was the day the Welfare women came and you had to write that letter to Ross that I suddenly realized I'd fallen in love with you.'

'But that was before May died,' she said.

'Exactly. Long before.' He bent to kiss her, as if he knew she needed to know she had never been second-best. 'You can't imagine how hard it was for me that night when we got back from her funeral. I was terrified at the thought of losing you. I wanted to seduce you, I even thought of forcing you into it with me because I thought if I did you might not go.'

'I probably wouldn't have,' she admitted. 'But then I'd have been so stricken with guilt about Ross I don't suppose I'd have been very good for you.'

'I didn't take your sheets off the bed for weeks,' he said with a smile. 'I used to get into that bed and just sniff them, like a sad old dog. Stephan was the only person I could really talk to about it. He never said much, just listened to my ramblings and reminded me I still had an ace card in Noël, and that I should take him to Esperance for a holiday as I'd promised.'

Dulcie smiled at this. She had seen so often how Stephan

seemed to be able to look right into people's souls and identify with them.

'I'm very glad you did keep that promise,' she said. 'Sometimes it was only the thought of that visit that kept me going. I've often wondered if it was you coming that finally pushed Ross into telling me to go, or whether it would have happened anyway.'

The ringing of the telephone broke into Dulcie's reverie, bringing her abruptly back to the present, and she picked it up to answer it, smiling when she found it was Rudie.

'I was just thinking about you,' she said.

'I think about you all the time,' he said, using a mock reproachful tone. 'In fact I think about you so much I went into Sydney this morning to chase up your pictures.'

'Did they tell you anything?' she asked eagerly. Brown and Allbright, a children's book publisher, had had her portfolio for over three weeks now, and there hadn't been a word from them.

'Well, it would have been unethical for them to tell me anything before you, but they said they were putting a letter in the post to you today, and I didn't get the impression it was going to be a rejection. They were much too smiley and nice for that. Brown actually asked me into his office for coffee and probed for a bit more information about you.'

Dulcie's heart began to race with excitement. She knew Rudie wouldn't have even told her he'd been there today unless he was sure she was going to receive an offer from these people. 'I won't be able to sleep tonight thinking about it,' she said.

'Well, come round to me then,' he said. 'Sleeping isn't compulsory.'

Dulcie giggled. 'Okay, I'll come straight after work so I can put Noël to bed.'

'What were you thinking about me when I phoned?' he asked. 'Was it that I'd better marry him quickly before he changes his mind?'

'No it wasn't, though I suppose it is related – I was thinking about that night!'

'What night was that?' he asked.

'You'd better remember before I get round there,' she said in a pretend severe voice. 'I shall test you on it. Now I've got to go. I can hear Stephan saying goodbye to his patient. See you about six.'

Rudie put the phone down and looked at Noël playing with a toy train on the floor. He could see he was tired, they'd caught the ferry into Sydney this morning and he'd walked a long way.

'Dulcie's coming to see us later,' Rudie said.

A wide smile spread across the child's face. He was three now, tall for his age and sturdily built, growing more like his father every day, except that his dark eyes were very prominent without the slightly hooded appearance Rudie's had. 'For tea?' he asked. 'Can we go for a walk after too?'

'We'll see when she gets here,' Rudie said. 'But I think it's time for a little nap, otherwise you'll be too tired to play with her when she comes.'

Once Rudie had put Noël on his bed for a sleep, he went into his studio to carry on with some work, but instead of getting on with it, he stood at the window looking at the view of the bay.

He did of course remember 'that night' as Dulcie always called it. How could he ever forget it? It was the most memorable of his entire life. But though he remembered the love-making so well, the bliss of possessing her after such a long, long wait, it was what happened afterwards that had stayed in his mind most clearly.

They had been lying on the floor, cuddling and talking about how it was for him after Dulcie left Sydney to go back to the farm, and how Stephan had told him to keep his promise and go there. Then Dulcie asked why she thought Ross chose that time to let her go.

Rudie could remember so distinctly the stab of guilt he felt. He managed to say he thought his presence there might have greased the wheels a bit.

'It was such a brave and noble thing he did,' she said thoughtfully. 'I think it was the first time in his life that he'd put his own needs aside for someone else. All he'd ever learnt as a child was personal survival, no sense of morality really. He told me once that he would do any-thing, lie, cheat, steal and maybe even kill if necessary to keep going. I often wondered if he hadn't ended up in Bruce's barn, what would have become of him.'

She hadn't spoken of Ross for a very long time until that night. She would occasionally mention something from a letter he'd written, talk in general about the farm, but not about him. Maybe she was only prompted to talk about him then because she'd got the news of the annulment that day, but Rudie felt if she was in the right mood it was time he shook out a few skeletons.

'Are you ever going to tell me what happened at Bindoon?' he asked. 'Now and then I feel the weight of it hanging around in the air. Can't you tell me now?'

She had been so relaxed until then, naked and unashamed, but she suddenly sat up, grabbed his shirt and put it on. Somehow that seemed very symbolic to him, the order of the past coming back. Rudie moved to sit beside her, drawing her back against his chest, his arms around her. 'You're quite safe here with me,' he said gently against her ear. 'Just tell me.'

She did. Starting at the point when she and Ross left the farm for Perth, she described in detail all the events which led up to their eventual arrival at Bindoon. Her surprise at the beauty of the place, but the mounting, sickening horror as Ross showed her how it had been built, and his part in it. Finally she told him how it all came to a climax when they saw the tomb of Brother Keaney, that Ross became rigid and immovable with fear, and that she had to trick him into getting into the car. She stopped there for several minutes, crying silently, and it was all Rudie could do not to turn her around and say she didn't have to tell him the rest.

Yet he knew that whatever it was that came next, and he knew without a doubt it was the worst part, she did have to tell him, for if she kept it inside her it as Ross had, it would never be exorcized.

She gave a kind of shuddering sob and told him how she drove Ross away from there, stopping further down the road. Haltingly she described the lonely road, the heat, and how she held that broken man in her arms and listened to him baring his very soul.

She spared Rudie nothing. It was as if she had been a witness to the ugly scene in the dairy, and he could see, feel and smell that young boy's fear and pain. Terrible and shocking as the story was, for Rudie it was like a beam of light coming into a dark place and illuminating it. All those ideas he had about Ross, personal observations, intuition, hear-say from Dulcie, Bruce, and Mary up at Kalgoorlie, and indeed the prejudices he'd formed while Dulcie was here with him battling for Noël, all came together. He felt he fully understood now what lay at the very core of the man, and his heart went out to him.

'Do you understand why I couldn't speak of it to anyone?' she asked, twisting her neck round to look at Rudie, tears dripping down her face. 'I felt responsible for unleashing it all and causing the breakdown. Then I found I didn't even want him to try and make love to me any more, and that gave me an even bigger load of guilt, because it made the whole thing so cruel and unnecessary.'

It crossed Rudie's mind that maybe he could get rid of that bit of guilt for her by telling her that Ross had in fact had at least a partial cure in as much as he could have sex with other women. But he squashed that thought. It would only stir up things best left undisturbed.

'Tell me, do you still feel guilty about him?' he asked.

'No, it's all gone now,' she sighed. 'The way he let me go, not challenging the annulment, his friendly letters and time to reflect on it all, wiped it out. I just feel tenderness and pity for him, that's all.'

As he sat there with her in his arms, Rudie thought how incredibly forgiving she was. He still occasionally smarted at the treatment he'd had at school, even though it was nothing compared with what she had had to endure. Only a week or two earlier the subject of the Sisters at St Vincent's came up, and Dulcie said she felt sorry for them now. He had teased her, in fact tried to make her angry about them, but she only said she thought most of them were troubled women themselves, cut off from their families, stuck out in the middle of nowhere, with nothing ahead of them but a sad old age.

Rudie smiled as he looked out at the bay. The sun was sparkling on the water and it looked very beautiful. Dulcie had been so beautiful that night too, he'd carried her up to his bed later, and they'd made love for hours.

He remembered that she'd fallen asleep just as the sun was coming up, and he'd just lain there looking at her. Her hair was all tousled, she had smudges of mascara under her eyes, and her mouth was soft and vulnerable like a little girl's. He had wanted to creep out of bed and fetch his sketchbook, for she had one small breast peeping out from the sheets, and her bare shoulders were the colour of apricots. But he couldn't bear to drag himself away from the warmth and smoothness of her body, so instead he just stayed there and silently worshipped her.

Maybe his gaze was so intense it woke her, for she opened one eye and smiled. 'What are you looking at me like that for?' she said.

He said the first thing that came into his mind. 'Because I want to marry you.'

She made a kind of chuckle and burrowed closer to him. 'You don't have to make an honest woman of me,' she said. 'I quite like sin now I've tried it.'

Rudie turned away from the window and picked up a picture Dulcie had painted for him. He had brought it up here to frame. It was nothing like her other work, the colours were subdued, almost sepia-like, and worked in oils. It was of two little girls with blonde hair in pigtails sitting on a low wall, the house behind them red brick but tinged with soot. The smaller girl was laughing, the older one a little anxious-looking. They were of course her and May, and the house, their old one in London. The detail was incredible – weeds sprouting out of the wall, a scrubby, tired bit of hedge struggling to grow with no nourishment, net curtains at the window, and a milk bottle on the doorstep.

It wasn't an uplifting picture, for there was great sadness in it, as if Dulcie had relived the ugly scene that took place upstairs on the first floor while she was painting it. Yet it was a powerful, emotive piece of work, and he knew that if ever one day Dulcie was to have an exhibition of her art, this would be the biggest talking point, for anyone looking at the picture would sense there was a story behind it.

Reg and Anne Taylor were gone now, and Maud, the old granny Dulcie so often talked about. May too. So much tragedy in one family. He wondered whatever happened to Susan, her old teacher, for somehow he didn't believe she'd really lost interest in the girls. It was far more likely she'd been prevented from keeping in touch with them.

Should he put Dulcie out of her misery tonight, and tell her that Brown and Allbright did want her to illustrate a series of books? He had seen the author's manuscript this morning and her suggestions for the pictures, and he knew it was exactly the kind of work Dulcie would be brilliant at.

'No, you won't say a word,' he told himself aloud. 'You can't rob her of the joy of opening that envelope tomorrow and reading it for herself. You'll push her into setting a day for the wedding instead.'

He picked up the length of light ash he'd bought for the picture frame and held it against the painting to check it really did look right before cutting the angles. It was perfect, the light wood giving just the right amount of lift to the work. He would make the frame now as a surprise.

Epilogue

'Is Mrs Jameson there?' a gruff male voice asked when Dulcie answered the telephone. His voice was loud as if unused to the telephone and it also sounded vaguely familiar.

'This is Mrs Jameson speaking,' she replied. 'Who is calling?'

'Dulc! Strewth, have I got you at last? It's John from Frenches'.'

'John!' she exclaimed with delight. 'How are you, and how's Maggie? My goodness, what a surprise.'

The last time she'd had any contact with John was fifteen years earlier when Bruce died and she and Rudie went to Western Australia for the funeral. John had in fact left the farm some five years before that to run a guest-house with his new wife, and in a quick mental calculation she realized he must now be approaching seventy.

She tapped Rudie on the shoulder. He was sitting reading the paper, and when she mouthed at him that it was John, he too looked surprised.

'I've been trying to get hold of you for over three weeks,' John said. 'I rang there, and your other house, but there was no one there.'

'We've been in England,' she said. 'We only got back a couple of days ago. Noël's a dentist now, living in England. We went over to meet his fiancée Katrina and make plans for the wedding next year. Can you imagine he's twenty-eight now? It seems only five minutes ago you and Ross made that swing for him.'

'It's Ross I'm ringing about,' he said. 'Oh hell, Dulc, I don't know how to tell you this, see, he topped himself.'

Dulcie stiffened but thought she'd misheard. 'He what? Could you repeat it?'

'He's dead, Dulc. He shot himself.'

It was as though someone had just thrown a bucket of icy water all over her.

'Ross is dead? He shot himself?' she repeated.

Rudie got out of his chair and came over to her, his dark eyes wide with disbelief at what he'd just heard. He gently nudged her down on to the couch and sat next to her, taking her hand in his.

'I'm sorry to tell you over the phone,' John said. 'But I ain't much good at letter-writing. Are you all right?' he added, perhaps suddenly aware how big a shock this would be to her.

Dulcie was trembling all over. 'Just knocked sideways,' she said. 'But what happened, why did he do it? Last time I spoke to him, not long before we went to England, he was fine.'

'He seemed okay too when I last saw him, a couple of months ago,' John said. 'I thought at first the farm must be in trouble. But there's been people up there going through the books and all that stuff and everything's all right, better than all right, he's been doing great.'

Bruce's funeral was the first and last time Dulcie had seen Ross since they split up, though they had remained in contact by letter and phone both before and after. At the funeral Ross had welcomed Rudie as warmly as he had Dulcie, and asked that they stayed out at the farm.

Bruce died of a stroke, and upset as Ross was, he'd said he was glad Bruce went instantly for he would have hated to have been left an invalid. While they were still in Esperance they went to the reading of the will. Bruce had left Dulcie and each of her three children five thousand Australian dollars, and asked her to take her pick of Betty's handmade quilts. He had made generous bequests to John and Bob too, even though neither of them was working for him any more. To Ross he'd left the farm, with the proviso that a proportion of the profits was to go annually to Betty's nieces and nephews in Perth, and if at the time of Ross's death, he was still unmarried without children, the farm was to be sold and the money to go back to the family.

Grief-stricken as Ross was to lose his dear friend and employer of so many years, he took great pride in increasing the profits year by year. Dulcie felt it comforted him to know he was doing this for Betty's relatives, and they in turn showed great appreciation and treated him as if he was one of their family.

'I just don't understand it,' Dulcie said, tears beginning to stream down her face. 'It doesn't make any sense to me.'

'Nor me,' John said. 'He could have come down to my place at any time if he had problems. But I reckon he planned it some time before he did it. He'd put everything in order. Wrote letters, got his will done, he even did it in the barn so as not to mess up anywhere that mattered.'

Dulcie winced at the image of Ross lying dead on the floor of the barn.

'I'm sorry,' John said, perhaps realizing that was tactless. 'But I guess you need to know some of this stuff even if it hurts. He left a letter for you, and in his will he said he wanted you to have the furniture he made. He wrote me a letter too.'

'Did he make any explanation?' she asked.

'No, just thanked me for being such a good friend all these years, said me, Bruce and Bob were like his guiding lights. He asked me to take his dogs and find good homes for them, and to contact you. That's where I got the phone numbers from.'

'Have you read the letter to me? Might there be something in that?'

'Of course I haven't read it,' John said indignantly. 'It's private between you and him.' He broke off suddenly as if overcome by emotion.

Dulcie couldn't continue a conversation anyway, so she just asked him to send the letter on to Watson's Bay, asked for his telephone number and said she'd ring him back once she'd got the letter.

Once she'd put the receiver down Rudie drew her into his arms. She sobbed into his chest for some time before she recovered enough to tell all that John had said.

Rudie was sixty-four now, his once dark hair flecked liberally with grey and receding at the temples. His face was lined and he wore glasses, and as he had put on around thirty pounds in weight since they married in 1964, he had a bit of a paunch, but he was still young at heart, very fit and healthy.

Dulcie at fifty was a little heavier too and thicker round the waist, but her hair was still blonde, helped to stay that way with regular colour rinses. She had a few lines around her eyes, but they had retained their vivid blue and she was still a remarkably pretty woman.

Life had been very good to them. Rudie's success as an artist had spread beyond Australia, to New Zealand and the Far East. In 1972, when Noël was eleven, their daughter Louise five, and their son Ben four, they had bought a far bigger house up in the Blue Mountains, for the cottage in Watson's Bay was too cramped. But they kept it for holidays and weekends, and now Noël was in England and Louise and Ben both off at university in Melbourne, Rudie and Dulcie spent most of their time at the cottage.

'Why do you think he did it?' Dulcie asked. 'He seemed so happy and fulfilled.'

Rudie thought for a few moments before replying. 'He may have seemed that way, Dulcie, but I doubt he really was. Since he was a small child, hard physical work was all he'd known, it became his sole reason for being.'

'But he had several women,' she said. 'Bruce said just before he died he thought he was getting more like John every day, with different women tucked away all over the place, and that one day he'd surprise us and get married again.'

'But John's an uncomplicated, loving man, he didn't have the scars that Ross had,' Rudie said. 'I think those scars must have opened up again for some reason. And he couldn't cope with it.'

'Well, why didn't it affect me like that in England when we went back to Hither Green and Deptford and saw where the Sacred Heart orphanage used to be?' she said. 'All that did to me was make me see how much I've got now.'

'That's just it, you have got such a lot now,' Rudie said. 'Three happy healthy children, a husband who adores you, and you are a very well-respected illustrator. You have to remember, too, that for years now, since you made contact with Susan again, you've known that your father didn't give his permission to send you to Australia, and that the Sisters blocked all letters from him and Susan to you. You saw all those places again in the knowledge that you were loved. Of course that couldn't entirely make up for all the misery you and May had, but it certainly soothed it.'

Dulcie knew that much was true. It was Rudie who tracked down Susan, as a wedding present to her. He made contact with an old friend back in England and got him to make inquiries through another vet. Once he'd found the address in Yorkshire, without breathing a word of it to Dulcie, he wrote to Susan, told her some of the background and pointed out how important it was that Dulcie should have some of the questions in her mind answered.

Dulcie didn't think she'd ever forget the absolute joy she felt when she got the first letter from Susan. It was no guarded or suspicious response, but an emotional letter written straight from the heart. In it Dulcie was able to see that Susan had done her utmost to keep in contact with them, but she'd been lied to and fobbed off with so many false trails that in the end, for the sake of her own three children and her husband, she'd had no choice but to abandon the quest. Yet it was clear from her words that she'd never forgotten May and Dulcie, or forgiven the people responsible for shutting her out of their lives.

For years, letters had passed between Dulcie and Susan, for there had been no opportunity then to visit England. They shared each other's life stories, Dulcie relating her childhood memories of all those sad events, Susan shining light into some of the darker corners with her adult view on them.

It was a magical moment for Dulcie when she finally went back to England and walked up the path to the kind of quaint cottage that had remained in her mind for over forty years in Australia as quintessentially English. It didn't matter that Susan was now a widowed grandmother of sixty-seven, stout and heavily lined with white hair, and not the elegant young woman Dulcie remembered. What counted was to be embraced by the woman who had encouraged her reading, painting and drawing, become both her grandmother and father's staunchest friend, and who had over the years made sense of so much that had once puzzled Dulcie.

'Finding Susan was one of the best things you ever did for me,' she said, and hugged Rudie. 'I think if it hadn't been for that I might have had problems with telling the children about my past. But maybe that's what finally got to Ross. He never knew exactly why he was pushed into an orphanage, or what happened to his brothers.'

'I know one thing,' Rudie said, tilting her face up to his. 'Whatever reason Ross had for killing himself, you weren't in any way to blame. So don't allow even the tiniest bit of guilt to creep into your mind.'

It was five days before the letter arrived from Western Australia, and during the long wait Dulcie had thought of little else but what the contents might be. She had busied herself by cleaning the cottage from top to bottom, tidying drawers and cupboards, throwing out toys and old clothes that had been hoarded since the children were tiny.

The cottage wasn't so very different to the day she first saw it. The boat and plane mobiles had been moved to the boys' rooms in the Blue Mountains house, many of Rudie's paintings had been sold over the years and replaced by pictures by other artists they both admired. The couches were new, a modern stereo had taken the place of Rudie's old radiogram, and a colour television had replaced the small black and white one. But the flavour was still the same – bright colours, polished wood – and upstairs the studio was no different. But Noël's old room was Louise's now, with a pretty bed handpainted by her father, flower-strewn curtains and the wicker cradle she'd slept in as a baby holding her collections of old dolls and teddy bears. The room that had once been Dulcie's was very much a boy's room now, bunk beds with bright red duvets, cricket bats, footballs, posters of pop stars, and shelves over-flowing with toy cars, trains and carefully built Lego models.

Dulcie purposely kept the children's rooms that way, even though they were grown-up now, for to her it was like a scrapbook of happy memories. She loved to remember those early days with Noël, making love to Rudie for the first time, the births of Louise and Ben. The cottage had been their only home until Louise was five and it had been cramped, noisy, full of toys and very untidy. In the evenings she would be doing her illustrating work on the dining table, and it was often Rudie who went round picking up toys and clothes and despairing over the clutter and lack of space. Yet to her it was a real home, every corner filled with love and hope. She had even been reluctant to find a bigger house, afraid that by going up in the world she might lose everything that was precious to her.

Fortunately it didn't turn out that way, or maybe it was because Rudie encouraged her to share their good fortune with others. He had taken up an interest in state-owned orphanages even before they married, using his influence to chivvy the Welfare Department into checking them all far more rigorously. Once they moved to the Blue Mountains, they often had small groups of orphaned children to stay for holidays, and many of them, now young working adults, still kept in close contact with Rudie and Dulcie.

Through those children Dulcie had often relived her own childhood fears and anxieties, and discovered what a difference it made to her holiday guests to have someone they could confide in and trust. Their sad stories often brought back memories of Pat Masters. She had nothing but sympathy now for Pat, the poor woman had experienced the worst life could throw at her, with no resources to deal with it. Yet she had been brave enough finally to leave Bill, and Dulcie hoped that she had found happiness in Adelaide.

Stephan had once told Dulcie that learning to trust again was the cornerstone in any damaged child's recovery. Not just to place trust in others, but to trust their own judgements and emotions. Dulcie believed that she had fully learned to do that and to help others achieve it too, but she suspected Ross never had.

She and Rudie were eating their breakfast when the letter came. It was the only letter that morning, and even the way the letter-box rattled as it was pushed through struck an ominous note. Dulcie jumped up and ran to pick it up, relieved to see John's familiar large scrawl on the envelope, yet half afraid to open it.

'Go on, open it,' Rudie said encouragingly. 'I don't think it's going to contain anything you don't already know.'

Inside the envelope was a letter and a couple of newspaper cuttings folded up and secured with a paper clip. She put these to one side and read the letter first.

Dear Dulcie, she read. *By the time you read this you will already have heard of my death, and I'm sorry if it upset you. I'm writing now to try and explain because I know unless I do you will always be wondering if there was anything you could have done to prevent it.*

You couldn't have done. It wasn't anything to do with you and me. You've always been special to me, a true friend. I want you to know that I valued that over everything else. I don't know if you remember but I told you once after I had that breakdown, that all going back to Bindoon did was oil the hinges on the door so I could open it and close it easily. For years after we split up, I did open the door and look at it sometimes, the more I looked, the more I thought I'd beaten it. I was doing fine at the farm, I had girlfriends and a few good mates. Even when Bruce died, I felt strong, I didn't go out and get drunk, I just rode it out and everything came all right again.

But then a couple of years ago there were some articles in the Western Mail, and they made me feel uneasy, one was about kids like you and May being sent to Australia, another one was about Bindoon. You'd think I'd have been glad that someone had finally woken up to the sort of hell us kids were put through, but it just made me scared. I had this feeling that I was going to be pushed into that room again, the door closed on me forever, I found I was thinking about it every bloody minute.

Then that book came out called Lost Children of the Empire, it was written by a couple of Poms, all about all the orphan kids England sent to other countries, including here. I got it and read it, but though it mentioned Clontarf being a grim place and kids getting beaten for bed-wetting and stuff, it was only the sort of general stuff that people have been saying about orphanages for years.

Then one weekend about three months ago up at Kalgoorlie I ran into a bloke I knew at Bindoon. I wouldn't have recognized him, he looked so old, but he knew me right off. We downed a few beers, and then he tells me he's written a book about Bindoon. He said he was going to blow the whole thing open, and make the bastards pay for what they'd done to us boys.

Since then my life has been hell, I can't get it out of my mind, every little detail keeps coming back, I've been having nightmares so bad I'm scared to go to sleep. I'm drinking too much, I'm angry all the time. I feel menaced. I knew if I phoned you and told you about it, you'd have told me it's better that it all comes out. Well, maybe it will be for some of those poor bastards who suffered the same as me, but not this one. I can't risk another breakdown, it would be the nut-house for me if that happened. So I'm taking the coward's way out.

Don't judge me too harshly, Dulcie. Unless you were to get inside my skin and head you couldn't know how ugly it is in there. I can almost hear you telling me to be brave and stand up and be counted, when the shit hits the fan. But I can't. All I can offer in place of courage is that you keep this letter, and if, and I know it will, the truth comes out about Bindoon, you use it in any way that might help the rest of the boys to face up to their demons, or to stop any more Brothers and priests beating and buggering little boys and getting away with it.

Don't cry for me, Dulcie. I was always glad that Rudie gave you the happiness you deserved. He is a good man, and I hope your three kids inherit both of your kind hearts and gentle ways. I've got this picture of you in my head as you were that first time I met you when you were running away from the Masters' place. Such a skinny little girl, with big eyes full of fear. I never told you before, but I saw myself in you that day. We came a long way didn't we? I'm sorry I won't be around to hear how you got on in England, or when your kids get married and have some of their own. I want you to have the furniture I made, give each of them a piece, and tell them I made it with love for you.

I wish you and Rudie a long and happy life together. Goodbye.

Ross

Dulcie sobbed as she read it, imagining Ross sitting at that jarrah desk in their old house writing it, his dogs about his feet. It was impossible for her to see him as a man of fifty-two. To her he would always be young, lean, with a mop of curly hair.

She handed the letter silently to Rudie and took the

paper clip from the newspaper cuttings. One had a headline, *The Lost Children Britain Sent Away to Australia*, the second was *The Nightmare of Bindoon*. The third said, *The Book That's Too Hot to Be Published*. This was the newest cutting and clearly the old friend Ross had spoken of was pushing to get it published.

Then there were several other smaller cuttings where institutions other than Catholic ones were featured, including the Fairbridge Farm Schools at Pinjarra, but it was the Catholic ones which came under the most fire, with an ex-Christian Brother quoted as saying, 'It was unbelievable the things that went on at Bindoon, including sodomy.'

'The poor, poor bastard,' Rudie sighed as he finished the letter. Tears were trickling down his cheeks, and he took Dulcie's hand across the table. 'It's so cruel that he could never get over it. I just hope he's at peace now.'

'Stephan once said that there were some things no one could ever forgive or forget,' Dulcie said sadly. 'He had two patients who were survivors of the Holocaust, and they seemed fine for years after counselling. Then one of them killed themselves, the other went off into the outback and became like a hermit, living alone in an old shed. I suppose it was much the same for Ross.'

Rudie picked up the newspaper cuttings to read them. 'I think Ross was right in one thing,' he said when he'd finished. 'These few articles are just the start of it, there's bound to be more. I wouldn't mind betting that before long old boys and girls from orphanages all over Australia will begin to speak out. Maybe too those responsible for ruining their lives will be taken to task.'

'Don't count on it, Rudie,' she said, her voice full of cynicism. 'The Church will shelter their own, and there'll be plenty of Doubting Thomases out there who assume all orphans are human rejects and not to be believed.'

Rudie got up from the table and came round to her and pulled her up into his arms.

'When the time comes, you must speak out then,' he said, kissing her nose.

'I couldn't,' she said, appalled at the thought.

'Oh yes you could,' he said firmly. 'Not for yourself perhaps, but for the Mays and Rosses, and all those countless other boys and girls, British and Australian, who had their lives blighted by the cruelty and lack of care in institutions.'

'But Ross was afraid of just that. Won't it make things worse for other people like him?'

'He wanted you to do something, it's there in the letter,' Rudie pointed out. 'For all we know, those atrocities could still be going on. Could you stay quiet while little children were still being hurt?'

'But they can't be, surely, Rudie. This is the eighties, people are enlightened now.'

'Are they, Dulcie?' he questioned, looking at her with one eyebrow raised. 'Maybe those big orphanages like the ones you went to are a thing of the past, but child molesting isn't. Paedophiles target vulnerable children in every level of society, and I believe everyone should be aware of that.'

Dulcie broke away from his arms and went over to the window. She knew Rudie was right, but there was still a tiny place inside her where the hurts of the past lived on. Even in all the happiness she'd known in the last twenty-six years it remained. She didn't speak of it, not to Rudie, Stephan or her children, but it was there.

She leaned her forehead against the cool glass and remembered how she used to do the same thing at the Sacred Heart, staring out of the playroom window in the hope that someone might come along to rescue her.

Of course her need to be rescued had gone many, many years ago, but Ross's letter had brought it home to her that there must be thousands of other men and women who still had that need. Ones who hadn't been as fortunate as her, where the hurt wasn't tucked away in a very small place but dominated and poisoned their lives. She knew from her own contacts in the Welfare Department that lack of self-esteem was a major cause in turning people towards drink, gambling, crime and vice. That hurt people went on to hurt others, unless they could find a way to rid themselves of it.

She sighed deeply, knowing she was no Joan of Arc, able to rush headlong into battle. But she did have the ability to listen, to care, and unlike the many do-gooders who would doubtless rattle their sabres at the first rallying call, she truly understood the nature of the terrible scars these people bore.

Turning back to the table, she picked up Ross's letter, folded it with the newspaper cuttings and placed it in the box where she kept photographs of May and her old letters. It was only in the past few years that she'd put the photographs of her wedding to Ross and her certificate of annulment in there too. Even at the time she'd sensed something symbolic about putting them together.

May was gone, and now Ross, both deaths precipitated by their sense of worthlessness. She had loved them both, understood their pain. Maybe if their stories were told it would help others to overcome theirs.

She looked up to see Rudie was watching her curiously. 'They belong together,' she said by way of an explanation, wiping a tear away from her cheek. 'Okay, when the time comes I'll be ready to fight for their cause.'

Afterword by Bruce Blyth

British children transported to Australia – documents forged and names illegally changed – families torn apart – incarcerated in slave camps, exploited, starved and denied education – publicly flogged, humiliated, abused and sexually assaulted.

These atrocities belong not to the nineteenth century but to a period within living memory, with many of the children now in their fifties and sixties. In the middle of the twentieth century, the Child Migration Scheme was intended to relieve pressure on British orphanages straining under the upheavals of six years of war and at the same time populate the colonies with 'good white British stock'. Australia in particular was crying out for British migrants, and who, it was thought, would make better 'Aussies' than young children languishing in UK orphanages? And what twelve-year-old, incarcerated in a dank and dreary English orphanage, would not be tempted by promises of a land of sunshine and beaches, of kangaroos and horses, where fruit falls off trees? In 1945 the Minister for Immigration told the Australian Parliament that the government intended to bring 50,000 orphans to Australia during the next three years.

In fact, between 1947 and 1955, 2,324 orphans were transported from Britain to Australia, their fate in the hands of men and women who wore black robes and habits and worshipped a Saviour who said, 'Suffer little children to come unto me.'

And how those children suffered! Four hundred and fifty of them were incarcerated in four orphanages in WA, which we now know, half a century later, were no more than slave camps where thousands of children, mostly Australian, were exploited, starved, denied an education and subjected to physical and sexual atrocities. Bindoon is particularly notorious following revelations of the horrific crimes committed during the rule of its founder, Christian Brother Francis Paul Keaney. Keaney was revered by an unsuspecting public and shortly before his death in 1954, he was awarded the MBE and ISO. Thousands of admiring citizens, many prominent in public life, paid tribute at his funeral, and in the main forecourt at Bindoon a life-size bronze statue was erected in his honour. Today, the atrocities committed by Keaney and other Christian monks are difficult to comprehend, but every victim is still living with the brutal realities of a childhood mutilated by tyrants like Keaney.

In July 2000 a group of Bindoon survivors wreaked a belated revenge on the monk who had blighted their lives for fifty years. In a howling gale in the dead of a winter night, they hacksawed the head off Keaney's statue, an act of vandalism which André Malan, a leading Australian journalist, called 'a funny form of symbolic justice and half a century too late. But Brother Keaney', Malan wrote, 'has finally got what he deserved.'

But with no one to turn to for help or sympathy, many survivors never recovered. For decades they lived through agonies of misplaced guilt and shame and could not reveal to anyone the childhood nightmares which stalked them every day of their lives. It was to be forty years before a survivor of Bindoon was able to put his story on paper. But who could believe it? Not the big publishers who rejected it because, according to an Australian senator, it was 'too hot to publish'.

As a small, independent publisher, the senator's comments aroused my interest. I sought out the author, took his manuscript home and sat up all night reading it, unable to put it down. From that moment my life changed, never to be the same again. After reading thirty pages I knew I had to do something with it. It was a shock. Could nuns and clerics really savage children so cruelly? Was it a credible document? But every word and every line echoed with the ring of truth. It hit me hard. With a loving, caring childhood to remember and a long and happy marriage and two adult children to be proud of, I, like most others, admired and respected the dedicated nuns and Brothers who struggled on behalf of the poor, unfortunate orphans placed in their care. Why would anyone think differently?

Geordie Welsh, the author, was no ordinary man. He had spent five years at Bindoon under the notorious Keaney, followed by years as an alcoholic on skid row across Australia. He introduced me to men who had stories just as terrible and just as authentic as his own and my resolve to publish was strengthened by every one. *Geordie – Orphan of the Empire* was the first book written by a survivor and was widely reviewed in the Australian media, Geordie becoming a well-known character on radio and TV. But just as importantly, it aroused interest among his fellow survivors. At last the truth was out. My office quickly became a rallying point. Every day men poured out their secret stories of childhood terrors which had haunted them for as long as they could remember.

Those early days were emotionally loaded. Over the telephone, I listened to life-hardened men break down in mid-sentence, and as I waited for them to recover, I was filled with anger, horror and disgust. Nothing in life had prepared me for this onslaught. Letters flowed in, letters pages long, painfully written by men who had never written more than a few words at one time.

Out of this turmoil was born VOICES. Three hundred men in Perth, Western Australia, joined together not only to seek justice but to expose the truth. For six long years we fought a bitter battle in the media, through the courts, in parliament and with the support of the public: 30,000 West Australians signed a petition of support. Every inch of the way we had to fight the wealth as well as the power and influence of the Roman Catholic Church. But for these survivors of the infamous Bindoon, Clontarf, Castledare and Tardun orphanages the truth was emerging, and at long last people were actually believing them.

The truth, however welcome, was not always kind. The Christian Brothers were not the only ones to suffer as their wicked deeds were finally uncovered. As the truth unfolded, it had to be told through the media. Dark secrets never whispered even to loved ones had to be revealed to the whole world. Facing up to the glare of the TV camera and telling the world that as a child of nine or ten you were raped by a lecherous monk is an act of extraordinary courage. Next day at the local supermarket, the stares and pointed fingers hurt and are hard to ignore. Even harder, perhaps, is the sneering jibe and ribald gesture in the Aussie-macho workplace.

The truth hurt at home too. Wives told me how they were caught unawares, that they knew nothing about the atrocities inflicted on their husbands so long before. One tried to explain to me her anguish and helplessness as her husband broke down beside her as they watched *The Leaving of Liverpool* on TV.

Another wife, who later became a VOICES committee member, wrote:

. . . one night he told me about his childhood at Castledare and by the time he had finished he was crying and so was I. He told me that every day of his life it had been with him – he could not get it out of his mind. At first I felt cheated. I could not understand why he had not told me before, but the more I thought about it, the more I realized how hard it must have been for him to tell me at all . . . It will never go away. I still cry for my husband and I know he cries too. Sometimes his tears are silent, it is hard to hide one's feelings.

In the cruel, bleak and isolated orphanages there was no mother to love and cuddle a crying child; not a grand-mother's knee to climb up on in search of a comforting hug – just sex-starved Christian Brothers wielding monstrous leather straps and committing evil deeds upon innocent boys in the dead of night. In 1948, three inspectors of the Child Welfare Department reported:

> Castledare is catering for children who are still little more than babies, who need love, affection, care and attention which a child of such age would get from a mother ... there is an immediate necessity for the touch of a woman's hand.

Another inspector visiting Bindoon reported: ' ... the home is entirely lacking in the necessary female staff.'

There is no doubt that the lack of a female presence in childhood has had a detrimental and lasting effect upon the survivors. Many men and their partners say how difficult their lives have been as a result of the husband's upbringing. While many have found it impossible to establish and maintain relationships, the parental bond with children has also been difficult.

One man told me that when his wife died after their fifteen-year marriage, he stood by as his fourteen-year-old son and only child wept with grief. He said:

> I knew I had to comfort him, put my arms around him, console him. He was my son, but I couldn't bring myself to touch him. In the orphanage, no one touched us out of genuine love or affection and as my son sobbed in front of me, I was still trapped by the loathsome hand of the orphanage.

In fact, the wounds inflicted in the orphanages never heal. Paul Bennet, a Canadian therapist who treated boys abused by Christian Brothers, wrote: 'None of these guys will ever be cured and they will probably spend the rest of their lives trying to recover ... many of them carry tremendous rage, anger, confusion, guilt and shame.'

This volatility is never far below the surface and is often more wounding to the victim than to those who are subjected to it. Man after man has explained to me how they cannot control the anger which flares up with little reason and no warning. Those they love and those who help them are particularly vulnerable.

A leading Australian forensic psychologist who treated many of the men associated with VOICES spoke of typical symptoms such as flashbacks, chronic sleep disorders, an inability to form and maintain relationships, increased anxiety, low self-esteem and intense feelings of shame, guilt and suicidal tendencies. 'By and large many of them are ruined human beings,' he said.

Many of the men have led lonely and deprived lives. Many succumbed to alcohol, some have known the hell of skid row, many have been in gaol, while one of the most common burdens they carry is a lack of education.

When VOICES took its case to the NSW Supreme Court, an eminent QC acting for the Christian Brothers suggested that the motive for the men's legal action was money. Under this savage grilling one middle-aged man, on the verge of tears, exclaimed to a hushed court, 'No, I wasn't after the money at all. I am not after any money. I want to learn how to read and bloody write.'

Girls in the care of the Sisters fared no better than their brothers. Discussing conditions in orphanages run by the Sisters, a 1998 House of Commons report speaks of severe floggings with thick leather straps and of the fifteen-year-old girl stripped naked and savagely flogged in front of fifty other girls, suffering unbearable pain and humiliation. One survivor told the Australian Forde Inquiry:

Living at that hellish place has left me with enduring nightmares, emotional pain and torture, resentment, insecurity and self-loathing. I have never shaken the feeling of worthlessness. They [staff] told me I was no good — that's what I believe. I cannot express how these feelings have affected my life. I cannot shake feelings of self-hatred and guilt. My education and marriage have suffered, I could not be the mother I wanted to be to my children. On occasions, I know I have let them down by lacking the strength to stand up for the right thing. I get so depressed sometimes, because I know there wasn't any way to change how things turned out for me, and for those who depended on me. [The orphanage] took away my childhood. It left me no hope.

The House of Commons Committee investigating the Child Migration Scheme heard of one victim's first experience in Australia: 'Where it hit me particularly was when they dragged the brothers and sisters from one another, I can still hear the screams.' In its report, the same House of Commons Committee commented on how survivors often referred to the Christian Brothers as Christian Buggers and the Sisters of Mercy as the Sisters without Mercy.

The scandal of the Child Migration Scheme and the evil which pursued the unfortunate children into the orphanages is a sad story which can never have a happy ending and *Trust Me* reflects that sadness. But Lesley Pearse has a special gift which enables her to capture the personal turmoil in moving, gritty, authentic terms. Dulcie, May and Ross are real people permanently scarred by their childhood experiences. *Trust Me* may be fiction, but every word is engraved with the truth.

REMEMBER ME

Acknowledgements

To Pam Quick in Sydney, New South Wales, not only for all the information, books and pictures you passed on to me about the First Fleet, but for being there for me too. Without your keen interest, generosity with your time, unflagging help and support I could never have finished this book. When I come back to Sydney I owe you a slap-up dinner at least. Bless you.

I read dozens of books in my research for *Remember Me*, but these are the most outstanding ones.

To Brave Every Danger by Judith Cook. Truth is often stranger and more heroic than fiction, and Judith Cook's meticulously researched book on Mary Bryant of Fowey is truly inspiring and a must for anyone with a passion for history.

Fatal Shore by Robert Hughes. A fascinating, fabulous book on Australia's early years.

The First Twelve Years by Peter Taylor. Amazingly informative without being dry or dull. Good pictures too.

Orphans of History by Robert Holden. An often tear-jerking story of the forgotten children of the First Fleet.

The Floating Brothel by Sîan Rees. The story of the transported women who sailed on the *Juliana*. Shockingly informative.

Boswell's Presumptuous Task by Adam Sisman. A wonderful work on James Boswell.

Dr Johnson's London by Liza Picard. Wonderfully readable, an incredibly vivid image of London in the eighteenth century.

English Society in the Eighteenth Century by Roy Porter.

The Voyage to Botany Bay.

NORTH ATLANTIC OCEAN

London

Santa Cruz, Tenerife

AFRICA

Cape Town

SOUTH ATLANTIC OCEAN

Rio de Janeiro

INDIAN OCEAN

DUTCH EAST INDIES

Batavia

JAVA

Straits of Sunda

AUSTRALIA

NEW SOUTH WALES

Botany Bay

SOUTH PACIFIC OCEAN

Equator

Tahiti

Norfolk Island

--- Track of the 'Charlotte'

DEVON

Exeter

Plymouth

Devonport

Fowey

CORNWALL

Miles

Spring Cove

North Head

South Head

Rose Bay

Dawes Point

Sydney Cove

Port Jackson

Botany Bay

Captain Cook's Landing Place

N

Miles

Chapter one

1786

Mary gripped the rail of the dock tightly as the judge came back into the courtroom. The windows were small and dirty, letting in only a meagre light, but there was no mistaking the black cap over his yellowish wig, or the expectant hush from the gallery.

'Mary Broad. You will be taken from this place, back to whence you came, and there you will be hanged by the neck until dead,' he intoned, not even looking directly at her. 'May God have mercy on your soul.'

Mary's stomach lurched and her legs buckled under her. She knew only too well that hanging was the usual punishment for highway robbery, but a small part of her had clung to the belief that the judge would be merciful because she was such a young woman. She should have known better.

It was 20 March 1786, and Mary Broad was just a few weeks short of twenty. She was an average girl in every way, neither particularly tall nor short, not outstandingly pretty but not plain either. The only thing which set her apart from the other people on trial that day in the Lenten

Assizes was her country girl appearance. She had a clear complexion, which even after weeks of incarceration in Exeter Castle still had a faint glow. Her dark curly hair was tied neatly back with a ribbon and her grey worsted dress, though soiled from the gaol, was a plain, serviceable one.

A babble of noise broke out all around her, for the courtroom in Exeter was packed to capacity. Some of those present were friends and relatives of other prisoners to be tried that day, but the majority were mere spectators.

Yet the noise was not one of sympathy, nor outrage at such a severe sentence. Mary hadn't one friend in the whole room. A sea of grimy faces turned towards her, eyes alight with malicious glee, the slight movement wafting up the smell of their unwashed bodies to her nostrils. They wanted a reaction from her, be it tears, anger or a plea for mercy.

She wanted to cry out, to plead for her life, but the defiant streak in her which had led her to rob someone in the first place urged her to hold fast to her dignity if nothing else.

A guard's hand clamped down on her shoulder. It was too late now for anything but prayers.

Mary was barely aware of the ride on the cart back to Exeter Castle, the gaol she'd been held in since she was brought up from Plymouth following her arrest. She hardly noticed the rasp of the iron shackles on her ankles which connected to another heavy band around her waist, her seven fellow prisoners in the cart, or the jeering from the crowds in the streets. All she could think of was that the next time she saw the sky above her would be the day when she was taken to the gallows.

She lifted her face up to the weak afternoon sun. This morning, as she was brought out to go to the Assizes, the spring sunshine had almost blinded her after the darkness of the cells. She had looked about her eagerly, seen new leaves unfurling on the trees, heard pigeons cooing in a mating display, and foolishly taken all that as a good omen.

How wrong she was. She would never see her beloved Cornwall again. Never see her parents or sister Dolly either. All she could hope for was that they would never find out what she'd done. It was better that they should think she'd abandoned them for a new life in Plymouth, or even London, than endure the disgrace of hearing her life had been ended by a hangman's noose.

The sound of sobbing made Mary look at the woman sitting on her left. Her age was impossible to ascertain for her face was ravaged by pock-marks and she clutched a tattered brown cloak around her head to try to conceal it.

'Crying won't do no good,' Mary said, assuming the woman was to hang too. 'At least we know now what's coming to us.'

'I didn't steal anything,' the woman gasped out. 'I swear I didn't. It was someone else and they got away and left me to be blamed.'

Mary had heard that same story over and over again from other prisoners since her arrest in January. She had believed most of them at first, but she was harder now.

'Did you tell them that today?' she asked.

The woman nodded, her tears flowing even faster. 'But they said they had a witness to it.'

Mary had no heart to ask for the full story. She wanted to fill her lungs with clean air, fill her mind with the sights and sounds of the bustling town of Exeter, so that when she got back to the filthy, dark cell she would have some memories to draw on. Hearing this woman's tale of woe would only bring her down even further. Yet her natural sympathy wouldn't let her ignore the poor creature.

'Are you to be hanged too?' she asked.

The woman's head jerked round to look at Mary, surprise registering on her ravaged face. 'No. It was only a mutton pie they said I took.'

'Then you're luckier than me,' Mary sighed.

Once back in the Castle, thrust into a cell with around twenty other prisoners of both sexes, Mary silently found herself a space against the wall, sat down, adjusted the chains from her shackles so she could pull up her knees, wrapped her cloak around her tightly and leaned back to take stock of her situation.

It was a different cell to the one she'd been taken from this morning, better in as much as fresh air was coming in through a very high grille on the wall, the straw on the floor looked marginally cleaner, and the buckets weren't yet overflowing. But it still stank, with an all-pervading stench of dirt, body fluids, vomit, mould and human suffering which she inhaled with every breath.

There was an ominous hush. No one was talking loudly,

4

swearing or screaming abuse at their gaolers, as they had in the previous cell. In fact they were all sitting much as she was, submerged in thought or despair. Mary guessed that meant they were all sentenced to death, and as stunned by it as she was.

She couldn't see Catherine Fryer or Mary Haydon, the girls she'd been caught with, although they'd all been taken together to the Assizes that morning. She had no idea whether they were still back there waiting to be tried, or if they'd escaped with a lighter punishment than her.

Whatever the reason, she was glad they weren't there. She didn't want to remember that but for them she would never have considered robbing anyone.

It was too gloomy to see her other cellmates clearly, the only light coming from a lantern in the corridor the other side of the grilled door. But at a cursory glance, aside from the fact that there were men there too (her previous cell had been all women), they didn't appear very different from those she'd been imprisoned with for the last couple of months.

The age range was wide, from a girl of about sixteen, who was sobbing on an older woman's shoulder, to a man of perhaps fifty or even older. Three of the women might have been whores, judging by their colourful and even quite elegant gowns, but the remainder were very ragged, women with hard faces, bad teeth and stringy hair, and gaunt-faced men staring silently into space.

There were two women from her previous cell. Bridie, in a red gown with a tattered lace collar, had confided in Mary that she'd robbed a sailor while he slept. Peg was much older, one of the very ragged women, but she had steadfastly refused to say anything about her crime.

Mary guessed from the experiences in that cell that however subdued they all were now, within a few hours the naturally dominant types, like Bridie, would rally themselves to take charge. Much of this was bravado – it was necessary to appear strong if you were to survive prison. Fighting, shouting and demanding food or water from the gaolers was one way of sending out a message to your cellmates that you weren't to be pushed around.

Mary wondered if there would be any point in anyone asserting themselves now. She certainly didn't feel inclined to do so herself; all she wanted was to know how many days she had left to live.

Seeing Mary, Bridie hitched up her chains and hobbled across the cell towards her. 'Hanging?' she asked.

Mary nodded. 'You too?'

Bridie squatted down on the straw, her woebegone expression confirming it. 'That bastard of a judge,' she spat. ''E don't know what it's like for us. What good will hanging me do? Who'll look after the old folks now?'

Bridie had told Mary soon after she was brought to Exeter that she'd taken up whoring to keep her old parents from the parish. But there was something about her colourful clothes and even more colourful nature that suggested she hadn't had much of a moral struggle. Yet ever since Mary's first night in prison, Bridie had been kind and protective towards her, and Mary felt she was at heart a good woman.

'I thought you'd get off though, what with yer innocent

face an' all,' Bridie said, reaching out her dirty hand to caress Mary's cheek lightly. 'What happened?'

'The lady we robbed was in court,' Mary said sadly. 'She pointed me out.'

Bridie sighed in sympathy. 'Well, let's hope they get it over quick. There ain't nothin' worse than waiting to get a body down.'

Much later that night, Mary lay on the filthy straw-strewn floor among her fellow prisoners, who all appeared to be sleeping soundly, and found her thoughts slip back to her home and family at Fowey in Cornwall. She knew now that she had been born more fortunate than many of the women she'd met since leaving there.

Her father, William Broad, was a mariner, and although there had been hard times when he had no work, somehow he'd always managed to make sure his family never went hungry or lacked a fire. Mary could remember being cuddled up in bed with her sister Dolly, hearing the sea crashing against the harbour walls, yet feeling safe and secure, for however long her father was away at sea, he always left enough money to tide them over until he returned again.

Just thinking of Fowey with its tiny cottages and cobbled streets made a lump come up in her throat. The bustling harbour and town were never dull, for she knew everyone, and the Broads were a well-respected family. Grace, Mary's mother, set great store by respectability; she kept the tiny cottage spotlessly clean, and tried to instil in her daughters her high standards in cooking, housekeeping and sewing. Dolly, Mary's older sister, was the dutiful, obedient one, happy to follow her mother's example, and her dreams were only of finding a husband and having children and a home of her own.

Mary did not share Dolly's dreams. It was often said by friends and neighbours that she should have been a boy. She was clumsy with a needle and household tasks bored her. She was happiest when her father took her out sailing and fishing, for she felt at one with the sea and could handle a boat almost as well as he. She preferred male company too, for men and boys talked of exciting things, of lands overseas, of war, smuggling, and their work in the tin mines. She had no time for giggling, simpering girls who cared for nothing but gossip and the price of hair ribbon.

It was a thirst for adventure which made her want to leave Fowey, and she fully believed she could make her mark upon the world if she was just somewhere else. At the time Mary left, Dolly had said somewhat unkindly that it was just because she'd never had a sweetheart, and she was afraid no one would ever want her.

That wasn't true. Mary had no real desire for marriage. In fact she felt pity rather than envy for the girls she'd grown up with who were already saddled with two or three children. She knew that their lives grew tougher with each new mouth to feed, that they lived in fear of losing their husbands through drowning at sea or in an accident in the mines. But then life was hard for everyone in Cornwall, unless you were gentry. Work was either fishing, mining or going into service.

Dolly was in service with the Treffrys of Fowey as an under-housemaid, but Mary had stubbornly refused to follow her example. She didn't want to spend her days emptying slop pails and laying fires, at the beck and call of a hard-faced housekeeper. She'd seen no future in that. But the alternative was gutting and salting fish, and although she'd done that since childhood, and enjoyed the freedom to chatter as she worked, and the camaraderie of her workmates, no one ever got rich gutting fish. You smelt disgusting, and it was freezing in the winter. Mary would look at the bowed backs and gnarled fingers of the women who'd spent their whole life doing it, and knew it meant early death.

She had heard about Plymouth from the sailors. They said there were fine shops and big houses there, and opportunities for anyone with determination. She thought she might get work in one of the shops, for even if she couldn't read and write, she could add up quicker than her father.

Her parents had mixed feelings about her leaving. On the one hand they wanted to keep her at home in Fowey, but times were hard and they were struggling to support her. Perhaps, too, they hoped that a couple of years away from them in a respectable trade would settle her down, that she'd find a sweetheart and eventually marry.

Mary couldn't wait to get away, yet now as she lay on the hard cold floor of the prison cell and recalled the day when she left her home, she was filled with remorse.

It was very early in the morning, a beautiful July day without a cloud in the azure sky, and the sun was already warm. Her father had sailed off for France just a few days earlier, and Mary had insisted that only Dolly should come down to the harbour to see her off. She didn't want any further lectures from her mother about behaving like a lady on the boat, or being wary of strangers.

Her mother had never been given to displays of emotion, so it was a little unnerving as Mary went to kiss her cheek at the door to find herself suddenly being hugged tightly.

'Be a good girl,' her mother said, her voice cracking. 'Say your prayers and don't get into any mischief.'

Mary remembered how she hurried away with Dolly, giggling with excitement. It was only as she got to the end of the narrow street and glanced back that she saw her mother was still standing in the doorway, watching them. She looked so old, small and oddly vulnerable, for she hadn't yet braided her hair up for the day. It was as grey as her dress, making her almost disappear into the stone of the cottage. Even without being able to see her face clearly, Mary knew she was crying. Yet Grace still managed to wave a cheerful goodbye.

'I don't know why you think Plymouth will be better than here,' Dolly said waspishly as they got down to the harbour and saw the boat waiting. 'I bet you could go right round the world and never find anywhere so pretty.'

'Don't be like that,' Mary retorted, thinking Dolly was jealous. Her sister was far prettier than her, her eyes as blue as the sky above, her complexion clear and pink, and she had a dear little upturned nose. But Mary had a feeling that Dolly often wished she was more daring, and perhaps resented that her life was already mapped out for her.

'I can't help it,' Dolly replied in a small voice. 'I'm going to miss you so much. Don't stay away too long.'

Mary remembered how she'd hugged her sister then, and said something about how she would make her fortune and send for Dolly to join her. If she had known that was going to be the last time she'd see her, she would have told her how much she loved her. Yet that sunny morning she couldn't get on the boat fast enough. It didn't even cross her mind that she might fail in Plymouth.

What Mary hadn't anticipated was that hundreds of girls came off the boats in Plymouth every week looking for work, and it was the literate, the prettiest and the ones with good references who got the best positions. All she landed was a job in a seamen's ale house, washing the pots and scrubbing the floors. Her bed consisted of a few sacks in the cellar.

It was around Michaelmas when the landlord threw her out. He said she'd stolen some money, but that wasn't true. All she'd done was refuse to let him have his way with her. Without a reference she couldn't get another job, and she was too proud to go home to Fowey to hear 'I told you so'.

The moment she met Thomas Coogan down by the harbour, she knew that she was on the way to hell in a handcart. Surely no decent young woman would allow a complete stranger to buy her a dinner, let him hold her hand, and not run a mile when he suggested she stayed with him until she found another job? But there was something about his lean, bony face, the sparkle in his blue eyes, and the stories he told her of voyages to France and Spain that captivated her.

Thomas wasn't bound by any of the rules Mary had been brought up with. He cared nothing for the King, Church, or indeed any authority. He had a gentlemanly manner and was fastidious about his appearance, and he was more fun to be with than anyone she'd ever met before.

Maybe it was partly because he seemed to desire her so much, to hold her and kiss her. No man had ever wanted her that way before, they saw her just as a friend. Thomas said she was beautiful, that her grey eyes were like a brewing storm and her lips made to be kissed.

That first day with him was utterly magical. It rained hard and he took her into a tavern by the harbour and dried her cloak in front of the fire. He introduced her to rum too. She didn't like the taste, or the way it burned her throat, but she did like the way he leaned forward and licked her lips lightly with the point of his tongue. 'It tastes like nectar on you,' he whispered. 'Drink up, my lovely, it will warm you all over.'

He made her feel so wanton, her whole body seemed to glow, and it wasn't just the rum. It was his wit, the feel of his hand in hers, the suggestion that she was on the brink of something dangerous yet wonderful too.

With hindsight she ought to have suspected there was something amiss when he never attempted to bed her. He kissed her passionately and told her he loved her, but it never went any further than that. At the time Mary had

12

foolishly believed his caution was out of love and respect for her, but it was only later she discovered the truth.

Thomas Coogan cared for no one but himself. He was a pick-pocket, and when he'd spotted her crying down by the harbour, he knew her well-scrubbed, innocent country girl appearance would make her an ideal accomplice. All it took was a few sympathetic words to win her trust.

It never crossed Mary's mind in the first few weeks after meeting him that as they stood arm in arm looking in shop windows or strolled around the market, he was often engaged in helping himself to someone's pocket-book, fob-watch or other valuable with his spare hand. She was too enamoured with his charm, excited by his interesting friends and acquaintances, and bowled over by his generosity to her to study him closely.

By the time she did become aware of it, she was so entrenched in his easy, fun way of life that he could have told her he was a grave robber and she wouldn't have turned a hair. When he disappeared just after Christmas, leaving her in the dwelling-house he'd taken her to, she was inconsolable.

The chances were that he'd been caught by the constables, and that was what made her fall in with Mary Haydon and Catherine Fryer. She didn't want to lose face with these two cut-purses, whom Thomas had held in such high esteem. They appeared so worldly, so very daring, and she needed money to pay the rent on Thomas's room for when he came back.

At first she was just a lookout while the other two

snipped off purses in the crowded streets and markets. Sometimes she caused a diversion by pretending to faint or claiming that she'd had her own purse snatched. But the day came when Catherine said it was time she took on some of the danger herself, and when they saw the small, neatly dressed woman walking home through the main street with her arms full of parcels, it appeared to be the perfect initiation.

Maybe if Mary hadn't been so anxious to prove her courage, she would merely have tripped the woman up and sped off with just one of her parcels. But instead she grabbed the woman's pretty silk hat with one hand, and scooped up everything she dropped in alarm, throwing the parcels to the other Mary and Catherine before running for it. Unluckily for them, people gave chase, cornered them in an alley and called for the constables.

Most of the details of Mary's arrest and imprisonment in Plymouth were hazy to her now, for the journey to Exeter later on eclipsed everything else. It took four days in an open-topped cart where she was shackled to three other women, two of whom were her supposed friends but berated her most of the way for getting them caught too. It was January, and the icy wind swept across the bleak moors, almost cutting them in half with its ferocity. If they wanted to relieve themselves, all the women had to get down together, with the guard leering at them. Every step was torture, for the shackles dug into their tender skin and they weren't yet practised at moving together. At nights they were thrown into a stable at an inn, with bread and water the only nourishment they received.

Mary thought she would die of the cold, in fact she hoped fervently that she would, if only to shut out the scorn and ridicule of her companions and the knowledge that her crime, highway robbery, was a hanging offence.

On her first night at Exeter Castle it was Bridie who had comforted her and assured her she would become accustomed to the rats, lice, dirt, stale bread and using a slop pail in front of everyone. Mary supposed that she had now, in as much as she accepted that was all part and parcel of prison life and she deserved punishment for what she'd done. But she couldn't accept that she was to die in a few days' time, and would never be free to walk country lanes, to watch the sea breaking on the shore, and see the sun set again.

She wept then, for failing her parents and bringing shame to the family, and for not listening to her conscience when she knew that stealing was wrong.

It was a well-known fact that as many as half of those sentenced to death would get some sort of reprieve. In the next three days Mary's fellow prisoners talked of nothing else, everyone hoping they would be among the lucky ones.

But Mary was no fool. She knew you needed friends on the outside, a concerned and kindly master or mistress, a member of the clergy, or even a friend with money to plead for you. As the hours and days ticked slowly by, it became clear which of her companions were that fortunate. They were the ones who got food, drink, money and even clean clothes sent in.

Mary looked enviously at the young girl and the woman she knew now to be her aunt, as they ate hot meat pies brought in by one of the gaolers. They had been charged with theft from a lodging-house, but had been protesting their innocence ever since their arrest. Now, judging by the pies and the blankets they'd been given, maybe they had been telling the truth, for someone on the outside was obviously working for their release.

Yet some of the prisoners, even those without any hope of reprieve, had become quite jovial in the last couple of days. Maybe it was because in their eyes a quick death was preferable to the misery of a long prison sentence, or a lingering death through gaol fever. There was also a certain amount of status in being hanged, for huge crowds gathered to watch. If they could go to their death with dignity and courage and get the admiration of the watching rabble, they might become heroic figures, maybe even a legend.

Dick Sullion was one man who felt this way, and he had cheered Mary considerably with his humour and his philosophy of life. Like her, he had been charged with High Toby, the common name for highway robbery. But Dick's crime fitted the description more accurately than Mary's did, for he'd lain in wait on isolated roads for unwary travellers, taking not only their valuables but their horses too.

He was a big man, close to six feet, with a ruddy face, wide shoulders and an irrepressible sense of humour. The first morning after her trial, Mary had woken to hear him singing some bawdy ale-house song about going to the scaffold drunk. She had of course assumed he was drunk then, for those who had money or goods to bribe their gaolers could be inebriated all day and night. But as she sat up, he smiled at her, and his blue eyes were clear and bright.

'No sense in lying around moping,' he said as if to explain himself. 'I've had a good life, and I reckon it's better to hang than lose my wits and looks in a place like this.'

'Some of us would rather sleep than think on that,' she retorted.

Mary had learned in her first few days of imprisonment back in January that it was advisable to befriend someone tough and wily as a protector, and as Dick appeared to fit the bill in every way, she allowed him to move closer to her, and talked to him.

She soon discovered that Dick had no money left to buy drink or extra food. He told her he'd blown all he had in the first few weeks before his trial. But even if he couldn't make her last few days more comfortable in a physical sense, he was strong, tough and knew the ropes, and his chatter and laughter cheered her.

Dick was Cornish too. It was good to be able to talk about home with him, and it wasn't long before she told him how she felt about her crime and letting her family down.

'Ain't no good worrying about that,' he said, his local dialect as thick and reassuring as her father's. 'We all do what we gotta do to survive. It's the government's fault we've come to this. The high taxes, the Enclosures Acts, they rob us blind at every turn and live in palaces while us lot starve. I took from those who could afford it, so did you. Serves 'em right, I say.'

Mary, who had been brought up to be honest and God-fearing, didn't entirely agree with him about that, but she wasn't going to say so. 'Aren't you afraid of dying though?' she asked instead.

He shrugged. 'Been too close to it so many times, it don't have no meaning any more. What's hanging compared with a naval flogging? I had my first when I was only sixteen, now that's summat to be scared of, pain so bad you cry out to death. Hanging's quick. Don't you worry, little one, I'll hold your hand right up to the end.'

Mary took some comfort in Dick's words. She made up her mind that if she was to die, she'd do so bravely.

Four days after her trial, around ten in the morning, the gaoler came to the cell door and called out for Nancy and Anne Brown. They were the aunt and niece accused of robbing a dwelling-house. He said they had been acquitted due to new evidence and were free to leave.

Despite her own predicament, Mary was delighted for them, and got up to hug and kiss them goodbye. She'd talked to the two women at some length in the previous couple of days and was sure they were as innocent as they claimed to be. They had barely left the cell when the gaoler called out a further four names, three men's and Mary's.

'You lot come with me,' he said curtly.

Mary turned to Dick in dismay, thinking she was to be led to the gallows then and there.

Dick put one big hand on her shoulder and squeezed it. 'Don't reckon it's that,' he said confidently. 'At the end of each quarter session they go through the list and pick out likely folk for transportation. My guess is that's what they want you for.'

The gaoler roared at them to follow him, giving Mary no time to say a proper goodbye to either Dick or Bridie.

As she shuffled along the dark passage behind William, Able and John, her fellow cellmates, their shackles clanking against the rough stone floor, she heard Dick's voice boom out behind her. 'Seven years, that's all it is till you're free, my little one. Be brave and strong and you'll see the end of it.'

Able, a sickly-looking man in his thirties, glanced back at Mary. 'What does he know?' he said dourly. 'I heard tell they ain't sending no more felons to the Americas now the war's over.'

Mary had heard the same thing too while she was in Plymouth. If it was true, it would be a relief, for she'd been brought up with horror stories passed on by sailors of the terrors that lay in store in that far-off land. Convicts there were treated the same as the black slaves, starved, beaten, made to work on the land till they dropped dead from exhaustion. Yet if not to America, where would they be sent, and would it be any better?

Once out in the yard, Mary saw other prisoners lined up, including Mary Haydon and Catherine Fryer, her old partners in crime. There were five women in all, and some fifteen or sixteen men. Mary Haydon tossed her head and looked the other way when she saw Mary, but Catherine glowered at her, so clearly they still held her responsible for their plight.

A judge, or at least Mary assumed that's what he was, by his wig and gown, came down the few steps into the yard, flanked by a couple of other men, then read aloud from a piece of parchment.

Mary could make no sense of what he was reading. She heard 'At Assizes and general delivery of the gaol of our Lord the King,' then what sounded like a string of 'Sirs' who were all unknown to her. It wasn't until she heard her own name mentioned that she began to listen more intently. At the words, 'His Majesty has been graciously pleased to extend the royal mercy on them,' Mary's heart leaped. But as the judge read on, her heart sank again, for it was as Dick had said, mercy on condition they be transported for seven years.

After the judge had left the prison yard, leaving the prisoners there alone with the guards, they turned to one another, their delight that they weren't to be hanged mingling with an acute fear of what transportation would mean.

'I never met anyone who ever came back from it,' one man said gloomily. 'They must have all died.'

'I know a man that did come back,' another man retorted loudly. 'He had money in his pockets too.'

Mary tried to make sense of the babble of conflicting opinions around her. While she personally felt that a seven-year sentence, however hard, had to be better than hanging, every single person in the yard appeared to be more knowledgeable on the subject than she was, so there was no point in her volunteering that opinion. But as the woman standing next to her began to cry, she put her arm around her to comfort her.

'It's got to be better than dying,' she said softly. 'We'll be out in the fresh air, we might even be able to escape.'

Able, who was standing in front of her, must have heard what she said for he turned to her, a scornful expression on his face. 'That's if we don't die on the voyage,' he said.

Mary thought privately that he wasn't long for this world anyway. He had a hacking cough, he was very thin and the only one of them in the cell who showed no eagerness when the daily mouldy bread was dished out.

'As long as I'm still breathing, then I'll still hope,' she retorted staunchly.

Less than an hour later, doors in the prison yard opened and two large horse-drawn carts were led in.

The prisoners had all pondered on why they had been left out in the yard, but no one had anticipated they would be moved from Exeter Castle that same day. But that was what was planned, and without any further delay, they were chained together into groups of five and ordered up on to the carts. Once again, Mary found herself alongside Catherine and Mary. On the other side of her was the woman she'd comforted earlier, whose name was Elizabeth Cole, and another called Elizabeth Baker. Behind their bench were five men, one of them Able.

For the first hour, as the cart slowly trundled its way out through Exeter, Catherine Fryer and Mary Haydon kept up a volley of abuse towards Mary.

'It's all your fault,' Catherine repeated again and again. 'You brought us to this.'

Elizabeth Cole, who went by the name of Bessie, squeezed Mary's hand in sympathy, and finally called a halt to it.

'Shut yer mouths, you two,' she snapped at them. 'We're all in this together now, whether we like it or not. There ain't no sense in blaming Mary, you'd have been caught before long anyway. Besides, none of the rest of us wants to hear all that stuff.'

Mary was touched by Bessie's intervention. She was an odd-looking woman, red-haired and fat, with a cast in one eye and several teeth missing, but the fact she'd been brave enough to speak out suggested she wasn't as downtrodden as she looked.

There was an echo of agreement from the men sitting behind them, and perhaps that finally persuaded the two women to stop, for they lapsed into silence.

After a little while one of the men in the back prodded Mary. 'Sweet-talk the guards into telling you where we're heading,' he whispered.

'Why me?' she whispered back.

'You're the bonniest,' he replied.

Up until that moment Mary had fully believed she had absolutely no assets – no money or property she could bribe anyone with, no influential friends. All she had was the clothes she was wearing and they were worn and soiled. But as she glanced at the row of women, she saw she was younger, healthier and stronger than all of them.

Mary and Catherine had been living by theft for years before she met them. Back then she'd been fooled by their gaudy clothes into thinking they were superior to her in every way. But cheap silk didn't wear well, not in prison, and their pinched features and grey skin, the hollow look in their eyes and their gutter language showed up what they really were. As for Bessie and Elizabeth, while she didn't yet know what crimes they had committed, or anything of their family background, they both had that worn-out appearance she had observed so often among the very poorest back home in Fowey.

All at once she saw a chance for herself. She was young and strong, no man had spoiled her, she knew she had a quicker mind than most, and she had determination.

She waited until Bessie asked to relieve herself, and once all the women had climbed down from the cart, Mary positioned herself so that she shielded her squatting friend from the guard with her skirt, and smiled warmly at him.

'Where are you taking us?' she asked. 'Is it back to the prison in Plymouth, or straight to a boat for the Americas?'

He was a hard-looking man, with brown, broken teeth and a battered hat pulled down over his slanty eyes.

'You're bound for the prison hulks at Devonport,' he said with an evil grin. 'Don't reckon you'll get much beyond there.'

Mary gasped involuntarily. She might not have seen a

prison hulk but she knew their evil reputation. They were old warships, moored in estuaries and creeks, the government's answer to overcrowding in prisons. The responsibility for running them was passed over to private individuals whose only interest was making as much money as possible from each prisoner. It was said that the unlucky felons who got sent to them would die either of starvation or of overwork within the first year. For the sideline of these notorious hell-holes was that the prisoners were forced to do slave labour on land, usually building 'hards' along the river bank.

'I didn't think they sent women there,' she said, her voice trembling.

'Times are a'changing,' he grinned. 'You'd better pretty yourself up if you want to make it off there alive.'

Mary gulped and looked him in the eye. She knew gaolers and guards were punished too harshly to dare let anyone escape, however 'nice' a prisoner was to them. But he probably thought she was stupid enough to be ignorant of this and hoped she might make up to him imagining he would help her in return.

'But the judge said it was transportation.' She forced herself to squeeze out a few tears.

'They mean it to be,' he said, his voice softening. 'But they can't send no one to the Americas since the war. They tried Africa, but that didn't work. There's talk of a place called Botany Bay, but that's on the other side of the world.'

Mary vaguely remembered the sailors in the ale house she'd once worked in talking about a man called Captain

Cook who had claimed for England a country that was on the other side of the world. She wished now she'd listened properly, but at the time it held as little importance for her as whether King George was really mad, or what grand ladies wore to balls in London.

'Do you think that's where we're bound then?' she asked.

He shrugged and scowled at the other women who were crowding around Mary to hear what he was saying. 'Get back on the cart,' he said curtly. 'We've got a fair few miles to cover before dark.'

Once back on the cart, Mary decided there was no point in thinking upon anything more than the present. It might be uncomfortable in the cart, but it was better to be out in the spring sunshine than in a stinking gaol. She would keep herself poised for an opportunity for escape.

She doubted there was any hope of that before Devonport. If the guards on this journey kept to the same routine as those on the way from Plymouth to Exeter, she and her companions would remain shackled together constantly.

But there was a faint possibility that the chains would be removed when they had to get into the small boat to be rowed out to the hulks. If so, she could jump out and swim for it. She smiled inwardly. It was a very faint hope, for surely any guard worth his salt would anticipate such an attempt, but then few people knew how to swim, even sailors like her father couldn't. The thought of swimming was pleasing, to be able to wash off the prison stink and make for a stretch of coastline she knew well. It was worth any risk, and even if she couldn't do it then, maybe she could jump from the side of the hulk at night.

But as the afternoon shadows lengthened and it grew colder, Mary's spirits began to sink again. Even if she could escape, where would she make for? She couldn't go back to Cornwall, she'd be caught again in no time. And how would she get anywhere else with no money, wearing filthy clothes and boots with holes in them?

By dusk Mary was in too much pain to think beyond lying down. Even the slightest movement from herself or one of her companions made the iron shackles bite into her ankles. She had torn a strip off her petticoat to act as a bandage beneath the iron, but the cotton was stiff with dried blood now, and it rasped against the wounds rather than protecting them. She had hunger pains in her stomach, her back was so stiff she doubted she could walk, and she was shivering with cold.

Four days later, when the cart eventually reached Devonport, Mary's companions were too deeply demoralized even to react to their first sight of the prison ship moored out in the river. It had been raining solidly for the past two days, and they were all soaked through to the skin. Many of them were feverish and everyone was exhausted through lack of sleep due to the cold in the barns and sheds they'd been locked into overnight.

There had been no conversation on the cart today. The only sounds were groans, sneezing, coughing, sniffing and the clank of chains as they vainly attempted to get more comfortable. Able was now seriously ill, unable to sit upright, and with each strained cough he brought up blood.

'That's yer new home, the *Dunkirk*,' the guard said, turning in his seat to grin maliciously as he pointed at the old hulk moored out in the river. 'She ain't a very pretty ship, that's for sure, but then you lot ain't so pretty either.'

Mary had suffered as much as her companions, but whether it was because she was the youngest and the most healthy at the outset, or just because she had kept her mind active by thinking about escape, she appeared to be the only one affected by the sight of the hulk.

With its masts cut down to mere stumps and surrounded by wispy sea mist, it had the eerie look of an ancient wreck waiting for one good storm to dismember it. But worse still than its appearance was the putrid stench wafting from it on the wind.

Mary was already shivering so violently that her teeth were chattering, but she felt an even icier chill run down her spine, and her empty stomach lurched with nausea. This, she sensed, was going to be real hell, a hundred times worse than Exeter Castle.

She thought she'd been in hell there, and was glad when they'd first left, delighting in the fresh air and sunshine. But all too soon she'd found herself wishing she was back in the Castle. Late the previous night, cold, wet and hungry, every bone in her body screaming in pain, she would even have accepted a noose being put round her neck to end it all. Now it seemed there was even more horror in store for her.

'Ain't no use looking like that,' the guard said, and leaned back in his seat to give Mary a poke with the stick. He'd already struck several of them when they took too long getting off and on the cart. 'That's the wages of sin out there. You lot deserve it.'

A few days earlier Mary would have cursed him, spat in his face or even lashed out at him, but she had no fight left in her.

'Are we to be taken out there now?' she asked instead, her quick mind telling her she'd better keep on the right side of him.

'No, it's too late,' he said, touching the horses with the whip to get them to move. 'You got another night in a warehouse first.'

It wasn't just the occupants of the two carts from Exeter who spent the night in the warehouse. They had hardly got inside and slumped down on to the dirt floor when the doors opened again and another couple of dozen people joined them.

They were in an even worse state than Mary's party, having come all the way from Bristol. Their clothes were mere rags, they all looked feverish, and gangrene had clearly taken a hold of a gaping wound in one of the men's legs, for the smell was unmistakable.

There was a feeble attempt at conversation, questions asked about friends who had been incarcerated in Exeter Castle and Bristol's Bridewell, but the main thing everyone was concerned about was how long they would be kept in the prison ship before being transported.

'I heard a party escaped from Gravesend,' one fierce-looking man from Bristol claimed. 'The guards opened fire on them and killed a couple, but the rest got away. Since then they've kept everyone in chains.'

Bessie, sitting next to Mary, began to cry. 'We might just as well been hanged,' she sobbed out. 'I can't take no more.'

The same thought was in Mary's head too, but faced with Bessie's utter dejection she swept it away. 'We will be all right,' she insisted, putting her arms around the woman and hugging her tightly. 'We're just cold, wet and hungry now, we can't think straight. In a day or two everything will look different.'

'You're so brave,' Bessie whispered. 'Aren't you scared too?'

'No,' Mary replied without a second thought. 'Not now I know I'm not going to be hanged.'

Later that night as Mary lay in a huddle with the other women, desperately trying to draw some warmth from their bodies, she realized she really wasn't scared. She was angry that people could treat others so cruelly, ashamed of the crime that had brought her to this, apprehensive about what would come next, but not scared. In fact, when she thought about it, she'd never been fearful of anything. She had taught herself to swim at six by just plunging into the sea. After she'd discovered she could keep afloat, the sea held no terrors for her. Nor did anything else. She was the one who always took dares, found risk exciting. Even when she first found out how

Thomas made a living she wasn't horrified – it just seemed daring, a bit of a lark.

She remembered then how her father had always remarked on how sharp she was. She had always been much smarter than Dolly and her friends of a similar age. She grasped things quickly, was curious about how things worked, and retained the information. She could almost hear her father boasting to the neighbours that Fowey was too dull for Mary, and that he had no doubt she'd come home one day having made her fortune.

How was he going to hold his head up when her recorded crime and punishment was seen in the *Western Flyer*? He couldn't read himself, but there were plenty of people in Fowey who could and would be only too glad to pass on such a shocking piece of news.

Knowing she was only about forty miles from home brought on an unbearable pang of homesickness. She could imagine her mother sitting on a stool in front of the fire, some mending in her hands. Mary took after her in looks, the same thick curly hair, which she braided tightly round her head, and the same grey eyes. When Mary was small she could remember her mother undoing the braids at night, running her fingers through them till her hair fell in a dark shiny storm on her shoulders. It transformed her from being just an ordinary woman into a beauty, and Mary and Dolly often asked why she didn't leave it loose for everyone to admire.

'Vanity is a deadly sin,' she'd reply, yet she always smiled as if it pleased her to have a beautiful secret, unseen by anyone but her own family. She kept her feelings secret too, and the girls had learned from a very early age to gauge them purely by her actions. When she was angry she banged pots and poked the fire vigorously; when worried she was silent. Her way of showing affection was no more than a tender stroke of the face or a squeeze of the shoulder. Yet now that Mary knew she would never see her again, those little gestures seemed so precious and important.

She remembered how her mother had hugged her as she left home that last morning in Fowey. She hadn't really hugged her back, for she was impatient to leave. The last memory her mother would have of her was that. A daughter who went off giggling carelessly. Never to be seen again.

Chapter two

Thankfully the rain had stopped when the prisoners were ordered out of the warehouse the following morning. But the sky was still grey, with a keen wind blowing off the river which made them all huddle together for warmth.

Breakfast had been nothing more than water and a lump of stale bread, and as Mary looked across at the prison ship *Dunkirk*, and saw it really was as decrepit as it had appeared at dusk yesterday, she guessed the provisions there would be no better.

Yet her spirits were a little higher than on the previous day. Despite her wet clothes, she had slept quite well, and at least there was no further travelling today. She thought escape was out of the question for the time being. Apart from her shackles, which she now doubted would be removed, the quay was busy with watchful Marines, all carrying muskets.

Dozens of boats of all sizes were bobbing around on the water, ferrying passengers across the river and carrying goods to the bigger ships anchored at deep water. Mary couldn't smell the prison ship today, but whether that was because the wind had changed, or she had imagined the smell last night, she couldn't guess. It was good to breathe in the salty air, and if she ignored her fellow prisoners and her hunger, and just drank in the sights, sounds and smells, it was almost like being back in Fowey.

At midday Mary was still waiting on the quay, still chained to her four companions. So far several small groups of male prisoners had been rowed out to the *Dunkirk*, and they had watched them climb up the ladder to the deck, then disappear from view. But the women's interest in this procedure had long since waned. Most were trying to improve their appearance, combing or plaiting their hair, attending to wounds on their ankles from the chains, and any who were carrying belongings were sifting through them, sorting out another dress or petticoat.

Mary had no belongings beyond a comb, and that had been given to her by another prisoner at Exeter, so her grooming could go no further than trying to remove as many lice as possible from her hair. They had been provided with a bucket of water to wash their faces and hands that morning, but she longed to be able to strip off her dirty clothes and wash herself completely. She hadn't done that since before her arrest, and she felt she must stink.

None of the other women seemed that concerned about their filthy state, but then Mary had discovered almost as soon as she left home that the high standard of cleanliness her mother had instilled in her was rare. When she confided in Bessie about how she felt, the other woman looked at her askance. 'We can't look that bad,' she said. 'Those Marines over there are giving us the glad eye.'

Mary glanced at the group of men surreptitiously and observed that she was being singled out for particular attention from them. She thought that red jackets, well-fitting white breeches and highly polished boots gave almost any man, however homely-looking, an unfair advantage over civilians. But she wasn't going to delude herself that they were looking at her because she was outstandingly attractive.

Mary had been around seamen all her life, and she knew the first thing they did when they got off a ship was look for a woman. Mostly they landed up with whores, and with that came the near certainty of disease.

These Marines were in a slightly different position to seamen. They would be guarding the prisoners, both male and female, here and on the transport ship later. Mary guessed they knew they'd get little if any shore leave. It stood to reason they were all hoping that amongst this ragged, demoralized bunch of women, there would be some eager to meet their sexual needs. A young, fresh-faced and disease-free country girl would be their ideal. Mary thought she'd sooner throw herself off the *Dunkirk* in her chains than be used that way.

It was mid-afternoon before Mary's group were rowed over to the hulk. The chains linking them together had been removed, but they were still shackled from their ankles to their waists. As they drew closer to the prison ship, Mary saw the sides were green and slimy with weed, and the smell of human effluent gradually increased until the women were gagging.

Once up the slippery ladder, they were lined up to be examined and measured, and their crime recorded.

'Mary Broad,' a young Marine called out, and ordered her to stand in front of a rule marked on the broken-off mast. 'Five feet four,' he called out to another man who was recording it. 'Grey eyes, black hair, no visible scars. Crime highway robbery. Seven years' transportation.'

As soon as the whole group had been similarly dealt with, and each of them been handed a worn, stinking blanket, a hatch was opened and seamen pushed them roughly through it, down a steep companionway. Bessie tripped on her shackles and fell the last few feet, letting out a cry of pain. They were in a narrow area which appeared to lead on to the guards' quarters, then another hatch was opened.

The stench that burst out hit the women like walking into a brick wall, and they all moved back involuntarily, horror on every face. Each one of them had grown used to filth in all its forms in the past few weeks, but this was something far beyond anything they'd experienced previously.

'Get in there,' the guard shouted, hitting at them with a stick to make them climb down the stairs. 'You'll soon get used to it. We have.'

Mary resisted, but the guard hit her on the shoulder and forced her down through the hatch into what must have been the hold when the vessel was still sailing. The first thing she glimpsed was a sea of ghostly white faces, and when her eyes grew more used to the gloom, she saw a series of wooden shelves which were to be their beds, four women to each. There was some air and light though, coming from open hatches on the seaward side of the ship and a further grille at the far end through which Mary could just make out the male prisoners' quarters. The evil smell came from the floor, which was awash with the contents of overflowing slop buckets. Clearly this was one place which was never cleaned.

Mary realized this meant that rats, bugs and lice would be living here in their hundreds with the women. Just to look at their haggard grey faces, stringy hair and bony bodies was proof that the diet was one of starvation. Fever could sweep round in one night and under these conditions would claim them all.

She thought she would be lucky if she survived long enough to be transported.

An hour or two later Mary was as despairing as everyone else. All around her was moaning, groaning, crying and the occasional demented scream from a woman who appeared to have lost her wits. One woman was suckling a newborn baby, and Mary was told it had been delivered down here by the other women.

The beams were too low for them to stand up, so there was no alternative but to sit or lie on the wooden shelves. When the evening meal, a thin floury soup and stale bread, was brought in, the women fought to get it, and by the time Mary managed to reach the pot, everything was gone. The rats didn't even wait for total darkness to fall, they scuttled along the beams and under the bed shelves, and even jumped across bodies.

But to Mary, the most terrifying prospect was that she could expect nothing better. She had learned they were never allowed up on deck, their quarters were never cleaned, they couldn't wash their clothes, and the slop buckets were emptied only once a day.

She fell asleep eventually, tucked between Bessie on the inside, closest to the ship's hull, and a girl called Nancy who was only fourteen. Taking up the outside position on their shelf was Anne, a woman of over fifty.

Mary's last thought before sleep overcame her was that there had to be some way to escape. The other women had insisted there wasn't, but from what she'd observed of them, they were all dull-witted.

She would find a way.

Over the next few days Mary watched and listened to her fellow prisoners. While her whole being wanted to hammer on the door, scream for release, even to insist that she'd rather be hanged than endure this, she knew she had to control herself. By staying quiet, learning about the running of the hulk and observing the other women, she would arm herself with knowledge.

She noted that many of the women were so deeply immersed in their misery that they barely moved from their sleeping places and hardly spoke at all, and she guessed they hoped that death would come speedily to release them.

At first Mary had every sympathy with them, but as she began slowly to accept her imprisonment and get to know those women who still had a spark of life and hope in them, so her feelings for the remainder turned to scorn and irritation.

Almost all of the women who talked and even found something to laugh about now and then had been convicted of theft. Nancy, the fourteen-year-old, had taken some food home to her family from the house in Bodmin where she was a scullery maid. Anne had taken a dress from the laundry where she worked in Truro. There was a woman who had acted as a look-out for a cut-purse, and another had helped herself to a blanket left out on a washing-line to air. Yet another had stolen a couple of silver teaspoons. None of the women were hardened criminals, they had all committed opportunist crimes, out of need.

When Mary admitted she was convicted of High Toby, she saw awe on the faces of her audience. Back in Exeter Castle, she had learned the hierarchy of crime, and a highway robber was at the top of the pile. To Mary it seemed a little absurd that snatching a hat and parcels should be considered in the same light as waylaying a stage-coach. But she supposed she had technically robbed on the highway, as opposed to stealing from a shop or dwelling-house.

While she knew that in reality she was exactly the same as most of these women, just another country girl who had fallen by the wayside, she saw immediately that it would be smarter to keep that to herself. Status was as crucial to survival as food and drink. She would make it work for her.

Another thing she observed was that not all the women were filthy and in rags. Four of them had fairly decent clothes, their hair looked as if it had been washed recently, and they were plumper, less strained and hollow-eyed. Because of their appearance, and the fact that some of the prisoners gave them the cold shoulder, it didn't take long for Mary to realize these women had friends among the guards and Marines. Clearly they were trading their bodies for extra comforts.

'They ought to be ashamed of themselves,' one old biddy exclaimed, pursing her lips in disgust. By the way she coughed she had to be in the grip of consumption. 'Dirty whores!'

Mary had always believed that any woman who sold her body was beyond redemption. In Plymouth she had seen whores grappling with seamen in alleys, and heard about the terrible diseases they passed on, and she felt almost faint with disgust.

Yet as the days slowly passed on the *Dunkirk*, and the horrors seemed to grow greater rather than diminish, she found herself looking at the whole question a little differently. While she still thought that offering her body in return for food and a clean dress would be the surest way to hell and damnation, surely she was in hell already? She intended to survive at all costs, and if sacrificing her chastity would prevent a slow death from starvation, she was prepared to do it.

It wasn't just the desire for more food and the chance

to get out of this stinking hold into fresh air once in a while. Escape was most prevalent in Mary's mind, and for that she needed her chains to be removed. While there was no certainty that a lover would do this for her, she hoped she could persuade him to. Maybe if he grew to like her enough he'd even help her escape.

Sadly, she had no idea how to go about getting a 'friend' on the upper decks. The ugly brutes who came to collect the slop bucket or bring the rations had to be the lowliest of the crew, and they were the only ones she had any contact with, and that only briefly.

At the end of her third week she was growing desperate. Her twentieth birthday had passed at the end of April, and May Day, with all its happy memories of village celebrations, had made her spirits plummet even further. She would stand all day at the open hatch, looking out seawards, watching the sunshine glint on the water, aching so badly to be out in it that she thought she would lose her reason.

She knew all forty women's names, where they came from, their crimes and about their families. She had even seen a change in Catherine Fryer and Mary Haydon's attitude towards her, perhaps because they saw she was stronger and quicker-witted than anyone else, and it was better to be on a winning side than a losing one.

Mary had spoken to some of the men prisoners too, at least shouted to them through the barred grille. Because they were often taken out to work ashore, she'd learned from them the names of the few humane officers on board.

Lieutenant Captain Watkin Tench was the one who had captured Mary's interest. The men said he was young, and that they found him fair and reasonable, an intelligent man, who had been held prisoner himself during the American war. He sounded perfect for Mary's plan, but as yet she had no idea how to get his attention.

She had gone out of her way to befriend all the women who were labelled as whores. It wasn't difficult as they were only too glad of someone taking an interest in them, and Mary discovered that in the main they were very like her, a bit daring, more amusing than the other women, and warm-hearted.

But although they often gave her titbits of food or a new ribbon for her hair, and passed on rags when she was menstruating, they were all tight-mouthed about their men and how they got themselves picked in the first place. Mary could understand why. They weren't going to take the risk of losing their lovers and the comforts that came with them to another prisoner.

She had thought of picking a fight with another woman, to create such a big disturbance that she would be hauled out of the hold. But it was likely she'd be flogged for that, and even if she got to meet Tench, under those circumstances it was hardly likely to endear her to him.

One evening, the pot of soup and bread were brought in as usual, and as always, the strongest pushed their way forward to grab the lion's share. It was only the fear of dying of starvation that made the women fight to get to the soup. It was invariably cold and watery, mainly barley with a few bits of vegetable and strands of rank

41

meat. It had taken Mary several days to overcome her nausea before she felt able to elbow her way in to get her share.

That evening, she was up by the door talking to Lucy Perkins, a girl from St Austell, when the men unlocked it to come in. For once she was in a strong position to get a better helping, but as she took her place, and the women behind her began to push and shove, she glanced backwards.

It was a shock to see the plaintive faces of those who were too sick and weak to get off their beds to collect their share. Some were holding out their bowls, their feeble cries for help drowned by the clamour, and their distress unnoticed by anyone but herself.

Mary hated injustice. Even as a small child she had despised bigger children who bullied younger and weaker ones. Knowing that healthy women capable of fighting their way forward were sentencing the sick ones to death by depriving them of food, she suddenly saw red.

Turning in the queue, she held her arms out wide, blocking the way to the soup pot. 'Let the sick ones have their share first,' she commanded.

There was a hush, surprise on every grimy face. 'We should take care of the sick,' she said in a loud, clear voice. 'They might treat us like animals down here, but we are women, not savages.' Seeing Bessie at the back of the queue, she shouted to her, 'Get their bowls and bring them here, Bessie. When they are served everyone else can have theirs.'

Mary heard the rumble of dissent, and it frightened

her. But she had no intention of backing down. She was aware that the guards were watching from the grille on the door, and she hoped that if the stronger women rushed her, they would step in.

'Who d'you think you are? Fuckin' royalty?' Aggie Crew, one of the most ragged and dirty of the women, shouted out.

Mary had crossed swords with this woman on several previous occasions. In Mary's opinion she was totally brutalized. She stole from others, she didn't even attempt to wash her face and hands when the morning washing bucket was brought down. She belittled anyone with a shred of decency left. She had sneered at Mary for washing out the rags she used when she had her menses, and for her attempts to rally some of the other women to join her in asking for buckets of water and mops to clean the floor. Now Aggie's thin face was alight with malice, and she was clearly spoiling for a fight.

'I don't think I'm anyone other than a woman who doesn't want to behave like an animal,' Mary said, looking hard at her. 'It isn't right to act like this. The food should be shared equally, and I'm going to see it is.'

Bessie squeezed through the crowd with the sick women's bowls. 'Fill them, Jane,' Mary ordered the very young pregnant girl who was standing right by the soup pot, her hand on the ladle. Mary had talked to Jane a great deal, for as if it wasn't enough to be transported for stealing a candlestick, the parson who had made the complaint to the constables had also raped her.

Jane dutifully began to ladle soup into the bowls, and

Mary ordered those standing nearest to take them over to the sick ones. 'You'll get your share next,' she said by way of an inducement.

For a while it seemed as if Mary had won the day. The sick got their rations, and the other women were queuing properly for theirs, but as Mary turned to look at the soup pot, to make sure there was enough to go round, she was suddenly hit over the head with a bowl. She fell forward, knocking another woman off her feet, and all at once Aggie Crew was screaming blue murder, trying to entice the other women into hitting Mary.

The door flew open and in came the guards, lashing out with their sticks. They hauled Mary to her feet and unceremoniously dragged her out.

She knew they must have watched the whole proceedings through the grille on the door, but she also knew better than to hope they'd be on her side. Back in Exeter Castle, Dick Sullion had explained to her that the whole business of running prisons was put out to private tender to save the government money. As he pointed out, it was a good business for those who had no scruples; they hired the most brutish men as gaolers, ones who weren't above cutting corners with the rations. And in turn the owners turned a blind eye to their men taking bribes and treating their charges with the utmost brutality.

The two who held her by the arms now were typical of their breed, with their ugly, foxy faces and broken teeth. There was no light in their eyes.

'Why me?' she asked them when she'd caught her breath. 'It wasn't me who hit anyone.'

'You were inciting riot,' one said. 'Bloody trouble-maker.'

'Take me to Lieutenant Captain Tench,' she said boldly. 'I'll explain it to him.'

They didn't reply, just dragged her on along the passage and up the companionway, out on to the deck. Mary was sure she was going to be tied up somewhere for a flogging but at that moment, as her lungs filled with the sweet, fresh air after breathing effluent for so long, she didn't care.

She saw the night sky, sprinkled with a million stars, and the moon cutting a silver path across the dark waters of the river to the shore, and it seemed to be a sign that this was her moment, the opportunity she'd hoped for.

'I want to see Tench,' she screamed out at the top of her lungs. 'Get him now.'

One of the guards struck her, knocking her down on to the deck. 'Shut up,' he hissed at her, and added a stream of profanities.

All at once Mary saw what they were about. They hadn't dragged her out of the cell for formal punishment. They were intending to have their way with her, then shove her back later, with no one the wiser.

Determination was one of Mary's strongest attributes. While she might be prepared to be bedded by someone who would feed her, allow her to wash and perhaps show her some affection, she wasn't going to let herself be taken by a couple of rutting animals. She guessed too by the way they'd tried to silence her that there were men on the *Dunkirk* who didn't approve of prisoners being raped. So she yelled again and again, and when one of them tried to cover her mouth, she bit his hand and punched him, screaming still louder for Tench.

'What's going on?' a voice boomed out, and as the two men let go of her, she saw a slim male figure silhouetted in an open doorway to one of the many sheds that were built on the deck.

'Mr Tench?' Mary yelled out. 'They dragged me out, I've done nothing wrong. Help me, please.'

'Stop that yelling and come in here,' he said. 'And you too,' he added to the men.

The shed was part ward room, part office. At the centre of it was a table littered with papers and lit by a couple of candles. It looked to Mary as though this man had been writing, for there was an open notebook and an inkwell in front of the stool he'd obviously just vacated.

Mary had no way of knowing if this was Watkin Tench. But the gold braid on his well-fitting red jacket and his spotless white breeches proved he was an officer, and he spoke like a gentleman. He was of slender build, with dark crinkly hair and brown eyes, and she thought he was around twenty-four or -five. His face was unremarkable, with small, neat features and clear and glowing skin. While he looked irritated at being disturbed, he certainly didn't give the impression of being bad-tempered by nature.

'Your name?' he asked curtly.

'Mary Broad, sir,' she said. 'I was trying to make the women let the sick ones have some soup,' she added quickly. 'Some of them didn't like it, and one hit me, then these two dragged me out.'

'She was trying to start a fight,' one of the guards claimed. 'We had to separate her.'

'Wait outside, you two,' the young officer said.

They left, one muttering something under his breath. Once the door was closed, the officer perched on his stool and looked hard at Mary.

'Why were you calling out my name?' he asked.

Mary felt a sense of relief that she had found the right man. 'I'd been told you were fair,' she said.

Tench nodded noncommittally, and asked Mary to explain what had happened.

Now that she had a platform to air her complaints, she spared him nothing. She said how the strongest women got the food while the weakest were starving, and that in her opinion there wasn't enough food to keep so many women alive.

'Our punishment is supposed to be transportation,' she said heatedly. 'Surely it's wrong to try and kill us before we ever get put on a ship?'

Tench had been surprised enough to hear his name being called out, and even more so by this woman's obvious intelligence. But most of all he was touched that she had the courage to speak up for her weaker fellow prisoners.

He had been a prisoner of war himself in America and had feared he would die from the terrible conditions there. When he arrived at this posting on the *Dunkirk*, he was horrified to find his fellow countrymen were capable of even worse barbarities. To his distress he found there was nothing a Marine officer could do to prevent it. The

47

hulks were run by private companies, and the Marines were merely there to keep order, without any control over the management.

When he had voiced his strong feelings on the matter he'd been severely reprimanded, and as he was only a junior officer without anyone higher up in agreement with him, there was nothing more he could do, and in truth he had become apathetic. When he took men to work outside, he was kindly to them; he tried to make certain the guards were giving the full quota of rations to the prisoners, and when someone was brought to him for punishment he was always fair. But he knew that wasn't enough.

Mary's Cornish dialect sliced through his apathy. He had spent his childhood in Penzance and had a store of happy memories of its natives. He felt compelled to find out a little more about this woman before dismissing her. Realizing she must have foregone her own supper during this skirmish, he put his head outside the door and ordered one of the men to bring something from the galley.

'Am I to be flogged?' Mary asked, once he'd shut the door again. She didn't hear what he had said to the men, and assumed he'd sent one of them to fetch someone of a higher rank than himself.

'No,' he said. 'And in future I shall order the guards to make sure the rations are shared out equally.'

'While you are about it, could we have more?' she asked cheekily.

Tench had an overwhelming desire to laugh. The

woman reminded him poignantly of many Cornish miners he'd known, dogged, tough and fearless. He remembered from the records that she had assaulted the woman she'd robbed, yet her calm grey eyes and gentle manner belied a vicious nature. Likewise, the innocence in her face sat uneasily with her impudent demands. A woman to be watched, he thought. But a rather admirable one for all that.

The guard brought in a plate of bread, cheese and pilchards. Tench pulled up another stool at the table and told Mary to eat.

It was so long since she had tasted either cheese or pilchards that it was all she could do not to cry. She wolfed down the food, holding on to the plate with one hand, afraid Tench might snatch it before she'd finished.

He poured her a little rum too, and topped it up with water, taking a glass neat himself. As he watched her bent over the plate, he noted that although her hair was alive with lice, her neck was very clean, an extremely unusual sight in a prisoner.

'I'll get someone to take you back now,' he said when she'd finished.

Mary had always found it easy to talk to men, but she had no idea how to flirt with them, nor would she know if a man found her attractive. As she looked into his soft brown eyes she thought she read curiosity in them, and she wished wholeheartedly she was in a clean dress with her hair newly washed, at least to give herself some sort of chance.

49

'Can't I stay a while longer?' she blurted out impulsively.

He smiled, and his eyes twinkled. 'No, you can't, Mary,' he said. 'I have work to do. But why do you want to stay? I've given you food, you aren't to be flogged.'

'Because . . .' she began, but to her horror she felt tears welling up in her eyes. She couldn't find the words to explain what it meant to be out of that stinking hold, or how it felt to have a full belly. And she certainly couldn't say it had been her intention to offer him her virginity in the hope she would get some privileges.

Perhaps he understood at least some of it, for he put his hand on her shoulder. 'You have to go back,' he said gently. 'But we'll talk again.'

Watkin Tench's kindness comforted Mary that night. As she lay between Bessie and Nancy, she wasn't so aware of the moans and groans, the coughing and the sobbing from the other women. Nor was she so aware of the stench or the rats scuttling around. Instead she was able to immerse herself in the thought of the amusement in his eyes, the shininess of his hair, and his gentle manner. For just a few brief minutes she'd felt clean, forgotten she was a felon. It was a form of escape, and a very welcome one.

Mary didn't know whether it was as the result of Tench's influence or not, but a couple of days later she, Bessie and two other women, Sarah Giles and Hannah Brown, were called out of the hold for work. There had already been a marked improvement in the food sharing, as the guards stayed in the hold to check everyone got fair shares, whether sick or not. To Mary that was enough. And to be called out for work was an unexpected bonus.

The job they were given was washing clothes, mainly shirts. It wasn't an easy task as they had to carry the four heavy wooden tubs out on to the deck from a store-room, which was difficult wearing chains, then lower buckets on a rope to the river to fill them with water. But it was good to be out in the sunshine, to be able to look over to the shore and see the lush green of fields and woods, and even if the guards did watch their every move, at times leering at them in a frightening manner, it was a million times better than being cooped up in the hold.

'Do you think we could wash ourselves when we've finished all these?' Mary whispered to Sarah as they scrubbed at the dirty shirts with blocks of hard soap.

Sarah was one of the women the others called whores. Small and pretty, with red-gold hair, she was twenty-five, a widow with two small children. Her fisherman husband had been lost at sea when his ship went down in a storm, and Sarah had left the children with her mother in St Ives and gone to Plymouth. Her story was very like Mary's – she'd turned to stealing because she couldn't get work – and she'd already been on the *Dunkirk* for eight months.

'You can if you want,' Sarah said, and laughed as if it was funny. 'But I hope you ain't intending to do it with nothing on.'

'Of course not.' Mary coloured up. 'I'll just get in the tub with my dress on and wash that too while I'm about it.'

'Chains and all?' Sarah raised one eyebrow.

'Well, I can't get those off,' Mary said offhandedly, and looked round at Bessie. 'What about you? Fancy a bath?'

Bessie began to giggle, and it infected them all. Sarah rubbed soap into her hands and blew bubbles, Hannah splashed Mary with water, and Mary retaliated by slapping her with a wet shirt. If the guards noticed they didn't intervene or stop them, and all at once it was as if they were just girls at a Sunday school picnic. They giggled, chatted and sang. Bessie even did a little dance, rattling her chains in time with her feet.

Once the washed shirts were hanging up on lines to dry, the women were completely hidden from the guards' view. 'Go on then if you're going to,' Sarah urged Mary. 'Before we empty the tubs.'

While Bessie and Hannah looked on, tempted to join her, but afraid of being caught at it, Mary stepped into the tub, gasping at the cold. Elated by the almost sensual touch of water on her skin, she began to laugh. 'It feels wonderful,' she gasped out, crouching down so that the water came up to her middle and looking to the others to join her in their tubs. 'Do it quickly if you're going to, before we get caught.'

Bessie and Hannah got into theirs without any hesitation; only Sarah held back, claiming she was keeping watch. The three women scrubbed themselves and their clothes eagerly, aware they hadn't long to finish the task, yet smiling with delight as they saw the dirt floating away from them.

After soaping her hair, Mary dunked herself right under

the water several times. As she came up for the last time, to her horror she saw the two guards and an officer staring down at her. A quick glance revealed that Bessie and Hannah were already out of their tubs, trying vainly to wring the water from their dresses. Sarah was white-faced and agitated.

'We weren't doing no harm, sir,' Mary said, addressing the officer. He was a portly man with a big nose and he looked astonished. 'Just using up the water before we threw it overboard. We've done all the washing.'

Mary could see no good reason why bathing should be considered something punishable. But one glance at her two wet friends alarmed her. Their dresses were clinging to their bodies, showing clearly the curve of their breasts and hips, and the guards were looking at them with naked lust. Aware that her own body must be similarly displayed, she was stricken with embarrassment.

'I'm sorry, sir,' she said as she struggled to get out of the tub. 'But you can't blame us, we're never given enough water to wash properly.'

'Why is it that you women always take advantage of any situation?' the officer asked.

Mary glanced at her companions and guessed they were tongue-tied with fear. The officer was older than Tench, perhaps thirty or more, his voice high-pitched and clipped. Yet she could see no cruelty in his eyes, only puzzlement.

'Wouldn't you?' she retorted. 'What else are we to do? That hold you keep us in wouldn't stink so much if we were allowed to bathe and come up here for exercise, and if it was scrubbed out now and then. If you kept animals in such a place there'd be a riot.'

One of the guards sniggered, and the officer silenced him with a stern look. 'Take those three back,' he said, pointing to Bessie, Sarah and Hannah. 'I'll deal with this one.'

The other women were pushed away through the lines of washing by the guards, leaving Mary alone with the officer. She vainly tried to wring out her skirt as she waited for him to speak.

'Your name?' he asked.

'Mary Broad, sir,' she said. 'Am I allowed to know yours?'

She thought she saw a glimmer of a smile, and she ran her fingers through her hair and smiled back defiantly. Her mother and sister had often remarked how pretty her hair was wet, as it sprang into ringlets, and she hoped that was true because the wind felt chill now she was wet, and she wouldn't look anything more than pathetic if she began shivering.

'Lieutenant Graham,' he said. 'It seems to me, Mary, that you haven't quite grasped the gravity of your situation.'

Graham was a name she'd also heard from the men prisoners. He was reputed to be dangerous when crossed, but decent enough most of the time.

'Oh, I have, sir,' she said boldly. 'I can see that I won't be alive to be transported, not unless I get a lucky break and a chance to have a bath and some extra food from time to time.'

He gave her a long, appraising stare which seemed to go right through her clothes, and she knew in that moment that he wanted her.

She had set her heart on Tench as a prospective saviour, and Lieutenant Graham would be an extremely poor substitute. His face was fat and flabby and she suspected he had little hair under his very well-cared-for wig. But there was no harm in having someone in reserve in case Tench couldn't be tempted. And Graham wasn't entirely repulsive as his teeth and skin were good. Besides, she wasn't looking for true love, only to survive long enough to escape.

'Are you trying to suggest something?' he said, his eyes narrowing. They were a muddy brown, not the kind which could keep her awake as Tench's did.

'It's not for me to suggest anything, sir,' she said, making a bob of a curtsy and grinning impudently. 'I was just saying how it is for me.'

He ordered her back to the hold at that, but as the guard roughly pushed her down through the companion-way, she felt Graham was watching with interest.

Down in the hold, the afternoon's bath was being discussed by all those women still strong enough to be interested in the others. As Mary was pushed inside, they broke off their chatter to look up at her.

'What happened to you?' Bessie asked, wringing her hands with anxiety. 'We were afraid you'd be punished, or . . .' She broke off, not wanting to add the word 'raped'.

'I told him we need more food, fresh air, and this hovel cleaned out,' Mary said. She didn't feel inclined to discuss it any further as her wet clothes were making her cold and she wanted to talk in private to Sarah.

Her chance didn't come till much later that evening. She took off her wet clothes, hung them from a nail on the beam to dry and huddled in her blanket, but each time she looked across the hold, Sarah was talking to Hannah.

It was almost pitch dark when Mary saw Sarah move towards the bucket. By then most of the women were lying down ready to sleep. Mary got up and shuffled over to her, holding her blanket round her.

'When you've finished, can we talk?' she whispered.

In the gloom she saw Sarah nod her head.

The bucket was the best place to stay, furthest away from any of the women, but without room to stand up. When Sarah had finished, they perched on a beam. 'What is it?' Sarah asked.

'Who is your lover?' Mary asked. She saw no point in being more subtle.

Sarah hesitated. It was too dark for Mary to see if she was angry at being asked.

'Is it Tench or Graham?' Mary persisted.

'No, neither of those,' Sarah whispered. 'But you shouldn't ask such things, Mary.'

'Why not? I have to, if only so I know who not to make up to,' Mary whispered back.

'Tench can't be drawn into such things,' Sarah said with a sigh. 'Most of us have tried. And I wish you luck if you're going to try Graham, he's a hard man.'

'How do I go about it?' Mary asked.

She felt rather than saw Sarah's shrug. 'Give him the

glad eye whenever you see him, that's usually enough for them to call you out on a pretext. But don't hope for much. You'll only be disappointed.'

'Does your man remove your chains?'

'Sometimes, not often,' she said wearily. 'Now, go to bed, Mary, I don't want to tell you these things, it's not good.'

Mary heard the sadness in Sarah's voice, and knew instinctively it was only desperation that had driven her to such an arrangement and she wanted no part in seeing another girl follow her lead.

'We have to do what we can to survive,' Mary said, taking Sarah's hand and squeezing it. 'That's all it is, Sarah, nothing more. I don't see any shame in that.'

'You will when the others turn their backs on you,' Sarah said, her voice breaking.

'Better a turned back than dying of hunger,' Mary insisted.

For over a week Mary waited, each day hoping she would be called out again for work. The weather had turned really warm and the hold was stifling. A woman called Elizabeth Soames died one night and was only discovered dead at daybreak, but what shocked Mary most was that no one had anything to say about her. She'd been locked in here for months, yet she hadn't made one real friend and no one seemed to know anything about her.

'She was already here when I came,' Sarah said when Mary pointed this out. 'She was sick then, she barely spoke. She was old anyway, don't fret about it.'

Mary did fret about it. She wondered where the guards took Elizabeth's body for burial, whether the woman had any relatives and if they'd be told. It also made her own desire to escape even stronger.

The only comfort she could find was reliving memories of home. She found that if she sank into them far enough she could forget the heat, hunger, smells and the other women. Sometimes she would imagine herself walking down the path to Bodinnick with Dolly and their mother to catch the boat up to Lostwithiel. Mary could only recall going there twice, the last time when she was about twelve and Dolly fourteen, but both occasions were hot, sunny days, and she remembered sitting in the boat trailing her hand in the cool, clear water.

For much of the boat journey the river ran through steep, thickly wooded banks where the trees grew right down to the water's edge, their roots reaching out into the water like gnarled fishermen's fingers. It was a journey of enchantment, dragonflies hovering over the water, herons standing patiently in the shallows, and often timid deer peeping out from the trees. Kingfishers perched on the tree roots, waiting for an unwary fish to swim by, and then they would swoop, a glorious flash of turquoise, and come back up with their silver prize in their beaks.

Lostwithiel was the farthest Mary had ever been from home until she went to Plymouth. It might have been no bigger than Fowey, but to her it was thrilling because coaches thundered in from as far away as Bristol and London. She watched bug-eyed as the passengers alighted, marvelling at the women's beautiful clothes and pretty hats, and wondering why, if they were rich and important enough to travel so far, they didn't look happier.

Last time they'd gone there, Father had given her and Dolly tuppence each to spend. While Mother was buying material for new clothes, they looked in every single shop and examined each and every market stall before they decided what they would spend their money on. Dolly bought some artificial daisies to put on her Sunday bonnet, and Mary bought a kite. Dolly said she was stupid wasting tuppence on something she could make at home for nothing, and anyway girls didn't fly kites.

Mary didn't care about being the only girl to fly a kite, and she thought Dolly was foolish wanting daisies on her bonnet. Besides, kites made at home were too heavy to fly well; hers was made of red paper, with yellow streamers, and the string was waxed so it slid through her hands smoothly.

The very next day after church, Mary took the kite up on the hill above the town to fly it. Dolly came with her, but only because she wanted to show off her newly trimmed bonnet. As always on a fine day with a strong breeze there were many boys flying kites, and they all looked enviously at Mary's when it took off effortlessly, soaring up into the sky way beyond all their homemade ones.

Dolly overcame her prejudice about it being a boy's game, mostly because there were several boys she liked up there, among them Albert Mowles whom she was sweet on. Mary might have known she shouldn't have allowed Dolly to persuade her to let her hold the kite. She only wanted to do it so she could attract Albert's attention.

A gust of stronger wind came, and to Mary's horror, Dolly didn't hold the string tighter, but let it run right through her fingers. The kite was off, swept along on the wind in the direction of the beach at Menabilly.

Everyone gave chase, some abandoning their own kites to rescue the superior one. Mary remembered how she ran like the wind, determined to beat all the boys, and they were all whooping and shouting at the unexpected excitement.

The kite came down suddenly and dramatically as the wind dropped, landing on some rocks to the side of the little beach. The tide was out and Mary didn't stop to think about her Sunday clothes and shoes, but ran full tilt across the seaweed, sand and mud, her mind only on rescuing her kite.

She tripped on a half-submerged rock and fell face down. It was Albert who reached the kite, then turned back to help her up.

'You can run faster than most boys,' he said in admiration.

Now, as Mary lay sweating in the stinking hold, she thought she ought to remember the wallop she got from Mother when she returned home soaking wet and smeared with mud. Perhaps too she should remember Dolly's baleful look when Mary was the recipient of Albert's praise. Maybe she would have been wiser to have taken note of her father's lecture that girls who acted like boys came to a sticky end.

Yet none of those things were important to her then, or now. Nothing could detract from the thrill of seeing the red kite soar up into the sky, feeling the warm sun on her face and the soft grass beneath her feet, experiencing the joy of running wild and free, the beauty of that little beach where she so often caught crabs and mussels. It was even more important now to hold on to those memories, to think of herself as that kite, straining to be free. For hadn't she been told at Sunday school that if you prayed hard enough for something, it would come to you?

But it was hard to believe God listened to her prayers. Did He know or care that she was terrified she'd never see Fowey again? Was it too much to ask to go back to stand on the hill and look down at the pretty little town as the sun was setting? To watch the fishing boats come in, laden with their quivering silver pilchards, or hear the men singing in the tavern by the harbour?

Tears came into her eyes as she reminded herself that she had lost the chance to make her mother and father proud of her. That she'd never be able to dance at Dolly's wedding. Mary knew they despaired of her for being a hoyden, but she had always known they loved her. What would it do to them when she didn't come home again?

Just as Mary was beginning to believe that the hot weather would never break and she was going to be stuck in the hold for all eternity, she was called out for work again. This time it was just herself and Sarah.

It struck Mary that Sarah must have had some hand in it, as she'd spent two nights out of the hold since the wash day, but if she had, she didn't let on. Once again they were instructed to wash shirts, and as they were lowering buckets over the side they saw a group of male prisoners being brought up for work too.

Although Mary often spoke to the men through the grille and could put names to the different voices, she had no idea what any of them looked like. But the moment she saw a big man, well over six feet tall with wiry, fair hair, a thick beard and pale blue eyes, she knew with certainty that was Will Bryant, the man most of the other women liked best.

Mary liked him too, mainly because he was Cornish and knew Fowey well. They had talked on several occasions, but once the initial delight of finding someone to share her memories of her home town had worn thin, she'd found him to be something of a braggart. He boasted he was one of the few men to be convicted of smuggling.

This seemed odd to her, for it was a crime that was usually ignored because everyone in Cornwall, from the poorest people to the gentry, were involved in it to some extent. As he was a fisherman by trade, with a boat of his own, he would know the rugged coastline well, and certainly have all the necessary skills for bringing contraband ashore, but Mary didn't believe that was all he'd done. Nor did she like the way he considered himself to be the cleverest, toughest prisoner on the *Dunkirk*.

But seeing him in the flesh, she had to admit he was handsome. Even grime couldn't spoil his strong features, or the loose shirt hide his muscular body. His fair hair shone in the sunshine, there was a sparkle in his blue eyes, and his skin was golden-brown from working outside. He was probably only a couple of years older than her, still fit and healthy despite having been on the hulk for over a year. Clearly he'd found a way to get extra rations, which proved he was resourceful.

'Who are you two?' he shouted, as if they were at the market place, not prisoners in chains.

'I'm Sarah, this is Mary Broad,' Sarah called back. 'A good day for working outside!'

'It's worth breaking my back to see you two beauties,' he replied impudently, making the other men with him laugh. 'If you can get away later, I'll meet you at the tavern and buy you both a drink.'

Mary had to smile. A man who could still make jokes when he was about to start a ten-hour stint of shifting rocks was someone to be admired.

'I'll buy you two each, me darlin's,' another man called out. He had an Irish accent and Mary knew right away he had to be James Martin, the man who made all the women laugh with his florid and often suggestive compliments. But whereas Will was better in the flesh, James was disappointing. His large nose dominated his gaunt face, his brown hair was stringy, and his ears stuck out. His shoulders were stooped and his teeth were very brown.

'I thought a horse thief would look more dashing,' Mary remarked to Sarah as the men climbed down the ladder into the waiting boat.

Sarah laughed. 'That one's got more cheek than an elephant's behind,' she said. 'I don't think he needs looks too to attract women.'

'Who were the other two with Will?' Mary asked. One had bright red hair and freckles and looked about the same age as herself. The other was younger still, perhaps only sixteen. He was very small and nervous looking, with sharp, bird-like features. 'The young one had a nice smile.'

'They arrived about the same time I did. The one with the ginger hair is Samuel Bird. He's a bit gloomy, not one to brighten up a girl's day like Will and James,' Sarah said with a grin. 'The little one is Jamie Cox. He don't say much, too shy I guess. He's lucky Will and James Martin keep an eye on him, it don't bear thinking of what some of the brutes in that hold would do to him otherwise.'

Mary asked what she meant.

Sarah shook her head. 'If you don't know, then I'm not going to be the one to tell you,' she said. 'There's some things men do that are better not mentioned.'

It was quiet up on deck after the male prisoners were rowed ashore. The sun was hot on the women's arms and heads, and a heat haze shimmered on the water. They scrubbed at the clothes in companionable silence, and there seemed no need for conversation as both of them savoured the light breeze, the sound of the seagulls and the gentle movement of the hulk in the water.

Later, once they'd rinsed the first load of shirts with fresh water, both women bathed in the water, giggling delightedly as they helped each other to wash their hair. The two guards, who were lounging on crates further back on the deck, smoking pipes, made no comment. Perhaps the hot sun had mellowed them too.

The women's clothes dried quickly as they hauled up fresh water for the second load of washing, but Mary was horrified to see how faded and flimsy her dress was becoming – another couple of washes and it would fall apart.

'What will we do when these clothes are just rags?' she asked Sarah. Many of the other women were already semi-naked, clutching the last vestiges of their rags around them to hide their bodies.

'My man gave me this dress,' Sarah said, her eyes downcast. 'Hold out for clothes and food, Mary, don't let him have you for nothing.'

Mary looked thoughtfully at her friend for a moment. Her dress was blue cotton, nothing fancy, and it was too big for her slight shape. But it was by far the best one down in the hold. She guessed that Sarah had been quite a head-turner back in Penzance, for her red-gold hair was pretty and her dark eyes smouldered.

'Is it terrible?' she whispered. 'I've never done it.'

Sarah sighed. 'I thought lying with my husband was wonderful,' she said, her voice cracking. 'It hurt a bit the first time, but he was so gentle and I loved him. It won't be like that for you, I fear, the men here that want a woman won't care about your feelings. You are nothing but a warm body to use any way they like.'

'Is there any way I can make it better?' Mary asked nervously.

'Don't struggle, try to pretend you like it.' Sarah sighed. 'But don't think he'll love you, we're only convicts after all.'

Chapter three

Around noon Watkin Tench came back to the hulk in a small boat. Mary's heart leaped as she heard his voice calling out from below. But she continued bailing out the wash tub over the side, waiting for him to appear.

As he clambered on to the deck, she smiled. He was wearing a white shirt and breeches and his face was shiny with perspiration. He looked hot and tired, but to Mary that only made him more desirable.

He nodded when he saw the two women. 'Good day, Sarah, Mary. I hope you are behaving yourselves today?'

It was clear by his light tone and the hint of amusement in his voice that he'd heard about the bathing in the wash tubs. Mary wondered what he'd have to say if he knew they'd repeated it today. But their clothes were nearly dry now, and they were spinning out the remaining washing to delay the moment when they had to go back to the hold.

'We'd behave still better with something to eat,' Mary called out cheekily. 'Any chance?'

She saw Sarah turn away and guessed her friend thought she was being too forward.

'Isn't it enough you've got out of the hold for a few

hours?' Tench asked, taking a few steps closer to them. There was no real irritation in his voice, and Mary decided she had to charm him now or lose the chance for good.

'Oh yes, sir, we really appreciate the chance to come up here, to look at the woods and fields, hear the birds singing, and feel the sun on our faces,' she said, trying not to laugh because she was aware she sounded insincere. 'I wouldn't complain about anything ever again if we had work like this every day.'

He smiled then, his teeth very white against his tanned face. 'Tell me about yourself, Mary,' he asked, then added, 'And you too, Sarah.'

It seemed to Mary that Fate was smiling on her for once, for Tench sat down on a crate and looked relaxed as he talked to them both. No guards came near and there were no distractions of any kind; they could have been two ordinary girls chatting to a friend after work.

Mary let Sarah talk first. She spoke of her husband's death and the children she was afraid she'd never see again. She went on to explain that her parents were past the age when they should be bringing up children, and if they should die, the children would go to the workhouse.

Tench really listened. Mary saw him clench his lips as if he was incensed that Sarah's family circumstances hadn't been taken into consideration when she was sentenced.

Mary's own story was very short. She told him about her family in Fowey and how she'd left for Plymouth to get work.

'I wish to God I'd stayed at home now,' she said

ruefully, as Sarah tactfully moved away to check the drying washing. 'It pains me to think that I'll never set foot in Cornwall, or see my family ever again in this life.'

She half expected Tench to insist she would, that seven years weren't so long, but she knew by his grave expression he could hold out no hope for her.

'It is more difficult for women convicts to return,' he said. 'Men can sign on a ship coming home when their time is up.'

He didn't have to add that there was no such opportunity for women, and therefore they were forced to stay. Mary heard it in his voice.

'I'll get back,' she said with determination. 'Somehow. But do you know where we are to be sent?'

He shrugged his shoulders. 'There's talk of Botany Bay, in New South Wales, the country Captain Cook discovered. But no one else has been there to confirm or deny it's a viable proposition. America is out of the question now since she gained her independence. They tried Africa and that failed.'

'If we stay here on the *Dunkirk* we shall all die,' Mary said dolefully.

Tench sighed. 'I agree it's bad, but what can the government do? Every gaol is overcrowded.'

Mary was tempted to comment that if they didn't send people to prison for petty crimes like stealing a pie, there would be no overcrowding. But she wanted to keep Tench's interest, not have him scuttling away in haste.

'Tell me about you yourself, sir,' she asked instead. 'I heard you were in the war in the Americas?'

'I was,' he grinned ruefully. 'Taken prisoner of war too. Maybe that's why I'm a little more sympathetic to prisoners here than the average Marine. I grew up in Penzance too, so I also know how hard life is in Cornwall for most people.'

Mary sat on the deck by the wash tub entranced as Tench told her of his happy childhood memories of Penzance. He had of course come from an entirely different world to her – a big house with servants, a boarding school in Wales, a family with a good name and money. But there was common ground, their love of Cornwall, his interest and affection for ordinary people. He could paint vivid pictures with just a few words of his life with the Marines, of America and of London.

'I have to go now,' he said suddenly, perhaps aware he'd stayed talking to her for far too long. 'You empty that tub and clear away. I'll bring you up a little something to eat.'

'He's not the kind to take a woman,' Sarah said sharply as soon as Tench had walked away. She had remained silent all the time Mary was talking to him, only nodding and smiling from time to time. 'You won't get what you want from him, Mary.'

'How do you know?' Mary asked, hurt because she thought the older woman was ridiculing her.

'I know about men,' Sarah said simply. 'He's the kind who will save himself for the woman he'll marry. A rare breed.'

Mary thought Sarah was mistaken when Tench came back to give them a lump of bread, some cheese and an orange. But as he hurriedly walked away, urging them to finish up and go back to the hold, Sarah looked at his slender figure retreating down the deck and sighed.

'He's a kind, good man,' she said. 'No doubt if you can keep his interest he'll always help you, Mary. But don't hope for love, or even sharing his bed. His kind don't fall for convict women.'

The bread and cheese were both a little mouldy but that didn't matter, it was solid food after all. It was the orange which thrilled them even more, for such fruit had always been a rare treat even before imprisonment. They ate it all greedily, even the peel, licking every last drop of juice from their chins and laughing at each other.

They had just emptied the last of the washing water over the side when Lieutenant Graham appeared. He was in full uniform and looked very hot and tetchy.

'Time you were back in the hold,' he said curtly.

'We were just going to take down the dry washing and fold it,' Mary said.

She had caught the sun on her face and arms, she could feel the familiar sting and knew it would be tender for days. But up here she felt free and even happy and she didn't want to go back down to the hold just yet.

'My men will do that,' he said, giving her a piercing look. 'I know what you women are like, you probably aim to steal a shirt or two.'

'You are mistaken, sir,' Mary said indignantly. 'We just wanted to finish the job properly.'

He leaned back against the sawn-off mast and sneered.

71

'Is that so? I think it's more likely you'd sell your souls for a new dress, food or a drop of rum.'

Mary glanced at Sarah, saw her anxious expression and guessed she had already passed a message that Mary could be tempted into becoming a bed partner. After talking to Tench, Mary had no real interest in Graham any longer, but her common sense told her she mustn't wipe him right out of the picture.

'I wouldn't sell my soul,' she said pointedly. 'And I haven't considered selling my body either, not yet.'

'You women are all whores,' Graham said nastily. 'Now finish up and get back.'

His words stung, but as they lifted the tub to empty it completely, Mary felt Graham's eyes on her legs. She had tucked the sides of her dress up into the chain around her waist and forgotten she'd left it like that.

She looked round at him and winked cheekily. She had no doubt he could be lured, even if Tench couldn't.

Over the next few weeks, Mary was called out for work regularly. Sometimes it was just with Sarah, often with other women. But she wasn't slow to notice she was always picked, whether it was for washing, mending or peeling vegetables. Sadly, she had no way of knowing whether it was Tench or Graham who was putting her on the list.

She saw both men on nearly every occasion, and although Tench didn't stop to speak again for as long as he had before, he almost always slipped her something to eat. Graham on the other hand lingered longer each time, often calling Mary away from the other women under a pretence of chastising her for something.

The man puzzled her. He could be so curt and even nasty, but now and again he showed a touch of real kindness, like the occasion when she got a splinter in her foot from the deck planking. Several of the women had attempted to get it out for her without success. By the end of the day she could barely stand on it, and when Graham saw her limping, he called her over.

'What's wrong with your foot?' he asked.

She explained, and he asked her to let him see it. She turned her back on him and with some difficulty because of the chains, lifted her foot up by bending her knee.

'It's embedded,' he said. 'I'll get a needle to dig it out.' He then ordered the other women back to the hold and told Mary to stay where she was.

'Sit down,' he said sharply as he came back with a needle and a small bottle of liquid.

Mary did as she was told, and Graham squatted down on a crate before her and lifted her foot on to his knee. It hurt as he prodded the needle in, but he eventually got the splinter, then rubbed a dab of the contents of the bottle on to it, making it sting. Mary squealed with pain.

'That's to kill any infection,' he said. 'Now, put something round it, and don't walk around in any muck until it's healed.'

'Difficult down in the hold,' she retorted.

'Don't you ever give up on complaining?' he asked, but he was still holding her foot in his hand.

In that moment Mary knew for certain he did have a

real interest in her. 'If you think that's complaining, just let me get into my stride,' she said with a wide grin. 'What would you like to hear about? The filth, the stink or the lack of decent food?' She laughed then, to soften her words. 'But I don't want to put you off your supper tonight. It was very kind of you to see to my foot.'

He said nothing, but his hand strayed on to her leg, just above the shackle, smoothing the skin. 'You keep yourself cleaner than the others,' he said, his voice suddenly lower and more intimate. 'I like that about you. I wouldn't want to see you get a poisonous wound.'

'Keeping clean is one way to survive this hulk,' she retorted. 'That's my aim, to survive it, whatever I have to do.'

He smiled then, a warmth coming into his plump face, and for a brief second he looked almost handsome. 'Whatever you have to do?' he asked, raising one eyebrow.

Mary couldn't look at him. She sensed he wanted her to spell out to him that she was available. Knowing that he could, if he wished, take her by force made her feel a little tender towards him.

'I've never been with a man,' she said softly, keeping her eyes down. 'I always intended to wait till I was wed. But that's not going to happen now. I could easily die of starvation before I see the country they plan to send me to. So if a man was to offer me food and a new dress, I think I would do what he wanted in return, as long as he was kind.'

'You don't mind if it's not love?'

That seemed a strangely sensitive question to Mary.

Not what she would have expected of a man of his class.

'Love doesn't come to women like me,' she said. 'I'll settle for kindness.'

He ordered her back to the hold then, but as she got up he gave her a strip of cotton to bandage her foot. 'Keep it clean,' was his only comment, but his eyes said a great deal more.

That night Mary was in a quandary. It was Watkin Tench she wanted: for him she could feel very much more than mere gratitude. But she felt Sarah was right in saying he wouldn't ever take a woman he wasn't married to. Yet if she allowed Graham to have his way with her, and Tench found out, he'd be bound to despise her for it.

All the following week she could think of nothing else, agonizing over whether it was nobler to allow herself to starve to death than lose her self-respect, or fight with the only weapons she had for survival.

The long hot spell broke with a fearsome storm. The old hulk bucked and shuddered, the timbers groaned as if it was about to break up. The hatches had to be closed, and remained that way day after day as heavy rain continued to bucket down. As the women lay on their benches in complete darkness, listening to the cries of those who had become sick, the already fetid air was so thick and heavy it was difficult even to breathe.

Baby Rose, who had been sickly from birth, died first, followed a day later by her mother and the woman who shared the same bed. Within twenty-four hours a further eight women were running a fever, and a dozen more, including Mary, were vomiting and had diarrhoea. Most were so weak they couldn't even make it to the buckets and just lay in their own mess.

Mary saw for herself then that the only women who weren't suffering so badly were the so-called whores. They were the ones still healthy enough to be able to wipe another woman's fevered brow, to offer a few words of comfort. Even Mary, who had considered herself so strong, barely had the strength to crawl to the bucket.

She made up her mind then that survival was far more important than morality.

Eventually the rain abated, and the hatches were opened again, to reveal a foot of bilge water beneath the sleeping shelves, vomit and excrement floating on it. The sickness among the prisoners persisted, claiming yet another two souls. The men called through the grille to the women, but they were suffering just as badly. Mary heard that Able, her cellmate in Exeter, had died, as well as a young boy, barely fifteen years of age, and two of the older men.

Mary spoke to Will Bryant one morning. Even he didn't sound as brash and full of confidence as previously.

'If it's gaol fever that's come amongst us, we'll all die,' he said gloomily. 'We've got to find a way to make them swill out these holds. There's more rats than ever and I fear for us all.'

'I'll try and do something,' she said.

'What can a little thing like you do?' he retorted arrogantly.

'I can try pleading for us,' she said, more determined because he doubted her.

'You can try, but it won't get you anywhere,' he said. 'They want us all to die, then they'll fill the hulk with new 'uns who'll die too. Save 'em a fortune it will.'

'You bring shame to Cornishmen,' she shouted at him. 'Talk like that won't help anyone.'

'I'll marry you if you get the holds swilled out,' he called back, and gave a raucous laugh.

'Be careful I don't hold you to that,' Mary yelled at him.

Sarah smiled weakly as Mary told her what she intended to do.

'The guards won't get Tench or Graham down here,' she said. 'They'll just ignore you.'

'I've got to try,' Mary insisted.

There was no point in banging on the door, no one ever answered. So Mary waited until the guard came down to order two of the women to bring out the slop buckets, and as soon as he unlocked the door she pounced on him.

'I've got to see Lieutenant Captain Tench or Lieutenant Graham,' she insisted.

'Bugger off,' he said, pushing her away with his stick. 'You'll see no one.'

'I will,' she said, grabbing him by the arm. 'If you don't take a message to one of them from me, I'll see you punished.'

'*You* get *me* punished?' His narrow eyes became even

77

narrower. 'D'you think anyone up there would take the word of a bloody felon?'

'Ignore me at your peril,' Mary replied menacingly. 'I'm telling you, give them the message, or take what will come to you.'

'Bugger off,' he repeated, but this time with less conviction. He ordered two women to take the buckets, holding Mary back with his stick.

'Tell them,' she yelled out as he slammed the door and locked it. 'Tell them or be damned – it's important.'

Mary tried again when the women came back with the buckets, but with the same response. As the hours crept by and still no one came, she stared out through the hatch at the dark grey sky above and cried. More women were going down with the fever, and she feared that if they were left like this they would all be dead within a week.

'You did your best,' Sarah said in an attempt to comfort her. 'It's just like Will said, they don't care if we die.'

'That may be true of most of them but I can't believe it of Tench or Graham,' Mary said. 'I won't believe it.'

She had no idea what time of day it was, as there was no sun to tell her, but it felt like late afternoon when a guard came in and called her name.

'Up there with you,' he said.

It wasn't the same man she'd threatened earlier, but she felt he knew of it because for once he didn't whack her with his stick. As Mary reached the top of the companionway she took a deep breath of clean air, and it made her giddy.

Lieutenant Graham was standing on deck. 'You wanted to see me?' he asked.

Mary poured out what was wrong. 'The holds must be scrubbed out,' she pleaded. 'We'll all go down with fever if they aren't.'

He remained impassive, and it infuriated her. 'If we all get fever it will spread to all of you too,' she said heatedly. 'In God's name do something, you don't want the death of a whole ship's company on your conscience.'

He gave her one of his long, penetrating stares. 'And what will you do for me, if I do what you say?'

Mary gulped. She hadn't expected him to bargain with her.

'Whatever you want, sir,' she replied.

'I don't want you unwillingly,' he said, and for the first time ever Mary saw a trace of nervousness in his face.

'I don't want you to help those down in the hold unwillingly either,' she said.

He looked away from her, over towards the sea, and Mary could see he was struggling with his conscience. Not so much whether it was right to let prisoners die for want of clean air, but whether it was right to bow to Mary's demands because he wanted her.

After what seemed an interminable silence he turned back to her. 'I'll pass the order that the holds are to be cleaned,' he said sternly. 'You will come to me as the other women are sent back.'

It was dark by the time the scrubbing of the women's hold was completed. The women had been brought up on deck, and the evening soup and bread were dished out there while the guards went down to do their task. For some of the women who had never been out of the hold since they were originally put there, it was almost too much. They crouched on the deck fearfully, shivering in the brisk breeze, their eyes dull as if they were partially blinded by the daylight.

Mary was shocked by the condition of some of them. In the gloom of the hold she hadn't been able to see the full horror of it. Some were nothing but skin and bone, and all were pale, gaunt and listless, dirt so deeply embedded in their skin and hair that it would take more than one bath to clean them. She saw ulcerating sores where their leg irons rubbed, the lice crawling on them, the bites on skinny arms and legs which could only have come from rats. Sadly, she sensed that the cleaning of the hold wouldn't help them unless they were given better food. She doubted that all of their number would survive to be transported.

As the guards returned on deck, sweating profusely from their efforts, the smell of vinegar sharp in the evening air, Mary began to tremble with fright at the thought of what was coming to her.

She knew what love-making entailed. In the tiny cottage at Fowey there was no privacy, and she had heard her parents at it in the darkness. During her time in Plymouth she had seen it going on all around her too, so the act itself wasn't frightening. Thomas used to kiss her passionately, and she would have gladly let him go further if he had pressed her. But there was a great deal of difference between being seduced and being compelled to submit to it.

Apart from her fear of being taken by a man she scarcely knew, there was the information Sarah had passed on. She said that although the officers turned a blind eye to one of their number taking a convict woman, that didn't always stop them from banding together to flog a woman afterwards if they had some grievance against her. Mary guessed she would be a marked woman now for daring to complain about the holds.

Lieutenant Graham appeared just as the guards were ordering the women back below. He gestured for her to follow him to the stern of the ship, and disappeared into one of the shed-like structures up there.

He closed the door and locked it as soon as Mary was inside. It was very like the room Tench had taken her into before, tiny, with a bunk, a desk and a couple of stools. Graham lit a candle on the desk, and it was then that Mary saw the small bath of water on the floor.

'For me?' she asked.

'Yes. You stink,' he said, looking faintly embarrassed. 'Wash yourself all over, including your hair. I'll come back later.'

'Will you take these off?' Mary indicated her chains.

He hesitated for a moment, which suggested to her he hadn't done this before, then taking a key from his pocket released both her ankles and drew the chain from around her waist. He left her without another word.

For a moment Mary could think of nothing but the sheer joy of being released from her chains. To be able to move easily and not to hear the hated clank she'd lived with for so long was bliss. But she regained her wits within minutes and sprang to the door to try it. It was locked of course, just as she'd expected, and the two porthole windows were far too small for her to get through, so she peeled off her clothes and got into the bath.

To her delight it was warm, and the soap he'd left wasn't the rough stuff they used for washing clothes. The bath was too small to do anything more than squat in it, but it felt so good, especially without the hated chains weighing her down.

She was drying herself with the towel he'd left when she spotted a looking-glass on the wall and took a look at herself, almost falling back with shock at what she saw. Hollows had taken the place of her plump red cheeks and her eyes seemed to be bulging out of her head. When she looked down at her body she saw that was emaciated too, her ribs sticking out below her breasts. Stranger still were her brown face and forearms when the rest of her was ghostly white.

But her newly washed hair did look pretty, hanging in dark shiny ringlets to her shoulders. She rubbed at it hard with the towel, and combed it through with Graham's comb to remove the lice, then washed that too in the bath water and put it back where she'd found it.

As she heard the sound of Graham's feet coming back she dived into the bunk, quickly covering herself with the blanket.

Graham came in slowly. He was carrying a small tray

which he put down while he locked the door again. Mary felt too shy to speak, but at the smell of the food, she couldn't resist sitting up.

'Is that for me?' she exclaimed, hardly able to believe her luck, for it was some kind of pie, the pastry all golden the way her mother used to make it, with a rich gravy poured over it.

'I guessed you were still hungry,' he said gruffly, without looking at her, as if embarrassed.

'That was kind of you, sir,' she said.

'You don't have to call me sir in here,' he said, passing her the tray and sitting down on the edge of the bunk. 'My name is Spencer, now eat it up before it gets cold.'

Mary didn't need to be told twice, and fell upon it with glee. It was rabbit and vegetable pie, the best she had eaten since she left Fowey, and even though the food meant more than the man who brought it to her, she couldn't help but notice he seemed to be enjoying her obvious delight.

The Lieutenant was surprised by his own emotions as he watched Mary eat. He had expected either to feel guilt that he was betraying his wife's trust in him, or so lustful once he got back to his cabin that he wouldn't be able to give Mary time to eat the dinner. But instead he felt able to put aside both his guilt and his lust, because the way she ate the food made him feel good. She hadn't noticed as she was eating that her breasts had become exposed, two small perfect little mounds with pale pink nipples. A little gravy had run on to one of them, and it was all he could do not to lean forward and lick it off.

He had married Alicia, his second cousin, at twenty, ten years ago now. They had played together as children, learned to dance and ride together back home in a village near Portsmouth, and there had always been an understanding that they would eventually marry. Alicia had come to live in his parents' home, and she was very much the daughter of the house. She painted, sewed and played the piano, was gracious to all their guests, never complained when he was away for long periods. She even produced first a son, then a daughter, without losing her shapely figure.

Graham considered it a very successful marriage. They were in harmony with each other, and he knew that other men envied him such a pretty and vivacious wife. He didn't understand why he sometimes felt disappointed.

Yet as he watched Mary eating, he realized why. Alicia was like biting into fruit, delicious and good for him, but not satisfying in the same way as a meat pie could be. Alicia never argued with him, everything he said was right. She always looked lovely when she welcomed him home on leave, but there was never any passion, no real emotion.

Mary was not even close to being as pretty as Alicia. Even if she were dressed in the most expensive silk gown, her hair arranged in an elegant coiffure, she would still look what she was, a simple country girl with no social graces.

Yet she was so very desirable, especially now, scrubbed clean and her dark hair flowing on her shoulders. She had a defiance he'd never seen in Alicia; she was proud, daring, wilful and outspoken. It would be a challenge to make this convict woman love him, and he felt that if he succeeded he'd discover something marvellous and sustaining. It even thrilled him that he was risking his career in the Marines by bringing her to his cabin. He'd never done anything so daring in his life before.

'That was wonderful,' Mary said, surprising him that she could be so grateful. 'And the bath, that was wonderful too.'

She felt she was up to sharing his bed now. Warm and clean after the bath, with a belly full of food, she was ready for almost anything. Somehow she didn't think he'd be very rough with her, not if he thought to bring her such good food.

'Would you like some rum?' Graham asked.

'Just a little,' she said. She didn't really like the taste, but she enjoyed the warming effect it had on her. Besides, Sarah had warned her to drink whatever she was offered, saying it would help to numb her.

Graham handed her some rum in a glass and began to strip himself of his clothes. Mary gulped down her drink as she saw his white, hairy legs, suddenly afraid she couldn't go through with this. The fear grew greater still as he threw aside his shirt: he had a pigeon chest and a fat white belly which quivered as he moved.

All her life she had been used to seeing semi-clothed male bodies. Fishermen and sailors were often stripped to the waist in the hot weather and they had hard, lean bodies rippling with muscle. That was how she thought all men were, and Graham's unexpected white, flabby flesh made her feel suddenly queasy. But there was no backing down now, so she wriggled down under the blanket, leaving room for him beside her, and averted her gaze.

He was on to her within a second of getting into the bunk, pressing her into the mattress under his weight, his hands moving wildly all over her body and his lips clamped to hers like a limpet. Mary had no idea how to respond; her only experience had been with Thomas, and he'd given her gentle, sensual kisses that left her aching for more.

Graham's mouth moved from her lips to her breasts, sucking at them so hard it hurt, and his breath came hard and heavy like a horse's after a long gallop. She could feel his penis against her belly, hard and hot, but mercifully it appeared to be small. Within seconds, with his face buried in her neck, he was prising her thighs apart and forcing his way into her.

It didn't hurt, but it wasn't pleasant either, just the sensation of a pole being shoved into a dry tube which was barely large enough to accommodate it. She didn't like the way he gripped her buttocks, grunting like a pig.

But thankfully it didn't last long. The grunting grew gradually louder, his body grew hotter and more sweaty, then all at once he sighed deeply and was still, his face buried in her neck.

It was only then that she felt a slight tenderness towards him. After all she had been through in the past six or seven months, it was good to be held, and to lie in a warm and comfortable bed. She lifted one hand and caressed his neck and shoulders, wondering if she should say something.

But what could she say? Not that she loved him or that he thrilled her. Nor could she ask if he intended to do it again to her, tonight or any other night. That was another reminder of her status, a wretched convict woman who had no rights and was considered to be without feelings or needs. She was pretty certain that most people imagined such women were incapable even of thought.

He moved down the bunk a little, cradled his head against her breasts and almost instantly fell asleep, his arm tightly round her.

Mary lay there for some time. The air coming through the porthole was clean and fresh, only Graham's gentle breathing breaking the total silence. It was good to know that no rats were likely to run across her in the night as she slept, and no hunger pains would wake her. Yet she couldn't sleep, for it suddenly occurred to her that she might be able to escape.

Graham had locked the door when he came in, and she was sure he'd put the key in his jacket pocket. Could she possibly get out of the bunk and find her clothes and his keys without waking him? Would there be a guard posted outside?

The last question was answered when she heard the tread of heavy boots pass by the door. She listened closely for some time, mentally seeing the route the guard was taking around the deck. As he approached the cabin door for a second time, she counted out the seconds before he made a complete circuit. Ninety seconds, but on the third circuit he stopped somewhere, perhaps to smoke a pipe, or rest.

She realized then that there were too many unknown quantities to deal with to try to escape tonight. She didn't know how heavy a sleeper Graham was, she wasn't certain where the key was, nor had she checked the sides of the hulk to find the best place to climb down to the water. Jumping over the side would be foolhardy; she'd alert the guard in a second with the splash. All she could hope for was that Graham would want her again, that she could build up his trust in her, and meanwhile take careful note of the deck layout and best escape routes.

Mary dreamed she was at home in bed with her sister Dolly, waking to find that the hand caressing her belly was Graham's, not her sister's. She feigned sleep, hoping he would drop off again too, but to her surprise she heard him lighting a candle.

It was so tempting to open her eyes to see what he was doing, but if she did he might send her back to the hold, and she was too warm and snug to relish that. She felt him move the blanket back, and felt the slight heat from the candle coming nearer her.

All at once she became aware he was sitting up, the candlestick in his hand, studying her body. It was unnerving, but still she didn't open her eyes. He gently probed at her private parts with one finger, parting the hair, then with two fingers held the lips apart.

It was even harder to pretend sleep, knowing he was looking at a part of her no one but herself had ever seen. She wondered why he wanted to look at it. Had he never seen one before? Or was he checking her for a disease?

But as his finger slid over her there, the strangest sensations washed over her. It felt good, the way Thomas's kisses had, and involuntarily she opened her legs a little wider. The hesitant rubbing became a little stronger, and she knew he was looking at that part of her, not at her face, because she could feel the warmth of his breath on her belly. She half opened her eyes and saw that he wasn't holding the candlestick as she supposed; that was resting on the side of the bunk. He was rubbing his penis with one hand while stroking her intimately with the other.

She shut her eyes tightly. She didn't want the image of his fat belly to spoil the pleasure he was giving her. While it seemed peculiar that a man would prefer to do such things to her while she was asleep, rather than awake and responding, she had no real idea what lovers did to one another anyway.

Again and again his finger slid into her, and it was all she could do to lie quietly and not call out. She could hear his breath becoming more laboured, his hand moving faster and faster on his penis, and then just as she was about to reach for him, urge him to put it inside her, he made a grunting sound and was still.

He got back into bed beside her a few seconds later, and again fell soundly asleep. Once more Mary lay awake, disturbed by the feelings he'd aroused in her, and even more puzzled by his actions. Was he being caring by not waking her for what he wanted to do? Or was it some deviation of normal male behaviour?

She must have fallen asleep eventually, for the next thing she knew he was shaking her. 'Wake up, Mary,' he said. 'It's time for you to go back.'

It was barely dawn, just a faint pink glow in the east, as she walked across the deck, the chains back on her. Graham was in front of her, and as he reached the first of the two doors to the hold, he turned back to her.

'Do not speak of this to anyone,' he said, his face tight with tension. 'If you are asked to explain your absence tell them you were locked up on deck as a punishment. Next time I will try to have a dress for you.'

He said nothing more, just unlocked the first door, then went down to the next and unlocked that, gently nudging her in without a word of farewell.

If anyone heard or saw her come in, they said nothing. Mary made her way to her bench, nudged Anne over as she had taken up her space, and lay down. After the warmth and softness of Graham's bunk, the planks seemed very hard and cold. But she noticed it smelt far more pleasant in the hold, and that pleased her. Yet Graham's last words had made her feel uneasy, for it was obvious he didn't know how the other women would react to one of their number going missing for a night. They wouldn't ask where she'd been, they'd just ignore her.

To Mary's utmost surprise there was no animosity towards her when she woke again later. In fact her status appeared to have been raised to one of heroine. 'Did they flog you?' Anne asked first, and with that every single woman, even the sick ones, raised themselves to thank Mary for her courage in demanding to see Graham. Only Sarah gave her a knowing look, and she grinned when Mary told the story that she'd been chained up on the deck until dawn.

All the women seemed much less apathetic now the hold was cleaner, and throughout the day Mary was unable to get to speak to Sarah for them complimenting her, asking questions, and remarking on how no one else had ever dared do such a thing. The men were cleared out of their hold that morning too, for cleaning, and later, as they came back, Mary was subjected to shouted praise from them too.

Will Bryant called her over to the grille. 'You're a plucky little lass,' he called out. 'Bless you for it.'

'You got to marry her now,' James Martin shouted, and Mary laughed along with the men, amused as much by their ribald remarks as their praise for her.

'I won't be holding you to it, Will Bryant,' she called back. 'I know you're all talk, and besides, I've got no wedding finery in here with me.'

While it felt good to receive so much admiration, Mary felt guilty too. The next time Graham called her out, not only would she lose all this respect, but they'd hate her for deceiving them.

After dark she managed to slip on to Sarah's bench to talk to her. 'I was with Graham,' she whispered. 'What do I do now about all this?'

'But for you there would be many more deaths,' Sarah whispered back. 'Besides, they'd all be offering their fannies if they thought there was anyone up there wanting them. But never mind that, what was it like?'

'Not so bad,' Mary replied. Much as she would have liked to share her experiences with her friend, she couldn't out of loyalty to Graham. He had after all been kind to her.

Four days later Mary was called again by Lieutenant Graham. This time she had been set to work cleaning the galley alone, and when she finished the filthy job, Graham appeared and ordered her into his cabin. It was late afternoon, and seconds after the door was locked behind her, she heard the male convicts arriving back from their outside work.

Again he removed her shackles, and again there was water for her to bathe in. But he didn't stop to undress, and took her swiftly, before she was even dry, and when he had finished thrust a clean dress and petticoat at her.

'You can't stay up here,' he said. 'It would be noted. Put these on and be gone.'

'Can I have something to eat?' she asked as she put the petticoat on. It was very worn, but soft and clean. The grey dress was equally worn, but it looked wonderful to her as her old one was in shreds.

'I thought you'd steal food while you were in the galley,' he said with a sneer.

'Our arrangement wasn't for me to steal what I need,' she said sharply. One of the guards had watched her most of the time she was in the galley, and to her disappoint-ment all she'd managed to get her hands on was a bit of cheese. 'I've kept my part of the bargain, so you keep yours.'

As she put the new dress on he turned away and opened a tin box. 'Very well,' he said, his back turned to her. 'But keep your mouth shut about this. If word gets out I'll have you flogged.'

He handed her a cold pasty and an apple.

'Thank you, sir,' she said, and made an insolent curtsy. 'I won't be boasting about it. I'm not proud to stoop this low either.'

As he bent to lock her chains, she felt his hurt. She might have added something kinder, but she was too busy eating the pasty.

The weeks and months passed very slowly into autumn and finally to winter, bringing with it the prospect of freezing to death. With only one blanket apiece, the women huddled even closer together at night. There were several more deaths among the older ones, but a new influx took their places, and still there was no news of the transportation.

Will Bryant had been on the *Dunkirk* for two years already and he often joked to Mary through the grille that his seven-year sentence would be up before they set sail.

Mary was still every bit as desperate to escape. She knew the layout of the upper decks intimately: who patrolled at any given time of the day; the times when there were fewer guards on duty. But no feasible opportunity to escape had presented itself yet, however vigilant she was. She certainly wasn't going to attempt it in a foolhardy way, for if she was caught she could expect a hundred lashes at least.

So, like Will, she had learned to bear her imprisonment, concentrating her energies on finding ways to alleviate the misery and stay alive and healthy. Whilst her continuing good health and her work up on deck, and nights away, did create some jealousy among the other women, she still commanded their respect for being their spokeswoman when required. She also helped herself to anything useful which came her way – rags for the women's menses, soap and small amounts of food when she could get it – and gave it away to those who needed it most.

Mary Haydon and Catherine Fryer, along with Aggie as their vociferous mouthpiece, did their best to make the other women turn against Mary, but the only real charge that stuck against her was she was aloof and proud. Mary didn't mind them saying that of her – pride to her wasn't a fault – and as for being aloof, she supposed she was, in as much as she kept her own counsel and tried to rise above the petty squabbling some of the others went in for. But no one ever called her a whore, though she was well aware that was in fact what she'd become, even if it was only with Lieutenant Graham.

Once, sometimes twice, a week she slept in his cabin. He slipped her extra food, gave her clean clothes now and then, and showed her a certain amount of affection. But she was still nowhere nearer understanding the man.

At times it seemed as if he was in love with her, at others he appeared to loathe her. She now knew he was married with two children, and when he did speak of his wife Alicia it was almost with awe. Yet he persisted in bedding Mary, and seemed desperate for her to say she loved him. At times he gave her some pleasure, but more often his love-making was like the first night, fast, furious and without any feeling.

Mary's feelings for Graham were based on pity more than anything else, for she sensed he was a complicated man, who didn't appear to have any true friends. He had no real love for the Marines and had told her many times he wished he could resign his commission. Mary sensed he was a coward, and that he lived in fear of being given new orders to go somewhere dangerous. Yet he liked the power he had as an officer and knew there was no place for him in civilian life.

Mary suspected that even the marriage he claimed was such a happy one survived because husband and wife were apart so much. Lieutenant Captain Watkin Tench, whom Graham belittled at every opportunity, was a far happier man.

Tench was Mary's other problem, for she felt she had fallen in love with him. While she doubted she would ever have looked his way if she'd met him when she was free, right from the first night they talked, she'd been smitten. It wasn't for his looks, which weren't that remarkable, nor because he could be relied on to give her extra food. It was because he cared about people, even convicts. He could command without brutality, and had a sense of humour too.

She loved his ready smile, a certain eagerness for life,

his generosity of spirit and his lack of prejudice. She had long since given up any hope of him as a lover, but she counted him as a friend.

She knew now that it was he rather than Graham who put her on the list for work up on deck. He always spoke to her kindly, and listened sympathetically when she went to him with complaints. While mostly he couldn't reduce the hardships the prisoners had to bear, for decisions were made much further up the hierarchy, he did what he could.

Tench was well aware of Mary's arrangement with Graham, but he did not appear to despise her for it. He was an intelligent and adventurous man, who had already seen more of the world than anyone else Mary had known. He liked order and calm, but he was courageous too, loyal and dutiful to his King and Country. Mary doubted he would ever lie or take a bribe, yet he had compassion for those who did.

He loved books, and had told Mary that he kept a meticulous diary which he hoped might be published one day. Mary often wondered if he mentioned her in his writings, for she felt he was fond of her. He had said once that he wrote a great deal about his view of the penal system, because it would be of interest in the future to historians.

One day just before Christmas, Mary was called out for washing duties with Bessie. It was a bitterly cold day, and for once Mary would have been glad not to have been chosen. Bending over a tub of washing, up to her armpits in icy water and exposed to the elements, was not something to be desired. Only the prospect of possibly seeing Tench made it bearable.

It was even worse than she feared. The wind from the sea cut through the poorly clad women like a knife. Bessie began to cry within minutes of putting her hands in the cold water, and however much Mary tried to take her mind off it, she couldn't be cheered.

They didn't wash the clothes as thoroughly as they had during the summer and by noon the job was completed, the whole deck festooned with wet shirts which would freeze on the lines.

As they made their way back to the hold, Tench appeared. 'I want a word with Mary Broad,' he said to the guard. 'I'll take her back myself in a few minutes.'

To Mary's surprise and delight, he ushered her into his cabin on the deck and gave her a cup of tea to drink. She clasped the cup with her two hands to warm them.

'Bless you,' she said gratefully. 'I'm so cold I thought I might die in a few more minutes.'

'I didn't just bring you in here to let you get warm,' he said. 'I have some news for you. Your transportation has been arranged.'

'When and where to?' she asked, hoping it was to be soon, to somewhere warmer than here.

'We are bound for New South Wales,' he said.

Mary could only stare at him for a moment. He had told her what he knew of this country on the other side of the world in a previous conversation. Captain Cook had reported on a place there he had named Botany Bay, which it was thought might be suitable for a penal colony.

97

But at the time Tench told her this, he considered New South Wales was unlikely to be the final destination of the convicts on the *Dunkirk*.

'"We" are to go?' she said. 'You mean you too?' She didn't think she'd mind being sent to hell if Tench was to be there along with her.

He smiled. 'Me too, they need Marines to keep you all in order. I am excited at the prospect. It's a new country, one I very much want to see. England needs a presence in that part of the world, and if this country is all that has been reported, it could become an important place for us.'

Tench's enthusiasm warmed Mary even more than the hot tea. As he went on to speak of the fleet of eleven ships being sent, of convicts building towns, of farming and being given free land when their sentences were up, she shared some of his excitement. She had always wanted to travel, a long voyage by sea didn't daunt her, and if they were to be the first people to land at Botany Bay there could possibly be good opportunities for someone as quick-witted as herself.

'Swear you won't tell the other women,' he warned her. 'I'm only telling you because I hoped it might cheer you. I watched you earlier out there in the cold and my heart went out to you.'

He went on to tell her that Botany Bay had some native people with black skin, that the government believed there was flax and timber there, and the climate was good, far warmer than in England. He said Captain Cook had reported many strange animals and birds, including a large furry beast that bounded along on its back legs, and a huge flightless bird. But though Mary was interested to know more about this new country so far away, it was Tench's words, 'my heart went out to you', that resonated in her mind.

'When will we sail?' was all she could ask.

Tench sighed. 'We have orders to take you to the ships on the 7th of January, but I suspect it will be some time before we set sail. Captain Phillip, who is commanding this operation, is not yet satisfied with the supplies of goods and food to be taken with us.'

'Will I be on the same ship as you?' Mary asked.

'Would you like to be?' he asked, his dark eyes looking hard at her.

'I would,' she said bluntly, seeing no point in being bashful.

'I think I could arrange that,' he said, and smiled. 'Now, not a word to anyone, especially Lieutenant Graham.'

'Is he going too?' she asked.

Tench shook his head. 'Does that sadden you?'

Mary smiled. 'No, not at all. I don't think he's a man for an adventure.'

Tench chuckled, and Mary wondered if that meant Graham had in fact refused to go. 'No, he's not one for adventure, Mary. But you and I are, and perhaps we'll see things we never dreamed of.'

Chapter four

The prisoners were not informed of the date of their transportation until the morning of 7 January, the day they were to be moved to the *Charlotte*.

Ever since Tench had told Mary when it would be, she'd been in a state of agitation, made far worse because she was unable to share it with anyone else. One moment she was hugging herself with glee that her days on the *Dunkirk* were numbered, the next she was terrified that the sea voyage and the land at the end of it would be even worse.

As the days slowly passed and she'd still heard nothing official, she began to think Tench might be mistaken. She couldn't even ask Graham to verify it, for he would undoubtedly take Tench to task for telling her.

Lieutenant Graham was behaving very strangely though. More and more, he fluctuated wildly between tenderness and malice. This in itself seemed to confirm Mary really was leaving.

'You are just a whore,' he said with venom one night. 'You might think you are different from the rest of the women in the hold, but you aren't, just a damned whore like all the rest.'

Yet on another occasion as she was getting dressed to go back down to the hold, he fell down on his knees before her and clung to her with his face buried in her breast. 'Oh, Mary,' he gasped out. 'I should have done more for you, not used you the way I have.'

On Christmas night he was very drunk and he told her he loved her. That night his love-making was gentle and very tender; he kissed the marks on her ankles made by the shackles and with tears in his eyes, begged her to forgive him for his moments of cruelty to her.

'There's nothing to forgive,' she said. His previous insults hadn't really hurt her, at least not if she stacked them up against the good things he'd done for her.

'Then tell me you love me,' he begged her. 'Let me believe you came to me for something more than food and clean clothes.'

'Of course I did,' she lied, feeling sorry that he wasn't able to accept their arrangement as she did. 'But you aren't free to love me, Spencer, so please don't give me false hope by saying such things.'

She didn't love him, she wasn't sure that she even liked him, yet that night he had moved her, touched some inner part of her. As she made her way back to the hold the following morning, with another, newer grey dress, she wondered whether if they'd met under different circumstances it could have been different.

On the night of 6 January he called her out again, and she expected it was to tell her about the move the following day. But he said nothing about it, offered no endearments, further apologies or good wishes for her future.

He just took her roughly, and curtly ordered her back to the hold. If she hadn't known better, she might have thought he didn't know what was coming for her.

It was barely light when the guards opened the door of the hold and read out the names of the women who were to go up on deck. Mary wasn't surprised by the brusque order, but she was startled to hear just twenty names called, and some of those the old and infirm.

The reaction of the women called up on to the deck in a sleet storm was understandable. They were suspicious, puzzled and dismayed, clutching their ragged clothes about them and huddling together for warmth. Mary had to act just like them, for if anyone was to guess she knew where they were going, she'd be in trouble for not telling them. Yet as she stood there shivering on the deck, she was at least glad that Sarah and Bessie had been called, and Aggie, her old adversary, left behind.

Mary Haydon and Catherine Fryer were on the list as well, something Mary viewed with mixed feelings. They made a show of friendship now and then, but she sensed they would always be waiting for her downfall. Among forty women Mary had been able to keep her distance from them, but now the number was down to twenty it would be harder.

Thirty men were called out too, six of whom looked so sick and frail that they could barely be expected to stand, let alone survive a long voyage. But Mary was cheered to see Will Bryant and Jamie Cox among them, though disappointed that James Martin and Samuel Bird were not. Mary had grown to like all four men during her chats with them through the grille: Will and James both made her laugh, and Jamie had become like a younger brother. His crime had been stealing some lace valued at only five shillings, and he worried about how his widowed mother was managing without him. He was so mild and gentle that she was very relieved he could stay under the mantle of big Will's protection. She hoped James and Samuel would look out for each other when their other friends had gone.

The news that they were to be moved immediately to the *Charlotte* came from a man Mary had never seen before. He wore civilian clothes covered by a thick cloak, and a three-cornered hat trimmed with gold braid, and seemed ill at ease addressing felons. Perhaps his nervousness was because he expected his announcement would be met with anger. And it was: the majority of the prisoners let out a wail of outrage, for many had already served over half their original sentence and had husbands, wives or children they now feared they would never see again.

As always, protestations were ignored, and the guards moved menacingly closer. Only Mary dared to raise her voice with a question.

'Sir, are we to receive clothes for this voyage? Some of our number have little more than rags to wear, and I fear they will die of cold before we reach warmer climates.'

The man lowered his spectacles and peered over them at her.

'Your name?' he asked.

'Mary Broad, sir,' she called back. 'And some of the

women are already sick. Will there be a doctor to see them before we leave?'

'Everyone will be checked,' he said, but there was no certainty in his voice. He made no reply to the request for clothes.

It was dusk before all the prisoners from the *Dunkirk* were ferried out to the *Charlotte* in Plymouth Sound. Mary's only thought as she saw the ship was surprise that it was so small, just a three-masted barque perhaps a hundred feet long. But it looked sturdy, and she was so perished with cold that she was incapable of taking anything else in.

The belief they were to set sail within a few days was soon dashed. It seemed the rest of the fleet wasn't ready and there was a problem with the seamen's wages. The conditions on the *Charlotte* were superior to the *Dunkirk*'s in as much as rations were larger, and the twenty women were not joined by any other prisoners, so they had more space. The men were not so lucky, for they had been joined by prisoners from elsewhere in England, making a total of eighty-eight. But as the *Charlotte* was anchored out in the Sound, and the hatches to the holds were closed because of bad weather, many of the women suffered from sea sickness immediately. Within days the conditions were almost as foul as those on the *Dunkirk*.

Week after week passed with no news of sailing. As they were still chained and kept in darkness for most of the day, with the ship wallowing in the waves, any optimism the women had felt at first was soon replaced by despair. Many of them took to their bunks and sought refuge in sleep. Those who found themselves unable to do this squabbled among themselves.

There were times when Mary fervently wished she was still on the *Dunkirk*. She desperately missed her conversations with Tench and the male prisoners, and even her visits to Graham. Tench was on leave, and on the rare occasions the women were allowed up on deck, the few Marines and sailors on board ignored them.

The brief periods on deck were a torment to Mary. While it was wonderful to breathe clean, salty air, to be able to stand upright and walk, the sight of Cornwall on the horizon was almost too painful to bear. And it was worse still to be forced to return to the stinking hold, never knowing when she'd get out again.

She found herself recalling the most inconsequential things about her home and family as she lay shivering on her bunk. The way Dolly and she used to brush each other's hair at night, laughing at how it crackled and sparked. Father chopping up wood for the fire, shouting through the window that he should have had boys so they could do it. Mother straining her eyes threading a needle by candlelight. She wouldn't sew and mend by day when the light was good because she felt it was sinful to spend daylight hours doing something she enjoyed.

Mostly these memories were tender ones, but now and again Mary would be stricken by a bitter one too. Like the time her mother beat both her and Dolly because they'd gone into the sea naked.

On the day it happened Mary hadn't understood why their mother was so angry. It seemed totally illogical to her. It was after all a very hot day, and surely if she and Dolly had spoiled their new clothes with salt water, that would have been much more serious.

Of course it wasn't Dolly's idea: she couldn't swim, and a paddle was all she wanted. Mary made her do it.

Mary could see them both now. Dolly was about sixteen, and had the Sunday afternoon off from her job in service, so they'd gone for a walk to the beach at Menabilly. Both girls were wearing new pink dresses. Their uncle Peter Broad, who was a mariner and rumoured in the family to be making a lot of money, had brought back the silky material from one of his voyages overseas, and Mother had spent weeks making them.

Dolly was absolutely thrilled with her new dress. She adored the colour pink and the style was a very fashionable one, with a nipped-in waist and a small bustle. Mary wasn't struck on pink, nor did she want to be dressed identically to her sister. It was bad enough that Dolly always managed to look perfect, whatever she wore, for she was naturally neat, but when they were dressed the same, Mary thought her own defects showed up more. They were very alike in as much as they both had the same dark curly hair, but Dolly was much daintier, with a tiny waist, a graceful way of walking, and big blue eyes that enchanted everyone. Next to her Mary felt plain and awkward.

By the time they got to the beach they were very hot,

and Dolly was disappointed that there was no one there to see her in her new finery.

'It was silly to come here,' she said peevishly. 'Now we've got to walk all the way back in the heat.'

'Let's cool down in the sea then,' Mary suggested.

Dolly was worried about their dresses of course, but after some persuasion Mary convinced her that they could go beyond the beach and through the woods, then come out again at the water's edge, take their dresses off and paddle.

One thing led to another. Once they were in a place where they couldn't be seen, Dolly saw no point in getting her petticoat or shift wet either, for she was sure Mary would splash her. Maybe for that one time she wanted to be as daring as her younger sister, and when Mary took off every stitch of clothing and went in for a dip, Dolly followed her willingly.

It was the most fun they'd ever had together. Mary held Dolly under her stomach and tried to teach her to swim. She couldn't get the hang of it, so Mary pulled her along in the water by her hands. They were so engrossed in playing that they forgot to keep an eye out for anyone watching.

Later, dressed again, they giggled all the way home, and Dolly told Mary funny stories about some of the other maids where she worked.

Their mother was standing outside the house when they got home, and even from a distance they knew she was very angry. Her mouth was set in a straight line and she had her arms folded across her chest.

'You little hussies,' she shrieked at them as she came closer. 'Get inside at once and explain yourselves.'

It seemed a fisherman in his boat had seen them bathing, and passed on the information to someone else, who hastily reported back to their mother.

'The shame of it,' she kept saying over and over again as she clouted them up the stairs and ordered them to remove their clothes.

She beat them with a stick across their bottoms and backs, drawing blood on Dolly. Then she banished Mary to bed without any supper, and Dolly back to her employers.

Mary had thought then that her mother was a cruel kill-joy. She couldn't see what harm there had been in swimming naked. And she continued to blame her mother when Dolly never seemed to want to go anywhere with her again.

Mary sighed as she remembered that day. She had been so innocent then, barely aware of her own budding breasts, let alone of how desirable Dolly was. She certainly didn't have any idea that her mother was afraid of what might have happened if her daughters had been spotted by a couple of sailors.

But she knew now, and understood what animals men could be. It seemed to her that almost everything her mother had tried to warn her about had happened. Even the absence of the menses.

Mother had always been vague about what happened between men and women, but she had warned them about what she called 'funny business', and said when the menses didn't arrive it meant a girl was having a baby.

Mary tried to convince herself this couldn't be so, that perhaps it was only the result of the anxiety of waiting for the ship to sail. But by March she was forced to face the possibility that she was expecting Graham's child, and she consulted Sarah.

'I reckon you are,' she said, looking at Mary thoughtfully. 'You poor cow, I'd throw myself overboard in the chains if I thought I was. I've heard tell you can get a reprieve from hanging because of your belly, but I never heard of anyone getting off transportation because of it.'

Mary's heart sank even further then, for she had expected Sarah to pooh-pooh her fears. 'Well, if I am to have it, I'd rather have it here than on the *Dunkirk*,' she said defiantly. She had witnessed Lucy Perkins giving birth there and the horror of it hadn't left her. Lucy was not released from her chains, and after some twenty hours of labour her baby was stillborn. Lucy died a few days later. No doctor was called, the only help she'd had was from the other women. Sarah had been one of them. 'Besides, you'll help me, won't you?'

'Of course I will,' Sarah said quickly, perhaps remembering that birth too. 'You're strong and healthy, you'll be all right.'

Mary lay awake all that night worrying. Not so much about the birth, but what Tench would think of her when he found out. She would never stand a chance with him now.

*

It was the start of May, just after Mary's twenty-first birthday, when they finally heard they were to sail on Sunday the 13th to join the rest of the fleet. There would be eleven ships in all, four of them carrying nearly 600 convicts and a full company of Marines, some with their wives and children, and the rest carrying stores and provisions for the first two years.

During the long wait, most of the other prisoners had written home, or if they couldn't write, had others write letters for them. One day back in April while Mary and the other women were allowed up on deck for exercise, Tench had suggested writing one for Mary, but she refused his offer.

'It's better they don't know where I'm bound,' she said, looking sadly towards Cornwall across the choppy sea. A green haze of spring had suddenly appeared on the land in the last few days, and she thought nostalgically of primroses on grassy banks, birds nesting, and newborn lambs out on the moors. It seemed unbelievable that she was to be torn away from the land she loved so well. 'Better for them to think I don't care about them any more than to imagine me in chains.'

Tench glanced down at her chains and sighed. 'Maybe you're right. But I think my mother would sooner know I was alive and thinking of her, even if I was on a prison ship.'

Mary felt even sadder at his words. Before long her belly would be swollen and he'd see she was having a baby. She doubted he would want to continue to be her friend then. She could just about cope with never seeing her family again, but she didn't think she could stand to be rejected by Tench too.

As the *Charlotte* finally weighed anchor and slipped out of Plymouth Sound, many of the women were crying and saying their goodbyes to England forever.

'I shall come back,' Mary said firmly. 'I swear it.'

While many of the women grumbled even more about sea sickness, the sound of the wind in the sails, and the cuts and bruises they got from falls in bad weather, Mary found herself exhilarated once the ship got underway. The sound of wind in canvas was like music to her and she delighted in watching the bows cleave through the clear water.

The captain of the ship, a Royal Naval officer called Gilbert, was a humane man and he ordered the prisoners' chains to be removed, and only put back on as punishment for bad behaviour, or when they reached port. And as the ship sailed down the coast of France and the weather improved, the hatches were opened up again and the stink in the holds gradually dispersed.

Mary had always loved sailing, but she had never been in anything bigger than a fishing boat, and then only for a few hours at a time. It was very different on a big ship, for you could move about and even find quiet hideaways between coiled copes and lockers to get away from everyone else.

All at once she understood why her father had always eagerly anticipated his next voyage. It was exciting to feel the deck roll beneath her feet, and there was a kind of awe in seeing the wind harnessed to drive the ship along and the way everyone from the lowest sailor to the captain worked as one to maintain her speed and direction. The *Charlotte* was one of the slowest ships in the fleet, and the men had to work hard to keep up. Yet striving to hold their position was a challenge, and Mary could see the pride in their faces each time they managed to outrun the *Scarborough* or the *Lady Penryn*.

But it was the freedom to be up on deck for long periods which Mary appreciated above all else. She could cope with the hold at night, lying wrapped in a blanket between Bessie and Sarah; it wasn't so terrible if she'd been outside nearly all day.

Up on deck she was free from the carping and squabbling of the other women. She could feel the wind in her hair, the sun on her face, and she forgot the filth and smells below. Her fears for the future vanished like a feather tossed up into the wind. She felt as free as the seabirds who followed in the ship's wake.

The sounds on deck were almost as clamorous as those below: the roar of the sea, shouts from sailors, the rasps of pulled ropes and the creaking of sails. But they were good sounds, and the wind and sea spray were so clean and pure that she felt intoxicated.

She was glad most of the women found the sea frightening and the wind too cold to stay up there for long. Alone, gripping the deck rail, she could pretend to herself that she was an heiress taking a trip to Spain or even America. She could tell herself truthfully that she was doing what she'd always wanted to do, travelling the world.

Once they were underway, Mary found the sailors very much like the men back in Fowey, strong, wiry, friendly souls who grinned at her cheerfully. Without other women around she sometimes got opportunities to talk to them and ask them questions about the route to Botany Bay. Some of them were only too happy to tell her about the ports along the way they had visited before, and explained that they had to go right across the Atlantic Ocean to Rio, instead of down the African coast, to take advantage of the Trade Winds. Mary wondered how many of them had originally been press-ganged into the Navy, for they seemed to have some sympathy for the prisoners, and resentment towards most of the Marines who had precious little to do on the voyage.

Many of the Marines had brought their wives and children along too. The women looked fearful whenever they took a walk along the decks, and Mary felt sorry for them even if they were too snooty to smile. They were as much prisoners as she was, but while she knew just how harmless most of the real prisoners were, these women probably imagined they were all desperadoes, waiting for an opportunity to take over the ship and kill every soul on board.

Mary was glad that she seldom saw Tench on deck, for she could feel her body changing, even if it wasn't apparent to anyone else. Her breasts were fuller, her belly had a curve to it. She was dismayed that her liaison with Graham had led to this predicament, something she'd never really considered could happen to her, but she was becoming resigned to it. Part of this acceptance was because she'd been brought up to believe that all babies were a gift from God and therefore must be welcomed wholeheartedly. Whilst she had some fears about the delivery, and her own ability to be a good mother, she felt strangely warmed by the prospect of having someone all her own to love and nurture. In good weather she would find a sheltered place to sit up on deck, and lapse into day-dreams about her child. She hoped for a boy, and imagined him a little like Luke, a son of one of the Marines.

Luke was seven, a sturdy boy with dark hair and blue eyes, who smiled at her when his mother wasn't looking. Mary liked to watch him trying to help the sailors – he was clearly as keen on sailing as she had been as a girl. As the ship sailed down the coast of France to Spain and the weather became warmer, Luke's mother often sat with him on deck, helping him to read and write. Mary wished then that she had such skills to pass on to her child.

It was fear for her baby's safety that finally made her approach Surgeon White. Her father had always said that ships' surgeons were either butchers or drunks, but she had never seen White drunk. His jovial face, and his gentle manner when he checked her health just before sailing, didn't appear to belong to a butcher, either.

She hadn't told anyone but Sarah of her predicament, and she was certain no one, especially not Tench, had guessed. But however embarrassing it was to admit it to the doctor, she realized she must face up to it.

'I think I'm with child,' she blurted out, after first asking him if he could give her something for a cut on her foot which wouldn't heal.

He raised one bushy grey eyebrow, then asked her a few questions and got her to lie down so he could feel her belly.

'Will I be all right?' she asked when he made no comment.

'Of course you will, a birth at sea is no different to one anywhere else,' he said a little sharply. 'I'd say it is due in early September, so we'll be somewhere warmer and more congenial by then. You are strong and healthy, Mary, you'll be fine.'

Mary realized then that she had probably conceived at Christmas, the night Spencer Graham had been his most loving.

'Who is the father?' the surgeon asked, his sharp dark eyes boring into her as if he'd read her thoughts. 'You must say, Mary, for the father must be made responsible. If it is another convict you can be married, and a Marine can be made to give the child his name.'

It was surprising to Mary that anyone should care who'd got her pregnant, and even more so that they would take any man to task for it. But she wasn't prepared to name Graham. Without him she wouldn't have survived the *Dunkirk*, and then there were his wife and children who didn't deserve the hurt of knowing he'd been unfaithful.

'His name, Mary?' White said more firmly.

'I don't know who the father is,' she said, folding her arms in a gesture of defiance.

'I don't believe that of you,' he said reprovingly. 'Some of the other women I might, but not you. Now tell me and leave me to deal with it.'

'I won't,' she said stubbornly.

White tutted. 'Your loyalty is admirable but misplaced, Mary. Do you want your child to have "bastard" on his record of birth?'

'It's no worse than having a convict for a mother,' she retorted.

White shook his head, then dismissed her, with only the parting shot that she must think on it and come back to him if she changed her mind.

The day following her visit to the surgeon, a storm broke out, and once more the hatches were battened down and Mary was forced to stay in the hold. After the freedom of the deck it was hideous to be trapped again in darkness with the women, most of whom were in the throes of sea sickness. The ship rolled and pitched, the slop buckets overturned, and icy sea water rushed in, soaking them all. All Mary could do was clutch her blanket more tightly round her, cover her nose against the smells, and pray for the storm to pass quickly.

It took three weeks to reach Santa Cruz in Tenerife, the ship's first port of call, by which time Mary had got to know a couple of the Devonshire sailors quite well. It was from them she learned that on one of the other transport ships the male convicts had broken through the bulkheads to get at the females, even before they sailed. They said too that the women who had been brought down from the London prisons were vicious, hardened criminals, always fighting among themselves, ready to sell themselves to anyone for a tot of rum.

This was frightening to Mary, for she had imagined the prisoners on the other ships to be no different to those on the *Charlotte*. Some of those were bad enough, she knew they'd happily steal pennies from a dead person's eyes. But at least she knew which ones to watch, and she felt secure in the knowledge that Captain Gilbert would never allow the male prisoners on his ship to threaten the women.

Although a humane man, he was very strict. On the few occasions when male prisoners were on deck at the same time as women, they were watched carefully by the Marines for any misbehaviour. And the threat of being put back in chains or receiving a flogging was enough to deter both male and female from taking any risks.

Yet like on the *Dunkirk*, there were illicit relationships, formed not with the officers, but the Marines and sailors. Mary Haydon and Catherine Fryer were two of the worst offenders, going with any man who would have them. Neither Mary nor Sarah chose to go down this route; they laughed together about it, and said if they couldn't have an officer then they didn't want anyone. The truth of the matter was that they didn't have to fight for survival any more. They had enough to eat now, water to wash with, and after a day on the deck in the sunshine it was preferable to go back to the hold at night than be humiliated and mauled by a rum-soaked sailor.

The only male prisoner that Mary saw often was Will

Bryant, and occasionally Jamie Cox was with him too. The rest of the men weren't allowed up on deck for long. Whether this was because they outnumbered the crew, or that Captain Gilbert felt the women prisoners and the Marines' families needed fresh air more, Mary didn't know, but Will got special privileges. It seemed he had talked his way into being allowed to do some fishing to supplement the ship's rations, so he spent a good part of every day on deck. Mary admired his resourcefulness, and thought they had a lot in common.

When the ship dropped anchor in Santa Cruz to take on fresh water and more provisions, the ship's company were free to go ashore, and once again the prisoners were chained and the hatches closed. It was June and the heat was suffocating, and to be forced to lie sweltering in the darkness after the comparative freedom they'd enjoyed before was intolerable. For Mary it was even more unbearable as now that her belly was swelling she found it impossible to get comfortable on the hard bench, and the lack of fresh air made her nauseous.

But as they set sail again to Rio in South America, the chains were removed and they were allowed on deck again. One afternoon, Mary was sitting dozing in the sunshine when she heard Will Bryant swearing because his fishing net was torn. She got up and made her way back to the stern where he was sitting and offered to mend it for him.

He had become even more attractive during the voyage. The increased rations had put flesh back on his body, his eyes were as blue as the sky above, his fair hair and beard bleached by the sun and his skin a golden-brown. He also had an impudent grin and a great deal of cheek.

'You know how to mend a net?' he asked, looking surprised.

'Would any girl from Fowey not know how to?' she laughed.

Mary thought that it was because she was usefully employed mending the net that no one came over and ordered them apart. She and Will spent the whole afternoon chatting together, mostly about Cornwall.

'You're looking very bonny,' Will said suddenly. 'When's the little 'un due?'

Mary was stricken with sudden embarrassment. She hadn't realized anyone other than Surgeon White and Sarah knew. If Will had guessed, maybe Tench knew too!

'September,' she murmured, blushing to the roots of her hair. 'How did you know?'

'I've got eyes,' Will laughed. 'It ain't something you can hide forever, not when the wind blows your dress close to you.'

Mary felt a little queasy. 'Does everyone know?'

Will shrugged. 'Dunno. Why? Are you scared?'

'A bit,' she admitted. 'I don't want folk to think badly of me, and I don't know much about babies.'

'Don't you trouble yourself about what folk think,' he said with a grin. 'There'll be plenty of other women having a babby afore we get there. As for not knowing about babbies, reckon that comes natural like. The other women will help you too, so don't you fret about nothing.'

Mary was touched that he could be sensitive, she'd

always thought of him as being something of a hard man. A little later he told her he'd heard that a convict on the *Alexander*, another ship in the fleet, had hidden on the deck in Tenerife and lowered himself into the sea later when it was dark and stolen the rowing boat tied to the stern.

'Damn great lummox gave himself away by going to a Dutch ship and asking to be taken aboard,' Will laughed. 'I'd have made for the town and hidden up till the fleet was gone.'

'I used to think about escape all the time on the *Dunkirk*,' Mary admitted. 'There's no point in thinking on it now, not in my condition. But as soon as the baby's born, I'll be watching for an opportunity again.'

'I'll wait to see what Botany Bay's like first,' Will said. 'If I can fish, build a decent place to live, grow a few vegetables, it might not be so bad.'

'But we don't know what the prisoners on the other transports are like,' Mary pointed out. 'All us lot are from Devon and Cornwall. None of us are real bad 'uns. But I've heard tell the women on the *Friendship* are a tough lot, mostly from London. They got put in irons for fighting among themselves. Once we go ashore in Botany Bay we'll have them to put up with.'

'Reckon you can handle most kinds of folk,' Will said. 'I can too. We'll get by.'

It was only a few days later that Tench spoke to Mary up on deck. He asked if she was enjoying the voyage, and explained that he hadn't had much opportunity to be on deck as he had many duties elsewhere. 'Are you feeling well?' he asked, looking at her intently. 'The surgeon told me you were expecting a child.'

Mary could only nod. While to some extent she was relieved it was out in the open, she was afraid that he would question her as White had done.

'I don't pass judgement on others,' he said gently, as if guessing what she was thinking. 'I'm just concerned about you. You are lucky White is aboard this ship, he's a good surgeon. Are you getting enough to eat?'

Mary nodded again. She didn't trust herself to speak.

'If you need anything, come to me,' he said, patting her on the shoulder. 'I'll try and get you some fruit in Rio. Scurvy is a menace on these long voyages. But Captain Gilbert appears to be more aware of all our needs than most sea captains.'

He walked away then, and as Mary watched his slim back, the neatness of his dark hair and the cleanliness of his white breeches, she wished it could have been his child she was carrying.

There were some terrible storms on the way to Rio. The ship pitched and rolled in the heavy seas, and water rushed into the holds, sweeping the women off their bunks. Again and again they thought they would all perish – every crack of the ship's timbers appeared to be evidence she was breaking up. Even Mary, who hadn't suffered from sea sickness before, fell prey to it, retching until she had nothing more to bring up, so weak she could barely move.

But the storms passed and then there were periods of

calm when the ship barely moved at all. It was on one of those days, as Mary stood at the deck rail watching the rest of the fleet, and keeping an eye out for dolphins and porpoises, that Tench suggested she looked among the male prisoners for a husband.

He didn't often get the opportunity to speak to her, and even when he did it was never for more than a few minutes, but since the day when he'd told her he knew of her pregnancy, he usually slipped her something when he saw her. Sometimes it was a piece of hard cheese, or a couple of ship's biscuits; on two occasions it had been a hard-boiled egg. That he cared about her health was enough for Mary. She didn't want him getting a reprimand from the captain.

'Have you considered how it will be when we get to Botany Bay?' Tench began, looking not at her but out to sea and the rest of the fleet marooned in the calm. 'I mean, have you considered how many more men there will be than women?'

She shook her head.

'There will be three to every woman,' he went on, frowning as if deeply concerned by this. 'I suspect it may prove difficult for you women.'

Mary realized with some shock that he was alluding to the likelihood of rape. 'Won't you Marines look after us?' she asked.

'We'll do our best,' he said seriously. 'But even with the best will in the world we won't be able to be every-where, all of the time.'

Mary shuddered. She knew from Will that many of the

men were very desperate characters, but then so were many of the women. Theft of food and belongings was the main thing she'd thought about, but now Tench had made her aware that stealing wasn't going to be the only problem.

'You'd do well to consider getting wed,' he said.

For one brief second she thought it was a proposal, and her heart leaped.

'Wed?' she repeated.

'To one of the prisoners, of course,' he said quickly. 'Your baby will need a father.'

Mary knew she was blushing and she hoped he didn't know why. 'I hardly know any of them,' she said indignantly.

Tench looked over his shoulder, checking to see who was watching them. 'I must go now,' he said. 'But think about what I've said, will you?'

He walked away before Mary could say anything more.

Mary did think hard about what Tench had said. The more she thought about it, the more sense his words made. Men who had been locked away from women for so long were likely to be dangerous, and so were some of the women too.

It was Tench she wanted, she felt she would love him forever and no other man could make her feel that way. But she was a realist; he might like her, maybe even have some romantic feelings for her, but it would take more time than she'd got to make him love her enough to step over the line and take a convict woman. Besides, he was due to go back to England after three years, and she'd still have another four years of her sentence to complete.

There was only one convict she'd seen that she could admire, and that was Will Bryant. He was strong and capable, and he could read and write, he had a real trade in fishing, and he shared her love of boats and the sea. He was also handsome, and he was a natural leader.

The more she thought about Will, the more certain she became that he would be the ideal husband. Of course he wasn't going to see her as much of a catch, she'd have a child which wasn't his for a start. Nor was she that pretty. But there had to be some way to make him see she'd be an asset to him.

All through the eight weeks to Rio, Mary thought of little else but how she was going to persuade Will to become her husband. Because of her condition, Surgeon White gave her permission to stay on deck all day in good weather and have a larger share of rations. This meant she saw Will almost every day, and she mended his nets, gutted the fish for him, often gave him some of her extra food, and flattered him.

Almost daily she found some new facet in Will. His bragging could be wearing, he thought he could do almost anything better than another man, but he was strong, practical and knowledgeable. Yet he had a gentle side too. He always inquired how she was feeling, and once he'd asked if he could put his hand on her belly to feel the baby kick, and looked astounded when he felt it. He was protective of those weaker than himself, and he was a jolly man, rarely down in the mouth about anything.

When the ship had docked in Rio, the chains went on again, hatches were locked, and the crew went ashore. From time to time the prisoners were allowed up on deck for short periods and those who had money could buy produce from the swarthy men who came alongside the ship in little boats to barter with them.

Some of the more fortunate convicts had relatives close enough to Devonport to bring new clothing, food, money and other items for them before the ship sailed. A few had money they'd managed to hang on to throughout their time in prison and the hulk. Will was one of these – he told Mary he'd kept it in a pouch hidden beneath his shirt. He bought oranges and gave half of them to Mary. He also bought a length of white cotton and handed it to her. 'To make some baby clothes,' he said with a strangely shy smile.

When Tench came back on board, a little fragile from all the drinking and carousing he'd done with the other men ashore, he too had a present for her. A blanket for the baby.

'Will bought me cotton to make some clothes,' she added after she'd thanked him, biting back tears of gratitude. 'I'm lucky to have two such good friends.'

'Will's the man you should marry,' Tench said abruptly, taking her completely by surprise.

'Marry me!' she exclaimed, as if such a thing had never crossed her mind. 'Why would he want me when there's prettier women without a child on the way?'

'Because you're clever, good company and steadfast,'

he said, his brown eyes twinkling. 'Those are the attributes I'd look for in a wife.'

'What about love?' she asked, wishing she knew how to flirt the way she'd seen other women do to lure the man they wanted.

'I believe love comes when two people are completely in tune with one another,' he said earnestly. 'I think many people mistake lust for love. The two are very different.'

'But don't they go together?' she asked.

'Sometimes, if you are very fortunate,' he smiled. 'Sadly most of us get one or the other, not both. Or worse still, feel all that for someone who just isn't suitable.'

Mary had a feeling he was trying to tell her that was how he felt about her.

'But surely if you feel that way they can become suitable?' she said wildly.

'Maybe.' He shrugged his shoulders and looked across the harbour to Rio. 'If you could take that person to some new place where your backgrounds didn't matter.'

Their conversation was halted abruptly by Captain Gilbert coming aboard. Tench had to go and greet him, and Mary slipped back to the stern of the ship to gaze at Rio across the bay and wonder if Tench had wished he could take her there.

But if he had, why was he encouraging her to think of Will? Surely that wasn't what men did? But Mary had long ago realized that Tench wasn't like other men.

They sailed out of Rio harbour on 4 September, and three days later, in the evening, Mary went into labour.

It wasn't so bad at first. She lay quietly next to Bessie and even managed to doze. But by the early hours of the morning she was in real pain, and she had to get up and hold on to one of the ship's beams to alleviate it. Surgeon White was called at mid-morning, but he pronounced everything to be normal and said first babies always took a long time. His only preparations were to order two women, who just happened to be Mary Haydon and Catherine Fryer, to collect some straw for Mary to lie on.

The ship was rolling in a heavy swell, and Mary and Catherine were entirely unsympathetic towards Mary. To make matters worse, the hatches were closed because of high winds, so the hold was dark and stuffy.

'You 'ad the pleasure,' Mary Haydon said spitefully. 'Now you got to suffer the pain.'

Mary had always been aware that these two women had continued to hold her responsible for their plight, however much they had insisted in the past that it was done and forgotten. Every time Mary had received gratitude or praise from the other women, she had sensed their jealousy. She guessed they saw her labour as a chance to get even, hoping she'd make an exhibition of herself and lose some of the admiration the others had for her.

But Mary wasn't going to give them the satisfaction of that. When the next pain came she gritted her teeth and bore it silently.

On and on it went, each pain a little stronger until she was forced to lie down and cling to the knotted rope one of the older women had thoughtfully tied around a beam for her to pull on. Sarah sat beside her, bathing her head, and making her take sips of the brackish water.

'It won't be long now,' she whispered encouragingly. 'And if you want to scream, you do it, don't pay no mind to those two witches.'

Mary thought she might die of the agony, and wondered in a brief moment between pains how women could bring themselves to have more than one child. But then, just as she felt unable to bear any more, there was a new sensation, one of wanting to bear down.

She had heard other women, including her mother, speak of this part, and knew it meant the baby was fighting its way out. Suddenly she felt a wave of tenderness for the child within her, and a determination to expel him or her as quickly as possible.

'It's coming now,' she whispered to Sarah, and as the next pain came she clenched her teeth together, brought her legs up, pulled on the rope and bore down hard.

She was vaguely aware that the other women were having their evening meal beyond the blanket Sarah had thoughtfully hung up to give her some privacy – she could smell the stew and hear them chewing. The rolling and the bucking of the ship seemed to echo what was going on with her body, and she was glad of the darkness hiding what she knew must be a very ungainly sight.

She heard Sarah order someone to go and get the surgeon, but it was some time before he came, and he left almost immediately after giving Sarah some curt instructions and a lantern to see by.

'Don't leave me,' Mary screamed as he walked away.

'The women will deal with it,' he said sharply. 'I can't stand upright in here.'

'Bastard,' Sarah spat at his retreating back. But she leaned over to wipe Mary's face tenderly. 'You still got me,' she said soothingly. 'I know what to do, love, you'll be all right.'

The pain was red-hot, and it seemed to Mary she could almost see it glowing through her skin as Sarah washed her bottom and thighs with cool water. As she gave one long huge push she felt the baby coming, and heard Sarah's cry that she could see its head.

Mary had the sensation that a big slippery fish was being drawn out of her. The pain had ceased, and she could hear voices from behind the blanket curtain.

'You've got a little girl,' Sarah crowed delightedly. 'A fine big one too.'

The light from the lantern was dim, but Mary could see Sarah holding up what looked like a skinned rabbit. Then all at once its cry burst out, an angry, defiant yell as if dismayed to find itself in a dark ship's hold.

'She'll make it,' Sarah said with relief in her voice, and put the baby in Mary's arms. 'Now, what are you going to call her?'

Mary couldn't reply for a moment. She could only stare down in awe at her baby. She had a shock of black hair, she looked purple in the dim light, and her little fists were pummelling the air. It seemed unbelievable that this angry little scrap was something which had grown within her.

'I'll call her Charlotte,' she said eventually. 'After the

ship.' Then, as she got a flash of Graham's face looking tenderly at her the night their baby was probably conceived, she added, 'Charlotte Spence.'

'Spence?' Sarah asked. 'What sort of name is that?'

Mary didn't trust herself to answer that one. 'Could I have a drink now? I'm parched.'

It was very late at night when Charles White got back to his cabin, having returned to the hold to find that Mary's baby had arrived safely. He poured himself a glass of whisky, then sat down to write up his diary.

'8 September,' he began. 'Mary Broad. Delivered of a fine girl.'

He sat for a moment, unable to think of anything else that had happened during the day. Mary, lying cradling her baby in that filthy, stinking hold, filled his mind to the exclusion of all else. He had been called to many births over the years, from women of quality in fine houses to peasant women in hovels, and he'd helped them all and been touched by the wonder of new life. He felt some shame that he'd left Mary to fend for herself, for she was clearly a good woman, a cut above her companions with her intelligence and her calm, reserved manner.

Perhaps it was because he knew it was unlikely the infant would survive more than a few weeks. Infant mortality was high enough on dry land, but on a ship with rats, lice, foul water and every kind of disease lurking, waiting to find some weakened recipient, a newborn baby stood little chance. There had been surprisingly few deaths so far, most of those attributed to sickness brought with the convicts from the prison hulks. But there was still a long way to go before they reached Botany Bay.

And when they arrived, things would get far tougher. There were houses to be built, land to be tilled and planted. The natives might be hostile, the weather inclement. It was hardly an ideal environment in which to rear young children.

But he thought Mary would make an excellent mother, she had so many remarkable qualities. He wondered again who the baby's father was, and considered Tench, for he had been on the *Dunkirk* with Mary. He had obviously been waiting for news of her, and his eyes had lit up when White told him about the new arrival. He'd been eager to hear the sex and name of the baby and whether Mary was well.

Yet for all that, he couldn't see Tench as the kind to take a convict woman. He was an upright, honest young man, with a great deal of natural dignity, more interested in putting the world to rights than philandering. But he did have some feelings for Mary Broad, that much was evident. Understandable really, when even a crusty old surgeon like himself found her intriguing.

Charles sighed deeply. There were so many unknown factors in this grand idea of emptying out the prison ships and sending all the undesirables to the other side of the world. No one really knew about the country's climate and its native people, or whether the land could be cultivated. It was a huge gamble, not just with the prisoners' lives, for precious few people back in England cared a jot about them, but with those who were sent to keep them in line.

Captain Arthur Phillip, the commanding officer of the whole fleet, had himself expressed concern that there weren't sufficient provisions, tools and clothing in the supply ships, and that the quality of them all was poor. Nor were there many skilled craftsmen among the prisoners.

Charles stared gloomily at his unwritten diary. If all the prisoners had been like Mary Broad and Will Bryant, intelligent, resourceful people, then the project might have a chance of success. Sadly, a huge proportion of them were complete scoundrels, the slime at the bottom of England's barrel. In truth, the idea was doomed before it had even started.

As the ship sailed towards the port of Cape Town five weeks later, Mary stood at the rails with Charlotte in her arms and marvelled at the beauty of the scene before her.

The sun was setting, the sky pink and mauve, and all eleven ships were close to one another now, their sails billowing in the wind. The sea was turquoise, and a school of dolphins were leaping and diving around them, as if putting on a special show. They had been seeing dolphins and whales too for some days now, a sight Mary never tired of.

'And you aren't even watching,' she said tenderly to Charlotte, who was fast asleep, wrapped in the blanket Tench had given her.

The horrors of her daughter's birth were quite forgotten now. Mary had ample milk and Charlotte was thriving. But then Mary devoted her entire attention to her child.

She never would have believed that she could feel so much for her baby. She rarely put her down, for she didn't trust the other women not to stick their dirty fingers in her mouth, or drop her if they picked her up. One of the sailors had made a little crib for her to sleep in, but though Mary would put her in it up on deck during the day, with a cloth hung over it to keep the sun off, at night she was too worried about the rats, and kept Charlotte firmly in her own arms.

Captain Gilbert had said she could be baptized when they got to Cape Town, as the clergyman for the fleet would be coming on board there. That had touched Mary: she had expected that a prisoner's child would be treated with disdain, as if it wasn't quite human.

'We'll be able to see Table Mountain by tomorrow morning, I expect,' Tench said suddenly by her elbow. Mary hadn't seen or heard him coming towards her. 'It looks just like a table too,' he went on. 'Flat on the top, and when there's mist hanging around it makes a tablecloth, at least so I'm told. I haven't been to Cape Town before.'

'You'll be able to explore it,' Mary said wistfully. 'See all those wild animals and things.'

She knew Tench liked exploring and writing in his diary about where he had been and what he'd seen. She had never met a man with so much enthusiasm for new places and strange things.

'You won't always be a prisoner, Mary,' he said, his

133

voice soft with sympathy. 'Once the settlement in Botany Bay is thriving, and your sentence is up, there will be opportunities for a woman like you to make good.'

'You'll have gone home by then,' she said, trying to keep her tone light.

'I expect so,' he said. 'But you'll be part of a new community, and I've no doubt you will be married too. Perhaps little Charlotte will have a brother or sister.' He bent his head closer to the baby in Mary's arms and kissed her forehead. 'Go for Will Bryant, Mary, he's the best man for you.'

Tench had said nothing more about Will since long before Charlotte was born, but the fact that he'd obviously kept it in his mind proved to Mary he was completely serious about it.

'How would I go about it, just supposing I thought that was a good plan?' she asked.

Tench thought for a moment. 'I'd lay my cards on the table. Point out the advantages for him having a wife. Especially one like you.'

Mary half smiled. 'Back home I would've been thought of as the worst possible choice for a man. I'm not good at cooking and sewing or womanly things.'

'There won't be much call for domestic talents in Botany Bay,' Tench said with a wry smile. 'It will be the toughest, the most adaptable that do well there. You've got backbone, Mary, and plenty of determination. Will knows that, he admires you. I don't think he'll take much persuading.'

'How would you feel if a woman asked you to marry

her?' she asked him, smiling as she asked, as if it was only banter.

'Now, that would depend who asked me,' he laughed. 'If she was rich and beautiful I'd be flattered.'

'So a poor, plain convict girl would have no chance?' she said, trying to sound as if she was joking, but she could hear a plaintive note in her own voice.

He didn't answer and Mary was shamed.

'I'm sorry, I've embarrassed you,' she said.

To her surprise he turned to face her and laid the palm of his hand gently against her cheek. 'I said I'd be flattered by someone rich and beautiful asking me. I'd also be just as flattered if it was a convict girl I really liked. But I wouldn't agree to either,' he said, looking right into her eyes. 'Not because I didn't care enough for her, or thought she was too lowly for me, but because I'm not the marrying kind, Mary. There's too many places I want to see to settle down with anyone.'

'You might end up a lonely old man,' Mary said, swallowing down a lump in her throat and fighting back tears.

'Yes, that's true, but at least I wouldn't have left a wife lonely without me while I explored the world,' he said, and smiled. 'Or children without a real father.'

Charlotte's baptism took place after they had been anchored at Cape Town for three days. The Reverend Richard Johnson came aboard on Sunday morning during a service for the entire ship's company and the prisoners.

Mary was the only prisoner not in chains. Hers had been removed for the duration of the service, but would be put back on immediately afterwards. She had made an effort with her appearance, washing her hair till it shone, and wearing the grey cotton dress given to her by Graham on the *Dunkirk*. She wished it wasn't so crumpled as she'd had to conceal it in the hold when given a 'slop', the shapeless, rough dresses doled out to the women prisoners.

The Reverend Johnson directed his sermon to the prisoners, saying that Botany Bay was a golden opportunity for them all, if they turned away from the wickedness which had caused them to be sent there. He urged the men to choose a wife, for only in matrimony would they find true happiness and contentment.

Mary became aware of Will's eyes on her as she stepped forward holding Charlotte in her arms for the christening ceremony. As the Reverend Johnson poured some water on the baby's head and she began to howl lustily, drowning his words, Mary offered up a silent prayer, not just for Charlotte's safety, but that Will would want her for his wife.

It was a week before Mary had any opportunity to speak to Will as they had run into some rough weather and had had to stay below deck. It was still a little precarious climbing up the companionway with a baby in her arms as the steps were slippery, but she was desperate to get out into the fresh air.

Will was on deck fishing again. Hearing footsteps behind him, he looked round and grinned. 'Good to be out of there, eh!'

'I couldn't stand another minute of it down there,' Mary said with a laugh. 'It's like breathing week-old soup.'

'You and I are made of the same stuff,' Will said, looking at her in approval. 'How's the little 'un?'

'Doing fine,' Mary said, looking down at the sleeping baby she had tied across her in a shawl for safety. 'I wonder if there's any babies on the other ships?'

'Several, I heard,' Will said. 'So at least Charlotte will have some playmates when she's bigger.'

'And if folk get married like the Reverend suggested, there'll soon be more,' Mary added.

Will laughed. 'A lot won't wait for a wedding service. Reckon we'll be overrun with babbies afore the first year's over.'

'But there's three men to every woman,' Mary said pointedly. 'I reckon wives will be in great demand.'

She felt nervous now, sure this was the moment, but afraid to say what was on her mind.

'I'll do all right,' Will said. 'I'll have them lining up for me.'

Mary felt a stab of irritation at his arrogance. 'You'd better choose carefully then,' she said sharply. 'From what I've seen below these decks few of the women have any common sense, and the ones on the other ships may be even more stupid.'

'You wouldn't be a bad prospect for any man,' Will said unexpectedly. 'You've got a good head on you, and you ain't a slattern like most.'

Mary took a deep breath to steady herself. 'I'd be a good prospect for you,' she blurted out. 'I know boats and fishing. We come from the same place, the officers like us both.'

Will seemed staggered at such a suggestion. He stared at her open-mouthed.

'Are you wanting me to wed you?' he said at length, his voice a little strained.

'You could do a lot worse,' she said, blushing furiously. 'I'm healthy and strong, I can work hard for what I want. I know I've got Charlotte and maybe a man doesn't want another's around . . .' She stopped suddenly, unable to think of any other good reason why he should choose her, and ashamed she had to beg.

'Well I never,' Will exclaimed, but he grinned broadly. 'I thought you was too proud to bend to anyone.'

'I'm not bending,' she said quickly. 'I like you, and it's practical.'

'I'd want a wife who does more than just like me,' he said. 'I want her to be hot for me.'

Mary was prepared to go to some lengths to get Will to agree to her proposition, but she didn't feel able to pretend a great passion for him. Faced with his smug grin, she felt foolish and inadequate.

'We've been good friends for over a year,' she said after a few minutes' thought. 'Would you want a friend to lie to you?'

'Of course not,' he said, though he was still grinning smugly. 'But I'd still like a wife who was hot for me.'

'Maybe I could be, in time,' she said wildly, blushing scarlet because she was sure he'd rush off to the other men and tell them what had passed between them. 'We haven't had a chance to get to know each other like that yet.' But before she could say anything further, a sudden shout of warning came from one of the Marines – clearly they were too close together for the man's comfort.

'I've got to go,' Mary said quickly. 'Think on it.'

The weeks that followed were hard, with violent storms and squalls, contrasting with periods of calm when the ship barely moved. The fresh-water ration was cut to conserve it, the food was becoming rotten. Mary had times of extreme anxiety when her milk looked as if it might fail, and she was frightened too of what lay ahead.

Most of the other women were so empty-headed they appeared to imagine they were going to a place that would be ready for them. Mary knew they would be living in tents, and that it was likely some of the foodstuffs taken with them would have perished on the voyage, the same way as many of the animals had. Before Charlotte's birth she had never dwelt on the possibility of the ship being wrecked, but now the fear was with her in every storm. The waters they were sailing in were barely charted, none of the crew had been there before. For all anyone knew, the natives in Botany Bay could be cannibals, there could be wild animals that would tear them apart.

But even worse in one respect was that Will hadn't said another word to her about her proposition. She didn't know if that meant he was still thinking about it, or if he found it too ludicrous to contemplate.

Chapter five

1788

Mary was just coming up the companionway with Charlotte in her arms when she heard the cry 'Land ahoy'. A surge of wild excitement grabbed her and she rushed up the last few steps and across the deck, to join crew members and other prisoners at the rail.

It didn't look much like land to her, just a slightly darker line on the far horizon which could easily be cloud, but she knew the sailor up in the rigging who had spotted it was unlikely to be wrong.

It was January, a whole year since Mary had been transferred to the *Charlotte* from the *Dunkirk*, eight months of that time spent at sea. Charlotte was now five months old. Five male prisoners and a Marine's wife on the *Charlotte* had died, but their deaths were attributed to diseases they carried with them from England, rather than lack of care on the voyage. In the main the prisoners were healthier than when they'd boarded the ship, thanks to fresh air and better rations. Few people had escaped some kind of accident, however, whether a broken limb or mere cuts and bruises, for the ship's deck and steps were dangerously slippery during foul weather.

On the whole, Mary had found the voyage an enjoyable experience. While she was often terrified in the worst of the storms, and despaired at the spite and depravity of some of her fellow prisoners, this had been balanced by the happiness Charlotte had given her. Contrary to all the gloomy predictions, she was thriving. She seemed to charm everyone, from the officers, Marines and sailors right down to the other prisoners, with her ready smiles and placid gurgling. She had given Mary real hope for the future, but now they were nearly at their destination, Mary's natural excitement was also tinged with anxiety.

Tench had told her back in Cape Town that the fleet would be split, the fastest ships going on ahead to prepare the settlement, but she knew that hadn't happened. Bad weather and unfavourable winds had slowed the first ships down, and the others, which included the *Charlotte*, had caught up with them. Mary could see all the ships now, and it was daunting to know there would be nothing ready for them, and that for all they knew the natives could be hostile.

Will Bryant and little Jamie Cox were at the rails, and Mary joined them. ''Tis a grand sight,' Will said with enthusiasm, making an expansive gesture with his hands at the other ships. 'I feared we might lose at least one of them, but they've all made it.'

The prospect of shipwreck had been in everyone's minds during the bad storms, and doubly so for Mary with Charlotte to protect. She had always found it comforting after a bad night to see at least one of the other ships close by in the morning. Will's remark suggested he felt this too.

'Aren't you scared of what's to come?' she asked.

He shrugged. 'Only that there won't be enough food to support us till we've grown some,' he admitted somewhat reluctantly.

'And you, Jamie?' Mary asked.

He smiled shyly. 'The natives mostly. What if they're cannibals?'

'You won't make much of a meal for them,' Mary laughed, and prodded him in the side. Jamie had put on a little more flesh during the voyage, but he still looked like a skinny child to her.

'So what are you scared of?' Will asked Mary.

'The other prisoners we don't know, mostly,' she said. 'And whether I'll be able to keep Charlotte safe and well.'

'I'll be looking out for you,' he said, patting her on the arm with one great paw.

Mary wondered exactly what that remark meant. Although she had gradually picked up the old friendship she'd had with him before her proposal, she'd never mentioned it again, and neither had he. She had to assume he didn't want her as a wife, and that silence was his way of not embarrassing her further.

'I hope you mean that,' she said with a smile. 'But I expect you'll be kept busy taking your pick of all the women. So I won't count on it.'

*

It was another three days before the *Charlotte* sailed into Botany Bay, for the wind had been against them. But there were no cheers, smiles or laughter from the seamen, Marines, officers or prisoners as they got their first view of the new land they'd come so far to populate. For once they all reacted in the same way, shocked into silence.

It looked utterly desolate, and parched by the burning sun. There was none of the expected green pasture, the few trees were scrubby and stunted. Yet even more daunting was the sight of the very black, stark naked natives who brandished spears menacingly at the ships. It was quite clear they weren't pleased to see white strangers invading their territory.

Most of the fleet had got there before the *Charlotte*, and a party of officers and Marines had already gone ashore to try to find a suitable site for their camp. But the prisoners were not allowed to stay on deck to watch the proceedings; once again they were made to return to the holds where they were locked in.

It was weeks later that Mary heard what had happened during the long days when she and her companions were incarcerated below decks in the suffocating heat. One story that would have amused them was that the natives hadn't known which gender the white officers were, and one of the group was asked to drop his breeches to show them.

It seemed that Captain Arthur Phillip had managed to divert the natives' hostility with gifts of beads and trinkets, but he'd been alarmed to find Botany Bay could not support over a thousand people and all the animals. The soil wasn't fertile, and the water supply was in the wrong place. So, with a small party, he set out in the ship's boats to try to find a more agreeable place further down the coast, leaving the rest of the company to clear trees in case he couldn't find anywhere better.

He came to a place called Port Jackson which he understood from Captain Cook's report to be a mere cove. As it was late afternoon he ordered his men to row in through the two giant headlands to check it, and once inside discovered it was not a cove at all, but a huge natural harbour, the best he'd ever seen anywhere in the world.

Delighted to find such a jewel with many sheltered bays, trees and fresh water, he pressed on and came to a place where the water was deep enough for the ships to come close to shore. He named it Sydney Cove after Lord Sydney, Secretary of State, to whom he sent his despatches. It even appeared that the natives were more friendly there too. So Sydney Cove was where the first settlement in New South Wales would be.

Mary and the other prisoners knew nothing of all this. Sweating and gasping in the heat of the holds, all they knew was that they'd been landed in a hellish, barren place peopled by fearsome savages. It was no wonder that many of them believed their long voyage had been for nothing and now they were going to die.

It was only on 26 January, when the prisoners heard the weighing of the anchor and the sound of sails being hoisted, that they felt a renewal of hope for their future.

By the time the *Charlotte* reached Sydney Cove it was night-time and too dark to see anything. The prisoners were not told that the flag-ship *Sirius* had arrived much earlier in the day, and that its officers had gone ashore, raised the English flag and held a simple ceremony where they fired a volley and toasted the royal family and the success of the new colony. But it was obvious to all the prisoners from the joyous shouts coming from the ships' companies anchored out in the bay, that this was where they would be settling.

Down in the steamy, fetid darkness of the holds they couldn't share in the excitement. They felt relief that they would soon be walking on solid ground and sleeping in tents, but they were fearful too, for this new prison which they had yet to build was so remote that they knew it was unlikely they would see England and their loved ones there again.

At first light the following morning the sound of axes felling trees filled the air and the women rushed to the hatches to look out.

'Looks better than that other place,' Bessie said cheerfully.

'It does too,' Mary agreed. The early-morning sun was glinting on the turquoise sea, and on land there were many trees, some quite large ones growing on the hills behind the bay. While there wasn't what could be called pasture anywhere that she could see, this place certainly didn't have the same desolate appearance as Botany Bay.

As they watched, they saw boats being lowered from the other ships, and male prisoners on the *Friendship* climbing down to them.

'I wonder when we'll go ashore,' Bessie said longingly.

'I hope it's soon,' Mary sighed. 'It's far too hot for Charlotte down here.'

It was over a week later that the women left the ships. They were allowed up on deck during that time as the men put up tents, cut trees and built store-sheds and a saw-mill, but they were told they had to stay on board until there was more order ashore.

Excitement grew with each day. It reminded Mary keenly of the sense of expectation before May Day back home. Women who had other clothes stored got them out and went through them to find something more fetching to wear, but most of them, like Mary, had arrived on the *Charlotte* with only the clothes they stood up in.

A new generosity bloomed, however, and ribbons, pieces of lace and small trinkets were offered to others who had nothing. They helped one another wash and curl their hair, and those who could sew were eager to assist those who couldn't.

They could hear the women on the *Lady Penryn* engaged in much the same way. Their laughter and ribald comments wafted across to the *Charlotte*, and the rigging was festooned with drying clothes in every colour of the rainbow.

Although Mary felt every bit as excited as the other women, she was nervous too. Just a glance across to the

Lady Penryn was to know that all those London women were going to be more worldly than her, and undoubtedly more attractive. On board the *Charlotte* she had a sort of distinction, admired for her ability to speak up for the women and her sense of fair play, and for being a mother. Her friendship with Will would almost certainly protect her from any harm amongst his large group of friends. She was also respected by most of the officers and Marines. She'd even gained the trust of their wives and children.

But on shore she would have to start all over again. She would need to be on her guard all the time. She was afraid that Mary Haydon and Catherine Fryer might seek to malign her to anyone who would listen, and enjoy seeing her humiliated. Officers from other ships wouldn't give her the trust and freedom she'd grown used to. She would be just a very small fish in a big pond, with no one to protect her and Charlotte.

On Sunday, 3 February a church service was held for the men by the Reverend Richard Johnson, under the shade of a big tree. Like all the women, Mary watched from the ship's deck, a little awed to see around 700 men, prisoners, officers, Marines and sailors gathered together in prayer. Will stood taller and broader than most of the men, his fair hair bleached almost white in the sun. Jamie Cox stood next to him, so small he looked like a child compared to Will.

A mop of red hair in the crowd made Mary look more intently and to her surprise she saw it was Samuel Bird.

Looking again, she saw James Martin beside him, his stooped shoulders and big nose unmistakable.

She was thrilled, for it was almost like seeing family members again, and she had to assume they'd been put on one of the other transport ships, maybe even separated from Will purposely to prevent them from inciting any kind of rebellion together.

Tench stood with the other officers, his hat tucked under his arm, and just the distance between prisoners and officers was a further reminder to Mary that the friendship between herself and Tench was unlikely to continue now the voyage was over.

Three days later the women went ashore. The excitement had been building up gradually over the last week, and as they were rowed to shore, Mary felt as giddy and giggly as her companions. It was wonderful to see everyone so happy, after the hardships on the voyage, with flushed cheeks and bright eyes, just like a bunch of bridesmaids at a wedding party.

For Mary, the prospect of walking on dry land again, to be rid of the smell of slop buckets, and to escape the nightly menace of rats was enough to start her heart pounding. But she was aware that for the other women it was mostly the men waiting on the shore that had them fired up.

As the boat got closer to the shore and Mary could clearly see the men waiting for them, she felt suddenly afraid, and hugged Charlotte closer to her breast. The expression on the men's faces reminded her of when a ship came into Fowey harbour after weeks at sea. She had observed that same hungry look then, and although she hadn't understood at the time why her mother always called her and Dolly indoors, she did now.

Sailors had a kind of rough charm, they were fit and strong, scrubbed up to look their best for shore leave. But these men waiting for the women prisoners were ragged and dirty, more like a vast pack of wild dogs than human beings.

Some of the women began to shout crude things to them, pulling their neck-lines lower and blowing kisses. In another boat coming from the *Lady Penryn*, one woman actually stood up and lifted her dress to show her private parts.

Marines pushed the men back as the boats were grounded on the beach and the women climbed out, but it seemed to Mary that the Marines were almost as bad as the convicts. They were laughing, winking, grabbing at the women's hands, and there was certainly no sense of them being there to protect the fairer sex.

Mary elbowed her way through the crowd, Charlotte's small crib under one arm, the other defensively round her child, almost deafened by the cat-calls, crude remarks and appeals for a kiss. It was exhilarating, like all the fairs and festivals she'd ever been to rolled into one, but frightening at the same time. It seemed odd to her that the officers were just standing by watching after all their stringent efforts to keep the men and women apart during the voyage.

Other boats came in, depositing more and more women on the beach, and the hubbub grew louder, the pushing and shoving more aggressive. But it was as much on the women's part as the men's – some of them were even running over to the men to kiss and embrace them.

Mary wanted so much to take off her boots, to run barefoot along the sand, to look at the strange birds watching them from the trees, to revel in her new-found freedom. But she could see this wasn't an option right now, she had to stay in the safety of a group.

Seeing a small bunch of women with children, standing apart, Mary ran over to them.

'Lawd have mercy on us,' she gasped out. 'It's getting out of hand!'

A tall woman in a plain dark brown dress and bonnet, holding a small child in her arms, responded. 'We asked to be taken to a place of safety some time ago,' she said. 'But our husbands seem distracted.'

Mary realized then that these women were Marines' wives and families, and as she'd been treated with some kindness by those who travelled on the *Charlotte*, she assumed this group would be the same.

'May I stay with you?' she asked. 'I'm afraid for my baby.'

The woman's expression stiffened. 'Join the other women from your ship,' she said curtly. 'That's where you belong.'

Shamed, Mary turned and walked away, realizing that brief encounter had shown how things were going to be here.

A little more order came later when the Marines fired a warning volley over the prisoners' heads, and the women were led to the tents allocated to them. But even as they were marched along, Mary overheard comments and giggles that suggested most of the women were too excited by the eager men to be kept under control for long.

Mary, Bessie and Sarah managed to stay together, but the other three women they were to share the tent with were strangers. The leader of the three, who announced herself as Cheapside Poll, was a tall, skinny woman with hard blue eyes, wearing a striped dress and a battered red hat. She deposited a carpet bag by the tent pole and glowered at Mary and her friends.

'Any of you so much as think of digging in there and I'll slit yer nostrils,' she said. She looked round at her companions and urged them to tell what she was capable of.

'She done it to a woman in Newgate,' a fat one with a pock-marked face said gleefully. 'Never 'eard screams like it afore.'

'We aren't thieves,' Mary said, even though technically she supposed they were. She was frightened now; all three women had harsh voices and a way of speaking which was very different to her own. As she knew Newgate was the infamous prison in London, she supposed that was where they came from.

'Keep that brat well away from me,' Poll said viciously, pointing to Charlotte. 'I can't be doing with a screamer.'

It was perhaps fortunate that the three Londoners were anxious to get out of the tent as quickly as possible. After laying their blankets down, they disappeared.

Mary sat down to feed Charlotte, but it was clear from the way Sarah and Bessie were fidgeting that they were anxious to get out too. Both her friends looked much better now than they had back in England. Sarah was plumper, with pink cheeks and shining hair, while Bessie, who had been fat when they arrived at the *Dunkirk*, was a couple of stones lighter, and her once grey complexion peachy with health.

'We'll just look around,' Bessie said, primping up her hair. 'We'll be back when we've found out where we get our rations from.'

Mary had been looking forward to going ashore as much as anyone, but now she felt close to tears. It was so hot, sweat was already soaking her dress, she needed to find water, both for a drink for herself and to cool Charlotte down. All around her she could hear strident, coarse voices, but the language they spoke wasn't English as she knew it. She guessed it was the Newgate prison cant she'd heard about in Exeter, for odd words had a familiar ring to them. She hadn't expected that she would have to learn a new language on top of everything else.

On the ship she had known exactly what was expected of her, a daily routine that seldom varied. She was one of only twenty women, an individual with a name and a character. Now she was to be one of some 200 women, thrown in together without any clear-cut rules of behaviour. If Cheapside Poll was an example of what she could expect of the rest of the women, she knew she would need to find new strengths for survival.

Tears dripped down her cheeks as she held Charlotte

to her breast, and the words she'd so often heard in church at Easter-time came to her: 'Lord, why hast Thou forsaken me?'

Darkness came suddenly, taking Mary by surprise. There appeared to be no twilight period like back in England. The noise which had grown louder and louder throughout the afternoon reached fever pitch.

Mary had plucked up courage to explore the row of women's tents to seek out her old companions and get food and water. She had spotted James Martin with Samuel Bird, but though they waved and shouted out greetings, Mary didn't go and talk to them as they were with other more desperate-looking men. She did try to join in the revelry for a while, but the underlying menace in it drove her to join some of the older women who were as nervous as she was.

Again and again the Marines had tried to separate the men from the women, with little success, but as darkness fell all attempts to control the prisoners broke down, and couples were seen scurrying off into the bushes.

Mary was just laying Charlotte down in her crib in the tent, when a flash of lightning lit up the entire bay. Thunder followed it, so loud it was like a cannon, making Charlotte scream out. More thunder and lightning followed, and then came rain, heavier than Mary had ever seen in her life. Within minutes the hard ground was awash, water running through the tent like a river.

Mary expected that the storm would at least dampen the spirits of the revellers as it put out the many fires burning along the beach. Yet as she crouched in the shelter of the tent looking out, to her horror she saw that the storm was only inflaming people more. Each flash of lightning lit up acts of obscenity, women pulling off their clothes, men rushing to grab them and taking them there in the mud. But if such acts were horrifying, they were at least mutual; elsewhere she saw men rushing like ravaging beasts, pulling down women who were running for their lives, their screams reverberating around the camp. It wasn't only the convicts either, some of the men were Marines, and as she stood with her hands clamped over her mouth in horror, she saw old women, too frail and bent to run, being knocked to the ground and raped.

It was like a scene from hell she'd once seen a picture of at Sunday school in Fowey, the men demonic in their lust, some women spurring them on with gleeful shouts, others screaming in terror. She saw one woman get up unsteadily from the ground as her rapist left her, so thickly coated with mud she had no features, only to be leapt upon by a second man, while another stood waiting for his turn.

Mary didn't know what to do. To run from the tent would be folly for she would surely be caught by someone, and if she took Charlotte with her she might be dashed from her arms and killed. Yet the tent offered no protection. Even as she hesitated, another flash of lightning revealed a band of men coming along the rows of tents looking in each for new prey.

Grabbing Charlotte from her crib, she wriggled under

the back of the tent and cowered there for a moment, considering which direction would be the safest. Going inland appeared to be the best choice, with luck there might be bushes to hide under, so hitching Charlotte under one arm and holding up her dress with the other, she ran for her life into the shelter of the trees.

She stubbed her bare feet against stumps of felled trees and tripped over dead branches, but somehow she managed to hold on to her baby. Just as she thought she was well away from the mayhem on the beach, however, she saw two men in front of her.

'Lookee here,' one of them shouted. 'Fresh meat.'

'Don't hurt me,' Mary screamed out in terror, for she knew whichever way she ran, one of them would catch her. 'I've got a baby with me.'

'We ain't after hurting a baby,' one of them said. 'Just put it down and be nice to us.'

Mary screamed and clutched Charlotte even tighter to her. But one of the men grabbed her shoulder and pushed her down to the ground.

Flat on her back, still holding Charlotte who was now screaming too, Mary fought with the only weapons she had, her legs and feet. It was too dark to see, but she felt the heel of her foot land in a soft place and the yell that followed it suggested she'd struck his belly.

'Get off me, you brutes,' she yelled. 'There's plenty of willing women back there.'

One man pinned her down by the shoulders, the second one grabbed her by the knees and forced them apart. She could smell their sweat and rancid breath.

'Damn you to hell,' she screamed out, still bucking frantically. 'Help me, someone!'

The man who held her legs apart was pulling her on to him as he knelt in front of her, the other one was still holding her shoulders in a grip of steel. She heard someone crashing through the bushes even over Charlotte's screams, but that increased her terror further as she thought it would be another man wanting to join in.

'Let her go,' a male voice bellowed out, and to her shock she recognized the voice as Will's. She saw nothing more than a dark shadow, then heard a crack, and the man about to rape her toppled back on to the ground.

There was another loud crack and the hands on her shoulders fell away. 'That's my woman,' Will roared out, and all at once he was pulling her up and holding her in his arms.

'There, there,' he said gently, disengaging himself slightly so Charlotte wouldn't be crushed. 'You're safe now.'

Taking her arm, he led her away. Mary had to suppose he had knocked the two men out with some kind of cudgel, but she didn't turn to look.

'Did they do it?' he asked breathlessly.

'No,' she gasped out. 'You were just in time.'

Will took her much further into the trees, and when they came to one that offered some real shelter from the heavy rain, he stopped and made her sit down.

'Are you or the babby hurt?' he asked, sitting down beside her and putting his arm around her.

'I don't think so,' she replied, rocking Charlotte in her arms to soothe her.

All at once she was crying as she had never cried since her trial. All the hardships, deprivations, the cruelty and humiliations she had endured for so long seemed to come to the surface, just because one man cared enough to comfort her.

'You're safe now,' he whispered, holding her tight and rocking her. 'I won't let anyone touch you again.'

A little later it stopped raining as suddenly as it had begun, and the moon came out from behind the clouds. Will continued to hold Mary as she offered Charlotte her breast to calm her. They were soaking wet and covered in mud, but at least it wasn't cold.

'I came looking for you when it all got nasty,' Will explained. 'I'd seen Sarah and Bessie earlier and they said you was back in the tent putting Charlotte down. I should have come to you then.'

'I was scared almost as soon as we came ashore,' Mary admitted. 'Everyone was so wild.'

'It was like a madness caught them all,' Will said, his tone hushed and shocked. 'I've never seen the like afore.'

'How did you find me?'

He was silent for a moment, and she guessed his conscience wasn't entirely clear either.

'I saw a gang going through all the women's tents,' he said eventually. 'I guessed if you were in there you'd get out the back and run for it. So I went that way, and I heard a babby crying.'

'Will it always be this way?' Mary whispered. She was

shivering with shock, the vivid pictures of what she'd seen down on the beach still dancing before her eyes.

'I don't reckon so,' he sighed. 'Tomorrow the officers will take control, there'll be floggings for some, chains for others, it will settle down.'

'I hope you're right,' she said. 'But I don't like the thought of living with those London women, they scare me to death.'

'You scared?' he teased. 'A girl who is brave enough to ask a man to marry her?'

'I wish I hadn't now,' she admitted. 'It must have seemed so forward. It was just that we appeared to have so much in common, I really like you and as tonight proved, women do need some protection here.'

'They do indeed,' he said thoughtfully. 'But I think us men will need a good woman beside us too. So we will get married.'

'You want to marry me?' She was so surprised it dried up her tears instantly.

'Well, I don't want one of those London harpies full of pox,' he said with a chuckle. 'You were right, Mary. We'll make a good team, you and me. They'll need someone to fish, a lot of the food they brought with us is rotten. I think I can bargain for us to get a house of our own, my mind's a bit sharper than most of the others.'

Mary was very aware he wasn't saying he loved her, only that he thought she was clean and useful to him. Yet he had fought off those men for her, he'd comforted her just when she needed it. This place was going to be a living hell, and she doubted she could survive it alone.

She didn't expect or need romantic love, she'd settle for protection.

Four days after that terrible night, Will and Mary were married by the Reverend Johnson under the shade of the big tree where he'd held his first service. They weren't alone, other couples married too, perhaps for the same reasons as Mary and Will.

Mary had no finery to wear, just the same shabby old grey dress freshly washed, and an artificial flower in her hair, lent to her in an unusually generous gesture by Cheapside Poll.

Mary had no real expectations, either of her marriage or of this new country. In the four days since coming ashore she had observed that the vast majority of the convicts were bone idle and devious. They would steal anything, cared nothing for the idea of working for the common good, and many were already bartering rations or belongings with the Marines for drink. The Marines were every bit as bad, and there was a lack of organization on the part of the officers and the powers that be who had sent them out from England.

Will had been right in saying some of the food was rotten. Mary had had to eat rice crawling with maggots and the salted beef was almost inedible. Tools were of inferior quality, there were too few women's clothes, and a complete lack of skilled men.

She wondered how they could farm this desolate place when there were but two men out of hundreds who knew anything about farming or animal husbandry. How could a town be built without skilled carpenters or brick-makers? Captain Arthur Phillip had his house erected, a superior canvas one, a store-house had been built to lock away the provisions, and a few tents had been put in isolation as a hospital.

But the animals brought with them were in poor health, and dysentery had already broken out among those weakened by the voyage. Captain Phillip might be proud that only forty-eight people overall had died on the way here, but how many more would perish before the year was out?

An eighty-year-old woman hanged herself from a tree on that first night ashore. Many women still had black eyes and a hunted look. There were snakes, spiders and many flies and other insects, any of which could be dangerous. As for the natives, the officers seemed intent on getting their cooperation, when even an illiterate girl like herself could sense they bitterly resented this swarm of white people who'd taken it upon themselves to oust them from their land. Mary wondered how long it would be before their curiosity turned to real anger and they began killing.

But Will had been as good as his word. Not only had he pledged to marry her, he'd already made a deal that put him in charge of fishing and allowed him to build a hut for himself.

Mary glanced at him standing next to her, and smiled. He looked so handsome in a clean shirt and breeches; he'd even shaved off his bushy beard, and his blond hair was as bright as ripe corn. She knew most of the women envied her, for he was without doubt the most attractive and capable of all the male convicts. She might have her work cut out keeping him faithful to her, and perhaps his bragging would be wearing, but she did like and trust him. That was enough.

As the wedding ceremonies ended and everyone drifted back to their tents or the huts they were building, Lieutenant Tench stood for a little while watching Mary and Will walk away up the beach.

He was in a state of confusion about everything. Nothing was as he'd expected – not the country, nor the organization, nor the officers from the other ships. Even the stores they'd brought with them were inadequate. It was a shambles, in fact. And from what he'd seen of the convicts so far, it was going to be an uphill struggle to get any of them to work.

As far as he could see, only a handful of officers shared his will to make this place work. As for his men, most of them were behaving appallingly, every bit as devious and idle as the convicts.

He had thought he would feel more positive after the weddings today. They were, after all, one way of injecting a little joy into a new community, a show of hope for the future. Yet he had felt no joy at seeing those couples married. What he felt was utter sadness.

His mother always cried at weddings. She believed the more she cried, the happier the couple would be. But he knew his mother's tears weren't sad ones, they were pure emotion at a public declaration of love between two people.

Perhaps that was the cause of his sadness, knowing the couples married today were not in love. The women wanted protection and security, the men wanted sex.

He had thought he'd be happy to see Mary under Will's protection. But he hadn't considered till now that meant she would be her husband's in every way.

He turned sharply and walked away towards the store-sheds. Maybe if he found something constructive to do he'd overcome these ridiculous feelings milling around inside him. Mary looked pretty and happy. Will was a decent enough man. They were right for each other.

'It will be a nice little place once I've finished it,' Will said later that same night, as he laid their blankets on the hard-packed dirt beside Charlotte's crib.

They were in their new hut, which at present was nothing more than a few poles hammered together and the walls interwoven branches, with a piece of sacking tacked on a stick for a door. The roof was not yet on, and when Mary sat down on the blankets and looked up, the night sky strewn with a myriad stars looked very beautiful. Their bellies were full, as extra rations had been dished out to honour the weddings today, and Will had managed to get hold of some rum to celebrate.

Rules had been made since that first night ashore. Male convicts were banned from the women's area, and guards were on duty to make sure no one slipped in. There was also a dusk curfew when everyone was supposed to be back in their own quarters. It didn't actually work, men did get in with the women, but at least it was covert, and the women willing.

'Plenty of fresh air,' Will said, and laughed. 'I can stand upright too. Beats that stinking ship anyways, or a tent with the men. Now, come here and give your husband a kiss.'

Mary needed no urging; since Will had announced their wedding plans she'd found she had status, and for that she was extremely grateful. Even Poll and her two cronies, three of the most foul-minded women Mary had ever met, were awed that she was wanted by the most desirable convict in the colony.

There were good things here. It was hot, the sand on the beach soft and white, the sea so blue and clean, and there were hundreds of beautiful birds. Even the trees had a lovely smell that cleared your nose. It beat a prison back in England any day.

Now Mary had a home, well away from everyone else, and even if it hadn't got a roof yet, nor a stick of furniture, and the first storm would knock it down, it was theirs. Will had managed to get her a cooking pot, a bucket for carrying water, and a few other essential pieces of household equipment from the stores to start married life.

He'd already kissed her several times today, and he did so tenderly. She hadn't expected to want him, but she found she did; in fact for the first time in over a year she was really happy to be where she was.

'You're such a little thing,' he said gruffly as he helped her out of her dress. He cupped his big hands round her

163

breasts and squeezed them, then sliding his hands down to her buttocks squeezed them too. 'A bit skinny, but I never was one for fat women.'

He lifted her up in his arms then and laid her down on the blankets. Mary expected nothing more than for him to pull off his clothes, a quick coupling, then for him to fall asleep. But to her surprise Will made no attempt to undress himself, only to caress her. She had once heard him bragging to a sailor on the *Charlotte* that once he'd bedded a woman they always came back begging him for more. She believed it now, for she was afraid that any moment he might stop. His touch was so sure and slow, his fingers found exquisitely sensitive places to touch that until now she hadn't even known existed.

The hard ground beneath the rough blanket, the crudeness of their unfinished house, even the hardship she'd been through were forgotten as Mary gave herself up to the bliss of his love-making. When she opened her eyes and saw the stars above, she could have been lying on a feather bed in a royal bedchamber, the stars just a decoration on the ceiling. Will made her forget she wasn't pretty, or that there were lice in her hair; for once she was beautiful, desirable and loved.

She never could have believed she could behave like a wanton, begging for more, asking him to show her what pleased him, and doing it all too eagerly. At the peak of it all the thought crossed her mind that it was worth crossing the world in a prison ship to feel like this. She didn't care about the future, she just wanted this night to last forever.

'Are you glad you married me?' Will whispered later, after he'd covered them with the blanket to keep off the insects.

'The happiest woman alive,' she whispered back, her cheeks wet with tears of joy.

'We'll make something of our life here,' he murmured. 'We'll plant ourselves a little garden and grow some vegetables. We'll never go hungry while I can fish, and we'll have other children for Charlotte to play with.'

'Will we go back to England when our time is up?' she asked.

'Sure, if you want to,' he said, and laughed. 'Or we might stay as free men and take some land for ourselves. Anything's possible.'

Chapter six

1789

Mary was standing waist-deep in the sea, holding tightly to the fishing net, looking as all the other helpers were towards Will in the small boat, waiting for his signal to pull the net tight.

She was very hungry, but hunger pains and the dizzy spells which went with them were just a fact of life now. After a whole year here at Port Jackson she couldn't even remember what it was like to be without them.

She was much thinner than she'd been back on the *Dunkirk*, her skin leathery and brown from constant exposure to the sun and wind, her hands hardened like the women's who gutted fish back in Fowey. But her looks weren't something she ever thought about; just keeping herself and Charlotte alive was of far greater importance.

Will gave the signal and everyone holding the net began pulling and moving back to the shore. Mary's heart leaped when she saw the abundance of fish squirming in the net. It wasn't often they were that lucky.

The colony was close to dying of starvation. The rations

had been cut again and again because no further supplies had arrived from England yet. A great many of the provisions brought out with them were spoiled, and the original hope that within a year they would be producing home-grown food was shattered. Had draught animals and ploughs been sent out, along with men from a farming background, maybe the ground could have been tilled and cultivated quickly. But all this had been overlooked. The weather and the lack of fodder for the animals soon decimated their numbers, cereals withered in the ground and vegetables didn't thrive.

Building work had been the priority at the start, houses for the officers, Marines, and then the convicts. But along with the lack of carpenters, an outbreak of scurvy, together with dozens of other diseases, kept the men from work, and so the building was painfully slow.

As the rations were cut, more people risked stealing food. Flogging was the punishment for this crime, but 100 lashes failed to be a deterrent, and Captain Phillip increased it to 500, and eventually to 1,000. When that didn't work either, he finally resorted to hanging. Just the previous week Mary and Will had watched as Thomas Barrett, who was only seventeen, was hanged from the newly erected gallows for stealing some butter, dried peas and salt pork from the stores. Mary couldn't even weep for the boy, for he'd been imprisoned for theft at the age of eleven, and she thought that death was preferable to the kind of life he'd had.

'Come on, Mary, put your back into it,' Will yelled at her from the little boat.

Mary laughed, for Will didn't really mean she wasn't pulling her weight – that shout was their secret code for 'We'll be eating well tonight.'

'I don't know what you've got to laugh at,' the woman next to her said sharply as they hauled the net back on to the shore. 'If I was in your shoes I'd be crying.'

'Why's that?' Mary asked.

She didn't trust Sadie Green an inch. She knew the only reason the woman had come down to the nets to help was in the hope of stealing a couple of fish for herself. She was one of the Londoners, foul-mouthed, cunning and lazy. And she bitterly resented that Mary appeared to have a better time of it than her.

'Will's gonna leave you soon,' Sadie said, her mud-coloured eyes sparkling with malice. 'He keeps telling the other men he isn't legally wed to you.'

'Is that so?' Mary retorted with heavy sarcasm. Will had told her he didn't believe their marriage was valid, not like a church wedding at home, but all the same she was hurt he'd bandied it about among the other men to reach the ears of people like Sadie. She wasn't going to show that hurt though.

'Just don't wait around for him, Sadie, you might be waiting a long time,' she said with a forced chuckle.

She saw the woman's face tighten with anger. Sadie could only attract the most desperate of the male convicts. Although only about twenty-four, she had the grey look of gone-off meat, and smelled much the same. She never combed her wispy straw-coloured hair, much less washed it, and dirt was ingrained in her skin. There were no beauties in this colony, the sun and starvation saw to that. But Sadie was probably born plain, and a life of prostitution had done the rest.

'Why, you stuck-up cow!' she snarled, showing the blackened stumps of her teeth. 'What makes you think you're better than the rest of us? You've got a bastard kid that ain't Will's.'

Mary hesitated. She was very tempted to hit Sadie, but that was just what the woman wanted, so she could say Mary started the fight and get her punished.

'Leave me alone, if you know what's good for you,' Mary replied wearily. 'This place is bad enough without picking fights.'

'But it ain't bad for you, is it?' Sadie put her hands on her hips and glowered at Mary. 'You've got a nice little hut, Will's got the best job, and I bet he gets extra rations too. Lieutenant Tench is always sniffing round you too. I bet he's the bastard's father.'

Mary was saved from answering by an officer coming along the beach to check the catch. Sadie gave Mary a menacing look and smirked at him, then left her place on the net and flounced off.

An hour later Mary was back at her hut, having collected Charlotte from Anne Tomkin, her neighbour, who minded her while Mary was helping with the nets.

The hut was now much improved. Because of Will's status they had been allowed planks from the saw-mill for both roof and walls. The furniture was of the most basic kind: a rough-hewn bed, with rope tied across it like a hammock, a small table made from a tree trunk with a board nailed to its top, and two stools fashioned out of wooden crates. The floor was still hard-pressed dirt, though Will intended to put some planks down soon, and the only decoration some pretty sea shells on a shelf. Another held the few cooking pots, plates, mugs and a tin bowl to wash in. Yet however primitive, it was Mary's haven, a place of comparative safety and peace for both herself and Charlotte.

At seventeen months Charlotte was a bonny child, with pink cheeks, black curly hair and well-rounded limbs. Her wide, joyous smile was worth a king's ransom to Mary, and she gave shape and reason to her life. Yet at the same time, keeping Charlotte safe and well under such appalling conditions was slow torture.

While she was still a babe in arms, feeding from her mother's breast, it was relatively easy, but once she began crawling and then walking, Mary saw danger everywhere. Aside from the most obvious things — insects, snakes, the sea and fires — there were the hidden hazards. Who knew what was buried in the sand Charlotte played on, which she could pick up and swallow. Other mothers here were very casual about their offspring, allowing them to wander and showing no anxiety if they got sunburnt, fell over, or ate something that made them sick. But Mary couldn't be that way, she had to have Charlotte near her at all times. She tied a piece of rope around her waist to keep her close when she was mending nets, and gave Anne some fish or part of their rations to mind her when she was helping to haul them in. Even in the evening when Charlotte had fallen asleep in the bed all three shared, Mary wouldn't go beyond her own door, even though other mothers went out to visit friends.

While waiting for Will to come home with their rations and hopefully some fish, Mary filled the bowl with water, peeled off Charlotte's dress and began washing her. She didn't like to dwell on the fact that the dress was merely rags now, held together by a few threads. Or that it would have to be washed tonight and put on again tomorrow because it was the only one. Nor did she want any reminders that she hadn't any friends to visit.

She couldn't win in this place.

Marrying Will had been a wise choice. He had protected her from the other men, built them this hut, and had come to love Charlotte as if she were his own. But Mary hadn't anticipated that his fishing skills would make him so important in the colony, and it was that which had brought her problems.

When they first landed, the convicts from London and other cities were suspicious of fish and refused to eat it. This was understandable, considering that where they came from it was probably at least a week old and stinking. But by the time the rations had been severely cut and starvation was a real possibility, they quickly overcame their objections. Will was elevated to hero status because he was the man who not only introduced them to something tasty and filling, but also supplied it.

Yet as Will basked in the warm glow of admiration and gratitude, Mary had lost the strong position she'd once held with the other women from the *Charlotte*. With Mary

Haydon and Catherine Fryer dripping poison in the ears of the trouble-making women from other ships, it wasn't long before most of the women were suspicious of her. Even Bessie and Sarah, whom she thought she could count on forever, had turned against her. They called her a 'dark one', as if she was guilty of some treachery, when the plain fact was that they were jealous of her.

Mary understood why. They were mostly sleeping six to a hut, while she was tucked up in a strong, weatherproof one, well away from the noise and trouble in the main camp. She ate better in those early days because Will was allowed some of each catch for himself. Nor did she have to work as a servant for one of the officers as the other women did. Added to this, the women saw Mary as a 'nark', because officers talked to her.

Tench often came to see how she and Will were getting on, and he liked to help with the fishing at night. It was reported that even Captain Phillip had remarked that the Bryants were the model family, industrious, sober and clean.

In the early days in the colony, Mary had made a good friend of Jane Randall, who sailed on the *Lady Penryn*. She too had a baby en route, though it was born while they were berthed in Cape Town. Initially it was because Charlotte and Henrietta were so close in age that Mary and Jane became friends; they had the same anxieties for their babies, and they minded each other's to help out. Jane was sweet-natured and fun to be with, and like-minded too about making the best of it here.

Then Captain Phillip decided to start a new settlement

on Norfolk Island, 1,000 miles away. It appeared to have a better climate, and the ground was more fertile, so some of the convicts, Jane among them, were sent there to alleviate the food shortages. Mary still missed her badly. Jane had never been jealous of her, she was always glad fortune seemed to shine on her friend.

Mary took the view that many of her former friends could be just as fortunate as her if they only used their brains. In the early days, Mary had tried to make them at least see the logic of appearing to be industrious. It was so easy to do, the officers only poked their noses in if there was any trouble, and to her mind the majority of the Marines were half-wits. Likewise, keeping yourself clean and tidy, and not running around hunting for men and drink, got you privileges and respect.

But sadly, one by one her old friends had fallen into apathy and allowed themselves to be influenced by a few forceful characters who thought they were proving their toughness by fighting and stealing. Nothing was safe from these women, and they recruited new members into their band by offering the drink they acquired through theft or prostitution.

Mary understood why Sarah had gone that way. She'd been raped on that first night, and found herself pregnant afterwards. Her baby was stillborn, and that brought back all the pain of the two children left behind in England. Drink was the only thing which made her life a little more bearable.

But most of the women hadn't got such a good excuse. They had become filthy slatterns who neglected their children, preyed on those weaker than themselves, and went with any man for a shot of rum.

Mary was like a pricking conscience. They sneered at her because she bathed in the sea every day, cleaned her hut and kept Charlotte constantly beside her. But Mary knew that most of their spite and scorn was purely because she had the man they all wanted.

Will was attractive in every way. His looks, height and muscular body were almost enough on their own, but added to this he was a kind man with a jovial, cheeky nature that endeared him to everyone. He was also strong and clever with his hands, so it wasn't surprising that everyone, from Captain Phillip right down to the lowest of the prisoners, held him in high esteem.

But what they didn't know, and Mary would never divulge, was that Will was in fact quite weak. He might be able to read and write, but he didn't use his brain and was unimaginative. Left to his own devices, he would be much like all the other men, living in squalor, getting drunk as often as he could, and bemoaning his bad luck.

Mary was the strong-willed and wily one. It was she who realized the importance of fish for their survival, and she talked Will into seeing his skill as the trump card to improve their life here. Will's bargaining for a hut in a good position, the use of the only small boat, and a portion of each catch for himself, was all her doing. In return, Mary made their hut more homely so that he would want to be there, and pandered to his vanity so that he felt important.

If only he had listened to her when a new rule ordering

that the entire catch should go into the stores was made. Mary had wanted him to go straight to Captain Phillip, not only to dig his heels in and insist on keeping his original rights, but also to discuss her plan with the captain. This was to build a bigger boat which would then be able to go further out into the sea and get catches big enough to feed everyone well. She also suggested they used surplus fish as a fertilizer for the soil, something she'd seen done back home in Cornwall.

But Will wouldn't do that. He might brag to his friends that Mary's ideas were his, as it made him look cleverer than them, but in reality he was too scared of losing his popularity with the officers to speak out. So instead he resorted to stealing what fish he needed.

Mary sighed deeply as Charlotte began groping for her breast under her dress. She had little milk left now, and each time the rations were cut further she was fearful Charlotte would become sick as so many others had.

It was the very young and the very old who were dying in ever-increasing numbers each week. The hospital building was always full now, the path to the cemetery so well used that a new funeral wasn't remarked on any longer.

Shouting and chatter outside made Mary start. Through the window they had plaited with twigs in place of glass, she could see the sun was very low, and Will should have been home by now. She stood up, and holding Charlotte in her arms, went to the door.

The commotion was coming from further along the beach closer to the main camp. Mary thought she saw a glimpse of Will's blond hair, so wrapping a piece of cloth around Charlotte, she went to look.

She had gone no more than two hundred yards when she saw Sarah.

Her once pretty face was gaunt. Her strawberry-blond hair was matted and filthy, her blue eyes were dulled by drink and she'd lost her two front teeth in a fight. Her slop dress still had bloodstains from the birth of her child and it was split on one side, showing her scrawny thigh.

'Your Will's been caught stealing,' she called out. 'He'll be for it now.'

Mary's heart quickened. She had of course eagerly eaten the fish Will brought home, and to help him remain undetected she had made the sacking bag to put them in. He hung this on a hook on the boat's side below the water-line to retrieve later after the rest of the catch had been weighed and taken to the stores.

It had appeared to be a foolproof plan, but Mary guessed that Will had been stealing more than he told her, selling the surplus off to others or exchanging it for goods.

'My Will's no thief,' Mary said sharply. She couldn't look upon it as theft – after all, fish were free to anyone who could catch them.

'I don't think Captain Phillip will see it that way,' Sarah said, her grin a touch malicious. 'He'll say you've been robbing the rest of us.'

Mary looked at her former friend coolly. 'Will's one of the few men here who provide anything for us to eat,' she said. 'But for him most of us would be too weak to be nasty.'

It hurt that Sarah had turned against her. Mary could not forget how close they'd been on the *Dunkirk*, and that Sarah had helped her with Charlotte's birth on the voyage. But it had never been a one-sided friendship. Mary had always made sure she saved food for Sarah, comforted her in the aftermath of the rape, and even gave her some of the fish Will got. But perhaps the horror of the rape had killed off something inside Sarah.

All the way into the town, people called out to Mary. A few, like James Martin, Jamie Cox and Samuel Bird, Will's closest friends, offered help and words of sympathy, but from the others it was mostly spiteful remarks. Mary remembered how back in the early days everyone would have stuck together if something like this had happened. But hunger and deprivation had changed them all. There was no sense of honour any more, people would peach on almost anyone in return for drink or extra food. And they took pleasure in seeing anyone they considered favoured brought down.

Mary kept her head up and ignored them all, but her insides were turning over with a combination of fear and hunger. The town didn't consist of much, just two rows of squalid little huts for the convicts, slightly larger ones set further back for the Marines and their families, and the guarded store-sheds. But Mary's eyes were drawn to the gallows. She remembered only too well the warning that anyone found stealing food would receive no mercy.

Watkin Tench came out from behind one of the store-sheds, surprising Mary for she'd thought he was away at Rose Hill, a new settlement inland where the soil was more fertile. Tench had been put in charge of it, and they were building a new Government House here too.

'Mary!' he exclaimed, his tanned lean face etched in concern. 'I assume you've been told?'

Even he, who had always been so elegant and spruce, was looking worn. His boots were rarely highly polished any more, his red jacket was threadbare and his breeches stained. But the compassion was still there in his dark eyes.

Mary nodded. 'Is it true?' she asked.

'Caught red-handed,' he shrugged. 'I'm afraid there's little I can do to help him, however much I wish I could. The Governor will have to treat him just like anyone else caught stealing food.'

'They won't hang him, will they?' Mary felt faint now, and her voice was little more than a whisper.

Tench glanced round to check who was watching, then moved closer to her. 'I certainly hope not,' he said. 'It would be folly to lose any of the skilled men.'

His first reaction to the news as he rode in from Rose Hill had been anger at Will. Will was more fortunate than any other prisoner, he did a job he enjoyed, he had privileges and a decent hut. And he had Mary for a wife. Tench knew in his heart that Will hadn't taken fish just for himself and his family, he'd been taking a great deal and trading it for rum. This incensed him, for it was not only breaking down the very fabric of the community, but cheating Mary too; no doubt she was oblivious to how much her husband needed drink.

'Could I speak to Captain Phillip?' Mary asked in desperation.

Tench hardly knew what to say. He certainly couldn't bring himself to hammer home what kind of man Will really was. 'Captain Phillip has probably already made his decision,' he said after a couple of moments. Then, seeing the terror in Mary's eyes, he weakened. 'But perhaps if he saw you with Charlotte in your arms, he might be persuaded to change it.'

'Please take me to him,' Mary pleaded, and she reached out and clutched at his arm. 'Will doesn't deserve to die just for feeding his family. Surely any man would do the same?'

Tench looked at her for a moment. There had been so many times when he wished he had never suggested Will as a husband for her, for he knew now that Will was weak, easily led and very boastful. He guessed Mary felt mortified each time it got back to her that Will had claimed they weren't legally married. Or that he intended to be on the next ship home when his time was up.

He wished too that he could get Mary out of his mind. He had hoped that being sent to Rose Hill would help. But now, faced with her distress, he knew the feelings he had for her hadn't abated at all. 'Any man would do the same for you,' he said, putting his hand over hers briefly.

Captain Phillip's house was some distance away from the town, up on a hill. With its two floors and veranda along the front, it stood out as being the residence of the most important man in the new colony, but this was not because it was grand, only that it had an appearance of sturdy permanence in comparison to all the other building work.

Mostly everything else was made of clay and wood, for even though there was plenty of stone around, and a brick-making kiln too, no lime to make mortar could be found anywhere. Mary, like many of the women, had been set to collect sea shells, then grind them up and burn them to make lime. She supposed all those many hundreds of bucketfuls she'd collected had barely made enough for the foundations of Phillip's house, so it would be years and years before the real town he envisaged, complete with a church, shops and paved streets, could be built.

As Mary followed Tench up the hill, she held her head high and ignored the coarse remarks and stares. Will had always claimed that no one would ever peach on him, but that was yet another of his failings, a stupidly vain belief that he was special. He'd probably bragged about the fish to someone, and it hadn't occurred to him that when jealousy reared its head, friendship and loyalty vanished.

Mary had to wait out on the veranda while Tench went inside the house to get permission for her to speak to Phillip. Charlotte was wailing with hunger now, and Mary jogged her soothingly in her arms as she looked back down the hill towards the town.

Darkness had fallen on the way there, and for once the town looked pretty, lit only by the many campfires. Mary could see the silhouettes of women cooking on them, and the flames highlighted trees and cast a twinkling orange glow on to the sea beyond.

She sighed, for although she always told anyone who asked that she would be on the next ship back to England when her sentence was up, she had grown to quite like this strange new land. Of course she hated what it stood for, a place where all the degenerate, desperate and wicked people from England were dumped. But it had some good points. The heat of the summer was sometimes too much, but there was always the warm sea to take a dip in. She loved the sandy beaches. Winter was nothing like as severe as at home, and however peculiar-looking most of the trees were, she liked their pungent aroma. Then there were the wonderful birds. To see flocks of the grey ones with pink bellies flying brought tears to her eyes. There were also the sulphur-coloured cockatoos that sat up in the trees squawking out what sounded like insults. Birds here were every colour of the rainbow, so vivid she could hardly believe they were real. She still hadn't seen the animal Tench called a kangaroo, or the big flightless bird; perhaps they were too timid to come close to people and she'd need to go further inland.

But whether or not she much preferred the land to which she belonged, Mary was a realist. Hunger back in England was exactly the same as hunger here, except it was better to be hungry and warm than hungry and cold. Unless a miracle happened, she would never amount to anything more than a servant in England. Here she stood a chance. When she was free she could claim land of her own, and the challenge to build something out of nothing appealed to her.

Often at night she thought about having a few animals, growing vegetables and fruit, and sitting on a porch in the evenings with Charlotte and Will, gazing at their land. Will had always pooh-poohed such ideas, he wanted to live in a fishing village with a tavern at the centre of it. But as she'd often retorted, he could build his own tavern here.

'You can come in now, Mary,' Tench said softly behind her. 'I have to warn you, Captain Phillip is very angry and disappointed. I don't think you can sway him from hanging Will.'

Mary knew Tench would have done his best for her and Will, for even the hardships here, which were almost as bad for the officers as for the convicts, hadn't changed his caring nature. Mary still had that same yearning for him, which marrying Will hadn't made go away. In a year here she had seen many officers who were once above taking convict women into their beds, succumb to the temptation. And in her heart she knew that if Tench was to weaken, she would go all out to be with him, regardless of her marriage.

But she knew somehow that Tench never would. He cared for her, she saw it in his eyes every time he stopped off at her hut or looked for her amongst a group of women, and in the tender way he petted Charlotte. Just knowing he cared for her helped. It was something good to dream about at night, a reason to keep herself clean and neat, another reason to stay alive.

It also gave her the courage to face Captain Phillip, and the same defiant streak which had prevented her from crying out when she heard her own death sentence, rose in her as she marched into the house. She didn't intend to watch Will hang while she still had breath in her body.

Captain Arthur Phillip was seated at his desk, a pen in his hand, as Mary came into the room.

'Thank you for agreeing to see me, sir,' she began, and bobbed a little curtsy.

Rumours went around the town that Phillip's house was very impressive inside, stuffed with fine furniture and silver plate. But to Mary's surprise it wasn't even as grand as the rector's house in Fowey. He had his desk, the chair he was sitting on, and there were a couple of armchairs by the fireplace, but apart from a silver-framed picture of a lady who was almost certainly his wife, there was little else, not even a rug on the bare boards.

Captain Phillip wasn't much to look at either, fifty, slender and small, all the hair on the top of his head gone. But he did have lovely dark eyes, and Mary thought he wore his naval uniform well.

'I suppose you've come to plead for your husband?' he said coldly.

'No, I've come to plead for everyone in this colony,' Mary said without any hesitation. 'For if you hang Will, they will surely all die, yourself included.'

He looked startled by such a claim, his dark eyes widening.

'Without the fish he brings in we will starve,' Mary continued, hitching Charlotte higher into her arms and willing her not to cry. 'There is no one else as skilful as Will. If you hadn't taken away his rights to take a few fish home for us, this would never have happened.'

'That couldn't be helped, it was an emergency situation,' Phillip said tersely, irritated that she had the audacity to question his orders. 'And your husband hadn't just taken a couple of fish. He had a great deal. He has been bartering them for provisions stolen from the stores. Each time someone steals from there, it leaves even less for the rest of the colony. It is an extremely grave offence.'

'Wouldn't you do the same if your wife and family were facing death?' Mary said, glancing at the picture of his wife.

'No, I would not,' he said firmly. 'The provisions are rationed fairly. I only have the same as you.'

Mary doubted that, but didn't dare say so.

'So what good will hanging Will do?' she asked. 'I'll be left to bring up this child alone, the people who steal from the stores will still do it, and every one of us will be even hungrier.'

Phillip looked at Mary, noting that she was every bit as ragged as the other convict women, but that she was clean. Even her bare feet were only dusty, not filthy as he'd observed many of the other women's were.

Lieutenant Tench had often spoken of this woman, whom he considered intelligent and forthright, and claimed had been a good influence on the other women on the *Charlotte*. There hadn't been any complaints about her behaviour, in fact he had himself commented on the Bryants being model prisoners.

'Go home now,' he said. 'He will be tried tomorrow. Tonight he stays in the guard-house.'

Mary moved towards the door, but turned before leaving and gave Phillip a penetrating stare. He saw deep fear and desperation in her eyes as she held the child out to him.

'Please, sir,' she pleaded. 'Look at my child. She is bonny and healthy now, but without Will she may not stay that way. I'll make sure Will never goes wrong again. Please, for the love of God and this child, spare him!'

She left then, slinking off into the night like a cat.

Phillip sat for a while deep in thought. The woman was right. Hanging Bryant would bring the spectre of starvation even closer.

'Damn those fools in England,' he muttered. 'Where are the provisions asked for? How can I be expected to make this colony self-sufficient when I haven't been given even the most basic equipment or men with the right skills?'

He had deep anxieties about almost every facet of this experiment: the infertile soil, the fast-dwindling stores, the behaviour of the felons, and the natives. It was predictable that the felons wouldn't pitch in and help themselves. They were townsfolk in the main, and they were more familiar with a jug of ale than a plough. They had no morals – dozens of the women had given birth or were expecting a child, and they moved from one partner to another without a qualm. They'd rather stand about chatting than work, would rather steal vegetables than grow them. Phillip could understand them, they had after all been sent here for good reason. But he was very disappointed in the natives.

Phillip had believed that if they were treated with kindness and friendliness, they would reciprocate. Sadly, this didn't seem to be the case – over the last few months several convicts working away from the camp had been brutally murdered. He still wanted to find a way to communicate with these people, to discover where the big rivers and fertile land lay, to learn about the native animals and birds, but all his efforts had come to nothing.

In truth, by the first anniversary of the colony, Phillip was a very worried man. He had the settlement at Sydney Cove, the one in Norfolk Island, and now Rose Hill too, but the convicts showed little inclination to reform, the Marines grumbled constantly, and the situation with the natives appeared to be getting worse rather than better. Without more food and medicine, the death toll would rise even more steeply. He found it hard to sleep at night for anxiety, and he couldn't see an end to it.

Mary bit into her knuckles as Judge Collins stood up in the guard-house to tell Will what his punishment was to be. As she had expected, someone had informed on Will, and she guessed it to be Joseph Pagett, a man who had been on both the *Dunkirk* and the *Charlotte*. He had shown signs of jealousy during the voyage, and she could recall him giving Will a baleful look the day they were married.

Charles White, the surgeon from the *Charlotte*, had spoken up for Will, but even so Mary was sure he was to be hanged. She knew Will thought so too, for his face was drained of all colour, and he was biting his lip and trying very hard not to tremble.

'I sentence you to a hundred lashes,' Collins said. 'And to be deprived of the direction of fishing and the boat. Also to be turned out of the hut you are now in, along with your wife and family.'

Will shot a glance at Mary, his face registering some relief, but anxiety at how she would take the loss of the hut.

Mary couldn't think about that now. While she was relieved Will wasn't to be hanged, and 100 lashes was a light punishment compared to some she'd witnessed, any flogging was still terrible, and she felt her stomach heave with nausea.

'Take him away for punishment,' Collins said.

All the prisoners were rounded up to watch Will's flogging, even the children. They took their places in a semicircle before the big wooden triangle, which was manned on either side by a Marine drummer. In front of the triangle stood the Marine who was to administer the flogging. He had stripped down to his shirt and was already wiping sweat from his brow with the back of his hand, for it was yet another very hot day. In his other hand he held the cat-o'-nine-tails, each strand tarred and knotted.

The Marines began to drum, and Will was brought into the circle. His guards removed his shirt, then tied his hands to the upper parts of the triangle. There wasn't a sound for a moment, not a whisper from a concerned friend, nor a cry from a child. Everyone was entirely focused on the hideousness of what they were to witness.

Will's punishment was announced again, and one of the Marines who had brought him out of the guard-house gave the signal count of one.

Mary had witnessed some thirty or more floggings, of women as well as men, and it had always appalled her, even when she thought the victim deserved punishment. Some were given 1,000 lashes, 500 one day, the rest saved for when their backs healed up. Some people died before they got even half-way, and those who survived would bear the scars for the rest of their lives. Mary felt sick even before the Marine lifted his arm for the first lash. She had caressed that broad brown back, knew every knob in Will's spine as intimately as she knew her own hands.

Will didn't flinch at the first lash, he even tried to smile at Mary as if to prove it didn't hurt. But just that one stroke had left a red weal, and his smile, however brave, didn't fool her.

The counting was slow, half a minute between each lash, and by the eighth blood was drawn. Will couldn't smile any longer, his body jerked with each lash and he was biting his lips as he tried not to cry out.

On and on it went, flies homing in on the fresh blood which spurted out all over his back like water through a sieve. By the twenty-fifth lash, Will was clinging to the triangle, his handsome face contorted with agony. Mary held Charlotte's face close to her chest, and shut her eyes each time the drum was beaten. But she could still hear the whip whistling through the still air, and the sound of the Marine's boots on the ground as he spun round to give each stroke more impact. She could also smell Will's blood and hear the buzzing of the flies gorging on it.

It took over an hour in all, many of the crowd almost passing out from standing beneath the hot sun. By fifty lashes Will was insensible, the sinews on his back showing white through the lacerated skin. He hung by the ropes around his wrists, his legs sagging like a drunk's.

Mary was crying now, hating the system which ordered such brutal punishment and despising those Marines who had often talked and joked with Will and were now his torturers.

The drum and the count finally stopped. Will was released from the triangle and he slid down it to the floor. His breeches and boots were soaked with blood, and ants were already carrying off small pieces of his flesh on their backs.

Mary ran to him, imploring someone to get cloths and salt water to bathe his back. Will was unconscious, his face still contorted with pain, and she crouched down beside him, Charlotte still in her arms.

'Let me take Charlotte?' a familiar voice asked.

Mary looked up and was surprised to see it was Sarah with a bucket of water and cloths. She had streaks from tears down her dirty face and it seemed that Will's suffering and Mary's distress had reminded her of their old friendship.

'Bless you, Sarah,' Mary said gratefully as she handed

her child over. She washed Will's face first, then looked up at Sarah again. 'I ought to get him out of the sun but I haven't got anywhere to take him now that they've confiscated our hut.'

'We'll take him to mine,' Sarah said, leaning down and patting Mary's shoulder. 'Hold on, I'll get some men to help.'

As Sarah walked away with Charlotte in her arms, Mary leaned over and put her lips close to her husband's ear. 'Can you hear me, Will?' she whispered.

He didn't reply, but his eyelids flickered. 'I swear to you we'll escape from here,' she whispered, hate for Captain Phillip and everyone else responsible welling up inside her. 'We'll find a way, you'll see. I'll never let this happen again.'

It was later that day, as Mary crouched by Will's side in the small hut, gently bathing his back, that she considered her old vow to escape. She hadn't thought of it once since her arrival, and now it seemed incredible to her that she had begun to accept this terrible place, even to like it. But she couldn't bear it any longer. Somehow she was going to get Will and Charlotte and herself away from here and do so as fast as was humanly possible.

Chapter seven

'Move over, Mary,' Sarah hissed in the dark. 'You aren't in bed with Will now.'

Mary half smiled, wishing she was in bed with Will, back in their own hut. But however cramped it was sharing this hut with five other women, plus Charlotte, she was very grateful to Sarah and her friends for letting them stay. In cynical moments she put their kindness down to her being back on their level. But mostly she preferred to believe that Sarah, at least, had had such a shock at seeing Will's flogging that she had regained her old standards of compassion and generosity.

Will was in a hut with James, Samuel and Jamie, and Mary hadn't had many chances to see him since the day of the flogging, as he'd been sent to work on the brick kilns the day after. His back still wasn't healed. Mary was incensed at the further cruelty of forcing a man to do hard physical work when his back was torn to shreds. She had gone to meet him after that first day, and she'd cried at the sight of him. He was dragging himself along, his shirt soaked in blood, his face contorted with the pain. He went into the sea for a swim, hoping that would heal it faster, but he could barely move his arms, and his face went so pale that Mary thought he was going to pass out again. The wounds didn't heal with all the bending and lifting, and dirt and dust had got into them and caused infections. Will was scarred for life now, both physically and mentally.

It seemed to Mary that she was in a dark tunnel without even a chink of light at the end of it. She'd been separated from her husband and lost her hut; rations had been cut again, even more people were getting sick and each week the death toll increased.

It had once been the custom that all work stopped for a funeral and everyone attended, but not any more, otherwise no work would ever get done. Death was commonplace now, no more remarkable than a reported theft or accident. Word would go round that Jack, Bill or Kate had gone, but the only real interest was in who would get their personal effects. That was, if they hadn't already been stolen even before the man or woman passed away. Children's deaths had even less impact; to everyone but the mother it was just one mouth less to feed.

Mary had been pressed into laundry work the day after Will's flogging. Although washing the officers' and Marines' clothes wasn't particularly hard work, the vigilance required was exhausting. Shirts were at a premium and if left to dry unguarded, would be stolen by other women. But it was always the laundress who was punished if a shirt went missing, even if she wasn't found with one in her possession.

Only the thought of escape kept Mary going now. It filled her mind from dawn till dusk, distracting her from hunger, the funerals and the depravity all around her. Four women had run off into the bush, but they were soon recaptured; others who escaped were either killed by natives or died unable to find food and water; sometimes their bodies were found later. Many more just returned with their tails between their legs, only to be put back in chains.

Mary knew from Tench, who had done a lot of exploring inland, that there was nothing there to run to, just mile after mile of barren bush land. Some men had stolen a boat a while ago, but they weren't sailors and capsized it and were soon picked up.

But Mary was familiar with boats and sailing. She knew she'd need a sextant, a great deal of provisions, and charts of the waters around here. Above all, she needed to know where the nearest civilization was, and find a boat suitable for rough seas.

She had said all this to Will a few days ago, but he'd just laughed at her. 'A boat, a sextant and some charts! Why don't you ask for the moon too, my lover?' he said.

Mary was well aware of the difficulties involved, but she didn't agree that it was impossible just because no one else had dared to do it. She knew that Captain Phillip and his officers had tried to communicate with the natives and got nowhere, but she had made inroads in that direction herself and been successful.

She attributed this to Charlotte. While the natives might be intimidated by men in uniforms, they weren't frightened of a small child almost as naked as one of their own. While walking along the beach and around to the next cove, collecting wood for a fire, Mary had become aware she was being watched by a group of women natives and their children. She sat down with Charlotte on her lap and sang some songs to her, and to her delight she heard a voice joining in. It was that of another small girl, and when Mary turned and smiled at her, the child came closer.

Mary did the same again for three consecutive days, and on the fourth the little girl came and sat beside her, the mother standing a little way back, watching. It wasn't long before other children joined them, and after only a few more days, they all knew some of the words to Mary's songs.

She showed the native women some leaves of 'sweet tea', the vine-like plant the convicts used as a drink. This was the closest thing they had to a cure-all. It seemed to alleviate hunger pains, it comforted and revitalized, and it was believed to ward off diseases as those who drank nothing else seemed to suffer less from dysentery. The convicts had exhausted all the sources of the plant close to the camp, and Mary hoped the natives would show her where there was more. They did, taking her there so fast she had to run to keep up with them, and they even picked it for her.

In general the convicts hated the natives. This was partly because these people were so free, while they had to work, but more because they felt they were inferior beings. Convicts were used to being looked down on as the lowest of the low, and to their minds the natives were lowlier still. They bitterly resented the way the officers gave these savages presents and insisted they were to be treated with deference, while the convicts were subjected to cruelty, with no allowances made for their needs.

Mary had never felt this way, although she didn't see the natives as beautiful people. To her mind the stink of the fish oil on them, their splayed noses and the ever-present bubbles of snot nestling above their thick lips made all but the children ugly as sin. But she was intelligent enough to realize that they probably thought white people just as ugly, and furthermore this was their land, and they were perfectly adapted to it. Her interest in them had been furthered by Tench's enthusiasm. He believed that the way truly to settle this new country was to learn to understand its people. Mary, however, didn't want to understand them in order to settle here; she was hoping for their help in her escape.

She persisted in making friends with them. And with a warm smile, and showing interest in their children, it wasn't hard. She told them her name, they reciprocated. They touched her hair and skin, laughingly holding their own black arms against hers to show the difference. Mary drew crude pictures of native animals in the sand and they told her their names. She drew a picture of one of the boats, then a very long wavy line to show them how far the white people had come to get here. She wished she could illustrate how different her homeland was from theirs, but that was too difficult. She wondered too if they had any conception at all of the nature of the white man's colony, and what the word 'convict' meant.

As Tench had pointed out, until the white man came

these natives wouldn't even have understood the notion of theft. They weren't acquisitive people, and they left their tools, canoes and other items lying around. Much of their hostility was due to white men taking their belongings, and who could blame them for retaliating with violence?

Mary continued to cultivate this little group of natives, day after day. They appeared healthy and well fed, and although she knew much of their diet was fish, which they caught from their canoes, she guessed they supplemented this with other things. She wanted to know what, for they didn't grow or rear anything. She thought such knowledge would help in her escape.

To her shock, the women showed her grubs and insects which they dug out of rotting tree stumps. Although Mary's empty stomach heaved at the very thought of it, she bravely tried some and found they weren't as bad as she expected.

Heavy rain prevented her from going to talk to the natives for almost a week, and when she did eventually venture back into the next cove, she couldn't see anyone. This disturbed her, for although she knew that these people didn't stay in permanent camps, wandering about as the mood took them, she was aware that this was a favourite fishing spot.

She walked farther than she normally did, until a buzzing of insects and a wheeling of birds overhead halted her. Ahead, she could see something lying up by the bushes above the beach, and to her horror she realized it was a dead native, covered in a swarm of ants. Snatching

Charlotte up in her arms, she ran as fast as she could back to the camp.

She was still running when she saw Tench. He must have come back from Rose Hill the previous night. He smiled at her warmly. 'You're in quite a hurry,' he said. 'Something wrong?'

'There's a body around in the next cove,' she blurted out.

'Anyone you know?' he joked.

Mary couldn't laugh, for she was afraid the body belonged to one of the group she had befriended. 'I think it's one of the natives,' she said. 'I didn't go close enough to be sure. Surely they don't leave their dead lying around unburied?'

'I wouldn't think so,' he said, looking concerned. 'I hope it is a natural death, not an attack by one of our people, we've got enough trouble without that. But I'll go and check it out now.'

After advising Mary not to stray so far from the camp again, he walked off.

It was several days before Mary had a chance to speak to Tench again. She'd seen him sailing off down the harbour with a group of Marines the day after she told him about the body, but he could have been going to the lookout on the Heads at the end of the bay.

She was just coming out of the stores with the rations for herself and Charlotte, when she saw Tench coming down the hill from Captain Phillip's house. She thought he looked very worried and upset.

'What's the matter?' she asked as he drew near to her. 'Didn't you have a present for him?'

This was a long-standing joke between them. In the early days Tench usually brought a gift of food when he dropped in to see her and Will. It was never anything much, maybe an egg for Charlotte, or some vegetables, but when times got harder and he didn't bring anything he always apologized and looked embarrassed. Mary would tease him then and say he couldn't expect a welcome without a present.

This time Tench gave her only a ghost of a smile. 'The captain's not happy with my news,' he said. 'There's dozens of dead and dying natives around the bay. Just like the one you saw.'

Mary instinctively clutched Charlotte tighter.

Tench saw her fear and put one hand on her shoulder. 'Don't worry, Surgeon White hasn't got any similar cases here. It must be something that only affects them. But keep away, just to be safe. Captain Phillip is sending someone down there to see what he can do or find out.'

Telling Mary not to worry was like asking the sun not to shine. She was terrified that this disease would spread to the camp and kill Charlotte, so her whole being urged her to flee now, any way she could.

Just a few days earlier, the *Supply*, the smallest ship of the original fleet, had returned from Norfolk Island with news that twenty-six of the twenty-nine convicts there had devised a plan to lure the crew away from the ship and sail off in her. By all accounts this plan was a first-class one and would have succeeded but for someone informing on them. While this meant on the one hand that Mary's idea was feasible, it also meant that all security would be tightened still further now, and punishments for any misdemeanour would be harsher than ever.

This was borne out just a few days later when six Marines were hanged for stealing from the stores. It seemed they had been doing it for months, having made keys for the locks, and when one of them was on guard duty he let his friends get in to plunder.

Most of the convicts were delighted that Captain Phillip was coming down on his men just as hard as on the convicts. But to Mary it suggested that Phillip was panicking because he knew the stored food wasn't going to last until more came from England.

As usual when a punishment took place, everyone had to be there. As Mary watched the rope put round each man's neck, and heard the sound of the gallows floor pulled away beneath him, leaving him dangling in space, she had never felt so desperate and afraid.

To her there was nothing good about this place – corrupt guards, women getting thirty lashes just for fighting, and all the time they were slowly being starved to death. It seemed to Mary that she was trapped in hell with several hundred lunatics.

In April, however, things looked up slightly for Mary and Will, as Captain Phillip was forced by food shortages to let Will go back to the fishing, under supervision. Mary smiled grimly to herself for she had been right, they couldn't manage without him. The catches had been tiny without his skill, and although Will very much resented being watched over, at least he had proved he was indispensable, and they got their old hut back.

Whatever the epidemic was which killed half the native population around the bay, it didn't spread to the new colony. Only one white man died, a sailor on the *Supply*. Surgeon White seemed to be of the opinion it was small-pox, but how it had come was a mystery. If they had brought it with them on the ships, it would have shown up far earlier.

Then in early May the gloom in the whole colony was lifted for a while by the arrival of the *Sirius* from Cape Town. Although she was mainly carrying flour, not sub-stantial provisions like meat, she brought good news that other ships were on their way, and long-awaited mail for those lucky enough to have friends and family who could write.

Yet the sight of the ship anchored out in the bay seemed to have a bad effect on Will. Mary found him on the shore on many an afternoon before he went out fishing, just staring out at the *Sirius*. When she tried to speak of it he snapped at her, and when he wasn't working he didn't come looking for her and Charlotte as he once did.

One day, early in the afternoon, Mary was taking the clean washing back to the barracks, having left Charlotte playing with another child, when she heard Will's loud voice coming from James Martin's hut. Mary guessed they'd managed to get some rum from somewhere.

Mary had conflicting opinions about James, the Irish horse thief. She had been delighted to see him again, and Sam Bird too, for the friendships formed on the *Dunkirk* were the basis of a kind of family here. James was a very amusing and charming man, intelligent and articulate, and able to read and write. But he was a devil for the drink, and women.

Mary recognized him as the sort who led others into trouble but usually managed to wriggle or charm his way out of any blame. He wasn't bound by loyalty; James Martin looked after himself first and foremost. She felt he was a bad influence on Will.

Mary wasn't by nature a snoop, but Will worried her when he drank, as he became boastful and often quite belligerent. She also wanted to find out how he and James had acquired the drink; if he was stealing fish to get it she wanted to know in advance.

There wasn't anyone else around, so Mary crept round the back of James's hut. If anyone came by she would make out she had just come out of the bushes after relieving herself.

James was talking about some of the men going after the native women. He took the view that a man wasn't right in the head to do such a thing.

'I reckons you'd at least be safer than with some of the pox-carrying hags here,' Will said, and laughed heartily. 'That's why I picked Mary, I knew she were clean.'

Mary wasn't sure whether to take that as a compliment or not. It had a kind of double edge to it.

'She's a good woman,' James said almost reprovingly. 'You're a lucky man, Will, in more ways than one.'

'I'll be luckier still once I get out of this accursed place,' Will retorted. 'And I'll be off on the first ship when my time's up.'

'Won't you wait for Mary?' James asked, his tone

slightly arch, making Mary suspect they weren't drinking together after all. Maybe Will had come visiting after getting some spirits elsewhere.

'No, I bloody won't,' Will burst out. 'Firstly no ship will take me on with a woman and a child, secondly I can do better than her.'

Mary felt as if someone had punched her in the belly. It was one thing for Will to tell others he didn't consider himself legally married, quite another to say he could do better than her. She turned and fled, trying very hard not to cry.

Will didn't come back to their hut before going fishing that evening, so Mary cooked up some rice on the fire, for once barely noticing the maggots that floated up to the surface as the water got hot. She had nothing more to add to it, as they had already eaten their tiny ration of salted pork earlier in the week. But Mary had no appetite, she was only cooking for Charlotte's sake. She felt weak with misery that Will intended to abandon her.

Charlotte sat right by the fire, as she always did when food was cooking, her dark eyes never leaving the cooking pot. That distressed Mary still further, for a small portion of rice wasn't anywhere near enough to keep a child growing and healthy. She could already see in her daughter the tell-tale signs of under-nourishment that she'd observed in children from desperately poor families back in Cornwall: the distended belly, sunken cheeks and lack-lustre eyes and hair.

If Will left her and went home, escape would be well-nigh impossible. She might be able to plan it, get her hands on all the necessary equipment and handle a boat well, but it was Will who had the navigation skills. There wasn't another man in the whole convoy likely to take his place.

The prospect of being left alone here terrified her. She'd lose the hut, the women would jeer at her, the men would pester her. She wouldn't be able to protect Charlotte from the depravity that was all around. The best she could hope for was to become a 'lag wife', the mistress of one of the Marines or officers. But that would only last until he too went back to England.

Mary's emotions ranged through despair, fear and then anger that evening, but by the time Charlotte had devoured the rice and turned sleepily to her mother's breast, she had a plan. Just as she'd coolly planned finding an officer lover on the *Dunkirk* in order to survive, she was now going to use the few assets she had again.

As Will made his way back to his hut it was almost dawn. He was chilled to the bone and wet through for it had started raining and turned very cold around ten o'clock the previous evening. He was also exhausted and aching with hunger, for they'd fished all night and all they had to show for the hard work was around a dozen fish. He had experienced all that a thousand times before, both here and back in Cornwall, but what had really got him down tonight was the attitude of the two Marines sent out to watch him.

'Bastards,' he muttered, and spat noisily on the sand. But for the fear of another flogging he would have knocked them over the side. How dare they suggest the lack of fish was because he didn't know as much about fishing as he claimed! And that he was drunk when he came aboard. He had had a few tots of rum, but that didn't impair his judgement. There just weren't any fish in the bay. If they'd been prepared to sail through the Heads like he wanted to do, they would have caught thousands.

As he drew nearer the hut, he was very surprised to see a fire and Mary bending over it.

'Why the fire? Is Charlotte sick?' he asked as he got nearer.

'No, she's asleep,' Mary said. 'I thought you'd be cold and hungry so I made some breakfast for you.'

Will's spirits lifted. He had expected Mary to be sullen because he'd gone off fishing without seeing her first. If she had found out he'd bought some rum instead of something they could all eat, she'd have been even madder.

'Breakfast?' he said incredulously.

Mary touched his wet shirt. 'Take that off and hang it up to dry,' she said, her face soft with concern. 'Wrap the blanket round you to warm you up. I could only fry a bit of bread for you, it was all I could get.'

Five minutes later, sitting on a stool in the doorway of the hut, with a cup of sweet tea in one hand and a big piece of fried bread in the other, Will felt much better. The first rays of light were coming into the sky and the bay looked beautiful with a cloud of mist just above the water. It was his favourite time of day, the birds just waking to sing, the ugliness of the camp not yet visible. It might be winter here, but it was as warm as a spring morning back home. In fact, looking across at the *Sirius* wreathed in mist, with the grey-green of the other side of the bay behind her, he could almost fool himself he was in Falmouth harbour looking out to St Mawes.

He missed Cornwall so much – the little winding cobbled streets, the houses huddled together, that blinding clear light in summer, the big fires in the tavern on a winter's night. When he thought of the risks the Cornish took with smuggling, it made him smile. Straining at the oars against waves as tall as houses, watching for the warning lanterns on the cliffs that said the excise men were coming – it was a game with high stakes, and only those with speed, nerve and strength dared play. But the winners tossed back glasses of French brandy, fishermen, miners and farm labourers equals with the country squire if they had played their part well.

The lasses there were pretty as well – rosy cheeks, big breasts and sweet shy smiles. The first time he saw Mary, through the grille on the *Dunkirk*, she was like that too. Now she was rake-thin, with hollowed cheeks, and she rarely smiled.

But she'd got up to make a fire and fry him some bread. She kept herself clean, and she didn't go after other men.

'Penny for them?' Mary startled him by coming up behind him and putting her arms around his neck.

'They aren't worth a penny!' he chuckled. 'I'll tell

you them for free. I was thinking about Cornwall, the smuggling and the taverns.'

'Want to know what I'm thinking?' she asked, kissing his neck.

'Go on,' he said.

'That we get into bed,' she said. 'And I warm you proper like.'

Will smiled, and it went right down inside him. Even before the flogging there hadn't been much love-making, hunger and exhaustion saw to that. But since then it had gone completely; his lacerated back, working on the brick kiln, and further cuts in rations had knocked all the passion out of him.

'Now that's a real good idea, my lover,' he said, turning to grab her for a kiss. 'It's been far too long.'

Mary smiled to herself later that day as she washed clothes down at the water's edge. She'd almost forgotten how special Will could make her feel. It was worth getting up so early, she'd even managed to forget how hungry she was.

In early September Mary knew she was definitely pregnant again. She was thrilled, not just because she'd reached her objective and found a way to prevent Will from leaving her here alone, but because he was genuinely delighted at becoming a father. Yet as always in the colony, any happy moment seemed to be erased by something bad. This time it was a soldier raping a girl of eight. To Mary it brought Charlotte's vulnerability sharply into focus. Up until then she'd hardly considered what the future for her child would be – keeping her alive was enough to concern herself with. But when the soldier wasn't even hanged, but sent off to Norfolk Island, she found herself sobbing with rage.

'Don't take on so, Mary,' Will said, trying to comfort her. 'He'll be out of the way there.'

'But there's children there too,' she reminded him. 'Including little Henrietta, Jane's baby. You explain to me why you can be flogged just for insolence, but hurting a little girl isn't thought a real crime.'

'I don't know,' Will said, shaking his head. 'Any more than I don't know why they still keep sending a couple of men out to watch me fish. If they weren't there, I'd sail right out the bay and get a better catch.'

'We have to think again about escape,' Mary said fiercely.

'How can we do that with a little 'un on the way?' he replied, tenderly patting her belly.

'Because of this little 'un,' she retorted. 'Don't you want something better for him?'

In November the whole colony buzzed with the news that Lieutenant Bradley and Captain Keltie of the *Sirius* had captured two natives on Captain Phillip's instructions.

The captured men were called Bennelong and Colbee, and it was discovered they had no wives or children. Lieutenant Bradley, the officer responsible for their capture, got an orphaned native boy who had been taken in by Surgeon White to explain to the men that they weren't going to be harmed.

Mary watched the whole proceeding with amazement. She had always thought that abducting anyone against their will amounted to harm. She was also sure that the two natives would be even more alarmed when they were subjected to being washed, shaved, dressed in clothes and shackled to prevent their escape.

Just a few days later, news got round that both men had managed to free themselves from their shackles. Colbee got clean away, but Bennelong was caught. The majority of the prisoners found all this highly amusing. They didn't consider Bennelong to be a person with feelings, more an animal which had to be caged. But Mary was sickened by it – there was something about the tall, well-built black man that touched her. She could imagine his confusion at the peculiar world he'd been dragged into. His people weren't confined in any way. Home was the temporary shelter of a cave or a mud and bark 'humpie'. They didn't have kings or princes in their tribes, every man was equal to the next, so how could he possibly understand the white man's class distinctions, or his lust for wealth, power and possessions?

Mary saw Bennelong as being in a very similar position to herself, and as such they could be allies. It struck her that if she could show him ways to use his captivity to his advantage, in return he might be persuaded to help her and Will escape.

The weeks went slowly by, and with each one Mary felt more desperate. There were no extra rations here for pregnant women as on the *Charlotte*, and she was so hungry that she often went searching for the grubs and insects the natives had shown her. During December and January it was blazing hot, she would be wakened at dawn by the sun beating down on the hut's roof, and there was no respite all day until sunset.

Only the relationship she was forming with Bennelong gave her a little hope. With words of his language she learned from the children she had befriended, she was able to suggest to him that if he played along with Captain Phillip his leg irons would be removed and he could become important to the white man. Bennelong seemed to understand what she meant; on one occasion he showed her half a bottle of rum he'd been given and grinned broadly. He appeared to be happy to stay in the settlement as long as more of it was forthcoming.

Mary knew it was too soon to attempt to enrol his help in any escape plan. Besides, it was impossible when she was so heavily pregnant. There was no possibility of collecting and storing food either, and anyway there were no ships in the harbour. Both the *Sirius* and the *Supply* had gone, taking ninety-six male and twenty-five female convicts, as well as twenty-five children, to Norfolk Island in an effort to eke out the rations a little longer. The *Sirius* was then going on to China to try to get desperately needed provisions.

When they set sail from England they had enough food for two years, and now that time was up. Even though the farm at Rose Hill had produced a good harvest of wheat, there was only enough food to last a few more months, with rations cut yet again. Everyone from

Captain Phillip to the lowest criminal was waiting expectantly for a ship to arrive with more food. Daily, people trudged down to Dawes Point, where they could just about see the flag mast on the South Head at the end of the bay. If the flag was struck it would mean a ship was coming, but day after day they were disappointed.

The fear of dying of starvation was very real now. It showed in every convict's face, from the bleakness of their eyes to the hollows in their cheeks, and in the slowness of their movements. With so many of their original number taken away by troops to Norfolk Island, and the countless deaths during the two years, Sydney Cove looked like a ghost town, and empty huts were being allocated to people who had previously shared. With a further cut in rations, no one had the physical strength to work a full day. An order was issued that they need only work until midday; the afternoons could be spent working their own gardens. At last Will was told he could fish without a guard, because there just wasn't the manpower to spare for fishing duties.

Mary had her first labour pains during the early evening of 30 March. She didn't recognize them as labour at first, assuming they were merely hunger cramps. Will was out fishing and it was raining so hard that the ground was a sea of slippery red mud. She put Charlotte to bed and got in herself, but the pains continued, just strong enough to prevent sleep.

All through the night she lay there, staring up into the darkness, listening to the steady dripping of water coming in through the roof. By then she realized the baby was coming, but in her weakened state she felt unable to get up and trudge through the mud and rain to seek help.

For the first time ever, she hoped for death. She was exhausted by the daily struggle to survive, and she felt unable to meet the further demands a new baby would place on her. Even the little cries Charlotte made in her sleep didn't stir her conscience. She hoped that by lying there, ignoring the child struggling to find its way out into the world, it would just fade away and so would she.

But as she closed her eyes and tried to will herself into death's dark valley, her mother's face came into her mind. Mary had tried her best to forget her parents and sister. She had long since given up trying to recall their faces and the sound of their voices or wondering if they ever spoke of her. She had even steeled herself not to think about Cornwall and compare it with here.

Yet there was her mother's face, as clear as if she was standing in the daylight before her. Her grey eyes were full of concern, her mouth slightly pursed as if in disapproval, wisps of grey hair escaping from her linen cap. Her expression was one Mary remembered very well, the one she'd always worn when berating Mary for unfeminine behaviour. Mary remembered then that her mother had always been strong, she'd never shown her anxiety to Mary and Dolly when their father's ship didn't return when expected. Somehow she always managed to put food on the table and keep the fire burning.

It seemed to Mary that her mother was trying to send her a message that she must fight for life, for her children's sake.

With great difficulty she got out of her bed, fumbled in the dark for a piece of sacking to put around her shoulders, and went out into the rain.

The nearest hut was only twenty yards away, but the pains were too fierce to stand up. On her hands and knees, Mary crawled through the mud in agony to get help.

The first dawn light was just coming through the open door of the hut as Mary's baby finally fought his way out, in the none too certain hands of Anne Tomkin.

'It's a boy!' Anne exclaimed with more weariness than jubilation, as she held the baby closer to the door to examine him. 'And he looks healthy enough.'

This was borne out by a lusty, angry scream. It was Mary who had to tell Anne to wrap her son in a piece of cloth, to tie the cord and cut it. Anne had no children herself and her husband Wilfred who had gone for more experienced help hadn't arrived back.

Yet as Mary took her baby in her arms, she forgot the pain, the hunger and even her blood- and mud-caked body. God had given her the boy she wanted, He had spared her life, and that had to mean there was hope for better times.

'I'll call him Emmanuel,' she said softly to herself.

Chapter eight

'He's a beauty,' Will said reverently as he cradled his son in his arms. He'd only just got back from fishing all night, and despite being wet, cold and exhausted he was thrilled to find Mary had borne him a son. 'And he's brought us luck! I've got a fine big mullet for us.'

When Mary shot him an anxious glance, Will grinned. 'It's fair do's. They gave it to me because of the babby. I reckon things will get better for us now.'

Mary relaxed again and smiled. Will had always been affectionate towards Charlotte right from her early days, but he was almost incandescent with pleasure now as he looked down at his own baby. 'Do you like the name Emmanuel?' she asked.

'It's a real good name,' he said, looking tenderly first at his son and then at Mary. 'A hopeful one, and I'll make sure he learns to write it too.'

That day was a golden one for Mary. The rain stopped, the sun came out and Will carried her down to the sea to wash her. There had been many sweet moments between them in the past, but never this degree of tenderness and care. He made her comfortable in a makeshift bed beneath a gum tree by the hut, tucked Emmanuel into Charlotte's old crib, then cooked the mullet over the fire with a couple of potatoes he'd managed to get from somewhere. Later he took Charlotte for a walk to tell Surgeon White about the new baby, leaving Mary to sleep.

She didn't sleep, despite the comfort of the food inside her. Will wasn't the kind of man who spoke of love, but his actions had told her how he felt. There had been times during her pregnancy when she had felt guilty she was trapping him, but that feeling had gone now she had seen his delight in having his own child. They were a complete family now, and whatever life had in store for them, they would cope with it together.

Tench came to visit later that afternoon.

'I heard your baby was born,' he said, looking down at Mary cuddling Emmanuel under the tree. 'I thank God you are both safe and well.'

'Isn't he the bonniest babby you ever saw?' Will asked as he dandled Charlotte on his knee. 'I never saw a more lusty one.'

Tench laughed and leaned down to stroke the child's head. 'He favours you, Will. The same fair hair and strong body. Mind you take good care of him.'

'Me too,' Charlotte said indignantly. They all laughed, for she'd clearly picked up the idea today that her place might be about to be usurped.

'I'll always take care of you,' Will said, picking her up and throwing her into the air. 'You're my little princess.'

'Don't place too much importance on the rumours that Will is going to run out on you when his time is up,' Tench said to Mary after Will had wandered off to boast to a few more friends about his son. 'I don't believe he's brave enough to ever leave you.'

Mary wasn't surprised that Tench had heard the rumours. People stopped at nothing to pass on information here. She wondered what he would think of her if he knew the baby was her secret plan to hold on to Will.

'I don't listen to what people say,' she said stoutly, for she felt so happy today that nothing else seemed to matter.

'You can apply for land of your own when Will's free,' Tench said.

'What would we do with land?' Mary replied with a smile. 'We aren't farmers. Will's only happy fishing.'

'Then he could build his own boat and start his own fishing business. Maybe you could open the first fishmonger's in New South Wales!'

'Maybe,' she replied. She wished she could believe as Tench did that one day there would be a real town here. He seemed to think that once the present problems were solved, the country would attract free settlers, to farm and trade, just as America had. 'And maybe a ship will arrive tomorrow with animals, ploughs, seed, fruit trees, food for us all, medicine and material to make new clothes,' she added with more than a touch of sarcasm.

'The ships will come soon,' he said, as he always did, but this time there was a lack of conviction in his voice. 'I really can't believe England would leave us to perish here.'

*

Emmanuel was baptized a few days later on 4 April, under the same big tree where Mary and Will had been married. As usual on such occasions, everyone was present.

Mary had considered herself poorly dressed for her wedding, but that grey dress had long since fallen apart with wear and become napkins for Charlotte. Its replacement, an issued 'slop', a shapeless sack of a dress in coarse cotton, was almost as worn out. One of the more kindly Marines' wives had given her a red ribbon for her hair, and a piece of flannelette to make a gown for Emmanuel – but for that he would have been wrapped in a piece of rag.

As Mary looked around at the rest of the congregation she saw how much they had all diminished since arriving here. They had in the main been healthy then, eyes bright with excitement and mischief; there was exuberance and hope, even when they were complaining vigorously. Their voices were strong, they argued, fought and laughed, pushing and shoving each other like impatient children. Mary remembered how she had once thought she would never learn so many names.

But it was easy to name every single one now. Death had claimed so many, and the recent removal of scores more to Norfolk Island meant there were perhaps fewer than 150 remaining. Only the number of children and babies had increased, but they were a sorry sight, nothing but huge mournful eyes set in pale, bony faces, legs and arms like little sticks, most sucking their fingers with hunger.

There were no bright eyes anywhere now, not even

among the officers. No pushing and shoving or loud voices, just apathetic, gaunt faces, aged radically by the sun and malnutrition. Laughter was a rare sound too, for those who still managed to get their hands on drink no longer wanted merriment, only oblivion. Even the bright colours of clothes were absent, for the finery some had sported that first day had long since turned to grey rags.

Mary thought they had all become like this savage land. As dull and arid as the scrubby bush, with its grey-green gums, as stunted and hopeless as the vegetables they had struggled to grow.

She would have liked to have put the blame on the officers, but even they were thinner and worn-looking too. As for the Marines, she felt even sorrier for them and their wives and families, for they had the same rations as the prisoners, their uniforms were in rags, and they were dying just as fast.

Watkin Tench went out to Dawes Point early the following morning to check the flag pole out on the South Head. He hadn't slept well, for the christening of Emmanuel Bryant the previous day had unsettled him deeply. While it was good to see Mary and Will's joy in their little son, a bright spot in an otherwise desperately grim period, if the child didn't survive, Mary was going to be devastated.

Tench wished he didn't care so much for her. He had told himself a thousand times that he only felt a bond of friendship with her, but the truth of the matter was that each time he saw her his feelings for her grew stronger.

His heart quickened at the sight of her. He felt helpless in the face of her great need for food and decent clothes. She was proud, she didn't beg for favours, and made light of the deprivation she suffered. Indeed, she made the best of the little she had.

He had even hoped Will's flogging would harden him in the way it had other men, that he would become a real trouble-maker and Mary would lose her loyalty to him. But instead of prising them apart it seemed to have had the reverse effect, baby Emmanuel being part of it.

If only he could stop weaving such futile day-dreams about taking Mary home with him when his term of office was up. If he were to tell anyone his thoughts of finding a little cottage for them somewhere well away from Plymouth, and telling his friends and family back home that she was the widow of a Marine serving here, they would laugh at him.

But that was what he dwelt on. He imagined Mary blossoming again with good food, lying in his arms each night in a feather bed. When he got to that point of his fantasy he would find himself aroused, imagining himself kissing those small breasts he'd so often glimpsed as she suckled Charlotte.

Tench broke off abruptly from this reverie when he saw the flag had been struck on the flag pole. This signified a ship was either anchored in the cove, or had been spotted out at sea.

In great excitement he ran to the observatory where an astronomical telescope had been erected and hastily trained it on the flag pole. He could see only one man strolling by the pole and to his intense disappointment he knew it couldn't be a ship from England, or there would be more frantic activity. It had to be the *Sirius* returning from Norfolk before making her trip to China.

He ran all the way back to find Captain Phillip to report it, and when the Governor said he would take his boat out to meet the ship, Tench begged to be allowed to accompany him, for at least it was a diversion from the normal routine and thinking about Mary.

They were about half-way to the Heads when they saw the longboat from the *Supply* being rowed towards them. Tench recognized Captain Ball making frantic gestures with his hands and his heart sank.

'Sir,' he said, turning to Captain Phillip, 'prepare yourself for bad news!'

Will came haring along the beach to where Mary was washing some clothes. She looked up from her task anxiously at the sound of his pounding feet. 'What is it?' she yelled, hoping against hope it was news of a ship carrying provisions.

'The *Sirius* has been shipwrecked,' he shouted back.

It was some time before Will regained enough breath to explain what he'd heard down at the harbour. The *Sirius* had just lowered its boats loaded with provisions in Sydney Bay at Norfolk Island, when the ship drifted on to sunken rocks. Captain Hunter tried to avert a disaster by dropping the anchor, but he was too late. Before the anchor chain had tightened, she struck the coral reef that ran parallel to the shore. As the sea tore into the holds, the crew cut away the masts to lighten the ship, so she might float free, but by then there was little hope of this.

'They sent out lines to get the men ashore,' Will gasped out. 'Worked till it was too dark to see any more, so I heard. Next morning they got the rest off.'

Mary was deeply shocked. Losing the *Sirius* was a mortal wound to the colony. How would they get provisions from China now?

'Is everyone safe?' she asked. Some of the women and children who had been sent there were people she'd come to care for.

Will nodded. 'Thank God for that small mercy.' His face broke into a smile then. 'Some of the convicts were sent out to the ship to get the remaining animals off. They found some grog, so they lit fires and settled down for a party.'

'Oh, Will,' Mary sighed. 'That's not funny!'

'We have to laugh otherwise we'd go under,' he retorted indignantly. 'And there's another funny story too. Lieutenant Clark got knocked off the raft by a convict falling in. The convict couldn't swim so Clark rescued him and brought him safely to shore. Then Clark beat him with a stick for jeopardizing his safety.'

Mary giggled. That to her mind was typical of Lieutenant Ralph Clark, whom she had never liked. He was a mean-spirited hypocrite who had spent most of the first year here calling all the female prisoners whores, and boring Tench and the other officers to death with tales of his wonderful wife Betsy back home. But then he'd had the nerve to take a lag wife, after all he'd said about the convict women! He was even absurd enough to name the child borne of that union Betsy, after his beloved wife. He'd been sent off to Norfolk Island to take control and as far as Mary was concerned, the harder he found it the better.

'But what will happen to us now?' she asked Will. 'The *Sirius* was our only chance of getting more supplies.'

Will frowned. 'Phillip has called a special meeting of all the officers for six o'clock.'

Mary knew from Tench that Phillip wasn't in the habit of confiding in anyone. He maintained his aloofness at all costs, so he must be extremely worried to call his men in.

'There's going to be even harder times ahead, that's for sure,' Mary sighed dejectedly. 'But let's try and look on the bright side, Will. If a ship doesn't come from England soon, Phillip will be even more dependent on your fishing. It's time you insisted on a portion of the catch for yourself again. Your skill will be the only thing which will keep everyone alive here.'

Captain Phillip was indeed a very worried man as he stood before his assembled officers at six o'clock. For so long he had lived in hope of a ship coming from England to solve the colony's problems, but now he had to face the reality that he had to take other drastic measures or be a witness to wholesale death through starvation.

'A further cut in rations will be necessary,' he began, his voice trembling slightly because he knew that a daily ration of two and a half pounds of flour, two pounds of very old pork, a pint of dried peas and a pound of inedible rice, divided between seven people, just wasn't enough to sustain life. 'We must supplement this with more fish and meat if we aren't to perish. My plan is to requisition all private boats for fishing and to form hunting parties.'

The officers looked at one another in consternation, knowing they were expected to volunteer their services. With the exception of Tench, they all considered supervising such expeditions unpleasant, for they did not like working with the convicts.

'Are you suggesting, sir, that some of the convicts are to be given arms?' one of the more senior officers asked, a look of horror on his florid face.

'Yes,' Phillip said wearily. 'Some of them are good marksmen. I believe if we show trust in them, they will respond with a real effort for the common good.'

He moved on to say he had no choice but to send the *Supply* off to Batavia, in the Dutch East Indies. Captain Ball would charter another ship there to bring back supplies. Philip King, the previous Governor of Norfolk Island, would also leave on the ship to take despatches and Captain Phillip's account of the state of the colony back to England.

The officers were even more concerned at this for the *Supply* was a little ship of only 170 tons, and for her to sail alone in unknown waters would be dangerous. Furthermore, if she was lost at sea they would have no vessel left here to take supplies to the settlement in Norfolk Island.

A murmur of dissent went round, but Phillip silenced it with a stern look.

'We have no choice,' he said bluntly. 'We have no supplies to take to Norfolk Island anyway, and to leave a ship in the harbour waiting for help from England which might never come would be catastrophic. I ask you all to give me your support.'

Fear reigned over the colony after the *Supply* sailed out of the harbour in April. The officers feared for the little ship's safety, and became aggressive. The troops dreaded an attack from the natives now firepower was so low. And the convicts were terrified of everything.

Before the *Supply* left a rumour circulated that the officers and troops were going to sail off in her, leaving the convicts to fend for themselves. They all knew they wouldn't last long alone.

Despite the best marksmen being sent out hunting, all they shot was three very small kangaroos. With all the extra boats and men, and the absolute necessity of catching more fish, the catches improved for a while, but then they began to dwindle again. The officers took back their small boats, and in sheer desperation Captain Phillip allowed Will to use his own cutter.

Mary was never one to allow an opportunity to go by without attempting to make use of it.

'This could be our big chance,' she urged Will one night as they lay in bed. 'With the use of that boat we could make our escape.'

'Don't be foolish,' Will said wearily. He was so weak

with hunger and tired from the strain of trying to bring enough food back for everyone that he wasn't inclined to listen to his wife's wild ideas.

'I don't mean now,' she said, sitting up beside him and leaning over to kiss him. 'We can't do it without instruments, charts or a store of food. But what you can do is win the Governor's confidence. Take the boat out further and further each time, but always come back. He's trusting you now, think how much more trust he'll have in you if you seem to be playing the game his way!'

'I can't see the point,' Will said irritably. 'Even if I did get him to trust me well enough so I wasn't watched, I wouldn't even know which was the best direction to go in to find a port.'

'Tench was telling me about the Dutch East Indies the other day. There's a busy port called Kupang,' Mary said. 'He said it was over the sea at the top end of this place.'

Will made a sort of guffaw. 'Over the sea at the top end of this place!' he scoffed. 'What kind of directions are those? Does he know how many leagues it is? Has anyone sailed to it afore? Don't talk daft, girl!'

Mary slumped back down, angry that he was mocking her. 'I don't know yet, but I'll find out,' she said with grim determination. 'We have to escape, Will. If we don't, Emmanuel and Charlotte will die.'

'No, Mary,' he said, turning his back on her dismissively. 'They won't, food will come, you'll see.'

'Maybe it will,' she said, but she ran one finger down the deep scars from the flogging on his back. 'Perhaps the children will even be lucky enough to survive all the outbreaks of fever, to avoid being bitten by a snake, and they won't be corrupted by the other convicts. But let's hope neither of us lives long enough to see Emmanuel tied to the triangle to be flogged.'

She felt Will stiffen under her fingers. She knew he still had nightmares about the flogging.

'I'd kill anyone who tried to do that to him,' he said.

'You'll be too weak by then,' she said gently. 'Old before your time with the struggle to survive. So will I be. That's why we have to go soon, while we're still capable of protecting the children.'

He sighed deeply. 'I'll think about it,' he said.

'And while you're thinking about it, do what I said and win the Governor's trust,' Mary said. 'Once we have that, we're half-way there.'

Mary lay awake long after Will had fallen asleep. She watched and listened constantly, whereas Will went around with his eyes and ears closed. He might think there were adequate provisions for many months yet in the stores, but she knew better. When the officers dined with the Governor now, they had to take their own bread, and the fare at Government House was little better than her own. One evening they'd dined on dog!

Just a few days ago an elderly convict had died while getting his rations in the store, and when Surgeon White examined his body he found his stomach to be completely empty. The only reason Mary still had some fight left in her, and milk in her breasts for Emmanuel, was because of fish Will brought home from the day's catch, and the grubs and berries the natives had introduced her to.

Bennelong had finally made his escape from the settlement, once the food and rum he had become used to grew short. Gardens, even the Governor's own, had been constantly plundered for vegetables, despite the severe flogging that resulted if the culprit was caught. It wasn't only convicts that did it, a seaman from the *Supply* was caught, and one of the Marines. Will had been compelled to dig a hole under their hut to keep their own meagre rations safe. He'd made it like the ones smugglers used back in Cornwall, lined with wood, and a false floor laid down on it.

Yet Mary thrived and still managed to feed her family because she refused to give way to utter despair as some were doing. As she told Will, it was just a case of hanging on, being helpful and pleasant to the officers so that when ships did arrive, as they surely must, she and Will would be in positions of trust. That way they could make opportunities to get the things they needed.

The days crept on, the misery of hunger growing more acute with each one. The weather turned very cold too, the wind eerily rustling the paper-dry leaves of the gums, and all public work ground to a halt because there was no one fit enough to do it any longer.

The convicts merely shuffled around now, every gaunt face illustrating the nature of real starvation. At night Mary often heard small children wailing pitifully from hunger. It was the worst sound she'd ever heard.

Will had appeared to heed Mary's advice, for he made himself increasingly popular with the officers and troops by his diligence in fishing. For this he was rewarded with a share of the catch, and being allowed to pick his own helpers. James Martin, Jamie Cox and Sam Bird, his most trusted friends, often went with him, and although there were usually a couple of Marines along too, this wasn't always the case. Will fished the waters beyond the Heads frequently, sometimes going several miles out to sea. He also struck up friendships with some of the natives as they fished from their canoes. Often it was they who directed him to large shoals.

Will sometimes saw Bennelong as he sailed down the harbour. He would paddle out in his canoe and occasionally climb aboard the cutter for a chat. Mary was sure that if she and Will managed to get their hands on some spirits, he could easily be bribed into helping them escape.

Just when it looked as if all hope of rescue was gone, in the afternoon of 3 June the flag was struck on South Head. As the cry went up that a ship was coming, pandemonium broke out. Men downed tools and cheered, women came hobbling out of their huts and hugged one another.

Watkin Tench, along with Surgeon White and Captain Phillip, took his boat and went off down the harbour. All three of them were as excited and emotional as the rest of the settlement, despite the discomfort of heavy rain and a stiff wind. As they drew closer to the Heads and saw the big ship coming in flying English colours,

Phillip transferred on to a fishing boat to go back, leaving Tench and White to go and collect welcome news from home.

'Look at that magical word on her stern,' White said, pointing to the painted sign that read 'London'. 'I had begun to doubt I would ever see such a thing again.'

The ship was the *Lady Juliana*, and because of the strong winds she was forced to anchor in Spring Cove just inside North Head, but Tench and White went alongside and called out a welcome to the ship's officers.

'You can't know how welcome you are,' Tench called out. 'We feared we'd never get the provisions we need so desperately. Can you tell us what you are carrying so we can take the good news back to the settlement?'

'Two hundred and twenty-five women felons, whores every one of them,' came the shouted reply from one of the officers.

Tench laughed, he thought it was a joke. But his laughter stopped abruptly when a group of tow-haired women suddenly appeared on deck, shouting obscenities.

'You have provisions too?' White yelled, aware that Tench was too stunned to resume any further questions. 'And the medicine we need?'

'Seventy-five barrels of flour,' the ship's officer called back. 'That's all. We set sail with the *Guardian*, she carried the stores, but she got holed by an iceberg.'

By nightfall all the convicts were in despair.

Captain Phillip had returned to the harbour with a beam on his face, confirming to them that it was exactly as the fishermen had reported, a big English ship, anchored at Spring Cove.

The convicts waited, expecting Lieutenant Tench and Surgeon White to arrive back an hour or two later looking happier still. Many of their number hastily ate the last of their rations, in the belief that by the following day they would be given more than they usually ate in a week.

But Tench and White came back grim-faced and silent, going straight up to Government House without a word to anyone. When one of the men who had been on the cutter reported that there were over 200 women on the new ship and no provisions, they were not believed. Some laughed, assuming it had to be a joke. Yet as they watched other officers speeding up to Government House, and no sounds of revelry wafting out, they slowly realized that it had to be true.

The male convicts were far too weak with hunger to be excited by a huge number of new women descending on them. Their reaction was only fear that their rations would be cut even more drastically. But to most of the women it was a calamity. Bad though it was to be forced to share rations with strangers, the prospect of new women stealing their men away was even worse.

A relationship with someone, whether you were legally married or not, eased the misery of life in the colony. In most cases the partnerships were a compromise, especially for the women. Back home few of them would have chosen the mate they had here. But choice was limited, plain girls were grateful for being wanted, the prettier girls felt safer with a protector, and where a baby was a result of the arrangement, it gave some purpose to their life.

Mary was more nervous than most when she heard the news of the *Juliana* and its cargo of women. She knew it wasn't her beauty or her cleverness that had kept Will with her for two years. He had stayed with her purely because there was a shortage of women, and by the time he'd got to know the prettier ones better, he found most had serious flaws in their characters.

Death, and men being moved to Norfolk Island, had decimated their numbers. There weren't more than seventy men left here now, and a great many of those were physical wrecks. Among 200 new women who had been cooped up on a ship for months, there were almost certainly going to be dozens who would set their sights on Will.

Chapter nine

Every single woman in the settlement turned out to see the women from the *Juliana* being rowed ashore. Apart from the weather, it was almost like a re-enactment of their first day here, for they could hear the same kind of excited laughter and the ribald remarks they'd made themselves. But whereas they had arrived in early February, which in this upside-down country meant summer with blazing sunshine, so hot that many of them ran into the sea to cool down, the new arrivals were experiencing winter. The sky was grey, a keen wind was blowing, making the sea choppy, and it was very cold.

There should have been sisterly concern for the new women. After all, they had been through a long, gruelling voyage, and now they were about to enter hell. Yet just the way they looked, even from a distance, was enough to make the old-timers forget any kindly thoughts and band together in antipathy and resentment. The new arrivals' clothes were vivid colours, many wore hats trimmed with flowers and feathers, they were plump and healthy, and they looked for all the world like a troupe of actresses, not convicts.

Mary clutched Emmanuel closer to her breast in fear.

Her first exposure to the convicts from the other transport ships in the fleet was printed indelibly on her mind. They had all seemed so much tougher than her, conniving and ruthless too. Time and the hardships here had made all the survivors equal now, but she was afraid these new women would alter everything.

'Lots of ladies,' Charlotte said, looking up at her mother with undisguised glee. 'Pretty ladies.'

At her child's innocent words Mary felt a pang of shame. They were, after all, just women like herself. All of them had known chains and the horrors of prison and had been wrenched from their families and friends. She didn't want Charlotte to grow up in a climate of bitterness and hate. She decided she must put aside her fear and jealousy and welcome the newcomers.

'I thought we might have had a few fights on our hands,' Surgeon White said to Tench over dinner at White's house the following evening. 'But thanks to the actions of Mary Bryant the new women appear to be settling in well.'

The two men had become friends on the *Charlotte*, despite a twenty-year age gap. Their interests and family backgrounds were similar, and though the surgeon was more concerned with the general health of the colony, and Tench with the challenge of making it a success, they were both intensely fascinated by this new, as yet unexplored land. They had gone on several exploratory trips into the bush together, and shared the same curiosity about its natives. Both of them also had compassion for the convicts, something few of the other officers felt.

By candlelight, White's dining room would pass for being much like any country doctor's back home in England, with its whitewashed walls, snowy table-cloth, plain, serviceable china, laden bookshelves and a couple of treasured landscapes on the walls. By daylight, however, the crudeness of the building showed. The walls were wattle and daub, and in heavy rain holes often appeared. The floor beneath a rug was uneven boards. But whatever its shortcomings, it was a haven of civilization for White and his dinner guests.

While Charles White often regretted his decision to come out here with the fleet, it was mainly because of the lack of medical equipment and medicine rather than the absence of comforts. A widower for over ten years, he had grown used to the bachelor life, and he had two convict women, Anne and Maria, who cooked and kept house for him. He also had little Nunburry, the native boy he'd adopted, to take care of, and some very good friends. Tonight his mood was mellow. He had managed to acquire a bottle of brandy, and he and Tench had dined on a first-class sea bass, with some carrots and potatoes from White's own garden. It was truly miraculous that the vegetables hadn't been stolen, but perhaps by showing Anne and Maria a little kindness, and giving them some extra food, he had gained their loyalty.

'Mary's a good woman,' Tench agreed. 'I daresay she remembered how hard it was for her to adjust when she first arrived here. If only all the women had her practical nature and generosity of spirit!'

He had been surprised and touched to see Mary helping with the allocation of huts for the new arrivals. She seemed to be making a real effort to make the new women feel welcome. He wished her attitude was a general one; already there had been reports of clothing and other personal possessions being stolen.

'There's a fair few trouble-makers among the new ones,' White sighed, remembering the two women he'd separated for fighting and the profanities they'd screamed at him. 'According to the reports, they carried on their whoring with the sailors all the way here. A great number of them are with child. But they are healthy at least, save for the pox of course.'

Tench smiled. White was always ranting about the scourge of venereal diseases. They were rife here of course, but Tench couldn't believe as White did that the whole future of this new land was at risk because of it.

'At least the *Juliana* brought news,' Tench said cheerfully. 'I am amazed to hear of the revolution in France. When I was in Paris I confess to being appalled by the excesses of the aristocracy. And good news too that King George has recovered from his madness. What do you know of this sickness he suffered?'

'Very little. I'm just an old saw-bones,' White shrugged. 'But I am glad Farmer George is well again. As glad as I was to find the *Juliana* has enough rations for two years for her convicts.'

Tench smiled. That news had been the very best, a huge relief for everyone. It was just a shame they hadn't been told immediately, then there would have been less hostility towards the new arrivals. Now everyone was hoping that the *Justinian* from Falmouth, which was apparently fully loaded with stores and equipment, would arrive before the next huge influx of convicts.

But personally Tench was most grateful for the letters from home that were brought out by the ship. He felt he had stood up remarkably well to all the discomforts and deprivations of the settlement, but the sense of isolation from his friends and family had almost broken him at times. Indeed, if he was truthful, there had been times in the past two years when he feared he would never live to see them again.

'Let's drink a toast to the light at the end of a very dark tunnel,' he suggested.

White filled their glasses. 'Light to banish the darkness,' he said, and chuckled. 'Though with another three transports, and a thousand convicts on their way, we'll need a great deal of light to banish that darkness.'

Mary and Will stood together at the harbour, quaking as they looked out across the bay to the *Neptune* and the *Scarborough*. They could see the longboats being lowered to bring the convicts ashore. But the terrible stench coming from the ships was enough for them to know that what they were about to see was going to be utterly appalling.

It had been bad enough on the previous day, helping the sick from the *Surprise* to the hospital. Many of those convicts were so frail that they were unable to walk, having lain in their own vomit and excreta for most of the voyage. But today was going to be even worse.

The *Justinian* had arrived on 20 June, bringing joy to everyone in the settlement as she carried ample provisions and much-needed equipment, along with animals. She had left England some time after the *Surprise*, *Neptune* and *Scarborough*, the three transport ships carrying another 1,000 convicts. But she had overtaken them and made the voyage in only five months. Full rations were issued once again, and working hours put back to normal. The *Justinian* left again as soon as her cargo was unloaded, to take provisions to Norfolk Island.

On the 23rd the flag was struck again, but it was two days before the ship which had been signalled sailed into the bay. This was the *Surprise*, carrying 218 male convicts and a detachment of the newly formed New South Wales Corps.

It was shocking to hear that there had been forty-two deaths during the voyage, and another hundred were sick. And when the Reverend Johnson went aboard, he reported back that the convicts were lying almost naked in the holds, too sick to move or help themselves.

Mary and Will, along with many other convicts, had come forward willingly to help, but the sights and smells were so awful that many of the volunteers turned tail and ran. Few of the women helpers could stop themselves from crying openly. It was patently obvious that these new arrivals had been half starved and kept below decks for almost the entire voyage. Many of them would never recover.

They had barely got those men washed, fed and under blankets, before the other two ships arrived. The Reverend Johnson went aboard the *Scarborough*, but was advised by the captain not to go below decks. The terrible stench coming from the holds was enough to deter him, and he didn't even attempt to board the *Neptune*.

Tents had hurriedly been erected in front of the hospital, and there was food, water, clothes and medicine in readiness. The night before, as Mary tried to sleep, the smell from the ships at anchor made her stomach heave. It was a hundred times worse than anything she'd experienced on the *Dunkirk*. Although her heart went out to the poor souls in their suffering, she had felt she couldn't possibly help again today.

But by dawn, the anger she felt at men putting profit before human life made her strong again. According to conversations she'd overheard between officers, transportation had been put out to private tenders. As the government offered £17 7s 6d a head for rations, the less the convicts were given to eat, the more food the ships' owners could sell off once they arrived here. If convicts died en route, this made it even more lucrative.

Mary heard one officer comparing the transport owners unfavourably with the slave traders. As he pointed out, at least the traders were motivated to keep the slaves fit and healthy, for the better the condition they were in, the more they could be sold for. There was no such incentive even to keep convicts alive.

'They say Captain Trail of the *Neptune* kept them all chained together,' Will said in a subdued, shocked voice. 'When one of the number died, the prisoners kept quiet about it to get the man's rations. Imagine being so desperate for extra food that you'd lie next to a decomposing body!'

Mary didn't answer him, for she knew from personal experience that she would probably do absolutely anything, however repulsive, to keep herself alive. Now she had two children to care for, her survival instinct was even stronger.

The loading of the longboats began. They watched the first few people climb slowly and hesitantly down the rope ladder, and even from the shore they could see how difficult it was for them. But they were the lucky ones; before long the sailors and troops were practically hurling people into the boats, as if they were sacks of goods, because they weren't capable of walking, let alone climbing.

As the boat rowed in closer, a gasp went up, for the people were like skeletons. There was no eager expectancy on their faces, and they lolled as if close to death – indeed, one was dead on arrival. Two more were to take their last breath as they lay where they'd been placed on the wharf.

'I can't believe what I'm seeing,' Will said, the horror in his eyes matching his cracking voice. 'God save us from men that would let this happen.'

'They aren't men,' Mary said in a loud, clear voice, feeling she could strangle those responsible with her own bare hands. 'They're beasts.'

Her anger fuelled her, stopped her considering the risk of infection to herself or even caring about the smell any more. The convicts were almost naked, their bodies covered with sores, wriggling maggots and faeces. She bent over one man to try to get him to drink some water, and he tried to cover his exposed penis because she was a woman.

'I've seen plenty of those before,' she said gently, touched that even in such a terrible state and close to death, he could still concern himself with propriety. 'You're safe now, there's food and drink, water to wash, but you've got to fight to get better. Don't you dare give up on me!'

'Your name?' he asked, his cracked lips splitting open with the effort to speak.

'Mary,' she said, wiping his face with a wet rag, 'Mary Bryant. And yours?'

'Sam Broome,' he whispered hoarsely. 'God bless you, Mary.'

The sights grew worse as the day progressed, men with dysentery so bad that the fluids ran out of their bodies where they lay. Surgeon White said they were all suffering from scurvy too and ordered men to go out into the bush and pick quantities of the 'acid berries' he'd found had anti-scorbutic properties.

It seemed 267 people had perished before even reaching Port Jackson, and many others had died since. In fact the bodies of those who died after coming through the Heads were thrown overboard. Of the survivors, 486 were desperately sick, and most of them were not expected to recover. Mary heard as she helped one woman with a tiny infant that she hadn't even had her shackles removed for the child's birth. She was to be told that again several more times during the day.

Later that evening in the drawing room of Government House, Captain Phillip sat with Captain William Hill of the *Juliana*, and raged about the obscenity he'd seen that day.

'I have spoken to the captains of the *Neptune* and the *Scarborough*,' William Hill said. 'In my opinion they should be hanged.'

William Hill was considered a hard man, but he had made sure the women convicts on his ship were well cared for. Some of their number had been old and feeble when they embarked, and he'd had a handful of deaths, but the rest of the women were probably better fed than they'd ever been in their whole lives. In Hill's opinion it would have been far more humane for the courts back in England to have sent all these people to the gallows than to allow blackguards like Captain Trail of the *Neptune* to profit by their slow and painful deaths.

'I understand there was a question of the prisoners on the *Scarborough* plotting to take over the ship,' Phillip said, his small face purple with anger. 'That would necessitate putting the ring-leaders in chains. But the conditions on the *Neptune* beggar belief. The ship should never have been considered seaworthy, she took on water constantly. The prisoners were actually up to their waists in water for part of the voyage. No fumigation of their quarters, none of them brought up on deck for exercise and fresh air.'

'I shall voice all this when I return to England,' William Hill said forcefully, banging his fist on the table. 'In my opinion these men are murderers, far worse species than you have in this colony.'

Arthur Phillip went over to the window. Below, the town was quiet, fires burning like little beacons in the darkness. He thought of all those lying in the hospital and the tents in front of it, and wondered how many more would be dead by dawn.

He was close to complete exhaustion. He had taken the position as Captain of the Fleet and then as Governor General because he believed he could make this penal colony a success. He had hoped that he could convert his criminal charges into men and women who would grasp the opportunities open to them and make something of themselves.

Sadly, he seemed to have failed. He knew now that the offer of free land at the end of their sentences would only be taken up by a few. Most were too lazy and incompetent to farm. The survivors of the Second Fleet would be prejudiced against the colony from the outset, and who could really blame them?

He was staring into the abyss again. Today he'd heard a Third Fleet was on its way with another 1,000 convicts. Many of his good officers would be returning home then. He'd done his very best, he'd tried to govern with humanity, but even a gardener couldn't hope to grow something of lasting beauty without basic equipment, good seed and fertile conditions.

'You seem troubled, Arthur,' William said from behind him. 'Today's events are no reflection on you.'

Phillip turned to Hill and pulled himself up erect. 'I think they are a reflection on all of us,' he said wearily. 'On those who stand by and watch the guilty go unpunished, just as much as the guilty themselves.'

'You're very quiet this evening, Mary,' Will said. It was Christmas Day, and he supposed she was brooding on Cornwall, and imagining her family sitting around the fire with a roast goose in their bellies. Lately he'd often heard her telling Charlotte about Fowey and her relatives there. As time went on she seemed to think about them more, rather than less.

'It's too hot to talk,' she said, but smiled at him and affectionately reached out from her stool to pat his thigh. 'It's a wonder the little 'uns can sleep.'

It had been fearfully hot for weeks now, the animals and poultry had taken to lying down in any shade or water they could find. Will considered himself lucky to be off fishing every day, at least out in the bay there was always a breeze.

'I thought maybe you were thinking of home,' he said.

'About how to get home,' she corrected him, and grinned. 'I think I know how to get the stuff we need.'

Will rolled his eyes with impatience. She never let up about escape. Even when she didn't talk about it, he knew she was thinking about it. He'd never known a woman as dogged as Mary.

Will was happy enough in the colony, though he would never admit that to anyone, least of all Mary. While they were all starving, he would gladly have gone, but the colony had got back on its feet since the Second Fleet arrived.

The help he and Mary had given the sick convicts had been noted by the officers, and as the convicts got better, they too were grateful for the kindness they'd been shown. They had nothing to reward him with except their admiration and loyalty of course, but that was enough for Will. It made him feel important.

He had the freedom to come and go as he liked within the settlement. He did a job he loved. He could treat Captain Phillip's cutter as his own. He could get practically anything he wanted in exchange for fish. He even had a fair stash of money too, for the crews of the Second Fleet were all sick of salted pork and were glad to pay him for fish. But above all he enjoyed his status here: men looked up to him, women lusted after him. He had it all.

'So where are you going to get it?' he said wearily.

'Captain Smith,' she said.

Will was so surprised he nearly fell off his stool. Captain Detmer Smith, a Dutchman, had only been here a few days. He was the owner of a snow, the *Waaksamheyd*, that Captain Ball of the *Supply* had chartered while in Batavia. Smith had sailed in on 17 December with provisions for the colony, after an appalling voyage in which sixteen of his Malay crew had died of fever.

There was some sort of wangle with regard to the provisions going on between Captain Phillip and Smith, and it appeared that none of the officers in the colony liked the Dutchman. Will did, however. Smith had none of the stuffiness of the English captains, he was warm, open and friendly.

'Are you mad?' Will asked Mary.

'No, just devious,' Mary replied. 'Detmer likes you and me. And I shall make sure he likes us even more before I talk him into parting with charts and a sextant.'

'He'll never do that,' Will scoffed.

'Why not?' Mary retorted. 'He's being treated shabbily by all the officers, he's lonely and far from home. He's not English, so why should he mind helping a couple of English convicts escape?'

Will always slapped Mary's ideas down as a matter of principle. Women weren't supposed to be the clever ones. Yet deep down he knew her mind was sharper than his. She'd once asked him to teach her to read and write, and he said he couldn't, not without books. She never asked him again, and somehow he knew that was because she'd seen through him. He didn't want a wife who could read and write. It would diminish him.

But then Mary could see through most people. She watched and listened, she took in things Will would never notice. She might even be right about Detmer Smith.

Will made love to Mary that night, and took great care to please her, for he really wanted her to forget about escape. His sentence would be up in March, and though he often told other men he would be on the first ship home, that wasn't what he wanted at all.

He only got nostalgic for Cornwall when he was drinking. He would remember the good parts, the soft climate, the moors and the woodland, the laughter in the tavern, the camaraderie among the fishermen.

But sober, he remembered it wasn't quite like that. Without a fishing boat of your own, you were dependent on the man who had one, hauling nets all night in freezing conditions for a shilling or so. He'd been hungry there too, and no place looked pretty to a man with an empty belly.

At least it was warm here, even in the winter. He might have got cold and wet many times when the weather was bad, but it wasn't the kind of cold that got right into your bones so it almost paralysed you.

It was said that men would be offered free land here when their time was up. Land was of no use to him, what he wanted was his own fishing business. If he could sell his catches to the store he'd soon be a rich man. Then he could build a fine house for Mary and the children. In time, Emmanuel would come into the business with him.

'Was that good?' Will whispered when he'd done. He was soaked with sweat, so hot that it was almost torture to hold Mary's equally hot body in his arms.

'Wonderful,' she murmured against his chest. 'But it's too hot. Let's run down to the water for a dip!'

She didn't even wait for him to agree, but wriggled out of his arms, took his hand and pulled him out of bed.

Then with a little giggle she ran out of the hut and down to the water.

Will smiled. One of the things he liked best about Mary was her spontaneity. She got an idea and she wanted to put it into action right away, not think about it first. Maybe that was what had got her into trouble in the first place, but he wouldn't change that part of her.

She was passionate too, something he had never expected of her, for she looked so chaste and shy. She was always eager for love-making, responding quickly to just a kiss or a cuddle. Time after time she'd taken his mind right off hunger with her sensual touches, the way she wanted to please him.

The moon was bright, catching on her girlish, slender body as she dived into the sea as gracefully as a porpoise. Few other women here could swim, or men for that matter; they walked in up to their waists looking fearful, as if they expected the sea to swallow them up. Will found that daring quality about Mary as sexy as well-rounded breasts or silky skin.

She waved, beckoning him to join her, and Will ran eagerly down the beach. They swam together a little way, then Mary turned on her back and floated, her hair like strands of seaweed around her face.

'We've never done it in the sea,' she said, and giggled softly.

'We might drown if we try this far out,' Will retorted, but he reached out for her, treading water and holding her afloat as he sucked at her nipple.

'First one back to the shallows gets to be on top,' she

said, flipping herself over and making off to the shore.

For once Will didn't try to beat her, he liked her being on top, and watching her face as she came.

'I don't think my John Thomas is all that eager,' he said as he swam over to where she sat in just a foot or two of water. He thought she had never looked so pretty as she did tonight, her wet curls glistening on her bare shoulders. He knelt and showed her his penis, which had shrunk in the cold water so it looked like an old man's.

'I have ways of reviving him,' she said with a grin like a whorehouse madam's. 'Would you like me to show you, sir?'

Will loved it when she played the whore. It made him feel powerful and lusty. He assumed when she reached out for his penis that she was just going to stroke it, but to his shock and delight, she wriggled closer in the water and took it into her mouth.

Will had heard from other men of high-priced whores doing such a thing, but he'd never bedded a woman who would do it. As Mary's warm mouth closed over him he gasped, for it was the sweetest sensation he'd ever known. He was erect immediately, and he was terrified she would stop, but she didn't. Instead, she held on to one of his buttocks, cradling his balls with the other hand, and moving her lips and tongue up and down the length of him. He could barely keep his balance on his knees, and when he looked down and saw himself disappearing into her eager mouth, her naked breasts undulating against his thighs, he almost toppled over.

It was the best thing he'd ever known. All at once he

was no longer in a penal colony, a man stripped of all decency and pride, but transported to a moonlit tropical island, where he was a rich gentleman. He imagined himself in a ruffled silk shirt and velvet knee-breeches with silver buckles, and Mary as an exotic beauty wearing nothing but a garland of flowers, his willing slave.

'That's so good,' he moaned, catching hold of her head and bringing her even closer.

'How good?' she asked, breaking away from him for a moment and looking up at him with an impish grin.

'The best in the world,' he sighed. 'Don't stop now.'

'I haven't told you the price yet,' she said.

'Whatever it is I'll pay it.' Will's voice was cracking with passion now.

'Escape is the price,' she murmured. 'Are you willing to pay it?'

Will was willing to promise her anything. 'Yes,' he groaned. 'Just do it some more.'

Mary smiled to herself as she continued. She had him now. Will might make himself out to be tougher and braver than he really was, but she'd found he always kept promises. She was very grateful to Sadie from the *Lady Juliana* for passing on her secret weapon to get men to obey her. The funny thing was, Mary had expected to find it repulsive but it wasn't, in fact she liked doing it.

Chapter ten

As Will lowered the sack of rice into the hiding place under the hut floor, he thought he must be in love. Why else would he be going along with this madness of Mary's, when in another month he'd be a free man?

He sat back on his haunches for a moment after he'd put the false floor back in place. Anxious as he was about the plan, he couldn't help but smile. Whether or not he was a free man, it would be sweet revenge for all the injustices and humiliations to sail out of the harbour in the Captain's cutter, taking not just Mary and the children, but his friends too.

The Dutch East Indies sounded a fine place to Will, a tropical paradise where a man could live like a king. Of course it was a huge distance, mostly uncharted, and daunting that no one apart from Captain Cook had ever sailed there from here. But in a strange way the danger made the voyage even more attractive to him, the kind legends were made of. Will wanted to be talked of in awed tones even after his death.

It was mid-February, and Will knew they must leave by the end of March or risk running into violent autumn gales. But there was still so much to do, including asking Detmer Smith for assistance.

Mary was with Detmer now, delivering back his clean washing, and no doubt she was charming him for all she was worth. Will didn't mind her doing that, it was necessary, but he didn't like the way she was trying to take complete control of the plan.

She had insisted he shouldn't ask his friends to join them until the last minute. She had to know what hell it was not to be able to confide in them, he wanted a man to talk to about it, not just a woman. Mary said one of them might forget himself when he'd been drinking and start talking. They all had women and Mary's reasoning was that these women might peach if they knew they were going to be left behind. So all Will could do for now was sit it out, get the stores together, and work on Detmer and Bennelong.

Will still often saw Bennelong when he was out fishing. He was naked again, and proudly showed Will new scars he'd acquired in fights. He remembered quite a bit of the English he'd learned while in captivity, and with that, and signs, Will found he could communicate with him quite adequately.

Back last November Bennelong had returned to the settlement, wearing the clothes he'd originally been given by Captain Phillip. This appeared to be a sign that he was willing to be an interpreter, as long as no one tried to chain him up again, and so the Captain gave him a hut to live in and food from the stores.

In Will's opinion, Captain Phillip had bitten off more

than he could chew with Bennelong. The man's real interests were fighting and women; all he wanted from the settlement was the drink the newcomers had introduced him to. Already he'd made a nuisance of himself by getting drunk and wild at Government House, and if Phillip thought that by giving him a house he'd become his lackey, he was mistaken.

Will really liked Bennelong, for his childlike enthusiasm, his wide grin and his curiosity about white men. When he came out fishing with Will he'd taught him some of his language and customs.

It was curious that in Bennelong's culture, if someone wanted a woman they usually hit her with a club and carried her off. Remaining faithful to just one woman seemed absurd to them, yet Bennelong revered Mary. His face lit up when he saw her, he was very anxious to please her, and Will was fairly certain that if Bennelong ever saw him with another woman, he would fight him.

Mary had been right in surmising that many of the natives knew a great deal about navigating the waters round here. They might only have the flimsiest canoes, but the skilful way they manoeuvred them and the speeds they reached were incredible. Bennelong had also shown Will ways of finding water, and which plants made good eating. Will had no doubt he would be only too happy to swim out to the cutter at night and tow her to the shore for their party to get aboard. He had no real loyalty to any of the officers, but he had to Mary and Will.

Although he knew he could count on Bennelong, Detmer was going to be more tricky.

Will and the Dutchman had a great deal in common. They were both big and blue-eyed, with fair hair; both were gregarious men who made friends easily. They were also both, for different reasons, out on a limb.

Since the settlement got back to full rations, many of the original convicts seemed to have forgotten that Will was the one who had saved their lives with his fish. As for the new arrivals, many of them were jealous of his freedom to come and go as he pleased, and often made sarcastic comments about him being the officers' 'boy'.

Detmer was isolated because he hadn't played by the rules with Captain Phillip. There was short weight on the stores he'd brought in, which made the officers distrust him, and now he was driving a very hard bargain with the charter of his ship. Phillip desperately needed it to send some of his men back to England, and Detmer was being foxy. As a result, he was ostracized by the officers, and sharp little Mary, always quick to take advantage of an opportunity, took it.

At first it was a few smiles, a little conciliatory chat, an offer to do his laundry, and finally to share supper with her and Will at their hut. Will didn't object to Detmer coming when he was there; he was good company, and he always brought a bottle of rum with him. But Will was aware that people were beginning to talk about Mary chatting to Detmer on the wharf and sometimes going out to his ship.

Only today someone had suggested she was 'making up' to the man. Will was jealous by nature and he didn't like the idea of his wife alone in any man's company. Yet he knew Mary was far more likely to get Detmer to agree to help them than he was, so he supposed he would have to turn a blind eye as to how she accomplished it.

Will got up from the floor and went out of the hut. Mary was just coming along, with Emmanuel in her arms and Charlotte skipping beside her.

Will thought they made a pretty picture, Mary with her black curls all around her face, Emmanuel chubby and fair-haired in her arms, and Charlotte, a tiny version of her mother, kicking up the sand with her bare feet. The *Lady Juliana* had brought cloth from England. Mary had managed to talk Tench into getting her a length and she'd made a dress for herself and things for the children. Will knew that by his mother's standards back home, Mary's blue striped dress was crudely made, but after seeing her and so many other women just in rags for the last two years, he thought she looked very fetching.

'You were a long time,' he said reprovingly.

'We got talking,' she said, and nodded pointedly in Charlotte's direction, her way of saying that what she had to report mustn't be in front of the child.

Mary heated up some water on the fire and made them a cup of sweet tea, then sat down to nurse Emmanuel. As soon as Charlotte had wandered off a little way, she beckoned Will to come nearer.

'I've asked Detmer to help us,' she whispered.

'You told him our plan?' Will was shocked that she'd done this without him being there.

'The time was right,' she said with a shrug. 'He'd had a row with Phillip again, and I knew it was the moment.'

'What did he say?' Will got a chill down his spine when he thought what would happen to him if Detmer peached.

Mary didn't answer for a moment. The truth was that Detmer's first reaction had been to laugh at the plan. He also said he couldn't see why Will wanted to risk his and his family's lives when he had everything set up here. Mary had to plead with him, explain how she was afraid Will would abandon her when his time was up. She even implied that she was willing to do anything for Detmer in exchange for his help.

His expression was imprinted on her mind. Lips set in a cynical straight line, yet laughter in his eyes. He was seated on a coil of rope in the bows of his ship while she was standing at the rail, half turned away from him because she wasn't quite brave enough to look him in the eye. He was wearing a clean white shirt and tan-coloured breeches that clung to his body like a second skin, his long fair hair blowing in the breeze.

He was similar to Will in looks, sharing the same colouring, height and size, though he was probably as much as ten years older. But Detmer had a polished look which Will could never hope to emulate. His skin was a golden-brown, his hair silky, and his teeth were still very good, white and even. His heavily accented English was attractive too – whatever he said he sounded as if he was trying to woo her.

'Come on, tell me,' Will exclaimed. 'Charlotte will be back in a moment and we can't speak of it in front of her.' Charlotte was very talkative now at three and she was inclined to repeat things she'd overheard.

'He said he would help us,' Mary said. The truth of it was that Detmer had asked, 'How far are you prepared to go to gain my assistance?'

'Why should he want to help us?' Will's eyes narrowed with suspicion.

Mary shrugged. 'Because he likes us. Because he wants to get back at Captain Phillip. Because I was persuasive. Take your pick.'

'Did you tell him what we need?'

Mary leaned closer to Emmanuel so Will wouldn't see her blushing. She had been shameless, just as she'd been with Lieutenant Graham on the *Dunkirk*. But what made it worse in her mind was that she actually wanted Detmer, and if she hadn't had the two children with her, she might very well have let him have his way with her, then and there.

'Yes, I told him, and he'll sell us a sextant and a compass,' she said. 'And he'll throw in a couple of old muskets, some ammunition and a water cask. You can agree a price with him for those.'

'What about a chart?'

'That too, he's going to look it out. He'll need to talk that over with you.'

'So I have got some role in this then?' Will said sarcastically.

Mary wanted to slap him for always wanting to be the big man. If she'd sat back and let him try to organize this escape, he'd be in irons by now because he couldn't keep his mouth shut. Even Detmer, who had only known Will for a relatively short time, had been worried about his reputation for having a loose tongue. But she had to hide her irritation. Everything depended on keeping Will sweet.

'You have the biggest role,' she said, reaching out to stroke his face in a display of affection. 'You are the navigator. Detmer says only a good one like you could manage to sail through the reefs without holing the boat.'

Will was appeased at that. 'I'll whip one of the new seine nets tonight,' he said. 'They won't miss it.'

Mary looked to see where Charlotte was, and, satisfied she was out of earshot, making mud pies, she continued, 'We ought to decide now who we're going to ask to go with us.'

'James Martin, Jamie Cox and Samuel Bird, of course,' Will said. 'They're my mates, been with them right from the *Dunkirk*.'

Mary nodded. She had expected Will would want them. She wasn't too pleased about Samuel Bird, he was such a gloomy man, but then she hadn't tried very hard to get to know him, put off by his red hair and pale eyelashes. 'Yes, but we did think William Moreton would be a good choice too, he knows about navigation.'

Will wrinkled his nose. 'I don't like him.'

Mary didn't like the dark, bull-like man either. Like Will, he was a big-head, full of his own importance. But he could navigate, he was strong and able to keep his mouth shut.

'We need another navigator,' she said firmly. 'You can't do it all alone.'

'Very well, him too, and maybe Wilf Owens and Pat Reilly.'

'Wilf Owens is a fool,' Mary said dismissively. 'And Pat Reilly can't keep his mouth shut.'

Will looked hurt. Wilf and Pat often came out fishing with him and he liked drinking with them.

'So who do you think then?' he snapped at her.

'Sam Broome, Nathaniel Lilly and Bill Allen,' she replied.

'We can't take that many,' Will exclaimed in horror. 'Besides, they aren't our mates, they're all from the Second Fleet. We hardly know them.'

'We'll need that many when we have to row,' she insisted. 'Besides, the boat's big enough. And they can all handle it. What does it matter if you haven't known them long? They are all trustworthy and capable.'

Will didn't mind the idea of Nat and Bill. Nat was another young kid like Jamie, who hung on his every word. He looked like a cherub with his fair hair and big eyes and Will liked having him around.

They called Bill the Iron Man. When he was flogged for theft from the stores, he never cried out once, and walked away at the end of it without even wincing. Compared to most of the men here he was a real criminal, convicted of a serious assault and robbery. Common sense said he was a good choice, they'd need more tough men if they had any trouble with natives.

'Yeah, Bill and Nat can come,' he nodded. 'But why Sam Broome?' he asked, looking at Mary with suspicion. He thought the man a rum sort of cove, he kept himself to himself, didn't like drink, and he was as skinny as a rake.

Mary had taken a liking to Sam from the day she gave him water as he lay close to death on the wharf. She had visited him in the hospital tents until he was well enough to be moved to a hut, and they had become friends. She liked his gentlemanly ways and his reserve, and it was flattering that he obviously adored her.

While no one would describe Sam as handsome – he was too thin and his sandy hair was disappearing fast – he had a strong face, and there was determination in his tawny-coloured eyes. He was also practical, a good carpenter, and steady. Mary needed him as her safety net if Will failed her.

She wished she didn't have these qualms about Will. In many ways he was the very best of husbands. But she had to be realistic, consider every possibility. If they were to reach a safe haven, and Mary was absolutely determined that they would, she couldn't guarantee that the success wouldn't go to Will's head. He liked the drink and it made him belligerent. She had to have some sort of backup plan for that eventuality; she didn't intend to risk her own life and those of her two children for a life that might turn out worse than anything she'd endured so far. She knew Sam Broome would step into the breach if need be.

'Sam has skills we might need,' she said firmly. 'He's a carpenter, remember. He's also a calm, steady man who will get on well with everyone else.'

Will made a kind of snort, implying he didn't agree, but he said nothing further.

Over the following days, Will asked each of the

chosen men to the hut to put his plan to them singly. For now, he wasn't telling any of them who else was in on it. Each one of them was wildly enthusiastic, grateful to be included, and made promises to bring things for the stores. Mary sat back while Will talked his way through it, never interrupting once. It wasn't until each man was about to leave the hut that she gave them her warning.

'You must swear that you won't breathe a word of this to anyone,' she insisted fiercely. 'Not your best friend, your woman, no one. For if you do and our plan is discovered, I swear I'll kill you.'

Bill Allen and William Moreton thought that it was crazy of Will to take a woman and two small children along on such a potentially hazardous escape bid, but even though they were both the kind who normally spoke up when they didn't agree with anything, neither of them dared to with Mary sitting there. When they heard the passion in her voice and saw the chilling determination in her grey eyes, they soon realized that she was no sleeping partner. Without her spelling it out, they knew this was her idea, her plan, and she meant exactly what she said.

Towards the end of February the secret store under the floor of the hut was full of provisions. Two old muskets, ammunition, a grappling hook, various tools, cooking pots, a water cask and resin to caulk the water should the boat spring a leak were hidden in various places around the settlement. The plan was to make their escape after the *Waaksamheyd* had departed for England; that way there would be no other vessel left in the harbour capable of giving chase or informing anyone else that convicts had escaped.

Bennelong had readily agreed to swim out to the cutter on the chosen night and bring it in to the shore for them. There was only one thing left to do now, and that was to collect the compass and sextant from Detmer and pay him the money Will had agreed.

Will hadn't had much problem getting his hands on money. He'd had some saved since he got here and there'd been nothing to spend it on. The rest he'd raised the same way he got the salt pork, rice and flour, by selling fish. A great many of the Marines were only too happy to buy fish, for like Will they had nothing else to spend their money on. They exchanged it for drink mostly, and the officers who ended up with the fish didn't ask questions.

But Detmer insisted it must be Mary who paid over the money and collected the goods, saying it was much less risky. Maybe concealing the money in clean washing and collecting some more dirty clothes with the sextant and compass tucked inside was a sound idea. But Will didn't like the way it looked to the others – he was in charge of this escape, not Mary. He was afraid that before long the other men might start thinking it was all her idea.

Will was brooding about this when he went off fishing one afternoon. Only the previous evening he'd wanted all the men to come to their hut and talk about the escape together. Mary would have none of it. She claimed that such a large gathering would be noticed, then they'd be watched more closely. She ruled that they must only ever continue to meet up in threes or fours.

Even James Martin, Will's closest friend, agreed with Mary. It made Will sick that James would take her part rather than his.

Will was on the cutter, with six other men ordered to help him that day, and about to cast off, when Bennelong came along the wharf. He had his sister and her two children with him, along with Charlotte who often played with them. When Bennelong made signs that he wanted them all to go out on the boat, Will's first thought was to refuse. He didn't like having so many people aboard, and anyway he was in no mood for company. But he knew it was a good idea for Charlotte to get used to the boat, and besides, Bennelong might take offence if he refused him, and then withdraw his promise to help in the escape. He really had no choice but to agree.

It was a pleasant day, much cooler than of late, and Will's bad mood left him once they were out in the bay. When Bennelong excitedly pointed out a quantity of seabirds hovering close to the west side of the bay, Will knew he was saying there was a large shoal of fish there.

Bennelong proved to be right, and it wasn't long before they pulled in the seine and found it full of fish. It was the best haul they'd had in some weeks.

Will was delighted, he kept thumping Bennelong on the back and telling him what a good fellow he was.

'Good fellow,' Bennelong repeated with a wide grin

which showed off his perfect teeth. 'You get good fellow rum?'

'I'll drink some with you,' Will laughed, and made signs to suggest they had a party. With such a good catch he'd be able to keep back a big quantity for himself, and he was in the right mood for getting drunk.

They were sailing back towards the wharf, the bottom of the boat full of wriggling fish, still laughing and congratulating each other on their good fortune, when suddenly a stiff wind came up, catching Will off his guard. The boat gathered speed, heading straight for some rocks, and Will couldn't go about fast enough. There was a crunch, the hooks holding the sails snapped, tipping the boat up, and all at once water poured in.

If there hadn't been so many people on the boat, Will could have dealt with it, but two of the convict men, both inexperienced, panicked, and suddenly the boat keeled right over and everyone fell out.

Will's first thought was for Charlotte as he hit the water, but John, one of the crew, already had her in his arms. She was screaming at the shock, but seemed unhurt. Bennelong's sister had both her two children too, clinging to her back, and with just a shout to her brother, she began to swim back to the shore with them.

'I'll take Charlotte,' John yelled. 'You get the men.'

Bennelong stayed long enough to help Will with the other five men, only two of whom could swim, then he too made off for the shore. As Will helped the floundering non-swimmers catch hold of the capsized boat, he swore to himself. He had lost the entire catch, he knew Captain

Phillip was going to be very angry, and even worse, it probably meant their hope to escape in the next couple of weeks was scuppered.

As Will stayed with the boat, the other men coughing and spluttering, Bennelong reached the shore and called to some other natives. Within a few minutes they were dragging their canoes down the beach to come to the rescue. Some came straight out to the boat to take the crew to safety, others began collecting up the oars and other equipment thrown out of the cutter, and another couple of men came out with ropes, which Will secured to the hull, and they towed the boat in to the wharf.

When Will got back to the hut with Charlotte much later, he found Mary had already heard the news. He expected her to rage at him, and was ready to give as good as he got, but to his irritation she seemed more concerned about Charlotte.

She took the child from his arms and wrapped her in a blanket. 'There, there,' she said as Charlotte began crying again. 'You'll be all right once you are warm again. I'll have to teach you to swim, won't I?'

'That's right! Comfort her,' Will spat at her. 'Don't think about me! I could get flogged again. As for the hope of escape, that's gone.'

Even as he said this, Will knew he was being completely unreasonable. But to have all his hopes dashed when they were so very close to leaving was too much.

His clothes had dried quickly in the wind but he felt chilled to the bone. He knew too that many of the people who resented his freedom would take great delight in his misfortune.

'Don't be such a fool,' Mary retorted, giving him a contemptuous look. 'Why should they flog you? It was an accident.'

Her sharp words seemed to suggest to Will that she wasn't bothered about him in any way. All the resentment which had been building up in him for some time flared up and spilled over, and he lashed out, slapping her hard across the face, knocking both her and Charlotte, who was sitting on her lap, to the floor.

'You cold-hearted bitch,' he yelled at her. 'You don't care about anything but yourself.'

Charlotte was screaming, and Mary quickly picked her up again and got to her feet. She didn't attempt to run out of the hut, but faced Will defiantly with Charlotte in her arms.

'I'm going to put that slap down to shock,' she said haughtily. 'But should you think of hitting me ever again, don't think I'll be so understanding a second time.'

Will had never hit a woman before, and the moment he lashed out he felt ashamed. But he wasn't going to apologize, not when she couldn't behave like a real woman and cry. Instead he turned on his heels and walked out of the hut.

Will came back much later, so drunk that he lurched through the door and fell flat on the floor. Mary had been lying in the dark, awake, but she didn't get up to help him. She suspected he hadn't come back of his own free will, but because his body had a natural homing instinct.

She wondered how he had got the drink, and what secrets he'd revealed under the influence of it.

She couldn't sleep, she felt too wretched. Will didn't seem to have considered that when she first heard the boat had capsized, she thought Charlotte had been drowned. She didn't know John had grabbed her for at least an hour after the event. After going through that kind of agony, a foiled escape meant little.

Yet once she knew Charlotte was safe, the hideousness of this place seemed even more pronounced. While she was waiting up on the wharf, she'd looked around her and seen it for what it really was – a shanty town, built by the sweat of men who had been dehumanized. Everything about it was ugly, from the crudeness of the buildings, the flogging triangle, the bleak, already overcrowded cemetery, to the people trapped here. There was an all-pervading stench about it, a combination of bodily wastes and rotten food. An atmosphere of hopelessness and oppression.

She could not bring her children up here. How could she fight against the squalor, the degradation, the utter despair of it? How could she teach children it was wrong to steal, when it was the only way to survive here? Or that fornication was a sin, when for most of those here it was the only small comfort they had? Nearly all the children were bastards, many of the mothers couldn't even say with any certainty who had sired their child. In years to come these offspring might even unwittingly commit incest.

All Mary's senses were offended by this place. She

was appalled at seeing drunkenness, debauchery, laziness, disease and utter stupidity. Daily, her ears were bombarded with the most vile language and sounds of human misery. The smells nauseated her. Even touch, that most personal of the senses, was distorted here. Wood was jagged and full of splinters, what looked like soft grass was as sharp as needles, her own skin and Will's was hard and rough, it itched from insect bites and often erupted in boils.

How she longed for all those things which were part of everyday life back in Fowey! To smell fresh bread baking, the lavender, roses and pinks in the tiny garden. To see strawberries, apples and plums still glistening with dew. A jug of cold milk, putting on a clean petticoat still fragrant from drying outside. To see her feet pink and soft after washing. To lie on the billowy softness of a feather mattress and watch the curtains fluttering in the breeze.

Only her children gave her a sense of all she'd left behind. Their skin was still silky, their voices soft and melodious to her ears, their breath as sweet as spring water. Apart from their rags, they were no different in nature to children born to the nobility. But just as she couldn't expect them to retain their baby looks, she couldn't hope to shield them from being corrupted either. Soon they would witness the floggings, the rutting behind bushes and the drunkenness, and they would consider that normal. Without something of beauty or worth to show them, how would they ever know the difference between good and evil?

They were innocent of any crime, yet by being born to a convict they became convicts too. And unless she got them away from here, that stigma would be attached to their children, and their children's children. She couldn't let that happen.

The following morning Mary got the children up, fed Emmanuel and made Charlotte some fried bread for breakfast, without waking Will. He was still lying on the floor where he'd fallen the previous night, and the hut stank of rum.

She heard the drum for work sound while she was on her way to collect dirty washing from the officers' houses. Although she wondered whether the loss of the cutter would mean that Will would be expected to report for work like the other men, she certainly wasn't prepared to go back and wake him.

She had a bundle of washing slung over her shoulder, Emmanuel balanced on her hip, and Charlotte skipping ahead of her, when she heard Tench call out her name. She hadn't seen him, even at a distance, in weeks, for his work at Rose Hill kept him there. He was coming out of Surgeon White's house, and she guessed he'd stayed the night there.

'How is Charlotte?' he asked as he came nearer. 'I heard she was in the boat yesterday?'

'She's forgotten it already,' Mary said. 'But it gave me a terrible fright before I heard she was safe.'

'And Will, how is he?' he asked.

'Sleeping it off,' she said, leaving Tench to guess

whether she meant the shock of the accident or drink. 'Or he was when I left.'

'The repairs will be started today,' Tench said, looking over towards the wharf. 'He should be there.'

'Repairs?' Mary's heart leaped.

Tench smiled, reaching out to stroke Emmanuel's cheek. 'Of course. Captain Phillip wants it back in use as soon as possible.'

'Is he angry with Will?' Mary asked.

'Why should he be?' Tench frowned. 'Captain Hunter saw the whole thing and reported back. It could have happened to anyone, after all it happened to Hunter himself on the *Sirius* at Norfolk Island. Phillip is also very heartened by the way Bennelong and his native friends helped out in the rescue.'

'Will is expecting to be flogged.' Mary half smiled.

'I'll go and see him then,' Tench said. 'He has nothing to fear if he throws himself into repairing the boat.'

Mary walked part of the way with Tench, and they talked about Bennelong, and how he'd helped out once before when Captain Phillip was speared by one of the natives.

'It's my hope that in years to come all our people will embrace the natives wholeheartedly,' Tench said.

Mary normally agreed with his views, but today, somewhat jaded by her own fears and despair, she couldn't help thinking he was being naive and even ridiculous.

'They won't,' she said. 'My guess is that there will come a time when the government will want to wipe out all the natives because they don't fit in with their plans for this place.'

Tench looked appalled. 'Oh, Mary, no!'

'That's what they do to anyone who has different values to themselves,' she said defiantly. 'The rich and powerful got that way by trampling on the less able. Even when us convicts have served our time, do you really think our past will be forgotten? My guess is there'll always be a two-tiered society here. Convicts, natives and ex-convicts at the bottom, people like your sort at the top.'

'I don't know what you mean by "your sort",' he said indignantly. 'All men are born equal. It is individual choice whether they rise or fall.'

'It's a damn sight easier to rise if you are educated, with a rich family to steer you,' she snapped. 'But that's not my point. Us convicts are no better than slaves to your sort. The more they send here, the more attractive this country will become to the moneyed classes back in England. I expect in time they'll come here to grab land, and who will work it?' She paused, waiting for him to give her a straight answer. But he said nothing, only looked hurt.

'Us convicts,' she said triumphantly. 'That's who! Don't deny it won't happen, sir, you know it will. Some people might feel badly about capturing a black man and forcing him to work for nothing. But no one at all cares if a bunch of convicted criminals are worked to death.'

Tench was staggered. In all the time he'd known Mary she'd never before shown such bitterness. 'I thought you were quite happy here with Will and your children,' he said weakly. Yet even as he said this he realized he was making the assumption that most of the officers made: that convicts had no finer feelings.

'Happy!' she laughed mirthlessly. 'How can I be happy when Charlotte cries with hunger? When I am afraid for her and Emmanuel's future? They have done nothing wrong, yet they are sentenced to life imprisonment too.'

'I'm so sorry, Mary.' Tench's voice shook, and his eyes swam. 'I wish —'

'Wishes don't come true,' she said, cutting him short. 'Prayers aren't answered, not for women like me. I have to make my own luck.'

Tench stood for a while as Mary went on down to the shore to wash the clothes. He felt impotent, for he knew deep in his heart that every word she'd said was true. When the *Scarborough, Surprise* and *Neptune* got back to England, who would care about the number of felons who died on the way out to New South Wales? Or all those who had died here from the First Fleet? None, he suspected. Yet there would be thousands waiting eagerly to hear the reports on what this place was like, with a view to grabbing land here. Maybe most would be put off by the hardships involved, but opportunists would think of the free labour and be prepared to take a gamble. Just as they'd done in America.

Tench watched as Mary sat Emmanuel down on the ground beside Charlotte, then knelt by the water to begin the washing. He was reminded of the first time he spoke to her on the *Dunkirk*, when she was incensed by the filthy conditions in the hold.

She was truly remarkable. She had struggled bravely to make the best of her lot in life ever since that day. Plenty of other young and sparky women like her had just given up. Her friend Sarah was a drunken slattern now, as indeed were most of the surviving women from the *Charlotte*. Seven had died, and God only knew whether some of those might have lived if there'd been a ray of hope that conditions would improve here.

He felt deeply for all of them, but suddenly to hear and see Mary's bitterness, when she had once been so optimistic, was unbearable.

Why couldn't he find the courage to tell her how he felt about her? Put aside all those lofty plans for his future, and urge her to leave Will and come to him? Other officers like Ralph Clark had taken lag wives, and Clark had a wife at home waiting for him, whom he professed to love. It wouldn't be so difficult. Will's time was nearly up, he'd go happily on the next ship without looking back.

But much as Tench wanted Mary, he knew he couldn't do it. He was too bound by convention to take a woman and her children from another man. It wouldn't be right not to give her the security of marriage. Nor could he bear to see her slighted by his friends and family, as they surely would if they knew her history.

Besides, he could be fooling himself that she felt as he did. She had never said anything to suggest she felt anything more than friendship towards him.

He looked at her slight figure bent over the water, and there was determination in every inch of her body. She would find some way to help herself. Somehow he knew she wasn't destined to be anyone's slave.

Chapter eleven

1791

'You have the money?' Detmer asked in his heavily accented English.

Mary nodded and held out a bundle of clean washing. 'It's in a handkerchief,' she whispered. She lightly touched the bundle he was carrying. 'Are they in there?'

It was 26 March, Detmer was due to set sail back for England in two days' time with Captain Hunter and his crew from the wrecked *Sirius*.

Mid-morning on the wharf was busy and noisy. Detmer's seamen were rolling along barrels of fresh water for loading, Marines patrolled, male convicts building a new shed hammered and sawed, and a gaggle of women convicts returning from cleaning duties in the officers' houses were shouting to one another. There were many children too, dirty, semi-naked little urchins boldly climbing on the many packing cases for loading. From time to time someone would shout and order them off, and they'd disappear like rats down a culvert, only to appear again within minutes.

The cutter had been repaired, just as Tench said it would

be. As it turned out, the accident had been fortuitous, for now the boat was in far better shape than it had been previously.

'Yes, they are in there. A sextant and compass. I wouldn't cheat you, Mary,' Detmer said, his smile slightly reproving. 'Will you come out to the ship for a farewell drink?'

'You know I daren't,' she said, glancing around her. She was very aware that Detmer's ship was being watched closely, for there had been stowaways on the *Scarborough* when it left Sydney Cove. They were discovered before the ship got to the Heads and were immediately put ashore. But since then all the troops and officers had been far more watchful. She could see a couple of officers coming down from Government House, and knew it would be advisable to get away from the wharf and suspicion as quickly as possible.

'I wish I could do more for you,' Detmer said with a sigh. 'Had I met you anywhere else in the world, I believe there would have been a different outcome.'

Mary blushed and lowered her eyes. She never knew how to take Detmer and his often very personal remarks. Some days she felt certain he did have strong feelings for her – why else would he risk so much to help her and Will? Yet at other times she felt she was just a pawn in his game to upset Captain Phillip.

'Look at me, Mary,' he said, his voice soft and insistent.

She looked into his clear blue eyes and felt that all too familiar tug of desire for him. He looked even more handsome than usual today – his fair hair had been trimmed, he had shaved and his white shirt was spot-less. Even his long boots were highly polished, and she wondered if all that was for her.

It was extraordinary that once again she should be attracted to a man so far above her. For two months now Detmer had invaded her thoughts and dreams in the same manner that Tench always had. But whereas Tench would always have a special place in her heart, and she intuitively knew that his feelings mirrored hers, with Detmer it was purely physical.

He came across to her as a man who had never been answerable to anyone. She felt he had salt water in his veins and was happiest out at sea battling against the elements. He was as deep as the ocean, and perhaps just as dangerous.

'That's better,' he said, and smiled. 'I will not be able to see you again before I leave. You must return this washing to one of the crew.'

Mary nodded, not trusting herself to speak. Whatever his motives for helping her, he had been entirely honour-able. No blackmailing her into his bed – he had treated her as a lady, not a convict. She would be forever in his debt.

'I am so afraid for you, and your children,' he said, low-ering his voice to a whisper. 'I hope to God you make it.'

'If determination counts for anything, we will,' she said, then hesitated. She so much wanted to convey the depth of her gratitude to him, yet she knew if she attempted it she might start to cry. 'Bless you, Detmer,' she managed to add.

'And may God bless you,' he said softly. 'I won't forget you. I'll make inquiries to discover how you fared.'

They exchanged the parcels, and his hand covered hers for a second. 'I must go now,' she said, taking a step back away from him. 'I'll return the washing tomorrow.'

At two in the afternoon of the 28th, Mary and Will stood on the shore together silently watching the *Waaksamheyd* sail down the bay towards the Heads. Seabirds flew in its wake, and they could hear the wind in her sails.

Up on the wharf almost the entire settlement was watching her departure, Mary could hear their cheers and shouted farewells in the distance. Captain Phillip would be among them, and for the first time Mary felt a pang of sympathy for the man.

He must almost certainly wish he was sailing home with Captain Hunter. They had been friends, and had been through a great deal together. In many ways Phillip was as much a prisoner as Mary was, chained to this desperate place by a sense of honour and commitment. Now that her escape was so close she could see clearly that he was in fact a good man. He had been humane, fair and dignified at all times, mostly under the most impossible conditions. She could even find it in her heart to wish him well.

'Just seven hours and we'll be on our way,' Will said with a faint tremor in his voice.

Mary knew he was thinking of what would happen if they were caught. They might very well be hanged; they'd certainly be flogged and put back into irons too. However good their plan was, however careful they'd been, there was always a chance that someone with a grudge had got wind of it, and would give them away.

Mary slipped her hand into Will's and squeezed it. She was scared too, not for herself but her children, for she knew only too well that she was taking a gamble with their lives.

Yet she had to take that gamble. If they stayed here the chances were that the next epidemic or the next cut in rations would carry them off, just as it had so many other children. It was surely better to take their chances with the sea. At least if they drowned, they would all go together. A quick, clean death.

'The cutter is in fine shape now,' Will said, as if to reassure himself. 'Even the weather is on our side.'

Mary looked up at the sky. It was cloudy, and unless it suddenly cleared it would obscure the moon tonight. The breeze was very light, but that hardly mattered as they would be letting the tide carry them out of the bay – oars would make too much noise and sails would be too conspicuous.

'We're going to do it,' she said firmly. 'I know we are.'

It was dark by six, and in the next couple of hours, the men arrived one by one and left silently, each with a sack of goods to be taken further down the shore to the agreed departure point.

Emmanuel and Charlotte were both sound asleep in bed. Mary had no fears that Emmanuel would wake when she picked him up, but Charlotte was a different story. She had been tiresome all day, whining and throwing tantrums. Clearly she had sensed that something was going on, and if she woke to find herself in a boat, she might start screaming.

Mary's mouth was dry with fright as she saw the last sack taken from the secret store under the floor and she was left alone with the sleeping children. Sam Broome would be back soon to help her with them. She would carry Charlotte, he would take Emmanuel, for Will would be waiting for Bennelong to bring in the boat.

She knelt down by the bed and offered up a last-minute prayer for their safety, but her attention wandered to all that this little hut had meant to her in the last three years.

It had been a haven, the one place where she felt an element of peace and safety. She had found joy in love-making with Will, there had been the happiness of Emmanuel's birth, and so many different milestones in Charlotte's development, from her first steps to her first words. Now they were leaving it for the unknown.

'Mary!'

She jumped at the sound of Sam's whisper, and turned to see him in the doorway. 'I'm sorry,' he said.

She realized he was embarrassed at interrupting her prayers.

'It's all right,' she whispered as she got up from her knees. 'Have you see Bennelong yet?'

Sam came right into the hut and looked down at the sleeping children. In the light from the flickering candle his lean face had an almost skeletal quality. He was not a handsome, confident man like Will, but the tender way he looked at the sleeping children touched Mary.

'Will thought he saw him swimming out to the cutter,' he said. 'I couldn't make out anything though, it's too dark, but he said you were to come now.'

Mary lifted up Emmanuel, wrapped him more securely in his blanket, then passed him to Sam. Picking up a sling she'd made from some canvas, she tucked it round the sleeping baby. She tied one set of straps around Sam's waist and the other two were put over his shoulders, crossed at his back and then secured in the front.

'It will leave your hands free,' she said by way of an explanation, afraid he might be irritated at her treating him like a nursemaid.

He gave her a faint grin. 'I'm scared. Are you?' he whispered.

Mary shook her head. Her stomach was churning, she was breaking out in a cold sweat, and the greater part of her wished she'd never dreamed up this plan. But she wasn't going to admit to any of that.

'We will do it, Sam,' she said with more bravado than conviction, and turned back to the bed for Charlotte.

As she lifted the child up into her arms, Charlotte muttered in her sleep, but her head drooped down on her mother's shoulder and she didn't wake. Sam picked up the blanket and tucked it round the child, then smiled at Mary. 'Ready?'

'Almost,' Mary said, and leaning down to the little table picked up a cloth bag.

'What's that?' Sam whispered as the bag rustled.

'Sweet tea leaves,' Mary said, and smiled. 'I have to take the one thing that we liked about this place, don't I?'

They stole silently from the hut, pausing every now and then to check no one was about. Further back towards the town they could see the faint glow from dying fires, but the only sounds were the usual night ones of a sentry's boots up on the quay, snoring from huts, the odd muted cough and the water lapping on the beach. Charlotte stirred in her mother's arms, but Mary wrapped the blanket round her tighter to keep out the cool air, and walked faster to keep up with Sam.

Once Mary's eyes had grown used to the dark, she could just make out the cutter coming towards the shore and Bennelong swimming before it, invisible except for a flash of white teeth every now and then.

She knew that if anyone had discovered their plan, it would be in the next few minutes that they would be stopped. Her ears ached with the strain of listening for running feet, every muscle was taut, and she expected to hear a musket fire with every step. When Will stepped out of the bushes in front of her she nearly jumped out of her skin. It was so eerie: the dark beach, the eight men all standing as still as statues, and the bundles lying like so many boulders. No one said a word, everyone watching as the cutter came closer and closer in.

Will waded out a little way, then swam almost as silently as Bennelong to help him bring the boat in closer. It glided in, just a few feet away, and James Martin waded into the water, climbed into the boat and signalled for the others to bring out the bundles.

Mary's nerves were now at almost breaking point, for every small sound seemed magnified. She rocked Charlotte gently, willing her not to wake, and wished the men could be a little quicker with their loading.

'I'll take her now,' William Moreton whispered to Mary, holding out his arms. 'You go and get in.'

It was the moment Mary had been dreading most, for the child was bound to wake if she was moved from her arms. Yet she knew she couldn't hold her and climb into the boat too. But William took Charlotte as gently as if she were his own child, and nodded to Mary to go.

Hitching her dress up high, Mary waded out silently, then taking a seat she held out her arms for Charlotte again. William Moreton handed her over, then got in. Next came Sam Broome, with Emmanuel, seating himself beside Mary.

Bennelong was grinning, his teeth and eyeballs flashing like white lights as he held the boat steady for the other men to get in with the muskets wrapped in oil cloth. Will sat at the tiller, Nat Lilly and Jamie Cox on either side of him, Bill Allen was the last. Bennelong gave the boat a hefty shove, and they were off.

Bennelong swam with them for some distance, pushing the boat until it caught in the current and began to drift slowly down the bay. Then he broke away, waved his hands in farewell and disappeared into the darkness as silently as a fish.

It was some time before Mary realized she had been holding her breath.

It seemed like many tortuous hours before they finally saw the Heads looming up ahead, like twin black mountains, although in reality it couldn't have been more than three. Everyone remained absolutely silent, for if they were spotted or heard by the lookout he would raise the alarm and shots would be fired.

All at once the water became choppier, they felt the current surging, dragging the heavily laden boat towards the gap between the Heads, and Will was wrestling with the tiller to get them safely through. Charlotte woke, sat straight up on Mary's lap and looked around her in astonishment.

'Hoist the sail,' Will whispered. 'Freedom is ours!'

The sail billowed out, the wind caught it, and all at once they were speeding along, the moon suddenly coming out from behind thick cloud as if to join them in their celebration. James Martin, always the most voluble of the men, gave a low rumble of a laugh, and was quickly joined by the others.

'We're free,' Will said in a shaky voice, as if he could hardly believe it. 'By God, we're free!'

Mary couldn't speak, only smile. She turned her head to look back, but could see nothing but the black rocks and the passageway they'd come through.

She felt no sadness at leaving, it wasn't in her nature to have regrets. Ahead was all that counted. But she did have a picture in her mind of Tench asleep in his bed, and that gave her a little pang of sorrow.

She had never seen him sleeping, shaving, washing or without his clothes. In her mind he would always be in his red jacket, white breeches and long, highly polished boots, striding along the quay. She would remember his soft brown eyes too, and the way his hand felt when he touched hers. All those many little kindnesses.

If she had a regret it was only that she hadn't said goodbye, told him just once that she cared for him. But such thoughts were foolish, because he wouldn't have been able to be party to an escape.

She glanced back once more, sending a silent message to him on the wind, knowing she would never see him again. Then she turned back and made a loud whoop of delight at their freedom.

While she had no idea if they could make it all the way to Kupang, it was enough that the plan to get out of the harbour had worked. She looked around at the eight jubilant male faces, and knew that in her own way she'd won a victory. She might not be able to read and write, or navigate like Will could, and perhaps none of the men would ever acknowledge her part in the escape, but she knew the truth, and come what may, she intended to see they found safety and permanent freedom.

She pressed her lips into Charlotte's forehead, aware that in the weeks ahead she would have to be constantly on guard over her children.

'Haven't you got anything to say about my ingenious plan, Mary?' Will shouted out.

For a brief second she considered pointing out the plan was hardly his. But as her father had often said, 'A battle is won by strategy, not by superior force.'

'Well done, Will,' she said, and smiled at him with affection. 'You are a clever, brave man.'

Chapter twelve

After two days at sea, Mary found herself feeling exactly the way she had on the cart from Exeter to the *Dunkirk*. Just like then, she had started out with so much enthusiasm, then came the aching all over from sitting in the same position for so long. At night she was chilled to the marrow, by day the sun and wind made her face raw. Yet on the trip to Devonport she hadn't had children to placate, amuse and control too. While Emmanuel at least stayed in one place, mostly on her lap, Charlotte kept trying to move around.

Mary had fallen asleep for a couple of hours at a time, once the children were sleeping, but she kept waking with a start, afraid that whoever was at the tiller had dropped off too, and that they were drifting on to rocks.

Yet despite the discomfort, she certainly hadn't found herself wishing she was back in Sydney Cove. The weather was good, with steady north to north-east winds driving them along, and all the men were still in high spirits, discussing endlessly how different people back in the settlement would have reacted to their escape.

'Cap'n Phillip will be wild with fury, to be sure,' James Martin said gleefully.

'I hope Sarah wasn't too sore at me when she found my note,' Jamie Cox said with a touch of sadness.

'You did well not to give in to temptation and tell her before we left,' Mary said soothingly. She knew Jamie was very fond of Sarah Young, and it must have been hard for him to leave her behind.

Although Mary thought she had known all the men quite well before they left the settlement, she had soon discovered they all had aspects to their personalities she hadn't been aware of before. James Martin, the ugly Irishman, had always been amusing, a funny man who could tell a great story, but something of a rake, chasing women and drink, and always ready for a fight. Yet she had found him to be unexpectedly fatherly, often taking Charlotte or Emmanuel into his arms to give her a break.

Red-haired, freckle-faced Samuel Bird had seemed to her a very morose man, and she had never really understood why Will thought so much of him. Yet now they were free he was laughing as much as anyone else and though he didn't say much, he listened to the others and responded.

Bill Allen and Nat Lilly were the ones she knew least, and they were complete opposites. Bill was stocky and bald-headed, with a pug nose that looked as if it had been pummelled with fists. In fact he looked every inch the 'Iron Man' of his nickname. Nat, with his cherubic face, big eyes and long blond hair, wasn't tough at all, in fact Mary had considered him a bit of a nancy boy. But he fitted in with any group of men he was set to work with, and everyone liked him. He was also very loyal to Will.

Both Nat and Bill had been in better health than any of the other men who arrived with the Second Fleet, and Mary had never discovered why. In Nat's case it was probably better not to ask.

It was this ability to survive which had made Mary pick both men for the escape. Yet now she saw they were both surprisingly sensitive. On the very first morning they had fixed up an awning to protect the children from the sun, and took charge of doling out the food fairly.

William Moreton was undoubtedly one of the more intelligent prisoners. He was also unattractive, with a large domed forehead, bulging eyes and a tight, narrow mouth. Sadly, he wasn't improving with knowing; he was very argumentative, and Mary was a little afraid he was going to put someone's back up before long.

Even Jamie Cox and Sam Broome, both quiet, thoughtful men who had appeared to be content to be led by the nose by the others, had asserted themselves a little. At one point Jamie had been brave enough to tell Will to stop bragging, and Sam Broome had told James Martin to mind his language because of Mary and Charlotte. Mary had no doubt that in the next few weeks she would find out even more surprising things about everyone.

Now and then the men would talk dreamily about what they would do when they got back to England. They all knew that it would be foolhardy to attempt going to their home towns, for fear of being re-arrested. London was the favourite destination, there they would be inconspicuous, and with a new name they could start all over again.

Mary couldn't bring herself to think that far ahead, it

seemed like tempting Fate to her. The reality of it was that they had no money, their clothes were in rags, and they'd need a tremendous amount of luck to avoid turning back to crime.

Yet despite her qualms sometimes she couldn't help but lapse into a little day-dream in which she found herself walking up the cobbled street from Fowey harbour holding her children by their hands. She imagined standing at the open door and seeing her mother inside the house, bent over the cooking pot on the fire. She would turn her head, see them and almost faint with surprise and delight. It was of course an unrealistic and fanciful day-dream, but it helped Mary's aching back and warmed her very bones.

The weather turned on the third day, with rain and a stronger blustery wind, and Will became concerned at the boat being rather overloaded. 'We must find somewhere to land until it passes,' he said.

A little later William Moreton, who was up in the bows, suddenly bellowed out that he could see what looked like a good spot.

Everyone looked to where he was pointing and saw a small cove with a pebble beach. Will went in closer to check for rocks under the water, and as there were none, agreed it was ideal.

'Let's hope there's a tavern,' James exclaimed.

That made everyone laugh, even William Moreton who hadn't appeared to have been amused by James's sense of humour up till now.

Will brought the boat in as close to the beach as he could, then James swam ashore with a rope to pull her into the shallows.

'Natives have been here,' James said, once they were all safely on the beach. He pointed to the charred remains of a fire and a great many fish bones.

'Well, they aren't here now,' Will said, scanning the cove carefully. 'Besides, I know enough of their words to tell them we mean no harm.'

The rain stopped, the sun came out again, and Mary chased Charlotte along the beach, laughing at the sheer joy of a night on dry land. There was a stream of fresh water from which they refilled their water cask and washed their salt-encrusted faces, and Mary found a plant that looked like cabbage. While Will, Bill and James took the seine net to fish, William lit a fire, Samuel Bird and Nat collected wood, and Sam Broome and Jamie Cox made a crude shelter under the trees.

The fishing was good, the men came back with a quantity of grey mullet, and along with some of the rice they'd brought with them, and the cabbage leaves, it was quite a feast.

'But for the dire lack of beer and some buxom wenches, I could be happy here,' James said, as he lay back on the beach after the meal.

Mary giggled. She hadn't always approved of James in the past, but she was growing to like him more with every hour that passed. His sense of the ridiculous warmed her and he could make time pass so quickly with his stories. She had always thought him a strange-looking man before, with his very bony, lopsided face, large ears and nose, and thick dark eyebrows that met in the middle. Her mother had always said that was a sign that a man was 'born to be hung', and perhaps he was, for he had only escaped it by a hair's-breadth. But his lack of good looks was compensated by his personality. She didn't find it so odd now that many women back at the settlement were after him.

That night they all slept well, huddled together in their shelter, the fire just outside. As Mary lay there, waiting for sleep to overtake her, Will curled against her back and the children tucked in between her and Sam, she felt warm, well fed and really happy. It wasn't just that she was freed from the penal colony, more that something inside her had been set free.

As a child she'd always wished she'd been born a boy, purely so she could go fishing, climb rocks and have adventures. Girls just didn't get opportunities to do anything more than ape their mothers, waiting on the menfolk. She supposed that when she went off to Plymouth that would change, but of course it didn't. All these years since she was first imprisoned, she'd had to yield to men's superiority, just to survive. But here she was with eight men, and she knew in her heart that in the weeks to come they were going to become dependent on her. She already sensed their admiration for her. She saw in their eyes and their manner that they knew she had dreamed up the plan, however loudly Will boasted otherwise. When she'd taken her turn at the tiller, they realized she knew boats almost as well as Will.

But her trump card was her passionate determination to get to Kupang. The men might believe they shared it, but Mary knew they weren't driven by anywhere near such a powerful force as she was. That force was her children, and she would put up with any hardships, brave every peril to keep them alive to find permanent safety. She slid her arm right over both Emmanuel and Charlotte, the warmth from their small bodies comforting her and adding to her determination.

'How long have we been sailing now, Will?' Nat Lilly asked one afternoon, his voice weary and jaded. He no longer looked so cherubic, his once golden hair was matted and dull with salt, and his fair skin was a mass of blisters from the sun and wind. 'It seems like a year.'

Will kept a log, which he assiduously wrote up every couple of days, and but for him none of them would have known what day or even month it was.

'It's well over a month,' Will replied, pulling hard on the oars as there was little wind that day. 'It's the 2nd of April today.'

'So how much more of this coastline can there be?' Nat asked, his full lips curling petulantly as he looked towards the shore. Not an hour since, he had pointed out that it rarely looked any different however far they'd gone in a day.

'Don't ask damn fool questions like that,' Will replied irritably. 'How would I know, it's not charted is it?'

'Well, whoever sailed it before must have known if it was one thousand miles, or five,' Nat said sullenly.

'Daresay they did, but they didn't bother to mention it,' Will said tersely. 'Now, shut up and row faster.'

Mary was at the tiller, Emmanuel on her knee, and Charlotte at her feet, playing with a doll James had made her from a piece of rope. She heard what passed between Nat and Will, just as she'd heard each of the men at other times questioning exactly how far Kupang was. They all needed a rest and she hoped against hope they would find somewhere soon where they could stay for a couple of days.

Since they made their first stop in what they'd called Fortunate Cove, they had stuck to a pattern: a few days' sailing, then a rest for two days when they found some-where with fresh water. Tension grew all the time while they were on the boat; they got stiff, cold and sharp with one another. But as soon as they got ashore all the bad feeling seemed to vanish.

Will was getting more and more worried about the boat, though, for it was taking on water badly now. William Moreton kept mentioning the monsoons too, he said he thought they were sailing towards one. The boat might have been fine sailing around Sydney Bay, but it wasn't intended for a long voyage packed with so many people.

Late that same afternoon they came to a big bay as fine as Sydney, and everyone immediately became more cheerful.

'We'll have to get the boat out of the water and caulk her seams,' Will said, then looking at Mary he added, 'You can wash everyone's clothes, my girl.'

Mary smarted, but said nothing in reply. She would have washed everyone's clothes anyway, but ordering her to do it was Will's way of admonishing her.

She knew exactly what was wrong with him; he was losing his spirit. The men had stopped praising him for getting them away. Perhaps too he was dwelling on how if he hadn't escaped, his sentence would have been up now. And of course he was worried about the boat's ability to hold together long enough to get them to Kupang.

Mary thought he'd probably be relieved if someone was to suggest they stayed for the rest of the winter months in a bay like this one. But he wouldn't suggest it himself for fear of looking cowardly. Also, he didn't like the way the men acted towards his wife.

It had begun with James getting a splinter from an oar in his hand about a week into the voyage. Mary had dug it out and he kept calling her 'Mother Mary'. Since then, every time someone had something wrong with them, they asked her opinion on it. To Mary, this was what anyone would expect – she was the only woman after all, and she'd picked up quite a lot of basic medical knowledge from Surgeon White, both on the *Charlotte* and in the settlement. But Will seemed to think it was because they had designs on her.

He had also made a fuss about how all of them, save William Moreton and himself, vied to be next to her in the boat, and took charge of Charlotte when she was feeding Emmanuel. Mary knew perfectly well that none of them did this as a prospective lover. It was just brotherly, and maybe sitting next to her as she nursed Emmanuel reminded them of how it had been with their own mothers. Perhaps, too, they were weary of acting tough the way Will did all the time. Talking to her, they could drop their guard for a while. She couldn't understand why Will saw anything more sinister in it.

Bill had confided in her that he'd been a brute to women in the past, but perhaps that was because his father had always hit his mother. Nat had admitted that he had allowed some of the sailors to use him like a woman on his transport ship, for it was the only way of obtaining extra food and getting out of the holds. Sam Bird had told Mary he stole rations from other people's huts when things were really bad, and now he felt terribly ashamed.

She didn't think any the less of the men for telling her these things, even if they were ugly. She felt shared confidences bound them closer together.

Once they were ashore, a shelter erected and a fire lit, Mary put Emmanuel into his sling, tied it around her, and leaving Charlotte playing on the beach where the men were hauling in the boat, she went off to look for things to eat.

She found some more sweet tea leaves, and some of the acid berries Surgeon White had set so much store by, but having failed to find any of the leaves that were like cabbage, she turned back.

All at once she saw a group of natives watching her from beneath a tree. She was momentarily alarmed as she was some distance from the men, but she waved her hand, which the natives back in Sydney had seemed to understand as a friendly gesture, and smiled at them. She sensed they were just baffled by her, not hostile, so she walked back to the men on the beach.

The following day the natives came closer. They crouched further up the beach, watching intently as the men repaired the boat. Mary was doing the washing, and each time she got up to hang a garment over a bush to dry, she smiled at them.

'What are you playing at?' Will suddenly snapped at her. 'Isn't it enough having eight men around you? Or do you want a few of them too?'

'Don't be a fool, Will,' she said wearily. 'I'm only smiling to show we mean them no harm, as well you know.'

Will continued to be sullen with her for the rest of the day, even though they'd caught enough fish to eat well that night and have some over to salt some down for the future. After Mary had put the children down to sleep in the evening, she sat for a short while by the fire. The men were discussing once again how much farther it was, a conversation she didn't join in. Feeling very tired, she got up from the fire to go and relieve herself before settling down to sleep.

It was a beautiful night, with a full moon, and instead of going straight back to the shelter, she sat down on a rock just to enjoy the quiet. Quiet times were something of a rare treat for Mary. Right from the day she was arrested back in Plymouth, there had always been noise and tumult around her. Even in her hut back in Sydney, she rarely got a chance to be entirely alone.

On the boat every single thing she did was in full view of the men. They were polite enough to look the other way when she relieved or washed herself, but they were there, just feet away from her. There was always someone talking, arguing, singing or even snoring. Even her body wasn't her own: Emmanuel was either at her breast, climbing on her or sleeping on her, and Charlotte demanded her attention most of the waking hours. Even the men used her as a cushion to lean against.

Looking up at the stars, with the sea lapping gently at the shore, she could pretend she was back in Cornwall. She lapsed into a day-dream again, imagining herself in a little cottage, the children safely in a real bed upstairs, and Will out fishing. She could see it so clearly – a candle burning, the fire glowing red and little sparks catching on the soot making pictures.

When she and Dolly were small they had always competed to see the best picture in these sparks. Dolly saw things like people going to church, dancers round a maypole, while Mary had always seen fish, animals or birds. She wondered what Dolly would make of the tales she had heard about the strange animal they called the kangaroo here, or those big birds that couldn't fly but ran faster than a man. Then there were all the millions of pretty birds, so exotic and brightly coloured they took her breath away.

'He isn't coming!'

Mary nearly jumped out of her skin at the sound of

Will's angry-sounding voice. She hadn't heard anyone coming towards her.

She got up and turned, and he was striding towards her. 'Who isn't coming?' she asked.

'Sam, of course, as if you didn't know,' he snarled at her. 'I caught him creeping off to meet you, and flattened him.'

'I didn't come out here to meet anyone,' Mary said indignantly. 'Don't you think I get enough of people all around me every day?'

He struck her so quickly that she didn't have time to move or even duck. The punch caught her on the cheek and knocked her backwards down on to the beach.

'You're my woman,' he hissed at her and threw himself down on top of her, pulling up her dress.

It was enough of a shock to be hit by him, but when she realized what he was trying to do, she was horrified and frightened.

'Don't, Will,' she implored him. 'Not like this.'

She tried to fight her way out from under him, but he was too strong and heavy. All at once he was forcing himself inside her, biting at her neck like a savage animal, his fingers digging into her buttocks as if to hurt her more.

When he was done, he got up and walked away, without even an apology.

Mary stayed where she was for a few moments, too stunned to move. Later she walked down to the sea and washed herself. Her eyes were dry but inside she was weeping, for she had never imagined her Will being capable of such a bestial act. Gentle, sweet love-making had been the one thing they'd had between them that made life bearable in the settlement. It eased hunger, physical pain, and the hopelessness of their situation. If he had wanted her tonight, he need only have said, and she'd have joyfully slipped away with him out here.

She knew what he'd done wasn't uncommon, she'd seen plenty of women with split lips and black eyes back in Sydney. She knew from confidences from some of them that they'd never known any other kind of love-making but the rough sort. But their men were in a different class to Will, low types, who would steal food from their own children without a qualm.

Mary heard a faint sound and turned to see Will had come back and was standing a little way up the beach. 'Come on back with me now,' he called out.

He was holding out his hand to her. It was too dark to see the expression on his face, but his stance was uncertain, as if he was ashamed of himself.

'Why, Will?' she said as she walked up to him. She felt no hatred, not even anger, just a huge well of disappointment.

'I don't know,' he said in little more than a whisper. 'I got all fired up about Sam, I suppose.'

Mary said nothing as they walked back to the shelter. She needed time to think this through.

When Mary woke up the following morning, she was alone in the shelter with the children who were still asleep. Will was already working on the boat repairs with William and James. She couldn't see the other men and guessed they'd gone off to try to catch some shellfish.

Gingerly, she felt her cheek. It was puffy and sore, but the skin wasn't broken.

A little later when she was kneeling trying to light a fire, Will came over to her. He just stood by her for a second or two, looking down at her. She ignored him.

'Do you hate me?' he asked eventually.

'Do you expect me to?' she retorted, looking up at him. He looked rough. Of course they all did, what with wind- and sun-burnt skin and little sleep. All the men needed their hair and beards trimmed, but it looked odd on Will who normally took pride in his appearance.

Yet it was more than that. Will's eyes were dull and sunken, Mary could only remember them looking that way once before. That was after the flogging.

He shrugged. 'I don't know.'

'We've been through a lot together,' she said. 'We've got a lot more still to come, and if we don't pull together we won't make it.'

'So you'll forgive me then?' he said, looking a bit puzzled.

'I don't know about forgiveness, you have to earn that,' she said sharply. 'But I'll put it to one side.'

He made a sort of exclamation with his hands. 'What sort of a woman are you? You don't cry, you don't shout. I don't understand you.'

'I understand you,' she retorted. 'And I don't cry or shout because there's nothing to be gained by it.'

She did understand him. She knew he was afraid she

was usurping the position he'd always held, that of leader. Raping her was his way of making her submit to him. But she wasn't going to.

The natives came back again during the afternoon. The men gave them some of the fish they'd caught and they in turn offered a gift of a couple of large crabs.

The following morning the natives came down the beach and helped them relaunch the boat, waving as they left. It was to be the last time they were to encounter friendliness when they put ashore.

The luck which had held for a month suddenly gave out. The weather turned bad, with strong winds and heavy rain, and though they saw many inviting beaches, the surf was too high to chance trying to go in. The boat was still taking in water, and when they eventually found a bay, natives appeared at once, throwing spears to warn them off. In desperation the men fired the muskets over their heads, and the natives ran away, but they were back in larger numbers the following morning, so there was nothing for it but to flee.

A violent storm caught them unprepared. The waves were like huge green mountains, tossing the boat up and down like a toy. Mary kept Emmanuel strapped to her chest, and held Charlotte tightly for fear she would be washed overboard. She doubted that any of them would see the sun rise again.

It was like the worst sailing nightmare which just went on and on. The sky was so black that even day seemed almost as bad as night. Emmanuel and Charlotte screamed with terror, then when exhaustion overcame them they merely quivered, too petrified, cold and wet to sleep.

The fresh water was nearly gone, but they were unable to go ashore for fear of wrecking the boat on rocks beneath the surf. Will anchored offshore and two of the men bravely swam ashore with the cask to fill it, but natives with spears appeared again and they had to retreat quickly.

Over the next couple of days Mary saw that Will was sinking into an apathetic state. He left William Moreton and James to take charge, and sometimes the wind blew them so far away from the shore that they lost sight of it altogether.

'Pull yourself together, Will,' she shouted at him one day. 'We're heading towards the reef and we'll be holed.'

He muttered something about needing speed to beat the monsoon, which sounded crazy to her, so she took the tiller and headed back towards the relative safety of the shore. By now the boat was filling with water, from both above and below the water-line, and they were in real danger of sinking.

Just when it looked as if all was lost, they saw the mouth of a river. Will rallied round then, took over at the tiller and skilfully negotiated the boat through shoals where the water was only five or six feet deep. At last, close to complete exhaustion, they managed to pull the boat up on to the river bank.

There was plenty of fresh water, but they were unable to catch any fish or find anything else to eat.

Yet even with only rice and the last of the salted pork, just to get dry and be able to stretch out and sleep was enough.

The following morning the men set to work to repair the boat again. The resin they'd brought with them was all gone, but resourceful James came up with the idea of using soap instead. They knew they would have to move on quickly to find food, and Mary was very anxious now about Emmanuel and Charlotte who didn't appear to be recovering as the adults had. They seemed listless. Charlotte took only a couple of mouthfuls of rice and fell asleep again. Emmanuel lay in her arms, not even attempting to suckle.

'They'll be all right,' James said comfortingly to her. 'They're just worn out. Let them sleep.'

They had only gone a couple of miles the following morning when the monsoon finally caught up with them. Torrential rain hammered down, the wind stronger than they'd ever known it before. Once again the sea was mountainous, and they lost sight of land altogether as the wind sped them along.

For the first two days and nights Mary concentrated all her efforts on her children, trying to shelter them with a tarpaulin, singing to them and rocking them. But when she saw all the men were losing heart, she knew she had to induce them to fight for their survival.

'We can do it,' she yelled at them. 'It's no good just giving up. At least this wind is carrying us fast, let's lighten the boat by throwing out all the surplus stuff.'

They threw out spare clothing and personal possessions, and when water still poured into the boat, Mary took off her hat and began bailing it out.

'Come on,' she screamed at them. 'Bail, every one of you. Your life depends on it now.'

One by one they joined her, apathetically at first, but as they saw the boat rise in the water, they worked faster. 'That's right,' she yelled. 'Come on, Sam, Jamie and William, do you want to end up as fish food? You can kill yourselves if you've a mind to when we get ashore, but don't let it happen out here just because you're tired.'

For eight days in all they couldn't see land. Still the rain came down, and still Mary shouted at the men. Her arms felt as if they were coming out of their sockets with bailing and her voice was hoarse, but she knew she was winning. Not one of the men would stop while she was bailing, and the boat was speeding along.

They saw the shore again just as night was falling, but the surf was so high they couldn't attempt to go in. Will dropped the anchor and used the grapnel to hold the boat faster overnight, hoping that by morning the wind would have dropped enough for them to get ashore.

In the early hours of the morning, as they tried to get some rest, they heard the ominous sound of the anchor being dragged along the rocks, and all at once the boat was drifting out towards the reef.

'It will be holed and we'll all drown,' Will shouted hysterically above the sound of the roaring wind. 'Oh God, why did I attempt this?'

Mary scrabbled her way to the mast and pulled herself up. She looked down at the cowering, frightened men, and snarled at them. 'It's just water, wind and rain,' she shouted above the wind. 'We've got this far, we're not going to let it beat us. Don't turn lily-livered on me now, pull up that anchor and we sail on.'

Dawn came as they battled against the elements, and as the sky lightened so the wind dropped a little.

'Keep bailing,' Mary yelled, her voice just a croak. 'We'll get ashore, I promise you.'

'Thank God,' James murmured a few hours later as they sailed into a bay ringed with white sand. 'And thank you, Mary, for having the courage to make us battle on.'

Mary smiled weakly. She felt sick with hunger and she was almost frightened to look at Emmanuel and Charlotte under the tarpaulin in case they were dead instead of sleeping. Maybe it was a victory, but right now she felt utterly defeated.

She had no recollection of coming ashore. The last thing she remembered was sailing close to the shoreline and then waking to find herself on soft, warm sand.

She sat up cautiously and looked around her, puzzled because the sun was in the east. She felt her clothes and they were dry, but stiff with salt. Alarmed by the utter silence, she tried to get up, but she was so stiff she could barely move.

As she turned her head she saw the men asleep under the shelter, Charlotte and Emmanuel tucked in between Will and James. There was the remains of a fire with a huge pile of mussel shells close to it, and the water cask was placed under a tree, a deep track in the sand showing how it had been rolled there after being filled.

All at once Mary guessed she must have fallen asleep or even passed out the day before, and the men had let her sleep undisturbed while they found food and water before finally falling asleep themselves.

That little kindness brought tears to her eyes, and gave her the strength to overcome her stiffness, to stand and stretch, then walk slowly over to the water cask. She drank greedily, mug after mug, until her stomach felt bloated, then she gobbled down the cold rice left in the cooking pot. Looking around, she saw it was a beautiful bay they'd come to, white sand, clear blue sea, and lush green vegetation all around.

Her heart seemed to swell up with gratitude, and she dropped to her knees to thank God for their safe deliverance from the storm.

Chapter thirteen

Sam Broome and James Martin stopped in their search for shellfish in the rock pools and sat down wearily.

'Mary's a hard task-master,' James said with a hint of laughter in his voice. 'But she's a grand woman for all that.' His breeches were so ragged now that they were hardly worth wearing, for most of his legs and parts of his buttocks were uncovered. Sam's shirt and breeches were still in one piece but so threadbare that one more dip in the sea would probably see them float away.

Sam looked back along the beach where they could see Mary hanging washing on some bushes to dry. She'd insisted they were to fill the sack with shellfish or not return to the camp. 'Aye, but she's harder on herself than us,' he replied. He knew Mary wouldn't rest all day. When the washing was finished she too would be out looking for anything edible to supplement their provisions.

James nodded in agreement. He found it incredible that Mary could be so calm and controlled after what they'd all been through in the last couple of weeks. Just last night he had woken from the most terrifying nightmare, and been too scared to shut his eyes again. Even Will, who had put to sea many times in the foulest weather

Cornwall could throw at a fisherman, admitted he'd never known anything like as bad. James believed they had looked into the very face of death that night when the anchor broke away from the sea bed, and it wasn't surprising most of the men were reluctant to set sail again.

'We would have all drowned but for Mary,' Sam stated, his voice shaking with emotion. 'Her courage and endurance puts us all to shame.'

James knew this was true, but it would make him feel uncomfortable to agree with Sam.

'Aye, but you were always sweet on her,' he teased instead. 'You'd better keep your thoughts about her to yourself, Sam. Will can be a dangerous man when he's crossed.'

'My thoughts about Mary are pure,' Sam protested. 'But for her I wouldn't have been alive to come on this escape. I was close to death when they dumped me like a sack of rice on the wharf. I saw other women stealing the clothes of those too weak to protest, they passed me by, not even giving me water because I was in rags. But she came to me, God bless her.'

Sam's passionate statement pricked James's conscience. He hadn't cared enough to help with the sick on the Second Fleet and he remembered he'd hidden himself away with a bottle of rum he'd stolen while helping to load goods in the stores. During the next week or so there was a great deal of talk about how hard Mary had worked with the sick, while he'd even been callous enough to tell her it would be better for all of them if they died.

Looking back further, he could recall his reunion with

Will when the men came ashore that first day in Port Jackson. Will had not known that Samuel Bird and James had been sent out on another ship of the fleet, and he was thrilled to meet up with them again. James remembered talking excitedly about sharing a tent with him and other men from the *Dunkirk*, but Will confounded him by saying he intended to marry Mary and built a hut of his own.

James thought the man had taken leave of his senses. He couldn't believe Will would choose to live with one woman and her child when he could be with his old mates and have a different woman every night of the week.

Yet James had come to envy Will before long. The women prisoners were in the main a disappointment, either conniving bitches or pathetic wretches, and there wasn't much fun to be had when a man was constantly hungry.

Mary had proved to be an inspired choice as a wife. She was bright and cheerful, she kept herself and Charlotte clean and decent. And just to look at big Will, who remained fitter and stronger than anyone else, was enough to know she took care of him in every way.

But then, just as he'd been wrong in his initial judgement of Mary, he'd been wrong about Will too.

''Tis not a good thing to idolize anyone,' he said, thinking aloud. 'Oh, I'm not meaning Mary,' he said quickly as he saw Sam's surprised and rather indignant expression. 'I'm talking of Will.' He didn't think he would ever forget how the big man had sat cowering with fear that last night at sea. Or how Mary'd screamed like a banshee to make them all exert themselves. 'You see, right since I first met him on the *Dunkirk*, I surely believed he was indestructible.'

'A man who has to boast about his strength or cleverness isn't sure of it,' Sam said with a self-satisfied smirk. 'And a man who will lay another out just on suspicion he wants his woman is a fool.'

James shrugged. He might be disappointed in his old friend, but he wasn't about to let some Johnny-come-lately slander him. 'Watch what you say,' he warned. 'Will and I go back a long way.'

'I know,' Sam said carefully. 'But you are no fool, James. You know as well as I do we need a strong leader if there is to be any chance of making it to Kupang. I'm not so sure Will is up to that any longer.'

'Surely you aren't thinking a woman with two babbies can be that leader?' James retorted. He admired Mary himself, but it was not in his nature to believe a woman could be tougher and more resilient than himself or any other man.

Sam chuckled. 'Of course not. We'd have mutiny on our hands.'

James had often called Sam 'the Parson' back in Port Jackson, because of his appearance, mild manners and disapproval of drink. But in the past weeks he'd come to see that the man was strong-willed and resourceful. He had an idea that Sam had some sort of plan of his own, and he thought it best to winkle it out now, so he'd know where he stood.

'What if Will suggests we stay here till the bad weather's over?' he asked tentatively. Will had only hinted at this, and if James were to be totally honest, the idea had some real attractions.

Sam half smiled. To him, this bay they'd christened White Bay was paradise. The soft sand, the lush vegetation and the mild weather were all so seductive. 'I'd gladly stay if we had more provisions,' he admitted. 'I'm no more anxious than anyone else to risk drowning again in a storm. But were we to stay, the flour and rice would run out, and there's a chance a ship might come by and haul us back to Sydney.'

'We could fish and hunt,' James retorted. 'As for a ship coming by, how likely is that?'

'Not very,' Sam agreed. 'But the whole point of our escape was to find a new life. The longer we put it off, the weaker we'll all become.'

'You got that from Mary,' James scoffed.

'Maybe, but that doesn't stop it being true. I think we've got to press on.'

'What if Will doesn't agree?' James said.

Sam shrugged. The gesture implied he thought those who wanted to go had a perfect right to take the boat and leave the others stranded.

James got up and began prising mussels off the rocks with a knife. He wasn't shocked that Sam would cheerfully leave Will here, he'd probably do the same if he could gain something by it. To him loyalty was just a concept men embraced when a mob could have more power than an individual. Mostly James looked after number one and to hell with anyone else.

He was also lazy by nature. He had always taken the

easiest path open to him. On the face of it, the easiest one right now appeared to be to stay here. But was it? They wouldn't be risking their lives, not unless some natives came and attacked them, but they'd need to build real shelters or huts, and they had only a few tools. With only one woman among eight men, they'd soon be fighting one another. Besides, he yearned for city life, for noise and bustle, to be able to get drunk, eat what he chose, ride a horse and charm the ladies.

He remembered how in the first year of the settlement, some misguided fools had run off into the bush thinking if they kept going they would get to China. He had laughed aloud at that, but then he was one of only a handful of men who could read and write, and he had a pretty good grasp of the world's geography.

He knew from Detmer Smith that from Kupang he could get a boat to China, or Africa, even South Africa. Those were all places where a lazy, cunning Irishman might find an easy life.

William Moreton wanted to press on, if only to prove he was as good a sailor as Will. Mary most certainly did, and Nat Lilly would side with Sam Broome now because they'd formed a strong allegiance. Bill Allen was likely to want to get to Kupang quickly, which left only Jamie Cox and Samuel Bird likely to side with Will.

James knew there was a lot more to be gained by siding with Mary than with Will. A plucky, resourceful little woman like her could be very useful to him when they made it to Kupang.

*

That same evening the whole party was clustered round the fire, for it had turned cold once darkness fell. William Moreton had brought up the subject of when they should move on. He wanted to leave the very next morning.

'What's to be gained by staying here?' he said forcefully. 'We've had a rest, dried our clothes and mended the boat.'

William irritated everyone. He had no sense of humour, he was pedantic and believed he knew everything. Nat, who had a mischievous streak, often goaded him by asking why, if he was so clever, he'd managed to get himself caught stealing. But he did have some clout with the group because of his navigation skills.

'I say we stay a while longer,' Will said stubbornly. 'The boat can't take another bad storm.'

All the men had had something to say, but Mary had made no comment so far. She was watching their faces and trying to gauge what each one really wanted. Sam Broome, Jamie Cox and Samuel Bird had almost blank expressions, and she guessed this was because they were weighing up the opinions of the more dominant group members. Then they'd side with whoever they trusted most.

James Martin was liked by everyone. He was good in a crisis, his humour had saved the day many times, he did have leadership qualities, but he wasn't the most rational of men.

Bill was also a good leader. He would row far longer than anyone else, chop wood quicker, light a fire almost instantly, and was sympathetic to those weaker than himself. But he was no sailor.

A month ago all the men would have gone along blindly with whatever Will decided, but he'd lost his hold over them since they'd seen him afraid and unsure of what to do.

Mary felt saddened that they were turning away from Will. They were all terrified during the storms, which were more than any human being could cope with, and she didn't think Will should be judged so harshly because he lost his nerve. But for Charlotte and Emmanuel she too would have panicked; the fact that she didn't was only down to a fierce maternal instinct to protect her children at all costs.

Mary was torn two ways herself. While she desperately wanted to press on to Kupang, to find permanent security, a home for her children and a tranquil life free from anxiety, Charlotte and Emmanuel weren't too well. The sea voyage, the cold and the constant soaking had taken a lot out of them. They were gaunt-faced, fearful and thin, and food was going straight through them. They really needed more time to recuperate. But Mary's milk was drying up, the rice they'd brought with them wouldn't last more than another three weeks, and she didn't know if a year-old baby's stomach could cope with a diet of mainly shellfish.

She thought that most of the men shared her conflict, not for the same reasons of course, but because they were scared of running into another bad storm.

'I agree with William,' Sam Broome said. 'We should go on, as fast as possible. There's nothing to be gained by waiting here till the provisions run out.'

Sam had become popular with the others for his calm practicality and his ability to listen, but since the night Will hit him, he had changed. While still measured, he asserted himself more. Mary sensed he had weighed up the other men and found most of them wanting in some way, especially Will. She didn't think Sam hated Will, or would like to see William Moreton become their leader. But she guessed he wanted some re-alignment of power, perhaps with himself as second in command.

'We can hunt and fish here,' Will argued, his face flushed with anger as no one seemed to be considering him their leader any longer. 'Didn't I keep everyone fed back in Sydney?'

The four men who had come on the Second Fleet hadn't experienced the near-starvation rations prior to their arrival, so Will's claim meant little to them. Only Jamie Cox and Samuel Bird nodded to confirm this was true.

'What about you, James?' Sam asked the Irishman. 'Go on, or stay?'

James couldn't bring himself to oppose his old friend openly. 'I'd like a few jugs of ale and some women,' he said with a contrived carefree air. 'And no amount of waiting around here will produce that.'

Some of the men laughed, but Will looked as if James had just stuck a knife in his back.

'That sounds like you want to go on,' Sam said, avoiding looking at Will. 'Anyone else got anything to say?'

Nat Lilly cleared his throat and spat noisily into the

sand. 'We should go on right enough, but go ashore each time the weather turns.'

Jamie Cox kept his eyes down. He was the youngest of them, and he'd told Mary once that he wouldn't have survived the *Dunkirk* without Will's help. He was slightly built and his sharp features which had reminded Mary of a bird at their first meeting were sharper still now. He clearly didn't care whether they left or stayed, as long as he was still with Will.

'Bill, what do you think?' Sam asked.

'Go on,' he growled, glowering at William Moreton as if to warn him not to try to take command.

Samuel Bird still had a blank expression.

'Mary! Where d'you stand?' William asked her.

Mary hadn't expected to be asked and she hesitated, not wanting to oppose her husband. Yet William Moreton had been the most outspoken about the foolishness of taking a woman and her children with them. If he cared what she thought, then she had a duty to voice it.

'I agree with Nat,' she said. 'We should press on, but stop if the weather changes.'

'So we're to listen to a bloody woman now, are we?' Will exploded. 'What does she know.'

Jamie Cox looked up in astonishment. Bill narrowed his eyes, looking daggers at Will. Sam bristled visibly.

'I'd say she knows more than all of us,' James remarked in a languid drawl. 'But for her we'd be fish food now. But let's have no more of this. Put it to a vote.'

William Moreton looked at Will, perhaps expecting

him to make some kind of speech to regain the loyalty of his former followers. But either Will believed he didn't need to do that, or he knew the outcome already, for he folded his arms sullenly.

'All those in favour of going on tomorrow, raise your hand,' William said.

Only Jamie Cox and Will kept theirs down.

'Motion carried,' William said, and smirked with self-importance.

'Don't cry to me if the boat don't make it,' Will said with a shrug. He then turned to Mary with a look of pure malice. 'And don't you blame me, girl, if the babbies die!'

There were times after they left White Bay when Mary was tortured by the memory of Will's words, for there were many more terrific storms which came on so suddenly they had no chance of getting ashore. Each time she saw her children's stricken faces and heard their shrieks of pure terror, she asked herself what had possessed her to gamble with their lives.

Yet the need to protect them gave her the strength to fight back when she saw the men weakening. Jamie, Samuel Bird and Nat were the worst. They were all small men, with much less muscle than the others, and they couldn't swim either, which made them even more frightened. In turn she praised, implored, bullied and goaded them. She swore at them from her position at the tiller, screamed that they were to bail and keep bailing if they didn't want to die.

But just when she was beginning to think, as the men

clearly were, that it was just a matter of time before death claimed them all, they came into calmer waters. On their left was the shore, to their right a huge reef, and the sea between was calm as a mill-pond.

'Thank the Lord,' William Moreton shouted in an unexpected display of emotion. 'I really thought we were done for.'

Yet even this new calm sea wasn't without hazards, for there were dozens of tiny islands and coral atolls to run aground on. They went ashore on one of the islands, only to find no fresh water, but they cooked up some rice with the remaining water, and when the tide went out set out across the rocks to look for more.

To their astonishment they saw dozens of giant turtles going up on the shore to lay their eggs. The men quickly killed some of them, and as the tide came back in, they hauled them back to their island.

That night they dined well on the first fresh meat they'd eaten since setting out from Sydney. As they fell asleep with full bellies for once, they were rewarded further by the sound of rain filling the upturned shells they'd hopefully left out.

In the days that followed, as James and Will caulked up the boat again with soap, the others caught more turtles and smoked the meat over the fire to take with them.

Bill had done a lot of poaching in his youth, and when he saw a kind of fowl that nested in the ground, he set out to catch them, with Nat as his accomplice. Mary found herself laughing as she watched them, for they certainly made the oddest partnership. Pugnacious, muscular Bill with his bald head glistening in the sun crouched down on the ground making hand signals to pretty boy Nat to drive the birds towards him. But they made a good team, and caught many birds, and Bill taught Nat the art of plucking them too.

Mary found more cabbage leaves, and fruit. She didn't know what it was, but it tasted wonderful, and the children, who were both in a poor, listless condition, began to revive.

After six days' rest they took off again, stopping every now and then to search for more turtles. They didn't find any, but there was shellfish and plenty of fresh water.

Everyone had long ago stopped asking Will when they would come to the end of this gigantic land mass. Where they would make for in England was a subject of the past too. They were all suffering from apathy now, not really expecting ever to find any kind of real civilization. When they saw the Straits ahead, as marked on Will's chart, they looked at each other questioningly, then as it slowly dawned on them that they were actually there, they began to laugh hysterically.

Once through the Straits, they found the gulf beyond was dotted with small islands, and they knew they must go ashore to refill the water cask before the last leg of the journey across the open sea. But as they tried to land on one of them, a group of natives watching them from canoes brandished spears and began paddling out to them.

The men were forced to fire their muskets to warn

them off, but then to their consternation they saw the natives pick up bows and fire arrows at them. Mary blanched as several of these eighteen-inch arrows with a barbed point landed right in their boat, and the men had no choice but to row like mad to get clear of them.

These natives were bigger and blacker than any they'd met before, and they came roaring after them in their canoes. But just as it looked as though they would catch them, enough wind came up to fill the sails and they escaped, all very shaken.

'We have to get water before we go across the gulf,' Will said later. 'It's some five hundred miles at least, and even with a full cask we'll still have to ration it.'

He was obviously right, and Mary was glad to see him taking charge again.

The following day they took a chance and moored at an island, despite a sizable village close by. They filled the water cask and left hastily, then returned to an uninhabited island to spend the night.

The following morning, elated by their success the previous day, they decided to go back for more water and to look for some fruit and cabbage leaves too.

The village looked as peaceful as it had the previous day, but as they sailed closer into shore, all at once two huge war canoes, with thirty to forty warriors on each, came hurtling out of nowhere, making straight for them. They had never seen boats like this before: they were sturdily made, with banks of paddles, sails made of some kind of matting, and a platform which was clearly for fighting.

Will swung the boat around. 'Row like buggery,' he yelled to the men, and quickly pulled up the mainsail.

Mary's heart was in her mouth and she hardly dared to breathe. The natives' faces and bodies were painted with a white pattern, they were chanting something, and she had no doubt it was their intention to kill every one of the intruding white men. They were so close now that she could smell their sweat and see the hatred in their faces. Even worse, there were more canoes coming out to join them.

Will showed them all then what a first-class sailor he was. He tacked back and forth to catch the wind, and once he'd got it, the boat sped forward just in the nick of time before the natives were in range to fire more arrows.

'We'll go straight across the Gulf now,' he shouted. 'Hold on to your hats. We're leaving this Godforsaken country for good!'

The natives followed them for some miles, until they knew they couldn't outstrip the cutter. As they finally turned to go back to land, Will cheered loudly. 'We've beaten the bastards,' he yelled, his smile as wide as the stretch of water in front of them.

Mary joined the men in complimenting Will on his expertise. She was proud of him, not just for his skill, but because she saw he had his old spirit back.

'You did so well,' she said, moving to sit beside him at the tiller.

'Couldn't have done better yourself?' he said, raising one salt-encrusted eyebrow.

'None of us could,' she said truthfully, and kissed his cheek.

'We'll be a bit light on water and food,' he said warningly.

'Then we must ration it,' she said. 'Have you any idea how far it is now?'

He shook his head. 'It's all uncharted now. You'd better start praying, my girl.'

Three weeks later, in the middle of the night, Mary gazed up at the stars and prayed. The many prayers she'd offered up previously, that they should find land soon, had not been answered. Now she was begging God to let her children die before she did, so at least she could hold them to the end.

Emmanuel was in her arms, Charlotte was lying with her head in her mother's lap. They were so thin and weak that they could no longer cry. They just lay there with their dull eyes constantly fixed on her. Mary had thought she was familiar with every kind of suffering, but knowing that she was responsible for her children's slow and terrible death was new and far worse.

The last of the food had gone several days before, and the water ran out at noon the previous day, when Emmanuel and Charlotte were given the last drops. No one had spoken today, for they had all lapsed into a kind of torpor, their eyes fixed on the horizon. They weren't even scanning it for land any longer, just avoiding looking at one another, for the sight of how weak they all were was too distressing.

Everyone but Mary and Will was asleep now. William Moreton sprawled against the empty water cask, Sam Broome and Nat Lilly were curled up like a couple of dogs in the bows, the others lay sagging against each other. Nat and Samuel Bird had suffered the worst from sunburn because of their fair skin, and their faces looked monstrous – red, swollen and blistered. Bill too had his share of sunburn on his bald head, but for the last few days he'd wrapped a piece of rag round it like a turban.

Will was hunched up at the tiller, but when Mary glanced at him she saw a stranger. He appeared to have shrunk, his once fleshy face now skeletal, and his eyes and mouth appearing much too large. It was just as well the wind was favourable, as it had been since they left the Gulf, for no one would have had the strength to lift the oars, much less row with them.

Mary wondered how the stars and moon could still shine so brightly at such a time. They twinkled in the calm, dark water like candles in a shrine. It seemed to her they were telling her to let the children go and spare them any further suffering.

She lifted Emmanuel higher into her arms. He weighed so little now, and she remembered how heavy he had been when they set out all those weeks before. He was all eyes now, for as his flesh disappeared, they had become more prominent. He didn't even turn his head towards her breast the way he used to, as if he'd finally accepted there was no food there now.

'I'm so sorry,' she whispered, kissing his little bony

forehead. She wished they could have survived to see him walk, to hear him talk, to know that he would become as strong as his father when he was fully grown. It wasn't fair that his short life should have been such a hard one. But as she turned her body slightly on the seat, intending to lower him into the water, she felt his fingers curl round one of hers.

It seemed to Mary he was making a silent plea to stay with her until the end. She clutched him tighter, bent her face to his little head and cried inwardly at her own cowardice.

'Mary!'

She woke with a start, to find Will tugging at her dress.

The first rays of light were coming into the sky, and her first thought was that Will was expecting a storm and she must get bowls ready to catch the rain to drink.

'Mary, are my eyes deceiving me, or is that land?' he asked hoarsely.

Mary looked. It did look like land, a darker, wavy shape on the horizon.

A wild excitement ran through her. 'Can we both be deceived at once?' she asked. 'It looks like land to me too.'

She moved along the seat, still holding the children, to be closer to him, and clutched hold of his hand.

'Oh, Will,' she whispered. 'Can it be true?'

They held hands for at least an hour, watching and hoping against hope it wasn't some kind of cruel joke of nature. But the dark shape remained constant, growing closer with each minute, until finally they were convinced it was in reality trees.

'Well, my girl,' Will said, beaming at her, 'I got you there. Today's the 5th of June 1791, and I've got to write in the log that I sighted land. It's sixty-seven days since we left Sydney, and I thank God for our deliverance.'

'Shall I wake the others?' she asked. 'Or let them sleep on?'

'Bloody well wake them,' he said, his once power-ful voice a mere husky croak, a tear running down his whiskered cheek. 'God knows it's something worth waking for.'

Chapter fourteen

It was late that same afternoon when Will sailed the cutter into a harbour. None of them knew or even cared if it was Kupang. It had buildings and people, which meant food and water, that was enough.

They were all in a pitiful state. Their clothes were ragged, their skin and hair stiff with salt, their skin peeling from long exposure to the elements. They sagged in their seats, too weak and exhausted even to smile at the prospect of salvation.

Mary's tongue was swollen from thirst and she barely had the strength to hold Emmanuel in her arms, but when she saw the throng of people gathered on the wharf looking curiously at the unkempt occupants of the cutter, her mind sharpened again.

'Whatever happens, remember to stick to the story,' she hissed at the men. 'If we let the truth slip we'll be sent back there.'

She didn't think this could be Kupang, as Detmer had said it was owned by the Dutch. She couldn't see anyone white, they were all brown- or yellow-skinned, but at least they bore no resemblance to the savage natives back in New South Wales.

'Water!' William Moreton called out. 'Water!'

His cry, whether actually understood or not, had a galvanizing effect on the bystanders. One man came forward with a hooked pole and guided the boat into a berth. A small, half-naked brown man leaped down on to the boat, taking the rope and throwing it back to his companions on the wharf. Then, miraculously, a wooden bucket of water was passed down.

All the men lunged at the bucket, rocking the boat furiously. But Will filled a mug and passed it to Mary. She let Charlotte have the first drink, and she glugged it down so fast that much of it ran down her chest. Emmanuel was almost unconscious, so Mary had to coax him by dipping her fingers in the water and getting him to suck them until he rallied enough to drink. Finally Mary got some, and nothing in her whole life had ever felt so good as the sensation of cool water running over her parched, swollen tongue and throat.

Although she couldn't understand a word of what the crowd were saying, she sensed by their frantic gesticulating and the tone of their shrill voices that they were in total sympathy with her, her children and the men. She tried to stand but she was so weak she fell back, and from then on everything became disjointed and hazy. She sensed rather than felt arms lifting her. It seemed to her she was laid down on solid ground, and then more water was given to her. Something pungent-smelling was thrust close to her face. She could hear a babble of voices around her, then she was lifted again, to be put down on something softer, and she could no longer see the sky above.

'Charlotte, Emmanuel,' she called out in panic.

A brown-faced woman was leaning over her, wiping her face with a cool, damp cloth. She spoke in a foreign tongue, yet whatever the words meant they were as soothing and kindly as the cloth, and Mary felt that at last she was safe enough to sleep.

She woke some time later to find herself lying on a mat, Emmanuel on one side of her, Charlotte on the other. A candle was burning on a low table, and she raised herself slightly to see a woman with glossy dark hair and brown skin asleep on another mat across the room.

Although the candle shed little light, Mary sensed by the peaceful way the children slept that they had been fed and washed. The room appeared to be a hut, larger than the one she and Will had lived in back in Sydney Cove, but similar. Tears of gratitude welled up in her eyes. A stranger had taken them in and cared for them, and she wished she knew this woman's language to be able to thank her.

The following days were something like being lost in a fog, which now and then cleared enough for Mary to know she was being fed drinks and soft, mushy food. Through the fog she heard voices and dogs barking; she smelled food cooking and sometimes she even thought she heard Charlotte laughing. But she couldn't quite manage to open her eyes and look around her.

She was finally brought out of it by Will. She heard his voice and that of James Martin.

'She must get better,' she heard Will say. 'Wanjon wants to see her.'

'She's just worn out,' James said. 'There's no hurry, he'll wait.'

Mary had no desire to see or talk to anyone, she was happy in her little twilight world where no pain and anxiety could touch her. But Will's voice struck a chord somewhere inside her, reminding her that she had responsibilities.

'Will?' she muttered, trying to focus her eyes and see him.

'That's my girl,' he exclaimed, and knelt down beside the mat and took her hand in both of his. 'You've been scaring us all. We thought you were lost to us.'

His hands were rough and callused, but the tenderness in them touched something deep inside her. 'Charlotte, Emmanuel, are they dead?' she asked.

'Would I be sitting here grinning at you if they were?' he replied.

She saw his grin then, the same cheeky one which had made her smile on the *Dunkirk*, but it was a minute or two before she realized what was different about him.

'Your beard,' she exclaimed. 'It's gone!'

He rubbed his bare chin. 'A change was in order,' he said.

He looked much younger without it, and although his face was very bony and gaunt, he looked much better. His eyes had regained the sparkle she had noted so often in the early days, and apart from flaking skin, he looked none the worse for their ordeal.

'Where are we?' she asked.

'In Kupang, where else? Aren't I the wonder boy getting you here?'

328

Mary smiled weakly, for his bragging assured her she wasn't dreaming. 'Where are the children, and the others?'

'All close by, nothing to worry about,' he said. 'Emmanuel's still weak, but he's getting better by the day. You're the one that had us in a spin.'

Mary sat up gingerly. She looked down at herself and found she was wearing a kind of shirt, long, loose-fitting and striped.

'How long have I been here?' she asked in bewilderment.

'Ten days now. You've been waking and taking food, then going off again. But you've got to take notice now. The Dutch Governor, Wanjon, wants to see you.'

Will and James helped her up and took her outside. Mary stared around her in utter surprise. Although she hadn't consciously formed any picture of the surroundings beyond the walls of the hut, she'd assumed by the amount of noise that she was in a town. In fact it was just a group of round huts, the roofs made of broad leaves. They were encircled by tall trees and thick bushes, like nothing she'd ever seen before. Around a dozen or so small, naked, brown-skinned children were playing together, and a few chickens, a couple of tethered goats and a group of old people sitting together completed the picture of a peaceful village.

'That's jungle,' James said, pointing to the trees. 'Through there,' he pointed to a well-trodden track, 'is the beach, as pretty as a picture.'

'I thought there was a town.' Mary frowned in

bewilderment. She vaguely remembered warehouses and brick-built houses at the wharf. Lots of people, hustle and bustle.

'There is, back there.' Will waved his hand vaguely. 'You and the children were brought here after you passed out.'

Will helped Mary to sit down on a log, and then, sitting with her, he and James explained what had happened. After being given some food and drink and a night's rest, they were taken to see the Dutch Governor, Timotheus Wanjon. They told him the story they had rehearsed while at sea, that their whaling ship had been wrecked back in the reef, and they'd taken to the cutter and sailed here.

'He swallowed it,' Will grinned. 'Like I told you, being first mate of a whaler, I could have my wife and kids with me. I told him I thought the captain and the rest of the crew were in the other boat and maybe they'll turn up too before long. I told them my name was Broad, wouldn't do to use Bryant in case they get to hear of the escape from Sydney.'

James then went on to say that Wanjon, who seemed an understanding, decent sort of cove, had agreed they needed clothing, food and accommodation, and as Will was a merchant sailor he could sign for whatever he needed and all bills would be passed on to the English government for payment.

'This place is heaven on earth,' Will chortled with unconcealed glee. 'Everything a man could want is here for the taking.'

For some odd reason that remark made Mary feel a

moment of disquiet. She asked Will to get the children and bring them to her, and the moment he'd gone she turned to James.

His beard was shaven too, but apart from that he looked exactly as he always had, skinny, wild-eyed and mischievous.

'I hope Will has been behaving,' she said.

'He's very full of himself,' James admitted. 'Especially when he's got the drink in him.'

'He's been getting drunk?'

'So would any red-blooded man who'd expected to die,' James replied.

He had said just what she expected, yet she sensed a faint note of sarcasm in his voice.

'Has he been bragging?'

James shrugged. 'Only to us. We humour him mostly. We all know who really got us here.'

Mary blushed, knowing he meant her. 'He did get us here,' she said staunchly. 'Maybe I bullied him, but it was his knowledge and skill that did it.'

'The loyal little wife to the end,' James said, giving her a wolf-like grin. 'Will's a lucky man.'

The moment Mary saw her children and held them in her arms again, she began to recover. Charlotte was just like any other four-year-old again, lively, inquisitive, full of mischief and prattling away about anything and everything. As the native women found her utterly beguiling she led a charmed life, being constantly fed with titbits, played with and petted. Although still very thin, she had colour in her cheeks again, brightness in her eyes, even her hair was beginning to thicken and shine. She seemed to have forgotten what she'd so recently come through.

Emmanuel took much longer to recover. His stomach could only cope with the blandest of food, and he slept erratically. Before they left Sydney he had been taking a few hesitant steps, but this was arrested by being on the boat, and he still preferred just to sit rather than try to crawl or pull himself up on anything. But he was a very happy baby, smiling broadly at anyone who made a fuss of him, and everyone adored him because of his blond hair and blue eyes.

As for the other men, they had all recovered. Nat and Samuel Bird still had scars from sunburn, and Jamie had been weakened further by dysentery, but was now on the mend. Bill and William Moreton looked particularly well, for their darker skins had turned a rich brown, making them look almost like the natives. They were happy too, working in the dock, loading and unloading ships by day, coming back to the peaceful village by night where the native women would giggle flirtatiously as they cooked for them.

It seemed to Mary that God had not only answered her prayers and got them all here safely, but was showering her with extra blessings. The climate in Kupang was perfect, hot but not overpoweringly so, there was an abundance of food, and its people were happy and generous. It was so beautiful too, with the white sandy beaches, crystal-blue sea and lush green jungle.

Yet over and above the kindness and comfort they enjoyed now was the admiration and respect shown to Mary. Word had got around that it was she who had provided the men with the will to make it here, and everyone, from Wanjon right down to the poorest of the natives, had taken her and her children to their hearts. She had never known admiration before. As a girl in Fowey she had been constantly rebuked for being unfeminine. When she went to Plymouth she was laughed at for being so unworldly. Then, after her arrest, she was treated with utter contempt and cruelty. Even when Will became something of a hero in Sydney, she was vilified as being in some way unworthy of him.

All at once she was a person in her own right, considered brave, steadfast and intelligent. When the Assistant Governor's wife gave her some new clothes, she was even told she looked beautiful by several men. Mary couldn't put into words what it meant to put on a pretty pink dress, to wear a petticoat soft as thistledown beneath it. She might have lost her peachy bloom of youth through the sun and wind, she might be as skinny as a stray dog, but she no longer looked like a felon or a beggar.

She felt feminine now, somehow worldly-wise and special. These good people who smiled at her with such warmth didn't know she had been in chains, or forced to barter her body just to stay alive. And she could forget that too, for she had saved her children from a life of hunger and degradation. Her plan to escape from New South Wales had worked, without loss of life. She had achieved what most people would consider impossible.

To Mary, Kupang was everything she'd ever dreamed of and more. The busy port had much in common with Plymouth, in as much as ships came in from every quarter of the globe. Because it was a major trading centre for the Dutch East India Company, it also had a rich and diverse brew of every nationality and religion. Up on the hills were grand houses where rich merchants' wives sat gossiping in beautiful exotic gardens. There were elegant townhouses where Mary saw dusky maids with almond eyes and snowy-white aprons polishing the door knockers and sweeping the steps. And while it was true that there were far more of the crudest of shacks for the workers than grand places, and disreputable boarding-houses, brothels and bars frequented by the sailors, it all gave the place more colour and vibrancy.

She would remind herself when she saw the many beggars here that at least they weren't cold and wet like their counterparts back in England. They could sit in the sunshine smiling at those who dropped alms into their bowls, they could sleep on the beach in comparative comfort, and fruit grew in abundance, free for the picking.

Mary had fallen in love with Kupang for giving her and her children back their health, for the kindness she'd received. She wanted nothing more than to stay here forever, to live the simple native life, fishing, collecting honey, swimming and bringing up happy, healthy children. She felt drunk on the aroma of sandalwood, which wafted through the village on the lightest of breezes. It clung to her clothes and skin, and she heard it was the island's main export. She felt she and Will had a future here, and they could live happily forever.

'Pssst!'

Mary was just putting Emmanuel down to sleep in the hut she and Will had been given to live in, and she jumped at the hiss from the doorway. She turned to see James Martin beckoning to her. 'I'll be with you in a minute,' she said, assuming his reluctance to come inside was from propriety. 'Has Will sent you with a message?'

Will had been absent a great deal in the past three or four weeks. He usually claimed this was through work in the port, but she knew perfectly well he was in a bar somewhere getting drunk. She just hoped James hadn't come to tell her that he'd signed on a ship and left her. That was what he'd threatened to do several times.

'No. But come outside.'

Mary bent to kiss Emmanuel, and after tucking a blanket around him she joined James outside. Her smile froze when she saw James's expression. He looked haunted.

'What's wrong?' she asked.

'Everything,' James snapped, and taking her arm pulled her away from the hut towards the jungle surrounding the village. 'A group of English sailors came into port just now in open boats,' he whispered. 'They were shipwrecked back in those Straits we came through.'

'So?' she exclaimed.

James rubbed his hands over his face distractedly.

'Don't you see? As soon as they are taken to Wanjon,

he's going to assume they are the rest of the crew from our supposed wreck. Bloody Will, he could never tell a story without adding some embroidery.'

Mary winced. She had been cross with Will when she heard he hadn't stuck to the exact story they'd planned while out at sea. He should have said that the whaler sank and they were the only survivors. That way it would all have been cut and dried. But once Will had Wanjon's sympathy he couldn't stop embellishing the story and added there were other survivors in another boat. Why he said this Mary didn't know, but as a result Wanjon would be duty-bound at least to make inquiries about the missing men.

Mary's heart skipped a beat. James was right, this was likely to be their undoing.

'Have they come from Port Jackson?' she asked.

'No. From Tahiti in a ship called the *Pandora*. Captain Edwards, the master of the ship, had been out searching for the mutineers from the *Bounty*. He's still got ten he captured. The rest went down with the *Pandora*.'

Mary gasped. They had all heard about the mutiny on the *Bounty* from Detmer Smith back in Sydney, and they were even more intrigued when they arrived here in Kupang to discover that coincidentally this was where Captain Bligh and eighteen of his men landed two years earlier, having been cast adrift in an open boat by the mutineers.

While Mary had no way of knowing whether Captain Bligh deserved his plight or not, one thing she did know was that if the English Navy had sent out another ship to bring the mutineers in, the captain wasn't going to be a soft touch like Wanjon.

'We'll be called in for questioning,' she said, her stomach turning over. 'Oh God, James! What are we going to do? It's easy enough to fool someone who doesn't speak much English, but it won't be so easy with an English sea captain.'

James half smiled. One of the things he liked most about Mary was how quick she was to grasp things. 'If we just stick to our story, we might be all right. Four months is far too short a time for the news of our escape to have reached England, and I doubt this Captain Edwards could have heard it anywhere else.'

Mary thought for a moment. If James did the talking, she was pretty certain he could convince anyone they were the crew of a whaler. But an English captain would want to know where the ship came from, the name of its owner and a great deal more information than they could plausibly invent. Then there was Will!

'What if Will gets drunk and starts bragging?' she asked.

'That's what I really came to talk about,' James said, putting his hand on her arm. 'Mary, you've got to take him in hand, make him stay away from the bars, and the port too, until these men sail off.'

'And how am I going to do that?' she asked.

'You're a clever woman,' he smiled. 'You'll find a way.'

After James had gone to round up the other men and warn them of the danger they were in, Mary called

Charlotte, who had been playing with some other children, and put her to bed with Emmanuel.

It was growing dark now, and she sat with the children until Charlotte fell asleep. As she looked down at their peaceful little faces, tears trickled down her cheeks. She had put them through so much, taken them almost to the jaws of death, and now there was a further threat to their safety.

Was she jinxed? Had some evil spell been cast over her at birth that meant her whole life would be an endless round of suffering and anguish? She had reconciled herself to the fact that Will might leave her. She didn't want him to, for despite his faults she cared deeply for him, but she knew she could cope with that. She had also realized that she was unlikely ever to get back to England, with or without Will. But that didn't seem to matter either. The only really important thing to her was to keep her children safe, happy, healthy and well fed. Until now she had believed she could do that here, with or without Will, for she knew that the other men, particularly Sam Broome and James Martin, held her in high regard.

It was strange, considering she wasn't a real beauty, that she had some kind of inexplicable power over men: Lieutenant Graham, Tench, Detmer Smith, and Will too, though he fought against it. Was it likely to work on this Captain Edwards, or even Wanjon?

She went outside later and sat down on a low stool by the door. It was dark now and very quiet, just a few people sitting by their fires, talking in low voices. A crescent moon hung above the palm trees, and Mary could hear waves breaking on the shore in the distance. It was paradise here, and until James had told her this disturbing news, she would have been only too happy to stay for ever.

Should she go now and try to find Will? She glanced back at the hut and decided against that. It was too late to ask someone to keep an ear out for her children, and if Will was drunk he would only be abusive.

She wondered if he had a woman in the port, as he often didn't come home at all. Now she came to think of it, he hadn't made love to her once since they arrived here. Was that because she had been sick? Because he was afraid she might get pregnant again, or just because he felt he wasn't the big man now she was the one who was admired and respected?

Mary had never been above using sex as a lure to get Will to fall in with her plans before, but she wished she had some other option now. Why should she have to appease him just to get him to listen to her? Surely any decent man faced with a potentially dangerous situation for his wife, children and friends would happily stay sober, lie low and keep quiet until it had gone away?

It was some hours later that Mary heard him stumbling down the path into the village. She knew by the unsteadiness of his feet that he was very drunk, and it would be wiser to wait until morning to tackle him. He fell into the hut, crashing down on to the floor, not even making it to the sleeping mat, and was out cold within seconds.

Birds singing and squawking woke Mary up. It was barely dawn, but just light enough to see that Will was stretched out on his back, a few feet from her. He stank of sweat and rum, and his shirt and breeches were filthy, perhaps, as he so often claimed, from unloading a ship.

Swallowing her revulsion, she moved nearer to him and snuggled into his chest, unbuttoning his shirt and running her fingers over his chest.

'Get off,' he growled. 'Can't a man sleep in peace?'

'Take your clothes off and come on to the mat with me,' she whispered, kissing his chest and moving her hand down to the buttons on his breeches.

'Leave me alone, woman,' he snapped, pushing her away harshly. 'If I wanted that I could get it in the port.'

'So this is just a place to sleep, is it?' Mary retorted angrily. 'If you don't come back here to see me and the children, bugger off for good.'

Even as she said it she knew it was a mistake. He leaped up and kicked out at her, sending her flying back to where Charlotte and Emmanuel lay asleep.

'You're a she-devil,' he yelled. 'My luck ran out when I got stuck with you. What you want is a lap-dog. But I'll never be one. I'm off on the next ship to be free of you.'

His boot had caught her in the ribs and it hurt badly, but it was the venom in his voice which hurt more.

'Shut up and listen to me,' she insisted. 'There's some English naval men arrived in open boats. Didn't James find you last night to warn you?'

She saw a flicker of something flash across his face, and knew James had found him, but Will had probably been too drunk to take in what he'd said.

'We're all in danger,' she went on, her voice cracking

with fear. 'This is no time for being spiteful. We've got to plan what we're going to say. You've got to stop drinking and keep your head clear.'

For a moment she thought he was going to calm down, but instead an angry red flush swept across his face. He had put on weight in the two months they'd been here, and he looked like a giant as he glowered down at her.

'I'm sick of you telling me what to do,' he snarled. 'You can lead the others round by the nose like prize geldings, but not me. I'm not afraid of some arse of an English officer. No one's going to put me in chains again, especially you.'

He wheeled round and left the hut, taking a swipe at the door post as he left, which trembled from the force. She could hear him muttering as he went off up the path to the port, and her heart sank.

For the next few days Mary lived in acute fear, expecting at any moment to be summoned to Wanjon's house. He had been very kind to her at their only meeting after she had recovered from her sickness. He had praised her for her fortitude, made a fuss of the children, and asked her to come to him if she needed further help at any time. She felt he was the kind of honourable man who, if she had been able to admit the truth about herself in the first place, might very well have protected her now. But men like that weren't likely to feel much sympathy when they felt they had been duped in the first place.

To make matters worse for her, Will continued to stay away. The other men told her he was drinking even more, swaggering around the town as if he was a ship's captain. James Martin, William Moreton and Samuel Bird had all tried to make him see sense and retreat back to the village and keep out of sight as they were doing. But Will would have none of it; he even said that he'd completed his sentence so no one could touch him.

'The bastard doesn't care that he'll bring us all down,' William Moreton admitted to Mary one evening. 'I wish to God we'd left him stranded in White Bay.'

Mary looked at each of the men grouped around her and her heart ached at their fearful expressions. They had become like brothers to her in the weeks at sea, each sharing some personal story with her, whether about their mother, the crime for which they were sentenced, or a girl they loved back home in England. They had behaved like gentlemen to her, and Emmanuel and Charlotte would go to any one of them for comfort as easily as they went to Will. They weren't bad men, just boys who went astray for a while and had surely paid the full price for their crimes. They had been semi-starved, savagely flogged and sent to the other side of the world in terrible hardship.

Mary knew she couldn't just watch and wait while her husband, their so-called friend, acted like a fool and put them all in jeopardy. She had to stop him.

'I'll try to talk to him again,' she said. 'Stay here with the children. I'll go up to the port.'

Mary found Will in the third bar she looked in. He was sprawled on a bench, a half-empty bottle of rum on the table in front of him, and several days' growth of beard on his chin. There were five or six other men near him, yet from Mary's viewpoint, looking through a dusty window, they didn't look like real friends, just drinking companions.

It was the first time she'd been to the port after dark, and her heart was pounding with fright, for she'd already been accosted twice by foreign sailors. She knew that most if not all of the women out on the crowded streets were whores. She was frightened to go into the bar, for she couldn't count on Will protecting her.

Taking a deep breath and tightening her shawl over her shoulders, she walked in and went straight up to Will.

'Please come home, Will,' she begged him. 'Emmanuel's ill.'

She knew he would be angry when he discovered this wasn't so, but it was the only thing she could think of which might make him come with her without an ugly scene.

He looked at her suspiciously, his eyes barely focusing. 'What's wrong with him?'

'He's got a fever,' she said quickly. 'Please come, Will, I'm worried about him.'

There was a titter of laughter from the men he was drinking with. Mary realized they probably didn't speak English and therefore they might think she was a whore offering herself to him. 'Please, Will,' she pleaded. 'Come now.'

His lip curled back disdainfully as he glanced at his

companions and the bottle of rum. Thankfully it seemed his son had a greater value, for he got up unsteadily.

'I'll be back,' he said self-importantly to the other men, and they grinned, showing rotten teeth. One made a crude gesture with his fist.

Out in the noisy, crowded street, Mary sped on ahead so Will couldn't question her, leaving him lumbering along behind. But when they reached the narrow path to the village, Mary had to slow down in the pitch darkness, and it was only then that she became afraid of how he'd react when he found she'd dragged him away from his drink on false pretences.

'He's coming,' she said as she got into the clearing where the men were sitting by the fire waiting for her. Nat's big eyes were even bigger with fear, Jamie was white-faced, and even Bill, the tough one, was chewing on his knuckles. Mary made a kind of hopeless gesture with her hands, hoping that would warn them she hadn't yet had an opportunity to talk to Will, and she didn't expect him to be receptive.

'Will!' James exclaimed as he came staggering out into the clearing. 'Where've you been hiding? We need to talk to you.'

'Not now, Emmanuel's sick,' Will retorted, his face tightening to see them all there.

'He's not sick,' Mary said quietly. 'I said that to get you back here.'

'You did what?' Will said, glowering at her.

'I had to, it was the only way,' she replied, taking a step back from him in case he took a swing at her. 'We're all worried. It isn't just your freedom you're risking, it's all of ours.'

'That's right, Will,' James agreed. 'We're all in this together. Or so we thought.'

Will looked slowly round the group of men, then shrugged. 'I promised to get you away from the camp. I did that, brought you here. Do you expect me to wet-nurse you forever too?'

'None of us need wet-nursing,' Bill growled at him, getting to his feet and clenching his fists. By the light of the fire he looked menacing, but Will didn't appear to notice. 'There's questions being asked about us all around town,' Bill went on. 'You're drawing even more attention to us all by getting drunk and shooting your mouth off. You should be staying here with Mary and your children.'

Will turned to Mary, his face dark with fury. 'You bitch,' he spat out. 'Thought you'd trap me here by getting them all to side with you, did you? Can't you get it into your thick head I'm sick of you? Next boat out I'll be on it.'

Without drawing breath once, Will embarked on a cruel verbal onslaught. That he wasn't legally married to her, that she was a nag, a whore and she brought him down. He claimed he could have sailed off with Detmer Smith but he didn't because he'd promised to get his friends to freedom. 'And I did,' he finally roared out. 'It was me who sailed us here, and you've even robbed me of that by making out you planned the whole thing and kept us all going.'

'I've not said a word about anything,' Mary said

truthfully. She was afraid of Will now, she'd never seen him quite this angry before.

'That's right, she hasn't,' Sam Broome spoke up. 'But we all know the truth about what went on at sea, Will. We couldn't have made it without her. She might not have navigated, but she sure as hell gave us the spirit to keep on. You're a bag of wind, Will. And that wind will get us all hanged.'

Will drew back his fist and punched out at Sam, knocking him to the ground. 'Let's see who's a bag of wind,' he yelled. 'You want her, then take her, you're welcome to the scheming little witch. Like I said, I'm off on the next ship.'

Bill and Sam grabbed Will, both of them desperately trying to hold him fast until James could talk some sense into him. But Will shrugged them off and backed away towards the path to the port.

'Don't come near me,' he roared. 'I'm sick of the lot of you, clinging to my shirt-tails one minute, doing me down the next. I can sail out of here, my skill is in demand. None of you have anything without me.'

He turned and went off up the path, and Bill started off after him. 'Don't,' Mary said, putting a restraining hand on his arm. 'It will only make him more determined.'

'What shall we do?' Jamie Cox asked, his voice trembling.

'Let's hope he does get the next ship out,' Mary said, and went to help Sam up off the ground. 'He's more trouble than he's worth.'

*

It was two days later, soon after dawn, that Mary heard the ominous sound of tramping boots coming towards the village.

She had woken earlier with a strange sense of foreboding, and when she heard the sound she immediately recognized it as soldiers marching. There was no other plausible reason for them to come to the village, it had to be for her and the men.

Her first thought was to grab the children and flee into the jungle, but she quashed this desire immediately, for it would only confirm they had something to hide. So she put on her pink dress, put her feet into the shoes she'd been given and never yet worn, and quickly brushed her hair. Then, picking Emmanuel, still sleeping, up in her arms, she went out to greet the soldiers with what she hoped was an innocent-looking smile on her face.

Chapter fifteen

'There is no point in denying it, Mary.' Wanjon sighed in exasperation. 'I know you escaped from the penal colony, your husband told me.'

At Wanjon's words Mary felt as if she was tumbling into a black, bottomless pit, from which there would never be any way out.

She and the children had been separated from the men as soon as they arrived at the Castle gaol, so they had no opportunity to confer about what they were going to say. They didn't know either whether Will had been arrested too. But Mary found herself being treated gently by the soldiers, the cell she was put in was clean, and she was brought water, bread and some fruit, so that gave her every hope.

Yet as she watched the sun rise through the tiny grilled window overlooking the port, and gradually move directly overhead, without anyone coming to her, her heart began to sink.

'Why have we got to stay here, Mumma?' Charlotte asked. She had accepted the situation patiently so far, but now she was getting restless. 'I don't like it here, I want to go home.'

'We have to stay because a man wants to ask us some questions,' Mary said, distractedly running her fingers through the child's hair. 'Now, be a good girl and let's play with Emmanuel.'

But Mary had no heart to encourage Emmanuel to toddle between the two of them, and tell him what a clever boy he was for walking unaided. She was terribly afraid that this tiny cell, less than four feet wide by six feet long, was going to be their home for the unforeseeable future.

Charlotte looked so pretty now, dark curls framing her small sun-tanned face, her bare arms and legs plump and dimpled. She reminded Mary very much of her sister Dolly, for she had the same pouting lips and turned-up nose. All the care and attention over the last two months, and the company of other children, had given her more confidence; she'd even learned many of the native words.

It seemed to Mary that Charlotte had left babyhood behind and become a little girl now. Only a few days before she had refused to put on the dull grey dress she had been given when they first arrived here, and insisted on wearing a brightly coloured one her mother had made from a length of locally produced material. Mary had wanted to keep it for best, as she did her own pink dress, but Charlotte had made such a fuss that she'd given in.

Clearly Charlotte had forgotten that back in Sydney Cove she had only one dress, so worn, faded and patched it had fallen apart on the boat. Mary was very glad her daughter appeared not to remember the colony, or how they all were when they arrived here, fainting with hunger and thirst, their skin and hair crawling with lice. Mary had managed to blank it out too, but now, faced with the possibility they might be sent back there, it was back in the forefront of her mind again. It was bad enough imagining herself living that way again, but how could Charlotte stand it now that she knew a different kind of life? As for Emmanuel, his little stomach couldn't possibly take a harsh prison diet. He wasn't strong, just the slightest variation in his food brought on sickness again.

Later, when both he and Charlotte had fallen asleep, their heads on her lap as she sat on the floor, Mary stroked Emmanuel's blond hair back from his eyes and choked back her tears. He was almost too pretty to be a boy, with his pure blond hair touching his shoulders, eyes like periwinkles, and translucent fair skin. She had kept him alive by sheer will-power on the boat, but if they had to stay in this gaol, or be sent back to the colony, how could she find that strength again? She knew that back home in Cornwall he'd be one of those babies people called 'a special one'. That meant the child had the look of an angel, and therefore was not long for this world.

Mary could tell from the length of the shadows outside the window that it was about five in the afternoon when the gaoler unlocked the door of her cell. He was swarthy-skinned, with almond eyes, and he said something unintelligible to her, beckoning for her to follow him. Holding Emmanuel in her arms, and taking Charlotte by the hand, she was finally taken to Wanjon.

He was in one of the upper chambers of the Castle, a

gloomy, cool room which presumably was his office for along with a desk there was a lamp and books on shelves, and many personal items, like a painting of a woman who was perhaps his wife, and a snake made of beads adorning a wooden bowl of fruit.

The white jacket Wanjon had been wearing the previous time she met him was slung on the back of his chair, his white shirt was crumpled and he smelled of sweat. Mary had thought him very personable and pleasant at that first meeting, but now he looked tired, hot and irritated. He was small and stout, with jet-black hair slicked down with oil and parted in the middle. She assumed from his name, almond eyes and coffee-coloured skin that he was native to this country, but he must have been well educated, probably in Holland or even England, as he could speak both English and Dutch fluently, along with the local language.

He began to ask her questions about the whaling ship: how many hands there were, the master's name, where the ship was registered, and the last port they'd called into before the ship was wrecked.

Everything except where the ship was registered had been rehearsed by them all back in the cutter. But even as Mary began to spill out that the master was from Rio de Janeiro, his name was Marcia Consuella, there were eighteen hands, and they'd sailed out of Cape Town, she knew none of it would stand up to close scrutiny. When Emmanuel began to cry, she hoped that Wanjon would be irritated enough to give up.

Sadly, the only effect it had was to make him stop

wasting any more time and come out with what he really believed.

'This is all lies, Mary,' he said, getting up and pacing up and down the room, his hands behind his back. 'You were not on a whaler. You have never been on a whaler. You stole the boat back in New South Wales. You are escaped prisoners.'

Mary jogged Emmanuel up and down in her arms as she protested he was badly mistaken. And it was at that point that he informed her Will had told him everything.

It took Mary some time to come to terms with the shock. She had asked the guard earlier if her husband was being held here, and he'd said he wasn't. Of course the guard had only a word or two of English, and her knowledge of his language was about the same, yet he appeared to understand what she asked. Will stood out in Kupang because of his size and blond hair, and Mary was sure that if he was in the Castle, everyone would know. She'd begun to think he might have made good the threat he'd come out with two nights ago and signed on a ship.

'My husband, though it grieves me to admit it, likes to brag,' she said wildly. 'Perhaps he thought that was a more exciting story to tell than the truth.'

'I have seen the log he kept,' Wanjon responded wearily.

It was all Mary could do not to scream when she heard that, for she had begged Will to destroy the log, even before they arrived here.

'This is all somewhat embarrassing for me,' Wanjon went on as he continued to pace around the room. 'You see, but for the arrival of Captain Edwards, I would have put you all on board the very next ship bound for England. But Captain Edwards wanted to know more about you all, so I had to bring in your husband and he told me everything.'

'Will peached on us?' she asked incredulously.

'Peached?' Wanjon frowned. 'What does that mean?'

'Told on us. Turned King's evidence,' Mary said.

'Yes, he told on you,' Wanjon nodded. 'Some men have no loyalty when they think they can save their own skin.'

Mary broke down then, she could no longer hold back her tears. 'Please, sir,' she pleaded with him, 'don't send us back there. Emmanuel still isn't well, Charlotte has only just recovered. They'll die if we have to go back.'

'My dear, this is beyond my jurisdiction,' Wanjon said with a dismissive wave of his hand. 'Your English naval officer, Captain Edwards, is the only one with the authority to decide what is to be done with you.'

He opened the door and gave an order to the guard.

'You will go back to your cell now,' he said, turning back to Mary. 'You will be brought food and water. I am not a cruel man, Mary. You and your children will be treated well during your stay here.'

Wanjon stared out of the window for some time after Mary had been led away and his heart felt heavy. He had accepted the men's story about how they made it here after their ship was wrecked, purely because it was so similar to what had happened to Captain Bligh two years earlier. It didn't even cross his mind that they might have escaped from the penal colony in New South Wales. Who would think a bunch of mere convicts could make a journey of some 3,000 miles in an open boat?

Even Captain Edwards, for all his seamanship, had come to grief in the Torres Straits, but then he was a bull-headed man who thought he knew enough to sail through such dangerous waters at night. The man clearly had no heart, for he had put his fourteen captured mutineers into a box-like structure on the deck, leaving them there in all winds and weathers, their legs and arms shackled. When his ship was going down he refused to let any of the crew unchain them, and it was only thanks to one of the men who ignored the order that ten of them survived.

Wanjon sighed deeply. It grieved him to hand Mary and her companions over to Edwards, for he knew they would suffer sorely at his hands. Mary was an exceptionally courageous woman, and whatever the crime that led her to be transported, she had already paid dearly for it. As for those innocent little children, they had been a hair's-breadth from death when they arrived here in Kupang. What right had any government, be it English, Dutch or any other nationality, to send them somewhere where their early death could be the only outcome?

It was over a week before Mary got to see any of the men. She was told by one of the guards who spoke a little English that they were being kept in one cell, Will included.

Wanjon had been as good as his word to Mary. She'd

received wholesome food for herself and the children and was even brought a sleeping mat, a blanket and water to wash with. Daily, she was taken down to the yard with the children so they could have some fresh air and exercise in the Castle courtyard. Sometimes she even allowed herself to believe the Dutch Governor would intervene and let her go free. For surely a man who could treat her and her children with such kindness would not send her away to be hanged, and leave Charlotte and Emmanuel orphaned?

So when the guard told her she might visit the men in their cell, she couldn't help but think that this was the first step to being released. The English captain hadn't come to see her, perhaps he'd even left Kupang.

The men's cell was much lower down in the Castle than hers, a big, dark, dank room with its slit-like window too high up in the wall to see out. They crowded round her, kissing and hugging the children, asking how she had been treated, and it was a minute or two before she noticed Will had remained sitting on a stool, his back to her.

'Don't you want to see Emmanuel and Charlotte?' she asked.

'He doesn't deserve to see them ever again,' Bill growled. 'He peached on us.'

Mary looked hard at her friends, pleased to see that they all still looked well and their clothes were clean. But their glances towards Will were malevolent. Even Jamie Cox and Samuel Bird, who had followed him blindly for so long, looked as though they hated him.

Mary had had time to consider what Will was supposed to have done, and she'd come to the conclusion that he was unlikely to have gone purposely to Wanjon to inform on them. He would know that he would be counted as guilty as the rest of them, and though he might not be hanged for escaping because his sentence was already up, stealing Captain Phillip's cutter would still warrant a death sentence.

'I really can't believe that of Will,' Mary said, moving closer to him. He still hadn't turned to look at her. 'Tell me. Did you inform on us?'

'They all believe I did,' he said in a low voice. 'So you might as well too.'

Mary caught hold of his chin and jerked him round so she could see him. She gasped. He'd been badly beaten, she assumed by the other men. Both eyes were hidden by purple, swollen flesh, his lip was cut, and his shirt was covered in bloodstains.

'You deserve that for ignoring my warnings to keep out of sight,' she said sharply. 'You're a louse, Will Bryant, a loud-mouthed, full-of-yourself, no-good bastard. But I still can't believe you'd turn us in.'

'I didn't, I swear I didn't,' he said hoarsely. 'I was drunk, some English sailors came in the bar, and we got swapping stories.'

Mary nodded, she could imagine it. The other men had talked about what they'd been through in their open boat after the shipwreck, and Will had to go one better and boast he'd been through worse.

Still she was furious with him – if she'd come face

to face with him the day after they'd been arrested, she would have tried to kill him with her bare hands. But time, and the belief that Wanjon might still intervene on their behalf, had calmed her down enough at least to try to understand why and how Will had got them into this.

'So, when were you brought here?' she asked.

'That same night,' he said weakly. 'I was just leaving the bar and the guards grabbed me. They took me to Wanjon early the next morning. He said you were all on your way here. He'd already got my log of the voyage from the place I was staying in. I couldn't do anything but tell the truth, he'd got me cornered.'

Mary closed her eyes in an effort to calm herself. She felt confused by conflicting emotions. She had always cared a great deal for Will, and it was tragic to see him brought low like this. Although he should have kept his big mouth shut, she also knew none of them would have stood up to close and prolonged questioning. Their story was too full of holes.

But she certainly didn't blame the other men for beating him. Both James and William had said he should destroy the log, and she knew exactly why he hadn't. He saw himself as a hero, and he wanted the whole world to acknowledge him as such. Even if he hadn't blurted it out here when drunk, he would have shouted it out sometime. The log was proof of his incredible feat. He probably hoped he could make money out of it too.

'Why couldn't you be satisfied with what we had?' she

357

asked bitterly. 'We were safe, Emmanuel was getting better. We were all happy, for God's sake. But you had to have more. Drink, other women –'

'I didn't have other women,' he interrupted her.

Mary gave a hollow laugh. 'I'd bet anything that you were staying with some whore. She'll be the one that handed the log to Wanjon or one of his guards, for a bit more money than you gave her.'

He turned his head away and she knew then that that much was true. It hurt so badly that she felt sick.

'I might not be the prettiest, cleverest woman in the world,' she said brokenly, 'but I was true to you, Will. Even when we were starving back in the camp, you never had to fear I would steal some of your rations, or your money. I made the best of what was there, and I should have killed to keep you and the children safe.'

'I'm sorry,' he whispered.

'Is "sorry" going to help Charlotte and Emmanuel when we are hanged?' she asked, her face contorted with anguish.

'We won't be hanged,' he said.

'We will be if we get sent back to England,' she retorted. 'And if we get sent back to New South Wales we'll be flogged and put in chains again.'

She turned away from him, unable to cope with the picture either of those punishments brought to mind. She would rather have died at sea than live to see the day when her husband would put fame and money before her, their children and his friends.

*

On 5 October, Mary, Charlotte and Emmanuel were brought out of their cell to sail with the men on the Dutch ship *Rembang*. Captain Edwards had chartered this ship to take them, his eighteen crew members from the *Pandora* and the ten remaining captured mutineers to Batavia. Mary had no real idea where this was, all she knew was that it was another island in the Dutch East Indies with a big port. It seemed Captain Edwards planned to get another ship from there to Cape Town, then on to England.

In the two months they had been gaoled in Kupang Castle, Mary had clung to the hope that Wanjon might let her and the children stay here. She knew she had his sympathy for he sometimes let her and the other men out of the prison, always just in pairs, but it meant Mary could go to the village, let the children play on the beach and talk freely with whoever accompanied her.

She was never allowed to go with Will, however, perhaps because Wanjon thought that was too much of a risk. The only time she saw Will was in the Castle yard, and his endless apologies only served to upset her further. He was not the man she'd known so well any more. Being ostracized by the other men, especially James Martin, Jamie Cox and Samuel Bird, once his closest friends, had made him withdrawn and inclined to emotional, often nonsensical outbursts. He would frighten the children by holding them too tightly, and when Charlotte ran away from him or Emmanuel hid behind Mary's skirts, Will would cry like a child. He would tell Mary he had always loved her, and beg her to forgive him. Wearily she would say she had, but in her heart she felt she never could. Often she wished she was able to ignore him as the other men did, but pity for him got the better of her.

They were only told a few days before the *Rembang* was due to sail that they'd be on her. As Mary had found one or two people who spoke some English when she was let out of the Castle, she could only view this with further dismay.

She had learned about Captain Edwards's fearsome reputation. The tale about the *Pandora*'s 'box' where the mutineers were held and four died was common knowledge. It seemed that the *Rembang* had an extra deck. It didn't take much imagination to see that this structure, with no portholes or hatches in it, just small holes along the roof, was yet another 'box'. And that was where Captain Edwards intended to hold her and the men.

She had also been told that Wanjon had asked Captain Edwards to honour the many bills for food, accommodation and clothing Will had signed for. Edwards had refused, and Wanjon told him that he would be given no provisions for the month-long voyage unless he paid up. Mary knew that meant Edwards would have a grudge against them right from the start.

All in all, Mary knew that the trip to Batavia was going to be just like being back on the prison hulk in England, with little food, in darkness, and in chains. She was right on all counts. The extra deck had been divided into three, the front for the escaped convicts, the middle for the crew of the *Pandora*, and the aft for the mutineers. Yet even more frightening than the dark was the 'bilboes', a long pole fixed to the floor, from which sliding shackles were attached to their ankles, rendering them unable to move at all.

Mary took one last look at the port before she was shoved into their new cell. It had rained during the night, and the whole town glistened in the sunshine. She saw women from the village with babies in their arms waving to her from the wharf where stalls were piled high with fruit and vegetables. Fishermen were carrying huge baskets of freshly caught fish, and the young boy she had so often tried to converse with, who trundled a small cart laden with coconuts, called out to her. The smell of sandalwood hung in the air like an aromatic, invisible cloud, and her eyes filled with tears at saying goodbye to the place which had become so precious to her.

'Why is he doing that to you, Mumma?' Charlotte asked as one of the ship's crew fastened the shackles around Mary's ankles. 'How can you walk now?'

Mary couldn't answer, she was too overwhelmed by the impossibility of caring for both her children under these conditions. But Charlotte's questions were halted when the door was slammed shut and bolted, leaving them in pitch darkness. She let out a piercing scream, and falling over the pole in the darkness, she landed in Mary's lap on top of Emmanuel.

'The captain had a cabin for you and the children aft of the ship,' Jamie Cox said from across the darkness of the cell. 'That bastard Edwards said you had to stay in here with us. He wants his pound of flesh because he's disappointed he didn't catch all the mutineers from the *Bounty.*'

'I'll cheerfully swing for him,' James Martin growled, then after a moment's pause spoke to Will. 'Well, you've got your ship at last, big man,' he said jeeringly in the darkness. 'How d'you like your cabin? How does it feel to have yer missus and babbies with you?'

Day by day the agony of that dark cell grew worse. When the sun shone outside, it was so hot they felt they were being cooked alive; when a storm broke out, they were soaked through. They were given only the bare minimum of food and water to keep them alive, and the way they were shackled meant they couldn't even move to relieve themselves. Mary screamed for mercy, if only for Charlotte and Emmanuel, but if anyone on the ship heard her, they ignored her. On the rare occasions the door was opened, she saw for herself that the improvement in her children's health in Kupang had been undone. They sat crying in bewilderment, caked in the filth all around them, and after only a few days Emmanuel went down with fever.

The men hardly spoke. When Mary could see their faces, their eyes were haunted. Nat and Jamie whimpered in their sleep, Bill swore, and James seemed to be constantly awake, his eyes glowing in the dark. Only Sam Broome tried to pretend everything would turn out all right, but Mary knew he was acting that way for the children's benefit.

They ran into a cyclone, and water poured in, threatening to drown them. As the ship pitched and rolled, thunder crashed and lightning momentarily lit up each of their terrified faces. Mary prayed then that the ship would go down and put an end to their suffering.

They heard the crew of the *Bounty* shouting and swearing as they pitched in to help the *Rembang* men. Much later she was to hear that many of the Dutch crew went below decks to play cards while the English struggled to keep the ship off the rocks.

Will caught the fever too, crying out in his delirium for his mother. Mary could do nothing to help him, for she couldn't move and had both the children in her arms. Jamie came out of his anger at his old friend sufficiently to give him sips of water, but the mood of the other men was ugly towards Will.

'Die thinking of what you brought us to,' William Moreton shouted out on several occasions. 'I hope you burn in Hell, you bastard.'

The *Rembang* sailed into Batavia on 7 November. A whole month at sea had seemed more like a year to them. Apart from the foul conditions they were chained up in, which became worse daily, and the hunger and thirst, it was almost like being blindfolded too, for they had been unable to see out. They didn't know whether they had passed other islands, big land masses, or whether they were just sailing on the open sea. They had lost all sense of time and distance too.

Hamilton, the ship's surgeon, came into the hold briefly, holding a handkerchief over his nose against the smell but retching anyway. He barely looked at the men, but ordered that Emmanuel was to be taken to the hospital, and Mary would go with him. The remaining convicts and mutineers were to be moved to a guard ship until such time as a ship bound for England could be found.

'Charlotte must come with me too,' Mary pleaded, fearful for her little girl being imprisoned in another ship without her protection. 'She'll get sick too without me.'

Hamilton was a hard-faced man with a bushy beard. 'She'll get sick in the hospital even faster,' he said. 'They call this place the Golgotha of Europe, and the hospital is a stinking hole. But take her with you if you must.'

Mary didn't understand what he meant then as she had imagined Batavia would be much like Kupang. A month's sea voyage must mean it wasn't so very far away, and she'd heard Batavia was the centre of the Dutch East India Company's operations. But she was soon to discover the difference. The first thing she saw when she was taken up on deck was dead bodies floating in the water, and she vomited over the side.

Kupang was a place Dutch East India Company employees felt fortunate to be posted to. It might be noisy and crowded with people of every nation, but the air was clean and invigorating, the climate perfect. It was also very beautiful just beyond the town, with jungle, mountains and idyllic beaches.

But Batavia sweltered in a hot, steamy atmosphere. The Dutch had built canals through the town, and the stagnant, putrid water bred diseases that killed Europeans like flies. Mary saw that the ship's crew were reluctant to go ashore, a sure sign it wasn't a good place. She overheard one of the English sailors who had been here before claim that even the healthiest ship's crew would be decimated by fever within weeks.

As Mary was led away by two guards, carrying Emmanuel in her arms, with Charlotte trailing along behind, she looked back at her friends on the deck and tears filled her eyes.

They were all gaunt and filthy. The only touch of colour in the group was Samuel Bird's red hair, but even that was muted by dirt. Nat Lilly and Jamie Cox, the two smallest, looked like little boys. Bill Allen was making a show of looking tough, and James Martin was rubbing his eyes with his fists. Sam Broome and William Moreton were supporting each other. Then there was Will standing apart from them all, swaying on his feet with the fever.

Mary's heart sank. They all looked so sick that she felt sure she was never going to see any of them again. But the guards dragged her away, and she felt even more demoralized, for the teeming hordes of small, brown-skinned natives who milled around them were sickly-looking too.

The surgeon's words about Batavia came back to her as she saw crudely constructed shanties instead of fine houses. The sticky heat, the revolting smells and the flies which bombarded her made her feel queasy and terrified for her children.

Her first impression of the two-storey hospital was that the builders had left it only half built. A few windows were shuttered, but the rest were just holes. There was a foul-smelling bonfire smouldering in the yard in front of it, and at least a hundred people were sitting or lying outside. Many of them had filthy, bloodstained bandages around their heads or limbs, flies had settled on those too weak to swat them off, and the sound of their wailing and groaning was terrible to hear. Charlotte clutched her mother's dress, whimpering with fright, but the guards prodded Mary on through the door, which suggested to her that the people outside were in better condition than those within.

The smell inside made Mary recoil in horror. It was utterly evil, so thick she could barely breathe. She knew then that nothing short of a miracle could prevent Emmanuel from dying. Even on the ship he'd given up crying, he just lay in her arms staring up at her. She had kept trying to make him drink, but he couldn't keep anything down. One moment he was so hot she could have fried an egg on his forehead, the next he was shivering violently.

An aging nun with a filthy apron over her white habit came forward. The guards said something to her in Dutch, and she peered at Emmanuel, making a tutting sound with her tongue, and indicated that Mary was to follow her.

As they passed several rooms, Mary saw that each held thirty or forty adult patients lying on mats, but she was led into a room at the far end of the hospital where there were only babies and small children being nursed by their mothers.

The nun left after pointing out where the spare mats,

washing bowls and buckets were kept. There was no explanation as to where the water was, whether a doctor was coming, or where food came from.

Mary put two mats in a corner, laid Emmanuel down and sat Charlotte beside him, telling her not to move. Then she picked up a bucket and asked the nearest woman in sign language where she could get water.

As night fell Mary lay down with the children. She had got water from a well outside to wash all the ship's filth off them, and found a grimy kitchen from which she could get a daily meal of rice. Anything else had either to be bought from a formidable-looking native woman who presided in the kitchen, or brought in from outside.

She heard the familiar sound of rats scuttling around the room, even above the moans and cries of the mortally sick, and put her arms protectively around Charlotte and Emmanuel. Her last thoughts before she fell asleep from exhaustion were to wonder how you got food and water if you were a patient without friends or relatives, and if a doctor ever came near the hospital.

She found the answer to her questions in the next day or two by observing and communicating in sign language with the other mothers. A doctor visited occasionally but saw only those with money to pay him. A handful of Dutch nuns did what they could, but faced with the huge numbers of sick people, it was like trying to empty a lake with a thimble.

It was soon apparent to Mary that this was more of a pest house than a hospital. People were sent there in an attempt to contain infection. Those outside in the courtyard were suffering from injuries rather than disease, and often had to wait up to a week to be examined. Most of the inmates died without ever being spoken to, let alone examined, and very few made a recovery. The children's room was kept reasonably clean by the mothers, but a glance into the adult ones revealed a horrifying sight. Vomit and excreta lay on the rough wood floors, walls were splattered with blood and pus. The cries, screams and delirium of the patients were ignored.

Mary sold her pink dress on her third day there, to buy soup and milk for Emmanuel, and to have some meat and vegetables in the rice for herself and Charlotte. She thought about running away, for it would be easy enough to slip out and mingle with the crowds outside. But she couldn't bring herself to subject Emmanuel to being carried about in the hot sun, and at least in here it was cooler, with a plentiful supply of water. She had to make his last days as comfortable as possible.

Her isolation was the worst aspect of the hospital. There were as many nationalities as there were in Kupang, but no one she had met so far spoke English. There was no one to turn to for help. Dying children were a fact of life here, it seemed, and even Emmanuel's ethereal appearance extracted no sympathy. She bathed him with water to cool him down, wrapped him in blankets when he shivered, squeezed water into his mouth drop by drop, but each day he grew weaker.

She desperately wanted to share her anxiety for him with someone. She was terrified to think of what would become of Charlotte if she caught the fever herself. It was no place for a healthy child to be either – daily, Charlotte was subjected to sights that would make even an adult turn pale. It wasn't fair that she had to spend every day surrounded by desperately sick children. In many ways it was worse for her than being on the ship – at least there she'd had the men to tell her stories and sing to her.

Sometimes Mary thought she might go mad with the noise, smells, heat and filth. She wondered too what she'd do when the money from selling her pink dress ran out. All she could do was blame Will, and vow to herself that when she got out of here she'd kill him.

Towards the end of November, one of the nuns who spoke a few words of English told her Will had been brought into the hospital too. Even if Mary had wanted to see him, she couldn't, for Emmanuel was far too sick. She had begun bribing one of the other mothers to get the rice and water for her because she didn't dare leave his side.

On 1 December, Emmanuel died in Mary's arms. She was rocking him and singing him a lullaby, when he just stopped breathing.

'What's wrong, Mumma?' Charlotte whispered, as she saw tears coursing down her mother's face.

'He's gone,' was all Mary could say brokenly. 'Gone to live with the angels.'

She had expected it. She had believed she was prepared. Day by day she had seen his flesh shrink until he looked like a little wizened monkey, yet even in his sickness, his small fingers had felt for hers. Now suddenly those fingers were motionless and cold, and she wanted to scream out her pain.

He hadn't even survived to see his second birthday, yet in the short time he'd lived, he'd given her so much joy and hope. It wasn't right that his whole life had been overshadowed by suffering, and that he should have died here in such an ugly, dirty place.

His body was taken from her by one of the nuns, to join others who had died that day, in a communal grave. Mary expected they'd come back for her when the service was due to start. But there was no service, a nun told her later. Too many people died here for that.

The following day, Mary sent Charlotte out into the yard, telling her to stay there till she came back. She was full of rage, and she wanted to find Will to tell him she held him responsible for his only son's death, before she had to go back to the guard ship.

She found him in a room at the far end of the hospital. The smell coming from it was so evil that she had to cover her nose and mouth when she looked in. There were at least fifty men inside, far more than in any other room she'd seen. They were squashed up together so tightly that they were lying in one another's vomit and faeces. The groaning and retching was so awful that she was about to turn away when she spotted Will. He was the only one not lying down.

He was almost skeletal, sitting huddled up in a corner wearing nothing but a pair of breeches. His fair hair and beard were matted with filth, his once bright blue eyes pale and red-rimmed with fever. He was twenty-nine, but he looked like a very old man.

Mary had told herself she would laugh if he was dying, she would speed his end by berating him for what he'd done to her. Yet as she stared at him, she wondered why it was she didn't feel appeased by finding him in such obvious misery.

A memory shot into her mind of him carrying her down to the sea to wash her after Emmanuel was born. He'd been so gentle and loving with her, making her forget she was a convict. That day, and on many more besides, she'd felt equal to any honoured wife and mother back home.

It had become very easy for her to believe Will was all bad. She had made herself forget that he had saved her from rape, married her to protect her, and that his skill and hard work at fishing had kept her from starvation. He had often given Charlotte part of his supper, pretending he wasn't hungry. She had been proud to be his wife, and despite Will saying he was going to get a ship home when his sentence was up, he didn't.

All at once she knew she must nurse him. Maybe she wouldn't be able to forgive him entirely, but for all that they had been to each other in the past, he deserved better than to die like a dog without one kind word.

Mary picked her way gingerly through the filth and bodies to his corner.

'It's me, Will,' she said softly as she reached his side.

She was appalled that such a big, strong man could end up like this. It reminded her of the way the convicts on the Second Fleet had been when they got them off the *Scarborough*.

'Mary!' he said weakly, trying to lift his head. 'Is it really you?'

'Yes, it really is me, Will,' she said, bending towards him. 'I've come to take care of you. First I'll get you some water, then I'll get you into a room which isn't quite so dirty and crowded.'

He caught hold of her hand. 'Emmanuel! How is he?'

She was touched that his first thought was for their son.

'He died yesterday,' she said abruptly.

'Oh no,' he groaned, squeezing her hand tighter. 'I am to blame.'

Part of her wanted to agree, to ease her own pain with spite, but the greater part of her felt soothed by having someone to share her grief with.

'No,' she whispered. 'It was the cruelty of that Captain Edwards, this stinking place, and bad luck.'

He opened his eyes wider and tears ran down his cheeks. 'You can say that after the way I treated you?'

Mary didn't trust herself to answer that question. 'I'll get some water,' was all she said.

'Charlotte! Where is she?' he asked, looking stricken.

'She's fine. I told her to wait outside while I came to see you.'

'Thank God for that,' he said, crossing himself.

She got Will drinking water, helped him into a cleaner room, then washed him all over. It was horrifying to see his once big, strong body so emaciated, and she browbeat one of the nuns into giving her a clean shirt for him so that at least he still could have some dignity.

Mary knew he was going to die; since being in this place for three weeks she'd learned the signs. But she told him he would get better, stroked his forehead until he fell asleep and then crept away to get Charlotte.

As she went out into the backyard by the well, she paused for a moment, suddenly aware that this was a perfect time to escape, before Emmanuel's death was reported and Captain Edwards sent guards for her. She could sell her good boots, buy some provisions, then take off into the jungle with Charlotte. She had made friends with the natives in Kupang, and she could do the same here. Maybe in a few months, with a false name and a plausible story, she could get on a ship out of here.

Mary took a few steps towards Charlotte who was sitting on the ground making mud pies in the damp earth around the well. She was dirty, thin and pale-faced and moved lethargically. She hadn't been that way in Kupang, and it hurt Mary to see what the prison regime on the ship had done to her. It was another very good reason to run for it now while they still could.

'Did you see the man?' Charlotte asked, looking up.

That question caught Mary short. All she had said to the child when she told her to stay out here was that 'she had to see a man'. If Charlotte had known who the man was, she would have wanted to see him too. She had been asking, sometimes several times each day, when they were going to see Dada again.

Will had always treated Charlotte as if she were his own daughter. When Emmanuel was born he'd made no distinction between the two children. Even when they had rows, he never once used Charlotte's parentage as a weapon. Will loved Charlotte, and that was evident today when, sick as he was, he wanted to know she was safe.

So how could Mary run out on this man and leave him to die alone?

She lowered the bucket down into the well, filled it and pulled it back up.

'Let me wash you,' she said, pulling a rag out of her pocket. 'We're going to see Dada.'

The heat seemed to increase with every day, and Will became weaker and weaker. Mary sold her boots to buy food for the three of them, but he never managed more than a couple of spoonfuls before falling asleep again.

When he was awake he would lie there looking at Mary, just the way Emmanuel had. He found it too much of an effort to talk, but he would smile when Mary told him stories about her old neighbours in Fowey, of smuggling yarns she'd heard from her father, and described the harbour and the people who worked there.

Every day, at least two people in the room died, and their places were quickly filled again. When Will was asleep, Mary would wash the others and give them water. It made no difference to her whether they were natives, Chinese or Dutch, they all had that same pitiful, childlike expression in their eyes, and at least when they took their last breath they weren't alone.

The nuns looked at Mary as if they thought her mad. Yet sometimes they brought Charlotte an egg or some fruit, which seemed to indicate they also had some sympathy for the English convict woman who was risking her own health staying in such a hell-hole to nurse her husband.

'Is it Christmas yet?' Will croaked out one evening just as the light was fading.

'Three more days,' Mary said.

'Ma always used to make a plum pudding,' he said.

Mary smiled, for she could visualize her own mother stirring ingredients in a big basin at the kitchen table.

'And mine,' she said.

'Ma used to tell us all to make a wish as we stirred it,' Will said in little more than a whisper. 'If I had one now I'd wish that I told you I married you because I loved you.'

Tears prickled at Mary's eyes and she wished she could believe him.

'I'm telling you the truth,' he said. His eyes were red-rimmed and sunken with the fever and he looked old and haggard, nothing like that big, handsome man she'd married. 'I fell for you on the *Dunkirk*. Even if all the beauties in England were lined up for me to choose from, I'd still have picked you.'

Mary's tears began to fall faster. If this was true, why couldn't he have told her before?

'I'm such a fool,' he sighed, as if knowing what she was

thinking. 'I thought if I told you, you wouldn't value me. That's why I used to say I was getting a ship home too. I wanted you to say you couldn't live without me.'

'Oh, Will,' she sighed, and took his hand and kissed it. She knew it was true now, Will wouldn't dare go to his death with a lie on his conscience.

He drifted off into unconsciousness again then, clearly the effort of talking was too much. Mary lay down beside him and held his hand for some time, thinking over what he'd said.

When she was a young girl, she'd always imagined this thing people called love hit you like a ripe apple falling on your head. Her wild desire for Tench confirmed this idea. Yet was that really love? Wasn't it more likely that she only felt that way about Tench because he was kind and interested in her at a time when she desperately needed something lovely to take her mind off reality? Would she have continued to feel such passion for him if they'd been able to live together forever?

The circumstances that led up to her marrying Will were hardly romantic. Yet despite her belief it was purely a marriage of convenience, there was passionate love-making, a warm and comfortable relationship, they could talk about anything together, they laughed a great deal. They were friends.

She thought most intelligent people would define that as love.

The first rays of daylight were slanting through the window when Mary felt Will tossing and turning. She touched his forehead and found he was burning hot again, yet shivering at the same time.

'I'm here,' she whispered, sitting up and reaching for the cloth and the bucket of water to cool him down.

'I'm so sorry about what I did,' he gasped out.

'It doesn't matter any more,' she whispered back, laying the cooling cloth on his brow and stroking back his hair. 'I've forgiven you.'

All at once she realized she had. Like love, it had crept up on her unnoticed.

'Keep Charlotte safe,' he managed to get out with great difficulty.

She knew then that this was the end.

'I married you because I loved you,' she said, and kissed his hot, cracked lips. 'I still love you, and I don't want to live without you.'

She didn't know if he heard the words he'd always wanted to hear, for he slipped into unconsciousness again. She stayed beside him holding him, her head so close to his heart that she felt it when it stopped beating an hour or two later.

Chapter sixteen

It was nearly four months after Emmanuel and Will died in Batavia that the *Horssen*, a Dutch ship, sailed into Cape Town with Mary and Charlotte aboard.

'I think that's the ship that's going to take us home, Mary,' Jim Cartwright said over his shoulder while pointing towards the harbour. 'Come and look! The sight of one of His Majesty's ships will cheer you.'

Mary smiled weakly. Jim was one of the crew from the wrecked *Pandora*. In the last few weeks of the voyage from Batavia, when both she and Charlotte came down with the fever, he had taken it upon himself to try to cheer her. Sometimes it was with different fruits or nuts, but more often it was with jokes or chat. Mary was very grateful for his kindness, but because of her fears for her daughter, she often found it difficult to respond.

Leaving Charlotte lying on a mat on the deck, Mary went over to the rail to look. It was cheering to see Cape Town again, for she had good memories of Charlotte's christening here. Of course she had hope then, to be a pioneer in New South Wales had seemed more of a huge adventure than a punishment.

But the thirst for adventure was long gone. All

she hoped for now was that Charlotte would recover, and to be treated kindly on the last leg of the voyage home.

Yet despite her jaundiced views, she couldn't help but feel some emotion at seeing an English ship. The *Gorgon* was graceful, its deck scrubbed almost white, rope neatly coiled and brass gleaming in the sunshine. She reminded Mary of similar ships she had admired in Plymouth — foreign vessels never seemed to be so spruce and polished. With Table Mountain as its backdrop, she couldn't imagine a prettier sight. Yet however lovely the *Gorgon* looked, the chances were she would have to endure hardships aboard just as great as those she'd experienced on the way here.

She did see Will buried, and heard a prayer said over him, even if it was a communal grave and the prayer in Dutch, so she couldn't understand it. But just as she was putting her few remaining possessions together and thinking of escape again, the guards appeared. They chained her, right there in the hospital, and took her and Charlotte to the guard ship where the other men were being held.

Mary's grief at Emmanuel's death, which she supposed she'd contained while she nursed Will, erupted as soon as she was locked up again. James and the other men were distraught at the death of Emmanuel, but they had no such sympathy for Will. To be imprisoned with them again, in stifling conditions, for almost a month, with water rationed to only a couple of pints a day and hearing them constantly blaming Will for their predicament, was too much to bear. She got so low that she even wished for death.

She rallied a little when she heard that she and Charlotte were to go on the *Horssen* to Cape Town, along with the crew of the *Pandora*. James and the other men, along with Captain Edwards and the mutineers from the *Bounty*, were to go on the *Hoornwey*. Despite the strong bonds she had with her friends, she was relieved that she and Charlotte would at least be alone together, away from the men's bitterness.

But fever had slunk aboard the ships, along with the provisions for the journey, and it showed no distinction between prisoners, officers, their wives and children, or crew. Almost daily Mary heard that yet another man, woman or child had gone down with it. It wasn't long before both she and Charlotte became ill too.

Fortunately for Mary, the captain of the *Horssen* was humane, and brave enough to defy Captain Edwards's orders that all prisoners were to be shackled and kept below for the entire voyage. When he was told that Mary and Charlotte were sick, he had Mary released from her chains so she could take care of her child.

It was only then, touched by this act of kindness, that Mary began to worry about how her friends were faring on their ship. All of them had looked appalling back in the guard ship and it was some wonder, after being kept below for weeks in fetid conditions, that they hadn't already succumbed to the fever. She knew Captain Edwards wouldn't show any of them mercy, and she was desperately afraid that not all of their number would survive to see Cape Town.

'You'll be going home with your mates,' Jim said cheerfully. 'So buck up now, and let's see that pretty smile.'

Mary wondered what this pint-sized sailor with red hair had between his ears, for however kindly he was, he appeared not to see the gravity of her situation. Charlotte was very sick with fever, and they were going home to England for Mary to be hanged and Charlotte orphaned. Could he really believe she ought to see the last leg of the journey as some kind of party?

'Are you always so jolly?' she asked, hoping he wouldn't note the sarcasm in her tone.

'Jolly Jim, that's what me mam used to call me,' he laughed, clearly taking it as a compliment. 'Now, you'd better get your things together 'cos I reckon we'll be going aboard the *Gorgon* very soon.'

It could have taken less than a second for Mary to gather together her few belongings. But she spun it out, examining each and every item, even though they had no value. A blue cotton dress, given to her in Kupang. The length of brightly coloured cotton from which she had intended to make another dress for Charlotte, but instead used to wrap Emmanuel in when he was in hospital. She held it to her face, hoping it still smelled of him, but that was gone now, just as he was, and the colours were faded from the many times she'd washed it. A string of blue wooden beads given to her by James Martin in Kupang. A lock of Emmanuel's blond hair, tucked into a folded piece of brown paper. The blanket Watkin Tench had given her here in Cape Town, for Charlotte.

It had been white and fluffy then, now it was brown with age, so threadbare it resembled a cobweb, but just holding it brought back many memories of both her babies. There were a couple of pretty shells, picked up on the beach in Kupang, and finally the bag holding sweet tea leaves.

She didn't really know why she'd held on to them all this time. They were the last of those she'd picked back in the colony. They were brown and crackly now, and she doubted they had any flavour left. But she couldn't throw them away, they too held good memories. She could see herself sitting by the fire with Will outside their hut, sipping at the hot tea as they planned their future. That tea had kept hunger at bay, it had warmed them when they were cold, comforted them when everything looked black.

She would put on the blue dress, for even if it was ragged, it was clean. She'd worn it all the time at the hospital in Batavia. She wished she still had the pink dress and the smart boots, or even her shawl and sun bonnet, as they would have made her feel a whole lot better going aboard the new ship. But if she hadn't sold them, they might not be alive now.

Charlotte had even fewer possessions, just a little shift and her colourful dress, now faded to just a blur of pastels, the stitching coming apart on the seams. She had stopped complaining about wearing the plain grey one back in the hospital. Now Mary came to think of it, she hadn't complained about anything since then – not the lack of food and water, or even when she was taken sick.

Mary glanced down at her. She was lying on the bench where they slept, curled up like a small dog, using her two hands as a pillow. Her face was pale and drawn, she was pitifully thin, and her eyes looked haunted.

'It will be better on the new ship,' Mary said, smoothing back her dark curls from her face. 'You'll get well again.'

Charlotte merely sighed. It was the sound of disbelief, and it hurt Mary more than a sharp retort.

Jim Cartwright was right about which ship they were going home on, but wrong that they would go to it immediately. They sat at anchor for over two weeks. The crew went ashore, but Mary was kept aboard. She wasn't put in chains again, but she was locked back in the hold with Charlotte, and even refused a couple of hours a day on deck for fresh air and exercise.

Daily, Charlotte became weaker, burning up with fever, and all Mary could do was bathe her, try to get her to drink, and curse a system which would allow an innocent child to suffer such cruelty.

Carrying Charlotte, who was barely conscious, Mary staggered up the gang-plank of the *Gorgon*, too weak even to respond to the sound of English voices.

Jim had told her the *Gorgon* had come from Port Jackson, and that the whole ship was filled with plants, shrubs, animal skins and even a couple of captured kangaroos.

He'd been impatient to see these wonders for himself. But Mary was more intent on being reunited with her fellow deserters, as they were now labelled, than concerning herself with whether there would be anyone else on board that she knew.

She was dizzy with fever and the heat. Shouting, thumping, squeaking and banging bombarded her ears, and her limbs ached intolerably. The glare of the sunshine on the water hurt her eyes, and the smells of spice, fish and human sweat made her feel nauseous.

The dizziness suddenly grew far worse as she stepped off the gang-plank on to the deck, which was crowded with people and boxes. Her legs felt as if they were made of rubber and, afraid she would drop Charlotte, she stopped, leaned against a packing case and closed her eyes for a moment to gain her equilibrium. Then she heard someone calling her name.

The voice was so familiar, but in her befuddled state she couldn't place it. She opened her eyes, but everything was a blur.

'Are you sick, Mary?' she heard the voice say as if from a great way off. 'Let me take Charlotte.'

She could only suppose she fainted, for the next thing she knew she was lying down on the deck and someone was dabbing at her forehead with a wet cloth.

'Charlotte!' she called out in alarm, trying to sit up.

'She's being taken care of,' a man said. 'Drink this.'

The drink was rum, and the man offering it to her had to be a sailor, judging by his white ducks and shirt. He had curly fair hair and a sun-blistered face. Mary was in a patch of shade now, and her vision seemed to have returned to normal.

'Who was that who spoke to me and took Charlotte?' she asked.

'That 'ud be Cap'n Tench,' the man said.

'Tench!' she exclaimed. 'Watkin Tench?'

'That's right, me lovely,' he said with a broad grin. 'And I take it you're the one he's been fretting about since we got told you was to sail 'ome with us?'

Mary lay on a bunk, Charlotte asleep beside her. She was bewildered, unable to make up her mind if she was really in a cabin, complete with open porthole, or if she was dreaming.

The cabin certainly looked real enough, very small with just the bunk, a kind of washstand, and a couple of hooks on the wall for clothes. Her bundle was on the washstand, beside it a pitcher of water. Through the porthole she could see barnacle-covered timbers, which had to be the sides of the wharf.

If it was a dream it was a lovely one, for she seemed to think the sailor who gave her rum had said Watkin Tench was on this ship.

She certainly hadn't dreamed about the rum, she could still taste it in her mouth. But maybe she'd drunk it too fast, for the events after that weren't clear at all. Could Tench have been one of the two men she'd heard talking by her? She was sure that one of them said, 'She's been through enough. I want her put in a cabin with her child. That way at least they'll stand a chance.'

Mary lifted herself up a little to look at Charlotte. Her breathing was laboured, her skin felt hot and dry and she was so thin every bone in her small body stood out. It didn't look to Mary as if she stood a chance. She had the same look Emmanuel had towards the end, and Mary had become all too familiar with the signs of approaching death during her time at the Batavia hospital to believe it was mere coincidence.

A rapping on the door woke Mary later. 'Come in,' she said weakly, surprised that anyone would treat an escaped convict with such deference.

The door opened, and there was Watkin Tench, looking exactly the way she remembered, slender, lean-faced, his dark eyes full of concern. Tears filled her eyes. So it hadn't been a dream! He had come back into her life to rescue her.

'Mary!' he exclaimed, and moved closer to her, leaving the door open. 'You cannot imagine my shock to hear you were travelling home on this ship. It is the most extraordinary coincidence.'

To Mary it was far more than coincidence. Only God could have worked this miracle.

'I thought I was dreaming when I heard your voice,' she admitted. 'Then I found myself in this cabin.'

'You have Captain Parker to thank for that,' Tench said. 'He is a good man, and when he heard the circumstances and saw how ill both you and Charlotte were, he gave the order. The surgeon will be along to see you both soon, and much as I want to know everything that has happened since we last saw each other, you must rest.'

'Do you know that Emmanuel and Will died?' she asked.

He nodded gravely. 'I am so sorry, Mary. I wish I had the right words to comfort you in your loss.'

The sincerity in his voice made her cry. In the past he had comforted her in so many different ways, for so many different reasons, and to find he was close by again when she needed a friend so badly was almost too much to bear.

'You were always such a good friend,' she said through her tears. 'And here you are again.'

'I missed you a great deal after you'd gone from Sydney Cove,' he said. 'It just wasn't the same place without you. You can't imagine the rumpus you caused.'

Mary tried to control herself and wiped away her tears. 'James, William and the others, are they here too?' she asked.

'James Martin, Bill Allen, Nat Lilly and Sam Broome are,' he said.

The hesitancy in his voice alerted her that something was wrong. 'And the other three?' she asked.

He looked away for a moment, as if afraid to admit the truth.

'They're dead, aren't they?' She slumped back on to her pillow in utter dejection. 'Was it the fever?'

He nodded. 'William Moreton and Samuel Bird died soon after leaving Batavia,' he said, reaching out to touch her arm in sympathy. 'Jamie Cox jumped overboard in the Straits of Sunda. Maybe he was trying to escape, but it's more likely he was maddened by the fever.'

Mary looked at Tench in horror. 'Oh no,' she croaked out, 'not Jamie!'

Jamie had become like a member of her family, he'd shared so much with her and Will. On the *Dunkirk* and then the *Charlotte* and in Sydney Cove he'd been Will's shadow. He had always seemed more of a boy than a man, even when he shared a hut with Sarah. He had a sweet innocence about him that set him apart from the other male prisoners. It was horrible to think of him ending his life in such a way.

'The other four are in poor shape,' Tench went on, 'but I believe they will soon recover. James told me everything about the escape, and that they all owe their lives to you. They send good wishes to you and Charlotte. They hope once we sail they'll be able to see you both.'

Mary turned her head towards Charlotte who lay asleep in the crook of her arm. 'I don't think she'll live to see them, let alone England,' she whispered.

Tench didn't reply, and when she turned her face to look at him, she saw tears in his eyes.

'Fate has treated you extraordinarily harshly,' he said in a low voice, 'and you have been so very brave. A line should be drawn now. You have suffered enough.'

'Did I hear right?' she asked. 'Did that sailor call you Captain Tench?'

He touched her face gently. 'How like you, Mary, to think of someone else at such a bad time for you. Yes, I'm Captain Tench now. I'm just glad my higher rank gets me a few more privileges, like this cabin for you.'

And with that he left suddenly, and Mary hugged Charlotte tighter and cried. Would Tench ask why they escaped? Or would he understand?

She had left New South Wales with eight healthy men and two children. Maybe she hadn't known some of the men very well then, and some she'd grown to like more than others. Yet they'd become a family, they had pulled together and made it to Kupang. But now there were only four left: cherubic Nat, funny James, stalwart Sam and pugnacious Bill. Half their number gone. And one of the children. Now Charlotte was mortally ill too, and the remainder would be hanged.

She had prided herself on being the mastermind behind the escape. In fact she'd led them all to their deaths.

The *Gorgon* sailed out of Cape Town on 5 April. Mary had her porthole open, and heard the shouted farewells from the wharf, but she was once again bathing Charlotte with cool water and didn't even look out. Her only interest was in making her daughter well again.

As the ship got underway, Mary found herself treated with the utmost kindness. Food and water were brought to her, the ship's surgeon visited her each day, and she was allowed up on deck at any time.

There were many familiar faces aboard other than Tench's, for they were all people who had been in the penal colony and were now returning home after their term of duty was up. Among them was Lieutenant Ralph Clark, the hypocritical man who had spoken to the convict women as though they were dirt under his feet, yet took up with one himself, and there were dozens of Marines with their wives and families.

Mary was far too despondent to talk to any of these people and ask how old friends like Sarah and Bessie had fared after she left. She could see a kind of irony in her situation. Had she become a lag wife to Tench or any of the officers, instead of marrying Will, she would have been left behind when they sailed. A widow here, or a widow there, whichever road she'd taken would have ended the same.

Mary doubted Ralph Clark had any sympathy with her – when she ran into him on deck he pointedly looked the other way – but everyone else was kind. Captain Parker's wife visited her once, bringing her a green and white striped dress, and a night-shirt for Charlotte. She was cool, but then Mary didn't expect a woman of her status to be friendly. It was enough that she'd overcome her fear of the fever to bring clothes.

Mary was gradually recovering her own health, feeling a little better each day, but Charlotte continued to sink. Some days she would swallow a little soup or mashed-up fruit, and stay awake long enough for Mary to sing to her or tell her some stories, but at other times she was delirious and unable even to sip water.

It became hotter and hotter in the next couple of weeks, and Mary was told by the surgeon that other children belonging to the Marines were sick. By Mary's twenty-seventh birthday at the end of April, five children had died and were buried at sea.

Tench came whenever he could, and his deep concern for Charlotte was very touching. He often brought messages from James Martin and the other three men, who were just as anxious about her.

'Kiss her for me,' Tench said, reading from one of James's notes. 'Tell her all her uncles are waiting to see her.'

'Are they well?' Mary asked. Half of her wanted to see her friends, but the other half was afraid in case they started on about Will again. But as she didn't like to leave Charlotte even for a minute or two she had the perfect excuse.

'Much recovered,' Tench said with a smile. 'Eating like pigs. James teases and flirts with the ladies. He is as much of a success with them as he was with the women back in Sydney. He is also talking about writing his memoirs, which should make interesting reading. Bill plays cards with the crew, Sam and Nat are always dozing.'

Mary smiled. It was good to hear they were being treated well too. She was also very glad they were able to put aside what lay ahead for them in England, if only for a few weeks.

During the night of 5 May, Charlotte finally gave up her long struggle and died in her mother's arms.

Mary continued to hold and rock her small body for over an hour, sobbing out her anguish. She wound her fingers into the dark curls so much like her own, and looked back at all the milestones in her short life. Her birth on the *Charlotte*, her christening, first teeth and

391

wobbly steps. But it was the time in Kupang Mary lingered most on, for there Charlotte had been truly happy, well fed for once, as free as any other child, and adored by everyone who met her.

At least now she wouldn't have to suffer the loss of her mother when she was hanged, or be subjected to the miseries of an orphanage or workhouse. She would join her little brother in heaven.

Yet even though Mary could claim a dozen good reasons why she ought to be glad her daughter died at sea, her heart felt smashed into a thousand pieces. Everything Mary had done had been for her. Charlotte gave her reason to go on, and without her there was nothing.

Charlotte's body was committed to the deep that afternoon with almost the entire ship's company, the passengers and the other convicts looking on.

It was Sunday, and raining, and Mary stood bare-headed and stony-faced as Captain Parker led the prayers. She had sewn Charlotte's body into the piece of sackcloth herself, and cried the last of her tears over it. She was empty now, nothing left, and she couldn't understand why her own heart kept on beating so stubbornly.

Even as the small package slipped over the side, she didn't cry out or turn to James or Sam for comfort. She wanted to join her daughter in a watery grave. Yet she knew if she tried to run forward and throw herself in, someone would try to stop her, and failure would make her feel even lower.

*

Agnes Tippet, one of the Marines' wives, watched Mary walk away from the service, and turned to the women next to her. 'She didn't care one bit,' she said in shocked tones. 'No tears, nothing. I've never seen anyone bury a child with such a hard face.'

Watkin Tench heard Agnes' remark. 'Be quiet, you foolish woman,' he snapped at her, incensed. 'You have no real idea what she's been through, or how she feels inside. Count yourself lucky your children are well, and don't make judgements on another.'

As Tench strode away, he could hear the women whispering among themselves and he choked back tears of sadness and frustration.

He knew Mary so well. She would not burden anyone with her grief, least of all him. He had seen the desolation on the faces of James, Sam, Nat and Bill, and he knew it wasn't only for the little girl they'd all come to love and look upon as their own, but for her mother as well. Mary had saved their lives, been a friend, sister and mother to each of them, and they all knew this latest tragedy had broken the last of her spirit.

Back in Sydney a year earlier, their escape had been a huge shock to Tench. He had believed he knew Mary and Will well enough to guess if they were hatching something like this up, yet he hadn't had the faintest suspicion.

He didn't have much faith that they would make it to the Dutch East Indies, for by all accounts it was a long and dangerous voyage. Yet he understood why they felt they had to attempt it, and greatly admired their courage.

He had missed Mary so much. Hardly a day passed

without him thinking about her. He offered up prayers for her safety, and a small part of him believed she must have survived, because he was sure he'd feel it if she were dead.

Even as he packed up his belongings to leave Sydney Cove, Mary was still on his mind. He could see her small, eager face in his mind's eye, the way her eyes used to light up when he called at her hut. He could still see her slender but shapely legs as she tucked her dress up to wade into the sea and help with the seine net, and her dark curly hair tumbling about her face as she washed clothes. Yet it wasn't the physical things about her he missed the most, it was her inquiring mind, her dry sense of humour and her stoicism.

Even if he had known she'd survived, he would never have considered he might run into her again. When Captain Parker told him in Cape Town that they would be taking deserters from Port Jackson back to England for trial, then named them, Tench was utterly astounded, almost disbelieving.

It seemed to him then that his fate and Mary's were linked. That God in his infinite wisdom had always intended them for each other. This belief grew even stronger when he talked to the surviving men and learned of the voyage, and how Will and Emmanuel had died in Batavia. He was of course distressed to think that Mary had lost her husband and her little son, but according to the other men Will had betrayed them all, and he hadn't got to know Emmanuel as well as he had Charlotte.

Then Mary came aboard, so weak that she collapsed,

and sweet little Charlotte, the child so many of his men believed was his, was mortally ill. Under the circumstances it wasn't appropriate to tell Mary what was in his heart. All he could do was make sure she and Charlotte got whatever they needed to recover, and that he was around when she needed a friend.

Yet it had become even less appropriate to tell her how he felt since Charlotte's death. She had survived the hulks, the long voyage to New South Wales, and four years of near-starvation in the penal colony. She'd had the audacity to plan a fantastic escape plot, and by sheer force of will got to the planned destination. Then she was betrayed by her own husband and found herself once again a prisoner, facing execution back in England.

Tench knew in his heart that it wasn't any of these things, terrible as they were, which had broken her. He had no doubt that if her children had survived she would have plotted yet another daring escape, and carried it out. But those children were her Achilles' heel. Once Emmanuel became sick she had to nurse him. Likewise with Charlotte. Now they were both gone, freedom was worthless. Mary would go to the gallows without fear. Death was the only escape she wanted now.

'You can't give up on her,' he muttered to himself. 'You've got to find a way to put some fight back in her.'

Several days later Tench came upon James Martin and Sam Broome on deck. They were sitting leaning back against a locker, to all intents and purposes just enjoying the sun and fresh air. They were both painfully thin, the horrors they'd endured still showing in their eyes, and they looked much older than they had back in New South Wales. But though they seemed relaxed, Tench picked up some animosity between them. Guessing it had something to do with Mary, he stopped to talk to them.

After some general conversation about there being little room on the deck because of the boxes of plants and shrubs from New South Wales, and whether or not the two kangaroos would survive in a colder climate, Tench mentioned Mary.

'Have you seen her on deck today?' he asked.

'She was up here for a while,' Sam said. 'She don't seem to want to be with us now.'

There was a note of real despondency rather than complaint in his voice, and Tench guessed he was in love with her. He knew it had been Mary who nursed Sam back to health when he came in on the Second Fleet, and probably any man would love a woman for that. Tench liked Sam, he was calm, good-hearted and a talented carpenter, and Tench couldn't help thinking that perhaps he would have made a better husband for Mary than Will, if he'd been on the First Fleet.

'She doesn't want to be with anyone,' Tench said soothingly. 'That's the way grief takes some people.'

'Or they only want to be with people who'll be useful to them,' James said with a slight smirk, looking pointedly at Tench.

'She isn't like that,' Sam said, his face flushing with anger.

All at once Tench saw the problem between James and

Sam. James was assuming Mary was as calculating as himself.

Tench hadn't ever really liked the wily Irishman that much. He was amusing and intelligent, but as cunning as a fox. 'Sam's right, Mary isn't like that,' he said firmly. 'You should know better, James.'

'I'm not blaming her for it,' James shrugged, his ugly face taking on a slightly remorseful expression. 'If there was anyone around who I thought could save me from the long drop, I'd lick their arse if that's what it took.'

Later, alone in his cabin, Tench found himself thinking about what James had said. The man was wrong about Mary of course, she wasn't talking to anyone, not for sympathy or any other reason. She was a prisoner inside herself right now.

But James had made a good point too. Mary could do with someone influential on her side. Tench was prepared to go to any lengths himself for her, but he was just a Marine, recently promoted to Captain, and he hadn't got an ounce of influence back in England.

He went through a mental list of everyone he knew, but none of them were in any better position to help her than himself.

Turning to his journal as he always did when he was troubled, he flicked back over the pages, reading parts of it at random. The penal colony in New South Wales was history in the making, and he had wanted to produce a work which in years to come would be a valuable source of information about the colony's first years. It wasn't ever intended to be a personal account of his own part in it, but a broader view.

Overall he considered he had done that rather well. Maybe when he retired from the Marines he'd take to writing articles for newspapers on the subject. And then suddenly, a thought came into his mind like a thunderbolt. That was it! A way to get influential help for Mary. He'd write a full account about her to the newspapers in England!

Despite his usual calm and controlled manner, he felt very excited. He couldn't write under his own name of course, there was bound to be some kind of law against a serving officer divulging information. But no one would guess it was him if he wrote the Bryants' escape story in a florid and sensational manner. Newspapers the length and breadth of England would devour such a story. Men would love the daring of it, women would weep for Mary losing her husband and children. Surely no one with a heart would want to see her hanged after going through so much pain already?

Tench's smile spread from one ear to the other. It could work. He had to make it work.

Mary sat in a sheltered nook at the stern of the ship, looking out at the fast-approaching coast of England with a mixture of pleasure and trepidation. It was a beautiful June day, warm, sunny and with just enough wind to send the ship scudding along at a good speed. Perfect sailing weather, and she could recall so many other days just like it, out in a boat with her father.

She had thought about her parents and Dolly so much over the years. Had they found out what happened to her? If they hadn't, maybe they thought she had forsaken them for high life in London. Or even supposed she had died! Whatever they knew, or believed, it was going to distress them terribly if they discovered that she was awaiting trial in London's Newgate prison.

She hadn't understood at nineteen what it was to be a mother. Mothers were people who nagged, wanted you to be ladylike, to cook and sew as well as they did, and to marry a respectable man so they could be smug and pat themselves on the back for bringing their daughters up well. They didn't want their daughters to have fun or adventure, because they didn't have any themselves.

Mary knew better now. All any woman wanted for her child was for it to be safe and happy. All that nagging was only an attempt to prevent harm. A way of showing love.

She wished there was a way of letting her mother know she understood that now. She also wished she could reassure her that death by hanging didn't frighten her. It was what she wanted, to rid herself of the terrible burden of guilt for her children's deaths.

Everyone on this ship had been so kind to her, but it would have been better if someone had called her a murderess, for that was what she knew she was. At the time she planned the escape she thought it was preferable to risk her children drowning at sea, a clean and quick death, than to watch them die slowly of hunger or disease in the colony. She still stood by that. Yet despite all her efforts they had in the end suffered a far worse fate than could ever have befallen them back in New South Wales. And she was to blame for putting them in that position.

A shadow falling on her made her look up. It was Tench.

'So thoughtful,' he said with a smile. 'Will you share them with me?'

Mary couldn't tell him she was thinking about her children, so she played safe. 'I was thinking about my mother.'

'Would you like me to write to her for you?' he asked, squatting down in front of her.

Mary shook her head. 'She can't read, she'd have to take it to someone else.'

'Maybe I could call on her at some time then,' he suggested.

'I can't put that burden on you,' she said, imagining how her mother would view a gentleman like Tench. She would be embarrassed to have him call at her humble home, so she'd be curt with him, as if she didn't care about Mary. Then she'd weep for days after he'd gone.

'I just hope I get tried and hanged quickly and no one will know about it. That's the kindest thing for everyone concerned.'

'Not for me it isn't,' he said, looking horrified. 'I believe there will be public sympathy for you and I hope you'll be set free.'

Mary gave a tight little laugh. 'That's foolish. You know perfectly well I'll be hanged or sent back. I just hope it's hanging.'

Tench didn't make any reply for a few moments. He

had been on an emotional see-saw with Mary for so long, sometimes he didn't know for certain how he really felt. She looked pretty today in her green and white dress, her hair neatly tied back with a white ribbon, her cheeks pink from the sun and wind. She had regained a little weight since Charlotte's death, and she looked a world away from the waif in rags he'd known back in Sydney Cove.

But her grey eyes looked dead now, no sparkle, no fire. Even her voice was muted. He couldn't bear it.

'It's difficult to find anything further to discuss after hanging has been brought up,' he said, afraid he might make a fool of himself and cry.

'Maybe it's because there isn't anything more to say,' she replied. 'We've had an odd sort of friendship, haven't we? It was always an uneven one, you with the world in front of you, me with nothing.'

'I never saw it like that,' he said sadly and with just a touch of indignation.

'Neither did I, once.' She sighed. 'But then I'm better at seeing things as they really are now.'

Tench felt helpless. He remembered her audacity back on the *Dunkirk*. He'd been fully aware she was always looking for an opportunity, whether that was escape, work on deck, extra food or clothing. It was that ingenuity and daring that initially attracted him to her. He couldn't believe she'd lost it all. But maybe if he told her how he really felt about her, some of it might return.

'I don't think you are that good at seeing everything,' he began cautiously. 'My feelings for you in particular.'

She looked at him inquiringly and it gave him heart.

'I love you, Mary, I always have,' he blurted out. 'I wish I had told you so long ago, and never let you marry Will.'

Mary just stared at him. Not disbelieving, nor scornful. She simply looked at him as if she was seeing right down into his soul.

'It's true,' Tench insisted. 'I want to find a way to get you released so you can share your life with me.'

She remained silent for another couple of moments, and Tench held his breath, waiting for her reply.

'I'm not for you, Watkin,' she said at last, her voice soft but firm, and her use of his Christian name sounded odd. 'You want me to have hope.'

'Of course I want you to have hope. For a future together, marriage, and a real home,' he said passionately.

She smiled wearily. His dark eyes had all the fire in them she once dreamed of, but it was too late now. 'I have hope for you,' she said. 'I hope you'll have a long and distinguished career, and a wife suitable for your station who loves you with all her heart.'

'But don't you see that it was Fate who brought us together again?' he said fiercely, catching hold of her hand and pressing it. 'We're meant to be together, I know it.'

'I think Fate brought us together only to give me a little comfort in seeing a dear face once again,' she said, putting her hand on his cheek. 'You have been the very best of friends.'

'But is that all?' he asked, his face full of hurt and disappointment.

Mary thought for a moment. She wasn't sure whether telling him the truth would hurt him more, or comfort him. Yet her mother would have said the truth is always best.

'It was you I wanted, right back on the *Dunkirk*,' she said with a sigh. 'Charlotte should have been your child. I carried that loving with me right through the voyage to New South Wales, even through my marriage. If you had said you wanted me as your lag wife, I believe I would have left Will for you.'

'Well then,' he said triumphantly. 'There's nothing to stand in our way now.'

Mary shook her head slowly. 'There is, Watkin. I'm not the same person any more,' she said almost wistfully. 'I have a thousand ugly pictures in my head. I'm all used up.'

'I don't understand.' He shook his head, dark eyes boring into her. 'If you were set free all that would go.'

'Some of it maybe,' she said, tears forming in her eyes because she wished what she was telling him wasn't the truth. 'But you love the old Mary, and that isn't what you'd get.'

'I don't understand,' he implored her, clutching her hand and lifting it to his lips.

'The Mary you loved was a scheming little minx,' she said with a half smile. 'She cared only for survival, she made things happen. But too much happened in the end. Things you can't even imagine. The old Mary died back in Batavia. All you see now is an empty shell.'

Tench looked into her eyes, saw the bleakness there and instinctively knew she truly believed what she said. 'Let me kiss you,' he whispered, not caring if anyone was watching them because he was sure it would change her mind.

Mary nodded. It seemed fitting to her that she should end this with the one thing she had so often dreamed of.

He slid his arms around her and drew her to him, his heart aching with the need to bring back the mischievous and audacious girl who had captured his heart and held it for so many years. Her lips were soft and yielding, but disappointingly her kiss was one of farewell. Tender, clinging, yet without passion, just a goodbye. He knew then there was nothing more he could do or say which would persuade her.

He cupped her face in his hands. 'I'll do my best for you,' he said fiercely. 'I'll write and come to visit you.'

'No, Watkin,' she said firmly. 'I don't want you to. You've been one of the best people in my life, I have a hundred bright memories of you in my head. If I'm to be hung they will sustain me. Let it be at that. Find someone from your own class who can bring you happiness.'

Of all the many traits of Mary's personality Tench had come to know and admire over the past years, her resolution was the most powerful. He knew it was that which had kept her alive and helped her make the best of what was thrown at her.

He knew she was resolved now. Even if by some miracle he could sweep her away from Newgate and the gallows, she would not allow him to sully his family name or his career by marrying her. Tench knew he had never known anyone so heroic and unselfish.

He stood up and moved to the ship's rail. He wanted

to find a persuasive counter-argument, yet knew there wasn't one. 'We're nearly at Portsmouth,' he said eventually, looking towards the shore. 'I have to leave the ship there while you go on to London.'

He couldn't stand the thought of it. He knew that very soon she would be put back in chains, just the way she was when he first met her.

'God go with you,' she said from behind him, her voice shaking. 'You are destined for greatness, Watkin. And I'll always count myself fortunate to have had you as a friend.'

Chapter seventeen

Late in the afternoon on a fine, sunny day at the end of June, Mary shuffled dejectedly along behind the Newgate gaoler, her four friends behind her. They had been processed and now they were being led along a narrow, dark stone passageway into the prison itself, to be locked up until their trial.

Mary's ankles were raw and bleeding from the chains that had been put back on her earlier in the month when the *Gorgon* docked at Portsmouth. They had remained on for the last part of the voyage to the London docks. She was also hungry, for she hadn't eaten anything since dawn when she, James, Bill, Nat and Sam left the ship, shackled together to wait to be escorted to Newgate prison.

Mary had felt very much as she had when she left the prison in Kupang to be transferred to the ship which would take them to Batavia. The difference was that the voices around them were now English ones, and more poignantly, four of the men and the two children were missing.

They hardly spoke as they waited on the busy wharf for the prison cart to arrive. They just sat in a row against a wall, clutching their small bags of belongings on their laps, each wrapped in their own private thoughts. Mary could understand why people passing through the wharf looked at them so curiously, for they must have been a strange sight. Chained convicts were usually ragged, dirty and malnourished, whereas they were clean and healthy. The men had all been issued with canvas breeches and shirts, and Mary was wearing the green and white dress given to her by the captain's wife. Muscular Bill with his bald head and prize-fighter's features might look like a dangerous man, but Nat, with his angelic face, blue eyes and blond hair shining in the sunshine, had more in common with a page or a choir boy. As for James and Sam, they gave the impression of being two impoverished, scrawny aristocrats. James looked arrogantly down his long nose at anyone who glanced his way, and Sam was in a world of his own, tawny eyes fixed on the distant horizon.

There was nothing to say to one another. No comment on the hurly-burly of the wharf, where piles of goods were being loaded and unloaded into ships. They didn't react to casks of wine and spirits being rolled over the cobblestones, nor to the shouts of porters and dockers, nor even to half a dozen horses being led nervously on to a ship.

The long voyage from Cape Town had restored their health, and the horrors of past imprisonments had begun to fade. But as they waited to be taken to Newgate, which by reputation was the hardest and cruellest prison in the whole of England, all of them were struggling to control their fear.

The cart didn't arrive until mid-afternoon, and it was only once they were in it, trundling slowly away from the frantic activity on the wharf, that Bill broke the silence.

'I'd forgotten what horse shit smelled like,' he exclaimed, as their cart joined a throng of others carrying goods along a narrow road between tall, grimy warehouses.

'It smells like Dublin,' James retorted, giving an exaggerated loud sniff. 'Do you think if we asked the driver nicely he'd take us to an ale house?'

Mary half smiled at their show of bravado. She knew they were every bit as scared as she was. She had finally made it to London, the place she'd dreamed of since she was a child, but it wasn't in her dream to see it from the back of a prison cart, or to die there, dangling on a rope.

Yet despite the knowledge that Newgate lay at the end of the cart ride, all five of them found much to distract them on the way there. The streets, whether wide and elegant or narrow and dingy, teemed with people from all walks of life. Ladies in silk gowns and fancy hats, on the arms of gentlemen in wigs and frock coats, strolled nonchalantly past blind beggars, drunken slatterns and bare-footed street urchins. It was pandemonium, carts and carriages charging along at breakneck speeds, strident-voiced street vendors offering everything from fly-blown meat pies to posies of flowers. There were organ grinders and men playing tin whistles and fiddles. She saw market porters carrying huge tottering piles of baskets on their heads, a fresh-faced dairy maid with pails of milk supported on a yoke across her shoulders, and a bow-legged man with his hands clenching live, fluttering chickens by their claws.

The shops were as diverse as the kinds of people who passed by them. One sold nothing but silverware, the next displayed great pink hams, pheasants and rabbits laid out on white marble slabs. A milliner's selling hats that could surely only be worn by royalty, and then in complete contrast a shop with mountains of secondhand boots and shoes.

Mary could hardly believe that women could go out on the streets wearing such low-cut gowns, displaying their breasts for the whole world to gawp at. Yet they appeared to be ladies of quality, for all had a soberly dressed maid or footman with them. In Plymouth only a whore would show so much naked flesh.

The clamour, dirt and evil smells ought to have shattered Mary's long-held illusions that it was the city of miracles. But until she saw Newgate, some hours after they'd left the docks, she was still clinging to them, expecting that any moment she would be rescued.

But no rescue came. The bony horses even picked up a little speed at the sight of Newgate's forbidding grey stone walls, relieved perhaps that they could now shed their heavy load.

Suddenly all those stories Mary had heard back in Sydney Cove of public hangings at Tyburn Tree, where huge crowds gathered to watch as if it was a sideshow in a fair, took on a new and horrific meaning.

As the gates opened to let the cart enter, the smell hit them. It wasn't just the familiar stench of human waste, more the certain knowledge that this really was the absolute bottom of the barrel of life.

Even James, who had joked and chatted most of the way from the docks, was silenced as the cart trundled into a small, cobbled, tunnel-like area with more heavy doors beyond. The two burly gaolers who had opened the outer gates closed and locked them behind the cart, then, picking up a cudgel each, stood by as the cart driver unlocked and pulled out the chains that had secured the prisoners together.

Mary was terrified as they were shoved into a small room off the yard. She remembered other women telling her back in Sydney Cove how the gaolers here would knock you out even for asking a question and body searches were just an excuse to humiliate prisoners. She was dreading the moment, too, when she would be separated from the men.

But there was no search, perhaps because they'd come directly from a Royal Navy ship. The only questions asked were for their names, which were duly marked down in a ledger, and after a brief wait, they were led down the passageway to another door.

There Mary glanced behind her at the men. She expected that this would be the point when they were separated. She wanted to say something, but the prospect of awaiting trial apart from them was so daunting that she was robbed of speech.

The gaoler opened the door, and the unexpected waft of warm air and sunshine beyond made Mary gasp. But if it wasn't enough of a surprise to find herself stepping out into an open courtyard, the sight that met her was so totally astounding that she stopped in her tracks.

'Holy Mother of God!' James exclaimed behind her.

It might be a yard within the prison walls, but the scene within it was more like a carnival than a place of punishment. At least a hundred people were milling around enjoying themselves. The noise of drunken revelry was as loud as in any of the taverns they'd passed on the way here.

Mary rubbed her eyes, thinking it was some kind of hallucination. It couldn't be prison, she could see no chains, no evidence of starvation, many of the crowd were even in fine clothes, men in wigs strutting around like gentlemen, women in what, to Mary at least, looked like ball gowns, bedecked with jewellery. One woman in turquoise satin, surrounded by men in velvet and brocade jackets, was actually fanning herself with a feathered fan as if she was at a private soirée.

Where were the poor wretches in chains they'd expected? The diseased, hollow-eyed old whores in rags, the pathetic young girls who had been led astray, and the scarred brutes who'd finally got their just deserts? These people cavorting, drinking and chatting certainly weren't being punished.

'Move along now,' the gaoler said impatiently, prodding her with his cudgel. 'It ain't like you never was in a prison afore.'

'I've never been in one like this before,' Mary retorted, glancing back at the men to see their reaction. But they looked as staggered and unbelieving as she.

Drink obviously played a major part in the festivities. They could see people coming out of a door carrying brimming tankards. There were even a few women dancing a jig accompanied by a man with a black patch over one eye, playing a fiddle.

Noise came from every quarter. Mary looked up at the grey prison building and saw many people craning their heads out of small barred windows and shouting to those below or either side of them.

As the gaoler urged them forward, suddenly a hush fell on the crowd, all eyes turning to Mary and her group.

'It's them!' someone shouted. 'Give 'em a cheer!'

As wild and frantic cheering went up, Mary suddenly felt like a bride who had turned up at the wrong wedding. She saw no reason why anyone would want to cheer them. It had to be a case of mistaken identity.

The crowd were coming towards them with shouts of welcome, broad grins, and hands outstretched to greet them.

'It's a pleasure to welcome you to Newgate.' A man in a stained black frock coat bowed and doffed a battered top hat. 'There's plenty of us know we're bound for Botany Bay, it gives us heart to hear of your escape.'

'They've found out what we done,' Sam said incredulously, holding on to Mary's arm as if he thought she'd faint with shock. 'God's teeth! I never thought we'd be famous.'

Clearly fame didn't preclude locking them up, for they weren't given a chance to speak to anyone, ask how they knew about them, or anything else. The gaoler pushed them on up a couple of flights of winding stone stairs and into a cell, slamming and locking the door behind them.

Temporarily stunned by what they'd seen out in the yard, and the welcome they'd had from the other prisoners, no one spoke for some minutes. The five of them just stood there, speechless.

Mary pulled herself together first. The cell was very small, the straw was dirty, and the only light came from a small slit window, too high up to see out. But compared with the conditions on the *Rembang* and in the hospital in Batavia, it was quite decent. To Mary, the best thing of all was that they were all together, and they weren't sharing it with anyone else.

'This is better than I expected,' she said, breaking the silence first. 'But I'd like to know why those people in the yard aren't chained.'

'I can tell you that, me darlin',' James said with a grin. 'It's money. Didn't you ever listen to any of those back in Port Jackson who'd been in here?'

'I listened, but I couldn't understand them,' Mary said, recalling how the Londoners with their flash lingo had sounded as if they came from a foreign land. By the time she'd learned enough of it to understand, they had moved on from talking about their old prisons to their plight in the new one.

'Well, they said you had to pay for what they call "easements",' James said with a shrug. 'They had it in Dublin too. You slip the gaoler something and off come your chains. You can get food brought from outside too.'

Mary nodded. She remembered now that that had also been the case with food and drink back in Exeter.

'I expect if you've got enough money, or at least something to sell, you can have a room on your own and a servant to bring you food and drink,' James said with a hollow laugh. 'But as we haven't got anything, this is all we can expect.'

The men slumped dejectedly down on the floor. Nat fell asleep almost immediately, and Mary was reminded of the women on the *Dunkirk*. Some of them managed to sleep almost round the clock, it was their way of escaping from the cruel reality of prison.

Mary sat down, arranged her chains so they didn't dig into her, and hunched her knees up under her dress. Leaning back against the wall, she considered her friends' plight.

Her own meant nothing to her, she wanted death to rid herself of the mental torment she felt. She might have regained her physical health on the voyage home, but she couldn't recover from the crushing guilt at taking her two children on such a hazardous journey and causing their deaths. Real hell to her was being sent back to New South Wales, and she would escape from it by jumping overboard at the first opportunity.

But the men hadn't become reconciled to the certainty of hanging. James had some kind of blind faith he was safe, for his original sentence was up now. Sam believed that if he showed enough remorse they would let him off.

Bill and Nat tried to blank out the possibility by sleeping or talking about something else.

Yet seeing London today had sparked something inside Mary. It hadn't made her want to live again, or lessened her grief, but it had brought the men's predicament sharply into focus for her.

None of them were bad men, and they'd already suffered so much. Mary couldn't hope to save them from hanging, but if she could just think of some way to get those 'easements', that might make their last few weeks a great deal more bearable.

She thought about it for over an hour, and then smiled as she came up with a solution.

'What've you got to smirk about?' James asked curiously, moving nearer and squatting down in front of her.

'I've had an idea,' she said.

'If it involves ropes and files, forget it,' he grinned. 'I did an inventory of our belongings before we left the *Gorgon*. We haven't even got a knife between us.'

'I'm glad you've still got your sense of humour,' she said, patting his bony face affectionately. 'That might come in handy for my idea. You see, I've been thinking. If we are famous, maybe we can wring some money out of it.'

Nat continued to sleep, looking like a sweet child in the dim light. But Bill and Sam sat up. James only raised his eyebrows questioningly.

'Will thought he'd make money from our story, that's why he hung on to his log,' Mary explained. 'We've still got all the stories in our heads. So why don't we sell them?'

'To who?' he said sarcastically.

'To anyone who cares to hear them,' she said, feeling a little of her old self coming back now she had a challenge again.

No opportunity presented itself to Mary before it was dark, but the following morning, when she heard the gaoler coming along the row of cells to unlock them so they could empty the night bucket, she was ready.

She brushed the straw off her dress and ran her fingers through her hair as the key turned in the lock.

'Come on, get that bucket emptied,' the gaoler shouted, far more loudly than was necessary. He looked the way Mary remembered the gaolers back in Exeter, fat and unhealthy, with shifty eyes and rotten teeth.

'How much for having the chains struck off?' she asked.

He sucked his rotten teeth, eying her up speculatively. 'That depends.'

'Depends on what?'

'Whether I want to or not,' he replied, and cackled with laughter.

Mary took hold of the front of his greasy shirt menacingly. 'You'd better want to,' she hissed at him. 'We've fought with cannibals and killed animals with our bare hands, and we're going to hang for daring to escape from New South Wales. So we won't think twice about slitting your throat. Now, do you want to be our friend or our enemy?'

His eyes rolled back in his head in alarm. Mary couldn't see the men behind her, but she had to hope they were doing as she'd ordered and looking fierce.

'W-w-what's in it for me?' he stuttered.

'That depends on how you go about it,' she said. She let go of him and smiled sweetly. 'I want you to put the word about that we're ready to receive visitors. They'll have to pay of course. Enough for the shackles to come off, for food, drink and hot water to wash with.'

It was a gamble. Mary had no real idea if anyone in the prison or outsiders visiting it had enough interest in them to pay for the privilege of meeting them.

'I don't know,' he said, still looking scared. 'Did you say cannibals?'

'I did, they had metal-tipped arrows this long,' she said, holding her arms out wide.

'I'll see,' he said, and moved back as if to lock the door.

Mary grabbed the night bucket. 'Empty this before you go,' she said, and thrust it at him. 'Rinse it out before you bring it back,' she added, 'I don't like the smell.'

He walked away with it as meekly as a child ordered to go and buy bread, and Mary turned to the men and giggled. 'I think we've got a deal,' she said.

By noon the shackles were off, they were eating mutton pies, and had a large flagon of small beer between them. The gaoler, whom they now knew as Spinks, was as resourceful as he was greedy, and they had already received two groups of four people, all desperate to meet the escapees and hear about the cannibals.

James was the story-teller and he did it well, embellishing the true story about the native warriors who chased them in a war canoe, to hand-to-hand fighting on land.

'In their village they had dozens of human skulls on poles,' James lied cheerfully. 'We saw piles of human bones. They wore the teeth as necklaces and used human skin to cover their shields.'

After the second group left, Mary and the men dissolved into laughter.

'Well, they could've been cannibals,' James said indignantly. 'I mean, we didn't stay around for long enough to find out, did we?'

Mary thought how good the sound of laughter was, which she hadn't heard since they were captured in Kupang. Even on the *Gorgon* they'd been very subdued. Yet she couldn't help feeling just a twinge of sadness that Will wasn't still with them. He would've loved an opportunity to tell such tales, and he would probably have made it even more exciting than James had done.

'You are a wonder, Mary,' Sam said a little later, as he licked his fingers clean of the meat pie. 'None of us could have thought up such a cunning plan. When James got to that bit about you hitting one of the cannibals over the head with an oar, I almost believed you'd really done it. I reckon you'd think of something to save us even if they were just putting us in the cooking pot.'

Mary smiled. It was good to have the men's admiration again. And even better to see them lifted out of their gloom. 'We mustn't go too far with the stories,' she warned them. 'We want sympathy, not people calling us liars.'

It was on the following day that they discovered how the other prisoners had found out about them. A forger by the name of Harry Hawkins came to see them. Like many others in Newgate, he expected to be transported. He was a slimy character, small and thin, with a beak-like nose and strangely unkempt long hair for a man who dressed well.

'I read about you in the *London Chronicle*,' he said, and proceeded to prove it by fishing a dog-eared cutting from his pocket.

All of them had assumed the news about them had merely passed by word of mouth, that was the usual way in prisons. It was a shock to find someone had written about them in a newspaper.

James read it aloud, then passed it back. 'It's not completely accurate. It was the Governor's boat we stole, not Captain Smith's,' he said airily.

Mary was astounded that James could be so blasé about such a florid and admiring account of their escape.

'Who wrote it?' she asked. She hadn't for one moment expected anyone in England to be sympathetic to them.

'It don't say,' James replied, looking at it again. 'But whoever it was, he knows a lot. He might have got it wrong about who owned the cutter. But everything else is right.'

The five friends had no further chance then to discuss where all this information came from, because Harry Hawkins wanted to talk about his plight. It was clear that what he wanted from them was inside information about officials in Botany Bay.

It amused Mary somewhat that this man, and everyone else waiting for transportation, still thought the settlement was in Botany Bay. Apparently no one here knew that place had been rejected by Captain Phillip. In fact it seemed that very little information had yet reached England about the colony. Mary suspected most of it had been withheld purposely as the government wouldn't want to publicize their terrible mistakes. That made the situation even better for her and her friends.

'It isn't like this place,' she said with a wry smile. 'You can't buy a better hut or bigger rations, the only way you can advance yourself is by having a skill they need.'

Hawkins looked disappointed. 'But you must've had some inside help, or slipped someone a back-hander!' he retorted.

'We didn't,' James said indignantly. 'It was all down to Mary charming the Dutch sea captain for the navigational instruments and charts.'

Hawkins gave her a disbelieving look and Mary blushed. She supposed he couldn't imagine a plain and worn-looking woman being able to charm anyone.

'The captain was lonely,' she said by way of an explanation. 'Me and my husband used to talk to him. He would come and have supper with us sometimes.'

'So he'll be the one who paid for you to have this cell?' Hawkins asked with a touch of sarcasm.

Mary and her cellmates looked askance at each other.

'Paid for this cell?' James exclaimed. 'No one paid for it.'

'Someone did, before you even got here,' Hawkins said, looking a bit uncomfortable. 'You'd have been put on the common side otherwise.'

An hour later, when Hawkins left, Mary turned to her friends. 'Who could have paid for it?' she asked them.

Hawkins had been happy to explain the prison system to them. Everyone, unless someone had intervened on their behalf prior to their arrival, got put in with the common criminals, hence the name 'common side'. These cells were filthy, stuffed to capacity and hotbeds of infection. The prisoners were at the mercy of the insane and the dangerous, and you'd be lucky to wake to find you still had your boots on your feet. Young women and boys were certain to be raped on their first night, and rarely by only one person.

Hawkins then went on to explain that as long as a prisoner had some money or goods to sell they could buy their way into somewhere cleaner and safer, and get the extras they'd already discovered for themselves. The merriment in the courtyard was proof of all this; the people they'd seen were either wealthy or had rich and influential friends. But once a prisoner had run out of money, it was back to the common side for him or her.

Hawkins had cited a highwayman who had his own feather bed brought in, hot water for a bath brought up to him each morning, his shirt laundered, meals with fine wine, and during the afternoons he was visited by his mistress. He was eventually hanged, but as Hawkins pointed out, bribes couldn't get you out of everything.

'Do any of you know *anyone* in London?' Mary asked the men in bewilderment. None of them had any idea who their mysterious benefactor could be.

'I used to know a few people,' James replied. 'But not the kind who'd even buy me a pint of ale, let alone a decent cell.'

'Maybe it was someone who felt sorry for us after reading that in the *Chronicle*?' Sam suggested.

'That would be it,' Bill said, stroking his beard thoughtfully. 'There was a man murdered in Berkshire when I was a boy, he left a wife and five children, and when people heard the story they sent money for them.'

'That's fair enough. But who told the story about us in the first place?' James asked, looking puzzled. 'That paper was four or five days old. We were still on the ship in the English Channel. How could they have got the story?'

'Someone must have talked when the ship docked at Portsmouth,' Sam said, and his face broke into a wide grin. 'Captain Edwards left then, and he would have informed the authorities about us. A big number of people left the ship there too, anyone of them could've talked to a newspaper.'

All at once Mary realized the story could only have come from Watkin Tench. Captain Edwards had no sympathy with them or the mutineers he'd caught, so any information from him would have cast them in a very bad light. As for any of the other officers who went ashore at Portsmouth, their accounts wouldn't have been so accurate.

Tench would also know about corruption in prisons

from his time on the *Dunkirk*, and how to go about fixing a cell for them in Newgate.

Instantly Mary decided to say nothing to the others. She was a little surprised they hadn't considered Tench, but then none of them had been as closely involved with him as she had. To tell them what she thought now would only raise questions she didn't want to answer. Besides, if Tench had done it in secret, he wanted it to stay that way – it might put his career at risk if it got out. Better that they continued to think it was a benevolent stranger.

'Luck's smiling on us again,' James chortled gleefully, not even noticing Mary had made no comment about it all. 'Maybe if the money keeps rolling in we'll end up like that highwayman, sleeping in feather beds.'

'Bless you, Watkin,' Mary thought, and she had to turn away from the others so they didn't see the tears of gratitude in her eyes.

In the days that followed they had many visitors to their cell. Some wanted to hear only of their escape, but more were facing transportation themselves and wanted to know what to expect.

Mary felt a little guilty that they were taking money from these people. It was bad enough for them to face parting from their loved ones, without compounding their misery by telling them of the dreaded flogging triangle, of hunger and unremitting heat. But as James said, it was better for them to spend some of their money on preparation for what lay in store for them than to drink it away, and she supposed he was right.

The first time they were allowed out into the prison yard, Mary felt she was entering a select party. People greeted them with genuine warmth, offering drink from the tap-room, advice and friendship. James and the three other men accepted this with alacrity, especially the overtures from women prisoners. But Mary hung back.

While it felt good to be admired, rather than scorned or pitied, her emotions were too raw to want to talk and laugh with strangers, however well-meaning. All she wanted was to sit quietly in the sun, but this was denied her, for everyone wanted something of her.

Some were after details of the escape, others asked her about their friends and relatives who had been transported, some women even wanted to know her experiences in childbirth. Then there were men either trying to court her or making lewd suggestions.

Within a few hours Mary had seen and heard enough. She didn't want to be a performer in this circus, or even part of the audience.

She had never before considered her feelings about the criminal world which she'd belonged to for so many years. Whether on the prison hulk, on the ship or in the penal colony, she was just another convict serving her time, doing whatever was needed to survive. As such she was loyal to her fellow prisoners, covering up, aiding and abetting sometimes in thefts from the stores and other wrong-doing, because that was the code by which they all lived.

But losing both her children had opened her mind wider.

She had never really been sorry she stole that woman's bonnet in Plymouth. She was sorry she was caught, angry with herself for being so reckless. But she'd never put herself in that woman's shoes and imagined how it was for her to be struck and robbed.

Now, when she thought about it, Mary felt deeply ashamed. She wasn't actually starving at the time, she didn't need the bonnet. She could look back on good people she'd known in her childhood, like Martha Dingwell in the baker's who gave the unsold bread at the end of the day to those unable to buy any, or Charlie Allsop, the gravedigger, who would do little unpaid jobs for the bereaved, his way of showing his sympathy. These two, and others like them, had little enough themselves, and there were those who had sneered at them. But Mary could see now that the Marthas and Charlies of this world enriched life. Criminals only made it frightening and ugly, contaminating everything with their selfish lust for money and goods they hadn't worked for.

As she looked around the prison yard, all she could see was people who cared for nothing but themselves. They had no remorse about lying, cheating, stealing or killing. The fact that they had money to bribe their way out here to boast drunkenly about their crimes proved that.

These were, she thought, without doubt some of London's worst villains and thugs, hard-bitten whores and the most cunning of thieves. Whether from wealthy backgrounds or the gutter, they all used that flash lingo, the underworld language she'd become so familiar with in the colony. She could also sense a dangerous undercurrent flowing around in the yard – jealousy, sexual frustration, pent-up violence and unsettled old scores, simmering as people drank.

Mary was no prude. She knew drink was a powerful remedy for alleviating misery and fear. But however desperate she felt, she knew she would never sell herself for a glass or two of gin, and allow the sexual act to take place in full public view. That was what some women were doing, and with their own children looking on.

She had averted her eyes several times during the afternoon as men rutted like beasts with women so drunk they were almost unconscious, but it appeared some of them had a taste for children too. An elderly woman, who came and sat by Mary for a while, told her that some of the men bribed the gaolers to bring them a constant fresh supply of children from the common side. She had cackled with laughter, and Mary might not have believed it, but later she saw a burly man fondling a ragged little girl of no more than six.

Mary's heart ached at the number of young girls in the yard. They reminded her of herself at the same age – the same fresh complexions, that same curious mix of innocence and courage. They were too busy flirting with the more gentlemanly prisoners to talk to her. Perhaps they thought the elegantly dressed fops would take them with them when they bribed their way out of Newgate.

Mary knew better. The girls would have lost their innocence after a week or two in here, and their courage would fail them on the transportation ships. A few years out in Sydney and they'd look like her. A bag of bones, all hope and spirit gone.

They had all been in Newgate for over a week when Spinks came to the cell and told Mary a gentleman wanted to see her.

Mary had struck up a wary kind of friendship with Spinks. She couldn't really like him, he was too wily, always on the lookout for a way to bleed money out of the prisoners. Yet when he'd found out about her children dying he'd shown real sympathy. He often came along when she was alone, sometimes bringing her a mug of tea or a piece of fruit, and for these there was no charge, he just wanted to chat for a while. Perhaps he was as lonely as she was.

Spinks found her alone more often than not, for after seeing a stabbing on her second visit to the yard, she had decided the gloomy cell was a better place to be. She was alone that day too, for the men were all down in the yard.

'Who is this gentleman?' she asked. Spinks called all men with money 'gentlemen'.

'By the name of Boswell,' he replied with a smug grin. ''E said 'e's a lawyer.'

'You mean he's from outside Newgate?'

'Well, we don't get many lawyers staying in 'ere,' Spinks retorted, and laughed at his little joke. 'Now, do yer want ter see 'im or not? Makes no difference to me.'

Mary sighed. She didn't feel like talking to anyone, but someone from outside might distract her from her melancholy. 'Bring him up,' she said wearily.

'That's my girl,' Spinks said affectionately. 'Now, why don't you comb that pretty 'air of yours while I'm gone? Look, I've brought you a ribbon fer it too.'

He pulled a red satin ribbon from his pocket, thrust it into her hand and was gone. A lump came up in Mary's throat as she ran it between her fingers, remembering her father. He always brought her and Dolly ribbon when he came back from sea. She'd been such a tomboy then, and she never really appreciated it. But she did appreciate this one; she needed something bright and feminine to cheer her.

'Good afternoon, Mrs Bryant!'

Mary spun round at the sound of the melodious voice. She was so engrossed in tying the ribbon at the nape of her neck that she hadn't heard the man coming along the landing.

Spinks was right for once, this one was a gentleman. Perhaps fifty or so, very stout with a red-tinged face, of middling height and wearing very fine clothes – a dark green three-cornered hat trimmed with gold braid, and a coat made of fine brocade. He was also out of breath and wheezing from the stairs.

'I'm known as Mary Broad now,' she said sharply, glancing down at his spotless white stockings and shoes with fancy buckles. 'Why have you come to see me?'

'I want to help you, my dear,' he said, and held out his hand. 'Boswell's the name, James Boswell. I am a lawyer, though better known for my book on Dr Samuel Johnson, my dear departed friend.'

Mary recognized his accent as being Scottish, for there had been a couple of officers in Port Jackson who spoke just the same. But the part about his book on his dead friend meant nothing to her. She was more impressed by his gold watch-chain and extravagant silk waistcoat. She thought even the King couldn't be dressed so well.

She shook his hand, and was astounded by any man having one so soft. It felt like a piece of warm dough. 'I'm beyond help,' she said. 'But it's kind of you to offer me some when I am unable to even offer you a chair.'

He smiled, and she noticed his eyes were large and almost luminous dark pools. As he wore a wig, she couldn't see what colour his hair was, but she guessed by his bushy eyebrows it had once been as dark as hers.

'I don't believe you are beyond help,' Boswell said stoutly. 'I wish to defend you. So I would suggest you tell me your story. All I know is the extraordinary tale I read in the *Chronicle*.'

Chapter eighteen

James Boswell strode away from Newgate prison, his feathers ruffled because Mary hadn't fallen at his feet and seen him as her saviour. It hadn't for one moment occurred to him that she wouldn't welcome his offer of help.

'Damn her,' he muttered. 'A heroine she may be, but she's clearly lacking a brain.'

A dear friend had once claimed years ago that 'Bozzie' was addicted to lost causes. He was referring to his passion for whores in that instance, but it was a well-known fact that Boswell was extraordinarily sympathetic to anyone he considered was being treated unjustly. He had often defended poor people without charge, and took on cases that no one else would.

In truth, nothing excited him more than a case everyone said he couldn't win, or a woman who was hell-bent on self-destruction. And Mary Broad was both rolled into one.

What all his worthy friends who poked fun at him didn't really appreciate was that he felt he had a great deal in common with his clients and his whores. He knew what it was to be forced into an unwanted career; he was often misunderstood, he made errors of judgement, and he was reckless.

His father, Lord Auchinleck, a judge in the Supreme Courts in Scotland, had insisted his son become a lawyer, despite his desire to join the Guards. As soon as he'd finished school, Boswell ran away to London and became a Roman Catholic, which appalled his dour Presbyterian family. Indeed, he flirted briefly with the idea of becoming a monk too. But a Catholic couldn't become an Army officer or a barrister, nor even inherit his father's estate, so he soon abandoned Catholicism and reluctantly went along with his father's wishes and entered the Inns of Court. But this wasn't a real change of heart, it was more so he could stay in London and use his allowance to cut a dash in society.

Boswell himself would concede that he was a poor student. He spent more time in the theatre, at the races, and drinking and picking up women than he did at his studies. His father also expected him to make an advantageous marriage, but Boswell disappointed him there too by marrying his cousin Margaret, who had no money of her own. But he married for love, and that to him was far more important than money.

Then his friendship with Samuel Johnson was misunderstood. People claimed he was worming his way into the great man's affections for self-advancement. They said Boswell was a snob, a social climber, a womanizer, a drunk and a hypochondriac.

It was true that he liked women and wine. He couldn't resist a pretty chambermaid or whore, but surely that was only the sign of a zest for life? What his critics failed to see and understand was that he spent the greater part of his life planning, compiling and collecting material for his work, *The Life of Samuel Johnson*. To do it justice he had to enter into the circles that Johnson moved in, to watch, listen, and see through Johnson's eyes. He enjoyed it of course, and maybe he did make use of some of the contacts he made. But he never used Johnson's friendship for self-advancement; he loved the man, and wanted the whole world to share his wisdom, intelligence and humour.

In his heart, Boswell knew he had produced a brilliant biography of his friend, and he was sure that in years to come his name would be up there with other great literary figures. Even if he wasn't getting the kind of rapturous praise and adulation that he felt he was due, he had made a considerable amount of money from his book. He had an elegant home just off Oxford Street, and fine clothes. He ate and drank well, had a great many friends, and his beloved children were a great comfort to him. All in all, he supposed that should be enough for any man.

Yet he still had a yen to do something sensational before putting down his pen and hanging up his wig and gown. He was fifty-two, widowed, no longer in the best of health, and time was running out for him. He wanted to be remembered as 'the Greatest Biographer of All Time', but it would give him immense satisfaction to confound those who considered him a mediocre lawyer too. To win one big, dramatic case was all he wanted; to be looked back on as a man who was the champion of the weak and oppressed.

Boswell smiled to himself, aware that he was being somewhat egotistical. It was absurd really that he felt so strongly about the case of Mary Broad, for until this very morning he had known nothing of her and her companions' plight. To be strictly truthful, something his father had been a stickler for, he had never before even considered the welfare of the felons sentenced to transportation.

In his view transportation was both humane and practical, for it removed criminals to a place where they could do no more harm to society. A far better solution than hanging. When he was a young man he had watched the public execution of a highwayman and a young thief called Hannah Diego, and the horror of it had never left him.

Yet there he was that morning, drinking a leisurely cup of coffee at home and reading the newspaper, merely passing some time before visiting his publishers to see how his book was selling, when he happened to come across an account of the escape from Botany Bay.

It was the quote from Mary herself which captured his interest. 'I'd sooner be hanged than sent back there.'

Clearly Botany Bay wasn't quite the tropical paradise which the newspapers had led most people to believe. Boswell had to read on.

He was shaken that Mary, eight men and two small children had sailed some 3,000 miles in an open boat. Even more disturbing was that four of the men had died after capture. But it was the loss of the two children which really plucked at his heart. As a man who adored his children, and felt blessed that they were all close to him, he couldn't imagine anything more tragic than to lose even one of them. This poor woman had lost everything, her husband and her children, and now she was likely to lose her life too.

In his mind's eye he again saw Hannah Diego struggling as she was dragged to the hangman's noose. He could smell her fear, hear the ghoulish roars from the watching crowd, and remembered the nightmares he'd suffered for so long after that day.

He felt a surge of sickness and anger. He couldn't stand by and let Mary Broad share that fate. It was barbaric. She had suffered enough.

Boswell was also curious about the character of the woman. She surely had immense courage and determination to lead those men to freedom, such strength to survive fever and starvation. He wanted to know more, to meet and talk to her. With that he suddenly put down the paper, called for his coat and hat, and set out for Newgate.

In his imagination, Boswell had pictured Mary Broad as a big woman, strong and lusty, just like his favourite whores. It was something of a surprise to find her small, thin and softly spoken. She looked old beyond her years too, weighed down with grief, her grey eyes already showing a resignation to death.

She told him her story very simply, as if she was weary of recounting it yet again. There was no attempt at trying to gain his sympathy, no shocking details of hardship, deprivation or cruelty. The only time tears sprang to her eyes was when she spoke of Charlotte's burial at sea. Even those she brushed away quickly, and went on to say that she was treated with kindness on the *Gorgon*.

Boswell found himself immensely touched, sensing all the horror Mary had left out. He had been in Newgate many times before, so he had come prepared for lies, exaggerations and distortions of the truth. Like most of his contemporaries, he believed in a criminal class, a stratum of people who were pre-ordained to undermine a decent society. They could be identified easily by their brutish manner, their idleness and their lack of principles. Down in the prison yard he'd seen so many of them, strutting around as if in a private and very select club.

Mary certainly wasn't one of them. She had more in common with the debtors, who sat disconsolately in small groups, bitterly ashamed of the events which had brought them into prison, all hope and spirit gone.

Yet the shiny red ribbon in Mary's dark hair, which was a little incongruous when her dress was so shabby and stained, suggested that the indomitable spirit which had kept her alive through so much hardship was still there, even if subdued for now. She'd asked boldly if he was prepared to defend her four friends too. When he'd stated that he felt it was only her cause he could fight, she'd turned away as if the interview was over.

'Then I cannot accept your help,' she'd said finally. 'We are all in this together, they are my friends, and I will not abandon them.'

It was inconceivable to Boswell that anyone in such desperate straits would put friendship before her own life. He pleaded with her, explained that he could win her case as public sympathy would be on her side because of her children. What he also thought, but couldn't admit, was that he saw her trial as a kind of showcase for his talents. He wanted it to be emotionally charged, he saw himself making a dramatic and heart-rending closing speech. But if he had to defend the four men too, all of whom were probably dubious characters, the sympathy he'd built up for Mary would be very much diluted.

'I have nothing left now but those four friends,' she said simply. 'We have been through hell together, and they are like brothers to me. I'll take my chances with them.'

'Do you think they would do the same for you?' he asked her. 'I think not, Mary, each one of them would do anything to save his own skin, regardless of what happened to you.'

'Maybe,' she sighed. 'There was a time when my own survival counted for more than anything else on this earth. But that's in the past. I don't value it very highly any more.'

James was impressed by her sense of honour, but he supposed she'd lost her common sense along with her spirit.

'Just how are you going to restore her spirit, Bozzie?' he asked himself, tipping his hat to a pretty maid walking with an elderly chaperone.

He paused and turned to look back at the girl, noting her tiny waist, the pert bow on the bustle of her pink gown and her bonnet trimmed with daisies. Veronica and Euphemia, his two older daughters, had many such gowns and bonnets, and nothing cheered them more than new ones. Perhaps Mary would begin to hope again with something pretty to wear?

The air in the small cell in Newgate was tense, the four men staring at Mary with cold, suspicious eyes.

'Don't look at me that way,' she said indignantly. 'The only reason I didn't tell you of his visit was because he can't help us.'

The men had come back to the cell late in the afternoon and they were all very drunk. Had they been sober she would probably have told them about the visit from Mr Boswell, but while they slept off the drink she came to the conclusion that there was nothing to be gained from such a disclosure. Mr Boswell only wanted to help her, not them, and if she told them that they'd only be hurt.

Unfortunately she hadn't realized that a visitor from outside would attract so much attention and speculation among both prisoners and gaolers. By the time the men sobered up and went back to the tap-room, it seemed the whole prison was talking about the lawyer gentleman who'd called on her.

'What scheme are you cooking up?' James burst out, his lean face flushed with anger.

'There is no scheme,' Mary retorted. 'Spinks brought

him here, he was curious about us all, but not interested enough to defend us.'

'You let a lawyer come and go without getting me?' James roared at her. 'I could have made him interested.'

Mary shrugged. 'When you were drunk? He would have been even less inclined to help us.'

'I can hold my drink, talk anyone round, drunk or sober,' James snarled. 'I'll wager you didn't even try to persuade him. You might welcome a rope around your neck, but none of us do.'

Mary looked appealingly towards the other three. 'Surely you know I'd do anything in my power to help you? Has cheap gin rotted your minds?'

They all looked a trifle sheepish.

'But James is right, you should have come and got us,' Bill said mulishly. 'He's the one who is good with words. You just don't care any more.'

'I might not care about myself, but I care about you,' Mary retorted heatedly. 'And if you want to know, I think you are becoming like everyone else in this place, drinking yourselves stupid and fucking anything that moves.'

'Is this man coming back again?' Nat asked hopefully.

'I doubt it,' she said curtly. 'There's nothing he can do for us.'

They heard Spinks coming down the passage, locking the cell doors for the night. Mary retreated over to her corner of the cell and lay down, hoping that the fast-fading light would put an end to the bitterness. James and Bill carried on talking for some time in low voices. Mary didn't even attempt to listen for she was bone-tired and dejected.

Mr Boswell had been such a nice man. Apart from Tench, no other man had ever shown such a keen interest in her. Maybe she ought to have tried a bit harder to persuade him to help all of them? What if she'd pleaded tearfully, clung to him, or even offered herself to him?

'No man would want you, not the way you look now,' she thought to herself. She knew without even seeing herself in a looking-glass that she was no prize. Exposure to hot sun and wind and a poor diet had made her prematurely old; she had no curves, no softness about her. Even Sam, who she knew had had romantic feelings about her in the past, seemed to have lost them since their capture in Kupang.

She could hear a woman screaming in the distance. It sounded like the agony of childbirth and it made Mary's stomach contract in sympathy. It seemed so strange to hear that after all the terrible things she'd seen in the past years, the hurts and humiliations, she still felt others' pain. She ought to be entirely numb by now, unconcerned whether a newborn baby would survive. But she did still care; each time she passed the doorway to the common side of the prison, she felt guilty that those poor wretches were starving, filthy and sick, while she was able to go outside, eat, drink and sleep in a decent cell.

The screaming stopped suddenly. Mary wondered if that was because the mother had finally delivered, or had died. Perhaps for her sake she should hope it was the latter, for the woman's troubles would surely only increase if she lived.

Three days passed, and slowly the men returned to their old easy manner towards Mary. On the fourth day they were taken to the court to be brought before the magistrate, Mr Nicholas Bond.

All five of them had become very nervous as soon as their chains were put back on. Then, as the prison cart rumbled through the crowded, noisy streets, nervousness turned to terror at what lay ahead. Nat's blue eyes were wide with fear, Bill clenched his fists so hard his knuckles were white, Sam appeared to be muttering a prayer. Even James was silenced for once, and when the cart was suddenly surrounded by a horde of people, all shouting at them, he clutched at Mary's hand.

All at once Mary realized this wasn't a mob baying for their blood, quite the reverse. Their shouts were 'Bravo', 'Good luck' and 'God go with you'.

Someone threw a sprig of white heather into the cart. Mary picked it up and smiled. 'They are on our side,' she gasped.

They had all got used to their notoriety in Newgate, but it hadn't occurred to them that their story would be of interest to ordinary people too. Clearly it was, and had touched their hearts too, for so many to have made their way towards the court to show their solidarity with Mary and her four friends.

*

As they were led up to the dock, they saw that the gloomy and dusty courtroom was packed to capacity with spectators. Among them Mary glimpsed James Boswell.

'Mr Boswell's here,' she whispered to James, assuming he and the others would start on at her again if she said nothing. 'The fat man in the fancy jacket.'

James looked, half smiled at the man and passed on the whispered message to the others.

The magistrate, who had a thin face and spectacles perched on the end of a very sharp nose, questioned them one by one, and seemed remarkably attentive to their replies. This in itself was a further surprise, for all five of them had experienced complete indifference from their judges during the trials which led to their transportation. And they all knew people who were shoved through the courts and sentenced without any real evidence or witnesses being produced.

When it came to Mary's turn, the magistrate was far more than just attentive, he was clearly truly interested and committed to getting a real picture of the events. Nervous as she was, she looked right at him and spoke in a clear voice. The only time her voice cracked was when she was questioned about the deaths of her children.

'It was all my idea to escape,' she admitted. 'I planned it and got hold of the charts and navigational equipment. I bullied my husband Will into going along with it, and made him persuade the others to join us.'

She sensed the men looking sideways at her. Clearly they were surprised she should put herself forward as the instigator.

'How long were you planning this escape before you actually left the colony?' the magistrate asked, peering at her intently.

'It was in my mind to escape almost from my first day there,' she said. 'But it was when my husband was flogged for nothing more than keeping back a couple of fish he'd caught that I became determined we should go. We were starving, people were dying all around us, yet my Will, the only man who was supplying any food, got a hundred lashes. It wasn't right.'

His questions went on and on, and Mary answered them all truthfully. Finally the magistrate asked her if she had repented of the crime that sent her to New South Wales.

'Indeed I have, sir,' she replied. 'Not a day went by out there when I didn't regret it.'

A murmur of approval at her words rippled round the courtroom.

'But tell me, why did you choose to risk your two small children's lives on such a long and perilous journey in uncharted seas?' he asked.

'The perils were every bit as great in the colony,' she said resolutely. 'I believed it was better for us all to die together in the sea than to die slowly one by one of starvation or some terrible disease.'

The murmur of approval from the spectators became a roar. When the noise had died down, the magistrate announced that he was not ready yet to commit them to trial and so they would be returned to the prison and brought before him again for further examination in a week's time.

As the five were led away, they were bombarded with more shouts of sympathy. They were put into a cell beneath the court to await their return to Newgate.

'Can you believe that crowd?' James said gleefully, his eyes dancing the way they used to back in Kupang. 'They are all on our side. Surely we won't hang now?'

Mary said nothing. To her, spending a great many more years in prison was a far worse prospect than hanging.

'You were wonderful,' Sam said to her, grinning from ear to ear. 'But you shouldn't have taken all the blame.'

Mary shrugged. 'It was all true, I did bully Will and got him to involve you.'

'You're a brave woman and no mistake,' Bill said in a shaky voice. 'I'm sorry we thought badly of you the other day.'

Before Mary could reply, she suddenly heard the unmistakable sound of Mr Boswell's voice. He was at the end of the stone passageway, demanding to be let in to see her. Mary's heart sank. If he made another offer to defend her in front of the men they would think her a liar.

All at once he was there in front of the grid, resplendent in a dark blue jacket and embroidered waistcoat, his round red face wreathed in smiles.

'Mary, my dear, you gave such a good account of yourself,' he boomed out joyfully. 'The crowd took you to their hearts. Within days people everywhere will read the newspapers' report on today's events, and everyone in England will be behind you.'

'Not just me, I hope,' she managed to say, hoping he'd have the sense to realize her predicament with the men. 'We are all in it together, and you haven't yet met my friends.'

'Of course, of course. They felt for you all up there,' he said, then held out a box containing a considerable sum of money. 'There was a collection for you to help with expenses while you are in Newgate. I am overjoyed for you all.'

James introduced himself and the other men. 'Does this mean you are prepared to defend us now?' he asked, taking the box from Boswell's hand.

'Now that the public has joined Mary in twisting my arm, I have reconsidered and think I can defend you men too, that is, if Mary is prepared to reconsider.' Boswell beamed, looking to each of the men's faces and apparently not seeing Mary's frantic gestures from behind them. 'I hope you appreciate your loyal friend! And now we must talk about the next stage. I believe there is no possibility of the death penalty now, just prison. But I'm determined to get you all a pardon.'

He didn't wait to see how they took this news, but carried on, 'I'll be there for all of you next week, and meanwhile I'm going to see Henry Dundas, the Home Secretary. He's a dear friend of mine.'

The moment Boswell had gone, James let out a whoop of joy and jingled the box of money. 'He knows the Home Secretary,' he gloated. 'And people made a collection for us. We're going to be set free!'

444

Sam looked at Mary reflectively, making her blush. 'He offered to defend you alone and you turned him down, didn't you?' he asked in an awed voice.

The other three men frowned, not understanding. Nat asked Sam what he was talking about.

'Don't you see?' Sam shook his head at their stupidity. 'That lawyer wasn't here by chance. He came to see Mary again. The reason she didn't tell us about his visit the other day was because he only wanted to defend her. She turned him down because of us!'

'You did that?' Nat said, his blue eyes wide with incredulity.

'Holy Mother of God,' James exclaimed. 'And we laid into you!'

Mary blushed furiously. 'It doesn't matter now,' she murmured.

'It does matter, Mary,' Sam said, putting his arm around her. 'That crowd up there collected the money for us because of what you said in the dock. I'm sure that's why the lawyer changed his mind about us too. Once again you've saved our lives.'

Mary couldn't sleep at all that night for her mind was whirling with 'what ifs'. What if they stayed in prison for months or even years until the public lost interest in their fate? They would never get a pardon then. What if Boswell was just a braggart like Will and didn't really know the Home Secretary? What if she did get pardoned? Where would she go, and how would she live?

If the public's imagination was fired up about her plight

as Mr Boswell said, then her family would be bound to hear of it. Her mother would surely die of shame to know her daughter's name was in the newspapers. Mary couldn't help but be amused to think of her worrying about that, after all she'd been through. But her mother's feelings were still very important to her. And she badly wanted to see her and the rest of her family.

At the second hearing in the magistrates' court, the five returned escapees were told officially that they would not be hanged. They were to receive an indeterminate sentence without a trial. To the men this was good enough; they had fame and enough money to be comfortable in Newgate, which after some of the other prisons they'd been in was paradise. It would of course be wonderful if Boswell got them pardoned, but they weren't counting on it.

But Mary couldn't see it the same way. She wanted to be hanged or to be freed, no half measures. She could wait for freedom, but she needed to know exactly how long it would take before she could walk on grass again, swim in the sea, smell flowers and cook her own meals. She couldn't spend her days in a gin-soaked stupor, the time-honoured way of Newgate.

Boswell was right in saying everyone in England would hear about them. The story had spread far and wide. But Mary took no pleasure from her fame. Each day people came to the prison to meet her. A few were from organizations who were firmly against transportation, others were journalists, but in the main they were just curious people, wanting to look at the woman who was in the news as if she was a freak in a side show.

Mary couldn't refuse to meet any of these people. She knew she and the men were dependent on public opinion to get a pardon. But it was painful to keep on telling and retelling the story, and have people raking up things she would rather forget.

James loved it all, especially the grand ladies who kept returning to visit him. Mary knew they didn't really care about his plight. Visiting Newgate was a diversion from their otherwise dull lives; it was exciting to go somewhere so dirty and dangerous. James turned on his Irish charm and he flirted with them, telling them shocking things they could repeat in whispers to less daring friends over afternoon tea. In return they brought him food, new clothes and books. He had also made a start on writing an account of their escape which he hoped he could sell for enough money to go back to Ireland and breed horses.

As for Nat, Bill and Sam, they felt important for the first time in their lives. They too had women admirers, and as each day passed they seemed to need Mary less.

Then there was Mr Boswell. Mary liked him – he was clever, entertaining and very kind – but she didn't know what he wanted of her.

James Martin had made it his business to find out everything about the man, and some of it was a little frightening. While he was a famous and much admired writer, and mixed with the aristocracy, he was also a rake who drank heavily and consorted with whores. He might be a good and loving father to his children, but it was said he neglected his wife, to the extent that he hadn't gone home to Scotland when she was dying. He wasn't even considered a very good lawyer.

Mary thought he was similar to Will in character. He gave the impression of great capability, of intelligence and daring, just as Will did. Of course Mr Boswell was much older, well-educated and a gentleman, but if she could strip him of his years, his book learning and fine clothes, he and Will had a great deal in common. He talked of friends in high places, but were they really friends or just passing acquaintances? He boasted, too, of cases he'd won in courts, and of his success with women, and how he was a descendant of Robert the Bruce.

But Mary could smell drink on him, whatever time of day he visited her, and the redness of his complexion was a sure sign he over-indulged in it. Drink had been Will's weakness too, and she couldn't forget the part it had played in their downfall.

Yet during Boswell's visits Mary believed in him totally. It was so easy to, for his melodious voice with just a hint of a Scots accent was easy on the ear. He painted a new world for her of dinner parties, ladies' gowns and country houses. He made her laugh with his vivid descriptions of people he knew. Yet for all that showiness his kindness was apparent too. He hated injustice, he had real understanding of weakness, especially in women. He loved children, he wanted a fairer society, and schools for the poor.

While he was with her, the room felt warm and full

of light, his conversation stimulated her, she felt hopeful. But the moment he'd gone, the shadows came back. What did he really want with her? Somehow she couldn't quite believe that he was doing so much just out of kindness. He had to have a motive, people always did.

Early in August, just over a month after they'd arrived in Newgate, he came to see her, this time in a small room downstairs in the prison which was furnished with a table and chairs.

'Dear me, it is *so* hot today,' he began, wheezing from the exertion of his long walk to the prison in the hot sun and wiping his brow with a handkerchief. 'I am off on holiday tomorrow. To Cornwall, my dear, but I have put things in hand on your behalf and it is my belief we shall have good news on my return.'

He launched into an explanation about a letter to Henry Dundas, to which he still hadn't received a reply. It seemed to Mary that his earlier claims at what a good friend this man was were probably exaggerated.

But then Boswell put the brown parcel he was carrying down on the table. 'Something for you, my dear. It isn't new, but I hope it will cheer you.'

Mary opened it, and gasped in surprise to find it was a dress, probably a cast-off from one of his daughters, she thought. It was pale blue and the low neckline was trimmed with white lace.

'It's lovely,' she said, blushing with embarrassment. It was in fact the kind of dress any woman would dream about, but it was surely intended for a lady of quality taking afternoon tea or a walk in a park, not for a prisoner in Newgate who had lice in her hair. 'Thank you so much, Mr Boswell, but I'm not sure it's suitable for me.'

'My friends call me Bozzie,' he said reprovingly. 'I consider you a friend. And of course it's suitable for you, you are still a young woman, and with freedom ahead of you. I shall enjoy seeing you wear it.'

'Will I really be freed?' she said, putting the dress to one side and sitting down. 'And if I am, what will I do?'

'I am certain you will walk free,' he said firmly. 'And I am your friend, so I shall make arrangements for somewhere for you to stay. It will give me great pleasure to be able to show you London properly.'

'I couldn't expect you to do that, sir,' she said, a little alarmed. 'I'd be more than happy to get a job as a housemaid or seamstress.'

He put one of his soft podgy hands over hers. 'You will need a little pampering before you can work,' he said, looking into her eyes. 'You are skin and bone, you need feeding up, a tonic to purge your blood. You will also have to learn London ways.'

Mary had a sudden, sharp picture of Lieutenant Graham. Did Mr Boswell believe he was going to take her as a mistress?

While she knew that if he did get her pardoned her gratitude would compel her to go along with it, the thought revolted her. He was fat, his breath smelled of drink, and she didn't think she could even bear to kiss him, let alone lie with him.

'I must make my own way in the world,' she said after a second's thought. 'I am so grateful to you, Bozzie, but if I do leave here, I shan't lean on you.'

He laughed, and tickled her under the chin. 'Smile for me, Mary. You are a pretty woman when that doleful expression vanishes. Do not be too hasty, for London is a harsh place without a friend.'

He changed the subject then, much to Mary's relief, and spoke of his planned holiday to Cornwall.

Just the mention of Cornwall was enough to evoke vivid mental pictures of home for Mary. It was just about seven years since she'd boarded the boat for Plymouth, and Dolly's words, '*You could travel the whole world and never find a place as pretty as Fowey*', came back to her.

She had travelled the world now, and it was true, she had never seen anywhere so pretty. If she shut her eyes she could see the sea sparkling under the summer sun, smell the seaweed, hear the gulls.

'I've never been to Truro, Falmouth or Land's End,' she said, when Boswell told her these were places he intended to visit.

'No!' he said in surprise. 'Really?'

'You will understand why when you visit them,' she said, and smiled because despite his age he had a very boyish enthusiasm for life. 'They might not be far away in miles from Fowey, but the roads are bad, little more than tracks.'

'There have been riots in Truro,' he said with a sigh. 'The Army had to be called to quell them. But then there have been riots everywhere since you've been away.

England has been affected by the revolution in France, I suspect, so much dissatisfaction and unrest.'

Mary knew Boswell read a great many newspapers. One of the things she liked best about his visits was the chance to talk about what was going on outside the prison walls. She might have her four friends for company, but their conversation was very limited. She was tired of discussing their escape, and the people they knew back in New South Wales, and she had even less interest in discussing the other prisoners here.

'I wish I could read,' she said regretfully. 'I am very ignorant of world affairs.'

He put his hand on hers again. 'Mary, you can learn to read if you wish for that. But do not say you are ignorant, for you have a greater intelligence and wisdom than many people I know who consider themselves clever.'

He got up then. 'I must go now. Try not to fret, and be sure you will be on my mind all the time I am in Cornwall.'

He kissed her on the cheek. 'Wear the dress, Mary, it might make you remember the days before your young life turned sour.'

Mary did wear the dress, a great deal. And Boswell was right, it did make her remember her girlhood. She thought of running to meet Thomas Coogan in Plymouth, the way he used to catch her in his arms and spin her round, and the heady delights of kissing him.

There were no looking-glasses in Newgate, but she could tell by the way men looked at her in the dress that she wasn't as worn and plain as she had previously thought. Knowing that helped her; she found herself thinking of freedom more and more, and despairing sometimes that it would never come.

Chapter nineteen

'What ails you, Mary?' Boswell asked, reaching across the table in the Newgate visiting room to take her hand. 'You've hardly said a word to me today!'

Mary had been imprisoned for seven months now, and it was a bitterly cold February day. She was wearing a man's great-coat, one of two that had been given to James Martin by his lady admirers. She had thick woollen stockings, and mittens on her hands, but she was still so cold she felt she might just die from it. But it wasn't only the cold which was making her so morose, she had lost heart.

'Will we ever get pardoned?' she asked in a small voice. 'Tell me now if it isn't going to happen, Bozzie. I can't go on waiting and hoping like this.'

Each time Boswell came to see her he told her how busy he'd been on her and her friends' behalf. He said he was making a nuisance of himself to everyone, browbeating Henry Dundas and anyone else who was influential. But as the months crawled by, Mary couldn't help but suspect Boswell's promises were empty ones.

'It is seven years now since you were first arrested,' Boswell said gently. 'You have borne that with such fortitude. Surely you can be patient for just a little longer? Or is it that you've lost faith in me?'

Mary didn't want to admit that was the case, for she was very aware of how little she knew of the world outside the prison gates, or of lawyers, judges and Home Secretaries. Boswell tended to talk to her as an equal, telling her about famous people he'd met, parties he'd been to, the theatre or concerts, assuming she knew who or what he was talking about. But how could she? She was an illiterate country girl. The closest she'd come to a concert was seeing a marching band in Plymouth. Not once in her life had she sat down to dinner at a table laid with silver knives, forks and crystal glasses.

When Boswell spoke of Lord Falmouth, Evan Nepean and Henry Dundas, people he was seeing on her behalf, they were just names. She didn't know who or what these people were. For all she knew he could be inventing them to make himself sound busy.

Her father used to have a saying: 'In the kingdom of the blind, the one-eyed man is King.' She had only come to understand what was meant by that when she was in Port Jackson. There she was smarter than most of the other prisoners, many of the Marines, and indeed some of the officers too. She had come to believe she was astute about people and capable of coping with almost anything.

But London and Newgate were a very different kettle of fish to Port Jackson. Everyone was sharp here, they might not have any more book-learning than she, but they were cunning. All of them, convicts, gaolers or visitors from outside the prison walls, had far more breadth of knowledge and experience than she did.

She might have been to the bottom of the world and back, but since arriving in Newgate, she had seen how limited her own abilities really were. She could catch a fish, gut it and cook it. She could sail a boat, help build a hut too, but there wasn't much else. She had pinned all her hopes on Boswell because he was clever and educated, but maybe she'd been foolish to do that.

'I think it's myself I've lost faith in,' she said with a sigh.

'That is very understandable,' he said, his dark eyes softening with sympathy. 'Newgate tries to destroy all that comes in through its doors. But you must fight against it, Mary. Look around at the women who sell themselves for a glass of gin, the men who would steal a man's boots while he sleeps, and remind yourself you are not one of them. You, because of your courage and forbearance, have captured the hearts of a nation. Each day people ask me how you are, they press money into my hands for you.'

'They do?' Mary said in surprise, and then her eyes narrowed. 'So where is it?'

Boswell chuckled. 'I'm keeping it safe for the time when you will need it. It wouldn't be wise for you to have it here, but I jot every penny down, and when you are released it will go towards lodgings, clothes, food and transportation to wherever you wish to go.'

She nodded, taking heart that he had said 'when' rather than 'if'. 'Can you tell me how many more weeks before I know for sure?'

Boswell shook his head. 'I can't, Mary. I'm doing everything I can to force the hands of those with the power to get you released. I can do no more.'

After Boswell had left, Mary went to the tap-room in search of the men. Despite her aversion to the place, she was loath to wait alone in the cell for their return.

As always, the fumes of cheap spirit, tobacco and human odours almost knocked her back as she opened the door. The room was small, a cellar-like place with grey stone walls which felt cold and wet to the touch. It was lit by a smoking lantern and the only furniture was a couple of rickety benches. Fresh air only came in via the door, but the regular drinkers appeared to have adapted to the smog-like conditions.

It wasn't as crowded as it normally was, perhaps because gaol fever was raging on the common side. But there were still around sixteen men and four women, two of whom Mary thought might be recent arrivals as she hadn't seen them before. One of them, gaudily dressed in a purple and blue striped dress, was perched on a man's knee, letting him fondle her breasts as she swigged at a bottle.

As always when she had occasion to come in here, Mary's stomach churned. It wasn't that she disapproved of people drinking here or anywhere else – drink was just as valid a way of coping with being in prison as prayer was. But the tap-room seemed to bring out the very worst in people. They boasted, they whined, they tore other people's characters to shreds. Sexual fumbling, often with a running commentary from the perpetrator, was a regular occurrence. She had come in here once to see a man push a woman off his lap, having just completed the sex act, and another man grabbed her and used her too, while people applauded him.

Plots against unpopular prisoners were hatched in here as well, and as jealousy was usually the reason behind most of the vicious attacks in Newgate, Mary often feared for herself and her friends.

'Mary, my little darlin'!' James exclaimed as he saw her in the doorway. 'Come and have a drink with us!'

James had undergone a quite dramatic change since their arrival in Newgate. The notoriety, his ability to read and write, and his natural charm had set him apart from the other prisoners almost immediately. But his image had been further enhanced by the stream of ladies who came to visit him. In smart new clothes, clean-shaven and with his hair neatly trimmed, he now had the persona of a member of the Irish aristocracy. He could never be called a handsome man, with his big forehead and nose, but he wore the new clothes with style, and his humour and warmth were very attractive.

Mary's heart sank when she saw his face flushed by drink and the way he staggered as he moved towards her, but far worse than the drunkenness was the company he was keeping. Amos Keating and Jack Sneed were real scum, as ugly in their appearance as they were in their hearts. The pair of them had bludgeoned a wealthy old widow to death when she caught them robbing her house. Even now, awaiting their execution, they showed absolutely no remorse, they even bragged about it. Nat, Bill and Sam weren't in the room, and Mary suspected they'd left because they didn't wish to mix with the likes of Amos and Jack.

'I just wanted to talk to you, James,' she said, backing away. 'But it will keep.'

'Too high and mighty to drink with us?' Amos, the smaller of the two men, leered at her, showing his rotting teeth.

Mary hesitated. It wasn't in her nature just to walk away silently from such a remark. But her hesitation was her undoing, for Jack, Amos's accomplice, a six-foot brute with a face like raw liver, was across the room in two strides and caught hold of her round her waist.

'I like 'em 'igh and mighty,' he said. 'They've always got the tightest cunts.'

He lifted Mary up, holding her in a vice-like grip, and tried to kiss her. Mary slapped out at his face, but he only laughed.

'That's right, you fight me,' he roared out in delight. 'I don't like me women too willin'.'

Mary struggled, but he was holding her too tightly to let her get free and, spurred on by strongly voiced encouragement from the other drinkers, he wasn't going to relinquish her.

'Let me go,' she shouted, pummelling him with her fists. 'James, help me!'

Mary saw him lurch forward, but Amos caught him around the neck to hold him back, and she knew in that instant that she was in real danger.

The majority of men in Newgate, whether prisoners or gaolers, believed all the women were theirs for the taking. Mary had always considered herself reasonably safe because of her elevated status as an escapee and her four male friends who stayed close to her. But Jack and Amos clearly weren't in awe of her, and believed she was easy game.

'A woman who lets herself be shared by four men shouldn't mind someone new having a turn,' Jack hissed in her ear, before flinging her down to the floor. He unbuckled his belt and leaped on top of her, the sour smell of his filthy clothes making her gag.

Mary screamed to James again, and she caught a fleeting glimpse of him as the other drinkers closed round to watch what Jack was going to do. James's face looked stricken, but she guessed he was still being held back by Amos and could do nothing.

Mary fought Jack, pulling his hair and scratching his face, but he caught her two hands with one of his, while the other groped frantically under her clothes. He was hampered a little by her heavy great-coat, and she was wriggling like an eel.

'Get off me, you filthy bastard,' Mary yelled, spitting into his face. She tried desperately to get a grip on the floor with the heels of her boots in an attempt to force his body off her, but the surface was too slimy. She continued to scream at the top of her lungs, but that only seemed to inflame Jack more, along with all the other men watching. Desperately, she remembered that screams in Newgate were too commonplace for anyone to come to her rescue.

She could feel the sudden charge in the air as the onlookers grew excited, and if Jack got his way with her, she had no doubt other men would follow him. But she wasn't going to succumb to rape after all she'd been through. She'd sooner die.

She fought him with every vestige of strength, getting her hands free again to claw his eyes with her nails, and pulling at his greasy hair until a handful came away in her hand. As he tried to suppress her with a kiss, she bit his lip hard.

'You little hell-cat,' he exclaimed, almost in admiration, pausing for a second to wipe blood from his mouth.

Mary took the opportunity to buck under him, and managed to get a few inches away to her left. But Jack was too quick; he grabbed her tightly again, pinning both her body and her right arm down, and pulled off his belt with his left hand.

'No, you bastard!' she heard James yell out, and perhaps he tried to get closer to help, though Mary couldn't see. But if he did, he didn't succeed, and Jack was clearly intending either to beat her into submission with the belt, or use it to tie her hands.

In a way the sight of the onlookers was even worse than what Jack was planning to do to her. The light from the lantern was dim, but she could still see the malicious glee on their faces clearly enough. Her terror grew into fury at their depravity and made her all the more determined not to give them the kind of entertainment they wanted.

Mary had always been observant, and over the last

seven years this had become even more finely honed out of necessity. She had noticed empty bottles lying on the floor when she'd been here before. It was too dark to see if there were any there today, but she stretched out her free arm and swept it quickly across the floor until she felt one.

Jack had now got his breeches unfastened, and his penis stood out like a purple-tipped barber's pole. He lunged towards her again, his belt in his hand, and she guessed his intention was to choke her into submission and silence.

She screamed again to divert him, squeezing her legs together so he would be forced to let go of one end of the belt to prise them apart. He faltered, not quite knowing which end of her to attack first. Mary seized the opportunity to tap the bottle sharply against the floor, leaving a broken jagged edge, then with one swift movement she thrust it into his neck, just below his ear, with as much force as she could muster.

Jack let out a bellow of pain, jerking up on to his knees, his hands going to his neck. Mary leaped up off the floor and stood with her hands on her hips, panting from the exertion, looking contemptuously down at her attacker.

The tap-room fell silent. Jack was still on his knees, blood spurting out between his fingers. His eyes were rolling fearfully, and he was making a horrible gurgling noise in his throat.

'Let that be a lesson to you,' Mary said between her teeth, and kicked out at him so he keeled over.

She turned to the rest of the crowd, the broken bottle still in her hand. They moved back a step or two, assuming by her bared teeth that she was going to attack them too. For a moment she wanted to, but they reminded her of the rats in the hospital in Batavia. Like them, these people all had sharp features and a furtive manner. They preyed on the weak too. They were despicable and beneath her contempt.

'If any one of you even thinks of touching me again, I'll kill you,' she snarled at them. 'Now, get help for him. And James, you come with me.'

The other three men were not back in the cell, even though it was nearly dark now. James, who had been apologizing profusely all the way up the stairs, slumped down on to the straw, drew his knees up to his chin and lowered his head on to them.

'You look as if you think I'm going to hit you,' Mary said sharply. 'Perhaps I should, for keeping company like that.'

'What if he dies, Mary?' James bleated out, his face chalk-white in the gloom.

'Do you think anyone will care?' she exclaimed as she lit a candle. 'He's a murderer and due to be hanged. But he won't die from what I did, it was only a flesh wound. If it keeps you out of the tap-room for a week or two, I won't have done it for nothing.'

James was silent for some time. Mary sat down and leaned her back against the wall. She felt very cold and shaky now, aware it was rather more luck than strength or superior intelligence that had enabled her to overpower Jack.

'Do you hate me?' James asked after a little while, his voice quavery and weak. Mary thought the shock had sobered him up.

'Now, why should I hate you?' she retorted. 'It wasn't you that tried to rape me.'

'I should have found a way to stop him. I let you down.'

'All men let me down,' Mary said, and suddenly she was crying. She hadn't once resorted to tears since they'd arrived in Newgate. She had told herself that after losing her children, nothing could make her cry. But once again she had been forced to fight for herself, and it seemed to her that her entire life had been one long fight, which she was now too tired to continue.

'Don't, Mary,' James said, and quickly moved across the floor to comfort her. 'I can't bear to see you cry.'

'Why?' she asked bitterly, tears running down her cheeks. 'Are you afraid if I crumple there'll be no hope for any of you?'

She had replied without thinking, but all at once she saw it was true. She had had people leaning on her, sapping her strength, right from the days back in the *Dunkirk*. She remembered setting up camp in Port Jackson, with everyone asking her how to do this, how to do that. They wanted her to listen to their problems, enlisted her help in everything from nursing a sick child to pleading with the officers for a blanket or a cooking pot. It never let up, right through the escape and afterwards.

But who did she have to lean on when things were

bad? Mary was forced to keep a grip on herself because she knew she couldn't count on anyone.

'We would flounder without you, that's for sure,' James said ruefully, as if he'd read her thoughts. 'But you do know how much me and the others love you?'

'I don't know that I believe men can love,' she sobbed. 'When men can use the very same act when they say they love a woman, as they do to show her how much they despise or hate her, I can't believe they have hearts.'

James put his arms tightly around her and rocked her against his chest. 'That's a very cynical thought, Mary. I've done a lot of things I'm ashamed of, but I've never taken a woman by force. And a man can love a woman with no thought of lying with her. Me, Nat, Bill and Sam, we all feel that way about you, you're like a sister to us.'

'But where are you every day if you care so much?' she burst out. 'I'm in here alone for hours on end. You leave me to see Mr Boswell, it's me that bargains for the food from Spinks, gets our washing done. What do any of you do but drink?'

'We leave you to see Boswell because we know it's you he wants to see,' James said indignantly. 'You get better deals from Spinks too because he likes you. And if we leave you alone it's because we thought that was what you wanted.'

'Is that so?' she retorted.

'You certainly know it's right about Boswell and Spinks,' James replied defensively. 'Was it something Boswell said that made you come to the tap-room for me?'

Mary thought for a moment. She had all but forgotten what had passed between her and Boswell. 'I think I was just upset because he had no news of our pardon,' she said, wiping away her tears with the back of her hand. 'I'm beginning to think there will never be one.'

'Then maybe it's time I wrote to the newspapers,' James said. 'A little reminder we are all still here, it might prompt some action.'

Mary was aware that the men weren't as desperate as she was to be freed. They wanted it of course, but they had grown used to Newgate, and as long as money came to them for drink and food, they were content. But in Mary's opinion James was living in a fool's paradise. He'd had ambitions when they first got here, of writing a book and going home to Ireland to breed horses, but all he did now was drink the time away. He didn't seem to realize that none of the women who found him so fascinating now would want to know him or help him once he was released. He had to start thinking about that day, now.

She sat up and caught hold of his face between her two hands. 'Listen to me, James,' she insisted. 'You've got to stop going into the tap-room. The people you meet in there aren't doing you any good. Please spend your time writing your book, reading, anything other than drinking, or when we do get out you'll get yourself in trouble again and you'll end up back here.'

'Don't preach, Mary,' he said, shrugging her away. 'I know all that.'

'Do you?' she asked. 'Then you are a great deal cleverer

than me. You see, I've thought about it constantly, and I still don't know how I'm going to live. I ask myself, what can a woman do to make an honest living when she can't read or write? I wonder what right-minded person would want a convicted felon working in their fine house.'

'There's always someone,' he said blithely.

Mary raised one eyebrow questioningly. 'Oh really? You believe that the stink of prison will disappear the moment I walk out the gate? That there'll be a kindly person waiting for me, ready to take me to their house and run the risk I might run off with their family silver?'

James winced. He never liked it when Mary reminded them all that they were convicted thieves. 'Mr Boswell will help you. Besides, some fine fella will come along and marry you, maybe you'll have children again too.'

Mary gave a harsh little laugh. 'I look like an old crow, James, what man would want to marry me?'

'I would,' he said, taking her hand and squeezing it. 'Sam too. You are beautiful, Mary, you are strong, brave, good and honest. Any man with half an eye would be joyful to have you.'

It was on the tip of Mary's tongue to point out that if she chose to marry either of them, her problems would be doubled rather than solved. But she realized James had intended it as a compliment, and it would be churlish to demean it. 'You could charm most of the women in London speaking like that,' she said with a watery smile. 'But not me, James, I know you too well.'

'But you don't know yourself very well,' he said, leaning over to kiss her cheek. 'Believe me, you are a prize, Mary. Worth far more than you know.'

James Boswell stood warming his backside by the fire in his drawing room, a glass of brandy in his hand. It was past seven in the evening and he felt drained, both mentally and physically.

It was a week since he'd seen Mary, and her despair had made him redouble his efforts for her. Since ten this morning he'd been calling on his most influential friends and acquaintances to secure their involvement. While most had heard him out and had even shown enough sympathy to give him a donation for her fund, not one had been sufficiently moved by her plight to offer their time or expertise to get her freed.

He moved over to his armchair and sat down heavily. As he leaned back in the chair and sipped his brandy reflectively, he had yet another sharp mental picture of Mary. Her large grey eyes which reminded him of stormy seas. That mane of thick dark curly hair, the pert little nose and lips that so easily curved into a warm smile. She was too thin and sallow-skinned to be a beauty, hard times had left their mark and the elements had aged her prematurely, yet there was something indefinably arresting about her.

They had had so many meetings, both alone and with the four men. Boswell knew the escape story inside out now, the individual character of each of those involved, including the ones who had lost their lives after the capture. He had learned to tune in to what lay behind Mary's words, for she always simplified a tale, usually leaving out her own crucial part in it. She had said what day in December Emmanuel had died in the Batavia hospital, and also mentioned how Will arrived at the hospital before then. Only a chance remark later, about when she rejoined the other men in the guard ship, made him see that she had stayed on at the hospital with Will until he died.

Boswell knew how the other men felt about Will, and why. Mary too felt he had betrayed them all. When he asked why she stayed with him until his death, she shrugged. 'I wouldn't leave anyone to die alone without some comfort,' she said.

To Boswell, that was the core of Mary's character. She didn't see such action as noble or generous, to her it was basic humanity. Most women who had just lost their baby would want the father to suffer even if he was only partially responsible. Mary could certainly have used that valuable time to escape with Charlotte, but she didn't. She stayed and cared for Will.

It hadn't been easy to really understand Mary. She was adept at changing the subject, making light of incidents and giving others credit when it ought to have gone to her. But Boswell was tenacious and also had a very good memory, and by fitting things the men had told him about Mary with what she had said herself, the truth emerged.

Her courage, endurance and intelligence were all remarkable. There was something decidedly masculine about the way she showed so little emotion under stress,

yet she was very feminine in other ways. She was passionate in her anxiety about babies born in prisons, and the
lack of care for the mothers. She would admire Boswell's
fancy waistcoats, tears had welled up in her eyes when he
brought her a posy of snowdrops, and she showed real
concern when he arrived out of breath. He had noted her
tenderness towards her friends, and the way she kept
herself and their cell clean and tidy. In Newgate, that was
almost unheard of.

It was well below freezing outside, but Boswell's drawing room was warm from the blazing fire, and very
comfortable. Shutters and heavy brocade curtains kept
out the draughts, his armchair supported him perfectly.
He had only to ring the bell and his housekeeper would
bring him anything he wanted – a plate of ham or cheese,
a bottle of port, or even a blanket to put round his knees.
She would warm his bed with a hot brick before he got
into it and his night-shirt would be hung by the fire to
warm too. In the morning he was woken with a tray of
tea, the fire would already be lit, and hot water ready for
his morning wash.

Tonight in Newgate it would be bitingly cold, and he
could hardly bear to think of Mary trying to sleep huddled
on straw. Yet she never complained about the conditions,
in fact she showed gratitude that she had been spared the
common side of the prison. It was only when she recalled
her native Cornwall that he saw a hunger in her eyes for
fresh air, the majesty of the pounding sea and the wildness
of the moors.

His own trip to Cornwall had made sense of some of

Mary's traits. While he had in the main found it a wet and cheerless place, with worse poverty in some areas than London, when the sun came out and he had seen the spectacular scenery, he had felt humbled.

The way the tiny fishing villages had insinuated themselves into the shelter of the cliffs spoke reams about its natives' tenacity. They fished, went down mines and farmed. However poor they were, the Cornish didn't kow-tow to the wealthy landowners. James had a sense all the time he was there that the common folk had the heart and the courage to rise up and take back what was rightfully theirs, if they so chose. Mary was Cornish through and through, sturdy and wild as a moorland pony, as tenacious as the limpets in rock pools, and often as deep as its pit shafts.

But last week he'd thought she was sinking, that she was unable to take much more of everything she'd endured so stoically. He was afraid that her low state would make her vulnerable to infection, and she'd have no strength left to fight it.

Perhaps he had initially looked for glory by defending her, but he certainly cared nothing for that now. He wanted so much to lead her from that dreadful place, to watch her blossom with good food, pretty clothes and freedom.

A friend had teased him recently by asking if there weren't enough whores in London to satisfy him, without rescuing a convict. Once he would have laughed off such a remark, and in the past his ultimate aim would have been to bed the woman once she was free. But Mary had touched something deep inside him that had nothing to do with lust. It stung that his friends didn't see this.

Mary, he believed, was his chance to redeem himself for past carelessness with women. He had truly loved his wife Margaret, but he had neglected her and been unfaithful many times. All those scores of whores, serving maids and often innocent young women he'd bedded! He wasn't guilty of callousness, for many of them had engaged his heart. But he had been like a butterfly, sipping nectar here and there, moving on as soon as the sweetness faded.

He wasn't going to lose interest in Mary, though – for once in his life he intended to see this through, whatever the cost to him. His aim went beyond getting her and her friends pardoned, he was going to help Mary on to a secure and prosperous life as well.

He swallowed the last of his brandy and reached out for the decanter to pour himself some more. He couldn't have picked a worse time to plead for Mary. For the past three years, the whole country had been in a state of unrest. The poor had good reason to feel bitter, the Enclosures Act forced many of them off the land into the cities, and craftsmen were finding that their skills were no longer needed as new manufacturing processes came in. They voiced their discontent in huge riots, and with men like Thomas Paine inciting rebellion with his belief that the monarchy should be abolished and the working classes rise to take control, the government was running scared.

Rioters were being arrested, charged and transported

before they had a chance to infect others with their inflammatory views, and although Henry Dundas had originally agreed that the five returned transportees should be pardoned, quite recently, when James asked him to fulfil his promise, he had denied making it and accused him of having a vivid imagination.

Boswell had gone to Evan Nepean, the Under Secretary of State. This man had been responsible for organizing the First Fleet of transport ships, and it was said he had been appalled to hear so many convicts died on the ships of the Second Fleet. There was no doubt that Nepean did care in general about the welfare of convicts, but he took the view that the government had already been lenient in not hanging these five, and saw no reason why they should be pardoned.

James felt a little ashamed now that he'd allowed Mary to believe Henry Dundas was an old and close friend. Their only connection was that they'd been at school together but they hadn't even liked each other. He would contact him yet again tomorrow, though, and write to Lord Falmouth too.

'I cannot, will not give up,' James muttered to himself. 'Right must triumph if I remain persistent.'

As James dozed later that evening in front of his warm fire, Mary was lying awake in the dark, her face wet with tears. She was so cold she could no longer feel her toes or even shiver, and every bone in her body ached.

She could hear someone wailing in the distance. It was a cry not of pain but of sheer hopelessness, and the sound echoed her own feelings. She was so weary of fighting that once again death looked desirable. She could no longer remember why survival had once been so important to her. What was there to live for?

Chapter twenty

'What's the date today, James?' Mary asked, turning on the crate she was standing on to see out of the cell window. She couldn't see anything more than the roof of the part of the prison opposite and the sky beyond, but it was infinitely better to look at the clouds and birds than at the cell walls.

James was sitting on the floor writing. He stopped at her question and looked up. 'The second of May,' he replied. 'Any special reason you want to know?'

It was mid-morning and they were all in the cell, Sam whittling an animal from a piece of wood. Nat busy sewing a patch on his breeches, Bill laboriously plaiting straw into fancy shapes. He called them 'corn dollies', and said that in the Berkshire village where he grew up they were considered fertility symbols. James had more than once joked that if there was a sudden increase in births in the prison, Bill would be responsible.

Since the attack on Mary in the tap-room, they all spent much less time there. Jack had survived his wound, but he was hanged for his crimes just a couple of weeks later. Since then Mary had found herself treated with extreme caution by the existing prisoners. But there were new arrivals every day, and many of them were even more dangerous than Jack, so the men had taken Mary's advice and kept out of the way.

They had all become adept at finding ways to fill the daylight hours. Mary was knitting a shawl, they played cards, they visited other prisoners in their cells, on fine days they went out into the yard. They also reminisced a great deal about New South Wales and their escape, as James was finally writing his book about it. When they did visit the tap-room it was only for a couple of hours in the evening.

'The second of May!' Mary exclaimed. 'Then it was my birthday two days ago, and we've been here nearly eleven months.' Her birthday meant little to her other than it came the day before May Day, which had always been special in Cornwall. No one had even mentioned that in here, so perhaps Londoners didn't celebrate it.

'It seems we've been here a whole lifetime, and they say it's bad manners to ask a lady's age,' James said with an impudent grin.

'You're older than me,' she retorted, and jumped down from the crate to sit on it.

'I have difficulty keeping track of years now,' Bill said thoughtfully, scratching his bald head. 'I'm not sure if I'm thirty-two or -three.'

'I'm still the youngest at twenty-five,' Nat chipped in.

Mary was loath to admit she was now twenty-eight. It seemed so very old. But then she felt old, and she'd been in Newgate for so long that almost everyone she'd met when she first came here had been hanged, died of fever, or been taken away for transportation.

'Someone's coming,' Sam said, looking up from his whittling.

He was right, they could all hear brisk footsteps coming along the passageway. It wasn't Spinks, who had a kind of shuffle, and the other prisoners walked slowly. Mary had found that odd at first, until she discovered herself doing it. What was the point of rushing anywhere when you had a long, empty day to fill?

The footsteps stopped outside their cell, and the door was pushed open. It was one of the guards from the gate, a tall, broad-shouldered man with a pock-marked face. They had seen him on their arrival here, and when they had been taken to court.

'Mary Broad!' he said, looking to her. 'You are wanted below.'

Mary exchanged a puzzled glance with the men. Normally when a visitor arrived for one of them, Spinks came to tell them.

'Maybe it's the King,' James said, and laughed at his joke.

Mary picked up her shawl and followed the guard down the stairs, across the outside yard and into the small office she had come through on her arrival.

'Mr Boswell!' she exclaimed when she saw him waiting there. He looked even grander than usual in a dark red jacket trimmed with black braid, and he had a cockade of red feathers in his three-cornered hat. 'I had expected something bad. Why didn't the guard tell me it was you?'

477

'Because this is an official visit,' he said, glancing at the guard, then suddenly his face broke into a joyful smile and he pulled a sheet of paper from behind his back. 'This, my dear, is your pardon!'

Mary was too stunned to respond. She blinked, caught hold of the edge of the desk for support and just stared back at Boswell.

'Well, say something,' he laughed. 'Or won't you believe it till I read it to you?'

He cleared his throat, made a sweeping bow as if about to deliver a proclamation to royalty, then held up the sheet of paper.

'*Whereas Mary Bryant, alias Broad, now a prisoner in Newgate,*' he read aloud, and paused to smile.

'Go on,' she whispered, afraid she might faint with shock.

'*Stands charged with escaping from the persons having legal custody of her before the expiration of the term which she had been ordered to be transported, and whereas some favourable circumstances have been humbly presented unto us on her behalf, inducing us to grant our Grace and Mercy on her and to grant her our free pardon for her said crime.*'

Boswell went on reading and finished up by telling Mary that the letter was signed by Henry Dundas at His Majesty's command. But she could barely take it in: the only two words which really meant anything to her were 'free pardon'.

'Oh, Bozzie,' she gasped as he finished. 'You did it! I'm free?'

'Yes, you are, my dear,' he beamed. 'As from this very

moment. You can walk out through the gates right now with me. You have spent your last night in Newgate.'

She rushed to hug him, kissing both his cheeks.

'You are a wonderful, wonderful man,' she said joyfully. 'How can I ever thank you enough?'

Boswell's face was always so red it was hard to tell if he was blushing, but he caught hold of her two hands and squeezed them hard, and there was an emotional tear in his eye. Mary had never kissed or attempted to hug him before, and he had expected her to take the news with her customary coolness. To see her so moved by joy was enough thanks for him.

'You can thank me by getting your things quickly and then we'll go off to celebrate,' he said.

Mary took two steps towards the door, then stopped sharply and turned to him again. Her smile had gone, replaced by a look of extreme anxiety.

'What about the men?' she said in little more than a whisper. 'Are they pardoned too?'

This was the moment Boswell had been dreading.

'Not yet,' he said carefully, afraid she might not want to leave without them. 'But they will get one in due course. I am promised that.'

She hesitated.

'Mary, they will be freed,' he insisted. 'I am sure they will be glad for you. You can do more for them on the outside than by sticking here with them.'

She left then, but walked away slowly, her head bent as if in thought.

*

479

Mary blurted out her news from the cell door, and began to cry when she got to the part that the pardon was only for her, and they'd have to wait a little longer. She thought they would be angry, hurt and resentful, and covered her face in expectation of a volley of verbal abuse.

James was stunned, but as he saw her gesture he felt ashamed that she anticipated jealousy at her good fortune. She deserved her freedom more than any of them, for her losses had been so much greater.

'That's all right with us, ain't it, boys?' he said, giving them a warning glance not to say anything mean-spirited.

'But I wanted us all to go together,' Mary said, tears running down her cheeks. 'How can I leave without you?'

As one, the four of them leaped to their feet, each man moved by her unswerving loyalty to them.

'Don't be a numbskull,' James said. 'We always expected you to go first, so bugger off and enjoy it.'

'You deserve it more than any of us,' Sam said, his warm smile softening his gaunt features. Nat patted her affectionately on the shoulder, while Bill gave a whoop of delight and punched the air.

Mary wiped away her tears, touched that they could be so joyful for her and hide their own disappointment. 'We've been together for so long I don't know if I can manage without you,' she said.

'Get away,' Sam said, waving her to the door in an exaggerated gesture. 'We'll be glad to be rid of your nagging.'

'We'll turn the cell into a midden, we'll drink all day, and we'll invite whores up here,' Bill growled, but his lips were trembling.

'I'll take your blanket,' Nat chirped up. 'It's thicker than mine.'

Mary looked at their faces with tear-filled eyes. Four brave smiles, four warm hearts, each one so very dear to her for a thousand or more different reasons. They had seen one another at their best and their worst. They had fought, laughed and cried together. Now she had to leave, and learn to live without them.

'Don't get drunk or fight, and James, you finish your book,' she said weakly, falling back on motherly advice because she knew that if she tried to tell them how much she loved them she would break down. 'I'll be back to see you, and we'll all celebrate together when you get your pardon too.'

She slipped off her old dress and put on the blue one Boswell had given her, then, tipping the straw out of the linen sack which she'd brought from the *Gorgon* and had been using as a pillow, she put her few belongings into it.

James came up behind her and fastened the buttons at the back of her dress, then turned her round to tuck a stray curl behind her ear. 'God bless you, Mary,' he said, his voice cracking with emotion. He kissed her cheek, then held her close. 'It'll surely be a lucky man who gets you.'

Wordlessly, Mary broke away from James to kiss and hug the other three, lingering just a little longer with Sam.

'Don't go wrong again,' she whispered to him. 'And find a woman worthy of you.'

She paused at the door, taking one last look at them. She could remember how disreputable and ugly she'd thought James was when she saw him marching off to work with Will from the *Dunkirk*. He was the last link with that stinking hulk, yet through his ability to charm ladies, he looked more like a gentleman now than a convict.

Nat had seemed suspect when she first met him. She had noted the shine on his hair, the smooth flesh on his bones, and guessed how the pretty boy had survived the *Neptune*. It saddened her to think she had judged him for that. It was no different to what she did with Lieutenant Graham.

Sam hadn't had the looks to trade his way to comfort on the *Scarborough*. He'd been close to death when she gave him water on the quay. He'd fought to live, just as he'd fought the elements with her to get them to safety.

As for Bill, she'd been impressed by his toughness when he walked away from his flogging, but she hadn't actually liked him until after they'd escaped. But time had proved there was a kind and decent man under that rough exterior.

She couldn't even claim that any of them had burst into her life like a fire cracker. They were just four seemingly unremarkable men who through desperation had become like her brothers. Every aspect of their characters was etched in her heart, she would hold each dear face in her mind forever.

'I love you all,' she said softly, her eyes filling with tears again. 'Please don't any of you break the law again, I want you to be honest and happy.'

She fled then, tears streaming down her face.

'I have found rooms for you in Little Titchfield Street,' Boswell said as he settled her into a hansom cab. He had noted her tearstained face, and guessed she was upset at parting from her friends. But he felt the separation could only be a good thing. He wasn't entirely convinced that the men would become honest and hardworking on their release, and he wanted no bad influences around Mary now she was free.

'Now, I have money for you,' he said, taking a notebook from his pocket to show her. 'Over forty pounds, a princely sum. I shall pay for your lodgings from it, and you will need clothes too. But for now you must just enjoy your freedom.'

The sadness at leaving her friends behind was eased by the excitement of freedom and seeing London. Boswell pointed out that the view of it she'd seen before when brought from the docks to Newgate was a rather squalid part of the city, and she was now going to a respectable area.

Mary could only stare in silent wonderment. It was a bright, sunny spring day, and the streets were crowded, forcing the cab driver to slow the horses to a mere walk. The iron-rimmed wheels on heavily laden carts, cabs and carriages made a racket on the uneven road surface. Sedan chairmen nimbly bypassed the many piles of horse dung, and wove in and out of the heavier traffic.

Ladies out shopping were wearing gowns and pretty bonnets in every colour of the rainbow, men in frock coats and hats like Boswell's hurried as if on urgent business. Street traders yelled out their wares in strident voices. There were thin little flower girls with baskets of primroses, small boys selling newspapers, and burly tradesmen unloading goods from carts or carrying everything from ladders to pieces of furniture.

But it was the buildings which took most of Mary's attention. Whether private houses, banks or other places of business, they were all so grand. Marble steps, pillars, stone carving such as she'd only ever seen on churches before, so many different designs, pushed up together as if the builders had been short of space, yet each one striving to outshine everything around it. Some places looked very old, half-timbered buildings that leaned out precariously into the streets. Then there were elegant new ones, three or four storeys high, with splendid long arched windows.

There were many smart carriages too. Some had dashing scarlet wheels, on others the graceful horses wore feather plumes, some even had footmen resplendent in gold and red livery.

Boswell pointed out things he thought might interest her – men carrying sides of meat coming from Smithfield market, the Inns of Court where he had studied to be a lawyer, Lincoln's Inn Fields, and many fine houses belonging to people he knew. He told her about the Great Fire of London, and how the city was rebuilt afterwards.

'Look!' Mary interrupted him as he was talking about a coffee house where he used to meet Dr Johnson. She pointed at a woman pushing what could only be called a baby carriage, for a small child was sitting inside the splendid large-wheeled vehicle, waving its little hands in excitement. Mary had never seen anything like it before. 'Are folk so rich here in London they wheel their children around?'

Boswell chuckled. He thought it was so like a woman to be more interested in a child in a wheeled conveyance than hearing about his great friend. He supposed, too, that when a person couldn't read or write, they wouldn't understand why anyone would bother to write a dictionary, or even need to use one.

'I see nursemaids wheeling their charges around the London parks so often that I don't find the carriages remarkable,' he said. 'But I suspect it's not only the cost of them which deters most mothers, they are a little unwieldy.'

'But it's a good idea,' Mary said. 'Especially if you had two or three little ones.'

'I daresay ordinary women with several children would like water coming into their houses in pipes, even more than baby carriages,' he said. 'That would save so much drudgery for them. Some of the rich people have rooms just for bathing in, and the dirty water is disposed of easily by opening a sluice.'

Mary looked at him in disbelief. 'They do?'

'Oh yes,' Boswell said. 'Whole terraces of houses have been built with water brought in by elm pipes, and drains to take away the waste. Maybe one day when these conveniences spread throughout the city our streets will be pleasanter places to walk.'

Mary began to laugh, for just ahead of them she saw a maid tipping the contents of a pail out of a second-storey window.

'I've been unlucky enough to be drenched that way dozens of times,' Boswell said ruefully. 'I think proper drains are something that the government ought to see as a priority.'

'I didn't think London would smell as bad as Plymouth,' Mary said, wrinkling her nose. 'But it does.'

'What can we expect with all these horses?' Boswell remarked, waving his hand to indicate at least thirty of them within their view. 'On a wet day the cart and carriage wheels splash their muck up all over you. They have tried to stop cattle being driven through the city, but to no avail.'

'At least London people seem to be mainly plump and well,' Mary said.

Boswell sighed. 'This is a respectable part of the city,' he said. 'There are other parts like St Giles which tell a very different story. But I'm not going to show you poverty and squalor, you've had quite enough exposure to that.'

The lodgings Boswell took Mary to in Little Titchfield Street were in a narrow but tall house in a terrace, with a gleaming brass knocker on the door and the whitest steps Mary had ever seen. She had a moment's panic as Boswell paid off the driver, for surely he didn't think someone like her should stay in such a place?

But the apple-cheeked woman with a lace-trimmed cap who opened the door and was introduced by Boswell as Mrs Wilkes didn't seem shocked or surprised by Mary's appearance.

'Come in, my dear,' she said. 'Mr Boswell has told me all about you, and I'm sure we'll get along famously.'

Without stopping to draw breath, she commented on the fine weather, and told Mary that she provided breakfast and supper, was happy to do her laundry, and that she must think of her rooms here as home.

'I have water heating for your bath,' she went on, though dropping her voice as if this was a delicate matter. 'Mr Boswell said that would be what you wanted. I only ask that you carry it up yourself because the stairs are too much for me.'

Mary could do no more than nod, for the closest she'd ever come to such startling comfort and splendour was peering through windows of the grander houses in Plymouth. From the narrow hall with its polished wood floor, she could see a thick fringed carpet, upholstered chairs and a shiny wood table with dozens of small ornaments. Yet the way Mrs Wilkes kept looking at Boswell, as if seeking his approval, suggested he was accustomed to even greater things. Mary felt weak with shock, terribly aware that she must stink of Newgate and had undoubtedly brought many of its smallest inmates with her.

'I will leave you to settle in now under Mrs Wilkes's

tender care,' Boswell said, and took hold of Mary's hand to pat it. 'You need another woman now, and some rest and quiet. I shall return at six-thirty to take you out to supper.'

A couple of hours later Mary lay on her bed, too thrilled to sleep even though she was tired.

She had two rooms at the top of the house. The one overlooking the street was a living room, with a table and chairs and two wooden armchairs, one of which rocked.

Her bedroom at the back contained an iron bed, a closet for clothes and a washstand. Compared with what she'd seen downstairs, the rooms were simply furnished, with similar items to those she remembered from home in Fowey. But after so many years of hardship and terrible discomfort it was like a palace, and almost everything she looked at made her want to cry.

She had gladly lugged up the pails of hot water, laughed aloud as she stripped off her clothes and climbed into the tin bath. She couldn't remember when she last had hot water to wash with, let alone submerge herself in. Nor could she remember when she last had a door she could shut others out with. As she scrubbed off the prison smell from her skin and hair, she felt reborn.

Mrs Wilkes was comfortingly blunt, once they were alone.

'I think it's best I burn all your clothes,' she said. 'Mr Boswell brought some things round for you last night, his daughter's I think. And in a day or two we'll go out and buy others. You'll find everything you need in the closet. But you make sure you wash that hair properly.'

Afternoon sunshine streamed in through the bedroom window, and as Mary sat up on the bed to look at her reflection in the looking-glass above the washstand, she was astounded to see that her hair shone the way it had when she was a girl. Mrs Wilkes had brought her up some fresh water with a little vinegar in it, as a rinse. She claimed it would make her hair shine, though Mary suspected it was really to kill off any remaining lice. But whatever the reason, it had performed a miracle, and her hair had never felt so soft or looked so pretty.

It would have been good to have found her face prettier than she imagined, but sadly that wasn't so. Her complexion was grey and coarse, there were lines around her eyes, and her cheeks were hollow. But Mrs Wilkes had made her swallow a huge spoonful of malt, and she insisted that with fresh air, good food and plenty of sleep, in a week or two Mary wouldn't know herself.

Yet happiness was already bringing a little colour to her cheeks, she thought. She'd had to enlist Mrs Wilkes's help not only to lace up the stays, but to take her advice in which order she had to put on all the undergarments. The dainty soft chemise which smelled of lavender and reached to her knees went on first, the low neckline drawn up over her breasts with a ribbon. Then came the petticoat trimmed with lace, and a skirt of blue cotton before the stays. Mrs Wilkes had to show her how the front pointed part of the stays went over the skirt, with small tabs fixed inside the waist. Finally the blue and white dress which had panniers over her hips went on almost like a coat, leaving the stays, chemise and much of her small breasts on view.

'That's the fashion in London, my dear,' Mrs Wilkes assured her when she saw Mary's bewildered and anxious expression. 'At least they've done away with those ridiculous hooped skirts I had to wear when I was your age. Now, let me help you with your hair, you can't wear it all wild like a gypsy.'

Mary put her hand on the bedcover and smiled with delight. It was a simple woven material the colour of oatmeal, but to her it could have been silk. Would Mrs Wilkes realize that she hadn't slept in a bed with sheets and real pillows since she left home for Plymouth eight years ago? Even there they'd been a rare luxury for ordinary people, and Uncle Peter had brought them home for her mother from one of his trips abroad. Would Mrs Wilkes understand, too, how strange it was for her to be in a room with furniture, when she had sat on either a dirt floor or a stone one covered in straw for so many years?

Mary didn't think even Boswell would fully appreciate how miraculous, strange and even frightening everything would be to her for a while. How could he? She hadn't even realized it herself until he brought her here.

'Who is this gorgeous creature?' Boswell joked when he arrived back to take her out for supper. 'Surely there is some mistake, madam? Your name cannot be Mary Broad!'

'It is indeed, sir,' Mary giggled. 'London water, it seems, has magical powers.'

She knew her transformation wasn't merely the result of a bath and new clothes but the spirit of freedom. She had stayed in the lodging-house all afternoon, but the thought that she could, if she wished, walk out of the front door and mingle with the crowds in the streets was like a tonic. To lie on the soft bed, knowing the airy, fresh-smelling room was just for her was so thrilling that she felt she could stay there forever and never be bored.

But Mrs Wilkes had fixed up her hair with some combs and a little lace cap, and she was wearing blue stockings and a pair of shoes with gilt buckles. Now she must go out and test her newfound freedom.

'I don't think I can do this,' Mary said in panic as Boswell helped her down from the cab in a busy street full of shops.

'You can't eat supper?' he exclaimed.

'Not in there,' she said, looking at the sparkling windows of the supper rooms he was intending to take her into. She could see a lady and gentleman sitting at a table by the window. The lady wore a pearl necklace and she was elegantly sipping wine from a glass. Mary thought that to go in there would be like bursting into Captain Phillip's house uninvited when he had other officers for dinner.

'Why on earth not?' Boswell laughed.

'It's too grand,' she blurted out. 'I'll make a fool of myself and embarrass you.'

'No, you won't,' he insisted firmly, and tucking her hand through his arm he led her purposively towards the door. 'All you have to do is smile, and copy what I do. I promise you there's nothing to it.'

Boswell may have thought there was nothing to walking into a place like that, with every single face turning to look at you, but to Mary it was more terrifying than a storm at sea. She realized by the curious stares, the smiles and nods at Boswell and the buzz of muted conversation that they all knew who she was.

Mary felt herself growing hotter and hotter. Her face felt as if it was on fire, for even though the other people didn't continue to stare at her once she was sitting down, she guessed they were watching her out of the corner of their eyes and talking about her.

Boswell was studying the bill of fare and commenting on various dishes he'd eaten here before. He didn't seem to be aware how uncomfortable she felt. 'What would you like to eat, my dear?' he asked. 'The beef pudding is very good here, but so is the rabbit and the duck.'

Mary had been ravenous before they left Mrs Wilkes's house, but that had gone now and she felt sick instead. Her stays were digging into her and the new shoes were too tight. Yet after all the years of living with constant hunger she couldn't possibly refuse a meal.

'You choose for me,' she whispered.

She tried to remind herself that she had been out to supper before, back in Plymouth with Thomas Coogan.

It hadn't been such a smart place as this, there weren't white tablecloths, but she hadn't disgraced herself there, so she wouldn't here. That was over nine years ago, though, and since then she'd become accustomed to gobbling down anything that came her way, whether it was ship's rations slopped into a bowl, or whatever she'd managed to cook in one pot. Choice had never come into it.

The whole idea of sitting at a table to eat was alien to her now. When she looked at the silver cutlery she blanched because a spoon and a knife were all she was used to, and she'd often had to eat with her hands.

'I expect everything feels a little strange to you,' Boswell said solicitously as he filled her glass with wine, 'but you'll soon get used to it. Now, drink up and enjoy your first night of freedom.'

Mary couldn't enjoy it, however. She was more on edge than she had been on her first night in the hospital in Batavia. There it was rats she was watching out for, now it was for people watching her.

The supper arrived, and it looked and smelled wonderful, but it seemed that every time she managed to get a mouthful of food on to her fork, the way Boswell ate, someone would come up to the table to slap him on the back and compliment him on his outstanding success in getting Mary pardoned.

They meant to be kind, their smiles were warm, and they wished her a long and happy life. But she was tongue-tied, and all she could do was force a smile and murmur her thanks.

'You can't blame them for wanting to meet "the girl from Botany Bay",' Boswell said, after it had happened several times. 'Everyone in London is talking about you.'

Mary couldn't bring herself to complain. She thought he had a right to take pride in what he'd achieved, and to bask in his friends' admiration. So she pretended she was every bit as happy as he was, and kept it to herself that she wanted to go home.

When they finally left, Mary was a little unsteady on her feet. She had drunk far more than she'd eaten, but she felt she'd managed to get through the evening without letting Boswell down.

'Goodnight, my dear,' he said, as Mrs Wilkes opened the door to them. 'Sleep well and savour your newfound freedom. I'll call on you tomorrow.'

Mary could hardly wait for Mrs Wilkes to light her a candle to see her way up the stairs to her room. Yet as soon as she'd shut the door, she felt afraid. For nearly a year she'd shared a cell with four men, often cursing them for their snoring or coughing at night. But now this sweet-smelling room with the comfortable bed seemed so eerie by candlelight and too big for her to sleep in all alone.

'Don't be foolish,' she told herself. 'Surely you wouldn't rather be back in Newgate than here?'

Chapter twenty-one

A month after Mary's release from Newgate, she was strolling with Boswell one afternoon in the sunshine of St James's Park.

Visiting London's parks had become one of Mary's greatest pleasures. It was so good to get away from the noise and dirt of the city's streets and see grass, trees and flowers. Many had enclosures with deer in them and there were sheep and cows too. She found it amusing that the cows in St James's were led back to Whitehall in the afternoons to be milked, and you could buy a glass of milk for a penny.

During the week the gentry used the parks to meet friends and be seen in their most fashionable clothes. They didn't appear on Sundays, however, as that was the day the common people came in their hordes. Stay-makers, milliners and shop girls had a chance to enjoy their day off and perhaps meet a handsome young clerk, or even a dashing soldier.

St James's Park was Mary's firm favourite, as the only riders or carriages allowed to use it were from the Royal Households. There were ducks, swans and geese on the lake and the flowerbeds were a riot of colour.

'I think I should find some employment now,' Mary said thoughtfully as she and Boswell stopped to watch some children feeding the ducks with stale bread. 'That money won't last forever.'

He patted her hand tucked into his arm. 'No, it won't, my dear, but it will last for a good bit longer yet, and you have to decide what you want to do, and where you want to go first.'

Mary was tempted to argue with Boswell, maybe even to tell him she wasn't entirely happy about her increasing dependence on him. But in the light of everything he'd done for her, that seemed ungracious.

It seemed absurd to Mary now that she had been so afraid when she was first released. Now she woke up each morning and gave thanks to God for His mercy and for sending James Boswell to her. But for the first week there had been many times when she'd almost wished herself back in Newgate.

It was wonderful of course to feel clean, to be free, to have a comfortable bed and good food to eat. Yet freedom was terrifying too, especially when Boswell drove her headlong into it, as he had at that first supper, making no allowances for her lack of knowledge of the world he lived in.

Boswell's friends were all gentry, and when he took her to visit some of them in their homes, she felt she would rather be left below stairs with their servants than be studied as if she were some curious specimen brought from overseas.

There was guilt too. Many nights she'd lain awake in her comfortable bed and all she could think of was Emmanuel and Charlotte. It didn't seem right that she was living so well now, when their short lives had been so wretched. Even now, a month later, she couldn't get away from that thought, it cropped up again and again whatever she was doing. She would go over every part of their lives, looking for something she'd done, or hadn't done, which had caused their deaths. And it always came back to the same thing. If she had stayed in Port Jackson, they might have survived.

These thoughts didn't only come when she was alone. She could be riding in a cab with Boswell and see a mother and child together, and she would feel a stab of pain. When she saw little girls of Charlotte's age in rags, out on the streets, she felt a surge of anger at a society which cared so little for its youngest members.

She also missed James, Sam, Nat and Bill desperately, not only for their company and the shared memories, but for the position she held in their group. She was the leader, the one whose intelligence, practicality and knowledge were valued. Outside Newgate she was an oddity, and people talked down to her as if she was dim-witted.

As the days went by she gradually adjusted. She accepted she would have to learn how to fit in with normal people again, that she would have to learn to make small-talk, and to live within the boundaries expected of women.

She found the courage to cross busy roads, weaving in

and out of the carriages. She learned how to use a fork by practising at home and to put her hair up the way Mrs Wilkes taught her. She even mastered lacing up her stays by herself.

Mrs Wilkes was such a kind, good woman, old enough at over forty to be motherly, but still young enough to understand just how inadequate and overawed Mary felt sometimes. She admitted she sometimes found Mr Boswell a little too bumptious for her taste, but she put that down to his breeding and fame as a writer. She would make a cup of tea, invite Mary to sit with her in the kitchen and get her to talk about anything that worried her.

Mrs Wilkes explained anything Mary was embarrassed to ask Boswell about. She understood why Mary didn't want to be put on show to his friends, and suggested ways in which Mary could make this clear to him. But above all she knew how strange it was for Mary to suddenly find herself out of her real station in life.

'Don't allow it to swamp you,' she advised. 'Learn as much as you can by watching and listening. Enjoy your fame without wondering how long it will last. After what you've been through, you deserve it. But above all, Mary, hold on to your courage, that's what makes you so fascinating.'

When Mrs Wilkes wasn't offering tea and advice, she dosed Mary up with malt, made her drink lemon juice for a clearer complexion, and took her shopping for new clothes. Even though Boswell believed he alone was teaching Mary how to be what he called 'a middling sort', a big step up from the poor but respectable roots of her childhood, in truth it was Mrs Wilkes who taught her most.

Yet along with the painful and bewildering moments there were many more joyful, happy ones. Mary had been to the Tower of London and seen the lions there, she'd visited St Paul's and the Monument and seen the royal palaces, and had been by river to Greenwich. She loved the parks, the busy shops in the Strand, the markets, and just looking at all the fine houses. Mostly Boswell took her to see the sights, but she loved exploring on her own too. He might need a cab because he was getting older, but she liked to walk, to stop and gaze at people, street scenes and buildings.

Now, a month after her release, she could probably fool some people into believing she'd always lived this way. She saw poor people every day, sweeping streets, selling flowers and begging on street corners, and she was very aware that this comfortable life she'd landed in more by luck than her own initiative wasn't secure. She knew she had to find some way of making it so.

She was far too astute to think that a few pretty clothes would land her in a good position. People wanted their housemaids young. They wanted real cooks, capable of coping with large dinner parties, not someone who had gained their experience throwing anything vaguely edible into one pot over an open fire. Housekeepers had to know everything, from how to care for linen and silver to keeping accounts. Mary knew none of that, and she had no references either. The more she looked around, the more she saw there were few work opportunities for any woman.

Even Mrs Wilkes, whom Mary had thought of as gentry, had no choice but to run a boarding-house. She had been widowed ten years earlier, and when the little money she was left with ran out, she'd got a position as a companion housekeeper for an old gentleman at that same house in Little Titchfield Street. When he died, leaving his money to his nephew, Mrs Wilkes inherited the contents of the rented house. Taking in lodgers was the only way she could manage to stay in the home she'd come to love.

Mrs Wilkes's answer to Mary's problems was marriage. She had hinted that Boswell might make the ideal husband. He was after all a widower, very fond of her, and a man of means.

There had been brief moments when Mary toyed with the idea. She liked Boswell very much, he was kind, entertaining and generous. Sadly, however, she knew she could never go willingly to his bed. He was getting old and fat and his teeth were rotten. He was also a very clever man, with children he thought the world of, so he certainly wasn't going to risk their disapproval for an ex-convict who hadn't already proved her love and passion for him.

'I think I would like to live by the sea again,' Mary said as they walked over the little bridge across the lake. London was exciting, but she often found herself longing for the serenity of the moors, the fresh wind from the sea and a calmer life.

'Then perhaps we should make contact with your family,' Boswell said. 'You will remember I met the Reverend John Baron of Lostwithiel while I was in Cornwall. A good man!'

Mary nodded. Boswell had mentioned this man, but as she had only been to Lostwithiel twice in her life, she didn't know him.

'He would call on your mother and father if I asked him to,' Boswell said. 'Shall I write to him? He was very sympathetic to you.'

'I'm afraid they would show him the door,' Mary said dolefully. She remembered only too well her mother's loudly held views on those who broke the law. Mary thought she must be thoroughly shamed by her daughter's notoriety. She wasn't going to like a man of the cloth pleading with her to forgive and forget. In fact it would probably set her even further against Mary.

'It's worth a try,' Boswell said.

'No,' Mary said firmly. 'It's up to me to throw myself on their mercy, it's cowardly to get someone else to act on my behalf. I'll go when the men are pardoned.'

Visiting the men in Newgate was one thing Boswell had refused to let her do. He said it was because of the danger of infectious diseases, but she guessed it had more to do with keeping her away from any harmful influences. As he had been so good to her, she felt she couldn't disobey him, so she had to make do with passing messages through him.

'That might not be for some time yet, Mary,' Boswell warned her. 'You know I am doing my best for them, but the law drags its feet, especially in summer.'

'Then I'll wait,' she said.

He smiled and squeezed her arm. 'Good, there's so much more of London still to show you. And don't worry about money. You still have more than enough.'

The remainder of June, July and the first two weeks of August were an exceptionally happy time for Mary. People's curiosity in her had waned, and she found herself far more comfortable in her new life. She helped Mrs Wilkes as much as she could, going shopping with her and often doing the washing and preparing the supper.

Yet every now and then a strange kind of melancholy came over her. She would think of Will, Tench and Jamie Cox, and all those she'd liked but left behind in Port Jackson. She would dwell on little moments she'd shared with them, and often found herself crying. It irritated her that people in England neither knew nor cared how grim or badly run the colony was. Yet conversely she often wanted to tell people that New South Wales was beautiful and intriguing. And she wondered why she could still think so after all that had happened.

She would be caught short, too, by the extreme contrasts in her new life to the old one. One day Mrs Wilkes asked her to throw away some meat which was going bad. Mary had to fight with herself not to eat it, for the thought of wasting food after experiencing starvation was terrible. It seemed ridiculous to her, too, that as a lady she was expected to be weak, helpless and squeamish, when she had collected and eaten grubs, hacked up turtle meat and been the driving force behind a 3,000-mile voyage in an open boat. A lady shouldn't mention bodily functions either, and certainly not in mixed company. But she had coped quite well with having to perform hers in the company of eight men, and after living with them in such close proximity for so long, there were no mysteries about men left for her to discover.

But as time passed Mary found herself looking back far less. While her children were always in her mind, she found other memories were fading, and she was living in the present again. The weather was good, and Boswell continued to call on her frequently, taking her out to the parks, on river trips, and to the countryside surrounding London.

One day in August, he took her out in a cab to the village of Chelsea. He appeared to be very much amused by poems about them which were being widely circulated around the town. It seemed the writers believed they were lovers, and in one of the poems they met their deaths on the gallows together.

'Perhaps I should marry you, my dear,' Boswell said jokingly. 'It would confound all those poetic simpletons.'

'I think your daughters might find that a little distressing,' Mary said with a smile. 'I am not the stepmother of any girl's dreams.'

'Your heart is still with Captain Tench?' Boswell said, raising one eyebrow quizzically.

Mary had often mentioned Watkin Tench, but had

never given Boswell any indication of how she had felt about the man. Even her four friends in Newgate knew nothing of that. So she was amazed to hear him say this. 'I don't have a heart,' she said flippantly.

'Untrue,' he retorted, but he laughed all the same. 'I found out he paid for your cell, Mary. You see, he stopped paying when you were pardoned, and the men had to make new arrangements.'

Mary had met her equal in quick wits with Boswell. Like her, very little passed him by. 'So! We were friends, he helped me, that doesn't mean I was in love with him.'

'I think it means he was in love with you,' Boswell said sagely. 'Marines aren't known for their largesse as a rule. But he strikes me as a gutless wonder for not coming to London to claim you if he knows you are free. He's on HMS *Alexander* now, part of the Channel Fleet.'

Mary's heart quickened at this news. She'd always imagined Tench had sailed off to some faraway place again.

'Aha,' Boswell chortled. 'I see a faint blush. Now, would that be because he's still close to England?'

Mary decided there was no point in trying to pretend any longer.

'I did have strong feelings for him, and he for me,' she said with a shrug. 'But it could never be. And he's not a gutless wonder. I insisted that he wasn't to try and contact me.'

During her time in Newgate Mary had tried not to hope Tench might turn up to see her. And in the prison it was easy to see he belonged to a different world.

However, now she was free, looking for all the world like a respectable widow, she couldn't help but drift into little day-dreams of him coming up to London to claim her and whisking her off to a country cottage. At times she even believed she'd changed so much that she could become the perfect wife for an officer.

'You are right. It couldn't be,' Boswell agreed, disappointing Mary somewhat. 'I've had my share of falling for unsuitable ladies, and it brings nothing but grief on both sides.' He took her hand and squeezed it in sympathy. 'Grief is something we should all try to avoid. Whatever our age or circumstance.'

Although on the face of it his remarks were only about her relationship with Watkin Tench, Mary had a feeling Boswell meant more. The earlier mention of marriage had been a joke, but she had a feeling he was also trying to sound her out to see if she expected him to propose to her. She thought it would be wise to make it clear that wasn't her aim.

'Well, tell me, O Wise One!' she joked. 'What sort of a man is likely to make me happy?'

Boswell pondered on this gravely for a moment or two. 'A sea-going one, I'd say,' he said eventually. 'A well-set-up mariner. Perhaps a widower, who would be less likely to feel aggrieved that you have a past. Not more than thirty-five. Young enough to want a family.'

'You wouldn't happen to know him already?' she asked laughingly, for he spoke as if he knew the very man.

'No, my dear, sadly I don't,' he chuckled. 'I'm just a romantic old fool who would like to see a happy ending for you. But to my mind, one of the best things about life is that one never knows what is around the next corner.'

Chapter twenty-two

'That wretched man again!' Mrs Wilkes exclaimed in exasperation at the hammering on her front door. 'Only yesterday I tried to tell him he wasn't doing your reputation any good by calling here at all hours. And here he is again, on a Sunday!'

It was 18 August and very hot. Mrs Wilkes and Mary were sitting out in the cool of the backyard with some sewing. They had been talking about Mary's friends still in Newgate. Mary had become a little tearful, afraid that their pardon would never come and that they would begin to believe she had stopped caring for them.

Mrs Wilkes, like Boswell, thought visiting was a bad idea, given the high risk of infection, but she offered to write them a letter for Mary. At the moment they heard the rapping on the door, Mary was thinking of all the things she had to tell them.

Mary smiled at her landlady's outburst, for she knew perfectly well that Mrs Wilkes enjoyed having neighbours gossiping about Boswell calling so often. He was, after all, famous and a gentleman, and noon, whether it was Sunday or not, was a respectable time to call.

'I'll go,' Mary said, getting up. 'Shall I tell him to go away?'

'No, of course not,' Mrs Wilkes said hurriedly. 'You must take him into the parlour and I'll bring you in some tea.'

But Boswell was not alone this time. He had a burly, florid-faced man with him, who in a somewhat loud checked jacket, matching breeches and a very poorly fitting dull brown wig, looked like a tradesman.

'Good day, Mary,' Boswell said, lifting his hat. She thought he looked flustered. 'This is Mr Castel, a glazier by trade, and a native of Fowey. He wishes to give you certain news of your family, and he insisted we came right away to see you.'

Mary looked from one man's face to the other, noting how hot and agitated they both looked. Boswell clearly wasn't happy about this man's insistence on coming to see her, and she guessed he suspected some kind of confidence trick. There had been several occasions previously when people had come to him claiming they knew Mary and asking for her address. So for Boswell to have brought this man to her door, there had to be some kind of credence to his story.

Mary invited them into the parlour and once they were sitting down, she looked hard at the man. 'So you are from Fowey, Mr Castel?' she said. 'I don't know any family of that name.'

'I left many years ago, when you would have been just a little girl,' he said calmly. 'But I know your sister Dolly very well.'

Mary gasped, despite herself. 'You know Dolly? How? Where is she?'

'I have only known her since she came to London,' he said, mopping perspiration from his face with a handkerchief. 'She is in service for Mrs Morgan of Bedford Square. I met her there when I was replacing some glass, and we got to talking about Fowey.'

'Dolly's here in London!' Mary could hardly believe what she was hearing, and even though Boswell was giving her a warning look as if he didn't want her to get too excited, she couldn't help but be.

'It seems Mr Castel wants your permission to write to your family in Fowey and inform them about you,' Boswell butted in, with a very cynical tone in his voice. 'He claims he also knows a relative of yours there, Edward Puckey.'

'Ned!' Again Mary gasped. She and Dolly had been bridesmaids at her cousin Ned's wedding.

'You have a relative called Edward Puckey?' Boswell asked.

Mary nodded. 'My cousin,' she said.

Mr Castel looked at Mary and his frown indicated that he felt aggrieved. 'It seems Mr Boswell doesn't trust me. I knew Ned Puckey when I was a lad, though he's a few years younger than me. It was through that connection that I got to know Dolly so well. All I want now is to see two sisters reunited and pass on news that could be advantageous to you.'

Setting aside Mr Castel's clothing and the ill-fitting wig, which did suggest questionable taste, Mary thought he had an honest face. He looked directly at her, he wasn't licking his lips or fidgeting nervously. He had also retained his Cornish accent.

'What news?' she asked suspiciously, and glanced at Boswell. He was tense, sweating profusely, and his frown suggested he wished to silence this man.

'That your family have come into a fortune.'

Mary laughed out loud and rocked back in her chair. 'I can't believe that, even if I wish to believe you know Dolly,' she said.

'It's true,' he insisted. 'Dolly told me. Your uncle, Peter Broad, died while you were in Botany Bay, and he left a fortune to your family.'

Mary stopped laughing suddenly. Her uncle Peter, her father's brother, was a master mariner, which meant he was hired to take control of a ship, unlike her father who was just an ordinary seaman. She had not known Uncle Peter very well as he was away at sea for very long periods. But whenever he came home she remembered that he always came visiting with presents of food, sweetmeats and other luxuries. It had been Uncle Peter who brought the pink silky material her mother had used to make the dresses she and Dolly wore the day they went swimming naked. It was always said around Fowey that he was rich too, in fact whenever her mother spoke of wanting something out of the ordinary, her father had always said jokingly, 'You'd better bide a while, my dear, until Peter comes home.'

'I don't know what to say,' Mary exclaimed. 'This has come as a shock, Mr Castel.'

'I'm sure it has,' he said. 'But believe me, there is no mischief in my desire to impart this news to you, only to try and bring a family together. You see, Dolly and I are friends. We met some four years ago and she told me she had a sister who had gone off to work in Plymouth and hadn't been seen since. She said her parents still fretted about you, not knowing whether you were alive or dead.'

'They didn't know what happened to me?' Mary wasn't sure whether this pleased or saddened her.

Mr Castel shook his head. 'According to what Dolly told me, your father went looking for you in Plymouth, but without success. Dolly had the idea you'd come to London, and that was mainly why she took a position here, hoping she'd run into you one day. But as the years passed that hope faded. I saw how important you were to her, that first day I met her. The moment she heard my voice and knew I was from Cornwall, she went out of her way to talk to me.'

Mary nodded. That sounded logical to her. For if she met someone with a Cornish accent she knew she'd immediately want to talk to them. 'Did you know then where I was?'

Castel shook his head. 'Indeed not. With a girl like Dolly you wouldn't ever think she could have a sister that might have been transported.'

'Why?' Mary asked.

'Well, she's so . . .' He stopped, clearly unable to find the right words.

'Honest?' Mary decided to help him out. 'You didn't think she could have a sister who was a thief?'

Castel looked embarrassed. 'I didn't mean that,' he said hurriedly. 'Dolly's timid and industrious. I imagined her sister was just like her.'

Mary was sure now that this man knew Dolly. 'Timid and industrious' was a good description of her. Mary had often described her to people as a mouse!

'So why has it taken you so long to come forward?' Mary asked. It was some fourteen months since the news of her arrival in Newgate had been in the newspapers. The pardon, when there had been more news, was over three months ago.

'You can call me slow if you like,' he said, and looked sheepish. 'Because I read all about "the girl from Botany Bay" in the newspapers, even noticed your name was the same as Dolly's sister. But I didn't think for one minute it could be the right Mary Broad.'

'You didn't?' Mary said in some surprise.

He fingered his stiff collar nervously. 'It was too extraordinary. No one knowing Dolly would think her sister could be that daring. Besides, Mary Broad is a common enough name and the paper I read didn't say you were from Cornwall.'

'So what finally made you think I might be her sister?' Mary asked curiously.

'A poem,' he said. He looked at Boswell as if hoping for some support, but Boswell didn't offer any.

'A poem?' Mary said. She guessed he meant one of those that Boswell had mentioned, though he'd never read one of them to her.

'They've been sticking them up all over the place since your pardon,' he said awkwardly. 'But I never really read one properly till they put one up by my shop. I can't explain why exactly, but I got this feeling about it which wouldn't go away. I didn't want to show it to Dolly, in case she got upset that her sister might have been transported. Or that the poem suggested you were more than friends with Mr Boswell. So I went round to his house this morning to ask his opinion.'

Mary looked at Boswell questioningly.

'The first thing he asked me was if you were from Fowey,' Boswell said with a despairing kind of shrug. 'I agreed you were, and then he told me of Dolly. I wanted to come alone to see you, but Mr Castel is a persistent man, my dear. Now, my suggestion is that I check out his story, and return to you when I have proof.'

Later that same day, Mary was helping Mrs Wilkes wash the supper things when someone knocked on the front door again. 'I'll wager that's Boswell again,' she said with a worried look. 'Maybe he's found out more about Castel.'

Mary had been anxious all day. She wanted to believe Mr Castel, but as Boswell had seemed so suspicious about his claims, she had tried very hard not to build up her hopes.

She hurried down the hall, removing her apron as she went, but as she opened the door, her knees went weak.

There was Mr Castel again, and by his side was Dolly.

There was no mistaking her sister, she looked just the same as she had nine years ago, when she stood waving goodbye to Mary as she took the boat to Plymouth. She had kept the image of that small upturned nose, and those blue eyes locked inside her all these years. All Mary could do was gasp and cover her face with her hands.

'Mary!' Dolly said softly. 'It really is you! I was so afraid Mr Castel was mistaken.'

All at once Mary was enveloped in her older sister's arms, and they stood on the doorstep rocking each other, both sobbing out all the years of separation.

'Now, will you please come inside?' Mrs Wilkes said firmly from behind them. 'This is all very heart-warming, but I don't wish it to be the talk of the street.'

Once in the parlour, the two women could only hug each other and cry for some minutes. Then they began to laugh hysterically through their tears. Everything was jumbled, half questions only half answered, a nonsensical struggle to bridge the gap of nine years.

Mr Castel had explained to Dolly some of what had happened to Mary, but his version, which had come from newspapers, wasn't accurate. Although Mary tried to give her sister the truth of it, Dolly was clearly too shocked and bewildered to take it all in.

'I look so much older than you now,' Mary said at one point, gazing at her sister with pride.

They had always been alike in as much as they both had dark curly hair like their mother's and the same sturdy build, and were a little taller than most other girls in the village. But Dolly's eyes were blue, not grey like Mary's, and then of course there was Dolly's more pronounced upturned nose.

The differences were in their characters. Dolly had always been the meek, practical, obedient one. For as far back as Mary could remember, she had always looked neat and tidy, her hair braided tightly back off her face, her pinafore spotless. She skirted round mud, avoided brambles, and would sit quietly on the doorstep watching as Mary played rough games with boys and tore and muddied her clothes.

Dolly was still dressed in a sober and neat manner, as befitted her position as a lady's maid. Her blue pin-tucked dress had a high neck with tiny pearl buttons and she wore well-polished black button boots and a small straw hat with just a plain blue ribbon round it. Mary knew her to be thirty, but she looked closer to twenty, her complexion clear and unlined.

'I haven't had the hard times like you,' Dolly said, her eyes awash with tears. 'You are so thin, Mary, I remembered your face being plump and bonny.'

With Mr Castel and Mrs Wilkes looking on, it was impossible for the sisters to talk frankly. Dolly started to ask about the two children, but stopped half-way through. Likewise, Mary wanted to ask so much about her mother and father, and whether Dolly had a sweetheart, but she couldn't in front of Mrs Wilkes and Castel.

Then, in the midst of it, Boswell came back.

Mrs Wilkes opened the door to him, and Mary heard her telling him that Dolly was already here. 'Oh, it's wonderful,' she gushed. 'They've been crying and laughing fit to bust.'

Boswell looked petulant when he came into the room. He had asked Castel this morning to let him arrange the meeting between Mary and Dolly. An hour ago he had gone to Bedford Square to see Dolly, only to find that Castel had already been there, and had brought the young woman here. But faced with Mary's joy, he recovered his natural good humour and apologized to Castel for doubting him. He then turned his considerable charm on Dolly, flattering her with compliments and saying that if he had appeared obstructive it was only because he had to protect Mary.

Mrs Wilkes opened a bottle of port wine to celebrate, and suggested that maybe it would be wise for the two men to leave Mary and Dolly to talk.

'But I promised Mrs Morgan I would escort Dolly home,' Castel said quickly, and from the adoring way he looked at her, it was obvious to everyone that he was sweet on her.

'I can't stay much longer anyway, I'm afraid,' Dolly said, turning to Mary. 'Mrs Morgan expects me home by half past nine. But I can spend my day off on Wednesday with you.'

'Well, perhaps, Dolly, before you have to go, you'd like to tell Mary about the inheritance from your uncle?' Boswell suggested. 'It's impertinent of me to ask, but I think it's something Mary would like cleared up.'

'It's quite true,' Dolly said, clutching at Mary's hand as if afraid that if she let go her younger sister would disappear again. 'Uncle Peter did leave all his money to Father. A considerable sum too. Father got Ned to write to me, explaining it all and urging me to come home as there was no longer a need for me to work.'

'So why didn't you go, Dolly?' Boswell asked. He couldn't quite bring himself to ask crassly how much money there was, especially in front of Castel.

She blushed. 'I like London,' she said, 'and my position. I'm very happy with the Morgans. I didn't want to be an old maid in Fowey.'

'I doubt if you would remain unmarried for long,' Boswell said gallantly.

'Mary would understand,' Dolly said, looking to her sister for support.

'Do you, Mary?' Boswell asked.

'I do,' she said, giving her sister a wry smile. 'All the years I've been away I've always imagined you married with a parcel of children. That was what you wanted as a young girl. But whatever the reason you left, you've made a good life for yourself. To go back would be like burying yourself alive.'

'That's just how it would be,' Dolly agreed earnestly. 'I couldn't change my station in life just because Father had money. We might live in a bigger house, have better clothes and food. But who would I have as friends? My old ones are poor. They would avoid me. The rich people would turn their noses up at me.'

Mary nodded in sympathy. She thought this was very likely. But there was also the question of fortune hunters. Dolly would want a man to love her for herself, not for her money. Mary guessed it could be quite difficult to be certain of a man's real feelings until well after the wedding.

'You don't ever intend to go back?' Boswell asked Dolly. He wondered if there was already a man in her life. Castel clearly had designs on her, but Boswell didn't think the attraction was mutual.

'Maybe in a few years,' she said, then looking at Mary she smiled. 'But I think Mary should go. At least to see our folks. They will be so overjoyed to know she is safe and well.'

Mary asked if she was sure their parents didn't know about what had happened to her.

'They certainly didn't when I heard from Father last year. You see, he mentioned you, and said he hoped it was a husband and children which had prevented you returning from Plymouth.'

Mary thought on this for a moment. It seemed almost laughable that her parents had imagined her just forty miles away in Plymouth, when in fact she had been right round the world. If she were to go home, how on earth was she ever going to be able to explain everything she'd done and seen? It was hard enough to deal with her memories, the contrasts, and the sheer distances she'd covered in her life, herself. She didn't think her mother, who'd never been further than twenty miles from Fowey, could possibly grasp it.

'Might Father have discovered about me since the letter he sent you?' she asked.

'Maybe,' Dolly said with a frown. 'Mr Castel told me there was much about you in the newspapers. But if I didn't hear about it, here in London, why should they, so far away?'

Mary sighed. 'Perhaps it's better that they never know about me, Dolly. It's too shocking.'

'Better to be a little shocked than to go through life

believing their daughter deserted them or is dead,' Dolly insisted.

Boswell left with Castel and Dolly later, and the two sisters arranged that Dolly would come again on her day off. After they'd gone Mary went off to her room, for she very much wanted to be alone.

She sat by the open window, looking out into the darkness. Sounds of carriage wheels, chatter, laughter, babies crying, and the tinkle of a distant piano wafted up to her on the still, warm air as it had on many an evening since she'd been with Mrs Wilkes. It was the sound of family life going on all around her, and until tonight she had always felt terribly alone when she heard it because fate had estranged her from her own.

Sometimes she had even had cynical thoughts about her freedom. She had thought that although she could walk around the town, she was still shackled mentally by guilt, shame and grief. She knew too that she was utterly dependent on Boswell, and that made him another gaoler of sorts. A kindly one, of course, but he decided everything, where she would go, who she would meet, and provided for her too. Until now she hadn't been able to see any way that she could step out of that dependency and into a life that was truly her own.

That chance had come now.

'But are you brave enough to go home?' she murmured to herself. It was one thing to tell it all to Dolly, she was still young, without any hard-held prejudices. Her father would probably be as understanding too, for he had sailed to many different countries, met men from all walks of life.

But her mother was a different story. Her world was a tiny one, bound by the church and her neighbours. Would she be able to open her mind wide enough to accept that Mary had received far more punishment for her original crime than it warranted? Could she forgive and remain resolute in the face of village gossip?

Mary doubted it. Grace Broad had never been a forgiving or tolerant person. As a child Mary had been considered odd because she liked to hang around the fishermen, went swimming, climbed trees and wandered away from home. Her father had laughed and said she ought to have been a boy, but her mother's face had always been dark with disapproval.

Yet Mary could understand why that was now. Becoming a mother herself had made sense of many things which once seemed so odd. A mother's role was to nurture and protect, showing praise and disapproval were merely ways of guiding a child to keep them safe. She had no doubt now that her mother had been frightened by her daughter's wilfulness. Maybe she always feared it would get Mary into serious trouble. And she was right of course.

Mary also doubted that the gossips in Fowey would see heroism in the daring escape, as people in London did. They would brood on the aspects of prison hulks, chains and the shadow of the gallows, whisper that she'd spent much of her time with a gang of men, and that would be interpreted as her being a wanton woman.

A tear trickled down Mary's cheek. She knew she'd been foolhardy and selfish as a young girl, but all that was gone now, and she so wanted to be taken back into her family. She had never been able to speak to anyone about the agony of losing her two children, but perhaps if her mother enfolded her in her arms, she'd be able to tell her. She wanted to tell the whole family the place they had in her heart throughout her imprisonment. Perhaps as an adult she could make amends for all the sadness and worry she'd brought them.

Mary also felt that she needed the familiar peace and loveliness of her own village to cleanse her soul of the ugliness trapped within it. She may have had forgiveness from the King and the government, but that meant little without the forgiveness of her own people.

During the next few days Mary's thoughts became even more confused. The day spent alone with Dolly was one of the best in her whole life, as they talked through everything that had happened to them both in the last nine years.

Dolly had always been held up to Mary as a paragon of feminine virtue. Her skill with the needle, the care she took in cleaning and laundry, her ability to cook tasty meals from almost nothing, and of course her lack of insolence and her sweet nature had all served to make her seem dull company in the youthful Mary's eyes. Yet nine years on, Mary found her older sister had a far more lively mind than she had supposed.

Dolly had used her position as lady's maid to become

acquainted with all aspects of the gentry's way of life. There was little she didn't know, from how to dress a fashionable woman's hair to the running of a large household. But she had picked up a great deal more than domestic skills from her master and mistress. She knew their secrets, their views on everything from religion to politics. Through them she had become educated, and she was no longer an innocent country girl. She might still be timid, in as much as she wouldn't speak out of turn or go out alone at night, but she had had two lovers.

She confided in Mary that one was a younger brother of her master, and it had made her realize that an intelligent woman could control her own destiny. She said she had no intention of marrying a humble footman or even a tradesman like Mr Castel and spending the rest of her life bringing up children in reduced circumstances. She said that if she didn't find a gentleman as a husband within the next few years, she intended to start up her own business, perhaps a bureau for domestic staff.

Dolly said that her father wouldn't reveal the size of the bequest for security reasons. In the letter he'd had written for him, all he would say was that it was enough to live on very comfortably and that if she required a 'nest egg' to advance her own position, she had only to ask.

As Mary listened to Dolly, she had no doubt that her sister could start her own business. Beneath her sweet, calm exterior there was a great deal of determination and good sense. So when Dolly insisted that Mary should go home to Cornwall, she was inclined to believe she was right.

Dolly had foresight and imagination. She said that with just a little capital, Mary could run a boarding-house down in Cornwall. She suggested Truro as many people passed through there, or even Falmouth where she could cater for ships' officers and their families. Another idea was that their parents might be persuaded to buy a small farm, and Mary could grow produce to sell.

'I might even join you in it if London begins to pall for me,' Dolly laughed. 'What you've got to keep in mind, Mary, is that you aren't an ordinary woman, you are brave, strong and sharp-witted. That's more than enough to succeed. If you stay in London, the only positions open to you will be lowly ones, like kitchen maid. You'll hate it. You can't kow-tow to a grumpy cook or a snooty mistress, you've seen too much for that. Be brave once more and go home.'

September came in with glorious weather, and whenever Dolly could get away from her mistress for a few hours, she spent them with Mary. The shared laughter, the pleasure of discovering how much they had in common, eased Mary's grief for her children, and she felt her old optimism and strength returning.

Mr Castel, with Boswell's help, had written to Ned Puckey to ask him to pass on the news of Mary to the Broads. Boswell had written to his friend the Reverend John Baron of Lostwithiel, seeking his help too in making sure Grace and William Broad were willing to receive Mary home.

Yet long before either the Puckeys or the Reverend Baron could have received these letters, one arrived at

Boswell's home from Elizabeth Puckey, Ned's wife. It seemed her family had only heard about Mary when she was pardoned. At that time the story about her transportation and subsequent escape was in a Cornish newspaper. Now they were very anxious to know how and where she was. Elizabeth urged that Mary should come home to her family, who as she put it *'were now in very different circumstances, due to a sizeable inheritance'*. She said Mary would have the warmest of welcomes from all members of the family and that William and Grace Broad were very relieved and happy to know their younger daughter had survived her terrible troubles.

While that letter assured Mary of her family's affection for her, and made her wholeheartedly wish to see them, she was still torn. She liked London, she wanted to stay close to Dolly, Boswell was such a good friend and such stimulating company, and then there was Mrs Wilkes too, of whom she'd grown very fond.

Boswell showed her a life which didn't exist in Cornwall. He took her to the theatre, coffee houses and restaurants. With Dolly she could recapture her girlhood, discuss men, clothes and the many differences in their lives now to the one they were born to.

Mrs Wilkes was a mother—aunt figure. She was wise and kind, knowledgeable and refined too. Mary sensed she wanted her to stay with her, and help her run her boarding-house. This was very appealing to Mary, for she felt safe there, but as Dolly pointed out, she would have to do the rough work, emptying slop pails, carrying hot water, doing laundry and scrubbing floors. Dolly said she should aspire to more than that.

Then there were the men still in Newgate. Mary didn't feel able to leave London while they remained in prison. Soon after she met up with Dolly again, despite advice from both Boswell and Mrs Wilkes, she went to visit them. After living in such comfortable surroundings, she was horrified and appalled by Newgate, and it seemed impossible that she could have borne those terrible conditions for the best part of a year. Whilst she knew Boswell was still battling for her friends, there was no pardon in sight yet.

Sam was so demoralized that he'd applied to enlist in the New South Wales Corps, a body of men who were to take over the role of the Marines and police the new colony. His reason for this change of heart was that he'd come to see England had nothing to offer men like him, and out in New South Wales as a free man he would be given a grant of land.

James was still working on his memoirs. He said Nat and Bill had a different idea every day for what they were going to do when they became free. Mary was terribly afraid that day would never come, but the men insisted it would, that they were happy enough, and that she must get on with her own life and not be held back by thoughts of them.

It was Sam who managed to convince her that she must separate her life from theirs. He walked her to the gates alone and talked to her.

'We will be pardoned,' he insisted. 'But you must not wait for that, Mary. Us four won't stay together when we are released, we've been held together this long by circumstance, not by choice. I want to go back to New South Wales, James talks of Ireland. Bill will go to Berkshire and Nat back home to Essex. We have shared the biggest adventure and the hardest times imaginable, but once free that will be just a memory, nothing more.'

Mary knew he was telling her that they'd only become so close because of adversity, and that was the only thing they had in common. She guessed too that he wanted to distance himself from the others because he was afraid they could become a liability. Deep down inside her she shared that fear, though she wouldn't have voiced it.

'You saved my life on the wharf in Port Jackson,' he said, his voice growing thick with emotion. 'I hope one day I'll be telling my children about you. But go now, and don't come back to visit again. You've done enough for all of us.'

Mary cupped her two hands round his bony face and kissed his lips lightly. 'Good luck, Sam,' she said tenderly, remembering how she'd once seen him as her safety net. She knew now that she didn't need one.

Towards the end of September the glorious weather ended suddenly with a huge storm, uprooting trees in the parks and flooding the streets. It continued to rain even after the gales had abated, and all at once Mary saw for herself the conditions Boswell had described on her release from Newgate.

The streets were treacherous, cloying mud mixed with human and animal refuse, showering anyone rash enough to attempt walking anywhere. Fever sprang up in the poorest districts and Boswell told Mary that the pits where the dead were taken for mass burial were filling rapidly. An evil stench hung in the air constantly, along with a sulphurous fog that swept in each night.

Mary was virtually imprisoned in the house in Little Titchfield Street, and it came to her that unless she left for Cornwall soon, before winter set in, she would be here till the spring. Her parents were getting old, and she would never forgive herself if something happened to either of them before she got there. And then there was the call of Cornwall itself, a siren that sang its beguiling song each night when she closed her eyes, urging her to return to where she belonged.

She would imagine herself standing in the bows of a ship coming into Fowey harbour just as daylight was fading and the autumn sun like a huge fiery ball sinking slowly into the sea.

She could see the small town rising up the hill from the quay. Grey stone cottages clustered together, with glimpses of the cobbled streets between them, where children were hurrying home before dark.

Down on the quay the fishermen would be getting ready for the night's fishing. The landlord of the tavern would be lighting his lamps, and the old men of the town would be hobbling slowly down towards it, raising their caps to any women who might still be abroad.

Mary could almost smell pilchards cooking, she could

hear the slap of the waves against the quayside, the shriek of the seagulls and the wind in the trees above the town. She wanted to fill her lungs with that clean, salty air, to hear those Cornish voices, and submerge herself in the simplicity of village life. She didn't belong in London.

'I think I must get a passage back to Cornwall,' Mary said to Boswell one evening when he'd called to see her.

He didn't say anything for a while, just sat looking quizzically at her. 'Yes, you should,' he said eventually. 'But I don't want you to go.'

'Why?' she asked, thinking perhaps he thought she would have a brighter future in London.

'Because I'll miss you,' he said simply, and to her utmost surprise she saw he had tears in his eyes.

Mary didn't know what to say. Was he implying he was in love with her? If so, what was she supposed to say or do?

'You won't miss me. You can go and visit all those grand friends you've neglected for so long,' she said flippantly.

'I've neglected them because they are all shallow compared to you,' he said, his voice quivering. 'You have given me a purpose in my life, opened up so many new vistas.'

'That is a lovely thing to say,' she said, a little overwhelmed. 'But I have even more to thank you for. You gave me back my life.'

He shook his head a little, looking down at his lap. 'I've been something of a fool for most of mine,' he said in a small voice. 'But I feel honoured that Fate singled me out to help you. Mary, you are the most astounding person I have ever encountered. You have taken what life threw at you with courage and fortitude. I have never heard you utter a word of blame against anyone.'

'There *is* no one to blame,' she said tartly. 'Only me for doing wrong.'

He began to laugh. 'Oh, Mary,' he spluttered, 'that is the absolute essence of you. If the whole world was to share your attitude, it would be a far better place. All my life I have been surrounded by those who seek to blame someone for their misfortune. I too have blamed my father, my mother, my dear departed wife, whores, drink, lack of money and even food for my failings. I wish I were a younger man and could start out on the road through life with you at my side.'

He ran his fingers over her hair affectionately, then, picking up a curl, he took a pair of scissors from Mrs Wilkes's sewing basket on the table beside him and snipped it off.

'A little memento,' he said, tucking it into a small purse he took from his pocket.

'I'll keep all my special memories of you in here,' Mary said, putting her hand over her heart. 'And make sure you get my friends pardoned or I will blame you.'

'It will come soon,' he assured her. 'Henry Dundas has it in hand.'

On the evening of 12 October Mary and Boswell were at Beals Wharf in Southwark where Mary was to board the

Anne and Elizabeth, due to sail to Fowey on the early morning tide.

It was a windy, wet night, and they hurried into a tavern nearby for shelter. When Boswell had called to collect Mary and her box of belongings from Little Titchfield Street, he had brought James, his fifteen-year-old son, to meet her.

Young James Boswell had the same beautiful dark eyes and full lips as his father, but he was taller, slender, graceful and clear-skinned. He was understandably shy, but eager to meet her. He said his father had told him and his sisters her whole story, and that they all wished her well for the future.

James arranged to meet up with his father later that evening, and as the cab rattled along the wet, windy streets towards the Thames, Mary was silent, her mind whirling with misgivings. She wasn't so sure now about returning to Cornwall, and especially about leaving Boswell, her dear friend and saviour. She glanced at him many times during the journey, sorrow welling up unbearably within her. She knew he wasn't in the best of health. His high colour and the stiffness of his limbs suggested to her that infirmity was catching up with him.

She would see Dolly again, maybe Mrs Wilkes too. But she had a feeling that the few remaining hours before she had to board the boat would be her last with Boswell.

In the tavern, Mary removed the heavy dark green wool cloak Mrs Wilkes had given her. She felt almost as indebted to the kind-hearted woman as she was to Boswell, for she had taught Mary so much. No one in this waterside tavern would take her for a whore or a felon. Everything, from the cloak and bonnet to the warm woollen dress and sturdy boots gave a picture of a genteel governess. Yet Mrs Wilkes had not only chosen the clothes because they were warm and serviceable, but because they made her look attractive too. There was a ruffle of cream lace on the high-necked dress, more lace on her petticoat, and her stockings were a fashionable red. Mary had many more clothes in her box too, and she found it hard to equate the pretty woman she saw reflected in a looking-glass, with the same poor wretch who had once worn rags and fetters.

As they drank rum, sitting side by side on a settle by the roaring fire, a tender current flowed between them. Mary wished she could find the right words to tell Boswell how she felt about him. Boswell, unusually silent, kept his hand covering hers on the settle, a gesture that showed he wanted to hold on to her for as long as he could.

The place reminded Mary of the taverns in Fowey and Plymouth, the flag-stone floor wet from men's boots, the air thick with smoke, the smell of wet clothes overpowering. Yet it was snug, a friendly place where sailors swapped stories, found a willing woman and drank their hard-earned money away. To Mary it was fitting that they should spend their last hours somewhere she found so familiar. The following day Boswell would be back where he belonged, dining in elegant places, drinking coffee with his illustrious friends or sitting at his desk writing again, while her boat battled its way through heavy seas to Cornwall.

'I have arranged with the Reverend John Baron in

Lostwithiel to give you an annuity of ten pounds a year,' Boswell blurted out suddenly. He took a five-pound note from his pocketbook and pressed it into her hand. 'This is for the first half year, and you must go to him next April for the next half, and sign your name as I taught you.'

'But Bozzie,' she exclaimed in consternation, 'why? I won't need it, and I know you aren't a rich man.'

Even though Boswell was wealthy in comparison to ordinary working people, Mary had discovered he had spent most of his life lurching from one financial crisis to another. Again and again he had come very close to ruin. It was only luck and good friends that had saved him from it.

'It will give you some security,' he said. He didn't add that it was in case things didn't work out for her in Fowey. Perhaps he was reluctant to point out that was a possibility, but Mary knew that was what he meant.

She thanked him, the lump in her throat making it impossible to say more. She put the bank note into the little reticule Mrs Wilkes had embroidered for her as a leaving present, and drew out a small package tied with a red ribbon.

'This is a keepsake from me,' she said softly, pressing it into his hands. 'It isn't of any value, but it was the only thing which comforted me during the bad times in Port Jackson.'

Boswell looked curiously at her, noting the tears in her eyes, and then opened the package carefully. All it contained was a few dried crumbling leaves.

'That was what we called "sweet tea",' she explained.

'I picked the leaves on my last day there before our escape. I kept those last few back throughout the voyage, through Kupang and Batavia, right home to England and Newgate. I wish I was able to give you a gold watch with your name engraved on the back, but these mean more, however humble. Look at them now and then and remember me.'

Boswell retied the package and put it into his pocket. 'I will keep them forever,' he said, his voice quavering. 'But I do not need them to remember you, Mary, you have a very special place in my heart.'

He picked up her hands and held them to his lips, his dark luminous eyes scanning her face as if imprinting it on his mind.

'I have vowed love to so many women in the past that I hesitate to do so again for fear of trivializing what I feel for you, my dear,' he said. 'But true friendship, the purest kind, is sprung from love. It never dies, never tarnishes. It remains even after death.'

Suddenly a loud cheer interrupted the tender moment and both Mary and Boswell looked up to see the men in the bar greeting another two coming in. One was a small, wiry man of about forty-five, the other tall, fair-haired and perhaps ten years younger.

'The older man is the master of the *Anne and Elizabeth*, by the name of Job Moyes,' Boswell said. 'I met him when I booked your passage. The other is his first mate. I shall invite them over for a bowl of punch. We mustn't spend our remaining time together in sadness.'

*

Job Moyes and his first mate, John Trelawney, greeted Boswell and Mary with great warmth, and it was clear they knew all about her.

'It will be a pleasure to have you aboard, Miss Broad,' Job said, his blue eyes twinkling. 'We know we'll be able to call on your sailing skills if we run into heavy weather.'

John Trelawney looked at Mary with frank admiration. 'You are a great deal smaller and prettier than I expected,' he said. 'I hope you'll tell me of your adventures during our voyage.'

Mary felt a warm glow from his compliment. He was a striking-looking man, with amber-coloured eyes that reminded her of a cat's, high cheek-bones, very white teeth and thick blond hair tied back at the nape of his neck. His voice was easy on the ear too, deep and resonant, with just enough of a Cornish accent to remind her of home.

The bowl of punch arrived at the table, and Boswell raised a toast to Mary's future. As he asked Moyes some questions about his cargo, John was looking at Mary in a way that made her heart flutter.

She had fully believed she was incapable of feeling romantically attracted to any man again, and it seemed preposterous that she should feel it now on the eve of her departure from London.

'What part of Cornwall are you from?' she asked.

'Falmouth,' he said, and smiled, showing his beautiful teeth. 'But I've no one there now, my parents passed on a few years back and my brother has gone to America.'

'So where do you call home?' she asked.

'The *Anne and Elizabeth*,' he chuckled. 'But if I was to settle down in one place, Fowey is where I'd choose.'

'No wife or sweetheart then?' She raised one eyebrow questioningly.

He shook his head. 'I never met a woman who was prepared to accept that the sea was my mistress.'

That phrase jolted something long buried within Mary. She looked at him curiously.

'I stole that line from your uncle,' John said. 'Peter Broad. I sailed under him when I was a lad. He was a good man and taught me all I know.'

Mary gasped. 'You sailed under my uncle?'

John nodded. 'And your father too, Mary. He is another good man, and I'm proud to be taking you home to him.'

'What's that?' Boswell asked, picking up the tail-end of the conversation.

'Just telling Mary I sailed under both her uncle and father, sir,' John said. 'But then you know that.'

'Bozzie,' Mary said reprovingly, 'is that why you were so adamant I had to go on this boat?'

His smile was a mischievous one. 'Would I entrust such a precious cargo to just anyone?' he asked. 'I spoke to several ships' masters before I found Job. I wanted one you would feel at ease with.'

They filled their glasses again and Boswell made the men laugh with a very funny account of what he called 'his Cornish jaunt' the previous year.

Mary was happy just to watch and listen. It was good to see the way Boswell sparkled as he told a tale. He had a gift of being able to describe a scene and the people there so well that the listener entered into it too. She was going to miss him, but her trepidation about going home was gone now. Cornwall was where she belonged.

It was after ten when they finally left the tavern to walk to the boat. John carried Mary's box, walking a little ahead with Moyes, while Mary followed, holding Boswell's arm.

'Leave me here,' she said to him as they got to the boat. 'Don't come aboard, you must go back to meet up with James as you promised.'

The wind had blown itself out and the rain had stopped. For once there was no fog, and the moon and stars were clear and bright, making twinkling lights in the inky river. The sound of water slapping gently against the hull reminded her poignantly of that other desperate voyage, something she hadn't thought of for a very long time.

'Will you be all right?' Boswell asked her, his customary confidence deserting him.

'Of course I will,' she said, kissing him on the cheek. 'The sea holds no terrors for me.'

Boswell caught her by the forearms fiercely, his face suddenly more youthful in the blaze of a lighted torch by the boat. 'If ever you need me, send a message,' he said.

She nodded. 'You take care of yourself, Bozzie,' she said. 'And say goodbye to James, Bill, Nat and Sam. Tell them I'm sorry I couldn't be there to celebrate their freedom.'

Mary heard Moyes or John cough and knew they were waiting for her to go aboard. 'Goodbye, my dear friend,' she said, kissing him again, this time on the lips. 'I shall never forget you. You gave me back my life.'

She left him quickly, not trusting herself not to cry. As she reached the deck she turned and waved just once. He was just standing looking up at her, the silver buttons on his coat and his gold watch-chain glistening in the light from the torch. He raised his three-cornered hat and bowed majestically, then turned and walked away.

'Will you miss London?' John said at her elbow.

Mary turned to look at him and smiled. She had a feeling that his real question was would she miss grand people like Boswell, not the city itself.

'No, I don't think so,' she said truthfully. 'I'm glad I've seen it, but I prefer a simple life, and people I can be myself with.'

Suddenly, she had the oddest feeling of having been here before. Puzzled, she looked around her, but in the darkness she could see little but the gleam of brass and the whiteness of coiled rope.

'What's the matter?' John asked. 'Don't tell me a born sailor like you is disturbed by the movement beneath your feet?'

'No, of course not,' she said, then laughed because John's Cornish burr was enough to jog her memory. The smell of river water, and a man who attracted her, completed the picture from the past.

She was on the deck of the *Dunkirk*, a girl in rags and chains, setting her heart on an officer with a faint Cornish accent.

'Let me show you to your cabin,' John said. 'You'll get cold up here.'

All at once Mary felt completely liberated, far more so

than when she was released from Newgate. She was going to a cabin, not the hold. Tomorrow at dawn they would set sail, she would eat meals with Moyes, John and the other seamen. And she could use a spoon if she wanted to, because no one here would mind. They would drink rum and swap sailing stories, and she would be the men's equal.

She began to laugh as she climbed down the steep steps to the cabins.

John stood at the bottom with her box in his arms and laughed too. 'Are you that happy to be aboard?' he asked, tawny eyes twinkling. 'I'm very happy about it. But we expected you'd have had enough of ships to last a lifetime.'

'I thought I had too,' Mary replied, with laughter still in her voice. 'But this one feels like I'm already home.'

Postscript

I confess that I never looked at these people without pity and astonishment. They had miscarried in a heroic struggle for liberty; after having combated every hardship and conquered every difficulty.

The woman had gone out to Port Jackson in the ship which transported me thither and was distinguished for her good behaviour. I could not but reflect with admiration at the strange combination of circumstances which had brought us together again, to baffle human foresight and confound human speculation.

An extract from Watkin Tench's journal, 1792

Afterthoughts

It was hard for me to leave Mary on the deck of the *Anne and Elizabeth*. I had become so attached to her that I would have loved to have written an entirely fictional account of her falling in love with John Trelawney on the voyage home. I would also have loved to have taken you to view the joyful reunion with her parents in Fowey, and later to go on to a romantic wedding for her and John, then the birth of a couple of healthy, bonny babies.

But Mary's story is a true one, and though I have added my own imagination to her personality, her friends and the many hardships she endured so bravely, I have stayed within the historical facts about her and the other main characters who played major roles. Therefore it would be wrong to misrepresent her life after leaving London.

Sadly, nothing is known of what happened to Mary after returning home to Fowey. We know she did collect her annuity from the Reverend John Baron, and this gentleman also wrote to James Boswell on Mary's behalf to thank him for his kindness, and recorded that she was behaving herself. But there are no records of marriages, births or even deaths that set her firmly in Fowey.

But I think such an intelligent and daring woman would

not have wanted to stay for ever in a place where she was gossiped about. If James Boswell's account of her family's legacy was true, and there is no reason to doubt it, I think she would have moved away, maybe even overseas.

I do believe too that a woman who was liked and admired by all the men close to her would have married again. I certainly hope she found a good man, and had other children.

James Martin, Sam Broome (who was also known as Butcher), Bill Allen and Nat Lilly finally got their pardon in November, soon after Mary left London. They went straight from Newgate to see James Boswell to thank him for his kindness.

Sam did join the New South Wales Corps, and went back to Australia. Nothing is known of the other three. But I like to think that James Martin either returned to Ireland, having made enough profit from his memoirs to breed horses, or went off to America.

As for James Boswell, sadly he died on 17 May 1795. His family cancelled the annuity to Mary, and although he recorded in his diary that he wrote four pages about 'the Girl from Botany Bay', these pages have never been found. But I am sure James rests happily knowing that *The Life of Samuel Johnson* did indeed become known as the very best biography of all time.

Watkin Tench went on to become something of a hero. He was captured in France, and supposedly escaped from the prisoner-of-war camp. He reached the rank of Major-General. I smiled when I discovered he married an Anna Maria Sargent. Sargent was my maiden name, and my father was a Royal Marine. Watkin and Anna Maria had no children of their own, but adopted his sister-in-law's four children when her husband died in the West Indies.

Watkin Tench's journals survived along with those of many other officers who went out to Australia with the First Fleet, and there is no doubt that he was an intelligent, compassionate and fair-minded man.

Mary never divulged who Charlotte's father was, for Lieutenant Spencer Graham was my own invention. Some people think Watkin Tench was responsible, but I doubt that very much, for he would surely have recorded his anguish at seeing Charlotte's burial at sea.

I like to think that the good men on that First Fleet, whether felons, officers or Marines, would be proud and pleased to see what a wonderful country Australia is now.

Who knows, maybe Mary slipped back there under another name and her descendants are still there, as brave and resourceful as she was.